W9-BVA-960

The Kent Family Chronicles

THREE VOLUMES IN ONE

The Kent Family Chronicles
NOVELS IN THE SERIES

The Kent Family Chronicles

THREE VOLUMES IN ONE

THE BASTARD

THE REBELS

THE SEEKERS

John Jakes

AVENEL BOOKS • NEW YORK

This edition contains the complete and unabridged texts of the original editions.
They have been completely reset for this volume.

Copyright © 1986 by John Jakes and Book Creations, Inc.
This omnibus was originally published in separate volumes under the titles:
The Bastard copyright © MCMLXXIV by John Jakes and Book Creations, Inc.
The Seekers copyright © MCMLXXV by John Jakes and Lyle Kenyon Engel
The Rebels copyright © MCMLXXV by John Jakes and Book Creations, Inc.

All rights reserved.

This 1986 edition is published by Avenel Books, distributed by Crown
Publishers, Inc., 225 Park Avenue South, New York, New York 10003, by
arrangement with Book Creations, Inc.

Printed and Bound in the United States of America

Book design by June Marie Bennett

Library of Congress Cataloging-in-Publication Data
Jakes, John, 1932–
    The Kent Family chronicles.
    I. Title.
PS3560.A37K432 1986   813'.54   86-7986
ISBN 0-517-61822-2

h g f e d c b a

Contents

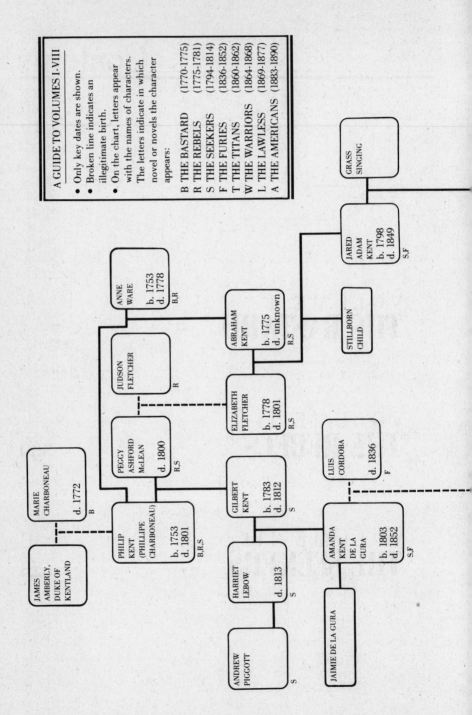

A GUIDE TO VOLUMES I-VIII

- Only key dates are shown.
- Broken line indicates an illegitimate birth.
- On the chart, letters appear with the names of characters. The letters indicate in which novel or novels the character appears:

B THE BASTARD   (1770-1775)
R THE REBELS   (1775-1781)
S THE SEEKERS   (1794-1814)
F THE FURIES   (1836-1852)
T THE TITANS   (1860-1862)
W THE WARRIORS   (1864-1868)
L THE LAWLESS   (1869-1877)
A THE AMERICANS   (1883-1890)

GRASS SINGING

JARED ADAM KENT
b. 1798
d. 1849
S,F

ANNE WARE
b. 1753
d. 1778
B,R

ABRAHAM KENT
b. 1775
d. unknown
R,S

JUDSON FLETCHER
R

ELIZABETH FLETCHER
b. 1778
d. 1801
R,S

STILLBORN CHILD

PEGGY ASHFORD McLEAN
d. 1800
R,S

LUIS CORDOBA
d. 1836
F

MARIE CHARBONEAU
d. 1772
B

PHILIP KENT (PHILLIPE CHARBONEAU)
b. 1753
d. 1801
B,R,S

GILBERT KENT
b. 1783
d. 1812
S

AMANDA KENT DE LA GURA
b. 1803
d. 1852
S,F

JAMES AMBERLY, DUKE OF KENTLAND

HARRIET LEBOW
d. 1813
S

ANDREW PIGGOTT
S

JAIMIE DE LA GURA

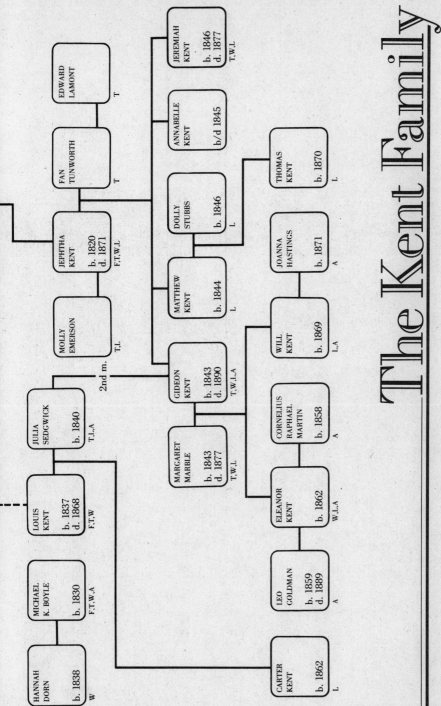

The Kent Family

HANNAH DORN
b. 1838
W

MICHAEL K. BOYLE
b. 1830
F,T,W,A

LOUIS KENT
b. 1837
d. 1868
F,T,W

JULIA SEDGWICK
b. 1840
T,L,A

2nd m.

MOLLY EMERSON
T,L

JEPHTHA KENT
b. 1820
d. 1871
F,T,W,L

FAN TUNWORTH
T

EDWARD LAMONT
T

GIDEON KENT
b. 1843
d. 1890
T,W,L,A

MARGARET MARBLE
b. 1843
d. 1877
T,W,L

MATTHEW KENT
b. 1844
L

DOLLY STUBBS
b. 1846
L

ANNABELLE KENT
b/d 1845

JEREMIAH KENT
b. 1846
d. 1877
T,W,L

CARTER KENT
b. 1862
L

LEO GOLDMAN
b. 1859
d. 1889
A

ELEANOR KENT
b. 1862
W,L,A

CORNELIUS RAPHAEL MARTIN
b. 1858
A

WILL KENT
b. 1869
L,A

JOANNA HASTINGS
b. 1871
A

THOMAS KENT
b. 1870
L

THE BASTARD

The eight novels in this series, carrying the story of an American family forward from its beginning in Revolutionary times to the two-hundredth anniversary of the Republic, could only be dedicated, book by book, to the eight Americans I love best of all. And so, Rachel, this is for you.

"The gentleman *tells us that America is obstinate; that America is almost in open rebellion. Sir, I rejoice that America has resisted . . .*

"The gentleman asks when were the colonies emancipated. But I desire to know when they were made slaves . . .

"They are subjects of this kingdom, equally entitled with yourselves to all the natural rights of mankind, and the peculiar privileges of Englishmen; equally bound by its laws, and equally participating in the constitution of this free country. The Americans are the sons, not the bastards, of England."

1766:
WILLIAM PITT THE ELDER,
BEFORE PARLIAMENT,
IN SUPPORT OF REPEAL
OF THE STAMP ACT.

Contents

BOOK ONE
FORTUNE'S WHIRLWIND

1
The Beating

THE WOMAN'S face burned, glowed as though illuminated by a shaft of sunlight falling from a high cathedral window. But the woman was no madonna, unanimated, beatific. Her face showed violent emotion.

He fought to turn away from the searing brilliance, but he could neither run nor move. The old, strangling dread began to tighten his throat—

The woman stared at him, accusing. Her black eyes shone nearly as bright as the highlights in her black hair where it crowned her forehead and cascaded on either side of her oval face. Behind her was darkness, nothing but darkness. It intensified the frightening radiance of her face, emphasized the whiteness of her teeth. Unlike most women of her years—she was three less than forty; he knew every dreadful detail—by some miracle of inherited health, her mouth was free of gaps and brown rot.

He struggled to hide from the face and could not even avert his head. The dread quickened. He heard his own strident breathing. It grew louder, because he knew she would speak to him—

And she did, the words frightening as always, frightening because he could never be certain whether she spoke from love or rage.

"Don't try to run. I told you—*don't*. You will *listen*."

Run. God, as if he could! He was held in that vast darkness where her face burned so fiercely; and her eyes—

"There will be no Latin. Do you hear? *No Latin!* You will study English. The reading and writing of your own language, and English. And how to figure sums—something I never learned. But I had no need of it, acting in Paris. You will. There's a different role for you, Phillipe. A great role, never forget that—"

Like coals on the hearth of a winter midnight, her eyes were fire, hypnotic. But they held no warmth. He was all cold sweat, terror, crippled immobility—

"I'll tell you what the role is when I feel the time is proper. Till then, you must obey me and learn English as your second tongue—and also such things as how much an English pound is worth. That way, you'll be ready to take what belongs to you. Let the fools around here chatter about the glory of France. The greatest empire the world's known since Rome lies across the water—where you must go one day, to claim what's yours. So let the little church boys learn their Latin from that bigot priest and his helper!"

Stabbing out, disembodied white things, white claws, her hands reached at him. Closed on his upper arms. She shook him, shaken herself with the ferocity of her passion.

Trying to deny her, negate her, he was able at last to turn his head from side to side. The effort required all his strength. But she would not release him. Her face floated closer, wrenching into the ugliness that brought the old, silent scream climbing into his throat.

"You will learn your English from Girard!" she cried. "From good, decent books—none of those filthy, blasphemous things he hides in his cupboard. Do you hear me, Phillipe?"

He tried to speak but his throat somehow remained clogged. Nothing but a feeble hiss of air came out between his teeth.

She shook him harder, then harder still, as a wind from the limitless dark tossed her lustrous hair. The wind added its keen to the rising shrillness of her voice; its blowing and buffeting seemed to shimmer the burning image of her face like a candle-flame in a gale—

"Do you hear what I say, Phillipe? *Do you hear me?*"

At last he brought forth sound: a howling, animal cry of fear and pain—

The wind-roar broke off like an interrupted thunderclap. He tore himself from the clutching hands, fled through the darkness. Away from the white claws. The face. The eyes—

But the darkness to which he fled was without substance. His legs churned on emptiness, as he fell, and fell, and *fell*—

This time the sound from his throat was a scream for mercy.

II

HE AWOKE sweating. Sweating and—after a moment's realization that it was over—enraged.

The dream came on him from time to time. He should be used to it. But he wasn't. Always, the dream brought unaccountable terror.

In those first muzzy moments, his anger turned to shame. He rubbed his eyes to rid himself of sleepiness. The roughness of his knuckles against his eyelids was a reassurance.

His body was slick with sweat. Yet at the same time he was cold in the garret room above the inn. He knuckled his eyes harder. A little more of his drowsiness sloughed away. And more of the fear. He tried to laugh but made only a rough, croaking sound.

The dream's details were essentially the same on every occasion. Her face. Her eyes. Her hands. Her implied accusations, couched in the long, jumbled harangue. He'd heard bits of it before, often. In sleep. And awake too.

She always insisted that England was the rising star in the world's constellation of powers, and now he wondered again whether she said that because she had been treated so shabbily by her own people.

She always insisted that he was better—much better—than any of those among whom they lived.

But she refused to say precisely why. Whenever he pressed her for specifics, she would only smile—how haughtily she could smile!—and reply:

"In good time, Phillipe. In good time."

The garret smelled of straw, and his own sweat. He rolled on his side, toward the little round garret window that looked out onto the basalt hillside touched now with the glint of starlight. Under his left arm, the stiff corners of book spines jabbed him through the prickly wool of the knee-length shirt that he merely tucked into his breeches when it was time for the day's work to start.

Uncomfortable, he tugged the precious, carefully hidden books from under his body—the books whose contents he understood so poorly; the dangerous books Girard had been slipping to him for more than a year now, always with the caution that he keep them concealed.

One of the volumes, by an Englishman named Locke whom Girard much admired, had been helpful in Phillipe's study of the second language he had learned. But *Two Treatises of Government* also puzzled and confused him in many places. As did the other two books.

The first was a slim volume called *Le Contract social*. By a Swiss writer Girard called one of the *philosophes*, whenever he didn't refer to him with a wry smile as the mad Master Jean Jacques. The largest and bulkiest book was one of Girard's two most cherished possessions. The first volume of something called *L'Encyclopedie*—a compendium of the world's knowledge to date. Mind-numbing essays on everything from politics to the nature and construction of the heavens. Two more of those admired *philosophes,* a thinker named Diderot and a scientist named d'Alembert, had assembled the vast work, Girard said.

The first two volumes of the work had been suppressed the moment they went on sale because, as Girard put it, quoting with acerbity some official of the French government, the compendium "tended to destroy the royal authority, to encourage a spirit of independence and revolt and to erect the foundations of error, the corruption of manners, irreligion and impiety." Somehow a few copies had been privately circulated before the official suppression. Girard had been lucky enough to get hold of one of each of the initial volumes.

As Phillipe buried the books underneath the straw, his mind turned back to the dream. Perhaps he deserved it, as punishment. On every possible occasion when more legitimate works—safer works—were not under study, Girard patiently tried to exlain some of the vast, hard-to-grasp ideas Phillipe could read but could not fully understand. Voltaire. Montesquieu. The mad Rousseau. They were all represented in that precious big book Phillipe slid on top of the other two and hid with straw. They were all, Girard maintained smugly, unarguably great. They were all rattling the world to its foundations—

And turning Phillipe into one corrupted by error?

If she only knew! How often would the dreams come then?

Probably never, he reflected with a small, weary smile. Very likely she wouldn't let him sleep but would lecture, lecture, lecture—

All three books safely out of sight, he relaxed a little. Breathed more slowly and deeply, for the first time since waking up. He sniffed the damp mist of fall drifting down from the Puy de Dome in the north. The tang of the autumn night

was a kind of tonic, restoring his senses by shoving him hard into reality again—the reality in which he always doubted the dream and all it contained.

Another cold, difficult winter would soon wrap around the Velay plain and freeze the Allier, which flowed northward to join the Loire. The dreary days would pass, and he would shiver and work and sleep his life away at a moldering inn that no longer attracted many customers.

He stuck a straw between his teeth and chewed the end absently. He was supposed to believe there was some marvelous, shining future waiting for him? In *England?* The homeland of France's traditional enemies?

He bit on the straw and let the corners of his mouth wrench up in another sour smile.

The very idea was laughable.

But it was also an explanation of why he had no friends his own age. Though he hardly believed the shrilled promises of the dream and the daytime harangues that carried the same promises, he knew he sometimes acted as if he believed them completely. Others sensed that unconscious arrogance—

God, he could make no sense of it. Especially not now. He was sleepy again, wanting to escape into dreamless rest. He was totally exhausted. He lay back on the straw, bumping the hidden books before he wriggled and got comfortable. He pulled up the ragged blanket that stank of smoke and age.

A splendid future? For *him?* Who was he, after all? A tavern boy, nothing more.

And yet, when her face came to him in the frequent dream—when she hectored him—he *would* wonder just a little, as he started wondering again now, whether there was something in what she said.

"In good time, Phillipe."

Was there something not yet revealed? Something waiting—as winter was waiting—to descend at its appointed moment? Something mysterious and exciting?

He didn't know. But of one thing he was utterly certain.

He feared and detested the dream. He hated being afraid of the savagery in the eyes of his own mother.

III

RAMSHACKLE, ITS wood sign creaking in the ceaseless wind of Auvergne, Les Trois Chevres clung to a hillside above a narrow road some three kilometers below the hamlet of Chavaniac. Four persons lived at the inn, tending the common-room fire, sweeping the rooms and changing the bedding, cooking the meals and serving the wine. They drew a meager living from the occasional coachloads of gentry bound farther south or heading eastward, toward the dangerous Alpine passes to the sunshine of Italy, which he imagined, in his most realistic moods, that he would never see.

Such a mood was on Phillipe Charboneau in the misty dawn following the nightmare. He felt he would probably spend his whole lifetime in the rocky country that was the only homeland he could remember.

With eyes fully open and his mind turning to the cheese to be fetched for the coming week, he displayed no sign that he believed the promises his mother shrilled at him in the dream. No sign, that is, except a certain lift of the shoulders and a touch of a swagger when he walked.

Of course, a short but strongly built boy of seventeen could be expected to stretch and swagger some. There were wild, powerful juices flowing at that age.

Phillipe's mother, Marie, ran the inn. It had belonged to her now-dead father, who was buried, as befitted a good Catholic, in the churchyard at Chavaniac. Years ago, Marie had run away to Paris to act in the theaters, and found herself automatically excommunicated from the Mother Church.

Phillipe helped her with the place, as did the hired girl, Charlotte, a buxom wench with a ripe mouth and wide hips. Charlotte's people lived a kilometer farther south. Her father, a miller, had begotten seventeen children. Unable to keep them all, he'd sent some of the brood to find employment where they could. Under Marie's guidance, Charlotte did most of the cooking.

The fourth resident at Les Trois Chevres was Girard, the tall, thin, razor-nosed man who had wandered by some four years ago, a pack of precious books tied to a stick over his shoulder. He had been persuaded to stay on because, at that time, Marie needed an older, stronger male to help around the place. Coming downstairs to the common room this morning, Phillipe found Girard mopping up sticky wine stains from the one table that had been occupied the night before.

"Good day, Phillipe," Girard greeted, in French. "We don't exactly have a bustling trade again this morning. May I suggest another lesson?"

"All right," Phillipe answered. "But first I have to go buy more cheese."

"Our sole customer of last night ate it all, did he?"

Phillipe nodded.

"He was a scrawny sort for a traveling tinker," Girard observed. "On the other hand—" He clinked sous down in his greasy apron. "Who am I to question the man's choice of vocations? He paid."

"Is my mother up yet?" Phillipe asked, starting toward the old, smoke-blackened door to the kitchen. Beyond it, he smelled a fragrant pine log burning on the hearth. "I heard no sound from her room," he added.

"I imagine she's still sleeping—why not? Our tinker took the road early." Girard rolled his tongue in his cheek. "I believe the charming Mademoiselle Charlotte's back there, however. Take care that she doesn't attack you." One of his bright blue eyes closed in a huge wink. "It continues to be evident that she'd like nothing better."

Phillipe flushed. The subject Girard hinted at excited him. He understood what men and women did together. But in actual practice, it still remained a mystery. He stopped a pace from the kitchen door. Yes, he distinctly heard Charlotte humming. And for some reason—his ill-concealed excitement, or nervousness, or both—he didn't want to face her just now.

Girard perched on a corner of a table, amused. He was an oddly built man of about thirty. He reminded Phillipe of a long-legged bird. Origins unknown—destination and ambition in life, if any, also unknown—Girard seemed content to do menial work and teach Phillipe his lessons, orthodox and otherwise. Fortunately, master and pupil liked each other.

"Go on, go on!" Girard grinned, waving. "A warm bun and the ample charms of Mademoiselle Charlotte await. What else could a chap want on a nippy morning?"

But Phillipe shook his head. "I think I'll go after the cheese first. Give me the money, please."

Girard fished the coins from his leather apron, mocking him:

"Your virtue's admirable, my boy. Eschew temptations of the flesh! Cling to

the joys of the soul and the intellect! After all, are we not privileged to be living in the greatest of all ages of man? The age of reason?''

''So you keep saying. I wouldn't know.''

''Oh, we're grumpy this morning.''

''Well—'' Phillipe apologized with a smile. ''I had a bad dream, that's all.''

''Not because of Monsieur Diderot and company, I trust.''

Phillipe shook his head. ''But there are some more questions I want to ask you, Girard. Half of that business about politics, I just can't understand.''

''But that's the purpose of education! To *begin* to understand! Then to *want* to understand!''

''I know, you've said that before. I got a little of what some of those writers were talking about. Enough to tell me that what they're saying doesn't—doesn't sound *right,* somehow. All that about kings no longer having God's authority to run other people's lives—''

Girard's emphatic nod cut him off. ''Exactly.''

''But we've always had kings!''

''Always is not forever, Phillipe. There is absolutely nothing inherent in the structure of the universe which dictates that any free man should be expected to obey authority unless he wishes to—for his own benefit, and by his own consent. Even the best of kings rules by tradition, not right. And a man must make up his own mind as to whether he's willing to be ruled by the authority in question.''

''Yes, I got that much.''

''Our mad Swiss was even more blunt about it. He once observed that if God wished to speak to Monsieur Jean Jacques, He should not go through Moses.'' Girard paused. ''Scandalous stuff I'm teaching you, eh?'' he said with a twinkling eye.

''Confusing, mostly.''

''Well, save your questions until we devote a little attention to something more conventional. When you return we'll try an English play. There are witches in it, and old Scottish kings who murder one another. You'll find it stimulating, I think. Learning ought not to be dull, though God knows it is the way the priest peddle it.'' With mock seriousness, he concluded, ''I consider it not just my job but my sacred obligation to sweeten your preparation all I can, my young friend.''

At the inn door, Phillipe turned. ''Preparation for what?''

''That, dear pupil, is for madame the actress to tell you.''

Phillipe frowned. ''Why do you always speak of her as madame?''

''For one thing, she insists upon it.''

''But she has no husband. I've no father that I know about.''

''Nevertheless, I consider your mother a lady. But then''—Girard shrugged, smiling again—''when she's in a bad mood, she herself calls me an unconventional, not to say dangerous, fellow. And she's not the only one! Pity I can't force myself to stick to sums and English where you're concerned. I can't because you're a bright lad. So before you keep on pestering me with questions, remember what I've told you before. Some of my philosophical ideas could land you in serious trouble one day. Consider that the warning of a friend. Now hurry along for the cheese, eh? Or I can't guarantee you'll be safe from Mademoiselle Charlotte!''

So, ON a gray November morning in the year 1770, Phillipe Charboneau left Les Trois Chevres. He had never, as a matter of record, seen a single goat on the premises, let alone the three for whom Marie's father had named the establishment.

He set off up the rock-strewn road in the direction of Chavaniac. As the morning mist lifted gradually, the sun came out. Far on the north horizon he glimpsed the rounded gray hump of the Puy de Dome, a peak, so Girard had informed him, that was surrounded with pits which had once belched fire and smoke. Small extinct volcanos, said the itinerant scholar.

Phillipe walked rapidly. On the hillsides above him, dark pines soughed in the wind blowing across the Velay hills. The air of Auvergne could shiver the bone in the fall and winter months. The inn was seldom warm this time of year, except when you stood directly at the fireside.

He wondered what it would be like to dwell in a splendid, comfortable chateau like the one near Chavaniac. The Motier family—rich, of the nobility—lived there, his mother said, usually hinting whenever the chateau was mentioned that he would experience a similar sort of life one day. In the stinging wind, Phillipe was more convinced than ever that she was only wishing aloud.

His old wool coat offered little protection from the cold. He was thoroughly chilled by the time he turned up a track through the rocks and emerged on a sort of natural terrace overlooking the road. Here stood the hovel and pens of du Pleis, the goatherd. Higher still, behind a screen of pines, bells clanked.

A fat, slovenly boy about Phillipe's age emerged from the hovel, scratching his crotch. The boy had powerful shoulders, and several teeth were missing. Phillipe's eyes narrowed a little at the sight of him.

"Well," said the boy, "look who graces us with his presence today."

Phillipe tried to keep his voice steady: "I've come for the week's cheese, Auguste. Where's your father?"

"In bed snoring drunk, as a matter of fact." Auguste grinned. But the grin, like the mealy dark eyes, carried no cordiality. The boy executed a mock bow. "Permit me to serve you instead, Sir."

Phillipe's chin lifted and his face grew harder. "Enough, Auguste. Let's stick to business—" He took out the coins, just as another, taller boy came outside. He carried a wicker-covered wine jug.

The new boy belched. "Oh. Company, Auguste?"

"My cousin Bertram," Auguste explained to Phillipe, who was studying the older boy. Bertram bore a faint scar on his chin. From knife fighting? He wore his hair long, not clubbed with a cheap ribbon at the nape of his neck, like Phillipe's. Bertram had dull, yellowish eyes, and he swayed a little as Auguste went on:

"This is Phillipe Charboneau, Bertram. A noted innkeeper from down the road. And far better than any of us. The little lord, some people call him."

"A lord of the horse turds is what he looks like," Bertram joked, lifting the jug to drink.

"Oh, no!" Straight-faced, Auguste advanced on Phillipe, who suddenly smelled the boy's foul breath. "Though his mother's place isn't prosperous enough to have even a single horse in its stable, he's a very fine person. True, he's a bastard, and that's no secret. But his mother brags and boasts to everyone

11

in the neighborhood that he'll leave us one day to claim some fabulous inheritance. Yes, one day he'll brush off the dirt of Auvergne—''

Auguste swooped a hand down, straightened and sprinkled dirt on Phillipe's sleeve.

''Don't laugh, Bertram!'' Auguste said, maintaining his false seriousness. ''We have it straight from his own mother! When she lowers herself to speak to lesser folk, that is.'' He squinted at Phillipe. ''Which brings up a point, my little lord. At the time my own mother died—just last Easter, it was—and yours came up to buy cheese, she didn't say so much as one word in sympathy.'' He sprinkled a little more dirt on Phillipe's arm. ''Not a word!''

Tense now, Phillipe sensed the hatred. Bertram shuffled toward him, swinging the jug. Phillipe knew that what fat Auguste said was probably true. But he felt compelled to defend Marie:

''Perhaps she wasn't feeling well, Auguste. That's it, I recall it now. At Eastertime, she—''

''Was feeling no different than usual,'' Auguste sneered. To Bertram: ''She was an actress on the Paris stage. I've heard what that means, haven't you?''

Bertram grinned. ''Of course. Actresses will lie down and open themselves for any cock with cash.''

''And for that she's not allowed inside a Catholic church!'' Auguste exclaimed, hateful glee on his suet-colored face. ''Very unusual for such a woman to be the mother of a lord, wouldn't you say?''

Bertram licked a corner of his mouth. ''Oh, I don't know. I hear most of the really grand ladies at the court are whores—''

''Damn you,'' Phillipe blurted suddenly, ''I'll have the cheese and no more of your filthy talk!'' He flung the coins on the ground.

Auguste glanced at Bertram, who seemed to understand the silent signal. Bertram set the wicker jug at his feet. The cousins started advancing again.

''You've got it wrong, little lord,'' Auguste said. ''We'll have your money. And perhaps some of your skin in the bargain—!'' His right foot whipped out, a hard, bruising kick to Phillipe's leg.

Off balance, Phillipe fisted his right hand, shot it toward Auguste's face. The fat boy ducked. A blur on Phillipe's left indicated Bertram circling him. The taller boy yanked the ribbon-tied tail of Phillipe's dark hair.

Phillipe's head snapped back. But he didn't yell. Bertram grabbed both his ears from behind, then gave him a boot in the buttocks.

The blow rocked Phillipe forward, right into Auguste's lifting knee. The knee drove into his groin. Phillipe cried out, doubling. Bertram struck him from behind, on the neck. The ground tilted—

A moment after Phillipe sprawled, Bertram kneeled on his belly. Auguste started to kick him.

Phillipe writhed, fought, struck out with both fists. But most of the time he missed. Auguste's boot pounded his legs, his ribs, his shoulders. Again. Again—

In the middle of the beating, one of Phillipe's punches did land squarely. Bertram's nose squirted blood onto Phillipe's coat. The older boy spat out filthy words, grabbed his victim's ears and began to hammer his head on the ground.

Phillipe's head filled with the strange sound of the heavy breathing of his two tormentors, the distorted ring of the goat bells from up beyond the pines. They beat him for three or four minutes. But he didn't yell again.

From inside the hovel, a querulous man's voice asked a question, then repeated it. The man sounded angry.

Auguste scooped up Phillipe's money. Bertram lurched to his feet, picked up the jug, brought the neck to his bloodied mouth and drank. Groaning, Phillipe staggered up, barely able to walk a straight line.

Auguste kicked him in the buttocks one last time, driving him down the track toward the road. The fat boy shouted after him:

"Don't come back here till your whoring mother can speak to her neighbors in a civil way, understand?"

Phillipe stumbled on, the sharp north wind stinging his cheeks. His whole body throbbed. He considered it an accomplishment just to stay on his feet.

V

EXHAUSTED AND ashamed of his inability to hold his own against Auguste and his cousin, Phillipe stumbled back to the inn along the lonely, wind-raked road. His sense of humiliation made him steal past the tavern perched on the hillside— he was grateful no one was looking out to see him—and seek the sanctuary of the empty stable behind the main building.

Hand over bruised hand, he pulled himself up the ladder to the loft and burrowed into the old straw, letting the blessed dark blot out the pain—

"Phillipe? Phillipe, is that you?"

The voice pulled him from the depths of unconsciousness. He rolled over, blinking, and saw a white oval—a face. Beyond, he glimpsed misted stars through cracks in the timbers of the loft. Down on the stable floor, a lantern gleamed.

"Sweet Mother of the Lord, Phillipe! Madame Marie's been out of her mind all day, worrying about your unexplained absence!"

"Charlotte—" He could barely pronounce her name. His various aches, though not unbearable, remained more than a little bothersome. And waking up—remembering—was not a pleasant experience.

Charlotte climbed off the ladder and knelt beside him in the straw. He licked the inside of his mouth; it failed to help the dryness. Charlotte swayed a little, braced on her knees and palms. He thought he smelled wine on her. Probably filched from the inn's cellar—

And it seemed to him no accident that Charlotte's position revealed her bare breasts all white where her soiled blouse fell away. For a moment, he thought she was ready to giggle. Her eyes seemed to glow with a jolly, vulpine pleasure. But her touch of his cheek was solicitous.

"Oh, my dear, what happened to you?"

"I had an accident," he said in a raspy voice. "Fell, that's all."

"Down ten mountainsides, from the look of you! I don't believe it for a minute." The girl stroked his cheek again; he was uncomfortably aware of the lingering nature of her caress. Nor could he overlook the feel of her fingertips. She must have been in the kitchen. She hadn't wiped off all the lard.

"Who beat you, Phillipe? Brigands? Since when have poor boys become their game?"

"Not brigands—" Each word cost him energy. But he managed to sit up, groaning between clenched teeth. "Listen, Charlotte, never mind. I came back and wanted to sleep so I crawled in here."

She began to finger his arm. A light, suggestive tickling. Ye gods, was *that*

what she had on her mind? At a time like this? He was too stiff and sore, end to end, to be much excited.

But for her part, Charlotte was closing like a huntress.

"Poor Phillipe. Poor, dear Phillipe." He caught a flash of her white leg as she hitched up her skirt to descend the ladder again. "You need a little wine."

"No, honestly, I don't really—"

"Yes, wait, you just let me help you, Phillipe. I've some wine hidden in one of the horse stalls."

So she was stealing from the inn supplies, he thought, hardly caring. He had an impulse to totter down the ladder after her, and flee. But he didn't. Wine might not taste bad. Might help revive him—

Charlotte made rustling sounds in the stall below. Then Phillipe's eyes popped open—a second after the yellow light of the lantern went out. From the ladder, he heard a single delighted little syllable—

My God. She *was* giggling.

Feeling trapped, he started to roll over and rise to his knees. Aches exploded all over his body. He groaned and leaned back, trying to forget the humiliation and hatred the pain produced—the residue of the morning. Once more Charlotte uttered that strange, pleased sound as she maneuvered from the ladder to the loft.

This time, she didn't even try for grace as she tumbled out next to him— permitting him, in the process, an ample feel of her breasts against his forearm. She pressed the bottle into his hand and didn't take her own hand away. Because his cut lower lip had swollen, he still spoke thickly:

"How did you find me?"

"Well—"

She stretched out beside him with a cheerful little wriggle of her shoulders. She turned onto her side, facing him, so that his arm nestled between her breasts. He shifted his arm. She immediately moved closer. The wench was not sober, he realized with a sudden sense of confusion.

She ran her palm over his forehead, said abruptly, "Are you warm? You feel all icy."

"Yes, I'm warm. Very warm."

"That's a dreadful lie, your teeth are clicking!"

"My teeth are cold but I'm warm everywhere else. I asked you—"

"Drink some wine. That'll help."

She practically forced the mouth of the bottle to his lips. The inn's wine was poor and sourish. He coughed and spluttered getting it down. But when it reached his stomach, it did indeed warm him a little, and quickly.

Charlotte hitched her hip against him. Though he was conscious of aches in his belly and groin, he was suddenly conscious of something else. A reaction in his loins. Unexpected; startling. And—*God help me,* he thought with some panic— not entirely unpleasant.

But he still felt like some cornered fox.

"To answer your question," Charlotte explained in a whisper, "we don't have a single customer tonight. Not one! The worrying in the kitchen got so tiresome—your mother and Girard saying this happened, or that happened—I just got thoroughly sick of it and crept out here for a drink from the bottle I keep put away. Isn't that lucky?"

Her laugh this time was throaty. That alarming, exciting hand strayed to his collar, teasing his neck. He didn't even feel the lard residue because he was

feeling too much that was surprising elsewhere. *What in heaven's name was happening?*

He tried to sound gruff: "Who gets the rest of what you steal? Your family?"

"No, I drink it all! Drink it—and have the loveliest dreams of—a certain young man—"

"I don't believe that."

"The dreams? Oh, yes! They are lovely!" She leaned her head in closer so that her curls tickled his cheek, accelerating the peculiar transformations taking place in his body. "What a pity they stay dreams and nothing else—"

"I mean I don't believe you about the wine, Charlotte."

"Well, I do take *some* home." She brushed his cheek with her lips, the kiss a soft, quick, smacking sound. "You will keep my secret, won't you? Please?"

He answered with a confused monosyllable. But it seemed sufficient to make her happy—and even more interested in his welfare, or something else. She burrowed closer.

"Phillipe, you're freezing."

"No, sincerely, I'm p-p-perfectly—"

"You need more wine!"

His protest ended in a gulp as she forced it on him. The strong-smelling stuff ran down his chin. Gasping for air, he asked:

"Charlotte—you didn't finish—how did you find—?"

"Oh, yes, that: Well, when I came in, I heard you thrashing and muttering in your sleep. Are you still hurting so much?" One of her hands slipped across his hip. "Can you move at all?"

"Uh—yes, I can move. In fact I should go inside and—"

"Oh, no!" she cried softly, pushing his chest with both hands. "Not until the chill passes. If you go out in the air, you might catch a fever. You need more wine!"

This time he hardly resisted at all. The sour stuff tasted better by the moment. It was relaxing him—except in a certain critical area over which he no longer seemed to have any control, thanks to Charlotte's constant wriggling and stirring and pressing and touching. In the darkness, she seemed to be equipped with numerous extra hands, many more hands than were customary for a normally built human being. They were all over him. But after the first shock of fingers straying down his stomach and hesitating an instant, he got so caught up in this peculiar, half-fearful, half-exciting encounter that the torment of the beating quite vanished from his mind.

"My turn," she giggled, prying the bottle from his faintly trembling hand. She drank. Somehow the bottle slipped, thudded to the dirt floor of the stable.

"Oh dear," Charlotte sighed. "Whatever will we do to warm you now?"

"Charlotte, thank you, but I'm sufficiently warm—"

"No, your poor sweet hands are still like ice!"

She's tipsy, he thought. His head buzzed. She wasn't the only one.

"We *must* do something for your hands. A warm place—"

She seized them, pressed them between her breasts. He now felt his bruises hardly at all. But he felt the other sensations with mysterious and mounting ferocity.

"Goodness no, that's *still* not good enough! Oh, you'll think me too forward, but—in the interests of your health, you sweet boy—"

Giggle. Then she somehow got her skirt up—guided his hands to a place new and warm, furred and mind-numbing.

"Ah—better," she purred. His hands seemed to have absolutely no control because she was doing certain equally new and amazing things with them. All at once she kissed him on the ear. Strange heats burst inside him, little fires, as she tickled his earlobe with her tongue.

"Love warms the blood too, Phillipe, did you know that? Unless you hurt so much—"

"I ache, I was stoutly beaten, Charlotte. I don't think we—"

"Oh, don't tell me! You don't care for girls?"

"Actually, I haven't been thinking much about that tonight—"

"Well, *think!*" Another kiss on his ear. "You darling boy—you'll feel so much better afterward. I promise!"

And before he knew it, her mouth came down on his, and he tasted the wine on her tongue. In some miraculous, crazy way he no longer ached—from the blows, that is.

"Oh, I'm just *suffocating*," Charlotte gasped.

A moment later, with another of those mental explosions, he comprehended the bareness of her breasts against the hairs of his arm, not to mention her fingers at the waist of his breeches.

Then the breeches were gone. And the mystery unfolded itself at last in the eagerness of her body.

"Here, here, dear Phillipe. Here—no, not quite—there, that's better—oh, you *are* warmer. I can feel you're warmer already! Oh thank goodness, the treatment's working—!"

"God, yes," he croaked, and let every other consideration go except the heat of her mouth and the strange, wondrous rhythm that began from the almost unbearably pleasant joining of their bodies. Charlotte seized the back of his neck and held fast. Somewhere a door opened and closed.

The rhythm quickened. The girl's hands worked up and down his back. He could feel her broken, work-blunted nails. The scratching only made him breathe more and more frantically. Uncontrollable surgings began in the depths of him, then roared outward in what his addled mind crazily decided was a most consuming, astonishing and remarkable cure for bruises and bad memories.

VI

THEY DROWSED pleasurably, arms intertwined. Then, without any warning, light blazed below. He heard something kicked over—the blown-out lantern?

"Phillipe? *Charlotte?*"

Rousing, Phillipe made a noise. Charlotte tried to shush him. A moment later he heard his mother's voice ordering them down.

Feeling trapped, he pulled up his breeches hastily. Charlotte was going, "Oh! Oh!" softly, fearfully. He touched her hand to reassure her. But her eyes looked stricken, her cheeks dead white in the glow of the other lantern at the foot of the ladder.

Phillipe climbed down first. He stepped off the bottom rung and groaned. The pain was back.

Charlotte joined him, smoothing her skirt, which appeared to be on sideways; the tie straggled down her left hip. Obviously terrified of the glaring woman with the lantern, she began, "Please, Madame Charboneau, let me say—"

"Be quiet, you little slut."

Charlotte started to cry. Phillipe's mother lifted the lantern higher, fixing her eyes on her son.

"My God, did you get caught in a rock slide? Or did she rake you like that?"

Marie Charboneau was a handsome woman with a wide mouth, a fine aristocratic nose, and the dark hair and eyes of Auvergne that her son had inherited. As Charlotte continued sniffling, Marie addressed her quietly:

"Go inside and tell Girard he's to give you wages for the week. And escort you home tonight. Don't come back."

"I'm not good enough for Phillipe, is that it?" the sobbing girl burst out. "What a noble attitude for a woman like you! A woman who can't even get past a church door because—"

Marie's slap was swift and vicious. Charlotte cried out and stumbled back, terrified, one hand at her cheek.

"You will leave," Marie said.

"Look, Mama, that's not fair," Phillipe said. "She was only trying to comfort me because I'd been in a fight—"

But even as he spoke, a shadow flitted past him; and Charlotte was gone. Crying or cursing, he couldn't tell which.

Marie Charboneau studied her son.

"Is this the first time with her?"

"Yes."

"With anyone?"

"Yes. For God's sake, Mama, I'm seventeen! There's no crime in—"

"Who beat you?" Marie interrupted.

As matter-of-factly as he could, but omitting all reference to the slurs against her, he explained. Then he looked straight into her eyes.

"I want to know why they call me a little lord. I've heard it before—and always with a sneer. I want to know what's wrong with a girl like Charlotte. She was kind, I was hurting, she brought me wine—"

"To trap you," Marie said.

"That's no explanation. What if I said I wanted to marry Charlotte? Boys in Auvergne are sometimes fathers at fourteen!"

Marie replied, "Phillipe, you will come inside. There are things I must tell you now, before you mire yourself in trouble and error."

Turning, her lantern held high and her step somehow assured, she walked out of the stable. In a turmoil, he followed her—to learn whatever secrets she had at last decided to reveal.

2
Behind the Madonna

"I WANT to tell you of your father," said Marie Charboneau, in the stillness of the large, sparsely furnished room she occupied at the head of the stairs. She kept the room spotless. Or rather insisted that Charlotte do so, in the hope that an

overflow of guests might require its rental. That happened perhaps once a year. In a good year.

Phillipe thought briefly of Charlotte; she was gone now, with Girard. He recalled the indescribable sensations of their coupling; swallowed, his cheeks warm.

His mother was obviously awaiting his response to her statement. He perched on a little stool at the foot of her high bed, tried a small smile.

"I always assumed I had one, Mama."

Marie did not smile in return. More soberly, Phillipe continued, "I imagined he might have been English, too, since you speak so highly of that country. But I don't know how a French woman could meet a man from a land that's always been our foe."

She stepped toward a dark corner where the glow of the single candle burning on her washstand barely penetrated. In that corner were clustered the room's only ornamentations. On the wall, two small, crudely done miniatures of an elderly, fierce-eyed man—his grandfather, Paul Charboneau—and his grandmother, a tiny woman, Marie had told him once. But even at the age at which she had been painted, the woman possessed that dark, lustrous hair that her daughter, and her grandson, had inherited. The portraits had been done by an itinerant artist who could only afford bed and board by bartering a few days of his time and mediocre talent.

Just beyond the miniatures was an oversized niche containing a Madonna and two small votive lights in amber glass. Although his mother had long ago been barred from Holy Church by her choice of profession, the statue had occupied its place in her room for as long as Phillipe could remember. He had never seen her praying before it, however.

Now she moved the Madonna aside. From the darkness behind, she lifted a small, leather-bound casket with nailed corner pieces of mellow yellowing brass.

"It was not difficult for me to meet an Englishman when I was twenty, and playing Moliere on the Rue des Fosses-St. Germain." He kept staring at the cracking leather of the casket as she went on, "Do you recall the coach that stopped here in August?"

He certainly did. "Four very elegant and nasty English. Gold thread on their coats. Powder in their hair. And all of them not more than a year or two older than I am. But each one had two servants of his own—and they were almost as foul-mouthed as their masters. I'd have hit a couple of them for the way they talked about Charl—things here, except they were spending a lot. Girard and I spoke about them afterward. How they ordered everyone about as if it were their right. Girard said that before many more years go by, the nobility will no longer be allowed to behave that way."

Annoyed, his mother sat near the foot of the bed and leaned toward him. "Girard is engaged to teach you mathematics and English speech—"

"I know both tolerably well already."

"—*not* to fill your mind with his radical rot. Those young gentlemen are of a class to which you will belong one day." As if to emphasize the point, she set the casket firmly on the duck-feather comforter. Then her features softened a little.

"Besides, not all men of noble birth are as ill-mannered as those four. But do you know why their coach stopped here for the night? Where they were bound?"

"Over the Alps to Rome, I heard them boasting."

"On the island of Britain, it is the custom for wealthy and titled young men

to take what's called the Grand Tour after finishing their university education. They visit Paris, Berlin, Rome—the great capitals. The museums, the theaters. That was how I met your father. In Paris, when I was twenty and he was just a year older. He came to the Comedie-Française, where I was playing. He didn't watch from the pit, with the drunken fops who baited the players loudly while soldiers stood by, their bayonets ready in case of a riot. Your father sat in one of the rows provided for the gentry right on stage. He didn't jeer or joke or indulge in the kind of nasty games that enraged too many of our hot-tempered company and got them clapped in prison at For-l'Eveque, courtesy of the Chamber of Police.

"When I withstood the rage of my father—your grandfather—at age nineteen, and went to Paris, and apprenticed to a company, I knew that play-actors were not considered persons with rights. I knew the risks. Jail at the pleasure of any drunken duke in the audience, who could hurl the vilest insults without reprisal but call for the arrest of any hapless actor goaded into answering with a taunt in kind. I also knew about the immediate barring from the Church—"

Her tone had grown bitter. Outside, the night wind began to creak the eaves, a melancholy sound.

"I cared about none of that because I'd had enough of this place. I felt that to stay here would be to waste my life. Despite the perils—the low status of men and women of the theater—I was convinced that in Paris I had a chance at something better. I went to jail twice myself for refusing to let ugly fools with titles sleep with me at their pleasure—did I ever mention that?"

Held fascinated by this tunneling back toward his own dimly perceived beginnings, Phillipe could only shake his head. Marie spoke again:

"But then came that glorious night when your father visited the playhouse and sat on the stage, watching me. I ruined half my lines because he was so handsome and seemed to look at no one else. At that moment, I knew again that the filthy jails, the scorn of the priests, my father's anger and my mother's broken heart were all worth it. He was on the Grand Tour, you see. More than seventeen years ago—and one year before the great war started. Before France and England began brawling all over Europe, and in the Americas too. I think I fell in love with your father on sight. He remained in Paris for nearly two months while the rest of his friends went on to Rome. It was the happiest time of my life. I wanted nothing more than to bear his child. And I did. I bore you."

"What—what was his name, Mama?"

"*Is*, Phillipe. His name is James Amberly. His title is sixth Duke of Kentland. It's because of him that you must not throw yourself after cheap little strumpets like Charlotte. Noblemen's children—even bastard sons—can marry well, if they've the money. Your father is alive today, in England. He cares about you. He writes me letters inquiring after your welfare. That's why I have prepared you to speak his language far better than I ever learned to. I believe he'll want to see you someday. And you must be ready. Because, Phillipe—"

Marie's roughened hands, perhaps soft long ago when they flitted a stage fan in Paris, clasped tightly around the leather casket. She lifted it like some kind of offering.

"You father intends for you to inherit a substantial part of his fortune."

II

OUTSIDE, THE wind groaned louder around the inn. Phillipe walked to the window, unprepared for all he'd heard, and shaken to the center of his being.

He pushed the shutter out and hunted for stars, for any sign of the world remaining stable. But the northern wind had brought heavy mist rolling down. The stars were gone. Cold dampness touched his face.

He turned back to Marie. She slumped a little, as if at last relieved of a burden.

"I thought," he said slowly, "that when boys like Auguste teased me—called me a little lord—it was only their stupid joking."

She shook her head. "I'm afraid I am reponsible for some of that. Now and then, when I'm feeling blue, I indulge myself in a glass too many in the village. Sometimes things slip. I don't think the fools around here have ever believed what I've hinted at, though. I'm sure they consider any comments about you just more of what they refer to as my 'airs.' "

"An English lord!" he exclaimed, unable to keep from clapping his hands. He wished Auguste could hear; how stupefied he'd look!

Phillipe rushed to the bed, sat close beside his mother, all eagerness. "You say his name's Amberly?"

"But the family title is Kentland. They own a splendid estate and have many important connections at the court of George III. Your father served in the military when the war broke out in fifty-four. He rode at the great battle of Minden in fifty-nine."

Phillipe nodded. He'd heard of Minden, one of the historic clashes between the alliance of France and Austria on one hand, and Prussia, Hanover and Britain on the other. Marie continued:

"But for all that, Phillipe, he was—and is—a mild man. Kindly. At Minden he took a saber in the side. A bad wound. It happened when the men in his unit, the Tenth Dragoons, charged of their own accord after their cowardly commander, Lord Sack-something, refused to commit his horsemen to the battle even though he'd been ordered three times. After the battle, your father was forced to return to England. His letters say the wound still troubles him."

"Is he married? I mean—he never married you, did he? Even secretly?"

She shook her head. "Both of us understood, during those two months in Paris, that it wouldn't be possible. In fact, he didn't so much as kiss me till he'd explained that he could never marry any woman except the one already chosen for him. I didn't care. I was full of the joy of being with him. And despite the reputation of actors as willful children who never grow up, I understood the realities very well. I came from nothing. From the dirt of Auvergne. And in the eyes of the magistrates and the prelates, I was no better than a street harlot. So what chance had I for marriage? As I say—it didn't matter. Your father, being a decent man, is dutiful to his wife. But he has always cared for me in a special way—"

Slowly, then, she opened the casket.

By the dim glow of the candle, Phillipe saw ribbon-tied letters. Written in French. Marie pulled one from the packet.

"I will not show you all of them. But this one's important. It's the only reason I came back to this hateful place after Paris. To wait. To raise you properly—"

She dropped the finely inked parchment into her lap amd seized his shoulders, her black eyes brimming with tears that mingled sorrow and happiness.

"I tell you again—it is no shame to be a nobleman's bastard. Your father loves you like any son. And this very letter is the proof!"

III

THEY TALKED almost until morning. Marie's revelations helped Phillipe to understand various matters that had been puzzles before: her fury over a possible liaison with Charlotte, her haughtiness toward others up and down the valley.

He had long imagined that he might have been fathered by some foreigner—perhaps even a runaway soldier who'd somehow happened along during the turmoil of the Seven Years' War. But an English lord! She had every right to put on airs! And no wonder she never reprimanded him for his occasional unconscious swaggering.

As she filled in details of the story during the long hours before dawn, Marie made it clear that she had loved this James Amberly, Lord Kentland, freely, completely—but with no claim on him. Phillipe realized the depth of that love when she told him that, after Amberly's departure from Paris, she had made a conscious decision to return to Auvergne even though she suspected she was already pregnant.

"I knew I would have a son," she said. "I knew—and I came back to this dismal place for that child's sake. You see, James promised me that he would acknowledge our child at the proper time, in order to leave him a portion of his inheritance. So I returned and made peace with my father as best I could—"

She gestured in a sad way, pointing to the cracked miniature of the old man hanging near the niche.

"A week after you were born, I wrote—in French, which of course your father reads well—that his son had come into the world. Since then, he has sent money faithfully each year."

"Money?" Phillipe repeated thunderstruck. "For me?"

"For us. The equivalent of ten sterling pounds. A handsome sum these days. Enough to let us get along even when no coaches roll through for days at a time. Enough to enable me to hire a tutor when I could find one. Girard was heaven-sent."

"So the reason for the English lessons is to help me when I eventually meet my father?"

"Yes. It may be many years before that happens. I may be long buried. But this will guarantee that it happens. This will carry you out of this accursed land for the rest of your life."

She lifted the letter again, carefully unfolding the crackling parchment so that he could read.

The letter was dated in December of 1754, one year after his birth.

> *My beloved Marie,*
>
> *I have spent a substantial sum to ensure that the courier bearing this missive reaches you despite the outbreak of hostilities. This is the letter which I promised you in Paris, and it is dispatched with all my faith and devotion. I rejoice in the birth of our son, whom you have named Phillipe. I wish to send you my*

*assurances concerning his future long before this. But, in candor,
my wife encountered difficulties, and indeed nearly perished, in ˅
the delivering of our newly born son, Roger.*

Phillipe glanced up, frowning. "He has another boy? Born after I was?"
"Of course. The hereditary title must be continued. Read the rest."

*Because of the aforementioned difficulties, the learned physi-
cians inform me that my wife shall never again in her lifetime be
able to accomplish woman's natural role. This makes it all the
more imperative, my dearest, that I fulfill my pledge to you. By
the witnessing below, this letter becomes a legal document. My
two friends have signed in confidence, thus testifying that my
natural son Phillipe is hereby acknowledged by me, and, upon my
death, shall receive, in accordance with the laws of the realm, an
equal share in my estate, save for Kentland itself—*

Again Phillipe's dark head bobbed up. "Kentland?"
"That is also the name of the family residence. Go on, finish and I'll tell you
the rest."

*—which, by custom, must pass to my legitimate son's eldest
male issue. I declare in sight of Almighty God and the presence of
my two worthy friends, who shall add their names below mine,
that this is my true and irrevocable intent, the whole declaration
being freely made by my own choice. Because, dearest Marie,
even though I cannot honorably write the details of it here, you
are fully aware of the lifelong devotion of him who shall remain*

> *Ever yours,*
> *Jas. Amberly*
> *Duke of Kentland*

Below the signature appeared two other, unfamiliar ones. Phillipe stared at his
father's name for a long moment. Then, exhilarated, he jumped up. In his haste
he brushed the parchment against the bedpost. A corner of the brittle letter broke
away, making his mother exclaim:
"Be careful with it!"
She seized the letter with urgency, yet with delicacy too, and began to re-fold
it along the old creases.
"This is your passage to freedom and position, Phillipe. As you read, the
woman he married could bear no more than one child—the son he named Roger.
You've half you father's wealth. Half!"
Carefully, she slipped the letter back into the ribboned packet, returned the
packet to the casket, the casket to the Madonna's niche. She straightened the
statue so that it once more concealed the box.
"Now," she said, "let me explain how it's possible for that half to be yours."
Briefly, she outlined her knowledge of English inheritance law, which she had
made it her business to learn.

Lord Kentland, she told him, could not will his title to a bastard. Nor could his home, his landed properties go to any save the eldest son of his son Roger, who was thus prevented from disposing of same and squandering the proceeds while he lived. By means of intricate legal arrangements, Roger, in effect, would become the lifetime tenant of the estate, unable to sell or mortgage it except by means of a troublesome and costly procedure involving special dispensation from the English Parliament. In this way, great family land holdings, were preserved.

"The remainder of your father's wealth," Marie continued, "principally money—of which he has a great deal—is divided in equal shares between his children. You see what that means? Thanks to his letter, you are acknowledged. There is only one other heir—and so half the money automatically falls to you. Believe me, you will be a rich man. The finest drawing rooms will be open to you. Not to mention a choice of wives! Perhaps you can marry in England. A titled lady might not have you. But a prosperous merchant's daughter is another case entirely. Your father has written that the mercantile classes are coming into great power in their own right. What father of a girl who stood to inherit—oh, say a tannery—wouldn't relish the addition of half a duke's income?"

Phillipe turned cold at the last remark. Perhaps it was the lateness of the hour. Or his increasing weariness. But he sounded quarrelsome when he said:

"Mama, I've no wish to marry some woman just because her father owns a leatherworks!"

That angered her. "An example, nothing else! Do you miss my point altogether? I have given my life—all of my life; here in this place I despise—so that you might go where you want in the world. Away from Auvergne. To walk among gentlemen of wealth, and be one yourself! I don't care who you take up with so long as it's a woman who is your equal. Since you will be a person of station in your own right, your marriage must advance your fortunes even further."

He rebelled against the callous way she put forth the idea. But he kept silent this time, because her eyes were so intense. She gripped his shoulders hard.

"Remember this above everything, Phillipe. The greatest crime a human being can commit is to allow himself to be humbled into poverty, into obscurity, into—" She let go of his arm, swept the room with a gesture at once damning and sad. "This. I committed that crime so that you will never need to. Swear that you won't, Phillipe. Swear!"

He seemed to be staring at a woman he did not know. A woman of agate eyes, a woman full of grief and hatred. He was afraid of her.

"Yes. I swear."

At once, she softened, hugging him to her breast. "Then it's time we slept, my little lord. It has a good sound, doesn't it? And now you know it's the truth."

Motherly again, she comforted him as she led him toward the door.

"I suppose I should have told you years ago, but I saw no reason. As I said, you may well wait a very long time until James Amberly dies. But you won't wait in vain. That's why you mustn't squander your future by entangling yourself with a penniless peasant girl. Perhaps I acted in haste, sending Charlotte away. But it's done and I feel better for it. Go to sleep now. Only don't forget the oath you swore."

As if he ever could!

He lay in the garret with gray light already beginning to break outside, his dazzled mind playing with details of the story as if they were wondrous toys. In imagination he saw himself dressed in a gold-frogged waistcoat, a splendid,

beautiful lady on his arm. They were passing through a crowded street, receiving the cheer of a crowd. He recognized a face—Auguste—and spat on his boots. Auguste did not dare to react.

He finally drifted to sleep thinking of what his mother had described as the greatest crime a human being can commit. For him, Marie Charboneau had committed that crime.

For her, he never would.

___IV

"So," REMARKED Girard, picking his teeth, "now you know. The scholar is not a noble humanitarian but has remained here these four years because he's been paid. Actually it hasn't been a bad bargain. I am basically out of step with the world. I study the wrong things—and frequently believe them! If I loafed around Paris, for example, I'd probably wind up drinking too much, proclaim my libertarian views—and get clapped in prison for it. Or worse. I've told you how Master Jean Jacques has been hounded from country to country—and he has an international reputation! Important friends, like Diderot. Imagine how a common fellow like me would be treated!"

Girard and his pupil sat at the top of the rock escarpment overlooking the inn and the winding road. Several days had passed since the revelations in Marie's room. She had obviously communicated the fact of the talk to Girard. He had behaved in a somewhat more relaxed way ever since.

It was a stunningly bright morning, all the mist burned from the tumbled hills. But Phillipe still felt winter's bite in the stiff wind. The backs of his hands were numb from gripping the little book they'd been studying, the play about the misadventures of a Scottish king called Macbeth. At his feet, shielded from the wind by his boots, were Girard's three precious volumes. Phillipe had carefully smuggled them from the garret up to the site of instruction, in the hope that Girard would be willing to amplify some of the puzzling ideas the books contained.

But for the past hour, the tutor had insisted on fulfilling his regular obligation to Marie. Phillipe had read aloud from the play while Girard corrected his pronunciation of the familiar words.

"Don't ask me about the unfamiliar ones—sweet William's Eizabethan cant. How should I know what *that* means? The play's an antique. And fashions change, in everything from metaphors to monarchies."

"Yes, but it's still English."

"And truthfully, you don't speak it badly after four years of practice—though I admit that for the first two, I just about gave up. Today, however, if you crossed the Channel, they'd recognize you for a foreigner. But you could communicate well."

At the lesson's conclusion, Phillipe asked, "Have you ever been to England, Girard?"

"Yes. I prefer not to discuss the circumstances."

Phillipe pointed to the topmost volume stacked behind his heels. "Is that where you found this book by Monsieur Locke?"

"No, I purchased that in Paris. But visiting Monsieur Locke's homeland was, at least in part, almost like a holy pilgrimage." The bright blue eyes gleamed

with mirth. "Provided an unholy chap like myself is permitted such an experience. You mentioned a day or two ago that you had some questions about
Locke—?"

Phillipe sighed. "I've forgotten half of them already. His English is hard for
me to follow. Too deep. I read some passages two and three times before I got
the notion that he didn't believe kings ruled by God's will."

"And so they don't. Among men who gave death blows to the theory of a
king's divine right to hold a throne, Locke was one of the foremost. If you'll
study him a little more closely, you'll discover he actually put forth one of the
ideas for which Monsieur Rousseau is receiving much credit."

"You mean that business about some kind of contract?"

Girard nodded, turning the tip of his boot toward the stack where gold letters
stamped on the binding of a slim volume spelled out *Le Contract social.*

"Locke actually espoused the contract theory as part of his justification of
constitutional monarchy. Stated that a king's role was one of steward, not tyrant—and that the ultimate test of a government was whether the subjects were
happy and prosperous. If so, the ruler should be obeyed. If not, he should be
booted out."

"So the best kind of king is one of those"—Phillipe fumbled for the term—
"enlightened what?"

"Despots. Enlightened despots. Yes, that's a popular theory. But even those
who give it credence do so with reservations. Here, pass me *L'Encyclopedie.*"

Phillipe did, and Girard leafed through until he found the passage he wanted.
He showed Phillipe the page.

"Have you read this?"

"No."

"Well, Monsieur Diderot is no flame-eyed revolutionary. Yet he recognizes
the dangers inherent in having a hereditary king—even a good one. Pay attention—"

Girard cleared his throat, began quoting from the page:

" 'It has sometimes been said that the happiest government was that of the just
and enlightened despot. It is a very reckless assertion. It could easily happen that
the will of this absolute master was in contradiction with the will of his subjects.
Then, despite all his justice and all his enlightenment, he would be wrong to
deprive them of their rights even in their own interests.' "

Phillipe shook his head. "But if there are to be no kings at all, who does have
the authority in this world?"

Quickly Girard flipped pages. "This is Diderot too. 'There is no true sovereign, there can be no true legislator, but the people.' "

"You mean kings rule by their consent."

"By *our* consent. Who are the people if not you and me and even poor,
love-crazed Mademoiselle Charl—come, don't pull such a face! Is it really such
an astonishing idea?"

"Yes. I can see it leading to all sorts of trouble. Fighting—"

"And why not?" Girard exclaimed. "Once, man swallowed every opinion or
order that was handed him—" The scholar spat. "So much for the age of faith.
Then, slowly, and with greater acceleration in the last hundred years, man began
to perceive the power of his own reason. His power to ask *why*. To find logical
answers in every area of human endeavor. Once unleashed, such a force can't be
halted. I venture to say that by the time your titled father passes to whatever waits
on the other side of the grave—oblivion, is my opinion—the world may be

radically changed, thanks in part to these fellows—our mad Jean Jacques most of all.''

Pointing to the gold-stamped book, Phillipe said, "But honestly, a lot of that seems just gibberish.''

"That must be overlooked! Rousseau has fired the world's imagination. Who can say why some writers can, and others can't? But he has! I understand he's very popular on the other side of the Atlantic, for instance. I agree, a lot of his notions are drivel. Or rehashes of what others have said before. Yet from time to time, he puts down with masterful precision some of the most astute statements on the subject of government and men's freedoms I have ever encountered.''

Phillipe squinted into the bright wind, his thoughts, and hence his words, coming slowly:

"It seems to me he doesn't like *any* kind of government.''

"Quite true. He considers them all evil and unnatural. He recognizes, however, that unlimited freedom, no matter how desirable, simply won't work. So, he compromises.''

"The contract idea again?''

"Yes, but carried even further. Here, the book—''

The man's obvious delight made Phillipe smile; Girard was like an infant with a shiny new play-bauble as he hurried through *Le Contract social*, hunting the section he wanted. Turning pages, he explained:

"Master Jean Jacques actually distilled much of the political thinking of the past hundred years. He states that not only does no man in a government hold power by personal right, but that he has no authority independent of those he governs. Ah, yes—''

He read:

" 'I have demonstrated that the depositories of the executive power are not the masters of the people, but its officers. That the people may establish or remove them as it pleases. That for these officers there is no question of contracting, but only of obeying. That in undertaking the functions which the state imposes on them, they only fulfill their duty as citizens, with no right of any kind to dispute the terms—' ''

Phillipe whistled. "No wonder he's notorious.''

With a shrug, Girard closed the book. "I repeat, much of the man's work strikes me as idiotic. His novels especially. Silly romantic fancies! But on politics—ah, on politics—!'' He kissed the tips of his fingers.

"I'm still surprised he hasn't been arrested,'' Phillipe said.

"Well, for one thing, the time's right for his ideas. More and more people are coming to realize that we are all born in a natural state of freedom—and that power is therefore *not* something which descends in selective rays of light from heaven, to touch only a few of the especially appointed. Such as our good King Louis XV up in Paris—'' Girard grimaced. "Or the Hanoverian farmer who holds the throne of England. *They* don't care for the notion that power and authority are the results of contracts between the people and the rulers—or that the people may break those contracts at any time.''

Mock-serious, he tucked the Rousseau work into his capacious side pocket. "Oh, it's dangerous stuff.''

"I wonder.''

"What?"

"Maybe it's just a lot of words. Soap bubbles—''

Girard started to sputter. Phillipe continued quickly:

"I mean—one of the things I really wanted to ask you was—has any of this actually changed anything?"

"*Changed* anything!" Girard rolled his eyes. "My dear pupil! It's stirring new winds all over the world. Have you ever heard travelers at the inn mention the former British Prime Minister? Monsieur Pitt?"

"Yes. With curses, mostly."

"Of course! The Great Commoner, as his people affectionately called him, directed England's effort in the late, unlamented Seven Years' War—and stole most of France's territory in the New World in the bargain. A few years ago, the ministers of King George attempted to levy various niggling taxes—in such forms as an official stamp on all legal documents, for example. These taxes were to be levied only in Britain's colonies in America. And Pitt himself—already an earl—actually stood up in Parliament and challenged the king's right to enact such a tax! He proclaimed injustice being done to England's sons across the water. And he helped get the stamp tax repealed! How's that for being a steward of the people? At the same time, there was an Irishman in Parliament—a Colonel Barre, if I recall. He likewise praised the colonists for refusing to pay the taxes because they had no representation in London. He termed the contentious Americans 'sons of liberty.' Don't tell your mother, but I like that touch. Phillipe, do you realize that a hundred years ago, both of those spokesmen for ordinary people might well have had their heads on the block?"

"I'll take your word for it."

Smiling briefly, the tutor went on. "It amounts to this. *Because* of books like the ones you've been struggling to understand, there's a test of wills coming in the world. The people against the rulers. It's reached England already. It will reach France one day."

"Well," said Phillipe, a little smugly, "my mother—and father—chose the side I'm to be on, I guess."

Now it was Girard's turn to squint into the sunlight, unhappily. "For the sake of your future—and your mother's ambitions—I trust it is not the wrong one."

"Do you seriously think it could be?"

Girard stared at him. "Shall I answer as your paid tutor? The fellow hired only to instruct you from noncontroversial texts?"

"No," Phillipe answered, oddly chilled. "As yourself."

"Very well. Although this may be envy talking, I don't believe I'd be comfortable belonging to a titled family just now. As I suggested, the British have always loved their liberties a little more fiercely than most Europeans. And done relatively more to secure those liberties—at the expense of their kings and their nobility. When intellectuals such as our mad Master Jean Jacques thunder that contracts between governors and the governed may be broken by the will of the people, should the governors grow too autocratic—and when British statesmen stand up, question the propriety of laws written by a king's own ministers, and take the part of a king's defiant subjects—well, I shall only observe again that there are strong winds blowing. Who knows what they may sweep away? Or whom?"

Phillipe asked, "In a contest like that, Girard, which side would you be on?"

"Isn't it obvious? The side to which I was born. My father was a farmer in Brittany. He was stabbed to death by the saber of a French hussar when the hussar 'requisitioned' our only milk cow for his troops. In the name, and by the authority, of King Louis. My father refused, so he was killed. If it were in my

power, I would forever shatter the contract with a king who would permit that kind of murder."

Girard's expression had grown melancholy. What he had just revealed was the first—and last—bit of autobiography Phillipe Charboneau ever heard from the tutor. Now Girard went on:

"Yes, gentlemen such as Monsieur Rousseau are subtly nudging common folk to the realization that, together, they can simply say, *"We are finished with you!"* to any monarch who serves them ill."

"But I still can't imagine a thing like that would really happen."

"Why? Because you don't want to? Because it might spoil your splendid future?"

Irritated, Phillipe shot back, "Yes! Here, I've finished with your books."

Girard took the other two volumes, said quietly, "The point is, Phillipe, they haven't finished with you. Whether it pleases you or not." He sighed. "Ah, but let's not quarrel over words. When I started giving you these books months ago, I only meant to shed a little more light into a bright young mind—"

"And instead, you've got me thinking the world's going to be blown apart."

"Well, it's true. There are whispers of it—no, much more than whispers— from those same British colonies I mentioned. And the Commoner—and others in King George's own government—applaud! Doesn't that tell you *anything?"*

Phillipe overcame his annoyance, grinned. "It tells me I'm lucky I'm going to be rich. I'll have money enough to build a big house with safe, thick walls."

But Girard did not smile back.

"Since I am fond of you, Phillipe, let us devoutly hope there are walls wealth can build thick enough to withstand the winds that may rise to a gale before you're very much older."

3
Blood in the Snow

AT NOVEMBER'S end, word circulated in the neighborhood that old du Pleis the goatherd had died. His son, Auguste, disappeared. The hovel up the track was abandoned. And Phillipe was spared further encounters with his now-vanished enemy.

Since the beating, he hadn't gone back to the hillside terrace, walking instead the full three kilometers to Chavaniac to replenish the inn's supply of cheese. But each time, as he passed the point where the track turned upward from the road, he still felt an echo of the humiliation—and regret that he hadn't found a means to settle his score with the goatherd's boy.

He walked into the village with considerably more confidence now. His mother's revelations had given him that. He was even able to pass by the tiny Church of Saint-Roch without experiencing more than a touch of the old boyhood fear that the priest would suddenly appear and recognize him as the unredeemed child of the unredeemable actress.

He set out on one such trip to the village on an afternoon a couple of weeks

before Christmas. The first furious snowstorm of winter was howling out of the
north, driving white crystals into his eyes above the woolen scarf he'd tied over
his nose and mouth. He had wrapped rags around his hands and boots. But even
so, he quickly grew numb as he trudged through the already-drifted snow.

Yet in a curious way, he relished the unremitting fury of the wind. It reminded
him of the winds of which Girard had spoken. And of other, more fortuitous
gales: the winds of luck, of changing circumstance, that had suddenly plucked
him up and were hurling him toward a new kind of future. Fortune's wind might
be savage, he decided. But to be seized and swept along by it was much more
exciting than to live forever becalmed.

Leaning into the blizzard, he fought it like a physical enemy. He was determined to reach the village and return home in record time, just for the sake of
doing it. Concentrating on making speed, he was totally unprepared for an
unexpected sound.

He halted on the snowy road, listening. Had the wind played tricks?

No. He heard voices crying out.

One was thin; a boy's, perhaps. The others were lower. Harsh.

Directly ahead, he saw where the storm had not yet concealed the tracks of a
horse. The tracks led off to the right, into the great, black wind-tormented pines.
The thin voice sounded again—

From back in those trees!

Phillipe began to run.

Following the cries and the drifted horse tracks, he quickly passed into the
forest. Not much farther on, he spied a boy defending himself from two ragged
attackers.

The boy wore a long-skirted coat and a tricorn hat, the hat somehow staying
on his red head as he darted from side to side, fending off the lunges of the other
two by means of a sharp-pointed. lancelike weapon that looked all of seven feet
long. In the swirling snow beyond the struggle, a small, tethered sorrel horse
snorted and whinnied in alarm. Phillipe kept running.

"You little sod!" shouted one of the attackers. The boy had slashed the lance
tip from right to left and caught the stouter of the two brigands across the face.

The injured man reeled back, cursing. As he stumbled, he turned. Phillipe saw
him head on. Even with a mittened hand clasped to his gashed cheek and a
shabby fur hat cocked over his forehead, his face seemed to leap out at Phillipe
through the slanting snow.

Auguste

"Circle him, circle! Grab that damned thing!" the other attacker screamed.
Phillipe recognized the voice of cousin Bertram.

The boy—twelve or thirteen at the most—darted to his left, manipulating the
lance with trained grace. Bertram ran at him, a knife gripped in his right mitten.

"The hell with holding him for money!" Auguste yelled over the wind. "He's
ripped my face to pieces—do the same to him!"

And that was just what Bertram intended, it seemed, as Phillipe ran the last
yards to the clearing and shouted, "Here! Stop!"

The cry distracted the boy, whose clubbed red hair was the only patch of color
in the gray and white scene. Phillipe saw a face frightened yet determined. But
when the boy turned suddenly, he lost his footing.

While the boy slipped and slid, Bertram seized the lance shaft, wrenched it
from the boy's grasp and threw it away behind him.

Phillipe ducked as the lance struck pine boughs near his cheek, showering him

with snow. Bertram slashed over and down with the dagger. But the boy dove between his legs and the cut missed.

Then Phillipe looked at the closer of the two attackers. Auguste drew his mitten away from his bloody face, gaping. The three-inch wound below one startled eye glistened pink where the skin had been laid open. As he recognized Phillipe, his face grew even more ugly.

"You'd have been wiser not to answer his cries for help, little lord."

Blood spattered on the snow from the point of Auguste's chin. His red mitten fumbled at his waist, producing a dagger similar to the one Bertram kept stabbing at the intended victim. The boy's tricorn hat had finally fallen off as he jumped one way, then another like an acrobat, trying to avoid the slashes.

Hate and hurt in his dark eyes, Auguste charged. The knife was aimed at Phillipe's belly.

Phillipe had no time to think. He simply reacted, reaching for the nearest weapon—the lance fallen nearby. He thrust with both hands, hard.

Auguste screamed, unable to check his forward momentum. His run impaled him on the head of the lance. Phillipe let go, jumping backward as Auguste fell, raising powdery clouds of snow.

Blood spurted from all around the vibrating lance. The fabric of Auguste's coat had been driven into his wound. Bertram checked a lunge, goggling at his fallen cousin. Auguste writhed onto his side, staining the immaculate snow a bright scarlet.

"Christ preserve us," Bertram quavered. *"Cousin?"*

Then he glanced at Phillipe with raging yellow eyes. The red-haired boy ran to the little sorrel, opened a sheath and drew an immense pistol.

Bertram pointed at the unmoving body. "Murderer. *You killed him!"*

With audacity Phillipe could hardly believe the young boy showed Bertram the muzzle of his pistol.

"You'll find yourself in a similar condition if you're ever seen near Chavaniac again. My aunts told me Auguste du Pleis had taken to thievery after his father died. But I didn't asume that included snatching rabbit hunters."

Phillipe stared at unblinking hazel eyes in the freckled, young-old face. The boy's voice sounded assured. Though he was three or four years younger than Phillipe, and slightly built, he handled weapons—the lance and now the pistol—with perfect familiarity.

The boy took a step toward Bertram.

"Don't you understand me? Get away from here or I'll shoot you. I'm giving you a chance. Take it."

All at once Bertram read the lesson of the pistol's eye. A moment later he was gone, boots thudding away into the wind-bent pines. Then not even that sound remained.

Phillipe moved shakily toward Auguste. "Is he really—?"

"I'd say so," the boy interrupted, planting a boot on Auguste's neck. "An officer doesn't carry a spontoon into battle for show. They're killing instruments."

With no trace of emotion, the boy twisted the gory head of the lance until it came free of Auguste's belly. Then he indicated the pistol he'd thrust into his belt.

"It's lucky those two knew nothing of firearms. I couldn't have got a ball off in this damp. The powder would have flashed in the—here! Stop looking so nervous! I've scared the other one off. We won't see him again. And you killed

this one in my defense. Let's drag him deeper in the woods. When he's found next spring, not a person around here will know how he died—or care.''

Despite the boy's words, Phillipe had started to shake with reaction to the struggle. He had slain another human being. And apparently the red-haired boy was not the least upset.

The boy tossed the spontoon aside. He reached down for Auguste's collar, then glanced at Phillipe with a touch of irritation.

"Look, will you help me?"

Phillipe wiped snow from his eyelids. "Yes. Yes, I will. But—how old are you?"

"Thirteen, if that matters."

"You handle weaons like a soldier."

"Well, I've been up to Paris for two years now. I only came back for Christmas, to visit my aunts and my grandmother. In the city, I've been schooled in the use of swords and pistols by an old officer who's one of the best. De Margelay's his name. When spring comes, I'll be a cadet in the Black Musketeers."

Again that stare of annoyance when Phillipe didn't respond. "Surely you've heard of the regiment that guards King Louis!"

Phillipe shook his head. "I don't know about such things. My mother keeps an inn near here. The Three Goats."

"Ah! I've ridden by it."

"Why did those two attack you? Hope of ransom?"

"Undoubtedly. It's no secret that I return home for the holy days. I was searching so hard for rabbit tracks, they took me by complete surprise. But you won't be punished for killing this one. I can assure you of it. In fact, what happened makes us blood comrades. In the military, there's no stronger tie. Now come on, let's move him."

Phillipe's shock and fear were lessening moment by moment. He and the boy hid the body in a drift some distance from the clearing. The young soldier kicked snow over Auguste's ghastly face. Then he resettled his tricorn on his head and asked:

"Were you headed home?"

"No, to the village."

"Then mount Sirocco with me. Two can ride as easily as one. No objections, please—I insist!"

It struck Phillipe that the youth wasn't accustomed to having anyone go against his wishes. Remarkable. Especially for a thirteen-year-old. Without a word, he followed the red-haired boy back toward the stamping sorrel.

II

"THE CRIME was theirs, not yours," the boy shouted over the roar of the wind, while the sorrel pounded through the snow toward the village. "Any soldier has the right to kill his enemy in battle."

"I'll try to remember that," Phillipe yelled, hanging onto the boy's waist with one hand and gripping the spontoon across his shoulder with the other. But his mind still swam with ugly visions of Auguste bleeding.

Snow stung his face. Ahead, he discerned the first of the cottages at the end of Chavaniac's single winding street.

"I must get off soon," Phillipe cried. "I walked to town to buy cheeses for—wait! Slow down!"

But the boy nicked the sorrel's flank with a spur, and the horse bore them up the short cobbled street, soon leaving it behind. The boy turned the sorrel's head westward.

"Where are we going?" Phillipe demanded.

"To my home. It's just ahead. There'll be a warm fire, and some wine, and I can show you a trick or two with the lance. You've had no training in arms, have you?"

"None. My father was a soldier, though."

The remark came out unbidden as the sorrel plowed through drifts beneath the limbs of bare, creaking trees. All at once Phillipe knew where he was. But he didn't believe it.

"So was mine," the boy shouted in reply. "He fell at Minden in fifty-nine. Hit by a fragment of a ball from a British cannon. What was your father's regiment?"

"I can't remember." The sorrel bore them past the facade of an immense, blockhouse-like chateau at whose corners two towers rose. "He's no longer with our family, you see."

"Can you remember your own name?" the boy asked, amused.

"Phillipe Charboneau."

"You must call me Gil. The whole of my name is too tedious to pronounce."

"Tell me anyway."

"Marie Joseph Paul Yves Roch Gilbert du Motier. And since my father's death, Marquis de Lafayette. See, I warned you! Make it just Gil and Phillipe. Fellow soldiers," he finished, turning the sorrel into a spacious stable behind the chateau—

Which belonged to the Motier family. Richest in the neighborhood. Each hour, it seemed, the winds of fortune were blowing him in new and astonishing directions.

III

THE RELATIVELY calm air inside the dark, dung-smelling stable came as a relief. Gil nosed the sorrel into a stall and leaped fom the saddle. Then the young marquis took the spontoon from Phillipe's hand, knelt and began rubbing at some dried blood still visible on the head.

"As to the story we must tell," he said, never glancing up from the work, "you discovered me at the roadside. Floundering in the snow and hunting for Sirocco, who stumbled, fell, unhorsed me, then ran off. After some delay, and with your assistance, I finally located the animal."

Gil looked up. "Agreed?"

Held by the steadiness of those young-old hazel eyes, Phillipe murmured, "Agreed."

Light flared from the far end of the stable. An old groom with a lantern hobbled toward them. He spoke with a clicking of wood false teeth:

"So late home, my lord! How was the hunting?"

"Poor," Gill replied. "Except that I found a new comrade. Give Sirocco an extra ration of oats, please." He took Phillipe's elbow with perfect authority and

steered him out of the stable. They crossed the yard through the whipping snow, then entered the chateau, where new wonders awaited.

___IV

"I DON'T believe the tale for a minute," said Girard, much later that night. He was warming his stockinged feet at the fire in the common room. "You stole the cheeses, Phillipe."

"I tell you I didn't! His aunts gave them to me. Saint-Nectaire. The most expensive kind!"

With a flourish, he slapped coins down on the table. "Go on, count. You'll find every last sou I took with me."

Girard fingered the coins. "We thought you'd fallen victim to brigands. But it turns out that it was only a marquis."

Despite the teasing, Girard's blue eyes couldn't conceal a certain admiration. As for Marie, she was jubilant, using a cheese knife to slash through the wrapping cloth with almost sensual joy. She slipped a piece into her mouth, chewed, exclaimed:

"Saint-Nectaire it is! I had some only once before in my life. Phillipe, how did you get on with the marquis? Easily?"

"Yes, very. And I don't think he was being kind just because I helped save— save his horse. We're friends now. I'm to visit him again tomorrow. And as many times as I wish before he returns to Paris after the holidays. His mother died last spring, you know," Phillipe added with the slightly condescending tone of one privileged to reveal a bit of gossip. "In Paris, he's to be a cadet of the Black Musketeers."

They said nothing. With outright loftiness, he informed them, "The regiment which guards the king himself!"

Flash went the blade, deep into the cheese. Marie wielded the knife almost as if she were striking an old enemy.

"You see, Girard? They got along famously because my son was born to that sort of life. Blood tells! In the end, a man finds his rightful place."

Sampling a morsel of the cheese, Girard glanced at Phillipe. The latter was too excited by memories of the splendid chateau, the incredible gilt-decorated rooms, the kindly aunts, to notice the dismay in the eyes of the lank scholar.

___V

LONG AFTER the fire had gone out and they'd locked the inn for the night, Phillipe lay shivering, trying to sleep. He was kept from it by recurring memories of Auguste's blood staining the snow bright red.

Again and again, he recalled Gil's reassurances. Gradually, the worry about discovery—punishment—diminished. But he was still disturbed by one aspect of the personality of his new friend the Marquis de Lafayette: the casual way Gil took a life—and hid the deed.

Did the nobility consider another human life worthless when their own lives

were threatened? Did they dispose of their victims secure in the knowledge that their position would shield them from reprisals? Did his father, James Amberly, behave the same way? If so, Phillipe could well understand Girard's approval of rebellion against such high-handed actions.

Troubled, he drifted into chilly drowsiness. His mind turned to the things he might learn from Gil before the young marquis returned to Paris. On balance, perhaps the day had been more good than bad.

I must forget the dead boy the way Gil forgot him, he thought, close to sleep. *I must remember what is the greatest crime of all. That is the only crime I must never commit.*

▬ VI

IN THE days that followed, Phillipe—with his mother's blessing and encouragement—became almost a daily visitor at Chateau Chavaniac.

Gil's aunts and his feeble, elderly grandmother treated him with polite kindness. And there were so many exciting things to do, and see, and learn, that Phillipe never noticed how the aunts now and again glanced at one another; how they smiled in wordless amusement when Phillipe upset a wine glass or tramped across a luxurious carpet in snow-covered boots.

Gil proudly showed off his military uniform. It was scarlet and gold, with a blue mantel that bore a cross encircled by a ring of fire, the devices sewn in silver thread.

In the stable yard, where the snowbanks glared white in the winter sunlight, Gil demonstrated the rudiments of self-defense with a sword. Of course they didn't use real swords, only stout sticks. But Gil didn't seem to mind demonstrating thrusts and parries with the beginner's implements from which he'd graduated long ago.

Then, two days before the holiday commemorating the birth of Christ, Gil took Phillipe down to the frozen lagoon near the chateau. From oiled cloth, he unwrapped his most prized possession.

"My military tutor bought it in Paris, for my birthday," he explained. "They're damned hard to come by, you know."

He thrust the shimmering walnut-stocked musket into Phillipe's hands.

"It's the finest military weapon in the world. Brown Bess. See, even the barrel's brown. They treat the metal with a secret preservative."

The incredible gun was more than five feet long. Phillipe held it gingerly, awed, as Gil produced a cartridge box from his pocket and initiated his friend into the step-by-step ritual that preceded a shot.

"Most of King George's redcoats can load and fire in fifteen seconds," he commented. "That's why, militarily, the French hate Georgie *and* his muskets."

In less than an hour of teaching, Phillipe learned how to pour powder into the muzzle, drop in the ball and ramrod the crumpled paper which held the powder.

Next—lift the firing-pan frizzen. Bat the barrel with the heel of a hand, to send a little powder through the touchhole—

With the Brown Bess at his shoulder for the first shot, he nearly blundered. Gil cried out, "Don't keep your eyes open! In a bad wind you could go blind from a flareback from the touchhold. Just hold it tight, aim in the general direction you want to fire, shut your eyes and pull the trigger."

Phillipe followed instructions. The thunderous impact knocked him flat. A pine branch across the lagoon cracked and fell.

"Not bad at all," Gil nodded, smiling.

Phillipe stood up, dusting off snow and shaking his head. "Gil, I don't understand how a soldier can win a battle with his eyes closed."

"When a thousand British infantrymen close their eyes and fire together, they can destroy anything standing in front of them. If we had such muskets, we could rule the world. Lacking them, we've nearly lost it. Try another shot." He smiled across the sun-gleaming brown barrel. "You hold her as though born to it. Must be the blood of that soldier father of yours."

Phillipe smiled back, friendship and his secret both serving to warm the bitter day.

___ VII

BUT AS quickly as it had begun, the friendship ended with Gil's return to Paris.

The return was signalled on the eve of the New Year, 1771, by the *clop-clop* of a horse climbing to the inn door. Marie peeked out, clasped her hands, excitedly.

"God save us, Phillipe, it's your friend the marquis! And this place isn't even swept properly—*Girard!*"

Her cry brought the gangling man from the back of the inn, just as Gil entered, afternoon sunlight making his red hair shine beneath the tricorn hat.

Flustered, Marie curtsied. Girard sighed and began to swish the broom over the floor. Phillipe rushed forward to welcome his friend.

"I expected to see you later this afternoon at the chateau!"

"But my grandfather wants me back in Paris two days hence. The coach is departing in an hour. Here, I've brought you a gift. I've been saving it for the last day we spent together."

"My lord," said Marie, "may I offer you a little wine?" Phillipe winced. Her expression was almost fawning.

Gil waved the offer aside courteously. "Thank you, no. I must ride back almost immediately. There's only time enough to present this to Phillipe."

He held out a long, slender package wrapped in oiled cloth.

"In token of our friendship. Perhaps you'll find it more enjoyable to practice with than a stick."

Touched, Phillipe laid the parcel on one of the scarred tables, carefully undid the wrapping. A bar of winter light falling between the shutters lit the slightly curved steel of the blade, the warm brass of the cast hilt.

"Dear Lord, what a beautiful sword!" Marie breathed.

Phillipe could only agree. The hilt had a bird's-head pommel and a single knuckle-bow and quillon. The grip was ribbed. Picking up the amazing gift, Phillipe discovered a second, separately wrapped parcel beneath it. Even Girard expressed admiration for its contents: a scabbard of rich leather, tipped and throated in brass.

"There's a staple and strap for carrying it," Gil pointed out, obviously enjoying his role of benefactor. "Now you have a *briquet* like any good French grenadier."

"I don't deserve such a splendid present, Gil."

"But you do! I think you have the natural abilities of a fighting man, should you choose to develop them."

"But—I have nothing to give you in return."

The hazel eyes seemed to brighten a moment. Gil's reply, though seemingly casual, communicated clearly.

"You have given me a great deal, Phillipe. Companionship during what would otherwise have been a typically dull visit with my dear aunts and grandmother. And the pleasure of teaching some fundamentals to an apt pupil. Now I must go back to being the pupil"

"I hope to have the honor to meet you in Paris one day," Phillipe said.

"If not Paris, then somewhere, I have a feeling. A battlefield? Well, who can say? But comrades in arms always keep encountering one another. That's a truth old soldiers know with certainty."

With a last, piercing look—the renewed swearing of secrecy—he stepped forward and seized Phillipe in an embrace. It was affectionate, yet correct. It left the older boy with tears in his eyes.

"God grant His favor to you all," Gil said, waving as he departed. Outside, he mounted Sirocco and hammered away north through the snowdrifts toward Chavaniac.

"He embraced you like an equal!" Girard exclaimed.

"I told you my son's breeding was recognizable to any man with wits," Marie countered.

"But—comrades in arms? That's a peculiar term for a friendship between boys."

Phillipe closed his fingers around the ribbed hilt-grip of the shining sword. "It's because I helped him find the sorrel in that snowstorm. It's just his way of speaking. Everything in military terms."

"Um," was Girard's reply. Phillipe turned away from the blue eyes that had grown just a shade curious—and skeptical.

"Shut the door, it's freezing in here!" he said loudly.

To his astonishment, Girard did.

VIII

THE YEAR 1771 brought more of the buffetings of fortune—and this time, the winds were bitter ones.

As touches of green began to peep between the basalt slabs of the hillsides of Auvergne, a courier on horseback galloped to the inn. Refreshing himself with food and wine, he informed Marie Charboneau haughtily that he had been hired to ride all the way from Paris to this godforsaken province to deliver *this*—

He proffered a rolled pouch, ribboned and sealed with maroon wax. Into the wax, a sigil had been impressed.

Marie retired to the kitchen to open the pouch. Though he hadn't been told, Phillipe suspected the sigil belonged to his father. He guessed it from the way she touched the wax with faintly trembling fingers, then from the courier's remark about the pouch having been forwarded across the Channel.

Phillipe was busy hustling up more wine for the irritable messenger when Marie screamed his name, piercingly.

He found her white-faced beside the kitchen hearth. She pressed a letter into his hand. Written in French, he noted. But not in Amberly's masculine hand.

"It's from your father's wife," Marie whispered. "He's fallen ill. They fear for his life."

Phillipe read the brief letter, whose cold tone suggested that it had been penned by James Amberly's wife on demand of her husband. Phillipe's dark eyes grew somber by the time he'd finished.

"She says the old wound from Minden has poisoned his system."

"And he wants to see you. In case he di—"

But Marie could not speak the word. She rubbed fiercely at one eye, fighting tears.

All at once Phillipe noticed something else. A packet of notes lying on the trestle table. Franc notes. More than he'd ever seen in his life.

Suddenly Marie Charboneau was all composure, decision:

"The money is ample for our passage to Paris, then by ship to England. We'll leave immediately. Surely Girard will keep the inn for us—"

She rushed to her son, wrapped her arms around him, pulled him close.

"Oh, Phillipe, didn't I promise? I've lived for this moment!"

Then he felt the terrible tremors of the sobbing she could no longer control.

"But I don't want him to die. *I don't want him to die!*"

4
Kentland

THE COASTING vessel, a lugger out of Calais, slid into the harbor of Dover in bright April sunshine.

Phillipe gripped the rail, staring in awe at the white chalk cliffs rising behind the piers and the clutter of small Channel vessels anchored nearby. Gulls wheeled overhead, crying stridently. The air carried the salt tang to open water.

Phillipe had seen so many new sights and wonders in the past fortnight, he could hardly remember them all. Especially now. He felt a tinge of dread because he was entering his father's country both as a stranger and as a traditional enemy: a Frenchman.

Beyond that, Marie had not weathered the journey well. During the one night they had spent in the splendid, teeming city of Paris, she had been confined to her bed at a shabby inn on a side street. Phillipe had wanted to roam the great metropolis, see as much as possible before the coach departed for the seacoast. Instead, he'd sat the whole night on a stool beside the bed where Marie lay wracked with cramps and a fever.

Perhaps the cause was the strain of the trip. Or—the thought struck him for the first time that night in Paris—perhaps the hard years in Auvergne had drained away her health and vitality.

He saw further evidence that this might be true when the lugger put out from Calais. Complaining of dizziness, Marie went below. She vomited twice during the night crossing, much to the displeasure of the French crew, who provided a mop for Phillipe to clean up the mess personally.

He gave his most careful attention to the cheap second-hand trunk they'd

bought in Chavaniac before departure. He mopped it thoroughly, even though the work—and the smell—was sickening.

Marie lay in a cramped bunk, even more pale than when she'd received news of Amberly's illness. She alternately implored God to stop the churning of the waves—the Channel was rough that night—and expressed her shame and humiliation to her son.

He finished cleaning up the ancient trunk and stared at it a moment. The trunk contained what little they owned that was of any value. Save for the inn, of course. That had been left in the care of Girard.

Marie's few articles of good clothing were packed in the trunk. Her precious casket of letters. And Phillipe's sword.

Why he'd brought the weapon he could not fully explain. But somehow, he wanted it with him in the land of the enemy—

Now he leaned on the lugger rail, squinting up past the gulls to a strange, tall tower on the chalk cliff. His confidence of the preceding months was all but gone.

He saw figures bustling on the quays. Englishmen. Would his limited knowledge of their language serve him well enough? He and his mother still had a long way to travel to reach his father's bedside. No instructions had been provided in the letter written by Lady Jane Amberly. Perhaps that was deliberate. He looked again at the cliff tower, strangely forbidding, as the sails were hauled in and the lugger's master screamed obscene instructions to his crew scampering around the deck.

The mate, a man with a gold hoop in one ear, noted Phillipe's rapt expression and clapped a hand on the boy's shoulder. He said in French:

"Busy place, eh? You'll get accustomed to it. The captain would probably have my balls for saying this, but I don't find the English a bad sort. After all, there's a lot of old French blood running in the veins of these squires and farmers."

The mate then proceeded to point out some of the structures high on the cliff, including the Norman keep and the strange, tall tower. Of the latter he said:

"There were two Roman lighthouses up there long ago, not just the one. Their fires guided the galleys of the legions into the harbor. And Caesar's troops fathered plenty of bastards before they pulled out. So whatever your business in England, my lad, don't let the locals put you down. Their ancestors came from all over Europe and God knows where else. Besides, we're at peace with them. For the present."

As he started aft, he added, "I'll be glad to help you and your mother find the coach. Shame the sailing wracked her so. She's a handsome woman. I'd court her myself if I didn't have two wives already."

Phillipe laughed, feeling a little less apprehensive. He went below.

He found his mother sitting in the gloom beside the shabby trunk. Her white hands were knotted in her lap. He closed his own hand on top of hers. How cold her flesh felt!

"The mate said he'll assist us in finding the overland coach, Mama."

Marie said nothing, staring at nothing. Phillipe was alarmed again. Distantly, he heard the lugger's anchor splash into the water.

II

THE MATE led them up from the quay into town. He carried the trunk on his muscular shoulder as though it contained nothing at all. In the yard of a large, busy inn, he tried to decipher the English of a notice board that listed the departure times of various "flying waggons" bound for towns with unfamiliar names.

"Flying waggon is intended to be a compliment to the speed of the public coaches." The mate grinned. "But I understand that's nothing but the typical lie of any advertisement. Bah, I can't read the ungodly script! I'll ask inside. What's the name of the village you want?"

"Tonbridge," Phillipe said. "It's supposed to lie on a river west of here."

The man with the gold ear hoop disappeared, returning shortly to report that they wanted the coastal coach, via Folkestone, departing in midafternoon.

The mate kept them company while they waited, stating that he'd only squander money on unworthy, immoral pastimes if he went off by himself. He was a jolly, generous man, and even bought them lunch—dark bread and some ale—at a public house called The Cinque Ports.

Then he saw them aboard the imposing coach, whose driver kept yelling, "Diligence for Folkestone, m'lords. Express diligence, departing at once!"

The mate had helped them change some of their francs for British money. Now he picked the correct fare out of Phillipe's hand and paid the agent. He waved farewell as the diligence rolled out of the yard.

Five of the other six persons packed inside the coach chatted in English as the vehicle lurched westward. Phillipe and Marie sat hunched in one corner, saying nothing and trying to avoid stares of curiosity. Among the passengers was a cleric, who read his Testament in silence. But a fat, wigged gentleman in claret velvet talked enough for two men.

Apparently he had some connection with the weaving industry. He complained about the refusal of the "damned colonials" to import British goods—in protest against some of those taxes of which Girard had spoken, if Phillipe understood correctly.

"But damme, we've the King's Friends in power now!" the fat gentleman sputtered. "North shall bring those rebellious dogs to heel. Eh, what do you say?"

The merchant's mousy wife said she agreed. Oh yes, definitely. The fat man became all smiles and smugness. Dust boiled into the coach windows as it lurched along the rough but supposedly modern highway leading southwest along the coast.

III

THEY ARRIVED in Folkestone late at night, and Phillipe engaged a room. His English proved sufficient to the task, even though his pronunciation did elicit a momentary look of surprise.

The landlord treated his French guests with reasonable courtesy, however, and at dawn he helped Phillipe hoist the trunk into the luggage boot of another coach. Shortly after sunup, Marie and her son were bouncing northwestward, through a land most pleasant to gaze upon. Gentle downs, green with spring, unrolled

vistas of tiny villages set among hop fields and orchards whose pink and white blossoms sent a sweet smell into the coach. Marie even remarked on the welcome warmth of the sun.

Phillipe got up nerve to ask an elderly lady what the district was called. She replied with a smile, "Kent, sir. The land of cherries and apples and the prettiest girls in the Empire!"

Near the edge of a great forest called The Weald, the coach broke an axle. They lost four hours while the coach guard, leaving his blunderbuss with the driver for protection of the passengers, trudged to the nearest town. He returned with a replacement part and two young wheelwrights, who performed the repairs. Finally, on the night of Phillipe and Marie's third day in England, the coach rolled across a bridge into the village of Tonbridge, a small, quiet place in the valley of the Medway.

They found lodging upstairs at Wolfe's Triumph, an inn evidently renamed to honor the heroic general who had smashed the French at Quebec. In Auvergne, the general's name was jeered and cursed.

The inn's owner was a short, middle-aged man with protruding upper teeth. Phillipe went downstairs to find him late in the evening. Marie was already in bed. Not asleep, but unmoving. As if the trip had proved too great a strain.

A fragrant beech fire roared in the inn's inglenook. The spring night outside had grown chilly. A crowd of Tonbridge men packed the tables, drinking and gossiping about local happenings. Most of the men were fair, ruddy-faced, in sharp contrast to Phillipe's dark hair and eyes. But he was growing accustomed to drawing stares.

As Phillipe approached, the innkeeper turned from an ale cask. He handed two mugs to a plump serving girl, who switched her behind and smiled at Phillipe as she walked off.

"Well, young visitor," said the proprietor, "may I serve you something?"

"No, thank you. I am not thirsty." Phillipe was careful to speak each English word clearly. But the answer was a lie. He felt too insecure about the future to squander one precious coin.

"Too bad," said the older man. "I meant the first one to be a compliment of the house."

"Why—in that case, I'll accept. With thanks."

"That woman who arrived with you—is she your mother?"

Phillipe nodded.

"Is she quite well?"

"She's tired, that's all. We've come a long way."

"Across the Channel. You're French, aren't you?" The man drew a frothing mug from the cask, replacing the bung with a quick, deft movement, so that very little spilled. "Good English ale," he said, handing Phillipe the mug. "I don't hold with serving gin to younger folk. It's the ruination of thousands of little 'uns up in London."

Phillipe sipped, trying to hide his initial dislike of the amber brew. "Mmm. Very good. To answer your question—" He dashed foam off his lip with his sleeve. "I am French. But I have a relative who lives near here. My mother and I need to find his house so we may go see him."

"Well, sir, Mr. Fox knows most if not all of those in the neighborhood. What's the name of this relative?"

"Amberly."

At the nearby tables, conversation stopped. Eyes stared through the smoke

rising from clay pies held in suddenly rigid hands. A log fell in the great walk-in hearth.

Mr. Fox picked at a protruding upper tooth with one cracked nail. "Amberly, eh? Is that a fact?" Someone snickered.

The landlord surveyed Phillipe's shabby clothes. Then he asked: "You mean you have kinfolk serving the Amberlys, don't you?"

"No, sir. I'm related to the family itself. How far is their house from this town?"

"If you mean their estate, lad—only us ordinary folk live in measly houses—" Laughter in the room. "Not far. A mile up the river. The Duke lies ill, did you know that?"

"Yes. Is there someone I could pay to take a message saying we've come?"

"My boy Clarence, I suppose." Mr. Fox sounded both amused and skeptical. "But in the morning, eh?"

At the appointed time, Phillipe paid a ha'penny and waited. By noon, his hope was failing. But then Mr. Fox came clattering up the stairs to knock and announce:

"Clarence has returned! Lady Amberly is sending a cart for you and your mother at three this afternoon."

Mr. Fox was, without a doubt, dumbfounded.

___IV

THE CART clacked along the towpath beside the clear-running Medway. On the banks, green willows drooped their branches into the river. Phillipe and Marie sat in the cart's rear seat. They were dressed in their finest. And Phillipe was conscious of just how threadbare that was.

The elderly carter, by contrast, wore clothing far more elegant. Orange hose; a frogged coat of yellow velvet. Castoffs, perhaps. But rich garments nevertheless.

Shortly after they left the village, Marie asked, "Can you tell me anything of the Duke's illness?"

The old fellow hesitated. "Well, 'tis really Lady Jane's role to speak for conditions in the household. But I will say Dr. Bleeker's much in evidence. I understand he bleeds the Duke regular. The Duke's bedroom is kept dark. He's never seen out of it. A shame, a terrible shame!" the man exploded suddenly. "Him having so many friends at court, I mean, and being talked about for an assistant secretary's post, now that Lord North's prime minister. For days, we've been expecting His Lordship to call personally. We had no word of other visitors," he finished, pointedly.

No, Phillipe thought, *I'm sure my father's wife would not announce our unwelcome arrival too widely.*

The cart horse ambled around a green hillock. The driver volunteered another bit of information:

"There is much turmoil at Kentland, you must understand. Lady Jane engaged the famous Mr. Capability Brown to redo all the landscaping just before her husband fell ill. No matter how important you think your business may be, I'd advise you to make your visit brief."

Coloring, Marie started to retort. Seated beside her, Phillipe shook his head. The carter did not see the woman's mouth and eyes narrow down.

Hatred? Apprehension?

Or both?

But she accepted her son's guidance. He suddenly felt much older.

The carter jogged up the pony. The towpath curved around another hillock. Marie let out a soft cry.

Kentland overlooked the river Medway with serene authority. The old, yellow Tudor brick of the vast, two-story main house shone mellow in the sunshine. The house was situated at the center of a grassy parkland alive with scurrying figures. Men carrying small trees with the roots wrapped, or turning the earth with spades. Phillipe was awed by the immense, rambling place. He counted six outbuildings as the cart rolled up the long drive.

The carter let them off at the front door and drove away without looking back.

____V

AFTERWARD, PHILLIPE decided that every detail of their reception had been planned to intimidate them.

The intimidation began with the delay after his knock. The door did not open for several minutes.

Eventually a footman in powdered wig, white stockings and satin livery answered. He turned away without waiting for them to state their identities. Apparently he already knew.

The footman led them to a vast, airy room on the southern side of the house. There, great windows with tall mirrors between them opened onto green expanses leading down to the river. The drawing room boasted carved doorframes, a chimney-piece painted in brilliant white, and chairs and tripod tables of gilt wood with needleworked cushions.

In one of these chairs directly beneath a huge crystal chandelier sat a woman of about Marie's age. She did not rise as the footman ushered the visitors in.

An austere, graying man lounged beside an open window where the scarlet damask curtains blew gently. He had a prim mouth, indifferent eyes. He wore black, with only white cuffs showing.

But it was the woman who riveted Marie's attention, and that of her son. She had gray eyes and rather sunken-looking cheeks. But obvious beauty could not be completely hidden by her masklike expression. Blue tinting powder in her wig caught random sunlight. The powder matched the rich blue of her long gown with Turkish sleeves.

Marie did not wilt under the impact of the woman's stare. Standing squarely, like a peasant ready to bargain, she announced in accented English:

"I am Marie Charboneau. I have brought my son, Phillipe."

Lady Jane Amberly inclined her head slightly. Her quick inspection of Phillipe said a good deal concerning her feelings about having Amberly's bastard in her drawing room. She addressed Marie.

"I was not certain you would be able to converse in our language. Since you can, we may conclude our business with greater dispatch. I will not offer refreshments since this is not a social occasion. I wrote you only at my husband's insistence."

Perhaps Marie drew on some reserve of inner strength. Or on her training as an actress long ago. Either way, she sounded fully as haughty as Lady Jane when she answered:

"A correction please, my lady. I am not here primarily for business, as you term it. I am here first of all because your husband wishes to see his son.''

"Since I wrote you, circumstances have changed. That may not be possible.''

The damask curtains stirred again. Phillipe felt a sudden, inexplicable chill. The gentleman in black stepped forward with an air of authority.

"Lady Jane is quite correct. The Duke's wound is severely inflamed. Poisonous. The suffering drains him of sense and energy. He is seldom awake.''

Once more the blue-tinted wig inclined just a little. Lady Jane sounded weary, as if each word were an obnoxious duty:

"Dr. Bleeker is one of the most respected physicians in London. He is staying at Kentland to attend my husband. I do not wish the Duke to die, but the possibility exists. We must all accept it. And behave accordingly.''

Phillipe studied the black-garbed doctor, thinking, *From London? The expense must be staggering—*

Silence, then, save for the rustle of the curtains, the tinkle of the chandelier and a shout from one of the small army of gardeners laboring outside.

Finally Marie challenged the silence:

"Does James know his son is here, my lady?''

"He was informed shortly after your message arrived this morning. He was awake briefly at that time.''

"Then in spite of his perilous condition, I ask that we be taken to him without delay.''

"Permission for that,'' said Dr. Bleeker, "I cannot grant. The doors of the Duke's bedroom are expressly closed to all but those few whom I personally admit. At the moment, a good friend and spiritual adviser to this family, Bishop Francis, is with him. Praying while he sleeps.''

"The face of his son might be better medicine than prayers!'' Marie said.

"As to this young man being my husband's son''—Lady Jane's gray eyes touched on Phillipe again and dismissed him—"I have no evidence.''

"But I have a letter, my lady. A letter from your husband granting Phillipe his rightful share of James Armberly's estate!''

Suddenly Lady Jane rose. "I will have no loud voices in this house, madame. I fulfilled my husband's request. Reluctantly, but I fulfilled it. That is all I intend to do. If there comes an appropriate time for this boy you claim is the Duke's illegitimate son to see my husband, well and good. If not—'' She shrugged.

"I *claim* nothing!'' Marie retorted. "Nothing except the truth.''

"Will you in the name of God lower your voice and speak in a seemly fashion? Don't you understand? You are intruders! Having stretched my conscience to its limits and told him you've come, I will not have him disturbed further unless Dr. Bleeker approves.''

Bleeker said, "For the immediate future, the prospect is doubtful.''

Marie looked shaken. "Then we will retire to the inn at Tonbridge—''

Lady Jane's eyelids flickered, hooding her gray pupils as she frowned at the physician. For his part, Bleeker acted amused. Marie's labored English had brought the name out as *Town-breedge.* Phillipe felt a raw impulse to use his fist to eradicate the doctor's supercilious expression.

As Lady Jane controlled her brief show of anger, Marie concluded in a somewhat stronger voice:

"But we will not leave until my son has met with his father.''

Lady Jane said softly, "To wait might not be prudent.''

Marie caught her breath. Like her son, she sensed the threat that seemed to

hover just beneath the surface of the remark. The breeze whispered at the windows. The moving curtains of scarlet damask created slowly changing patterns of sun and shadow that seemed somehow sinister. Phillipe felt cold.

Was there a threat in what Lady Jane had said? Or was his reaction only a product of his own imagination, as he confronted a tense and difficult situation—?

He managed to say, "I'm not certain I entirely understand your meaning, my lady."

"Oh—" A delicate shrug of Lady Jane's shoulder; a false, waxen smile instantly in place. The gray eyes were all at once bland, unreadable. "I only meant I am aware that your funds must be severely limited. Even considering what my husband sent you."

Was that all she'd meant? Somehow, Phillipe doubted it—

Dr. Bleeker broke the silence: "And I must repeat, the wait may be not only lengthy, but entirely fruitless." He turned his shoulder to them, in dismissal, staring outside with a languid expression.

"The decision is of course yours," Lady Jane said to Marie. "I should, however, like to examine the letter which you say you possess." Her voice had an unmistakable catch in it. Phillipe felt a point scored.

She knows from my face that I'm his son, he thought. She *knows* the letter exists. *And she's afraid.*

There was a brief, vengeful pleasure in the realization. By what right did this elegant woman continue to stare at Marie Charboneau as if demanding obedience from a servant?

He heard Marie reply, "I do not have it, madame. It is put safely away."

"Then at some future time you will certainly permit me to see it. Verify its doubtful authenticity—"

"There is nothing doubtful about—" Phillipe began loudly, only to be interrupted by a commotion of voices.

He spun around, angry again. The laughter of the new arrivals told him that Lady Jane's words about the grave situation at Kentland were at least in part a sham; a sham to intimidate the peasant woman and her peasant son.

A young man of around Phillipe's age burst into the drawing room, holding the hand of a girl of perhaps nineteen. Or, more accurately, he dragged her along after him. The pair stopped suddenly. The young man exclaimed:

"Why, God save us! The French visitors? My supposed half-brother—what, what?"

Phillipe could only gape. At first glance, the young man might have been a subtly distorted mirror portrait of himself.

Yes, the mouth was thinner. The shoulders wider. And the new arrival stood half a head taller, even though he was at the moment affecting a somewhat limp posture. But the resemblance was still marked.

Not in terms of costume, of course. In contrast to Phillipe's plain garb, the boy was dressed in a long, checkered coat much like a dressing gown. His outfit was completed by loose Dutchman's breeches and shoes of pink satin. He clutched a tall, varnished walking stick with a huge silver head. The carry-cord was looped around one wrist.

The young man's wig was stuck through with pearl-headed pins. Phillipe had never seen such a peculiar figure. Only much later did he learn that the apparel was, according to the lights of the macaronis—youthful noblemen who adopted

the latest fads and aped the sputtering "What, what?" of the king—conservative.

For perhaps a heartbeat's time, Phillipe was tempted to burst out laughing at the young man's bizarre appearance and studied pose of boredom. But two things checked the mirth—the first being the total lack of any softening humor in the boy's eyes. Focused on Phillipe, those eyes belied the pearl pins and pink shoes and limp wrist draped over the stick head. They were ugly eyes—

Ugly as the small, purplish birthmark Phillipe saw at the outer end of the young man's left eyebrow.

The mark was shaped roughly like a U, and tilted, so the bottom pointed toward the left earlobe. Then Phillipe noticed a cloven place in the mark's lower curve. He decided the mark didn't resemble a letter so much as a broken hoof.

No more than a thumbnail's height in all, the mark was still livid, disfiguring. Phillipe recalled the words in his father's letter about the difficulties Lady Jane had encountered bearing Amberly's legitimate son. Phillipe had no doubt about who the young man was—or why he stared with such open animosity.

The scene held a moment more—as the girl drew Phillipe's attention. She was beautiful, so softly beautiful, in fact, that he almost gasped aloud at his first close look at her.

She was about the same height as her companion, but slimmer. High, full breasts were accented by her military-style riding costume. The double-breasted coat was dark blue, faced with white. A froth of white cravat showed at her throat. She wore no wig, her tawny hair bound in back by a simple ribbon. She tapped a crop against her full skirt, from under whose hem peeped the polished toes of masculine jackboots.

The girl's sky-blue eyes engaged Phillipe's with frank interest. And without the obvious dislike with which the boy continued to regard him.

Slowly, then, with a curling little smile, the girl glanced away—

But not before Phillipe's startled sense caught a similarity between her gaze and Charlotte's. Like Charlotte, she was a creature of the flesh, some instinct told him. But she was not common. A whore at heart, perhaps. But a gilded one—

Obviously the two young people had been outdoors, engaging in some strenuous activity such as horseback riding. The young man gave off an aroma of sweat as he swaggered toward Phillipe, hitting the floor with the ferrule of his stick at each step, *rap, rap.* His grin remained lopsided, relaxed—unlike his eyes. The girl pretended disinterest, half-turning from the two young men. But she continued to watch in an oblique way, a faint sheen of perspiration glowing on her upper lip.

Rap, rap, rap—

The young man stopped two paces in front of Phillipe. Stared. The lopsided grin straightened out; disappeared, leaving his mouth stark with distaste.

With unmistakable reluctance, Lady Jane at last broke the prolonged tension:

"May I present my son, Roger, and his fiance, Alicia, daughter of the Earl of Parkhurst?"

Roger whipped up his stick. Phillipe had to step back a pace, quickly, to avoid being struck by the tip. He didn't miss the flicker of pleasure in Roger's eyes. Roger pointed the stick at Marie.

"This is the Charboneau woman?"

"Yes, that's correct. I've forgotten her boy's name."

Rage boiled inside Phillipe as Marie burst out, "You know his name is Phillipe."

Studying Phillipe through tawny lashes, Alicia Parkhurst remarked, "I do think there's a resemblance."

Lady Jane's gray eyes went to flint. Roger saw his mother' fury, and as if some unseen signal had passed between them, whirled on the girl, slamming the stick's ferrule on the floor.

"None! None at all!"

"Oh, but Roger my sweet, use your eyes!"

Roger's mouth wrenched. His color darkened as he went to Alicia in three swift strides. The mark at his eyebrow seemed more black than purple as his voice savaged her:

"Mine are perfectly clear, Alicia dearest. Yours, however—well, one would think you'd been indulging your excessive fondness for claret. You're babbling."

The girl's face turned pink. Her shoulders trembled. Her expression changed from anger to humiliation, then to fear as Roger lifted his free hand to tweak the point of her chin. Not lightly, Phillipe saw. He hurt her. The girl's eyes blazed again as Roger said:

"Pray be silent, Alicia, while we conclude this tiresome private matter."

Shut out, intimidated, the girl seemed on the point of attacking him; her fingers around her riding crop had gone dead white.

But under the impact of Roger's furious stare, she wilted. Though still angry, she turned her back. What had made her surrender? Phillipe wondered. Fright? or something more?

Rap—

Rap—

RAP—

Very slowly, in control again, Roger Amberly returned to stand before Phillipe, feigning a smile.

"No," he sighed, "no resemblance. Except one. We smell about the same. But then, I've been for a frisky ride, what—?" He jabbed lightly at Phillipe's armpit with the heavy silver head of his stick.

Phillipe's hands flashed out. He jerked the stick so hard, the carry-loop broke. He flung the stick without looking. It skittered and clacked across the floor, landing at Dr. Bleeker's feet.

"Don't prod me like some animal," Phillipe said.

The birthmark over Roger's eye darkened as he lunged forward. "You filthy French clod, how dare you touch a hand to anything of mi—"

"Roger."

Lady Jane's voice, steel, brought her son up in midstride. A blood vessel stood out in Roger's throat. He took another step forward but Lady Jane intercepted him.

"Roger—you will not. I will handle this."

He obeyed her. But not easily. Balked, he glared at Phillipe—and over Roger's shoulder, Phillipe thought he saw Alicia Parkhurst's eyes brighten with a moment's delight. It was quickly masked as Roger stormed toward Bleeker, snatched up his stick in a sudden wild arc. The stick's ferrule struck a small porcelain vase on one of the tripod tables, shattering it.

Once more Lady Jane stared at her son. A last piece of the vase clinked to the floor. Roger let out a long, heavy breath, as if something in him had been given

release. With mingled dread and curiosity, Phillipe speculated as to whether the boy's marked face was somehow a sign of a deeper, more damaging mark on his mind—From the hard birth, perhaps?

Lady Jane addressed Marie in a toneless voice:

"Be so good as to take yourself and this brawling boor out of my house."

"There's some doubt about who is the brawling boor," Phillipe said. Roger's eyes narrowed, hateful.

"I will leave," Marie replied. "But I will stay in the village until Phillipe stands at the bedside of James Amberly and is recognized as his son."

"On both counts, madame," said Lady Jane with that impeccable control, "there is much doubt about the outcome."

"I have his witnessed letter! You cannot destroy the truth of that!"

Marie wheeled and walked away. Face hot, Phillipe started to follow, only to have Roger dart forward:

"Hold one moment!"

Phillipe turned, waiting.

Roger was younger, he had decided. But by no means lacking in physical strength. Roger held his stick in one hand, fingering—almost caressing—the heavy, scroll silver head.

"Under the law," Roger said with venom, "I could have you maimed for attacking me."

"If that's so, then your laws are as worthless as you."

Roger stiffened, hand dropping from the silver head that winked deadly bright in a shifting gleam of sunlight. Phillipe expected an attack, tried to ready himself—then grew aware of Lady Jane again warning her son off with those strong gray eyes.

The corners of his mouth tight, Roger said, "But I won't call the law down, my little French bastard. If there's any punishing to be done, I'll do it. Thoroughly and well!"

Swallowing his fear of this crazed young man with the rampaging temper, Phillipe retorted, "Perhaps there'll come a time when we can test the truth of that boast."

"If you stay in Tonbridge long, I'm certain of it."

All at once Lady Jane was between them again, a hand on her son's arm.

"This is not a London cockpit! I will have that remembered."

Dr Bleeker took out a tiny snuff case. "Shall I summon assistance to have the boy removed, my lady?"

"Oh, no! Such boldness shouldn't be punished!"

Phillipe and everyone else swung around, startled by Alicia Parkhurst's merry little laugh. The girl let her sky-blue eyes linger on Phillipe—

Admiringly? Or was that merely hopeful self-deception?

Still smiling, she addressed her husband-to-be:

"I wouldn't venture to be too bold, Roger—"

"Shut your mouth."

Alicia rolled with the verbal blow, hardly blinked. She was afraid of Roger, that Phillipe sensed quite clearly. Yet she would not be easily humiliated. Under her lilting words, there was malice:

"But I mean it, dear Roger. The boy appears a match for your own hot temper. And brother against brother—that would be shameful."

Her head came up, defiantly. "Striking him would be like striking yourself. He does have your good looks, after all. Perhaps he's even a shade handsomer,

I can't quite decide—" She was daring them—any of them—to deny her right to speak.

"Can you, Lady Jane?" she asked. "You, Dr. Bleeker?"

Phillipe both admired her courage and deplored her foolhardiness. Lady Jane now looked nearly as wrathful as her son, though she said nothing. Parkhurst must be a name fully as illustrious and powerful as Amberly, he thought.

But insult for insult—cruelty for cruelty—the atmosphere in this breezy, sunlit room was all at once too foul and dangerous to be borne. He stalked toward Marie at the doorway, aware of a smoky, sidelong glance of speculation from Alicia.

As he reached Marie's side, she spoke, implacable:

"We will wait in the village. As long as necessary."

"At your peril," said Roger.

Hearing Lady Jane's sibilant burst of breath as she tried to still her son, Phillipe concentrated on taking Marie's arm and leading her out of the room of enraged faces. Still half-blind with anger himself, he seemed to see but one image: Alicia Parkhurst's sky-colored eyes, vivid and intense in the moment he passed by her—

Lady Jane's voice was raised behind them. It did no good. Roger shouted anyway:

"Your son will be dead before anyone calls him my lawful brother, you French harlot!"

Phillipe swung around, making a guttural sound. Marie's hand on his arm restrained him. Fighting his anger, he stumbled after her.

He didn't know whether the encounter had been a victory or a defeat. But there was no doubt that new perils had developed in the confrontation. As if to convince the world—and himself—that he wasn't afraid, he slammed the front door thunderously on the way out.

5
A Game of Love

THAT NIGHT, back at Wolfe's Triumph, Phillipe expressed a worry that had troubled him ever since the stormy confrontation at Kentland.

"How long can we wait?" he asked Marie. "Lady Jane was right—our money won't last indefinitely."

"Then we will find a way to get more."

Phillipe couldn't see his mother's face when she answered. He was lying on the truckle, pulled from underneath the higher bed into which he could hear her settling. Downstairs, the sounds of laughter and friendly argumentation emphasized again just how isolated and vulnerable they were in this alien land. Vulnerable especially to the temper of Roger Amberly—

But his mother's reply seemed to take no account of that. After a moment she went on, "We will not leave this place till your father has seen you, and you have seen him. No matter what it costs us." With a sharp exhalation of breath, she blew out the candle on the stand beside the bed.

Hands locked under his neck in the darkness, Phillipe reckoned that it had cost a good deal already.

After leaving the Amberly house, he and Marie had found no cart waiting to return them to Tonbridge. So they walked—not a long walk, at least not for him. Despite the attempted humiliation by Lady Jane and her son, he could take pleasure from the fact that she had not quite been able to conceal her fear of Marie Charboneau's presence—or his.

But Marie had made the trip to Tonbridge with difficulty. She grew short of breath, asking often that they pause and rest. In the low-slanting light of late afternoon, her face had an unhealthy pallor that disturbed Phillipe considerably.

In the sultry darkness of the room at Mr. Fox's establishment, he voiced his concern:

"Are you positive you're well enough to stay here for some length of time, Mama?"

"Why do you ask that, Phillipe? Because the boy threatened you?"

"No!" he burst out. "I'm not afraid of him—he's probably all bluff." In truth, he didn't completely believe either statement. He finished, "It's you I'm worried about."

"I am stronger than she is! You'll see. Now go to sleep."

Over the noise from below-stairs, Phillipe heard a far-off rumble. The first thunder of a spring storm. Coming from the north, the great city of London. Blue-white light flashed across the sky outside the open window.

Lightning flashes filled his uneasy dreams.

And an enraged face branded with a purplish mark.

And a vase shattering—

And the sky-blue eyes of an aristocratic girl.

II

NEXT MORNING, early, a knocking at the door roused him.

He clambered up from the truckle bed, aware that the sleeve of his coarse nightshirt was damp with rain. A shutter banged in the chilly breeze.

As he stumbled over to close it, he glimpsed the river winding near the High Street, all gray in a mist of morning. Tiles and thatching on the roofs of cottages in the village glistened from the storm that had drenched Tonbridge all night long.

Directly below the window, he saw a team of matched grays standing in the mud. The team was hitched to a splendid gilt-and-blue private coach with a coat of arms on its door. Two men huddled on the rear step while the driver complained about the sudden end of the fine weather. One of the men at the back of the coach picked at mud spatters on his white stockings and wondered rhetorically how long they might be forced to wait.

The knocking sounded again, waking Marie. She came muttering up from sleep, as though still partially in the grip of a bad dream. Phillipe touched her arm to calm her. Her dark eyes opened wide, suddenly full of fear as the knocking was repeated a third time, loudly.

As Phillipe strode to the door, he glanced at the trunk, wondering whether he should quickly unwrap his sword. But he decided to go ahead and slip the door latch, blocking the opening with his body.

A moment later, sounding relieved, he said to Marie, "No danger. It's only the landlord's boy."

Young Clarence Fox, a towhead with teeth equally as protuberant as his father's said in a hushed voice:

"You have visitors below. They want to speak to you private. My father and I are to stay in the kitchen. They ask you and your mother to come down as quick as possible. You'd better do it, because Father can't afford to anger the most important folk around here."

Tense, Phillipe asked, "Who are the visitors? People from Kentland?"

"Lady Jane herself. And some churchman wearing purple. My father treated 'em plenty polite."

Marie was sitting up, covering her threadbare nightgown with the comforter. Her dark eyes were clear and alert now. Her faint smile showed satisfaction.

Phillipe took his cue from that. "Go down and say we'll attend them as soon as my mother is dressed, Clarence."

As he shut the door, Marie laughed. It took no words to explain why. Lady Jane Amberly would not have bothered to seek them out if there was no validity to Marie's claim.

III

BUT THE brief period of exhilaration vanished the moment Phillipe and his mother went down to the common room.

Mr. Fox and Clarence had indeed retired, leaving a wedge of cheese and two apples on a serving board at the table where Lady Jane sat motionless. The hood of her pearl-gray cloak was pulled up over the powdery pile of her hair. Her hands were clasped tightly atop the handle of an umbrella of waxed silk.

Fox had built a small fire in the inglenook. Silhouetted against the flames was an obese man of middle age. Wearing purple, as Clarence had reported.

The man turned as Marie preceded her son into the room. The man's full moon of a face matched Jane Amberly's for severity. Small blue eyes that scrutinized the arrivals seemed to lack any emotion, save a remote distaste. But perhaps Phillipe was deceived by the flickering light of the fire—

All at once the man licked his thick, already moist lips and smiled an unctuous smile. Thready purple veins showed in his fleshy nose. Still, he radiated affluence, importance, authority. And once in place, his smile never wavered.

Marie maintained the pretense of politeness:

"I am sorry for the delay, my lady. I was not yet awake when the boy knocked."

Lady Jane offered no similar courtesy, coming to the point at once. "Last night, madame, I reflected for several hours on the unpleasantness which took place at Kentland. I then sought counsel from Bishop Francis."

She indicated the obese man standing at the hearth with hands clasped behind his back. So this was the prelate supposedly praying for James Amberly. Phillipe thought the man looked more acquainted with the ways of the flesh than with those of holiness.

With an air of sympathy, the bishop spoke in a deep, honeyed voice:

"And I naturally advised Lady Amberly to bring the matter to a speedy and amiable conclusion—for both your sakes. Affairs at Kentland are troubled

enough, as I'm sure you understand." A tiny pursing of the bowed lips. "If you are truly concerned for the welfare of the Duke—as well as your own—you will be receptive to my lady's proposal."

"I am concerned for his welfare but also for that of his son," Marie shot back with a sharp gesture at Phillipe.

"Yes, yes, of course, but don't you mean his *alleged* son?" Bishop Francis asked with the merest flicker of his eyelids. "The matter *is* in dispute—"

"Not as far as we're concerned," Phillipe said.

Lady Jane lifted one gloved hand from the head of her umbrella. "Please. Let us come to the solution without quarreling over the problem itself." To Marie: "You must realize that your presence places additional strain on our entire household. I have come here in the hope of persuading you to leave, thereby removing the extra burden. At the good bishop's suggestion, I am prepared to make a favorable reaction to my request worth your while."

Instantly, Phillipe suspected the game. So did Marie. Her cheeks turned chalky white. But her acting ability helped her keep control.

She walked to a chair near Lady Jane, sat down gracefully. Her dark eyes met the other woman's; held. Bishop Francis continued to smile sympathetically. But the little blue seeds of his eyes showed worry. He already sensed resistance.

"You have come to make us an offer of money?" Marie asked.

"Entirely and solely for the sake of forestalling further unpleasantness, my dear lady," said the bishop.

Marie whipped around to face him. "No. To ensure that my son will have no share in his father's estate, should the Duke's illness prove fatal."

Lady Jane maintained her composure with effort. "Madame, your crudeness is an affront."

"Does the truth affront those of your class, my lady? What a pity."

Lady Jane stood up. Bishop Francis stepped away from the hearth, raising one fat pink hand. His voice oozed conciliation:

"Let us have no un-Christian words when a man's immortal soul lies threatened." He walked toward Marie, fingers unconsciously stroking the purple folds draped across his large stomach. "The offer is most generous. Remove yourself and your boy from Tonbridge within a reasonable time—a day or two—and my lady is prepared to turn into your hands the sum of fifty pounds. Why, do you realize how much that is?" His smile was touched with irony. "Some of our village curates survive comfortably on two or three pounds a year."

All of Marie's theatrical talents focused in her contemptuous laugh.

Lady Jane looked as if she'd been struck in the face. Bishop Francis' eyebrows shot up. Folds of fat appeared between the lines in his forehead. Marie said:

"A mere fifty pounds? For a young man who's the rightful heir to part of James Amberly's fortune?"

"Oh, but my dear woman, we have no proof the Duke fathered him!" Francis said. "None whatsoever."

"Then I'll show you the proof!" Marie cried, running upstairs.

In moments she was back, carrying the brass-cornered casket. Phillipe had withdrawn to a place several tables removed from Lady Jane's. From that vantage point he watched Bishop Francis inspect the casket with eager curiosity. Like his mouth, the bishop's eyes looked moist.

All at once Francis noticed Phillipe's scowl. The prelate turned back to the fire, sighing and daintily rubbing at one eyelid with a sausagelike middle finger.

Lady Jane was breathing faster. Even though the bishop smiled again, his

pendulous lips glistening in the firelight, Phillipe felt an inexplicable sense of danger.

Marie set the casket on a table and opened it. From the packet she took out the topmost document.

"This is written in the Duke's own hand. And witnessed by two friends, for the sake of legality. The letter promises Phillipe his portion under English law. Since James has only one other male issue, that portion is half. Not fifty pounds. Half!"

Bishop Francis extended his right hand. "Would you be so good as to let me examine the document?"

Defiantly, Marie started to give him the folded letter. Phillipe saw Lady Jane glance from the letter to the fireplace. He ran forward and snatched the letter out of his mother's hand:

"I'll show it to him."

Phillipe unfolded the document carefully, held it top and bottom. Bishop Francis lowered his extended hand, all expression gone from his suet face for a moment. Then, hunching forward, he scanned the letter. He said to Lady Jane:

"My knowledge of French is no longer what it was in my student days. But I recognize the handwriting as your husband's. And the letter is indeed witnessed."

Phillipe carried the valuable possession back to the casket, folded it away and shut the lid. Bishop Francis fingered his jowl thoughtfully.

"In view of those facts, my lady," he said, "perhaps we might show a larger measure of Christian generosity. Obviously this woman and her son are not well off. A hundred pounds—?"

"Half and nothing less!" Marie exclaimed.

The tip of the bishop's tongue roved over his lower lip. He looked almost grief-stricken. "You reject my lady's offer?"

"Completely!"

Abruptly, Lady Jane made a quick gesture of disgust. She started out, her gray eyes venomous. At the doorway, she turned.

"Madame, you are attempting to deprive my son of his full inheritance— exactly as you have deprived me of my husband's affections for years. I cannot predict what will befall the Duke as a result of his illness. But regardless of the outcome, Roger will receive his full share of the estate—now or later. I nearly gave my life to bring my son into this world. His welfare has always been my paramount concern, because he is the only child I could ever bear. For almost a year after his birth, we were not even certain that he would survive—indeed, the midwives and the physician who attended my confinement had some suspicion that at birth he was harmed in some unknown way. When he did survive, and grow, I thanked the Almighty, and vowed he would receive my constant attention all his life. So I do not take any threat to his future lightly. Be warned."

And she stormed out, straight to the coach, where the footmen sprang down into the mud to open the door.

Bishop Francis paused a moment, a gross figure against the gray morning mist. His smile remained sad.

"Madame—young master—permit me to speak as one whose holy charge and duty it is to be sensitive to the situations of all human beings, regardless of their station. For your own sake—your own safety!—do not, I beg you, challenge the power of this family. To do so for any prolonged period would be extremely ill

advised. And I would be saddened by what must surely be the inevitable consequences. Heed me—and reconsider.''

Marie said, ''No.''

With a sigh and a shake of his head, Bishop Francis left in a swirl of purple. Phillipe couldn't decide whether the churchman was sincere—or a wily charlatan.

After the lavish coach had pulled away, Marie pressed her palms against the sides of the casket. She was jubilant.

''Do you realize what all of that signified, Phillipe? The claim is valid! She knows it! We will wait to see the Duke, no matter what happens. We're not dirt to be kicked aside as she pleases—or bought off for a pittance!''

Phillipe said nothing. In principle, he agreed. But he hoped it was not a foolhardy decision.

Distantly in the stillness, he thought he heard the Amberly coach thundering out of Tonbridge. He resigned himself to more waiting.

Among those who were now clearly enemies.

IV

THAT SAME day, Phillipe drafted a short letter to Girard. He wrote that they would be delayed longer than expected, and requested that Girard continue management of the inn as best he could. Mr. Fox helped dispatch the letter via coach post.

Phillipe had no idea what the next move in the game would be. He was convinced that Lady Jane would somehow keep track of their continuing presence. And indeed, it wasn't long until he had another proof of their peril.

Two days had passed. To fill the hours, he'd taken to helping young Clarence with chores around the inn. It was from Clarence that he received confirmation that he and Marie were being spied upon.

''A groom from Kentland stopped this morning,'' Clarence reported.

''What did he want?''

''He asked my father whether a French woman was still staying here. A French woman and her son.''

''Is that all?''

Clarence gnawed his lip a moment. ''No. The groom said that if anyone from Kentland caught the son alone anyplace, they'd break his head for sport.''

Down on his knees scrubbing the grease-spattered stones of the kitchen hearth, Phillipe ignored the look that hoped for an explanation. Once again he realized he and Marie were pitted against powerful antagonists in a strange and silent war. Who would surrender first?

More important, when would they face the next direct attack?

V

AS THE sweet month of May filled Kent with the green of tree buds bursting open and the colorful splash of flowers blooming in cottage gardens, Phillipe, despite the open and implied threats, began to roam the countryside. The wandering

filled the time when he wasn't helping Clarence pitchfork straw or polish tables; it filled the emptiness in which no word, no sign was received from Kentland. The war held static, as if the opposition forces were pondering basic strategies very carefully.

Tactics, however, were a different matter. Those were all too clear—and menacing.

On an early morning tramp in the direction of his father's estate, Phillipe encountered three grubbily dressed servants trudging toward the village with hampers. Though they wore no livery, he guessed at once that they must be from Kentland. Instant recognition showed on their faces.

He stood immobile at the edge of the towpath, watching the three come to a halt a few yards off.

"Why—'tis the French bastard!" sneered the youngest of the trio. "Still daring to show his dial in daylight!"

One of his companions crouched down quickly, snatched a stone, hurled it hard.

Phillipe didn't dodge swiftly enough. The stone struck his forehead, left a stinging gash that bled.

Growling under his breath, Phillipe started to charge the servants—and only checked when he saw two of them go for bigger rocks and the third drop his hamper and reach into his boot for a skinning knife.

The blade flashed in the low-slanting sun. Confronting bullies was one thing. But dashing unarmed toward suicide was quite another. What if he were seriously wounded? Even killed by these nobodies? Though it galled him to hesitate, he knew he shouldn't risk the danger of his mother being left with a dead or injured son on her hands. Not when she had poured so much of her strength and hope into bringing them this far—

He thumbed his nose at the trio and gave them a good, obscene cursing in French as he turned his back.

In response, he heard laughter, jeers, English oaths fully as blue as his own. His face reddened as he quickened his step and angled for some trees on the side of the path away from the river. He knew what he was doing was right. But it was still humiliating.

Trying to pelt him with stones, the servants gave chase. But only for a short distance. Once into the woods, he eluded them easily. He negotiated his way back to Tonbridge over the downs, stopping only to wash the blood off his forehead in a brook.

All the way to Wolfe's Triumph, the taunts tormented him.

He kept reminding himself that he must keep his eye on the larger purpose. It had taken more courage to flee than might have been required to attack the servants and jam their insults back down their ignorant throats.

Or so he rationalized, to ease his conscience.

When Marie asked him about the clotted cut over his eye, he gave her an evasive answer. He'd tripped, sprawled out, that's all. No use letting her know of the new evidence of their continuing danger—

But he was damned if he'd let intimidation from the Amberly household deter him from wandering wherever he pleased. He would not—could not—surrender that completely.

So if anything, the aborted attack only made his ramblings bolder and more frequent.

One bright afternoon he took another long stroll beside the Medway, then sat

down to rest at the edge of a large, shadowy grove on the summit of what the locals called Quarry Hill. Seeing no one, menacing or otherwise, in the vicinity, he yawned, leaned back and dozed off.

Hoofbeats wakened him.

Below, on the towpath, a rider reined in. A splendid, glistening black stallion pointed its muzzle up the hillside. He scrambled to his feet, alarmed until he saw tawny hair flash in the sun—

It was Alicia Parkhurst.

She had evidently recognized him asleep against the tree trunk. Phillipe's forehead felt warm all at once.

He walked forward as the girl dismounted, holding the black's reins with one hand. She looked down the hill, then swept the horizon with a glance, as if to make certain she was not being observed. She wore the same fashionable riding costume in which he'd first seen her, and again he noticed the way it emphasized the swelling fullness of her breasts.

"Good afternoon, Master Frenchman," she said with a coquettish nod. "I've never spied you on Quarry Hill before."

"Oh," he grinned, "have you looked?"

She feigned annoyance. "You have a saucy tongue."

"My apologies. Do you ride this way often?"

"Not as often as I'd like. Every few days—if I'm lucky."

"Well, I've never stopped here before. But I've seen enough of Tonbridge to last awhile. So I've been exploring. May I ask whether there's any news of my father?"

Alicia Parkhurst shook her head. "The situation's little changed. That ghoul Bleeker lets more and more blood. But still the Duke seldom wakens. They do fear for his life."

Phillipe swallowed hard. "I thank you for that much information—they've sent us no further word." He decided to avoid the subject of the attempted bribe.

"Nevertheless," Alicia said, "Lady Jane is very much aware that you are both still here."

"Yes, I've learned she has—informants, keeping track. I ran into what I presume were three of them on the towpath some days ago."

"But you haven't seen Roger," she countered; it was more of an assertion than a question.

"No, not so far."

"Because Lady Jane is restraining him. He'd like nothing better than to ride to Tonbridge and thrash you—for a start. You do realize how dangerous he can be?"

Phillipe's eyes looked bleak as he nodded. "He has what you call a fragile temper, doesn't he?"

"And you upset him so, that first day. You positively drove him to the limit!"

He wanted to comment that she'd had some hand in that too. But he refrained, asking instead:

"Why is his mother keeping him leashed? I can't imagine it's because she's concerned about my well-being."

"Certainly not. I think she's convinced you'll give up waiting and go away eventually."

"She's wrong. I intend to see my father."

"I knew you were determined the first minute I looked at you. So did Roger, I believe. Perhaps that's what prodded him into that awful display at Kentland."

Again Phillipe held back a comment. Alicia's brilliant blue eyes slid obliquely across his face. Her next words, couched as a request, were really more of a subtle command:

"Will you walk with me back in the trees where it's cooler? I love to ride hard but it tires the poor horse—" She stroked the animal's neck, but looked at Phillipe. "I can't linger too long. I'm really not ever supposed to ride about the countryside unescorted. But Kentland's so tiresomely gloomy—and I reach the point at which I'll gladly bear Lady Jane's criticism in return for a little freedom—"

She walked under the low-hanging branches, leading the black. Phillipe followed. Alicia seemed to relax the moment they were safely concealed in the green darkness at the heart of the grove.

"You're staying with the family for an extended period?" he inquired.

"A month or two—into the early summer, at least."

"Are you making plans for the wedding to Roger?"

"Of course. We're to be married next year. It's the way large estates are made larger in England. The Amberly lands added to those of my father will leave an inheritance of increased size to my children. Provided—"

Smiling in a sly way, she tied the sweating stallion's rein to a branch.

"—provided I can induce—or should I say—seduce?—Roger to carry out his duty. The dear boy has his father's occasionally hot temper—you share some of that, don't you—?"

"I hope not to the degree Roger does."

"—but I do believe he also inherited some of his mother's coolness toward more—intimate pursuits."

She didn't look at Phillipe as she said it, bending instead to touch a patch of emerald moss growing near a gnarled root. The leaves in the grove rustled. For a moment, Phillipe was both stirred and shocked to discover that aristocratic young English ladies would even allude to the subject of sex. The revelation brought to mind one of Mr. Fox's recent diatribes against the loose morals of the nobility. Mr. Fox was of the relatively new, Methodist persuasion.

Deciding to explore his discovery a little further, Phillipe picked up the conversation with, "Intimate pursuits, you said—are you well acquainted with such pursuits, Miss Parkhurst?"

The sky-blue eyes took on a smoky look. "What is your opinion?"

His cheeks felt flushed. He managed to shrug. "I'm not sure. I'm no expert on English manners. Or English girls—what they do and don't do. However"— he kept his gaze unblinking, a half-smile on his lips—"I do believe that with your eyes and certain other little—mannerisms—you want to make it seem that you're quite experienced. Maybe that too is the fashion here—?"

"La, how bold you are!" she said with a bright laugh. "Such perception! How old are you, Master Frenchman?"

"Eighteen soon."

"I'm nineteen."

"That accounts for the look of experience," he joked. Then, more soberly: "How old is Roger?"

"A year younger than you. He should have a splendid career—if he doesn't fall into some silly quarrel over cards or a bear-baiting wager and get himself killed. Lady Jane worries about that constantly. She's quite protective—"

"So I've noticed."

"—which I believe is the reason she has imposed her will and forbidden Roger

to look for you in Tonbridge. Thus far, she's been successful. I think she's the only person on earth of whom Roger is honestly afraid.''

Phillipe plucked a blade of grass, ran it absently between his index and middle finger. ''Tell me more about your future with Roger, Miss Parkhurst. What kind of career are you counting on for him?''

''Oh, first I imagine he'll serve in the army. Purchase a commission, of course. One can't achieve high rank quickly any other way. The army is a good steppingstone to a political career, so afterward, I imagine we'll live in London. No doubt Roger will enter one of the ministries. Those in politics have many avenues for increasing their fortunes. The closer they can position themselves to His Majesty, the more numerous become the avenues. I look forward to a fine, prosperous life—''

Phillipe's curt laugh made her scowl for the first time.

''What do you find so amusing?''

''You seem to have forgotten how Roger humiliated you the day we met. Hurt you, in fact.''

Her lips set. ''I haven't forgotten. But larger considerations make it prudent to show no public distress.''

''Larger concerns.'' He nodded. ''Roger's future. Roger's fortune—''

''Exactly.'' The word hung between them, flat, final.

Then, with another of those smoky looks at Phillipe, Alicia seated herself against the trunk of a beech, gracefully settling her skirts. She sighed what sounded like a contrived sigh, remarking:

''Of course, even when Roger and I are married, I shall have to find lovers.''

Phillipe laughed again. ''That's the fashion too? One husband isn't enough?''

She brushed back a lock of hair, laughing with him. ''Poor ignorant foreigner—!'' she teased, patting the ground next to her riding skirt.

He sat down beside her, then felt annoyed that he'd obeyed her pantomimed command so promptly. Despite many differences, he saw traces of Lady Jane in Alicia, foremost being her unspoken assumption that, because of her position, her whims would always be gratified.

Still, he couldn't deny that she was lovely.

Alicia leaned her head against the bark and closed her eyes, musing on:

''Among our class, Master Frenchman, marriage has little if any relation to more diverting pastimes. Except on those occasions when an heir must be gotten, of course. Oh, I shouldn't say that categorically. Much depends on the quality of the husband.''

Edging a bit closer to her, he asked, ''What are your feelings about Roger's quality?''

''Didn't I hint at it? He's cold with a woman. I've yet to discover his— quality.''

Her voice lent a shade of vulgar meaning to the final word. Phillipe felt warmer than ever. And aware again of Alicia Parkhurst's skill in sensual games. He asked:

''Would you like to?''

''What a frivolous question!'' She ran her pink tongue over the edge of her teeth. ''Shouldn't the wise person sample an apple before buying the bushel?''

She was leading him down a contradictory path all at once, a path that had little to do with the other one winding, presumably, to wealth and position as the spouse of the next Duke of Kentland.

"Then—" Phillipe's gesture was wholly French, eloquent. "Why not sample, Miss Parkhurst?"

"Heavens, I've already told you that he hesitates to touch me! Besides, it's really quite impossible on a practical basis. I mean—watched day and night at Kentland by gossiping servants—"

Another wistful sigh; artifice. Layer on layer of artifice—it had been born into her, he supposed; and more of it taught as she grew. Yet her behavior both unsettled and excited him.

"I rather suppose," she concluded, "that at best, Roger will be a crude lover. Unsure of himself, and therefore crude and rough. Only seeking to be done quickly—satisfy himself—never sensitive to the desires of"—a small catch of breath; the sky-blue eyes pinned him—"a partner. Tell me something, Master Frenchman." She inclined her head nearer to him. "Would you hesitate to touch me?"

"No." A pause. "Not if I wanted to."

"Ah, wicked!" she laughed. "Venomously wicked!" There was a hint of anger in the way she tapped his cheek. It reminded him of Roger's use of the silverhead stick. He closed his fingers on Alicia's wrist, gently but firmly thrust her hand away.

With a pretty pout, she pretended hurt. He let her go.

"I expected better manners from you," she told him.

"It will take some of my father's money to polish off the rough edges."

"Then you and your mother do intend to press the claim?"

"To the finish."

"Well, you're liable to cause no end of difficulty—and you'd better stay out of Roger's way if Lady Jane's leash ever snaps—"

She left off rubbing her wrist when she saw Phillipe was paying no attention. He was looking directly into her eyes. The smile of the genteel harlot teased at him again.

"But we've quite lost the drift of our conversation—"

"I believe you said I disappointed you."

"Yes. You're a lord's bastard—and a Frenchman to boot. I was entertaining the notion that you might be quite unlike your half-brother in the way you behaved toward a woman. Gentler—yet at the same time more impassioned. We're told that the French are experts in matters of love."

All at once, Alicia's physical presence and the intimacy of the rustling grove started a deep, now-familiar reaction in him. He was infuriated by the mannered way in which this haughty girl toyed with him, playing her romantic word games. At the same time, he was tempted.

In no more than seconds, he succumbed:

"Were you also thinking of indulging yourself in the novelty of finding out?"

For the first time, she was taken aback, pink-faced. The subject changed instantly.

" 'Indulging yourself.' There's yet another pretty turn of phrase. You speak our language surprisingly well."

"I had a special teacher, because I knew I'd be coming here to claim the inheritance."

Alicia touched his wrist. The feel of her warm fingertips excited him even more. She, too, hesitated only a moment.

"Have you had special teachers in Cupid's discipline as well?"

"A few."

He placed his own free hand on top of hers, nervous, yet somehow compelled. Her own grip tightened just a little. He looked into those remarkably blue eyes.

"And you?"

"Oh, yes—many."

Something told him she was lying. But he only said, "Miss Parkhurst—"

"My name is Alicia."

"The conversation's wandered a long way down an unfamiliar path—"

"Shall we turn back, Master Frenchman?"

From her expression, her tone, her touch that brought him to stiffness, her meaning was unmistakably clear.

"It depends on the reasons for going on. I don't want to be used as a means for you to strike back at Roger for what he did to you at Kentland."

Her quick intake of breath said he'd struck the mark again. She started to pull her hand away, ready to rise and leave, angered. He caught her fingers, felt their heat once more, refused to release her as he finished:

"That is—if it's the only reason."

For a moment her eyes darted past his shoulder, full of the fear of chance discovery. Then she looked back to his face. Their gazes locked, held a long moment. A lark trilled somewhere at the edge of the grove. The stallion stamped. Slowly, she leaned her face toward his.

"No," she whispered. "It isn't—"

Phillipe kissed her. Hesitantly at first. Her warm, sweet breath cascaded over him. All at once his hands were on her shoulders, pulling her close. Her lips parted. Her kiss became eager, hungry. He thought his tongue tasted wine; through his mind fleeted a memory of Roger scoring her for an excessive fondness for claret—

They tumbled over onto the grass, arms twined, kissing. They began to let their hands explore. Very shortly, he discovered that young ladies of the English nobility wore silk drawers beneath their underpetticoats. Not to mention scarlet garters elaborately trimmed with lace.

The greenish darkness had turned steamy as a jungle. After much fumbling and struggling, Alicia's shoulders were bare; then her breasts. He bent to kiss the soft valley between. He moved his head to one side, kissed again. She uttered a small cry of surprised pleasure. Was she, then, mostly artifice and little, if any, experience—?

The play of hands and mouths grew more intense. Soon he was crouching above her, gazing down at her tumbled beauty through the green haze that seemed to surround them. Her upper lip was moist with perspiration. Her garments all a-tangle around her slim hips—the silken drawers had been cast aside— showed him a delicate golden place above her white stockings and her garters.

She looked at him with wide, almost alarmed eyes. She started to speak. He laid his fingers gently on her lips.

"Shall I stop, Alicia?"

"What's fair for me is fair for you. Only—only if you're just attacking Roger—"

"I've forgotten all about Roger," he said, and wrapped his arms around her so violently that her head accidently struck the tree trunk.

She let out a low exclamation of pain, then another, sharper one a moment later when he forced his entrance. The lark trilled. The stallion clopped his hoofs. The green darkness seemed to light and glow with a fire that might have been kindled within Phillipe's own flesh—

At first, it was awkward; her body was still not prepared for him, although it had already received him. And something said over and over that, despite her talk of it, she'd never had a lover. That excited him even more. He kissed her eyelids, her cheeks, stroked her back—

Until finally the awkwardness passed in favor of a matched steadiness whose speed increased and increased like their breathing until she was hugging him convulsively and crying softly for him to press her even harder.

She clung to his neck with both arms, driving herself as close as she could to meet flesh with flesh. He gasped—and her answer was a strident, lingering moan of joy that slowly faded under the lark's singing.

___VI

DRESSED, REASONABLY composed and ready to ride away on the rested horse, Alicia looked at him differently. She tried to smile and play the courtesan but her eyes betrayed her.

He asked quietly whether he'd in any way hurt her.

"No," she murmured. "Oh dear God—no. I—" A little gasp when she tried to laugh. Another brush at a stray lock of tawny hair. "—I found my answers about Frenchmen, too. And I think, I do think the Amberlys have finally met an adversary worthy of them."

"What a strange way to form a judgment," he teased.

She shook her head. "Not really—" All pretense seemed stripped away as she leaned forward to let their mouths touch quickly, passionately.

He experienced strange feelings. He knew she was still a creature of skills and deceptions. Yet he hadn't the heart to force her to admit whether she had ever lain with a man before. He wasn't sure—but asking was a cruelty he couldn't perform. A half-hour ago, yes. But not now.

Nor did he care much whether, at the start, she'd been goaded into this game of love by a desire to secretly spite the man who had hurt her.

"I want to see you again, Alicia."

"I don't know—"

"While the spring lasts—while I'm here—I want to see you."

"It will be so difficult—" She mounted, steadying the restless black. "I told you how I'm watched."

"You must find ways to get around that. Dammit, you must! Unless you were lying to me, and just wanted to revenge yourself—"

Her voice turned husky:

"No!"

"Then come to Quarry Hill when you can. I'll be here as often as I can. You can do it if you want to badly enough."

"I suppose," she said, sounding uncertain. Their eyes met again. "I mean to say I suppose I can do it. I'll try. I want to come again, Phillipe, even though I think having met you could prove—very dangerous."

"For whom?"

"Both of us."

"Tomorrow? The same time?"

"I don't know for certain."

"I'll be here."

"But if it's not possible for me to leave Kentland—"

"Then I'll be here the next day. And the next." His voice was low. He was as shaken as she was, because he too sensed that they were plunging into something far more entangling than a casual liaison—

"All right," she said suddenly, leaning down again to caress his cheek. "At the first possible moment."

She wheeled the black stallion away, cropping him savagely all the way down the hillside.

6
"A Perfect Member of the Mob-ility"

THE END of May brought a spate of changes to the south of England—and to Phillipe, who was growing aware that he was not the same person who had stepped so hesitantly off the lugger at Dover.

He fretted about the dwindling supply of money Marie kept hoarded in her casket. Even at Mr. Fox's modest rates for bed and board, it would not last much longer.

On top of that, every few days Clarence reported that some servant or other from Kentland dropped by the hostelry—and did not depart without making an inquiry about the French woman and her son.

Though Phillipe still had not explained the reason for this unusual interest, he had gained Clarence's confidence to the point of convincing the boy that it was important Clarence keep him informed about the watchers. So Clarence kept a wary eye out, and an ear open. Phillipe had hoped the spying would stop. Apparently that was not to happen.

Blended with the anxiety these circumstances produced was the hope and the joy he felt each morning at the prospect of perhaps meeting Alicia.

Assignations had proved difficult, as she'd predicted. Somehow, though, the protracted periods of waiting between their furtive meetings on Quarry Hill only intensified his emotions—and the shattering satisfaction when a rendezvous did take place.

After that first tempestuous afternoon, he'd gone to the hill four days in a row—and no sign of her.

The third and fourth days were agony. On the fifth, he slipped back to the grove convinced he would never see her again, save perhaps at Kentland—and there she was, tearfully clinging to him, overflowing sweet, sad apologies.

She would never be able to ride off alone oftener than every three or four days, she told him after they made love. However, she believed she had found a system to at least minimize the potential danger to herself—and, she quicky reassured Phillipe, to him.

By paying close attention to household gossip—closer attention than she usually paid, she was frank to say—she could pick up hints of plans for the next day or the day after. Would Roger be off hunting? Lady Jane entertaining the bishop between prayers? When such situations developed, Alicia would now employ the services of a girl named Betsy.

Betsy was the one lady's maid Alicia had brought with her from home. She felt she could trust the girl—particularly when a few extra coins were slipped from hand to hand.

After Alicia had outlined her plan, she and Phillipe searched and found a felled oak with many rotted places in its lightning-blasted trunk. Phillipe scooped out one such place, which was designated the message spot. Here Betsy, sent on some fictitious errand, would leave a slip of paper with a crudely printed word or two on it—*Tuesday twilight*—so Phillipe might better know when to expect the tawny-haired girl.

After their third rendezvous, Phillipe noticed that she looked drawn, weary. He questioned her about whether the strain of outwitting and eluding dozens of people, from Lady Jane and Roger down to the pantry and stable help, was too taxing.

"Taxing, yes," she replied. "But worth it, my darling. And after all, haven't you told me I do exceeding well at games?"

She kissed him with lips parted. But not before he saw the shadow in her eyes, the shadow that said she was meeting him at the price of raw nerves.

One mellow evening when she brought a bottle of her favorite claret in a hamper—she drank twice as much of it as Phillipe—she speculated aloud that it might be amusing to let Roger know she'd acquired a lover.

Her eyes twinkled with hard merriment as she said it. Then she saw Phillipe's scowl, touched him.

"Though you know I wouldn't—ever."

"That first time, Alicia—"

"Yes?"

"You did let me make love to you because he hurt you, isn't that right?"

"You know me too intimately, Master Frenchman!"

"But you did."

"Partly." Her voice was thickened by the wine. "Only partly—" She kissed him.

The supressed streak of cruelty in Alicia was an aspect of her personality he intensely disliked. But it was an aspect that dwindled to insignificance alongside the overpowering reactions she produced in him, mind and body, when he was away from her, anticipating their next stolen moments together.

The message-tree system worked reasonably well. Yet there remained occasions when he would wait hours past the appointed time, then trudge back to Tonbridge when she failed to arrive. On those lonely walks, he experienced what he realized must be one of the first signs of full manhood. He knew the full meaning of sorrow.

During one such frustrated return to Wolfe's Triumph, he came close to losing his life.

In the mist of early evening, he was passing a copse when a blunderbuss blasted. He dropped instinctively, flattening in the tall grass—

Balls hissed through the tops of the nearby grass stalks, spending themselves. A bad shot, he decided. With a weapon of too short a range.

Still—

Who had fired?

Hunters? Yes; he heard them hallooing in the copse as he raised himself cautiously to hands and knees.

Rooks cawed their way into the sky's yellow haze, flushed from the thicket by the shot. Phillipe remained still, presently saw four riders emerge from the trees

and canter away toward Kentland. As the figures vanished, he identified the livery of the Amberlys.

He doubted the attempt had been deliberate. He had seen no one following him earlier, and he was always careful on his walks now, surveying in all directions as he moved. More than likely the servants had spotted him by chance while pursuing the bird among the trees.

But the very fact that they'd fire at all said much about Roger Amberly's feelings. How pleased the Duke's son would be if there were a report of a fortuitous accident—!

Phillipe reported nothing of the incident to his mother or Alicia. But his apprehension deepened.

There was another change in him as well. His conscious decision to keep the affair hidden from Marie. He didn't want to flaunt the conquest of the heiress of Parkhurst, drag it into the open for his mother to examine as another twisted proof that her son rightfully belonged among his so-called betters.

When Marie asked questions about his frequent walking trips, he gave evasive answers. Excuses: Boredom: no work to be done at Wolfe's Triumph. The deception was but one more signal that his feelings for Alicia were growing more serious than he'd ever intended.

It was, all in all, a May of changes.

Thunderous weather struck the Kentish countryside. Swift-flying spring stormclouds blackened the sky. The world did not glow. That seemed appropriate, because he knew his time with Alicia would pass all too soon.

II

"ALICIA?"

She answered with a sleepy murmur. They were deep in a dell they'd found, two days after the first of June.

They lay together on a mossy bank, Alicia with her bodice unfastened, Phillipe with his head resting between the pink-tipped hills of her breasts. Across the dell, bluebells nodded in the oppressive air. High up in the sheltering trees, raindrops patted tentatively on leaves just beginning to stir in the wind. Thunder boomed in the north.

When he didn't speak immediately in reply to her murmur, she stroked his forehead, as if to soothe away the hesitation she sensed. He rolled onto his stomach, touched the coral tip of her left breast and watched it rise. At last he said:

"Lovers shouldn't have secrets, isn't that so?"

"That's so." She pressed his caressing fingers against her body. "Secrets are only for husbands and wives. I'm not even wed to Roger yet, and think of the bagful I've hidden from him."

Completely true. By now there was no intimacy Phillipe and Alicia had not practiced.

"Go on, speak your mind," the girl urged softly.

"All right. Do you know what I thought of you that first day we met?"

"Tell me."

"I thought you were a fine lady—and a proper slut."

"What a horridly truthful young man you are, Phillipe! Of course you're

perfectly right. Earls' daughters are taught to practice feminine wiles. How do you think I got Roger to agree to the match our parents arranged? Still, isn't knowing the art of love a good thing—for lovers?''

"For lovers," he agreed. "But what about those who fall in love?"

She sat up as thunder echoed along the river valley. "You mustn't say such things, Phillipe."

There was no reproof in her remark. Only sadness. She avoided his gaze. He pulled her head around gently, stared into her eyes.

"You mustn't," she insisted. "We have no chance together."

"What if Lady Amberly was finally forced to acknowledge my father's pledge?"

"It will be a long time happening—if it ever does. You see how skillfully she resists. Letting you sit and sit, wait and wait, cooped up in the village—"

"Damme, how I hate her for that!" he exploded, jumping up. "Then other times, I have doubts—"

"About what?"

"Doubts that I don't know my proper place."

"Lady Jane would concur with that opinion," Alicia told him, though not with any malice. She tried to gesture him back to her side. But he stalked across the dell, scowling. She let her hand fall back to her side.

A moment later she began to lace her bodice. The mood was broken; they had strayed onto perilous ground.

"In my opinion, Phillipe, the reason you feel doubt is just because you're still trying to decide who and what you are. I'll admit my own feelings are tangled, now that we've started—well, you understand. I don't care for Roger, although I should, since I'll marry him. I love to be here with you like this, although I shouldn't."

Phillipe went back to her, kneeling and closing his hand on hers. "Alicia—"

"What, dear?"

"I've wondered since the beginning whether you've said similar things to other lovers."

Her blue eyes never blinked. "And I've wondered when you might ask me that."

"Is there an answer?"

"Yes—never. You were and are the first. Do you wonder I've been shaken so? And risk these rides—the stares and questions afterward? You don't know what you've done to me, Phillipe. Now I have nights when I can't sleep at all. Nights when I lie weeping and dreaming it was all different. When I wish to God I could board a ship and run off—perhaps all the way across the ocean, to live with a family like the Trumbulls and never have you torment me again."

He asked her who the Trumbulls might be. She explained that her mother's sister—Aunt Sue, she called her—had married and emigrated to the American colonies. Aunt Sue's husband, one Tobias Trumbull, had become exceedingly wealthy as the owner of the largest ropewalk in Philadelphia City. He lived in a fine house, endorsed the policies of George III and his ministers and was altogether a right-thinking Tory gentleman.

"There, at least," she concluded, "I'd be safe from what's happened. Something I never imagined would happen at all. For as I told you, anything beyond meeting this way is quite impossible. I am not strong enough to follow any course except the one planned for me. Marriage with Roger."

"Remember what I told you that first time? You could do whatever you wanted—if you wanted it badly enough."

"Badly enough? Oh yes, there's the problem—!"

Then she flung her arms around his neck, clinging to him and crying. It was a facet of her personality he'd never seen before. It touched him. Made him— yes, why not admit it?—love her all the more.

The rain began to drip through the leaves. She broke away, ready to ride back to Kentland. The parting lent urgency to his sudden question:

"Tell me one thing. Are they tricking us? Is my father really so ill?"

"Oh, yes. That doctor with his bleeding basin seldom leaves his side."

"Then if you care for me at all, help me this much. Use your skills to persuade Lady Amberly to relent just a little. My mother's nearly out of her mind with worry. She feels we're being deceived."

"Not deceived," Alicia said, adjusting the ribbon in her hair. "Fought. On very genteel terms. But fought nevertheless. Lady Jane is particularly afraid of you. I understand why. I told you a moment ago—you haven't decided what you want to become. A proper nobleman's bastard. Or a man who spits on noblemen."

"That's beside the point. Can't you persuade her to let my mother see the Duke for even a moment?"

Alicia pondered. "I can try. It must be discreetly done. A seed planted one day, then nourished little by little. She's not an evil woman. Only protective of what she considers is rightfully hers—"

"Like my mother."

"—and it is possible she might bend to a suggestion from her future daughter-in-law."

Alicia's eyes grew somber. "But it would have to be arranged for an occasion when Roger's away. That might happen quite soon, however."

"How so?"

"Lady Jane's leash is wearing thin. She realizes it. Roger storms about in a perfect rage most of the time. And whenever he talks about going to Tonbridge, there's a fearful row. Even behind locked doors, he and Lady Jane practically shake the house. I know she's trying desperately to persuade him to take a holiday in London. You see, it's as I said—she does fear you. Not only because of the claim but because of the harm you might do to her legitimate son. Yes"— she nodded suddenly—"what you suggest could be possible."

"Please do what you can. We're nearly out of money."

She lifted her face to the wind stirring the leaves. The afternoon had grown heavy with stillness before the storm. "And time. Time's our enemy, Phillipe. Sweet Christ, I sometimes wish you'd never come here! Forcing me to a choice I want to make and can't—!"

She turned and ran.

"Alicia!"

The cry died away. He was left alone in the dell as the rain slashed down through the treetops suddenly.

For a moment he felt thoroughly miserable. He suspected some of her motives one instant, and the next cursed the system that had locked her into a preordained future. But despite the torment, he couldn't deny it—he loved her.

From the edge of the trees, he watched the mounted figure receding into the black-clouded distance. He trudged back to Tonbridge feeling utterly alone.

III

ALICIA'S SEED, planted on his behalf, took three weeks to mature.

One afternoon on Quarry Hill, he found a note in the message tree telling him to come that night to a different spot—a willow grove along the river between Tonbridge and Kentland. Wary over the possibility of a trap, Phillipe nevertheless kept the appointment—though he surveyed the grove carefully before setting foot into it.

Alicia was waiting. She had only moments to report that Lady Jane had won out. In a day or two, Roger, at his mother's absolute insistence, would be off to town—London—to select items for a new fall wardrobe and learn the latest gossip in the coffee houses.

Further, Lady Jane did show small signs of yielding.

But Alicia had to exert pressure carefully, she said. She must not seem too unlike herself; not show too much interest in the welfare of the claimant and his mother. She'd positioned the suggestion as a possible means of ridding Kentland of the presence of Marie and her son. Once having seen the Duke lying comatose, she argued, the unwelcome visitors might realize their wait was hopeless.

For his mother's sake, Phillipe was encouraged. For his own—just the opposite. Alicia had all but admitted falling in love with him. Yet she was still protecting herself with exquisite care.

On a showery Saturday, the arrogant old cart driver appeared at Wolfe's Triumph. Lady Amberly requested their presence at the estate, he said.

She personally met them at the door and ushered them to the stair leading up to the second floor. Of Alicia there was no sign. But she had done her work, as Lady Jane's remark to Marie testified:

"Though it should not, my conscience began to bother me. I wondered whether you thought I was perhaps not telling you the truth. This visit will put your mind to rest on that score, certainly."

Marie's cheeks showed patches of scarlet. She looked as if she wanted to run up the steps. Following the two women, Phillipe was conscious of footmen below staring scornfully.

At the head of the stairs, a maid waited with a candle. She led them down a dim corridor that had a dank, unhealthy reek. Near the corridor's end, a shadow seemed to dissolve out of the wall. Phillipe recognized Dr. Bleeker, in black as always.

The physician eyed the visitors with disapproval. Standing in front of carved double doors, he said:

"You may not enter, only look at him from here. I've granted that much at the request of Lady Amberly. I wouldn't have done so on my own."

Marie's right hand dug into Phillipe's wrist as Bleeker opened one of the doors.

At first all Phillipe could see were the flames of two candles flanking the great bed in the draped and darkened room. The air gusting out smelled even more foul, a mingling of smoke and sweat and the bitter tang of some balm. Marie let out a low cry, took a step forward.

Bleeker shot out his black sleeve as a barrier. Marie's hand flew to her mouth. Lady Jane turned away, gazing at rain-washed leaded windows at the end of the hall.

The candles flanking the bed quivered a little. At last Phillipe discerned a

white face on a pillow. He might have been looking at an older version of himself.

Then came the sound—an incoherent muttering from the man lying in the stifling room. Details leaped out. A trace of saliva trickling from the corner of James Amberly's mouth; the glitter of sweat on his waxen forehead. Phillipe's legs felt weak.

Marie grasped Bleeker's arm. "Please let me go near him. Just for a moment!"

"I forbid it absolutely. You see his pathetic condition. Even when awake, his mind is not his own."

Marie stared into the room again. In a moment, Bleeker shut the door.

"I trust we have extended ourselves sufficiently for your convenience, madame."

Marie didn't hear. She was weeping. Phillipe wanted to strike the insufferable doctor. He went to his mother instead, anxious to take her out of this place of sickness and horror. *We shouldn't have come,* he thought. *It's worse for her to see him this way than not at all.*

Quickly he hurried Marie toward the stairs. She was trembling but she'd gotten her sobbing under control. He would never dare tell her that he had arranged the viewing. He'd hoped that the sight of James Amberly would lift her spirits. The effect was exactly the reverse. And he was to blame.

As fast as he could, he helped her down the staircase and across the foyer. They were but halfway to the front door, Marie still clutching at him, when Lady Jane spoke from behind:

"Now that you have gotten your desire, madame, I trust you'll trouble us no further. Leave England. Do you hear what I say!—*leave England.* He cannot answer you. He cannot speak to your claim. I am the Duke's voice now. And while I live, I will deny the contents of that letter with all my power. Finally— you know quite well how my son feels concerning this alleged claim—and the claimant." Her glance at Phillipe was pointed. He shivered. "I cannot forever guarantee to hold my son's natural instincts in check. Good day."

A footman had glided forward to open the door, as if to hasten their departure. Looking back at Lady Jane, Phillipe felt rain spatter his neck. He heard the noise of a coach rattling up the drive. *Now* he understood why Alicia's seed had fallen on fertile ground.

Lady Jane had summoned them not out of kindness or conscience but out of a desire to intimidate them even further—this time with the threat of direct intervention by Roger.

Phillipe suspected the threat might be a bluff. But it would be rash to accept that assumption completely.

In any case, Amberly's helplessness, Lady Jane's determination and the absent heir's vengeful temper were now openly ranged against them—and would defeat them. That was the message the encounter had been meant to convey. It did no good for Phillipe to remind himself that he and Alicia had actually been responsible for Lady Jane gaining her desired end by suggesting the strategy to her. The point was, she had seized on it eagerly.

And when Marie stumbled on the steps leading down to the drive, Phillipe knew how well the strategy had succeeded.

He couldn't catch her in time. She landed on her knees in the mud. He helped her up, filled with humiliation and rage.

MARIE'S SKIRT was filthy with spattered mud. As Phillipe lifted her to her feet, he saw a splendid coach-and-four arriving, its wheels throwing off more mud as the liveried driver braked and reined in the white horses.

Astonished, the senior footman called into the house, "My lady—unexpected visitors!" He darted down the steps to assist the liveried postilion just opening the gilded door.

Leaning on her son, Marie seemed to be regaining her composure. For his part, Phillipe was fascinated by the sight of a plump, wigged gentleman alighting from the coach. The only word for his apparel was magnificent, from the buckles on his shoes and the ribbons fastening his breeches at the knees, to the ruby-and-emerald-studded hilt of his sword and the intricate frogging around the golden buttons of his plum-colored coat.

The footman, the coach driver and the postilion gave Phillipe and his mother angry looks, because they still stood near the coach's right front wheel—at the foot of the steps up to the front door.

Lady Jane appeared in the doorway. "My lord, we've been anticipating your arrival for weeks. But we finally assumed that matters of state prevented a visit. We're not prepared—"

"I realize my presence is long overdue," answered the new arrival, pausing on the coach step. "And I cannot stay long—indeed, you can see my journey was made in extreme haste, without my customary full retinue. But I seized the moment because I am anxious to extend my sympathies and learn of my good friend the Duke's condition."

The coach driver whirled on Phillipe and Marie. "Stand aside, if you please."

His clothes daubed with mud, his emotions still chaotic because of the grim scene upstairs, Phillipe glared at the new arrival. The man remained on the coach step, only a twitch of his pink lips revealing momentary displeasure. The bedraggled woman and her son effectively blocked his way to the stone steps.

"Stand aside!" the driver demanded.

Phillipe said, "Why?"

"My lord, excuse these ill-mannered foreigners—" Lady Jane began.

Now the new arrival looked faintly amused. He lifted one ringed hand to stay the angry servants, stepped carefully down into the mud and around a puddle, confronting Phillipe face to face.

The man might have been a cousin to Bishop Francis in the general shape of face and figure. But his countenance was different in one way: it lacked oozing piety. Indeed, it had a certain merry charm. Yet the eyes were not those of a light-minded man. They met Phillipe's in a direct, challenging way.

"Why stand aside, sir? Because these good people believe some small deference is due the Prime Minister of England."

The senior footman seized Phillipe's arm. "You ignorant sod, this is Lord North!"

Savagely, Phillipe threw off the footman's hand. "And I should therefore step aside?"

The second most powerful man in the British Empire looked mildly astonished. But he managed to maintain a surface geniality.

"Yes, sir, that is essentially the reason."

"Well, I don't give a damn who you are," Phillipe shot back, too over-

wrought to let reason exert a calming influence. Stunned and furious, Lady Jane
was rigid in the doorway. The Prime Minister said to her:

"I detect a trace of the French in his accent. Do you suppose we have here a
disciple of the infamous Rousseau?"

"I've read him, yes," Phillipe said.

"The pernicious Locke too, I suppose?"

"Yes."

Lord North sighed. "Well, we may thank the Almighty that the former no
longer graces our realm, but has taken himself and his mad ideas back to the
continent—while the latter is at least forever buried. Would the same could be
said of his writings!"

"I find nothing wrong with the writings of either man, my lord."

"Oh-ho!" exclaimed North, warming as if to an oration. "I suppose we shall
be informed next that you are also a pupil-in-correspondence with that horned
devil, Adams? It must be so, since one mischievous idea only lures its believer
toward more and more of them! Tell me, young sir, are you truly one of those
who holds that the countryman, let us say, has the same rights as the king? That
the power of the former matches that of the latter?"

Phillipe managed to screw up his nerve to reply, "If a king oppresses people,
then the countryman should throw the king over. And has the right."

Lord North became less amused. "Lady Amberly, you have indeed attracted
a perfect member of the mo-bility, as we call the rabble over in our rebellious
province of Massachusetts Bay."

He turned to Phillipe once more, hectoring him now.

"Though I do not make a habit of discoursing with commoners in the rain, my
young friend, I must advise you of one fact. Englishmen enjoy the fullest liberties of any race under the sun. But liberties are not license. And those who
question the natural order of society do so at their peril. As the members of that
infamous Boston mob-ility are learning! Wherever you caught this wicked disease of false libertarianism, purge yourself of it before you come to disaster.
Now, if you will be so kind as to remove yourself from my path, I will get on
with the business of my visit."

But Phillipe still refused to budge.

Lord North flushed in anger. Finally, though, manners won out. He stepped
around Phillipe with such elegant contempt that the servants snickered openly in
approval.

Phillipe saw Girard's face in memory, shouted at the broad back ascending the
stairs:

"By what right does one man call himself better than another? Or rule
another? Kings rule because the people *let* them!"

North turned and peered down, this time with open hostility.

"Young man, I fear the noxious doctrines of Locke and Rousseau have mortally infected your soul. You'll come to no good end."

And with that, the Prime Minister vanished inside.

The door closed on Lady Jane's hasty apologies and angry denunciations of
Phillipe.

Pushing back his tricorn hat with its decoration of white Tory roses, the coach
driver exclaimed, "By God, I've never witnessed such audacity. Lucky for you,
my little sport, that Lord North is a mild-tempered gentleman."

"And a puppet of your German king!" Phillipe sneered. Even as he guided
Marie away from the coach, he was aware of the postilion slipping up behind

him. "I've heard what they say in the public house. King George hoists the hoop and North jumps through."

"Speak the name of him who said that and his tongue'll be out 'fore midnight!" vowed the coachman. He reached high to the seat and snaked down a coiled whip. "Anyone who repeats it deserves something only a mite less harsh." He uncoiled the whip with a single snap.

Phillipe wasn't averse to a fight. But he realized that he was outnumbered by the driver and the circling postilion. In a clumsy fray in the mud, Marie might be a chance victim. So he suppressed his anger and urged her down the drive, while the coachman played with his whip and called them obscene names.

Finally, out of range of the jeers, Phillipe slowed up. "Lean on me, Mama. The mud makes for hard walking."

Her face shone with pride. "Before God, Phillipe, you have a real fire in you!"

"Only when we're treated as nothing. I really don't have any desire to start brawls and bring down trouble. But why are we less than they are?"

"That's always been the order of things, as the man told you. Imagine—Prime Minister himself! I don't blame you for anger. But use it wisely. To gain your ends, not endanger your life."

She seemed almost her old self again, even though she held his arm for support as they made their way along the towpath that had become a quagmire. She added another bit of advice:

"Remember, you must take your place among people of that class, not alienate them."

Phillipe shrugged. "Evidently I'm already consigned to—what did he call it?—the mob-ility. But who's the 'horned devil,' Adams? I'll have to ask Mr. Fox. He seems well up on political affairs."

As they trudged along through the rain, he was swept again by a mood of discouragement. He recalled the blunderbuss firing from the copse, Lady Jane's warning that she might not be able to hold Roger at bay much longer. He found himself saying:

"Perhaps all this is useless, Mama. My father can't speak on my behalf—and even leaving Roger out of it, we both know Lady Amberly could hire whole armies of lawyers to argue against the claim. Should we go back to Auvergne?"

Her face turned bleak. "No. Not as long as I own that letter."

But as they tramped the towpath, muddy and tired, Phillipe began to wonder whether his mother was leading him—or pushing him—toward a destination where he would never be welcome and would never fit.

7
Brother Against Brother

"MR. FOX," said Phillipe two mornings later, "I must speak to you about the arrangements for our quarters. My mother and I have nearly come to the end of our money."

"Then, sir," answered the graying owner of Wolfe's Triumph, "I must let your quarters to others. Much as I'd like to extend you charity, I can't."

The two stood in the yard of the inn, near the arched gate through which the coach for London had departed only a few moments earlier. The yard smelled ripe from horse droppings.

Mr. Fox negotiated his way around several such fragrant mounds and dropped onto a bench against the inn wall, to rest. Inside, Clarence could be heard saucing one of the serving girls. Overhead, the morning sky was blue and sultry.

"It's necessary that my mother and I stay on—" Phillipe began.

"That may be. But I ask you in all candor, is it safe?"

Standing in the sunlight, Phillipe still felt a brief chill. "I can't let that influence the decision, Mr. Fox."

The innkeeper's lined face looked startled. "But arent't you aware that you're the talk—and in some quarters, the scandal—of the neighborhood? Because of the way you braced the Prime Minister himself? With what I understand are dangerous liberal opinions? You're fortunate his lordship's of an even humor, or God knows what obscure law he'd have invoked against you."

Fox peered at him shrewdly. "You have some hold on the Amberlys, don't you? It makes the family loathe you, yet tolerate your presence. I know you claimed to be related—"

"I am."

"I'd like to know how."

Phillipe glanced up at the closed shutters of the room where Marie was still sleeping. The homely, toothy inn proprietor sensed his uneasiness, laid a kindly hand on his arm.

"Come, lad, I've no great affection for the Amberlys myself. I'll keep your answer private, I promise."

The reassuring touch of the man's hand somehow drained Phillipe of his tensions. It was a relief to step from the already hot sun, slump on the bench beside Fox and, for better or worse, share the secret that dominated his life:

"James Amberly is my father, although he never married my mother. The Duke summoned us, before his illness grew so serious that he can't speak to anyone. Lady Jane hates me because the Duke promised me part of his fortune."

Mr. Fox let out a long, low whistle. "That explanation never so much as popped into my head. Yet it accounts for everything that's been puzzling me. Lady Jane condescending to call here—on two foreigners who speak imperfect English. The endless parade of servants dropping in to inquire about you—well, well! Bastardy in the Amberly woodwork. Imagine that!"

When he got over his surprise, the landlord asked, "Have you anything to substantiate this claim of yours?"

"A letter, written by my father. My mother keeps it hidden away. I think Lady Amberly knows the letter's genuine. She may despise me, but I don't believe she's quite ready to take action against me." He hoped it was the truth. Roger, of course, was another factor entirely.

"I trust that's right—for your sake." Fox scraped a grimy nail against one of his protruding teeth. "You're staying in the hope your father will recover, then?"

"Yes, and receive us, and say the claim will be honored."

"I can understand that. Still, it doesn't get 'round the subject on which we began."

"I could work for you," Phillipe said. "Not just a little, as I've been doing,

but all the time. All day long and into the night. Just don't turn us out now, Mr. Fox!''

The older man pondered a moment. "I'd have to move you to my smallest room—''

"Even the stable if you'll let us stay!''

Fox was amused at the seriousness of Phillipe's expression. "No, the small room will do. As I suggested, Lady Jane's no favorite of mine.''

"Mr. Fox, I can't thank you enough!''

"No thanks necessary. I'll get my due in hard work.''

Phillipe frowned. "There's only one thing—''

"Sir?''

"By staying here, are we in any way exposing you to risk?''

"Lady Jane,'' he returned emphatically, "would not dare overstep that far. The laws of England are a right good tangle these days. A poor child's hand can be lopped off for pinching a cherry tart, for instance. But mostly, the laws are good. They protect Englishmen. During his ministry, Mr. Pitt remarked that even the King himself couldn't set foot inside the humblest cottage in order to violate the owner's liberties. And thank God. Such principles are the strength and glory of this country. Also the reason why our cousins over in the colonies are so exercised by His Majesty's ministers,'' he added wryly.

That brought to mind Lord North's reference to "the mob-ility.'' Phillipe asked Fox about it, and the innkeeper proved knowledgeable on the subject:

"The nub of it is, the colonists consider themselves Englishmen just like me. They want the same rights. German George sees it different. He's determined to have all the power in his hands. The Hanoverians on the throne before him were lazy, profligate men. So when the King was very small, his mother drummed one idea into his head. *'Be* a king, Georgie!' As a result, he's had one prime minister after another. And he's kept searching for others even more willowy and pliant— the ideal being a man who'd execute the King's policies without question. In North, he's found him. And North's packing the government with his own kind.

"I think George would stamp on the rights of people in these very isles, if he thought he could. But he does appreciate the consequences that might ensue. Englishmen fight when they feel something's unjust.''

As an example, Mr. Fox cited mobs burning turnpike gates across the land in protest over the high road tolls levied by this or that nobleman who had secured control of a turnpike.

"Some Americans are protesting their grievances in much the same fashion,'' Fox went on. "But that, George will not allow.''

"The Prime Minister said I sounded like a pupil of someone called Adams. Who is he?''

"The longest, sharpest thorn in the side of His Majesty. Samuel's his first name, I believe. Said to be the most adamant and reckless of those who've opposed the King's policies in the Royal Province of Massachusetts.''

Then Mr. Fox went on to sketch some of the events that had produced increasing hostility between George III and his colonial subjects over the past few years.

The trouble had really started at the end of the Seven Years' War. The financially exhausted government had reached the perfectly logical conclusion that, since British troops had defended and secured the safety of the American colonies during the struggle that had raged from India to Canada, it was only right that the colonies begin paying a proper share of the war debt.

Various taxes had been levied on the Americans by a succession of pliant and accommodating ministers. Mr. Fox referred to a sugar tax, then a tax in the form of royal stamps ordered to appear on various colonial documents. Phillipe recalled Girard's mentioning the latter.

The taxes raised the question of whether the King's government in London had the right to impose such levies on the colonies without their consent.

"The crux of their complaint is that they have no voice in Parliament. Therefore they reserve to themselves the right to say what's taxed internally and what isn't."

Colonial protests, Fox explained, ultimately forced revocation of the stamp tax. But then, Chancellor of the Exchequer Townshend—"Champagne Charley," Fox called him with pious distaste—put through a program of new taxes on all glass, lead, paints, paper and tea imported into America.

"And do you know what happened then, lad? The good Englishmen of the colonies got together and said, 'Be damned to your merchandise! We don't need it.' Trade dropped off like a stone falling into a chasm. There were other, more violent protests—attitudes aren't all that clear-cut, you see. Many American subjects of the King want only fairness. Agreement to the principle that they alone control internal taxation. A good example of that position is one of their trade representatives who's in London right now. A learned man called Doctor Franklin. Other's though—especially the Massachusetts crowd—hate the whole idea of a king telling 'em what to do. Adams is reputed to be the worst of the Boston hotheads. He created so much mischief in sixty-eight, royal troops were sent in to garrison the place.

"Surprisingly, though, when the colonies stopped importing, the loudest squeals came from this side of the water. From the merchants of London and the other cities. And they're influential enough to be listened to—so when North took office last year, he threw out Champagne Charley's duties. All except the one on tea. That was kept merely to show America the King does have the power to tax, and the colonials had best not forget it.

"Things seemed to be getting back to normal till Adams and his friends stirred the pot again. The Boston mob provoked the troops one winter night. There was a street riot. Five colonials shot down in the snow. Altogether, it's a troubled land. On one side, good Englishmen totally loyal to the King. In the middle, others still loyal but arguing for fair dealing. And the rest—radical like Adams—crying that even redress of grievances isn't enough.

"That dangerous man may actually want complete freedom from the Crown's authority! Of course he'll never get it, short of fighting. Because King George *is* a strong-willed man in spite of that soft Dutchman's face of his. He'll have his way. That's why he keeps the soldiers in Boston-town. That's why he chooses an accommodating fellow like North for prime minister.

"It's a curious thing," concluded Mr. Fox, rising, "but travelers bringing news from London say the colonials by and large believe the King to be their friend. Their difficulties, they think, spring from the character of his high-handed ministers. But it's not the ministers who arrange things, it's His Majesty. For some reason, the Americans don't understand that."

"What's your opinion of the right and wrong, Mr. Fox?"

After a pause, the other answered, "I suppose it might be fair to allow the colonists a certain say in how they're taxed. Beyond that, I draw a line. Even Pitt drew it. The King is the king. If the Americans refuse to bend to the reasonable exercise of his will, they must be punished.

"Ah, but I've dawdled too long. Time we got on with more practical things."
He pointed to the horse turds littering the yard. "Such as shoveling."

Phillipe got to work cleaning up the dung. He had enjoyed listening to Fox.
And he would have liked to discuss the theories expressed in the books Girard
had given him. Especially the notion of the contract between men and their
monarchs, the contract that could be broken if the rulers proved too autocratic.

Phillipe really didn't know where he stood on the whole complex of questions.
His outburst at North had been more personal anger than moral conviction. He
really didn't want to be classed with the "mob-ility." If he could negotiate the
perils implicit in the confrontation with the Amberly family, he would much
prefer to be well-dressed, well-fed, rich and secure.

At least that was the state of his thinking on this sunlit morning in June 1771,
while he was shoveling up horse manure.

━━II

THE KENTISH summer turned steamy, June melting in to July, then August.

Phillipe's secret meetings with Alicia Parkhurst continued, though less frequently, because Mr. Fox kept him busy at Wolfe's Triumph. He and Marie had
moved into a single tiny, airless room. Marie worked in the kitchen. The activity
didn't seem to lessen her general despondency. She spoke little, even to her son.

The summer heat and the waiting grew oppressive. Phillipe's only respites
were the occasional nights he could arrange to slip away to Quarry Hill, but even
those became less than satisfactory.

Alicia brought occasional reports that Amberly was no better. And she began
to act distant, guarded. Phillipe picked up unsettling hints that she was reverting
to her old self, hiding deeper emotions that might threaten her future.

As they lay together after one particularly long and ardent period of lovemaking,
Alicia reached out through the darkness of the dell to fondle him with a kind of
callous intimacy. He couldn't see her face. But her amusement was unmistakable—and her speech slightly thickened; when he'd kissed her at the start, he'd
smelled claret again.

"If only Roger know how this sweet, strong machine pleasures me. His
expression would be priceless, I think."

Phillipe pulled away, upset. It was the gilded whore talking. He gripped her
shoulder.

"You promised you'd never tell him."

Fireflies glowed golden in the dark. She sounded annoyed as she answered.
"Why, not unless you abuse me in an ungentlemanly way. As you're doing
now."

He let go, tried to kiss her to make amends. She permitted it. But she wouldn't
abandon her original subject.

"Roger thinks he's such a perfect master of his world. The condition only
grows worse after he's strutted around London awhile—"

"He's back, then?"

She nodded. "I really think it would be charming to shatter his illusions. But
don't worry, my dear. I meant what I said before. We'll keep the secret. I was
only teasing you."

Still, the remarks troubled him for days afterward—until other events intruded
with devastating abruptness.

Phillipe was serving a platter of mutton to evening diners. He was out of sorts; he'd gone to the message tree four days in a row and found not so much as a note. He presumed Roger's presence had sharply curtailed Alicia's freedom. He fervently hoped there was no other reason for her silence.

All at once, he overhead a remark by one man in a coarsely dressed group at a corner table:

"—given wages and told to leave for the rest of the day. I guess Amberly will never have the pleasure of seeing the fine greenery we've been laying out according to Mr. Capability's plan."

Phillipe turned cold. He approached the table.

"Sir? What's this you speak about at Kentland?"

"The black wreath hung on the door," said the laborer. "We were told his lordship died shortly after noon."

The platter dropped from Phillipe's shaking hands. Some of the juices spattered the laborer's breeches. But Phillipe paid no attention to the cursing as he streaked toward the ktichen to find Marie.

III

THEY RAN down the now-familiar towpath through summer darkness pricked by heat lightning along the northwest horizon. Marie seemed obsessed with one thought, which she kept repeating aloud:

"We were not told. She wouldn't lower herself to tell us!"

As they dashed up the long drive, Phillipe noted that most of Kentland's windows showed lights, as if the household were in a state of commotion. A death wreath did indeed hang on the great door. Marie broke into tears at the sight of it.

Phillipe hammered the door. The senior footman answered, recognized him, said:

"This household is in mourning. Private mourning."

"I am entitled to see him!" Marie sobbed.

"Be quiet, you vulgar slattern," snarled the footman, starting to close the door. Phillipe's anger quickened. But before he could move, Marie hurled past him, a fist striking the footman's cheek.

"I will see his body! *Let me in!*"

Her hysteria drove all concerns but one from Phillipe's mind—the desire to spare her humiliation. He seized her arm, tried to pull her back.

"Mama, I know how you feel. But there are certain courtesies to the dead—you mustn't carry on this way. Let's go back to Tonbridge. We'll come tomorrow, when you're feeling—"

"Let go! He was your *father!* I have a *right* to see him!"

All at once the footman vanished. The door swung inward. Phillipe caught his breath at the sudden sight of Lady Jane Amberly.

The Duke's wife was dressed in black. She seemed to tower against a background of shocked faces—the horrified servants. Then Roger appeared, crossing the foyer, equally somber in a black suit much like that worn by the physician Bleeker.

Roger's face was wrathful in the light of the candles illuminating the doorway. The hoof-shaped mark at his left eyebrow looked nearly as black as his clothes.

He carried his varnished walking stick. Its huge silver head reflected the candle flames in glittering highlights. At the sight of Phillipe, he shook visibly. But not from fear.

Gripping the edge of the door with one pale hand, Lady Jane said, "Madame, you exceed the bounds of all decency. Leave at once! And take this information with you—my husband woke briefly before he died. He charged me to care for his son. His *legitimate* son. He never mentioned your name, nor that of your boy. You have no claim on us. The matter is closed."

The horizon lit with white light. Roger's face lowered over his mother's shoulder like a branded skull.

"If they won't walk away, I'll see they crawl away—"he began.

Lady Jane's stern eyes and upraised arm held him back. Then she started to shut the door.

Stunned, Phillipe inadvertently relaxed his grip on Marie. He realized his error too late. With another cry, she threw herself at Lady Jane and would have knocked her down if Roger hadn't stepped quickly in front of his mother to shield her.

"Leave this house, you French scum!" he screamed, and struck Marie in the side with the silver head of his stick.

Marie stumbled back. Roger Amberly wore no wig tonight. His hair was virtually the color of Phillipe's, contrasting with his white face, accenting the death's-head pallor of his cheeks. This came as a blurred impression while Phillipe tried to catch his mother as she fell.

He wasn't quick enough. Marie sprawled on the top step and exclaimed in pain.

That sound drove through Phillipe like a knife. He grabbed Roger's throat with both hands and dragged him outside.

Roger rammed the silver head of his stick against Phillipe's chin. Phillipe let go, staggered back, his foot missing the top step. He flailed, then tumbled all the way down to the drive.

Dizzy, he heard Roger's shoes clatter on the stone. Two male servants shouldered past Lady Jane, to help their master. Roger whirled on them, the brandished stick a blurred arc.

"Stay back, all of you! *I said stay back!*"

The servants hesitated, withdrew past Lady Jane as Roger leaped down the steps, loomed over his dazed half-brother, almost cooing:

"No one shall give the bastard his comeuppance but me—"

Face twisting with savage glee, Roger whipped his arm up. Frantically, Phillipe rolled aside. Holding the stick by its ferrule end, Roger sought to smash the huge silver knob down on Phillipe's head.

Roger's blow struck the ground instead, missing Phillipe by inches. He scrambled up, listening to the sibilant, almost deranged sound of Roger's violent breathing. Lady Jane cried out for her son to be careful, not to injure himself on a worthless nobody—

Roger paid no attention. Neither did Phillipe, circling away from his antagonist. In the yellow candlelight spilling from the house, half of Roger's face took on a jaundiced, poisoned color.

"I'll kill you for tormenting my mother," he said, taking a firmer grip on the stick. Then his voice dropped lower. "And for Alicia. Oh, yes—she's told me. Flaunted you! Her little French lover—"

Panting for breath, Phillipe tried to assimilate what he'd just heard. One of his

worst fears had been realized. Alicia had revealed the liaison—but why? *Why, when she'd promised—?*

Roger kept circling, poking at him with the silver stick head. "You're afraid of me, aren't you?"

Thrust.

"I can see it in your face, bastard. You're afraid—"

Thrust.

"Well, by God, *you have good cause!"*

Abruptly he grasped the stick with both hands, club-fashion, and brought it whipping down toward Phillipe's head.

Phillipe tried to dodge. The silver head glanced off his temple, bringing immediate dizziness. Lady Jane cried out again—some caution or warning, Phillipe didn't know. He was trying to outmaneuver Roger's foot in the uncertain light. But the kick caught him in the groin, doubled him over, dropped him to his knees.

He heard the warning hiss of air, stabbed both hands upward, deflected the stick blow that would have smashed his skull.

Then four hands gripped the stick, wrestling for it as Phillipe lurched to his feet.

Roger was mouthing incoherent obscenities now. But he was strong. The two figures swayed back and forth.

Roger drove his knee into Phillipe's genitals again. As Phillipe reeled and let go, Roger spat in his face, then swung the stick in a sideways arc. Phillipe ducked; ducked again, as the winking head whipped back the other way.

The spittle sticky on his face, Phillipe rolled his right shoulder down and bowled into Roger full force. He crashed his half-brother to the ground, kneeled on his throat. Roger squealed and clawed at Phillipe's eyes, his cheeks purpling till they were almost the hue of the clover mark—

But Phillipe got hold of the stick.

With one hand he seized Roger's right arm. With the other, he brought the stick down head first on Roger's pinned fingers. He struck the open palm once, twice, then again, again, the silver head hammering, each blow bringing the release of more hatred and frustration.

Smash.

SMASH—

Marie shrilled his name in warning. He twisted his head around, saw servants with branched candelsticks—and one with an ancient saber—boiling down the steps. Marie's streaked face shone like a coin in the windwhipped glare of the candles. Concern for her son had brought her back to reality. She tugged at him while Roger writhed on the ground, gripping his right wrist with his left hand. Spittle foamed on his lips—

The skin of Roger's right palm was broken. The fingers were bloody and oddly angled. *God help me,* Phillipe thought in terror, *what have I done?*

One of the footmen almost caught him. Phillipe tore away, ran with Marie down the driveway full speed. Two servants gave chase. Over his shoulder, Phillipe saw the antique saber flash—

Then he heard Lady Jane call out:

"Let them go! See to my son first, all of you. Do you hear me? *See to my son!"*

With oaths of disgust, the pair of pursuers fell back. Phillipe and Marie dashed on through the darkness.

When they reached the junction with the towpath, Phillipe looked back.

At the door of Kentland, candlesticks still bobbed and fluttered. He thought he could make out the bent, pain-wracked figure of Roger being helped inside. He urged Marie to run faster, away from the sight of the great door closing, the entrance darkening to black.

Fear swallowed him as they fled to Tonbridge.

___IV

"I WOULD say the situation for you is very desperate." Mr. Fox spoke with sad frankness, having heard Phillipe's gasped-out story.

Noting the appearance of Marie and her son when they stumbled back to Wolfe's Triumph, Mr. Fox had immediately hurried them into the kitchen and sent Clarence out, along with the serving girls. Now he brought them a tankard of ale each and blocked the door to the common room with his back.

Phillipe gulped the ale. It did little to wash away the taste of fright and ruin.

"You say Lady Jane's son struck first?" Fox asked.

"He did. He struck my mother cruelly hard."

"But they have witnesses, and you have none. They have status—and you have none. For your own safety, you must leave Tonbridge at the earliest opportunity."

"For the coast?"

"No, they'll expect you to go to Dover. Go to London instead. Lose yourselves in the town awhile. It won't be easy, but it's better than surrendering your lives."

"In God's name, how can we get to London?" Phillipe stormed, the tankard still shaking in his hands.

Mr. Fox tried to remain calm. "On the diligence that leaves at half past eight o'clock tomorrow."

"But we have no money!" exclaimed Marie.

"I will advance you some, though I can ill afford it. Let's hope morning won't be too late. Perhaps not, if young Roger's the paramount concern right now. I'm sure Lady Jane is convinced she can have you taken any time she wishes. Otherwise, she wouldn't have let you go."

"I think I destroyed his hand," Phillipe said, unsteadily. "I didn't mean to do it. But he was attacking me—he'd have killed me if he could—"

Because of Alicia.

And he'd trusted her! To repay the trust, she had bragged about their affair! Mr. Fox's steady voice interrupted his confused thoughts. "I'll put Clarence on watch, to alert us in case of surprise visitors. Try to get some sleep if you can. And if French folk pray to the deity, I'd suggest a prayer asking that confusion at Kentland and assistance for Roger spare you the attention of the Amberlys for another twelve hours."

But it was not to be. The Amberly coach arrived at the inn at half past seven in the morning.

__8
Trap

AT THE appearance of the Amberly coach, Mr. Fox came racing to their cramped room to warn them.

Marie started when she heard the news. She nearly dropped the brass-cornered casket which she'd been about to pack into the open trunk. Phillipe heard horses stamp, a coach door slam.

"Who's in the coach?" he asked, already reaching for Gil's wrapped sword.

Fear chalked Mr. Fox's face as voices sounded down below. "I didn't wait to see or inquire! Put down that damned sword and run for the back stairs. If you hide in the stable, perhaps I can convince 'em you've gone. Quickly, *quickly!*" He pushed Marie.

Phillipe left the sword. As he rushed out of the room, he thought about going back long enough to hide the casket; it lay in full view on the bed. But he didn't because Mr. Fox was in such a state of agitation.

Fox hurried them down the rickety steps and out across the rear yard. The morning sky showed unbroken gray clouds. As Mr. Fox gestured frantically from the stable door, a whiff of a breeze sprang up, bringing the first patters of rain.

The landlord rolled the creaky door aside, pointed to the dim interior where green flies buzzed over the straw.

"Go in the last stall. Don't make a sound, in case they search. Don't even draw a loud breath till I come back to tell you it's safe." He rolled the door shut and left them in darkness.

Phillipe led the way to the hiding place Fox had mentioned. They crouched behind the splintered partition. His initial alarm had begun to fade, replaced once more by anger. He squatted with his back to the partition, staring at Marie's face, a face he hardly recognized.

She looked beaten. Gone was the strength that had tautened every line of her features when she first drew the casket from behind the Madonna in Auvergne. Her dark eyes avoided Phillipe's. Veins stood out as she clasped her hands together.

Praying?

But he knew of no gods mighty enough to protect them from the wrath of people like the Amberlys.

Overhead, rain drummed the roof thatching. The sound was counterpointed by Marie's strident breathing. A dismal voice deep inside him said, She's surrendered. To illness. To strain. To fear of the Amberly money, position, power—

With a terrifying creak, the stable door rolled open.

Phillipe searched the stall for a weapon. A stone. A bit of wood. He saw nothing. Footsteps scurried in their direction.

Marie cowered visibly. Phillipe resigned himself to fighting with his hands—

Suddenly Clarence appeared at the end of the partition. Popeyed with astonishment, he reported, "The coach brought only that fat churchman. He wishes to see you. In Father's room—he said it must be private. He pledged no harm to either of you. Father's greatly relieved. But he asked you to hurry, so as not to anger the visitor."

All at once Phillipe began to feel a little more confident. He helped Marie to

her feet, guided her out of the stable and across the yard through the showering rain.

They climbed the rear stairs again, to the commodious sitting room Mr. Fox reserved for himself. Seated in a armchair next to a chipped deal table on which a single candle burned, Bishop Francis awaited them, his porcine hands folded in his lap, his moon face piously sad. Of Mr. Fox there was no sign.

Clarence went out and closed the door. The prelate's small blue eyes studied mother and son a moment. Then, in that syrupy voice, he said:

"I beseech you to cooperate with me in making this meeting as brief as possible. Grave spiritual matters require my presence at Kentland. Let me, then, go immediately to why I have come here."

He adjusted a fold of his robe. "Around midnight, I was awakened and made aware of grievous news. The tragic, untimely death of Lady Jane's husband. I proceeded to the estate with all due speed—sending prayers ahead. On arrival, I learned how sorely such prayers were needed. I found circumstances that compound an already tragic situation. Young Roger was being treated by Dr. Bleeker. His mangled hand may never straighten again."

At the conclusion of the mournful pronouncement, the bishop's tiny eyes flicked momentarily to Phillipe. More compassionate than condemning—

Unless the bishop was trying to gull them. Phillipe was suspicious. Perhaps from tiredness, tension—

"Roger has no one but himself to blame for what happened," Phillipe said. "He struck my mother."

Bishop Francis raised his hand. "Such a remark is unnecessary. Did not our blessed Savior forgive, no matter what the sin or its cause? Following His precepts, my purpose is not to wrangle over who is guilty. As I believe I remarked on my previous visit, the Church must play the role of conciliator. Peace maker. Binder of wounds. That is my mission—in addition to enumerating certain distasteful but unfortunately relevant facts."

Phillipe's distrust mounted. It wasn't rational; but it was there nevertheless, gnawing in his mind.

"I arrived at Kentland to discover young Roger raving and screaming in his bed. Oh, a most heart-rending sight! Despite the young man's pain, he made his intentions quite clear. He wished to pursue you—" He indictated Phillipe. "When Dr. Bleeker categorically stated that Roger's injuries made such action impossible, and I interjected that the action would be morally reprehensible, Roger still threatened to employ surrogates—armed servants—to carry out his desire to shatter one of God's prime commandments—"

"In other words," Phillipe interrupted, "he wants to kill me or have me killed."

"Sad to say, you are correct."

"That's nothing new."

The bishop ignored the bitter comment. "Only with prayers and fervent persuasion at the bedside did I manage to turn him from that course."

Phillipe trembled a little, hearing the mellow pulpit voice speak of murder. Francis went on:

"I could not stand by and permit such bloodshed! But from a practical standpoint—and this is the part distressful to my soul—Roger would, of course, be safe from reprisals."

"Safe?" Marie burst out. "He could kill my son and not be punished?"

"Not even accused or troubled by an inquiry—under the secular law. Believe

me, madame, striking at the Amberlys, you have struck very high. Such a family is all but invulnerable. No one in the neighborhood—no one in the realm, I venture to say—would concern himself about your son's death. As the sparrow falls, God's eye is upon it. But not, alas, the eyes of a magistrate. However—" Francis hitched forward slightly, his lips and forehead beginning to glisten. "My intercession and prayers showed Roger Amberly and, more importantly, his mother the moral folly of Roger's desire. True, my restraints may be no more than temporary—"

Phillipe spoke with a clarity that matched the cold rage he felt inside:

"Let me understand you, bishop. You're telling us that because I'm low-born, and Roger a nobleman, he can have me murdered and not be punished?"

"That is the unhappy fact, yes."

In that case, Phillipe thought, then Girard was right. It was indeed time for storm winds to blow away the rotten structure of the aristocracy.

Said the bishop: "After winning Roger's assurance that he could not act in haste—and seeing him finally asleep with some of Bleeker's laudanum—I took counsel with Lady Amberly. As you might suspect, her situation has become intolerably tormenting—"

"No more tormenting than ours!" exclaimed Marie.

"Yes, yes, madame, I fully appreciate your state of stress," he soothed. "But do remember—Lady Jane has not only lost her husband, she has seen her son possibly maimed for life. She is not the sort to accept all that lightly. But she *is*, we may say with thanks, at heart a Christian woman. Able, ultimately, to overcome her natural instincts and listen to a higher voice—a higher doctrine than the doctrine of Cain."

Sweet, flowing words. Almost hypnotic—

And yet Phillipe kept sensing a trap being set behind the pious, blubbery face.

"In short," Francis concluded, "after much soulful struggling, I wrung a concession from Lady Jane. She is prepared to let the past be forgotten—provided you both agree, finally and unequivocally, to certain terms—"

Phillipe almost laughed aloud. He had suspected before that he and his mother had in their possession the means to force a victory. Now the bishop's words assured him of it. Relishing the realization, he got a jolt when he heard Marie say:

"Go on."

"In the coach, dear woman, I have a pouch containing notes in the amount of two thousand pounds sterling. Lady Amberly has reluctantly agreed to that sum—and no action against you—" The blue seed eyes focused on Marie, picking up reflections of the candle in their depths. "—if—if you and your son will renounce all claims upon the family and return to France. Permanently."

"Two thousand—?" Stunned, Marie was unable to finish the sentence.

"I beg you to accept the offer!" Francis struggled to his feet like some purple mountain rising from a tremoring earth. The sausage-fingered hands spread in pleading eloquence. "It's not only a just settlement but—realistically speaking—handsome. Handsome indeed! Lady Jane is anxious to bring an end to the disputation, the turmoil. Join her in that endeavor! I can see the sad ravages of this wrangling in your face, madame—the toll it has taken. Why harm yourself further? Why risk your safety or your son's? Depart, and you can live in modest comfort for the remainder of your days! I plead as much for your welfare as for Lady Jane's—accept!"

"No," said Phillipe.

Marie glanced sharply at her son. Bishop Francis bit his lower lip, teeth sinking deep into the wet pink flesh for a fraction of time. Then he recovered, his melancholy seeming to deepen.

"Oh, God's wounds, sir!—is this another Cain who confronts me? I've wrestled one already tonight! Haven't I explained the alternative to acceptance—?"

"Yes, but the facts are no different than when we first knocked at the door of Kentland. Amberly was my father, the letter is legal, she knows it and apparently she'll do anything to see that Roger takes the whole inheritance. What if I wait another few hours? Will her price go higher?" Phillipe said contemptuously. "It can't be high enough unless it's the amount full due—half!"

Abruptly Francis faced away, concentrating on Marie:

"Madame, you are my last hope. I come here with the best of motives—and find Satan's imps of greed and error have preceded me. Talk to your son, madame. Open his eyes!"

Looking worn out, Marie said, "We can at least consider the offer, Phillipe—"

"Yes, yes madame! That's being sensible. Besides"—Francis turned back to Phillipe, the skirt of his purple gown belling—"if you wait, as you put it, for the price to go higher, there is no guarantee you will be alive to receive the payment. May I be forgiven in Heaven for alluding to such a grim reality, but it's the truth."

Marie gave a small, humbled nod. To his horror, Phillipe saw that the bishop—and the Amberlys—had broken through her defenses at last.

His jaw set. "Mama—"

"Don't you understand what the good bishop's saying, Phillipe? I won't risk your life!"

"And by accepting, you will save and enrich your own!" the churchman exhorted. "Roger will recover. Lady Jane may waver. I cannot constantly, constantly be in attendance, urging restraint—" He pressed his palm against his eyes suddenly, as if sezied by a dizzy spell. And in that moment of postured overstatement, Phillipe knew there *must* be a trap.

"Be damned to Roger and his threats!" he shouted. "I'm not afraid of him."

"But I am," Marie Charboneau said wearily.

She faced the bishop, her shoulders slumping. Phillipe started to argue. She was quicker.

"Two thousand pounds will last many years—we will accept the offer."

"Mama, listen! You're selling out everything you wanted, everything you—"

"I will not sacrifice your life. We will accept the offer."

Heaving a long sigh, Bishop Francis intoned, "Blessed be God's holy name. Wisdom and virtue have prevailed."

II

PHILLIPE STARED at the prelate's round face. The jowls shone with dozens of tiny diamonds of sweat. The battle of words had been an exertion. He thought bitterly, *No, power has prevailed.*

Showing more animation, the bishop seemed to collect himself.

"I will go down to the coach and bring you the money. I ask only the

opportunity to read the document at the heart of the dispute. You'll recall that when I tried to examine it before, I was not permitted to touch it.'' The blue eyes voiced Phillipe's on that point. ''Thus I saw only that the handwriting appeared to be the Duke's, and that the letter was duly witnessed. Before bringing this matter to its happy conclusion, it would be poor stewardship if I did not assure myself of the letter's contents.''

Marie gave a forlorn little nod. ''Fetch it, Phillipe.''

''I don't see why that's necessary, Mama. Lady Jane knows the contents of—''

''Fetch it,'' Marie said, her voice hoarse, her eyes exhausted.

He wanted to refuse. He didn't. The will to fight had gone out of his mother. Nothing he could say or do would overcome her fear for his safety.

He left Mr. Fox's sitting room and returned shortly with the casket. Bishop Francis was removing a tie cord from a pouch that contained a thick packet of notes. As he did so, he said:

''On Christian as well as material grounds, madame, I could not be more pleased. This sum will indeed keep you in comfort many, many years—'' For the first time, the unctuous smile Phillipe remembered from the first interview tugged up the corners of his mouth. ''A moment more and we're done. The letter—''

His right hand lifted, palm up. Phillipe saw sweat-diamonds glistening on the fat and in the deep folds. Again he was deviled by his conviction about a trap. Swiftly, he looked at Marie. Tried to explain, plead, warn with a glance—

She didn't see. Or did, and chose to ignore it. She turned away.

Swallowing, Phillipe opened the casket. He removed the folded letter carefully, handed it to Bishop Francis.

''Thank you, my son.''

The bishop inclined his head to study the French script. He held the letter in two hands, blinking abruptly—squinting—as if having difficulty with his eyesight. He lowered the letter to waist level, his concentration still fixed. A bead of sweat ran down from his left ear. Phillipe's mind screamed a wild warning—

He shook his head, angry. *What was happening to him?* Bishop Francis was still reading. Nothing was amiss.

The bishop held the letter only by its right margin now. He turned his flabby body toward the deal table, as if to provide more illumination on the document—

The bishop's right hand kept moving.

Toward the light.

Toward the candle—

''Mama!'' Phillipe shouted. In that wasted instant, Francis thrust a corner of the document into the candle flame.

Francis still smiled. But his eyes were triumphant.

For a harrowing moment, Phillipe was too startled to move. He was mesmerized by that vicious smile. By the thread of smoke rising. By the faint crackling. He drove himself forward, dropping the casket—

But Marie, her eyes wild as any harridan's, was quicker. And more savage; she had fallen all the way into the snare.

She seized the bishop's right wrist with both hands, jerking the fat arm toward her. Charring at the edges, the letter came out of the flame. Francis' left hand, an un-Christian fist, rose with startling speed. He smashed the side of Marie's head, knocking her over—

Ugly-faced, Francis started to kick her as she went down. Phillipe leaped on

him from behind, digging his fingers—his nails—into the folds of white fat at the nape of the bishop's neck. Francis shrieked like a woman.

His right hand opened. The letter fluttered toward the floor, still afire. On hands and knees, Marie had presence enough to reach for the burning document, slap out the glowing edges even though she gasped in pain doing it.

"You stinking, hypocritical bag of pus!" Phillipe howled, whirling the bishop around by the shoulder and hammering his fist into the veined nose. The fat man staggered, upsetting the armchair, then the deal table and the candle. The candle winked out.

The light of the rainy sky filtering through the shutters turned the bishop's face gray as rotten meat. He reeled clumsily along the wall, mouthing one filthy oath after another. Outside, Phillipe heard hallooing coachmen, wheels creaking, hoofs clopping away.

Francis wiped a sleeve across his bleeding nose. Gone was all pretense of piety. The small blue eyes glittered like a snake's.

"Impious whoreson!" he spat. "Hell take you for striking a man of the cloth!"

"As it's taken you already," Phillipe retorted. "She sent you here, didn't she? But never for the purpose you pretended. She sent you with tricks and sweet words to get the letter and destroy it—because we'd never suspect that of a man who pretends to serve God. It nearly worked the first time, so she sent you back again—*get out of here before I break your damned neck!*"

Face contorted, the bishop suddenly comprehended the rage that turned Phillipe white. A terrified look flashed over the bishop's face. He bolted for the door.

Phillipe took two steps after him, reached down and seized the pouch of money. He threw it after the retreating churchman.

Snuffling, his robes stained with blood and mucus, Francis picked up the pouch and disappeared down the stairs. Moments later, Marie and her son heard the sounds of a second coach departing.

Phillipe went to his mother's side. She was unfolding the burned document. The lower edge, including the last few letters of the right-hand witnessing signature, crinkled to black ash and fell away. A section of the upper edge was likewise destroyed. But the central message remained intact.

Boots clattered on the stair. Mr. Fox burst in on them:

"You young madman! What did you do to the bishop?"

"Hit him," Phillipe growled, righting the overturned chair and sinking down in it, fingers against his temples.

"In God's name, lad why?"

"The only purpose of his visit was treachery. He pretended to make a settlement with us—just the way he did on the first occasion. He claimed to be protecting me from Roger's revenge. All the time, he wanted nothing but that letter. You can see where he tried to burn it."

Fox shuddered. "Then the Amberlys are desperate indeed."

"He offered us money," Phillipe raged. "Two thousand pounds if we'd go away—"

"And I agreed!" Marie said. "I *agreed!* I never dreamed they could buy a holy man."

Sadly, Fox shook his head. "Madame, I've tried to give you some notion of the reach of that family. There is nothing they cannot order, or cause to have done. They'll probably have this place burned to the ground because I've harbored you," he added in a rare moment of self-pity. He stalked to the window,

clouted the shutters open to reveal the roofs of Tonbridge under a slanting gray shower.

Phillipe rushed to his side. "Mr. Fox, you've showed us only kindness. We'll leave at once."

"Easier said than accomplished," replied the older man, staring miserably out over the village. "Didn't you hear the other coach? The one for London—departing right on schedule? And," he finished after a moment, "there's not another till tomorrow morning, same time."

He rubbed his eyes, then looked chagrined.

"I'm sorry I turned on you, lad. I won't worry about losing this place till it happens. What must concern us is your welfare. I wonder if you dare risk waiting for the next coach?"

The late summer rain pattered in the silence. From the High street came the ringing of a bell and the cry of a baker's boy hawking buns. Finally, Phillipe said:

"No, I think we'd best go immediately."

"Go where?"

"The country. We can hide in the woods. That way, if they come hunting, you can prove we've gone."

"Phillipe's right, Mr. Fox," Marie agreed. "We can't let your generosity bring you to harm."

Fox licked one of his protruding upper teeth. Then a certain determination sparkled his glance again.

"I appreciate that, madame. On the other hand, is it fit that a piece of real estate take precedence over human lives? I can compromise my cowardice one more day, I think. I prefer that to feeling like a hypocrite at the Methodist meeting."

He tried to give them a show of cheer; an encouraging smile. Phillipe realized how great the effort must be.

"If you want to chance it," Fox said, "I'll offer you the same fine quarters you enjoyed earlier. I mean the stable. Should anyone come inquiring, I'll say you left the inn this morning—which will be true. Then you can slip aboard the coach at half past eight tomorrow—my offer of fare still standing."

Marie Charboneau flung her arms around old Fox's neck, hugging him and weeping her thanks in French. The landlord looked acutely embarrassed.

Phillipe said, "I think we'd best pack the trunk and haul it to the stable with no further delay."

III

CLARENCE BROUGHT them bowls of cold porridge and two mugs of ale an hour later. Then he rolled the door shut and sealed them in again.

Phillipe was already wishing they hadn't stayed. The place grew oppressive with its smell of moldy straw and horse droppings. He watched a spider weaving a web in the corner of the stall. He thought of Jane Amberly, Duchess of Kentland. And wondered whether the poor and powerless of the world were always at the mercy of those in authority.

Somehow, there should be another way.

Again he recalled Girard's talk of the storm winds sweeping the world. No

breath of them seemed to reach Kent. Then where did they blow, cleansing the evil of those who manipulated men's lives to their own ends?

A small sound from Marie broke into his thoughts. She looked waxen, leaning back against the side of the stall with her eyes closed.

She put down the ale without drinking. She hadn't touched the lumpy porridge, either. "I am sorry for this, Phillipe. My ambition for you has led us into a game we had no chance of winning."

He touched her hand. "Perhaps there's still a way when we reach London." He tried to sound optimistic; inside, he was anything but that. "We might find a charitable, decent lawyer to help us press the case. We could offer such a man a portion of what we finally recover."

Marie stared at him a long moment. "I'm glad there is still some hope in you. Those people have all but destroyed mine."

He clasped his fingers tighter around her cold-flesh. "I swore you an oath, remember?"

Eyes still closed, she gave a faint, embittered nod. The rain kept up its beat on the roof.

Phillipe felt troubled again. In attempting to reassure Marie with false words, he came to the unanswerable question again. Did he really want to become like the Amberlys? *Did he?*

Tormented by the dilemma, and chilled to drowsiness by the dampness of the stable, he roused abruptly when the door creaked. Mr. Fox appeared.

"A hired boy brought a message—"

"Summoning me to an ambush, no doubt."

"It's possible," Mr. Fox agreed.

"What's the message?"

"There is a lady waiting in a willow grove a half-mile up the river. Her name wasn't mentioned. But she claims she must see you—it's most urgent."

"Who hired the boy? The lady?"

"No, some servant girl from Kentland. She met the boy delivering milk at the edge of the village, and—"

Phillipe scrambled up, clutched Fox's arm. "Did the boy tell you the name of the servant wrench, by chance?"

"I believe it was—yes, Betsy. That's it, Betsy."

"And what did you say to the boy?"

"Exactly what we agreed. That you'd left the inn. He didn't care one way or another. He'd already been paid, and he was all in a rush to get back to his milk pails—here! You're not going?"

"Yes, I must."

Phillipe turned to speak to Marie, saw she'd fallen asleep. As he started for the stable door, Fox cautioned him:

"By your own words, you could be walking into their trap."

"I realize. I'll be careful. When my mother wakes up, tell her I'll be back in good time—"

"Go through the trees along the shore, then," Fox shouted after him. "For God's sake stay off the towpath!"

The words faded as Phillipe ran through the gray morning, toward the Medway and the one person he hoped would be waiting there.

9
Flight

HE KNEW the location of the grave well enough, having met Alicia there once before. Taking Mr. Fox's advice, he avoided the towpath, running instead among the trees on the riverbank below.

He jumped little inlets where the Medway had cut into the lush banks, moving so fast that his chest began to hurt. At the same time, he kept an eye on the towpath in case a cart should appear—or pursuers dispatched from the estate, perhaps.

The supple willow branches lashed his cheeks as he rushed along. He saw the grove ahead. Nearby, the towpath curved away from the river, toward the green hillock from whose far side he'd first glimpsed his father's estate.

The willows in the grove grew close together. But in the gray-and-green of the stormy summer day, he thought he detected a black horse moving behind the screen of overhanging branches. That reassured him a little, though he remained wary of surprise attack.

He leaped a last channel, pushing at the living, green-leafed curtain—

"Alicia?"

"Here."

"He plunged into the dim heart of the grove. Rain began to pelt again. The towering willows offered protection.

He came on her suddenly, waiting beside her splendid black stallion. She wore the same familiar riding costume. But her tawny hair was disarrayed, the ribbon at the nape of her neck half undone. Her cheeks were flushed. And one was marked with a nasty blue-black bruise.

She saw him notice it immediately, smiled in a forlorn way.

"A small remembrance from my intended. It's of no importance. Phillipe, I can stay only a few moments. This time I literally had to creep out of the house like a thief—after sending Betsy ahead. I only managed it because all the attention's on the bishop and"—sudden fear on her face—"plans for you." Tearful, she looked into his eyes. "Oh, Phillipe—what possessed you to attack Francis?"

"The pious bastard tried to trick us. On Lady Jane's orders, I imagine. He tried to burn my father's letter."

"The coach brought him back to Kentland in a perfect rage. Face all bloodied—and his language! Foul enough to make a fishmonger blush. You've got to leave Tonbridge, and quicky. That's why I had to see you. Warn you."

Bitterness twisted his mouth. "Salving your conscience for telling Roger about me?"

She turned pale. "How did you know?"

"He told me the night he attacked me."

"I don't imagine you'll soon forgive me—"

"No."

"It did happen by accident. At dinner. I drank too much claret—"

"A habit of yours, it seems," he said, harsh. Then he regretted it. He could understand a little about why she had to dull her senses so often.

For her part, Alicia was quick to answer him:

"He provoked me in the extreme, Phillipe! It was right after he returned from

London. He began boasting of an orange girl he'd dallied with. He met her one night at the theater—''

"So you, in turn, had to cut him down with an account of your own amusements? I really wonder if you weren't planning to do that from the start.''

She nodded, as if tired. "Perhaps I was. Perhaps—even despite my promise to you. Well—'' She fingered the blotched bruise. "I got my reward. Roger saw to it—in private.''

"And you're going to marry a monster like that?''

"Yes,'' she answered, a whisper. "There are—disagreeable parts to any bargain.''

"Christ in heaven! That's not a bargain. That's sentencing yourself to—''

"Don't Phillipe. It was settled long ago. Long before Quarry Hill—''

She touched his cheek. Her hand was warm. And capable of arousing memories, emotions, that quelled some of his anger.

"But what we shared was far more than amusement, my darling. Don't you know that by now? If it wasn't so, would I risk coming to tell you that Roger's up, and readying his plans to dispose of you? His hand's all wrapped in batting, like a mitten. My God, I've never seen him so angry—like a madman. This very minute, he's organizing some of the household men. To send them after you and your mother. At the very least they'll attack you and take the letter. At worst, they may kill you. I tell you he's completely out of his head!—you destroyed his hand, even Bleeker admits that. I—''

She hesitated, turning away. Never before had he seen so much as a trace of shame on her face. Now he saw it.

"—I know I'm partly responsible for what happened. Because I drank too much—and refused to bear his bragging.''

Phillipe still wondered whether her regret was wholly honest. There was no pleasure in Alicia's blue eyes. Yet he could vividly imagine its presence when she'd flung the truth of her liaison at her intended husband.

He cared for her. Deeply. But he knew, with a sadness, that his original impression of her was still, in part, valid. There was a whore in her.

True, the whore was elegant and soft-eyed. But underneath, calculating. And with the quick temper of her kind.

He rubbed the shiny flank of the restless black horse. The animal turned its head to nip. Phillipe stroked the stallion's muzzle to calm him, saying:

"That's done with. Obviosuly I'd better be concerned about the present. My mother and I plan to leave Tonbridge in the morning, by the London coach.''

"You don't dare delay that long! Believe me! Get out of the village. Hide in the fields. Along the river on the other side of Tonbridge—anywhere—but hide.''

He shook his head in disgust. "They're ready to kill me—when they should be making preparations to bury my father? What a despicable lot they are.''

"You've pushed them too far. As to preparations for the burial—''

A peculiar stiffness seemed to freeze her features. She turned away again, gazing down between the overhanging leaves at the Medway dappled with raindrop rings.

"—those can wait awhile,'' she finished. "Until the more important business is accomplished.''

He puzzled about the change in her expression a moment ago. He'd learned to recognize when she was concealing something. But his emotions made him forget that. Almost against his will, he slipped his hands around her waist and up

her back. He pulled her close to savor her warmth; the sweet breath he'd known so intimately.

Very softly, he said, "I wish you could come away with me, Alicia."

"In spite of the grief I've caused, telling Roger?"

"God help me—yes."

The blue eyes brimmed with tears. She bent her head into his shoulder. He stroked her tawny hair while she cried.

"I—I wish I could too. But I've told you I'm not strong enough for that. I'm what I was born and taught to be. The Alicia who drinks too heavily, and spills out secrets that should stay hidden. I will be Roger's wife next year."

He sounded bitter again: "I realize I have far less to offer. No inheritance except on a piece of parchment they mean to destroy. No pack of servants to call up to do murder at my bidding—"

"Please!"

She wrenched away, in agony.

"You knew what I was from the beginning, Phillipe. Do you realize how much I've thought about leaving everything to be with you? How close I am even now? So close it terrifies me! That's what you've done. That's how you've shaken and changed me."

"But not enough." Rage passing again, he drew her close. "Not enough."

His own eyes had grown blurred with tears. He fought them back as he lifted her chin, gazed at her a long moment before kissing her. Alicia clung to him with all her strength, bending his head into an almost painful embrace.

He didn't want to shatter the suspended moment. All the realities—the danger from Roger Amberly; the soft rustling of the willow leaves in the rain; his mother waiting back in the village—had faded to the background.

But one by one, those realities claimed his mind. He broke the embrace gently.

"I loved you, Alicia. Nothing that happens can ever change the truth of that."

"Loved, Master Frenchman?" Once more she tried to smile through the weeping. This time, she almost brought it off. Her shoulders lifted, though the jauntiness was still false and forced. "Can't we keep it in the present tense? Do you think a woman—even a woman like me—can ever forget the first man she really cared about? Or gave herself to? I love you and I always will. I swear I'll feel you close even when I'm with another man, for all the rest of my life. If I've never spoken the truth before, I swear by Almighty God I'm speaking it now. Be thankful we had the summer. Now go—before I decide to come with you."

Whirling, she dashed to her horse and mounted, pulling the rein so fiercely the black whinnied against the bite of the bit. She ducked under the branches and drove the stallion up the slope through the willows to the towpath, and out of sight.

Phillipe touched his face. Wet. With tears. And rain. The shower was driving hard enough to penetrate the trees—

As he walked out of the grove, he marked down one more score against the Amberlys of the world. They offered what he could not. The property and position that, in the end, had lost him a woman with whom he might have spent the rest of his life, knowing her weaknesses but loving her uncontrollably in spite of them.

LESS THAN an hour after Phillipe Charboneau crept back into the village of Tonbridge, he and his mother had left it for the last time.

Walking through clover meadows still damp with the morning showers, their plan was to strike north-westward, toward the hamlet of Ide Hill. At Phillipe's belt hung a tied kerchief with five shillings and some bread inside; the landlord's way of helping their journey.

Mr. Fox had apologized for the smallness of the gift, then issued warnings about the dangers to which they must be alert. Highwaymen on the public roads. Fees to be paid at the turnpike tollhouses if they went that way—or dodged, if they didn't. Suspicious country folk who might recognize them as foreigners and, very likely, fugitives of some kind.

Mr. Fox had advised that they might filch apples from orchards and find creeks with sweet, drinkable water, but they would be wise to avoid towns of any size until a week's walking, give or take a day or two, brought them near the city of London. Because of the necessity to travel swiftly and lightly, living off the land, the trunk was left behind at Wolfe's Triumph. Phillipe carried Gil's wrapped sword, Marie the small leather casket. They took nothing else.

By the time they neared Quarry Hill, Marie already looked weary. Despite the anguished memories the hill held, Phillipe decided to wait there until dark before pushing on, both for Marie's sake and to give them the cover of night.

The showers had cleared. A peaceful blue late afternoon sky replaced the earlier gray. Crickets began to harp noisily in the fields.

"We must go faster till we reach the hill," he urged, aware of their high visibility in an empty pastoral landscape. Marie countered with a question about the identity of the woman who had sent for him.

Phillipe kept his face expressionless. "I didn't realize Mr. Fox had told you—"

"Certainly. Who was she?"

He answered with an elaborate lie. It was a kitchen wench from Kentland. She knew one of Mr. Fox's serving girls. Phillipe had met her when she'd come to the inn to visit. Embellishing the falsehood, he added that he'd even passed some hours strolling with the young lady out in the country during the summer.

Being a kindly girl, he finished, this morning she'd arranged to warn him of Roger's planned action, at some personal risk.

Face wan, eyes remote as they trudged through the fields, Marie Charboneau accepted the explanation without question. But she said in a hollow voice:

"There was another girl. A beautiful girl—with the young man, the first day we went to Kentland. Remember?"

He kept his face impassive, scanning the horizon in the lowering light. A speck moved on a distant road snaking across the top of the hill. Only a farmer's cart, he realized a moment later, relieved.

Marie went on with her toneless reverie:

"She was the kind I wanted you to marry. Rich and beautiful and of good station. I had such hopes of a good marriage."

To try to cheer her, he smiled. "I'll make a match like that yet. My claim still stands." He tapped the casket which she crooked in her arm protectively.

They reached Quarry Hill as sunset came on. Settled on the damp ground well back among the trees, Phillipe broke the coarse, crumbly bread Mr. Fox had given them. He handed the larger half to Marie. She was shivering. She'd

brought only a plain woolen cloak to wear over her already muddied clothing. He could hear her teeth chatter when she tried to bite the bread.

He sat beside her, pulled her head close in against his shoulder, to let the warmth of his body reach her if it would. And suddenly, he felt the strange reversal of their roles, a reversal that had come about without his realizing it.

She was the child now, and he the adult, her strength.

He helped steady her hand as she brought the bread to her mouth. She chewed it slowly, like an old woman.

In the distance he heard the sound of horses, traveling fast.

He left her and slipped to the edge of the trees.

Below, in the red light of the August evening, half a dozen men rode in the direction of Tonbridge. He recognized their liveries. The sunset flashed on the belled muzzle of a blunderbuss carried by the leading rider. As he watched them pass, his stomach began to ache.

When the horsemen disappeared, he crept back into the woods to find Marie dozing. He touched her forehead. Warm.

He sat awake most of the night, feeling like a speck—nothing—beneath the twinkling summer stars.

Yet if he were nothing, why did he feel so much fear?

And so much hate?

BOOK TWO
THE HOUSE OF SHOLTO AND SONS

1
Swords at St. Paul's

THE GREAT city of London stank and chimed and glittered.

And as he first observed it with feverish eyes in the mellow light of early September, Phillipe Charboneau thought he'd never viewed anything half so marvelous and awesome.

They had approached through the southern sections, coming at last into the tumult of Southwark. Phillipe's fair command of English gained them the information that to reach the Old City, they must cross the Thames River. As they were doing now, near sunset, by the Westminster Bridge.

All around, crowds jostled; iron-tired coaches rumbled; and the great river below, alive with barges plied by shouting watermen, mingled its tang with the more pungent aromas of those passing to and fro on the bridge.

Marie walked listlessly. Her eyes were half-closed. Phillipe carried both the casket and the wrapped sword. Their money was long gone, spent carefully for tart cider or sugared buns, at small, poor inns they'd felt free to visit only after dark.

But now the long, exhausting journey on foot seemed to fade behind the panorama spreading in front of Phillipe's astonished eyes.

London. A sprawl, a hurly burly of wood and brick buildings of all conceivable styles, shapes and heights, bordering the river upstream and down for what appeared to be two or three miles. Splendid church domes shone dull gold in the autumn light, despite the pall of smoke accumulating from thousands of rooftop chimney pots. One dome in particular, eastward around the curve of the Thames, glowed with special magnificence.

Phillipe stopped a pair of boys. Both carried short brushes fully as black as

their cheeks and ragged clothing. He inquired about the imposing dome in the distance.

"Country lout, not to know Master Wren's greatest church!" jeered one of the boys, giving a wink to his companion. "St. Paul's! 'Ware you don't get sold a piece of the river!"

The sweeps were hidden suddenly behind a sedan chair whose liveried carriers jostled Phillipe and his mother out of the way. Inside the chair, a wigged gentleman fondled the brocaded breasts of a woman who laughed and slapped his wrist lightly with a sequinned domino on a stick.

"Mama—" Phillipe was force to speak loudly because of the incessant din. Church bells predominated, clanging and chiming from all quarters of the stained sunset sky. "We'll have to sleep where we can again tonight. There's a great church yonder. If we make for it, perhaps we can find shelter."

Marie's lips barely moved, the only sign she'd heard him.

Soon they reached the end of the bridge. Phillipe discovered that negotiating their way to the landmark dome had all at once become impossible. They were plunged into streets that took abrupt turnings. Buildings hid the skyline. Creaking wrought-metal shop signs effectively shut out the little remaining daylight.

The cobbled streets were perilously narrow, too. A drainage channel ran down the center of most of them. After a few minutes on such thoroughfares, Phillipe began to make sense of the patterns of foot traffic.

Those more elegantly dressed, or more robust, or armed with swords or sticks, kept to the sides of the street closest to the walls. Shabbier, less bold pedestrians made their way down the middle, walking as best they could through and around the mess in the drainage channels—fruit peels and vegetable garbage, human turds and puddles of urine, even an occasional rotting cat carcass.

But the head as well as the feet had an occupation—to stay wary, and dodge and duck when a bone or a heap of refuse came sailing down from above without so much as a cry of warning.

Phillipe's hair soon stank from being pelted with soggy garbage. Yet so alive and exhilarating was the spectacle around him that he learned the lesson without great anger. He started to keep sharp watch, and congratulated himself when the contents of a pot for human waste came showering down—and he pulled his mother safely out of the way.

Of all the sensations driving in upon him in one magnificent blur, the greatest, perhaps, was that of continual noise.

Stage coaches and wagons creaked and clanked in nearby streets. Young boys hawked newspapers, bellowing through tin horns. Rag pickers and post collectors rang handbells to announce their presence. Linkboys with torches already lighted against the descending darkness shouted for those ahead to make way.

When this happened, Phillipe and Marie had to fight for space along the wall, bumped here by a barber prancing along with a load of wig boxes, there by an old toothless apple woman shoving ancient-looking fruit at them with a plea that they buy. Then the linkboys would pass, preceding a sedan chair from whose windows there looked out yet another finely dressed member of the gentry, safe above the turmoil and the filth.

A cadaverous young man with yellow skin and foul breath thrust a sheaf of printed sheets under Phillipe's nose, fairly screaming, "New songs for sale! Latest ballads and amusements of the town!"

When Phillipe tried to back away, the balladeer clutched him. Phillipe broke into French, with gestures of noncomprehension. The vendor spat an obscene

word, turned away and, grinning instantly again, accosted the next potential customer.

Phillipe and Marie struggled on. He was afraid they might be going in the wrong direction now. He approached two women at a corner. Their backs were to him as he said:

"Pardon, but is this the way to St. Paul's church?"

He expected young faces. To his horror, he saw old ones, all white paste and rouge. One of the women grabbed at his trousers, began to shamelessly manipulate his penis so hard that he quickly came to erection. The stringy-haired slut whispered, "Ye'll not get a fancy fuck in that place, young sir. But step up the way a bit and we'll accommodate ye. We'll put yer auntie into the trade, too, if yer's pressed for a livelihood—"

Once more Phillipe resorted to French and helpless gestures as a defensive weapon. The tactic incurred curses even more flamboyant than those of the song vendor. Up the lane from the corner, Phillipe glimpsed a pair of hulking men lounging in the shadows. He suspected that something more than a "fancy fuck" awaited anyone foolish enough to accept the invitation of the two sisters of the street. He and his mother hurried away.

As darkness deepened, merchants shuttered their shops. Other windows began to glow. Coffee houses, taverns, eating establishments. They had passed into a section he was told was indeed the Old City, dating to Roman times. The crowds thinned out. Phillipe grew more wary.

And more lost.

He and Marie wandered through a square of elegant brick homes, then along several more lanes to a broad avenue where huge market wagons groaned in from the country with fragrant loads of melons and cabbages and apples. The wagons lighted sparks with their iron tires. Another cart passed, full of butchered cow quarters crawling with flies.

Finally, unable to catch so much as a glimpse of the great dome above the rooftops, Phillipe accosted an old gentleman standing on a ladder at a lantern post in another square.

"Which way to St. Paul's?" he shouted, dodging drops of hot oil that came sputtering down from the fresh-lit wick inside the box.

"That way," waved the old gentleman, climbing down and looking annoyed because Phillipe acted confused by the generality of the instructions. *That way* was a dozen streets, or a hundred; who could tell in this incredible urban maze?

"Keep straight on the way, ye're going!" the lamplighter barked. "Ye'll know the place from the immoral songs, and the beggars. I'd sooner visit hell at night."

Grumping, he lugged his ladder to the next lantern post. Such lighting devices, Phillipe noticed, were located only in areas like this one—tree-filled squares surrounded by prosperous homes. Once back in the narrow lanes and stews, light vanished, save for that of the ubiquitous linkboys preceding their masters, who walked or rode in chairs.

Phillipe pressed on—eastward, if he reckoned directions properly now that the sun had dropped out of sight. He was stinking dirty, and dizzy from fever, lack of food, or both. Marie was no more than a voiceless weight clinging to his arm. Yet he was continually excited by it all. By the wagon noise which, if anything, increased after dark. By the yells and bawdy laughter from the taprooms and coffee houses. By the occasional cries that might have been pleasure—or pain. He even caught the sound of two distant pistol shots.

How many hours he and his mother wandered, he had no idea. He heard loud bells chime to the number of eleven when they finally turned a corner and saw a wide paved area. At its far side towered the magnificent architecture of the church he'd glimpsed from the bridge.

St. Paul's Yard, sure enough. On the ground near numerous shuttered stalls, booths and business establishments ringing the open area lay a host of cripples and semi-invalids. Some rose to surround him and stretch out their hands— "A farthing, gentle sir. Remember the poor and save them from the curse of prison!"

Phillipe pushed a path through a half-dozen of these remarkably agile wrecks of all ages and degrees of uncleanliness. He stepped between Marie and one scabrous, slimy hand that pawed at them. He made threatening gestures. The beggars retreated, spitting at his feet, cursing him. He helped Marie up the great stone steps of the church to the doors, pulled at one of the rings.

The church was locked for the night.

He turned and surveyed the Yard. One lantern shed feeble light on a couple of seated balladeers. They passed a gin bottle back and forth between choruses featuring the most blasphemous, scatological quatrains Phillipe had ever heard.

The air had grown chill. The din of London receded. He realized how friendly a background the noise had become during the time they'd walked the mazy streets. Coach wheels grumbled and halloos rang only occasionally now, from far off. Other than the lanterns of the beggars, lights were few. A linkboy's brand winked like a firefly down some distant lane, then vanished.

And out in a darkened section of the Yard, Phillipe heard a shuffling that prickled his scalp.

He helped Marie sit down against one of the porch pillars. She mumbled an incoherent syllable or two. Phillipe rubbed her forehead. Burning. His own wasn't much cooler. His belly, though long accustomed to the pains of shrink-age, hurt again. His mouth was dry. The reek of his own body offended him.

He was glad to see Marie already dozing. Her torn woolen cloak provided her only protection against the night air. Again he heard a *shuffle-shuffle* of rag-wrapped feet—and sibilant voices.

The beggars.

He smelled them before he saw them. They advanced slowly up the steps in the darkness, stinking phantoms festooned with rags. He heard quavery old voices. Younger ones, too. *Shuffle-shuffle* went the feet as they came on.

Abruptly, one voice became audible:

"—lettle box. Could be jewelry. Also a long bundle. Might be a sword, General."

"An' the poor need 'em things more than the strangers do, ain't that so?"

"True, General, true," another man replied. Phillipe heard a raspy laugh.

The balladeers had extinguished their lantern and gone to sleep. St. Paul's Yard was silent.

Inside the church, there might be protection, other human beings. Out here, there were only human predators, chuckling and shuffling up the stone stairs as Phillipe fumbled to unwrap Gil's sword while there was still time.

II

HE COUNTED eight or nine surrounding him in a half-circle. They looked shaggy because of their town garments. The gleam of the stars above the rooftops revealed little more than their shapes. But here and there, a detail stood out. The glisten of a pustular sore on a cheek; the paleness of light-colored facings on the old uniform coat of the one who styled himself the General.

Phillipe could see nothing of this man's features. He was of good size, though. The top of his head gleamed faintly silver. A dirty wig. Stolen, probably. The wig hung low over his left ear, lending the General's head a peculiar, cocked look.

Metal winked in the General's right hand. A sword? But so short—

Then Phillipe realized the blade was broken off halfway to the hilt. A wicked weapon.

His breath hissed between his teeth as he let the wrappings of his own sword fall between his feet. He kicked them behind him, waiting to see how the game would play out. One of the beggars fluttered a hand in his direction.

" 'E's got a proper sword indeed, General. One we might fence for a nice sum."

"Here, sir!" the General announced, advancing up another step and flourishing his broken weapon. "Will you surrender 'at prize to me army of poor? We're only a hop and a step away from debtor's chains in the Fleet, don't ye realize? 'Em valuables, sold off, will keep me troopers warm an' cozy till Christmas or better."

"Get away," Phillipe warned, sidestepping nearer the pillar where his mother dozed. Marie muttered in the night's cold. Phillipe feared for her exposed position. But he was glad the fever screened out the reality of the immediate situation. He repeated his warning:

"Get away!"

"Funny sound to his talk, ain't they, General?" asked one of the others. "Ha' we caught ourselves some Frenchified rat what swum the Channel?"

"Even more reason for surrendering to 'is Majesty's sojers," allowed the General, moving up one more step. He was now just two down from Phillipe. "Hand us 'em things an' there'll be no military reprisals 'gainst that old lady with you."

Two of the raggy phantoms at the right of the ring—Phillipe's left—suddenly scampered up the stairs, hands shooting out for the casket in Marie's lap.

Phillipe had no chance to recall even the rudiments Gil had taught him with sticks. He had time only to pivot and bring his sword arm hacking down.

The blade bit to bone. One of the pair shrieked and dropped to his knees, wrist half severed.

"Then it's no terms!" cried the General, sounding almost happy. "Attack, men—*attack!*"

The command was wholly unnecessary. With the exception of the injured beggar who fled down the stairs wailing oaths, the rest advanced as one. The ring closed with the General at the center, so close Phillipe could smell his unbelievably putrid breath.

Phillipe whipped the sword up to block a downward stroke of the General's blade. Metal rang. Sparks flew.

Hands caught at Phillipe's legs, his ankles, tripping him off balance. He fell

on the stairs, head striking stone. A beggar stamped on his belly. The General gouged at his eyes with the broken end of his sword.

Despite the pain in his middle, Phillipe managed to wrench his head aside. The General's blade raked more sparks from the stair. Phillipe thrust out with his right arm, took satisfaction when Gil's sword slid through rags to a thigh. Another beggar howled and scrambled away.

But the rest piled onto Phillipe, sitting on his legs, his abdomen. The General kneeled next to his head.

One rough-nailed hand caught Phillipe's hair, lifted, then smacked his head down on the stair. The other beggars spread-eagled him, pinned his right arm out and began to scratch and claw his wrist. Phillipe's fingers opened. He lost the sword.

The General's crooked wig loomed, clearly defined by a suddden wash of ruddy light behind him. "Cut both their shitting throats!" the General panted, driving the end of his blade at Phillipe's neck. Simultaneously, another voice shouted from the foot of the stairs:

"Let be, Esau! It's none of our affair!"

Phillipe wrenched his head again, violently hard. The General's blade gashed the left side of his throat, a fiery track of pain. At the same time, Phillipe heard a loud, solid thwack.

The General fell on Phillipe, struck from the rear. A frayed epaulette tickled Phillipe's nose as he fought out from under the burden.

The General rolled off, staggered to hands and knees, his lowered head weaving from side to side. His wig, even further askew, hung down over his left eyebrow.

"Bleeding balls of the martyrs, who be hitting me?" he groaned. More weight lifted from Phillipe's arms and legs; the beggars jumping up, scattering down toward the Yard—

Through blurred eyes, Phillipe glimpsed two sturdy figures. One, on the stairs, lashed about with a heavy stick, knocking a head here, a shin there.

The other man down in the Yard took no part. He was a motionless silhouette against the source of the ruddy light—a linkboy's torch.

The attacker with the swinging stick thudded and thwacked the beggars, bawling. "You scum would pick the very linen of Christ on the cross!" He bashed one slow-moving fellow in the side of the head. The man went down in a floundering heap.

Phillipe sat up, a little more clear-headed. Suddenly a noise drew his attention toward Marie.

The General had managed to hold onto his broken blade, shifting it to his left hand as he crouched and reached for the casket. Phillipe saw his own sword being carried off by a beggar whose tatters fluttered as he ran.

Ignoring the warm, sticky wash leaking down his neck into his collar, Phillipe lurched after the thief. He caught him in the Yard and tackled him around the middle.

A-tumble, they rolled back toward the bottom of the stairs. Phillipe used his fist to bludgeon the back of the man's head, heard teeth crack on the paving stones. Then he was on his feet with Gil's sword secure in his sweaty right hand.

The big stranger had caught two more of the hapless beggars and was trouncing them in turn. Mere boys, Phillipe saw by the guttering torch. But he felt no pity—nor had he time for any. The General, one hand clutching his half-sword,

the other Marie's casket, was pelting down the steps toward the sanctuary of the darkness beyond the torchlight.

Phillipe drove himself into a run, caught up with the older man and killed him with one sword stroke through the back.

The General crashed onto his belly. The side of his face flattened against the pavement. His mouth flopped open as his bowels emptied, a terrible stench.

The big stranger on the steps paused to search for more enemies; saw none. He jogged down toward Phillipe, slapping his stick against his tight breeches while his companion and the linkboy approached to bend and stare at the General.

Phillipe retrieved the casket. Unbroken, he saw with relief. The stranger who hadn't fought said thickly to the other:

"Now there's murder done, Esau. To whom do we explain that?"

"To no one, Hosea. Because no one cares. Vermin squashed, that's all. They're a ruination of the neighborhood anyway. The good fathers locked up safely inside Paul's can decide what to do with the body in the morning. Let them be thankful decent citizens are protecting their holy sanctuary."

"But the boy—"

"Our linkboy saw nothing. Heard nothing." The big young man with clubbed hair swung toward the shabbily dressed carrier of the torch. "Did you, now?"

"No, Mr. Sholto. I've your money in my pocket to assure I didn't."

"Then let's go home," mumbled the other stranger, still with that slightly thickened speech. He bore a strong resemblance to his companion with the stick. He had the same wide shoulders and heavy, squarish jaw, though he looked to be a year or so younger. Perhaps twenty-one or twenty-two. Rather petulantly, he added, "You'd have us rescuing half the poor in London, I suppose."

"Only those unjustly preyed upon, Hosea."

The young man with the stick approached Phillipe. He had a blunt jaw, a broad nose, thick brows—and a suddenly amiable grin. "I heard the hullabaloo as we rounded yon corner, sir. I saw you put up a nice fight, considering the way they outnumbered you. I am Mr. Esau Sholto. This somewhat tipsy gentleman's my brother, Hosea. He's a good boy, but not of a temperament for street brawling."

"I'm grateful to both of you," Phillipe said. "I think they'd have killed us." He bent down and wiped Gil's blade on the patched back of the General's filthy uniform.

For a moment he glanced at the hideous wound left by his blade. Perhaps because of his feverish condition, or his exhaustion, he felt nothing. He'd changed a great deal since the woods where he'd accidentally killed Gil's would-be kidnapper. Well, so be it. That, apparently, was the price of survival.

Clutching casket and sword, he saw Mr. Esau Sholto flick a speck of dirt from the lacy ruffle at his throat as the latter said:

"Yes, sir, they would have killed you. For that reason, sensible folk stay shuttered indoors at night. Save when one brother must go with another to see he doesn't wager away the family business at the new quinze table in White's public rooms. Were you sleeping by yonder pillar?"

Phillipe nodded. "We came to town this afternoon. A church seemed a good place—"

"No, not any London church or street, after dark," advised Esau Sholto. "But you've learned that lesson, eh? Your speech isn't regular English. Do you come from France?"

Phillipe knew he must be careful. "Originally—some months ago. Then last week, we decided to journey up from—" he hedged the rest—"from the south."

His vision began to swim. He saw a double head on Mr. Esau Sholto's burly shoulders. He blinked away the illusion as Hosea thrust himself between them.

"Good God, Esau, will you have us chatter all night on top of a fresh corpse? Even the scruffy singers who were sleeping yonder have more sense than you. They ran off."

Esau laid a hand on his brother's shoulder. "We'd not have met any trouble at all, I wager, if it had been my kind of evening."

Hosea snorted. "Spring—Vauxhall Gardens open—an hour of that dreadful orchestra music—and home to bed, early and bored."

"Hosea, you are a narrow young man, thinking only of gaming and skirts. If you weren't my brother you'd be a thoroughly detestable fellow. As it is, I find you merely half-detestable. Do the Sunday sermons never bore past your ears?"

"Well, I'm usually dozing, so—"

"How many times has our father read the story of the Samaritan aloud?"

"Thousands," Hosea Sholto sighed. "To savor the King's English—"

"*And* drum some moral precepts into your thick skull. He's failed miserably."

Hosea took the rebuke in embarrassed silence. Esau asked Phillipe, "Have you some means of employment in town?"

"No, sir. But I expect I can find some. You've been of great help, don't trouble yourself furth—"

"I'll trouble myself as long as I please, thank you! Permit me to give you another quick piece of advice. Sleep somewhere else tonight. Far from here. The beggars of St. Paul's are a curious brotherhood. They remember faces. Even voices. They *never* forget grievances. It's the way of the ruined, gin-crazed poor. If you run into some of them again, it won't go easy with you. Or that woman you were protecting. Who is she?"

"My mother."

"Still sleeping," Esau said, sounding surprised.

"She's not well."

Hosea rolled his eyes toward the stars as Mr. Esau Sholto dug thick fingers into his waistcoat pocket.

"Perhaps I can spare a coin for lodging tomorrow night. I don't know a respectable landlord who'd admit you this late. I suggest you and your mother go back west, out toward Mayfair where the beggars seldom rove—"

All at once, St. Paul's Yard began to reverberate with the heavy clang of bells. Hosea stamped one buckled shoe. "Damme, Esau, it's twelve of the clock already."

"All right, all right, coming!" Esau extended two copper pieces to Phillipe. "Here, and good fortune to you. Let's hope other nights in London prove more hospitable than this one's been. There's work for industrious youngsters—"

"Younger in years, maybe," Hosea grumbled. "Look at his eyes. Living to four-and-twenty hasn't given you a corner on keen observation, you know."

With a tolerant chuckle, Mr. Esau Sholto dropped the coppers into Phillipe's hand. Somehow he lacked the power to close his fist. All at once his teeth were clacking. Waves of weakness, then nausea, wiped out his strength. He lurched forward.

Phillipe crashed against Esau Sholto, dropping the casket, the sword, the money. The coppers rang on the paving stones as he slipped to his knees at Esau's feet.

"Here!" exclaimed the big young man. "His mother's not the only one in bad health, it seems." Phillipe felt a callused palm on his cheek. "Why, his head's hot as the bottom of a kettle."

Phillipe mumbled apologies, tried to stand, couldn't. Esau's voice seemed to echo from a far distance:

"And that slash on his neck badly needs dressing—"

"Oh, damme, I suppose you'll summon the most expensive physician in London!" Hosea complained. Phillipe's skull rang and hummed. He saw only a blurred glow, as if the linkboy's torch had been lost in a fog. He scrabbled blindly till one hand bumped Marie's casket.

"And why not?" Esau Sholto retorted. "You won at cards for a change. We've plenty of empty rooms. You go fetch the woman, you mean-souled wretch. Be quick, or I'll give you the kind of knocking I gave those beggars!"

Hosea's voice retreated: "Dear God, what would I be without you for a conscience?"

"A sot, flat broke, afflicted of the whore's pox—not to mention detestable."

Big hands supported Phillipe under his arms. He let the foggy orange delirium give way to the dark of unconsciousness.

III

A BEAMED ceiling, dark with age. Beneath his head, a feather pillow of amazing softness.

He felt other sensations. The scratch of some kind of wool garment against his legs. A nightshirt? The thickness of a plaster dressing on his neck, where the General's broken blade had gashed.

The bed was a place of incredible warmth and comfort, thanks to the feather-filled blanket. But the bedframe vibrated occasionally from heavy thudding somewhere below.

He smelled something hot and fragrant, focused on a china cup held in the tiny hand of a small, mobcapped woman whose face was a crisscross of wrinkles.

"Can you drink this?" the woman asked. "Esau said you speak English although you're French—do you understand me?"

He nodded, astonished that he found himself in such luxurious circumstances.

"I doubt you've eaten in a while," she said.

He shook his head to agree.

"That's the reason we'll begin gently, with some black Bohea."

She cradled the back of his head with one hand, held the cup to his lips. He gulped, then spluttered. The woman laughed.

"Slowly, slowly!"

Thus, still feverish, Phillipe was initiated to his first taste of a beverage that, later, came to symbolize the essence of the haven he'd found. A haven whose full nature and identity he did not yet know.

He drank more of the strong tea, thanked the woman, said, "My mother was with me—"

"She's asleep on the other side of the wall. She'll mend with rest, I think. I bore Mr. Sholto five children. But only my two sons lived. The three little girls died early. Since we bought this house for a sizable brood, we've no lack of space."

The little woman said all this without a hint of pity for herself. As she left his bedside, she added:

"My son Esau has his father's good sense. Hosea is a good boy too, but he drinks too much. In fact Mr. Sholto caned him six times for being so reluctant to help last night. Hosea apologizes. Now try to sleep if you can."

With that she vanished, closing the door behind her.

Phillipe drifted back to drowsiness against the pillow, marveling at the comfort, at how safe he felt. Most miraculous of all was the renewed realization that the world was not entirely populated by Amberlys.

The occasional thudding continued below. Speculating on the cause of it—such a tame problem for a change—he slept.

___IV

MRS. EMMA SHOLTO would not let him get up, except to use the chamber pot, for three days.

Big-shouldered Esau appeared a few times, wearing black-smeared breeches and an equally stained jerkin over a full-sleeved shirt. And Hosea visited too, once, rather sheepishly. He was equally black-stained and smeared.

Hosea stated that he hoped the visitors were receiving good care and recovering their strength. Then he said with a guilty smile:

"Esau keeps reminding me I've no capacity for port. You do understand I was somewhat drunk in the churchyard?"

"You really didn't show much sign of it." Phillipe smiled back.

Hosea looked chagrined. "Some fall down. Some puke up their guts. But I walk around like a perfectly normal fellow—paying no attention to anyone but myself. I got Mr. Sholto's cane across the ass several times, by way of chastisement."

"Your mother mentioned that."

"I also got extra evening work, which I suppose is good. I won't squander so much of what I earn at the clubs. We'll produce our new editions more speedily. I'm not altogether certain whether Mr. Sholto's insistence that I work more hours is chiefly in the interest of punishment or profit."

Phillipe hitched higher in the bed. The plaster aside his neck itched. "Editions? Do you mean books?"

"What else? Don't you recognize this hellish black paste?" He displayed his smeared hands. "It takes hours to scrub it from under the fingernails. I thought you'd have heard the press thumping, too."

"I did, but I couldn't identify the sound."

"We work downstairs, live upstairs. This is Sholto and Sons, Printers and Stationers, of Sweet's Lane. Only a few paces from where we found you. Well— I'm under orders not to tire you out. Just wanted to make amends for the other evening—"

Phillipe grinned. "Not necessary."

With a wave and a smile, Hosea left.

Reflecting on his new circumstances, Phillipe again drifted into deep, relaxed sleep.

V

On the evening of Phillipe's fourth day in the Sholto household, the patriarch himself appeared for the first time. At least if the man had looked in before, Phillipe hadn't been aware of it.

In truth, he probably wouldn't have known if a coach thundered through the room. He had been luxuriating in sleep and security.

Mr. Sholto was a small person, lacking the breadth of shoulder of his sons. Both of them appeared with their father, standing behind him as he took the only chair in the modestly furnished bedroom.

Mr. Sholto's most prominent features were his oversized stomach, all out of proportion to the rest of him, his stern brown eyes and his aroma of ink.

The printer subjected Phillipe to a careful scrutiny, as if totting up his impressions before starting a conversation. His tiny, wrinkled wife appeared with a tray. Crisp-crusted mutton pie, a roast apple, a cup of the inevitable Bohea.

"Well, sir, I am Solomon Sholto," said the grayhaired man at last, as Phillipe dug into the mutton pie with ferocious hunger. "You are French, I understand. You have a mother in our next bedroom, and both of you were beset by the ungodly rascals who loiter at St. Paul's after dark. That's most of what I know. Are you well enough to tell me anything more?"

"First, Mr. Sholto, that we'll be in your debt forever for your kindness. I wish we could repay you."

"Who has asked for payment? We do our duty to our fellow men, according to the precepts of the Scriptures." The brown eyes darted momentarily to Hosea, who had wandered to the far corner of the bed, perching there until his father glanced his way. Immediately he stood up. He clasped his inky hands together, first at his waist, then behind him. Leaning against the wall, big Esau covered a smirk with one black-nailed hand.

"You mother has wakened once or twice," Mr. Sholto said. "But the fever still claims her. And so far, we don't know your names."

"Mine's Phillipe Charboneau, sir. Of the province of Auvergne."

"A long way from London," the elder Sholto observed. "What brings you to the city?"

Phillipe hesitated, the teacup at his lips; he was already beginning to like the strange, strong brew.

"Come, sir," Mr. Sholto chided firmly. "Enlighten us! French people don't simply pop up from nowhere. Unless you're an escaped murderer destined for hemp out on Tyburn Road, you've nothing to fear."

Phillipe thought a moment, then said carefully, "We came to England because of an inheritance."

"Somehow connected with that box you guarded so well?" Esau wanted to know.

"Yes, it—where is the casket?" he asked abruptly.

"Safe in the wardrobe in your mother's room," Mrs. Emma Sholto assured him.

"Along with that French sword," Hosea put in. "I'd give a deal to be able to hang that elegant sticker at my hip next time I visit White's."

"You and the fleshpots of St. James's Street," grumbled Solomon Sholto, "will not become reacquainted for quite some time. Would God that those infernal dens would shut all their rooms to the merchant classes, not just their subscription rooms. But extra presswork will serve the same temporary purpose.

And allow time for reflection on the sins of drunkenness and vanity, which permit no thought for the well-being of others.''

Hosea cringed. Esau again looked amused, only this time he let the amusement become a guffaw. Solomon Sholto silenced him with a glare equally as stern as the one he'd thrown Hosea. Then he continued to Phillipe:

''We do not pry into the belongings of our guests, you may be certain. So whatever's in the leather box, only you know.''

But his straightforward gaze as he hunched over, one ink-stained hand on his knee, indicated that he would very much like the information.

Phillipe glanced from face to face. Esau. Hosea. The small, strong wife. And finally the heavy-bellied head of the household—

Danger seemed remote. He offered a hint to test that conclusion:

''My mother and I fled from a village in Kent because we incurred the wrath of a great family. My life was threatened. We thought we'd be safer in the city crowds.''

Mr. Sholto said nothing, merely continued to stare. Warmed by the food and by these plain open faces, Phillipe felt resistance and suspicion melt. It was a relief to speak.

He told them most of it, omitting only the primary reason for the fateful struggle with Roger—Alicia.

At the end, he leaned back on the pillow with his hands around the still-warm teacup, awaiting a reaction.

''*Amberly!*'' Mr. Sholto exclaimed with sudden animation, hopping up and pacing the plank floor. ''I don't wonder you fled from that high-handed Tory crowd. This house is of a different persuasion. The Whig persuasion, which does not fully approve of the antidemocratic policies of the King or his puppet ministers—that little clique of King's Friends. From all I know of Whitehall gossip, your father would have been welcomed to that group with enthusiasm, had he not suffered an untimely death.''

''My mother speaks nothing but good of James Amberly,'' Phillipe protested. ''It was the same with the landlord and several others in Tonbridge.''

''Yes, well—the dead are the dead. Why haggle over their politics? I rather admire your audacity in challenging such a family. But I sense you have discovered what I could have told you merely from knowing the Duchess of Kentland's reputation. You waged a lost battle from the start. Nor would you be any more successful here, I expect. For every twisty-tongued lawyer you could buy, they could buy a baker's twelve, plus judges, magistrates—and thugs of every ilk, if that became necessary. When a woman like the Duchess wishes to refuse your claim, it *will* be refused, fair means or foul. Babies from the wrong sides of noble blankets can be found on every street in London. Some very few are lucky. Press their causes to successful ends. But most fail. For your own safety and peace of mind—as well as your mother's—I'd advise you to give up your quest, find a means to earn enough money to pay your way back to France, and forget the whole matter. Above all, say absolutely nothing about your claim—and your origins—outside this house. You'll never become rich, but you'll live longer.''

Emma Sholto rested a tiny hand on her husband's shoulder. ''He's tiring, Solomon.''

''Nonsense, he's a stout young man.''

''Still, I insist we let him go to sleep.''

Garrumphing, Mr. Solomon Sholto pushed the chair back to its place. He herded his sons toward the door. Both stared at Phillipe with new appreciation.

After the printer's wife had gone, Esau and Hosea lingered in the hall while the elder Sholto paused in the doorway.

"Should you decide to follow my advice, young man, and wish to do honest labor to accumulate that passage money back to France, we might be able to make a place for you here."

"I wouldn't want special favors, Mr. Sholto."

"None given, sir! You'd be in for hard work, I guarantee."

"Don't London craftsmen keep apprentices to help them?"

"Aye, and I've had two. Both have run off. I am demanding, but not cruel. The lads, however, considered me the latter. I wouldn't tolerate the swilling of gin by ten-year-old boys. Where they came by the stuff, I preferred not to know. Stole it? Killed for it?" He shrugged unhappily. "They were already so hardened before I took them on, they reminded me more of ancient dwarfs than children hopeful of learning a trade."

"Bad sorts, both of 'em," Esau agreed.

Phillipe broke in to say that the Methodist landlord of Wolfe's Triumph had mentioned the evils of gin drinking among the London lower classes.

"Then," said Mr. Sholto, "there's a point at which I, a High Churchman, and your friend of a Dissenting sect, may agree. But it's no wonder boys like that must besot themselves early in order to survive. They're brutalized from age seven or eight on up. With long hours. Backbreaking labor suitable only for grown men. The abuses of inhumane masters. I don't blame a lad who's known nothing but brutality and poverty for learning to drink, and drink hard, almost as soon as he can walk. For that reason, I did not order pursuit of either of the runaways—you realize there are severe punishments for the crime? Fingers or toes may be cut off. The two boys I lost one after another will be punished enough before their days run out all too soon. Ah, but I'm chattering on—Mrs. Emma will have after me in earnest. You've heard we have an opportunity here. Esau could teach you the fundamentals, I imagine—"

"Right quickly," Esau grinned.

"And it's a noble trade, because it promulgates that which neither kings nor armies can put down. The free traffic of the ideas of men's minds."

A small, protesting voice sounded from down the hall.

"Yes, Emma, yes—a moment more!" He looked at Phillipe. "To put it plain, we would welcome your assistance. Especially since some in the firm prefer virgins' sighs to vellum bindings. The offer is open."

The door closing hid the three—including Hosea, who had turned all red again.

VI

THE NEXT day, Phillipe made his way to Marie's room. He told her of the printer's advice, finishing, "I think I'd best accept Mr. Sholto's offer."

Marie protested instantly: "No! I will not let you give up the claim!"

"Just for a time," he said, with quiet authority. Inside his mind, a faint voice mocked him:

Or do you really mean forever?

Marie started to argue again, then looked closely at her son's face. It seemed older, showing the understanding of hard lessons recently learned. She put her head back on the pillow and turned away.

Phillipe left the room with a sense of sadness. Yet he was excited by a fresh sense of purpose, too. A purpose born of plain, homely kindness, of black tea— and the new world of presses and books waiting for him downstairs.

2
The Black Miracle

THE BUSINESS establishment of Mr. Solomon Sholto was divided into two sections. The smaller, occupying the front part of the main floor, opened onto the clatter of Sweet's Lane. This was the stationer's shop, where Mrs. Emma presided over the sale of an assortment of drawing and memorandum books, fine Amsterdam Black writing ink, quills, sealing wax and sand.

During the preceding year Mr. Sholto had expanded the shop with a new service—a lending library. Several similar libraries had become popular in recent years because, as Mr. Sholto explained it, only the rich could readily plunk down two guineas for a personal copy of a momumental literary achievement such as *The Dramatick Works of Wm. Shakespeare, Corrected and Illustrated by Samuel Johnson,* which ran to eight annotated volumes with deluxe Turkish leather binding.

Mr. Sholto bemoaned the popularity of "frivolous" fictional tales such as Defoe's *Moll Flanders,* Fielding's *Tom Jones* and Johnson's moralizing fable, *Rasselas.* But he was quick to recognize the commercial appeal of such works. As a result, his lending shelves had expanded to fill two walls of the tiny shop and were crowded with all manner of novels, as well as nonfiction. Phillipe was captivated by some of the lurid fiction titles. *Delicate Distress. Married Victim. Adventures of an Actress.*

But he had little time for reading. Mr. Sholto was, as promised, a demanding taskmaster. He kept Phillipe busy in the noisier part of the business, in the back.

Here, two tall, wooden flat-bed presses sat on platforms flanking a central work area. On these premises Mr. Sholto and his sons did the production work for their clients—booksellers in the Strand, Ludgate Street, Paternoster Row. Sholto's churned out editions on individual contract to each seller.

Mr. Sholto and his sons divided the labor according to the skills of each. Esau, who looked the least graceful because of his size, proved to have hands of amazing speed and dexterity. These hands plucked the metal type letter by letter, then locked it into the large chase. The chase held a form of four pages. Mr. Sholto had invested in presses of some size, to be able to print that many pages at one time.

The father and his other, more easily bemused son, were responsible for operating the two machines. Mr. Sholto was faster and more expert. But Hosea knew what he was doing. When Phillipe would lug one of the astonishingly heavy chases over to him, Hosea would lift it as if it weighed nothing.

Hosea would then seat the chase in the coffin, which sat on the rails of the horizontal carriage. He would place a dampened sheet of paper between the tympan and frisket hinged to the coffin, then snap his fingers for Phillipe to be at his work.

To the new employee fell the task of inking a pair of leather balls. The balls were used to apply the ink to the waiting type. Though the balls had handles, it was messy work. Phillipe's leather apron, as well as his face, hands and fore-arms, was constantly sticky and smeared.

On his first few tries, Phillipe failed to press hard enough, leaving several lines of type uninked. But all three Sholtos were patient. They sensed Phillipe's eagerness to learn. Within a couple of days he had the hang of it and could ink a form neatly with no difficulty.

As soon as Phillipe finished the routine at one press, he frequently needed to run to the other to perform the same job. Hosea, meantime, would clamp the sheet between tympan and frisket, and fold both down so that the paper showed through the frisket in four page-sized cutout sections. These cutouts permitted the paper to come in contact with the inked metal.

Next Hosea would slide the coffin under the massive vertical head of the press. Hauling on the screw lever lowered a four-inch-thick piece of hardwood on top of the closed coffin. The leverage thus applied brought the thick platen down with sufficient pressure to leave an impression on the paper.

Finally, the platen was raised, the coffin pulled back along the rails and the finished four pages removed as a single sheet and set aside to dry. A new sheet was inserted in the coffin and the process was repeated, with re-inkings as necessary, until the right number of sheets had been run.

Handling his chores on both presses, each of which creaked and thunked outrageously, kept Phillipe running from one platform to the other virtually all the time.

But in spare moments, he was also assigned the task of washing the ink from each form once Hosea or Mr. Sholto had finished with it. To do this, Phillipe used a foul-smelling alkali solution that not only removed the ink from metal—and his knuckles—but left his hands raw by the end of the long day. The print shop operated from before daylight till after sunset every day except Sunday.

As the winter of 1771 approached, Phillipe grew fairly skilled at his job. His hands became swift and adept with the leather balls. His arms strengthened from carrying big stacks of dried sheets printed on both sides. The sheets were taken away by the apprentice who worked for Mr. Sholto's bookbinder. Sholto had long ago decided that he could produce books more quickly by subcontracting the sheet cutting, the sewing of the binding and the mounting of the leather-covered boards.

What gave Phillipe the energy to endure the always tiring, often confusing weeks was his interest in, and admiration for, the process of which he'd become a small part. It struck him as downright amazing that so many black-inked pages, precisely alike, could be produced at such speed by the rattling presses.

One noon, the elder Sholto noticed the way Phillipe's eye kept straying to a stack of finished sheets, even while he paused to munch sections of an ink-smeared orange. Sholto came down from his press platform and waved at the stack:

"Gad, Phillipe, you look as though you were in church! That's only a small reprinting of the *Wild* novel, which is certainly one of Mr. Fielding's lesser works."

"But to see words duplicated so easily—it really is like a miracle. In Auvergne, if you wanted a chair, the furniture maker carved and glued it with his hands, one chair at a time."

"Machines are the coming thing. All over England, factories spin cloth—spit out iron bars. The age of handwork is gone."

Wiping his fingers on his apron, Mr. Sholto accepted a wedge of orange Phillipe offered.

"Despite the way I complain about the trashiness of so many books, I love the business. Reading's the means by which the lowest man can lift himself from a state of ignorance. You see how popular my little loan library up front has become. The masses are hungry for words and more words. Whether the words be for diversion or enlightenment, printing them, as I've said before, is a profession of which a man can feel rightly proud."

Popping a piece of orange into his mouth, Phillipe could only nod in agreement. Ideas multiplied mechanically, for all to share, certainly had to be one of those new winds sweeping the world. And he was delighted to be at the heart of the gale.

II

DURING HER first weeks in the Sholto household, Marie seemed to recover some of her health. Color returned to her cheeks. She even showed a certain animation when Hosea and Esau discussed affairs of the town at supper.

But she said nothing about the Amberlys, not even to her son. Phillipe didn't mind. He was too occupied with the exciting, tiring work downstairs even to think about the casket and the letter. It was Hosea who first brought the subject up again.

The family was gathered in the upstairs sitting room, an hour before the customary nine o'clock household bedtime. Mr. Sholto was reading a *Gazette*, a penny paper containing, among other items, the latest bad news about the great East India Trading Company. The company's mismanaged affairs had caused its stock to take another alarming dip, he reported. He was thankful he owned no shares. The household did not use the products imported by the firm. Mrs. Emma served cheaper tea smuggled in from Holland. It was sold everywhere.

The printer's wife sat doing embroidery while Phillipe, already yawning, sprawled at his mother's feet, listening to big Esau run through some melodic country dances on the flute he played with considerable skill. Hosea, who had excused himself to visit the jakes, walked back in to say:

"Phillipe, I've been making some inquiries in the coffee and chocolate houses—"

"Concerning which gambling establishments are the most lenient with credit?" asked his father.

Hosea flushed. "No, sir. About the man responsible for bringing our lively helper to England."

Esau took the flute from his lips. Emma Sholto frowned. Solomon Sholto folded the penny sheet into his lap. Only Marie failed to respond. She continued to stare into space as if still entranced by the music.

Hosea sensed the tension generated by his remark, and quickly defended himself: "I thought there might be some interest in what's been said about the Duke's passing."

That lifted Marie's head slightly. Phillipe saw remembered hurt in her eyes.

Speaking rapidly, Hosea continued, "The curious thing is—nothing's been said."

Mr. Sholto exclaimed, "What?"

"That's right. As far as I can discover, no word of Amberly's death has come up to town."

"You're not exactly in the circles that would be the first to know," observed Esau.

"Yes, but the public rooms are always full of gossip about the leading peers of the realm. No one's breathed a word. I—I thought it puzzling," he finished lamely.

Emma Sholto said, "Perhaps the Amberlys have retired to a long period of private grief. Perhaps they prefer to say nothing of the death outside the immediate family until a suitable mourning period is over. Loss of a loved one can affect an entire household for months, you know."

Mr. Sholto put one hand over his eyes. Was he recalling his three dead infant daughters? Phillipe wondered with a touch of sadness.

In response to Hosea's obvious embarrassment, Marie said, "You needn't worry about mentioning him in my presence. The kindness Phillipe and I have found in this house has healed the wounds of the past."

Phillipe was pleased at that. Whether his mother did or did not mean what she said—and he felt she didn't, fully—the sentiment was correct. Marie went on:

"The presence of my son and I taxed Lady Jane to the extreme. Perhaps the death did indeed affect her mind. They shut the Duke up in a foul, airless room while he ailed. I wouldn't wonder they've chosen the same kind of solitude for themselves. They're peculiar, twisted people."

Somehow Phillipe wasn't entirely satisfied with the explanation. But he could offer none better. He yawned behind his hand, anxious to retire. He thought the matter closed until he heard Marie say softly:

"However, Hosea, if any word should come to you on your rounds, I would welcome hearing it."

Scowling, Phillipe stared at his hands reddened by the alkali solution. The past was past. Why couldn't she let it go?

Esau noticed his expression, promptly took up his flute and began another country dance. Marie was soon lost in her private reverie.

Seeing what? Phillipe wondered sourly. Himself? Still as the little lord?

Well, he had other ideas now. He had already begun to formulate the first tentative plans for a possible future. A future far more realistic than that which had dragged them to England, and to grief.

III

As OCTOBER waned, the first brief snowflakes fell on the great city of bells. But immediately, the weather turned pleasant again. Phillipe and his mother began to go out and see the sights with the family.

On a Sabbath afternoon all flamed with sunlight falling through the coloring leaves, they strolled St. James's Park. On another unusually warm Sunday, after the printer and his wife had, as usual, worshiped at St. Paul's, they took a short barge trip down the Thames to view the Tower, whose history Mr. Sholto could describe in gory detail.

At one point on the return upriver, two elderly female passengers and their male escort paused next to Hosea, who was lounging against the rail and staring at the sky in a bemused fashion. Suddenly, with scandalized expressions, the ladies pointed to the water between the barge and the stately Parliament buildings on the north bank.

"Whoever it is, he should be prosecuted for profaning the Sabbath with vigorous activity!" declared one of the thin-lipped women.

As Hosea turned to follow the accusing fingers, the second lady gasped, "I believe his shoulders are entirely unclothed!"

The gentleman peered. "Perhaps the rest of him, too."

"Scandalous!" said the first woman.

Hosea smiled in a languid way. "He's traveling in the river—we're traveling on it. What's the difference?"

"If you don't know, then you are obviously an irreligious person," the first woman snapped. Hosea looked nonplused.

Along with a number of other passengers, Mr. Sholto and his party crowded around the outraged trio. Phillipe looked past the printer to see a most curious and unexpected sight: something which at first glance resembled a small white whale paddling and splashing downstream.

Only after he shielded his eyes against the sun's glare did the peculiar aquatic specimen take on definition. It was a man—and not a young one—swimming vigorously. On the embankment, a band of urchins followed the swimmer's progress, whistling and offering merrily obscene encouragement.

"It would serve the fellow right if he drowned!" the first woman said.

"Charity, Aunt Eunice, charity!" the man said. "It might be that he's suffering some mental lapse. There is nothing more pathetic than a gentleman of middle age who vainly attempts to behave like a youth. Don't scorn such derangement. Pity it."

At this, Mr. Sholto chuckled. "You're off the mark, sir. The gentleman is far from deranged. To the contrary—he's a scientist and diplomat of the first rank. Keen of mind. And he swims the Thames often."

"Damme, yes!" Hosea exclaimed with a snap of his fingers. "I thought I recognized him." He took no notice when one of the ladies appeared faint after he cursed.

"But—but the chap looks sixty years old!" the male escort sputtered.

"Very nearly," Sholto nodded. "He has a rugged constitution, however." The printer cupped a hand to his mouth and hailed, "Franklin! Ho, Dr. Franklin—over here!"

The racket made by the swimmer's youthful admirers on the embankment prevented him from hearing. He continued downriver, his thrashing arms and legs churning up water that sparkled in the sunshine.

One of the narrow-lipped ladies whirled on Mr. Sholto.

"Do you mean to say that is *the* Dr. Franklin? The godless wizard from the colonies?"

"I don't believe your adjectives are entirely correct, madam. 'Godless?' Perhaps. Certainly he doesn't observe the Sabbath as strictly as some of us." Mr. Sholto harrumphed for emphasis. "But 'wizard'? I think not. Rather, call him a genius. Of international repute."

"You seem well acquainted with him," the woman sniffed; it was far from a compliment.

"Yes, we take coffee together when my schedule permits. And he does visit

my bookshop on occasion—when *his* duties as business agent for the Massachusetts colony don't keep him running from one ministerial office to another—''

"Genius or not," the woman retorted, "I have read something about his tamperings with the divine mysteries of nature. 'The modern Prometheus,' isn't that what he's called in some quarters?''

"Aye, so the philosopher Kant christened him.''

"I still say anyone who meddles with the heavenly fire is satanically inspired!''

Annoyed, Mr. Sholto replied, "Then you are merely displaying your ignorance, my good woman. Of all the scientific thinkers of the modern world, it was that very Dr. Franklin—'' his hand shot toward the bow, and the diminishing glitter of water marking the swimmer's passage.—"who brought the study of what scholars term 'electricity' out of the province of superstition and into full respectability. Furthermore—''

Mrs. Emma tapped her husband's elbow. "Solomon, please.''

"No!'' exclaimed the printer. "I will not have a friend vilified. Are you not aware, my dear ladies, that 'Franklin' is the most famous American name in the civilized world? Are you not aware that our own Royal Society awarded him its highest honor, the Copley medal, for his *Experiments and Observations on Electricity* in fifty-two? He proved that lightning contains the same electrical forces which had previously been observed in laboratories at the University of Leyden and elsewh—''

But the trio of outraged puritans had turned their backs.

At first Mr. Sholto looked furious. Then, after his wife patted his arm several more times, he sighed, resigned. He gestured Phillipe, Marie and his family to another section of the deck, to prevent further friction.

Phillipe craned for one more view of the swimmer. He stared in fascination at the tiny figure still splashing down the great river.

"Solomon, that was not polite,'' Mrs. Emma chided.

"I know, but I can't abide stupidity. Franklin may not hold much brief for any sort of church, but he's no more devil than I am!'' Catching Hosea's start of a smile, Sholto added, "No remarks from you, sir.''

Marie wandered to the rail, indifferent to the conversation. Phillipe remained intrigued.

"And he's an American, you say?''

"Indeed. Nor was I exaggerating about his reputation. He's known all the way to the court of Imperial Russia. Do you know how he started his career? As a printer!''

Sholto's pride was obvious. Warming to his subject, he went on, "When he and his son performed their experiment at Philadelphia, and published the results, Franklin was immediately hailed throughout the world as a scientist of the first rank. But there's hardly a field of man's knowledge to which he hasn't added some improvement. When he couldn't find the proper type of spectacles to suit his weakening eyesight, he invented them. He was dissatisfied with the street lighting in his home city, so he created a better fixture. When his rooms got too cold, he built the famous Pennsylvania stove. And as deputy master of the colonial postal network, he overhauled the entire system, making it possible for a letter to travel from Philadelphia to Boston in two or three weeks instead of six or eight. Do you wonder I feel privileged to be his acquaintance?''

Phillipe looked thoughtfully past the stern of the barge. "I don't know a thing

about those scientific subjects. But yes, I can see why you'd admire him. It's plain he has an independent spirit. I'd like to meet a man like that. One who won't let himself be trod on by others—''

Solomon Sholto raised a cautioning hand. "Don't get the wrong idea. Dr. Franklin is a loyal Englishman. His own natural son William—''

"Must you bring up such indelicate subjects on Sunday?'' sighed Mrs. Emma.

"Well, Franklin makes no secret that his first-born's a bastard. By a woman whose name I've never heard him speak—'' Belatedly, Sholto caught his wife's glance at Phillipe and with some show of embarrassment exclaimed, "But he loves his son no less for that. If anything, he loves him the more! William Franklin's the royal governor of the New Jersey colony, Phillipe. So don't go thinking his father is the Crown's enemy. A stiff partisan of colonial rights, yes—but within the law.''

Phillipe wished again that he might have the chance to meet such a free-thinking gentleman face to face. He was ready to ask about the possibility when a yell from one of the watermen signaled their approach to the pier. In the rush attending debarkation, he had no chance to discuss the subject further. But the famous American was much in his thoughts in succeeding days.

In the lending library he located a copy of Franklin's study on electricity, which included an account of the celebrated "Philadelphia experiment.'' Phillipe was confused by a great part of the material, knowing nothing of the theoretical background or terminology. He did get the impression that considerable danger must have been involved when the doctor and his illegitimate son sent their kite aloft in a violent thunderstorm, then waited for the "heavenly fire'' to travel down the string to a metal key.

Mr. Sholto confirmed the danger. So potent was the force which Franklin believed was contained in lightning, he had literally risked instant death performing the experiment. Fortunately, when he touched the key at the critical moment, he felt no more than a repeated tingling in hand and arm—the "electrick spark'' that gave him international fame instead of an ignominious grave.

With such knowledge to be gained from it, London remained a constantly unfolding series of wonders and diversions for Phillipe. He spent another free afternoon strolling the far western reaches of the town with Esau. There, on the site of the great May fairs of the years past, fine new residences of the nobility were beginning to rise below the Tyburn Road. Esau discoursed on the new Georgian architectural style, which he much admired.

And one weekday evening, over Mr. Sholto's protests about trivial amusements, Hosea was permitted to take Phillipe and his mother to the gallery at Drury Lane. They watched a performance of a lively farce called *High Life Below Stairs*. Marie clapped and laughed with such animation that Phillipe felt she might be starting to free herself from the grip of the past.

Afterward, Hosea apologized for having chosen a play in which the great Mr. Garrick appeared only to speak the prologue instead of playing a leading role. But Marie was thrilled just to have seen the famous actor whose name had been well known in Paris when she performed there.

At Christmas, the family gathered for a festive dinner of roast mutton and many side dishes, all capped by plum pudding. Mr. Sholto matter-of-factly presented a gift to each of their boarders. Phillipe received a new shirt of white wool, Marie a set of tortoise combs. She wept happily at the table, and later was prevailed on to perform a lively dance in the sitting room, while Esau piped on his flute.

Outside, snow drifted down in Sweet's Lane. The bells of St. Paul's clanged in the lowering darkness of Christmas Day. Phillipe felt stuffed, warm and content.

But he realized it was time to begin giving serious consideration to the future. The few shillings Mr. Sholto paid him for his work in the print shop were beginning to accumulate in a kerchief he kept under his pillow. He needed to broach the subject of a return to Auvergne. He hoped to discourage Marie from going back to a life of managing a dilapidated wayside inn.

He had a better plan. Or should it be termed a dream? Either way, it filled most of his waking thoughts. To give it room to grow, he asked Hosea after the turn of the New Year whether he had yet heard anything about Amberly's death.

Hosea answered, "No, nothing."

Phillipe actually felt relieved. There was no doubt they would have to begin again. But why automatically back in France? Why not in another part of the world?

He had been borrowing books from the lending shelves in the front shop, where Marie helped Mrs. Emma from time to time. Late at night, he had begun reading about the American colonies.

____IV

IN EARLY February, a spell of bitter weather struck London. Mr. Sholto fell ill with a wracking cough, then fever. With the printing staff reduced to three, Phillipe worked even longer hours.

Esau still handled the typesetting because his hands were so skillful. But Phillipe took on new duties in addition to inking, washing the metal and lugging the finished sheets out to the binder's cart. Under Hosea's guidance, he began to operate the other press.

As with the ink balls, he was clumsy at first. He misaligned sheets between the tympan and frisket. He didn't lever the platen down far enough to produce the right weight and resulting good impression. But the mistakes were quickly corrected. And despite the elder Sholto's eternal remonstrances that Hosea was of light temperament, the young man proved a good and patient teacher. Phillipe's blood began to throb with the beat of the press.

Thunk, roll the coffin under the upright head. *Squeal*, pull the lever to tighten down the weight. *Squeak*, screw it up again. *Thunk*, retract the coffin and whip out the inked sheet. Then do it faster next time—

He no longer thought about the letter in the casket. He thought only occasionally about Alicia Parkhurst. Although her memory would never totally leave him, in the reality of his new life he recalled their love affair as if it were a dream. Full of pain and sweetness while it lasted. But ultimately unreal.

The rhythm of the flat-bed press created a new pattern to his days, a mounting hope. He gave voice to that hope one twilight late in February.

"No, Solomon! I forbid it!" Mrs. Emma cried, rushing down the stairs after her husband. The elder Sholto had appeared in his nightshirt, coughing and looking abnormally pale. "You're not well yet!"

"Cease, woman! If you want food on your table, I must look to the welfare of my business."

He closed the stair door with a bang, hiding his wife's dismayed face.

Sholto raised his eyebrows at the sight of Phillipe, smudged black from forehead to waist. Phillipe was tugging the lever to lower the platen for another impression.

"So we've a new hand on the press, do we?"

"And a mighty swift one he's turning out to be," Esau called from the type cases. His hands kept flying, independent of anything else.

"What's the work?" Sholto inquired, coming up the steps to Phillipe's press as the latter slipped a new, dampened sheet into place.

"A reprinting for Bemis in the Strand," Hosea informed his father from the other side of the room.

"It looks interesting," Phillipe said. "Written by a Mr. Dickinson of the Pennsylvania colony."

Mr. Sholto nodded. "It's a very lucid discourse on the position of the colonists in regard to taxes. A position supported by quite a few leading Americans—including Dr. Franklin."

"I'd have guessed that from what little I know about him," Phillipe nodded.

"Dickinson's book is already four years old. But it continues to sell nicely. He's a lawyer, by the way. Trained right here at the Inns of Court. He struck the proper tone in his arguments. Many in Lords and Commons heartily approved of his sentiments and his reasoning."

"Then I'll have to read what he says when I have time."

"Phillipe's gobbling up the library—every available piece of material on the colonies," Hosea said. "Good *or* bad."

"Nothing wrong with that," Sholto said to Phillipe, "so long as you understand that many who have taken up the quill to write about America have never been west of Charing Cross."

Phillipe said, "I've noticed that some of the books on the subject are fifty and sixty years old."

"And most of 'em paint a false, visionary picture of instant wealth for the hardy man who will but set foot on those shores. It's true in isolated cases. But as much depends on the man as on the country. For a more realistic picture, you'd do well to look through another monograph of Franklin's. One which he also wrote in the fifties. It brought him nearly as much recognition here and in Europe as the electrical discourse. By combining mathematics with sharp social insights, he produced a truly brilliant study of the potential for growth in the Americas."

"What's the name of the work?"

"*Observations Concerning the Increase of Mankind and Peopling of Countries.*" Sholto glanced at his elder son. "We own two copies in the front, do we not?"

"We did," Esau answered. "Both are gone. One fell to rags, and someone never returned the other." To Phillipe: "The book hardly came in but it was taken right out again."

"Perhaps we can turn up another copy. In any case, Phillipe, I think a realistic appraisal of the colonies is this. They do seem to be raising a new sort of person over there. Tougher. A mite more independent than those of us who've stayed home. And the land *is* bounteous. The southern colonies are rich from agriculture, the northern ones from commerce—you've heard how the merchants here exerted pressures on Parliament to repeal the obnoxious taxes about which Lawyer Dickinson was writing?"

Phillipe said he had.

"When the colonial trade fell off, all Britain suffered. That's proof the Americans are prospering. Becoming important to the Empire economically. For the time being, things are relatively calm over there. If that situation continues, I'm sure a good life—even riches—can be won. But not without diligence."

The printer stifled another cough and squinted at Phillipe. "Why does the subject interest you so much?"

"I've been thinking that one of the colonies might be a good place for my mother and me to settle."

"Ah—" Sholto smiled. "My guess was correct. But what trade would you follow?"

"Why, the one you and your sons have taught so well. You said your friend the doctor prospered in the printing business—"

"Hardly the word for it. He grew rich. First he ran a widely read newspaper. Then, with an eye on the commercial success being enjoyed by annual almanacs, he started his own. When he couldn't hire a suitable philomath for his publication—"

"A suitable what, sir?"

"Philomath. Resident astrologer. Predictor of the weather—giver of sage advice. Every almanac must have its philomath. Franklin couldn't find a scrivener capable of turning out work up to his standards, so he dreamed up Richard Saunders—and proceeded to write all of Poor Richard's pronouncements himself. Practically put the competing almanacs out of business, too. Poor Richard's aphorisms are universally quoted."

Hosea said, "The one I'm fondest of is 'Neither a fortress nor a maid will hold out long after they begin to parley.' "

"That is the one I would expect you to be fondest of," charged Mr. Sholto. "You conveniently forget many that are relevant to improving a person's character."

Esau nudged his brother with cheerful malice. " 'Experience keeps a dear school, yet fools will learn at no other.' "

Hosea turned pink. Mr. Sholto couldn't hide a faint smile. Phillipe spoke:

"All you're saying suggests there are a great many printing houses in the colonies—"

"Thriving ones. A lively book trade, too. The very Bemis for whom we're producing the Dickinson reprint supplies various American retailers with the latest titles by ship. Franklin says New York, Philadelphia and that troublesome Boston are particularly good markets. I also understand there are a great many penny papers and gazettes. Some support the Crown, others the radicals. No, there'd be no shortage of work for a young man handy at the press."

The upstairs door opened. Mrs. Emma appeared, carrying a cup of tea. She delivered it to her husband with a solicitous glance but no further advice or protests.

When his wife had disappeared into the stationer's shop, Sholto sipped tea, then remarked, "Never let a good woman know how much you depend on her. Spoils 'em—gives 'em a sense of excess authority. Now where were we? Ah yes, employment in the colonies. Have you discussed the idea with your mother?"

"Not yet."

"Do you feel you'd meet resistance?"

"Yes. A little or a lot, depending on her mood. I've had a hard time reading her mood lately."

"My wife and I also. Your mother's the soul of politeness. She works hard,

helping up front. But even though she never talks about the original undertaking that led you here, I have a feeling she broods on it privately a great deal.''

Phillipe's hands, hard and calloused by now, clamped on the lever handle, pulled, then released.

''That's what bothers me, sir. I hope she's still not clinging to some dream of gaining the inheritance. I'd sooner steer a course for a harbor that can be reached. And strange as it sounds, I think we might be better off to try the long voyage to the colonies, rather than go back to France. Life had nothing to offer there except false hope. You can't serve that at suppertime.''

''Agreed. Your course sounds sensible. When I'm over this accursed sickness, perhaps I can assist your endeavor. Introduce you to an American or two. We have 'em for visitors at the shop now and then—''

''I'd really like to meet your friend the doctor.''

''Capital idea—but as you've heard before, he's not been by in many a month. Too much to do looking after the interests of his constituents. If we can't put you in touch with him, we'll try someone else. At least you could see whether you think your temper would match that of the Americans. Also whether you would be willing to undertake the attendant extra risks involved in going there.''

Phillipe frowned. ''What extra risks, Mr. Sholto?''

''The problem Lawyer Dickinson argued has not been settled by any means. Only hid away for a time. It will be settled eventually. In peace, or with open trouble. Read those essays,'' he finished, pointing at the press. ''Between the lines!''

As he started across the room to inspect Hosea's work, he added, ''Dickinson and Franklin are men of reason. They openly and frequently avow their allegiance to His Majesty. But they are men of principle as well. I doubt such men will ever submit to what they consider tyranny. Weigh that—and all its possible consequences—before you decide.''

V

So AS the presses piled up the sheets during the gray, wintry days, Phillipe inquired further into the American character by means of the collection of essays first published in early 1768 under the general title *Letters From a Farmer in Pennsylvania to the Inhabitants of the British Colonies.*

The land-owning, law-practicing Pennsylvania aristocrat had been replying with firm but reasoned pen to the Townshend taxes. Dickinson conceded Parliament's authority to regulate American overseas trade. But he emphatically denied Parliament's right to tax within the thirteen colonies for the purposes of swelling the Crown's treasury.

He declared Townshend's duties—now already repealed save for the one on tea—as illegal. He hinted that such taxes must not be allowed for another reason. They might set precedents for a host of other levies, regulations and impositions of foreign rule.

To Phillipe, Dickinson emerged as a man implicitly loyal to King George. One passage read: ''Let us behave like dutiful children who have received unmerited blows from a beloved parent. Let us complain to our parent; but let our complaints speak at the same time the language of affliction and veneration.''

On the other hand, as Mr. Sholto had said, Dickinson also had steadfast

loyalties to what he believed was right. How such men would stand in the event of any further clashes of king's law and private conscience, the essays did not make clear.

Phillipe read the material with reasonable ease because of the expanded command of the language that his work for Sholto had given him. Thinking it over, he decided he was a definite partisan of Lawyer Dickinson and his American brethren, if only because they seemed opposed to the sort of high-handed behavior that had brought the visit to Kentland to such a tragic outcome.

If Dickinson fairly represented Americans, then Phillipe could only believe, with mounting excitement, that perhaps he belonged over there among them.

VI

BY EARLY March, Solomon Sholto recovered his health. Activity in the printing room returned to its original, pleasantly brisk pace. Feelings of hatred for the Amberlys began to trouble Phillipe less and less. The colonies were hardly out of his thoughts. He was convinced that he and his mother should emigrate.

What remained was to convince Marie. Somehow, he hesitated to bring up the subject. Perhaps for fear of refusal, he admitted to himself.

But one sunny day in April 1772, when a balmy breeze began to melt the last gray snow and send it rushing down the street channels, two unexpected visitors to Sweet's Lane took the decision about approaching Marie out of his hands.

3
Mr. Burke and Dr. Franklin

"WIPE THAT black mess from your hands, lad, and come up front at once!"

Startled, Phillipe nearly dropped the leather ink ball. Interruptions of the workday were rare; Mr. Sholto not only preached but practiced diligence. Yet there he was at the door leading to the shop, gesturing with some urgency. When Phillipe glanced at Hosea, the latter shrugged, equally baffled.

Phillipe grabbed a rag and cleaned his hands as best he could. Then he hurried to the doorway, where Sholto enlightened him a little further:

"I promised to introduce you to a colonial, didn't I? Well, Franklin's come by, out of the blue! In company with another of my good friends. Quickly, quickly!—we don't want to take too much time away from the press."

Phillipe followed the printer into the front shop. Two soberly dressed gentlemen were conversing with Mrs. Emma. Marie, busy dusting the bookshelves with a feather whisk, gave her son a surprised stare as he entered. Following Mr. Sholto, Phillipe didn't stop for an explanation.

The younger of the two visitors, a ruddy-cheeked man in his early forties, was speaking to Sholto's wife in lilting English that Phillipe later discovered was a hallmark of the man's Dublin origins:

"—we've missed your good husband's occasional presence at the Turk's Head. The Whig party is coming back to life over the coffee cups." The man turned to acknowledge the printer's arrival. "Even irascible Johnson, who thinks the first Whig was the Devil himself, has inquired after you, Solomon."

"Illness and work have kept me away," Sholto said. "When health prevails and profits are secure—*then* there's time for idling with friends."

But it was the other visitor at whom Phillipe stared in awe. The "godless wizard"; the internationally hailed genius, the lusty Thames swimmer—

Dr. Benjamin Franklin was a stout man almost twenty years older than his companion. He had jowls, receding gray hair, a paunch and keen eyes. Spectacles enhanced his sagacious expression. At once, Phillipe noticed a peculiarity about the lenses. The lower halves seemed to be of a different thickness from the upper. Could the spectacles be the invention to which Sholto had referred?

Franklin said to the printer, "I agree about work, Solomon. Hundreds and hundreds of times have I agreed!" He smiled. "Poor Richard said the same thing endlessly—whenever, in fact, I ran out of witty words for him. I long ago concluded that I have written overmuch concerning the virtues of thrift and labor. I'm supposed to be the very model of a dull, parsimonious drudge—and gad, how the reputation lingers! Let me so much as crack one jest among most Britons and eyebrows fly to heaven. But you know, my friend, I enjoy the presence of maidens and Madeira as well as the next."

"Better than the next," Sholto smiled.

"Keep my secret, Solomon. Meantime, let me echo Edmund. You have been too long away from our gatherings."

"And you from Sweet's Lane, Benjamin."

"Thank you. My sentiments also."

"There *are* other attractions at the Turk's Head besides political chatter," advised the Irishman, his eye merry.

"Quite so," Franklin agreed. "Doctor Goldsmith's been favoring us with readings from his new comedy. He hopes you'll land the printing commission after Garrack gets the play on. I predict it will be a solid hit. Very popular in the playhouses on our side of the Atlantic as well."

Sholto called a halt to the pleasantries by clearing his throat and glancing at Phillipe.

Both visitors focused their attention on the younger man. Phillipe was also aware of his mother watching him closely. He hated to have his speculations about America revealed to her in this fashion. But he saw little he could do about it.

A mussel seller pushing a barrow went by in Sweet's Lane, crying his wares as Sholto said, "This young man is a guest in my household. A sort of unofficial apprentice. His name is Phillipe Charboneau. His mother, Madame Charboneau, is there behind you."

The two gentlemen offered cordial greetings. Marie executed a stiff curtsy, still obviously confused. Phillipe didn't miss the way the older visitor adjusted his spectacles and boldly took note of Marie's still-shapely figure.

Sholto said to Phillipe, "Mr. Burke is an orator and pamphleteer of outstanding skill. Also a member of Commons from the pocket borough of Wendover. Doctor Franklin, I've already told you about. Phillipe shows an aptitude for the printing trade, Benjamin. He's most anxious to talk with you—and to read your *Observations Concerning the Increase of Mankind*. Our two copies, alas, are gone."

"Then come by my lodgings at Number Seven in Craven Street, young man—of an evening, preferably—and we'll accomplish both objectives. May I ask, however, the reason for your interest in my paper on population in America?"

Aware of Marie watching, Phillipe hesitated a second. Sholto answered instead:

"For various reasons, Phillipe's considering going there, rather than returning to his home in France."

Marie's intake of breath was sharp and sudden. Phillipe glanced her way long enough to see the anger in her dark eyes. He was caught off guard by Dr. Franklin's robust voice:

"Good for you! The opportunities are virtually unlimited. Particularly for an ambitious young fellow who can ply a press. Before I rose to my present position of eminence—" the twinkle in Franklin's eyes disclaimed any seriousness in the words. "—I was a printer myself. Philadelphia."

Phillipe nodded. "Mr. Sholto told me."

"I actually learned the trade in Boston, as an apprenticed boy. Never regretted it, either. I arrived in Philadelphia at age sixteen with absolutely nothing to my name but one Dutch dollar, a few copper pennies—and considerable hope. Thanks to printing, before too many years were out I was living well—and even making a modest mark in the world."

"Faith—'modest!' " Burke grinned. "The doctor's a man of parts, Mr. Charboneau. Inventor. Scientist. Founder of hospitals. Organizer of a society aiming to do away with the obnoxious slave trade—"

"He doesn't want to hear about me, Edmund," Franklin said. "He wants to hear about the colonies. Am I right, young man?"

"You are, sir. And I'll take you up on your offer to call in Craven Street."

"Excellent. I warn you—I may reminisce. I frequently wish I could go home, instead of wandering through the unspeakable maze of British politics. I formerly represented the commercial interests of Pennsylvania. Now it's Massachusetts Bay—but it's all the same kind of wrangling. And I had to leave my dear wife, Deborah, behind. She has an absolute horror of sea travel. Sometimes it's a lonely life," he concluded, with another glance at Marie.

Franklin's sighed complaint didn't match his lively eye. Marie wasn't interested.

"How much have you told the boy about America, Solomon?" Franklin asked finally.

"What little I've picked up from you. That there's hardly a city street corner where a hawker isn't peddling some broadside or penny sheet—"

"Did you also tell him that many of the publications are scurrilous and radical?" asked Burke in a tart tone.

"Who's to blame for that, Edmund?" Franklin retorted. "The longer His Majesty insists upon imposing unjust laws on Englishmen, the oftener the radicals like Adams and his engraver friend Revere will cobble together their inflammatory broadsides. The fault lies on your side of the Atlantic, not ours."

Edmund Burke returned a dismal nod. "You know I agree. Haven't I stood up in Commons many a time to plead for checking the excesses of the ministers? My position is conciliation. The government simply can't go on acting like a brutal father punishing a child."

Dr. Franklin smiled, raised a plump hand. "Edmund, you needn't impress me with your Irish oratory. I know your good intentions. I also know you're in the

minority—a steadily dwindling group that can no longer even count on Mr. Pitt's full support."

Burke agreed: " 'Twas a double tragedy when we lost him to the peerage, then to his mental disorder."

"And now," Franklin returned, "the King and his supporters have the votes, in both the Commons and the Lords, to do exactly as they wish, provided they can keep the British merchant class content and prospering. Even though there's a temporary stand-off, I am very fearful the government may again soon take up the same willful course that led to the massacre from which Adams made so much capital."

"There was a massacre solely because the Boston mobs provoked the troops!" Burke insisted.

"Damme, let's not argue like enemies, Edmund! We hold the same basic position, after all. And we both know one important fact which most of my countrymen do not. That it's really the King, not the toadying ministers, chiefly responsible for the vile taxes lying at the center of the trouble."

"Here, Benjamin!" Sholto said, dismayed. "That's a change of heart, isn't it?"

Franklin smiled sourly, "Many things change as a result of eavesdropping and maneuvering on the back stairs of Whitehall. Daily, I grow less and less enchanted with His Majesty—"

"Well, those taxes you mentioned may plague you again," Burke warned. "Have you heard the latest clack about the East India Company?"

"No, I haven't."

"It's rumored that because their fortunes have sunk so low, they may try to manipulate passage of a bill to give them a monopoly on the tea trade overseas."

"They'll do so at their peril." The keen eyes behind the peculiar spectacles showed a ferocity Phillipe found surprising in a man of such benign appearance.

Abruptly, Franklin turned his attention away from Burke. "I am supposed to paint you a cheerful picture, Mr. Charboneau. And here we are daubing out a gloomy one. But there's some sunlight among the thunderheads after all. Come by Craven Street and I'll show it to you."

"I look forward to it, Doctor."

"The colonies really have no desire to create problems, you see. The future tranquility of America rests solely in the hands of King George."

"Nonsense!" Burke protested. "Your friend Adams, for one, is anxious to provoke trouble. He can't wait to manipulate his mobs again, in order to feed the fire of his personal ambitions."

"Adams may run to excess on occasion," Franklin granted. "But if we do not share the same means, we share the same principles. We crave peace and harmony above all things save one." He paused a moment. "Our rights as Englishmen. I would have that warning repeated from the Turk's Head to your farmer king's own private cabbage patch. Yet I fear none will listen, except for a few good men like you, Edmund."

At that, Burke merely looked glum.

Phillipe noticed Marie watching him across Burke's shoulder and hastily averted his eyes. He realized that before the day was out, he would have to confront her.

Franklin became more animated again, producing a fobbed silver watch from his waistcoat pocket. Showing Burke the painted dial, he said, "I've an appoint-

ment shortly with the Secretary of State for the American Department. I must beg leave to go along.''

''I'll go as well,'' Burke said, ''now that we've concluded our main business—inquiring after Solomon's health.''

As the two visitors started for the door, the Irishman added, ''Rush orders or no, Solomon, your friends will be expecting you for coffee or chocolate at the Turk's Head within a fortnight. Uninterrupted work creates sour dispositions—''

''And wealthy printers.'' Dr. Franklin grinned. ''Mr. Charboneau, don't fail to call.''

''I won't, I promise. And thank you.''

The two men disappeared down Sweet's Lane, trailed by half a dozen urchins who suddenly materialized to importune them for gin money. Before the men and the noisy children had passed out of sight, Marie bore down on her son with a vengeful look in her eye.

''What is this plan you discuss with strangers when you haven't so much as mentioned it to me?''

Phillipe didn't flinch from the glare. ''I intended to speak to you about it soon, Mama.''

Solomon Sholto said, ''Your son wanted to investigate the idea first, Madame Charboneau.''

Marie's fists clenched. ''To labor like a nobody in some foreign land where everything's in a turmoil—is *that* your proposal?''

In an attempt to rescue Phillipe, Sholto stepped between mother and son. ''Madame, I remind you that we are in the midst of a working day. I appreciate that you and your son have matters of consequence to discuss. But pray do so later, when I'm not paying for it.''

With effort, Marie suppressed a retort. The front bell tinkled. Two bonneted ladies entered. Mrs. Emma bustled forward, saying much too loudly:

''Good day, Mrs. Chillworth! Come for the newest novels? Madame Charboneau will help you find them—''

For a moment Phillipe feared that his mother would explode with anger. But she didn't. Seconds passed. Mr. Sholto cleared his throat.

With a final glance at Phillipe that promised an accounting later, Marie turned and stalked off to aid the new customers.

Another welcome diversion, albeit one that made Mrs. Emma exclaim aloud, was a sudden crash from the back. Hosea bellowed, ''Oh, God damn and blast!''

Phillipe and Mr. Sholto dashed into the printing room. They found Hosea furiously kicking one leg of his press. The thick, all-important platen had split through the center.

At his type case, Esau was smirking. ''Too much pressure on the lever, dear brother. Where was your mind? Up some doxy's skirt?''

''We shall take all day replacing it!'' Mr. Sholto fumed, purple in the cheeks.

But as Phillipe followed the owner up the steps to where Hosea was swearing and rubbing his toe, he realized that no delays of any kind could prevent an inevitable—and inevitably unpleasant—confrontation with Marie.

II

MR. SHOLTO had to send all the way across the Thames to Southwark for a replacement platen. The part didn't arrive until well after dark. Installation took two hours. The family's customary eight o'clock supper was delayed. Phillipe was tired and edgy when he finally followed Sholto and his sons upstairs shortly after St. Paul's rang ten.

Marie was waiting for him.

"We will not eat until I have spoken with you, Phillipe."

He checked his temper with great effort. "All right. But at least we needn't disturb the household. We'll go for a walk."

"Careful of the streets at this hour," Mr. Sholto advised, moving on toward the kitchen, from which drifted aromas of steaming tea and new-baked bread. Phillipe nodded absently.

Marie fetched a shawl from her room. They walked down the outside stairs into darkness that had become thick with fog. Their feet rang hollow on the cobbles of Sweet's Lane. Phillipe was hardly conscious of which way they were going. His mother didn't speak. The tension mounted. Suddenly Marie slipped in the slime of the drainage channel.

He reached for her arm. She shook off his hand angrily. Then the outburst came:

"Your mind's been affected! You're ready for that asylum they call Bedlam! How can you even entertain the idea of traveling to another country when there's wealth—position—power waiting for you in this one?"

He could no longer treat the subject tactfully. "Mama, that's an illusion! Have you forgotten the trouble at Kentland? We've no chance of pressing the claim successfully."

Marie seethed; he could hear it in her rapid breathing. "What has turned you into a coward, Phillipe?"

He wheeled on her. "Nothing! I'm trying to look at the future like a grown man, not a bemused child!"

"I won't listen to—"

"You will! Do you propose that we live on charity all our lives? Clinging to the hope that some miracle will happen? The Duchess of Kentland won't permit miracles! And what's left for us in Auvergne?"

"Therefore—" He'd never heard such awful bitterness in her voice. "Therefore you intend to waste your life as a printer's boy? You, who swore an oath that you wouldn't let yourself be humbled into obscurity?"

Phillipe winced inwardly at that. Guilt lay heavy on him a moment. Marie was expert at striking at the most sensitive part of his defenses.

"I hadn't definitely decided to propose that we sail to America," he hedged. "It seemed worth looking into, that's all. Printing is a worthy occupation—"

"Being a tradesman is *worthy*? Faugh!"

"Dr. Franklin did well at it. His writings made him more than welcome among the nobility—"

"Oh, yes, I remember all the talk on the river trip. A genius!" Her tone grew cutting. "Are you a genius, my son?"

"No, no, of course not, I—"

"But you *are* a nobleman," she argued, as their clacking footfalls carried them deeper into the mist that beaded cold on his cheeks. "Even your American

122

genius can't claim that. It comes down to this, Phillipe. If you refuse to press your claim, then I've lived for nothing."

Phillipe's spine crawled. She no longer spoke with fiery conviction. She ranted, on the edge of hysteria:

"Will you do that to me, Phillipe? Will you destroy me after I've surrendered my whole life for you?"

"Mama, you know I'd never willingly hurt you. I love you too much. But you must be realistic—"

"Exactly. *Exactly!* Why do you think I've hoarded every shilling we earn helping the Sholtos? To buy passage back across the Channel?" Her harsh laugh unnnerved him even more. "No. Oh, no. I've been making secret plans of my own, Phillipe. When we have enough money, we'll find a lawyer here in London. One who can help us use the letter to advantage—"

Phillipe's voice was edged with irritation: "But I still plan to accept Franklin's invitation. Talk to him. Talking can't hurt—"

He realized Marie hadn't heard a word. She was caught up in her own wild monologue:

"—because I've no intention of sailing to a land peopled by tradesmen and farmers and those—those hideous red Indians everyone prattles about. I've no intention of leaving England until you have your full and rightful share of—"

"In God's name, woman, *let it die!*"

Die die die die rang the echo in the slowly swirling fog.

He hadn't meant to shout. Or call her by any other name than the one he'd used since childhood.

But he had done both. In an eerie way, that told him something new about their relationship.

His shout had cowed her a little. She spoke less stridently:

"Phillipe, what's happened to you? Don't you still have a desire to be like your father?"

He thought briefly of Lady Jane, of Alicia and, with hatred, of Roger. "Only sometimes," was the most honest answer he could give.

Marie Charboneau began to cry then. Short, anguished sobs that tore at Phillipe's heart. Miserable, angry with her as well as with himself, he lifted his head suddenly.

He'd heard another sound.

It came again, in counterpoint to her sobbing.

Shuffle-shuffle-shuffle.

The sound prickled his scalp and turned his palms to ice. It came from their left, but the source was invisible in the fog.

Then a second set of footsteps blended in. This time from the right.

Phillipe realized they must have wandered near St. Paul's Yard. There was a feeling of open space. High up, he glimpsed very faint lights in the murk. The small windows under the church dome. He groped for Marie's arm.

"Mama, I think we'd best turn back—"

Abruptly, an unfamiliar voice barked out, "I tell ye it's him! I knew when he yelled."

That voice came from the left, where the shuffling grew louder. Another responded from the right:

"Then old Jemmy weren't daft, saying 'e thought 'e'd seen 'em along Sweet's Lane. Let's find out fer sure—"

A lantern shutter clacked open. A sulfurous yellow flare lit the mist close by. Phillipe leaped back in alarm.

The lantern light revealed a graybeard with browned gums and one cocked eye. The apparition exclaimed, "Him, all right!"

Phillipe didn't recognize the hideous, leering face. But he wouldn't have known the face of any of those who had attacked him that first night on the church stairs.

Holding the lantern high, the beggar seized Phillipe's forearm with his other grimy hand. His one good eye glared. A second rag-festooned creature appeared behind him. A woman; a crone. Her sagging dugs were partially revealed by torn places in her filthy blouse.

The crone's mouth was just as toothless as the man's. Her eyes shone as she extended her hand, palm upward. The fingers wiggled suggestively.

"A penny to buy a posy for the General's grave?"

Phillipe stepped in front of the frightened Marie, tried to shake off the man's clutch as the crone shrilled:

"Just a penny. That's not much for a lad who works in a fine bookshop. Old Jemmy, he saw sharp. He recognized you!"

"Let go, damn you!" Phillipe pried harder at the dirty hand holding him. Suddenly the man with the crazed eye dropped his lantern, shot out both hands and closed them on Phillipe's throat.

"Can't buy a flower for a good man's grave?" he screamed. "You owe him! *You killed him!*"

Savagely, Phillipe drove his fist into the beggar's belly. One punch was enough to tear the broken nails from his throat. He practically jerked Marie off her feet, dragging her away as the old man and the crone began to shrill together:

"Murderer! *Murderer!*"

Their feeble shuffling followed Phillipe and Marie a short distance down Sweet's Lane, then faded.

Out of breath, they reached the sanctuary of the rickety stairs ascending to the Sholtos' second floor. They clattered up. Only the closing of the door behind them stilled Phillipe's hammering heart.

The beggars had really presented no serious physical threat. He'd been startled, that's all. Gotten alarmed all out of proportion to the cause.

Yet he was still shivering. He thought that somewhere out in the fog, he could still hear voices crying, "*Murderer—*"

Marie went to her room without speaking.

III

PHILLIPE SLEPT badly that night. In the morning he described the incident to Esau. The big-shouldered young man shrugged it off.

"It was only an attempt to bully you into giving them drink money. Do you really think they care when one of their own dies? The man you cut down—the General—was probably stripped and left to rot naked five minutes after Hosea and I brought you home."

Trying to take reassurance from the words, Phillipe was still troubled. The beggars knew where he lived. What if someone else came searching for him? Inquiring of the street people about a French boy?

Of course there hadn't been so much as a hint of any pursuit since the flight from Tonbridge. But he couldn't shake off the new worry.

Esau grinned at him. "Look here, stop scowling! Go ink Hosea's type or I won't be able to pick up my flute till midnight!"

Phillipe nodded, started to work. Yet the anxiety lingered with him most of the day.

He didn't mention his fear to Marie. In fact he avoided her. He didn't want to reopen the discussion—the argument—about their future until he'd hit on some way to persuade her that further involvement with the Amberlys was not worth the risk and was futile to boot.

By the next day, a warm but windy harbinger of spring, he had thrown off some of his apprehension. Though the gray sky threatened storms, he made up his mind to walk to Craven Street that very evening. He hoped he'd find Franklin home.

Marie retired early. Thus he was spared the need to tell her where he was going. He told the Sholtos, however. Once more they repeated their warnings about the unsafe streets. Out of range of observation by his father, Hosea slipped Phillipe a cheap dirk to stick in his boot.

"Don't ask me where I got the bloody thing—or how I use it. Just take it."

Phillipe thanked him and set out.

Thunder rumbled as he proceeded down the Strand. He glanced behind frequently but saw no sign of anyone following him. He located Craven Street, which led south to the river, without incident.

Going up the steps of the house at Number 7, he dismissed his anxiety about the beggars as foolish. By the end of the week, he was to discover that was a grave mistake. But as the night sky glared white and a thunderclap pealed and fat raindrops began to spatter down, he had no inkling.

4

The Wizard of Craven Street

EVEN AS Phillipe let the door knocker fall, lightning blazed again, raising white shimmers on the Thames, churning only a few steps further south of the brick residence. All at once the wind turned chill. The rain slanted harder. He huddled close to the building until someone answered.

A woman. Of middle age, but still attractive. She raised a candle in a holder as she peered at Phillipe from the gloomy foyer.

"Yes?"

"Good evening. Is this the house of Dr. Franklin?"

"No, it's the house of Widow Stevenson. But he lets rooms from me." The woman glanced past Phillipe to the dark doorways on the other side of the rain-swept street. Her eyes suspicious, she asked, "Are you a friend?"

"An acquaintance. Dr. Franklin gave me leave to call. My name is Phillipe Charboneau. If the doctor's at home, I'd be obliged if you'd anounce me."

Mrs. Stevenson's suspicion seemed to moderate. She stepped back, motioned him in. "Very well. But I'm afraid you'll be interrupting the doctor's air bath."

"His what?"

Phillipe's words were muffled by more thunder. Mrs. Stevenson didn't hear. Turning toward an open door on one side of the foyer, she continued:

"Normally he takes his air bath first thing in the morning. Today, early appointments prevented it." At the entrance to a well-furnished parlor bright with lamplight, the woman called, "Polly. Polly, my dear—"

In a moment, a pert, pretty girl appeared. She was about Phillipe's own age.

"Benjamin has a caller," said the older woman. "Mister—?"

"Charboneau."

"My daughter will show you up."

Phillipe thanked her, moved aside to let the girl precede him with the candle. Thunder boomed, then faded as they climbed the carpeted stairs. In the lull of silence, Phillipe heard someone singing behind a door on the second floor. He recognized the voice. Franklin's—acompanied by music unlike any he had ever heard before. Shimmering, almost eerie notes. The melody itself was plaintive; the words equally so:

> Of their Chloes and Phyllises poets may prate—
> I sing my plain country Joan.

"Oh," exclaimed the girl named Polly, "he's playing!"

"It sounds to me like he's singing."

"Well, of course—that too. What a foolish remark."

"Excuse me," Phillipe snapped. "I was told he was taking something called an air bath."

> Now twelve years my wife—still the joy of my life—
> Blest day that I made her my own,
> My dear friends—
> Blest day that I made her my own.

"Dr. Franklin can do all three at once!" responded the girl, her eyes positively sparkling in the candle's bobbing glow. "He's very accomplished on the fiddle, the harp—and his armonica." Her gesture indicated it was this last, unfamiliar instrument upon which Franklin was performing now. "He invented the armonica in this very house. Sometimes I sit with him and listen for hours." Young Polly Stevenson sounded smitten.

As they continued up the stairs, the strange, ethereally sweet notes grew louder. Franklin sang with gusto, yet with unmistakable feeling:

> Some faults have we all, and so may my Joan—
> But then, they're exceedingly small.
> And now I'm used to 'em, they're just like my own—
> I scarcely can see 'em at all,
> My dear friends.
> Blest day that I made her my own!

"He made up that song about his Philadelphia wife years ago," Polly declared as they reached the landing. "It's the only one he sings that I don't care for."

Phillipe readily understood why. Admiration had given way to jealousy in the girl's eyes. She knocked. The vigorous voice pealed on:

Were the finest young princess, with millions in purse
To be had in exchange for my Joan,
She could not be a better wife—might be a worse—
So I'd stick to my Joggy alone,
My dear friends—

Polly rapped louder. "Dr. Franklin! If you please!"

I'd cling to my lovely old Joan.

The last high notes melted to silence beneath the distant roar of the storm. Polly's third knock finally produced a response:

"That you, Polly my girl?"

"Yes. You have a caller."

"Male or female?"

"The former. A young man. He says he knows you."

"Then he may come in at once. But you stay out—I'm still bathing."

Polly giggled. She stood aside for Phillipe to enter. As he walked into the spacious sitting room, bright-eyed Polly was on tiptoe, craning for a view of the apartment's occupant. Phillipe turned to close the door, catching her. She looked acutely embarrassed. When he pivoted back in response to a boomed-out greeting—"Charboneau! Good evening to you!"—he instantly appreciated why.

Never in his days had Phillipe beheld such a bizarre combination of sights as in that chamber lit with lamps whose flames were shielded with chimneys. For good reason. All three windows overlooking Craven Street were wide open. The curtains blew, rain gusted in—and so did the wind, exceedingly chilly. The pages of a book lying open on a reading desk fluttered and snapped in the miniature gale.

But Benjamin Franklin appeared perfectly comfortable, seated on a bench near the opposite wall, in front of a totally incomprehensible device Phillipe took to be the source of the odd musical sounds. Franklin beamed cheerily.

"Have a chair. Help yourself to that Madeira. I'll be finished with my air bath in just a few moments."

He continued to smile with perfect aplomb, despite the fact that he was totally nude except for his spectacles.

Now just as embarrassed as Polly had been, but for a different reason, Phillipe made for the sideboard, and the decanter. He poured half a glass, sipped it hastily as Franklin rose, stretched, took several vigorous steps in one direction, then several the opposite way.

"Glad you fulfilled your promise, Mr. Charboneau. Please excuse my appearance. I've always believed fresh air has a salubrious effect on a man's health and longevity. Winter or summer, I throw open the windows and take the air in this fashion one hour per day—come, come! Don't look flustered. Is there any need for false prudery among gentlemen?"

"Well—ah—" Phillipe chucked down the Madeira, which hit his stomach with a sudden exploding warmth. He struggled for words. "No. *No!* But I've never walked into a room before and seen—seen—a device like that—"

Somewhat wildly, he pointed past Franklin's bare paunch to the peculiar instrument against the wall.

"My armonica? Performances on musically tuned glasses are all the rage over here, I found. I merely improved on the primitive arrangement generally in use. Here, I'll give you a demonstration—"

A mantel clock chimed the half-hour. "Ah, but time's up. Your momentary indulgence—"

He disappeared into a dark adjoining room, returned clad in a much-worn dressing gown and old slippers of yellowed lambswool. He bustled from window to window, closing the shutters and latching them. Then he crossed to his armonica, while Phillipe, now less nervous, poured another tot of Madeira.

He walked over to the bench at which Franklin had seated himself. He was beginning to notice other details of the room: books and portfolios of papers stacked everywhere; on the mantel, a trio of miniature oils in expensive gold frames. The central portrait was that of a plain-faced, even homely woman. She was flanked by a young, bright-eyed boy and a charming little girl. Franklin's children? Phillipe wondered briefly whether the young man was the bastard governor, William.

Franklin's fingers ranging over the armonica captured Phillipe's attention again. The high, shimmering notes faded away as cracks in the shutters admitted lightning glare. Thunder rocked the house. Phillipe bent forward to look while Franklin explained:

"Until the advent of my little creation, performers on the musical glasses simply had to arrange their vessels helter-skelter—and seldom within easy reach. I approached the problem a bit more scientifically, that's all."

He indicated the closely spaced glass hemispheres containing varying amounts of water. Each hemisphere resembled the bowl of a wineglass, but with a hole in place of a stem. Each hole fitted onto a peg on a spindle which, as Dr. Franklin demonstrated, moved back and forth at the touch of a foot treadle. Thus, certain glasses could be brought closer to the performer, or moved away. So precisely arranged were the hemispheres, not a drop of water spilled when the shaft changed position.

"Thirty-seven hand-blown glasses from three to nine inches—ranging through three octaves—and originally tuned with the aid of a harpsichord. Using a diamond, I engraved the note's letter on each glass."

Phillipe saw that when Franklin pointed it out. The older man moistened his fingertips in a bowl of water on a taboret beside the bench. Then he began to touch the rims of different hemispheres while operating the pedal. A surprisingly lovely tune rang forth, complete with simple chords that swelled and diminished as Franklin varied the finger pressure.

In mid-phrase, he laughed and turned back to the amazed younger man.

"That's enough musicology for the evening, I think. You're more interested in America. Sit down again, and let's have another glass of Madeira."

As a result of the two he'd drunk, Phillipe was already hearing a slight buzz. His eyes were a bit blurry, too. But he accepted the full glass Franklin poured and took the chair offered.

Franklin selected an even larger goblet for himself. He filled it to the brim, then relaxed in a second chair in front of jammed bookshelves, facing his visitor.

"I do recall I am supposed to give you a copy of my population essay before you depart. But tell me, Mr. Charboneau—where's your home? France, to guess from your accent."

"That's right, sir. My mother and I came to England from Auvergne."

"On business? To visit relatives? What?"

Phillipe was about to blurt that he was the son of a member of the nobility. He checked the impulse. Franklin might not be friendly with all the peers of the realm—and very likely not with the so-called King's Friends, among whom the

late Duke had been numbered. Still, he wasn't eager to have the story of his origins too widely circulated, especially not since the unsettling incident with the beggars. So he answered:

"Business, I suppose you'd call it. My mother was never married to my father, who was an Englishman of—good station." He saw Franklin's eyes dart quickly to the boy's framed portrait; unabashed affection showed before the doctor returned his attention to the goblet he was warming between his palms. Phillipe continued, "When my father died, I was supposed to receive an inheritance, but—well, let's say there were complications."

"Some pack of rascally relatives cut you off, eh?"

"You're very quick to get to the heart of it, sir."

Franklin waved. "It's an old story among the supposedly refined upper classes. So now your thoughts turn west across the sea—"

Phillipe nodded. "My mother's against it, of course."

"Handsome woman. Devilishly handsome! Can you persuade her?"

"I think so." It was a hope, not a fact. "Particularly if there's a more solid future than we'd find back in France."

"You couldn't have found better instructors in the fundamentals of printing than old Solomon and his sons. And the presses in the colonies do grow more numerous by the year. Commerce expands—that means more handbills, more advertising sheets. Literacy rises—the appetite for knowledge and news becomes voracious. Beyond that, we've a relatively open society over there—"

Phillipe shook his head, not understanding. Another intense glare through the shutters preceded a stunning roll of thunder. Franklin helped himself to more Madeira before going on:

"In America, a man's free to rise as far and as fast as his wit and industry permit. The colonies are largely spared the constraints of the antique European system of nobility and privilege—with which you hint you've had some encounter."

The shrewd eyes pinned him from behind the spectacles. Plainly the question was an attempt to draw him out. But Phillipe kept silent except for another nod.

Without thinking, he'd helped himself to more Madeira. The buzz in his ears had become pronounced. He wasn't sure he could tell the Amberly tale coherently if he wanted to. He was growing dizzy—from the wine, and from basking in the nearly godlike presence of this famous man who, in some ways, acted as comfortably common as his old lambswool slippers.

Seeing he'd get no answer, Franklin resumed, "Yes, a man can go far in America, no matter how humble his beginnings. That should continue to be the case unless, God help us, the Crown alters the course of colonial affairs."

"You discussed that trouble with Mr. Burke at some length—"

"Because it's seldom out of my mind. The future of relations between the colonies and the mother country depends entirely—*entirely*—upon the actions of His Majesty."

"Can you forecast the next year or so? Will conditions over there be so unsettled that it's foolish to entertain thoughts of a solid future?"

Franklin peered into his goblet in an almost cross-eyed way. He said somberly:

"I hope not. As do most of my countrymen, from the Virginia tidelands to the Maine lobster banks. By living where they do, they have already gambled on *their* futures. I wish I could be more specific, but alas—" A rueful pucker of the mouth. "As a prophet, Poor Richard Saunders is a pious fraud. I do know that Englishmen will not be driven to their knees. To sketch it candidly for you, I

would say America in the immediate future represents a unique combination of opportunity and risk. Opportunity to the extent I have already described—in plain terms, the air there is less stifling. On the other hand, German George— and many of his ministers who are supposedly Englishmen!—simply fail to understand the American temper. As you heard me tell Edmund, we seek justice, not enmity. But if they force the issue with their infernal taxes and fiats—that outrageous tea scheme, for example! I investigated Edmund's rumor—the scheme's certainly afloat. Should the high-handed ministers eventually push through a law granting an American monopoly to the half-wrecked East India Company—and should this government go on quartering royal troops among us at our expense—continue burdening us with aggravations and harassments of every devising—little 'innovations,' the wags in Parliament term them—*then*, Mr. Charboneau, you will see thirteen colonies pull and haul together as they have never done.''

Silence. The mantel clock ticked against the murmur of the rain. Abruptly Franklin stuck out his lower lip.

''No doubt I'm depressing you. I've certainly depressed myself. More Madeira!''

Before Phillipe knew it, both glasses had been refilled. He said, ''No, I'm not depresh—uh, depressed. I'm heartened. You've been honest. I think I'd welcome the free air in America. Whatever the dangers in the future.''

''Good! Remember—I may have overstated the grimness of the outlook. As long as there are no new assaults on our liberties, all may continue in relative calm—''

Franklin had barely spoken the last words when lightning blazed outside—and the loud, strident *dang-dang-dang* of a bell brought the half-tipsy Phillipe leaping out of his chair.

''Damme,'' Franklin exclaimed, ''I must have forgotten to unfasten the wire to the rod—''

He rushed toward the doorway where he'd disappeared before. This time, however, the black room beyond was illuminated by a ghostly light that made Phillipe's scalp crawl.

Franklin noted his visitor's white cheeks, chuckled.

''No need to be alarmed—the house is merely electrified from the storm. Come look.''

Dang-dang-dang-dang, the bell shattered the eardrums like some tocsin of judgment. Phillipe swallowed, wobbled as far as the doorway, looked in and observed Franklin silhouetted against a weird white aura glowing around a spot on one wall. *Dang-dang-dang-dang*—

''The natural force contained in the electrical storm makes them ring,'' the scientist shouted over the clatter. He resembled some white-lit creature of hell as he gestured to a little brass ball dancing in the center of that strange fire. The ball—and the white glow itself—appeared to leap back and forth between two bells mounted to the wall. *Dang-dang-dang-dang*—

''Normally I keep the roof rod grounded—the charge runs harmlessly through a wire into the earth. But on occasion, I connect the rod to the bells for the amusement of visitors.''

''Rod?'' Phillipe repeated in a blank way.

''The type of rod I devised to prevent lightning from damaging property. See where the wire comes down, suspending that ball by its silk thread?''

Phillipe stumbled forward through the semidarkness, past a table littered with

laboratory ware and tin-lined jars. The white glow was lessening. The ball moved more slowly; the bells rang with less stridence. Awed, Phillipe extended his hand toward the dancing sphere of brass.

"For God's sake don't touch it!" Franklin cried, seizing his wrist. "You might be fried where you stand."

Intoxicated and nearly frightened out of his wits, Phillipe took three long steps backward. He managed a weak grin.

"That—that's certainly a diverting demonstration."

By now the ball barely touched the bells. The white glow had all but disappeared. Franklin clapped an arm over Phillipe's shoulder, escorted him back into the sitting room.

"I imagine you'd prefer to be diverted by that book I promised you." He adjusted his spectacles, poked along the shelves, withdrew a slender volume— knocking several others on the floor in the process. Phillipe was relieved that he wasn't the only one feeling the wine.

Franklin handed the book to his guest. "Glean what facts you can from it. Then, since my friend Solomon is lacking a copy, donate it to him with my compliments."

"Dr. Franklin, I thank you most humbly for your time, your friendliness, your—"

"Electrifying discourse?"

Both laughed.

"Please keep me advised of your plans, Mr. Charboneau. Don't be discouraged or deterred by what *might* happen. America is a new, brave land—and her free air makes the risks attendant to emigrating there more than acceptable."

"I thank you again for the advice."

"It costs me nothing! And who knows? It may do the colonies a service by adding a citizen of worth. Truthfully, I can, and would like to be, of more practical help. Should you reach a decision to go, let me know and I'll write you a list of good printing establishments in the major cities. I'll also give you a note of introduction and recommendation."

"Sir, that's unbelievably kind. But I'd hate to trouble you—"

"Trouble me? I can do no less for a marked man."

Phillipe gulped. White spots seemed to dance behind his eyes. "*Marked—?*"

Franklin crooked a finger and walked to a front window. "To visit Craven Street is to be deemed dangerous," he said, pushing a shutter open and pointing. "At the next lightning flash, look across the way."

They waited for several moments. Then the sky glared, clearly illuminating a man lounging in a passageway between houses. The man was dressed as a seaman. A tiny ring in his earlobe glittered while the lightning flickered over Craven Street. Franklin slammed the shutter, his expression sour.

"I'll conduct you out the back way. For your own sake."

"You have spies watching you, Doctor?"

"Almost constantly. Certain members of Parliament even declare I should be hanged. And compared to Mr. Samuel Adams and some of the rest of that Boston crowd, *vis-a-vis* King George I am a moderate! Still want to take up with us Americans, Mr. Charboneau?"

Full of wine and excitement, Phillipe said to the great man, "Yes, I think so."

"I had that feeling shortly after we met. You're the right sort, young man. Yes indeed, the right sort."

The compliment, and another stout clap of Phillipe's shoulder, put him into a

state of complete euphoria. With the precious book tucked inside his clothes, he whistled and hummed all the way back to Sweet's Lane—and didn't realize until he arrived that he'd gotten thoroughly soaked.

But after an experience like tonight's, what did it matter?

II

HE FOUND Hosea drinking a pot of ale in the nearly dark kitchen. All but a few embers had gone out on the hearth. Esau perched on a stool, chin on his chest, snoring. His flute lay beside his right foot.

"Well!" Hosea grinned, tottering up. "The specter from the storm. No robberies?" Phillipe shook his head, tugging off his sodden shirt. "No assaults by wenches?" Phillipe shook his head. "Gad, what a dull evening."

"The most exciting evening of my life, Hosea. The man is—he's a giant!"

Hosea shrugged, weaving as he grabbed Phillipe's arm. "Listen. Himself is tucked up in his nightshirt. I smuggled this ale out of the cellar. Private stock. Join me—"

"No, I want to read."

"Read instead of drink?" Hosea leaned closer, blinking. "You must be drunk." He sniffed. "You are drunk. Pickled in the doctor's well-known Madeira. All right, if that's your pleasure, be unsociable!"

It wasn't a question of sociability, but of consuming eagerness to delve into the book. Phillipe lit a taper beside his bed, pulled off the last of his wet clothes, crawled under the blankets and turned to the first page. Within minutes, Franklin's prose began to light his thoughts almost as that electric display had lit the room at Craven Street.

In carefully structured phrases, and with precise logic, Franklin put forth his case for the coming greatness of the colonies. At the time he was writing—the fifties, hadn't someone said?—there were over one million Englishmen in North America. Yet only about eighty thousand had emigrated from the mother country since the start of colonization.

That fact alone established a fundamental difference between the Old World and the New. In Europe and the British Isles, population was more or less stable. But America, with its virtually unlimited land—land beyond the mountains of the eastern seaboard; land as yet unexplored except by soldiers and the hardiest woodsmen—gave families room to grow. The land provided them with sustenance as well. In Franklin's view, there was hardly any restriction on the number of people the American continent could support.

In fact, the mind-expanding essay predicted that America's population would double every twenty to twenty-five years—and a distant century in the future, "the greatest number of Englishmen will be on *this* side of the water."

Dawn's light found Phillipe still reading—drunk now on the words and their promise, intoxicated by the night just past, and by the force and vision of the man who had so patiently spoken with him—

Starting, he heard the dawn church bells. His head hurt. So did his eyes. He'd soon have to be up and working—a full, long day.

But it didn't matter. Nothing mattered except the sonorous word that rang and rang in his mind, a thousand times louder and more majestic than Franklin's electrified bells—

America.
America.
He blew out the taper and drowsed, murmuring the name.

5
The One-Eyed Man

THE FIRST hint that Phillipe and his mother were in danger came disguised as no more than an item of dinner conversation, three evenings after the visit with Franklin.

He was busy spooning the last of Mrs. Emma's delicious lentil soup from his bowl. Talk at the table was animated this evening. But as usual, Marie did not enter in. Whether this was because she felt secretly superior to the Sholto family or because she was still not at ease among English people, Phillipe could never decide.

As Mrs. Emma moved around the table, ladling extra portions of soup into the bowls of the three young men who had worked up their customary ravenous appetites in the press room, she said:

"The strangest person appeared in the shop this afternoon." An aside to Marie: "Just when you'd come up here to light the fire for tea time."

Marie responded with a faint nod. Her glance met Phillipe's briefly, slid away. They hadn't discussed their differences since the night the beggars accosted them in the fog. He'd been anxious to tell her about his remarkable evening at Craven Street, but thus far he'd lacked the opportunity—

Or was it the courage? They had been alone several times. But on each occasion, Marie's morose behavior quelled his enthusiasm.

He was growing concerned about her health again. She was wan, too silent all day long. He knew she was probably worried about their future, which would have to be decided eventually. But she seemed to be retreating into herself—as if, that way, the issue could be sidestepped altogether.

He heard Esau ask, "What was so strange about the visitor, Mother?"

"For one thing, he had a positively frightening phiz. Particularly his eyes. No, that should be singular. Eye. One was covered with a greasy patch of old leather. But the other had a distinctly mean glare. He was a tall chap. Imposing—though I've seldom seen cheeks so pitted with the marks of the pox. He kept darting glances every which way. As if he were ill at ease in a bookshop."

"How was he dressed? Was he a gentleman?" Esau wanted to know.

"A flash gentleman! Ill-assorted clothes. Old mended breeches. Jackboots. His coat, very dirty, might have been shot silk of bright orange—once."

"Orange was the macaroni color ten years ago," Hosea put in. "Today a gentleman dresses in more restrained hues."

Chuckling, Esau reached for his tankard of ale. "Naturally you speak from hope, not personal experience." Hosea scowled.

Mrs. Emma ignored the banter, seated herself next to her husband and continued, "Well, I certainly have little knowledge about high fashion. But it was

obvious this person wanted to look like a gentleman but couldn't quite bring it off. His sword had a very fancy French knot. He didn't appear wealthy enough to have bought it new.''

"From your description," said Mr. Sholto, "it sounds like he might have bought it on a coach road. At pistol point.''

His wife replied, "That's exactly how he struck me, Solomon! A thief in stolen finery.''

"Well, maybe some victim gave him books instead of rings, and he acquired a taste for literature," Hosea said between mouthfuls of bread. "I can't exactly see why such a fellow's worthy of so much discussion.''

Mrs. Emma gestured helplessly. "He—he frightened me, that's all. His beetling stare. His darted looks at every cranny and closed door.''

"Did he say anything ill-mannered?'' Esau inquired.

"No. No, but—''

"Then for once I agree with Hosea. What's the fuss?''

"Well, it occurred to me that perhaps our store was being examined for possible robbery!'' Mrs. Emma exclaimed. "The man did not belong here!''

Sholto asked, "How long did he stay?''

"Oh, ten minutes, perhaps. He spent most of his time at the bookshelves, taking down one volume and studying several different pages a long while. I finally got up nerve enough to speak to him a second time. I greeted him when he came in, of course. I got a hawkish flash from his good eye, and a bare nod. On the second occasion, he snapped the book shut and said he was searching for some diverting, fictional adventure. But the volume he'd been examining didn't measure up. With that, he walked out.''

It was one of those rare occasions when Solomon Sholto laughed aloud. "Emma, Emma, you are a dear nervous wren. Some gutter peacock leafs through a novel and you're alarmed—''

"But you still don't understand! The book to which he'd devoted so much attention was Mr. Chambers' *Cyclopaedia Britannica*. I'm positive the fellow couldn't read! And if not, what was he doing loitering in our shop?''

Phillipe lowered his spoon back into the bowl and sat stock still. He didn't so much as flicker an eyelash to reveal one possible answer.

Mr. Sholto pondered his wife's information and, after a modest belch, said, "Then it might be as you say. Maybe he was looking us over with robbery in mind. Puzzling, since any flash gentleman would have to fall quite low indeed to think about robbing a bookseller's. Looting one of the new mansions out in Mayfair would be much more lucrative. However, there's no accounting for the peculiarity of persons in London. Any big city attracts some strange ones. We'll lock up tight. Hosea, you put your pallet in the press room for a few nights, just in case.''

Hosea grumbled that he'd planned to be out late a couple of evenings during the week.

His father replied blandly, "That is why you may put your pallet in the press room instead. Guard duty will keep you out of your unsavory haunts—and perhaps prevent a misadventure. I'd just as soon not lose my book stocks to some deranged captain who's been temporarily forced off the highway.''

But after four nights of Hosea sleeping downstairs, and no robbery, nor even a reappearance of the peculiar stranger, the household relaxed and forgot him.

All except Phillipe.

MRS. EMMA'S fiftieth birthday fell on the last Saturday in April. The evening before, Mr. Sholto made a surprise announcement at supper. He would close his doors at three the following afternoon. Having hired a four-wheeled post chaise, he planned to drive them all out to Vauxhall Gardens, which had just opened for the season.

At the gardens they would eat a picnic supper and enjoy the music, while avoiding what he termed "the more salacious entertainments which I understand take place in the bowers and along the dark walls."

Mrs. Emma hugged him. Esau looked delighted. Even Marie showed some animation at the prospect of an outing; Mr. Sholto had made a point that she and her son were invited.

So, the next night, Phillipe Charboneau again glimpsed a world he was trying to forget.

The spring dusk smelled of thawed earth and the perfumes of the finely dressed folk dining in lantern-lit pavilions scattered around the vast pleasure park. Ladies in brocaded gowns and gentlemen in suits with sequinned buttons filled the twilight with much laughter and loud talk.

Admission to the park had cost Mr. Sholto a shilling per person. Mrs. Emma had therefore insisted on preparing her own birthday meal—which, Mr. Sholto privately revealed to his sons and Phillipe, he had planned for her to do all along, generosity having its limits.

Ignoring the food and drink available for sale on the grounds, they chose an open stretch of lawn from which they could hear the musical performance, spread blankets like many others around them were doing and enjoyed a splendid supper featuring minced chicken and two newly bought bottles of claret. The lilting strains of a string orchestra drifted from the far part of the grounds. And as full darkness settled, the garden walks livened with the scurrying footfalls of men and maids, not to mention other, occasionally sensual sounds. The only illumination came from the pavilions and from a few glowing lanterns hung from trees.

Soon Hosea began to display signs of impatience.

"May I have leave to wander a while, father? I don't have the ear for Mr. Handel's airs that Esau does."

"Yes, I suppose. But don't be gone longer than half an hour. I'm told those dim walks are dangerous places after the concert ends."

A moment or so later, Phillipe jumped up and announced that he wanted to walk too. The spring air, the sweet music, the muted laughter of lovers wandering the mazy paths had brought disturbing memories of Alicia Parkhurst. He hoped a little activity would dispel them.

He started off down the sloping lawn in the direction Hosea had taken. His mother, busy helping Mrs. Emma close the hampers, left her work and caught up with him.

"Look well at the places where the genteel folk are spending the evening, Phillipe." Her voice was low, but full of the intensity he remembered from Auvergne. "That's where you belong. And that's what you'll throw away if you keep entertaining this foolish dream of going to America. I promise you one thing. I'll never let you do it as long as I draw a breath."

She turned her back, leaving the soft steel of her words to twist in his mind.

Well, she'd given him the answer he'd wondered about ever since their first

argument. The lines of battle had been laid out. She'd only been awaiting the proper moment to deliver the first salvo.

Unhappily, Phillipe hurried down the slope to catch up with Hosea.

The two young men circled a large pavilion. Under its lanterns, a bewigged young macaroni was heartily puking all over the gown of his female companion. Other ladies and gentlemen in the party squealed in exaggerated shock. But several applauded drunkenly.

Phillipe hurried on by, wishing Marie could view the coarse scene. *That* was the world she wanted him to join?

Granted, it had its attractions. But sweet Christ, how could she overlook its darker side so easily? Those people lived with the assumption that any behavior, no matter how gross, could be excused—even approved—because of their wealth and position. Did Marie honestly prefer such standards over the simple decencies they'd found in an ordinary household like that of the Sholtos?

Of course, he realized his sweeping judgments were just that—and consequently, in certain instances, unfair. Hadn't Mr. Fox assured him that his own father did not conform to the pattern?

Still, Phillipe had conceived a hatred of all noblemen and their frivolous, painted women. He knew it was partly because he hadn't been good enough for one such woman, and because he'd threatened another—to the point where she retaliated through her son. But as he and Hosea ambled, trying to explain away the reasons for the hatred did little good. The hatred remained.

Shortly, Hosea was no longer content merely to amble. He literally hopped from one foot to the other, excited by something he'd spotted behind them. Phillipe came out of his reverie, heard feminine laughter.

"Shopgirls!" Hosea hissed. "Two of 'em—and damned pert looking. Come on, let's follow.'

Phillipe grinned. "I didn't think you slipped away from your father just to study the botanical plantings."

"Stop gabbing or we'll lose 'em, Phillipe!"

Tempted, Phillipe finally shook his head. "You go if you want. I'll meet you back where we saw that young beau amusing his friends by throwing up. Then your father won't suspect we've done anything but stroll."

Hosea needed no further prodding. He ran off after the two flirts, who had disappeared around one of the many turnings the path took between high hedges.

Phillipe wandered on. He inhaled the night air, watched the clear stars, listened to a nearby nightingale singing in harmony with the violas and cellos and French horns of the orchestra. No matter how he resisted, memories of Alicia flooded his mind.

Head down and pensive, he wandered deeper into the unlighted sections of the gardens. He failed to hear the footsteps until they were very close behind him.

All at once the back of his neck prickled. He realized that some solitary walker was approaching with unusual speed. He turned.

The glow of distant lanterns filtered across the tops of the hedges. Silhouetted against the faint light was a tall man. Phillipe could see nothing more.

The man reached him in three long steps.

"I have a present for you, sir," said the shadow-figure, who seemed to be rummaging in his right-hand pocket. "The one to whom you gave a ruined hand gives you this in return—"

The vague light between the hedges flashed on the barrel of a pocket pistol.

Phillipe only had time to fling himself forward and down as the pistol crashed.

A spurt of fire showed him the hem of the killer's dirty coat. Once it had been a vivid color. Orange—

The pistol ball hissed through the leaves directly behind the spot where Phillipe had been standing a moment before. On his knees, he grappled at the man's jackbooted legs. He knew the identity of his attacker now, even though tonight the man wore no sword.

The man cursed, pulled back, aimed a knee at Phillipe's jaw. Phillipe let go, wrenched his head out of the way, seized the heel of the viciously flying boot and heaved upward.

The man tumbled, dropping his pistol. His left hand dove into his coat for another.

Phillipe attacked, clumsily, but with power. He jumped on the bigger man's belly, driving his knee down hard, then again. At the same time he struck at the attacker's face.

The man slammed his head to one side, dodging the blow. Phillipe's fingers raked something leathery. An eye patch, he was certain.

On the far side of the hedge, he heard feminine cries of fright. The killer's left hand was coming up. For one dreadful instant the dim light again glared on a pistol barrel pointed directly at Phillipe's forehead.

He beat both fists against the man's wrist an instant before the attacker triggered the pistol. The cock fell; the powder flashed; the gun exploded. Phillipe wrenched aside, felt the sharp sting as the ball grazed his left temple. Only his fists, striking the attacker's wrist and angling the ball high and to the side, had saved his life.

The killer beat at the side of Phillipe's head with the butt of his empty weapon. One dizzying blow. Another—accompanied by blasphemous curses. Phillipe lunged backward, managed to gain his feet. He tried to jump in and stamp on the bigger man's throat. But by then, the outcries from nearby sections of the gardens had begun to multiply. Boots hammered the paths—

"Hallo, who shot?"

"Over this way!"

"No, to the left!"

The killer sprang up, kicked Phillipe's shin. The hard blow brought more pain. Off balance, he crashed into the hedge. The whole left side of his head was wet with running blood. He was certain the killer would come at him again.

Instead, the tall man hesitated, as if listening to the approaching runners. Then he ran himself, six steps taking him out of sight around a curve of the path. The hedges hid the belling skirt of his dirty coat of orange shot silk.

III

PANIC AND shock overwhelmed Phillipe as two men arrived from the direction opposite that which the one-eyed man had taken in flight.

"Here's the fray, Amos," yelled one of the arrivals, skidding to a halt and plucking something from the path. "Or what's left of it. A pistol. And the victim—or the cause?"

The man confronted Phillipe. "Who are you, sir? What happened here?"

About to blurt an answer, Phillipe's panic got the better of him. He snatched the pistol from the astonished man's hand and bolted off in the direction the killer had gone.

"Here, stop! The watch must look into this, sir. You must make explanation—!"

A foreigner make explanation of attempted murder by a thug employed by the Amberly family? He wanted none of that!

As he ran blindly through the pathways, he felt much as he had when he and his mother fled from Tonbridge. His hatred seethed because he knew again that he was a nobody, to be disposed of at their pleasure. How long had the search been going on while he foolishly thought himself secure at Sholto's?

A young couple barred the path ahead. " 'Ware his gun!" the affrighted young man yelled as Phillipe raced by them, accidentally bumping the girl. She began to scream:

"Blood! He's messed me with blood!"

Her scream shrilled up the scale, hysterical. Now that same blood was running into Phillipe's left eye. He plunged right, then right again, trying to find his way out of the warren of hedges, alert to the sounds of people searching for the cause of the commotion. Finally, he broke into the open. Off to his left he thought he recognized a pavilion near the lawn where they'd taken supper.

Moments later, he found the Sholtos and Marie.

They were all on their feet, wondering at the outcries and alarms. Marie let out a low scream at the sight of his bloodied face. Sholto exclaimed, "We heard two pistols discharge—"

"Both aimed at me," Phillipe panted. "By the one-eyed captain. But the Amberlys hired him."

At that, Marie seemed about to swoon. Mrs. Emma supported her. Phillipe threw his coat aside as Solomon Sholto demanded to know what had become of Hosea.

Pulling off his shirt and using it to wipe the blood from his face, Phillipe told them the younger son had gone off by himself. As he flung the shirt away, Mr. Sholto snapped, "Find him, Esau. And let's hide this."

Phillipe felt the pistol tugged out of his belt where he'd thrust it while he ran. He didn't even remember. "Bring Hosea to the chaise with all speed," Mr. Sholto called after his son. Then he bent to conceal the pocket pistol in his wife's hamper.

Next he picked up Phillipe's coat, draped it around the younger man's shoulders. "Everyone to the carriage—and quickly. In case we're stopped, we'll tell them the lad drank too much, fell and hurt himself—here, let's go to the left. Around that milling mob near the path."

They walked rapidly in a group, Phillipe in the center. Mr. Sholto's head swiveled constantly, surveying the situation. People dashed to and fro. Back in the hedges from which Phillipe had escaped, torches and lanterns bobbed. Mr. Sholto's nervous excitement showed in his almost nonstop speech:

"The devil who fired on you may still be lurking—we mustn't linger. But the park's crowded—and thievery's common—practically a robbery a night. We may be able to get away. We don't want to be questioned—"

Phillipe's eyes blurred. The lanterns in a nearby pavilion swam and grew hazy. He managed to say, "No, because I can't tell anyone the truth."

"Are you positive the man was sent by the Amberlys?" Sholto asked.

"Roger Amberly. He wasn't mentioned by name. But the man said my—my *present*, as he called it, came from the one to whom I gave a ruined hand."

He could barely gasp out the final word. His head ached violently. He felt

blood running again, staining the coat Mr. Sholto had wrapped around his shoulders. The printer cautioned him in a whisper:

"The gate watchman's eying us—" Loudly: "A casualty of the perfidious gin bottle, sir. The young scoundrel fell and cut his head. We must get him back to town—to a physician, then to a state of sobriety!" Sholto's smile was feeble and nervous.

But the guard seemed more interested in another subject: "Why all the lights and hallooing?"

"There's been a robbery, I think."

"Something new," said the guard, with sour amusement. "Pass on."

Phillipe's step was unsteady. He heard Mr. Sholto say, "The chaise is just ahead." But he never really saw it. He was only dimly aware of climbing inside.

Hours seemed to pass before he heard voices he recognized as belonging to the brothers. Mr. Sholto whipped up the hired team. The chaise clattered away from the lights and clamor in Vauxhall Gardens.

"Safe, thank heaven!" Mrs. Emma exclaimed.

Barely conscious and feeling sick to his stomach, Phillipe knew despairingly that the safety was illusory. Somewhere under the stars Phillipe could hardly see, the one-eyed man was still alive.

IV

ST. PAUL'S tolled one in the morning.

Near the lamp on the Sholtos' kitchen table, the dismantled weapon gleamed. A turn-off pocket pistol, its center-mounted box lock and the screw-on barrel lying separately.

Solomon Sholto had ordered the serving of a third bottle of birthday claret he had left behind when they went on their outing. Phillipe drank a little, feeling better physically. His head was wrapped in a clean linen bandage. The graze was not deep. It had clotted soon after Mrs. Emma cleansed it.

Hosea poked the coals in the kitchen hearth. The poker clanged loudly as he hung it up. Esau scowled an uncharacteristic scowl.

"You are *certain* the attack was made with a purpose?" Mr. Sholto inquired.

Phillipe sighed, nodded. "There's only one person in the world who could accuse me of destroying his hand. Roger, or his mother, or both of them, hired that one-eyed fellow. He probably searched a long time in London before he located me. Through the beggars around the church, I don't doubt." Phillipe covered his eyes. "I fought so damned clumsily. If I'd killed him, that might have been the end of it."

Big Esau snorted. "Stop that. We're ordinary folk, not soldiers. And men like that captain are skilled in the arts of murder. They strike by surprise, to protect their own cowardly hides. You said he ran as soon as the risk of capture presented itself."

Marie put down her wine, some of the old fire showing in her dark eyes. "The very fact they sought us, Phillipe, proves that they fear your claim."

Sick of hearing about the claim, he shook his head angrily. The starkness of his face, which hardly resembled a boy's any longer, made her catch her breath.

"They can strike down the claim by manipulating the law, Mama. It's me Roger wanted, in payment for what I did to him. And there's no use asking the

law's help to catch the one-eyed captain. If he were to be locked away, the Amberlys would only hire another like him—and another—until the work's done.''

Looking upset, Mrs. Emma asked, ''Then what do you propose to do, Phillipe?''

''Leave here. And quickly. We're not safe in London, any more than we were safe in Kent. I was a fool to think otherwise.''

''But we can't go running again—!'' Marie began.

''We can and we will,'' he said. For her benefit, he added harshly, ''The captain or his successor might strike this house next. I will not repay the kindness of the Sholtos by exposing them to that kind of peril. Doing it once to Mr. Fox was enough.''

Solomon Sholto scratched his chin, which was already beginning to sprout next morning's beard. ''A speedy departure is probably wise. I'm speaking for your sake more than ours, Phillipe—even though I appreciate your consideration more than I can say. Let us assume the Amberlys and their agent anticipate that you will flee the town. Where will they expect you to go?''

''Where they probably expected us to go before—and no doubt discovered we didn't. One of the Channel ports.''

''Which would be watched,'' Esau said.

Phillipe nodded. ''If Roger's as anxious for vengeance as it seems, he may have hired many more pairs of eyes than one. So—''

He barely paused. The decision had come to him only a moment before; inevitable.

''—we will go to the other direction. Take our chances on finding passage to the colonies.''

He saw rage light Marie's eyes again. Before she could speak he slammed his palm down hard on the table. The dismantled sections of the pistol rattled.

''Mama, there is no other way. Auvergne will be dangerous to reach. And what's left there anyway, except a dilapidated inn? You must listen to me now. It's my life they're after. And my right to save it the best way I know how.''

He regretted speaking to her that way. But he felt there was no choice. Every moment spent in London was another moment spent in jeopardy.

Esau nodded his agreement with Phillipe's decision. ''The best coaching service in all England runs west to the port of Bristol. You can be away in the morning from the One Bell in the Strand.''

''I have no idea what ship passage will cost,'' Phillipe said. ''Maybe I can work for it. Earn it for the both of us. I've probably saved enough to pay for the coach. But before we leave, I must get to Dr. Franklin's house.''

''Hardly seems like the time for a social call—'' Hosea began.

''That's not the purpose. When I visited him before—''

''You went to call on that American?'' Marie interrupted. ''When?''

''Some days ago. Of an evening. You were asleep—''

''You said nothing about it. Nothing.''

''I intended to. Each time I got close to it, I stopped short—because I assumed you wouldn't even listen to what he told me.''

''About those barbarous colonies? You're right.''

''There are big, growing cities in America, Mama! And Dr. Franklin promised that if we decided to go, he'd write a list of printing houses where I could apply for work. Also give me a letter of recommendation—''

Contemptuous, Marie was about to answer when Esau said:

"Damn decent of him."

Solomon Sholto shook his head. "No—just typical of his generous nature. Phillipe, you will be busy enough packing your belongings. Esau, you and Hosea go to Craven Street instead. Rouse the doctor. Explain the situation—"

"But please don't mention the Amberlys," Phillipe cautioned. "I hinted at the problem to Franklin but I didn't go into detail."

Esau nodded as his father said, "Speed back as quickly as you can. Start immediately."

As the brothers struggled into their coats, Phillipe received a fresh shock. Marie was watching him. For a moment it seemed as though her eyes brimmed with genuine hatred. Then the emotion—if it was actually there—dulled; her expression became one of slack-lipped resignation.

Her lips and cheeks were drained of color. She glanced away—brushed at a strand of loose hair with a vague, almost pathetic gesture. He could barely bring himself to look at her. He knew how she must be suffering—watching her one dream smashed beyond all repair.

Well, he'd lived with that kind of thing too; he'd lost Alicia and survived. She could learn to live with her ruined dreams, now that their lives were at stake.

One day she might come to understand that the decision forced on him tonight was made for both their sakes. One day she might accept—and forgive him.

Strangely calm, he realized he might as well go the rest of the way.

"While Hosea and Esau call at Franklin's, I'll borrow a quill and paper, if I may. I want to write a letter to Girard."

"Girard?" Mrs. Emma repeated.

"The man who's minding the inn for us. The place will become his—to keep or sell, as he chooses. We won't be going back to Auvergne for a long time. If ever."

Marie refused to look at him.

"I'll find the writing things," Sholto said. He turned to his sons. "On your way, on your way!—and take your sticks. Watch for anyone lurking. We want no more attacks by that vicious captain tonight. Your mother's had quite enough excitement for one birthday."

"For a lifetime of 'em, sir!" said his wife.

V

EXHAUSTED ALMOST beyond feeling, Phillipe still managed to complete the letter, sand it and wax it shut. Mr. Sholto promised to post it.

Phillipe leaned back and covered his weary eyes. He reflected ironically that once again they would be setting out with no more than the clothes on their backs—Marie's casket, the securely wrapped sword—and one dream of fortune now exchanged for another.

Mrs. Sholto packed them a small hamper of food as Phillipe dressed just before daylight. The elder Sholto once again dispatched his sons, who had come back from Craven Street. This time they were to survey the yard of the One Bell in the Strand, to see whether, by remotest chance, the one-eyed man had been noticed in the vicinity.

The One Bell was a major coach departure point. But only one of many. The captain could not be expected to survey them all personally, even if he suspected

that Phillipe and his mother might resort to immediate flight. Still, Mr. Sholto advised the precaution.

When the sons came back with the Bristol coach schedule—the first departed at seven—they reported no obviously suspicious persons on the premises they'd scouted. But Esau did remind Phillipe of his own words—that there was no way of telling how many watchers—or of what identity—the Amberlys' agent might employ.

As the family set out on foot together from Sweet's Lane—Mrs. Emma having insisted she would not be frightened out of seeing them off—it was just past six by the great bells. The narrow, twisting streets were still almost empty.

Esau pressed a pouch into Phillipe's hand. "The doctor sends you his commendation on your decision. He also expressed his hope that the list and letter will help secure you at least an apprentice's job at a good printing house."

"I'm sorry you had to waken him," Phillipe said.

Hosea grinned. "Oh, we didn't waken him."

Esau cleared his throat. "Dr. Franklin was—ah—entertaining."

"A damned smart-looking young flirt named Polly. His landlady's daughter," Hosea said. "Really, it was quite a scene. Franklin in his dressing gown—the wench in a filmy bed dress that would scandalize our dear mother. The doctor was ostensibly amusing the girl with tunes on a fiddle. But there was plenty of Madeira in evidence. I wonder if the old reprobate wasn't doing a little fiddling of a different kind—"

"Stop sounding so jealous," Esau said. "Dr. Franklin's relations with ladies other than his wife are entirely platonic."

"Or so he pretends in public," replied Hosea with a knowing smirk.

Annoyed, Esau changed the subject: "Have you any idea what your final destination will be, Phillipe?"

"Whatever the destination of the first available ship." Puzzled, he pointed to a second, smaller pouch Esau had taken from his pocket. "What's that?"

"As you asked, I didn't reveal the reasons behind your abrupt decision. Nor mention the name you wanted kept secret. But I did suggest that you had been threatened with harm. Franklin immediately gave me five pounds to help secure your passage—and cursed the air blue in the process."

Astonished, Phillipe asked, "Why?"

"You said yourself—you hinted to him that you'd encountered some trouble with persons of high station. Persons against whom you had no defense. He abominates that sort of thing. Also, he has a good opinion of you—and your ability to fit in where you're going. Yes, he was most flattering. Said he judged you to be strong, determined, intelligent—and now, obviously capable of quick action when circumstances demand it."

Gil said I had the makings of a soldier, Phillipe thought wearily.

Mama harped that I was a little lord. To Franklin I'm a printer's boy of determined character—just what the hell's it to be?

Then, with a kind of cold, weary insight, he imagined that the truth was closest of all to this: he would know what he was only afterward, when he'd seen how it had all come out.

"By the way," Esau added as they trudged along, "Franklin's not giving you a gift in perpetuity. He specifically charged me to tell you he expects the loan to be repaid one of these days. From the profits of your own printing house. He'll be back in America eventually—and will make a point of collecting. He was

smiling when he said it. But he wasn't joking. I'd consider that another compliment.''

"Franklin's estimate of my abilities, and of opportunities in America, may both be overrated. By his own admission it's not a peaceful country these days,''

"More peaceful than London—at least for you,'' Hosea put in. "Have a care. We're almost to the Strand.''

He ran ahead, jumping over two bawds snoring dead drunk against a wall. At the corner Hosea looked right and left. Then he gestured the rest of them to follow.

Phillipe began to feel a little excitement mingled with a sense of relief at being able to escape so quickly. The sun was starting to slant down between the rickety tenements now. The spring air was sweet and cool, tanged with the scents of the river and the smoke from London's chimney pots. A bit more confidently, he tucked Dr. Franklin's purse of money in a pocket and the pouch of papers in his belt under his coat.

Hosea ran back along the shops of the Strand to inform them, "The express is already loading. A four-horse coach—and it's packed. You'll be lucky to find places on top. Better hurry.''

They did, even Marie managing to keep up.

In the noisy, clattering yard of the One Bell, Mr. Sholto helped Phillipe pay the double fare. Eyeing the crowd, Hosea and Esau assisted Marie in her climb to the top, and an uncomfortable seat on the flat roof. She would have only rails for handholds.

Phillipe noticed that the interior of the coach was indeed jammed with passengers: a large family; two black-clad parsons. He prepared to climb up the wheel spokes before all the room was taken by a third passenger mounting the other side—a hulking blackamoor in a sateen coat and breeches. Evidently the black was the servant of a portly gentleman rudely squeezing inside the coach proper, over the protests of the others.

Mrs. Emma gave Phillipe a quick, forceful hug. She was crying, incapable of speech.

The sons, then stern-eyed Mr. Sholto shook his hand.

"I pray the Almighty protects you. And grants you a better welcome in the new land than you found in this one,'' the printer said.

Not looking back, Phillipe climbed the wheel to the roof of the coach.

6
The Bristol Coach

SHOUTS FROM the driver and a blast from the guard's brass horn warned of imminent departure. The guard hung his horn over his shoulder by a lanyard, hoisted himself and his blunderbuss up into position.

Phillipe settled cross-legged on the roof of the coach. He slid the wrapped sword beneath his thighs and deposited the precious casket in the diamond-shaped space between his legs. The blackamoor, whose tricorn hat contrasted

strangely with his apparel and the gold hoop that hung from the pierced lobe of his right ear, shifted a little to make more room. Phillipe nodded in polite acknowledgment.

The blackamoor broke into a big grin, displaying a huge expanse of even white teeth. The man thumped his chest with an immense fist.

"I be Lucas, sar," he said in peculiarly accented English. "We ride a long way to the sea town, so we hang on tight, yes?"

"I think you're right," Phillipe replied with amiable casualness. "The roads are probably none too smooth—Mama, hold onto the side rails!"

Marie sat with her knees tucked up near her chin, her hands locked around them. The hands looked white, bloodless.

And her lips were moving.

Phillipe's stomach tightened up. He leaned forward, touched her hand. She didn't respond. She was speaking French in a monotone. Her eyes stared past him at the morning sky and saw nothing.

Then he caught some of her words.

"—and when this coach arrives at their door, I'll tell them, 'This is the little lord. Treat him as he deserves. It's his birthright.' "

Terrified, Phillipe shook Marie's arm, said in French, "Mama, we're not going to Kentland. This is the coach to Bristol. For God's sake look at me!"

Slowly, as if returning with difficulty from contemplation of some remote landscape of the mind, she appeared to take notice of the surroundings. Bleak lines showed on her face.

"You must hold on to the rails or you'll fall," he warned, noticing that the Sholto family had all seen the peculiar expression on his mother's face. They watched her with obvious concern. A scrawny man whose greasy clubbed hair shone in the sunlight also gave Phillipe a curious stare as he turned his bay horse out of the One Bell's yard and clattered away up the Strand.

"Please," Phillipe pleaded, trying to pry his mother's hands apart. "You must hold on!"

Her eyes focused on his face. She said in French, "What difference does it make now?"

The driver uncoiled his short whip, gathered up the traces of the four impatient horses. Phillipe reached over, seized the man's shoulder:

"Wait! I must get my mother down inside."

The driver growled, "We've a schedule to keep. We should have left ten minutes ago. Besides, there's no room below."

"I'll make room," Phillipe said, already slipping over the side and skittering down the wheel spokes.

He yanked the coach door open, face to face with one of the children in the traveling family, a bonneted little girl, perched on her father's knee. Smiling, she was offering her small hoop to the portly man opposite. He in turn registered his dislike of children in general, and this one in particular, with an expression of pompous annoyance.

Phillipe said, "I beg your pardon, ladies and gentlemen. My mother's not feeling well. Is there space inside here, out of the wind?"

"No," said one of the parsons on the far side of the coach. "But we'll make some. Stay seated, Andrew," he added to his companion. "We'll take turns riding on top." He opened the door on his side and stepped out.

While the driver continued to grumble, Phillipe helped his mother down again. He settled her where the churchman had been seated, placed the casket in her lap.

She clutched it protectively. Then she began to mumble in French again. Phillipe heard the words *little lord* as he shut the door, clambered up and resumed his place along with the blackamoor and the shovel-hatted parson, who was already clutching the hat to his head with one hand while he gripped his testament with the other.

The driver flashed Phillipe a glare, muttering, "Damned cheeky foreigner." He uncoiled the whip, cracked it over the heads of his horses. With a jolt the coach rolled forward. The parson dropped his testament and seized the rail only just in time to keep from being toppled off.

The coach clattered away from the One Bell. Phillipe waved at the Sholtos as their figures diminished and then disappeared altogether. He could think of nothing except his mother down below. Had the decision to make for Bristol, and the colonies, finally undone her? Unconsciously he tightened his hand on the rail, cursing the Amberlys and cursing himself. The blackamoor stared in astonishment.

Phillipe paid no attention. Why couldn't his mother recognize that they were going to a place that might afford them safety, and a fresh start?

He knew the answer. It was not their ultimate destination that was at fault. He suspected she would have acted the same way if they'd returned to Les Trois Chevres. She had harbored her dream too long, to the exclusion of all others. Its destruction was in turn destroying her.

The morning wind blowing over the coach roof forced him to squint into the jumbled distance of streets and buildings. But he saw only Marie—her lips moving; her eyes vacant; her hands gripping the casket like claws.

He was desperately afraid for her sanity.

II

WESTWARD, THE crowded streets and lanes became occasional cottages and gardens—then open country, as the coach took the post road to Bristol.

The spring sun beat against Phillipe's back, making him sweat heavily. But the enforced concentration required to hold his place on top of the swaying, jolting coach helped push the worries about his mother to the back of his mind.

Lucas, the blackamoor, sat dozing, apparently quite at home with this risky mode of travel. The parson had tugged his shovel hat down next to his ears, and now used one hand to hold his open testament practically under his nose. How the cleric managed to read with all the bumps, the racket of hoof and wheel and driver's whip, and the blowing dust that clouded over them, visibly soiling the white lappets of the parson's collar, Phillipe couldn't imagine.

In an hour, though, he'd grown accustomed to swaying and bouncing and holding on. He even managed to relax a little. The sun's warmth helped cheer him, as did occasional friendly waves from farmers laboring in the hay fields or maneuvering their vegetable carts to the road's shoulder to permit passage of the speeding coach. The rolling, sunlit countryside brought Phillipe a sense of freedom, security—and direction—he hadn't enjoyed since the encounter at Vauxhall Gardens. He'd be sore and aching when they reached Bristol tomorrow. But if that was the worst that happened, he could be thankful.

He grew aware of the whites of the blackamoor's eyes. When had the big man wakened? Phillipe hadn't noticed. Lucas was watching the road behind them.

The wrinkles on the broad ebony forehead made it clear the blackamoor had spotted something unusual.

"Man on a horse, sar," Lucas pointed. "Not there a while ago."

As the black man tapped the driver's shoulder, Phillipe twisted his head around—and exhaled hard.

The rider was pacing the coach perhaps a quarter-mile behind. Phillipe could make out only essentials through the dust churning up from the rear wheels. The rider was scrawny, his mount a powerful bay. Phillipe remembered seeing such a horseman depart from the One Bell a few minutes ahead of the coach.

"Could be a gentleman jus' riding," Lucas shouted to his companions. "Or could be a road captain."

The driver preferred to take no chances. He immediately whipped up his horses.

"In the latter event," yelled the parson, "I will for once be thankful for the poverty of clerics. A highwayman would want nothing of mine."

Lucas surveyed the landscape skimming by on either side.

Thickets and low hills now. Not a sign of a farmstead, nor any other riders or wagons anywhere ahead.

The blackamoor growled, "Been robbed once before, on the Oxford coach. Sometimes, the captains don' ride alone. That happen, everybody certain to be poor after."

Alarmed, Phillipe thought of the talk he'd heard about highwaymen in London. Captured ones were summarily hanged from Tyburn Tree. But that didn't seem to discourage extensive practice of the profession. They were a desperate lot.

Phillipe turned around again. The rider on the bay was galloping to keep pace with the speeding coach. His hand came up. Suddenly an explosion split the morning air, louder than the thunder of the wheels.

From beech thickets flanking the post road just ahead, two other horsemen appeared, spurring to the road's center to block passage of the coach. Now it was no longer a question of outrunning a single rider.

The one behind had fired the warning shot. Both men ahead rode expertly, without gripping the reins. Between them they held four long-barreled pistols.

The coach guard flung the blunderbuss to his shoulder, then let it drop— because the driver was already kicking at the brake and hauling on the traces, unwilling to press his luck against a trio.

Phillipe's eyes riveted on the rider who had come out from the left side of the road. He sat very tall in his saddle, the silver side plates and butt caps on his pistols flashing in the sunlight. Even through the billowing dust, Phillipe could see that the highwayman wore a leather patch over one eye, jackboots and a dirty coat that had once been bright orange.

III

SHRILL QUESTIONS and cries of alarm rose from inside the coach as it swayed to a halt. The guard leaned over the side and yelled:

"Keep still and hand 'em all your valuables and we'll get off safe—if we're lucky."

Phillipe's scalp crawled with sweat. Perched in the open, he was quite aware

that the one-eyed man had spotted him. As the coach settled to rest, the two highwaymen trotted their horses toward it, joined by their companion from behind. He sprang from his saddle, jerked open the left-hand door.

Phillipe sat utterly still. He knew this meeting was not accidental. Perhaps there had been watchers at every coaching inn of importance. His palms grew as sweaty as his forehead. He realized once again the depths of Roger Amberly's animosity.

The one-eyed man gave the driver an empty smile and a salute with one pistol. At close range, the pock marks on his ravaged cheeks stood out clearly.

"Captain Plummer, sir, at your service. We'll trouble your passengers for whatever trinkets they may have. Then you shall be on your way again."

"Everyone out," ordered the scrawny man at the coach door, stowing both of his pistols in his belt. The four barrels of the two others still menaced driver, guard and passengers—sufficient firepower to guarantee success of the enterprise.

The family alighted first, the mother comforting her frightened little daughter. Next came the outraged fat man, then the other parson. Of Marie there was no immediate sign.

But Phillipe was more concerned with Captain Plummer. He brought his horse near the coach and once again smiled his false smile:

"If each one of you ladies and gentlemen obey the orders of my coves in good fashion, we shall have no unhappy accidents." His one glaring eye slid to Phillipe—and the smile froze in place. Phillipe knew full well what was going to happen. At least one "unhappy accident."

When Captain Plummer saw that understanding register on Phillipe's face, his smile became genuine. He wagged a pistol.

"If the passengers on the roof will also alight, please—?"

As the parson began to descend via the wheel spokes, the scrawny man said, "There's one left inside, cap'n. A woman."

Plummer nodded. "Yes, I wondered about that."

Phillipe's cheeks felt fiery. Under his sweated clothes, his heart hammered hard. He knew he had no chance to unwrap Gil's sword. Nor did he have any other weapon at his disposal. But unless he defended himself, he would die, the quickly forgotten victim of yet another highway incident.

Lucas' shiny face looked ferocious as he climbed down. A possible ally there, Phillipe thought, dropping into the dust behind the blackamoor.

"Assist our reluctant passenger," Captain Plummer ordered his scrawny helper.

The man dropped a sack he'd pulled down from his saddle, reached inside the coach toward Marie. For one moment, his body and outstretched right arm blocked the line of sight between Phillipe and Captain Plummer. Phillipe chose the moment because it might be his last chance. He struck for the scrawny man's exposed middle with both fists.

IV

THE SCRAWNY man doubled forward, uttering a furious curse. He clawed for the second, undischarged pistol in his belt. Phillipe heard the mother of the little girl shriek—and something else: the sudden clopping of Captain Plummer's horse as the one-eyed man positioned himself to shoot.

Phillipe whirled the dazed man by the shoulders. Captain Plummer's right-hand pistol boomed with a flash and a puff of smoke. Blood splattered Phillipe's cheeks as Plummer's close-range blew a hole in the scrawny man's neck.

The man let out a kind of choking sigh, sagging in Phillipe's arms, no longer a shield.

Phillipe released the dead man, leaped away as the passengers yelled and scattered. Plummer roweled his nervous horse viciously to hold him still, pointed his second pistol at Phillipe's head.

A clear target against the side of the coach, Phillipe had no place to run. The dark eye of the pistol muzzle followed him as he threw himself on the ground.

Captain Plummer was a professional. He would not be rushed into the shot for which he had undoubtedly been well compensated. Hitting the dust, Phillipe awaited the explosion, the thud of a ball into his flesh—

But it didn't come. The blunderbuss roared.

Captain Plummer began to swear, his oaths punctuated by groans of effort. Phillipe rolled frantically underneath the coach and out the other side. Just ahead of the horses, the third highwayman toppled from his saddle. A wound in his groin bubbled red.

That man had been the target of the blunderbuss, then. Phillipe ran toward him. Over the lathered backs of the horses he saw what had saved him. The blackamoor had fastened both hands on Captain Plummer's left arm and was holding on ferociously, even as Plummer tried to haul back in the saddle and transfer his still-loaded pistol to his right hand.

But the immense Lucas kept levering the highwayman's left arm down and back. Plummer's mouth worked in obscene rage, spittle on his lips, sweat on his pocked cheeks. With his right hand he hit for Lucas's eyes, to claw them out if he could. Lucas snapped his head back, laughed a big booming laugh that died abruptly as Plummer managed to gouge a thumb into his eyesocket.

Lucas's hold on the highwayman's left arm loosened. Plummer wrenched free and aimed at the nearest target—the black by his stirrup.

Phillipe had reached the fallen man, who was moaning in pain. He snatched up one of the man's pistols. He fired past the bobbing muzzles of the lead coach horses.

With a scream, Captain Plummer arched his back. Phillipe had aimed for the best and biggest target—the man's torso. There, over the left ribs, the shabby orange coat showed an immense black-edged hole from which blood poured.

Lucas pried the pistol out of Plummer's relaxed hand, drew back the cock and fired point blank.

Captain Plummer's leather eyepatch disappeared in a torrent of blood. The sight brought fresh screams and hysterical sobs from the mother and her small girl. The big blackamoor hit Plummer's horse on the flank and sent it bolting toward the trees. The sudden motion flung the highwayman's corpse into the roadside ditch, mercifully hiding the ruin of his head.

Wiping sweat and dust from his cheeks, the blackamoor grinned across the backs of the horses.

''A keen shot, sar.''

Phillipe waved weakly, dropped the hot pistol in the dirt. He heard the driver and the guard calling thanks and congratulations. With surprising lack of Christian concern for the dead thieves, even the parsons expressed delight at the outcome.

Phillipe walked back to the right-hand coach door, opened it to look at his mother. He started to speak, couldn't.

Marie huddled in the corner. Her fingers tapped nervously at the old leather of the casket. Her lips moved but produced no sound. Her eyes stared far beyond the wall of the coach. If she'd heard the pistol shots and the screaming, she gave no sign.

Phillipe spoke his mother's name.

Silence.

Slowly he closed the coach door and stumbled to the roadside ditch. There he bent over, violently sick.

V

PRESENTLY THE journey resumed, Phillipe back in place on the roof with his equally bedraggled companions.

Lucas hummed, striking his palm in rhythm against the sateen of his knee as the coach flashed under low-hanging branches that dappled Phillipe's vision with flickering shadows.

He'd tried to rouse Marie once more before the coach got under way. He had managed to produce a murmur that might have indicated she recognized him. But that was all.

In a way he was glad that she had missed the entire encounter. But her condition continued to frighten him.

He felt totally alone. Only he knew the true reason Captain Plummer and his henchmen had selected this particular coach for plundering. Plummer had planned to earn a double reward. His loot from the passengers, and whatever sum he'd been paid by Phillipe's half brother.

Phillipe tried to imagine the damage the fight with the silver-headed stick had worked on the young nobleman's hand. It must have been considerable to provoke such retribution. Of course—Phillipe was already familiar with this bitter lesson—Roger would have undertaken his scheme with few fears of paying any penalty. Phillipe only hoped there would be no further pursuit before he was able to secure their passage out of Bristol.

But there was no one to whom he could communicate his anxieties now. Not the driver, whose attitude had become overwhelmingly cordial; not the parsons; no one. His secrets, and his hatred, were prisoned inside, where their heat had begun to forge a new Phillipe Charboneau out of the one who had so naively crossed the Channel only a year ago.

As the coach jounced along, he realized he was nearing his nineteenth birthday. He'd lived nearly half a man's normal life span already. In Auvergne, he had known virtually nothing of the world. But in the last twelve months he had learned enough to more than make up. He only hoped he could put the experience to some use.

It troubled him deeply that he had now been responsible for the deaths of three human beings—four if he counted the scrawny fellow he'd thrust into the path of Captain Plummer's ball.

True, none of the killings were deliberate. All had been done in self-defense. And his success in each case was, in fact, the source of an odd, guilty pride.

Still, none of the deaths, not even Plummer's, rested easy on him. As he clung

to the roof rails, beginning to ache from all the bounces and jolts, he hoped to God he would never entirely lose that sense of life's value.

If he ever did, he would then have become exactly like Roger Amberly.

___VI

FINALLY, ABOUT an hour after the incident with Captain Plummer and his men, Phillipe shook off the horror of the attack and turned his mind to more practical things.

A ship out of Bristol offered not only sanctuary but hope and opportunity. So the ledger was not entirely without its credits. He recalled the money Franklin had advanced and searched for the purse to make certain he hadn't lost it in his scramblings. He hadn't.

But the pouch containing the list of printing houses and the letter of introduction was gone from his belt.

Urgently, he bent forward to the driver's shoulder. "Sir—back along the road when we stopped, I lost papers I was carrying."

"Sorry, lad," the man shouted. "Can't turn around. Can't stop except to change horses—I'm fined if we don't keep schedule. Even when the cause is a captain of the road."

"But the papers are valuable. I need them where I'm going."

"Then ye'll have to take another coach back, and try to get off and search," was the answer. An impossible answer, Phillipe knew. Funds were short enough as it was. And he felt he dared not leave Marie alone now that her health had taken such a strange, precarious turn.

He regretted his own stupidity in not taking the time to so much as glance at Franklin's list. Even a few remembered names might have been of assistance when—and if—they reached America. Establishing connections in a new city would be just that much more difficult now.

He smiled a small, bitter smile. Even in failure, Roger Amberly's agents had dealt a blow to his prospects.

But he reminded himself that he was no longer Phillipe Charboneau of Auvergne. He had become someone different; harder, perhaps.

And so he thought, *God damn them all. I will survive.*

___VII

THE BRISTOL coach stopped the night at a restful country inn. When Phillipe opened the door to help his mother alight, he was thankful that she seemed aware of her immediate surroundings, and his identity again.

Earlier, when the driver had halted a few minutes at a way station for fresh horses, Phillipe had circulated quietly among the passengers. At that time Marie was still sitting immobile inside. He told the passengers that due to recent strains, his mother was not herself. He suggested there was no point in alarming her later with references to the attack by Captain Plummer. Since Phillipe and the blackamoor had assumed the temporary stature of heroes, thanks to boldness and lucky shooting, the others readily agreed.

Even the portly and somewhat pompous man whom Lucas served grew more friendly. He invited Phillipe to share his table at the inn that evening.

The portly gentleman was named Hoskins. He lived in Bristol. He was quick to point out that he did not own Lucas outright, as a slave—as was the custom in some of the colonies. The blackamoor was a free member of the serving class.

"So he can join us, too," Phillipe said as the guard tooted his horn to signal that the coach was ready to get under way.

"Oh, no!" Hoskins returned, horrified. "He's still required to eat in the kitchen."

Climbing up the wheel, Phillipe recalled the Irishman Burke's remark about Dr. Franklin having organized a colonial society to oppose the institution of slavery. But he couldn't recall any mention of slavery in the numerous books and pamphlets he'd devoured. Perhaps the references had been there and had slipped by him; or perhaps the propagandists of the colonies preferred to gloss over the subject. At any rate, the reminder that a market for human beings existed in America tainted Franklin's glowing comments somewhat.

At their overnight stop, Phillipe and Marie sat opposite Hoskins. After a filling meal, of which Marie ate little, the traveling family retired for the night. The parsons withdrew to a private table, presumably to discuss rarefied theological subjects. The coach driver and the guard had eaten their suppers on benches near the cheerful fire. They were already drunk and busy poking and fingering the rump of the inn's cowlike serving girl.

"Have you and your mother any connections in Bristol?" Hoskins asked eventually.

"No, sir, none." Phillipe glanced at his mother. The fire lit her dark eyes with pinpoints of brilliance, threw patterns of scarlet and shadow on her cheeks. She stared at her mug of ale that had been heated with a poker. She'd managed a few yes and no answers during dinner conversation, but nothing more. Phillipe was terrified in the face of such continuing silent despair.

With effort, he amplified his short answer to Hoskins:

"We're anxious to find a ship for America, though."

Hoskins drank. He was already working on his third or fourth mug. "Oh, then you've connections in the colonies."

Again Phillipe shook his head. "We intend to sail to one of the colonial ports, where I mean to look for work as a printer."

"Which port's your destination?"

"We'll go wherever the first ship goes, probably. Do you know how much it costs for passage, sir? I have five pounds."

Hoskins drank more ale. "Not nearly enough. However—" He belched, wiped his blubbery lips with his sleeve. "Since you defended us so handsomely today, and I take you for a person of good, if humble character, I may confide a secret. I'm carrying a deal of money. Yes, a deal," he emphasized with puffed-up pride, fingering the thickness under his waistcoat. Phillipe had assumed it to be natural fat, not concealed wealth.

"'M a manufacturer of ironware. Hoskins' kettles and pisspots are the byword in the finest dining places and hostelries in London. Used in many of the very best whorehouses, too—oh. Your pardon, madame. Now I just sold a handsome lot of merchandise this trip. But I also ship to the colonies. Oh, yes, in quantity. And while I'm a loyal Tory—a supporter of His Majesty—I also prefer to see relations with America prosper at any cost. Any cost short of rebellion, that is. I'm glad the King's ministers repealed some of those damned

taxes. Might have been necessary, those taxes. But ruinous for trade—ruinous! Urged their repeal myself. Joined with many other important merchants and factory owners. Put the screws on that fat German—''

Hoskins belched even more loudly. Phillipe realized the overweight gentleman was tipsy.

"Beg pardon, His Majesty. Where was I? Oh yes. Colonial trade. Well. In Bristol, one of my first tasks is to immediately hie myself to the wharfs and see what American vessels are in port. For with this—''

Another thump of what had to be a money belt concealed under his clothing.

"—I can finance quite a shipment of Hoskins' finest to our American cousins. Yes. Quite a shipment.'' Belch.

Phillipe sat silent, letting the fat man ramble on.

"Here's the point, young fellow. I have wide acquaintance with the sailing masters who call at Bristol from Philadelphia, New York City and that blasphemous hotbed of treason—'' A double belch; a prodigious yawn. "—Boston. So if you care to follow me during my calls on the captains, perhaps I can use my influence to find you a working berth. Only alternative is to sell yourself to the captain for seven years, then hope he can re-sell your indenture contract to some decent gentleman on the other side. Let me see—'' A noisy fart "—Madame, beg pardon. Let me see if I can help you get around that unpleasant prospect. I do have influence. I ship large orders. Large! You saved me a deal of money. Grateful. Glad to swing my weight with the captains as best I can. They lose ship's boys all the time, they do. Boys squander their pay on wagers in the cock pits. Dally with whor—prostitutes. Lie drunk when their vessels sail. Shouldn't be hard. Not with a tot of luck. And Hoskins. All the captains know Hoskins. Successful merchant prince. Finest ironware—''

With a gentle *whoosh*, Hoskins settled his lips together, thunked his head against the high back of the bench and began to snore.

Phillipe had already made up his mind to accept the invitation. He would indeed dog Hoskins' every step when he called at the port to arrange his shipment.

Encouraged again, Phillipe slid off the bench. He bent over Marie, slipped an arm around her slumped shoulders, said softly:

"Mama?"

"What?"

"Are you tired now? Do you want to go up to the room and sleep?"

Still gazing at the mug of heated ale, she didn't answer.

A minute went by. Another.

Heartbroken, Phillipe pried her fingers loose one by one. He helped her stand up, all the while speaking to her in a low voice, soothing her as he would a child. She shuffled her feet as she walked, accepting physical direction of her body in a docile way. The parsons watched. Even the driver and his guard stopped their rowdy laughter, to stare with strangely sober expressions.

7
To an Unknown Shore

EIGHT MILES up the River Avon from the Bristol Channel, along the brawling, noisy Bristol docks, Phillipe Charboneau discovered that Hoskins was as good as his tipsy word. Under the brilliant blue of a May morning, Phillipe dodged among burly handlers loading and unloading cargo as he followed the portly ironmaker along the tar-reeking pier.

A thicket of masts stood against the sky. Great hulls creaked in their berths. Ropes and pulleys racketed, off-loading a bewildering array of goods from the newest arrivals in port.

They passed men bent beneath the weight of huge sacks of fragrant African cocoa beans. Phillipe saw a factor's agent slash open a canvas bale to inspect a bundle of light brown leaves the size of elephants' ears. Hoskins informed him that was tobacco in its native state, fresh from the tidewater plantations in America's southern colonies.

Hailing another factor of his acquaintance, Hoskins got permission to pluck a sample from a small mountain of stalks, each of which bore dozens of tubular and slightly curved yellow fruits. He handed the sweet-smelling sample to Phillipe, who immediately picked up Hoskins' cue that it was "passing tasty," and started to bite into it.

Hoskins' puffed up with shock. "Wait, you must skin it first! Have you never seen a West Indies banana?"

"Banana? No. I've never even heard the word."

"Well, then, Hoskins is giving you a liberal education in world commerce, damme if he isn't."

To which Phillipe could only nod enthusiastic agreement, though it was well nigh impossible for him to assimilate every detail of the busy wharf scene.

Strutting along, Hoskins made inquiries of several clerks and seamen. He seemed to be on familiar terms with many of them. At last he informed Phillipe:

"Excellent luck! One of the more reliable captains docked two days ago. Will Caleb out of Boston. I've shipped goods with him before. A God-fearing man who can be relied upon not to be grogged to the eyeballs during a squall. Profit is too precious a commodity to be risked with a sot. Come on, sir, a little more lively! That's Caleb's vessel second one down. We'll see whether I can strike a bargain."

Bustling ahead with a step surprisingly brisk for one of his girth, Hoskins led the way to the foot of the gangplank running up to the ship. She was three-masted, some eighty feet long and perhaps a quarter of that across. She bore the gilt-painted name *Eclipse*.

At the rail, watching a line of handlers loading large canvas-covered chests aboard, was a hawkish, white-haired man of fifty or so. He had thin lips and a face tanned and roughened by exposure to the elements. He wore a plain coat of dark blue wool.

Hoskins hailed him: "Good morning, Captain Caleb! Are you bound back for Boston?"

"Good morning, Hoskins," answered the sea captain, with a compression of his lips that passed for a smile. "I am that—when the hold's full."

"What are you carrying, sir?"

Captain Caleb replied that he had so far negotiated to freight fifty chests of green Hyson tea and a quantity of Lancashire fustian in assorted colors. He added:

"But I've room for more."

"Then by all means let's discuss an arrangement."

As he waved Hoskins aboard, the master of *Eclipse* glanced at Phillipe with a flash of curiosity. "Step to one side for Mr. Hoskins!" he shouted to the handlers. "Any man dropping a chest in the harbor will discover that a peace-loving captain can still use the cat!"

Hoskins bobbed his head to indicate that Phillipe should follow, which he did, causing Captain Caleb's white brows to shoot upward in puzzlement. Caleb shook the fat man's hand as the latter stepped on deck.

"You've lost Lucas, then? Replaced him with this young man since last I saw you?"

Hoskins shook his head. "No, sir, Lucas is presently at the Flagon, attending this young man's mother. She was not in proper spirits to come knocking about these piers."

Phillipe wondered how Marie was surviving the wait at the inn. Though listless, she'd seemed a little more herself when they arrived in Bristol.

"On the coach trip from London," Hoskins went on, "this chap, Mr. Phillipe Charboneau, provided handsome service—as did Lucas—in defending myself and other passengers from three infernal highwaymen. Since Mr. Charboneau has small funds, but a great desire to start a new life in the Americas, I brought him along in the hope of finding an available berth."

Captain Caleb's eyes displayed innumerable wrinkles at the corners as he scrutinized Phillipe again. "Well, my mess boy's felled with a flux. I should leave him behind—which I won't, since I know the plight of his widowed mother back in Marblehead. The boy may be up and about soon or he may not. I might be able to use a hand and I might not." His glance grew sharper. "However, I want no hands who are fleeing from the law or the debtor's prison."

"I'm fleeing from nothing like that, sir," Phillipe said as Caleb continued to evaluate his size and probable strength. The half-truth came easily because of the circumstances. "I'm only going toward something—starting with a passage."

Caleb thumbed his wind-roughened chin. "You don't speak pure English. What are you, French?"

Phillipe wanted to reply that the captain didn't speak pure English either, but rather, a strange, nasal version of it. Was that how colonials of Boston talked? Prudence made him simply nod instead.

"How much money can you pay?" Caleb asked.

"I have five pounds."

"For himself *and* his mother," Hoskins emphasized. "As I mentioned, Lucas is keeping watch over the lady right this moment. She is not herself. Certain problems of health—"

At this, Captain Caleb looked even more skeptical. "I'm not taken with sailing a sick woman to Boston. We make a hard crossing. Six, eight weeks, depending on storms and adverse winds."

"She can manage, Captain," Phillipe said. "She's as anxious to be away from England as I am."

"Well, five pounds is hardly sufficient—even if I used you in the mess, helping that Dutch devil Gropius with his so-called cooking."

Hoskins cleared his throat self-importantly. "Captain Caleb, I indicated that

Mr. Charboneau performed a brave service, and saved me considerable expense. If you're averse to passengers such as he and his mother, perhaps I should pass along the wharf and seek another vessel for my shipment.''

Standing on the gently rolling deck with the shadows of noisy gulls falling through the tangle of spars and lines above, Phillipe felt a tightening in his throat, an emotional response to Hoskins' bluff. He didn't want to lose this chance, even though he was more than a little intimidated by the immense unknown lying to the west along the glitter of the Avon.

''I was planning to ship a deal of kettles,'' Hoskins sighed. ''Yes, a deal. But I want to assist the boy as part of the bargain.'' He turned to Phillipe. ''We'd best make inquiries elsewhere.''

''Here, not so hasty!'' Caleb exclaimed, seizing Hoskins' arm.

Neither man smiled. But each had a glitter in his eye that signaled the enjoyment of hard bargaining. Caleb said to Phillipe, ''You go aft, lad.'' He was required to point out the direction to the nautical novice. ''So you don't interrupt those dock rats doing the loading. Hoskins and I will drop down to my cabin, where I keep a bit of Providence rum for special visitors.''

And, slipping an arm around Hoskins' shoulder, he led him away, murmuring, ''Now, sir, indicate to me the quantity of iron on which we'll open the discussion—''

They vanished below, leaving Phillipe to pace nervously for almost an hour.

When the two men reappeared, Hoskins was smiling.

''You and your mother are aboard, Mr. Charboneau. In a single, very small and airless cabin, I'm afraid. I couldn't wheedle two from a hard-headed Yankee like Caleb. But I filled his hold for him. We'll load tonight and the pilot will take *Eclipse* down the river on the tide tomorrow. Shall we fetch your mother?''

''Yes, sir, certainly. How can I ever thank you?''

''It's I who have a debt to pay,'' Hoskins answered as they dodged their way down the plank again. ''Thanks to you, I'm less poor than I might have been. Turning over a pound is all in life that matters. Keep that as your maxim in the colonies. Indeed, if you stick to commerce and avoid politics, you'll end up rich instead of hanged.''

Thus maintaining his pose of total unconcern for others—a pose his actions of the morning belied—Hoskins strutted away up the wharf. He assumed Phillipe would follow; he did not glance back. Phillipe smiled and tagged after him.

II

GRAY WEATHER greeted the one-hundred-fifty-ton schooner *Eclipse* as she left the western counties of England astern and cracked on canvas, her prow rising and plummeting through an already heavy sea.

The mess boy was still confined to his berth with the flux. Phillipe was put on duty at once. The ship hadn't been away from the mouth of the Bristol Channel two hours before he received six whacks of a stick from the bandy-legged ship's cook.

The Dutchman, named Gropius, spoke only a few words of English, and those mostly obscene. But Gropius' vocabulary and the stick were sufficient to indicate that Phillipe had committed his first error.

Gropius had handed him a kettle of stew to lug to the crew's mess. Phillipe

observed aloud that the stew seemed to include a number of recently cooked white slugs. That brought on the howls and the whacking.

Phillipe's anger flared at the first blow. But he accepted the punishment because he realized he was lucky to be sailing for the colonies so soon. He carried the kettle to the mess without protest, rubbed his butt on the way back and decided to say nothing about the weevils in the biscuits or the worms in the potatoes.

Besides, he had plenty to do just learning to negotiate the tilting decks and companionways without spilling the contents of such a kettle, or the tots of rum Captain Caleb allowed his New England crew in the evening.

The first day at sea—the ship rolling and pitching; tackle creaking; canvas snapping; men scrambling aloft to frightening heights as if born to it—brought Phillipe acute nausea and the conviction that he would never be a seaman. And as much as eight more weeks of this lay ahead!

To compound his problems, he was worried about his mother again.

When he'd accompanied her aboard *Eclipse* at sunset before the schooner sailed, he'd tried to ignore the continued listlessness of her movements, the way she spoke only in monosyllables and let her gaze wander up to the tips of the masts without seeing them.

During the second and third days at sea, the weather grew increasingly worse. Phillipe made frequent trips to the rail, to the loud amusement of the sailors. But he managed to recover fairly fast every time. Marie, in contrast, simply lay on her side in the single cramped bunk in their tiny steerage cabin.

Located on the port side of the schooner's berth deck, the cabin was even less appetizing than Hoskins had painted it. For one thing, it was noisy; similar cubicles for the boatswain, the carpenter and the captain's clerk were nearby, along the poorly lit fore-and-aft gangway. For another thing, the cubicle reeked constantly. It reeked of pitch, of the water in the bilges and of other stenches Phillipe didn't care to identify. And seeing anything clearly was almost impossible. A candle in a wrought-iron holder with a hook for securing it into the wood of the bunk provided the only light.

All through the third day, Phillipe looked in on Marie as often as he could. Her position in the bunk seldom changed. She clutched the leather casket to her stomach, her legs drawn up against the now-worthless treasure. Each time Phillipe urged her to eat a bowl of the stew Gropius grudgingly offered, she refused. It was increasingly evident that her precarious mental state and the rolling sea were taking a double from her already low reserves of strength.

Two more days, and Phillipe was almost frantic with fear. After dark, he got up his nerve to go to Captain Caleb's quarters in the stern.

He knocked, heard a voice answer above the crash of the waves and the grinding of the hull, bidding him come in.

Caleb's cabin was only about three times the size of Phillipe's. It was sparsely furnished with a built-in bunk, a locker, a small desk bolted to the bulkhead. A small, round table of oak and two chairs were similarly bolted to the decking.

A hanging lantern swung back and forth above the table. Seated there, Caleb glanced up from an open book which Phillipe recognized with some surprise as a Bible.

Caleb gestured to the other chair, then to a platter of biscuits. The swaying lantern threw shifting shadows across the New Englander's face as Phillipe sank wearily into the chair, declining the food.

"Some difficulty, lad?" the captain asked.

"It's my mother, sir. She's not well. Does anyone aboard have medical skill?"

"The first mate, Mr. Soaper, has some simple knowledge. But *Eclipse* is a commercial vessel. We don't often carry passengers. So we can't afford the luxury of a doctor."

Phillipe's face fell. Caleb leaned back, his eyes unblinking.

"I'm aware the hard weather must be troubling the lady, since she hasn't showed herself at table with the mates. Makes me regret you didn't take my warning about a rough crossing more seriously."

"It was important we leave England as soon as possible."

"Because you are running away from some trouble," Caleb said, so quietly he could barely be heard against the smash of the Atlantic on the hull. "I read it in your face the moment Hoskins brought you aboard. I accepted your word that it was otherwise because I wanted Hoskins' cargo."

Phillipe came close to pouring out the entire story to the captain. But didn't. He was just a little afraid that his tale of persecution by the Amberlys might sound like the ravings of a madman. Caleb was tough, practical, independent; a tangled story of a woman who had dreamed of her son becoming a nobleman could hardly interest him.

Besides, that part of Phillipe's life was past. His concern was the immediate moment.

"I felt my mother and I would be better off starting our lives over again in the colonies," he said. "Can we let it go at that, sir?"

"Since the British Isles are now well behind us—yes."

"Now it seems I made the wrong choice."

Caleb touched the page of his Bible without glancing at it. "What man doesn't, almost hourly? Can you tell me what ails your mother?"

He shook his head. "Not exactly. I'm afraid the idea of traveling to a country we know nothing about—a country where we'll be strangers again—has hurt her mind. She won't eat so much as one bite."

"You've tried?"

"Over and over. She just lies in the bunk. I don't know what I can do to help her."

"Say prayers to Almighty God," replied Caleb with perfect seriousness. "There's no way I can turn *Eclipse* back to England."

III

SEVEN DAYS onto the Atlantic, Phillipe came to the realization that Marie was in all probability dying.

When the thought struck, his first emotion was renewed guilt. Then came fresh rage at all those he considered responsible. Lady Jane. Roger. Perhaps, in a small way, even Alicia.

But the dominant reaction was guilt. It ate into his mind like some voracious monster.

The mate, Mr. Soaper, examined Marie in the cabin that now smelled sour with her feverish sweat. He stated that unless Phillipe could force her to take nourishment, she would indeed die. Another effort to pour a little broth between her clenched teeth failed.

"Perhaps dying is what she wants," was Soaper's brief and gloomy conclusion.

Phillipe took to staying in the cabin as much as his duties would permit. He hardly knew what hour it was, let alone the day. *Eclipse* continued to run through rough seas. He was able to live with that at last, although he knew he'd never like it.

He slept only for short periods, seated in the corner between bunk and cabin wall, hard planking for his pillow. Even in sleep he was half-awake, alert for changes in his mother's shallow breathing. He woke in the darkness of their tenth night at sea to hear her calling his name.

"Wait, Mama," he said, scrambling up in the black, fetid cabin. "Give me a moment to light the candle—"

"Don't! I know how I must look. I can feel the filth of my body. Come close to me."

On his knees, he crawled to the side of the bunk. He found her hand. It felt almost boneless. And feverishly hot.

"Phillipe—listen to me. I will never see this America of yours."

He wanted to cry then, unashamed tears. But he could not. It was a measure of how much he had changed in two years.

Instead, he stroked her hand, tried to speak in a comforting way:

"Yes you will. If you'll only eat. Help yourself to live!"

"To what purpose? Your father is dead. So is everything I held out as a hope for you. But—I know you made the best choice—the new country—that's what I have been trying to find strength to say before it grew too late."

The limp, fevered fingers fluttered over his face, found his mouth to still his words. She whispered on:

"I hated what's become of us, Phillipe. I hated how it all went wrong because of that accursed family. Worst of all, for a time, I—I hated you for refusing to keep struggling against them. But hating my own flesh—that is a sin. A mortal sin. Only—lately, on this wretched ship, did it come to me that you were right and I was wrong. We had no way to win against them. I should have seen that from—"

She stopped, stricken by a harsh cough.

"—from the first time we entered their house. But the blame is on them, not you. That's—what I have wanted to tell you. To forgive you for—for a crime you never committed—"

"Mama, Mama, what's this talk of crime? We did what was necessary."

"Because I forced us to go to England, where we didn't belong."

"In America, common people are not so helpless. There are no hereditary lords to oppress them—"

"And that's why you are right to make a fresh beginning. You have the youth—the heart for it. I do not. I followed the wrong hope. Saw it—saw it die away. There's nothing left for me—"

"There is, Mama. Life! Please, for God's sake listen. We can be happy again, if you'll only fight this awful defeat that's taken you—"

"I no longer have the strength—or the will. I—can barely make my tongue work even now, when I must. I—made you swear an oath. A wicked, hopeless oath and I know it. You must forget that. I only beg you for a promise—"

"Anything, Mama, if you'll just try to help yourself—"

He realized she wasn't listening. Her voice grew softer, the words more

slurred, almost inaudible against the crack of a great canvas sheet wind-whipped somewhere high above.

"—the greatest crime, Phillipe, is still the one of which I spoke in Auvergne. So if you can't take your rightful place in England because of them, at least— at least promise me that in this new land, you'll strive to be a man of position, a—man of wealth. Then someday, perhaps, you can return to England and repay them—"

She cried out stridently:

"Repay them, God damn their arrogant souls—!"

The last word broke off with a sharp exhalation of pain.

"Mama?"

He leaned forward, slid his hand across her cheek, felt her raging fever. Something lost and sad within him said, *God have mercy on this poor woman. She still has the same dream. The words have changed. But not the dream itself.*

Because he loved her, and because it cost him nothing, he said, "I promise."

The waves beat thunderously.

"Mama? Mama, I said I promise—"

Her hand slipped into his, pressed his fingers weakly. She had heard.

She started murmuring in French again. The indecipherable words became a fragment of a melody. She was humming an old, romantic air.

Several times more he tried to break through her delirium. She hummed and laughed, sudden little gasps of delight. Where was she? On the stage in Paris again? With James Amberly? Walking in some chateau of dreams where she was complete mistress, uncowed, unafraid? Her absolution of his guilt poured relief through him suddenly—

He stayed with her most of the night, although he knew it was pointless. She no longer recognized him. She wasn't even aware of his presence.

Inevitably, he thought back over the months that had passed since she first drew the casket from behind the statue of the Madonna. It struck him that, in a larger sense, she might have been right all along. The greatest crime could very well be that of allowing yourself to be humbled into poverty and obscurity.

At the same time, as she understood, events had forced a change in his perspective on the question. He no longer harbored any hope of gaining his inheritance. Nor of striking back at the Amberlys.

He had the hatred for it; the desire. That would never completely leave him. But there were certain practical limitations now. He was sailing toward an unseen shore that would hold more new challenges than he could possibly imagine. And opportunity, too.

Perhaps his mother was only wrong in the means she had chosen to avoid commission of what she considered man's most heinous crime. Through the wearying hours in which he leaned against her bunk and listened to the heart-breaking sounds of delirium—her feverish laughter; snatches of singing—he concluded with a certain coldness that the dream itself might be the right dream after all.

Wealth, status—that was what he wanted from the new land. He would find them. By God he would.

For himself. And for her. Nothing else mattered now. Nothing.

Phillipe Charboneau passed the next twenty hours in the cabin, with little sleep and no thought of food. At the end of that time, the woman of Auvergne was dead.

IV

CAPTAIN WILL CALEB asked Phillipe about Marie's religious persuasion. He replied with no apology that she had been a beautiful and excellent actress in her youth in Paris—and therefore excluded from her Catholic faith. Captain Caleb said that while he was a Congregationalist, all people were equal in the Maker's eyes. That belief was one reason his own grandfather had fled the English midlands for America. He promised he would try to find an appropriate text for the burial.

V

THE LATE May morning sparkled. *Eclipse* lay becalmed in the bright, windless weather. Fore and aft, to port and to starboard, the Atlantic resembled green glass.

Captain Caleb had turned out his entire crew. His master of sail had supervised the sewing of Marie's body inside a canvas shroud. Just before the last seam was closed, Phillipe returned from below deck. Caleb stepped to his side, white hair gleaming in the noon sunshine.

"Is that what you wish to bury with her?" the captain inquired.

"Yes, I remembered it at the last minute. I think she'd want—"

Suddenly something checked him. He was silent a moment. Then:

"On second thought, I believe I'll keep it. I have nothing else but these few personal letters to remember her by."

And he tucked the leather-bound casket with its long-dulled brass corner plates under his left arm.

VI

"LET NOT your heart be troubled. Ye believe in God, believe also in me."

Captain Caleb's resonant voice rolled out across the deck between the ranks of the assembled crew. They were clear-eyed, healthy-looking men, colonials every one, except for Gropius, who had not as yet removed his woolen cap. A glare from mate Soaper took care of that.

Phillipe stood beside Caleb at the head of two lines of men. The lines faced inward. Between, the shroud was being carefully lifted by four other sailors.

"In my Father's house are many mansions. If it were not so, I would have told you."

Phillipe felt the beginnings of tears sting his eyes. He glanced from the shroud rising toward the rail to the hard faces of the New England sailors. They were profane men; he'd heard them curse often enough as they clambered aloft in foul weather. They were ignorant men as well; most of them could neither read nor write. Yet in the presence of death they seemed to bear themselves with a certain dignity Phillipe had never seen in England. Could this subtle difference come from breathing what Dr. Franklin had called "the less stifling air?" If so, then Phillipe knew he had indeed made the right choice.

160

"I go to prepare a place for you. And if I go and prepare a place for you, I will come again, and receive you unto myself, that where I am, there ye may be also. And whither I go ye know, and the way ye know—"

All at once, the pages of St. John from which Captain Caleb was reading began to snap and flutter. The rice paper whipped over, causing Caleb to lose his place. He rifled back to find the verse. Phillipe noticed the quick shifting of the seamen's eyes. Mate Soaper actually glanced aloft, where the canvas had begun to flap faintly in the new breeze.

"Thomas saith unto him, Lord, we know not whither thou goest—and how can we know the way?"

Phillipe watched as the shroud was lifted high above the rail, slowly tilted forward by rope-galled, tar-blacked hands of surpassing tenderness. Caleb raised his voice a little as the Testament pages snapped again:

"Jesus saith unto him, I am the way, the truth, and the life. No man cometh unto the Father but by me. Amen."

The quartet of seamen released their burden. The shroud fell out of sight. Phillipe heard the splash as it struck the shimmering water. He closed his eyes, praying that his mother would at last find peace on her own unseen shore.

A touch on his shoulder broke the melancholy moment. He raised his head, opened his eyes. Captain Caleb was looking at him with a strange expression on his weatherbeaten face.

"I think a sip of Providence rum might go well," he said gently.

Phillipe followed him below without question. Soaper barked orders and men began to race aloft to prepare for the fair wind's rising.

VII

ALL SORROW seemed burned out of him as he sat in Caleb's cabin, sipping the strong, sweet rum. The captain contented himself with one of his biscuits.

The casket rested on the table between them. That, and Gil's sword, were the only items of consequence with which he and his mother had begun their journey, the only ones with which he would end this phase of it.

No richer and no poorer, he thought. *But wiser? God in heaven, let us devoutly hope so.*

Concentrating on his biscuit, Caleb asked, "What was the trouble that forced an obviously sick woman to undertake this voyage?"

With no hesitation, Phillipe told him.

He even showed Caleb the letter from James Amberly. After he had finished the narrative, he replaced the letter and closed the casket, saying, "But all that's over."

"Not quite."

Phillipe glanced up sharply.

"That girl of whom you spoke—you said something about her thinking of leaving England, didn't you?"

"Yes, but I don't see—"

"To come with you to America? Where she had relatives?"

"It was only a passing mention, Captain Caleb."

"The point is, lad, the thirteen colonies remain a part of the British Empire. You may not be entirely out of danger yet. Through the girl whom your half

brother is marrying—through her family connections in Philadelphia—the long arm of private or even public justice could reach out eventually. The chance isn't a likely one, I'll admit. But since you were sorely used in England and want to begin with as much in your favor as possible—the Almighty can testify that landing penniless in America, while not unusual, presents huge difficulties—I'd suggest one final separation from that ugly past you described. You have abandoned any hope of claiming part of your father's fortune. Then why not start as a new man entirely? Take a new name? One which would never give you away?''

For the first time in days, Phillipe Charboneau almost smiled. The suggestion was both surprising and exactly right.

"Thank you, Captain," he said. "The idea's excellent. I'll do it."

"Help yourself to the rum," Caleb said as he rose to leave the cabin. "But tell no one that the master of this ship allowed you more than a single cup or I'll have a mutiny. I must be up to the helm—I think we've seen the last of the calm that put us behind schedule. With any luck we can run straight to Boston now. Oh, and one thing more." He paused at the door. "To lose the woman who gives you life in this world is no easy thing. My mother's eighty-seven. Healthy and peppery up in Maine. I hope when she passes I can behave as you did today. You took it as a man."

VIII

THAT NIGHT, alone in the stench-ridden cabin for the first time, Phillipe was glad Captain Will Caleb couldn't see him.

He was unable to force himself to lie in the bunk. He took his customary place on the decking instead. He had lost track of time. He heard the ship's bell clang four bells. But of what watch, he didn't know.

He tried to fix his attention on something other than his mother's absence. On the schooner's creaking; on the soft, constant roar of breaking water just beyond the hull planks and the huge rib of rock elm that intruded into one corner of the cubicle. He tried and tried—

Useless.

Unbearable anguish built within him. He heard footfalls in the gangway outside, held back the low, half-uttered cry. The invisible walker hesitated, then moved on.

Just in time.

He wept as he had never wept in his life. Wracking sobs. They lasted five minutes. Ten—

And then he was empty of the capacity to weep any longer. His belly hurt. Something had burned to ash in the center of his being. Burned—and was now forever gone.

Phillipe leaned his forehead on the edge of the bunk and closed his eyes. But no sleep would come all that long, long night.

IX

NEAR THE end of the mid-watch on the morning of the sixth day of July, 1772, Phillipe stumbled up from the berth deck for a breath of air. The ship's bell rang seven times, telling him that in half an hour it would be four A.M. At least he'd

learned the system of bells and watches on the voyage, if nothing else.

Stepping out on the deserted deck, he walked toward the bow, away from the men standing watch at the helm, shadow-figures against the quarterdeck's hanging lanterns.

He knew why he'd wakened abruptly from a restless slumber. It was because of the talk the evening before. They should be sighting land soon, the old hands predicted. Perhaps tomorrow—

But it was already tomorrow, wasn't it?

From behind the bowsprit, he peered over the sea at limitless darkness. Slowly he craned his head back. There, at least, was light. Endless stars, thousands upon thousands, dusting the huge arch of heaven and shifting slowly in his vision with the schooner's pitch and roll—

The name. He should do something about the name.

He'd toyed with possibilities, found nothing satisfactory. What if they did sight land tomor—today? Who would he be?

All at once, under the immense canopy of tiny silvered lights, he felt small. Smaller even than on Quarry Hill, the night he and Marie fled from Tonbridge. The vastness of the sky, the sweep of black ocean seemed to press in on him; reduce his size; his hope; his courage—

She was gone. He was alone.

He was *alone*.

And out there somewhere beyond the carved figurehead—a buxom, bare-titted mermaid with painted wooden eyes—an alien country waited—

Suddenly he was almost dizzy with fear.

And why not? Nothing existed any longer to which he could cling. The books he'd read, the kindness of people such as Mr. Fox and the Sholtos and Hoskins, the encouragement of Dr. Franklin—all that was meaningless. Cut away as if it had never been. Lost and gone far behind the ship's faintly phosphorescent wake.

He felt smaller and more forlorn by the moment. He knew nothing of the realities of day-to-day living in these colonies toward which the schooner raced on the night wind. He knew nothing but words and more words—and all of those nearly forgotten. Part of another life, it seemed now. The life of someone who was a total stranger.

Nothing from the past applied to his new situation in this new world. No one could be relied upon because there *was* no one—except himself. Survive alone among these Americans? He who was doubly foreign? Not even able to claim the soil of Britain as his own? The whole of creation, sea of stars and sea of darkness, seemed to laugh with wind and wave at his incredible presumption—

Then, reacting to the fear, he felt ashamed.

He had withstood severe tests up till now. He could withstand more.

He lifted his head. He fought the dread born of the future's uncertainty. He repeated to himself what he had repeated before—

I will survive.

It helped—a little. But the stars and the dark remained vast and forbidding. *Well, by Christ,* he thought, *I can be a man outwardly, at least. Never let them see the way I really feel—*

Phillipe knew only smatterings of the Bible. But he was acquainted with the tale of Adam. As he brooded at the bowsprit, his mind fashioned an encouraging little conceit, to help put down the fear—

He was like a man being born in the fashion of Adam, new-sprung into the

strangeness of a creation whose details he couldn't possibly guess. All right—he would take control of that creation as befitted a man, not a boy. He *would*, by God—

But who will I be?

The problem kept him awake the rest of the night. Kept his mind occupied, at least—

But deep down, he was still afraid.

X

JUST BEFORE sunset of that same day, an outcry from the crow's-nest signaled land on the horizon. Caleb's older hands had been right.

He stood at the port rail in the stiff wind as Gropius howled inflammatory curses in Dutch and English about the new mess boy malingering again, even while the regular mess boy still lolled in his bunk.

He ignored the oaths, peering at the greenish-black line, still so very thin and far away, that separated the sky of the mellow summer evening and the white-crested Atlantic. Gulls wheeled and shrieked high above the topmen working aloft.

He held the rail tightly, fairly tasting the salt wind. He felt not only a tingling anticipation, but a coldness in his hands and in his soul. The fear—

At least he had a name now. He'd settled on it during the forenoon watch.

With every tie of consequence severed, his name was his only link to his past existence. And it was a tenuous link at that. But he needed something that belonged to both worlds. Something to help carry him through the gigantic transition rushing to meet him. An old box, a sword, a self-consciously jutting chin and a feigned expression of resolve were not enough.

He had decided to Americanize his given name to Philip. And, to remember at least part of his origins, he had shortened his father's hereditary title to Kent. Philip Kent. He would no longer think of himself, or be called, by any other name. He had already told Captain Caleb.

Thus, self-christened, a new man watched his new homeland rising under the orange-tinted clouds in the west, and wondered what lay ahead for him as *Eclipse* bore into the Nantasket Roads under full canvas.

BOOK THREE
LIBERTY TREE

1
The Secret Room

DURING THE night, *Eclipse* anchored two miles from the glimmer of Boston light. Before daybreak a pilot came aboard. He took the helm from Caleb and maneuvered the trading vessel through the narrow channel and past the islands dotting the harbor to a berth at Long Wharf.

The early haze of a summer's day promised intense heat. It blurred the hills and the rooftops of the town and the parapets of Castle William, the island fortress out in the harbor. But nothing could blur Philip Kent's sense of anticipation as the lines were snubbed tight and the plank dropped.

Anchored ships lined one side of the teeming pier, ramshackle commercial establishments the other. Philip took a tight hold on casket and sword, about to descend into the confusion of the quay. A hand gripped his shoulder.

"Lad, do y'know where you'll be going now?" Captain Caleb's face was patterned by changing light and shadow as men aloft furled sails between the deck and the sun.

Philip shook his head. "No, sir."

Caleb rolled his tongue in his cheek thoughtfully. "Might have been better after all had you bound yourself to me. With no certain destination—"

"Captain, that makes the possibilities all the more numerous and excit—" He flushed and, despite his best efforts, couldn't conceal a little anger in his voice: "You're laughing at me."

Caleb nodded, and his smile broadened. "No offense meant, Philip. It's just that there's been such a change in you—I'll be flogged if you aren't beginning to sound English already. A few months among these folk and they'll never take you for a Frenchman."

"Because I'm not," Philip replied, embarrassed by his display of temper.

Buoyed by the noise and spectacle along the pier, he said eagerly, "I'm like you now. A citizen of the Americas."

"But perhaps we should talk a few minutes about where you could go—"

"Thank you, Captain, no. I'll get along very well."

"So you're determined Mr. Philip Kent will be completely his own man?"

"Completely."

"Although our Mr. Kent is but how old?"

"Strictly speaking, Captain—a couple of days."

"That's right. In a new country, the fact that he's lived eighteen years—"

"Nineteen."

"—doesn't count for much. But this might. Our new gentleman of the Americas lacks even a basic knowledge of the town's geography."

"I'll find my way, sir, don't worry."

Caleb's face said he knew further attempts at persuasion were useless. "You're not only sounding like an Englishman—you're acting like a hard-headed Yankee! Well—" Caleb held out his dark, weathered hand. "Good luck and Godspeed."

Trying to ignore the look of concern that came unbidden into the captain's eyes, Philip shook hands. Then he turned and hurried down the gangway.

Swift movement was necessary. The longer he lingered aboard *Eclipse,* the more he would be forced to acknowledge that Caleb spoke the truth. He was absolutely alone, with no experience to guide him.

But then he reminded himself that, night before last, he'd vowed to turn his solitary condition from a disadvantage to an opportunity to begin anew. Risks and all. So be it. He *was* nineteen years old, and strong, and feeling fit. The sun warmed the back of his neck pleasantly as he pushed and shoved his way up Long Wharf, his entire store of worldly possessions tucked under his arms. Beneath the soles of his boots, the rickety boards that represented his new-found home felt more reassuringly solid every moment.

II

BUT BY nightfall, he began to think that heeding Captain Caleb's suggestion might have been prudent.

The onslaught of hunger sent him scavenging through a litter heap behind a waterfront tavern. He discovered half a dozen oyster shells, each with a tiny bit of meat clinging to the inside. Scraped loose carefully with his grimy fingernail, the gobbets of oyster served as his first sumptuous meal in his new country. *An event to remember,* he thought ruefully as he pocketed one of the shells and stole away from the crowded tavern.

He trudged down an alleyway hot with twilight shadow. *Oysters from a garbage pile. Something to remember indeed, when I've my own house one day, and silver for fifty guests—and a mantel over which I can hammer pegs to hold Gil's sword in a place of honor.*

The shining vision soon produced negative ones. Bitter memories of the past flooded his mind. Images of Marie, Roger Amberly, the murderous one-eyed man, Alicia. He put them aside as best he could, while thunder rolled over the lamp-lit town. A summer rainstorm was brewing in black clouds that massed above the chimney pots in the northeast.

Not knowing the name of a single thoroughfare or what his position was in relation to the place he'd landed that morning, Philip Kent slept the night in a haystack.

He found the haystack in the tiny yard behind a home on one of Boston's winding streets. On the other side of the warm, fragrant hay, penned pigs squealed miserably in the downpour. He burrowed deep into the stack, one hand curled around the oyster shell he'd kept from the litter heap. He'd discovered the shell had a sharp edge. Almost as keen as that of a knife. A handy weapon, especially for a stranger in a new city—

He awoke well before dawn. He was thoroughly soaked and shaking with the start of a fever.

III

BY MIDMORNING he found his way back to Long Wharf. He had made up his mind to admit his error of launching out hastily on his own, and he planned to seek words of counsel from Captain Caleb.

But the few sailors left aboard *Eclipse* reported that the ship's master had already issued instructions about disposition of the cargo to the mate, Soaper, and departed for his mother's home in Maine.

Grumbling Gropius, looking more than a little hung over from his first night on shore, gave Philip a hunk of weevil-infested bread and a cup of rum before the latter once more turned his unsteady step up the wharf to the town.

He studied passing faces. Some were coarse, some prosperous-looking. Some appeared beneath tricornered military hats. But soon, all began to blur in front of his feverish eyes.

His forehead streamed with sweat. His rain-dampened clothes clung to his body, smelling sour. But he kept on—

And trudged Boston for two days and two nights.

He stole garbage where he could; slept where he could; and, despite the illness that left him weak and short of breath, managed to fix a fair approximation of Boston's geography in his head.

At one taproom where he inquired for work, any kind of work, only to be turned down by the landlord's obese, mustached daughter, he paused long enough to ask about the size of the city.

The fat girl picked something out of her hair and regarded it with curiosity as she said, "Why, the *Gazette* reports we're fifteen thousand souls now. Too damned many of 'em lobsterbacks."

"Lobster what?"

"Redcoats. British soldiers."

"Oh, I see."

"Funny question for you to ask. 'Specially when you want work one minute and look ready to faint away the next. Where do you hail from? You've an odd way of speaking. Like a French mounseer who came here once—"

Too tired to engage in explanations, Philip left.

As he wandered, he began to be more conscious of those lobsterbacks she'd referred to. King George's soldiers wore splendid scarlet coats and white or fawn trousers. Each coat had its own distinctive color for lapel facings and cuffs—buff and yellow and blue and many more.

He'd noticed the soldiers before, of course. But paying closer attention, he saw how some of them moved along the streets with a certain air of authority that drew glares and snide remarks from many an ordinary citizen—although other Bostonians, usually better-dressed ones, treated the troops with politeness, even cordiality.

And the troops were everywhere, from the elm-dotted greensward of an open area identified to him as the Common, to the shade of a huge old oak tree, the largest of several in Hanover Square, where he watched a group of officers rip down some announcement nailed to the trunk. He saw redcoats from the North End to the double-arched town gate leading to the Neck.

The Neck was a long, narrow strip of land connecting the city with the countryside around it. It was no more than yards across at its narrowest point just outside the imposing brick gate. With the Dorchester Heights across the water to the east and the Charles River on the west, Boston resembled a sort of swollen thumb stuck up from the mainland—and linked to it only by the Neck.

The city's tolling church bells reminded Philip of London. But Boston had its own bustling style and distinct aromas. Predominantly fishy. But spiced by the pigs and cows kept in those small back yards, by rum distilleries and reeking outhouses and, near the waterfront, by shipyards and ropewalks that smelled fiercely of pitch.

Ill, Philip lost track of the days. Perhaps two more went by. Perhaps three. He grew filthy and hungry beyond belief. As a result, he found himself more and more the object of suspicious stares from well-dressed pedestrians and gentry on horseback. His inquiries about work—here at a smokehouse, there at a brewery—brought replies that were increasingly curt as his physical appearance worsened. His eyes took on the slightly unfocused glare typical of fever, which didn't help his cause either.

Shaking, teeth chattering, he was wandering somewhere in the city's North End again, just at sunset, when two figures whirled around a corner and crashed into him.

Philip stumbled, fell to hands and knees on the cobbles. His sword and the casket slipped out of his fingers.

He was vaguely aware that the splat of his palms in the mud oozing between the stones of the street had sent droplets of the sticky brown stuff flying—

Straight onto the spotless white breeches of a soldier who now loomed over him.

The man was silhouetted against the ruddy evening sky and the leaded windows of an inn a few steps away. "Damme, Lieutenant Thackery," he said, "the clumsy young bastard dirtied my trousers!"

"Then we shall make him pay for a laundress, Captain." The second man grabbed Philip's collar, dragged him up. "Come round to the headquarters of the Fourteenth West Yorkshires in the morning, boy. Bring sufficient money to— here, hold on!"

He reached forward to grab Philip again. The latter had pulled away to retrieve his two possessions. The lieutenant's fierce grip brought Philip out of his feverish daze—and face to face with eyes that were distinctly unpleasant:

"Pay attention when a King's officer gives you instructions. Unless you prefer to have the order delivered in a more memorable way." The lieutenant's other hand dropped suggestively to the hilt of his dress sword.

Philip glared at the slender officer, then at the beefy captain whose white

breeches did indeed display quite a few large mud spots. Something weary and uncaring made Philip utter a low growl and knock the restricting hand away.

"Damme, a scrapper!" cried the heavy captain, careful to back off and let his subordinate handle the altercation. Handle it he did, his mouth tightening, ugly.

Philip heard footfalls coming along the cobbles behind him. But he didn't dare look around. The lieutenant's sword slid from its scabbard and winked in the glow from the nearby tavern.

"He's probably sporting a liberty medal under those stinking clothes," the lieutenant said, flicking Philip's sleeve with the point of his blade. "He's certainly insolent enough to be one of 'em. Do I have leave to thin their ranks slightly, sir?"

The senior officer grumbled assent. But the lieutenant didn't even wait for it, whipping his sword up. The blade caught the late-slanting sunlight, started down on a path that would lay open Philip's face—

Feet planted wide, head ringing, Philip still had presence enough to block the glittering steel by spearing the lieutenant's right wrist with his left hand. Grunting, he held the sword arm off for an instant while his other hand plucked the oyster shell from his belt. He raked the shell's edge down the lieutenant's left cheek.

Howling, Lieutenant Thackery danced back on the slippery cobbles. Blood dripped on his buff lapels. The captain cursed and began to unlimber his own sword as the owner of the footsteps Philip had heard earlier ran up behind him.

The man seized his arm. "Need assistance, youngster?"

Philip stared into the lean, middle-aged face of a black-haired man with flushed cheeks. Philip could do no more than swallow and nod. Lieutenant Thackery was advancing toward them now, sword up, blood pouring down the left side of his jaw.

"Stand out of the way, sir, because I'm going to gut him through. You see what he did to my face—"

"Improved it considerably," remarked the black-haired man. His lilting speech sounded like that of the Irishman, Burke. "What started this, lad?"

"I happened to splash mud on the other one's trousers," Philip gasped out. "An accident—"

"God damn it, sir—move aside!" the lieutenant roared.

The gaunt, black-haired man shook his head. Positioning himself at Philip's elbow, he said, "Sirs, let me remind you of where you are. The Salutation—" he indicated the inn just up the street"—is crowded with my friends. If you truly wish to engage, I can guarantee that a substantial part of the North End will be after your heads before three blows are struck. You've heard the whistles and horns blowing before, haven't you?"

"The whistles and horns of your damned Boston mobs?" the captain fumed. "Indeed we have."

Unruffled, the other said, "Well, I've some ability at summoning them out. I am Will Molineaux, the hardware proprietor." His announcement, as well as his fiery black gaze, was clearly inviting a fight.

The captain swabbed his perspiring face. "Molineaux?"

"Yes, sir, the same."

"Leave off, Thackery," the captain ordered the lieutenant. "He's the leader of the whole damned liberty mob in this part of town."

The lieutenant flared, "Sir, I refuse to cower in front of—"

"Leave off, I say! Or you'll have a cut across your throat to match the one on your face."

Swearing bitterly, Lieutenant Thackery rammed his sword back in place. The unnerved captain gestured him to follow up the street.

But Thackery, his uniform cuff pressed to his cheek and already bloody, had to deliver a parting thrust.

"One of these days we'll have laws permitting us to hang you rebel scum!" he shouted.

"No, sirs," Will Molineaux shouted back. "Because we shall see you swinging from Liberty Tree first."

He laughed uproariously as the taunt inspired the fat captain to disappear around a corner, practically running. The bleeding lieutenant vanished into the gloom after him.

The older man turned to Philip. "That captain's a rarity. The King's own quartered in this town are not cowards. Tyrants, yes. Swaggering bullies, frequently. But not cowards. You did a bold thing, my lad. Some would have truckled."

"I—" Philip had difficulty speaking. His whole body felt afire. The Irishman's features grew distorted, elongated. "—I may have acted out of ignorance, sir. I've only come to Boston city a few days ago."

"And look half-dead from the experience. Where d'ye live, may I ask?"

"Nowhere. I've been seeking lodging—employment. I can find none at all."

"What's your name?"

"Philip Kent."

Molineaux's eyes narrowed. "Are you a runaway bondsman?"

"No, I am not."

"Can you prove that?"

"Just with my word."

Mr. Molineaux studied him a moment longer, then pressed the back of one hand to Philip's forehead. "You're sicker than hell, that's clear. I'm bound up the street to the Salutation. Some gentlemen who convene there are not friends of His Majesty—or His Majesty's military forces. Landlord Campbell holds those sentiments too. So come along and we'll see if he'll give you a bit of sweeper's work. He'll be pleased to do it, is my guess. He'll fancy a fellow who tweaks Tommy's beak the way you did."

Molineaux helped Philip retrieve his belongings and accompanied him to the Salutation's doorway, over which hung a creaking sign painted with the figures of two splendidly dressed gentlemen bowing to one another.

Virtually all those gathered in the cheerful taproom wore old, tar-stained clothing or nautical coats and caps. "A rowdy lot of sailors, hull builders, caulkers and mast-makers," Molineaux commented as he led the unsteady Philip through the smoke to the bar, where a stocky man presided over the kegs. "But a good, freedom-loving lot. Hallo, Campbell."

" 'Evening, Mr. Molineaux."

"Campbell, here's a chap on whom I hope you'll lavish your hospitality. Young Mr. Philip Kent."

Molineaux described the street incident in a rather loud voice. Those at nearby tables listened. At the end, Philip drew a round of applause. Campbell grinned, promised Philip a meal, lodging in the tavern's outbuilding, and a few days of manual work to earn his keep while he looked for other employment.

The tobacco haze and tar and alcohol fumes were making Philip more and

more dizzy. But he thanked Campbell, then turned to thank Will Molineaux. He discovered the latter already moving toward a shadowy doorway at the very rear of the taproom.

Molineaux had been joined by a shabbily dressed man of middle years. The man's hands and head trembled with palsy. Where the man had come from, Philip hadn't noticed.

Philip started after them. Campbell caught his arm. "Where you going?"

"Into that back room, to speak my appreciation to the gentleman who—"

Campbell shook his head, no longer smiling. "That's a private chamber, Mr. Kent. Provided so Will and Mr. Adams—" He indicated the palsied fellow disappearing beyond the closing door "—and a few other close friends can confer without disturbance. No one in my employ enters that room unless I sent them. Keep that in mind while you're 'round the Salutation. Now do you want to eat or do you want to sleep?"

"As a matter of fact—both."

"Come along then. I'll wake you at sunup and start you working. Even a Son of Liberty must earn his way. I'd say you've joined the organization whether you realized it or no."

With a comradely arm across Philip's shoulder, he conducted him to the kitchen and, soon after, to the welcome sanctuary of a smelly, rickety outbuilding. There, Philip dropped into exhausted sleep on straw, while a milk cow lowed nearby.

IV

WHAT BEGAN as a short stay at the tavern on the corner of Salutation Alley and Ship Street lengthened into a week. Then into another. As Philip's natural strength gradually overcame the feverish illness, he sought every possible means to make himself indispensable to the landlord.

He hammered up plank siding to repair the outbuilding where tipsy guests sometimes slept off their revels before tottering home to their wives. He clambered over the roof to nail new shingles onto the Salutation itself, Campbell having idly remarked that during heavy storms, water dripped from the beams near the taproom hearth.

Campbell obviously liked the young man's eager industry. But what held Philip at the Salutation with Campbell's unspoken consent was not merely finding a temporary haven, important as that was. What held him was a realization that had come to him when he woke the first morning after his arrival.

The seedy, palsied fellow glimpsed in company with Will Molineaux bore the name *Adams*.

He'd inquired about the man when Campbell had a moment's leisure. He was told the gentleman's first name was Samuel. So it *was* the same radical politician whom Mr. Fox had described at Tonbridge and Lord North had scorned at Kentland!

At first, Philip could hardly believe that such a frail, badly dressed person could be a serious threat to George III—let alone the fomenter of rebellion.

On the other hand, he supposed it took neither good looks nor rich apparel to produce a temperament opposed to royal tyranny. Perhaps the requirements were just the opposite: ugliness and poverty. In any case, the frequent visits of Mr.

Samuel Adams and like-minded men to the private room at the Salutation fired Philip with curiosity and a determination to get into that room at the first possible chance. So he searched for ways to keep himself busy, reported failure to Campbell after his occasional expeditions to look for work elsewhere—no lies required there—and awaited his opportunity.

It came one afternoon during Philip's third week on the premises. Embarrassed, Campbell confronted his helper with the news that he could think of no other work that needed doing. The opening gambit to politely asking him to move on?

Instead, Philip immediately suggested, "You could let me serve the gentlemen who meet in back, sir."

"What?"

"I can be trusted to say nothing about what I hear. And I want very much to meet Mr. Adams."

"For what reason?"

Aware of how incredible it would sound, Philip still brazened ahead: "The Prime Minister of England once told me I behaved like one of his pupils."

Polishing a tankard, Campbell gaped. "The Prime—?" He guffawed. "Oh, you had an audience with him, did you?"

"No, sir, a chance encounter. At my father's home in England."

Campbell squinted at him in the buttery yellow sunshine falling through the leaded windows. "You speak good English, Philip. I think I recognize some French overtones too. But I still find it hard to believe that a lad who arrived penniless in Boston could have encountered that sow-faced North."

"But I did, Mr. Campbell."

"Where do you really come from, Philip? More important—from what are you fleeing? Or should I say who?"

"From my father's family," he answered at once, deciding that candor was the only workable course now—and that the chances of being harmed by it were slim. "My father's a nobleman. I'm his son by a woman he never married. He promised me part of his fortune, but when I journeyed to England from my home in France to claim what was mine, my father's family tried to have me killed. I came to America to escape them."

"Why America? Why not back to France?"

"I worked in a London printing house for a time. I got to like the trade, and thought I might have a better chance to pursue it here. And I met a Dr. Franklin—"

"The trade representative for Massachusetts."

Philip nodded. "He convinced me to come to the colonies. He said that in America, people were resisting those who wanted to enslave and oppress others."

Campbell now looked thoroughly astonished. " 'Fore God! The Prime Minister and Ben Franklin too!"

"The doctor was extremely kind to me. I spent a whole evening in his rooms, talking with him about America."

Campbell studied his hands. "You visited his quarters on Marrow Street in London, then."

"No. Craven Street."

Campbell relaxed, nodded. "Of course—Craven Street. I was mixed up." But the words were a shade too casual; Philip knew he had been tested.

He went on, "The doctor really had many good things to say about the freedom here, Mr. Campbell."

"Preserving that freedom requires struggle, Philip. Just as important, it requires secrecy. What is said in that back room would not find favor with Governor Hutchinson. Or the Tory citizens of this town, for that matter. But damned if it doesn't sound like you have good credentials. I joked about it the night you arrived, remember?"

"I surely do."

"But now I really do think you have the makings of a fellow who might wear one of these—"

He tugged a chain from inside his shirt. At the end of the chain, a medal gleamed. Philip bent closer to see the symbols on it: a muscled arm grasping a pole, on top of which perched a peculiar-looking cap. Engraved on the medal were the words *Sons of Liberty*.

The street door opened. Half a dozen redcoats stamped in and headed for a table. Campbell hastily hid the medal, but not his distaste, as the soldiers loudly called for service.

Campbell ordered one of his girls to wait on the soldiers. This done, he scratched his chin and returned his attention to Philip. After a moment of silence, he said:

"All right. I'll risk it once and see what happens. The gentlemen plan to gather this evening. I'll send you in to serve the flip."

V

LATER, PHILIP would look back on that stifling night in late July and consider his entrance to the private room as a passage of great significance in his life. But at the time, his main reactions were immediate excitement and curiosity. If that closely guarded room was the meeting ground of men who had allied themselves against oppression represented by aristocrats such as the Amberlys, then he wanted to know more about such men—and their ideas.

Accompanied by Campbell, he went into the room about eight in the evening. He was carrying a heavy tray of tankards filled with a mixture of rum and beer fresh-heated with a poker.

The room was plainly furnished, windowless. Tonight it contained but five men. Philip had only seen two of them enter the Salutation. Then he noticed a rear alcove, a door in shadows. All five men turned as Campbell and Philip came in.

Will Molineaux saw Philip, gave the landlord a startled look. As Philip set the tankards on the table, Campbell explained quickly:

"I'll vouch for the trustworthiness of this young man, gentlemen. Will knows him too."

"Slightly," Molineaux said, on guard.

"Philip Kent's his name," Campbell went on. "He's newly arrived from England. And Samuel—he encountered Lord North by chance over there. The Prime Minister told him he already behaved as if you personally had taught him his political catechism."

"Indeed, is that so?" returned Samuel Adams. The man's clothing, Philip noticed, was as threadbare and disreputable as before. Food stains, and a smear

of what looked to be printer's ink, suggested that he cared nothing for his personal appearance.

Adams fixed Philip with a slate-blue stare. His pale hands shook continually. Now and again his head jerked. Yet those eyes held Philip's and burned. In a high, quavery voice, Adams asked:

"And how did this remarkable confrontation come about, sir?"

In much the same words he'd used with Campbell, Philip described the circumstances. Adams digested the story with no change in his expression. At the conclusion, he said:

"We always welcome recruits to the cause that must inevitably triumph. From what you say as well as what you don't, I infer you've no love for the English nobility."

"Not for those who treat ordinary folk like property."

"There are no other kind," Adams told him.

A light-haired, exceedingly handsome man in his early thirties, prosperously dressed in dark green velvet, chuckled and turned a long-stemmed clay pipe in fine, slender hands. "You've a foolish consistency sometimes, Samuel. You dismiss our friends like the Earl of Chatham—"

"*Principiis obsta,* Dr. Warren, *principiis obsta!*" Adams retorted, shaking a finger.

The man identified as Warren laughed again, glanced at Philip. "Samuel is constantly quoting Ovid to us. 'Take a stand at the start.' "

Adams' slate-blue eyes shone with that ferocity Philip had already found unsettling. Whatever his personal motives, the man had an unsmiling, almost fanatical air about him—one that did not seem common to the others, who occupied themselves with their tankards as Adams retorted:

"The first appeasement leads only to many more, be assured of that. And at the very moment when we've no issue to stir the citizens of Boston to our purpose—then are delivered two—*two!*—in June—" He swept the gathering with an accusing hand. "You hesitate! It's unforgivable!"

Campbell plucked Philip's sleeve, nodded toward the taproom door, obviously intending for the younger man to leave now that the introduction had been performed. But Adams jumped from his chair, strode toward them with quick, nervous steps.

"No, Campbell. Let him stay. If we hear our remarks abroad tomorrow, we'll know who to blame."

"And who a few members of the mob may wish to visit," Molineaux added with an easy smile. But his undertone of meaning was unmistakable to Philip. Here was another, more critical test of whether he was trustworthy. This one, he had no doubts about passing.

"Come, come—he seems the right sort," a new speaker put in. The man was short, square-jawed, with dark eyes and hair neatly clubbed. He wore plain clothing, considerably less expensive than that of the others.

Dr. Warren smiled. "I'd expect you to say that of a fellow Frenchman, Paul." To Philip: "This is Mr. Revere of North Square. Our resident silversmith—"

"More important," said Adams, "the one man among us who never sniffed the somewhat rarefied air of Harvard Yard. Paul alone has the ear of the huge numbers of artisans and mechanics in town—"

"Because I'm one myself," said the stocky man. He was in his late thirties or early forties, Philip judged. His blunt-fingered hands looked calloused, muscular, testimony to his position as a craftsman. "Mr. Kent, let me welcome you,

and suggest that if you're ever in the market for replacement of a fine silver button—''

"I'm afraid I don't have any of those, Mr. Revere."

"You have teeth," Campbell said. "Paul replaces them, too."

"A necessary sideline to feed all the mouths at my table," Revere shrugged. "Mr. Kent, you mentioned your home originally being in France. So was my father's."

"Where, sir?"

"Riaucaud, near Bordeaux. My father's people were Huguenots."

Philip nodded slowly. "We had few in Auvergne. But I know how the Protestant French were persecuted—driven out—"

"Which is why Monsieur Apollos Rivoire emigrated here, apprenticed himself to a goldsmith, and as soon as his first shop on Clark's Wharf began to prosper, changed his name to something more American. I suspect you've already done that?"

"Yes. Our family's name was Charboneau."

"You see?" Revere smiled at the others. "I told you he was all right."

Philip had taken an instant liking to the clear-eyed, forthright artisan, a liking intensified when Revere had the thoughtfulness to add, "You're no doubt confused by all this clack about recent affronts to the cause of Englishmen's rights—"

"I am, Mr. Revere. I'd be grateful for a little explanation."

"The first incident Samuel made reference to involved His Majesty's customs schooner *Gaspee*. In pursuit of smugglers—"

"Real or fancied," said Dr. Warren, with some cynicism.

"—she ran aground on a sandbar below Providence. Now you must understand, sir, that among we coastal colonists, smuggling of Holland tea and similar commodities is a highly respected occupation. But not to be brooked by the *Gaspee*'s most unpopular master, Lieutenant Dudingston. Before his unhappy grounding, he had, in fact, been stopping and searching our ships up and down the coast. Harassing American captains and crews viciously and vindictively. Well, sir, the *Gaspee* aground brought a swift reaction. The high-handed lieutenant and his crew were driven off. Then a group of patriotic citizens burned her to the waterline. As a result, it's been proposed that the offenders be tried in England. *If* they can be brought to justice."

The square-jawed man allowed himself another little smile. "Which is doubtful. Who among those who set the *Gaspee* afire will identify his neighbor?"

Dr. Warren put in, "The second issue Samuel wishes to seize upon is the announcement by the Royal Governor of Massachusetts, Hutchinson, that commencing next year, his salary will be paid not by our Provincial Congress, but by the Crown."

"Two provocations of excellent quality!" Adams cried. "We must exploit them!"

"We are all agreed on that," Warren retorted. "But the wish doesn't guarantee the deed. Since the last taxes were rescinded—"

"Not their damned tea tax!" Adams said.

Warren went on with forced patience, "Still, the rebellious mood has quieted considerably here. And virtually vanished elsewhere."

"But the June announcements are the most noxious threats against our liberty thus far!" insisted Adams.

Warren gave a weary shrug. "I can only proselytize so many from my sur-

gery, Samuel. And I cannot reach into all the other colonies. As Franklin once observed, the need is to make thirteen clocks strike as one. Not easy."

A heavyset man who had thus far remained silent spoke up:

"I've published articles—yours, Samuel—your cousin John's—Abraham Ware's—in the *Gazette,* and I'll continue to do so. But like Dr. Warren, I fear it isn't enough. The people have simply relaxed with the complacency of prosperity again."

Philip, who had been standing somewhat self-consciously with the serving tray dangling from one hand, perked up at once:

"You're a printer, sir?"

The stout man's nod was brief. "Benjamin Edes. The firm of Edes and Gill, in Dassett Alley behind the State House."

"I learned the printing trade in London—"

"Did you, now?"

"I also learned that it's a worthy, important trade. I told Dr. Franklin it's the one I mean to take up here, if I can."

Adams perked up. "You encountered Benjamin in London?"

"Yes, sir. He welcomed me at his rooms. In Craven Street."

He glanced at Campbell. The landlord smiled, realizing Philip had seen through the little test of veracity.

Philip had decided to say nothing of the lost list and letter. Instead, he told the men, "Dr. Franklin felt I could find work in this country. So if you've ever a need for a devil, Mr. Edes—"

"Constantly," Edes sighed. He ranged his glance up and down Philip, gauging him. "I can't hold 'prentices for long. Most of 'em are frightened of running afoul of the King's justice. It keeps my partner John Gill hovering far in the background, too. You see, I publish not merely a paper, the *Gazette*, but what many Tory citizens label sedition. Samuel, for instance, must cloak his articles under Latin pseudonyms such as Brittanus Americanus. So must some of our other authors. If you've a belly for that sort of risk—" A pointed look toward Campbell. "Perhaps our host didn't err in appointing you to help him serve."

Philip didn't ponder a decision for long.

"When may I come around to talk to you, Mr. Edes?"

The abruptness shocked the other man. But he recovered quickly.

"Why, on the morrow, if that pleases you. Meanwhile, I'm plagued thirsty." He shoved his empty tankard at Philip handle first.

Edes asked the others their pleasure. All wanted refills save for the silversmith. Edes' laughter stirred the tobacco clouds.

"Paul is our sober husband and father," he explained to Philip. "Also the man whose copper engravings illustrate the broadsides we nail up on the Liberty Tree. I suppose we should be thankful he prefers to keep his hand steady."

Revere smiled back. Philip started out.

"Mr. Kent!"

He turned to see Revere facing him.

"Pleasantries aside—what you've heard must indeed go no further. Lives are not yet forfeit in Boston for the kind of talk which takes place in this room. But that time can't be far off. We will protect ourselves at all costs," he finished quietly.

Philip shivered a little under the impact of the silversmith's forthright gaze. "I assure you I'll say nothing," he replied, adding to Edes, "and I'll visit you in the morning, sir."

As he left, he heard the querulous, yet somehow passionate voice of Adams resume:

"The problem is to seize the advantage! Confrontation—conflagration—must surely come. The sooner the citizens understand and *accept* that—"

"You are a manipulator, Samuel," Warren interrupted. "I do not agree that 'conflagration'—your prettified term for open rebellion—for war—is inevitable. Or need be made so by us!"

Philip pulled the door shut.

VI

HE PAUSED a moment, gazing out over the black-beamed taproom crowded with noisy North Enders. He noticed two British officers seated in the front corner, finishing platters of meat while they stared with open arrogance at those nearby.

The arrogance was returned with scowls. Philip felt another chill chase down his back. With a single step into the Salutation's rear room, he had plunged far deeper than he'd originally meant to.

True, he'd wanted to meet the radical Adams. But now he was linked to the group by an opportunity to seek work with a printer who spread the propaganda for the American cause.

He noted the British officers again, and felt cowed by the figures of authority, despite his best resolves not to be.

Well, the solution was extremely simple. Leave the Salutation. Never call on Benjamin Edes. Avoid further contact with the men who were, by their own admission, dangerous—

Campbell came through the door, stopped, looked at Philip. The landlord seemed to sense Philip's uncertainty, and his voice bore just a trace of threat:

"I trust you have no regrets about being admitted to that room, young man. It would prove awkward if you did. Molineaux's North End mobs are no longer rampaging quite the way they did a year or so ago, in company with Ebenezer Mackintosh's bullies from the South End. But the warning served inside was not given lightly. Should confidences be violated—even by accident—well, Mr. Adams knows the mob organizers intimately. And he is a determined man."

Philip stared at the bright scarlet coats of the British officers. He remembered his mother, the Amberlys, Girard's books and his talk of new winds blowing—

"Regrets, Mr. Campbell?"

His eyes hardened.

"No, sir. None."

2
Mistress Anne

THE PRINTING firm of Edes and Gill in Dassett Alley was not particularly prosperous-looking, equipped as it was with but one small flat-bed press in its cramped main-floor room. A few type cases sat nearby. Behind a partition was

a tiny, cluttered office from which the stout Mr. Ben Edes oversaw the publishing operation.

As he'd promised to do, Philip called on Mr. Edes at ten the morning following his admittance to the private room behind the Salutation. They soon concluded an agreement for Philip to be a general boy-of-all-work around the shop.

From time to time Edes' son Peter apparently helped out as well. But the boy was small, and Edes wanted an assistant of size and strength. And, he said, "One who won't cower and run off when Governor Hutchinson or some other damned Crown toady makes one of his frequent public denunciations of our sheet."

Before giving his final assent to the arrangement, Edes watched Philip work the press for nearly twenty minutes. At the conclusion of the test, he said, "You've practiced with excellent masters. Come, let's go back to the office and talk wages. Do you have a place to stay?"

Elated, Philip said as he followed Edes, "No, sir. But I'll find one immediately."

"We've an unused room down cellar where we can move in a pallet if you wish—no charge."

"That would be perfect."

"You'll have to catch your meals as you can, in the taverns in the neighborhood."

"No problem there, sir."

"Do you own a trunk? Any possessions you want to store? We can lock 'em in back. Or at my house."

"These—" Philip showed him the casket and wrapped sword "—are all I have."

Settled in the office again, Edes studied him. "Brought 'em along, did you? That's confidence. You came from England with nothing else?"

"Nothing."

"Then tell me what you want in this country. More specifically than you did last evening."

Philip thought a moment. "Frankly, sir, all I can think of at the moment is the chance to start working. Oh, and some new clothes. I'd hope to buy a proper suit from what I save. Without spending all of it, I mean."

"Got any ambitions beyond the job itself?"

"Yes, sir. I think I'd like to put myself in my own printing business eventually."

Edes grinned. "Competing with me already!"

"Well—" Philip nodded. "In a way, I suppose. A man needs to look ahead."

"Understandable, Mr. Kent, perfectly understandable. Let us hope the town of Boston's not burned to the ground in civil disorders or leveled by the King's artillery before you've the capital to take away my trade." He continued more soberly, "As you may have sensed last night, Sam Adams is bent on armed collision with the British government. He's failed in every business venture he's ever attempted. But the man's a positive genius at politics—wheedling here, whispering there, stirring mobs in secret to work his will. His hatred of the Crown isn't all pure idealism, though. Sam's father was ruined in the Land Bank failure a number of years ago. So, as you were warned, you'll be associating with less than respectable men if you join Edes and Gill. Are you still persuaded?"

"I am," Philip replied with an emphatic nod.

Ben Edes looked pleased. He reached for the pull of a desk drawer.

"Then let's have a tot of rum and haggle over the price of your service."

II

BEFORE MANY days had gone by, Philip realized that financial success was not the paramount goal sought by the proprietor of Edes and Gill and his seldom-present partner.

True, the establishment did a modest commercial printing business, over and above publishing its little Monday paper, the *Gazette*. In spare hours the press churned out handbills, shop window placards and anything else that might turn a profit. In this last category were several hand-colored copper plate engravings, joint ventures of Revere and Ben Edes.

The two best sellers both dated from 1770. One depicted the still-infamous Boston Massacre. The other was a less sanguinary *View of Part of the Town of Boston in New England, and the British Ships of War Landing Their Troops in the Year 1768. Dedicated to the Earl of Hillsborough.* When Philip asked why a member of the inner councils of the Sons of Liberty would dedicate such a work to any British nobleman, Edes answered, "You wouldn't catch him inscribing it in that fashion today. But Paul's got a houseful of youngsters—and he knows how to sell both sides of the fence to support 'em. His tongue was a good way in his cheek when he wrote those words, Philip. But his eye was on his purse."

Mr. Edes then went on to note that Revere, a self-taught engraver, made no claim to originality as a pictorial artist. All his engravings were "modeled"— stolen was the interpretation Philip put on it—after drawings by others. Revere merely duplicated them on metal with a few embellishments.

"But in working silver, he's entirely original—and many say he has no peer in all the thirteen colonies," Edes added on behalf of his friend.

Despite such frankly money-making ventures as the Revere engravings, however, it was evident that most of Edes' energies were devoted to the *Gazette*. His aim was to make it not only New England's most influential news organ, but the means by which the patriots of Boston town could speak their defiance of the King's edicts and issue their warnings and alarms to a temporarily placid populace.

The *Gazette's*—or, more correctly, Ben Edes'—political orientation was in fact the prime reason the other partner, John Gill, was seldom on the premises. He did not so much disapprove of Edes' approach as desire to protect his own neck. And, as Edes remarked once, in arguments concerning publishing policy, Gill always lost. "Because I can shout longer and louder every time."

As the summer of 1772 mellowed into clear, crisp autumn, Philip had little time for anything except the exhausting labor Ben Edes demanded. Just as he had at Sholto's, he worked a six-day week, resting only on the Sabbath. He usually spent half of that day sleeping off his tiredness in the small but basically comfortable cellar room Edes had provided for his use.

The printer soon recognized Philip's skill and expanded his duties to include not only inking and operating the press but setting type—a slow process at first.

But satisfying once Philip got the hang of it. He would never be as swift as Esau Sholto. But he was competent.

By now Philip was physically grown to manhood. Though not of great height, he was strong and powerful-looking, his shoulders thickly muscled from hauling on the press lever hour after hour. His dark, forthright eyes took in every new sight, every new face—and every word printed by Edes and Gill—with avid interest. Thanks to Sunday afternoon rambles about town, he soon became quite familiar with Boston—and his work acquainted him with the leading citizens involved in defending the cause of Englishmen's rights against the encroachments of the King and Parliament.

Samuel Adams was a frequent visitor to the print shop, usually arriving with sheets of foolscap on which his palsied hand had penned his latest diatribe against the North ministry. In the announcement that the Royal Governor's salary, as well as those of all Massachusetts judges, would soon be coming directly out of England's treasury, Adams had found an issue with which he hoped to excite his countrymen. He wrote about it incessantly. The *Gazette* printed the articles under his various pseudonyms—a continuing indication of the dangers inherent in such literary work.

Another frequent visitor was introduced to Philip as Abraham Ware. A Harvard-trained lawyer, Ware was a small, pot-bellied man with popping, frog-like eyes. He contributed essays almost as inflammatory as those of Adams, but he had only one nom de plume, Patriot.

Revere, the quiet, plainly dressed silversmith of North Square, also called occasionally, bringing bits of news or a crudely engraved political cartoon.

On the second floor of the Edes and Gill building, these men and others met by night. The chamber up there was called the Long Room. Philip was never admitted, even though he was by now a reasonably trusted employee. But Edes didn't mind identifying his nocturnal visitors for his young assistant—

That stout little lawyer from nearby Braintree was Samuel's cousin John. The handsome, rather dandified man in his early thirties, whom all visitors seemed to treat with special deference, was John Hancock, the merchant prince of Beacon Hill.

Edes said Hancock was no hothead. In fact, he occupied a position of such status that he might have fallen more logically into the Tory camp. Those who supported the King's policies and policymakers were a majority in Boston, albeit a relatively silent, inactive one.

But Hancock had somehow developed a quixotic interest in the ideals espoused by Sam Adams and the others. Then, so Ben Edes explained, in 1768, the Royal Commissioners of Customs had recognized the potential strength Hancock could lend to the cause of the Sons of Liberty. The commissioners had falsely accused him of smuggling Madeira on his sloop *Liberty*. His cargo was impounded.

The strategy backfired. Hancock suffered no financial loss whatsoever—thanks to the convenient and not at all coincidental intervention of one of the famous Boston mobs put together by the cobbler Mackintosh from the South End and hardware merchant Molineaux from the North. The savaging crowd rescued Hancock's Madeira, and from that time on, the wealthy man's devotion to the cause was steadfast. Although he remained less of a firebrand than Adams, he spent considerable personal money underwriting the extra printing expenses—the broadsides, the handbills—that the Sons of Liberty distributed and nailed up surreptitiously all over town.

Hancock, the Adams cousins and Revere—the only non-Harvard man in the group apart from Edes—met at least once a week in the Long Room. Working at the press by the light of whale-oil lamps, Philip could often hear contentious voices raised during those sessions. That of Sam Adams was usually the most strident.

In addition to the Long Room and Campbell's Salutation up north, the Green Dragon on nearby Union Street was another popular meeting spot for the patriots. Philip took many of his meals at the Dragon. He felt that patronizing the place somehow enhanced his association with the cause, even though he was not privileged to share the thinking of its leaders, except as it slipped off the press in the pages of the *Gazette* or in the broadsides run behind locked doors at night.

By early October, the drumfire of propaganda had succeeded in generating a certain amount of public concern about the threat posed by the salaries of the Governor and the judges being paid from England. Adams' next move was to press for the convocation of a town meeting. Its purpose was to establish permanent correspondence committees in Boston, as well as in other Massachusetts villages, to further communicate the position of the Adams group and seek support not only of neighboring communities but of like-minded people in New York, Philadelphia and other colonial cities.

In connection with the committee scheme, Edes dispatched Philip one morning on an urgent errand to the South End. He was to pick up copy from Adams at his home on Purchase Street; copy for a broadside destined for the trunk of the Liberty Tree and other highly visible spots around town.

Hurrying up Purchase Street not far from the Neck, Philip was astonished at the size and splendor of the Adams residence. It was multi-storied, even boasting an observatory on the upper floor.

He imagined the observatory would afford a fine view of the harbor. But he wondered how a man as financially distressed as Adams could maintain such a large home. In conversations at the Dragon and the print shop, Philip had learned that despite a promising start at Harvard, Samuel Adams had subsequently succeeded in mismanaging every single business opportunity life had presented to him.

Adams' father—the Deacon, he was called, because of his strong religious convictions—had indeed lost much money when the British government outlawed the colonial Land Bank he'd organized. But along with resulting lawsuits, son Samuel had inherited the Deacon's thriving brewery-distillery, source of some of the best beer and rum in New England. That firm, having been operated for several years by Mr. Samuel, was now defunct.

Adams' stint as Boston's tax collector had been equally disastrous. When he had stepped down in sixty-five, he was behind in collections to an amount exceeding eight thousand pounds. Governor Hutchinson accused him of malfeasance. Edes said Adams' real problem was "no head for figures—and a tendency to be generous to anyone with a heart-rending story." Philip readily understood how the Royal Governor had become one of Adams' favorite targets.

But after the business debacles, Adams, already into his forties, found his destiny and his lifelong career at last. Politics. Or, as he termed it, "the cause of liberty." At the moment, though, no one in Boston professed to know how he was able to support his family and conduct his busy political life. There were rumors that his younger cousin John, the successful lawyer from Braintree, paid him a dole as a "consultant."

Philip reached the metal fencing outside the Adams house. It became evident that, contrary to his first impression, the property was not being kept up at all. The fence badly needed painting; rust showed everywhere. Behind the fence, weeds that had yellowed in the first frost still stood knee-high.

The front-door knocker was tarnished. And the pretty but fatigued-looking woman who opened the door wore an old dress befitting the poorest-paid servant.

"Is Mr. Adams at home?" Philip asked. "I'm from Edes and Gill—"

"Oh yes, my husband's expecting you," the woman said, shocking her visitor with the revelation of her identity. Her smile was tired. "Step in, won't you? Samuel's in the study upstairs. He's having an early lunch. Would you like to have something with him?"

"No, thank you, I'm to hurry straight back with his manuscript."

The woman started to say something else, but was distracted by the rocketing entrance of a huge Newfoundland dog that badly needed bathing. Philip started up the stairs quickly, crunching spilled breadcrumbs under his feet. He noticed cobwebs in the ceiling corners, and scarred woodwork.

Despite the gloomy, run-down atmosphere, Mr. Samuel Adams was humming cheerily beyond the open door of the study near the top of the staircase. Philip walked toward the door. Adams looked up, his palsied head bobbing. His smile broadened. He laid down the quill with which he'd been writing, called out:

"Come in, Kent! Care for a bite of something while I finish up the copy?"

With a trembling hand, he shoved a plate to the corner of his littered desk, nearly upsetting his inkstand. He was wearing hose, breeches, a white long-sleeved blouse stained black in a dozen places. His left shoe was missing its brass buckle.

The politician noticed Philip's expression as the latter stared at the slimy-looking edibles on the plate.

"Raw oysteres—good for you! I have an absolute passion for 'em—sure you won't join me?"

"No—no, thanks," said Philip, a little queasy. When he'd been starving in the streets, he'd eaten gobbets of oyster from garbage heaps—and thankfully. This morning he could barely stomach the sight. Another sign his life had changed, he thought, fighting back a sour taste in his throat.

He glanced around the book-lined study as Adams began to scratch with the quill again. Most of the books had titles suggesting their subject was politics. Among them Philip recognized works by Locke and by Rousseau in translation.

Humming again, Adams finished the copy with a flourish, then began to blow on the manuscript.

"Ben Edes tells me you're working out well for him," the older man stated between puffs at the paper.

"I hope so, Mr. Adams. I very much like the job."

"I apologize for my somewhat rude behavior that first evening at the Salutation. But these are dangerous times. We can't be overly careful—"

He handed across the sheet, popped another oyster into his mouth, swallowed with relish. Philip winced.

He studied the copy Adams had given him. It was a strong appeal to Boston's citizens to promote the idea of the correspondence committees. The broadside ended with a warning:

*Those who Fail to Adopt the position of the Reasonable and
Fair-minded Mr. Adams will Earn our deepest Displeasure.*

The signature was one Philip had seen on other pieces in the shop—Joyce
Jun'r. He raided his eyebrows at that; the communications of Joyce Junior were
usually threatening, even sinister-sounding.

"Is this another of your pen names, Mr. Adams?"

"When a little honest fear must be stirred in the public breast—yes."

"I thought perhaps there really was someone by this name."

"You mean you don't know who Joyce is—or was?"

"No. I've asked Mr. Edes a couple of times. He always breaks out laughing."

Adams' slate-blue eyes sparkled. He laced his hands together, a bit of oyster
still clinging to one corner of his mouth. His head continued to bob, but the
twined hands shook less visibly. He said:

"Joyce Junior has been a legendary, if unreal, personage around Boston for
years. The real Joyce—Cornet George Joyce of the British army—was the chap
who captured that damned Charles I. An evil king if ever there was one! Some
say Joyce actually wielded the axe that lopped off the King's head, but that part's
apocryphal, I believe. On this side of the Atlantic, we call him Junior. And
reserve him for tasks or appeals that might be beneath the dignity of more
law-abiding citizens. 'Brittanus Americanus,' for example, would never think of
calling out a mob. But stout Joyce has, many a time." Once again the slate-blue
eyes held a cold brilliance that made Philip shiver.

"I don't doubt we'll be hearing often from the ghost of the good Cornet in the
days and months to come," Adams concluded. "Be sure you heed his advices,
Mr. Kent, or you'll find yourself in trouble."

Philip matched Adams' smile. "Out of a job, you mean?"

"That's part of it. But only part. No man can remain neutral in the coming
struggle."

Despite the surface cordiality, Philip was glad to say a quick good morning
and retreat from that cramped, musty little room where the politician hunched
over his plate, smacking his lips and lifting oysters to his mouth with a shaking
hand. As he hurried to the front door, Philip heard the dog barking furiously, a
child wailing—and Mrs. Adams crying out in dismay and frustration somewhere
at the back of the house.

Relieved to be on the street again, smelling the fresh harbor wind, Philip
thought it was no wonder those in power in England found Adams a dangerous
enemy, a man determined to unsettle the future. He might have failed in business, but he would never fail in his current mission—that much, at least, communicated itself in every glance of the almost eerie eyes. Philip felt that by going
into the Purchase Street house, he'd stepped into the center of a spider's web. He
hoped Edes wouldn't soon send him back again.

III

On a dark, gloomy morning later in that same month of October, Philip was alone in the shop. He was busy setting type for next Monday's issue of the paper, which would contain yet another piece by Adams proclaiming the value of the committees in promoting colonial unity. The bell over the door jingled. He looked up to see a young woman entering.

She acted unhappy to find Philip the only person present. Throwing back the cowl of her cloak, she pulled foolscap sheets from under the rain-spattered garment and asked:

"May I see Mr. Edes, please?"

"He's gone off to the Green Dragon, miss. Mr. Gill too."

The young woman scrutinized him. "Are you a new apprentice?"

Annoyed by the stare, Philip told her, "I work for Mr. Edes on wages. I am not bound to him."

The girl flushed a little at the sharp reaction. She was an inch or so taller than Philip, though about his age, he judged. Her eyes were brown, her hair chestnut, her mouth generous but firm-looking. Her skin had the lustrous, wholesome color of one who spent time outdoors. He noticed a few freckles on either side of her nose, as well as an ample figure beneath the cloak. Though not dressed with great elegance, the girl carried herself with a certain no-nonsense air that rankled Philip for no clear reason.

"Is there something I can do for you?" he asked finally.

The girl held out the foolscap. "I'm Mistress Ware. This is copy from my father, to be set immediately. He'd have come in person but he's meeting with a client."

Philip took some time to scan the three closely written sheets, noted the Patriot signature and the nature of the message: an appeal to the citizenry to openly support Adams' plan to establish the twenty-one-man Committee of Correspondence for promulgating the "Boston view" to the other colonies—and, as it said near the end, "the World."

He heard the girl give an impatient little sniff, glanced up, found the brown eyes sparkling with irritation:

"I trust the writing has your approval?"

"It seems excellent, yes."

"I'm so pleased. I wasn't aware an ordinary devil approved or disapproved copy. I thought his function was to set and print it, nothing more."

Philip placed the foolscap on a stack of freshly printed handbills, his grin a shade insolent. "But I'm not an ordinary devil, Mistress Ware. May I ask what's annoying you? The dark weather, perhaps?"

Red glowed in her cheeks. "Young women are not accustomed to being so smartly addressed by apprentices!"

Philip's grin hardened. "I told you—I am a free laborer, not an apprentice. But I do believe you knew that when you said it the second time." Then he moderated his tone. "I'll pass the material into Mr. Edes' hands the moment he comes back."

"Thank you." The girl looked embarrassed; Philip's accusation had struck home. She hesitated, then said, "I did address you sharply—"

"And I returned in kind. I apologize."

"So do I. This article's terribly important, you see. The town's buzzing with

184

talk about Mr. Hancock's reluctance to lend his support to the plan for correspondence committees.''

"I'm sure your father's usual fine phrasing will help persuade him."

Startled, she asked, "Are you familiar with his writing?"

"Certainly. I read most everything Mr. Edes gives me to set at the font. Some typesetters, I'm told, see only letters, never whole words. I'm not one of them."

"Then I indeed mistook you," the girl said, a little more friendly now. "The apprentices who've worked for Ben Edes before cared for nothing except counting the days till the Sabbath, when they could sleep."

"Well, I do that too. But I came a long way to live in this country. If I plan to make my future here, I should know its affairs."

"A long way?" Mistress Ware countered. "From where?"

"France. Then England. My name is Philip Kent."

Once the opening hostilities had subsided, he'd decided he rather liked the girl's prickly manner and her frank way of speaking. But the friendly overture in the form of his name produced no similar response. Mistress Ware had evidently learned as much about him as she cared to know. She tugged her cowl up over her brown curls and started for the door, saying:

"As soon as the material is proofed, my father would welcome a message to that effect. He may wish to make last-minute corrections. If you will so notify Mr. Edes—"

"Please."

"I beg your pardon?"

" 'If you will so notify Mr. Edes, please,' " Philip said softly but firmly. He was teasing, but not completely.

The girl stood framed in the doorway, the rain slanting down in Dassett Alley behind her. She gave him another of those challenging looks. The cloak shaped to her body showed high breasts; he felt a physical response that had lain dormant months now, except in sweating, unwelcome dreams of Alicia.

Mistress Ware's tart reply put an end to the possibility of getting acquainted:

"I thought I made a mistake about you. I was in error. You have the boorish mentality of an apprentice after all. Good morning."

She whirled and stamped out into the rain.

IV

BENJAMIN EDES returned shortly after noon. Philip delivered Patriot's latest article into his hands, then inquired about the first name of the daughter of the author.

Riffling through the copy, Edes answered absently, "Her name's Anne. Nice-looking girl. But inclined to a sharp tongue."

"So I discovered."

"In my opinion, Abraham's permitted her too free access to his library. A woman should keep to sewing and cooking meals. It'll take some man with backbone and a large fist to wed and bed that one. Anne's nineteen already— well past marriageable age. No regular beaux, to her father's chagrin. He fears she'll turn into a spinster. Too smart for her own good—and failing to fulfill a woman's natural role."

"I can't imagine that someone isn't courting her."

"True, though. Oh, she draws attention from some of the British officers. But she'd as soon spit on them as curtsy. In that respect, she's Abraham's flesh, all right."

A few moments later he handed the foolscap to Philip.

"Stirring, stirring."

"Ware's daughter said he wanted to look it over when it was proofed."

Edes nodded. "As soon as you've set it, take the galleys to his house in Launder Street. We'll run it on page one, in place of that item about the ropewalk fire. The outcome of the town meeting remains doubtful. Hancock is still balking at the committee idea. Says it's too overt and radical—"

He noticed Philip's distracted look, nudged him. "To work, boy! Don't stand staring at the rain or we'll never get the paper printed."

V

EARLY NEXT morning, with the sky clearing and a sharp nor'easter hinting of winter, Philip set off with the proof sheets of Patriot's call for support of the Committees of Correspondence.

Following Edes' directions, he located the prosperous-looking two-story home in Launder Street. But he was informed by the cook who answered the door that Lawyer Ware and his daughter had already left on errands. They might be found toward ten o'clock at a place where they frequently stopped, the London Book-Store of Mr. Knox in Cornhill, opposite William's Court.

The moment Philip walked in the door of that establishment, he wondered whether he'd been given wrong information. At first glance, the London Book-Store resembled a salon more than a commercial establishment.

The place was packed. Among the clutter of books, flutes, bread baskets, telescopes and rolls of wallpaper, finely dressed ladies and gentlemen of the town conversed with British officers in friendly, animated fashion. As Philip stood staring, he saw a fat, pink-faced young man speaking with an older officer. The young man wore a silken bandana wrapped around what appeared to be a crippled hand. A memory of Roger Amberly fleeted through Philip's mind.

The fat young man noticed Philip's lost look, bustled over to greet him:

"Something, sir? I am the proprietor, Mr. Knox."

"I'm from Edes and Gill. Hunting Lawyer Ware."

"In the back. Talking with the grenadier captain. I'm afraid the conversation is a bit one-sided. You'll be a welcome distraction."

The fat man waved and hurried back to the officer with whom he'd been speaking, an even fatter colonel of the Royal Regiment of Artillery, resplendent in blue coat with red facings. As Philip moved toward the rear of the store, he heard Knox say enthusiastically:

"I've a new work just in from the continent which contains some interesting theoretical material on the deployment of cannon. Be most interested in your opinion—"

Proceeding past the assorted merchandise displays—and ignoring the amused glances given his poor clothing by some of the chattering ladies and gentlemen and most of the officers—he bore down on the frog-eyed lawyer and his daughter. They were plainly fretting under the attentions of a tall officer in his mid-twenties.

The man's yellow-faced uniform identified him as a member of the grenadier company of the Twenty-ninth Worcestershires. Philip had learned enough about the British troops stationed in Boston to know that the grenadier units were the elite shock troops of every regiment. The men who filled the ranks of such companies were selected for great physical strength and stature. The officer in conversation with the Wares was no exception. Big, long-nosed, not unhandsome, the captain had a scar on his chin and an impeccably powdered wig.

As Philip approached, he heard the captain say:

"—would welcome your permission to call upon your daughter, Mr. Ware. Despite our political differences."

The man's humor was condescending. It produced a moue from Anne, who was pointedly focusing her attention on a display of vials. A placard announced that they contained *Hill's never-failing cure for the bite of a mad dog*.

Lawyer Ware replied, "As to that, Captain Stark, you don't need my consent so much as the young lady's."

"And the granting of that is an impossibility," Anne said in a cool tone.

The captain couldn't repress his distaste. He said to Ware, "You have no control over your daughter's behavior?"

"Why, of course he does," the girl replied. "My father supplies me with what Mr. Locke called 'a standing rule to live by'—"

"Locke!" the officer exclaimed. "That damned radical—they should have burned his books, and him too!"

The girl shrugged. "In your opinion. I feel he put it well. He meant his remarks for men living under a government, but they apply equally to children living with their parents." Lawyer Ware sighed loudly as his daughter continued, "Once I know the 'standing rule to live by'—the broad rules set down by my government or my father—then I want 'a liberty to follow my own will in all things where that rule prescribes not.' I won't be subject to the 'inconstant, uncertain, unknown arbitrary will of another man.' "

"Is that you speaking?" sneered the officer. "Or Mr. Locke?"

"Some of both, sir."

"By gad, you Whigs are a peppery, windy lot," the captain complained. "I thought Mr. Knox's emporium was considered neutral territory. Politics forgotten in lieu of more pleasant topics—"

Lawyer Ware's eyes seemd to pop even more than usual. "Well, sir, since you've mentioned politics—"

"No, sir, it was your daughter."

Ware ignored him: "—the abridgment of liberties can never be forgotten. Although the King's simple-minded ministers continue to seem unaware of that elemental fact."

Philip had stopped a few steps behind the captain's broad back, awaiting a chance to interrupt. He was struck by the sight of Abraham Ware's daughter. Her opened cloak revealed a simple but well-cut gown of sprigged yellow muslin that Philip found overwhelmingly lovely. The folds of the material couldn't conceal the ample swell of her young breasts.

He wondered whether his reaction was merely general—that is, the same as he would have felt in the presence of any attractive female—or whether it was due to the qualities of this one in particular. Speculation was cut short as Anne Ware noticed him, smiled with startling warmth and brushed past the elegant and powerful Captain Stark.

"It's Mr. Kent from the printing house," she said as she took his arm. "Good morning to you."

"Mistress Anne," he nodded politely, quite aware of her breast against his forearm and the fresh smell of lavender soap she radiated. He couldn't resist a sidelong smile and whisper:

"Your greeting is somewhat different today. For practical reasons?"

Her quick flush admitted guilt. But he didn't mind her strategy of clinging to him as they walked by the huge grenadier. The officer gazed at Philip as if he were something less than dung.

"Your daughter keeps company with mechanics?" remarked Captain Stark to the lawyer.

"That's correct, sir," Anne replied. "By preference."

Disliking the soldier's stare, Philip said, "I trust you have no objections to that, Captain?"

His tone made the grenadier stiffen his shoulders, as if to emphasize the difference between his overpowering height and Philip's relatively small stature.

"I might, sir, if we were to meet privately, and you were to continue your sarcasm."

The threat in Captain Stark's eyes was not merely the routine arrogance Philip had seen in many of the British troops in town. It was a personal, male reaction to Anne's deliberately insulting attention to Philip. She still gripped his arm as if they were the closest of friends.

Philip's chin lifted. "I wouldn't shrink from that kind of encounter. I've some small skill with a sword."

In response to the bluff, the grenadier's flecked green eyes grew uglier. "Every democrat apes the aristocrat here, it seems. Well, Boston is not a large city. Perhaps I'll indeed have the pleasure of meeting you again."

Cheeks red, Captain Stark bowed to Anne. "Your servant." With another glare at Philip, he stalked off.

Anne released Philip's arm, laughing delightedly. "Insufferable asses! They think their uniforms and their elegant manners make them the catch of the day. Our thanks to you, Mr. Kent. We simply couldn't get rid of him, even with outright rudeness."

Philip said, "I'm happy to make some slight amends for yesterday."

The meaning of that went right by Lawyer Ware. He stuck a pinch of snuff up his nose, inhaled and blinked his frog's eyes. "Annie's run into Stark before. I have it on authority that the man's a whoremaster of the worst sort. Beg pardon, Annie—"

She shrugged, not the least shocked by her father's choice of language. Her reply struck Philip as equally typical of her unusual personality:

"The term is accurate, I imagine. I've heard the same thing. Captain Stark reportedly prides himself on the quantity of his conquests, quality being immaterial. And he has a filthy temper." To Philip, with a genuine smile: "So I do appreciate your playing my little game. Nothing's ever devastated him quite so completely before."

Somewhat annoyed that he'd been deliberately used, Philip didn't remain annoyed for long. He couldn't. The warmth of Anne Ware's expression pleased him. He found himself glancing down at the scooped neckline of her sprigged yellow gown. How well the color went with her healthy, tanned skin—

Anne noticed where his gaze had wandered. Her brown eyes frosted just a little. She released his arm.

Reaching for his pocket, Philip said in a lowered voice, "I've brought the proofs, Mr. Ware. But this seems the wrong sort of place—"

Ware waved. "Ah, the red-coated fops who hold levee here every morning have nothing on their minds except their Tory lady friends. They'll think I'm reading a brief."

As he accepted the galleys, Ware added, "Annie tells me you pore over everything you set and print for Ben Edes."

"Yes, sir. Because I'm interested in colonial affairs."

Anne had returned to her examination of the display of Hill's mad-dog nostrum. Did she act a bit self-conscious, to be revealed as having talked about him? While Lawyer Ware examined the first galley, Philip went on:

"I was a little surprised by one of the closing lines in your article, Mr. Ware. The one expressing hope that the sword of the parent would never be stained with the blood of his children."

"Adams would have me strike that out," Ware said. "But some sops are needed to satisfy the less intemperate advocates of liberty. Johnny Hancock and Sam's cousin John, for instance. I'd remove the line myself, except for one consideration. We are not yet ready to strike a blow in return."

"Will the colonies ever be ready for that?"

"If the ministerial troops and that truckling Hutchinson don't change their ways, yes."

"When do you think it will happen, Mr. Ware?"

"Hard to say. If not this year, perhaps next. It's what Samuel's counting on— along with some of the rest of us," he added with a steady look that somehow removed all traces of the grotesque or the comical from his appearance.

Ware's statement jibed with the atmosphere that permeated Edes' print shop. Philip had the impression that certain members of the liberty faction would not be satisfied with anything less than open rebellion—were, in fact, striving to manipulate events to achieve that end. Perhaps they were right in doing so. Philip had so far formed no final opinions. He did realize that such a turn would bring a halt to his own ambitions, though.

But such abstract subjects didn't linger long in his mind with Anne Ware nearby.

Her father stumped to the back corner of the Book-Store, muttering phrases in Latin like any good attorney. He hardly attracted a glance from the socializing soldiers and ladies. Philip took the moment to approach Anne.

He indicated the portly Knox up near the front door. "Is that fellow partial to the Tory cause?"

"By no means."

"But he's certainly friendly with the officers. Look at him showing off his books."

Anne Ware's brown eyes grew serious. "Like my father, Henry believes a military confrontation is, if not yet totally inevitable, then certainly possible. Henry's a fox, Mr. Kent. He very cleverly picks the brains of the best officers who stop in here. Encourages them to do so, in fact. He draws them out on the pretext of exchanging opinions about military strategy and tactics. Henry's never served in a military unit. But he wants to be prepared. He's especially interested in the use of artillery. So he allows this place to become more Tory than Whig."

For a moment Philip experienced sharp uncertainty. Surely George III would never permit the situation in the colonies to deteriorate to armed conflict.

And yet, when he recalled the hard-learned lessons of England, the kind of people who held positions of authority there, he was not so sure.

"Mr. Kent?"

Startled, he realized Anne Ware had put her hand on his arm again.

"Yes?"

"I do thank you once more for rescuing me from a most objectionable situation. More important, I want to offer a complete and sincere apology for my own bad behavior yesterday."

Philip smiled, said, "I owe you the same kind. Will you accept it?"

"Of course."

He feigned a frown. "There is one small point—"

Despite herself, she bristled. "Concerning what?"

"You did tell Stark that you kept company with mechanics. Since I fall in that classification, I intend to take advantage of your admission. May I call on you some Sunday? Perhaps for a walk on the Common, or—"

"God's truth," she laughed, "you are without a doubt the most forward printer's boy I've ever met. I've trapped myself, haven't I?"

"Indeed so, Mistress Anne."

She challenged him with her brown eyes. "Depending on degree, Mr. Kent, audacity can be an admirable quality in a man. Or an annoying one."

As he'd done yesterday, she was teasing—but fully so? He couldn't be sure.

"Which is it in my case?"

"Frankly, I haven't as yet decided." She glanced at his clothes. "Do you have a decent suit?"

"No. But I'll get one. I already made up my mind to that."

"Oh? When?"

"After you walked out yesterday," he lied. "Having taken me for an apprentice."

"There is really something unusual here, Mr. Kent," she said. She sounded neither antagonistic nor approving, only speculative.

"Care to expand on that for me, Mistress Ware?"

"Well, for one thing, you spoke to the grenadier as if you considered yourself as equal."

"I am his equal," Philip said. "What's unusual is a woman making that same declaration."

"Oh," she said with a smile, "I thought if the boor had any sort of education at all, the mere mention of John Locke would infuriate him."

"But you were quoting with feeling—and application to yourself."

"So I was. Are we discussing me, sir?"

"I thought it was Locke. I've read some of his writings—"

She looked surprised. "No wonder you took on so about being classed as an ordinary apprentice. What do you think of Mr. Locke's ideas?"

"Sometimes I think what he said was very correct."

"Not all the time?"

Philip frowned. "No. Not all the time. Finish what you started to say. You called my behavior unusual because I took that captain for an equal. Why not? Isn't that one of the central beliefs of your father's group?"

"Yes, but it was more than that. A look, a haughtiness—oh, I can't properly explain it. All smeared with ink, you still carry yourself almost like a lord. Perhaps—" She paused, that challenge in her gaze again. "Perhaps that's why

I would be intrigued to have you call. Provided you can indeed afford a proper broadcloth.''

He stared her down. "Be assured I'll steal one if I can't.''

Her breasts rose sharply as she drew in a breath. Was that heat coloring her cheeks? *Strange, prickly girl,* he thought, feeling physical attraction and something more. He admitted privately that he'd enjoy confronting her with the facts of his origins. How would she treat him then? How would she react? He looked forward to finding out—

"All in order," Lawyer Ware said as he bustled up to them. He pressed the proofs into Philip's hand. Anne said to him:

"Mr. Edes' assistant has asked for permission to call, father.''

"Annie," Ware said with another sigh, "that prattle from Locke, Esquire, about a 'standing rule' is all very nice. But ever since your dear mother died, it's been increasingly obvious that I have no voice in such matters. I wish you luck, Mr. Kent. If she takes a mind, my daughter can be quite like gentle Shakespeare's beautiful shrew.''

"I'll stand the risk with pleasure, Mr. Ware," Philip answered, touching his forehead to the lawyer and directing a last bold glance at Anne as he turned to go. This time, she didn't seem to mind; she was watching him as if she still didn't know what to make of him.

On that score, he thought, they were decidedly even.

The last thing he heard as he passed through the door of the London Book-Store was the jovial Knox asking two artillery officers about the most effective ranges for mortar fire.

VI

PHILIP FOLLOWED the events of November 1772 by means of the stories he set and printed in the *Gazette.*

To the fury of Governor Hutchinson at Province House, Samuel Adams' town meeting convened on the second of the month, established a standing Committee of Correspondence and urged that similar committees be set up all over Massachusetts. Express riders pounding out across Roxbury Neck bore the news to other population centers.

By November's end, the Boston committee had begun to churn out a blizzard of position papers, which the *Gazette* duly summarized.

Adams himself penned a *State of Rights of the Colonists.* Dr. Joseph Warren, perhaps the most popular physician—as well as the most eligible and handsome bachelor—in all the town contributed a *List of Infringements and Violations of Those Rights.* Soon reports began to filter back into Boston that other committees were indeed being set up throughout Massachusetts, as well as in the large cities down the coast.

The men who tramped through the early winter snowfalls to meet up in Edes' Long Room were elated that they had opened permanent communications with men of like temperament in other colonies. Their excitement brought to mind Warren's quotation of Franklin's remark about thirteen clocks striking as one. If the clocks were not yet chiming in harmony, certainly they were all ticking.

Besides keeping track of political developments, Philip had more personal interests. He hoarded his shillings, visited tailor shops to price merchandise and

finally, impatient, asked Edes for an advance against wages that would put him in the printer's debt for nearly half a year.

A few days after the bells in the steeple of Christ's Church had rung the New Year of 1773, he was suitably outfitted in a modest but neat brown suit of broadcloth, his outfit complete with snowy neckcloth, hose and buckled shoes. On a Sunday afternoon of thaw and mellow sunshine, he turned into Launder Street to call the bluff—if bluff it had been—of Mistress Anne Ware.

As he climbed the stoop of the handsome house, a cloud crossed the January sun. In the brief, chilly shadow, he thought of Alicia. He thought of her with sadness—and a question.

Was his interest in the attractive and somehow formidable lawyer's daughter only a convoluted way of circumventing memories of Alicia? Memories that still disturbed him?

Finding no ready answer within himself, he knocked at the Wares' front door.

___3
September Fire

LOOKING SERENE and beautiful in a white gown, Anne Ware sat waiting in the parlor to which Lawyer Ware ushered the young caller. The afternoon sunlight slanting through the front bays from Launder Street lit her skin and made it glow like dark amber.

She gave Philip a cordial smile that might have concealed just a tiny bit of amusement at his expense. Philip's new clothing itched. His fidgeting showed it.

"Good afternoon, Mistress Ware," he said. His voice sounded hoarse.

She inclined her head. "Good afternoon, Mr. Kent. Won't you be seated?"

He rushed to one of the chairs with embroidered cushions placed around the room. Lawyer Ware acted almost as nervous as Philip himself, rubbing his hands, shifting his weight from foot to foot and blinking his pop eyes. He hurried to the hall door, saying:

"I'll see whether the tea's ready. We serve nothing stronger in this house on the Lord's day." With that, he vanished.

Dust motes swirled slowly in the sunbeams falling athwart Anne's white lap, where her hands lay folded, composed. She continued to regard Philip with that faintly amused expression.

"Your suit is quite handsome," she said finally. "I did wonder whether you'd keep your vow."

"When the goal's worth gaining—always." Damn, how the girl unsettled him!

Was this merely a charade on her part? A little diversion, to be joked about with friends later? He could almost hear her describing how a bumpkin of a printer's boy had twitched and quivered in her parlor, ill at ease and more than slightly red-faced. The angering thought produced a rash promise. He'd see that tanned and softly rounded body revealed—and submissive to him—before he was done.

Matching her smile as best he could, he asked, "I trust you had a pleasant Sabbath morning?"

"If you call a one-hour prayer and a four-hour sermon pleasant," she sighed. "We're Congregationalists. I think our preachers don't believe in overcoming sin so much as in making the faithful too exhausted to be able to think about it. Do you profess or practice a faith?"

"No, neither. My mother was French. Born Catholic. But because of her—her early career, she was excluded from the rites of the church. She was an actress in Paris," he added, with unmistakable pride.

"An actress! How fascinating. I've begged Papa to let me go see the traveling troupes that play Boston. But such entertainments are considered wicked worldliness in our denomination—"

"I thought you did as you pleased, Mistress Anne."

She colored just a little. "So I do—up to a certain point."

"And what determines that point, may I ask?"

"Prudence. Common sense. You expressed it a moment ago. Is the goal worth gaining?" Her quick glance held a meaning he didn't fully understand. "Is it worth going beyond the prescribed limit? Risking turmoil, disapproval—?"

As if she didn't like the path the conversation was taking, she veered off: "You mentioned Paris, I thought I detected a touch of an accent in your speech. I recall you said you came to the colonies from France—"

"After some difficult months in England. I was trying to claim an inheritance—"

"Where did you learn the language so well?"

"In Auvergne. My mother hired a tutor. He was the one who introduced me to Locke's writings. And Rousseau's. The preparation was wasted, though. My father was a member of the nobility. But he—" Well, why not admit it? "—he never married my mother. So his family—" Another wary pause "—refused to honor the claim. When they caused trouble for me, I took a ship here to start a new life."

He expected her to mock him with laughter, or at very least with the amusement which came so readily to her brown eyes. So he was unsettled even further when it didn't happen. Instead, she clapped her hands together and cried softly:

"You've just explained the very cloud of mystery I said hovered around you! The way you faced that loutish grenadier—the way you strut a bit—" She extended one hand quickly. The gesture tautened the white fabric across her breasts. "Please, I don't intend that in an insulting way. You have a pride about you that sets you apart. That's good. I'd love to hear more about your adventures in England. How do they color your outlook toward what's happening here? The agitation against the Crown, I mean?"

Quietly, Philip said, "I despise my father's family and everything they stand for. They destroyed my mother's health and peace of mind."

"Was she with you in England?"

"Yes. She died on the ship that brought us to Boston."

"Oh, I'm indeed sorry."

"If I could, Mistress Anne—"

"We can use first names, can't we, Philip?"

A stiff nod. Then: "If I could, I'd go back to England and take everything that's mine. And I'd cause the family pain doing it."

Anne studied his stark face a moment. All trace of her earlier amusement was gone. She asked:

"I don't quite understand. Do you want to be one of them? Or do you simply want to see them brought down? Humiliated?"

"A little of both, I think." It was the most honest answer he could give. And for a moment it produced troubling memories of pledges made to Marie. Pledges now almost completely forgotten.

Anne pondered his reply, said, "Even with your explanation, you're still a puzzle, Philip."

"In what way?"

"You work for Ben Edes, who is certainly no partisan of the aristocracy. Yet you suggest that if given the opportunity, you'd return to England—"

"Oh, there's no real possibility of that. I've made up my mind to find my place here."

"Out of desire? Or necessity?"

"I'll give you the same answer as before. A little of both."

"That kind of position may not be tenable much longer, you know."

"Because of the trouble Mr. Adams keeps predicting? And trying to bring about?"

She nodded. "He's only hastening the inevitable. The people of these colonies are going to have to make a decision. The King is determined to work his will. And for all his questionable methods, I think Mr. Adams is correct about one thing. A small oppression only precedes a larger one. A small nibbling away of liberty will only encourage King George's ministers to take a larger bite. And another, and still another. That's what the Committee of Correspondence is trying to impress on the other colonies—what happens in Boston could very well happen to them. So we must stand together."

She said it all quietly. But she impressed Philip with her seriousness. He thought briefly of Alicia, contrasting Anne Ware's calm-spoken idealism with the frank lack of it displayed by the Earl of Parkhurst's daughter—

A tea tray rattled. Philip looked up to see Lawyer Ware entering, followed by his cook, whom Philip had met at the door on his first visit to Launder Street. The cook was a young, buxom girl with bright red hair and a cheery face. Ware introduced her as Daisy.

The cook put the tray down and began to pour tea into delicate china cups edged with pale blue. When Daisy had finished and retired, Ware hoisted his cup in a small gesture suggesting a toast.

"Will you drink with us to the resistance of tyranny, young man? I should perhaps note that we are drinking smuggled Dutch tea. We'll have none of the damned stuff from England, so long as it still carries that intolerable threepence tax."

Nothing, it seemed, could escape the taint of politics, Philip thought as he raised the steaming cup to his lips, not even a rather awkward Sunday visit in a dark-paneled, comfortable old room from whose chimney piece an oil portrait of a bearded man in severe black stared down.

"I'll drink to your hospitality too, sir." Philip said, and did.

He stayed only half an hour longer. During that time, Lawyer Ware held forth on the various abuses and, as he called them, crimes of the North ministry. At the end of a pause in the diatribe, Philip stood up quickly and announced that he had to leave.

Ware rose in turn. "Your company's been most welcome." He started to the door with Philip. But Anne, rising smoothly from her chair, touched Ware's arm.

"Finish your tea, Papa. I'll see our visitor out."

Sun through the front fanlight lit her eyes and her chestnut hair as she walked with him to the entrance. He felt embarrassed by the entire experience. He didn't have the proper graces or training to hold his own in this kind of social encounter. He had an urge to flee as swiftly as possible, back to more suitable surroundings—the cellar room at Edes'.

Anne said, "I thank you for coming to call, Philip."

"I enjoyed it." His words were forced.

They stood close together for a moment, bodies nearly touching. Where was the shrew Ware had spoken of? he wondered. He saw only the whiteness of Anne's smile—the loveliness of her brown eyes.

She said, "You're welcome to come again."

To his own astonishment, he found himself replying, "Thank you. I will."

And as he set off through the slushy streets under the pale January sun, he felt exhilarated all at once. Ashamed of his earlier desire to run.

But one crucial question remained. What in heaven attracted him to the girl? Beyond the obvious physical excitement produced by too long a period of celibacy?

Anne Ware was aligned on the side of the patriots, of that there was no doubt. She had subtly but unmistakably challenged him as to where he stood. He didn't honestly know.

Well, perhaps that explained it—

Anne Ware was a kind of mirror. One in which he might, with luck, at last discern a clear image of himself.

On top of that, she was poised, intelligent, strong-minded. He was curious as to how she'd come by her independence of thought and action. She wasn't extreme about it—but if personal experience, her father and Edes could be believed, she was still clearly different from the typical young woman of Boston. The curiosity he felt added yet one more dimension of intrigue—

As did the fact that she was damned attractive.

Whistling, he quickened his step. *I'll bed her before it's done, damned if I won't,* he thought.

II

PHILIP DID not know the precise and complete implications of the word *courting,* a common term in the Americas. But in the months that followed, he gradually assumed that he was involved in the process.

He became a frequent visitor at the house in Launder Street. And the attorney's daughter, in turn, was almost always the bearer of Ware's essays delivered to the *Gazette*.

They walked abroad in Boston a good deal as the winter waned and the mild heat of spring lay over the city. In Sabbath twilight, they would often turn into Hanover Square, where the paper lanterns of the patriots glowed on the huge Liberty oak. The lanterns were constantly torn down by the royal troops or Crown sympathizers. But new ones always appeared to illuminate thinly veiled threats against the Tories from Joyce Jun'r., or broadsides carrying news of the patriot cause.

How the Virginia House of Burgesses had established an eleven-man Corre-

spondence Committee on the Adams model, for instance. That was important, Anne explained, because the more conservative planters of tidewater Virginia did not carry the taint of extreme radicalism that the New Englanders did. When men of property and status—she named *Henry* and *Jefferson* and *Washington* and *Richard Henry Lee,* all unfamiliar—heeded Adams' warnings and set up machinery to maintain communication with Massachusetts, the cause of liberty had been significantly advanced.

Once, as they were strolling at the Common on a late Sunday afternoon, a half-dozen British officers galloped by, racing their splendid horses across the open grass. One man thundered past, then reined in long enough to look back and verify the identity of Anne and her companion.

Holding his snorting horse in check, Captain Stark did not speak to them. But his glance at Philip said all that was necessary. The flesh around his chin scar looked livid white as he dug in his spurs and galloped off after his hallooing companions. A small, ragged boy who had been sitting against a nearby elm scooped up a stone and slung it after the rider:

"Dirty shitting lobsterback!"

Philip hadn't thought of the grenadier captain since the meeting at the London Book-Store. But today's chance encounter told him Stark had not forgotten their exchange. Nor fogiven Philip's insolence.

As the captain rode out of sight, Anne slipped her arm through Philip's—and smiled. He was immensely pleased. It was the first time, in all the weeks of their strolls and conversations, that she had touched him.

Given extra confidence by that touch, he attempted to kiss her when they returned to the dusky shadows of the stoop at Launder Street. She averted her mouth, so his lips only brushed her cheek. Then she slipped inside with a murmured word of farewell.

The kiss had been a letdown. Eminently unsatisfying. *Damn woman!* he thought as he trudged back to Dassett Alley. *Always in perfect control of the situation.*

Perhaps, he decided wryly, that was why he kept returning to see her.

And would no doubt continue to do so.

III

"MR. KENT where is Ben Edes? This must be printed immediately!"

The querulous voice brought Philip out from behind the press, to see Sam Adams at the door, shaking with something more than his perpetual palsy.

The man's breath smelled rancid. His threadbare waistcoat bore numerous wine and food stains. He looked, in short, as disreputable as ever. And yet he was a figure of commanding presence as he thrust a sheet into Philip's hand. The ink was still damp.

Outrageous Affront to Englishmen's Liberties! proclaimed the heading of the short composition. Philip said, "Mr. Edes is up in the Long Room talking with Mr. Hancock, sir—"

Adams snatched the paper back. "Then they must both see it personally. The damned rumors were true after all. North's inviting disaster—*and* giving us precisely what I've hoped for!"

"How, Mr. Adams?" Philip asked as the other scuttled for the stairs.

The older man wheeled back, his slate-blue eyes almost maniacal with glee.

"With tea, young man. With their Goddamn tea! A packet brought the news just this morning. A bill passed in London not thirty days ago—twenty-seven April to be exact—granting the rotten East India Company a virtual monopoly in the colonial tea trade. To shore up the company's foundering finances, the export duties which East India previously paid in England have been canceled. And hencefoth, no tea may be sold here save by the exclusively appointed agents of the firm. Even paying the threepence tax on this side, the company will be able to undercut the prices of both smuggler's tea and that sold by law-abiding Tory merchants. *Now* we'll see the damned conservative businessmen admit I've been right in saying danger to one citizen—or one colony—is danger to all."

"But why would they pass such a measure?" Philip asked. "It's bound to be unpopular."

"They want to test us again! And they have no guilt whatsoever about using the law to rescue the privileged scoundrels who've manipulated the East India Company into near-bankruptcy. Damme, it's an issue with real teeth—and they'll feel the bite, by God!"

In a transport of delight, Adams clattered up the stairs.

Philip recalled hearing Burke and Franklin discuss a proposed scheme to shore up the trading concern. Now the scheme had become a reality. Whether it would indeed provide Adams and his associates with the clear-cut issue they desired remained to be seen.

With a May breeze blowing through the open front door of Edes and Gill, Philip had trouble getting excited about the turn of events. The warm air, redolent of the salt sea and the green ripening of spring, filled his mind with erotic images of Anne Ware. The images persisted as he went back to the press and listlessly resumed printing a commercial handbill.

But in ten minutes, Ben Edes, Adams and the elegant Hancock came clattering downstairs. Philip was put to work setting type for a broadside that was nailed to the Liberty Tree by sundown.

IV

THE HEAT of early summer brought further intensification of the crisis of colonies against Crown.

In England, Dr. Franklin had somehow come into possession of a packet of letters penned by Governor Hutchinson and the Massachusetts Provincial Secretary, Andrew Oliver, to a member of the North ministry. The letters contained a frank, even brutal appraisal of the character and activities of the Boston radicals.

Franklin sent copies of the letters back to Adams, who was apparently supposed to honor Franklin's original promise to the supplier of the letters that they would be kept confidential.

But that was Franklin's promise, not Adams'. The latter read every one to a secret session of the legislature, then promptly set the Edes and Gill press to work printing the full texts.

The letters revealed and damned Governor Hutchinson as deceitful. They exposed him as a man who was publicly trying to maintain an image of sympathy with the colonists, while at the same time privately advising London to deal with

the rebel ringleaders in the only appropriate fashion—harshly. One letter contained the bald assertion that *"there must be some abridgement of what is called English liberty."*

Laboring night after night at the press, with Ware, Warren, Revere and other members of the Long Room group coming and going constantly with new pamphlets, broadsides, articles for the *Gazette,* Philip soon realized that Adams had indeed found sparks he could fan into a blaze.

The Hutchinson letters were kindling. But the real fuel was the tea monopoly.

Governor Hutchinson talked of appointing one of his nephews as the agent and consignee for Boston. Immediately, as Adams had predicted, Tory merchants found themselves economically motivated to add their outcries to those of the liberals. One merchant actually wrote an article for the *Gazette* which said, in part, *"America will be prostrate before a monster that may be able to destroy every branch of our commerce, drain us of all our property and wantonly leave us to perish by the thousands!"* Philip marveled. The temporarily converted Tory sounded almost as rebellious as old Samuel himself.

Anne Ware was exhilarated by what she called this major blunder on the part of King George's ministers. She predicted to Philip that Adams would orchestrate the issue to a crescendo of protest—and even to open hostilities. The mobs might be roaming Boston again very soon—

But it annoyed Philip considerably that the tea matter was virtually all Anne wanted to talk about when they took their Sabbath walks.

In an attempt to divert her from the constant preoccupation with politics, Philip counted his wages, decided he could afford to spend four shillings and invited Anne to go with him on a Saturday night in late June to view Mrs. Hiller's popular waxworks on Clark's Wharf. Early evening found them outside the stile at the door of the clapboard building, Philip handing the admission of two shillings per person to a ragged boy fidgeting on a stool.

The noise of the wharf faded as they turned the stile and pushed through curtains into the lamplit hall. Elegant duplications of England's kings and queens were ranged on pedestals, the sequins and gold threads and shimmering velvets of their costumes picking up the glow of smoky lamps hung from the ceiling beams. Anne and Philip walked slowly past the first of the curiously lifelike figures whose wax eyes stared unseeing into the lamplight and shadow. There was strong-jawed Arthur of legend, with Excalibur. A handsome Richard Lionheart in crusader's mail. A villainous, humpbacked John. And many more.

But Mrs. Hiller's had only a few customers tonight. Perhaps it was the weather. A muggy mist had settled on the harbor, and the atmosphere was twice as stifling inside. It seemed to affect Anne's mood. She was almost as remote as the frozen image of Queen Elizabeth in her starched white neck ruff. Anne stood staring at the queen, not really seeing her—

"This isn't appealing, is it?" Philip asked finally. He was sweaty and thoroughly uncomfortable in his good suit. "We needn't stay—"

"Oh, yes, let's see the whole exhibit," Anne responded, though without much enthusiasm, he felt. She pointed. "There's our current monarch. I'm surprised Mrs. Hiller hasn't thrown him off the end of the pier."

Two patrons moved past them in the half-light, casting grotesque shadows on the not too clean floor. Under another lantern, they paused before the pudgy-faced, pink-lipped statue of a young George III. He looked boyish, benign, utterly harmless in a splendid suit of pale blue satin and a neatly powdered wig.

The King's cheeks glistened. The wax melting in the heat, perhaps. On the pedestal someone had scrawled an obscene epithet.

Philip shook his head after a long moment of silence. "No, I think we'd better go. Your mind's elsewhere."

She turned, apologetic. "Truly, it is. I'm sorry."

He couldn't resist a little sarcasm: "Shall we stroll up the wharf and discuss tea again?"

"It's poor Mr. Revere I'm concerned about. He dropped in this afternoon with the porringer he repaired for Papa. He looked exhausted. I don't think he spoke ten words."

That, at least, Philip understood. Revere had been to Edes and Gill hardly at all during the preceding month. Early in May, his wife, Sara, had died. Ben Edes said her death had left him devastated.

"Sara Revere shouldn't have borne that last child in December," Anne said. "Isanna came into the world sickly, and my father predicts she won't live long either." She looked at Philip in a peculiar, searching way. "Mrs. Revere was only thirty-six. A year older than my own mother when she died. They say a married woman loses a tooth for every baby. Sara lost many more than that—and life too. That's too high a price to pay for being what the world expects of a woman."

"A wife and mother, you mean?"

Anne nodded. "I want a family of my own. But not at the expense of destroying myself."

"I did get the feeling you took exception to the way a young woman of Boston is supposed to behave." He meant it as a mild joke. The strained expression that came onto her face showed him he'd made an error.

"There's more to living than babies and kitchens and seeing to the furniture!" Anne exclaimed softly. "That's all my mother had. It killed her."

"When—" he hesitated, almost reluctant to ask, "—when was that?"

"In sixty-four."

"I never thought to ask you before, Anne—did you ever have any brothers or sisters?"

"One younger brother, Abraham, Junior. He lived only three months."

"What caused your mother's death?"

Again her eyes seemed to reach through him toward some haunted past.

"The smallpox. There was a terrible epidemic. Almost five thousand people died here in town. Nearly fifty of them from the preventive measure that was supposed to save them. My mother was one of those."

"What kind of preventive measure?"

Running her hand absently along the shabby velvet rope that separated them from the waxworks, she answered, "Back in the year 1721, another epidemic struck. A Dr. Boylston and the Reverend Cotton Mather argued that the only way to save lives was to give prospective victims a light case of the pox by a new method called inoculation. The selectmen of Boston considered that heresy then. But by sixty-four, they were willing to try the idea. My mother took the venom drawn from a pox victim. Took it in the prescibed way—on the point of a needle, directly into a wound cut in her arm. But she developed no light case. She died of it." After a moment, she finished, "Papa never blamed the physicians. The idea was sound. Many more were saved than perished. I think my mother was ready to die. I think she had died long before, really—"

Her voice trailed off as she stroked the rope, staring at Farmer George's

bulging wax eyes. Philip felt he might be close to some understanding of this girl's unusual spirit and independence, closer than he'd ever been before. He asked:

"Will you explain that, Anne?"

She looked at him. "Explain what killed her? The same thing that killed Sara Revere. Having the world limit what a woman is allowed to do. Rear babies. Supervise servants. Think no independent thoughts of any consequence—I vowed it would never be the same with me."

"Knowing you, I'd guess it won't."

"But it takes struggle, Philip. Society doesn't change quickly—" Her eyes fixed on his. "Would you like me to show you what destroyed my mother?"

Before he could answer, another female voice boomed out:

"Dear Annie Ware! For heaven's sake—!"

A stout, cheery-faced woman of middle age appeared from the murky shadows at the rear of the hall. Approaching, she clasped Anne's hand between both of her own.

"I haven't seen my favorite pupil in ages. How have you been? Why don't you ever call on me?"

"I do apologize, Mrs. Hiller. It's very nice to see you again." She inclined her head toward Philip. "Let me introduce my friend Mr. Kent. This is Mrs. Hiller, who owns the exhibit—"

Deflated, Philip said, "I should have realized—you've been here before."

"Many times," Mrs. Hiller smiled. "Though generally upstairs, where I conduct my private school for young ladies. Annie excelled in feather and quill work. Embroidery too. But her heart was never in it, I could tell. That's what comes of spending too much time among her father's books!" Behind her smile, the older woman was scolding.

"Yes," Anne said, "Papa's still disappointed that I learned the feminine arts but never do much about practicing them."

"No doubt that will change when you're suitably wed," Mrs. Hiller replied, glancing quickly at Philip. He felt hotter than ever. The stout woman went on, "Too much learning is a hindrance, not a help, in the pantry and the nursery and the drawing room, my dear. Just remember—a man of substance doesn't wed a woman because she has a dominant spirit. The opposite! Wives must be submissive."

Anne sighed. "Then I imagine I'm not destined to marry."

"That could well be your unhappy fate," Mrs. Hiller advised, "*unless* you alter your outlook." But she couldn't conceal her fondness for her former student. Patting Anne's hand again, she said, "Still, you were and are a fine, charming girl. Do come to visit some afternoon, won't you?"

"Yes, I'll try."

"Good. Now if you'll excuse me, I must go see whether that rascal at the stile has sneaked off for a gill of rum again—" Skirts rustling, she hurried up the aisle.

Philip said, "Anne, I wouldn't have brought you here if I'd known you'd seen the exhibit before—"

"Oh, I always enjoy it. And it's been a long while. As Mrs. Hiller said, I most often saw the schoolrooms on the second floor. Poor Papa. I'm afraid he wasted all that money. I detest embroidery!" She smiled. "I hope I haven't spoiled your evening, Philip."

"No. But you've shown me some more mysteries about yourself."

"Mysteries?"

He nodded, began, "Sometimes I think I understand you—"

"Which is more than I can honestly say about you," she teased. "I press and press, and you won't tell me a thing about your time in England."

On guard, he waved: "That's all past. Of no consequence. Let's get some air, shall we?"

They left the waxworks hall. But it was almost as humid on the pier outside. Torches had been lit at dusk. The warm, clammy mist off the ocean still obscured details. Pale yellow faces loomed as they walked; men and women and some youngsters gathered around a balance master performing on a pole nailed to a pair of kegs set far apart. Applause rang out, and a few coins were tossed on a barrel head as the pole walker executed a crisp turn on one foot.

The crowd faded into the mist behind. Far away, a bell buoy clanged. Anne stopped abruptly.

"I asked earlier whether you'd like to see why I've become such a scandalous person."

"It's something that can be shown, then?"

"In a way. We'll have to walk about half a mile up the waterfront—"

"Lead on. While we go, tell me how many different schools you attended. You mentioned grammar school once, didn't you?"

"Yes. And dame school before that. Dame schools are run by women for very young children. From grammar school, boys can enter a university. Girls must go to academies like Mrs. Hiller's. Papa thought he was doing me a service sending me there. His heart was in the proper place. But I learned as much or more from his library—starting with the required books for moral guidance. Mr. Bunyan's works. The Reverend Mather's sermons—"

"Then you graduated to Mr. Locke—and politics?"

"I did. I won't spend my life as my mother spent hers. I'll observe the proprieties when it's necessary. But that doesn't mean I can't think, can't have a role in something besides—besides childbearing that makes all your teeth fall out!"

Philip wanted to laugh. But that anguished tone had come into her voice again. He decided it might be better to let the subject drop until they reached the destination that would supposedly explain something about her free spirit, a spirit that her father clearly could not control beyond a certain limit.

As they walked along through the thick, swirling mist, he lost track of their surroundings. All at once he saw a spot of yellow ahead. The cobbled street ended. He heard water lapping nearby. It was nearly dark. Anne took his arm:

"Careful of the mud. I must stop at the watchman's hut before we go in."

Puzzled, Philip accompanied her toward the yellow blur that brightened to reveal a bent, white-haired man hobbling out of a rickety little shanty. The man raised his lantern.

"Who goes? Speak up!"

"Only me, Elihu."

The man had to be at least seventy. Watering eyes glistened in the lamp's glow. The wrinkled face broke into a smile of cracked teeth and ruined gums.

"Mistress Anne! You've not been here since a year ago—no, more like two. How are you, girl?"

"Fine. Just fine, Elihu."

"And your good father?"

"In excellent health, thank you. Though he still works too hard. This is a friend—Mr. Kent. May I show him a little of the yard?"

"Why, 'course," the watchman nodded. "I don't care who's supposed to own it—far's I'm concerned, the whole place is still Abner Sawyer's. Send up a yell if you lose your way."

"We won't," Anne smiled. "I know the yard too well."

Taking a firmer grip on Philip's arm, she led him from the hut toward a gate. A huge, crudely painted sign hung between the uprights:

SAWYER SHIP-YARD

Anne stopped just beneath the sign, pointed upward.

"My mother's maiden name was Sawyer. This belonged to her father—all of it. Once."

Slowly she disengaged her hand, walked on with a strange, melancholy expression on her face, as if the past, like the mist, was closing around her.

Philip followed. He passed tall stacks of lumber, great piles of raw logs, saw Anne stop ahead. He came up quickly behind her. She caught his arm again:

"Careful!"

This time she pointed downward. One more step and he'd have tumbled into a rectangular pit that looked nearly as deep as a man. Beyond it, great ghostly U-shaped ribs loomed up like the bones of some primeval monster. Only a moment later did he recognize what looked like the inside of *Eclipse*, minus its hull planking: the keel and ribs of a sailing vessel under construction on one of three timbered ways that inclined toward the unseen water.

"You nearly walked into the saw pit," Anne told him. "One or two men work down there, two more up here. With crosscut saws they turn logs into sixty-foot planks that'll eventually form the hull for that sloop."

"And your grandfather owned this business?"

She nodded. "He came from England in 1714, indentured to another yard owner. His home was Plymouth. His father and his grandfather before him had worked in the shipyard saw pits. I think that's how the family came to be called Sawyer. English families took names from their work—Carter, Miller, Carpenter—oh, there must be dozens. Even though my grandfather was a landsman, he loved the sea. He loved building ships. But Plymouth had all the yards it needed, so he sailed to America. By the time my mother was born in 1729, he had his dream—his own yard. He was only twenty-five, but he worked very hard to be a success. He was. But he and his wife had no other children except my mother. That was the difficulty—"

She started walking again, the mist swirling around her. They circled the end of the saw pit where crossbeams were planted in the ground to support the long logs to be cut by the saw working back and forth from above and below. Anne wandered toward the skeleton of the vessel on the ways. The huge ribs towered above them as Philip stood at her side, letting her speak because he somehow knew she had to:

"This was my mother's playground from the time she could walk. She loved the place so much, I suppose it was only natural she thought she would own it one day. She never bargained on my grandfather being exactly like most other Englishmen. Disappointed that he didn't have a son. And accepting without question the fact that a woman could never be responsible for this sort of business. Running a yard is man's work—" A somber pause. Then:

"She told me she only asked him about it once. She was fifteen or sixteen. She wanted to know when she could start taking over. Be his assistant. She knew the routine as well as he did. How to scarf the lengths of keel together. Exactly what had to be done to frame up properly. Planking, dubbing, caulking—she knew it all, because she'd helped the men do it. So she asked. She said Grandfather Sawyer never laughed so hard in his life. Laughed till the tears ran on his face. He simply couldn't believe she was serious. He meant no unkindness. He was a man of his times, that's all. But I think he started killing her that very day. Although it's the last thing he would have done on purpose—"

Musing, her voice turned sad:

"Strange, the way people hurt each other. Unknowingly. Because custom says they must. Well—"

With another small shrug, she threw off the mood. "My grandfather's rebuff was a turning point. When my father courted my mother—he was fresh out of Harvard—she married him because she'd already given up her dreams. My grandfather sold the yard to another owner the year before he died in fifty-one. He gave Lawyer Ware and his wife part of the profits. It was a handsome gift. Grandfather never thought twice about refusing my mother the one gift she wanted most—but couldn't have because she was a woman. When I was small, she brought me here time and again, just to watch the workmen. Those were the only times I ever saw her truly happy. When we were leaving to go home, she'd almost always cry a little."

"Did your father know?"

"I'm not sure. If he did, I doubt if it concerned him much. A man's work is a man's, period."

"But why did she marry him if she felt the way she did?"

"She loved him. And—" bitterness then, "—she realized it was her only course. That a woman would even daydream about taking over this kind of business—she finally understood it was unthinkable. It still is. An establishment like Mrs. Hiller's—well, that's a bit different. Running a girl's school is accepted. It falls into a woman's prescribed sphere. My grandfather, from all I know of him, was a kind, loving man. So is my father. But they killed my mother all the same."

"So you're going another way. Reading Mr. Locke. Involving yourself in politics—"

"I'll involve myself in my husband's work, too, when—" She turned away "—when I know who he is."

"Anne, you're a damned unusual girl."

She laughed. "It has its price. I have no circle of young female friends my own age. And no gentlemen who've called more than once or twice—except you," she teased. "And you're French, and new to America, and probably don't know any better! Even though I attend church dutifully and observe most of the outward conventions, I am not entirely respectable, Philip."

At that moment he wanted to reach out and take her in his arms. He held back, a little in awe even yet. Sensing the awkwardness of the moment, she said:

"It's dark. We'd better go."

They walked away from the eerie ribs of the ship on the ways. They passed the hut where old Elihu had fallen asleep beside his lantern, and still Philip kept silent. She had partially explained herself at last; he understood why Lawyer Ware had sighed when she quoted Locke at the ill-mannered grenadier.

They left the shipyard and the sign towering into the mist. As they reached the

solid cobblestones, he concluded that a girl like Anne Ware could very well prove too much for most ordinary men.

But then, had he ever considered himself as ordinary? he thought with an inward smile.

They walked in easy, companionable silence to her home, only the distant cry of the watch disturbing the night—*"Eight o'clock of a foggy evening, eight o'clock!"* He kept mulling what she'd told him. Somehow it only increased his fascination with her, his attraction to her, physically and otherwise.

At the steps in Launder Street, she seemed in better spirits, to the point of smiling with real feeling.

"I thank you for the pleasant outing, Philip."

"I apologize again for dragging you somewhere you've been many times before. You should have told me—"

"Not at all. I appreciate how hard you worked for those four shillings. But I have a feeling I talked too much—and too frankly. Are you sure you want to continue associating with a young woman who insists on having thoughts of her own?"

His reply was instantaneous:

"I'm sure."

She laughed, a warm, rich sound. She leaned forward suddenly to give him a gentle kiss on the cheek.

The kiss, prim as it was, left him happier than he'd felt in many a month. He stood on the steps in the mist long after the door closed behind her.

V

THE WATER of the Charles River purled against the bow of the small rowboat. Philip had hired the boat for the afternoon. As he rowed, Anne chattered from her seat in the stern. She wore the gown of yellow sprigged muslin, the one that had first taken his fancy. A wicker hamper rested at her feet.

Gulls wheeled in the mellow September sky as Philip angled the boat toward the grassy hills on the peninsula opposite North Boston. It was a Saturday. With work momentarily slow at the printing house, he'd asked Ben Edes for the afternoon free. He was delighted when Edes consented, because picnicking was not considered a suitable pastime for the Sabbath.

Philip rowed past the neat, sunlit houses and the piers of the little village of Charlestown. The village occupied the southern point of the peninsula. But his eyes were drawn constantly to the green hills beyond. Breed's and Bunker's were the names of two of them.

Only a few white farm buildings dotted the rolling land. Somewhere on those slopes, he planned to make his intentions known to Anne. The demands of his mind and body had grown nearly intolerable during the stifling summer months.

"—and Mr. Adams is certain other ports will be involved too," she was saying. "There's talk that as much as half a million pounds of tea will be shipped to the agents of the East India Company. And that silly ass Hutchinson continues to swear the monopoly scheme will be enforced. It's glorious!"

"Good God, we're back to that again!" he groaned, only partly in jest. "I'm fairly sick of hearing tea, tea, tea!"

"But it's the rallying point we've needed so badly!" she said, brushing back

a lock of chestnut hair blowing in the Atlantic breeze. Further out to sea, whitecaps rolled toward the harbor islands. A pair of boys fishing off a Charlestown pier hailed them. Anne waved back, then said in her now-familiar tone of teasing:

"Besides, Philip, what do we have to talk about that's more interesting? That evening at the shipyard, I bored you to death talking about my family—"

"No, you didn't."

"—but we never seem to discuss your side of things. For months, I've kept trying to lure you into telling me more of your mysterious doings in England. All I get in return is silence and portentous looks. Fair's fair. I've revealed everything, yet your past is still locked up tight as a spinster's dowry chest. Don't you think we know each other well enough for confidences by now?"

"We know each other," he replied. "But hardly well enough." His lingering glance at her breasts, coupled with his sudden, bold smile, brought scarlet into her cheeks.

She patted her hair again. Nervously, he thought. His hope increased that the golden afternoon and the isolation of one of the farmers' hillsides would bring the result he so badly wanted.

Abruptly, Anne touched his hand where it gripped tight on the oar. "I don't mean it the way I think you do. Truly, Philip, I've puzzled over you night after night—"

"Any conclusions?"

"That something haunts you. Drives you."

"And you."

"Yes, but I've explained my—what do the French say?—my black beast. Can yours be so terrible you won't speak of it?"

Resting on the oars, he deliberated. He'd guarded the past overcautiously, perhaps. So, resuming his rowing, he told her.

Not in great detail. But enough. He did omit mention of his involvment with Alicia Parkhurst, and converted the motivation of Roger Amberly's attacks to hints that they had been inspired by Lady Jane. But even the story thus distorted held Anne silent with interest. By the time he beached the rowboat on the northeast point of the peninsula, she was studying him with a new, thoughtful understanding.

"Then I wasn't far off in my chance remark."

"What chance remark?"

"The one about your lordly ways. You really do have some credentials there. I wasn't entirely sure when you said as much the first time you came to our house."

"Yes, I've credentials, as you call them. Useless ones."

"Do you still have the letter from your father?"

"In my mother's casket. I keep it in my room. Worthless too, I suppose."

"But there's a kind of distant hope in your voice when you say that. Did you realize it?"

"No," he lied, clambering out onto the pebbled shore. He took her hand, felt her breast brush his arm as he assisted her from the rowboat. As he reached down for the hamper, she said:

"What is it you want, Philip?"

"You've asked me that before."

"Yes, but you didn't answer. Realistically, anyway. You've escaped the

family's reach, surely. You should be moving toward something now, not simply away. So what's the goal to be?''

"Food.''

She laughed. "All right. Shall we try Morton's Hill? It's pleasant. But answer my other question, if you will.''

As they climbed through the fragrant long grass, he responded at last, "I'd say I want to be a man of property one day. Own my own printing house—''

"Then go back to England and flaunt your position to those people? As you told your mother you would before she died?''

"To be realistic, as you call it, I think that's out of the question.''

Half way to the summit of the hill, she touched him again, brought him facing around so that he saw her framed against the late summer green of the hilly pastures, and the church spires, the jumbled rooftops, the harbor masts of Boston across the river. Some of those masts belonged to an English naval squadron.

"Even yet you don't sound certain, Philip.''

"Well, then, dammit, maybe I'm not.''

"Do you recall what I've said before—echoing Mr. Adams? A time comes to everyone when a choice must be made. A direction must be taken. You can't evade that forever.''

He was disconcerted by the firmness with which she spoke; even though their ages were the same, at the moment she seemed the more adult. Perhaps it was because her own direction was already charted.

"Yes, I'm aware that you know where you're going. A husband you can live beside. Not just raising children but working with him to make a success of his trade, his profession—''

"Oh, but that won't come immediately,'' she said, starting to climb the hill again. "It can't, even if—the proper man should drop from heaven this minute. The future's too uncertain. The questions that obsess Papa and Mr. Adams and the others must be decided before any of us are free to pursue other ends. One of my goals is to see that happen. To help it happen, if I can.''

"You really do have conviction about the cause, don't you?''

"Yes. You know I won't retreat from the world like women are supposed to do. And I not only love my father, I respect most of his ideas. Except for the ones concerning the female's role!''

"You seem to have gotten around that obstacle,'' Philip said, wry. "He lets you have your head—go where you wish—doesn't he?''

"True. The dear man realized that battle was lost a long time ago. Seriously, Philip—when it comes to the law, politics, he's a solid thinker. That's influenced me to place importance where he places it. I've thought matters over for myself, too. Or tried. Resistance is right and proper. I should think all you experienced in England would bring you to the same conclusion. The world *is* changing. People won't permit themselves to be put upon by kings or persons of privilege any longer. You mentioned that tutor you had in France. He knew choice was inevitable, didn't he?''

Philip nodded. "I think so. I'll make mine one of these days.''

"Unless you wait too long and have it forced on you by the pressures of the moment. Believe me, I've read enough history in Papa's library to know that chance plays its part. But I think it's better that a man—or a woman—make a choice by his or her own will, not simply be thrust along by events, willy-nilly.''

"Anne—'' He scanned the shimmering hilltop, the hazed sky beyond, set the hamper in the grass. "I've made one.''

"What is it?"

"To tell you I care for you very much." The wind whispered through a moment of silence. "That I want you very much."

Flushing again, she picked up the hamper. "Let's go on to the top. The mutton won't be good if we don't soon—"

"Anne."

He tightened his hold on her forearm, then took her other arm as well. Slowly, he pulled her down beside him in the wind-rustling grass.

He slipped an arm around her shoulder, the excitement in his own flesh relentless now. From the tiny glisten of perspiration on her upper lip he guessed she was experiencing a similar reaction.

"I've waited months for a time like this, Anne."

"Philip, I can't. I mean—"

She stopped as he thrust her backward in the grass, cushioning her with his arm. She didn't resist. But there was a flicker of unhappiness in her brown eyes as he stretched out beside her, brought his face down close to hers and kissed her.

He touched her mouth tenderly, marveling at its soft warmth. Then he raised up on one elbow. She gazed at him, looking almost frightened. Her voice sounded small:

"I knew that if we came here—somehow I knew that we—*oh.*"

Giving that strange, almost sad little murmur of surrender, she closed her eyes and lay very still.

He bent close again, stroked the softness of her hair, the sun a fire on the back of his neck. The fire spread through him as he brought his hip against hers.

She still didn't pull away. But there was a resistance, a tension in her that he could feel. Fear?

He kissed her again. This time, her mouth responded. One of her arms stole around his neck. His shirt touched her breasts. She moaned softly, turning against him, clasping him tighter while they kissed with the ardor of the young and the heat of the golden September—

Hidden in the meadow grass, the world lost except for the faraway clank of a cow's bell, they kissed a long time. His mouth caressed her eyelids, the fragrant strands of her hair. The grass was heady with the perfumes of autumn, but no headier than her breath when, at last, her lips parted and he tasted her sweet mouth—

Another surprised little cry deep in her throat told him she'd felt the change in his body. Felt it because they lay so close together, nothing separating them except rumpled clothing. A boatman on the river hailed someone. The sun blazed, showering down gold light to drown them in warmth, to stoke the quick-breathing eagerness of mouths, the tremble of hands exploring—

For Philip there was no holding back. The blood-tide was running too high. He began to tug at the hem of her yellow muslin skirt. He thought she started to draw away, make a sound—perhaps a word of negation—but with the hammer of his own heartbeat so loud in his ears, he couldn't clearly tell.

The skirt came upward. His hands sought her. Warm, private places tingled his fingertips. He felt passion change her body, as his had changed—

The meadow grass rippled in the wind, a whispering. Cries of gulls drifted from the harbor. The hot light poured down as her own hands moved over him—and his grew bolder—

Jolted, he rolled back a second after she pulled away.

She thrust down her skirt as his eyes flared with anger. Sitting up, she brushed off her bodice. She wouldn't look at him.

"For God's sake, Anne, what's the matter?"

"Philip, this was foolish. Foolish and wrong. I shouldn't have come with you. I shouldn't have let you think—oh, dear heaven, please forgive me?"

A hint of tears showed in the corners of her dark eyes. He stood up, his hair ribbon loosened in the tumbling. The ribbon snapped in the breeze as he gazed down at her. He was trembling from fury, from astonishment, from the sudden chilling of the September sun.

"You're denying you want the same thing I do?"

"I—Philip—"

"You can't deny it."

She clasped her hands around her knees, bowed her head. Her voice sounded as he'd never heard it before. Unsure:

"No, I can't. But—"

Abruptly her head came up. The autumnal sunlight caught fire in the tears streaking her cheeks. Yet he still recognized the Anne Ware he'd met on that first day in Mr. Henry Knox's bookshop.''

"But I will not have it."

"Oh," he shot back, almost snarling, "a man working his will on you—is that it? Well, by Christ, you'll never get any man to touch you if you insist on—*ah!*"

Angry at himself, he pivoted away. "I'm sorry." He dropped to his knees beside her, took both her hands in his. "From the way you kissed me—Anne, I *felt* what you wanted."

"Yes," she said, unsteadily, "that's true. It's a bright, hot day. We're safe here, we'd never be caught, but—Philip, I've loved no man yet, not that way, not in nineteen years. I—I can't do it so casually."

"Can't because a *man* wants it?"

"I don't blame you for anger—"

He stood up. "I just don't understand."

"—and you'll think me a prude—"

"You don't kiss like a prude. Anything but a prude. Anne—"

"Listen, please *listen!* It was my fault. I was foolish and wicked to lead you on. I didn't mean to do that—" The words spilled out rapidly now, as she dashed tears off her cheeks. "But when the time comes, there must be—there must be some other reason besides the heat of a September afternoon."

Glum, he felt his wrath fading away. He knew all too well what she meant: "Love."

The grass bent and rustled in the wind. All joy had gone out of the day. Anne's face remained averted:

"Yes. Otherwise, it's like the rutting of a slut and someone who's paid her. Do you understand that, Philip?"

The cries of the gulls rang in the distance, forlorn.

"I do. You want another choice out of me."

"No, I didn't ask for—"

"But it's what you want. What you must have—though you'll forgive me if I can't square the wish with other things you say."

"What things?"

"That talk about your mother, for instance. She married because it was the accepted way. She put herself in bondage. That was also love, wasn't it? You said it was—"

"Yes."

"And she died of it."

"Yes."

"Yet you want that same bondage? From a man? And for yourself too? Is that your much-touted liberty, Anne?"

"For my mother, marriage was—surrendering."

"Which is precisely what you're getting at, isn't it?"

"No. No, there's a difference. I don't know whether I can say it correctly— I'm not saying anything correctly—yes, loving someone is a bondage. But that kind of bondage—to a person, or even to an ideal—you enter it freely. You go *toward* it, you don't use it to escape something—"

"Pardon me, but the difference is pretty Goddamn subtle. How do you decide which kind is which?"

"You—just know. Does it fulfill you, or—or destroy you?"

Too upset to cope with such thoughts for long, he made a sharp gesture. "Well, you may be right. But whatever sort of choice you're after—fulfilling, destroying—running toward, running from—it's one I can't make."

This time her nod was heavy with sadness. "I'm not half clever enough. I think I already knew. And I still said yes to coming here. Realizing what might happen. Wanting—" Her head lifted; her eyes brimmed with sorrow. "—wanting it more than a little."

"Don't lie to me."

"I'm not! It's the truth! But I was terribly wrong to let it go so far—"

Kneeling beside her again, Philip put two fingers on her still-warm mouth. He was troubled and utterly miserable. He concealed it in the protection of a curt laugh:

"Don't score yourself. The error's mine, Mistress Ware. I'd forgotten just how infernally strong a female you are. What positive ideas you have about every sort of human action. You want to be sure of certain things, but to use your words, fair's fair. Don't I get the same privilege?"

"Of course. Of course you do."

"I do apologize for trying to work my will, as they call it. A mere man, demanding—"

"*Stop it, Philip!* I told you that has nothing to do with it."

He knew it didn't; he was ashamed he'd attacked her that way a second time.

To calm the churning of his own emotions, he tried to smile; it was a grimace. "Best we drop it. Here—" He speared the hamper, held it high. "Let's not waste the mutton and good sunshine."

"I—I'm still afraid you're angry—"

"I'm absolutely enraged with you, my girl. And the crazy thing is, that makes me want you all the worse. So bad I ache—damned if I know why. I should row back to Copp's Hill pier and leave you stranded. I guess I won't, though—"

"I'm surprised," she said with a rueful smile.

"Are you? Don't be. There—" He couldn't pretend; he could only speak the painful truth of his own heart. "—there's something in you I admire even when you turn me away. Maybe I admire you *because* you turn me away—I'm plagued if I know enough about women to figure it out! But in your own way, you're tougher than old Adams at his wildest. Come on."

He extended his other hand to assist her. She kept her hands at her sides.

As they started to climb again, he went on, "I wish I could lie to you, Anne.

I wish I could pretend I can give you what you say you've got to have. That'd bring everything to a nice, neat solution—"

"But I'd know you were lying—if you were."

"Bet you would at that," he sighed. "Well, anyway, I can't do it. Making promises is impossible."

She stopped and looked at him, her eyes so intense that he felt they reached and wrenched at whatever soul or central essence lay in the depths of his being:

"For now? Or forever?"

His mind swirled with memories of Kentland, of his mother, of what he could have been—and might yet still be. Damn heaven, what *did* he want?

He said, "Anne—I don't know."

Turning, he stalked on up toward the searing light of the hilltop.

He wished he could lose himself in that fire, be consumed, destroyed, relieved of thinking, of decisions, of trying to unlock the riddles of the whole damned world—and himself—

He managed to calm down and occupy his attention with opening the hamper. In a few moments, Anne joined him. She seated herself beside the cloth he'd spread. Her cheeks were reddened but the tears were gone.

As Philip unpacked the food, he said in an offhand way, "I imagine you'll want me to stop calling after this."

Her smile, though forced, puzzled him until she said:

"That's the last thing I want, Philip. Like these colonies, you'll make choices. One way or another, something will become of you. I'd like to find out what."

She glanced away. "However, the decision is yours."

VI

THEY PASSED the remainder of the afternoon in repetitious speculation about the tea crisis and empty pleasantries about the beauties of the early autumn weather. While he rowed her back to Boston in the twilight, neither of them said a word. He left her at the door in Launder Street with a quickly murmured goodbye, and without touching her.

He slept very little that night. The September afternoon had focused the question to unbearable sharpness: What was his ambition? His future? And how much of the choice would be his and how much the result of events he could not control?

Tossing restlessly, he concluded that he must be falling in love with Anne. Nothing else would explain his feeling so forlorn, furious and confused.

VII

EXPRESS RIDERS galloping in across Roxbury Neck in late October brought news that a mass meeting in Philadelphia had forced the resignation of the tea agents appointed for that city. A similar meeting was convened locally. But Governor Hutchinson's nephew and two of his sons who had been appointed to the potentially lucrative posts would not relent.

Adams and his followers thundered denunciations of the tea consignees. Called them traitors, enemies of America. To no avail.

Then, on the twenty-seventh of November, *Dartmouth*, the first of three vessels reported on the way to Boston with the hated cargo, was sighted offshore.

The following night, Philip and Benjamin Edes labored almost until dawn. They set, proofed and printed copies of a sheet circulated throughout the town and nailed to the Liberty Tree next morning:

FRIENDS!   BRETHREN!   COUNTRYMEN!

That worst of plagues, the detested tea, shipped for this port by the East India Company, is now arrived in this harbor; the hour of destruction or manly oppositions to the machinations of tyranny stares you in the face. Every friend to his country, to himself, and posterity is now called upon to meet at Faneuil Hall at nine o'clock this day (at which time the bells will ring), to make a united and successful resistance to this last, worst and most destructive measure of administration.

Philip had no idea what Anne Ware thought about the atmosphere of tension and anger mounting hourly in the city. Since the day in September, he had not visited Launder Street once, and had arranged to be occupied in Edes' back office whenever he spied the girl turning into Dassett Alley on her way to the shop. By now he was not entirely sure whether his reaction came about because he was in love with her, and feared it, or because he wasn't.

The tea ship docking at Griffin's Wharf brought accelerated activity among Edes and his friends. It also provided Philip with welcome diversion from the weeks of painful doubt and introspection, weeks which had still produced no definite answers in his own mind.

VIII

HE COULD keep himself physically separated from Anne, it seemed. But he couldn't prevent her from coming to him in other ways. Two nights after *Dartmouth* anchored, he dreamed about her—a heavy, sensual dream in which he glimpsed her naked through mist or smoke.

He groaned, rolled over on the cellar pallet, coughed, smelled the tang of his dream in the damp darkness—

Smoke?

Instantly his eyes opened. In a panic, he fought free of the sweated blankets. The erection produced by the dream wilted under his sudden fear.

His wool nightshirt flapped around his knees as he stumbled for the stairs. The smoke stench was growing stronger. A splinter stabbed his bare sole as he took the risers two at a time. He was terrified by the roseate light at the head of the stairs. He heard a sound. Crackling—

He burst onto the main floor, dashed past the entrance to Ben Edes' office. Flames shot up from a stack of fresh-printed *Gazettes* near the press.

The fire was not large as yet; the still-damp ink produced the excessive smoke. He leaped for the burning papers, scorched his hands in the process of spilling the sheets off their pallet and away from the vulnerable wooden press.

The leaping fire showed him a fallen pine-knot torch and the front door half-torn from its hinges. The door's outer surface bore the scars of gouging and prying. He'd apparently been sleeping so hard that he hadn't heard the break-in.

"Fire, a fire!" he bawled from the doorway, hoping the hour was not too late.

Relieved, he heard the cry echoed a moment later by other men, some of the loafers hanging around the taverns close to the nearby State House, he suspected. He raced behind the press, seized the bucket of sand kept there for just such emergencies, emptied it on the scattered, burning newspapers with a hurling sweep. That helped—a little.

The voices grew louder in the close confines of Dassett Alley. Philip shouted at figures dimly visible at the door:

"Someone with boots help me stamp this out!"

A tottering tosspot with a red nose and a woolen muffler around his neck was pushed forward by his companions. "And one of you run to Mr. Edes' house and fetch him—quickly!" Philip cried.

By the time Edes arrived in a quarter of an hour, the blaze was well extinguished. A noisy, quarrelsome-sounding crowd now packed the alley, some with torches. Edes had to struggle and shove his way through.

Shivering in his nightshirt, Philip greeted him at the door. Edes surveyed the damage while Philip explained what had happened.

"Sharp work," Edes said finally, fingering the smashed-in door. "Thank God you saved the press."

"Apparently someone discovered the source of the new broadside hung on the tree."

The printer snorted. "D'you think that's any secret? I've had threats of this— and worse—more times than I can count."

Philip suggested that perhaps some partisan of the Tory cause had worked the damage. But Edes rejected the idea, searching the crowd outside.

"No, lad, the merchants who still kiss Farmer George's ass are too concerned about their own hides—and too scared of the Sons of Liberty—to risk villainy after dark. 'Twould be soldiers, most likely. Come over from the garrison at Castle William. The right honorable King's men."

He spat, turned and began picking up charred sections of the *Gazette*.

"They think they can silence our protests about the tea matter with a little hooliganism. 'Course," he added, managing a smile at last, "they probably got their inspiration from our own organization. We've burned before, when circumstances warranted. Well, we must print again tomorrow. It appears they destroyed about a third of the run—"

"And came close to destroying the only place I have to build a future, damn 'em to hell!" Philip said impulsively.

Ben Edes gave him a keen look of approval. He reached under his shirt, pulled off the chain bearing a medal like the one Campbell had shown. He looped the chain around his startled assistant's neck.

"A little gift, Philip. Wear it proudly. You earned it with what you did tonight. And what you just said."

"PHILIP, YOU know there's to be action tonight. We need young men. Are you with us? I should warn you—it may be dangerous."

Ben Edes spoke the words shortly after noon on a Thursday, the sixteenth of December. Outside, a thin early winter rain spattered Dassett Alley.

Philip wiped his ink-stained hands on his apron, met the inquiring gaze of the older man; he had no doubt about what sort of "action" Ben Edes referred to. Boston had seethed with talk of nothing else during the nineteen days *Dartmouth* had remained at Griffin's Wharf, her cargo still in her hold. During those same nineteen days, two sister ships, *Eleanor* and *Beaver*, had dropped anchor at the same pier. Both carried more tea.

At public meetings in late November, Samuel Adams had reiterated the demand that all the tea be shipped back to England. Adams' cohorts skillfully controlled the loud, vocal voting—in favor of the patriot resolutions.

But that made no difference to the Royal Governor. Hutchinson issued orders to the Customs authorities who patrolled the harbor that the tea ships could sail only on presentation of official documents to certify that the duty had been paid.

Tomorrow—December seventeenth—would mark the end of a crucial period. Twenty days after any ship's arrival, Customs men could board her and seize her cargo for non-payment of duties, *Dartmouth's* twenty days expired tomorrow.

In anticipation of that—so Edes had confided to Philip—three or four days ago, Adams had convened a secret session of Committees or Correspondence from Boston and four neighboring towns. The object was to prepare the plan that had to be carried out before the sun rose on the seventeenth—and the tea fell into Crown hands.

"The Governor won't relent?" Philip asked now. "I heard at the Dragon there was to be another last-minute meeting to press for it."

"Aye, there's a meeting. At Old South Church, beginning at three this afternoon. But it's doubtful Hutchinson will change his mind. If he does, several gentlemen I know will be exceedingly disappointed. The Governor obviously realizes trouble's coming. He's fled to his big country place over by Blue Hill in Milton."

"Yes, I heard that too."

"So the tea will be seized unless he permits *Dartmouth* to sail tonight. Which he won't."

"But what about the troops, Mr. Edes? Will they stand for what's been planned?"

"That's the question—and the risk. The soldiers could move in from the island garrison to block us. Worse than that, when we're at Griffin's, we'll be in range of the guns of the English squadron. If that damned Admiral Montague decides to throw a little grape or canister to discourage our—protest, we could be in for it."

"You think they'd damage the tea ships and the wharf?"

"To damage some patriots at the same time? I don't think it's impossible."

Philip shivered. In response, Edes said, "There's no guaranteeing anything, of course. With the town in its present mood, the lobsters might choose inaction. There's also a question of what orders would be required for the soldiers to act.

Orders to shoot us? We plan no harm to any person. Still—'' He shrugged. ''That's not to say bloody hell couldn't break loose. On purpose or by accident. So you're fairly warned, lad. What's your answer?''

The younger man grinned. ''Risk or not, do you think I'd miss it? Especially after they tried to burn us out? Tell me what time and where.''

Edes clapped him on the shoulder. ''My parlor. We've three groups organizing—one at my home. Lock the shop and be there before sundown. I understand those gathering at Old South will try one final time to force *Dartmouth*'s captain, Francis Rotch, to sail this evening. We'll wait for his refusal—then Sam's signal.''

With that, Edes bundled into his surtout of dark gray wool and hurried out of the shop.

Watching him go, Philip noted that Dassett Alley was enjoying more pedestrian traffic than usual this morning. Despite the wretched weather, the Boston streets teemed with people. Almost as if there were a fair, Philip thought wryly. The public mood hardly seemed suitable for a day when a clear and open blow was to be struck against the King's law. Peculiar people, these Americans.

═══ II

PHILIP ARRIVED at Ben Edes' home at quarter to five. The rain was beginning to slack off, the clouds to blow away as winter twilight came on. Edes' young son Peter admitted him to the house, conducted him to closed parlor doors.

''I'm not allowed in, except to keep the bowl filled with rum punch,'' he said unhappily.

The boy knocked. Philip heard muffled voices go silent suddenly.

A moment later the doors slid aside. Edes greeted Philip, gestured him in. He was unprepared for what he saw as Edes shut the doors again.

The room was crowded with young men, all of them unfamiliar. Most were mechanics; artisans, to judge by their clothing. They resumed conversing in lively fashion, joking and posing for one another in ragged costumes that ranged from tattered wool blankets to women's shawls. But the talk seemed too boisterous, as if it concealed each masquerader's apprehension—

The same apprehension Philip felt. Throughout the afternoon, worried-looking strangers had hurried into the shop, hunting Edes. Philip had sent them on to the printer's home.

All at once Philip did recognize one face in the gathering. Revere, the silversmith. He was bundling a blanket under his arm and tucking what appeared to be two wild bird's feathers beneath his coat.

Philip hadn't seen the craftsman of North Square in a month or more. Tonight Revere's dark eyes snapped, alert. His color looked excellent again. Philip reminded himself to remark on the happy reason for the change, if he had the chance.

At the moment Edes was leading him to a polished walnut table in the center of the room. On it were piled a good dozen axes and hatchets. The printer chose one, pressed it into Philip's hand.

''Tonight, my boy, you'll be a noble savage.'' Edes' smile faded. ''Don't be surprised if you're required to use this on something other than tea.''

Hefting the weapon, Philip frowned. ''Trouble coming?''

"Not sure. The district near the wharf is crawling with tommies. And everyone's lost track of that damn admiral—he may have got wind of this and be readying his guns. But Samuel won't call it off for a piddling reason like that."

Possible bombardment by English sea gunners hardly seemed to deserve the description "piddling." Philip said nothing, however. Edes pointed to a heap of frowsy clothing in the corner.

"Find some costume that suits you. Once we leave Old South, we'll add lampblacking or the ochre to our faces and—lo!—law-abiding townsmen turn into wild Mohawks."

Philip picked up a blanket and cocked an eyebrow as a flea hopped to the back of his sweating hand, then hopped off again.

"Why all this mummery, Mr. Edes? I mean, these outfits will hardly fool anyone—"

"No, but they just might keep you from being recognized if the troops move in and there's a fracas."

Paul Revere walked up, saying, "Some disguises will be more complete than others, Mr. Kent." As Edes moved off and Philip slung the blanket around his shoulders, the silversmith went on, "Look sharp and you may notice gentleman's lace at a cuff or two. Some who support our cause can't afford to risk discovery just yet. But they'll make good Indians nonetheless. And on top of what Ben said, these rags can be shed quickly if we've got to run for it. But come, nothing's happened yet! Let's celebrate while we have a chance."

Smiling, Revere signaled one of the young mechanics, who handed them both cups of rum punch. By now Philip could definitely detect the falseness of the glee turning the room noisy. The bogus Indians were pretending the evening was to be nothing more than a grand party. But it could turn out to be something entirely different.

With the wicked-bladed axe thrust into his belt, he definitely felt like a lawbreaker. He thought glumly of the English men-o'-war riding at anchor. Surely the admiral in command wouldn't be so thick-witted as to order the guns trained on the town. Surely not. But accidents could happen. Tempers could snap—

Trying to forget his tension, Philip hoisted his cup in salute:

"Mr. Revere, I haven't seen you to congratulate you on the happy event in October."

"Why, my thanks, Mr. Kent. A widower with a flock of children can't run a business and a household. Fortune smiled when she directed Miss Rachel Walker my way."

The said Miss Walker, only twenty-seven, had become Revere's second wife less than sixty days earlier. She was not supposed to be a great beauty. But she was called kindly, intelligent, capable. And Edes said that Revere became his old self during the short courtship.

"I was distressed to hear of the death of your youngest child, though," Philip added.

"Your sympathy's appreciated. Poor little Isanna—she wasn't meant to live. But a man can't mourn forever. I've turned my back on past sadness and I take delight in my new and happy state."

"Ben Edes told me you'd made up a clever riddle about the new Mrs. Revere—"

"About her name," the other nodded. " 'Take three-fourths of a pain that makes traitors confess—' "

Helping himself to a second cup of punch, Philip said, "That'd be 'rack,' I guess. And three-fourths? R-a-c?"

"With three parts of a place which the wicked don't bless—"

"H-e-l from 'hell'—that makes Rachel—"

"Time to leave!" Ben Edes yelled. "Time, gentlemen!"

Philip and Revere tossed down the rest of their punch, the latter saying, "The next two couplets give the name 'Walker,' and the last two are sheer romantic compliment. But she deserves 'em. So I'll accept an earnest wish that we all live long enough for me to enjoy my first anniversary.

"Gladly given," Philip grinned. "And many more."

His head hummed from the punch. His earlier fear was gone. When he hurried with Edes, Revere and the others down Marlborough Street shortly before five-thirty—no man making the slightest attempt to conceal the disguise he carried—thanks to the liberating effects of the punch, Philip shared the holiday mood. Under a just-showing sickle of moon, he laughed when loungers in doorways applauded and feigned shrieks of terror:

" 'Fore God, it's a Mohawk rising! Look at them tommyhawks shine!"

By the time they neared the corner of Marlborough and Milk streets, darkness was nearly complete. The intersecting streets were packed wall to wall, a larger crowd than Philip had ever seen at one time in Boston. More cheering, more yells of encouragement welcomed Edes and his followers as they shoved their way toward the doors of Old South.

But the crowd whistling and applauding outside was as nothing compared to the huge throng jamming the interior of the church.

Every pew and gallery was filled. Every inch of aisle space was occupied by standees. Edes and his group managed to squeeze into standing room at the very rear. Overhead, the church's chandelier candles flickered.

Philip scanned the restless audience. A man near Edes was whispering, "—oratory's been plenty hot so far. Adams and Quincy and Dr. Warren kept the crowd fired for two hours. But now they're impatient. Already been several motions for adjournment—"

From the pulpit, a man someone identified to Philip as a Mr. Samuel Savage was just gaveling down another such motion:

"I repeat—Captain Rotch has been sent on his way to His Excellency's home in Milton, and there is no reason to doubt the captain's good faith. Besides, our several towns are very anxious to have full information as to this matter, and are desirous that the meeting should be continued until Rotch returns."

Grumbles and catcalls greeted the statement. Philip's eyes kept ranging over the faces in the high galleries. Suddenly, he recognized two of them. Lawyer Ware and, beside him, Anne.

She was staring at him. He couldn't clearly read her expression. It seemed admiring, yet sorrowful. Perhaps the admiration was to acknowledge his presence, the other emotion more personal—

Another flea crawled down his collar. He scratched, then acknowledged Anne's look with a nod, a tentative smile. She nodded ever so slightly in return.

Studying her fair, bonneted face high up in the crowded rows, he felt a tug of emotion. He wished he could speak to her—

Abruptly, there was commotion at the side doors. A cry went up:

"Rotch is returning! Open the way!"

Everyone began talking at once. Savage hammered them to silence as a pale man in sodden, mud-stained clothing struggled through to a point just below Old

South's pulpit. In one of the rows near the front, Philip recognized the back of Sam Adams' unmistakably trembling head. Adams was half-risen in his pew, straining forward to listen.

Revere whispered, "I see you've spotted Sam. He'll give the signal if we're to go."

"Yes, Mr. Edes told me." Philip nodded.

Hammer-hammer-hammer. Finally, the immense crowd quieted.

"Captain Rotch," Savage said to the exhausted-looking man, "have you called upon the Governor?"

For an answer, Rotch gave a tired nod.

"And what is his disposition of the matter?"

The hush was complete. Across the packed pews, Philip heard the master of *Dartmouth* reply, "The same His Excellency indicated several days ago. He is willing to grant anything consistent with the laws and his duty to the King. But he repeated that he cannot give me a pass to sail from the harbor unless my vessel is properly qualified from the Customs House—with the duty paid."

Shouts of *"No, no!"* rang from scattered points in the church. Again Savage banged his gavel for silence.

"In that event," Rotch continued wearily, "I would be free to accede to—to public opinion, and carry the cargo back to England."

"In other words," Savage said, "you are not presently free to sail from the harbor?"

"That is correct."

"But it is the will of the citizens that the tea be returned. Unless you weigh anchor tonight, your vessel is liable to seizure. Therefore, sir, you must sail."

"I cannot possibly do so," Rotch said with a shake of his head. "It would prove my ruin."

From the west gallery, a raucous voice boomed, "Then let's find out how well tea mingles with salt water!"

Yells of assent, clapping, boot-stamping followed the cry. Philip glanced at Anne again, saw her shining face turned toward the pulpit. She and her father looked pleased—as did almost everyone else present.

Savage's gavel thwacked again, and still again, to quiet the clamor as Sam Adams rose from his pew.

Savage recognized him. The crowd quieted once more. The familiar, quavering tones carried clearly in the silence:

"I would remind the audience that Captain Rotch is a good man. He has done all that he could to satisfy the wishes of the citizenry—"

Adams turned a little, partially facing the rear of the church. Revere seemed to be standing almost on tiptoes. Ben Edes looked flushed. Adams' slate-blue eyes glittered with reflections from the smoking chandeliers as he continued:

"No matter what transpires from this hour forward, let it be remembered that no one should attempt to harm the captain, or his property."

Mopping his face with a kerchief, Rotch glanced up, frowned in genuine alarm.

Adams seemed to grow a bit taller, turning more directly toward the back of the hall as he said, "But this meeting can do nothing more to save the country."

Then he lifted his right hand to his waist, and moved it outward in a gesture of resignation.

Philip caught his breath. That must be the signal. The roar from the throat of Ben Edes confirmed it:

"Boston Harbor! We'll brew some harbor tea!"

Men and women surged up from their seats, roaring in approval. Captain Rotch cried, *"Wait—!"* The rest was lost in the tumult.

Revere spun Philip by his shoulder, thrust him in the direction of the doors, as several of the young men around Edes began to utter wild warwhoops. Philip draped the blanket over his shoulders, fastened it with a pin, pulled on a stocking cap he'd tucked into his pocket. Above the shouts and thud of feet in the aisles, he heard the gavel hammering again, a voice exclaiming, *"—meeting is dissolved."*

Pushed and pummeled, Philip finally reached the outer steps. Under the thin moon, a cold north wind whipped across the rooftops. But it couldn't chill the enthusiasm of the hundreds—perhaps thousands—now gathered in the streets.

"A mob, a mob!" they howled. "Boston Harbor a teapot tonight!"

And over the words shrilled the whooping of the bogus Indians, busy donning their ragged coats and blankets, thrusting turkey and goose feathers in their hair, daubing each other's faces with lampblack or ochre from hastily opened belt pouches.

Revere decorated Philip's cheeks with several quick streaks of blacking, then passed the pouch in order that Philip could do the same for him.

"Are we proper Mohawks?" the silversmith wanted to know when Philip was finished.

Philip nodded, nearly losing his balance as the mob crowding outward from Old South shoved relentlessly. Off to the right, he heard Ben Edes calling to his group. He started in that direction as Revere yelled behind him, "Then follow Ben to Griffin's Wharf!"

Just as Revere shouted, Old South's bell began to toll the hour of six.

III

WHOOPING, EDES' INDIANS struggled to rally at the head of Milk Street. It was an indication to Philip of how much secret preparation had been made when the crowd opened with fair speed and order to let the crudely disguised men through, then immediately closed in again and began to troop along behind.

As Edes and his followers started for the harbor, people popped out of doorways carrying whale oil lanterns. Before long, Philip could glance over his shoulder and see torches flaring as well. The mob sang, chanted, howled cheerfully obscene oaths against the King, his tea and his taxes—all in all, it was a carnival atmosphere.

Even Edes looked gay, striding along with hatchet in one hand, his cheeks ochre-streaked. He scanned ahead for the other groups supposed to be gathering on Hutchinson Street near Fort Hill—

But Philip was well aware that the partisan mob could and probably would disappear at the first sign of danger. The Mohawks, not those tramping behind them, would be the ones most easily caught and identified if the British reacted.

By now the effects of the rum punch had completely worn off. Philip felt the gnaw of fear again. So did those around him. There were furtive glances, scowls, teeth nervously chewing underlips because of something the raiders hadn't seen before. Red-uniformed men. Quite a few of them. In tavern doorways. On balconies. Pistols and swords were in evidence.

The watching enlisted men and officers did not draw their weapons or attempt to interfere. Nor did the mob molest them—except verbally. The British gave back a few curses and shaken fists, but nothing more. Perhaps they were awaiting a signal? Philip started to sweat again.

Another hundred Indians waited at the rendezvous point near Fort Hill. The whooping grew even louder as the raiders swept down Hutchinson Street, the distorted shadows of their feathered heads leaping out ahead of them along the walls of buildings. But the first ranks grew quiet suddenly as they swung into the head of Griffin's Wharf. The others following fell silent in turn.

The masts, spars and furled sails of the three tea ships stood out against the emerging white stars. Beyond, in the harbor, all could clearly see the riding lights of the squadron. Were gunners with slow-matches crouched behind the rails—?

By now quite a number of soldiers mingled with the throng following the Indians. Philip saw no muskets. Yet. He scanned nearby rooftops for possible points of attack. Nothing suspicious there—

But in spite of the apparent quiet, his tension grew.

Ben Edes called for his group to follow him aboard the vessel nearest the head of the wharf, Rotch's *Dartmouth*. Other groups charged on down the dock to *Eleanor* and *Beaver,* while the dock itself became more and more crowded with the people who had turned out to watch.

Philip saw men race by carrying coils of rope over their arms. And he did indeed notice a lace cuff or two, as Revere had suggested. In moments, Griffin's Wharf grew virtually as bright as day, lanterns and torches by the dozen held aloft to illuminate the spectacle of Edes and his men clambering up *Dartmouth*'s plank to confront an alarmed mate and a man whose uniform identified him as an official of the Customs House.

A total hush had descended on the wharf. Edes' followers gathered behind him as he approached the mate. Philip braced his feet on the gently tilting deck, heard Edes say over the laping of the water:

"Mr. Hodgdon, it will be to your advantage to stand aside and let this work be done. You know why we are here?"

Mate Hodgdon glanced nervously at the semicircle of torchlit, painted faces.

"Yes. Captain Rotch informed me that something like this might transpire. We will not interfere." *As if it were possible!* Philip thought.

The mate and the gaping Customs House man retired to the quarterdeck. There, together with a few astonished seamen, they watched as Edes spun to his followers.

"Remember—harm no one and nothing but the tea. Now to work!"

A young apprentice near Philip let out an ululating whoop. Edes silenced him with a glare. The carnival mood was gone. Eyes roved nervously toward the lights of the British warships as Philip and the others sped for the hatches and opened them.

Edes organized the activity. Philip soon found himself too busy to worry about danger. He was sent to the rail on the harbor side, as men who had dropped below helped raise the first of the canvas-covered chests by means of a hastily rigged tackle.

The chest was passed along by hand to the rail, and set down. Philip and two others proceeded to hack it open with their axes. When a cut of sufficient length was opened, they lifted the chest, tilted it and let the powdery contents spill over the side. Then they threw the empty chest over too, and went on to the next one.

The strange silence continued. It was punctuated by the heavy breathing of the men, the creak of the tackle, the thump of the chests, the hack of the weapons, the loud *plop* as the empty chests hit the water. Philip and his two associates sneezed repeatedly as the fine Bohea dusted into their nostrils, clogged their eyelids. But they kept working.

The mob on the pier lingered an hour, two. It showed no sign of diminishing. But the number of red military jackets increased. Sweating and breathing hard, Philip could discern the faces of the soldiers as little more than blurs. But here and there, closer to the tea ships, a few did stand out. Incredulous. Or, more often, enraged.

Once more he scanned the roofpeaks. *Was that a Tommy by that chimney—?*

He started to point and cry a warning. Then he realized his imagination had tricked him. The watcher clinging to his high vantage point wore civilian clothes.

The Boston citizens made no effort to bother the officers and soldiers who continued to arrive in twos and threes. Occasional jeers and curses continued to ring out, but the lobsterbacks, still outnumbered, could do little more than return looks of fury and loud promises of reprisals.

The wrecking and emptying of the chests went on for the better part of three hours. At the end of that time, Edes announced, "She's empty. Someone have a count—?"

"Eighty whole chests, thirty-four half-chests," came the reply.

Philip leaned on the rail, stifling another sneeze with his thumb before he thrust the axe back into his belt. In all his life he had never seen such a bizarre sight: the torches; the rapt faces of the silent watchers, friend and enemy; the water all around Griffin's Wharf afloat with ruined chests, some of which sank even as he watched. The firelit surface of the harbor seemed to gleam with a peculiar opaque scum—the tea. One whiff of the cold December air would have convinced anyone that he'd suddenly been plunged into a pot of the stuff—

Halloos from the decks of the other two ships indicated that work had been finished there too. According to accounts in the *Gazette*, the entire three-vessel shipment amounted to three hundred and forty-two full chests. That was a mighty lot of the King's duties ending up in the ocean, Philip reflected.

He honestly didn't know what to make of the whole affair, beginning as it had with a mixture of worry and loud revelry, and ending in this strange, eerie silence, as a few men used brooms to neatly sweep up the spilled tea remaining on the deck. He rubbed sweat from the corners of his eyes, squinted at the squadron lights again. No attack had come. He almost felt let down. The strain of waiting for possible reprisals was nearly as bad as outright hostilities—

Yawning, he watched Mr. Edes salute Mate Hodgdon politely to signal the departure of the exhausted Indians.

Certainly there would be repercussions, he thought as he stumbled down the plank to the pier, his arms aching, his nostrils still tickling. How could it be otherwise? But Adams and the rest had never seemed to care about possible consequences. Thinking back on the attempt to burn out the *Gazette*, Philip decided that perhaps they were right.

But all he really wanted to do now was go back to the cellar room, throw off the filthy, flea-ridden blanket, wipe the black from his face and sleep.

The crowd was dispersing. Fewer torches and lanterns were visible every moment. Singly and in small groups, the weary tea raiders passed the head of the pier where their group leaders waited to pass out compliments:

"Well done, gentlemen."

"A tidy night's work for liberty."

Edes caught Philip's shoulder as a fife began to shrill farther up the street. "Some of the company are assembling to march to the State House—"

"I'd just as soon go home, sir. I've tweaked the King's nose sufficiently for one evening. I'm worn out."

Edes smiled a thin smile. "Fair enough. Shed the disguise quickly, then. Go your own way—but I suggest the back streets."

Philip nodded, moving on alone as the crowd thinned still more. He turned into the mouth of Hutchinson Street, barely aware of a pair of red-coated officers staring at him from shadows by a wall. He was distracted suddenly by a commotion a few doors down: the clatter of a window rising, shouts from the Indians who were just passing in double marching file beneath.

"Sweet Christ, there's the admiral!" one of them pointed. As Edes dashed by, Philip saw a stout man lean from the second-floor window, wig askew. "The yellow dog's been watching from a safe hideout the whole time!"

"Indeed I have, boys," Admiral Montague shouted down. "And you've had a fine, pleasant evening for your Indian caper, haven't you?" A fat finger shook, the voice harsher. "But mind, you've got to pay the fiddler yet."

"Oh, never mind, never mind, squire," another of the ragtag Indians yelled back. "Just come out here, if you please, and we'll settle the bill in two minutes!"

The admiral of the squadron crashed the window down immediately. A second later, the lamp that had been burning in his chamber went out. Raucous laughter rang as the fife resumed, and the marchers continued their parade, in high spirits.

Philip managed a weary smile, started to trudge on. Suddenly he heard faster footfalls behind him.

He turned. Two British officers, hurrying—

The same ones he'd passed a few moments ago?

One of them pointed at him. Then he shoved a woman and her two small boys out of the way. Philip's belly wrenched.

He faced front, quickening his step. The tension and subsequent letdown had lulled him into false security. He'd wasted precious seconds after going by the two watchers without giving them a close look; walked when he should have fled at full speed—

Glancing back a moment ago, he'd glimpsed the face of the soldier who pointed. It was the tall, long-nosed grenadier with the white scar on his chin.

Walking faster, Philip twisted around again. He caught a flash of yellow lapel. Captain Stark shouted for him to hold up.

Philip flung off his cap and stinking blanket, left them lying on the cobbles as he ran. He heard the boots of Stark and his companion clatter in pursuit.

Philip hadn't gone two blocks before he realized he couldn't outrun them. He was too tired.

IV

DESPERATELY, HE turned to the right, into an unfamiliar alley. Once more Stark shouted for him to halt. The man's voice sounded peculiarly thick. Had he been drinking?

If so, it didn't seem to lessen the grenadier's steady pace as he and his comrade rushed to capture their quarry.

Philip's right boot slid out from under him, slicked with some animal's turd into which he'd stepped. He sprawled hard, his chin smacking the ground, snapping his teeth together. He heard and felt a cracking in his mouth. He spit out something that clicked and gleamed white on the stones.

The breath knocked out of him, he struggled to rise. His tongue told him he'd broken off most of an upper front tooth.

He pushed up with both hands, heard Stark cry:

"Down here!"

Turning, Philip saw a glitter at the alley's mouth; Stark drawing his sword.

The other officer protested that he couldn't keep up. A group of citizens with lanterns appeared in Hutchinson Street, hurrying home. Two of these men spotted Stark with his sword drawn, broke away, seized the second officer and began to jostle him. But Stark was too fast. He eluded the others and sprinted on into the alley's darkness.

On his feet, Philip started running hard again. His eyelids itched furiously from the tea. His shoulders hurt. The relentless thud of the grenadier's boots coming on tightened his belly with cold, sick fear. It was only one on one now— but Stark had the advantage of energy and determination.

The alley veered obliquely left. Philip dodged a refuse heap, jumped over a squalling cat whose eyes glowed like gems. Stark's companion was long gone from sight. But the big captain was gaining.

A plank fence loomed on Philip's left. Pretty high, but maybe he could clamber over. He leaped for the top—

But not with enough spring. Cursing, he fought for a handhold, lost it, felt himself falling—

He landed on his spine with a jolt, panting. The failure to scale the fence had cost him his only margin of safety.

Captain Stark loomed, checking his run. His blade, held out in front of him, gathered the starlight and shimmered.

Stark's chuckle sounded heavy. Philip smelled rum. The captain's eyes were invisible in the pits of shadow under his brows. But his face shone white as a skull in the semi-darkness.

Captain Stark took a step forward. Philip jumped up, backed against the fence.

"I thought I recognized you under that blacking," the grenadier said. "Not only do you insult His Majesty's officers—you flout his laws. I suppose I could haul you up before a magistrate. But I think I prefer more personal justice—"

Again Stark chuckled. This time, it was a laugh of humorless pleasure. He added:

"Especially since I doubt anyone will mourn long for an obvious lawbreaker. And while you're rotting here with the dogs picking over your bones, I'll call on the young lady again. Remember that while you're bleeding to death, eh?"

Without warning, he launched into a formal thrust.

Lightning-quick, his right knee bent as his boot slammed down. His long arm drove the sword forward like a streak of white fire.

Philip calculated his time, ducked at the last possible instant and flung himself forward at the grenadier's boots.

The sword point chucked into the plank fence. Captain Stark swore, pulled the blade free. By then, Philip had his arms wrapped around the man's right leg, pulling him off balance.

Arms windmilling, Captain Stark cursed again. Philip toppled him backward.

But the grenadier was superbly conditioned. Even as he toppled, he managed to use his left leg to kick Philip's shin, hard. Philip danced away.

Captain Stark scrambled up again, his scarlet-clad shoulders faintly white from the powder knocked loose from his wig. He lunged, simultaneously raised his right arm, then brought it whipping down—

Philip jerked his head aside. The blade glanced his temple, the edge nicking a long cut from hairline to cheek. Blood ran down the left side of Philip's face as he took two hopping steps to the side, managed to free his axe from his belt—

"Slippery little gutter bastard," Stark panted, right arm across his chest, blade ready to chop outward in a lopping horizontal arc. "Bragging and smarting about your swordplay—"

With a sibilant hiss the sword slashed the air. Philip ducked again, running forward bent over, his hand so tight on the axe handle that his fingers hurt. Because he knew the half-drunk Stark meant to kill him, he wasted no time on gentlemanly maneuvering. He darted under the next arc of the sword and swung the axe full force.

The blade chopped through white trousers into Stark's thigh. His left eye blind from blood, Philip barely perceived Stark go stiff. But he heard the grenadier yell in pain.

Stark clutched his red-sopped trousers with one hand, whacked at Philip's neck with the other. Philip ran backward without looking—

Another of those infernal garbage heaps tripped him up. He went down on his back among rotted cabbages and stinking fish carcasses.

The hard-breathing Stark hobbled forward, left hand gripping his thigh wound, right readying the sword for a last direct thrust. The refuse pile was slippery, no footing, no handholds—

Captain Stark had no need to proclaim his advantage, or his satisfaction. Philip could hear pleasure in the incoherent growl building in the grenadier's throat. The rum reek blended with the stink of cabbage and fish. For one awful moment, Philip seemed to stare up at some giant limned against the winter moon showing between the rooftops. Stark drove the blade's point down at an angle toward Philip's exposed throat—

Hacking over from the right with the axe, Philip felt the sword slice the air next to his face. The axe bit Stark's uniform sleeve, cut all the way to the bone. While Stark was bent forward for the finish of the stroke, Philip kicked him in the belly with his right foot.

The grenadier's hand opened. The sword dropped away as the severed muscles of Stark's arm failed him. He moaned, sank to his knees. He turned his head from side to side as if searching for his enemy.

"Lad—" he began—to appeal for mercy? Philip didn't wait to find out. He snatched up the sword and rammed it all the way through Stark's midsection until the point protruded from his backbone.

Stark crumpled slowly onto his side, lips and eyeballs glistening in the starlight. The grenadier let out one hideous grunt of pain between clenched teeth and shuddered, dead.

Numb, Philip listened.

He heard no sound save for some male voices singing drunkenly in the distance. Then a church bell chimed half after nine.

Philip had struck at Stark out of self-defense, not heeding or even thinking of what could happen to him afterward. Now visions of that spilled through his

mind with terrifying detail. He dropped to his knees and dug through the garbage till he'd cleared a place in which to hide the gory axe.

Let anyone who discovered Stark think he'd been felled solely with his own sword. By some robber, perhaps.

The same cat he'd encountered before strolled into sight as Philip heaped slimy cabbage leaves and fish heads on top of the axe, burying it. The cat licked his left hand with its rough tongue, pressed its head against his knuckles and meowed.

That commonplace sound somehow unnerved him completely. He bolted away, leaving the dead man to the cat and the darkness.

He could feel the blood drying on his left cheek. He must be a sight, lampblack and red and half of a tooth knocked out of his mouth—

He took side streets, pausing now and then to rest and let the nausea, the dizziness work themselves out. His teeth were chattering loudly by the time he reached Dassett Alley.

He dropped the key twice before he got the front door unlocked. He stumbled downstairs, lit the candle, took a step toward the basin of icy water and fainted.

5
Decision

A DISTANT rapping. Repeated—

Philip opened his right eye. The left one took a little longer. Caked blood had sealed the lid.

He squinted at straw near his nose, remembered what had happened. He'd fallen. Some time ago, to judge from the way the candle had burned down to a stub. With a groan, he dragged his knees under his body, pushed up from the floor as the knocking sounded another time. For a moment his eyes glittered with a wild, trapped look.

He knew his crime had been detected. Stark had told the other officer, the one who had fallen behind, that their intended victim worked for Edes the printer. Only that could explain the rapping at the upstairs door—

Philip's head began to clear. He ran his tongue over the broken tooth, waited, breathing softly. Perhaps the nocturnal visitor would leave—

The knock came again.

Philip left the candle burning, climbed the stairs as silently as possible. At the top, he stole toward the shop's rear door.

This time, the knock at the Dassett Alley entrance was accompanied by a voice:

"*Philip?*"

He whirled, ran up past the press, unlocked the door and jerked it open. A cowled figure shivered in the December wind, a shadow—but not threatening. Familiar.

"Anne!"

Behind her, the moonlit sky looked cold silver. She slipped past him as he

knuckled his left eye, trying with that physical act to drive the dull ache from his head. She blended into the shop's darkness as he shut the door and locked it.

He reached for her hand, felt a responding pressure of her fingers as she said:

"I had to see you. I waited until Father and Daisy were both asleep, then crept out of the house—"

"What time is it?"

"A little after three o'clock."

"And you came all the way from Launder Street by yourself? Good God, girl, that's dangerous!"

"Any less dangerous than what you did tonight?" Her voice was husky with emotion. "When I looked down from the gallery at Old South and spied you with Mr. Edes—well, I can't properly describe everything I felt. Surprise. Admiration. The truth about why—why I've been so miserable ever since that afternoon we rowed across the river. Why didn't you come calling again?"

He phrased the answer carefully, so it would carry the truth, yet not hurt her:

"I thought it best not to, that's all. You made your feelings clear. But I couldn't say what you wanted said. I—"

Yes, tell her. The moment demanded no less than complete honesty.

"I still can't. Now I think I should see you back home."

The dim white oval of her face seemed to move in the dark; she was shaking her head. "Not just yet—" She touched his left cheek, gasped softly. "What's that on your face?"

He winced at the pressure of her cool fingers against the clotted gash, drew back. As his eyes adjusted to the faint light filtering up from the cellar, he saw her own widen:

"You're cut! But I heard there was no trouble at Griffin's Wharf! No fighting, nothing—"

"I had an accident running home. I fell."

"So much blood doesn't come from a fall. I want to see it. Where's your room, and some light?"

In her tone he heard the prickly determination that had been one of the first qualities that had attracted him. And her presence—her concern—cheered him. Consequently, he didn't argue. He gripped her still-chilly hand and led her toward the stairs.

She threw back her cowl as they reached the cellar chamber, looked closely at his face. "Dear heaven! That's a sword mark. And you've lost part of a tooth!"

Anne's cheeks had gone pale. The freckles on either side of her nose looked almost black in the dim light.

"The tooth was my own fault. I was running, I fell—Mr. Revere can repair it, I imagine. God knows if anyone can repair the rest of the damage done tonight."

"You don't mean the tea, do you?"

He shook his head, took her hands in his:

"Anne, if I tell you what happened, you must promise to repeat it to no one. Not even your father, do you understand?"

Wide-eyed, she nodded. He released her hands, faced away toward the ledge where Gil's wrapped sword lay, and, in a niche above, Marie's casket.

"There were a few soldiers in the crowd when we sank the tea—"

"So Father reported."

"One was the grenadier Stark. He recognized me. He and another officer chased me. The first one fell behind. But Stark caught me in an alley. With no

one watching, he had his chance to do what he's wanted to do since that day at the Book-Store. He'd been drinking a lot, I think—''

"And you fought?"

"Yes. Before it was over, I—I had to kill him."

The dark eyes welled with tears. She rushed to him, bending her head to his chest. "Oh, Philip, what a terrible thing."

"For who?" he asked, a bit ironically.

"You, of course. And the captain. He was a vile man. But death is no light matter."

Absently, he touched her lustrous hair and realized again that she was an inch or so taller. "I've killed men before, Anne. But you're right—there's no joy in it. Just fear afterward. And shock. And knowing it will happen to me someday—in any case, I took a long time answering your knock because I thought I'd been identified. Perhaps by the second officer. I was starting to steal out the back way just as you called my name."

Silence. Anne seemed to be looking at him differently. With a trace of fright in her eyes. Then she drew on that strength she possessed in such amazing degree, and smiled.

"I'm sure you'll be safe. They'll probably think Stark was caught by some of the mob."

"The other officer was."

"There, you see? With Stark's bad reputation, everyone will assume he provoked his own killing."

"Unless Stark did identify me to his companion. There's no way to tell—until someone comes to arrest me."

"Worry about that if it happens. For the moment you're out of danger. Here, sit down and let me clean you up a little. God, you're fearfully smeared with blood. Is there a place where you can safely burn your shirt?"

"Yes."

"Then you must, first thing in the morning."

Pressing his shoulder with soft but forceful hands, she sat him on the stool by the pallet, then hurried to the stand with the basin of water. She unfastened the ties of her cloak, tossed it aside, soaked a towel in the basin.

"Pull your shirt off."

He did, noting her fresh surprise at the sight of the liberty medal hanging on his chest. One hand holding the wrung-out towel, she lifted the medal with the other.

"I didn't know you wore one of these."

"A present from Mr. Edes. For dousing the fire a few weeks ago—agh!"

His yelp was a reaction to the sudden cold of the water. Methodically, she scrubbed away the dried blood. Though she tried to do it gently, some pain was inevitable. But he made no further sound. In fact, he began to relax under her ministrations.

Then he grew conscious of an itch under the sole of his right foot.

As Anne worked, dipping and re-dipping the towel into the basin until the water took on a deep scarlet tint, he hauled off the boot. He tilted it—and laughed as a little cascade of black tea poured out.

"I think I should save this! A souvenir of my career as a Red Indian—wait, I know just the thing for it—"

Anne watched with an amused smile as he hobbled upstairs on one bare foot, returned a few moments later after rummaging in the shop. He showed her a

small green glass bottle, used to contain the type-cleaning solution. He'd emptied the bottle the previous week and opened a new one, so the bottle in his hand was dry inside.

Carefully, he poured the rest of the tea from his boot into the bottle. The tea formed a layer of half-inch thick in the bottom. He stoppered the bottle and set it on the ledge beside Gil's sword.

"Another Kent family heirloom. To show my grandchildren I attended Mr. Adams' tea party."

Anne directed him back to the stool, began scrubbing his left eyelid. Presently she stood back, surveyed her work, gave a nod.

"Clean at last. Carry the basin out to the alley and empty it while I try to find something to wrap the top of the wound—that's the deepest part."

"Think there'll be a scar?"

"A slight one. But no one will ever be able to say how you came by it." She took hold of his arm, turning him toward the stairway with that crisp, authoritative air that made him chuckle.

As he headed for the rear door, he reminded himself that he should take her home soon. He heard sounds of movement up by the press, where she'd gone to find a clean rag in the supply kept to wipe up excess ink. The night air bit his bare skin as he stepped out under the stars to empty the basin of its red evidence. Going back in, he re-latched the door.

Downstairs again, he resumed his place on the stool while Anne tore a rag in long strips. She wrapped his forehead, covering the worst of the gash, and knotted the bandage at the back. Hands on hips, she stepped away, satisfied.

"You're presentable, at least."

The candle was flickering out. For the first time since her arrival, he was conscious of her femininity, of the swell of her breasts beneath her plain gown of violet silk. He rose and reached into the niche behind the casket as Anne said:

"I've always wanted to see where you stayed, Philip."

He pulled another candle from behind the box. "I'll have a better place one day, I promise you that. Mr. Edes is holding my wages for me. He gives me what little I need for meals when I ask for it. I'm saving the rest. For a shop like this—"

He realized she was staring at something beyond his shoulder. He turned. The object of her curiosity was the leather-covered casket.

"That must be the place where you store the letter you told me about in September."

Turning away from the niche, he nodded. "But I'm beginning to think I've really put all that behind me, Anne." He touched the fresh candle to the stub, dripped a little wax up on the ledge and planted the new light in place. "When someone tossed that torch into the doorway, I reacted in a way I hadn't before. I was angry as hell. It wasn't only Mr. Edes they were trying to burn out—it was me! It's hard to explain properly, but that night I understood for the first time what Mr. Adams keeps saying. That a threat against one man, or one colony, can have consequences for many others."

Cheeks shining in the candle's glow, Anne sat on the stool, resting her hands on her knees. "Yes, you have it exactly right. We are all threatened—so we're all involved. You've seen how it's spread. At first Boston was the target of most of the King's wrath. Now the repression's reaching out further and further. Tea ships anchoring in other ports—" She paused, then added, "When I saw you at

Old South tonight, I did wonder whether you'd come to some decision on the whole issue."

Looking down at the engraved oval of bright metal on his chest, he replied, "It appears I have. I never planned on it. But I felt proud when Mr. Edes said I was fit to wear one of these things. When they organized the tea raid, I hardly hesitated. So—" He smiled, tried to push disturbing thoughts of Marie from his mind. "I am a rebel now, I guess." His eyes clouded; the smile froze in place. "Especially having killed a royal officer."

The girl stood up slowly. Her fingers stirred nervously at her sides. Without taking her eyes from his, she said in a quiet voice:

"One of the things I came to tell you tonight was that if you had made your decision, I had too. Since that trip across the river in September, I've tried to lie to myself. Tried to pretend I didn't feel what I do. As it did to you, something happened to me for the first time. You say I'm strong, but I'm no stronger than— what's inside my heart."

She walked toward him, looking shy, yet radiantly lovely. The implied meaning of her words filled him with surprise and excitement.

"I said I couldn't describe all my thoughts up there in the gallery tonight. I don't think you could guess half of them. But I had to come here and say one thing I've never said to anyone before—"

The color deepened in her cheeks. The sweet lavender scent of her body had grown almost overpowering.

"I want you for a lover, Philip. With no conditions, no promises, no pledges about tomorrow or a fine house, because there's no certainty of any of that after what happened with the tea."

Stunned, Philip protested, "I'm still the same person I was in September, Anne. Not sure—"

"I realize that completely." Her right hand slipped over her shoulder to the back of her gown. "I'll tell you again. No conditions. Even if it should be only this one night, I'd rather have that than nothing."

In the corners of her eyes, tears began to glisten. But she was smiling, too, as she unfastened the closures of the gown, pushed the bodice and sleeves down and her linen shift along with it.

"We have time," she said. "An hour or more before the dawn clocks ring—" She thrust the garments to her waist and ran to him, arms around his neck, mouth seeking his.

Her firm breasts touched his chest. As he slipped his hands to the small of her back, he felt the tips crush to his skin, hardening.

"Anne, Anne—" He stroked her hair, kissed her cheek. "I do care for you—"

"That's enough, then," she breathed. "More than enough for now—"

"I don't want it to be hurtful. You told me you'd never—"

The soft, seeking mouth stopped the rest.

He tasted the sweetness of her tongue as she pressed his back with her palms. She let out a little cry of delight when he pulled her tight against him and she felt his maleness. He'd never fully realized that under her sensible, capable exterior lay this potential for heat and passion—though he might have guessed it, he supposed, from the encounter on the September hillside.

In a way, he was tempted to break off the involvement before it went further. The reason was simple. He cared for her enough to admit that he didn't know

how much he cared for her. And that demanded that she not be hurt—physically or in any other way.

Yet the silence and isolation of the cellar room, the candle flickering on the ledge, her kisses and caresses and, most of all, the unguessable future, conspired to overcome his reluctance. They tumbled on the pallet. He bared her body, casting the gown and underthings aside. Then he reached up to pinch the candle out between thumb and forefinger, never feeling the heat.

Anne's hand touched the buckle at his waist. He helped her. He kissed her face, her eyelids, the gentle, warm valley between her breasts. And knew that all of it was still a pledge of sorts—

The darkness turned sweltering as she rolled against him, no longer shy but seeking him—with her hands, then her whole body—

The joining was painful to her; he could tell by the convulsive way she clasped his shoulders. And for him, the end was unsatisfying because it was overly quick, reached just as her flesh began to stir with first reactions. They fell back on the pallet, exhausted, her hair a lavender-scented webbing against his sweated chest. When they separated, she gave a last little cry. Pain or pleasure? He couldn't be certain.

"Dammit, Anne, I know I disappointed you—"

"No. No!"

"Yes. I was too soon. And I hurt you—"

"Isn't—" She still breathed hard. "Isn't it supposed to be that way the first time? The next time I'll know how. I'm not at all experienced yet—" Her laugh was embarrassed, yet totally female in its warmth. Her fingers kept moving on him, lovingly tracing the outline of his right hand where it curled around her naked waist to hold her belly. "Oh, if Papa realized his proper Congregationalist daughter had taken a lover—! But then—" she punctuated the teasing with tender kisses of his throat, his chin. "I've at least had the good sense to become involved with a man of the right political persuasion." She lifted the liberty medal, held it a second, then released it and pressed both hands to his cheeks, kissing him with passion.

They rested a while under two shabby blankets. Presently her exploring hand and wicked, womanly little laugh roused him again. When he took her a second time, she opened herself and clasped him eagerly, without restraint or fear, and responded with a rhythm and ferocity that fully matched his own. The dark of his mind burst alight, lit by a thousand blazing stars, and a thousand more. His body burned, sought—and so did hers.

Together, faster and steadily faster, they surrendered everything, one to the other. And when the last delicious, shuddering moments came on them both simultaneously—moments of impossible, unbearable straining, of sudden, cascading release, of joyful cries and whispers in the slow-cooling aftermath—there was no need for either to murmur an apology.

This time, it had been perfect.

II

YAWNING AND whispering and holding hands, they walked through the cold December morning to Launder Street. After an almost prim kiss, he promised to call on Sunday. Eyes aglow, she touched his face a final time and slipped inside.

The memory of her radiance lingered with him as he started back to Dassett Alley, whistling an air in spite of his tiredness. He kicked at a rime of ice in a low place in the street, thrust his chilled hands deep into his pockets and speculated on whether a man ever fully controlled his own destiny. It did not seem so. The encounter with Captain Stark had been an accident. And perhaps Anne Ware might not have given herself if the sword wound hadn't added an extra measure of sympathy and concern to push her across the emotional brink.

Striding along in the dawn with the sky turning opalescent, he could reflect that it had been a night of wonders. With significance for the future in many more ways than he could ever hope to enumerate.

Yet he was oddly content, even smiling as he bent into the northwest wind.

A decision, Anne had called it. A whole series of them, really. Small, casual ones, progressing from incident to incident—

His wrath after the abortive fire. Edes handing him the medal. His resulting impulse to join the tea mob.

The necessity to deal with the grenadier. His unwillingness, at the last moment, to refuse the gift of Anne's love despite his reservations about a permanent future with her.

Well, despite her assurances, he was partially bound to her now, just as he was bound to the patriot cause. Neither outcome had been foreseen.

His breath formed a plume ahead of him. In the stillness, a watchman called the half-hour after five, and a clear day predicted. He accepted the workings of his destiny without regret.

In fact he slept deeply and blissfully for an hour—until Ben Edes arrived to waken him for the day's work.

III

PRACTICALLY AT once, Edes inquired about his young assistant's chipped-off tooth, the bandage wrapped around his head, and the remainder of the gash showing below it.

Philip had already decided that the fewer who shared the secret, the better. He said he'd broken his tooth and gotten the wound while escaping from a couple of drunken British officers who had watched the tea thrown in the harbor and had been sufficiently angered to chase him and try to vent their feelings. It was the truth, if not all the truth.

"I outran them," Philip said. "I fell hard, right on my face, then scraped my head dodging around a corner in the dark, that's all."

Edes nodded and accepted the explanation without further question. He left the shop about an hour later. Philip used the opportunity to bring his bloodied shirt up from the cellar, rip it and burn it in the little wood stove that warmed Edes' office.

IV

ANNE WARE started coming to the shop with her father's copy again. Occasional speculative looks from Mr. Edes told Philip that perhaps their intimacy was obvious.

Anne always behaved in a ladylike way, of course. But there were moments when she let her hand rest against his as she showed off Patriot's latest indignant phrases. Edes didn't miss the byplay. But he made no comment.

Philip and Anne had no opportunity to be alone in the days that followed. When he called at the house in Launder Street on the Sabbath, Lawyer Ware was usually present, or at least the cook, Daisy O'Brian. The weather was too cold for finding a place to make love out-of-doors. And even though Philip's key would have made use of the cellar room quite easy, Anne didn't want to risk being seen entering the Dassett Alley establishment in daylight, or a Sunday afternoon. As she herself had said, she still had the good sense to respect certain proprieties.

At the same time, her cheeks had taken on a richer color, almost as though the winter could not fade her summer's tan. They both derived a great deal of private pleasure from sharing the secret.

"I think Daisy suspects," Anne whispered merrily, an hour before the new year of 1774 was to be rung in from the steeples of the town. "Have you noticed the way she stares at us?"

Philip turned from the window. Outside, a fluffy white snow drifted down, softening the glow of the lamps in other houses along Launder Street. In the Ware fireplace, beech logs crackled and flamed. Anne's father, who had proposed a toast to the coming year only five minutes ago, now snored like a somnolent frog, his skinny hands folded on his paunch. He kept slipping further and further down in his chair.

Philip had dressed for the evening in his one good broadcloth. He grinned at Anne and replied, "No, I haven't noticed your cook or her staring. All I care to see is you." He picked up his glass of claret and toasted her.

Anne walked to his side, took the goblet from his fingers, sipped from it, then leaned back against him. Philip glanced at the sleeping lawyer. Ware appeared ready to slide off his chair. He let out a snort but his eyes stayed closed. Philip slipped his arm around Anne's waist.

As they watched the snow fall. Anne went on, "Poor Daisy. She craves a husband in the worst way. Her widower father keeps a farm out beyond Concord. She thought the chances of matrimony were better in town. She's told me she'd even take up with a Tory, if only one would look in her direction. I never realized the true sadness of that kind of longing before we—well, you understand. Oh, Philip! How fine it feels to be close to another person. I'd like for Daisy to make a match—"

She set the goblet on a taboret, turned and laid her hands on either side of his neck. Lawyer Ware snored and bubbled his lips. Anne looked into Philip's eyes.

"I'd like her to be as happy as I am. Even though matrimony is *not* part of the bargain." She kissed him gently on the lips.

Warmed by the wine, he replied, "Yes, but no one said it was out of the question, either."

"I know. But never think you're bound in any way by what happened. I've said it before—the months ahead are too clouded. Too unsure. Let's take only as much as we can, while we can."

She darted one more glance at the slumbering lawyer. Then, eyes sparkling, she asked:

"Have you ever seen the little barn that stands behind the house?"

Keeping a straight face, he said, "Why, I don't believe so, Mistress Ware."

"The former owner put it up. We never use it, because Papa's not the sort to

fuss with milking a cow to save a penny. There's a big hay pile in the barn. If you wished, we could welcome the New Year in a more private fashion.''

"Anne Ware," he laughed, "you are indeed a scandalous woman."

"No," she said, "one in love." And, taking his hand, she led him to the parlor door.

They paused at the entrance to the kitchen to look in on Daisy. The buxom Irish girl had dozed off after drinking the claret offered by her employer.

"A whole household sleeping!" Anne exclaimed in a whisper. "A fair omen for celebrating seventy-four, wouldn't you say?"

"I would, Mistress Ware. Lead on!"

They stole across the back porch and through the powdery whiteness with an almost conspiratorial delight. On the roof of the tiny barn the snow had accumulated till it looked thick as a breadloaf. Inside, the hay proved warm and comfortable.

Tonight their lovemaking had less of the urgency of the first time. They shared little private amusements with a tenderness and frankness that made Philip ask himself whether marriage to this bright, eager girl might not be as endlessly satisfying as the moment they were sharing now. Alicia Parkhurst seemed an alien figure of the past, less than real.

For her part, Anne now had absolutely no hesitancy about showing physical passion. Though they made love with half their clothes still in place, and laughed about it, she still reached a full, joyous climax just when he did, a moment or two after the bells of Boston began to peal the arrival of the first day of January.

Shortly afterward, however, Philip was again reminded of the tougher, more practical side of her nature. As she smoothed her skirt, she said:

"Has Mr. Knox called to see you yet?"

"The owner of the book-store? No, does he intend to?"

"The other day I told him you might be a candidate for—oh, but it might be better if I let him explain in person."

"Explain what?"

"Henry will make that clear."

"Now see here, woman. You're teasing me again."

"Only a little." She gave him a long, level look. "When you accepted that medal from Ben Edes, you did make one commitment, Philip."

V

THE FAT Knox arrived at Dassett Alley within a matter of days. He was bundled in a snow-dusted greatcoat, his curly hair unpowdered and his manner business-like.

"Mr. Kent, are you aware that throughout the town and some areas of the countryside, militia companies are being formed?"

"Militia—? Yes, we've printed stories about it in the paper. Why do you ask?"

Knox stepped closer. "Because, sir, I am recruiting for the Boston Grenadier Company, Captain Pierce commanding. I am one of his lieutenants. Should there be trouble as a result of the tea dispute, we mean to be prepared."

All at once Philip studied the jowly man with new interest. Knox was obviously well educated, polished. His corpulent figure had a softness that suggested

anything except a fighting man. Yet his eyes were keen and determined. He continued:

"We need men for the ranks. Six feet tall if we can find 'em—less than that if we can't. I understand from—certain mutual friends that what you might lack in stature, you make up for in spirit and devotion to our common concern. We drill once a week, and the pay's insignificant. But I feel confident Ben Edes would grant you the time off. If you don't know how to load and shoot a musket, we'll teach you."

Philip realized that Anne's assessment of Knox had to be true. While pretending purposeless amiability toward the British officers who turned his store into an unofficial salon, he was learning their tactical and strategic secrets. Now he was putting them to use. Philip answered:

"I fired a Brown Bess a few times. But that was several years ago."

"The knack will come quickly if it was easy for you the first time." Knox lifted his silk-wrapped hand. "As you may have noticed, handling a musket is impossible for me, thanks to a hunting accident. I suppose," he added with a grin, "that's the reason they turned me into an officer. Oh, I should tell you before you decide that each member of the company is responsible for securing his own musket. They're not easily come by unless you're a rural man who keeps one pegged over the hearth. But we are not overly curious about how a man *acquires* a gun—so long as he gets one. Until he does, he drills with a stick."

Philip stifled a laugh. "A *stick*—!" Instantly, he knew he'd said the wrong thing.

"Be assured, sir, we are not playing children's games. You can and will learn the proper order for loading and firing the weapon, even though you do not have powder and shot or the musket itself. But then when you have them—" Knox's expression showed resolve. "—you will be ready to use them."

A shiver of apprehension chased down Philip's back. The step from orderly mobs destroying tea consignments to organization of military units was a long and significant one. Frowning, he asked the bookseller:

"Do you honestly think that we'll come to open hostilities?"

"Who knows what we can expect when Hutchinson's reports of the tea affair reach England—as they've surely done by now? Our basic position is preparedness. For any eventuality. You were recommended as one who would fit into our unit. If the recommendation was in error—" His unfinished sentence and challenging stare left no doubt about what his opinion would be if Philip responded negatively. The storm winds were blowing in earnest now, he thought. Buffeting him along—

"All right, Mr. Knox. I'll join. Provided Mr. Edes agrees."

Knox clapped him on the shoulder. "You can be certain of it! Once you've taken care of the formality of obtaining his permission, come 'round to the store and we'll arrange the papers."

VI

A FEW days later, Philip found a couple of spare hours for personal business. He visited Knox at the Book-Store to sign the required forms. Then he hurried toward the North End, where he hoped to see Mr. Revere.

A January thaw had set in. Midmorning sunshine gilded windowpanes and

glittered the ice melting on rooftops as he turned into North Square. From one end to the other, the Square teemed with citizens and tradespeople moving among flimsy stalls put up at sunsrise. Several days a week, North Square served as one of Boston's three chief marketplaces.

Philip pushed by single- and two-horse carts unloading vegetables or firewood fresh from the country, thrust his way around bargainers buying and selling firkins of country butter, baskets of fresh-baked gingerbread, gabbling turkeys. The shoppers were mostly townswomen with baskets on their arms. They haggled cheerfully with the farmers or their smiling but wary-eyed agents; some of these last, Philip noted, were black men. The noise of the market was loud but pleasant. And the aromas were a banquet: oysters and pickled pork, mackerel and rye meal, hams and haunches of venison.

Revere's small, peaked-roofed house fronted on the square. Philip was about to descend side steps to the shop entrance when he noticed a commotion a few doors down. He shielded his eyes against the sun, saw a small but rough-looking crowd—men, chiefly—gesturing and scowling at a second-floor window. He had no notion of the reason.

He watched a few moments longer, then went on. It was too fresh and sunny a day for such displays of bad temper, whatever the cause.

A bell over the door rang to announce his entrance. From an adjoining room, he heard Revere's voice:

"Right with you—just a moment—"

Philip was content to wait, bedazzled by the profusion of goods jammed on the shelves, counters, even the floor of the establishment. Clock faces hung in rows. And branding irons and sword hilts. Sunlight slanting through the street-level windows flashed from the blades in a case of surgeon's instruments.

And he had never seen so much silver in so many different shapes and sizes. Baby rattles and teaspoons, shoe buckles and chocolate pots, creamers and standing cups. The sun struck starry highlights from the products of Revere's metalworking skill.

The craftsman himself appeared a moment later, wiping his hands on his leather apron.

"Mr. Kent! Good day. What brings you to this part of town?"

"I'm in need of your services, Mr. Revere."

"Well, I've a diversity of those to offer! What's your choice?" His blunt-fingered hands ranged over a display. "A baptismal basin? Ah, but nothing's been settled formally with you and Mistress Ware, has it?" The smith's grin confirmed what Philip already suspected. He and Anne were the subject of amused gossip among the group that gathered at Edes and Gill.

Revere picked up a glittering length of silver links. "A chain for your pet squirrel, then? Or how about a whistle? An excellent silver whistle—" He blew a piercing blast.

Laughing, Philip held up a hand. "I'm calling on Mr. Revere the dentist." He opened his mouth, pointed. "I broke this the night we sank the tea."

Revere stepped closer, peered into Philip's mouth. Over the smith's neatly clubbed hair, Philip could see into the darker adjoining room. It was dominated by a brick furnace. The furnace's partially open door revealed glowing coals that gave off pronounced heat and cast a dull red glare on crucibles, an anvil, a heap of damaged silver cups and tankards, and other paraphernalia whose purpose he didn't understand.

"A good tooth lost in a good cause," Revere declared, straightening up. "I

can fit you with a more than satisfactory replacement. Sit you down—'' He indicated a peculiar-looking chair amid the clutter. Philip hesitated.

"We need to talk about the price first, Mr. Revere."

"All right. I have a different and much higher set of charges for Tories—don't get much trade from 'em, I confess. How much can you afford?"

Thinking of the sharp bargaining he'd witnessed in the square, Philip put on a doubtful expression. "Oh, no more than a few pence—"

"How few is few? Five?"

"Three would be better."

"Call it four and I'll guarantee to carve you a fine tooth no one will tell from the original. You're lucky you broke a dog tooth—they're easier. The price includes mounting with cement and the finest gold wire for extra permanence. I'll whittle the new one of the very best hippo tusk, too."

He began rummaging through the tiny drawers of a wall cabinet, found a large, curved tooth and displayed it proudly. Then, noting Philip's dumbfounded expression, he asked, "What's wrong?"

"Isn't a hippopotamus an animal?"

"Of course it's an animal. Where else d'you think a man gets a new tooth? The triangular traders bring me tusks from the West Africas regularly. I tried elephant a few times, but it yellows too fast. And sheep's teeth are all snaggled and crooked. Difficult to work. Sit down, sir, and let me put in the wax—"

"*Wax?*" Philip repeated in a somewhat strangled voice, as Revere thrust him into the chair and forced his head against a pair of pads projecting from an upright rod. Humming, Revere conducted another search under one of his counters, returned with a red chunk of the stuff.

"Open wide, please, Mr. Kent," he instructed, practically yanking Philip's jaws apart. He crouched beside the chair, peered upward at the damaged canine tooth, broke off a bit of the red wax, balled it between thumb and forefinger, then pressed the wax carefully up against the tooth's broken surface.

A moment later he pried the wax out. He carried it to the counter, deposited it in a clay pestle and used a quill pen to scratch some figures on a scrap of paper. The paper too was put in the pestle, which was pushed aside to a place near half a dozen silver pepper pots. Philip wondered how the man could keep all his various business enterprises in order in his mind.

"I'll have the tooth in a week, so drop back then," Revere said.

"Don't you need to take any kind of measurements?"

"I already did." Revere lifted a hand to point to one eye. "The most accurate measuring devices known to man—provided they're used properly. No, sir, we're finished—unless of course you'd like me to clean those teeth up a bit. Only costs an extra pence to make your dental equipment white and sparkling. I use a special dentifrice of my own devising. Several secret ingredients I'm afraid I can't reveal, plus saltpeter, gunpowder, crumbs of white bread, cuttlefish bone, broken crockery—"

Philip gulped. "You mean broken dishes?"

"It's all in how you grind and mix it, Mr. Kent. Does wonders in attracting the fair sex. But then you don't have that problem, do you?"

"Well—ah—thank you, but I don't believe I can afford—"

"*Paul?*"

A female voice from a curtained door at the rear of the shop spun Revere around and brought Philip out of the chair. He saw a slender, dark-haired young

woman in a plain frock and apron, a spot of flour whitening one cheek. She looked alarmed.

"What's the trouble, Rachel?" the smith asked.

"I was just out on the stoop—there's an awful row down the way. I fear a mob's going to do harm to poor Johnny Malcolm."

Instantly, Revere untied his leather apron, flung it aside. "The crazy old wretch will get himself killed with that tongue of his. There's been trouble brewing all morning. Someone out in the square told me a little boy accused Malcolm of upsetting his sled of kindling. Come on, Kent, let's have a look." Grim-faced, he hurried for the door.

Philip followed the smith into the January sunshine. At the house where he'd seen a few people earlier, he now saw a crowd three or four times the size. An angry crowd. Taunts were being exchanged with a cadaverous, white-haired old man who leaned from a second-floor window, brandishing a pistol in one hand and a broad-axe in the other.

Revere and his companion trotted toward the crowd. Philip noticed three men running up from the other direction, carrying a ladder.

"This Malcolm's a friend of yours, Mr. Revere?"

"Far from it. Crazy Johnny's a senile, vile-tempered fool. Likes nothing better than to bait people with his impudent and provocative jibes. Trouble is, he's a flaming Tory. In this neighborhood, that's not safe. The Sons of Liberty got blamed once before when some rowdies chastised him—"

As the two approached the edge of the crowd, the old man with the weapons shrieked down, "Ah, go to Hades, the lot of you! I'll push over that little wart's sled any time I damn please. His father helped drown the King's tea, don't think I don't know that. If I split the sprout's head, I'd get ten shilling sterling from the Governor. Twice that for the rest of you Yankee traitors—!"

The old man's voice was shrill. Spittle flew from his mouth. Philip disliked the fellow on sight. But at the same time, he realized the unfairness of the odds against Malcolm.

Revere shouldered into the crowd. "Let him alone. Let the old lunatic rant—"

Scowling faces swung toward the smith and Philip. "Tend to your cream pots, Revere. He bullied the boy, and he's no high son of liberty, either."

"But he's touched in the head. He can do no one any real harm—"

Revere's argument produced no response except for more yells directed at the old man in the window:

"Have a care with your nasty tongue, John Malcolm!"

"Aye, don't forget you were treated to the tar and feathers once before. If you don't shut up, we'll do it again—properly, this time."

Malcolm howled, "You say I was tarred and feathered and that it wasn't done in a proper manner? Damn you, let me see the man that dares to do it better!" He spat down on the crowd.

A coarse-faced woman cursed and wiped her forehead. That incited the mob to rage. There were cries for the ladder. Before Philip knew it, the ladder was jammed against the front of the house. Two burly men started climbing it, one after another.

"Stay away!" Malcolm screeched. "I'll shoot!"

"He's too draft to aim straight," someone jeered.

"Or load it right," another voice added. "Go get him!"

Revere fought through the press, grabbing arms, shoulders.

"Dammit, if you're friends of liberty, leave off baiting a helpless enemy!"

"Get out of here!" someone bawled. Philip watched Revere stagger from a fist that struck hard into his belly.

Pushing, Philip tried to go to Revere's aid. All around, he saw twisted mouths, vicious eyes, threatening hands. One, raw-knuckled, knocked him in the side of the head. He stumbled. Someone else struck the small of his back, hard.

One of the men on the ladder had already dived through the second-floor window, from which shrill yelps of fright now issued. The sunlight and the blows blinded Philip as he struggled to fight off those who pounded him, slammed boots against his shins. Somewhere near the house, Revere was down, exclaiming in anger. But the mob howled louder:

"Tar and feathers!"

"Tar and feathers for liberty!"

"We'll show the fucking lobster-lover—!"

Suddenly Revere burst through a break in the crowd, staggering. A bruise showed on his forehead. Blood ran from the corner of his mouth. His clothing was dirtied and torn. Men grabbed at him from behind. Revere swung a quick, clumsy punch that drove the leading attacker back, clutching his nose and spitting curses.

Revere reached Philip: "Run for it. They're madmen—"

"Yes, you'd better run, God damn you!" screamed the woman who'd been spit on. "You're no friend of Englishmen's rights, Revere!"

"And you don't understand the meaning of the term!" he shouted back.

Oaths. Another frenzied rush at Revere and Philip. A rock flew. Then more. Philip's ear stung painfully as one of the missiles hit him. All at once the hate-filled faces blurred out of focus and he saw Roger Amberly. A mob of Roger Amberlys, screaming, reaching, threatening—His rage and revulsion matched Revere's.

Equally plain was the smith's humiliation. He didn't want to flee from the crazed crowd. But neither did he want to lose his life in a hopeless struggle. Prudence won out. Dragging Philip by the arm, he dodged a chunk of brick, and the two retreated toward the stoop of the Revere house. A cheer went up from the mob. Almost immediately, there was another—

Disarmed, the pathetic Malcolm was dragged from his front door by the two who had entered to capture him. Malcolm's shrieks sounded incoherent now, mortally terrified—

Rachel Revere was waiting on the stoop. She let out a little exclamation of alarm when she saw her husband bleeding. He thrust her hand aside, watching the mob rampage across North Square, dozens of hands supporting a flailing, wailing Malcolm high in the air.

"Animals," Revere seethed. "God damn animals. To wreck our cause with their savagery—!"

"I thought Mr. Adams sometimes called up mobs," Philip panted, his head still buzzing from the blows he'd taken.

"There's not a man in that pack who wears a liberty medal!" Revere snarled. "All they want is cruel sport."

Philip wondered about the truth of Revere's first remark. The second one certainly seemed true, though. The mob had grown till it numbered hundreds. Shoppers and sellers alike left the stalls to follow, laughing and chattering. The

head of the column, and the hapless Malcolm, were finally out of sight on the far side of the square. It seemed to Philip, squinting into the January sun, that above the hubbub, he heard the old man scream in agony. But he couldn't be sure.

He was sure of one thing. The cheerful morning was ruined.

VII

BY NIGHTFALL, Crazy Johnny Malcolm's fate was the talk of Boston. Philip sat over supper at the Green Dragon, listening in disgust to a group of apprentices gleefully retelling how the old man had been loaded into a cart, wheeled to a nearby wharf, stripped down to his belt and painted with tar.

Next, feather pillows had been slashed open, the contents emptied over Malcolm's body. Until early afternoon—four hours or more—he was exhibited throughout the town, people in the crowd pulling the cart. He was displayed at the Liberty Tree, then on the Neck. There, somehow, tea was produced. The victim was forced to toast the health of all eleven members of the royal family. Philip could imagine the added pain that had caused. Describing it, the apprentices roared.

But quarts of tea forced down his throat on the Neck hadn't been the end of Malcolm's dark day. There was more parading. To the tree again, and King Street, and Copp's Hill. At these locations, a new element was added. Whips. Malcolm was flogged unmercifully, until the mob wearied at last, and abandoned him.

"A proper sight he was, too." The apprentice chortled, spreading his hands. "The tar an' the whipping took off hunks o' skin this big. First he pissed his pants. Then he yelped a while. But when we finished with him, he looked froze, an' stiff as a log."

Stomach turning over, Philip threw coins on the table and stalked out of the Dragon. The apprentices never even noticed his glare.

Ben Edes was as dismayed as Revere had been. The Malcolm incident, he said, was the kind of thing that only firmed the resolve of the British ministers—and the King—to deal severely with the colonials. What right had animals to be treated as anything else?

Early the next morning, Samuel Adams appeared in person with copy freshly penned for a notice. He too proclaimed outrage. But as Philip started to pull type for the announcement, he pondered the sincerity of Adams' wrath.

Anne had told him quite a lot about the troubled period of the last ten years. Savaging mobs had roamed before—and she knew for a fact that Adams had at least been indirectly involved in their formation. Had Adams adopted his new, more scrupulous attitude out of changed convictions? Or just from the practical realization that violence—for the present—brought no useful end?

Whatever the reason, Adams' words, printed and hammered to the Liberty Tree by sunset, declared the position of the Sons of Liberty:

BRETHREN AND FELLOW CITIZENS

This is to Certify, That the modern Punishment Lately Inflicted on the ignoble John Malcolm was not done by our Order. We reserve

that Method for Bringing Villains of greater Consequence to a Sense of Guilt and Infamy.

Joyce Jun'r.

Chairman of the Committee of Tarring *and* Feathering

If any Person be so hardy as to tear this down, they may expect my severest Resentment.

J. jun'r.

For days afterward, Philip continued to speculate about the purity of Adams' motives. In the past, how much blood had been callously scrubbed from the man's conscience, if not actually from his palsied hands?

One conclusion was certain. Governor Hutchinson's denunciations of the cruelty to Malcolm only widened the split between Whig and Tory opinion, hardened attitudes on both sides. In the sanctuary of his Purchase Street study, did Samuel Adams allow himself a smile now that one more branch had been tossed onto the slow-kindling fire?

At least one good result came from the memorable January day, though. As Revere had promised, Philip's partial tooth, carved and polished and fastened in place, could hardly be told from the real thing. Anne said she could only see the difference between the two sections when she came near, starting to kiss him.

And as soon as she closed her eyes, she saw no difference at all.

VIII

THE BOSTON GRENADIER COMPANY drilled weekly on the Common, in sleet, in bitter wind, in driving snow. Philip found himself one of the shortest members of the group, only eight or ten of whom actually owned muskets. Under Captain Pierce's direction, the rest went through the manual of arms using the already-mentioned sticks—or, in Philip's case, a broom handle Anne Ware happily supplied from the household kitchen.

Standing in the corner of Philip's cellar room, that plain, homely length of wood began to take on a kind of dreadful symbolism as the winter months ran out. Boston received word of impending royal retribution against Dr. Franklin's delivery of the Hutchinson letters into the hands of Sam Adams. Incoming ships in February brought specific information. Franklin had been subjected to a scathing denunciation by the Crown's Solicitor General. The good doctor had been publicly called a man lacking honor—a thief—and had been dismissed from his post as Deputy Postmaster General for the colonies.

Marching and countermarching on the Common as winter snow gave way to March rains, Philip sometimes asked himself another question. What sort of justice would be meted out if the death of Captain Stark was ever traced directly to him? Even Edes' newspaper had reported the "Sensational Fatality" of a Crown officer. But thus far, he had recovered no hint that he was in any way connected with the crime. As Anne had said hopefully, the trail might end at the point it began. In the alley where Stark died.

As time passed and that assurance began to look like a distinct possibility, he

still felt less than calm, though for quite another reason. He'd caught the prevailing mood of Boston. The entire town and surrounding countryside, alive with
drilling militia companies, was in a state of steadily increasing apprehension.

What *would* be the Crown's response to the tea affair?

When the air turned warm again and sunlit spring broke across Massachusetts,
the answer came—with force more stunning than had ever been anticipated.
Except, perhaps, by those few radicals like Adams, who remained convinced
that George III was Satan incarnate, and the members of the North ministry his
eager acolytes.

As Mr. Edes remarked, the events of spring proved there might be something
to that novel metaphysical theory after all.

6
The Sergeant

"I THINK, gentlemen," said Paul Revere as he unfolded the wrapping material,
"you'll find this appropriate to the situation. If you do, I'll transfer it to copper
at once." He laid his drawing on the table of the Long Room.

Handsome Dr. Warren studied it, nodded somberly. Puffing on his long-
stemmed clay pipe, he stepped aside to permit Molineaux and the others to
examine the artwork held down by the silversmith's work-roughened hands.
April rain pattered at the draped windows.

Philip had never been permitted up here before. It was a measure of the trust
he was now accorded by his employer that he was allowed to be present. Squeezed
in behind Edes, he looked at the grim symbols Revere had inked: the Phrygian
cap, one of the chief emblems of the liberty movement, done large and surrounded by a mourning wreath, the whole bordered with a pattern of skulls and
crossbones.

Edes turned to his assistant. "This will be the engraving on the front of our
handbill." He nodded toward Adams, who sat at the table's far corner, eyes like
blue agates in the lamplight. "Samuel's prose on the reverse. There'll be little
sleep for us during the next couple of days and nights, you may count on that."

Dr. Warren raised his pipe to signal Revere. "It's your intention to ride
express with the news and the handbills, Paul?"

"That's right. I have four other couriers waiting. Trusted men, every one.
We'll start as soon as the press run's finished. I'll take the south road to New
York and Philadelphia. The others will cover the towns to the west and north."
His calm, open face looked momentarily rueful. "Though I wish we might be
spared the necessity—" Adams glared. "I'd prefer to stay in North Square with
my engraving work for Mr. Rivington's new edition of Captain Cook's voyages.
However, I know the hour's much too late for that."

His tone brought headshakes of agreement and a melting of Adams' brief
hostility. Philip had never seen the Long Room conspirators so grim.

All at once, Adams slapped the table.

"The front as it stands won't do!"

"Why not?" Revere countered.

"We must have a message printed with the drawing. The other colonies must be shocked—assaulted!—with the implications of the damnable law. Even though the law's directed only at us, they must be made to see once and for all that the intent of the King's ministers is clear—to dominate and destroy *any* colony daring to resist."

He licked his lips, stretched out one veined hand to grasp a quill pen, then quickly inked a line at the lower margin of Revere's artwork. Philip craned forward to read it.

The Tree of Liberty Cut to the Root.

Will Molineaux snorted. "That's still an understatement, Sam. Hacked down, would be more like it. But I'm afraid the addition of a slogan won't help this province one whit."

"You'll discover otherwise, Will, as soon as Paul and his lads spread the word. The sister colonies will come to our aid. Rally around us with food, with supplies—"

"I pray God you're right," Dr. Warren sighed. "For if that's not the case, Boston's lost her life from this intolerable act."

"Lost her *life?*" Adams' lips jerked at the corners. "By no means! You know what the eventual outcome will be if the ministers dare to continue sponsoring laws to punish us. You know where that road will lead, as surely as sunrise follows the moon."

Will Molineaux's dark Irish face looked even more troubled. "You mean armed resistance."

"More than that," Adams corrected. *"United* resistance, by all the colonies. Then—independency."

Despite the heat of the lamps, the thick blue of pipe smoke, a sudden chill seemed to overwhelm the Long Room then. Adams had stated a possibility that Philip had never really contemplated before. Separation of America from the mother country—The very mention of it suggested an abyss of uncertainty and peril.

And yet, Philip could see the logic, the inevitability. So could the others, as their faces showed. No one looked happy. But no one looked startled, either. In fact, Molineaux smiled with grudging admiration, murmured:

"I've speculated on who among the group would be the first to speak that word. I imagine you've had it in your mind a long while, eh, Sam?"

Adams' head came to rest a moment. He glanced from face to face. With a small, prim smile, he replied:

"I have. I will accept nothing less."

II

THE EDES and Gill press hammered and clattered for the next seventy-two hours, pouring out the handbills that summarized the dire news from England. Over the objections of the elder Pitt, Burke and a few other conciliators who were shouted down, a new bill had passed Parliament, a bill reflecting the King's personal wish that the province of Massachusetts be punished for destroying the tea, as well as for her long and open rebelliousness against Crown authority in general.

The Boston Port Bill, proclaimed the handbill, forbade the loading or unload-

ing of any cargo in the harbor, effective June 1, 1774. The sole exceptions were military stores and some foodstuffs and fuel supplies given special clearance by the Customs House—relocated to Salem by the same bill. George III would reopen the port only when the duties on the ruined tea, as well as the tea itself, had been paid for in full.

Revere and his couriers sped out across Roxbury Neck, the only route of supply for the town, now that its all-important ocean commerce was to be cut off. Within days, the riders returned bearing communications that allayed the fears of the patriots that the other colonies would be indifferent. Edes' paper circulated the heartening news:

New York's Committee of Fifty-one went on record with its "detestation" of the bill.

The mild Quakers of Philadelphia urged moderation but swore support even to "the last extremity."

The Carolinas pledged rice and money. *They* recognized, Adams crowed, that it could just as easily be the bustling port of Charleston whose sea trade—whose life—was being strangled!

Flocks of sheep appeared on the Neck, driven in from New York, Connecticut and elsewhere, tangible signs that thoughtful men well understood the Port Bill's implications. Throughout Massachusetts, the other Committees of Correspondence began to implement the stockpiling and shipment of foodstuffs for Boston. The supplies were delivered in wagons and carts the public jeeringly called "Lord North's coasters"—wheeled replacements for the coasting ships that would be banned from the harbor anchorages after the first of June.

But an even more severe shock lay in store. Governor Hutchinson announced he would step down, return to England, be replaced by a newly appointed official who bore a triple title: Vice Admiral, Captain-General and Governor-in-Chief of Massachusetts. It was taken as a sure sign of worsening relations between colonists and Crown that the provincial government was to be turned over to a military man, General Thomas Gage.

With him, the last incoming vessels reported, he would bring fresh regiments from Britain. Not to mention warships of His Majesty's fleet to enforce the closing of the port. In hamlets throughout the province, Philip soon learned, the militia companies were organizing and drilling in earnest. And accumulating what muskets, powder and shot they could.

The troubled spring grew even more troubled as the days wore on.

III

RESPLENDENT IN his red uniform jacket, Captain Joseph Pierce called the Boston Grenadier Company to attention.

Up and down the length of Long Wharf, other local units snapped to—including Hancock's Boston Cadets, the merchant himself personally commanding. Fifes began to shrill, drums to beat out riffles and tattoos.

At the head of the wharf, a huge crowd of well-dressed Tories, many seated in carriages, started to applaud the wave handkerchiefs as the brass fieldpieces under the charge of Captain Paddock crashed smoky aerial salutes over the rain-dappled harbor. A nasty day made nastier by this false show of pomp and friendliness, Philip thought.

He was uncomfortable in the uniform procured, like all those of the Grenadier Company, with Hancock's financial assistance. He felt foolish and damp to boot, clad in a heavy red coat, white trousers and a tall, tapered black bearskin cap with gleaming brass frontplate. He wriggled his nose as the stench of perspiration and wet wool thickened moment by moment.

The rain fell steadily from a gray sky this thirteenth of May, all but hiding the furled topsails of the man-o'-war anchored out in the harbor. By turning his head slightly in that direction, Philip could just make out the cutter being rowed from the fighting ship to the stairs of the wharf. The thwarts were crowded with oarsmen and cloaked officers in tricorn hats. General Gage and staff.

When Henry Knox had issued the orders for the Grenadier Company to muster and join in the official welcome for the man responsible for enforcing the hateful new law, Philip and quite a few others had openly questioned the advisability of such a move. Wouldn't the company's presence demonstrate respect? Loyalty?

Knox was quick to dismiss the complaint:

"Several factors demand our attendance. First, Gage may not be so bad as Sam Adams would like him painted. He's a man of moderate temper, by all accounts. With a fondness for the colonies. His wife was born here. She's a Kemble, from the Jersey state. And while most of us share the current mood of outrage, many would still rather see some method of accommodation worked out between Massachusetts and London. If it can't be done—'' He shrugged. "You may all be certain of one thing. Our presence on Long Wharf day after tomorrow will be completely understood by our friends. The joy that will seem to reign will be recognized for what it is—expedient hypocrisy. Mingled, of course,'' he added with an amused expression, "with the Bostonian's inbred instinct for extending traditional courtesies to any gentleman. Until he proves himself otherwise.''

So here they were, miserable in the rain, as General Gage and his staff mounted the wharf stairs, accepted the salutes of the militia officers and proceeded down the line of ranked companies for an inspection.

Gage's broad, middle-aged face showed careful restraint of any emotion. But the expressions of his officers left little doubt about their opinion of the local military. From his place in the second rank, Philip saw eyebrows raised, small scornful smiles exchanged. Philip didn't bother to conceal his reaction.

Gage moved slowly toward the head of the wharf, where the Tory crowd had broken into loud cheering and clapping. A colonel behind Gage noticed Philip's insolent expression, paused and called Knox's attention to Philip's trousers:

"That man's breeches are disreputable, Lieutenant. I see mud spots. In England, he'd be flogged.''

"Yes, sir,'' Knox answered. "But we lack supplies of pipe clay for whitening, sir. And I beg the colonel's permission to remind him this is not England.''

The officer's cold stare traveled back from Philip to Knox.

"No, but it shall begin to seem more and more like England as the days pass, be assured of that.''

The colonel stalked off. Philip hawked and spat on the ground.

The colonel spun, scanned the ranks. Philip stared straight ahead into the rain. Knox looked dismayed. After a moment, the colonel uttered a controlled curse and continued on.

Members of the Boston Grenadier Company around Philip smirked and growled their approval. One man in the front rank even whistled sharply between his

teeth. The break in the colonel's stride showed that he heard the mocking sound. But he did not wheel to confront the offenders again.

As the drums and fifes struck up a martial air, the companies faced around to begin the dreary march to the State House as Gage's honor guard. Knox took the opportunity to fall in beside Philip and complain, "Kent, will it hurt you to behave with military courtesy for one hour?"

"I am not a King's soldier!" Philip said from the corner of his mouth. "And I can promise you that if we ever see action against them, I won't be wearing one of their own damned red coats."

"Nor will any of us," Knox retorted. He was obviously irritated by the continuing coarse comments from the men around Philip. "Sergeant!" he exclaimed suddenly. "Count the cadence for these hay-foots!"

With another glance at his prime troublemaker, he added, "For the moment I am persuaded it would be better if we're never forced to fight. Try to build an army out of an ill-tempered band of apprentices who won't take orders from anyone? I pity the general who's handed *that* assignment."

He strode away to the head of the column.

IV

THE COLONEL'S prophecy that Gage would enforce stronger Crown rule in Boston was soon fulfilled. The word "intolerable" started to appear frequently in the *Gazette's* pages, to describe a new series of Parliamentary decrees.

The Administration of Justice Act almost guaranteed a not-guilty verdict for any Crown official tried for employing violence in putting down an act of rebellion. On the recommendation of the Governor, such an official's trial could be moved to England to ensure "fair" judicial proceedings.

A second act, passed in May, virtually dismantled the Massachusetts provincial government. Judges, sheriffs and even justices of the peace would be Crown-appointed in the future. That meant juries could be packed with Tories, since they were selected by the sheriffs. Finally, in a move designed to rob the radicals of their single most important instrument of political persuasion, the traditional Massachusetts town meetings could only be convened with the Governor's approval—after he had ruled upon the permissibility of all items on a proposed agenda.

Like all the citizens of Boston, Philip and Anne Ware found that each day in the late spring and early summer seemed to bring some new development—or the sight of another man-o'-war bearing down from Nantasket Roads, loaded to the gunwales with more redcoats.

The day after the Port Bill went into effect, the Fourth Infantry—the King's Own—debarked, along with the Forty-third, fresh from Ireland. Up from New York sailed the Royal Welsh Fusiliers. A royal artillery company soon spread its tents on the Common. In all, nearly five thousand military men swelled the population.

And their arrival had a direct effect upon all the colonies, thanks to yet another Parliamentary measure passed in June. Its provisions applied not merely to Massachusetts but to every locale up and down the seaboard where royal troops might be garrisoned.

In private, Adams and the Long Room group gleefully celebrated what they

considered to be the King's latest, enormous blunder. But those who were directly affected by the provisions of the Quartering Act were less amused.

"A stinking lobsterback in my own house!" Abraham Ware exclaimed, fairly dancing up and down in front of Philip and Ben Edes one muggy day in late June. "Imagine!—I am commanded to feed him, to give him a bed, to treat him cordially at all times! Well, the only bed he'll get is in my barn, by God."

"You're not alone, Abraham," Edes told him. "The troops are being jammed into private homes all over Boston. Not to mention the taverns and warehouses. In fact, anywhere their damned officers choose. Has your—ah—guest arrived?"

Ware shook his head. "But I understand I'm on the list for quartering someone from the very next regiment coming in. The Thirty-third. By Jesus, just see if I so much as speak to the swine!"

"Well," said Edes with a rueful smile, "personal inconveniences aside, the Quartering Act's had one good outcome. There's the news of it, just in with Revere—" He gestured, and Ware followed him to the press.

The popeyed lawyer peered down at the type locked into the form. "I can't read your damned lead backwards Edes!" Philip helped out:

"It says that New York and Philadelphia have answered Boston's appeal—and in the fall, there'll be a great congress of representatives from all the colonies. The congress is supposed to decide what's to be done about the Intolerable Acts."

The information partially mollified the little lawyer. But he still left the shop grumbling about being forced to board a British soldier at his own expense. "The moldly hay in the barn is the best meal I'll offer him!" was Ware's pronouncement as he departed.

V

ON A blindingly sunny August morning, several hundred citizens—including Anne Ware and, with Ben Edes' permission, her frequent companion these past summer days—crushed into Bromfield's Lane. The crowd was awaiting the opening of the front door of the splendid home belonging to the speaker of the Massachusetts House.

Before the mounting block stood a handsome coach with red and yellow wheels and four chestnut horses. A liveried driver and groom sat on the box. Two black footmen in similar attire waited by the coach door. Four more servants on horseback controlled their mounts prancing nervously at the edge of the crowd. Philip noted the gleam of pistol butts in the holsters of this quartet of outriders.

Anne seized Philip's arm and pointed excitedly. "The door's open. There's Papa!"

The crowd broke into applause and cheering as Ware appeared, engaged in conversation with a fellow lawyer, the soberly dressed John Adams of Braintree. The next man to emerge from the site of the farewell breakfast was almost unrecognizable, so clean and opulent were his claret-colored suit and the snowy ruffles at collar and cuffs. Silver buckles on the shoes of Samuel Adams twinkled in the August light. The golden head of his long cane glittered.

All of these items, Philip knew, had been donated so that Adams might appear fittingly dressed when he attended the great Congress, to be convened at a place

called Carpenters' Hall in the Quaker City on the fifth of September. As the *Gazette* had duly reported, only one colony of the thirteen, Georgia, had balked at sending delegates to the meeting, whose express purpose was to agree upon a response to the repressive laws—especially the Quartering Act and the new Quebec Act of early summer. This last had expanded the boundaries of Canada to a distant western river, the Ohio. "Canada," as Philip understood it, now contained land to which speculators in Virginia and Connecticut, as well as Massachusetts, laid claim.

Soon Molineaux, the dandyish Hancock, the smiling Dr. Warren and others in the party came out to mingle in the crowd. Someone marveled that the Massachusetts contingent, including delegates, servants and outriders, would number close to a hundred men.

While Sam Adams conferred with his cousin John and with Hancock, who was remaining behind, Abraham Ware searched the crowd for his daughter. He located her, waved and fought his way forward. Philip drew aside to let Ware give Anne a farewell hug and a few admonitory whispers. At one of these, Anne's brown eyes flashed with delight as she glanced at Philip.

He experienced one of those rare moments in which he had no doubt about his enjoyment of their relationship. Being with Anne—strolling the town or gossiping in her kitchen about the latest turn of events—had become both natural and automatic. He seldom thought about the nature of their liaison, and he never discussed it. Nor did she. Each had accepted the other's terms. Whenever there was an opportunity for them to discreetly steal time for lovemaking in the Ware barn, they did so with pleasure, and without debate over the significance of the act.

Anne hugged her father one last time. Her face glowed, the freckles along her nose showing dark against the brown sheen of her skin. Philip realized Lawyer Ware was peering at him with a peculiar concentration. Pulling his daughter by the hand, the little man approached Philip to say:

"I've asked Annie to excuse us a moment while we have a personal word."

He released Anne's hand and guided Philip through the crowd applauding Sam Adams' somewhat ostentatious mounting of the coach step. Anne's look seemed to say she had no idea what her father wanted of Philip.

In the midst of the shoving, vocal crowd, Ware found the privacy he sought.

"You know I'll be away at the Congress for several weeks, Philip. And that my daughter and Daisy are alone on Launder Street with that soldier."

"Yes, Anne told me a sergeant was quartered with you now. I haven't met him yet."

"Poor lumpish creature," Ware said. "He's not a bad sort—for a Tommy. But I want to speak to you on another subject. I haven't questioned Annie keeping company with you—even though I'll frankly admit I would be pleased with a suitor of more substantial means and background. Don't take offense! That's a father's natural reaction. Besides, I'm uncertain about your intentions. But as I say, I haven't questioned your association with my daughter—"

"Though you obviously wanted to," Philip said, somewhat irritated.

"Indeed so. However, the truth is, she asked me not to do it."

"Why?"

"Your company gives her pleasure."

"Mr. Ware, I'm very fond of Anne. But—" He structured the falsehood carefully. "—you hit it yourself."

"Hit what?"

"The reason I can't state any—intentions, as you call them. I feel I don't have sufficient money. Or prospects for the future."

Ware digested this with a murmur and a bob of his head. Then:

"In confidence, I can say that Annie has mentioned both reasons. She's also expressed an opinion that neither is genuine. Now don't goggle and swear! Listen! My time's short, and this needs saying. While I gather you have never spoken anything on the subject, Anne's convinced there must be another woman somewhere in your history. Having lived with my own child since her birth, that kind of statement tells me how she really feels about you. Though the struggle goes unmentioned, she's locked in some kind of battle with—whoever or what-ever still holds a claim on you. Because she has—" He cleared his throat, obviously ill at ease. "—ah—set her cap for you."

Stunned, Philip looked through the crowd for the blaze of Anne's chestnut hair. He couldn't find her. That she had sensed the tearing in him—the pull of the past, of Alicia—only heightened his appreciation of her sensitivity.

"Ultimately," Ware went on, "a father, of all persons in the world, has the least to say about the disposition of a daughter's life. Outside the royal circles, of course. So I speak to you instead. Asking two things."

The little laywer's face revealed his concern for his child. "First, in my absence, call frequently at Launder Street. Look after Annie as only a man can. And secondly—whatever your final feelings about marriage—don't hurt her. If there's to be nothing permanent between the two of you, so be it. But when you make your mind up, should the decision be negative, tell her frankly—and quickly."

Ware's hand, surprisingly powerful, locked on Philip's arm. "Because if I thought it was dalliance, with no genuine feeling, I would have you flayed out of your skin. If I couldn't do it myself I would hire it done. I will, if you ever deliberately bring Annie to grief."

In as steady a voice as he could manage, Philip answered, "There'll be no need for that, Mr. Ware. I think too highly of your daughter."

"Fair enough. Come along and let's find her. I must be into the coach for Philadelphia."

___ **VI**

SERGEANT GEORGE LUMDEN was just under thirty years old. He had mild gray eyes, a large mole in the center of his forehead, crooked teeth. His manner was shy, almost humble.

Lumden had answered the summons of the recruiting drum in his native Warwickshire. The eleventh son of a smithy, he had chosen military life because it offered his only means of escape from poverty. But, as Philip discovered in conversation with the soldier in Ware's kitchen during the last days of August, Lumden was not pleased that the Thirty-third Infantry Regiment had been shipped to Boston.

"There's plenty in the regiment who feel the same way, too. In my case it's personal. I've got a relative—a second cousin—in these colonies."

"Indeed, where?" Daisy O'Brian exclaimed, bringing a heaping plate of hot biscuits to the table and setting them in front of Lumden with a flourish.

The cook's cheeks seemed exceedingly pink, Philip thought. From his vantage

point on a hearthside stool where he sat with hands locked around one knee, Daisy looked positively fluttery. She overflowed with gasps and exclamations and too-loud laughter at Lumden's slightest jest or sign of attention.

Philip glanced across to Anne. She was slowly stirring a fragrant kettle of fish-head chowder simmering on a chain over the logs. Anne returned his glance with amused understanding. Neither the enraptured Daisy nor the slump-shouldered Lumden noticed.

Lumden had both of his spatterdashes spread on the table. Using a little brush, he was applying moist white paste from a small jar. His uniform jacket with willowgreen facings hung over the back of his chair. His torso, already turning to fat, was clad in woolen underwear that appeared fiendishly heavy for summertime.

"I think the town's known as Hartford," Lumden said in reply to Daisy's question. "I want to visit there—provided all stays calm in Boston. It's my wish that it will. I have never served in combat and, damme, I don't want to," he added, without the slightest embarrassment. "Soldiering's a hard enough life without throwing in the risk of being killed. I mean—just consider! You're damp all the time. Even in summer, you're damp from collar to socks!"

Anne laughed. "I'll agree, Sergeant, those uniforms do look hot."

" 'T'isn't only the sweat," he said. "It's this damned pipe clay. Every inch of white we wear must be clayed day in, day out, or there are hellish penalties." Disgusted, he flung the brush down beside the jar of whitening compound. "When the pipe clay's fresh, you feel soggy because it's wet. When it dries it shrinks the material so tight you're half strangled—and you sweat all the more. Then there's the damn pewter buttons, each of which must wink and twinkle—" Reaching behind him, he flicked one of the offending buttons. "—or that's another fine or whipping. Or both, if you've a commander like ours."

"Got a tyrant in charge, do you?" Philip asked.

"Yes, sir. The man has the vilest temper I've ever seen. Regiments like the Thirty-third attract such types."

"And other regiments don't?"

"Not so much."

"I don't understand."

"Well, you see, the British army's composed of two sorts of regiments. Royal ones—always in blue facings, surely you've seen those in town—"

The other three nodded almost simultaneously.

"Then there's proprietary regiments like the Thirty-third. Hired to fight by the Crown. A real moneymaking operation for the nabob who can put one together. He virtually owns it, and even after expenses are met, he can bank on fattening his own fortunes. Take our actual commander. He's a gouty old far. . . —" Blushing, he glanced at Daisy, swallowed. "—Viscount. Name of Coney. He's never marched, never faced fire, never left England. So the man in charge of the regiment here, Lieutenant Colonel Amberly, he's not the real commander at all, if you follow—"

Lumden blinked, noticing the sudden tightness around Philip's mouth.

"Mr. Kent, did I say something to anger you?" He sounded apologetic.

Philip's scalp crawled. The palms of his hands had turned damp. He shook his head.

"Go on, Lumden. Tell me about this lieutenant colonel."

The sergeant scratched his chin, frowned in annoyance when he realized his

finger was still smeared with pipe clay. Daisy scampered for a cloth. As Lumden wiped the paste off his jaw, he continued:

"He's the sort you often find commanding a proprietary. Care nothing about the men—or the profession. Only wants a little experience to put on his record. Bought his commission, of course. Or his father did, I 'spose, that's generally how it works. There's no other way to achieve a high rank quickly. Like I say, Amberly's a bas—uh, a bad-tempered man. He can be plagued cruel. Turn on you in a second! On the other hand, he's not much worse than many I hear about. So maybe I shouldn't complain."

Philip said quietly, "Do you happen to know this Amberly's first name?"

" 'Course. It's Roger. Roger Hook-hand, some of us call him on the sly. He has this crippled right hand—"

Lumden held up his fingers, grotesquely shaped. Philip stared, his throat tight and hot. He jumped up with such suddenness that Daisy started. Lumden again look distressed:

"Ah, I'm sorry! I know it's not decent to mock a man's misfortune. But the lieutenant colonel's infirmities have crimped up something in his soul, damned if they haven't. A bad hand—the mark of a bad birth—" Lumden touched his forehead near his left eyebrow. "That's a hell-born combination, I'll tell you. No wonder he's taught himself to use the whip with his left hand. He enjoys handing out punishment when the mood's on him—"

"Does this commander of yours ever speak of a wife?" Philip asked.

"Yes, I've heard tell of one back in England. Mr. Kent, I've upset you, haven't I? My apologies. But I'm damned if I know how I—"

Philip spun for the back door, growling, "Never mind, it's nothing."

"Do you know the commander, is that it—?"

Philip slammed the door and clattered down the stairs into the mellow August sunshine.

He heard the house door open again. Head down, one knuckle rubbing against his mouth, he walked to the relatively cooler shadow inside the little barn. Without really seeing it, he stared at Lumden's spread-out equipment: his sizable pack, his cartouche, his Brown Bess with a swordlike length of steel mounted so as to extend well past the end of the muzzle. He felt rather than heard Anne enter behind him.

He turned to confront her. The daylight outside set her chestnut hair aglow.

"The name turned you white, Philip. Is it the same man you told me about?"

"It can't be anyone else. The first name might be coincidental, but not the hand and the birthmark." Searching back, he remembered a statement Alicia had made and he added, "When I knew him, there was talk that he'd spend some time in the army. With so many regiments being sent here, I suppose it's not unthinkable that he could wind up in Boston."

She glided toward him, touched his hand. "What do you intend to do?"

Fighting the memories of how Roger Amberly had been instrumental in arranging his near-murder, Philip said, "I intend to stay out of his way. If he caught sight of me by accident, I imagine he could trump up an arrest. He hated my mother and me enough to want me dead, and I doubt the feeling's lessened very much. He still carries that wrecked hand I gave him."

Anne gazed deep into his eyes. "You asked about a woman. A wife. Is she the one I've been struggling against all these months? I know there's something more than your father's letter binding you to the past—and holding you from any kind of future—"

He was ready to lie to spare her feelings. Then he recalled his pledge to Abraham Ware. He said:

"Yes, she's the one."

"Married to your father's other son. You never told me that part, Philip."

"I saw no need. Anne, I have to go back to the shop. Please don't say a thing to Lumden."

"Of course I wouldn't. But—when you questioned him, your face was as ugly as I've ever seen it. Do you still hate Amberly so?"

"He caused my mother's death! I'd like to kill him."

A weary expression overrode the starkness on his features then. His voice moderated:

"But I've become enough of a realist—like the sergeant—to want to stay alive. Deliberate contact with Roger Amberly would put all the odds on his side, and none on mine. Unless—" A harsh thought changed his face again. "—unless a killing was carefully done. The trouble is, in these times—well, I have allegiances to Mr. Edes. And plotting murder's no simple job. At least for me."

"Murder would only make you just what he is!"

He knew she was right. He almost hated her for saying it. "Let's not talk about it, Anne. I said I had to leave—"

"First tell me a little about his wife. Was she beautiful?"

"No, I won't tell you. She's married—and that's the end of it."

"Except inside you."

He whirled away from her, away from the dreadful accuracy with which she'd struck to the heart of his turmoil. He stalked toward the front of the property. When she called his name, he turned in the blue shadows at the side of the house.

Anne was standing in a patch of sunlight outside the barn. Her fists were clenched.

"I'll win against her, Philip. I swear I will!"

He thought he saw tears shining on her summer-ripened cheeks. He turned again and hurried away down Launder Street.

7
Betrayal

A NEW king, Louis XVI, reigned in France. But some in Boston town proclaimed that they too had been graced with a new monarch, a despot. For although Thomas Gage spoke mildly enough in public, he manipulated the royal troops with a firm purpose from Province House. On the first of September, a few picked companies marched to Cambridge in a surprise raid and seized quantities of powder and muskets belonging to the local militia.

Church bells pealing and small cannon exploding brought Boston citizens to an awareness that something extremely serious had happened. Serious for the colonials—but serious for the British, too, as it turned out.

Response to the raid had been swift, the *Gazette* reported. Clanging bells and couriers on horseback summoned several thousand farmers with their muskets,

their scythes—any weapon available—and drew them all toward Charlestown, where Gage's men were busy seizing a second storehouse of powder.

No military clash occurred. The soldiers prudently returned to the city just as the first countrymen came streaming to the site of the expected battle. When they found no enemies, they went home.

But Ben Edes, for one, considered the affair a victory of sorts:

"The general's afraid, Philip. And in fear lies the capacity for error. Thinking to gobble up arms meant to be used against his men, he practically gave a lesson on how he'll operate if he ever moves in force. You heard how quickly the militiamen rallied?"

"Yes."

"Well, it wasn't quick enough—the raid taught us that. We've got to set up new, faster ways of signaling and mobilizing the countryside. One day Gage will regret being such a generous instructor," Edes chuckled. "Sam Adams is a quick study."

So it proved.

Gage fortified the Roxbury Neck with guard posts during the first week in September. But Adams, Hancock and the other prime movers of the patriot cause came and went—if not unrecognized, at least unmolested. The general continued his policy of not moving openly against the rebel ringleaders, though he kept his regiments busy drilling.

The freedom of movement Gage allowed Adams and the others permitted the Massachusetts House to sit at Salem in early October. In open defiance of the Governor, the House approved formation of a new Committee of Safety, chaired by Hancock, with official power to organize, arm and summon militia contingents to action. Philip began to hear a new term used to identify those select companies now responsible for rallying to an alarm in a very short time. Minute companies, they were called.

Meantime, Abraham Ware's weekly letter to his daughter brought a running account of developments at Carpenters' Hall in Philadelphia.

In response to a set of Massachusetts resolves drafted by Dr. Warren, enacted at a convention of Suffolk County and then sent overland with Revere on horseback, the radicals and the conservatives in the great Congress pulled and hauled against one another, now rejecting Warren's firebrand call for arming the towns and imposing economic sanctions against Britain, now proposing more moderate resolutions opposing the Crown's position.

Finally—"Praise the Almighty as well as those who argue loudest!" Ware declared in one epistle—the Congress adopted a set of ten resolves. Among other things, the resolves declared the exclusive right of the provincial legislatures to regulate matters of internal policy, especially taxation. The resolves also stated that thirteen separate and distinct Parliamentary acts put in force since 1763 were in violation of the colonials' rights to "life, liberty and property." And the radicals won a key point in the form of the sought-for promise of economic reprisals until the Intolerable Acts were repealed.

Ware wrote Anne that the unprecedented assembly hoped to adjourn in late October, after drawing up a petition of grievances specifically addressed to the King. The representatives of the various colonies had already decided to meet again the following year if relief was not obtained.

'Tis not as much as Sam'l. or Dr. W.—or indeed, myself—would have wished," the lawyer said in one of the letters Anne showed Philip. "On the other hand, there is concert—agreement—and that in itself is fraught with meaning

for the future. To see the delegates, foregather at City Tavern at nightfall, and to hear such gentlemen as the very respected Col. Washington of Virginia voice the same concerns as the men of Boston—while we all indulge ourselves in Maderia and great heaps of baked oysters—that, my dearest daughter, is an experience not capable of being fully described, only savored in the proud heart.

November came. Anne looked forward to her father's return with mixed feelings. She missed him. But she would likewise miss the privacy afforded by his absence, privacy in which she and Philip could be alone in the parlor of an evening. They talked of everything except their own futures, while Daisy and Sergeant Lumden of the Thirty-third laughed and chattered in similar fashion in the kitchen.

The approach of winter made it increasingly apparent that the Port Bill would indeed prove disastrous. Gage interpreted the act as even prohibiting ferryboats from crossing the river. Thus the price of partridges or mutton or cod carted the long way around, by Roxbury Neck, grew astronomically. Decent quantities of firewood and sweet-smelling lamp oil could be afforded only by the very rich—mostly Tories, who were delighted to see the Whigs suffer, and who were not overly concerned when the poor did, either.

Philip, of course, never forgot the presence of Lieutenant Colonel Roger Amberly in Boston.

He questioned Lumden as to where the regiment's commander was domiciled, and learned that it was in a huge house on Beacon Hill, a house whose owner had strong Tory leanings.

Philip loitered outside the house on several different evenings, shivering in the dusk and hoping to catch a glimpse of the man whose death he planned in endless variations. He speculated on ways to arrange what would look like an accident. Other times, he thought of using what little money he'd put by to hire one of the South End mob men to act as executioner.

But luck never gave him so much as one look at his enemy in all the hours he stood in the bitter wind, pondering alternatives.

The answer to one major question still eluded him. Was he actually capable of doing what he told himself he wanted to do? The question unresolved, his plans remained just that.

He finally abandoned the evening spying and let himself be consumed by the routine at Dassett Alley—and by Anne. Perhaps, he thought more than once, he was hiding from his own weakness; from a basic inability to cold-bloodedly kill another human being—

After that first day in August when Lumden revealed the name of his commander, Anne never raised the subject of Amberly. Nor did she mention Alicia. Philip was grateful. He finally did admit to himself that he lacked the will to do deliberate murder.

A part of him cried out for it. But something else, equally strong, held him back.

II

"OH, GOD, there's going to be war, all right," Sergeant Lumden declared glumly one night in late December. "Have you heard the news from New Hampshire—wherever the devil that is?"

"Fort William and Mary," Philip nodded, turning the tankard of rum punch in his hands to absorb its warmth. "They're talking of nothing else down at the Dragon."

Red-haired Daisy hovered by the hearth. Much of her usual good humor seemed lacking this evening. Philip wondered why—until he caught up to the fact that she could scarcely keep her eyes off the mild-spoken British infantryman with the forehead mole. And she looked worried.

Philip drank a little, chose his next words carefully:

"In fact, I've even heard gossip that a Boston man, riding express for five shillings a day, carried a warning of the expedition to New Hampshire, so the stores could be carted off."

Gossip was hardly the right word. Philip knew full well that Revere had done the riding. But he wasn't sure how far Lumden could be trusted, likable as he might be.

General Gage had intended to strengthen the New Hampshire fort with several boatloads of troops slipped quietly out of Boston late one night. His plan had evidently been picked up by the alert ears of some informer at Province House. It was no secret that each side had its anonymous spies planted on the other.

A patriot named John Sullivan received the warning from Revere. He encircled the fort with a band of men, overcame the small British garrison without so much as a single injury to anyone. Gage's reinforcements arrived to find all the fort's arms and powder gone.

"And I agree with you, Sergeant," Philip finished. "It does bring war that much closer."

Lumden eyed Philip morosely. The latter changed the subject, saying to Daisy, "You've no idea when Mistress Anne and her father will be back?"

"No, sir. They left on some errands." She moved to the table. Philip noted that her breasts rose and fell quickly. Why was she nervous?

The pretty, red-haired cook pulled a stool to the table, sat down and leaned her elbows on the wood. She look intently at Philip.

"But I'm glad you chose to call, sir. Geor—the sergeant has been meaning to speak to you for several days."

Philip shrugged as if to say the sergeant should go ahead. Lumden did, but with difficulty, staring at the open pantry door, at the rime of frost on a window overlooking the backyard—everywhere but at Philip.

"Well, Mr. Kent, the truth is, I—I—"

"Don't hesitate now," Daisy urged. "Tell him!"

Lumden's gray eyes finally met Philip's. "I can speak to you in confidence?"

"Of course."

"I told you that!" Daisy sighed.

Lumden swallowed. "I have been thinking of leaving the army."

"You mean a resignation?"

"No," Daisy answered, clasping her hand over the sergeant's.

All at once Philip understood the girl's tension, the way her eyes lingered on Lumden's face. He recalled how the cook and the soldier had spent many an evening together in the kitchen in recent weeks. Their soft laughter took on a new significance. He said:

"Desertion."

Daisy nodded emphatically. "George and I wish to be married. We have resolved the matter of our different faiths—"

Philip grinned. "That's wonderful! Congratulations to both of you!"

Daisy flushed, prettily this time. Her bright red hair glinted with reflections from the crackling fireplace. Lumden put in quickly:

"I realize desertion's a damned detestable act. Though I hate being stationed here to repress fellow Englishmen, three months ago I would have struck any chap who suggested the possibility that I might run away. But I don't mind admitting my feelings for Daisy have changed my attitude."

Philip said, "George, you're smart enough to appreciate that you've been quartered in a household where sympathies for the Crown are not exactly at a peak—"

"Oh yes, I've picked up a hint or two," Lumden answered with a wry smile.

"So you don't have to apologize. I applaud your decision. I think Mr. Ware will too."

"More and more of the lads are doing it, you know," Lumden said. "Slipping out across the Neck dressed as countrymen. Or rowing for the Charlestown Ferry guard post on the pretext of some official errand—"

"I say bravo to that," Philip told him.

"You must realize it's not cowardice on my part!" Lumden exclaimed. Then he added more softly, "At least not entirely. I doubt if I'd ever have decided to do it, except for—for what I've found in this house. Affection. Tenderness—" He lapsed into silence, turning even redder than Daisy had a moment earlier.

Presently, he managed to go on, "Also, as perhaps I've indicated, I *do* have a liking for the people of Boston—!"

Philip suppressed a smile. "Yes, you indicated that a minute ago, George. You don't need to keep explaining or excusing—"

"In my own heart, I think the King and his ministers are fools, villains or both! They don't realize you colonials are strong-headed. You won't yield easily!"

"We won't yield at all, George."

"Just so! That means action and counteraction—one side against the other— till the fuse ignites *all* the powder, am I correct?"

"I think you are, George."

Lumden banged the table, making the tankards rattle. "But dammit, I've no stomach for going into battle against artisans and farmers whose only crime is holding fast to what rights they feel belong to 'em—and are being taken away!"

"Understood," Philip assured him. "Completely understood. But let's discuss the practical problems—"

"Leaving Boston, you mean?" Daisy asked.

"Yes. It's either the Neck or the river."

"I think it must be the Neck," Lumden said. "A smithy's son gets little chance to become acquainted with water. Been swimming just once in my life. We visited a distant relative's near the River Avon. I only had nerve to wade up to my ankles. Scared to death, I was! On the voyage across from England, I was sick nearly the whole time. Y'see?—it's true! I'm a swinishly bad soldier! Trained for just one thing—like every other fellow in a British infantry regiment. Trained to be fodder for the enemy's muskets and cannon! In the formations in which we march, a man stands every chance of being shot down in the opening volley—"

His eyes gazed into some grim distance, seeing the slaughter he described. Then, as Philip cleared his throat, Lumden veered the talk back to the subject with a sharp, distracted gesture.

"I can't chance the river."

"To cross the Neck, you'll need different clothes," Philip said.

Daisy put in that she'd already been gathering up items from serving girls she knew in other houses. "Discards, mostly. They'll do well enough."

Philip nodded. "But you won't dare speak, George. Your accent would give you away."

"We have a plan for that as well," Daisy told him. "All it requires is another person. I've some savings of my own—do you know a trustworthy lad we could hire to pose as George's companion? His son—his nephew? The plan's to work this way—"

She described it in a few sentences. Philip admitted that, while it contained some risk, it stood a chance of succeeding, because the British soldiers typically regarded Massachusetts farmers as oafish types unable or unwilling to put any kind of check on their consumption of spirits—especially rum.

"I don't know of anyone offhand," he told Lumden. "I'll make inquiries, though."

"God bless you for that, sir!"

"When do you want to leave?" Philip countered.

"As soon as the arrangements can be completed."

"Where will you go? To that relative of yours you mentioned? Connecticut, wasn't it?"

Lumden answered, "Eventually I'll go there, yes. For the time being I plan to hide at Daisy's home. A farm beyond Concord. I don't imagine they'll search for me too long."

Philip chuckled. "If they kept up a constant search for every Tommy who's deserted in the past few months, Gage's men wouldn't have time for anything else. And he'd soon run out of men to do the searching! I'd hazard that you'll be safe within a week or two—" A thought occurred to him. "What are you going to do with your uniform and equipment?"

Lumden thought a moment. "Burn the uniform, I 'spose. In that fireplace. As for the Brown Bess—"

"And the blade that fits on the end. The bayonet," Philip prompted. "That's a weapon the colonial troops don't have, and don't know how to use."

The statement was entirely accurate. More than once, Lieutenant Knox of the Boston Grenadier Company had declared that lack of bayonets, as well as lack of training in using same, would put the colonials at a bad disadvantage if they were ever up against British line regiments in a stiff fight. Most of the militiamen tended to scoff. They bragged about their accuracy with a musket, rejected the need for an additional weapon affixed to the muzzle for stabbing and hacking. But Philip respected Knox, and took him at his word. So he tried not to show his eagerness as he asked Lumden:

"What will become of those things?"

"I'll leave them hidden in the barn. Or ditch them in the river. If I tried to haul 'em along with me, they'd be recognized as Crown issue right off. And God save me, I've come to hate all they stand for. Any fighting I have to do, I'll do with my own two hands."

Philip's dark eyes shone with a sudden intensity. "Will you give me the musket and the bayonet?"

Lumden grinned. "In return for finding the reliable lad to help with our plan."

"Done!"

"I prefer not to speculate on what you want with those things," Lumden said. "If the time ever comes when you use 'em against men who might be friends of

mine, I hope I'm tilling a field in Connecticut and bouncing a youngster in my lap." He reached over to clasp his pale hand around Daisy O'Brian's.

She stared back with unashamed affection. Philip barely noticed. His mind's eye glowed with an image of the Brown Bess and its shining length of steel. With difficulty, he refocused his thoughts on the reality of the moment.

"One more thing. Who's to know this plan? Mistress Anne, for instance?"

"I have already described our intentions to her," said the girl. "I imagine Mr. Ware will need to be told, too. Beyond that, I've spoken to no one. I haven't sent a letter to my father—and even if I could find someone to write it for me, I won't. If George should be caught—"

"I'd be flogged at the least," Lumden put in. "Or, more likely, shot."

"So I figured it's best my father know nothing of it till George reaches the farm. I hear sending messages out of Boston can be risky these days."

"Agreed," said Philip, rising from the table. There were noises at the front of the house.

Lawyer Ware appeared momentarily, knocking snowflakes from the crown of his tricorn hat.

"Aha, some conspiracy brewing!" he said with a sly smile. "I can tell from the cats' grins you're all wearing." In spite of himself, Ware had taken a liking to Lumden.

Anne entered the kitchen. Philip moved a couple of steps so their hands could touch briefly. With his other hand, he lifted his tankard in mock toast.

"Yes, sir, we're conspirators, all right. We've just recruited a new man to the cause. Or at least subtracted one from the other side. We should celebrate."

"You're mighty free at celebrating with my own supply of spirits, Mr. Kent," Ware said with false seriousness. "What's the nature of this conspiracy?"

As soon as Lumden explained his decision, Ware clapped his hands in delight and demanded that they all drink several festive rounds.

"At my expense," he said with a look at Philip. "This time."

III

FOLLOWING THE advice of Ben Edes, Philip decided to hire his help at the Green Dragon. Edes said boys who worked there were none too scrupulous about how they earned extra pay.

The boy on duty when Philip dropped in was an unkempt, ragged lad, one Jemmy Thaxter. Recognizing Philip as a friend, the landlord stated confidentially that, yes, Jemmy was willing to do illegal work when sufficiently rewarded.

"But he's been on the streets since he was seven or eight. So drive a sharp bargain. And keep any necessary secrets to yourself."

Philip disliked the fox-eyed twelve-year-old from the start. He especially hated Jemmy's putrid breath and his noxious habit of licking his crooked, yellowing upper teeth.

But Jemmy listened carefully, then said sure, he could come by a rickety cart and a horse in the slums of South Boston where he lived. Some risk to the venture? Never mind—all he cared about was the ten shillings.

Philip didn't ask how the boy intended to acquire the cart and the animal. Steal them, probably. Nor did he outline details of the plan, or its purpose. Those

would be revealed only just before Lumden's departure, when it would be too late for the boy to betray them.

Jemmy shrugged, apparently unconcerned. "So long's I'm paid, I'll sup with Old Nick himself. When's this here cart and nag wanted?"

"When I tell you so and not before. Could be days. Could be weeks. I'll let you know." The timing, Philip had been told, was up to Lumden himself.

The whole scheme somehow made him apprehensive. He charged it off to the worsening mood of the city. The closed port put hundreds of men out of work at the shipyards, the sail houses, the ropewalks. Why build a vessel if she could only be launched to sit in the harbor? Quarrelsome bands of the unemployed roamed the streets, harassing Gage's soldiers. Attacks against the troops became more frequent and more violent. The unwary enlisted man or officer who ventured out alone after dark stood the risk of being found the next morning severely beaten or—in two cases Philip heard about—dead. The only relief from the general grimness came during the occasional moments he and Anne managed to steal for themselves.

On the last night of the old year, he visited Launder Street exactly as he'd done twelve months earlier. Anne teasingly suggested they welcome 1775 in the manner that had pleasured them both a year previously.

Accomplishing the suggestion proved a little harder. Lawyer Ware yawned and retired well before the clock chimed eleven. But Daisy and her sergeant kept the kitchen humming with their claret-primed merriment. Philip and Anne ultimately had to resort to the pretense of announcing a short stroll in the wintry air just before midnight.

Once into Launder Street, they slipped around through twisting alleys to the sanctuary of the tiny barn, where they shared each other's embraces with eagerness and delight. But because of the glow from the kitchen windows, they didn't dare linger too long. They returned to the house the way they had left, within half an hour after the tolling of the bells.

As the new year opened, food and supplies in the Ware home, as in all of Boston, became more and more limited. The Wares took to burning only a few sticks of kindling in the kithen hearth at night, and none in the parlor.

And although Philip repeatedly offered Lumden reassurances that the plan would work smoothly, he continued to feel less than certain. Conditions in the city generated that kind of pessimism. Everything seemed to be breaking down.

While the days went by, Lumden grew increasingly fretful. Philip was worried that the man's agitated state would draw suspicion from his senior officers. Almost daily, so Anne reported, the sergeant vowed that he couldn't wait any longer. But he refused to name a day and hour when he would actually desert. Clearly, a violation of military law ran against his principles. Even though he was sustained by Daisy's romantic encouragements, the whole business placed him under a severe strain, Anne said.

Visiting Launder Street the next time, Philip discovered she hadn't exaggerated. Lumden spoke in monosyllables. He paced the Ware kitchen, up and down, up and down, fingering the mole on his forehead. On one of her trips to Dassett Alley, Anne said:

"I think if the poor man delays much longer, he'll suffer some kind of seizure. Or blurt out his guilt to the whole town. Do you suppose we should encourage him to abandon the idea?"

Philip shook his head. "I want that musket."

A somber pleasure brightened Anne's dark eyes. "Papa and I may make a revolutionary of you yet, Philip."

Ignoring the remark, he said, "I agree with you that Lumden shouldn't keep waiting. Else he may well give the game away. We'll talk to him tonight. Try to force a decision. Speed, after all, is to his advantage. Adams is already predicting that Gage will move in the spring. Go after the militia stores out in the country in earnest. So if our sergeant delays and delays, he may be marching in battle formation whether he likes it or not."

Philip repeated the warning that same evening. The pale infantryman listened in silence. Wintering indoors in the city had turned his cheeks hollow but had added even more weight to his belly.

When Philip finished, Lumden gnawed his lip, said with effort:

"All right—Saturday. Tell the boy Saturday. When it's dark. I'll disappear after evening muster—"

"How soon will you be missed?"

"Not till late Sunday, I shouldn't imagine."

Daisy looked relieved. "I have all the clothing put by."

"Good," Philip said. "Saturday. Seven o'clock."

The next afternoon, Philip asked Ben Edes' permission for half an hour off. He trudged to the Dragon in a thin, sifting snow. He instructed Jemmy Thaxter to bring the cart and horse to Launder Street at the appointed time. Sniffling and wiping his nose on his sleeve, the boy promised he would.

Philip slept badly the two nights prior to Saturday. The day dawned dull gray and unseasonably warm. He had trouble concentrating on his work, the typesetting for Monday's edition of the paper. At closing time he locked the shop and rushed to Launder Street. He found Lumden again pacing the kitchen.

"Well, you do look the picture of a countryman," Philip nodded, taking in the sergeant's attire: a leather hunting shirt with decorative fringe; a flop-brimmed hat and a thick muffler of dark brown wool; dirty trousers that might once have been bottle green; worn boots with flapping sole pieces. Daisy had indeed secured the ultimate castoffs of other households.

"Smear some of that fireplace soot on your neck," Philip instructed. "Under your nails, too." He went to the parlor for a glance at the enameled clock. Nearly six-thirty already.

He lifted one of the draperies, peered into Launder Street. Why was he so damned jumpy? His mind swam with a memory of Jemmy Thaxter's foxy, opaque eyes.

At seven-thirty, standing beside him in the cold, lightless parlor, Anne voiced the fear that had become a certainty to Philip:

"Something's amiss. He's not coming."

"I'd better go find out what's happened—"

"Philip?" He turned on his way out. "Please be careful."

Nodding, he bundled into the surtout he'd purchased a few weeks ago for protection against the damp January winds. He tramped to the Green Dragon, pushed through the doors, blinked against the smoke—and clenched his teeth in fury at the sight of Jemmy Thaxter piling three new logs onto the irons of the blackened hearth.

The boy saw Philip immediately. He bolted for the back.

Philip ran after him, dodging among the startled patrons. "That's Ben Edes' devil!" one exclaimed. "What did Jemmy do this time, sell his sister and give the lad the pox—?"

Philip crashed out through the tavern's rear door, sprinted six steps along the alley, caught Jemmy's collar.

"Leave go!" the boy squealed. Instead, Philip shook him, hard.

"Seven o'clock's come and gone. Where's the horse? Where's the cart?"

Still struggling, Jemmy cried, "I don't want nothin' to do wif' a soldier running away!"

"Running—?"

Philip was so astounded, he nearly let the boy go by accident. But he held on. Jemmy coughed, a heavy, wheezing sound. Philip's mouth tightened. His voice dropped, threatening:

"How did you decide that's why the cart was wanted?" He shook Jemmy savagely. "Tell me or I'll break your damn bones!"

"I—I didn't think this was no straight deal from the start. I wanted to see wot I was gettin' into. So I follered you one night. From Edes' place to that house in Launder Street. I peeked in an' saw you talkin' to that lobsterback in the kitchen. He's goin' to ditch, ain't he? That's what I'm 'sposed to do, ain't it, help smuggle him 'cross the Neck? Well, I don't like bloody Tommy any better'n the next. But I ain't mixing in helping somebody from the Thirty-third run away. Ten shillings ain't worth it—nothing's worth it—you git a whip or a musket ball if you're caught—*quit holding me so hard!*"

Something in the boy's darting eyes started suspicion churning inside Philip. But he couldn't quite pin down what was wrong. Especially when his anger was running high, urging him to administer a beating. The frail, dirty boy disgusted him.

"So you haven't got the horse or the cart?" he asked.

Jemmy gulped, admitted it was so. Philip flung him away, cursing.

"Ain't you going to hit me or nothing?"

"Hell, why? The harm's done. But let me warn you, Jemmy. Boy or no boy, breathe a word to a soul and you'll be called on by some gentlemen in liberty caps. They won't spare you because of your age, you sneaking little bastard."

Coughing out a mist of spittle, Jemmy cowered back against the fence opposite the Dragon's rear door. "There won't be a word—nobody knows 'cept me. I haven't even told the lady, God's truth! I just decided not to go through with it, is all—"

"Why didn't you tell me that, damnit?"

"I—I was scairt to. I thought you'd beat me."

"Remember that you'll be beaten worse if you don't keep your mouth closed."

"I will—I swear."

Again Philip felt that sting of suspicion; again he failed to define the source. It was obvious he'd simply approached the wrong boy, and now Lumden's whole escape was in jeopardy. Once more he tried to read Jemmy's grubby face, darting eyes. He couldn't.

Turning, he sped off up the alley, intending to run all the way to Launder Street.

At least, he thought as he raced along with the night air stinging his cheeks, Lumden could return to his unit for the next muster and not be missed. But Philip also realized he'd have to call at the Dragon a few more times, to make certain he'd put sufficient fear into Jemmy Thaxter to ensure the boy's silence—

A silence which the next moments revealed to be a fraud.

Philip rounded the corner into the street where Lawyer Ware's house showed

lamplight at its parlor windows. He stopped in mid-stride, cold dread clawing his middle.

In front of the house, reins looped and tied to the ring of the mounting block, a horse fretted and blew out plumes of vapor.

Philip had seen enough wealthy people riding on the Common to recognize an expensive saddle. What person of means was calling on Abraham Ware just at the hour when Lumden's escape was supposed to be taking place? It was too damned coincidental for comfort—

Stealing toward the stoop, Philip suddenly recalled something else. Jemmy had specifically identified Lumden's regiment. That was what had been nagging his mind!

Perhaps the boy already knew which regiment wore willow-green facings. But if not, why would he go to the trouble of finding out? Unless—

Nerves taut, he crept up the front steps, crouched and peered through a slit where drapery and window frame didn't quite meet. Terror soured his throat as he caught a flash of scarlet inside—

An officer's tunic!

Waiting only long enough to confirm that with a second look, Philip whirled and darted back down the steps. The horse neighed, clopped its hoofs. Philip edged away, stole through the passage beside the house and across the tiny yard under the pale stars.

As he approached the closed barn door, his mind seethed with fury. What had happened had become all too evident.

First, he'd blundered, let himself be followed.

And Jemmy had been lying when he claimed he wanted no part of the desertion. The boy's gutter mind had simply recognized a chance for bigger profit. How much had he gotten from the officers of the Thirty-third for informing on the would-be deserter?

Starting to roll back the barn door, Philip again cursed his own foolish mistake. *Who was in the house? What was happening?*

With the door no more than half open, he heard quick movement. Something flashed toward his face. He ducked instinctively, drove his left hand up, battered Lumden's musket aside. A second slower, and the bayonet would have pierced his throat—

"Lumden—hold still!" The terrified sergeant kept trying to wrench his musket loose. *"God damn it, stop! It's me!"*

At last Lumden recognized Philip. He lowered the musket with a trembling hand, whispered:

"Kent—what in the name of Christ went wrong?"

"The boy sold us out. My fault."

"I thought I'd gone stark raving crazy when Daisy spied one of the regimental officers riding up to the front door—"

"Who is it?"

"I don't know, I ran out here to hide. Mistress Anne said she could get rid of him."

Philip prayed Anne's confidence would prove warranted. She, Daisy and Ware had carefully discussed and rehearsed the story they would tell if anyone from Lumden's regiment came searching for him. The story was to be simple and, therefore, easily kept consistent. They would merely state that Lumden had vanished without any explanation.

But though the household had planned on the certainty of an investigation,

they had *not* planned on it taking place until Lumden was well out of Boston. To have an officer pounce while the sergeant was still hidden on the premises was a development even the courageous and quick-witted Anne might not be able to handle.

Philip wished her father were home to help. But he knew that Ware, anticipating no difficulty with the departure, had left Launder Street at five, to confer, then dine, at Hancock's.

Chafing his hands against the cold, Philip kept glancing toward the rear of the house. He saw lights but no sign of movement in the kitchen.

He had to trust Anne. Depend on Anne. Her good sense, her bravery—

"Why is the officer here now, Kent? You haven't explained!"

"He's here because that little sod from the Dragon must have gone to your regimental headquarters. The boy pretended the plan was too risky. Said he followed me here, saw you inside, guessed it was a desertion—wanted no part of it at any price. Obviously that's not true. He saw a chance to get a higher price from someone else, just for reporting—look, we're wasting time. Gather up your gear. We'll slip out the back way. Go to the shop. Anne will be able to turn the officer away. But he'll probably want to verify any claim that you're not here—"

"But she may be telling him I *am* here!"

"I doubt it. She knows you'd be questioned. Hard. So you'd better not be around. Come on, I'll help you—"

He bent in the darkness, fumbled Lumden's pack straps into his hands—

And went rigid at the sound of a woman crying out in terror—or pain.

The scream came from the house.

Philip bowled past Lumden, snatched up the sergeant's musket. He loosened the bayonet from the muzzle in seconds. With the length of steel glittering in his hand, he dashed across the yard and up the kitchen steps as the cry rang out again.

This time he had no doubt that it was Anne's voice.

8
Journey to Darkness

PHILIP WASTED no time on silence. He kicked the porch door open, sped through the kitchen with barely a glimpse of Daisy O'Brian, round-eyed and uttering small, wordless sounds of terror.

She had good reason to be frightened out of her wits. As he reached the closed parlor doors, he caught the sounds of struggle on the other side.

His breath was a ghostly cloud in the chill darkness. The front hall was illuminated only by the faint light of the January stars through the fanlight. He pressed close to the carved wood of the doors, heard a pained exclamation from Anne—then a voice that dredged up memories of depthless fear and hatred:

"—will not lie to me further, madam! Has he fled or are you concealing him? Come, which is it?"

The familiar voice sounded heavy with sudden exertion. Anne let out another little cry.

"Other commanders may delegate unpleasant business like this, madam. But I punish personally. I punish both those under my direct command and any who abet their treachery—"

Philip pried the doors apart with his free hand and stepped into the parlor's dim lamplight.

He knew the voice—and the man—beyond all doubting. He saw other details only marginally—

Anne's gown disheveled; ripped down the right sleeve, where the officer held her with his left hand—

The man's scarlet tunic, seen from the back. But even from that viewpoint, Philip recognized the additional height, the wider shoulders—

The officer wore his sword in an unusual position. On his right hip.

Because he would have to wield the weapon with a hand that was not crippled—?

Anne glimpsed Philip across the officer's shoulder. She couldn't conceal her reaction. The officer heard Philip's quiet voice even as he started to turn.

"Yes, that would be like you, now that you no longer have to act secretly. Now that your uniform gives you the authority to strike in the open."

Like an image from a half-remembered nightmare, Philip saw the face at last. The features so like his own. The small, cloven U mark near the left brow. For a moment Roger Amberly's expression remained blank. Philip waited at the doorway, bayonet held near his waist.

The stunning recognition hit.

"My God in heaven. *Charboneau?*"

He saw the ruin of his half-brother's hand. The fingers were permanently tightened into a claw, much as Lumden had shown him. The hand had a shrunken, bloodless appearance, as if it had not only locked in its crippled position, but withered from lack of use. It looked tiny, dangling at the end of an otherwise normal arm.

The disfiguring mark turned darker, almost black. Roger Amberly's face became a show of confusion—disbelief and rage mingled as he struggled to comprehend the reality of the man confronting him. The young officer's splendid red coat with its cuffs and lapels of willow green stained the scene with vivid color.

Never taking his eyes from his half-brother, Roger relaxed his grip on Anne's arm. She retreated a step, watching tensely as Philip sought to control the rage in his own mind and heart.

"Charboneau?" Philip repeated. "You're wrong, Colonel. Charboneau died in London. Or was it on the Bristol road? If not one, then the other—as you intended, correct? Charboneau's mother is also dead—because of your harassment. It's a man named Philip Kent you must deal with now." He gestured savagely with the bayonet. "Get outside, so I don't spill your God damn blood in this house!"

To Roger's credit, he stood still, composed. "Philip—what?—Kent?" he said. His mouth took on its familiar, mean twist. "Well, a new name hardly conceals the insufferable bastard boy I met formerly. And I find you in a traitor's house to boot. Oh, yes—" The slight turn of his head was for Anne's benefit "—The dwelling of Mr. Abraham Ware is well known to the general's staff as a place where these so-called patriots hatch treason."

Very slowly, he reached across with his left hand, gripped his sword hilt, suddenly freed the blade with amazing speed. His eyes loomed huge and dark in the shifting flicker of the two lamps. His loathing poured like a torrent through one more sentence he spoke:

"It shall give me considerable pleasure to write my good wife, Alicia—with whom I believe you were briefly acquainted—that circumstances presented me with the opportunity to finally bring about your long-overdue death." Without warning, he ran at Philip, left arm extended, sword reaching out—

Philip had no time to think, only to react in order to save himself. He twisted aside. Roger's sword gouged into one of the doors. For a moment Philip smelled his blood kin: the scented powder in his hair, the damp odor of his woolen coat, the sudden sweaty odor that danger produces in all men. The half brothers stood no more than a foot apart for one frozen instant. Roger's midsection was fully exposed by the force and extension of his lunge. Philip brought his right hand up and stabbed the bayonet into Roger's belly and pulled it out.

Roger's mouth dropped open. His shoulders sagged. He did a peculiar step to the side, his boot heels clicking. Then he stared down at the pierced wool to the left of his brightly polished buttons.

A darker red appeared in the cut in the fabric—and spread, staining. Struggling for breath, Roger let out a labored exclamation.

Now that his initial thoughtless fury had been drained away in the single driving blow of the reddened bayonet, Philip turned cold. Roger was dying on his feet—

It took him a moment to fall. Blurring, his dark eyes seemed to search for Philip, his bravado replaced by a horror-struck look of hurt, by the realization that he might be mortally injured.

Philip felt weak, almost sick. His enemy no longer looked formidable, only helpless. Roger's sword struck the pegged floor to one side of the carpet. With a last, bubbling grunt of pain, he dropped.

Thrusting the bloody bayonet under his left arm, Philip cried, "Help me, Anne!"

She stumbled forward, grabbed Roger's right shoulder. The two turned Roger so that he lay on his back. Mouth open, eyes shut, he gasped like a beached fish. All at once Philip realized the full significance of what had happened—and what had to be done.

"We must get him out. He mustn't bloody the place, because someone will surely come to ask about him. I'll take him through the back. Dispose of the body. You—" He spoke with difficulty; he was still trembling "—you go to the street and untie his horse. Get it going—away from here."

"When—when Daisy announced him," Anne said in a faint voice, "I could hardly keep my hands still, they were shaking so badly—"

Philip held up one of his own. "Like mine."

"Yes. I knew who he was. But he was in such a fury he didn't notice immediately. How did he get here, Philip? How did he know—?"

"The boy from the Dragon gave us away. Probably took a higher price for telling Lumden's officers he planned to desert. Did you admit anything to Amberly?"

"Nothing. I denied having seen George all day. I denied any knowledge of his desertion. But your brother kept staring at me—he frightened me terribly. I think he knew I was lying. I could tell the first moment he walked in that he was all you'd said, and more."

"Well, we're done with him." The implication of those words still rocked him to the center of his being. "The horse, Anne. But quietly. So none of the neighbors are roused—"

Philip slid Roger's sword back in its scabbard, began to haul the still form by the collar. He dragged the body through the black hallway, seeing Anne limned briefly against the radiance of lamps alight in the house opposite. Then the front door shut.

By the time he reached the kitchen, he thought he heard horseshoes ring on cobblestones. He winced at the loudness.

Daisy rushed to the kitchen door when she heard him coming, looked at the closed eyes, saw the widening stain at the belly of the uniform and ground her knuckles against her mouth. She started those small, incoherent sounds again. Philip realized she might easily become hysterical.

His eyes locked with hers. "Daisy."

"Wh—what?"

"Make no sound or we're undone. I need George's help. I need his help to carry the body so we don't leave blood."

He let go of Roger Amberly's collar. There was a sickening thump when the powdered head struck the floor. Philip drew the bayonet out from under the arm of his surtout, walked by the round-eyed girl, laid the bayonet on the kitchen table.

"Daisy, fetch Lumden. And find me rags to wipe this thing clean. Then burn the ra—*damn you, girl, do what I say!*"

Still dazed, she stumbled out into the darkness. She returned in a few moments with the astonished sergeant.

Staring down at his commanding officer, Lumden seemed pleased—but only for a few seconds. His gray eyes misted with shock. And perhaps pity.

Still struggling against a feeling of numbness, unreality, Philip cleared his throat, said:

"We'll take him through the alleys. Several blocks—as far as we can go without being detected. Then we'll come back here, clean this place and get out."

"We?"

"I'm going with you. That's the only way you'll ever escape Boston now."

"Kent, it's not your affair. I mean—I'm the one wanting to desert—"

"But you can't get across the Neck by yourself. And Amberly must have told someone on his staff what he planned to do. Take his boots, man. Hurry!"

Philip bent, gripped the limp shoulders. He tried to keep his eyes away from the slack lips, the waxy eyelids, the bloodstain that had now spread beneath Roger's jacket to redden his white trousers at the groin and down the inside of his right leg. With a heave, the two men lifted the body, struggled it off the porch and carried it around the barn. After a survey of the crooked alley behind the property, they turned to the right.

They crossed a deserted street, running with their burden. They plunged into another alley. In about two minutes they carried the officer some three squares from Launder Street.

As they were about to dart across one more dark thoroughfare, Philip dropped the body suddenly. Hoofs rang out a couple of blocks away. Wheels creaked. A coach—coming at a good clip.

"We'll leave him here," Philip whispered, shoving the limp form against the

wall of a building near the alley mouth. He positioned the body so the head faced the brick wall. The approaching coach thundered—

There was no longer the remotest sense of satisfaction in any of this, only a desperate urgency. He and Lumden backed to the wall, stood elbow to elbow to hide Roger as best they could. Philip prayed the darkness was sufficient concealment—

The two-horse berlin rumbled by, hoofs and ironshod wheels raising sparks.

As soon as the coach had passed, Philip grabbed Lumden's arm. He shoved the slow-moving man back in the direction of Ware's house.

Rushing along, he tried to organize his tumultuous thoughts. In only a few ticks of time, the present had crumbled—and the future as well. He knew exactly what must be done. There remained the dangerous task of implementing the decision. He cursed Roger Amberly silently as he and Lumden ran along the barn wall and up the porch. Anne and Daisy waited in the kitchen, both of them still pale.

Philip kicked the door shut. On the table lay the bayonet, freshly wiped, free of blood. In the hearth a scrap of rag sent up a curl of smoke.

Well, that was a start toward salvaging the disaster of the past half-hour.

II

"I'LL GO to your father's farm," he announced to Daisy. He was sitting at the table. His head had started to ache horribly.

Her chestnut hair all a-tangle around her shoulders, Anne seemed about to offer an argument. Philip prevented it:

"It's the only way Lumden can leave Boston—and he must leave *tonight*. Where's the rum, Daisy?"

The red-haired cook hurried into the pantry and brought back the demiflagon set aside earlier to implement the escape. Philip took the jug, placed it on the table, holding it with both hands to mask the trembling of his fingers.

"Do you think your father will take us in?" he asked Daisy.

Wide-eyed, she nodded.

"How do we find the farm? It's out past Concord, you said—"

"Once you reach the village, you cross North Bridge. Keep on along the road going west. You'll passs a large farmhouse. It belongs to Colonel Barrett. About a half-mile beyond, there's another, not quite so big. That's my father's."

"All right." He glanced up. Anne was watching him. She looked exhausted, and far less assured than he had ever seen her.

"Anne, it will be difficult for you here, so try to prepare yourself. Another officer—perhaps several—will surely come from Lumden's regiment. Maybe as early as tomorrow. You did loose the horse—?"

"And saw him gone out of sight."

"We'll just have to trust our luck—which so far tonight has been very poor indeed. If none of your neighbors grew overly curious when they heard Amberly's horse arrive—*and* if none of them looked out their windows to see a British officer walk up to your door—there will be nothing to link him to this house. *Except* his intention to come here. Which he surely didn't keep to himself back at headquarters. So your story is this: He never arrived. Once we're gone, make sure there's no evidence of it. Check the parlor for blood. For traces of his hair

powder—out in the hall too, where I dropped him. Tell your father what happened. Be certain he's ready to deny, as you'll deny—and you, Daisy—any knowledge of the sergeant's plans to desert.''

"All right," Anne said.

"You never heard him speak of it, understand? Never."

"Yes."

"He kept to himself except at meals. If he intended to leave his regiment, the secret was his and nobody else's. Now—'' Thinking of what he was about to tell them, Philip's eyes grew ugly with frustration. Was there no end to the running? To the destruction of even the smallest hope for a future?

With effort, he mastered the self-pity, went on with what he'd started to say:

"In a day or two, when the danger's past, you must tell two people that I've gone. But only two. You needn't explain why. Just say I was in trouble and had to escape."

"Who must I tell?" Anne asked.

"Ben Edes and Henry Knox. Let them know I'll return to Boston when I can. Ask Edes to give you my sword and my mother's casket."

"And your bottle of tea?" Anne's effort at a smile failed.

"If you wish. I'd feel safer with those things stored here. Edes' shop may go up in flames one day soon—or be closed on order of General Gage."

Again the silent motion of her head agreed to his request. Philip laid his palms on the table, pushed up, feeling incredibly tired but a little less shaky than he had in those first moments when he realized he'd struck down his mortal enemy—and taken not a fraction of the pleasure from it that he had anticipated for so long. In fact, Roger's death had only added a further complication to an already peril-fraught situation.

George Lumden, who now looked reasonably alert and had been listening attentively, spoke up:

"Shall I get the musket from the barn, Philip?"

"No, leave it where it is," he answered, reluctantly handing over the bayonet. "And put this with it. The weapons and your equipment will help confirm Anne's story. Anne, be sure to show the musket to anyone from his regiment—''

"I will."

"If it's not confiscated you can arrange to give it to Knox for the Grenadier Company."

Philip still wanted the musket himself. But he had already ruled out taking it along. Possessing a Brown Bess would virtually guarantee their failure to pass the guard lines at Roxbury Neck.

He wiped his mouth with the back of his hand. He glanced from Daisy to Anne, including them both in his final remarks:

"We'll rely on you to send us word of conditions here. To notify us somehow if and when it's safe to come back. George—'' He bobbed his head at the red-haired country girl. "—say your goodbyes. But don't be too long about it. The quicker we head for the Neck, the surer we can be of getting across."

His words belied his doubt about the ease of the escape. They had no official papers of passage. Sometimes the troops let farmers through without them, sometimes not. They stood an excellent chance of being turned back.

But he said nothing. Things were bad enough already.

III

UNDER THE star-glowing fanlight of the front hall, Philip stole a few moments to take Anne in his arms, stroke her hair, whisper his own farewells. With his mouth pressing the warmth of her cheek, and her hands tight at the back of his surtout, he experienced a strange, almost melancholy emotion—

A conviction that not even in their most intimate moments had he ever felt so deeply about her—so concerned, so caring.

Was that love?

Well, whatever the name of the emotion, it brought an unashamed tear to the corner of his eye as they clung to each other in the darkness.

On their way to the front of the house, Anne had shut the parlor doors, as if the act could somehow obliterate what had taken place. But he knew it was not so easy as simply closing a door.

"Anne, I ask you to forgive me."

"For what?"

"For placing you and your father in danger. Danger that may last for days— weeks—perhaps months. I struck Roger without thinking—"

"Because he struck at you!"

"Yes, but that doesn't change—"

The pressure of her fingers against his lips stilled the rest. Her hand was cold, proof she was still very much frightened. But her voice remained calm:

"We'll see it through. The only flaw in everything you suggested is the possibility that someone did see Amberly arrive. I'll coach Daisy to meet that eventuality. She can be prepared to say she received him at the door and reported George gone."

"That's risky. When you're questioned, you may not know whether some of your Tory neighbors have already spoken with the investigators."

"It's a risk we'll have to face—and a situation we'll have to handle as it happens. We'll manage." Again she tried to smile. "Papa's a lawyer, you know. Artful dissembling's not entirely unknown in that profession. Perhaps the men who come won't be clever about their investigation. If we can pick up some hint of whether they've already visited other houses, we can fashion the response accordingly. Either say Amberly did stop, and went on when Daisy reported George gone—or use your story. Amberly never got here at all. Don't worry— women know how to improvise. Constantly fending off men, we have to learn that skill early!"

Her light tone failed to fit the moment. But he knew she was trying to reassure him, a reversal of the scene in the kitchen. He leaned forward to kiss her lips, hesitated as she added quietly:

"In a way, Philip, this night could mark an important turning. I know how the memory of that man ate at you. Now that page of the past is closed. You can go ahead—"

"To being a fugitive?" he said bitterly. "By God, that's not what I planned when I landed on Long Wharf!"

"What did you plan? To grow rich in the printing trade, as you've mentioned? Then go back to England and show them what a fine Tory gentleman you'd become? So you could see that woman again—?"

Her voice had risen. Abruptly, she stopped, averted her head.

"I'm sorry. I admit I've a jealous hatred of her. And a wish that you'll finally discover yourself to be what I think you are."

"It appears I have damned little choice about what I am. Things seem to have a way of getting out of hand these days—"

"The world's always been that way, Philip. There's something else happening now. Not chance alone destroying the future, but men."

Maybe she was right, he thought, holding her close again. Maybe that was the essential nature of the struggle Adams and Edes and the rest were waging: to free themselves from the capricious dictates of people who would dominate and destroy their lives in a test of wills, a test of an old, creaking system—

Ah, but what the hell good did such idealism—a noble cause—do at a time like this?

The gentle heat of Anne's warming cheek helped soothe away some of his turmoil. She whispered with her lips against his face:

"I'll send word to the farm as quickly as I can. Meanwhile, remember this. I love you." She kissed him with a desperate fierceness.

A noise at the rear of the hallway separated them. It was Daisy and Lumden, the latter lugging the demiflagon of rum.

"I think we'd best go the back way," Philip said.

Feeling alone and not a little afraid, he walked toward the barn with the nervous sergeant at his elbow. The dampness of the January night penetrated even the warm surtout. He turned briefly for a final look at the kitchen's cheery light—and saw Daisy and Anne watching together. Anne's hand lifted in a small gesture of farewell.

He straightened his shoulders and followed Lumden in the darkness. Somewhere the cadence of a regimental drum beating the night's tap-to echoed along the lonely streets.

Their route led them through South Boston, within a block of the Liberty Tree. On its great soughing branches a single, forlorn paper lantern burned. *Shining about as brightly as the hopes of Mr. Edes and friends for peacefully winning their battle,* Philip thought in a moment of deep pessimism.

Even as he watched, a gust of wind blew the lantern out.

IV

ON ORANGE Street, Philip called a halt in the shadow of a ramshackle building. In the distance, beyond the double arch of the town gate, torches winked at the guard post on the Neck.

"Now, George," he announced with a smile that had no substance, "the anointing. And don't forget—not one single coherent word. You may stumble. You may mutter. But don't let them hear you speak, I'll do the talking."

Tossing away the demiflagon's cork, he poured rum down Lumden's collar, sprinkled some into his hair, then handed him the jug.

"Don't drink. Just take in a good mouthful and hold it a minute, so you'll reek inside as well as out."

The sergeant dutifully tilted the jug, filled his mouth and shut his lips till his cheeks bulged. At last he spat the rum into the gutter. A scraggly dog that had come slinking around the corner caught some of the spray, reacted with a yapping bark. Philip picked up a stone and flung it.

The dog ran off a short distance. But it continued to bark, the noise unnaturally loud in the stillness of the night. Down at the guard post, Philip thought he saw

figures moving, aroused by the racket. He swore softly as he slipped his arm beneath Lumden's.

"Lean on me, George. Try to act drunk. Hum a little if you want—but not some Goddamn regimental song!"

They approached the gate and passed through. The moment they did, the wind struck them, whipping across the narrow stretch of land. Philip shivered. Lumden's teeth chattered.

The muddy road out of Boston was rutted from wagon tires, bore countless prints of men and animals. The figures at the barrier ahead took on more definition. Two—no, three British soldiers, one inside the jerrybuilt booth, the others waiting at the horizontal pole.

Philip and the sergeant walked slowly, erratically along the strip of land that connected Boston to the countryside beyond. Ahead, a few lamps in Roxbury burned yellow in the vast darkness. The Charles River lapped on one hand, the harbor on the other, redolent with the tang of the salt sea.

Philip could smell the rum, though. But could Lumden carry off the deception? For that matter, could he?

He had almost, but not entirely, lost the traces of his foreign speech. And if the sergeant accidentally spoke one word, the soldiers would know instantly that he was no Massachusetts man.

As they neared the barrier, Philip said in a loud, complaining voice, "Come on, stand up straight!"

He paused long enough to lob another rock at the dog, still pursuing, still barking. The stone hit the animal's hindquarters, sent him running with a yelp.

Despite the cold night air, Lumden's cheeks shone with sweat. *Damn. Not good*, Philip thought, half-carrying his tangle-footed companion toward the pole.

Two redcoats stood in the snapping glare of torches stuck into the wall of the guard booth. The soldiers brought their muskets up to waist level, bayonets shining. One looked to be no more than fifteen or sixteen. The other was older, a paunchy veteran.

Lumden mumbled and pretended to sag. Philip struggled to prop him up, growling, "Goddamn it, Ned, stand on your pins. I'll not carry you all the way to Roxbury!"

Lumden did a good imitation of drunken blathering as the heavyset redcoat prodded Philip's chest lightly with his bayonet.

"No passage to Roxbury till you answer a couple of questions. What be your names?"

Philip dredged up a last name Knox had mentioned once, replied, "George Kemble, sir. I farm land outside Roxbury. My cousin Ned here—Ned Kemble— he's got a fondness for the town whores. They got him drunk, as usual. I had to come in and fetch him out of one of the deadfalls."

The soldier peered into Lumden's face. Lumden affected a moon grin, letting slobber leak over his lower lip. The soldier looked disgusted.

"Have ye papers to prove your identity?"

"Papers?" Philip feigned a witless look, then a queasy smile. "Sir, neither Ned or me can write a line. Farming's what we know. When we sign, it's with a mark. Listen, I come into Boston at noon without anybody asking me for papers—"

"Coming in, yes. Going out's a different story. Bastards like that silver-maker Revere must have papers 'cos they might be on treasonous errands."

"Oh." Tense, Philip tried to look merely unhappy.

"Let go of your cousin, then," said the soldier. "Ye can't pass without a search."

Philip reluctantly released his burden. Lumden swayed and clawed at empty air. Philip grabbed him hastily, causing the sergeant to laugh and spit on the muddied road.

"Two of the colony's finest! Tell me, Kemble—" He laid his musket against the pole, started to poke and probe Philip's surtout. "—are you lads members of these militia companies we hear about? The fine units they say will take the field against us one day?"

"The Kemble family's loyal to King George, sir," Philip said with a toadying smile.

"Ah, yas—" The soldier's quick hand patted down Philip's breeches, squeezed his boots. "—every bloody one who comes to the barrier says that. Then we find daggers hid, or cartridges an' ball. 'Course, it really makes no damn difference. If ye ever do have a mind to fight the King's regiments, there's but one thing waiting for you an' the rest who march up an' down with them silly sticks on their shoulders—a grave, Kemble. A grave's waiting for ye. All right. How's the other one, Arch?"

The younger soldier who had been searching Lumden said, "Nothing on him except the smell of dirt an' rum."

Philip seethed at the way the paunchy soldier had spoken with such contempt for the military skills of the colonists. Perhaps if he knew a Henry Knox—!

But he didn't dare let his temper best him now. The paunchy soldier was reaching for the rope that controlled the pole—

The pole creaked as it rose in the wind. The torches snapped and sparked. Philip swallowed, propped Lumden up again, began to urge him forward:

"Walk, Ned, for Christ's sake! All full of drink, you weigh a short ton and you're saggy as a sack of shit besides—"

From the corner of his eye Philip saw the guard booth drop behind. And the pole. Lumden pretended to stumble in the mud. Philip cuffed his ear for effect, cursing even more floridly.

Another step.

Another. The darkness pricked by the lights of Roxbury seemed a reachable haven now.

One more step.

One more—

"Hold up."

Philip clenched his teeth at the sound of the younger soldier's voice. The third redcoat had emerged from the booth to lean on the pole as the boy and his paunchy comrade dodged under and hurried after Philip and Lumden.

The younger soldier grabbed Philip's shoulder roughly. He lost his grip on Lumden. The latter, acting with a vengeance, tumbled face forward into the mud. Harder than he'd expected. A single word burst out explosively—

"Damme!"

We're done, Philip thought as hands jerked his left arm up. The boy soldier said:

"Look there at what you missed! Noticed it when he was walkin' away. That's blood or I ain't never seen it."

"So 'tis, Arch," grumbled the older one, whirling Philip around. Lumden was pushing up from the oozing mud, clambering to his feet. Philip hoped to God that the distraction of the suddenly discovered bloodstain under the arm of

his surtout—where he'd gripped the bayonet—might have distracted the soldiers from realizing Lumden had cursed in pure, British English.

"Where'd you come by that, Kemble?" the older one demanded. "Let's have an explanation—and quick."

Philip wriggled free, still maintaining his fawning grin.

"Sirs—didn't I mention already? Ned got mixed up with some real sluts. They damn near clawed me to pieces 'fore I could drag him away. Least I imagine that's how the blood got there. One of the whores had a little knife. I took it away from her and kind of cut her—by accident, y'know?" He winked. "She bled a storm—"

The heavy soldier acted dubious. "Funny place for the blood to land, though."

"Admit it is. Just can't explain it any better. In the fracas I wasn't too particular about keepin' clean. I slipped and fell a couple of times. Maybe there was some of her blood on the floor of the crib, I dunno."

Philip could feel the sweat rivering down the back of his neck. The longer they were detained, the greater the chances they would be detained permanently— turned back. He tried one last, huge grin.

"Guarantee you one thing, though. I fixed that whore just fine. There's one less fluff in Boston to give you a dose of the pox."

That amused the heavy man. "Well, I'd say that's a real service to the Crown. I'm a man who likes his fuckin', but I had that French pox once. It makes you feel like you're bloody well pissin' needles." He stepped back. "Pass on."

"Yes, sir. Thank you, sir."

Supporting Lumden again, Philip fought the urge to run. He forced himself to walk away from the soldiers slowly, his eyes on the wagon-tracked ground ahead of his boots.

The ground grew darker—darker—

At last the periphery of the torchlight was left behind.

The mournful sounds of wind and rolling water filled the night. Roxbury was ahead—and a longer road beyond. Seventeen miles or so stretched between them and Concord village. The darkness began to seem forbidding, hostile.

And well it might, he thought. In order to help Lumden, he'd left Anne behind, her safety, her very freedom uncertain.

All at once Lumden started to blurt out his thanks. Philip hissed at him to keep silent. The thick, gummy mud pulled at their boots with sucking sounds. The night was growing decidedly colder. The wind slashed out of the Atlantic from the northeast.

Philip hardly noticed the string of in-bound carts creaking toward Boston with loads of fish. When the carts were gone, the road again became as empty and bleak as the future to which the disastrous circumstances on Launder Street had led him. Head down, hands deep in the pockets of his surtout, he kept walking into the enormous dark.

BOOK FOUR

THE ROAD FROM CONCORD BRIDGE

1
The Letter

A COCK crowed the morning. The second morning since the two fugitives had crossed Roxbury Neck. Shivering in the chill, his belly growling, Philip crouched in a roadside ditch and peered at the clapboard farmhouse, its weathervane just turning a sulfurous orange in the January dawn.

Behind the farmhouse stood two dilapidated outbuildings. The larger, a barn, was still indistinct in the shadow cast by the frost-whitened hillside immediately behind. Inside the barn, horses whickered. A cow lowed.

They had been watching the O'Brian farmstead for almost ten minutes. Philip said:

"Come on, George, for God's sake! Let's march up and wake him. I'll stand behind your explanation."

The sergeant fingered the mole on his forehead, his habit when in a state of nerves, Philip had observed.

"I wish I'd asked Daisy for some token," Lumden said. "Something her father would recognize as hers—"

Philip jumped the frozen water in the bottom of the ditch, climbed up the bank to the road.

"Well, I'm not waiting any longer. I'm damn near dead from hunger and just about frozen stiff from the wind. What's he going to do, shoot us for redcoats?"

"He might," said Lumden dourly. "I know for a fact Gage has sent out spies disguised as farmers." His teeth started chattering again as he followed Philip to the road.

They'd walked most of two nights and half the intervening day. They had traveled north from Brookline through Cambridge, then northwest to the hamlet of Lexington, and five miles more to larger Concord, which appeared to be a

substantial village, perhaps as many as a thousand or fifteen hundred souls. It boasted clusters of prosperous-looking homes, a grist mill situated at one end of a pond of some size, a meeting house and a tavern the creaking signboard identified as Wright's.

On their journey they had gone parallel to the main roads, avoiding the roads themselves, because of the chance that they might be pursued. So the trip had been slow going. Clad only in the fringed leather shirt, Lumden had suffered worst from the winter air.

Passing through Concord village just before first light, they crossed the purling Concord River via a narrow wooden footbridge northwest of town. The land here was different from the flatter country around Lexington. Ridges crested against the skyline. The road Daisy had told them to follow wound between low hills.

They passed the farm she had identified as belonging to someone named Barrett. The next place, poorer than the first, looked bleak in the cold orange glow just touching the eastern ridges.

"George, hurry it up, will you?" Philip grumped now, determined to delay the confrontation no longer.

As they crossed the road and started up the narrow track leading past the house, a figure emerged from the gloom around the barn. Philip and Lumden halted, caught in the open, fully visible in the light brightening the eastern hills.

The figure stood motionless near the barn door, strangely dark, even about the face. A shadow-man. Philip's heart beat faster. His hand came up, his mouth opened to hail the watcher, let him know they were not thieves—

The figure darted back inside the barn.

Lumden started to ask a worried question. Philip waved him silent, sprinting for the front of the house just in case his fears proved to have foundation.

They did. The shadow-man reappeared, a musket raised to his shoulder.

"Down!" Philip shouted, leaping sideways to tackle Lumden and roll him into the frozen grass as the musket exploded with a puff of smoke.

Philip heard the ball whiz past, strike somewhere out on the road, spent. He shot up a hand, waved.

"Wait! We're friends. Sent here by Daisy O'Brian—"

Already re-loading, the man by the barn hesitated. Within the house, Philip heard cursing.

The man from the barn loped forward, turning his empty musket and grasping it by the barrel, a club. Philip clambered to his feet slowly and drew in a surprised breath. He saw why the man had blended so completely with the barn shadows.

Black hands gripped the musket's muzzle. White teeth glinted between black lips. The Negro was middle-aged, plainly dressed in boots, old trousers, a coarse gray farmer's shirt. But he had a powerful, resilient look about him. Beneath the poll of grizzled hair, his dark eyes were not friendly.

"Honest folks don't come sneakin' into farmyards 'fore the light's up," he said, passing the corner of the house and coming to within a couple of feet of Philip and his companion. "But horse thieves do. Tell me who you be—and right now."

The farmhouse door opened. Behind a plume of breath, Philip glimpsed a short, rotund man in a nightshirt that hung to his bare ankles. The man's eyes and rosy face bore a certain resemblance to Daisy's.

"What the hell you shooting for, Arthur?" the farmer barked.

"Shooting at a couple very strange birds, Mr. O'Brian," said the Negro. "Spotted 'em creepin' across the road."

"We're friends—" Philip began.

"You're a damn liar." O'Brian scrutinized the pair with cold blue eyes. "I never seen either of you before."

"Mr. O'Brian, let me explain," Philip said, taking a single step toward the porch. Arthur tightened his dark hands on the musket muzzle, lifted it back across his right shoulder, ready to strike.

"It's true you don't know us. My name is Kent. This is George Lumden—"

"You still haven't told me anything. Where d'you hail from?"

"Boston. We both know your daughter."

"You do, eh?" A pause. "Which one?"

"The one in Boston of course."

"What's her name?"

"Daisy."

The farmer pondered. Then: "State your business."

"Mr. Lumden's a former soldier of the King's infantry. I helped him escape two nights ago. Daisy sent us here because—"

Well, why not out with it?

"—because Mr. Lumden and your daughter have plans to marry."

Philip thought O'Brian was going to faint. "*Marry*—? You come skulking to the house before the moon's down, and greet me with the news that this one is my future son-in-law? Blessed Mary! These are mad times—but not that mad."

Wary of sudden moves because the big Negro was still poised to attack, Philip slowly reached under his surtout. As he did, O'Brian snorted:

"Arthur, I think I'd best dress and load my squirrel gun. We'll haul these two loonies to Concord and have 'em locked up. Daisy's intended? Sweet God, d'you take me for a total idiot?" He scowled. "I'd wager the truth is more like this. You're King's men. In disguise and hunting military stores!"

"No, sir, that's wrong," Philip said. "Will you look at this? I think it'll help convince you—"

He pulled out the medal on its chain.

O'Brian shook his head. "Wearing a medal from the Mother Church doesn't prove a damn thing. There are plenty of Irish lobsterbacks, I hear tell."

"This isn't a holy medal, Mr. O'Brian. There's a Liberty Tree on it. Won't you look?"

For the first time, O'Brian appeared a shade less skeptical.

"You're one of the Boston band?" he asked.

"I am."

"Let me see."

Philip approached the lower step. O'Brian's thick, gnarled fingers turned the medal, examining both sides before he let go.

" 'Pears real enough. Could be stolen, though."

"But it isn't."

"He's telling the truth, Mr. O'Brian," Lumden said despite his chattering teeth. "I have deserted from the Thirty-third Infantry, in these clothes your daughter found for me."

"You really mean to say that you and my child—? That the two of you—?"

"Yes, sir. I was assigned to quarters at the house where Daisy works. Mr. Ware's house. That's how we met."

Philip waited tensely while O'Brian continued to study them. Then the farmer's features seemed to relax a little.

"Well, I'm damned. I'm waked from sound slumber by a musket banging and find two beggarly fellows shivering in my yard—and that's how nuptials are announced these days? Arthur—"

"Sir?"

"What d'you think?"

"It's mighty peculiar, sir."

"It's so goddamn peculiar, there must be a kernal o'truth to it. Let's fetch 'em inside and hear the whole fancy tale."

Still keeping a watchful eye on Philip and his companion, the Negro followed them through the front door and the heatless front rooms. In the kitchen, O'Brian stamped barefoot to the hearth and struck a fire under some kindling.

"Now," he ordered, "sit yourselves down and let me hear it from the beginning. Then I'll decide whether to march you to Concord and the stocks."

Philip decided he liked the crusty old man. He certainly couldn't blame O'Brian for his suspicion. At least they'd gotten out of the cold. He edged his stool a little closer to the crackling blaze and joined O'Brian in staring at Lumden.

"One o' you start talking!" O'Brian cried.

Turning red, Lumden said, "What my friend Kent has told you is gospel truth, Mr. O'Brian—" He got busy fingering his mole. "I am George Lumden, late of the Thirty-third. While I lived at the home of the lawyer, Mr. Abraham Ware, your daughter and I developed—" He turned redder. "A—a—" He mumbled the rest.

"Louder! Speak up!" O'Brian roared.

"A mutual affection for one another," Lumden said in a strangled voice. "At the same time, it became clear to me that I had no stomach for this colonial quarrel with fellow Englishmen. I say that to you without shame, sir—I want no part of it! I only desire to marry your daughter, be a good husband and provide for her for the rest of our lives."

O'Brian's blue eyes narrowed. "How?"

"Well, sir, in England, my father was a smith. I know something of that trade—"

"God's wonders! I'd say your head's cracked—or mine is!—except you really talk like all this blather is the truth."

"Sir, it is. Daisy and I are—" Scarlet again, Lumden mumbled the rest.

"You expect to marry my child without asking my leave?" O'Brian challenged.

"Indeed not! I—I'm asking it now."

"Well, I ain't giving it! Not yet." The farmer hunched forward. "What's your faith?"

"Church of England, sir."

"Oh, Christ help us—!"

"—but Daisy and I had agreed to marry and raise our offspring in her church!" O'Brian blinked. "You have?"

"Definitely."

Scratching his chin, the farmer turned to the Negro. "Arthur, what's your opinion now?"

"It's too crazy not to be true, Mr. O'Brian," said the grizzled black. "But I'd like to hear the other one talk some, too."

Before Philip could speak, Lumden said matter-of-factly, "I didn't know men in the colonies asked the opinions of their bond slaves."

Arthur slammed the musket butt on the pegged floor, glaring. For the first time, Philip noticed rings of thickened tissue on the inside of each black wrist. Shackle scars?

O'Brian made a placating gesture. "Arthur, he only speaks out of pagan ignorance." To Lumden: "We don't hold with slavery in the Massachusetts colony. Arthur is a free man of color. He works for his wages and board like anyone else—and can cease to do so and move on whenever he chooses. Bear that in mind when you speak to him."

Lumden flushed still another time. "I meant no offense, certainly. My apologies, Arthur—if I may address you that way."

"Guess so. Only name I got." But the black looked mollified.

Philip felt certain the shackle marks meant the man was a runaway. Perhaps from one of the southern colonies, where the peculiar institution so disapproved by many Boston liberals had long flourished with the assistance of Boston sea captains who brought human cargo from Africa as part of the vastly profitable triangular trade.

O'Brian resumed, "The blessed Lord saw fit to deliver nothing but females from the loins of my sainted, departed wife. Five of my daughters are already wed and living in various towns around the province. Daisy went traipsing off to Boston in the hope of improving her fortunes in similar style—" Another glance askance at Lumden, as if to say he wasn't sure she had. "So there's none but Arthur and me to run the place. If it's sanctuary you're seeking, the price is work."

"We'll gladly pay it," Philip told him. "George plans no return to Boston. And I can't go back for some weeks—if at all. I—" He hesitated only a moment. He felt he could trust the old farmer with at least a portion of the story. "—I encountered some trouble with one of His Majesty's officers. There may be arrest warrants out for me."

"Is Daisy in any danger?" O'Brian asked suddenly.

Philip didn't like lying. But he felt it best to spare the man undue concern.

"I am not aware of any, sir. She and Mistress Ware helped George find clothing for his escape, that's all. Your daughter directed us to come here, and said she'd send a message—"

"About what?"

"Joining us."

"How soon?"

"I don't know, sir."

"But you, the lobsterbacks want to arrest?"

"Possibly, yes."

At that O'Brian broke into his first genuine smile of the morning. "Well, that's a good recommendation!"

Already Philip felt better. The kitchen was warm now, flooded with the gold light of the winter morning breaking across the hillside behind the farm. The Irishman went on:

"And you're in top company. We understand the lives of such men as Sam Adams and Johnny Hancock aren't worth a shilling if they linger in Boston many more days. Fact is, we've been hearing they may seek sanctuary out this way. If you're all you claim, Kent, you'll want an introduction to my neighbor down the road. Jim Barrett—the Colonel. In charge of our Concord militia."

Philip nodded. "Indeed. I've already mustered with the Boston Grenadiers under Captain Pierce."

"Good. Arthur—hang up the porridge pot. Let's feed these scarecrows, and

ourselves too. I guess I'd best become acquainted with Tommy here, since it appears I may be stuck with him, like it or not. As soon as they've eaten, you can put 'em to work.''

At last the big black managed a grin.

"Mr. O'Brian, I'll keep 'em busy, don't you worry.''

II

ARTHUR PROVED a hard but fair taskmaster. He set Martin O'Brian's two unexpected boarders to hammering and sawing from sunup to dark, completing needed repairs on the siding of the rickety barn. Philip was grateful for the labor. It drained his body of strength by day's end, and the exhaustion helped drain his mind of worry about Anne Ware.

But no matter how tired he became from his chores, worry about Anne never escaped him completely. January turned into gray February, and still no message arrived.

During long evenings by the kitchen fire, O'Brian and his prospective son-in-law held lengthy conversations. They exchanged views on the seesaw struggle between Crown and colonies, impressions of British military capability in the event of open warfare. O'Brian was also fairly consistent with questions about the sincerity of Lumden's intent to become a Catholic convert.

O'Brian had by this time taken Philip down the road to the home of leathery Colonel James Barrett, who was readying the Concord militia and minute companies in the event of hostilities. Philip's sincerity and background convinced Barrett that the younger man was a worthy recruit. He drilled in Concord village with men of all ages. Some of the older ones were veterans of Rogers' Rangers in the French and Indian War—the struggle that had been called the Seven Years' War in that lost, dim time in Auvergne. Then, the men had fought on the King's side.

Out in the country, as Philip had heard, equipping the militia with muskets, powder and ball was no problem. The stockpiles had been building up for months. Barrett's smokehouse was a major storage point for arms. Other stores, including half a dozen cannon, were hidden in Concord's meeting house.

But because of the stockpiles, Barrett frequently reminded his companies, their quiet little village in the wooded hills where the Sudbury and Assabet flowed together to form the Concord might well be a major target of an expedition by Gage's soldiers.

Though security at the Neck was now reported tighter than ever, word of the heightening tensions in Boston reached Wright's Tavern with fair regularity. Patriots managed to row across the Charles by night to carry the news—

Revere had organized a secret company of mechanics to keep track of any sudden troop movements out of the city.

Ships newly arrived from England bore word that America's partisan, old Pitt, the Earl of Chatham, had responded to the declaration of grievances from the Congress. He had laid a plan of conciliation before Parliament. The plan included a provision for withdrawing all royal troops from Boston.

Pitt's plan was defeated. Next, it was rumored that while pretending to draw up a reconciliation program of its own, the North ministry was privately readying even more repressive and economically disastrous measures, including bills to bar New England ships from commerce in any ports save those in Britain and the

British West Indies, and to forbid New England fishing vessels from working the North Atlantic banks.

Most ominous of all were reports of another act, already said to be passed in London and awaiting only formal transmittal to Gage. It would authorize the general to use whatever measures he deemed necessary to enforce the various Crown edicts.

As the ice of February thinned under the first onslaught of March winds, the Concord patriots met in dark old Wright's to hear that despite the pleadings of men such as Pitt and Burke, both Lords and Commons had already declared the Massachusetts province *"in rebellion."* Gage seemed to act accordingly. He sent soldiers to Salem to seize the colonial arms stored there.

The night it happened, loud knocking at O'Brian's door roused Philip from his pallet. He grabbed his musket and ran all the way to Concord.

The provincial alarm system, a combination of mounted couriers and ringing bells in every village steeple, had been perfected now. All the Concord companies were ready to march within a couple of hours.

Then a horseman pounded in to report that the Salem supplies had been moved safely out of reach of the troops—and Gage's officers had chosen not to search and force combat in order to capture them.

But the patriots who made Wright's a rendezvous—Concord's Tory families wisely avoided the tavern—swore that it was only a matter of weeks, or perhaps days, before inevitable bloodshed.

In preparation, the Provincial Congress sitting at Cambridge under the direction of Hancock and Dr. Warren passed a resolve which put the militia companies on notice that any troop movements from Boston *"to the Number of Five Hundred Men"* would be considered grounds for mobilizing to a war-ready state.

Philip supposed he should take a more serious interest in all these dire tidings. But he was too preoccupied with the lack of any communications from Anne. O'Brian was equally worried about his daughter. As was Lumden.

By the second week in March, after discussing the situation with the Irish farmer and the ex-sergeant, Philip decided he would try to re-enter the city.

The very next morning, a cold, rain-spattered day, he was inside the barn preparing to saddle the sway-backed mare O'Brian had offered him. He heard wheels creak, hoofs plopping, looked outside—

The farm wagon appeared on the road at the front of the property. Arthur had driven to Concord for some flour and other staples. There was a second person returning with him. Squinting through the gray rain, Philip detected bright red hair—and shouted to the back of the barn where Lumden was sawing a plank:

"George! Daisy's here!"

Both men went racing through the drizzle as Arthur turned the wagon down the rutted track alongside the house. Laughing and weeping at the same time, Daisy flung herself down into Lumden's arms.

When the embrace ended, she ran to Philip and hugged him impetuously. "Mistress Anne's waiting for you at the tavern in Concord."

"You mean she came with you?"

Daisy nodded. "She and her father have taken rooms there. Adams has fled Boston for good—Mr. Hancock too. Sneaked out like criminals at night."

"The danger's grown that great, then?"

"So everyone says. Only that Dr. Warren stayed behind, Mr. Ware told us." She glanced around, wiping the joyful tears from her face while Lumden

simply stood, his saw forgotten in the mud at his feet. He beamed with almost comical happiness.

"Where's my father?" Daisy asked.

"Gone down the road to speak with Colonel Barrett," Arthur informed her. She turned to Lumden. "Have you—? That is, will he let us—?"

Lumden just grinned and nodded. Daisy squealed and rushed into his arms again. Philip started for the house to get his surtout. He called over his shoulder:

"Tell Mr. O'Brian I've gone to town to see—"

He stopped suddenly, looking at Daisy.

Holding Lumden's arm, she was staring at him with all trace of happiness momentarily wiped away.

"Daisy, what's wrong?" he asked.

She rushed to him, whispering:

"Mistress Anne will tell you."

"No, you tell me."

"There—there seems to be fairly certain evidence that the officer—well, the one who came to the house the night you left isn't—" She couldn't continue.

"Daisy, go on! Isn't what?"

"Isn't dead."

III

COLD FEAR, cold and slashing as the March rain, ravaged him as he swung into the saddle and headed the mare down the half-thawed road to Concord.

He saw O'Brian's horse tethered outside the colonel's house but pushed on without stopping. He clattered over the footbridge and through the center of the village to Wright's. The mud outside bore marks of the recent arrival of a coach.

Daisy's news had struck him with stunning force. And yet, reflecting as he dismounted, he realized that it was a turn of events he might have foreseen. He could not remember a single second during the haste of that bloody night on Launder Street when he had paused to determine whether Roger Amberly was indeed dead. He had assumed the bayonet stroke to be fatal.

The error could be fatal to him in turn.

Boots dropping clumps of mud, he stalked into the tavern. The landlord directed him up to the front suite of rooms. He burst into the gray, chilly parlor to see Abraham Ware hauling one of three trunks to one of the bedrooms.

Just throwing off her damp travel cloak, Anne turned. Her eyes grew wide. "Oh—*Philip!*"

He was not even conscious of crossing the threadbare carpet to wrap her in his arms and hold her.

"Anne, Anne. I've waited for word—!"

After a moment, they separated. He was alarmed to notice how wan she was. Despite the joy of the reunion, she acted oddly ill at ease.

Looking tired and peaked himself, Lawyer Ware harrumphed as he returned from the bedroom.

"Conditions have grown so bad in Boston, there was no way we could prudently communicate with you, Philip," she said. "The couriers do dangerous work—and have enough on their minds without the burden of personal messages."

"I was astonished to hear you were in Concord," Philip told him.

"It took a deal of finagling and some clever forgeries to come up with the papers that got us across the Neck." Ware indicated the trunks. "That's all we were allowed to bring. As to the rest—the house, the furnishings—well, the soldiers or the damn Tories have no doubt looted the place already. But it was run or face possible arrest for my activities. Only Warren insisted on remaining behind, and Revere—to coordinate the spying on the soldiers."

"We've heard Gage is getting ready to move against the towns," Philip said.

"He is. To seize the stores. There's supposed to be an authorization on its way by ship from the Colonial Secretary, Dartmouth."

"We've heard that too." Anne was watching him with a strange, bleak expression he wouldn't fathom.

Ware rolled his tongue in his cheek, continued, "Warren will arrange to get Paul and some others out with a warning if Gage moves. That's his plan, anyway. We've come to what Sam Adams wanted all along. Though it may be the only way, God take me, I'm frightened to my bones."

"How is Mr. Edes faring?" Philip asked.

"With difficulty. Distribution of the *Gazette's* all but forbidden. When Ben and I talked last—two days ago—he was starting to dismantle his press. He hopes to smuggle the pieces and a few fonts of type across the Charles. Perhaps to Watertown. He and Revere are holding conversations about money—"

Philip frowned, failing to understand the reference.

"The printing of it!" Ware exclaimed. "Should war come, the colonies will need their own financing. Paul's already drawing designs for the bills. But we've news of more direct concern to you, lad—" His protruding eyes harbored a new respect. "Concerning the officer who met an untimely accident in my parlor. Annie told me everything about it, of course."

"Daisy said there was reason to believe the man didn't die."

"Good reason."

Ware plumped himself on a rickety chair and peered gloomily through the yellowed lace curtains at the rain on the roofs of Concord.

"Thanks to Annie, we were prepared when other officers from the Thirty-third called at Launder Street. My daughter had rehearsed Daisy well. And the officers were careless enough to admit they had questioned some of our neighbors first. They told us Amberly was seen knocking at our door. Daisy led valiantly. Said Lumden disappeared that morning—I gather he's safe at her father's farm?"

"Yes, he is."

"Daisy told the redcoats she'd shown Amberly the equipment Lumden left in the barn. After which, he went away. She and Annie stuck to the same story although each was questioned twice more. I don't think either of 'em was fully believed—"

"I'm sure of it," Anne put in.

"The only saving factor was, Gage hasn't started torturing suspects for information. As yet! Maybe it's the influence of that American wife of his. The mysterious circumstances surrounding Amberly's whereabouts later might have helped keep us free of trouble, too."

Philip still couldn't fathom that strange, unblinking look on Anne's face. Her color had faded badly. Gray half-circles of fatigue showed beneath her eyes.

"What mysterious circumstances?" he said.

Anne replied, "Amberly was apparently found where you left him. Unconscious but not dead. He was removed from Boston a few days later."

"Removed!" Philip exclaimed. "Wasn't he put in a military hospital?"

"He should have been," Ware said. "And he was—at first. But someone interceded on his behalf. To arrange more suitable care."

"Explain what you mean."

"According to a lad on Revere's committee of mechanics whom I asked to keep watch and pick up information, Amberly—still in bad shape, mind—was loaded into a private coach by several men unfamiliar to my informant. Servant types, the boy thought. But not wearing a livery. The coach went out across the Neck with no hindrance."

Ware's mouth turned down, sour. "Evidently it's still possible to purchase special medical privileges, just the way prisoners in England purchase extra food, better quarters—and the way that damned fellow purchased his commission! Someone learned of his plight. Arranged for him to be attended elsewhere than in the military hospital—where he'd more likely die than recover. They're pest houses. The so-called surgeons are no better than butchers. It's all damned curious—"

He gave Philip a challenging look. "But Annie's brought you something whose outward appearance suggests it may serve to explain."

"What is it, Anne?"

"A letter."

"Which we didn't open," Ware advised. "The contents are your affair. Give it to him, Annie. I'm going down to the taproom and try to unfreeze my veins with some flip."

A moment after the door closed, Anne walked to the smallest trunk. She unlatched it, raised the lid. Among the folded articles of clothing Philip saw his mother's casket, Gil's wrapped sword, even the green glass bottle of tea. He was touched by the care with which Anne had obviously packed them.

She produced the letter from the bottom of the trunk, passed it to him.

Sealed with wax but bearing no sigil, it showed signs of much handling. The address, in a delicate, unfamiliar hand, read *Mr. Philip Kent, Esq.,* and was written in care of Ware's home in Launder Street, Boston.

He looked up. "How did you get this, Anne?"

"A private courier brought it to the door. Only hours before we loaded the trunks into the chaise."

"You mean you didn't see my name in the usual list in the paper? You didn't go down to the postal office for it?"

Anne shook her head. Her voice sounded hollow as she said, "Someone spent a great deal of money to hire a messenger and have it delivered faster than the regular service would have."

Somehow, then, Philip had an eerie sense of fate working. The plain room all gray with rainy light suddenly became a place where the gale winds of chance could reach and storm around him. He didn't know why he felt frightened holding the wrinkled letter. But he did.

He broke the wax hesitantly, unfolded the sheets inside. As he began to read the finely-inked lines, a lump congealed in his throat. The room seemed to blur.

The top of the letter bore the words *Philadelphia City,* and a recent date. The salutation was a hand from the past that clawed and held him remorselessly:

My darling Phillipe—

After much difficulty encountered in strenuous ocean travel, I

*have arrived here at the home of my Aunt and her Husband, Mr.
Tobias Trumbull of Arch Street. I write this to you in secret, by
the candle's light. In the next chamber Roger lies abed, barely
conscious and perhaps already in the thrall of death.*

*Before he took ship fron England with his regiment, we had
agreed that, in the event military duty in the colonies resulted in
any serious injury, he would if possible communicate with my
cousin by coach mail or private post rider. No matter their location in the Empire, the army hospitals are known to be places
where death for the badly wounded is a virtual certainty, due to
unclean conditions, poor physicians, and such like.*

*During a brief wakeful period after he was discovered lying
stabb'd in some publick thoroughfare and conveyed to one such
hospital—*

She *knew!* Philip thought, the hand of the past tighter now, making him
breathe hard, and with strain.

*—he managed to pay for a rider to Philadelphia. From here, my
good Aunt Sue dispatched a private coach northward to bring him
back. Many bribes were necessary to effect this departure. But as
funds are never lacking to Roger, it was accomplished. My Aunt
forwarded the dread news to me on the first fast packet. I have
come to Roger's side, landing in Philadelphia Harbor only yesterday. Last night my husband was awake long enough to talk
with me a while. He survived the journey over the rough roads,
though barely, and—*

The next words were underscored with quick slashing

*—he named his assailant. He told me where and how the act was
done.*

*He spoke both your new name and the older, more sweetly
familiar one by which I have addressed you. And so, my dearest
Phillipe, I come to write the truth of my heart—I have never
forgotten Quarry Hill, nor can I. I tell you from the depths of my
Soul that I want nothing more than to see you. Speak with you. Be
close to you—yes, I admit without shame—as close as we once
were.*

Horror crawled over Philip for a moment. He imagined her bent by a candle
in some dark, musty room that smelled of a suppurating wound.

*I do not know whether my husband also named you his assail-
ant before he was borne here. From all I can gather, I do not
think so. Perhaps, in his weakened state, he was first concerned
for his own welfare, and communicating with my Aunt.*

But I have no assurance. If there is never a response to this,

which I am sending to the Street in Boston City whose name Roger breathed out last night, then I will know.

Yet if by some miracle this letter finds you, I beg you come by any swift means to Philadelphia City so that we may meet and speak. You will be safe from any reprisals, believe that if you ever loved me. I only desire your sweet presence again. For though I may be damn'd eternally for writing it, my husband is what I knew him to be long ago. A cold, empty man. To marry him was folly which I have long since regretted. I beg you to answer my plea, Phillipe. Take all precautions you deem necessary. But come even if we may meet only for a day.

As token of my good faith and undying love for you, I close by telling you that I have asked the doctors attending my husband to make certain he receives heavy draughts of an opiate to relieve his sufferings—and also to prevent him from again speaking your name, which I alone heard in the privacy of his room last night. My Aunt and her Husband do not know of you, of that much I am positive. For God's sake come, my darling!

The letter ended with more savage underscorings of the last six words, and a single shattering signature—

Alicia.

Shaken as never before, Philip looked at Anne.

She must have guessed it was something like this, he thought. Her face was a study in pain as she took the letter from his numbed hand and began to read it.

2
A Death in Philadelphia

AT THE end, Anne re-folded the sheets, put them down on a small table, turned to stare out the window. When she spoke, her voice had an edge to it:

"And what will your response be, Philip?"

He couldn't tell whether she spoke in anger or sorrow, probably because he was so unsettled himself. The letter had reached across the years to rouse emotions he hadn't felt so acutely since Quarry Hill.

Anne sensed his uncertainty, spun to face him. He was again aware of how pale she'd grown. Was she ill, refusing to tell him—?

Her suddenly scornful look shocked him out of all such speculation. "She's a proper lady, isn't she? Arranging to meet her lover while her husband lies in the next room—perhaps dying. And she's going to drug him in case he should wake and interrupt the proposed assignation! Oh, yes—a woman of fine principles!"

"Anne—"

"You haven't answered my question. Are you going to run to her, the minute she commands?"

"I don't know."

"My God. You're actually considering it!"

He stood speechless—accused.

"Philip, do you know how far it is to Philadelphia? Will you travel almost four hundred miles just to let them arrest you?"

"Arrest—? I don't think that's part of her plan."

But he had to admit it well could be. Possibly Roger wasn't in serious condition at all. Perhaps he was recovering, and had prevailed on his wife to help set a trap for the one who had brought him to grief.

Contemptuously, Anne said, "On second thought, I doubt they'll even bother with legal formalities. They'll probably follow their more familiar course. Hire men from some gutter gang—to finish the work your brother started in England. Surely you won't let yourself fall prey to such a transparent plot. You can't be *that* brainless!"

Her voice rang loudly in the dim parlor. As the sound of it faded, the tap of the March rain on the shingled roof counterpointed the strained sibilance of her breathing.

Philip had trouble framing exactly how he wanted to approach a reply. He knew she was struggling against Alicia, as she'd vowed to do months ago. So she'd no doubt exaggerate the dangers inherent in answering Alicia's plea for a meeting.

Yet, the dangers might be entirely real. He said carefully:

"I'll admit everything you suggest is possible. Except for one fact. Alicia had no part in Roger's schemes in England—"

"She certainly didn't try to prevent them!"

"Yes, she did. In Tonbridge, it was only her warning that helped my mother and me escape in time. After that, I'm not even sure she knew what Roger was up to."

"Who are you trying to convince, Philip? Me? Or yourself?"

"Dammit, Anne, listen to reason—!"

"About a woman who wants to take you away from me? No."

"But you're not looking at it clearly—!"

"*Clearly!* That's the pot calling the kettle black! Who said I must, anyway?"

"Anne, if Roger were recovering, I think he'd have already arranged for the kind of men you described to visit Launder Street. To find me or, failing that, force an admission from you about my whereabouts. He wouldn't lure me all the way to Philadelphia."

"You keep saying all that because it's what you want to believe!" Anne cried, tears starting to show at the corners of her eyes.

"I'm trying to think it out!"

"Well, spare me! I've gone through quite enough for your sake these past few weeks. You seem prepared to forget that."

He understood the tactic painfully well, a womanly tactic, springing from her anger. He didn't blame her for the attack on his seeming ingratitude. But neither would he yield to it.

"You were also protecting Daisy and the sergeant. You helped hatch Lumden's plan, remember?"

"The plan never included killing Amberly."

"Or his arrival! Or the boy selling us out!" Philip countered, his voice louder.

"Don't deny the killing wasn't welcome revenge—"

"I will deny it!" He stepped close to her, reached for her arm. "He meant to hurt you. That was what went through my mind first and foremost—"

She flung his hand off, white with rage.

"You're lying! Lying and evading the truth! You've become an expert at it! Does everything that's happened to you in Boston mean nothing? All the work for Edes—was it a dumb-show, without any feeling, any conviction on your part?" Then she lost control completely. "And what passed between us—was that meaningless too?"

"No!"

He clenched his fists, regretting the shout. He lowered his voice, but it remained harsh. "But I told you clearly, Anne—I would not be tied—"

"Because you can't decide what you are!" Anne mocked. "A free man, or the trained pet of that—that British whore. Why would you even *consider* going to her?"

"If I tried to explain, you wouldn't—"

"A man of conviction would consign that damned letter to the fire instantly. But maybe I misjudged you. Maybe you really do want to be what she is. Maybe you aren't strong enough to bury all those sick, false dreams your mother poured into you—"

Face darkening, he exploded, *"Don't speak of my mother that way!"*

"I will! Because she's brought you to this—all her rantings about your rightful place as a little lord—"

"Shut your mouth."

"Not till I'm finished. One thing's certain. If you go to Philadelphia, you'll no doubt save yourself from the battle that's coming here. That may be the final proof of what you really are—a cowardly aristocrat like that woman's husband. Well, go and be damned. I'm sorry I ever had hope for you—or let you touch me!"

"I believe, Anne, that decision was *yours.*"

His enraged counterattack proved futile. She was trembling on the edge of hysteria. The last faint color had drained from her face. The half-circles of fatigue looked stark beneath her eyes. He wanted to strike her—

He jammed his fists to his sides, tried to speak calmly:

"Anne, you know I care for you—"

"Stop it! We've nothing further to talk about."

"Yes, we do. There's no other way to put the past to rest but to see Alicia one last time."

"Another lie!" she cried, letting the tears come at last.

"No, believe me—"

"You don't belong in Massachusetts, you belong in some stinking, perfumed manor house across the Atlantic. You're going exactly where you want to go—!"

In blind fury she shot a hand toward his throat. He jumped back, startled, as her fingers twisted under his collar, found the chain, tore it savagely.

He felt the chain part, cutting at the back of his neck. She lifted her prize up between them—the broken links, and the medal.

"But don't travel with this, Philip. You're not fit to wear it!"

She flung the medal. He heard it strike the wall, clink to the floor.

Anne looked at him hatefully. Her lips were tight together. Her breasts rose

and fell rapidly, taut against her gown. He wanted to take her in his arms, try to make her understand that only by confronting the demon of his past could he reach a final point of decision—

He couldn't put it adequately into words. He tried for a moment, but the result was only incoherent stammering. Anne turned from his outstretched hand.

At last he managed to say, "Just because I go doesn't mean I won't come back."

Her fury changed to sorrowing pity. "And still one more lie. Maybe you can't even recognize the way you lie to yourself any longer. If you go, Philip, I know I'll never see you again."

"By whose choice? Mine or yours?"

"*Both!*"

Covering her eyes, she ran. The bedroom door crashed shut.

A spatter of rain struck the window. He stalked to the door where she'd disappeared.

"Anne?"

Silence. He wrenched the knob.

Bolted.

Grim-faced, he surveyed the parlor. Saw Alicia's letter on the threadbare carpet, brushed from the small table. He bent slowly, picked up the letter, slipped it into his pocket. He heard soft, anguished crying from the bedroom.

He was angry, ashamed and bitter over the scene just concluded. A weary acceptance dropped over him suddenly. He could be no more and no less than what he was: a man caught in the present but pulled relentlessly toward a past he thought had died.

He lifted Gil's sword, the green glass bottle and his mother's casket from the open trunk. He walked out leaving the liberty medal where it had fallen.

II

As PHILIP clattered down the stairs, Lawyer Ware glanced up from his conversation with a group of Concord men in Wright's public room. Philip kept straight on toward the front door.

Ware rushed after the younger man.

"Kent, a word! Anne's been sickly of late. I have a suspicion as to why she—"

But Philip had already stalked out into the rain. He swung up on the mare's back, jerked her head toward the bridge and O'Brian's farm. He heard Ware shout his name, this time angrily. But he did not turn to look.

III

O'BRIAN PRESSED Philip on the reason for the journey. He got noncommittal answers, except for Philip's use of the term "urgent." Finally, O'Brian agreed to let him have use of the mare. But when he heard Philip's destination, he cautioned:

"Some of those Boston express riders claim they've covered the distance in eleven days round trip. Push Nell that hard and she'll die on you. No more than thirty or thirty-five miles a day for her, mind. And rest her often. Or you can't have her."

At that rate, Philip reckoned the trip one way would take more than ten days. But traveling mounted, though slowly, was preferable to the impossible alternative—trying to make it on foot.

"All right, Mr. O'Brian, I promise."

"This is truly a pressing matter?"

"Believe me, it is."

"Then ask Arthur to pack saddlebags for you. Bread and some of the apples from the root cellar. We've an old skin you can fill with the apple wine—"

"Thank you."

"Where will you stay at night?"

"Fields, barns—anywhere. I left what little money I've saved in the hands of Mr. Edes, the printer. God knows what's become of it with things as they are."

"Well," the blue-eyed Irishman said, "I doubt you'll be permitted to sleep in the streets of Philadelphia. I'll advance you a little money—with the proviso you pay it back."

"I appreciate it, sir. Of course I will."

"You do intend to come back soon?"

Philip hesitated a moment. "That's my present plan." He felt guilty about the half-truth. He had no clear idea of the outcome of the journey.

The farmer scratched his nose, scrutinized Philip closely. "Something's happened today—something very strange. I've never seen you so jumpy. Not even when you were dodging Arthur's musket that first morning. I'd still like to know what sudden emergency hauls you off so far."

The truth of it came automatically, and painfully:

"A personal matter I need to settle for good."

"Colonel Barrett won't be happy to lose even one musket man from the Concord company."

"Tell him I have no choice."

He left the farmhouse to search for Arthur in the barn, and say his farewells to Daisy and George Lumden. By early afternoon he was mounted and riding through the drizzle on the road back toward Lexington. Alicia's letter was folded into the pocket of his surtout.

He was still too shaken to know whether what he was doing was right. But he had told O'Brian the complete truth at least once:

He had no choice.

IV

THAT NIGHT, he tried to sleep in the lee of a stable belonging to some Cambridge farmer. He couldn't doze off. He was bedeviled by a sense of his own inadequacy and weakness.

And by guilt.

He'd acted unfeelingly, brutally toward Anne Ware, who had given so much of herself with so little reservation. Excusing himself with the argument that he'd acted in the heat of the moment helped not one whit. And though Anne's

accusations still tormented him, he was no longer capable of feeling angry. She'd said what she had because she loved him.

Huddled in the dark with the mare, Nell, standing head down nearby, he fell prey to guilt from another source as well. His own emotions.

He couldn't pretend that he felt no passion for Alicia Parkhurst. The passion had only been submerged out of necessity, and because of Anne's presence. But whether his feelings for the earl's daughter went beyond the physical, he was too weary and confused to decide. Perhaps, during the solitary trip to the city of the curious sect called Quakers, he could sort it all out.

The sorting, he decided, was long overdue.

And so, even though he was thoroughly wet and miserable, he began to be grateful for the enforced solitude of the post roads waiting to the south.

God forgive me—and you, Anne, if you can, he thought as he sat with his head slumped against the planking of the Cambridge stable. *Excepting a few rare ones like old Adams, it seems the way a man must go is never clear—*

V

THE WEATHER improved slightly as he traveled into the Connecticut countryside, following a rutted highway that ran parallel to the river of the same name. Mindful of his pledge to O'Brian, he took care not to push the mare too hard. But though he rode relatively slowly, he ended each day the same way—aching and butt-sore.

In the town of Hartford, he managed to cadge food and a night's rest in the public room of a tavern whose sign still bore a flattering image of round-faced King George. Anxious for news of events in Massachusetts, the landlord and his wife eagerly exchanged great chunks of hot bread and country butter and some deliciously roasted apples for what information Philip could provide. He was allowed to sleep on a bench by the hearth, warm for the first time since his departure.

But he was troubled by dreams in which Alicia's face changed to Anne Ware's, and back again—

By bridge he crossed to the northern end of the wooded island at whose southern extremity rose the thriving city of New York. He spent a morning in its streets, then used one of the shillings O'Brian had loaned him for ferry passage across the Hudson River to the Jersey shore. He pushed on southwestward to the town of Trenton, and paid again to be ferried over the Delaware.

On a late March day livened by a warm breeze hinting at the end of winter, the old mare set her hoofs on the soil of Pennsylvania. At Frankfort, five miles from Philadelphia, he realized with disappointment that the hoped-for solution to the riddle of his future hadn't materialized during the long ride. His quandry was as deep as ever.

He was also uncomfortably conscious of mounting excitement at the prospect of seeing Alicia.

Of the two women, Anne was by far the more sensible and solid. And no less passionate and giving of herself than the English girl. She'd make any man a fine wife—

But she also represented uncertainty, the peril of this struggling country.

Everyplace he had stopped on the long road south, anxious men had questioned him about the chances of war.

And while he might agree with the principles for which patriots like Adams were struggling, he was still realistic enough to understand that the security—the personal safety—of all who espoused the colonial cause was vastly uncertain.

Alicia, in turn, stood for everything he had been taught to desire during all the years in Auvergne. He knew much of her world was cruelty and sham. It was a world devoted to the ruthless employment of wealth and position and power to acquire more of the same—at the expense of others. Yet even now, a part of him still craved admission to that world.

To shun a chance for entrance had been, to his mother, the greatest crime a man could commit. Sometimes he shared that conviction fervently. Sometimes he was desperately afraid of a long life of poverty, anonymity, and all their attendant dangers.

Once, inspired by the example of the Sholto family, he'd imagined starting a printing enterprise of his own here in America. The craft fired his imagination then, and still did. He'd seen first hand the power of a paper like the *Gazette* to move men's minds and hearts on behalf of a cause—

But with conditions as they were, how could he count with any sureness on the opportunity to build such a business?

Ben Edes was being forced to suspend operations, Ware had said. In the turmoil and disorder of what seemed an all but certain confrontation, his accumulated wages held by Edes stood every chance of disappearing into the patriot coffers. Or of being confiscated if Edes were arrested. That little bit of money was all he had in the world. Only a very foolish person would envision a solid future in that kind of situation, he believed.

Indeed, he thought as he neared Philadelphia, if America as a whole dared to seek what Sam Adams openly desired—total independency—she would be, in a sense, what he had been from the beginning: a bastard child thrust into a dangerous world alone and unprotected; a bastard child exposed to countless risks the more timid and secure would never experience; a bastard child forced, on occasion, to kill other human beings in order to survive—

With survival itself completely in doubt.

He wondered in passing whether there would be as much blood on his hands—and his conscience—if he'd been born to a higher station. He thought not.

Finally, there remained with him the tantalizing memory of James Amberly's letter, now stored at O'Brian's farm. He had long ago abandoned any hope of ever putting that document to use.

Yet he'd saved it.

Why?

He approached the outskirts of Philadelphia on a road crowded with market carts. The warm March breeze blew against his grimy face. Danger might well wait for him at the home of Alicia's relatives on Arch Street. But there was still a relief in this coming, at last, to a meeting that had probably been ordained from the beginning. A meeting not so much with Alicia, he thought in another moment of sudden insight, as with himself. The compulsion to find and confront the truth of what he was, and what he wanted, was what had actually driven him onto his long road.

If only he'd been able to explain even a part of that to Anne—!

Phillippe Charboneau, the bastard heir of a nobleman, or Philip Kent, plain printer's helper—which was he?

Time, finally, to know the answer. Perhaps it would happen in that very city rising on the horizon this bright morning.

VI

THE CITY by the Schuylkill River was twice as large as Boston, he learned from a cart driver he caught up with just at the outskirts. The dirt tracks he'd followed from Massachusetts soon changed to smooth brick.

He took pleasure in letting the mare amble for an hour through the wide, tree-lined streets. He was impressed by all the splendid homes, churches and mercantile establishments. He also took note of the numerous street lamps, so unlike the dim, smoke-stained globes of Boston. The Philadelphia design featured four flat panes of glass, topped by a funnel, presumably to let the smoke rise into the air. He asked a stranger whether the lamps were Dr. Franklin's invention. The stranger told him they were.

On all the main thoroughfares, Philip saw well-dressed people. Gentlemen in velvet, with walking sticks. Young ladies with parasols; the most elegant wore vizards to shield their delicate skins from the glare of the noon sun.

Vendors hawked fresh vegetables and something called scrapple on the corners. By the busy wharves, Philip saw trading vessels of every size and description. Though he was exhausted from the trip, the noise and animation of the town buoyed his spirits.

But he remembered the need for caution the minute he began making inquiries about the whereabouts of Arch Street.

He located it near Chestnut, one of the main arteries of the town. This much done, he turned the sweating mare back to the riverfront. He quartered her at a seedy inn called The Ship, securing a small, airless room under the eaves. For one night only.

He waited until dusk on that Tuesday before making his way toward Arch Street on foot. On Chestnut, he spoke to a vendor just throwing a cloth over his half-emptied cabbage cart. The man was familiar with all the well-to-do residents of the area. He directed Philip to a large brick residence fourth down on the right-hand side of Arch.

"Everyone in town knows the Trumbulls," the bearded farmer commented. "The mister owns the biggest ropewalk 'twixt New York and Charleston. And a mighty loyal Tory he is, too. But the household's in mourning—"

Already starting away, Philip turned back swiftly.

"For who?"

The farmer spat on the lamplit bricks. "Why, lad, such fine folk don't confide everything in the likes of me! All I know's what I hear and what any eye can see. Walk up that way—you'll see it too."

Whistling, the old man shuffled off, pushing his cart.

First scanning the block for signs of watchers who might have been posted for his arrival, Philip strode along the walk next to the high black iron fences that protected each house. He was walking on the side of the street opposite the Trumbull home. When he was in position to get a clear look, he broke stride and caught his breath.

All windows in the two-story structure were draped, barely revealing the hint of lamps glowing inside. On the imposing downstairs door hung a somber wreath trailing black crepe ribbons—

For Roger Amberly?

He felt a brief, vicious satisfaction at the possibility. The emotion shamed him as he hurried on by, and returned to the rowdy waterfront inn.

Over a tankard of beer at a corner table, he scrawled a note to *Mrs. Alicia*

Amberly, in care of the *Trumbull Residence, Arch Street*. The message inside was simple—one sentence long:

A friend desires to know the cause of the household's bereavement.

Then, after chewing the end of the quill a moment, he signed *P. Charboneau*.

He hired the landlord's boy to carry the note, and gave him explicit instructions:

"That is to be delivered into the hand of the lady to whom it's addressed, no other."

"Right, sir."

"And you'll wait for any answer."

"Got it." The lad hurried out.

Philip hitched his chair around so that his back was to the corner. From that position he could peer through the smoke and the press of noisy sailors and dock workers and watch the door. The tavern clock chimed nine.

Philip bought another tankard of beer, drank it all. He grew drowsy as he rubbed his aching legs. His muscles were still not accustomed to the rigors of days on horseback.

The beer helped dull the discomfort. It lulled him into a doze that was suddenly broken by the footsteps of someone approaching his table.

He opened his eyes, startled by the sight of a tall, cloaked man in a tricorn hat. The man peered down at Philip with ill-concealed disdain.

The tavern boy stood behind the stranger, obviously apprehensive. The man threw his cloak back over his right shoulder far enough to reveal servant's livery—and a brass-chased pistol in his belt.

"Are you the gentleman who sent an inquiry to the Trumbull household?"

Philip's palms started to sweat. He didn't like the way the man's hand rested on the broad belt, so close to the pistol. He tried not to show his concern as he answered:

"I am."

"Charboneau—that's your name?"

"Yes."

"Tomorrow, there will be a room waiting for you at the City Tavern—are you acquainted with it?"

"No, but I'll find it."

The curl of the man's mouth suggested knowledge of some illicit purpose behind the note and its reply. "The lady to whom you addressed your inquiry wishes for me to acknowledge it. You will be contacted at the City Tavern at the proper time. You understand, of course, that it may not be for some days, due to the household's distress—"

"A death—" Philip began, still wondering whether it was all an elaborate ruse—and the servant might suddenly haul out the pistol and shoot him. He slipped his hands to the edge of the table, ready to overturn it as an impromptu shield.

But the man made no menacing moves. In fact, he behaved as if the entire conversation was beneath his dignity. Still regarding Philip with arrogant amusement, he replied:

"A death indeed. The lady's husband, Lieutenant Colonel Amberly."

It could still be a trap; lies. But Philip tried to look sympathetic as he asked:

"When did it happen?"

"This past Sunday. It appears the mourning period for widows is rather more brief than in England."

"If that's any of your affair."

"I wouldn't make the observation to anyone else. But your—association with the lady seems quite—personal, shall we say? Good evening. *Sir.*"

Wheeling, the man stalked through the crowd of noisy seamen and wharf workers. One growled a remark about Tories. The man hesitated, seemed on the point of reaching for his pistol—

His sly eyes moving quickly, the man assessed the numbers against him. He proceeded on toward the door, pausing only for a last, speculative glance at Philip sitting tensely in the corner. Then he went out.

Philip slept badly that night, alert for surreptitious sounds on the stair outside his room. But none came to disturb him. At last he drifted off.

In the morning, he paid for his bed and breakfast, then asked directions to the City Tavern.

The landlord laughed. "You came into a fortune last night, did you? Those are considerably finer quarters than my place. Distinguished gentlemen lodge there— some already gathering to plan the next Congress."

"Just tell me the way," Philip snapped.

The landlord obliged. Philip mounted the mare and set off through the clamor of Philadelphia's market day.

His cheap, travel-stained clothing attracted the same sort of stares from the staff at the City Tavern that he'd gotten from the servant who sought him at The Ship. But he was shown to a large, airy bedroom on the second floor without question. A stable boy took Nell, to rub her down and feed her. In fact it was soon evident that someone had gone to some trouble to finance a comfortable stay. When he inquired about the cost of lodging and meals, he was informed that his bill would be handled by another person—who wished to remain anonymous.

At nightfall a girl brought in a long-handled warming pan to heat the bed-clothes. Philip went downstairs.

Excellent though the food was in the busy main room, he found he had no appetite. All around him, he heard nothing but political discussion. He retired to his room at half past eight, settling into a comfortable rocking chair with a prodigious yawn. He didn't mean to fall asleep. But he was still worn out from the eleven-day ride, and he did.

Before he knew it, a sharp sound intruded at the edge of his mind. He lifted his head, listened, picked up only the hum of conversation from below-stairs. After a moment, though, the sound was repeated.

A soft knocking.

He stood up, silently slipped to the window and freed the latch. He had already determined that in the event he was still being drawn into some elaborate trap, the window would serve as a viable escape route. It was a long drop to the brick walk below. But at least it was a way out.

The lamp burning beside the turned-down coverlet cast a grotesque shadow of his head and shoulders as he crept toward the door. He honestly didn't know what to expect; it was possible that he might be confronted by armed men. The backs of his hands itched. His mouth had grown dry.

The knock came again, more insistently. One more step, and he reached out to open the door.

VII

THE LAMPLIGHT raised glints from the brasswork of the pistol in the belt of the tall servant. The knowing smile still quirked the man's mouth—almost as if it were part of a permanent expression.

"I'm to request you to come with me, if you please," the man said.

Wishing for a weapon as he scanned the dark-paneled hall behind the looming figure, Philip asked, "Where?"

The man gestured with a gloved hand. "Down those back stairs. To a coach waiting a few doors from here. It's not possible for the lady who wishes to speak with you to enter a public house by the main door. Especially not this public house. She would be noticed not only because of her mourning black but because of her political associations."

"I don't understand."

"Although the accommodations may be the best in the city, neither Mr. Trumbull nor his good wife would set foot in this viper's pit. As for me, I'd burn this place to the ground—and all within it who are busy hatching treason." The man's muddy brown eyes showed impatience. "Are you coming?"

"Yes. Just a second—"

Philip stepped into the room for his surtout, blew out the lamp.

As he preceded Philip down the creaking back stair, the servant chuckled, a lascivious sound. He didn't bother to hold the door, hurrying ahead through the warm night wind to the end of an alley. There, a high-wheeled coach and team waited, the horses fretting, the driver on the box swearing, one boot on the brake lever.

The servant handed open the coach door and stood aside. Beyond the rectangular opening, Philip could see nothing but darkness.

3
Alicia

FOR A moment he was tempted to run. If the Amberly family wished to bait a trap for Roger's slayer, none could be more perfect than this black coach silhouetted against the rooftop chimney pots and the blurred April stars beyond.

The tall servant kept his hand on the open door. But now shadows hid his face. The team whinnied. The driver swore again.

"Step in," the tall man prompted.

Inside, Philip thought he saw a figure stir. He couldn't be certain. From the City Tavern, a fiddle struck up a lively air. Annoyed, the tall man said:

"Sir—if you please!"

Suddenly the figure inside leaned forward just enough to reveal its presence.

"Do, Phillipe. You're safe. And there's little time."

"Alicia?"

"Of course."

He climbed the step and plunged into the black interior. He heard soft rustlings

just before the servant slammed the door. The coach creaked and swayed as the man climbed a wheel to the box. Alicia rapped the roof. The team started forward.

Philip still couldn't see her. But he could smell a faint, bitter sweet lemon fragrance—scent or soap—clinging to her skin. And he could smell claret, strongly.

As the coach swung out from the alley and turned to pass a row of lighted windows, her face glowed. It was as if all the time since Quarry Hill had never existed.

She looked at him, too moved to speak. The radiance of her face was in part due to the contrast with her widow's weeds: all black, from the skirt to a modish feminine variation of a man's tricorn. Strands of tawny hair glinted at the collar of her cape.

In the dim light from the homes going by outside the slow-paced coach, he saw again the blue eyes that had once gazed into his with such heat and pain. But the longer he looked at her, the more aware he became of subtle changes. A strained set to her mouth. A faint coarsening of the texture of her skin—too many damaging cosmetics?

And her voice had the ever-so-faint slur of too much wine:

"Dear God, there are still miracles in this awful world!" Her cheeks glistened with tears as her black glove sought his face.

Trying to ignore the changes he'd detected, he slid closer on the velvet coach seat. His hands circled her waist while she held his cheeks and brought her mouth to his, hungrily.

The kiss was long, full of the wine taste of her breath when she opened her lips to caress his tongue with her own. At last, laughing in a peculiar fashion—a lilting laugh, yet one with tears in it—she broke away.

"Hold me. Just hold me a while."

He cradled her against him, her face buried on his shoulder. Her small gloved hand pressed his arm.

Finally this embrace ended too. She pulled his hands into her lap, simply staring at him in silent joy as the coach rattled along. Stark shadows of still-bare elm branches flickered across the interior. He could now see her clearly. Her black clothing lent her face the quality of a shining cameo. As she ran her right glove down the side of his face, her blue eyes welled with tears again.

"You're not a boy any longer. There are marks on you."

"A long time's gone by, Alicia."

"You're looking at me in such a strange way—"

"I never expected you to come this soon. In fact, I had some doubts you'd come at all. I wondered whether this whole business might be a trap."

"Didn't my letter convince you?" she exclaimed softly.

"To be honest—no, not completely."

"I suppose what I wrote was terribly incoherent. That's how I felt the night Roger spoke your name. The old one. But Philip Kent's a fitting name too, considering who your father was—"

All at once she hugged his hands to her breasts. Even through the layers of her clothing, the touch triggered sensations in his body; a memory of how much he'd loved her.

Did he still?

She started chattering, her delight almost girlish:

"According to the proprieties, I should have waited a week or more before

setting one foot outside the Trumbull house. I simply couldn't. And I don't care whether my aunt and her husband are scandalized. Nothing matters except finding you again.''

''Where do these relatives of yours think you've gone this evening?''

''For the air. To escape from that stifling house—nothing but the stench of candles burning by Roger's bier. I'll have to take him home for burial. I don't know whether I can endure that—'' Her voice broke just a little. ''How did you come to bring him down?''

''Must we talk about it?''

''I'm curious, that's all. Roger never explained.''

''I'd rather not explain either. Unless it matters greatly to you.''

She shook her head. ''He never mattered. I knew that the last time I saw you. But I went ahead. The marriage—''

''Children?''

''No, none. Though not for his want of trying. I made a frightful mistake in England, Phillipe—do you mind my calling you by that name?''

''I suppose not.''

''I'm glad. I really can't think of you any other way.''

''You spoke about a mistake.''

''Yes. I should have come with you.''

''Why didn't you?''

''Oh, darling, I told you on Quarry Hill—I didn't have the courage. But after you left, I felt nothing for him. Nothing—ever. It may be a mortal sin to say that, with him dead no more than a few days. I can't help it.'' A pause. Then: ''But let's not talk of grim things. I had no idea you'd emigrated. I was astonished when Roger spoke your name. When did you decide on the colonies?''

''When I was in London. It seemed a better choice than crawling back to poverty in France.''

''Tell me what's become of you, living in that seditious Boston. Philadelphia's full of talk of armed rebellion—perhaps coming very soon. Have you been caught in that?''

''Some.''

''And your mother? How is she?''

''My mother,'' he said slowly, ''died on the voyage to America.''

''Oh, I am sorry. How did it happen?''

''Your hus—Roger hired killers to find us. In London, we got away. But they followed us when we took the coach for Bristol. The fear—the running—destroyed my mother's health and sanity.''

''What became of the men?''

''There's no need to go into that.''

Alicia looked at him, unblinking. ''Did you kill them, Phillipe?''

''Let's just say we managed to escape them.''

''I heard nothing of any such schemes after the household men lost you that night in Tonbridge.''

''I'm sure it's something Roger preferred to keep to himself. I wouldn't doubt Lady Jane knew about it, though. I think she was the one who feared me the most.''

''Feared? Perhaps. But she never hated you a tenth as much as Roger did after you ruined his hand.''

Philip shrugged: ''As you said yourself—why dwell on grim things? It's over.

What happened to Roger was the natural consequence of his own desire for revenge. His fault, not mine.''

"Ah, you've turned hard,'' she breathed. "The marks on you aren't only on the surface. Well, I have some of both kinds myself, my dear.''

Looking past her, Philip saw that the team had borne them to the riverfront. Warehouses loomed. From the other window, he saw the lights of trading vessels riding at anchor. The tang to the ocean drifted into the coach on the warm April wind.

They sat a few moments in silence. With his leg touching hers, Philip felt the familiar reaction stirring him. He wanted to hold her again. But he made no move.

An open tavern doorway lit her blue eyes briefly. He wasn't sure what he saw in that gaze. Love? Or speculation—an attempt to judge him? For some reason, he was disturbed.

Then he recalled that Alicia Parkhurst was nothing if not deliberate. She had proved that in England, by her decision to remain with Roger even when she professed that she loved only him—A first stir of suspicion came. He asked:

"Can these coachmen of yours be trusted?''

"I would hope so! Else I've squandered several expensive bribes. But I want to hear more about Boston. Have you really become involved with those treasonous people?''

"Wouldn't you suspect that, from what happened to Roger?''

"Yes.''

"There's your answer.''

"But where do your sentiments lie?'' She squeezed his hand. "Not that it's of any great importance, you understand. It's just that so much time has gone by, I can't help wanting to know everything. How have you lived? Have you taken up a trade?''

"I learned a little about printing in London. The experience got me a job in Boston. I worked for a man who publishes a newspaper that—well, is not exactly popular with your General Gage.''

"The military governor?''

Philip nodded.

"He's not *my* General Gage! I got fairly sick of Roger's ranting letters. All about the necessity to punish the partisans of the so-called liberty movement—''

"I'd expect that of Lady Jane's son,'' Philip observed.

"Well, I've no concern for politics—or the past. There will have to be the necessary observance of mourning in England. But when that's done—'' She leaned near, a strand of her tawny hair loosening and falling against his skin. "—I can be with you. That's how it should have been after we first met. You remember I thought of it—''

"Of course I remember. But as you said a moment ago—you hadn't the strength.''

"Time changes people—''

Stiffening abruptly, she sat back.

"Phillipe, what's wrong?''

The swaying of the coach over the riverfront cobbles filled him with a momentary dizziness, a gut nausea he couldn't control.

"Phillipe—tell me!''

"There is something damnably wicked in all this, Alicia.''

"Wicked? Why?"

"Because I killed your husband!"

"And I told you it doesn't matter! Of all people, why would you be guilt-stricken? You told me how many times he struck at you. More than I ever heard of, certainly—"

"Yes, that's true."

"All right, what is it? Did you attack him by surprise? Waylay him?"

"No. We met by accident."

"Then forget him. He's gone! He can no longer hurt you—or claim me. I was a sham wife to him anyway."

"In what sense?"

"The most important one. I took lovers. And every one was you. I'd close my eyes and see your face—always yours. Now that I've found you again, I won't let you go."

"Not unless I'm apprehended," he said with a humorless smile.

"No one here knows who killed Roger! He repeated your name only to me, I'm positive of that. So there's no danger. Provided you weren't detected in Boston—"

"I don't think so."

"So the secret will be buried with him. We're free!"

"Alicia—"

Again he stopped. Shook his head.

"Speak what's really on your mind, Phillipe. I don't believe it's Roger."

With those words, he caught a new, harder note in her voice. A lantern over the front of a chandler's store highlighted tiny pits in her cheek. His earlier judgment hadn't been wrong. Young as she was, her face was already showing the ravages of the pastes and ointments that had to be worn by ladies of fashion, no matter what the cost. For a moment, her blue eyes looked like agate—

Or so he imagined, as the coach rolled by the chandler's into a gloomier section.

All at once she clapped her black gloves together.

"Dear Lord, I forgot the most obvious question—which in turn gives me the answer." Her smile was the kind of coquetry at which she was so skilled. "You've wed some other woman!"

"No, I haven't."

"Very well—promised yourself. Who is she? Some coarse little merchant's daughter?"

Her mockery angered him. His mouth set. "Anything of that nature, Alicia, has no part in this talk. You say Roger's death can be forgotten. But there's no way of overlooking this. I'm still what I've always been. A commoner. Whatever—" Sarcasm crept in. "—presumptions I may have had at Kentland are gone. I've been forced to make my way without a title, or wealth, and I've done it. Not handsomely. But I haven't starved. Suppose we do feel about each other as we did in England. That doesn't change my circumstances—or my prospects."

"Nothing but excuses!" Alicia breathed, caressing his face with her lips. "I know the truth—you're involved with another woman."

"Alicia, listen—!"

"Do you think I can't make you forget her? I love you, Phillipe Charboneau. I'll love you as Philip Kent, if that's what you want. But I am going to do what I should have done long ago, and that's love you completely—"

Soft and moist, her mouth pressed his face while her gloved hand stroked the back of his neck. He felt the heat of her now. And strangely, he was both excited and appalled.

"I plan to marry you, Phillipe," she whispered. "I'll make you forget any other woman. Every day—and every night—"

Her gloved hand was on his hip, questing. He was aroused.

"—for the rest of our lives."

Alicia's mouth found his, open, hungry. The hand in the glove reached between his legs and closed, holding hard.

Abruptly, he abandoned his hesitation. Reached beneath her cape to feel the warmth and fullness of her breast. She began to moan and twist a little on the seat of the coach, the glove opening and closing, making his arousal almost unbearable.

He had an impulse to take her here, in the coach, with the bribed men riding above. Who gave a damn if they smirked at the sounds they heard in the windy April night? Wealth could buy anything. Their silence, conspiracy to defraud him of the inheritance that was his; murder—

She felt him go limp. She lifted her hand away. He heard rather than saw her rage.

"So it's not the same after all. You've forgotten your own promises back in England."

"Alicia—" He caught her hands again, feeling the tension in her fingers. "When you touch me like that, it's as if nothing's changed. No years have gone by. But I'm still not a rich man like Roger! I have no title, no money to speak of—"

"Surely you have ambitions!"

"Of course. But this plagued war they keep talking about may well ruin them all. Even if it doesn't, there's no way on God's earth I could ever match the wealth you were born to—no way I could buy you the kinds of things you grew up with—and that you take for granted. After six months of a marriage like that, I doubt you'd say any of the things you've said tonight."

She tried teasing him: "Are you so afraid to put me to that test?"

"Alicia, in Boston I lived in a cellar room. A small, grubby cellar room—with one candle for light! That's what you'd have living in America, at least for a few years—"

"You're not thinking clearly, Phillipe. What's to keep us from going back to England? I must take Roger there—surely we can find a ship before the trouble breaks out—"

"And what would your family think of that? I can just see them when you walk in with a printer's devil with one good broadcloth suit to his name."

"I don't *care* what they think, Phillipe! That's what I keep trying to make you understand!"

"But I care. Because eventually, the poverty would destroy everything between us. Suppose I were to become a reasonably successful printer. That would still be meaningless compared to the station of the men who've surrounded you all your life."

She dismissed him with a wave. But her strained smile was clearly visible against other lamps passing outside the oblong of the window.

"England's changing," she said. "My father detests the idea—refuses to admit it's happening—but it is. It's the mercantile class that's coming to power, because they control more and more of the money. Marriages between prosper-

ous businessmen and daughters of peers are becoming commonplace—oh, you don't seem to see it at all! We needn't *go* to England! I'll bury Roger and come back to you here. Nothing is of any importance save one fact—I *love* you!''

She threw her arms around his neck, kissed him—and he felt himself begin to surrender, his arguments melted by the warmth of her body, the touch of her hands and her hungry mouth. He forgot his suspicion that somewhere, somewhere in this patchwork-puzzle of frenzied emotion, there was an explanation she had not made clear. He forgot—and kissed her again, with passion, while the coach creaked on through the dim Philadelphia streets.

When they separated, she dabbed her eyes. Her laugh sounded both gay and sad.

''How amused they'd be at home. Parkhurst's daughter weeping like some ribbon girl over her swain. I could almost hate you for that, Phillipe—if I didn't love you so much.''

Another long, deep kiss. Then, tear-traces gone, she said:

''I do see there's still a battle to be fought.''

''With me?''

''Yes! To batter through all those defenses you've raised. Well, I warn you, Phillipe, you'll find me a fierce combatant. Because you and I are going to be husband and wife.''

Her directness left him startled and silent. She reached up, rapped the roof twice. The coach began to pick up speed, the heavy iron tires clanking noisily over the bricks.

''However, there are a few proprieties to be observed,'' she told him. ''Can you stay in Philadelphia a few days?''

He came close to saying no. There remained some element that troubled him deeply—and eluded his understanding. Was it Anne? Or feeling like a kept creature at the City Tavern? Damned if he knew—

She touched him. ''Phillipe?''

''Yes,'' he said, ''I can stay.''

''I'll come to your rooms next time. I can't do it immediately. But I'm sure it can be arranged before too long. Since the burial services must be held in England, I can move about the city making arrangements to transport the body. Aunt Sue's husband feels a new widow should remain indoors, grieving. I shall convince him he's wrong. At least in my case.''

She sounds supremely confident, he thought, marveling. It reminded him of the first day he saw her, fresh from the sunshine at Kentland, accompanying the man she was to marry and he was to kill. In his mind he'd called her an elegant whore. A woman who manipulated men to her own ends—

Her remark of a moment ago showed she hadn't entirely changed.

Why, knowing that, had he agreed to stay? He couldn't fully explain it. She had a power to weave spells—wake emotions—that overcame all reason—

She was whispering again:

''I want to be alone with you, Phillipe. I want us to be alone the way we were before. There are years to be wiped out. And more things I want to ask you about than I can begin to think of now.''

Her blue eyes picked up the gleam from the leaded windows of the City Tavern. The coach swung past the front of the building, on the way to the alley. She laid a gloved palm on his cheek.

''I'll marry you, Phillipe Charboneau, and God damn what any of the rest of them say.''

She brought her face close. The moist tip of her tongue crept into his mouth for one last caress. The coach stopped, swaying. He heard the tall servant grumble something to the driver. Boots crunched on the ground. The door was levered open.

The tall man's eyes, lewdly amused, slid to Philip's face. Philip climbed out. Had the man said a word, Philip would have hit him.

But the servant knew the limits. He mounted to his place on the box and signed the driver forward.

Philip stood under the April stars, his clubbed hair blowing in the wind. As the coach vanished around a corner, he thought he heard a low, lilting laugh—

A laugh of pleasure. Certainly—

Victory.

God, how easily she manipulated him too! *And yet you don't put a stop to it, do you, my friend?*

Nor could he put a stop to his uneasiness. Its source remained hard to define. Perhaps it *was* Anne—and the vivid image of the liberty medal cast inside. Or the shameful fact that Alicia's husband was not yet even in his grave—

He knew one thing. Only three or four years ago, he would never have raised a quibble about the future Alicia wanted. To have married an earl's daughter would have fulfilled his ambitions completely—

Then.

It was a mark of all the change that time and circumstances had wrought that at this moment, he hesitated—

Remember what she stands for. The same kind of power the Amberlys used against you. How can she give that up?

Of all the questions, that one troubled him most. He knew Alicia too well to believe in miracles of love. Either she had given way completely to passion, and didn't honestly realize the implications of all she'd said tonight—

Or—a return of his earlier suspicion—there was something else he didn't understand.

Instead of going upstairs, he walked around to the main entrance of the City Tavern. At a table in the public room, he drank three tankards of flip, trying to solve the engima of the night's developments. Failing, he drank one more to get rid of the nagging question marks.

He staggered up to his room half-drunk and vaguely ashamed. The landlord has refused money for the drinks. The sum would be added to his bill.

In the darkness, he flung the warming pan out of bed and sprawled, trying to think it through.

Instead, he slipped into sleep—dreaming not of Alicia but of Anne Ware.

II

A WEEK in Philadelphia's balmy April weather brought him a sense of the pace and mood of the prosperous Quaker City.

On Tuesday evening, the sonorous "butter bells" of Christ Church tolled for the coming of market day on Wednesday. But everywhere, talk concerned itself less with commerce than with the trouble in Massachusetts.

Taking a meal in the tavern's main room of an evening, he found that careful listening provided bits of news that were apparently being relayed by mounted courier to Philadelphia's patriot faction.

Companies of British soldiers, he heard, had once more marched from Boston, this time toward the village of Brookline. Philip assumed the force had numbered fewer than five hundred men. There was no word of hostilities.

But the well-dressed gentlemen who dined and drank and cursed the North ministry under the blackened beams seemed to share the opinion of most everyone Philip talked to: hostilities were now inevitable.

He listened to men at the City Tavern laud some Virginia orator named Henry. In late March, the man had addressed the House of Burgesses and declared that, with war a virtual certainty, he saw only two choices for men of conscience— liberty or death.

The ruffled and powdered gentlemen of the City Tavern also seemed to be among the first to receive overseas news from arriving ships. Yes, the King was determined to force a showdown. The gentlemen banged their sticks on the pegged floor and shouted, "Fie, oh fie!" until the smoky room fairly thundered with the racket of the ferrules.

And when some slightly tipsy patriot rose to quote excerpts of the Henry speech, the sticks thundered with equal ferocity. This time in approval.

Six days passed. Philip was continually worried about Anne Ware and her father. Once he saddled Nell, intending to ride to Arch Street, bid Alicia goodbye and return north.

But with the saddle in place, he unstrapped it again. As he laid it aside, he cursed his own indecision—and Alicia's hypnotic influence on his feelings.

I will see her one more time, he thought. *That will be the end.*

Yet he wasn't sure.

What if, through some strange chemistry of the emotions, she truly *had* decided Roger Amberly's world was not all she had once thought it to be? What if she really did want to be his wife, regardless of his prospects for the future? Time and events had changed him; why couldn't the same thing have happened to her?

As a result of this kind of self-questioning, he remained in Philadelphia—in limbo.

The tavern conversation was full of references to the Second Continental Congress, due to open in early May now that George III refused to give ground. On his seventh afternoon in the city, Philip asked directions to the site of the forthcoming assembly. He strolled through the mild April twilight under the elm trees beginning to show their buds, and reaching the imposing brick State House.

In the yard, boots tramped in rhythm. He looked in to watch a local militia unit drilling. Near them, half a dozen splendid saddle horses were tied.

As the militiamen executed a smart countermarch, Philip was troubled by a memory of Colonel Barrett and the Concord companies—as well as by thoughts of all those who had befriended him, adopted him to their cause—

Ben Edes.

Lawyer Ware.

Anne—

God! he swore silently. *That man was ever born to be torn and troubled by women!*

He absolutely could not stand to wait any longer. He resolved to get a message to Arch Street. Face Alicia, and see whether the encounter would lead to a resolution of the turmoil within him. One moment, he wanted her desperately. The next, he suspected her motives—

Yes, let it be a message to Arch Street! He'd hire another tavern boy and damn the furor it might cause among her relatives.

Vaguely aware of the *clip-clop* of hoofs behind him, he started away from the gate of the yard, determined to force the confrontation before the day was over—

"Sir—a moment. Aren't we acquainted?"

The voice broke Philip's concentration. He turned to see a man on horseback outside the State House gate. A stout, elderly man with spectacles and an all-but-bald pate—

It was Franklin.

The doctor had evidently come out of the State House and mounted one of the horses tied to the ring blocks in the yard. He was gorgeously clad in a suit of deep emerald velvet. White ruffles at the throat matched his white hose. Silver buckles decorated his shoes. Franklin nudged his horse with his knees and rode forward.

The sight of him carried Philip back instantly to Sweet's Lane and Craven Street. Dr. Franklin still wore those glasses with differing thicknesses in the same lens. But the jowly, keen-eyed face appeared to have aged a good deal. The lines were deeper. Franklin's smile as his horse trotted up seemed less natural than before, tinged with a puzzling melancholy—

"Warmest greetings to you, Dr. Franklin," Philip said.

"Mr. Charboneau, isn't it? I remember you distinctly from London."

Philip smiled. "That's mutual, sir. I remember you—and with much appreciation. Your loan of five pounds helped me reach Bristol and the colonies."

"That's splendid, splendid."

"But I've taken an American name here. Philip Kent."

"Capital! I was informed you were forced to leave London in some haste. I trust the list and letter were of assistance in establishing you in the printing trade?" Franklin pushed his spectacles down and peered over the top of the frames. "I mean, sir, I expect the loan to be repaid when your industry makes you rich."

Preferring not to tell Franklin how he'd lost both documents, Philip simply said, "It'll be repaid, you can count on it. I found a very good location with a Mr. Edes in Boston."

"Ben Edes of the *Gazette?* Then you're not set up here in Philadelphia?"

"No, I'm only in the city on—on business."

Gazing down from the expensive saddle of polished leather, Franklin gestured. "Sir, come along! You must let me buy you a mug of coffee or chocolate while you bring me up to date on news from our beleaguered sister city. How recently did you come from there?"

"Close to three weeks ago. I'm afraid any news I have is badly dated."

"Mmm, quite so. However, working with Ben Edes puts you on the proper side, doesn't it, Mr.—Kent, isn't that what you said?"

"Right."

"Good and proper American name. This way—there's a very excellent and popular place just a few steps from here. I insist you let me buy you a refreshment. I want to hear how you've gotten on. After all," Franklin added, still smiling that strangely forced smile, "I had something to do with persuading you to sail to this side of the ocean, I believe."

"You certainly did, sir."

"Perhaps now, with everything in such a catastrophic muddle, you've begun to regret heeding my advice!"

___4
Too Much for the Whistle

PHILIP WALKED beside Franklin's horse to their destination, The Sovereign Coffee-House, less than a block distant. The doctor frowned at the sight of several other horses tied up in front. Young black grooms held the reins of two more.

As Franklin swung down with a grace surprising for a man of his years, Philip glanced at the faded sign above the doorway. It bore yet another of those ubiquitous likenesses of the Hanoverian king. But some zealous individual had managed to stain the plump, painted face with what appeared to be dung. The Sovereign's proprietor hadn't bothered to remove it.

"Place looks more crowded than usual," Franklin muttered as he and Philip pushed through the door. "Hope my favorite spot's not taken—damme, it is."

He indicated a deacon's bench under the swirled bottle glass of a window to their left. Franklin scratched his chin while heads turned. There were whispers, pointing fingers. Philip realized he was in the company of a celebrity.

No one in the shop seemed inclined to offer the celebrity a place to sit, however. And Philip saw only one vacant table, a small one in a dingy rear corner.

But Franklin had a sly twinkle in his eye and didn't budge from the entrance. He signaled the landlord's boy, called sharply:

"Young man! If you please!"

Recognizing his important visitor, the boy rushed forward.

"Very sorry, Doctor, but we've only that back spot open—"

"I suppose we'll have to take it," Franklin shrugged. "By the way, my horse is tied out front, and he's hungry. The big roan—you know the one?"

" 'Course, sir."

"Take him a quart of oysters immediately."

"A quart of *oysters?*"

"You heard me—a quart of oysters!" boomed the older man. More heads turned. Eyes popped and conversations stopped. "You have them this month, don't you?"

"Yes, sir, got plenty."

"Then see to it. My horse craves oysters in the worst way."

Philip drew Franklin a questioning look, but the doctor simply proceeded majestically toward the little table in the back. Philip followed. By the time they reached the table, the boy had returned from the kitchen carrying a small copper pot. Two men rose from a table. Two more. Before a minute had passed, The Sovereign was virtually empty, most of the clientele having followed the boy outside to view the remarkable horse that consumed oysters.

"We can move up front now, Mr. Kent," Franklin said. "My favorite place is vacant."

And so it was. Philip chuckled as Franklin settled on the deacon's bench, remarking, "A little trick I learned when I first took over the postal system years ago. I traveled the routes personally to inspect them. Most country inns where I stopped were crowded of an evening. When I wanted the seat next to the fire and it was taken, I called for oysters for my horse. Never failed. The boy will be back momentarily to take our order."

304

Franklin's prophecy was correct. The landlord's young helper looked unhappy as he approached, his oyster pot empty. He indicated a red place on his forearm.

"That damn horse won't have a thing to do with oysters, Dr. Franklin! When I tried to feed 'im, he near bit my arm off. I spilled the whole blasted quart."

Franklin looked thoughtful. "Perhaps my horse suddenly lost his appetite."

"And I lost my seat," complained one of the men who had trooped back inside.

"Oh, I thought you'd departed sir," Franklin said in a bland tone. "Well, there are plenty of other places—boy, two chocolates here. And put the oysters on my bill, of course."

He turned his attention back to Philip, who could hardly control a guffaw as the tricked patrons stampeded through the shop, attempting to regain their former tables. Franklin ignored them. Sunlight through the bottle glass struck fire from his spectacles as he asked whether Philip's mother was satisfied with their new country. Philip told him of her death aboard *Eclipse*.

"Ah, that's tragic news. You have my deepest sympathies. I suffered a bereavement myself only this past December—" The boy arrived with warm mugs of chocolate, left again. "I was still in England when I received word that my dear Joan had died."

"Your wife? Oh, doctor, I'm sorry."

"At least I had my Philadelphia family to come home to—my daughter Sally lives here with her husband, Richard Bache." Philip wondered why Franklin made no mention of his illegitimate son. "And you've found a home too, Mr. Kent—literally, if not philosophically—with Ben Edes?"

"And met Samuel Adams, and Mr. Revere and Dr. Warren and many of the other patriot leaders."

"Excellent men, every one," Franklin nodded, sipping his chocolate. "I'm informed their lives are forfeit if they stay in Boston much longer, though."

"To my knowledge, all but Warren and Revere have gone out into the country. I helped a British soldier find a safe haven there, in fact."

"Helped him desert?"

Philip nodded. "He didn't have any stomach for causing trouble for other Englishmen. I took him to Concord. I've been drilling with one of the militia companies there."

Franklin pulled down his spectacles. "Is it committee business that brings you to Philadelphia?"

Redness colored Philip's cheeks. "No, it's—it's personal. In a way, it was a relief to get out of Massachusetts for a while. Things are so damned confused—Some people want independency, some don't—and most have no opinion but are scared as hell anyway, because everyone's convinced there's going to be trouble."

Sadly, Franklin bobbed his head to agree. "The irony is, just prior to sailing from England—not only in low spirits but in some disgrace, as you may have heard!—I had an audience with one of this country's last good friends. The Earl of Chatham. I told him that in all my years in the colonies, I had never, in any conversation, from any person drunk or sober, encountered a deep and genuine wish for separation. Or the suggestion that such a thing would be of the slightest advantage to America. Yet back on these shores, I find it's being discussed openly. Once, the word was merely whispered—and only by radicals, at that."

The alert eyes pinned him. "Have you a position on it, Kent? When the

second Congress convenes, there'll be much interest in the state of mind of our citizenry. So every opinion's valuable."

Thinking a moment, Philip shook his head in a glum way. "I had unfortunate experiences in England—"

"Yes, you alluded to those when you visited Craven Street. Something to do with a well-placed family, I believe—?"

"That's right. The trouble they caused didn't exactly give me a favorable feeling about the ruling class. On the other hand, all except the most extreme men in Boston—Mr. Adams, for instance—seem to favor some kind of reconciliation."

"Even at this late hour?"

"If it's possible. Maybe it isn't. But with a few exceptions, the soldiers have behaved with restraint. Certainly the Governor has. I mean—elsewhere, I'd guess that a man like Gage would arrest a man like Ben Edes, considering the attacks on the general that the *Gazette's* printed."

"That restraint," Franklin returned, "is one of the reasons Gage's star is already falling in Whitehall. I believe he'll be recalled before too long. The King and his flunkies want decisive action now that they've declared Massachusetts in rebellion."

"I'll admit none of it's pleasant to look forward to—I hoped for a chance to build a future here. Maybe that's why I'm still a little on the fence. I've worn a liberty medal, helped Mr. Edes, things like that. But I haven't supported the cause as completely as I might have. Who wants to see the future go up in musket smoke? And risk dying at the same time?"

"No one who is sane," Franklin said. "But times do come in the affairs of men when such a course can't be avoided. I realize many, many people in America would prefer safety to the perils of war—" Franklin set his chocolate mug down, his voice low, his spectacles like twin fires in the filtered sunlight. "But those who would give up essential liberty to purchase a little temporary safety deserve neither liberty nor safety." A pause. The melancholy look returned. "So we must go ahead, whatever the outcome—though I'm not at all certain a war would succeed."

"Well, that's one view I haven't heard before."

"You hear only the patriot side. Narrow, and admittedly partisan. I try to sound all quarters. I believe only a fraction of our population would support armed hostilities. A fourth, perhaps. A third if we were lucky. We have no army, and who knows how untrained farmers and artisans would behave against regiments that have distinguished themselves on battlefields all over the world? And yet," he went on earnestly after another pause, "I am still persuaded that we're traveling the only road we can. In my opinion there is no greater crime under heaven than for one man to allow another to place him—or his nation—in bondage. However"—He shrugged. "—that's a stand which each must take for himself."

Franklin's words struck Philip like a blow. Struck and drove deep into his mind. An image of Marie Charboneau drifted through his imagination. Her views were certainly in marked contrast to Franklin's. But as a result of the man's quiet, forceful words, Philip found himself agreeing silently.

A sudden, wrenching insight came to him:

What my mother wanted was no less than bondage of another kind. Voluntary bondage to the ways of the Amberlys. Not a fulfilling bondage, as Anne called it. A destructive one. Only my mother never saw that—

Against the murmur of talk that had resumed at nearby tables, Franklin said something else. Philip looked up. The doctor's eyes were hidden by the sun-glaring spectacles. Yet Philip had the uncanny feeling that Franklin was looking through him, toward some deep sadness.

"I beg your pardon, Doctor, I didn't hear what you said."

"Oh, I was only thinking of my Billy."

"Your son?"

Franklin nodded, said with faint bitterness, "His Excellency, the Royal Governor of New Jersey. Each man, as I say, takes a stand. Billy's taken his. I helped him obtain his position. Pulled every string I could in London, back in the days when relations with the colonies were more cordial. I wanted Billy to have an important post! But I also thought I'd drilled some sense into him when he was young—"

Franklin's hand clenched, white at the knuckles. "I sailed home only a few weeks ago with the highest hopes. I prayed I'd step off the ship and hear Billy had resigned in protest against the Crown's actions. Well, Mr. Kent, he hadn't. And I'm informed he won't. I love him above any person in this world save my dear departed wife, and I'm not ashamed of that. But, God help me, I love liberty more. Billy, it seems, does not. I hear he's grown extremely fond of the perquisities of his splendid life. It'll drive a wedge between us. Forever, if he persists."

Once more Franklin pulled down his spectacles, and once more Philip saw the sadness. Now he understood another reason for it.

"It's all choice, Mr. Kent," Franklin sighed. "How much are you willing to pay for the whistle?"

"The what, sir?"

"Oh—" A gentle smile. "That's just an old expression of mine. When I was growing up in Boston, a visitor to our house gave me some pocket change. Later that day, in the streets, I met a boy playing a whistle. I'd never heard such a sweet sound. I offered the boy all the money I'd been given—and tooted that whistle mighty proudly when I got home. My brothers and sisters broke out laughing. It came like a thunderclap when they, with my father's corroboration, convinced me I'd paid the lad four times what the whistle was worth. The whistle instantly lost its charm. As soon as I heard my family laughing, and thought of what I'd squandered, I cried with the vexation only the young can summon. Ever since, the incident's stuck in my mind. Whenever I'm tempted toward a comfortable but wrong judgment as opposed to the one that's difficult but right, I say to myself, 'Franklin, do not give too much for the whistle.' That's what Billy's done, you see. I—" Franklin seemed to speak with great effort then. "—I will very likely never see him again unless he resigns. And I don't think he'll have the courage. He's still enchanted with the whistle for which he's paid too dear a price."

Philip stared at his own hands. After a moment, the doctor let out a long sigh. "Well, that's all beside the point—we were talking of broader matters. I really wish I know where all the turmoil will end. We're a powerful people here in America. Unique in many ways. Should the ministers decide to test us to the limit, I think they will be mightily astonished—at first, anyway. In a long war—" A doubtful lift of the shoulder. "I've expressed my views on that."

"Do you think the ministers will test us, Doctor?"

"Given George's determination—yes, I believe it will happen. His Majesty's not an evil man. But he's a bad, misguided king. And there's not a person in his

administration who'll gainsay him. Not North, not Dartmouth, not Kentland, not—''

Franklin stopped, clacked down his mug.

"What's wrong, Mr. Kent? You're white as ashes.''

"You spoke a name—I'm not sure I understood—Kentland?''

Franklin nodded. "Aye, James Amberly, the Duke of Kentland. A member of the little clique known as the King's Friends. He's an assistant secretary for overseas affairs, in Lord Dartmouth's department.'' The jowly man peered over his spectacles. "You're acquainted with him?''

"I—I heard the name at Sholto's,'' Philip said quickly. "They said he was highly placed—but I also heard that he had died. Could there be two noblemen with that name?''

"There is one hereditary Duke of Kentland and only one, Mr. Kent. Come to think of it, though, I do recall that Amberly was gravely ill a few years ago. For months, he never left his country seat. He did recover eventually. Came up to the town and took a place in the government. That, I believe, had been his plan before an old war wound caused the illness.''

"He's alive? Today?''

"I can't speak for today. But I conversed with the Duke outside the House of Lords a fortnight before I sailed. A wise, humane man in all respects—save for his blind loyalty to King George. His wife's another case entirely. A regal bitch, with the emphasis on the latter. I'll admit Amberly didn't look too healthy when we spoke. But he's certainly able to get about and assist Dartmouth in the execution of foreign policy. I also understand his only son is serving in the military somewhere in these very col—*good heavens!*''

Philip had stood up suddenly, nearly overturning the table. His face was stark with the disbelief hammering in his mind.

They said he died. *They told us he died.*

The implications of the treachery left him in a cold fury, shaking. He could barely speak:

"Mr. Franklin—you'll pardon me—there's something I must do—''

"Wait, Kent! I remember what you told me in Craven Street—your father not married to your mother—*was Amberly*—?''

Leaving the doctor's question unanswered, Philip tore out of The Sovereign and broke into a run. He understood some if not all of it. But most important— the knowledge was like a white iron searing him—he thought he understood Alicia.

There would indeed be a confrontation now. One that would rattle the Tory teeth of the whole Trumbull family!

He ran through the streets to the City Tavern, dashed across the public room toward the stairs. First his surtout and saddlebags. Then his horse. Then Arch Street—

The landlord stopped him at the foot of the stairs:

"Mr. Kent, you've a visitor upstairs. Came in the back way, just after dark.'' The man's smirk widened. "The same benefactress, I believe, who's handling your bills while you're here. I'm not anxious to be known as a man who takes a lot of Tory money. But when a woman's as fair, and as rich, as the one who—''

Philip was gone up the stairs.

He found the door to his room locked. He pounded the wood till Alicia freed the latch to admit him.

II

HER SHOULDERS shone golden in the glow of the single candle burning beside a pewter tray. The tray held two goblets and a decanter of shimmering claret.

Alicia stepped back to let him enter. Her tawny hair, unbound, hung down over her shoulders. She clutched a woolen coverlet she's wrapped around herself, holding it at her breasts. But not so high that he couldn't see the pronounced shadow at her cleavage. One raking glance at the room revealed all the details she'd so prettily—and carefully—arranged.

The bed was turned back. The shutters were closed against the spring dark. Her clothes were a lacy spill in one corner.

Her bare feet whispered on the floor as she glided toward him. The sudden way he slammed the door banished the heated glow from her eyes.

Her mouth went round. She started to frame a question. He was faster:

"Why didn't you tell me Lord Kentland is still alive in England?"

"What?"

The woolen coverlet slipped, showing her right breast. He closed his fingers on her forearm.

"Why didn't you tell me my father never died?"

The aroused pink tip of her breast shriveled. She seemed unable to speak. His voice savaged her:

"Why, Alicia?"

"I meant to when the moment was right—" She struggled, backing away. His grip held her. His fingers left livid white marks on her skin. "Who told you?" she breathed.

"A gentleman recently arrived from England—if that matters. My father wasn't dead when my mother and I were turned away from Kentland. It was all a fraud, a hoax! The mourning servants, the pretended grief—good Christ, how stupid they must have thought us! Peasant clods from France. Willing to eat whole any story they fed us!"

"Phillipe, let me explain—"

"They were right, weren't they? Who arranged it, Alicia?"

"If you'll stop hurting me—"

He bent her wrist. "Tell me, God damn it."

"Please, Phillipe—" She was almost whimpering. "Let go."

When he didn't, she bent her head, the tawny hair spilling across her forehead. She tried to press her mouth to his hand, kiss it, even as she brought her other hand up to stroke his arm.

"Please. Please don't hurt me, darling—"

He shoved her, hard.

Stumbling, Alicia collided with the bed. She shot out one hand to cushion her fall. The coverlet had dropped to her feet. By the gleam of the candle she was like some carved figure, nipples and belly and triangle of tawny hair sculpted and shadowed by the light—

She started to get up from the edge of the bed. She looked at his face, thought better of it. Her quick, breathy speech revealed her terror:

"Lady Jane hatched the scheme. She never stopped fearing you and your mother and that letter the Duke wrote. When—when it became evident you wouldn't leave until you saw your father, Lady Jane decided to arrange things so you'd have no further reason to stay. No hope of a meeting—"

"And it was easy for her to buy black wreaths for the door of Kentland. Easy

to buy the mournful looks of the servants. Pay them enough and they'd go through any mummery—Lady Jane can buy anything or anyone, can't she? With money or with threats. Wealth and station—that's all it takes to create a little show to fool the stupid French boy and his mother.''

"She was *afraid!* She knew her husband would acknowledge you publicly as his son if he ever met you face to face. She realized she had to use desperate means to get rid of you—''

"Meantime letting Roger pursue his own preventive measures!'' Philip said, acid in his voice. "After she'd convinced us Amberly was dead and we'd run to London, she let Roger make sure we never walked out of the city alive. I never realized I had such power over her! On, my mother claimed there was great value in the letter. But I don't think I ever understood the full value until today.''

He walked toward her slowly. Still huddled on the bed, she seemed to grow smaller.

"What I found out today also explains several other cloudy issues. Up in London, we could never pick up any word of Amberly's death.'' His dark eyes narrowed as he remembered the willow grove beside the Medway. "And when you warned me about Roger, just before my mother and I fled from Tonbridge, you said something that struck me as very odd. Something about preparations for the burial. They could wait, you said. While Roger finished his business with us. Yes, of course they could wait.''

He dug his fingers into the scented skin of her shoulder. Her breasts shook as she tried to writhe away, crying out softly. He refused to let her go.

"You knew then that my father wasn't dead. You had courage enough to warn me about Roger—but not enough to tell all the truth. I thought you were hiding something. I never guessed what it was.''

Tears flooded her cheeks. In an almost hysterical voice, she begged him to release her. He did. But it was an effort to keep his hands off her throat.

She wept softly as he walked to the shutters, thrust them open a little way. He fixed his eyes on the April stars. He was fearful that he might do her physical harm.

Soft footfalls. Hands slipped around his waist, clinging. Her breasts, her thighs were fierce against his back and buttocks.

"Don't hate me too much. I tried to tell you about your father but I couldn't bring myself to it. I'm no more than what I was raised and taught to be. If you'd stayed—if you'd discovered the hoax—I was sure you'd meet Roger another time. Perhaps be killed—''

He seized her hands, broke the hold, whirled on her.

"Or kill him? And ruin your precious future? Lady Jane wasn't the only one who wanted me gone!''

"Phillipe, I love you—and I loved you then. Only the other night, I told you I'd made the wrong choices. It took years of living with Roger for me to appreciate that. I know I should have given you all the truth before. I couldn't because, in my own way, I was as fearful as Lady Jane. Yes, your accusation's true. But that's over. That's the past, sweetheart—''

She slipped her arm around his neck, brought her mouth near his, whispering: "You're the only one I care about!''

Wildly, her mouth pressed against his. Her breathing was strident as she kissed him, then again, moving her body so the points of her breasts rubbed against him—

"Lie with me, Phillipe. Now—on that bed. Let me show you the past doesn't

count any longer. Roger's gone—your father is alive—we've found each other—*please, Phillipe. The bed—''*

A final, icy comprehension spread through him. Once more he shoved her away.

''I think, Alicia, the past counts very much in your case. Especially the way it's linked to the change in your circumstances. Roger's dead. The Duke is living in England. And I'm his only heir.''

''That's your strength! Your advantage!'' she cried, a false joy on her face, an enthusiasm too bright, too insistent. ''If you return to London secretly—if you locate your father before Lady Jane gets word of it—and show him the letter—Phillipe, you do still have the letter?''

He noticed a sheen of perspiration on her upper lip. She no longer looked soft in her nakedness.

He said, ''What if I answered no? Suppose I sent it down to the sea with my mother's body?''

''Tell me the truth!'' Alicia cried, running at him, one small fist raised to strike.

A half-step away, she checked, sensing that she'd betrayed herself. Her tone turned pleading. ''Don't twist words and make sport, Phillipe. Not when that letter can mean a whole new world for you—''

''And you.''

''You said you wanted to be what your father was! It's within your reach!''

''I realize that.''

And it was a grievous burden.

A lifetime of longing—of being turned aside—of being wounded and counted no more than cipher—all that could be erased. Canceled forever. His pledge to Marie could be fulfilled. And his savored dream of seeing England again, this time as a man of property—

No, more than that. A man of property and *title*.

It was all possible.

To such fulfillment could be added the bounty of this sleek, golden-breasted girl. A woman to teach him. To counsel him, and smooth his passage into the courts and the salons where his mother said he truly belonged.

If all that was his, *why in the name of Almighty God did something in him turn aside?*

As if in answer, the fragmented past leaped to mind—

He thought of Girard and his promise of the new winds that would blow away the tottering structure of a society gone corrupt, a hierarchy past its time.

He thought of plain Ben Edes and the power of his clattering wood press, of the meaning of so many of the pieces by Patriot and the others that he and Edes had labored long into the night to set and proof and print.

He thought of the liberty medal, and the night of tea sifting into Boston Harbor.

And he thought of all Benjamin Franklin had said only an hour ago.

Philip stared at Alicia, his eye remote, strange. She was beautiful. *Beautiful.* But in his mind, a voice mocked—

And how much are you willing to pay for the whistle, my friend?

Alicia crept back to the bed, abruptly conscious of her nakedness. She covered her breasts and her pubis with the coverlet, her shoulders prickled with goosebumps. Philip smiled an odd smile. The spring air drifting through the half-open shutters was not all that chilly.

In the silence of his mind he said to Marie, *You were wrong. The greatest crime a man can commit is not bowing to poverty and obscurity but bowing to slavery. Allowing another to put you in ruinous bondage. Bondage of the body. Or bondage of the soul. Forgive me, if you can.*

Weight seemed to lift from him, a vast, encrusted weight of doubts, sometime hopes, vengeful yearnings. The weight broke and crumbled and he knew what Alicia was—

A creature exactly like the Amberlys.

How long, then, before he was transformed himself? Enslaved—and enslaving others in turn?

Slowly, he repeated the thought of moments ago:

"I do realize what's in reach, Alicia. But for some peculiar reason, I have a small doubt. One tiny doubt—"

He approached the bed. With one swift motion he stripped the cover from her body, hooked his hand down between her thighs, holding the hair of her, and the lips of flesh, for what they were—a marketable commodity.

"The doubt tells me you wouldn't offer this unless I had the letter. You wouldn't offer this, or all your endearments, or your vow that nothing else matters but our being married—"

She wrenched away, tumbled off the bed, fell to her knees. She was weeping again, this time in desperation:

"I love you, Phillipe. God as my witness—"

He extricated himself from the frenzied play of her hands.

"Forgive me if I don't believe that. Maybe you loved me a little in England. But never enough to tell me I was deceived. Never enough to leave Roger. You didn't love me enough to offer yourself until you were certain Roger was dying— and you realized I might, just might, still have a paper with monetary value. I never knew James Amberly. Perhaps he's not the same as the rest of you. But I intend to pass up the opportunity to find out."

"You incredible fool!" she cried, kneeling on the bed, her bare belly heaving, her embarrassment forgotten. "To walk out on riches—position—because I made one mistake—"

"Alicia, you made many more than one. At Kentland. On Quarry Hill and by the river. In the coach the other night—many more than one."

She screamed, "That letter is everything you wanted!"

"Once. Now, I don't want anything it can buy, including you. The price for using that letter is too high, you see."

"Price? What price? Phillipe—dear God, answer me!"

I must go, he thought. *Now—quickly—because I'm liable to kill her if I don't.*

Studying his own flexing hands, he avoided the sight of her kneeling on the bed. The tawny hair was a tangle around her shoulders. Her blue eyes were stunned and full of fear. Her shadow, cast by the guttering candle, was misshapen, hideous on the beamed ceiling—

Abruptly, he crossed to the corner where he'd left his saddlebags. He picked them up, still without looking at her. He walked toward the door.

"The letter can give you everything," she wept, rocking back and forth, small fists beating on her bare thighs. The mounting note of hysteria in her voice disgusted and saddened him. He kept on. Only four paces to the door—

"With the word of the Duke to verify your claim, you'll have what thousands of men dream of with never a hope—Phillipe? *Don't go—!*"

"Goodbye, Alicia."

"I'll go mad if you leave me—I'll kill myself—"

"Nonsense. You'll be married to another rich man within a year."

"I won't! I love *you!*"

"But not enough."

"Yes, now enough—more than enough—!"

"Goodbye, Alicia."

Screaming his name, she leaped from the bed, flung herself at him. She lost her footing, sprawled. Struggling up, she wrapped her arms around one of his boots.

Looking down at the tawny head, he felt pity. And a sense of walking through the dark, hostile valley where faint sunrise at last showed the path ahead. His urge to harm her physically drained away.

"You can't leave. I can't survive if you leave. *Phillipe—!"*

He was prying her fingers loose one by one. He didn't enjoy the sight of her agony, because he saw in her eyes the madness that can come of a lustful dream destroyed.

"Alicia, you've forgotten something," he said gently. "My name is Philip Kent. I'm not the man you wanted. I'm a Boston printer. The man who owned the letter—he died."

Lifting the latch, he went out quietly into the darkness of the corridor.

III

PAST TEN o'clock, pushing the mare as hard as he dared, he reached the Delaware and roused the old ferryman in his shanty. With a lantern hung from a pole at the prow, the barge put out.

The river was flowing swiftly. The April night had turned cool. Philip stood with one hand on Nell's muzzle, staring at the black of the far shore while, behind him, the old fellow grumbled at the tiller.

The deed's done, he thought. Done in haste, perhaps. Done in anger, too. And—yes—still done with some guilt, because of Marie.

He wished the purling water would carry the barge faster. *I must bury that guilt now,* he said to himself. *The guilt must go down to its death because I have lived her life too long—*

He had no illusions about the existence of a hereafter, the kind of which divines were fond of speaking. Yet in some silent, mystic way, he hoped that the change which had taken place in him tonight would be understood by the woman who had given him life—along with another gift he could no longer claim.

The barge coasted toward the Jersey shore, where the dim lights of isolated farms showed in the wind-soughing dark. He admitted privately that many a man would call him crazy for what he'd done.

Slowly, though, he took a new perspective on it. With Alicia, he had only spoken aloud the final resolution that had been building for months and months. He didn't want what the parchment in Marie's casket could obtain for him if it meant becoming like the Amberlys and their kind. Users of others. Masters of others—by decree, or tax, or deceit, or secret assassination. He despised them. He had become a different sort of man.

Looking back, he couldn't mark the hour when he had changed. But he felt that the outcome of the nightmarish scene with Alicia had probably been foreordained. Only his conscious mind hadn't known it until it happened.

The barge bumped against the rickety dock among the reeds. The old man tied lines, then hauled down the lantern. He had ruined yellow stumps for teeth, foul breath. But there was a certain sprightly gleam in his eye as he held the lantern aloft.

"Ye speak like a New England man, sir. Be ye riding home that way?"

"A New England—?" Taken aback, Philip smiled. When had the very sound of his voice altered?

He nodded in a friendly way. "Yes, I am. Out of Boston. I'm going there now."

"There's much talk o' fighting soon. Will ye be part of it? Or are ye Tory?"

"No, sir. I guess I'm what they call a Whig. I'll be on the fighting side."

" 'Tis a horrible thing—bloodshed. Battle. I lost a son on the Plains of Abraham, y'see—"

"I'm sorry to hear that."

"—even so, we can't give in to that fat old German farmer, can we, eh?"

"No, sir, that we can't."

Philip swung up on horseback, stepping the mare onto the splintered planks of the swaying dock. Hoofs thudded, hollow. Then the horse was on soft shore ground. Philip turned her head north under the April stars. Behind him, the old ferryman waved the lantern and cried Godspeed.

Philip kneed the mare's flanks, absolved, at peace with Marie. His only worry was one that reached into the bottom of his heart—

He must find Anne. Now, above all, he must find Anne.

What if she'd gone from Concord with her father? What if hostilities had already started, and in the chaos of men mustering, he lost all chance to see her again?

What if she no longer wanted to see him? Because of the way he'd left her, he wouldn't blame her—

Against all the advice of O'Brian, he urged the mare to greater speed. He soon had her galloping at the limit of her strength.

5
Alarm at Midnight

AFTER THE rising of the spring moon, Philip began to recognize familiar countryside.

The night was warm. The balmy spell had followed him all the way north from Philadelphia. Ideal weather, nothing worse than a couple of short rain squalls while he slept in the open. Tonight was no exception. Even so, he felt no lift in his spirits when he realized that he was less than ten miles from Concord.

He'd been riding ten days—or was it eleven? His skin was gritty. He'd washed his face and hands at spring-fed wells along the way—that is, he had whenever he'd been able to find a farmer who didn't mind a bedraggled stranger stopping on his property. Several times he'd been run off with threats and, once, with a blast of a musket.

As a result, he carried most of the grime of his journey with him—all over. His body ached from the up-and-down jolts of the ride. He'd long ago decided he would never be a good horseman, any more than he'd be a good sailor. He was a landsman, through and through.

Knowing it wasn't far now to the little village where, with luck, he might find Anne, he still couldn't throw off his lethargy. He slumped in the saddle, offended by his own sour smell. His senses were uniformly dulled.

The moon bleached the surrounding pastures dead white. Ahead, he glimpsed the houses in tiny Lexington. More than a few showed lamps. That was odd. Surely the time was close to midnight—

He yawned. All at once he blinked. He noticed miniature, moon-touched figures on the neat central green of the village. The figures, some with lanterns, seemed to be scurrying every which way.

Immediately he suspected some kind of trouble. A British foray, perhaps. A raiding party on the way, hunting military stores.

Or perhaps they'd already arrived. He decided to forego satisfying his curiosity. Tugging the mare's rein, he cut across a pasture, intending to bypass the village.

As he rode, another peculiar fact struck him. Once north of Boston, he'd observed a great many countrymen on the roads this evening. Most had hailed him cordially, receiving a tired hail in return. He really hadn't paid much attention, or wondered about it at the time. But now, thinking of the running figures in Lexington, he began to ask himself why so many people were abroad. Was this some special occasion? A holiday?

Actually, he didn't even know the exact date. April seventeenth? The eighteenth, maybe. He'd lost track. But he wasn't familiar with any holidays around that time. Perhaps the fine weather had brought people out. Sent friends to gather at the taverns. And young men to court at neighboring towns and farms—

Soon Lexington lay behind him. He located a break in one of the low stone walls that flanked the level road to Concord. Less than five miles now. He yawned again. Stretched. The insides of his legs were nearly raw under his breeches.

Almost drowsing, he suddenly sat bolt upright. He heard a racket on the road ahead. Someone whacking on wood—

He peered under overhanging trees, made out a farmhouse set back from the left side of the road, where the stone wall ended. He slowed Nell's pace, riding more cautiously. The night was redolent with the smell of spring earth. He discerned a horseman—

No, two.

Wrong again. There were three, sitting restless mounts in front of the house. One of the men hallooed and once more whacked the porch post with a crop.

A door opened. A candle gleamed. The householder wakened by the noise appeared as a blur on his doorstep. Reining the mare to a stop by the end of the stone wall, Philip sat dead still. He couldn't tell whether the mounted men wore uniforms.

"Curse ye for raising such a noise at twelve o'clock!" the farmer complained. "Who are ye? What do ye want?"

The tallest rider maneuvered his horse forward so the farmer's candle lit his profile and tricorn hat.

"You'll recognize me, Mr. Hunnicutt. Dr. Prescott of Concord—?"

"Oh, aye. But I don't know those two with you."

"Express riders out of Boston. I met them near Munroe's Tavern in Lexington. They came to alert the Clarke household, where Hancock and Adams have been staying. I told them that since I reside in Concord, I'd best ride along and verify their identities."

"All right, but why waken sober folk at midnight, Doctor?"

"Because, sir—" Philip stiffened, recognizing the new voice instantly. "—after arranging for sexton Newman to hang warning lanterns in his steeple at Christ's Church tonight, Mr. Dawes and I came out of town—he by the Neck, myself across the Charles in a rowboat with wrapped oars—to alarm the countryside."

"Alarm?" the farm repeated, sounding fully awake.

"Yes, sir. The regulars are coming out."

Philip's hand tightened on the reins as Revere went on:

"I fear you'll have noise a-plenty in a few hours. The British are moving across the Charles in boats."

"My God! Ye can't be mistaken?"

"No. They're coming. No less than five hundred and perhaps as many as fifteen hundred. Dr. Warren's intelligence said their destination is Concord."

"No doubt they're after what military stores are left there," said the man identified as Dr. Prescott.

"Arm yourself accordingly," Revere added.

With a touch of his tricorn, the silversmith wheeled his horse and started out of the yard. Philip nudged the mare forward as Prescott said to the farmer:

"One more thing, Mr. Hunnicutt. A patrol of at least nine British officers passed through Lexington a while ago. They appeared to be bound this way—advance scouts, perhaps. Did you by any chance hear them pass?"

Hunnicutt said he hadn't. He'd been sleeping soundly.

"Well, they still may be ahead of us," Prescott said. "Good night, Hunnicutt." He rode out beneath the trees where Revere and his companion waited, both turning now as Philip's horse approached.

Hunnicutt vanished indoors. His voice sounded loudly, shouting to his wife. Philip was too tired to feel fear over the grim news he'd heard. He clattered up to the trio barring his way in the road, saw steel wink—a dagger or hunting knife—in the hand of Dawes. The lanky man was a Boston cordwainer. Philip had seen him once or twice with Revere at the Dragon.

"Who is it?" Revere called sharply as Philip reined in a few yards from them.

"It's Kent, Mr. Revere. Philip Kent, from Ben Edes' shop."

The silversmith gigged his horse into an open, moonlit place in the road. "Come forward so I can see your face."

Philip did. Revere relaxed, saying:

"Edes told me you'd left the city. Where are you bound?"

"The same place as you. I've just come from Philadelphia."

Dawes slipped his knife out of sight. An owl hooted in a dark grove farther down the road. Young Dr. Prescott stepped his horse in closer to study the new arrival, asked Revere:

"You know and can vouch for this man?"

"Yes. He's a high Son of Liberty." Revere managed a tired smile. "Not to mention one of my dental patients."

"Then come along," Prescott said. "Time's running short."

With Dawes and Dr. Prescott riding abreast ahead, Revere fell in next to Philip, who said, "So the regulars are coming out at last?"

"In force." With cynicism, he added, "Are you surprised?"

"No, I guess not. But as I said, I've been away a while. I've no idea of what's happened in town—"

"Something's been afoot for several days. Officers combing the countryside, some in disguise, some not. Tonight our mechanics' committee detected the beginnings of a most peculiar activity. Light infantrymen and grenadiers of various regiments started turning out of their quarters and slipping off to boats that were recently moved to the Back Bay shore. There's been a lot of talk about a major troop movement. But no one knew exactly when it might come. This evening, we got our answer. One of my lads saw two mongrels lying bayoneted in the street."

Philip shook his head. "I don't understand."

"They're killing the dogs to prevent their barking. To conceal all signs of what's supposed to be a secret expedition."

"I rode around Lexington," Philip told him. "I saw lanterns—men running on the green—"

"The minute companies are being called out. Hancock and his whole retinue—plus Mr. Adams—are packing to leave. They'll have their necks in ropes if the soldiers catch 'em—"

Abruptly, Revere reined in, responding to the upraised hand of Dawes farther up the road.

Philip inhaled the soft scents of the spring countryside, heard the gentle nickering of the horses—and drew a deep breath, his lethargy shattered. In this mild night, all silver and peaceful, the dreaded confrontation was in the making.

The night should be wracked with storms, he thought. *Rains, lightnings, thunder-peals—somehow, it's all wrong in such pleasant weather—*

He heard a whisper from Dawes, who was pointing down the road to Concord:

"Two men riding, Paul. I thought I saw metal trappings. Could be some of those officers."

"If there are just two, then the nine have split into teams. Let's see what they're up to—"

Dr. Prescott started to object. But Revere was already spurring his horse forward between Dawes and the physician. The two followed, Philip bringing up the rear.

Momentarily, he caught the sound of hoofbeats ahead. He couldn't see the riders. Trees ached thick over the road here, weakening the moonlight. The distant ridges around Concord further solidified the darkness of the background.

All at once, Philip heard what sounded like a voice in the woods on his left. He turned his head as twigs crackled. Suddenly three mounted figures broke from the shadows. Philip stood in the saddle, shouted:

"Revere—!"

"Keep your horse standing where it is," said the foremost rider. His cloak was thrown back, making his scarlet jacket dimly visible. In his right hand he held a military pistol at full cock.

The two officers with him were similarly armed. One chuckled in a humorless way:

"A nice bag of rustics, eh? It's well we took different sides of the road. Where are the rest?"

"Seizing the two ahead," replied the first officer.

Shouts rang out. Philip's belly tightened as he saw four more British officers ride from the thickets on the right side of the road. They filed their horses one

by one through a gap in the stone wall, surrounding the others. Two more officers returned along the road to join them. One of the group called out:

"Major Mitchell? A catch here—"

"Good work!" answered the officer covering Philip with the glinting pistol.

Within moments, Revere, Dawes and Prescott had been driven back to where Philip sat captive. The four of them were ringed by the muzzles of nine side arms. Major Mitchell addressed the silversmith in clipped, proper English:

"May I crave your name, sir? And those of your companions?"

"I am Paul Revere of Boston."

"Revere! Gentlemen, we've made a fortunate catch." To the silversmith: "Who are your friends?"

"The others may speak or not, as they choose."

"They'll damned well speak or we'll blow their God damn heads off," another officer growled.

Mitchell raised his free hand. Then:

"What are you doing on this road, Mr. Revere? Riding express, perhaps?"

"I esteem myself a man of truth, sir. So to that, I can only answer yes." With audacity that astounded Philip, the silversmith went on, "May I ask the nature of your mission?"

Major Mitchell chuckled, genuinely amused. Philip couldn't help being surprised at the civility of it all. These redcoats were the enemy! Perhaps it was a measure of the reluctance of those on both sides to bring matters into open conflict that Mitchell deigned to answer at all.

"Why, Mr. Revere, we're out chasing deserters." His tone implied that he didn't expect Revere to believe the statement. He added, "And that's as much information as you'll get. But I expect a good deal more—"

He pointed his pistol at Revere's forehead, his voice less affable.

"I am going to ask you some questions, sir. If your replies are not truthful, I'll shoot you down."

Another of the men said, "There's moonlight back in the pasture, Major. We can get a better look at them there."

"Very well," Mitchell agreed. He indicated the prisoners. "Turn your horses about. Ride through that break in the stone fence beyond the trees."

Philip tugged the reins, fell in next to Dr. Prescott. The physician leaned over quickly to whisper something Philip couldn't catch. An officer thwacked Prescott's shoulder with the muzzle of his pistol.

"No talking!"

The young doctor swore under his breath.

As the four prisoners and their nine captors proceeded back along the road to the gap in the wall, another of the officers behind Philip exclaimed:

"By God, Mr. Revere, we've all heard of your riding. You will take your hands off those reins and let your horse walk."

The first officers reached the stone wall. They positioned their mounts to either side of the opening, waiting for Prescott to go through. With a yell, the doctor dug in his spurs. His horse leaped the wall.

A pistol exploded. Men cursed. Another gun went off, streaking the night with a bright powder flash. Then a half-dozen things seemed to happen at once.

Revere jumped to the ground, dodged between the startled officers and vaulted the stone wall on the other side of the road. Dawes, with an almost jovial shout, turned full about and spurred past Major Mitchell, clouting him with a fist as he raced by.

The major reeled in the saddle. His pistol discharged in the air. Smoke and the fumes of powder swirled. The officers' horses neighed and reared.

Philip saw the gap in the wall standing open. He kicked the mare forward, sighting on Dr. Prescott. Man and mount were a blur of silver out in the pasture, racing away from the stone wall.

Philip's horse plunged through the opening. He sensed rather than saw a pistol whip up on his left; an officer fought to control his horse and aim at the same time—

The mare almost stumbled in brambles as she cleared the wall. The pistol crashed, the orange glare blinding Philip momentarily. He felt the air stir behind his head where the ball passed. Bent over the mare's neck, he shouted to her for speed.

She escaped the brambles, sped across the loamy earth of the pasture, Philip still bending forward from the waist to present the smallest possible target. Another pistol exploded.

On the road—dwindling—sounds of confusion. Oaths. Commands bawled by one officer, then another. Revere had run off one way, Dawes had escaped another. They seemed to be the quarry Major Mitchell's party wanted most. At least, glancing over his shoulder, Philip saw no immediate signs of pursuit.

The ground swept by beneath the mare as she tried to respond to Philip's hammering boot heels. He could already feel her flagging. Ahead, where the pasture ended and a grove rose against the moon, Dr. Prescott had already disappeared.

Philip looked back again. One of the British officers was galloping after him, cloak streaming—

The mare reached the safety of the trees. Philip reined in. The pursuing officer stopped in the middle of the pasture, cursing loudly.

New shouts rang from the Lexington road. The officer in the pasture abandoned Philip for the more important fugitives, and cantered back toward the stone wall.

II

AFTER TWENTY minutes of walking the mare through the wood, Philip finally picked up the road to Concord again. He surveyed it in both directions from the screen of trees. Then he bore left toward the village cupped among the hills.

The brilliantly white April evening was still warm and sweet. But he was cold. Pistol fire and Mr. Revere's news—*The regulars are coming out*—had at last struck a heavy note of dread. Well before he rode into visual range of Concord, he heard the church bell begin to toll.

The alarm echoed from ridge to ridge, to wake the sleeping farmers, bring them hurrying into town. Philip recalled Dr. Franklin's grim reservations about the ability of country folk to stand against crack British regiments.

Clang and *clang,* the Concord bell pealed in the April stillness. He rode into the village to see a repetition of the sight glimpsed from the outskirts of Lexington. Men criss-crossed the street near Wright's Tavern, lanterns bobbing. Doors opened as young men and old turned out—with muskets. Dr. Prescott, then, had gotten through ahead of him.

In the confusion outside Wright's, he saw two boys on farm ponies start in the

direction of the South Bridge. Sent to summon militia companies from the neighboring towns, undoubtedly. Philip had seen it all rehearsed before. Heard it planned at the militia musters. Yet tonight, as men bawled questions, orders and milled uncertainly near the tavern, he could sense a difference. Voices were hoarse with strain. This was no rehearsal. Tonight—*clang* and *clang*—the regulars were coming out.

He hauled his aching frame down from the mare, pushed into the crowd. By a lantern's glare, he saw Dr. Prescott trying to answer a dozen questions at once:

"Yes, I think Mr. Revere is captured. Yes, he personally saw the regulars on the move. No, I don't know how many. More than five hundred, he was sure of that—what? No, not complete regiments. Flanker companies from different regiments. The light infantry, the grenadiers—"

That information produced a murmur of apprehension from the Concord men, perhaps fifty strong by now. Most had muskets. They understood the implication of Prescott's news. If General Gage had dispatched light infantry and grenadiers into the countryside, he was in deadly earnest. The flanker companies were the toughest, bravest fighters, the soldiers most accustomed to the heaviest combat—

A stocky man Philip recognized as Major John Buttrick, Colonel Barrett's second in command, fought his way to the stoop of Wright's. He raised his hand for silence. Gradually, the crowd quieted. Buttrick said:

"All those already armed remain here. Those not yet equipped, get your muskets and reassemble as quickly as you can. We have stores still to be moved here in town—we'll need every hand."

"Are we getting any help?" someone shouted.

"Yes! We've already sent to Lincoln for their minute companies. We should be in good force if the lobsterbacks get this far."

No one appeared encouraged by Buttrick's words. Everyone from stripling to graybeard knew full well that even several companies of militia could probably not stand for long against thoroughly trained British troops. But no one voiced the fear openly.

Buttrick continued to issue orders. Philip's attention was distracted. In the lantern light around Wright's stoop, hostile eyes locked with his.

Lawyer Ware.

His nightshirt was carelessly stuffed into his trousers. His thin hair blew in the breeze. The protruding eyes that could look so comical now looked anything but that.

At Buttrick's command, the crowd broke. Philip started for the tavern. Despite Ware's threatening expression, he intended to find Anne. Ware stood on the stoop, waiting. Never had the little man looked so formidable—or so full of wrath.

Philip had gone half the distance to the glowering lawyer when Buttrick caught his arm.

"You're Kent, aren't you? From O'Brian's place?"

"That's right."

"When you go to fetch your musket, make sure Barrett's heard the bell. Sometimes," he added with an empty smile, "Jim's fond of the rum jug and sleeps too deeply."

Then Buttrick was gone into the confusion of lanterns and shadow. Men were scattering to the various houses that held caches of supplies.

Lawyer Ware continued to stand on the step of Wright's. As Philip approached, the little man barked:

"Gone to Philadelphia, were you?"

"Yes, sir."

"Well, you've come back at a most inauspicious time. I'm sure you regret it."

"Regret it? Why?"

"I presumed you wanted to flee from danger—and your shameful actions."

Philip didn't fully understand Ware's scathing words. They angered him. A vein stood out on his forehead as he shot back:

"I went on necessary private business, Mr. Ware. Is Anne inside?"

"Whether she is or isn't makes no difference. I warned you in Boston, boy. I said I wouldn't have her hurt. What you did—and what you must have said when you left—have brought her such grief as I've never seen before. I pressed her, but she refused to give me any details—except to say there was nothing more between the two of you. Go carry out your commander's orders. And don't try to see her again."

"Mr. Ware—"

"Don't. Ever."

"Mr. Ware, listen! Anne understood I had to leave. Had to settle one matter before—"

"*Understood?* No, she didn't!"

Caught in the impulsive falsehood, Philip turned scarlet. He began:

"If you'll let me explain—"

"I want none of your damned explanations! Neither does she. Annie risked her life for you when the British investigated the death of that officer. And your repayment was to leave her and give her grief. I warned you against it!" he repeated, his frail shoulders trembling.

"Let Anne be the one to say she doesn't want to see me!" Philip said, reaching out to shove Ware aside. The lawyer's veined hand darted for a trousers pocket—

And Philip was staring into the round black circle of a gun muzzle.

The beautifully worked silver scrolling of the pocket pistol flashed in the lamplight. The lawyer's hand shook so badly that Philip expected the pistol might go off any second. Ware had it cocked. At close range, the ball could tear half his head away.

"I've kept this for emergencies," Ware said. "Thinking that if I was ever caught by redcoats wanting to arrest me, I'd use it on them. I'll use it on you if you don't leave. Don't ever let me see your filthy face again."

"Damn it, Mr. Ware, I don't understand why—"

"You don't eh? Then you're stupid! Wanting to protect you in some misguided way, Annie's hid the truth. But she can't hide the white look of her face. The spells of weakness that come on her more and more—"

Against the mournful tolling of the bell, Philip's thoughts flashed to the last time he'd seen her. He recalled the strange, unnatural pallor very well.

Ware said, "I will make you one last promise, Kent. If my daughter is, as I suspect, carrying a child—"

"A *child!*"

"—and if the child's yours, I'll find you, wherever you are. And I'll kill you. Don't make the mistake of doubting me."

He spun and walked up to the door of Wright's, wispy hair blowing back and forth across his forehead, the pocket pistol still shaking in his hand.

Stunned, Philip considered trying to lunge, disarm the little lawyer. At all costs, he needed to see Anne—

A voice bawled behind him, "Kent, damn you, get going to Barrett's! That's an order!"

Buttrick ran on. The door of Wright's slammed. The bell shattered the night, *clang* and *clang*—

Philip stumbled toward the mare. As he hoisted himself to the saddle, he glimpsed Abraham Ware peering from one of the front windows of the tavern, frail, yet somehow almost Biblical in his wrath.

A child, Philip's mind kept repeating, as if that would help him comprehend the astonishing fact. *Our child?*

He tried to recollect when it might have happened. Surely it had to be the night before New Year's. He had to see Anne! Suppose she and her father fled before morning. He might never find her again—

He almost turned the mare's head back. But he encountered Buttrick once more. Again the major yelled for him to hurry. So he kept on toward North Bridge, past silent, hard-breathing men rolling flour barrels to a new hiding place.

As the mare clattered over the plank bridge, the church bell finally stopped its wild pealing. One thought thundered in Philip's mind, so compelling he almost wept.

She knew the day I left her. She knew but she wouldn't use it to hold me—

And now, with the regulars marching somewhere beneath the paling stars, it might be too late. If the British came as far as Concord, men could die—

Philip Kent among them.

III

AT COLONEL BARRETT'S farm, lanterns burned in the barn. Philip found the militia commander assembling his gear. A bit addled and still smelling of rum, he had nevertheless wakened to the bell.

"Did Buttrick think I wouldn't, for God's sake?" Barrett belched. "That's one tocsin I'd hear even if I were down in hell. I'm glad you're back, Kent. Some said you'd gone for good. To the Tory side, maybe."

"I couldn't ever stand on the Tory side, Colonel."

"Good. Because we'll need every man if they're sending fifteen hundred to strip this farm of all we've hidden away. Good black powder in the attic with feather ticking over it. Cannon buried in the furrows of the back field—and d'you know how much is left in Concord?"

"I saw flour barrels being moved—"

"That's a fraction! There's nearly ten tons of musket balls and cartridges. Thirty-five half-barrels of powder. Gun carriages and tents and salt fish and beef and harness and spades and—well, plenty to make it worth Gage's while to search it out, I'll tell you. Worth our while to defend, too. A couple of days ago there was a rumor this raid might be coming. So some of the stuff's been hauled to towns west of here. But by no means all. Here, I'm talking too much—get going!"

NOT MANY minutes later, Philip turned the mare into the yard of O'Brian's. He found the whole household—the Irish farmer, Daisy, Lumden and Arthur— awake and wondering at the exact meaning of the alarm.

Because of the tense situation, Philip's sudden appearance elicited only momentary surprise, and the briefest of greetings. They all wanted to know why the bell rang. Philip explained. Arthur finished rounding up the arms for him and for O'Brian: a musket apiece and shoulder-strap cartouches packed with lead ball and paper-wrapped powder charges.

O'Brian hummed a military tune, checking his supplies with a sprightliness more appropriate to a man half his age. Lumden voiced the wish that a spare musket could be found. He felt obliged to be ready to defend O'Brian's house.

Arthur's teeth showed in a hard smile. "Don' fret, Sergeant George. Tommy comes this far, there's sickles and scythes in the barn. And a loft where you can drop down on 'em by surprise."

"By God, you can count on it."

Philip found a moment to draw Daisy aside.

"I tried to see Mistress Anne in the village. Her father wouldn't permit it. I don't want to put you in danger, Daisy, but is there any way you can get to her? Slip in and give her a message and then get out before there's trouble?"

Daisy didn't hesitate. "Of course I can."

"Then tell her—" A lump seemed to congeal in his throat. Already the musket felt dead heavy in his right hand. "Tell her she has my love. In case I don't see her again."

"All right," the red-haired girl whispered, awed by his stark look.

"And tell her I'm sorry I caused her any—"

"Kent! Let's move out!" came O'Brian's hail from the front of the house.

Nodding wearily, Philip started away. A thought crossed his mind. He called, "One moment more, sir—" He turned back to the girl, who was already pulling a shawl around her shoulders. "Daisy, are my things still stored in the clothes press?"

"Your sword and the tea bottle—?"

"And the box."

She nodded.

He leaned his musket against the wall, went to the clothes press, knelt and rummaged in the bottom until he located the leather-covered casket. He opened the lid, drew out the document on top, replaced the casket, shut the press doors and walked swiftly back past Daisy to the kitchen, where Arthur had already kindled a fire.

He stared at his father's witnessed letter for a few seconds. Then he put it in the flames. He retrieved his musket and left the house by the front door.

He drew a deep breath of the sweet morning air as he joined O'Brian out by the road. Behind the ridge, the eastern sky was already growing light.

6
"God Damn It, They Are Firing Ball!"

THE HOT morning sun beat against Philip's neck as he obeyed the command to load.

He braced the musket's butt on the ground. He tore one of the paper cartridges with his teeth, poured its contents down the muzzle, then dropped the ball in after it. Three twisting strokes of the ramrod and the load was seated.

He was conscious of sweat on his palms, the nervous expressions of the men around him. Several hundred by now. The Concord companies had been reinforced with units that had marched in from London, Acton, Bedford. And there were young and old men who belonged to no company at all, but who had brought their ancient squirrel guns, even a few pistols, in response to the couriers and the tolling bells that had spread the dreadful tidings across the countryside—

The regulars are coming out.

From the slant of the sun, Philip judged the time to be near eleven o'clock. He stood next to O'Brian on the Muster Field, a high hilltop place well back from the north side of the road that led west from the river bridge.

As the mounted officers resumed their conference, he wiped his sweating forehead. Squinted at the white clouds sailing calm and stately overhead. His mouth was dry, with a metallic taste. Was this how it felt when a man faced in battle?

Because there was no longer any doubt that the stage was set for conflict. Just down the hillside, invisible from the Muster Field to which the militiamen had retreated, British units in their brilliant, blazing red had crossed the bridge to the west side—

It still seemed unreal.

So did the whole morning. Since first light, he'd lived through a terrifying swift sequence of events. Events far different from any his wildest imagination had ever conjured in Auvergne. Or London or Boston, for that matter.

Through it all, he'd searched for Anne. He hadn't seen her—nor her father, thank God.

Perhaps he'd only missed her by moments. But that was no comfort. Not now.

II

HE AND O'BRIAN had arrived in Concord at dawn. People were everywhere: armed men tramping in from the hills, others still moving stores to new hiding places. In dooryards, women gathered with their sleepy children, whispering, their faces drawn.

About six o'clock, a scout brought news from Lexington.

Many companies of British soldiers were indeed on the march. At Lexington green, the arriving redcoats and Captain Parker's minutemen had exchanged shots. The scout had spurred his horse away at the first sounds of firing. Thus, he couldn't answer what seemed to be everyone's question—including O'Brian's:

Were the British firing ball or only noisy powder?

The scout swiped at his mouth. "I do not know. But I think it probable they were using ball."

The man could offer no more definite information as to who had fired first, the Crown soldiers or some hot-tempered colonial. But the stunning truth spread throughout the village in a few minutes, casting a new pall—

Shots exchanged.

A war of words had turned to a war in fact.

The Concord companies formed up and marched out toward Lexington before seven, to probe the enemy's strength.

A slender country fellow Philip knew as Hosmer beat time on his drum as they trudged east in the steadily brightening light. At that hour, the column comprised not many more than a hundred men, drab in their plain shirts, their farm-muddied boots and trousers.

Someone let out a yell, pointed. Away in the east, Philip and the others spied the head of what seemed a great red serpent crawling along the level road to meet them—

Several hundred grenadiers and light infantrymen at least. Preceded by their musicians thudding drums and tootling fifes. Bayonets glittered in the rising sun. Ornamental plates on the tall black caps of the grenadiers winked like mirrors. Crossbelts and pipe-clayed breeches showed brilliant white. The music and the sound of their coming filled the countryside.

Colonel Barrett reined in, scowling. A moment later he ordered his companies to turn about and countermarch. The men in the colorfully faced red uniforms pouring along the road far outnumbered Barrett's force. There might be as many as five hundred or a thousand approaching, their brave music louder by the moment.

So on Barrett's order, the Concord companies preceded their enemies back to the village, keeping in surprisingly good formation and showing no panic. But their own riffling drum and single fife were all but drowned out by the massed instruments behind them.

A strange procession indeed, Philip thought as he tramped back into town. He and his companions marched—even joked—as if that immense scarlet serpent didn't exist—

The officers spurred ahead to warn the women and old men to retreat to their homes. The flood of armed redcoats would be sweeping into Concord before another hour was up—!

The militiamen kept in their ranks and halted on command. Philip again searched the scurrying clusters of townspeople for a glimpse of Anne. He didn't see her.

He reflected with a grim amusement that the colonials had almost behaved like a sort of advance honor guard for their foes—music competing against music in the warmth of the April morning. Toward the end, Hosmer had actually picked up and matched the cadence of the British drums.

As the British tattoo grew still louder, officers and townsmen argued briefly. Some, the Reverend Emerson for one, wanted an immediate confrontation right in the village. Barrett finally overruled the hotter tempers. The supplies in town had now been reasonably well hidden, he said. No one as yet had a clear indication of how thorough—or how violent—the British search would be.

"And if it does come to battle, the longer we wait, the better. We'll have more men from the neighboring towns."

Many questioned Barrett's decision loudly and angrily. But no one disobeyed when he gave the order for the men to march.

They headed up the road in the direction of North Bridge and the high ground

of the Muster Field. On the way, scouts reported that the British bandsmen had broken formation. Retreated to the rear of the column. Some light infantry companies were leaving the road, scaling the ridge on their right to search for hostile forces—

Once across the bridge, Barrett ordered his officers to clear the hillside of a considerable number of townsmen and farm families who had waded the river to watch any forthcoming action. Looking back during the ascent to the Muster Field, Philip saw red and white uniforms through the trees lining the road from Concord.

Six or seven companies of light infantry, it looked like. Moving westward— no doubt to find the supplies at Barrett's farm.

The colonel left Major Buttrick in command as the country soldiers reached the hilltop. Barrett galloped off to his farm for a last-minute check of the hidden stores.

The sun grew hotter.

The British companies advanced across the bridge. Three deployed on the river's west bank. The other four marched on toward Barrett's, to the steady thumping of the drums.

Soon Barrett came riding back, having circled wide to elude the searchers. He dismounted on the brow of the hill and surveyed the situation down at the bridge.

All the time, more men arrived. From the south, from the north, they flowed in singly and in groups. The sun kept climbing toward the zenith.

Philip and the others fidgeted while Barrett spoke with his officers. The morning wind blew warm across the hilltop.

Word circulated that Barrett was gambling on the main thrust of search and seizure being aimed at his farm. Perhaps all that the redcoats left in town wanted to do was show their authority—by means of their presence.

Before long, however, he was proved wrong. About ten, a man slipped across the river. He reported that the leader of the expeditionary force, a Lieutenant Colonel Smith, had established a command post at Wright's. His soldiers were scouring the town for stores.

With restraint, the spy said. The townspeople were not being abused—or even touched. But sacks of bullets and barrels of flour were being pitched gleefully into the millpond by the redcoats. That remained the extent of the damage to the moment—

The whole action seemed hesitant, Philip thought. It was as if the British still hoped to bring the colonists to heel without violence. Could the report from Lexington have been exaggerated? The possibility helped him breathe a little easier—

Especially about Anne. Wherever she might be in town, her safety seemed more certain than it had a few hours ago.

Then, just before eleven, the black plume of smoke climbed into the sky.

From the Muster Field, it wasn't possible to see what buildings were afire. But the meaning of the smoke column seemed unmistakable. One of Barrett's adjutants confronted him angrily:

"Damn it, sir, will you let them burn the town down?"

A few moments later, Barrett gave the command to load with ball.

III

HOSMER STRUCK up his drumbeat again. In a column of twos, the country soldiers marched to the edge of the hill and started down.

From his position alongside Martin O'Brian, Philip saw the Irish farmer grin a hard grin. And realized Barrett's strategy had been sound. The double file trailing away ahead and behind surely must total five hundred by now. The three British companies on this side of the bridge appeared to number no more than a hundred or a hundred and twenty at most.

Barrett sat his horse at the crest of the hillside. As Philip and the others trudged past, he kept repeating a stern command:

"Don't fire first. If there's to be shooting, don't fire first!"

Philip's heart beat hard, almost matching the rhythm of Hosmer's drum. Below him, the head of the column reached level ground, turned in the direction of the bridge. The whole proceedings still did not seem quite real—

Except for that black pillar of smoke over the treetops that screened out all sight of the village.

"Hah, look! They're scurrying back!" O'Brian rasped cheerfully.

As the British officers shouted commands, the three companies hastily formed up and faced about. In a moment, their cadenced marching hammered the planks of the bridge. Hosmer's drum beat furiously in answer.

Barrett spurred down the hillside to the head of the column, his eyes narrowed against the April sun. Philip and O'Brian reached the road, turned left after the men ahead of them. Across the murmuring river, Philip could see little except a rush and flash of scarlet-clad forms. The light infantry companies were dividing, one moving to each flank of the third company, which now faced toward the far end of the bridge.

The men of this company were drawn up in streetfighting formation—three ranks, one behind the other. The sun shone on the brown barrels of their muskets, flashed from their bayonets as the first rank knelt. The second rank moved up close behind.

Barrett shouted, "Faster cadence, drummer!"

Boldly, the colonel headed his horse out ahead of the double file. The first in line were men from the town of Acton, Philip believed.

Barrett rode to within shouting distance of the bridge as half a dozen redcoats frantically started trying to rip up the planks on the far side.

"Leave the bridge alone!" Barrett bawled in a threatening voice.

Philip heard no order given. But suddenly the muskets of the kneeling front rank of the central British company exploded.

Smoke—spurts of fire—

At the head of the militia column, the captain of the Acton contingent pitched over.

Hosmer's drumming stopped in mid-beat as he toppled. Blood from his throat spilled red over his drumhead—

Barrett's horse screamed and shied from the thunderous volley. Somewhere Buttrick's voice rang out:

"Fire, for God's sake—*fire!*"

Drawn up two by two in the long column, only the foremost militiamen had a clear shot. But seconds after the British fired, and without any specific command, the men in the rear of the column broke for both sides of the road.

Philip ran to the right, O'Brian the other way. Over the racketing of the muskets, Philip heard the Irishman's enraged yell:

"God damn it, they are firing ball!"

Philip dropped to one knee in the marsh grass. He hit the musket's muzzle to send powder through the touchhole, braced the piece against his shoulder—and for one awful instant amid the shouting, the rattling fire from the militiamen, the confused yells and orders, the blowing smoke, his very will seemed frozen—

Across the narrow bridge, he saw an officer down. Another fell. The kneeling front ranks scrambled up, dropped behind to permit the second rank an unobstructed aim. Finally, Philip's finger tightened—

Tightened—

Taking an eternity, it seemed.

It had come.

In the cries of pain, the corpses of the drummer and the Acton captain, he heard and saw the end of the settled world he'd hoped for—

Gone. All gone this April morning—

He fired.

He reeled back against the musket's kick, saw a light infantryman at the far end of the bridge spin and sprawl on his face. Whether Philip's own ball had scored the hit, or a ball fired from another of the crackling muskets, he did not know for certain.

But he knew an era had ended and another had begun, for himself and for all the shouting, cursing Americans who leveled their weapons and continued firing on the King's soldiers across the river.

___IV

THE COLONIALS never fully understood the reason for what happened next.

Over the long months in which the conflict had been building to this climax, many who had openly predicted that war would come had, at the same time, reminded their listeners of one more fact. Haphazardly drilled, poorly equipped Massachusetts farmers would be no match for regimental troops that had fought honorably all over the world—and won.

And yet, with his own eyes, Philip witnessed the astounding aftermath of the exchange of volleys—one from each side.

Even as he crouched in the long grass and frantically rammed home his next load, he saw the crack British light infantrymen break ranks. Carrying or dragging their dead and wounded, they plunged back up the road to Concord.

Not in formation. Running—like a mob in panic. Their passage raised clouds of dust.

No one could explain the frantic retreat. Was it caused by the surprising courage of the double file that had marched down the hillside to confrontation without cover? Was it produced by the American musket fire, a thunder more intimidating in its noise than its accuracy? Or was it the result of the British simply never expecting any resistance at all?

Whatever the reason, the redcoats fled. Without plan and without pattern, they fled—while Barrett rallied his men, Philip among them.

The colonel led his troops over the bridge. At the east end, a young, tow-haired redcoat lay on his face, shot through the back. Caught by a ball when the front rank moved away so the second could fire? Who would ever know?

Philip trudged by the fallen soldier. The boy's shoulders moved slightly. He was still alive. One of the Americans spat on him. But no one touched him.

The militiamen followed Barrett, moving in ragged formation. Some three hundred yards from the bridge, the colonel led them up a hillside. On command, they sprawled in the long meadow grass behind a low stone wall, to await orders or the next action.

In the distance, Philip spied companies of grenadiers in their tall, glossy black caps moving out from the blowing smoke that still hid most of the village. The grenadiers—reinforcements for the bridge—met the noisy, panic-stricken light infantrymen running the other way. Perhaps there was some plan to re-form the entire force, return and confront the enemy. It never materialized. In a few minutes, all the troops had disappeared back into the smoke.

Philip lay with the grass tickling his cheek. He was still stunned by the significance of the brief battle. *They had fired on the King's troops.*

The other men resting behind the wall were equally stunned—and equally quiet. After their first triumphant yells at the bridge, a strange silence had settled on them. It continued as the tramp of more marching feet sounded from the direction of the river.

Philip raised on one elbow, caught sight of the companies that had marched to Barrett's re-crossing the bridge at quick-step. He glanced down the line of the wall, searched for an officer. But Barrett, Buttrick and the others in charge had disappeared.

He asked about them. A man four places down said they'd crept away along the ridge to survey the town at closer range. There was no one to issue a command to fire as the four companies tramped by along the road directly below—well within musket range.

Not a shot rang out. Barely a mumbled curse could be heard from the men crouched behind the stone wall. Did they all feel what he felt? Dread? One skirmish did not make a successful revolution—

The noise of the returning companies gradually died away. A jay circled in the hot, still air above the watching farmers. The bird shrilled at them.

By noon, the British expeditionary force had taken the road back to Lexington. Concord lay quiet in the April light.

V

EVERYWHERE, IT seemed, men were running again. Excited now, jubilant. Making bawdy, contemptuous jokes about the Crown soldiers.

The hilltops around Concord were black with running figures—musket-armed countrymen still pouring in from all points of the compass. Many marched in across South Bridge.

Receiving hasty orders in the village street, they hurried out again to climb and move along the ridges that overlooked the highway back to Lexington and Boston.

When the fact of the British departure was certain, Philip and the rest had descended the hillside and raced back to the village. There, along with other chagrined officers and men, they discovered the cause of the smoke that had precipitated the march from the Muster Field, and the subsequent volleys.

Far from burning the town, grenadiers under Smith's command had simply

found several gun carriages among the stores cached in Concord's meeting house. They had dragged the carriages into the open and set them alight. Philip stared ruefully at the charred, smoldering remains. He shook his head with a dour amusement. So easily did war begin. By a mistake, a wrong judgment—

All around him, men with muskets kept moving out toward the east. North of the village he saw them thick on the ridges. Someone in the crowd seized his arm.

He whirled, recognized O'Brian, his blue eyes fierce.

"Come along, come along, Philip! We're to give chase. We'll chivy them all the way back to Boston, damned if we won't!"

"Pack of strutting peacocks!" another man yelled. "Marching with their God damn fifes and drums—we showed 'em, I'll say!"

"Aye," a third agreed. "They fired ball and they'll get ball in return—from now on."

The trio, including O'Brian, disappeared in the dust and commotion.

Philip wiped his forehead. Sweat trickled beneath his shirt. He searched the faces of the excited people clustering outside their homes and near the meeting house—where the remains of the gun carriages finally collapsed into ash.

No sign of her. Not anywhere. With a weary sigh, he started for the east edge of town.

"Philip?"

He turned, blinking into the smoke and glare. He was afraid in the depths of his soul that his ears had played him false. And false hope was worse than none—

A patch of smoke cleared. He saw her.

Her plain gray dress was stained, torn at the sleeves, wet all around the hem. Her chestnut hair was tangled. Something seemed to turn and break inside of him. Tears welled in his eyes as he shouldered the musket and ran toward her.

She ran too, closing the distance between them with amazing speed. Dropping the musket, he swept his arms around her, kissing her tear-stained cheek, kissing her unashamedly in the smoky sunlight.

"Anne," was all he could say at first. "Oh, Annie, oh my God, Annie—I thought I'd never see you again. Your father turned me away from Wright's last night—"

"And told me about how he threatened you," she said, half-laughing, half-crying as she wiped her eyes.

"Did Daisy find you? I sent a message—"

"Yes, she brought it. That's why I've been searching for you all morning. Were you at the bridge?"

"I was. But I only got to fire one round before the redcoats ran."

Her hands seemed all over his face, his arms. Squeezing, touching.

"You're not hurt—?"

"No, no. Only two or three died on our side."

"I'm such a sight—I look so terrible—" Her face was still wet with tears. She spoke in short, almost incoherent gasps. "We've been at the millpond, pulling out the flour barrels. The poor grenadiers—they were so polite. They neglected to crack the barrels open. The flour around the lids sealed them shut. So most of the flour is good as new. Philip, that fat, frightened puppy—" Her laugh was ragged. "—Smith, the commander—he paid for wagons and chaises to carry his wounded back along the retreat route. *Paid* for them! Gentlemen to the end!"

"Some of those gentlemen are shot down dead," Philip told her. "I'm sup-

posed to go up the road and find Barrett's companies again. We're to follow the redcoats and harry them, Mr. O'Brian said—''

"Smith ranted about the delay of the reinforcements he sent for. There may be many more troops marching out from Boston—''

"Annie, forget the troops.'' He touched the freckles on her cheek, barely able to speak. "Last night, your father said—he told me—''

"That I'm going to bear a child? It's true.''

"Why didn't you speak of it before I left for Philadelphia? You knew it then, you must have!''

She answered quietly, "Of course I did. But I wouldn't have used that to hold you—''

"Just what I suspected!''

"I'd have no man without love, Philip. And I want no man except you—'' Her voice broke. She brushed at her tear-streaked face, embarrassed. "Truly, I never thought you'd come back. What—what happened in Philadelphia?''

A peculiar smile pulled up the corners of his mouth. "I almost bought a whistle. But it cost too much.''

"A whistle? Whatever are you talking about?''

"It's not important,'' he said, still smiling that strange smile.

"But the woman, Philip. What about her?''

He thought a moment, then said, "I'll tell you one day. When we're old and our child's grown up, maybe. All you need to know now is that it's done—and I know what I want and what I am.''

"What I hoped and prayed you'd turn out to be!'' she whispered joyfully, hugging him.

"Annie, there's nothing I can offer you—Christ, not even the certainty I'll come back today. Who knows what kind of fighting there'll be if we chase the British? But if I can come back, Annie, I want to marry you—''

"Not because you think you must,'' she said with a shake of her head. "Not because of my father. Or for any other reason except—''

"That I love you,'' he finished, kissing her.

Some passing men jeered and called him a yellow shirker, and why didn't he get a move on? He paid no attention, his hands fierce against Anne's back, holding her, feeling the warmth of her through the stained dress—and the trembling, too, as she wept her happiness.

She wrapped her arms around his waist, buried her face against his shoulder. "We'll raise good strong sons, Philip. You'll start a fine printing firm of your own and be a rich man—we'll have a splendid house—''

"Annie, Annie—'' He lifted her chin, caressed tears from her eyes. "That's a good dream. But not a certain one. The fire's broken out. Right here in Concord this morning. And in Lexington, they said—''

"Yes, eight or nine of Captain Parker's best were shot down on the green. But you saw how the people rose up in the countryside—came to fight—''

"Still, it's a terrible thing to think of what can lie ahead. The colonies locked in war with the strongest nation on earth—God knows what sort of future any man will have—''

"*I* know!'' she exclaimed, her face shining. "I know—now that you've chosen your side. You'll live, and we'll take what comes—and we'll still be together when it's done, you'll see. What Sam Adams wants will happen now, it must—''

"You mean independency?''

"Yes—maybe declared by that very Congress meeting in May. Philip, it has to come! A new country. Free of the old bonds just like you're free of them. But we'll weather everything—and turn the Kent family into something strong and fine."

He let himself smile a little, saying:

"Provided your father doesn't put a ball through me first. Where is he?"

"Down at the pond hauling out the flour barrels." She laughed. "I told him I felt an attack of female dizziness coming on. He's utterly confounded by such things. I said I was going back to Wright's to rest—but I was really coming to hunt for you again. By the time you return, I'll see that he's properly tamed—since you've decided to do the decent thing," she finished, teasing.

He kissed her for another long, sweet moment.

"Somehow, I think you're right, Anne."

"About what?"

He pressed her hand. "I think the Kents will turn out to be a very fine family indeed."

He retrieved his fallen musket and, after one final wave, started walking east.

VI

PHILIP HEADED out of Concord in company with other men. A great many sang. Some recounted the fight at the bridge second or third hand, or continued making obscene jokes at the expense of the royal troops. Philip's belly growled. How long was it since he'd eaten or slept? It seemed an age.

Yet there was a spring in his stride; a fresh sense of direction. Despite the uncertainties and dangers ahead, he was, for a few moments, completely happy.

The euphoria didn't last long.

How would England react now? he wondered. With armed might, surely. Unrestricted and unrestrained. Only in that way could the King hope to put down this rebellion in the cause of freedom—

No matter. He'd follow the road from Concord wherever it led. And come back to Anne, and see their baby born. The first one, then many more—

Dirty, weary, he still hummed a little as he left the highway and started to climb the hillside toward the ridge, where he thought he'd glimpsed some of the Concord contingent. The higher he climbed, the hotter the sun seemed to burn. Almost like a fire on his face.

He climbed toward the blue sky and the free air at the crest of the ridge and caught up with three men he recognized. He was soon out of sight of Concord, lost among the other Americans streaming east to fight.

Afterword

Several people deserve a generous share of thanks for their contributions to this book.

First, Lyle Engel, whose concept of the series provided the canvas for this panoramic picture of our beginnings as a nation.

Marla Ray merits special mention for her editorial help and continuing encouragement.

Norman Goldfind, vice-president and editorial director of Pyramid Books, who developed the concept with Mr. Engel, has lavished the kind of interest and attention on the project that, all too often, an author finds missing.

And Norman and Ann Kearns, senior editor at Pyramid, must be thanked for a host of perceptive suggestions that helped strengthen the final work immeasurably.

Finally, I must tender appreciation to my family, who collectively endured months of three different typewriters clacking at strange times, small mountains of research books cluttering up the otherwise orderly premises and periods of authorial gloom and doom alternating with nonstop monologues about Paul Revere's dentistry or Dr. Franklin's air baths that monopolized dinner-table conversations. My wife especially was patience personified when I kept the lights on and the coffee kettle whistling in more predawn hours than I'm sure she cares to count.

I often think that far too many Americans today do not know how and why this country came into being—and, more tragic, do not care. Perhaps in some small way, these novels will help remedy that unhappy situation—and prove, at the same time, as entertaining as only an epic adventure of the spirit can be.

To all those people named, who have been instrumental in my own personal rediscovery of our heritage—a rediscovery that has been, if I may be allowed to use the word in this cynical age, inspiring—I owe a lasting debt.

And Don—thank you for that very first phone call.

JOHN JAKES

THE REBELS

For my daughter Andrea.

"You will think me transported with enthusiasm, but I am not. I am well aware of the toil, and blood, and treasure, that it will cost us to maintain this declaration, and support and defend these States. Yet, through all the gloom, I can see the rays of ravishing light and glory. I can see that the end is more than worth all the means, and that prosperity will triumph in that day's transaction, even although we should rue it, which I trust in God we shall not."

JOHN ADAMS,
WRITING TO HIS WIFE ABIGAIL
FROM PHILADELPHIA.
JULY 2, 1776:

Contents

BOOK ONE

OUR LIVES, OUR FORTUNES AND OUR SACRED HONOR

1
A Taste of Steel

A BRITISH drum started a slow march cadence. Others joined in. The thudding spread across a broad front at the southeast end of the Charlestown peninsula.

For a moment the drums sounded abnormally loud in the hot summer air. There was a temporary lull in the crashing of the cannon from the Copp's Hill battery in Boston across the Charles, and from the ships that had ringed the peninsula in order to rake it from all sides.

On Philip Kent's left, a skinny black man with a squirrel gun grinned uneasily.

"Guess Tommy finished his dinner, all right."

"Guess he did," Philip said. Speaking was difficult. His throat was so parched he could barely whisper.

He twisted the ramrod twice more to seat the paper wad on top of the powder and the ball in the muzzle of his precious British-issue Brown Bess musket. He wished to God he could find a drink of water.

His stomach growled. Actually hurt from lack of food. All the rations he'd packed when they mustered in Cambridge at sunset last night were gone.

Besides that, he ached. My God, how he ached. All night long he'd labored with the other colonial soldiers on top of Breed's Hill, digging a redoubt after the officers settled their argument about the exact wording of the orders. Were the men to fortify Breed's Hill, or Bunker's, which lay northwest toward the isthmus connecting the Charlestown peninsula with land more easily defensible?

Finally, an engineering officer named Gridley settled it. Breed's. Concealed by darkness, the Americans dug their square fortification, almost a hundred and forty feet on a side, with an arrow-shaped redan jutting from its south side to overlook the sloping meadow that ran down to the Charles River.

The black man next to Philip in the redoubt had said his name was Salem

Prince. Philip had no idea where he'd come from. But then, he didn't know a fraction of the several hundred soldiers jammed down inside the dusty pit in the earth, where the temperature this blazing June afternoon had to be well above a hundred.

It was doubtful that the black man belonged to the Massachusetts regiments. Or the Connecticut forces under the old Indian fighter, Putnam, who were digging in behind them on a knoll on farmer Bunker's property. The black man had simply appeared one moment when Philip was crouched down, head covered, as a cannon ball screamed over. The ball had blasted a crater into the hillside leading down to the Mystic River on the left of the redoubt. When Philip looked up, the black man stood at his left, running his hand up and down the muzzle of his antique squirrel gun and smiling shyly. Though the American army was a ragged one, the black was even more ragged. Probably he was a free man of color who had slipped out to the peninsula on his own accord. The army, such as it was, didn't mind volunteers one bit.

Now Philip and Prince exchanged anxious glances. Both heard the drums. Both tried to shrug and grin cynically as if the sound didn't matter. Both knew otherwise.

Philip was nearly as dark as Salem Prince by now. Dirt stained his skin, his knee breeches and patched hose and loose, sweat-sodden shirt. In the confusion of men running in and out of the redoubt, there was no way of telling to which unit a man belonged. Few wore uniforms.

But the ebb and flow was constant. New volunteers arrived. Other men sneaked away, using the moment whan a cannon ball exploded and heads were covered to escape the hot, filthy fortification that somehow reminded Philip of a large, freshly dug grave.

The man on Philip's right craned up on tiptoes, peered over the earthwork. Another cannon ball struck, and another. Closer. Clods of dirt showered down on Philip, who had shut his eyes.

But he couldn't shut his ears. He heard the drum cadence growing louder.

A terrifying image swam in his thoughts. Bodies lying unidentified in this dirty, foul-odored pit. Christ, what if one of them should be his—?

Philip Kent, born near the village of Chavaniac, France, 1753. Died on a beautiful Saturday, the seventeenth of June, in the year 1775—

Anne—! he thought, anguished. Somehow, he would come through.

The drums thudded. Another cannon-crash shook the ground. At least they were getting accustomed to the roar of those iron monsters.

The American fortification had been dug by stealth, during the dark hours early on the seventeenth. The activity had been discovered by some sharp-eyed fellow aboard His Majesty's Ship *Lively*. The first round thundered from the ship at about four in the morning.

Some of the green troops screamed in outright terror. Not long after, another ball blew off the head of a man named Pollard working outside the redoubt. The corpse tumbled into the damp grass in the first faint light of morning.

Pollard's blood-gouting stump of a neck was a vivid warning—if one were really needed—prophesing what the day might bring to every man on Breed's Hill.

As the hot morning wore on, the realization dawned that the British guns in the river and over in Boston weren't angled properly to do much damage. Yet their incessant thunder had a power to rip the nerves and clutch the bowels with a universal message that could be seen on most every sweaty face:

Today I may die for daring to take up arms against His Majesty, King George III.

Now the cannonading increased again. Philip wanted to peek over the earthwork, see what he and his fellow soldiers would be confronting. For a moment he lacked the nerve. A shout brought him pivoting around:

"Oh, goddamn them shitting British—they've fired Charlestown."

Even before Philip raised up to risk a look, he saw the smoke and flames. Under an intensified bombardment of red-hot ball mixed with carcasses that shattered on impact, releasing their oiled combustibles, fires were already burning on rooftops in the little waterside town of two or three hundred houses. The town's frightened residents had already fled.

"The reinforcements have beached," someone said.

"Royal Marines," someone else added.

Another voice, shaky, put in, "The regulars have started up. Look—"

"Keep quiet so you can hear the command to fire!"

That hard, cracking voice belonged to the field commander, tall and graying Colonel Prescott of Pepperell. Through the tangle of men in the redoubt, Philip saw Prescott collapse a spyglass and head for the fortification's single rear entrance. Just one means of escape for all these hundreds. What if the redoubt were overcome? He felt more and more like a man already interred.

Suddenly, he caught an excited murmur:

"Warren—it's Dr. Warren—"

An exceedingly handsome and fair-haired man with musket and sword had just stalked into the redoubt. Dr. Joseph Warren, a Boston physician, was one of the prime movers of the patriot cause in Massachusetts. Philip had come to know Warren while working at the Edes and Gill printing house.

"Your servant, sir," the unsmiling Warren said to Prescott.

Prescott seemed taken aback for a moment. Recovering, he spoke over the drumming and the cannon-fire:

"General Warren." He saluted. "You're entitled to take command."

"No, Colonel, I'm here as a volunteer. My commission still exists only on paper, waiting to be signed. I'll take my place with the others."

Men nearby raised a brief cheer as the physician, a figure of supreme if sweaty elegance in his gold-fringed coat, walked through the dust to a position at the dugout earth wall. Prescott vanished at the redoubt's narrow opening, to take charge at the breastwork which ran down the side of the hill on the left.

The drumming grew louder. *I should look at the enemy,* Philip thought.

Just then, Warren spotted him. The physician hurried over, managing a smile:

"Kent?" He extended his hand.

"Yes, Dr. Warren, good afternoon."

"I hardly recognized you."

"The work in here has been a mite dirty."

"But well done, that's plain. So you're serving—"

"We all must, I guess."

"I hear you've a new wife. Lawyer Ware's daughter."

"Yes, sir, we were married a month ago. Anne's living in rented rooms in Watertown. Her father, too."

"Well," said Warren, "if we give Tommy a sharp fight, you'll get back to see her soon."

With a wave, the doctor returned to his place at the wall. His presence still produced gapes and admiring stares. Warren was one of the most important

leaders of the rebel cause. In concert with John Hancock, the Adams cousins, Samuel and John, the silversmith Paul Revere and others, he had been instrumental in pushing the Americans of Massachusetts to armed confrontation with the British. That a man of such prestige and position would come to this potential death trap to fight like an ordinary soldier seemed to have a heartening effect on those in the redoubt. It certainly did on Philip Kent.

What time was it? About three o'clock, he guessed from the angle of the sun. Despite the almost incessant pounding of the cannon, he stood up on tiptoe to look out toward Morton's Hill and see the challenge facing them this afternoon.

He gasped when he saw the red lines advancing across virtually the entire peninsula. His hand closed around the muzzle of his Brown Bess. His palm sweated, cold.

Scarlet. Everywhere, scarlet. A thousand or two thousand British soldiers at least. And the American forces must have shrunk to half that number by now.

The British advanced in orderly fashion, climbing stone walls, slipping past trees, maintaining perfect marching order. Their flags snapped in the sultry summer wind.

It was a parade march. Slow; steady. A march to the drumbeats that thudded between cannon bursts. The soldiers formed long scarlet lines stretching to the Mystic River. Company flanking company, they were marching against the redoubt; against the breastwork; and, further down, against the hastily erected rail fence where straw had been piled to stop musket balls. Still further down, more companies were advancing against the stone wall erected hastily between the fence and the river's edge. Behind the various fortifications, shabbily dressed colonials waited.

Philip turned in another direction, surveying the entire scene. Across the Charles River in Boston town, thousands of people watched from windows and rooftops as white blooms puffed from the muzzles of the Copp's Hill battery.

Almost hypnotically, Philip's eye was drawn back to the lines advancing up the hillside. Someone had said the troops were personally commanded by Major General Sir William Howe, one of the three officers of like rank who'd arrived in mid-May to bolster the command of General Thomas Gage.

"No firing," an officer shouted from the redoubt's far side. "Hold fire until you hear the signal. Let the bastards get close enough so your muskets can reach 'em."

It would take forever, Philip thought.

He counted ten companies across the broad British front. And ten more immediately behind. Hundreds and hundreds of red-coated men laboring in slow step. A scarlet wall. *Coming on—*

Sweat rivered down his chest under his soggy shirt, so he knew what the British must be feeling, stifled in their red wool and burdened with packs containing full rations, blankets—a staggering weight. Yet they continued to march steadily, breaking cadence only to climb over or go around obstacles. Philip began to discern features. A large scar on a man's chin. Bushy, copper-colored brows. Sweat-bright cheeks.

"Hold fire," came the order again. "Prescott will give the word."

Swallowing, Phillip rested his Brown Bess on the lip of the earthwork. The black man, Salem Prince, and the others took up similar positions. Down on the left, Philip glimpsed Prescott in the blowing cannon smoke. The colonel was striding back and forth behind the breastwork, ducking only when a ball whizzed over and crashed.

The drums throbbed. Philip recognized the uniforms of the crack troops marching up to crush the Americans who had been unwise enough to fortify one of the two chief areas overlooking Boston. In addition to regular infantry, the British barges had brought over the pride of their fighting forces—the light infantry and grenadier companies of various regiments. From behind the marching assault troops, small fieldpieces banged occasionally.

What terrified Philip Kent most was the determined, ceaseless forward flow of the soldiers. And, on the ends of their muskets, glittering steel—

The steel of bayonets.

Hardly an American on Breed's or Bunker's Hill had that kind of deadly instrument affixed to the end of his weapon. The colonials held the bayonet in contempt. Philip wondered now whether that attitude wasn't foolish—

After the first outbreak of fighting at Lexington and Concord in April, Philip had been among the hundreds of militiamen who had harried the shattered, astonished British expeditionary force all the way back to Boston, pinking at the lobsterbacks from behind stone walls, watching them drop one by one, the ranks decimated by a disorganized but deadly attack to which the British were not accustomed. Afterward, the Americans had been jubilant; supremely confident. Who needed precise formations and steel when a colonial's sharp eye aimed a musket?

Today it might be different. Up the hill came the world's finest military organization. Orderly. Fully armed and moving steadily, steadily higher toward the redoubt, and across swampy lower ground toward the rail fence, the stone wall—

If we have to go against those bayonets, Philip thought, *we're done.*

II

"GODAMIGHTY, WHEN they gonna let us shoot?" raged Salem Prince. Philip wondered the same thing. But again the order was passed by the officers:

"Colonel Prescott says no firing until you can look them in the eye and see the white."

Slowly, inexorably, the grenadiers and light infantry climbed through the long grass. Philip wiped his forehead. For a moment he felt faint.

He hadn't slept all long night. He was exhausted; starved. This whole confrontation seemed futile. That the colonies he'd adopted as his homeland would dare to challenge the armed might of the greatest empire the world had known since Rome was—madness. No other word would fit.

He looked out again. Faces took on even greater detail. Fat and thin; sallow or ruddy; young men and old. Clearly now, he could see the whites of nervous eyes—

Down behind the breastwork on the left, muskets erupted in a sheet of oily smoke and fire. All along the British front, men began to fall.

"*Fire!*" someone yelled in the redoubt. Philip pointed his Brown Bess—the musket was too inaccurate for precise aiming—and pulled the trigger. A moment later, he watched a light infantryman in his twenties—no older than Philip himself—drop in the grass, writhing.

Like some great leaden scythe, the American fire cut down the lines of the attacking British. But they kept marching. Kept climbing—

Now entire ranks were down, men thrashing and screaming while their comrades from behind marched past them, stepping over them—*on* them when necessary. The men still on their feet fired their muskets and re-loaded as they marched.

Philip heard the British musket balls go hissing through the air over his head and smack the rear earth wall. In the redoubt too, men cried out—but very few compared to the numbers of red-clad grenadiers and light infantrymen dropping all across the peninsula.

The Americans re-loaded as fast as possible, with speed, great speed, and continued firing. Philip had no time to think of anything save the repetitive routine of powder and ball and paper. *Load faster,* the officers kept urging. *Fire, goddamn it! Quickly, quickly—!*

"Look at that, mister! Looky!" Salem Prince shouted. Philip glanced up.

The British companies had halted their climb. Front lines turned on command, broke, retreated. Went streaming back toward Morton's Hill where they had eaten a leisurely lunch and smoked their pipes before beginning the assault.

In the redoubt, men started cheering. Philip didn't join in. He licked his palm, scorched by the hot metal of his musket, then leaned on the inner wall, panting for air.

Again he wished for a drink of water. There was none. Overhead, visible through the smoke that had thickened considerably, the sun broiled. With numbed fingers Philip checked his powder horn.

He'd loaded and fired so often, it was half empty. Others around him were grumbling over a similar lack.

"Hold your places," came the command. "They won't give up so easily."

Philip closed his eyes, tried to rest. He didn't want to die any more than the others did.

Near him, a Rhode Islander groveled in the dirt, gut-shot by a chance ball. A Massachusetts man was methodically relieving the wounded man of his musket, powder horn and crude wooden cartouche containing the precious wadding and ball.

The drumming had receded. But for how long?

The British would certainly try a new strategy next time, he felt. Advancing in perfect order, with perfect discipline, had given them command of the world's battlefields. Today, that method of fighting had proved disastrous.

But whatever their strategy, if they ever reached the American lines with those bayonets—

Philip tried not to think about it.

III

AFTER CONCORD, Philip Kent had experienced an almost euphoric joy that lasted several weeks.

The British had run—*run*—back to Boston. And an American army—ragtag, poorly organized, but still an army—had encircled the city where hostile attitudes between Crown and colony had built to the breaking point over a period of some ten years.

Once the siege lines were in place, the small local militia companies of the kind in which Philip had served in Concord were re-organized into larger state

regiments. Similar home or state guard units from other colonies arrived, the whole being commanded somewhat haphazardly by old General Artemas Ward. Ward was lying abed in Cambridge this June afternoon, trying to manage the military force while the agony of a stone burned in his flabby body. The Massachusetts men on Breed's Hill had volunteered to serve in the new regiments until the end of the year. The eight-month army, the officers called it. Not exactly with humor.

Other colonies sent reinforcements to Boston. Rhode Island and New Hampshire and Connecticut—Old Put, the Indian fighter, had brought in three thousand Connecticut men plus a herd of sheep for food. Meantime, matters political were directed from the temporary provincial capitol, Watertown. Cambridge served as army headquarters.

But control resided in Watertown. From there came the orders that sent Colonel Benedict Arnold of Connecticut westward in late April, to raise a new levy of Massachusetts men and join forces in early May with Ethan Allen, a rough-hewn fighting man from the Hampshire Grants. Allen led a contingent whose members styled themselves the Green Mountain Boys.

Continually wrangling over who had command of the expedition, Allen and Arnold still managed to surprise and force the surrender of the small garrison at Fort Ticonderoga on Lake Champlain. Not much of a victory in military terms, the officers around Boston admitted. Hardly more than forty Britishers captured. The value of Ticonderoga lay in its supply of military stores, the most important being cannon.

No one knew for sure how many cannon. But the prospect of even a few pieces in patriot hands was considered a blessing.

To the accomplishment of routing royal troops at Lexington and Concord—or the crime, depending on a man's political position—the colonials could now add the seizure of a royal fort and a quantity of royal artillery "in the name of Jehovah and the Continental Congress," as Allen put it when presenting the surrender demand. It was doubtful that the second Continental Congress, commencing to sit in Philadelphia in May, was aware that Ticonderoga's capture had been made in its name until one of the express riders pounding between the north and the Quaker City bore the surprising news. A rider making the return trip reported that the Congress intended to appoint a supreme commander to take charge of the Massachusetts siege.

But something far more important than military developments had contributed to Philip's happiness that spring. Philip and the girl he'd courted, Anne Ware of Boston, had been married in late April, in a small Congregational church in Watertown. Anne's father, a pop-eyed little lawyer who had written numerous essays supporting the patriot cause, gave the couple his grudging blessing. After all, Anne was already five months pregnant with Philip's child.

Like so many young husbands and wives, Philip and Anne faced a cloudy future. Philip's dream of establishing himself in the printing trade would have to wait until the armed struggle was resolved. It might end soon, in a truce; reconciliation along with redress of colonial grievances. Overtures in that direction were being considered by the Congress, Philip had heard.

But if firebrands like Samuel Adams had their way, the war could go on and on—a titanic struggle whose goal would be Adams' own: complete independency for the thirteen colonies.

Re-loading his Brown Bess now, Philip could hardly believe that this corpse-littered battleground was the same pastoral peninsula where, back in September

of '73, he had clumsily tried to seduce Anne. It seemed unreal, all that long past with its beginnings in the French province of Auvergne, the trouble in England with the high-born Amberly family, Philip's emigration to America and his work for the patriot printer, Ben Edes. Philip had come a long way in the rebel cause, from indifference to confusion to firm belief.

Still, a cause was one thing, reality another. He glanced up at the scorching sun behind the smoke, wiped his sticky forehead. He wanted to live. He wanted to see Anne again; see their child born whole and sound—

But he and Anne had agreed that he had to serve. In truth, Philip had been the first to raise the issue—at the same time he announced his decision. He was committed to the cause. Anne had fired him with her own zeal. So when he told her he would henceforth be living in the military barracks hastily converted from buildings at Harvard College, she had nodded and kissed him gently, holding back her tears—

Last night, around six, Reverend Langdon, the president of the college, had prayed for the men who mustered in Harvard Yard, bound for the Charlestown peninsula. The move was designed to counteract a British attempt to fortify the Dorchester Heights, rumored to have been scheduled for Sunday, June eighteenth.

With blankets, one day's provisions and entrenching tools, the Americans— no more than a thousand, Philip guessed—had marched into the darkness, leaving General Ward groaning in bed, and Reverend Langdon seeing to the loading of wagons that would carry the precious volumes of the Harvard library to safety in Andover. If the British ever stopped hesitating and moved out of Boston in massive numbers, those books could be burned—destroyed—just like Charlestown this afternoon—

On Breed's Hill, Philip felt none of the exuberant confidence he'd enjoyed in the days following the skirmish at Concord.

Wounded men moaned in the redoubt. Philip looked around as Salem Prince said quietly, "They coming again."

Philip closed his eyes and drew a deep breath of the fetid air. Prince was right. He heard the drums.

IV

THE SECOND attack was much like the first. Stupid on the part of the British, Philip thought. He and the others fired and fired and fired again. The withering flame that leaped outward from the American muskets devastated the steadily advancing soldiers a second time. Sent the survivors into retreat a second time. Now the colonials had real cause for cheering—

But it was short-lived:

"I've only powder for two or three more shots," Philip said to the black man after the second charge had fallen back. The smoke in the redoubt was thicker than ever.

"You better off'n I am," the black said, up-ending his empty powder horn. "Ball almost gone, too."

A passing officer spun on them. "If you have powder, fire anything you can find. Rocks—or this." He snatched up a bent nail left over from the erection of the redoubt's timberwork. He disappeared in the smoke, leaving Philip to stare in dismay at the nail.

How late was it? Four-thirty? Five? Philip peered over the earthwork, saw hundreds of fallen grenadiers and light infantrymen, flowers of scarlet wool and blood strewing the hillside. He squinted through the acrid, choking clouds, hastily grabbed the black's arm, pointed.

"General Howe, he finally got some brains," the black observed. But his eyes were fearful.

The re-forming British ranks looked different. The soldiers were stripping themselves of their cumbersome packs and field gear. They tossed aside their mitre-like hats or bearskin caps. Threw off their white crossbelts, red uniform jackets—

Down the line, Dr. Warren was likewise discarding his fine coat. "I think they mean to break through this time," he said. "Howe has all the powder he needs. He must know we're running short."

"Why the hell doesn't someone send for more?" a man complained.

"Someone did," Warren told him.

"Then where the hell is it?"

Warren shook his head. "I don't know. Perhaps the message was intercepted." His mouth twisted. "Or the messenger ran away. I've noticed that's not unusual this afternoon—"

The drumbeats resumed. Philip swallowed, reloading.

The British marched up the hillside and across the swampy patches in front of the rail fence and stone wall. This time, they looked much grimmer. They stepped over their fallen comrades without glancing down, the rage on their faces was obvious.

The soldiers kept coming, gaiters splashed with blood from the previous engagements. Up and down the line the Americans began firing. For a few moments, it seemed as if the pattern of the first two assaults would be repeated. The front ranks faltered. Men stumbled, pitched over, shrieking—

The smoke in the redoubt was suffocating. It settled over Philip and the others like a pall. He was frightened out of his wits when he used his last powder to shoot the bent nail. The Brown Bess might explode—

It didn't. But he couldn't see whether he'd hit anyone.

Bayonets shining dully in the smoke, the British went halfway up the side of Breed's Hill. Suddenly Philip heard a change in the level of sound—

Fewer and fewer American muskets were shooting.

"Fire!" Colonel Prescott screamed, somewhere out of sight down on the left. Hoarse voices answered:

"Powder's gone!"

Then Philip's heart nearly stopped. The loud gulp of Salem Prince was audible too. They and the others still on their feet in the redoubt heard a dreadful new sound almost like a mass chant on the other side of the earthwork. The British soldiers were calling encouragement to one another:

"Push on. Push on. Push on—"

Philip peered over the lip and knew what was coming; a direct breach of the redoubt. There was no longer enough firepower to repel the advance.

All at once a few British soldiers began to run toward the hill's summit. Then more. Soon the whole front rank was charging, bayonets thrust out ahead. Salem Prince leaned his elbows on the little ledge to steady them, fired his last ball with powder he had borrowed from Philip. The ball drilled a round red hole in a portly sergeant's forehead.

But they kept coming, on the run:

"Push on. Push on. Push on—"

In the last terrible seconds of waiting, Philip raised his Brown Bess like a club, grimly aware of its limitations as a weapon against bayonets. British discipline, instilled as a tradition not to be violated, had paid off after all. In the wake of two disastrous charges, they intended to make the third succeed:

"PUSH ON! PUSH ON!"

A bayonet flashed over Philip's head. Musket clutched in both hands, he fended the downward thrust of the British light infantryman towering at the edge of the redoubt. Philip smashed the musket against the soldier's left leg. The man pitched forward into the redoubt. His bayonet gored Salem Prince through the chest.

The black fell screaming. The British soldier floundered on top of him, struggling to rise. A bayonet raked Philip's left shoulder from behind. He dodged away, raised his musket by the muzzle, struck the fallen soldier's head once, twice, three times, panting as he hit. The soldier's skull caved in. He collapsed across the dead black man.

But there were hundreds more of the soldiers jumping into the redoubt now, those murderous bayonets slashing and stabbing. In the smoke it was almost impossible to tell friend from foe. Philip heard an officer's cry:

"Retreat! Retreat to Bunker's! Abandon the redoubt—!"

Hysteria then. Pandemonium.

Royal Marines who had reinforced the infantry regiments leaped into the redoubt, firing at close range. Philip kicked and clubbed his way toward the narrow entrance packed with frantic men. His chest hurt from breathing smoke. He coughed. His eyes streamed tears.

Another bayonet wielded by some phantom came tearing at his cheek. Philip kicked the unseen soldier, hit his calf, heard him curse. The bayonet slid by Philip's shoulder and into the eye of Rhode Islander behind him in the stampede. Blood gushed over Philip's filthy neck, hot, ripe-smelling. He wanted to scream but he didn't.

He saw Dr. Warren in the crush, brandishing a musket. Random sunlight made Warren's face gleam like a medal for a moment. A bayonet speared Warren's ribs. Then the doctor went rigid, as if a musket ball had hit him. Horrified, Philip watched the patriot leader disappear in the smoky carnage.

He fought ahead. Saw sunlight gleaming—the outer end of the entrance passage. He raised his Brown Bess horizontally, ducked and battered through, his only goal that patch of brilliant light beyond the earth walls.

His chest on fire from the smoke he'd inhaled, he broke out and began to run down through the orchard on the northwest slope of Breed's Hill. From the redoubt he still heard screaming, muskets exploding, and the howls of the redcoats taking vengeance.

V

THE SUN was dropping behind the smoke. It had to be almost six o'clock, Philip thought as he scrambled toward the top of Bunker's Hill. There, Old Put's men had dug another fortification—

Empty now.

Everywhere, the colonials were fleeing. Rushing toward the all-too-narrow

strip of land that was the only escape route from the peninsula jutting into Boston harbor. Philip headed that way, running for his life because that was the order he heard yelled from all sides:

"Retreat, *retreat!*"

The Charlestown Neck proved almost impassable. Men shoulder to shoulder beat and clawed one another to gain a yard's forward passage. Off in the Mystic river, the guns of *Glasgow* erupted. Cannon balls tore the Neck to pieces, shot up huge gouts of earth, blasted men to the ground. Philip felt something sticky strike him in the face. He glanced down, gagged. A hand blown from a body—

He wiped some of the blood away and struggled ahead, trying not to be sick.

Near him a weary Rhode Islander shouted with false jubilation:

"I hear Tommy lost a thousand'r more, and us but a hundred!"

It might be so, Philip thought, gouging and shoving his way over the perilously narrow piece of land. It might be so, but it was no American victory. Even if the British had paid with fifty times the number of dead, how could anyone call it a victory? Though the king's troops had died by the score in the first two charges, they had broken through on the third—with those invincible bayonets that still blazed in Philip's imagination—

All at once he felt totally discouraged, disheartened. Even more disheartened than he'd been during what was perhaps the lowest point in his life: the grim sea voyage on which his mother, Marie Charboneau, had died, and he had taken a new name before stepping foot on the shore of his adopted land. Years from now, Breed's Hill might or might not be deemed a victory of sorts. But he saw it as a clear defeat.

As he ran on in the smoky sunset, glimpsing safe ground ahead at last, he knew that he and his wife and their unborn baby confronted a future that had become utterly bleak in a single afternoon's two-hour engagement.

The thirteen colonies faced exactly the same future. At last, the might of Great Britain had asserted itself. Very likely the king would spare nothing to bring the Americans to their knees with fire and steel; that terrible steel—

The struggle of the patriots could be very long.

And doomed.

2
Sermon Hill

"JUD DARLIN'?"

He reached across her naked hip for the jug of rum they'd shared. The cabin was warm this June evening, accentuating the woman's smell: a faintly gamy combination of sweat and farm dirt that never failed to excite him, when he'd consumed sufficient rum.

"Jud?" she said again.

"What?"

"That all for tonight?"

"Not by a damn sight, my girl."

He drank; emptied the jug. Dropped it and heard it thud on the dirt floor. He rolled toward her, stroking a moon-dappled patch of thigh. She guided his hand up her hard belly to one of her breasts. She laughed; a coarse, harlot's laugh:

"Good. The old fool, he won't be back till the cock crows, I bet. Means to show the gentry he's doin' his duty, ridin' patrol with the best. If he only knowed he could meet some of the gentry right in his own bed—!" She giggled.

"Lottie, stop talking so goddamned much." He gave her a fierce kiss that was half passion, half punishment.

She complained that it hurt, shoved his exploring fingers away. The straw crunched as she shifted out of his grasp:

"You're not treatin' me proper this evening, Jud Fletcher. Like to took my head off with that kiss."

"Sorry."

He reached for the rum, remembered it was gone, swore softly. A ravening thirst still burned in him. But then, when didn't it?

"That all you can say? *Sorry?*"

"What else should I say, Lottie? Conversation's not one of your better skills, so let's get down to the one in which you excel, shall we?"

Once more he reached out to touch her nakedness. His hand was moonlit for a moment. It was a strong young man's hand with fine golden hairs downing the tanned back.

But he'd angered her:

"No, sir, I want to know where your head's at tonight, Mr. Judson Fletcher."

His laugh aped the crude guffaws heard at taverns, or around the gamecock ring. Like downing rum, that sort of laugh somehow came easy. He said:

"I'll show you where it ought to be, honeylove—"

He bent his bare back, his mouth seeking. Again she struggled away. She was beginning to irritate him considerably.

Pettish, she said, "Listen, you yelled out somebody's name last time."

"Oh hell no I didn't."

"Yes you did, I heard it, right there at the end."

"All right, I got plumb excited and yelled your name."

"No, sir, Judson Fletcher, it wasn't Mrs. Lottie Shaw you was yellin' about—" Another laugh; vicious. "You were givin' somebody else a hard ridin' and I don't take kindly to it."

Furious, he wrenched away. He stood up, naked in the moonlight falling through the curtainless, glassless window of the crude little farm cabin. "For Christ's sake, woman, you got what you want from me. What that old wreck your papa married you off to can't deliver—"

"I want a little respect too," the young woman whined. "A little feelin'—I don't want somebody pokin' around in me and callin' out "Peggy, Peggy!" "

He seized her bare shoulder. "Shut your mouth, Lottie."

"Leggo!" She writhed. "I heard it clear. *"Peggy!"* Think I don't know which Peggy that is?" She was growing shrill, matching his anger. "Think the whole damn county don't know whose head you wisht you could put horns on—?"

He found the rum jug and hurled it at her half-seen form. She yelped, dodged away. Outside, her husband's yellow hound began to bark.

Judson grabbed up his clothes, practically yanked them on. By then, Lottie Shaw had realized her error. She leaped naked through the patch of moon, doubled over in exaggerated penitence, pressed her cheek against his ribs as she

clasped his waist. While stuffing his fine lace-fronted shirt into his pants, Judson gave her an elbow in the nose, not entirely by accident.

Lottie hung on. Judson's blue eyes and fair, clubbed hair looked all afire in the light from the window. Lottie began to cry in earnest:

"Don't get mad, darlin'. I spoke too sharp. Come on back and love me again—"

Judson leaned down toward her in the patch of moonlight, a tall, elegantly handsome young man with a long, sharp nose and just a slight softness at the edges of his mouth. His fingers closed on her muscled forearm. He looked like some avenging angel of scripture as he said quietly:

"You ever speak her name again in my presence—or if I ever hear of you speaking it to anyone, Lottie, I'll come here and kill you. Now think about that."

Pulling loose, he yanked on his boots of costly Russian leather, picked up his rich coat of dark green velvet and stalked out of the cabin.

He shied a stone at the yellow hound to drive him away, then pulled himself up on the beautiful roan he'd tethered to a low branch of a scrawny apple tree the farmer was trying to grow in his dooryard. Still shaking with anger, he galloped out the lane and turned into the road leading toward the Rappahannock, and home.

It was a fine, balmy evening in late June. He reached behind him, pried up the flap of his saddlebag, wiggled his fingers down inside, let out an oath. He was half drunk and wanted to be completely so. And he was out of rum.

Lottie Shaw was another kind of medicine he took on the sly. Tonight, by catching him when he'd accidentally cried *her* name, Lottie had gone dry on him too.

He cropped the roan without mercy, thundering down the dirt road in the sweet-smelling night because fleeing from the pain of having uttered Peggy's name without thinking had plunged him into this star-hung dark and pain of a different sort, equally hurtful.

II

RIDING THE roads of Caroline County, Virginia, always reminded him of his one best friend of boyhood. George Clark, the second of farmer John Clark's six sons.

The bond between George and Judson had been a powerful one in the years when they were growing up together, even though George's father was relatively poor, while Judson Fletcher's was rich. Maybe the reason was simply that any human being of any age liked to find another who would act as pupil—and George Clark, though two years younger than his friend, had discovered early that Judson was something besides a typical tobacco planter's son. In fact, Judson loathed Sermon Hill. He much preferred studying what George, a boy who had roamed the Virginia woodlands since he could toddle, taught so eagerly.

The geography of the heavens, for instance. Even swaying in the saddle, Judson could pick out the pole star, and the Cross.

In their days and nights of wandering the fields and forests together, George Clark had taught him many things. How to discover a fly-up-the-creek, the little green heron that hid for protection on river banks. How to find hives full of wild

honey, and to tell which plants and berries were edible. How to look to the horizon and identify objects and details of terrain at twenty miles—or spot a nighthawk at dusk just on the other side of a meadow. Far sight, was George's name for it. He developed it with practice. He would need it where he was going, he always said.

They'd traveled to fairs in Richmond, too. Spoken with rough, buckskin-clad men who carried long squirrel guns and claimed to have tramped the wild country west of the shimmering barrier of the Blue Ridge Mountains—the Blue Wall, Virginians called it. Out there, the long hunters remarked while spitting tobacco in a delightfully ill-mannered way, was a sea of forest and grass, sky and cloud. Enough animals to last a man a lifetime, whether he trapped and sold their pelts, or ate their flesh to survive, or both.

Three years ago, in 1772, Judson's friend and mentor had disappeared out that way; crossed the Blue Wall. He seemed to have a courage Judson lacked.

Also, George Clark was not in love with a woman he couldn't possibly win.

Twice in the intervening time, George had reappeared for brief visits at his parents' home. On those occasions, Judson had been invited to share an evening meal—and George's wondrous tales.

He described how he'd reached a raw frontier settlement that had grown up near Fort Pitt at the fork where two rivers flowed into one much larger one—the beautiful water, the red Indians called it. *O-hi-o. La Belle Riviere,* according to the French fur trappers.

George Clark had gone down this immense river. Taken to the poplar, as the companions with whom he traveled termed it. He'd journeyed a long way down the Ohio, through a vast, hushed wilderness, paddling in that sixty-foot hollowed poplar log marked with bloodstains and the grease of pelts.

On his second trip he'd traveled the river again. And wintered with a tribe of Indians called Mingos. He'd learned their tongue. He spoke glowingly of the gentle wisdom and forest skills of their old tribal leader, Logan.

It was difficult for Judson to absorb all the amazing detail of these narratives. But it wasn't hard at all to be entranced; to have his imagination lifted, until his mind's eye built an immense wooded kingdom where dark-skinned savages slipped silently along the game trails. A kingdom where a man could claim land if he wished it. Or simply find room to do as he pleased. To be what he was, not what someone else expected him to be.

The western forest was the only part of the continent for him, George Clark averred on those all-too-brief evenings before he vanished again, sterner-looking than he'd been in youth. Toughened now. Lean. He came and went across the Blue Wall like some red-haired ghost, and each short visit somehow freed Judson of the confinements of his own life—if only for a few hours.

The visits saddened him, too. Perhaps he belonged in the western forest. A great many bold, enterprising fellows were drifting that way, George said. Some families as well. More and more land companies were being formed to explore—and exploit—the vast wilderness. On occasion Judson thought that maybe he was a fool not to pack and follow his friend—

There was just one problem. Judson had inadvertently brought it up tonight, when he should have been murmuring Lottie Shaw's name instead.

Judson saw George Clark's face in his mind as he thundered the Virginia roads under soughing trees. The eyes of his friend never seemed at rest. They always seemed to be searching past a man's shoulder—

For what? he wondered. Freedom? The constantly retreating horizon—?

"It's that goddamned red hair," Judson exclaimed thickly, just before a branch nearly took his head off. He straightened up again, reflecting that red hair was one painless way he rationalized George's boldness. In the Clark family, it was said that red hair marked a man. Set him apart. Destined him for remarkable deeds. Of John Clark's six sons, two had red hair. George Rogers, gone now there years, and the tad, William, still at the farm, only five.

Why in hell wasn't I born with red hair? he thought fuzzily as he rode. It was certainly a convenient excuse to relieve misery of the sort he'd encountered in Lottie Shaw's cabin. And the different kind of misery he found along the dark, earth-smelling roads. Roads alive with memories of the friend who possessed some intangible quality of which he, Judson Fletcher of Caroline County, Virginia, had been unjustly deprived.

III

JUDSON HAD ridden the roan so hard, the animal's flanks were lathering. A measure of sobriety returned when he noticed it. He reined in, dismounted at the roadside. He wandered aimlessly while the roan blew and stamped.

Judson belched, scratched his crotch under his fine gray trousers. Be just his luck to catch the pox from Lottie.

Suddenly he stumbled across something propped against the rail fence. He crouched, uttered a surprised oath, fingered a crude dummy of white rags and straw stuffing. A fragment of slate lay in the dummy's lap.

He carried the slate out from under the tree branches. Turned it this way and that. He finally made out the word scrawled on the slate. His spine grew cold.

"Buckra," he said. And again: *"Buckra."*

The West African word for white man.

He dragged the dummy into the road. By the light of the moon and a thousand summer stars, he saw what he'd missed before. A wooden stake driven into the dummy's chest. The hole was smeared with something dark.

Judson knelt, fingered the smeared cloth and whittled stake. Little sweaty places formed on his neck and behind his ears. He tried to still his alarm by talking aloud:

"Has to be chicken's blood. Or pig's—where'n hell you suppose it came from?"

Abruptly, he heard hoofbeats down the road. He whipped his hand to his right boot, where a discreet scabbard in the Russian leather accepted a slim dagger. A gentleman's protection. He retreated to the shoulder, unpleasantly sober—and cautious.

He saw lanterns bobbing around a bend. Half a dozen riders. He stepped into the road, hailed them: "It's Judson Fletcher—"

The horses reined in. It was the patrol that kept constant watch on the roads for runaway slaves, rotating its personnel nightly. Mounted on a fine sorrel at the head of the patrol was slender, gentle-looking Seth McLean. Behind him, shabbily dressed, a gray failure, Tom Shaw slumped on a sore-ridden nag.

Tom Shaw spoke first, pathetically polite:

"Evenin', Mr. Fletcher."

Judson's profile, lantern-limned, was sculptured arrogance. "Evening, Shaw." The reply was so brusque, Shaw looked visibly hurt. Judson accented the social difference by greeting the others more cordially: "Mr. Wells—Mr. Squire—Seth."

"Taking the air again, Judson?" Seth asked, his smile innocent.

"That's right." Ah, this was rich! The man he cuckolded regularly, and the one he wanted to cuckold above all, and never would. "I found something down here you gentlemen should see."

He led them to the stabbed dummy and the slate. Concern was instantaneous.

"I knew them niggers was up to somethin'," Tom Shaw exclaimed. "My Lottie, she sweared she heard a drum two, three nights ago. That way. From the river—"

"Impossible," Seth McLean said. "You know there's not a planter in the district who allows his nigras ownership of a drum. Too easy to signal with them. My hands get nothing but dried beef bones—those, they can rattle all they please." He addressed the others: "Gentlemen, would you continue the patrol without me? I'd like to speak privately with my friend Judson. He may be able to assist us."

In what way, Judson couldn't imagine. But the others seemed to understand, and readily agreed. Judson fetched his roan, mounted up, and was soon jogging beside Seth back along the road by which the horsemen had arrived. The patrol's lanterns vanished in the other direction.

"I didn't want to admit it to Tom Shaw," Seth remarked finally, "but there may be nothing wrong with his wife's hearing."

"I can't say. I never listen for drums at night."

Seth laughed. "I know. Only for the rustle of the skirts of married women."

Judson went rigid in the saddle. Seth slapped him on the shoulder and Judson relaxed. Apparently there was nothing personal in the joke. His friends in the district had treated him to variations of it on more occasions than he could remember.

"There have been rumblings about possible trouble," Seth said, serious now.

"You mean with the nigras?"

Seth nodded gravely.

"At your place?"

"Possibly."

Judson was surprised. Seth McLean was reasonably humane in his treatment of his three-hundred-odd field bucks and wenches.

"I don't see what it has to do with me," Judson shrugged.

"I'll explain over a glass of port, if you don't mind." Seth spurred ahead toward the lights of his elegant house near the shore of the Rappahannock. Judson studied the illuminated windows on the second floor. One was Peggy's room. He knew the location by heart.

He followed Seth McLean down a lane between dark, rustling tobacco fields. The green leaves were ripening toward the end-of-summer harvest. Seth's lean silhouette stood out momentarily against the lamps at his front door. Reining in a second later, Judson felt criminal. Seth was decent.

At the same time, Judson was amused in a perverse way. It's sort of like the fly inviting the spider home with him, he thought.

IV

A HUGE London-made clock ticked in the library; a quarter past midnight. The library doors were open to the candlelight in a cool, airy foyer two floors high.

Seth poured wine for himself. Judson begged off, helped himself to Rhode Island rum instead. Then he settled his long frame in a chair, trying not to appear nervous or reveal his guilt—he was getting pretty good at that by now. He'd crawled into bed with his first married woman when he was fifteen.

Judson heard footsteps. His heartbeat picked up until he realized the steps were too heavy for a woman's. A grizzled black man in livery glanced in the doorway.

Seth McLean looked at the black, his piece of property, said:

"Nothing further tonight, Andrew. I'll serve our guest."

With a polite murmur that might have been Judson's name—a servile acknowledgment of his presence—the slave withdrew. Seth McLean rolled his wine glass between his palms.

"Have you heard nothing about discontent among the nigras, Judson?"

"You know me, my friend. The skirts swish too temptingly. The dice clack, the horses run, the cocks scream—and my father, the old bastard, swears a good bit, too. At me." Judson's mouth wrenched. "There's altogether too much noise for me to hear anything significant. It's different with you, I gather."

"Well, as I said, there have been signs. Insolence out of the ordinary. My overseer has been forced to the whip three times this week."

"Ours is never forced," Judson said, the sour smile remaining in place. "He looks for opportunities."

"Shaw," McLean reflected. "Old Tom's younger brother."

Judson nodded. "Cruel, illiterate bastard. Not like your Williams."

"But even Williams is being pushed hard. These things go in cycles, Judson. I'm uneasy—I just fear the wheel's almost around again. I've questioned Andrew and his wife—they're very loyal. They don't know much about what's happening. But they do admit there's wide unrest. It has—spread."

Judson knocked back the rum, felt it scald his belly. Not with relief this time, but with an upsetting fire. The clock ticked loudly. The room's shadows became ominous somehow. Clotting in the corners; blurring the gold stampings on the couple of hundred books on the high shelves.

"Spread from here?"

"From Sermon Hill. Andrew has heard that a nigra named Larned is at the center of it."

"Larned—" Judson's mind saw a slab-muscled figure with blue-black skin. "Big buck nigger. Damn near gigantic. Just two years off the Richmond block. Came from the West Africas in a Boston ship. My father says he never made a better investment."

"Breeding stock?"

"Yes. And Larned's smart with the natural kind of smartness some of 'em have. That may be his trouble."

Seth McLean cocked a dark eyebrow that contrasted with his pale, almost ascetic face. "Or ours."

"You mean Larned may be fomenting rebellion?" Judson ambled to the sideboard for a refill of rum. "Possible. He took a mighty handsome wife. Young yellow girl named—let me see—Dicey. Up till three days ago, she was

this big—'' One hand sketched pregnancy in the air. ''She produced twin boys for Larned. I heard Shaw brag last Christmas time that he was fucking her, too.''

''Well, that's certainly cause enough for trouble.''

''I don't suppose Larned found out. Those wenches are always too scared to tell their men.''

''But Larned could have heard it round about. Anything else?''

Judson pondered. ''Shaw laid eight strokes on Dicey two weeks before her term was up. Some trivial excuse.''

''But not trivial to a particularly intelligent and resentful nigra.''

Judson nodded. ''I'll wager the excuse was just that. Shaw probably wanted to exercise overseer's rights and take Dicey with a full belly. If she refused, he'd find reason to whip her.''

''Another grievance for Larned.''

Judson had no comment.

Seth McLean sighed. ''Regardless of causes, the figure you found *is* pretty definite proof something's in the wind—''

Judson nodded again, uneasily. ''And you think it's centered at Sermon Hill.''

''I do. If it should break out as a full-fledged revolt—''

Seth's unfinished sentence conjured chaos. Judson glanced at the curtains blowing; the darkness outside. He didn't care for the responsibility being pushed onto him:

''Seth, I understand all you're saying. But Lord, man, what can I do?''

''I've spoken to your father several times in hopes of getting him to moderate his treatment of his nigras. I've had no luck.''

Judson guffawed. ''You think mine will be any better? Christ, Seth, you know he hates me.''

''No,'' Seth returned quietly, ''I don't believe that's true.''

''Bullshit. I'm the second son. Automatically second best.''

''But you and Donald are both his flesh.''

''And we're both traitors because Donald went to the Raleigh Tavern last year, and I went along. Spiritually, anyway,'' Judson added with a wry smile.

He was referring to the gathering of members of the House of Burgesses who had assembled in the Williamsburg tavern at the urging of Patrick Henry, gentleman lawyer of Hanover County.

Henry, a natural leader, was the chief spokesman in the Burgesses for the back-country people. Over the last ten years, that segment of Virginia's population had found itself almost constantly opposed to the more conservative tidewater planters.

Henry had stirred Virginia with his hot oratory against Crown infringements of colonial rights. And when the royal governor, Lord Dunmore, had temporarily dissolved the legislature in May of the preceding year, Henry immediately led most of the Burgesses to a rump session at the Raleigh. There they appointed a delegation to the first Continental Congress. Along with Judson's older brother and several other Virginians, Henry was presently away at the second Congress, where his stock stood high because of an inflammatory speech given in March of this year. In the speech, Henry had taken an inflexible stand against Great Britain. The alternatives for him, he'd declared, were liberty or death—no middle ground. Governor Dunmore promptly issued a proclamation branding Henry an outlaw, which only enhanced his status further among Virginia's patriot faction.

Judson continued to Seth, ''I think my father would have horsewhipped Donald

if Donald would have allowed it. At the moment there are a great many people on my father's list of political enemies. Donald, myself, Henry—even Colonel Washington of Fairfax County, because he went up to Philadelphia too. On top of that—''

Judson sloshed another slug of rum into his glass. He was growing tipsy again: ''The lord of Sermon Hill happens to consider me a drunken wastrel. A prodigal on whom he squandered a deal of money for an education at William and Mary. He's commented that the sterling notes would have served a better purpose if they'd been used for wiping asses in the outhouse.'' Judson toasted an unseen presence. ''So saith Angus Fletcher, in one of his less biblical moods.''

''Still, can't you talk to him?''

''Well,'' Judson said, drawling out the word, ''we do speak every month or so.''

''Suggest he say something to Shaw, then. Try to get the man to moderate his behavior until we isolate the cause of the problem, or it calms down.''

Glum, Judson shook his head. ''Seth, I repeat—I exert no influence whatsoever at Sermon Hill. I sometimes wonder why I'm even allowed to live there.''

''Because you're Angus Fletcher's son! Judson—for friendship's sake—and the tranquility of this district—*try*.''

Judson poured more rum. ''All right. I'll say something. A remark or two. I'd be rash to promise more.''

''It's a start.'' Seth pumped his hand. ''Thank you —''

''I must go.'' Judson finished his drink quickly, asking himself why he had given in to Seth. He knew the answer. It was a cheap way to purchase temporary absolution of guilt—

The shadow across the floor at the library entrance made him glance up sharply.

She stood there; slender, dark-haired, fair-skinned and lovely in a peach-colored night robe whose high collar and decorous lines still set off her figure to advantage. She was all grace and gentility; a perfect lady he had loved since he was seventeen.

But she had been Peggy Ashford, respectable, while he had been—still was—Judson Fletcher; something less.

Their two-year relationship before her marriage had scarred them both. In those tempestuous times, Judson had never touched her other than to kiss her, though it had been obvious they both desired much more than that. Perhaps that restraint was what compounded the agony now.

Seth knew very well that the two had courted. Meeting at cross-country hunts. Attending balls together at wealthy houses up and down the river. All with the growing disapproval of the Ashfords, as Judson's nature asserted itself in frequent public drunkenness and brawling.

Finally, the Ashfords forced Peggy to stop seeing him. It was heartbreaking for her. But she was a dutiful daughter. Presently Seth stepped in. When the marriage was arranged and solemnized, Seth expected his friend Judson to behave like a gentleman. Which Judson did, in atypical fashion, because, above all, he did not want to bring Peggy any further hurt or scandal.

Now Seth simply assumed that while Judson, being a man, might harbor certain lingering impulses that could lead to adultery, he would never permit those impulses to become deeds. Seth also considered Peggy above reproach—

And those stories about Judson's affairs with other men's wives—well, it was doubtful whether Seth fully believed them. Judson knew his friend failed to

understand how deeply his feelings ran—or how close he'd come to making advances to Peggy on several occasions. In business affairs, Seth was reasonably worldly. In human ones, no—

Still, Judson managed to keep his distance. To him, Peggy Ashford McLean was something of a shrine. Unsullied, as few things in his life were any longer. He had never been able to explain why he loved her. She was sweet, intelligent, attractive; but many women along the tidewaters were that. What was it in her special combination of dark-eyed glances, smiles and small feminine gestures that had continued to torment him after he lost her? Perhaps part of his passion sprang from a realization even during their courting that she would probably never be allowed to marry him. For a man like Judson Fletcher, permanent frustration had its twisted charms—

"Melissa told me we had a guest," Peggy said. "Good evening, Judson."

"Good evening." He managed a bow. "I'm just on my way—"

He hardly dared glance at her for fear he'd reveal his feelings. He had seen her often since the marriage, of course. At holiday fêtes, or the Richmond fair. On such occasions, he could never read her expression. He suspected that whatever she'd felt once was completely gone. Speaking marriage vows would have begun to destroy it automatically. Her code of behavior said that was only decent and proper—

Peggy turned to her husband. "You're home early, Seth."

"To speak with Judson. I'm seeking his help in regard to the unrest."

"I warned him he might as well ask for help from a woodpecker," Judson said with a merry laugh, walking quickly past the woman, still unwilling to face those well-remembered eyes. He went straight to the imposing main doors and out, with a hail:

"I'll be in touch if I've any results to brag about, Seth. Which I doubt."

Into the saddle, he tore down to the Rappahannock rippling silver under the stars. He never once glanced over his shoulder at Seth McLean's large, colonnaded white house with its rows of slave cabins at the rear, near the curing barns. But all the way to Sermon Hill, Peggy rode with him. The starlight that put highlights on the river glimmered on the tracks of angry tears on his cheeks.

V

SERMON HILL, five thousand acres of prime tobacco land worked by five hundred male and female slaves, fronted the river as McLean's did. But Sermon Hill boasted its own wharf, where the huge tobacco canoes tied up in the autumn to load the casks that carried eight hundred pounds of cured brown leaf.

That is, the canoes had anchored there every autumn for as far back as Judson Fletcher could remember, then floated down river with the casks lashed across their gunwales. Trading ships anchored in the navigable waters of the estuary took the casks to market overseas. Whether they would so do this year in view of the worsening trouble with England was a question no one could answer. News of exchanges of fire between royal troops and colonial militia in April, someplace up in the Massachusetts Bay area, had cast doubt on all commercial ventures involving overseas trade—and on the placid quality of life itself.

But Judson wasn't thinking of that two mornings later. By way of fulfilling Seth's request, he rose earlier than usual—at sunrise, for God's sake!—to take a stroll around to the slave quarters.

The slaves lived in two long rows of whitewashed cottages that faced each other across an expanse of dirt. At the head of the avenue sat the small house belonging to the overseer. Outside this house, Judson spied a crowd of field bucks and wenches gathered in the orange light of early morning.

Moving closer, he heard the cracking of a whip. Because of the crowd, he couldn't see the victim.

He ran. Past the windowless cottages where barefoot black children wandered in the tiny okra patches, or squatted, dropping excrement from their bottoms, or simply sat in the doorways, picking at their hair and examining the creatures they discovered. In terms of sanitation and living standards for slaves, Sermon Hill was no different—no better and no worse—than most major tobacco plantations along the river—

Except in the matter of Reuven Shaw, general overseer.

Judson dashed up to the slaves at the rear of the crowd. They recognized him, quickly stepped aside. He spoke to one strong-looking buck:

"Who's being punished?"

"Dicey. Shaw, he say she fit to work. Dicey, she say no."

"Jesus—!" Judson exploded. "Where's her husband?"

"Field already," was the reply.

For a moment Judson stared into brown eyes that seemed to add silently, *Good thing for Mist' Shaw.* Or was that only his imagination?

He shoved through the crowd, saw the skinny, ill-clad Shaw, younger brother of Lottie's husband, raise his long blacksnake to make another mark on Dicey's yellow-brown back.

Shaw looked up, threat in his eyes. It simmered less hotly when he recognized the man in boots, hose, trousers, shirt—one of the owner's sons.

Judson gestured at the wench, who had been forced to discard her ragged dress—Shaw liked to punish the wenches naked—and kneel in the dirt with her head bowed over her knees. Dicey's back bore three bleeding stripes.

"Want to lay on a few, Mr. Judson?" Shaw asked. It was said with thinly concealed contempt. Judson and the overseer had long disliked each other.

"You ignorant son of a bitch, I'll take the whip to you instead. That wench birthed twin boys only five days ago." Judson held up one hand, fingers spread. "Five!"

"Three's the most I 'low 'fore they go back to work," Shaw grumbled.

"Dicey, put your dress on and go back to your cabin," Judson ordered. " 'Till next Monday morning."

"Listen here! I'm in charge of—" Shaw began. Judson leaped forward, seized the whip and looped it around Shaw's neck. He yanked both ends:

"What'd you say?"

"N—nothing, Mr. Judson," Shaw gasped, pop-eyed.

God, how he stank. Judson shoved him. "Get their black asses to work and quit causing unnecessary trouble." With that, Judson let go of the whip and turned to walk away.

"The snake is all that's keepin' us from having' trouble—!"

Again Judson whirled, staring into the warped, resentful face of the sunburned white man.

"Did you have another comment, Shaw?" he inquired, almost whispering.

Shaw swallowed, watched Dicey gather her dress and flee barefoot. "No," he mumbled. "No, I dint." But Judson didn't miss the hate in Shaw's eyes—

Nor, for that matter, in the eyes of the bucks and wenches who stood aside to

let him pass back toward the rambling, two-story, twenty-three-room house where he intended to have his breakfast.

Strange, he thought as he walked, his fair hair shining in the morning sun, very strange indeed. Striding by all those silent blacks, he'd had the uncanny feeling that their hatred was directed as much at him as at Reuven Shaw. Perhaps just being white did it, he thought wearily. Just as being black got you bought, whipped or fucked at the pleasure of your owners. Somehow, moving up the cabin avenue and hearing the chatter of the group breaking into field gangs, he didn't care to look back.

At Shaw *or* the slaves.

___VI

THE SILVER service gleamed, then suddenly distorted, reflecting a wizened face, white hair, enraged eyes.

Lounging on the veranda, Judson glanced from the reflection in the bulge of the pot to the creator of the image: his father, a tiny-boned man with a pointed chin and skin like old leather.

Angus Fletcher never tried to look prosperous, not even on social occasions. This morning his hose drooped, there was a rip in the knee of his breeches, and his shirt was wet with sweat. He came into the veranda's shade, shot his head forward like a turkey, confronting his son:

"I just had a report from Mr. Shaw. Apparently you interfered with him while I was down seeing to the repairs on the dock."

"And I just had a letter from Donald." Judson used a smile to conceal his uneasiness as he lifted the document in question. "A hired courier brought it from Richmond not ten minutes ago."

"Wondered who that trespasser was," Angus Fletcher garrumphed. He sat down in one of the large basket chairs. "You may keep the letter to yourself. I've no interest in tidings from that nest of traitors up north. That my own son should allow himself to be influenced by those perfidious wise men of the East—"

Judson laughed at his father's use of the term that Tories, and even some rebels, applied to the influential patriot leaders leaders of Massachusetts. "Father, you'll have to put Colonel Washington even more firmly among the traitors now. Donald says that he and the other Congressional delegates appointed the colonel to lead the Continental armies. It happened just the middle of this month. Washington will have the rank of general and will go to Boston to take command."

He consulted the letter quickly, enjoying his father's fuming.

"And there's been more fighting. Some place called Breed's Hill. The British won the day, but our side acquitted itself well—"

"Your side, not mine!" Angus Fletcher leaped for the letter, flung it away. "Those fools will bring down ruin on all of us. We should be suing for peace before matters get worse." Again he shot his head forward. " 'Blessed are the peacemakers, for they shall be called—' "

" '—the children of God,' " Judson finished wearily. Of all his father's annoying personal characteristics, the old man's fondness for scripture offended Judson the most. Angus was especially partial to St. Matthew. So taken was he with the message and language of the Sermon on the Mount, he had re-named his own father's plantation on its low hill above the Rappahannock in honor of it.

"Shall we move to another text?" Judson asked. " 'Blessed are the merciful—' "

"I want to hear what in damnation angered Shaw!"

Judson stared at his father. Despite his age—he was nearly sixty—Angus Fletcher's slight frame suggested great strength. He worked diligently at the business affairs of Sermon Hill every day of the week except Sunday, when he attended church in the morning, prayed in the privacy of his bedchamber all afternoon, and forbade anything that smacked of light amusement on his property throughout the entire Sabbath. The old man did have a certain biblical majesty, Judson reflected as he studied the seated figure outlined against the river and the rolling, heat-hazed hills beyond.

But he could never remember a time when there had been tenderness or even kindness between father and son. Even in Judson's earliest recollections, it seemed that his father had treated him sternly; as a full-grown man. Wanting—demanding—more than a boy could give. Judson had resigned in defeat by the time he was ten. He could never be as clever, as strong, as pious as Angus expected him to be. Perhaps that was part of the trouble.

Of course, being the second son was another part. He could not inherit, hence was less important than Donald. Even so, the same kind of relationship existed between the old man and Donald, ten years Judson's senior.

Donald was gout-ridden at thirty-five. He downed great quantities of port and claret when Angus wasn't watching. Further, he never shrank from proclaiming how proud he was to be a member of the Burgesses chosen to represent Virginia at the Congress.

Of their mother Judson could remember next to nothing. She had died when he was four. Donald recalled as a kindly, religious woman who slipped silently through the house attending to her duties, totally in awe of her husband.

Resentful of Angus' outburst about Shaw, Judson said, "The text I had in mind will bring us to that subject. Remember, Father—the merciful 'shall obtain mercy.' Shaw's doing his best to see you get just the opposite."

Angus made a face, rang a handbell. In a moment, one of the liveried house blacks—they were a caste above the field hands—glided to the old man's elbow with a goblet of cold spring water. Angus Fletcher extended his hand. The goblet was placed into it. He did not look around. He expected the drink to be where it was supposed to be, and it was.

He sipped, then said, "Be more explicit, I have work to do."

"Shaw was whipping Dicey. I stopped him."

"You *stopped* him? You don't run Sermon Hill! And unless you change your whoring ways and your politics to boot, you won't even receive so much as one shilling when I pass on."

"I've heard that threat before," Judson returned. He was cool, but it took effort. "I think you're facing a more immediate one—"

Briefly, he described his conversation with Seth McLean, as well as the stabbed figure and slate he'd found by the roadside. The description seemed to unnerve Angus Fletcher slightly. At least, the wrinkled hand and the water goblet shook for a moment.

Solely to antagonize the old man, Judson crossed his boots, stretched and yawned. It worked:

"Go on, go on!" Angus exclaimed.

Judson still took his time before resuming:

"Seth heard a rumor that our buck Larned may be responsible for stirring up

some of the discontent. Since Dicey is Larned's woman, I stopped Shaw in the hope of preventing real trouble. I also stopped him because what he was doing was wrong.''

"Spare me your false piety, please!''

"Why, Father, I thought you thrived on piety.''

Angus colored.

"All right,'' Judson shrugged, "we needn't debate on moral grounds. I thought I was doing you a good service. Isn't a little restraint preferable to an outbreak? To seeing Sermon Hill set afire, for instance? Rebellions have happened before.''

"Never here. And they won't. I'll chain up every one of those unwashed sons of Ham before—'' He blinked twice as Judson raised a languid hand. "What, what?'' he roared.

"Your biblical scholarship is faulty, I'm afraid,'' Judson informed him. "The name Ham means swarthy, not black. If Noah's son had any real descendants— other than fairy-story ones, that is—'' Again Angus' cheeks darkened. "—they were doubtless the Egyptians, or those people called Berbers, not the poor bastards the blackbirders bring from the West Africas to do your hard work.''

"When did you become a biblical expert, may I ask?'' Angus sneered.

Judson smiled with great charm. "Why, at college. You paid for the lessons.''

"You're not only disloyal to His Majesty, you're a disgrace to the very flesh that bore you! To think I wasted hard money so your head could be filled with godless rot—''

"Any rot, as you call it, was probably acquired at Sermon Hill.''

Angus Fletcher flung the cold water in his son's face.

Judson jumped up. He almost went for the old man's throat. But he checked, big veins standing out in his strong hands as he sat down again and gripped the arms of his chair.

Angus Fletcher set the glass on a wicker stand, rose and walked toward his son. Despite his small stature he looked commanding, looming there in the shadows of the veranda. His voice shook:

"Month after month, I've prayed to God to make you realize what you have been born to, Judson Fletcher. On my knees I have begged God to help you understand how much struggle and toil has gone into building this estate—''

"Black struggle and black toil, you mean. And black blood.''

"Your grandfather labored and died to—''

"Oh, for Christ's sake, stop it.''

"Blasphemer! You take the Lord's name in—''

"Yes! Because I've heard that whitewashing till I'm sick of it!'' Judson thundered. "I've known the real story for a long time—others in this district are more accurate reporters. Your father was a catchpenny redemptioner from Glasgow—a criminal, most likely, since he never signed his real name to his indenture papers—and didn't even honor his contract. Two days after they landed him in Philadelphia, he ran away from the soul-driver trying to unload him for transportation plus profit! Years later, he bragged about it! He turned up here in Virginia and got a farmer's girl pregnant and had to marry her, and then the farmer died suddenly of a fall from a horse while just he and my grandfather were riding in the woods. Believe me, I know all about how the first land for this whited sepulcher was acquired! It's going to come down unless you stop thinking you're the anointed of God, ruling the impious. Those black bucks and wenches

are human beings! Dumb, dirty—but people nonetheless. Seth McLean understands that.''

"Seth McLean is a weakling and a fool. He owns a tenth of the land I do
because he's a tenth as canny.''

"A tenth as brutal!'' Judson shouted. "A tenth as immoral!''

Angus Fletcher tried to strike his son. Judson caught the thin wrist, easily
pushed it down. The old man was breathing heavily. For a moment Judson was
worried. But he quickly recognized the raspy breathing as a sign of rage, not
seizure:

"I've raised a liar, a drunkard, a lecher—''

"Who wishes to Christ—''

"You will not blaspheme in my presence!''

"—he'd never set eyes on this place.''

"Twenty-five years old and look at you! Dissolute—idle—your head full of
sin and poisonous idolatries! Well, go chase after your painted whores in Richmond. Go follow your crazy friend George Clark who's probably dead in the
wilderness by now. *Or go join your damned brother and the traitors in Philadelphia!''*

Judson Fletcher was so full of fury, he was afraid he might hit his father and
injure him. And the father would not be able to stay the son's hand. To protect
himself from launching an attack which he knew he'd ultimately regret, Judson
fought for control, tried the Bible again, with a forced smile:

" 'Agree with thine adversary quickly, while thou art in the way with him,
lest at any time the adversary deliver thee to the judge—' ''

"Hold your filthy tongue! You have no right to quote our Savior!''

"If you understood your Savior, old man, you'd do something about Reuven
Shaw.''

"I will. I'll order him to enforce even stricter discipline. To search the cabins
for a drum—and to give a hundred strokes to any nigger hiding one.''

Red-faced, Judson started away. "I'll inform Seth McLean of your decision.''

"I'm sure you will,'' the old man jeered. "So as to get another opportunity for
lewd concourse with his wife.''

Judson stopped as if he'd been bludgeoned. For the first time, Angus Fletcher
looked amused; master of the situation. He actually laughed as he resumed his
seat:

"If I have secrets which are public, so do you. Do you think I don't remember
how you felt about the McLean woman? How you still ride by her house night
after night? One more reason I brand your friend McLean a fool. If you came on
my property feeling about my wife as you feel about his, I'd put a ball in your
head.''

With grudging admiration, Judson said, "You old bastard. Sometimes I forget
how foxy you are. Figured me out, have you?''

"Aye, long ago. But I constantly find new examples of your sinfulness—to
my everlasting disgust. It came as no surprise to me when the Ashfords finally
refused to permit their daughter to see you.''

"Your faith in me is constantly overwhelming—!''

Angus ignored that; pointed a wrathful finger:

"What decent folk would want you as a son-in-law? For any woman you'd
marry, there'd be naught to look forward to save anguish over your debauchery.
And if she bore you a child, she'd go to her grave in despair because of the taint
you'd lay on the babe—''

Thunderstruck, Judson gaped at the old man. "What taint? *Your* taint—if any!"

Angus Fletcher shook his head in dogmatic denial. "Something in yourself has ruined you, Judson. Better to shoot any child you'd father than let him live his life with your devil's blood poisoning him and all his generations after hi—"

"Be damned to you, you sanctimonious hypocrite!" Judson fairly screamed. "If I've devil's blood, you've only to look in a glass to see who's the source!"

If the words affected Angus, he concealed it. His features hardened into that expression of smug piety Judson hated with such passion.

"You're carrying on like a raving fool," Angus declared, "because you know this for a fact—Peggy McLean should thank heaven she was prevented from marrying you."

"It—" Judson could barely speak. "—it must give you great pride and satisfaction to say that about your own flesh."

"It gives me great sadness."

"You vile, lying old—"

Unable to continue, he wheeled and rushed away down the veranda. Angus shouted after him:

"At least you can have the decency to keep yourself from her presence. She knows your wicked purpose for calling at McLean's! 'Ye have heard that it was said by them of old time, Thou shalt not commit adultery—' "

Scarlet again, Judson stalked straight ahead, fearful that if he turned back, there would be blows struck—or worse. It required an act of total will for him to continue toward the main door of the house as Angus' voice grew more and more shrill:

" 'But I say unto you, That whosoever looketh on a woman to lust after her hath committed adultery with her already in his heart—' "

Judson slammed the door, stormed past the startled house blacks who saw his thunderous look and glanced away.

He raced up to his room, tore off his sweated shirt in exchange for a new one. He hated his father. Yet surely some of the guilt for these dreadful confrontations was his. He took pleasure in tormenting the old man, in revenge for the old man tormenting him. *What in the name of God was wrong with him?*

Even Donald's faults were mild in comparison. In their father's eyes, Donald's chief sin was his conviction that the oppressive taxes and restrictive policies of Britain could no longer be borne. To that iniquity Judson added a score more, from adulterer to defender of slaves—

Ten minutes later, he was galloping one of the dirt lanes that crisscrossed the plantation. His saddlebags bulged with two unopened jugs of rum.

Judson saw black heads turn in the fields. One slate-blue face burned bright: the buck Larned, bare-shouldered, risen like some demonic figure from his weeding among the ear-shaped leaves of the tobacco plants.

Larned watched him ride on, and it seemed to Judson that his back was afire from the slave's venomous glare. Judson was a white man, and Angus Fletcher's son. No matter what he'd done for the wench Dicey, Larned would surely twist it so that it acquired a practical—a despicable—motivation: to preserve the wench for further work, perhaps. Or sex with Judson himself. What the hell was the use of trying to intervene if it generated so much hate from all of them?

That Judson understood how the whole slave problem had gotten so thoroughly out of hand in a hundred and fifty years didn't mitigate his sense of

outrage—or his sad conviction that the system would produce continuing friction and violence unless it was abolished.

The agricultural economy in which he'd grown up was based on grueling physical labor. So he really couldn't fault the people of the southern colonies for buying black workers in preference to white ones when the latter were far less desirable.

Men such as his grandfather, for example, could be counted on to work for their buyers only until the expiration of their indenture contracts. Of course his grandfather hadn't been willing to wait even that long!

The problem of finding a stable work force had grown still more difficult early in the century, when some combination of geniuses in the mother country had conceived the idea of clearing Britain of many of its undesirables—thieves, pickpockets, whores—whose crimes weren't quite serious enough to earn them hangropes. The answer was to transport them across the ocean at three to five pounds a head, to be purchased on arrival for negotiated periods of servitude. But just exactly like the man who voluntarily indentured himself, transportees eventually were eligible for freedom —earned legally or, sooner, by flight.

What planter who prided himself on efficiency—and ledgers that showed a profit—wouldn't prefer to purchase a cowed, completely unlettered black from Africa? A black whose legal status, from the beginning, was vague? And whose fatally distinctive coloration made him easier to detect if he fled his bondage? Even the meanest petty criminal from the London stews at least had a white skin to keep him relatively invisible if he succeeded in escaping.

But what had begun as a natural tendency to seek the most stable and permanent kind of agricultural labor force had degenerated into outright ownership of one human being by another.

It was a source of sardonic amusement for Judson to recall that the very first blacks on the continent—twenty—were put ashore and sold at the Jamestown colony by the largely British crew of a Dutch privateer. The date was 1619—one year before the arrival of the *Mayflower* at Plymouth, carrying forty-one stiff-necked Puritan families whose children and grandchildren prided themselves on being descended from "founding fathers." What a pity there were no genealogical tables to permit the offspring of the Jamestown twenty to dispute that claim!

In the early years of the colonial blackbird trade, the word *slave* had seldom if ever been spoken. Gradually, though, it came into common use as the more unscrupulous members of the landed class realized that New England shipowners were quite willing to supply a constant stream of African bucks and wenches, and that a combination of evolving custom and clever writing of new statutes could transform purchased black workers into permanent chattels with no hope of ever earning freedom—a condition the redemptioners and transported prison inmates never faced.

Now the institution had grown so entrenched—producing fear and repression on one side, submission and hatred on the other—that Judson could only foresee an eventual confrontation between those who listened to their consciences and those who heard nothing but the jingling voice of the pound.

By mid-morning, his reflections had put him in thoroughly miserable spirits. He lay in a grove at the edge of the plantation, glooming over the explosive potential of the situation with the local blacks, then experiencing even deeper depression over his own behavior.

Why in God's name was he driven to such excesses of word and deed, both

in his father's presence and elsewhere? Gazing out across the tobacco fields where heat-devils rippled the air, he saw the white walls of Sermon Hill rising on the crest of the low rise above the Rappahannock and wished he were anywhere but here.

He wished he were out beyond the Blue Wall with his friend, for instance. In empty country. No laws, no Bible-spouting hypocrites, no incipient rebellions, no pea-headed overseers, no—

No Peggy to haunt him.

His father's words came back to him with tormenting clarity.

Taint.

Poisoned.

Devil's blood—

Try as he might, he couldn't scoff away the uneasy suspicion that Angus had struck a vein of truth. One from which Judson turned in terror and loathing. The only way to blunt the fear was with rum. Slowly drinking himself insensible, he was able to convince himself that he only needed to escape Virginia to escape his demons.

He fell into a stupor that brought bizarre dreams.

He saw flame-haired George Rogers Clark stalking through the wilderness, standing as tall as the trees themselves. He saw Peggy naked, beckoning him with lewd gestures, a slut's teasing smile. He saw his father, fierce as Moses, hand raised to deliver a blow while lightning flashed in a sky of churning storm—

He awoke suddenly. Lying on his back in the grass, he felt chilly. Nearby, his roan stood head down, a statue against the first faint stars. In the west, red stained the horizon.

Judson licked the inside of his furred mouth. He heard a sound so faint that the slightest change in the direction of the breeze silenced it for a moment. But he recognized the sound.

The hollow boom of a hand drum.

The moment he identified the sound, it stopped completely. But he could have sworn the eerie thudding had drifted from the direction of Sermon Hill.

3
Birth

RAGGED AND and louse-ridden, Philip Kent trudged through the mud of what passed for a street in the camp of the American army.

He was physically exhausted. Not from working at digging and fortifying new earthworks; not from trenching out new vaults when the old ones overflowed with human waste. From boredom. The endless, uncertain waiting—

Constant worry about his wife Anne only added to the strain. He got to see her once or twice a week if he was lucky. Regulations were haphazard in the American siege lines surrounding Boston. Sometimes he could obtain permission to slip away to Watertown of an evening, sometimes not. He seldom knew in advance. Tonight he'd been fortunate, and gotten leave to go.

A drizzling mid-September rain fell, worsening conditions in the already wretched camp that had sprung up and spread as various volunteer regiments from all over the colonies arrived during the summer and settled in beside one another, helter-skelter. Since taking charge in early July, the new commanding general of the Continental Army, George Washington of Virginia, had been trying to bring some organization to the chaos. He hadn't made much progress, even though new orders relating to camp discipline or procedures came streaming out of Wadsworth House in Cambridge almost every day.

Philip Kent, a short, wide-shouldered young man with dark eyes and hair tied up in a queue, scarcely looked like a soldier as he slogged along in boots worn perilously thin on the bottoms. But then, few of the volunteers resembled soldiers.

There were some exceptions, of course. The Rhode Islanders with their neat tents, each equipped with its own front awning. Their encampment looked almost British. The same held true for the Twenty-first Massachusetts, men from Marblehead who had given up their occupations as shipwrights and fishermen but not their seafaring heritage. The Marbleheaders were outfitted in trim blue seacloth jackets and loose white sailor's trousers. But apart from a handful of such regiments, the Americans dressed and often acted like rabble. Their living places matched.

Most of the men, Philip included, lived in shelters made of whatever materials they had purchased, brought from home, or stolen. Philip's Twenty-ninth Massachusetts infantry regiment, camped between Cambridge and the earthworks at the center of the American line overlooking the Charles River, made do in shanties knocked together from warped boards. But as he walked, Philip saw many other types of structures, from sailcloth tents sagging under the drizzle to crude shelters of fieldstone chinked up with turf. Some units simply lived on the ground between constantly soggy blankets.

To add to the confusion, it was often impossible to tell officers from enlisted men. General Washington had tried to outfit the volunteer soldiers in some semblance of a uniform. Amid the flurry of organizational orders and new commissions issuing from the house formerly occupied by Harvard's president, he'd sent off a request to the Continental Congress for ten thousand smock-like hunting shirts. No action had been taken on the request before the assembly adjourned early in August. Washington had meantime authorized officers to adopt scarves, cockades, second-hand epaulets—whatever they could find to identify themselves.

Not that it made much difference to the men who served under them.

The army encamped at Boston consisted mostly of farmers and artisans, all waiting to see whether a full-scale war would break out, or would be defused by moves toward reconciliation already taken by the Congress that represented every colony except Georgia. The men who made up the army didn't understand military discipline and in fact resented it. Philip recalled hearing a prediction that this attitude might prevail, and prove disastrous. The prediction had been made by his friend Henry Knox, the fat Boston bookseller who was somewhere in the lines acting as a sort of supervising engineer in charge of artillery. Philip had not seen Knox all summer, though.

No one knew how many volunteers had arrived in Massachusetts since the outbreak of hostilities. Philip had heard figures ranging from twelve to twenty thousand. The reaction of these summer soldiers to the commander-in-chief's various orders forbidding such activities as gambling and "profane cursing,"

and demanding attendance at "divine services" twice daily, ranged from indifference to outright defiance.

A few shrewd commanders recognized the problem and tried to deal with it. One such was Iz Putnam of Connecticut, the old Indian fighter who had defended the king's interests during the American phase of the Seven Years' War. Putnam invented schemes to sharpen his men for combat and keep them diverted at the same time.

Since the terrifying shelling of Breed's and Bunker's Hills in June, most of the Continentals had learned they had little to fear from the barrages of the British batteries in Boston. But the artillery fire was almost constant in clear weather. So Putnam sent his men darting out of their earthworks to recover spent cannon shot, in short supply on the American side. The prize for each round was a tot of rum. An explosive shell earned two tots—provided it didn't blow up the man who went after it. Philip wished that the Twenty-ninth Massachusetts had that kind of imaginative commander.

Now, as he slogged along in the mud, his mind began to veer from camp life to the other world he lived in whenever he could. The world of Watertown—and Anne. He paid less and less attention to the men idly attempting to wipe their muskets dry inside lantern-lit hovels. He dodged the bones of an evening fish ration flung into his path. Unseeing, he passed two volunteers urinating in the open—the accepted custom. He went by tents and lean-tos noisy with quarreling, drinking and forbidden dicing. In some of the temporary dwellings, feminine giggling could be heard, indicating that "immoral practices"—likewise prohibited—were in full swing. Head down, hands in the pockets of his sodden coat, he thought only about his wife.

She was near her term; immense of belly. She'd been extremely weak the past month or so, abed most of the time in the rented rooms Lawyer Ware had taken in Watertown.

But even more disturbing, the Connecticut surgeon whom Philip had located with such difficulty in mid-summer, and hired to take over Anne's care on a once-weekly basis, had been shot and killed the preceding week after an argument about cards.

Philip had paid the cheerfully greedy doctor with money saved from his earnings at the Edes and Gill print shop. He'd gotten the money from Ben Edes personally. Edes, who had set up his patriot press in Watertown, had been keeping the funds for Philip. Now the money was of no use. The doctor was permanently unavailable.

In the past few days Philip had searched frantically for someone to replace the doctor. The quest so far had been fruitless.

Wiping rain from his cheeks, he turned a corner past another hovel. He glanced up suddenly at the sound of a brawl in progress between a double row of tents a few steps further down. Damnation! He should have watched his route more carefully. Avoided this most contentious section of the American center. Now he was caught.

He walked rapidly, determined to pass the twelve or fifteen men punching, kicking and yelling in the middle of the muddy street. He kept close to the line of the tents, eyed the combatants. Virginians to a man.

The Virginians had become the marvel of the camps when the first contingent reached Boston in July, boasting a march of six or seven hundred miles in three weeks, with no one ill, no deserters. They were tall, peculiar, violent men with skins the color of browned autumn leaves. Their clothing—especially their vo-

luminous white hunting shirts and their headgear: round, broad-brimmed hats or caps with dangling fur tails—excited comment wherever they walked.

The Virginians automatically pushed aside all men smaller than themselves, and many who weren't smaller. Their height and tough bearing gave them the authority. So did their strange weapons: guns much longer and narrower through the barrel than the familiar smoothbore muskets.

The backwoodsmen from Virginia called their weapons Kentucky rifles, though they claimed the pieces were manufactured in Pennsylvania. Using the rifles, they challenged all comers to shooting contests—and always won—shattering bottle targets at impossible ranges of two or three hundred yards. Philip's Brown Bess could barely fire half that distance before spending its ball.

Though the rifles took longer to load than muskets, and could not be fitted with bayonets, they were deadly accurate. So were the eyes that aimed them. Eyes that had supposedly gazed on distant country where blue mountains climbed toward a sea of cloud, and tribes of the red-skinned, savage Indians roamed.

This evening, the Virginians were having at each other again. That too was a familiar occurrence. Men gleefully booted the groins of their opponents, stepped on faces, bit ankles or wrists. Half the fighters were on their knees or backs or bellies, covered with gummy mud. But they kept slugging and thrashing and getting up again. And—to Philip's astonishment—for the most part, they were laughing.

He moved faster, determined to get clear of the brawl post haste.

He skirted the churning mass of men while other Virginians lounging near the tents eyed him with arrogant curiosity. Further down the camp street, a phaeton turned the corner, heading away from the brawlers. Suddenly one of the phaeton's three cloaked occupants lurched to his feet. He grabbed his driver's shoulder. In a moment, the team was charging back toward the fight, which continued without letup.

One side of the battle abruptly grew like a living organism, rolling outward until Philip was virtually on the edge. He had to jump aside to avoid a whizzing fist. Someone shoved the small of his back:

"Hey, Zech, if you need somebody to punch, here's one of them wise men!"

Philip had been pushed by a spectator. Off balance, he cursed and fisted his hands. He got angry when men from other colonies taunted the Massachusetts soldiers with the epithet applied to the Boston radicals. But before he could swing on the man who'd shoved him, he inadvertently stumbled into the melee. A huge, hard hand blasted into his stomach, doubled him over—

He dropped to his knees, madder than ever. But the burly Virginian who'd punched him had already turned his attention to one of his own—a tall, skinny, mud-slimed man with a mouthful of crooked teeth and one eye that pointed off at the oblique. Positively the ugliest specimen Philip had ever seen.

Philip's attacker kicked the tall fellow in the groin. The man grimaced as he lost his footing, toppled into the mud. He floundered on hands and knees. His burly opponent bellowed a laugh, laced his fingers together, intending to chop them down in a murderous blow to the other man's exposed neck.

Philip could have avoided further involvement by sneaking away. But he was tired, and thus not hard to provoke. Finding steady footing at last, he grabbed the burly man's shoulder, pulled hard.

The man wheeled, aborting his vicious blow at the tall fellow's neck. The burly man took one look at Philip, smiled an oafish, infuriating smile and

resorted to his favorite tactic—a lightning kick between the legs. Philip clenched his teeth to keep from screaming in pain.

"Dunno who the hell you are, little boy," the burly man growled. Philip realized the man was ugly drunk. "But this here's Virginny territory. You go play someplace else 'fore I spank you good."

Shaking, Philip said, "Come on and try."

The tall, ugly fellow darted up from behind and bashed his opponent in one ear. The burly man didn't appear to feel it. Only his eyes showed a reaction. He stabbed his hand down past a tangle of thrashing, mud-covered arms and legs. Instantly, Philip saw what he was after—

A spade someone had used as a weapon.

The man seized the spade's handle—but Philip wasn't the target. The burly man swung the spade toward the tall fellow, howling:

"I'll take yer head off, Eph Tait!"

Phillip made another two-handed lunge at the burly man's forearm. The Virginian with the cocked eye ducked and the spade hissed on through the air. Except for Philip's restraining grip, it would have completed its arc—

To smash into the face of the officer who had climbed from the phaeton.

The spirit seemed to drain from the burly man in a second. His mud-daubed face lost color. All he could breathe out was a raspy, "Oh, heavenly Christ—"

Philip was equally alarmed, to put it mildly. No man in the American lines could fail to recognize the towering officer. His thrown-back cloak revealed a dark blue coat with buff facings, a buff waistcoat and, above the white breeches, his purple sash of rank.

He had somehow lost his hat. Rain glistened in his clubbed reddish-brown hair. He was in his early forties, with huge hands, equally large feet whose size was emphasized by his big boots. In fact the man looked almost ponderous. But he moved with startling speed as he seized the spade and hurled it to the ground. Philip noticed a light pitting of pox scars on pale cheeks that bore traces of sunburn—or the flush of anger. The man's gray-blue eyes raked the brawlers:

"I expect better than this from Virginians! Where is the commanding officer?"

The fighting had all but stopped. One of the mud-covered men shouted:

"Dead drunk—as usual."

"To your quarters, every damn one of you. And think about this while you wait for the orders for punishment I intend to issue before this night's over. I have made a pretty good slam since I came to this camp. I broke one colonel and two captains for cowardice at Bunker's Hill. I've caused to be placed under arrest for trial one colonel, one major, one captain and six subalterns—in short, I spare no one, particularly men of my own colony, and you will find that reflected in the redress of this disgrace. *Dismissed!*" he shouted, suddenly pointing at Philip. "All except you."

Philip stood frozen, swallowing hard. The officer's temper had moderated. His speech took on a softer quality; the genteel, almost drawling quality of his native Fairfax County:

"You don't belong to this regiment, do you, soldier?"

"No, sir."

"What's your name?"

"Philip Kent, General."

"Your unit?"

"Twenty-ninth Massachusetts."

"Why aren't you with your unit?"

"I have my commander's permission to visit Watertown, sir. My wife's there—she's expecting a baby and not doing well—"

"I can vouch for this man's identity, General Washington."

The new arrival stumping up on fat legs brought Philip momentary relief from the absolute terror he felt under the blue-gray stare of the chief of the American forces. The new arrival was a pie-faced young man with a white silk scarf wrapped around his crippled left hand. He weighed close to three hundred pounds and wore civilian clothes.

Shooting a quick glance at Philip—a warning for him to stand fast—he continued:

"He served with me in the Boston Grenadier Company before the trouble broke out. If he says his wife's in Watertown, and that he's been given leave to see her, it's undoubtedly the truth."

"I'll take your word, Knox," Washington said. He smiled faintly. "Especially since this soldier's hand on that fool's arm—" He pointed at the burly drunk being lugged away by two companions, "—saved me from a broken skull. My thanks, Kent."

Washington whirled on the goggling laggards:

"Inside, the rest of you. Smartly—*smartly!*"

The Virginians ran, including the toothy, cock-eyed fellow who seemed to be trying to grin some sort of appreciation at Philip. Washington pulled his rain-drenched cloak down across his blue-and-buff uniform and turned to stride back to his phaeton. Henry Knox lingered, his round young face beaming:

"I'd heard you were out here, Philip."

"But not in officer's territory."

"Oh, I'm not there myself. Only on the border. Neither fish nor fowl, it seems. Still, I'm happy to serve where I can be useful."

"Your name's been widely circulated, Henry. I understand General Washington's impressed with your knowledge of artillery."

"I trust he will increase his reliance on what little I've learned," Knox said, no longer smiling. "Only cannon can defeat the British garrison in Boston."

"I've also heard you may be commissioned a colonel."

Knox made no comment. But he couldn't hide a prideful look. Before he'd shuttered his Boston bookshop to join the American army, Henry Knox had deliberately turned the shop into a haven for British officers of the occupying force. He had a purpose: to draw out the enemy's best thinking on the subject that fascinated him—the proper use of artillery. "Lucky you had a good reason for your presence," Knox observed finally. "The general's determined to birth an army out of this dismaying collection of ruffians. He was correct when he said he spares no one—least of all himself."

"Well, that may be true, but—" Philip hesitated.

"Go on with what you were about to say."

"Maybe I'd better not. It concerned the general."

"You can be candid. God knows everyone else in this camp is!"

Still Philip held back. Knox smiled wearily:

"Did you intend to tell me that most of your compatriots have doubts about the general's ability?"

Enbarrassed, Philip nodded. Knox waved:

"Don't worry, I've heard that ten times over—from high and low. I've heard it all. That he was nothing more than a militia colonel before. And that while

fighting the French and Indians, he lost several engagements. But I tell you this, Philip, judge him by what he does now, not by his past.''

"I suppose that's the fair way,'' Philip agreed. It was pointless to go into all the widely expressed reasons many soldiers considered Washington a poor choice for his high post.

Aware of the general watching impatiently from the phaeton, Knox himself changed the subject:

"So you're on your way to see your wife, are you?''

"That's right.''

"I do believe I heard you'd married Mistress Ware—''

"Back in April.''

"And she's with child. You're to be congratulated.''

Philip didn't smile. "As I said, she's been sickly—''

"Knox!" Washington's shout from the phaeton hurried the fat young man's departure:

"I hope that condition reverses itself promptly. Give Anne and her father my compliments. I'm glad to find you again,'' he added as he waddled off. "I might have need for a couple of quick-witted men for a scheme I'm hatching—''

With a wave of the silk-wrapped hand, he was into the phaeton, a cloaked mountain hulking beside the general and the other officer as the carriage vanished in the murk.

Philip turned and hurried away from the Virginia encampment. He had only a few hours—and he was already late.

II

"ANNE?''

Kneeling beside the bed, Philip kept his voice to a whisper:

"Annie? It's me—''

Slowly, Anne Kent's eyes opened. Her head moved slightly on the sweat-dampened bolster. The brown eyes reflected the flame of a candle by the bedside. Rain pattered the roof of the cramped upstairs bedroom in the house on a shabby side street in Watertown.

His mouth dry, Philip closed his hand around his wife's, felt its heat. Her chestnut hair glistened with sweat just above the forehead. The light dusting of freckles on either side of her nose—prominent when her skin was wholesomely tanned by sunshine—had almost faded into invisibility.

Suddenly Anne rolled onto her side, gasping while her hand sought and touched the great mound of her stomach beneath the comforter.

Fearful, Philip bent closer. He smelled the staleness of her breath. "I'll find you a doctor, Annie. I'm trying hard as I can—''

Her glazed eyes showed no sign that she heard. The hand on the comforter knotted convulsively.

Gradually the pain passed. She relaxed again. Philip's voice sounded hoarser than ever:

"Annie, look at me. Don't you know me?''

The brown eyes closed. Her breathing became more regular.

Despairing, Philip stumbled to his feet. In the shadows behind him, a sneeze exploded.

"I've caught a plagued disease myself! Guess I shouldn't be in here—"

Sneezing into a kerchief a second time, Abraham Ware stumped back into the lamplit parlor crowded with large and small trunks: the belongings of a prosperous Boston lawyer who had been forced to flee his home, and his livelihood, because of his patriot convictions. Philip heard his father-in-law walk into the other bedroom.

Gently, he stroked Anne's forehead. He wished she could speak to him. Wished she could listen to a pledge that he would desert the damned army, if necessary, to locate a physician. But she neither saw nor heard.

Just looking at her pale, drawn face was agony for him. Despite her youth, she bore little resemblance to the pretty, quick-witted and independent girl he'd first encountered in Henry Knox's London Book-Store. She seemed frail and altogether vulnerable as she muttered in her sleep.

Close to tears, Philip remembered the joyous moments of their courting. And the times when he had questioned his own feelings for her, tempted as he was by the daughter of the Earl of Parkhurst, who had almost lured him away from Anne in Philadelphia—

Then the past receded. Only the present counted. He loved his wife with every fiber of his soul. That love made his helplessness all the worse.

He uttered a frustrated curse, blew out the candle, tip-toed out leaving the door ajar. Abraham Ware, disheveled in an expensive suit that showed hard use, had returned from the bedroom with a fresh kerchief and was helping himself to what amounted to little more than a thimbleful of precious claret. With overseas trade at a standstill because of the hostilities, everything was in short supply—including money to buy life's necessities. Ware was spending his savings to shelter himself, his daughter and her near-penniless husband during these days when no man could accurately predict what would happen next.

Philip sat down wearily on the battered travel trunk in which Anne had carefully stored the sum of his worldly possessions—three items. The first was a small, worn leather casket with brass corners. It contained letters from James Amberly, Duke of Kentland, to the French actress from Auvergne whom he'd loved and reluctantly left in Paris. The Duke, still alive in England, was Philip's father.

Just the preceding spring, after fruitless and near-fatal attempts to claim the portion of Amberly's fortune which he'd been promised, Philip had finally burned one particular document from the casket. That document was a letter declaring Amberly's intention to share his riches with his illegitimate son. Philip had decided he wanted no part of Amberly's world, in which the rich and the powerful exploited others. Destroying the letter, he'd become an American in spirit as well as in fact.

Also in the trunk was a memento of his boyhood in the French provinces: a splendid sword. The grenadier's briquet had been presented to him by a young nobleman he'd helped out of a difficult situation. The nobleman's title was the Marquis de Lafayette. But Philip would always think of him by one of his given names—Gil. One day, he'd hang Gil's sword in a place of honor above the mantel in his house. Provided he lived long enough to build a house!

The last of the three items was a small bottle of green glass filled with flakes of dried English tea. He'd found the tea in his shoes on the December night in 1773 when he'd joined Samuel Adams' band of bogus Indians and helped destroy three shiploads of tea chests in Boston harbor, as a protest against one of the king's repressive taxes. The souvenir of that evening had another, much more

memorable meaning as well. That same night, in his cheap cellar room at the Edes and Gill printing house in Dassett Alley, he had first made love to the young woman he'd married—

The young woman whose condition now tormented him with anxiety.

"How long has she been feverish?" Philip asked his father-in-law.

"Since last evening." Ware's protuberant eyes were doleful. The man had lost weight. Appeared bent; shriveled. He extended the decanter. "You'd better down some of this yourself, lad. You look like you bathed in mud, and your teeth are knocking like a bride's knees."

Philip didn't move. From the hem of his soaked coat, a drop of water plopped to the shabby carpet. The rain beat on the roof.

"Damn it, there's got to be a doctor someplace!" he exclaimed suddenly.

"Not one. I've asked everywhere."

"But we've got to do something! I don't know how to tend a pregnant woman. Annie's liable to die from plain neglect!"

Ware drank, and shivered. "Do you think the possibility hasn't occurred to me? I am as worried as you."

"You're sure there are no doctors here in Watertown?"

"None. They've all gone off to the lines."

"A midwife, then."

"I located one. But she's taken to her bed, out of her wits with grief. Her son was bayoneted to death in the Breed's Hill redoubt. There's no telling whether she'll recover in time for Annie's delivery—and I'd hate to trust my daughter to a woman in such a precarious mental state anyway."

"God, I wish the whole abominable mess were over, so we could go back to living like human beings!"

Ware tried to smile. "Annie would scold you if she heard that, Philip. No, more than scold. Tongue-lash you—and make you like it, as only she knows how—"

His son-in-law didn't answer. Ware's forced smile faded.

Philip jumped up, began pacing. To take his mind off the seemingly insoluble problem of Anne, he asked, "Has there been any more word on the petition?" He referred to the so-called Olive Branch resolution drafted in Philadelphia before the Congress adjourned. A direct appeal to George III, the petition pleaded for the king to effect a reconciliation before further conflict developed.

Ware shook his head: " 'Twas only dispatched in July. With six to ten weeks of sea travel involved each way, we won't have the answer for a long while, I expect. Besides, you know what that answer will be. It's the king as much as his puppet ministers pushing this break to the limit. Too many fail to understand that fact."

What the lawyer said was true, Philip knew. He'd heard similar views expressed by everyone from Samuel Adams to Dr. Benjamin Franklin, the eminent scientist and diplomat whom he'd known in London and met again in Philadelphia just this past April. No, there wasn't any realistic basis for hoping the fighting would end before his enlistment ran out—

A moment ago, he'd decided not to drink any claret. Now he changed his mind, and poured half a glass. The wine warmed his belly but not his mood.

Ware stifled another sneeze. "I don't doubt that when and if His Majesty replies to the petition, it will be with a 'damned to you, sirs!' I encountered Hancock the other morning. Before the Congress closed its session, there were

already rumors afloat that His Majesty has dispatched confidential agents into Europe. To Brunswick, Anspach, Hesse-Hanau—''

Philip shook his head, not understanding.

''Those are principalities in Germany. There, the house of Hanover would find receptive ears.''

''Receptive to what?''

''A plea for troops, perhaps. Troops to crush the rebellion.''

''Would the Germans ally themselves with Britain?''

''For money they might. If that should ever happen, there would be no turning back.''

''Well, all I care about is Anne. I've got to find *someone*—''

''I will continue my inquiries. I don't hold out great hope. I—'' Abruptly, Ware was seized with a long, wheezing cough that drained every last bit of color from his sunken cheeks.

''Perhaps you ought to be in bed too, sir,'' Philip said.

Ware rejected the suggestion emphatically: ''I know you must return to the lines soon. I'll watch Annie after you've gone. Don't think you need stay here and chatter with me, Philip. Go where you want to be—in there with her.''

Philip thanked him and left the room.

He sat at the bedside for almost an hour, holding his wife's hand and listening to her stertorous breathing. She cried out whenever pains in her belly twisted her from side to side. Philip's own hands were chill and stiff by the time he heard the small parlor clock chime eleven. He'd be almost an hour late returning to the encampment—

''Annie. *Annie.*'' He felt so helpless, no other words would come.

She didn't answer. He crept out.

Lawyer Ware had fallen into a drowse, his mouth hanging open. Philip bundled himself into his damp coat and let himself out, sick with fright as he half walked, half ran through the rainy September darkness.

III

TWO DAYS later, the sky cleared and the British batteries started rumbling again.

In the mellow twilight, Philip sat on the ground outside his quarters, trying to bite through the petrified leather that passed for the day's ration of corned beef. Even washing the stuff down with the locally brewed spruce beer that was regular issue failed to make it more palatable. At least the royal troops in Boston were faring no better. The American soldiers had guffawed over a story about a prominent officer, the Earl of Percy. The Earl had given an elaborate dinner at which, by necessity, the main dish was roast colt.

On the ground next to Philip lay a scrawled note from Abraham Ware. The note had arrived earlier in the day. It reported that Anne's fever had broken but she remained weak, and was asking for him. It would be two more nights before Philip could get leave to return to Watertown—

An elongated shadow fell across his legs. He glanced up and started, spilling his mug of beer. An immense, gangly figure silhouetted against the sinking sun warned him of danger—

Until he recognized the face, and saw it bore no signs of malice.

A vast display of crooked teeth partially masked a certain shyness as the

Virginian with the cocked eye and unmercifully ugly countenance scratched at his scrotum and shifted from foot to foot. In one hand the man carried his Kentucky rifle. At last he said:

"Hello."

Philip's nod was cautious. "Hello."

A long silence. Then:

"Got sent to Cambridge with a dispatch. Got lost on the way back. Seen you sittin' there. Figured I should stop and say thanks for keepin' me from gettin' kilt the other night."

Philip waved. "I doubt that drunk would have done much damage."

"Listen, he could of busted my neck, coming at me like he did. I'm obliged to you."

"Did you boys get punished pretty severely?"

"Damn if we didn't," said the other, in slow, soft speech that contrasted with Philip's somewhat more nasal New England tone. "We're down to half rations and confined to quarters 'cept while we're on duty or 'ficial business. Next time any of us bust out, Squire Washington says he's gonnna put the cat on our backs. And when that man promises, he don't forget." The tall frontiersman spat once, eloquent emphasis.

"Gather you think he's a pretty good soldier."

"They don't make 'em no damn better. The difference 'tween the colonel— I mean the general—and some o' them peacocks on his staff like that Charlie Lee is this. When Washington takes the wrong fork once, he don't ever do it again. He ain't perfect, but he's got balls, and he knows woods fightin', too. That may count for more than all the fancy-dancy soldierin' that's been done by Lee and his crowd. By the way—" The ugly man extended a callused hand. "Been jawing and jawing and ain't even said hello proper. I'm Experience Tait of Albemarle County. Most call me Eph."

They shook. "Kent's my name. Philip Kent."

"Well, you're a little rooster, but you fight pretty good—" Tait grinned. "For a wise man."

"Thanks. From a Virginian, that's a real compliment."

"Well—" Tait spat again. "Guess I better haul shanks. 'Ficial business, y'know. And soon's I get back, I'm 'sposed to sew up a lieutenant's hand. Fuckin' fool can't handle his own sword proper—be seein' you, mebbe—"

Philip ran after the backwoodsman. "Wait a minute, Mr. Tait."

"Eph, I said it's Eph."

"You also said something about sewing up a hand. You—you're not any kind of doctor?"

"Only the back country kind," Tait shrugged. "I do smithing, barbering, mix up tonics to cure boils and minor complaints of the bowels, minister to expectant heifers an' women, includin' my wife—little of everything, guess you could say. In the Blue Ridge, a man's got to know a smatter of this and a smatter of that just to stay alive."

A lump had formed in Philip's throat. He was almost afraid to speak for fear he'd be refused. But the hesitation didn't last:

"Eph, would you have a minute to share a drink of spruce beer?"

Tait reflected. "Well—no more'n a minute. But I drink fast," he grinned. "Fast as I shoot with this thing—"

He lifted the long, beautiful muzzle loader with its grooved barrel: the rifling that imparted such speed, distance and accuracy to the balls it discharged.

Philip gestured. "Come on, then—"

Experience Tait cocked his one good eye at the entrance to Philip's shanty. "There's some of your friends inside, ain't they? Will we have a set-to? Much as I wouldn't mind one, I cain't afford 'nother fight."

"I'll fetch the beer and we'll drink it out here. I've a favor to ask, Eph—if you're really serious about thanking me."

"Shit, I ain't goin' to pay or nothin', if that's what you mean," Eph Tait returned with a grin abruptly tempered by suspicion.

"No, it's something else. And you're the man to do it."

"Don't sound good," Tait commented as Philip ducked inside. "They warned us to stay away from twisty wise men. Trick the buttons right off a man's pants, you Massachusetts fellas. Least that's what we got told—"

But he leaned on his Kentucky rifle in the sunset light, and waited for the beer anyway.

___IV

PHILIP WALKED up and down, up and down—just as he'd been doing for half an hour.

At first, between sneezes and swallows of the dwindling claret, Lawyer Ware had expressed annoyance. But when Philip showed no signs of calming down, the little man drained the rest of the decanter and went to sleep after a final tense glance at the closed door.

Philip had been alternately walking and sitting for about three hours. His eyes itched. His clothing stank. His stomach hurt. He hadn't eaten since early morning. The clock ticked loud as the strokes of judgment sounding—

Quit thinking such morbid thoughts! Philip chastised himself. But he couldn't help it. All he loved or cared about in the world lay hidden from his sight behind the bedroom door. Occasionally he heard a small sound. Water sloshing. A stifled cry from Anne. The murmur of another voice. His mind built monstrous imaginings—

Death.

Deformity.

An outcome so devastating, she would never want to have another—

A squall rooted Philip to the carpet. His scalp crawled. White-faced, he stared at the closed door.

The squalling gurgled away to silence.

Philip wiped his stubbled cheek, crossed the room to where his father-in-law was on the point of sliding out of his chair. Philip shook him.

Ware grumbled, smacked his lips. Philip shook him again, still staring in hypnotic fascination at that door. *Why was there no more sound?*

Suddenly Lawyer Ware bolted up. "My God, what's happened? Is Annie—?"

Before he could finish, the door was open. Experience Tait said:

"What's happened is, everybody done a good job—me and your wife and the Almighty and the youngster too. He come out kickin' and I'm thirsty as hell. If you ain't got any likker in this place, somebody go fetch some because I figure I deserve some kind o' reward for my first-class work." As he spoke, the tall Virginian wiped his hands and forearms on the large piece of rag tied around his waist. The lean hands and big-boned arms left bright blood on the rag. The long hilt of a skinning knife stuck up from his belt.

"Well, go on, go on!" Eph Tait waved to Philip, exasperated. "Don't you want to see your own child? An' you, you runt," he added to Ware, "go find me that drink!"

Ware licked his lips, bulging eyes on the doorway. "Is—is she—?"

"Fine, fine! But she wants to see *him*, not you. God!" he sighed to a still-stunned Philip. "You're some husband—get a move on!"

Philip looked swiftly at the clock. A quarter past twelve. At a quarter past twelve on the morning of September 29, 1775, in Watertown, Massachusetts, his son had been born—yes, Experience Tait had distinctly said *he*—

Philip pushed past the bloodied, craze-eyed woodsman lounging against the jamb. From the bedroom's dimness he heard the miraculous sound of an infant making moist sucking sounds.

"Annie?" he bellowed.

"Jesus blue lightning, don't jump all over her!" Tait shouted behind him. Philip paid no attention. For the second time in his adult life, loudly and without shame, he was crying.

V

ANNE WARE KENT was awake, propped up on the bolster and several rolled blankets. Philip knelt beside two basins of pink-tinged water. In one of them floated something that resembled a short piece of bloody rope.

Anne looked sleepy and pale. Yet there was a radiance to her face. In the crook of one arm she cradled a small, rag-wrapped bundle from which protruded a reddish gnome's head almost as sinfully ugly as Eph Tait.

Philip couldn't find words. He reached one trembling hand toward a miniature fist whose longest finger was shorter than his thumb from knuckle to nail.

"You can touch him," Anne said softly, smiling. "He's yours, after all."

Marveling, Philip stroked the clutching little fist. The child whose head was capped with dark fuzz promptly screwed up its face and shrieked.

Comforting the baby with wordless murmurs, Anne gazed lovingly at her husband. "We must name him, Philip. Have you thought—?"

"Some. I'd like him to be called Abraham, if that's all right."

"Papa would be pleased."

"Did—did you hurt a lot?"

"Oh, enough." Again the drowsy smile. "But Mr. Tait is a gentle man. His hands look so big but his fingers are as supple as a woman's. Where ever did you find him?"

"In the mud."

"What?"

"I'll tell you another time. He's a Virginian, just like General Washington."

"So he told me—I think. I don't remember everything."

"What's this?" Philip said, picking up a length of fresh-whittled wood from the floor. The wood bore teeth marks.

Anne focused on the wood with difficulty. "I had to bite on that when the pains were strongest. Mr. Tait doesn't believe in giving wine or beer during deliveries. But he must have quite a thirst himself. All he could speak of was hurrying matters along so he could swallow his pay. Philip—" Anne began to rock the infant gently. The fuzzed head all but disappeared under folds of rag. "How is it with you?"

"Bearable. Lonesome without you. The days just drag and drag—"

"No action on either side?"

"Shelling from the British, that's all. Washington sent an expedition against Canada earlier this month. I'm not sure whether it'll accomplish anything—or is supposed to. But all the men in camp—fifteen, twenty thousand by now— they're getting restive. Either the British will break out of Boston, or we'll overwhelm them and drive them out. It has to be one or the other, unless there's a settlement."

"A few days ago Papa said he thought any such hope was foolish."

"I think so too. But my eight months will be up at the end of the year, and it won't matter after that. I'll be with you all the time."

Her voice surprisingly clear, Anne said quietly, "What do you mean?"

"I mean when my enlistment's finished, so am I. The colonies can't win a war against Great Britain."

"I agree—not with men who go home." Her brown eyes sparked; the Anne he remembered.

"Annie, for God's sake—!" he protested. "I'm a father now. With responsibilities—"

"I doubt you're the only father in the colonial army."

"But we've the future to think about!"

"Exactly what do you propose to do, Philip? Turn Tory?"

"Annie—!"

"I mean it. What are your plans?" She was challenging him, and he knew what it must be costing her in terms of discomfort. Her body shifted frequently beneath the covers Eph Tait had tucked neatly back into place. "Do you want to creep back to Boston and set up a press to print pamphlets supporting the king? I'd hate to tell our son that, wouldn't you?"

"Annie, you know as well as I do—this rebellion has no support at all! Everyone says less than a third of the people in the colonies are in favor of it—"

"Does that make it wrong?"

"Of course not, but—"

"Does that give you leave to quit?"

"Dear God, you're stubborn!"

"Yes, because when you came back from Philadelphia this spring, you made a decision. You chose your side. Will you forget that so quickly when things grow difficult? The man I thought I married wouldn't forget it."

Stung, he colored. There was a moment of strained silence. Then Philip let out a long sigh, and nodded:

"I guess you're right. I'm sorry."

With one of those tart yet loving smiles he knew so well, she said, "You're forgiven. I don't blame you for wavering. Papa's told me about the wretched conditions and poor discipline in the army—"

"The *army* doesn't even deserve the name. It seems all you can think about in camp is the next minute, then the next one after that. You eat, sleep, dig, dodge cannon shot—you lose track of what it's all about."

Still smiling, she touched his face. "That's why you need a wife, my darling."

He laughed, the tension broken. Just as during their sometimes-stormy courtship, it was Anne who put his frequently muddled and imperfect thinking into

proper order and focus. That was just one of the many reasons he loved her so much.

She saw he was still troubled, though:

"Don't worry, we won't lose track of what we've planned for Abraham. A good house for our family—your own printing establishment—Kent and Son. How does that sound?"

"Grander than anything in this world." He hugged her. The baby began to squall again.

Humming a little, Anne soothed the newborn infant back to sleep. Awestruck, Philip stared at the lumpy bundle that represented his flesh and hers. He knew he was only one man among multitudes who had experienced the same supreme moment of joy and wonder down through the centuries. Yet he couldn't help feeling moved, as if he were biblical Adam gazing on creation's first-born son—

"By God," he breathed at last, "he is a big boy, isn't he?"

"Seven or eight pounds, Mr. Tait said. But I wish you wouldn't look at him quite so much."

Philip's eyebrows shot up. "Why not?"

Warm and loving, she caressed his face again.

"Because I'd like for you to kiss me."

VI

WHEN PHILIP and Experience Tait walked back toward the American lines at dawn, Philip told his new friend that he'd changed his mind. If the war should last beyond December, he would re-enlist.

Tait's crazed eye seemed to glow like a small moon in the first flush of eastern light. "Damn fool," was his reply. "That's how fine young girls like your wife turn into widders. Guess I'll do the same thing, though."

"You said you had a wife didn't you, Eph?"

"Yep. And fourteen youngsters back in Albemarle County."

"Fourteen! My Lord, you don't look that old."

"Started when I was fourteen years old. Besides, it ain't how old, it's how stiff." He gave Philip a lewd nudge in the ribs, and belched. Presently, noticing Philip's dour look, he asked:

"What the hell's got you down now?"

"Oh, just that I really thought about quitting—until Annie helped me see things straight again."

"Heck, don't feel bad. I'd sooner be back home huntin', far as that goes. The Blue Ridge is mighty pretty this time of year. And it's too dang cold up in these parts. But I guess I'd rather have my kin remember me as a fella who died free an' sassy, instead of kissin' that old Dutchman's royal ass just to stay alive."

"That's about how Anne put it," Philip told him.

"Oh hell no she didn't!" Eph said. "She's a lady. Ladies don't cuss half as colorful as us Virginians."

"You're right about that," Philip said with a tired smile. Far away, he heard the ominous thump of the Boston batteries beginning the day's bombardment. The sound erased the smile as if it had never existed.

4
The Uprising

DONALD FLETCHER'S hired coach brought the weary delegate back to Sermon Hill in mid-August. The father's greeting of his elder son was brief and perfunctory. What few meals the three family members took together in the long, airy dining room of the main house were strained and virtually devoid of conversation.

Donald, a steady-minded but phlegmatic man, took to spending most of his holiday in his younger brother's company. Whenever possible, the two snatched meals in the great kitchen, away from Angus. The company of the black housewomen who tended the huge iron stove and brick hearth was far more relaxing.

In Judson's opinion Donald didn't look well. He'd gained weight. His normally soft face was puffier than ever. His eyes were perpetually reddened with fatigue, and he could neither mount nor dismount without the assistance of a slave at the stirrup. From mid-calf downward, his left leg was swathed in heavy bandages. Yet he persisted in drinking the wine the physicians claimed only worsened his gout.

Donald had married late, at age thirty. His wife, the daughter of a prosperous tobacco factor with headquarters in Richmond, had gone to her childbed thirteen months later—and both she and her infant daughter had died there. After that, Donald's only pleasure or release seemed to lie in his involvement in the political affairs of the colony. This in itself guaranteed continual strain at Sermon Hill.

Angus Fletcher refused to discuss either politics or the management of the property with his older son, even though Sermon Hill, at least, should have been a subject of frequent conversation. Theoretically Donald would inherit when the old man died. In private, Donald told Judson that he suspected Angus had already entertained thoughts about altering his will. In fact, he believed Angus might well have Sermon Hill sold off after his death, the proceeds to be distributed among an assortment of distant relatives still living in Scotland. Their names and whereabouts were carefully recorded in the family Bible Angus kept at his bedside, Donald said. Angus had shown him the list of relatives several times. Perhaps as a threat.

Donald seemed resigned to whatever happened. Besides, he was interested in more significant matters. These came up for discussion one muggy day in early September.

The brothers were taking a turn around the countryside on their horses. Near noon, they ended the ride at the wharf beside the river. Three plantation wagons were being unloaded by blacks under the supervision of Reuven Shaw's drivers—specially appointed slaves who served as his assistants. As the brothers rode down the pier, Judson noticed many a black face turned in their direction. He also saw not a few resentful stares.

"Lord, you can almost smell the anger," Donald said, his voice heavy with the wheeze he'd developed in Philadelphia.

"Yes, but the old man won't stay Shaw's hand one iota."

"I understand they caught the nigger with the drum."

Judson nodded, his blue eyes ranging along the hazed river. By this time of year, the hand-hewn tobacco canoes should have appeared—forty feet long, five

381

wide and lashed together in threes and fives to carry big loads. Because of the trouble, no one as yet knew whether the canoes would come to load the casks. The agents of the factors—most of whom were Tory sympathizers—hadn't shown up at the plantations in the neighborhood to begin finalizing purchases.

"Who had it?" Donald asked.

"The drum? One of Seth McLean's field hands. Built it on the sly, out of woodshed scraps and a goatskin. Seth burned it, then had fifty laid on the culprit. The punishment damn near crippled the man. It wasn't much easier on Seth. But he said it had to be done."

Donald scratched his veined nose as Judson walked around and helped him dismount. In the process, Donald nearly fell.

Leaning on his younger brother, he hobbled toward the end of the wharf where the Rappahannock lapped softly. The sky was graying in the northwest, promising storm before the afternoon was over.

Donald tried his best to stand upright, bracing himself on the cane he always carried. Without looking at Judson, he said:

"You don't sound convinced that Seth did the right thing."

"Living around this place, how can you be certain of anything? Except the old man's dislike for the both of us."

Donald chose to let that go for the moment. "Is Seth of the opinion the slave problem's quieted, then?"

"Gone under the surface, would be more like it." Judson slapped a gnat on his sweaty neck, turned to stare into the west, a blur of hills beneath the blackening clouds. His expression conveyed his disgust over the entire situation.

Donald shifted his weight to favor his bandaged foot. If you find Sermon Hill so opprobrious, why do you stay on?"

The younger brother shrugged. "Where would I go instead?"

"That's what I wish to discuss with you."

Judson's head snapped up, his blue eyes hooding with suspicion; Donald had sounded almost schoolmasterish. He, in turn, saw Judson's temper flaring. He held up a hand to reassure him:

"Surely you've expected it. The old man's been quite pointed in the few talks I've had with him. You're drinking too much. And he says you're worthless— wait, that's his word, not mine—when it comes to running the place."

"I wouldn't deny that," Judson replied coldly.

"Then what does keep you here?" Donald's face showed sympathy. "McLean's wife?"

"Goddamn it, Donald, you know that's over!"

"On a practical basis, of course I do. But a man doesn't heal a wound in his heart all that easily. I speak from some experience," he added after a moment. "However, I won't press you if you prefer not to speak about it."

That was good, Judson thought sourly, because he'd only have been forced to tell more lies. And it was hard to lie to the one member of the family with whom he could discuss things on a halfway intimate basis. Hard, but not impossible. Very few actions frowned on by so-called respectable people were impossible for him any more.

"Jud," Donald resumed, leaning on his cane and staring at the river turning glassy under the fast-moving clouds, "this siege between you and Father will only come to a bad end. You need to leave Sermon Hill for a while."

"I repeat—to go where?"

"I've a suggestion about that. Nothing definite as yet, but I feel compelled to mention the idea for your sake as well as mine."

Judson sat down on the end of the Wharf, lolling one of his expensive Russian leather boots in and out of the water. Behind him, he heard the grunting of the blacks unloading the huge casks of cured leaves. One of the drivers shouted angrily. A whip popped twice. The offender yelped. Judson preferred not to turn and look. He waited for Donald to continue:

"As you know, I must return to Philadelphia in a week or two. The long hours of the Congress, the rich food, the drinking—they haven't served me well. I lay abed three weeks during the last session. I got about the rest of the time only with great difficulty. There's important work to be done when the delegates reconvene—particularly if the king rejects the petition on reconciliation. I'd like to go north confident that if my strength fails, someone trustworthy could be appointed to fill my seat."

Realizing at last what his brother was getting at, Judson almost burst out laughing. Donald's intense, pain-wracked expression checked the impulse. Judson said instead:

"You mean I'd be your replacement?"

"If a replacement became necessary, yes."

Stunned by the idea, Judson sat in silence. Finally he shook his head:

"I'm flattered you'd even consider me, Donald. But I doubt very much that the members of your delegation would welcome someone like me." A mocking smile. "A gentleman who's seldom sober, and hence surely doesn't deserve the name."

"But you are my brother. More important, your politics are proper."

"If not my morals?"

"See here, do you suppose the morals of the delegates are all that spotless? I've sat at table with Dr. Franklin and watched him turn to stone consuming Madeira. I'm not attending a conclave of angels, you know—only of men. So long as you create no public scandal—stay within the bounds of decency—"

Amused, Judson said, "For years I've been trying to find out where those are located. Every man places 'em differently, it seems." He pondered a bit longer. "You know, I wouldn't want to wish you ill—but I will admit the possibility's intriguing."

"Good."

"In fact I'd be more than happy to get away from this damned place for such a purpose. Still, can you just—just wave your hand and appoint me to attend in your stead?"

"Naturally not. You'd have to be duly elected to the delegation. But there's precedent. Richard Henry Lee saw to the election of his brother, Francis Lightfoot, when old Bland had to come home because of his infirmities. With words in the proper ears, I could swing it. I'm on good terms with Tom Jefferson of Albemarle County, for instance. He's highly respected despite his youth—yes, I could definitely swing it. Mind you, I'm not saying it *will* become necessary. But I'd rest easier up there knowing that if this blasted gout does lay me low again, my place would be occupied by a man who's as determined as I am to stand fast against the king and his ministers."

For a moment Judson was tempted; exceedingly tempted. To his private shame, he nearly wished that his older brother would be incapacitated. Then reality took over. He shook his head again:

"Oh, I don't think it would work, Donald. I have no experience in politics."

"I realize that. Some of the other delegates are pretty short on it themselves. I want to say something else, Jud. I say it as a brother who feels affection for you. Eventually, you're going to have to decide what you are—and where you belong. The kind of life you're leading now—surely it brings you no real pleasure—"

"I hate it, for Christ's sake," Judson said savagely. "But as to what I am— that's been settled up at the big house."

"Then at least don't shut out a possibility that might relieve the situation. All I want today is your pledge that I can depend on you if I need you."

Westward, fast-flying clouds showed flickering white light. Judson watched the bleached wood of the pier dot with the first raindrops.

"All right," he said with a wry shrug that concealed a feeling of futility. Donald had probed the painful riddle that Judson struggled with for hours on end. He knew he didn't belong here at Sermon Hill, where his father's disapproval and the nearness of Peggy Ashford McLean were constant torments. But just as certainly, he didn't belong in the learned councils of the patriots in Philadelphia.

Where, then?

Where?

He stared morosely at the lightning-ridden clouds on the western horizon, confronting again the damning truth:

He was a misfit. His father hadn't been entirely wrong when he claimed that devil's blood ran in his son's veins. And to make matters worse, not only did Judson not know where he belonged in the world, he didn't know how to find out.

The closing of Donald's fingers on his shoulder took him by surprise. The compassionate look in Donald's tired, reddened eyes startled him, then filled him with a warmth he hadn't experienced in—Lord, it must be years.

"Thank you," Donald said.

"You've made a wretched mistake, you know," Judson laughed with a false heartiness, helping Donald hobble back to the horses.

"Who can be sure? You might discover you have a flair for oratory and backstairs finagling. Besides, while the winters in Philadelphia are miserable, I understand the ladies are quite flirtatious."

"You understand? Haven't you persuaded even one to tumble into bed with you?"

Donald responded to the teasing with a grimace. "I fear these damned bandages would prove—hampering, shall we say? You, though—that's another story. See what you have to look forward to?"

"You haven't mentioned this to the old man, have you, Donald?"

"What would be the purpose? It's merely a contingency."

"Contingency or no, please do me a favor and keep it private. Otherwise I'll be rousted to camp in the fields."

Donald laughed. "I suspect you're right. I'll keep quiet."

The first of the empty wagons was pulling away as they mounted in the pattering rain. The huge casks were somber reminders of the canoes that might never come.

One buck in the second wagon glared at them when they rode by. Wincing with pain, Donald didn't see. Judson pretended he didn't either.

IN THE second week of September, Donald Fletcher left in a coach, heartened by a letter from his friend Tom Jefferson. The letter said that, for the first time, the Congress might soon represent all thirteen separate political entities up and down the eastern seaboard. Reluctant Georgia was apparently planning to dispatch a delegation at last.

After Donald departed, Judson was also the recipient of an unexpected communication: four closely written foolscap pages dated almost eight months earlier, and wrapped inside a pouch one of the Clark boys brought to Sermon Hill. The letter was one of a packet that had been sent east by Judson's friend George. The packet had been posted at Pittsburgh.

The Clark boy said George had informed his family that he was well and in good spirits. As a member of the Virginia frontier militia, he had scouted for the royal governor, the Earl of Dunmore, in sharp action against the "savages" late the preceding year.

Dunmore had personally gone across the mountains at the head of an expeditionary force numbering a thousand men. His purpose was to put down raiding by the Indian tribes. The raiding had been provoked by Dunmore's own seizure of land in Western Pennsylvania, and by the arrival of settlers in the country below the river with the Indian name—Ohio.

In the letter directed to Judson, George Clark wrote of a successful military engagement at a place called Point Pleasant. There, a Shawnee war chief named Cornstalk and his followers had been decisively defeated. Most of the rest of the letter concerned itself with the breathtaking beauty of the wilderness south of the Ohio.

On earlier expeditions, George Clark had looked at its dark, lush shores from a poplar canoe. But now, at last, he had set foot in Kentucky, and explored it.

The letter described strange, eerie marsh hollows where animals stole down to lick at frosty-white deposits of salt, and woodsmen marveled at bones thrusting up from the ooze. George wrote that he had personally seen time-bleached ribs as long as the roof pole of a cabin, and thigh bones thick as tree trunks:

> *I believe we gazed upon the remains of phenomenal Beasts which*
> *may have roamed our earth before the coming of the human kind.*
> *At least I have never heard of skeletons so immense, save in*
> *fanciful tales.*

Judson's mind couldn't quite comprehend such a bizarre curiosity. But he knew George Clark would never invent a story merely to impress him. He actually felt a thrill of awe down his spine as he read the passage.

Kentucky, already divided into three large counties which nominally belonged to Virginia, now boasted several white settlements. In 1769, a man from the back country of North Carolina had crossed the barrier mountains to explore the territory. Subsequently, he'd led members of his family to the rich new land. The Boone clan had journeyed through the notch in the mountains called Cumberland Gap, and established a few isolated stockades.

Inhabitants of the frontier outposts lived with constant danger. The reason was simple: Kentucky had long been a hunting ground for the Creek and Cherokee tribes who ranged up from the south—and also for the more ferocious Miamis, Shawnee and Wyandots who claimed the forests north of the Ohio. In spite of the

threat of Indian attacks from two directions, Clark saw the Kentucky wilderness as a promised land for men of free spirit:

> *Such spacious domains, my friend, have doubtless never before been viewed by Human eyes. Here is land where a man can breathe sweet, untainted air. Stroll all day through forests with branches that arch overhead like the vaults of Cathedrals. The limestone soil is fertile, and game astonishing in its abundance. Fat Turkeys of gold and purple—Buffalo grazing the canebrake which rises taller than a rider on horseback—Elk and Deer beyond counting—Paradise, notwithstanding its perils. In Kentucky a man relies solely upon Himself and a few trusted Comrades of like mind. It is here, I may say with conviction, that I have found both Beauty to entrance the Soul, and vast spaces whose exploration and defense give purpose to my Life at last.*

The letter closed with a brief but sincere wish that Judson was in good health, and that George Rogers Clark might again share his experiences in person, if ever the mounting conflict with England gave him reason to return to the Virginia colony which had taken so much of the western forest in its own name.

The letter fired Judson's imagination just as George's two visits had done. It also filled him with a heightened loneliness, and a sense of deepening confusion. At a river-front inn, he withdrew to a corner and read the foolscap pages again and again. Rum helped paint vivid pictures of his lanky, red-haired friend striding along under those immense green arches, smoothbore over his shoulder, listening to the wild bird calls and sharing the friendship of a night campfire. The names rolled sonorously in Judson's inner ear—

Pittsburgh.

Kentucky.

Ohio.

Shawnee.

By their very sketchiness in his own mind, the lands beyond the Blue Wall became richer and more colorful moment by moment; then day by day.

More painful to think about, too.

He took a trip to Richmond. The trip had no purpose other than to allow him to spend the better part of two days in bed with a cheerful whore who didn't constantly whine for demonstrations of affection, the way Lottie Shaw did. On the trip he heard that George Clark had indeed acquitted himself well in the battle at Point Pleasant. His name was mentioned in the taverns along with those of other well-known frontiersmen—Kenton, Girty, Boone. Thanks to men like George, Lord Dunmore's western war had been a success. God alone knew when Judson Fletcher would be able to say the same about his own existence.

III

IN EARLY November, Donald sent Judson a letter saying that grim news had arrived on a transatlantic schooner recently docked at Philadelphia. In August, George III had refused to receive the petition for reconciliation, and formally proclaimed the American colonies in open rebellion. Said Donald:

Such as John Adams of Mass. Bay are jubilant. It is plain that we shall soon be past the point of possible compromise, if we are not already. I was advised of the unhappy turn of events while at rest in my quarters. The d———d gout has once again confined me, together with what one of the local croakers diagnoses as a congestion in the breathing passages, brought on by exposure to a prolonged spell of wet, foul weather.

IV

"THE VILE, perfidious spawn of Satan!" Angus Fletcher cried, much too exercised to touch the hog cutlet and greens on his plate. "The wretched, deceiving miscreant!" The old man bunched his fingers and hit the polished dining table so hard the candle-glasses rattled. A spoon fell to the pegged floor.

Into his fourth or fifth glass of claret, Judson Fletcher lounged in his chair at the opposite end of the long dinner table. A nervous house black stepped forward to retrieve the spoon. He retreated when Angus glared.

Muttering private curses, the old man covered his eyes with both hands. The tall windows of the dimly lit room were open on the November dark. The evening was unusually warm; Judson's neck cloth was undone.

"And all along I thought you and His Excellency were kindred souls," he said.

Angus Fletcher whipped his hands down. "I need no clack from you, you damned young traitor."

Judson smiled. "Strikes me it's Lord Dunmore who's the traitor to those who thought him a friend. That he'd try to recruit a loyalist army is to be expected. But promising freedom to any nigra who deserts his master to join—that's a delightful fillip, to say the least. After Seth heard the news, he was talking like the hottest rebel."

Livid, Angus opened his mouth to reply. He was so upset, he couldn't say a word. Judson glanced away, momentarily ashamed of himself.

Yet he hadn't held back, had he?

The opportunity was just too rich. In one stroke, the Tory governor had undercut the very planters who were his strongest adherents. Men like Seth McLean could switch sides quickly when their economic position was threatened. But Angus, believing both in the slave system and the authority of the king, was not so flexible. He'd been suffering ever since the surprising announcement had been circulated in the neighborhood the preceding day.

"I'd expect you to relish my discomfort," Angus snarled at his son. "To gloat—because you've no brains in your head! No notion of the turmoil Dunmore may have unleashed. We put the lid on the kettle that was stewing all summer. Now the damn fool's pulled it off again. Only Jehovah in His wisdom knows what will—"

Boots rapped on the pegged floor. Judson swung around.

Looking apologetic, Reuven Shaw stood just inside one of the tall windows. His long blacksnake whip was draped over his left shoulder and under his right armpit.

"Blast you, Shaw," Angus said, "you're never to interrupt my dinner and you know it."

Shaw seemed unnaturally pale. "Yessir, I realize, but—" The overseer swallowed. "Number two curing barn's afire."

The room was absolutely still. Angus turned as white as Shaw:

"Afire?"

"Yessir. I been smellin' something comin' all day. The niggers been jumpy as hell. I got a gang working to control the fire, but—"

Angus leaped up. "The niggers set it?"

"Who else, Mr. Fletcher? Half the bucks ain't in their cabins. Sneaked out after sunset, I reckon—"

Judson felt no further impulse to laugh. Outside, behind the overseer, a dull red glare was rising. He heard strident voices through the November darkness.

"Sneaked out!" Angus thundered. "Don't you have anyone watching to prevent that? Who's your driver tonight? Why didn't he sound the alarm?"

Reuven Shaw wiped a hand across his mouth. "My driver tonight was Beau. You know Beau—a good nigger. I just found him by the pond. His body was lyin' on the bank, an' his head—his head was floatin' in—"

Shaw stopped, looking nauseated.

Well he might, Judson thought, chilled despite the mildness of the evening. There had been occasional slave rebellions throughout the southern colonies in the past. Not many. But each one was usually disastrous, at least at first, because the white owners and overseers were numerically inferior.

"You mean to tell me niggers are loose with field knives?" Angus whispered.

Again Shaw nodded, sick-faced. "Guess that's how they butchered Beau. Larned, he's gone for sure. I checked."

Judson saluted Shaw with his goblet. "Congratulations. I was told you hided him twice this afternoon."

"Sassy bastard kept braggin' he was gonna enlist in Dunmore's nigger army. I shoulda castrated him last summer, 'fore this got out of hand."

"Well, it obviously *is* out of hand," Angus seethed. "Why haven't I heard the bell?"

"I come to report first. There ain't much we can do to save number two barn—"

"Go ring the goddamned bell!" Angus screamed. "We've got to turn out every white man on the river before this spreads!"

The old man's profanity indicated the depth of his fear. The house black who had been waiting on table had disappeared, Judson noticed. Angus dashed from the dining room, headed for his office. His passage made the flames of the candles jump and cast distorted shadows of Judson rising from his chair.

On his way out, the overseer gave the younger man a questioning look.

"If you're counting on me to help slaughter the nigras—" Judson realized he was more than slightly drunk. He had trouble articulating the last word: "Don't."

Shaw scowled. "Like Mr. Fletcher said, we need every man—"

Judson waved. "Shit. I didn't bring this on. I won't help finish it."

Reuven Shaw trembled, but not from fear. He gathered spit in his mouth and blew a gob onto the pegged floor. Then he spun and ran into the red-glaring dark.

Judson tossed off the last of his wine. He was setting the fine crystal goblet on the polished table when he heard a hideous shriek from out on the grounds.

He bolted for the window, raced down the lawn toward the rear corner of the big house. Beyond it he saw flames leaping from the curing barn, and terrified bucks and wenches running to and fro, adding their hysteria to the din. Other

male slaves were trying to round up the frightened ones with profane shouts or, in some cases, drivers' whips.

Before Judson reached the corner of the house, his boots struck something in the neatly scythed grass. He halted, crouched down, tasted vomit in his throat—

Reuven Shaw, lying crooked as a doll. The overseer was dead. An immense gash had been cut in his throat. The distant firelight lit the still-wet blood drenching his right sleeve and the front of his coarse shirt.

Out back, the alarm bell on its great iron Y began to toll—but not before Judson heard a stirring up on his left, in the dark near the unlighted windows of the conservatory.

"Jesus God—!" he breathed, lurching to his feet as an ebony figure shot toward him from the shadowy concealment. Firelight glittered on one of the knives used to chop off the leaves at harvest.

The black man was red to the elbows. Judson's sotted mind screamed the danger. Somehow he managed to duck as the frenzied face loomed, white teeth and eyes glaring. The long knife slashed in an arc where Judson's head had been a moment before.

He dropped to his knees, grappled for the slave's ragged trousers. A work-toughened hand clasped his throat, cutting off his air. He heard the guttural breathing of his attacker, then the *whissh* of the knife hacking at his throat—

Wildly, Judson wrenched free and rolled. The slave jumped after him, hacked again. The blade struck Judson's left boot, cut through the leather but didn't break the skin. The renegade slave's downward stroke had thrown him off balance. Judson sprang up, used his head to butt the black in the stomach. In seconds, fright had torn the cobwebs out of his mind.

The slave pitched over backwards. He cursed Judson in West African dialect. The cursing ended in a yelp as Judson stamped on the slave's wrist. The gory right hand opened. The field knife was loose. Judson snatched it up, leaped back, panting—

A shadow fell across the lawn from the dining room. Judson whipped his head around, saw his father with his sword buckled on and a British-made horse pistol in each hand.

"Kill him," Angus ordered as the terrified slave struggled to rise.

Judson hesitated. Angus made a sound deep in his throat; a wordless condemnation. In two steps he reached the floundering slave, who blocked his face with his scarlet forearms, shrieking, "Mist' Fletcher—*don'*—"

Angus shoved the horse pistol against the slave's chest and fired.

Clang and *clang,* the Sermon Hill bell spread its message of terror through the still November night. Angus treated his son to one final glare of utter loathing, then disappeared around the corner of the house, on the run.

Judson turned his back on the grisly corpse with the huge, dripping cavity in the chest. The curing barn collapsed in a crash of burning timbers and sky-spraying sparks. The slaves were being whipped into submission by the black drivers; being formed up into bucket lines that stretched from the springhouse. He heard two more shots, new screaming—and then, off across the fields, a series of ululating yells that sent worms of horror gnawing through his mind.

The renegade slaves were loose not just at Shermon Hill, but out in the countryside—

That made him run like a man demented.

Upstairs first, for his own horse pistol and the knife for the sheath in his boot. Then through the red confusion to the stable, where he flung a saddle on his roan,

trying not to hear the pitiless crack of the whips beating the less able-bodied slaves back to their cabins.

The fire seemed under control now. It had spread to the roofs of the other curing barns, but slaves on ladders were dousing the flames with buckets of water. Judson mounted, jerked the roan's head savagely, galloped past the cabins and down to the main road.

At a crossroads he encountered a dozen men from neighboring estates, all summoned by the bell. They reined in, shouting questions at him.

"Stand aside!"

When they didn't, he booted the roan, jumped the roadside ditch and thundered by along the shoulder, tortured by what he saw through the trees in the distance.

Seth McLean's house. Ablaze.

He booted the roan still harder, the wind carrying those piercing howls to him twice more before he turned into the lane leading to Seth's property.

Riding fast toward the curving front drive, he saw that his original estimate of the situation had been wrong. Slave cabins, not the main residence, were afire. But the front door of the great house stood open. He heard terrified wails from within.

He jumped from the saddle and sped across the veranda between the tall white pillars. He heard mounted men back along the lane. He paused in the doorway, saw another eight or ten galloping toward the house, swords swinging from their hips, muskets and pistols in their hands. In the distance, the bell still clanged.

Judson wiped his sweat-blurred eyes, entered the foyer and gagged.

Hacked by a field knife, Seth McLean lay on the parquet. An ear missing. An arm. One foot. The sickening stench of blood filled the air.

Judson heard something stir in the darkened parlor. He aimed the horse pistol at the arch—

And watched two black girls in long dresses and kerchiefs come forward out of the gloom. Both were young—and weeping. House help.

"Upstairs," one pleaded in a feeble voice. "Love o' God, Mist' Fletcher—*upstairs.*"

In the drive, the plantation men were dismounting. Judson swayed a moment, drunk again. But not from wine. From the slaughter, from the unavoidable truth:

This is what happens when one man chains another. God damn my father for not understanding—

Somewhere on the upper floor, a woman screamed.

Judson climbed the stairs three at a time, maddened almost beyond sense. His heart hammered so violently his chest hurt. The memory of Seth lying butchered brought bile back to his throat. But he kept running, toward the source of that scream keening down the long corridor where two chimneyed candles flickered, islands of yellow in the darkness—

At the hall's end, a door on the left stood open. The screaming came from that room; mindless; mortally afraid. He shouted Peggy's name as he plunged toward the rectangle of light on the carpet, skidded to a stop outside, hate welling when he looked in.

She lay on the floor. Half her nightgown was in shreds, the rest completely gone. A young black bent over her, his trousers around his ankles. A field knife shone in one hand.

The slave turned at the sound of Judson's footsteps. His other hand held scraps of pastel fabric. Behind him, Peggy thrashed and wailed, her legs spread. A

moment's distorted glance showed Judson the secret place he'd thought about so often; the curling dark hair against the pale skin. He saw her small, firm breasts as well. But there was no excitement in it; only horror. Seth's wife shielded her face with her forearms as she screamed—

Desperately, the slave lunged with the field knife. His pants at his ankles made him stumble. Judson hammered the barrel of the horse pistol on the slave's wrist. The knife clacked to the floor.

The black swayed forward, afraid now. Judson used his free hand to catch the sweaty chin, prop the slave up. The weight put great strain on his arm and shoulder. His right knee buckled. But he needed only a moment more—

The young slave saw what was coming. His mouth opened like some ivory-lined chasm. Judson shoved the muzzle of the horse pistol between the black's teeth and pulled the trigger.

The black's body seemed to leap upward, then landed half on top of Peggy McLean. She recoiled from the weight she couldn't identify, tore at it with maniacal hands and kept on screaming. Judson tried not to look at the reddened gobbets of brain matter and bone the pistol ball had deposited on the rumpled bed and the wall behind.

He kicked the dead slave's body aside, laid the still-smoking pistol on the carpet, bent over the flailing woman. He started to speak, noticed something else: a few glistening drops of milky fluid in the black tangle between her legs. And drying stains inside her thighs.

He closed his eyes, bent his head, jammed one palm over his face until he was able to control himself.

Then, as gently as possible, he touched her hair.

"Peggy?" he whispered. "Peggy, look here. It's Judson."

The backs of his fingers accidentally brushed her cheek. She shrieked again, trying to hitch her bare body away from whoever was touching her.

"Peggy, you're all right. For God's sake look at me," Judson pleaded, unaware of the tears on his cheeks. He repeated it:

"Look at me!"

She opened her eyes; those beautiful, luminous dark eyes he'd coveted for so long. Her gaze was unfocused; opaque.

She lifted one hand, as if on the threshold of recognition. Then something quenched it. She recoiled, hand whipping over to shield her face as the screaming started again, louder and shriller than before. She bent her knees, hitched her hips away from the terror in her own mind—

Dry-eyed now, Judson ran downstairs and found the two shivering house girls. From behind the main building came the familiar crack of whips and discharging pistols.

"Go up to her," Judson ordered. "Lock yourselves in with her and take care of her. Don't open the door unless it's someone you know personally. A white man. If anything happens to her, I'll come back and kill you both."

They obeyed without hesitation as Judson ran out into the darkness.

V

SOME FORTY men answered the summons of Sermon Hill's alarm bell that night. Mounted, they stormed through the tobacco fields, youths with torches in the van. They shot, sabered or whipped any black they found running loose. Judson

traveled with one group and did his part, short of actually firing his pistol. He rode like a man half dead, only marginally conscious of details of what was going on.

Though not completely like the vividly remembered outbreaks of past years, the one that had ignited at Sermon Hill, McLean's and one other plantation further downriver resembled earlier uprisings in at least one way. It was fueled and given momentum by rage more than reason. Poorly organized and planned, it began to weaken as soon as the planters took to the saddle with their superior weapons and jangling shackles. It crumbled further as whites rode in leading chained slaves in twos and threes. It dissolved completely about midnight, when another group arrived at Sermon Hill with the corpse of big, blue-muscled Larned dragging on the ground, pulled by a rope around one ankle.

Larned had been shot in the back with a musket ball while attempting to swim the Rappahannock. His noisy thrashing attracted a passing party of whites. Down on the river bank, they killed him.

"Poor dumb nigger," remarked one of the party, without any real pity. "He was trying to swim across to the other side. Didn't have one damn idea of the way to Williamsburg."

Angus Fletcher ordered Larned's head cut off and exhibited on a pole in front of the cottage belonging to the dead overseer.

More and more slaves were rounded up in the hours after midnight. Most wailed for mercy, claiming that they had only done what they thought was right: "S'posed to go fight with Gummer Dunmo." To start the outbreak, Larned and a few co-conspirators had circulated word of Dunmore's outrageous offer.

Judson listened to the fearful, unlettered pleas and shook his head sadly. At minimum, each runaway would receive a murderous lashing that might cripple him for life.

One pocket of resistance remained. Half a dozen slaves, male and female, hadn't surrendered, yet hadn't been quick enough to escape from Sermon Hill after the diversionary fire was discovered. The slaves had thoughtlessly holed up in the smokehouse. Angus Fletcher issued orders for brushwood to be piled around the building. He had been informed that Larned's woman, Dicey, was one of those inside.

While Judson watched from horseback a few yards away, Angus lighted a torch. The old Scot turned his back on his son's obvious disapproval and applied the torch to the brush. Within minutes, there was a stench of scorching flesh. Cries of human pain mingled with the fire's crackling.

A charred door fell outward. Dicey appeared, soot-covered, pleading for mercy. Angus Fletcher ordered her shot. A planter with a freshly loaded musket put it to his shoulder and obliged.

Judson wheeled his roan away from the carnage, wanting the solace of alcohol. As much alcohol as he could consume, as quickly as he could consume it.

First, though, he made inquiries of the loyal house blacks. Yes, the situation at McLean's was under control. Peggy's mother and father had been summoned from the Ashford plantation.

Perhaps thirty blacks in all had been slain outright. Scores more would be maimed by their punishment. Still, that represented a smaller economic loss than if the rebellion had gone unchecked even for another few hours. Judson heard men laughing and congratulating each other as he headed upstairs.

He locked himself in his room and started to drink himself insensible. For

some reason it proved difficult. Long after he should have fallen into a daze, he heard the last dreadful cries from the smokehouse.

Or were they only in his mind?

Judson's chin sagged onto his chest. He speculated in a thick-witted way that the burning alive of six prime bucks and wenches would no doubt be considered a good investment by old Angus. An example to insure tranquility for months, even years to come—

Presently the rum did put him in a stupor. Yet even then, he heard the slaves' screaming.

And Peggy's.

___VI

SETH McLEAN's funeral was held at an immaculate white Presbyterian church six miles from Sermon Hill. The whole district attended—except for Seth's widow. Three days earlier, her father had taken her away from the McLean house in a closed coach, so that she might recuperate—if that were possible— among her closest kin. In the interim, McLean's overseer Williams was to operate the plantation.

Judson rode to the church ten minutes after Angus left Sermon Hill. He didn't care to share the old man's company.

When the pastor finished eulogizing Seth McLean and turned to speculating on Jehovah's mysterious and unfathomable reasons for taking human life in its prime, Judson rose up in a back pew. He had been drinking since dawn. In fact he had taken his last pull at the doorway of the little country church. He created a disturbance by shouting at the pastor:

"Jehovah didn't kill Seth. Or the nigras either. We did."

Several of the church elders converged on Judson and hustled him from the sanctuary. He laughed in a crazy, embittered way as they hoisted him onto his horse and sent him away up the road. Then the elders went back inside, shaking their heads.

There, Judson supposed as he groped for another jug in his saddlebag, Angus Fletcher would be seated in the very front pew, his head bowed in abject prayer for the forgiveness of sins—

Particularly those committed by his satanically inspired second son.

___VII

A GRAY December morning, with rain tapping the glass. Judson let the curtain fall on the misted view of the wharf beside the Rappahannock.

The wharf was empty. A factor had been found, and the canoes had come at last. This year's crop had brought a modest profit. Trade with the ports of England hadn't ceased completely. But most of the planters considered that inevitable—just as they now regarded war as inevitable.

Judson rummaged through the odds and ends of clothing remaining to be packed. He discovered he'd miscounted the pairs of linen underdrawers. He added two more to the pile.

He just wasn't thinking clearly. Images of Peggy McLean kept intruding. First the Peggy he'd courted, warm-eyed and laughing. Then the harrowing face of the screaming girl he'd discovered in the McLean bedroom—

Finishing his counting, he saw the second picture again. He began to shudder. Only one remedy for that. He relied on it almost constantly these days. Since he had to face his father shortly, that justified a second drink.

He set the jug aside and picked up the folded sheets of parchment. Carrying these, he lurched down the graceful curving staircase to his father's cramped corner office behind the conservatory.

Judson rolled back the sliding door and walked in. Then he rolled the door shut with a loud bang.

Framed against a window overlooking the slave cabins and the raw lumber already nailed up for the framework of a new smokehouse and curing barn, Angus Fletcher took his old clay pipe out of his mouth and scowled. The room reeked of Sermon Hill's own fragrant leaf.

"You know I don't care to be disturbed when I'm working on the accounts, Judson." The old man waved the pipe's long stem at several open ledgers.

"Appears to me you're smoking, not doing figures, Father."

Angus sighed. "May God forgive you for your neverending disrespect."

"Oh, I think He's too busy with more worthy folk to bother with the likes of me," Judson grinned. He held up the parchment sheets. "I thought you'd want to know the contents of Donald's letter. It came two days ago and you haven't asked—"

Angus cut him off: "The activities in that nest of vipers are of no interest to me."

"Well," Judson announced with another muzzy smirk, "you needn't count Donald among the vipers any longer."

That caught the old man's attention. With bitterness, Judson recognized concern breaking through the flint facade. *There'll never be such concern for me,* he thought.

Angus asked, "What does Donald say, then?"

"That the gout is afflicting him severely. And the pleurisy. As soon as he can arrange transportation, he'll be returning home."

One veined hand darted out. "Let me see—"

"Sorry, there are parts of the letter that are personal." Judson folded it and shoved it in his belt.

Angus Fletcher sucked on his pipe. "You delight in baiting me."

"I guess I do," Judson admitted in a moment of candor.

"It's your pleasure, your sport. Along with drunkenness—"

"For Christ's sake don't start that."

"How often must I tell you to refrain from blasphemy in my presence, Judson?"

"All right." A weary shrug hid his sudden hurt.

Despite their differences—and the serious imperfections of each—Judson knew he should love this old man. And be loved in return. Sometimes the fact that both seemed incapable of it produced pain that was damn near unbearable.

Judson quickly regained control. His customary mask of smiling arrogance back in place, he continued:

"Truth is, you won't have to suffer my blasphemies at all from now on."

"What do you mean?"

"I'm packing to go to Philadelphia. I'm to serve as Donald's alternate in the Congress until he recovers."

Angus Fletcher sat down in his hand-hewn pine chair, dumbfounded. But not for long:

"Apparently there is no limit to your waywardness."

Weaving on his feet, Judson replied, "Why, I'd say I've been an exemplar of virtue since that unfortunate business at the chapel—"

"An example of debauchery," the old man snorted. "Besotted every waking minute—"

"I told you, don't start—"

"—off at that slut Lottie Shaw's most nights oh, yes, I know about that, too." Reaching out as if he wanted to conceal something private of his own, the old man closed the ledgers one by one, then stacked them. "It's time we had an accounting."

"No accounting necessary, Father. I'm leaving, that's all."

"How will you travel?"

"On horseback." The purpose of the question eluded him.

Angus rectified that: "I can't spare a single nigger to accompany you. Not one, is that clear?"

"Oh, I see. Surely. I'll hire some piece of white trash, then. Send him for the trunk—"

"You are an abomination in the eyes of the Lord," Angus Fletcher declared. "A disgrace to your heritage, to your upbringing—"

"Dammit, I've had enough of your prating!" Judson exploded. "My politics are no different than Donald's!"

"Donald is a misguided innocent compared to you," his father told him. "You shame me in front of the church congregation, you scandalize the Fletcher name with your concern for widow McLean's welfare—no, don't argue! I know how you've had someone from the house bustling over there almost daily to inquire about her! If she hadn't been hurt the night of the rebellion, you'd never have ridden the fields to capture the niggers."

"You've certainly outlined the charges well," Judson said. If only the old man would speak to him kindly just once. *Once!* But that was a forlorn hope. And he recognized that effort was sorely lacking on his side as well. He went on:

"There's not much I can add to your expert presentation of the evidence. I stand accused. Proudly, sir. Proudly—"

"When will you stop your insolence?" the old man fairly screamed.

Judson smiled his most charming smile. "The day you're rotting in hell, which I sincerely hope is your destination."

Paling, Angus Fletcher blinked several times. Water appeared at the corners of his eyes. In a peculiar, strangled voice he asked:

"What is it that you have against me, Judson? Why is it that you hate me so?"

"I've often wondered the same about you, Father. Goodbye—"

As he started to leave, Angus' voice regained its old harshness:

"One moment more."

Judson turned back; recognized the familiar sternness of the lined face. That moment of hesitation and hurt in which they might have reached out symbolically to touch one another was gone. He felt overpoweringly thirsty.

In a level tone, Angus said, "You do not approve of my loyalties to the government which has made it possible for the Fletcher family to prosper. You do not approve of the system of labor that keeps this plantation operating profitably. You certainly never respond to my suggestions for improving your lax morals. It seems to me there is nothing more for you at Sermon Hill—"

He leaned over the desk, pressing his knuckles on the closed ledger on top of the stack:

"Am I plain enough? Nothing—not a farthing."

"I take it this is your way of informing me I'll have no consideration in your will?" It was an upsetting thought, though not entirely unexpected.

"That's correct. You have already tried me beyond all reasonable limits. Go to Philadelphia—step off this property for that purpose—and I will never permit you to set foot on it again."

"Oh—" Judson tried to muster another grin, couldn't. "A little bait dangled? If I repent, everything will be well?"

"What's the harm in that? I'd redeem your soul if I could, since you won't do it yourself." All at once the man sounded tired. "You seem bent on destroying yourself."

"Thoughts like that are too deep for me," Judson said with a loose shrug. Inside, something broke with tearing pain. He shut his eyes a moment. Then he reopened them, managing at last the kind of totally cavalier smile that could light his face. He reached for the door. "Goodbye, sir."

"You do understand what I intend, Judson?"

"Of course. 'And if thy right hand offend thee, cut it off and cast it from thee, for it is profitable for thee—' "

"Stop."

" '—that one of thy members should perish—' "

"*Stop, goddamn you!*"

But Judson kept on, loudly: " '—and not that thy whole body should be cast into hell.' All right, I'll do the service in hell in your place. For the moment! That way, you can keep fancying yourself spotless and sanctified. Until you arrive to join me." He walked out, rolling the door shut with a bang.

Rain rattled on the windows as he hurried through the conservatory. Suddenly he thought he heard a muffled outcry from the office. A cry of grief. His heart leaped—

He hesitated. Thought about going back—

But he didn't.

It was much too late.

VIII

HALF AN hour later, Judson Fletcher left Sermon Hill. His cloak belling behind him, his tricorn cocked low over his forehead to keep off the worst of the rain, he galloped down to the river and turned southeast in the direction of the ferry that would take him across to the road leading north. At a front window of the great house, one curtain was held aside by an unseen hand until Judson's flying cloak vanished in the December mist. Then the curtain was slowly put back in place.

5
The Guns of Winter

A BITTER gale off the Atlantic flung sleet through the November twilight. Philip turned in at the front gate of the Vassall house on Brattle Street, Cambridge. He was chilled clear through, and nervous. Only an hour before, one of his occasional visits with his wife and son had been concluded in unexpected fashion.

Philip had arrived in Watertown to find Anne feeding their stocky infant at her breast. Her color was good, her strength increasing daily. Apart from a continuing concern about the likelihood of full-scale war, what troubled Anne Kent at the moment was her father's poor health.

The lawyer had lain abed for more than three weeks. Wracked by chills and constant coughing, he lacked appetite and was steadily losing weight. During the hour Philip spent with his family, the raspy cough from Ware's bedroom was a worrisome counterpoint to conversation.

On his way back to his regiment, Philip stopped at the tiny shop near the Charles River where his former employer, Ben Edes, had reassembled his press after smuggling the pieces out of Boston in a rowboat. With a few fonts of type, Edes was struggling to publish his patriot newspaper, the *Gazette,* on a more or less regular basis.

But when Philip arrived, he found Edes setting up the press to print paper currency; special currency authorized by the Massachusetts provincial legislature.

There had already been talk in Philip's regiment that such money might be used to pay the soldiers. The possibility caused grumbling and resentment. Money made legal only by the legislative act of a colony in rebellion might not be worth much. Certainly it wouldn't be as readily spendable as the sterling pound. The new currency was being printed in desperation, to purchase needed supplies and materiel for the army. Edes, who looked tired, emphasized the point by showing Philip several plates for various denominations. When Edes turned the plates over, Philip recognized Revere engravings, prints of which had been sold at the old shop in Dassett Alley. Revere had worked one new design on the back of his popular depiction of the Boston Massacre.

"Even new copper for etching the worthless stuff can't be had," Edes complained, just as the front door banged open.

"Are you Philip Kent of the Twenty-ninth Massachusetts?"

Philip whirled to confront the gruff-voiced arrival: an officer of the Marblehead Twenty-first. The unit's trimly outfitted men had been chosen as personal guards for the commanding general's headquarters.

"I'm Kent, yes, sir."

"Christ, you roam around a lot. First I rode to your regiment, then your wife's rooms—come along smartly, if you please. I've a horse for you outside."

"Come along where?" Philip asked. "I'm due back in camp—"

The ruddy-cheeked man seemed skeptical of his own reply:

"No, you're to come with me. To General Washington."

Even Ben Edes looked flabbergasted.

During the uncomfortable ride to Cambridge, Philip's uneasiness increased. The officer said he had no information about the reason for the summons.

Presently they arrived at the large, imposing residence on what was coming to

be called Tory Row. Like many of his neighbors, Mr. Vassall, owner of the property taken over by Washington, had fled to sanctuary with the British in Boston. A few other loyalists who hadn't as yet departed had painted black rings around their chimneys, to signify continuing allegiance to the king.

As he tethered his horse, Philip decided that his involvement in the brawl in the Virginia encampment had somehow caught up with him, and he was due for punishment.

He slipped and slid up the sleet-covered walk. Three officers emerged from the brightly lighted house, arguing. Philip stepped aside, remembering to offer a salute. The officers returned it in perfunctory fashion, giving him over-the-shoulder stares as they hurried on to their horses. Their expressions showed their astonishment at the sight of a common soldier of the line approaching headquarters; a soaked, bedraggled soldier at that.

More apprehensive than ever, Philip moved on. Near the front of the house, wind tore at a swaying pole. At the top, a flag cracked and fluttered. A flag Philip hadn't seen before. Britain's Union Jack in the upper left corner was familiar, but not the red and white horizontal stripes. He counted thirteen, just before the armed Marblehead men flanking the doorway demanded identification.

Philip gave his name and unit. He was astonished when he was admitted instantly, with instructions to turn left and knock at the drawing-room door. He did.

"Come in, come in!"

Teeth chattering from more than the cold of the night, he obeyed.

___II

BEHIND A littered writing desk, General George Washington faced a wall map representing the Boston area. A few candles lent a soft glow to the room. Philip was startled to see a familiar figure all but hiding most of a chair.

Henry Knox.

Knox lifted his silk-wrapped hand to acknowledge Philip's presence while the third—feminine—occupant of the room set a tray on a corner of the desk. On the tray were glasses, a decanter of madeira and several oranges.

The plump-cheeked, diminutive woman was dressed in an elegant gown of pale blue. She glanced at Philip and smiled in a friendly way. The same couldn't be said of Washington or Knox. Both looked weary; under strain.

Philip said, "Kent of the Twenty-ninth Massachusetts reporting as ord—"

The tall, big-boned general in dark blue and buff cut him off with a gesture:

"We may eliminate the formalities. Time presses." His gray-blue eyes shifted to the woman, softening a little. "Our thanks for the refreshments, my dear. Now if you'll be so kind as to allow us privacy—"

"Of course," the woman murmured, withdrawing quickly and closing the door behind her. Philip assumed the woman must be the general's wife, only recently arrived from the family plantation on the Potomac River in Virginia.

Camp gossip about Martha Custis Washington was uniformly favorable; she was reputed to be a kind, gracious person who preferred to be at her husband's side instead of at faraway Mount Vernon. Everyone knew the general loved his estate, and the refined squire's life it afforded. Everyone also knew that if a British force ever penetrated up the Potomac, Mount Vernon would surely be burned.

Yet Washington's wife had placed her husband above her opulent home, and traveled north in bad weather over difficult roads to be with him. Unexpectedly, Mrs. Washington's arrival in Cambridge strengthened the general's own standing among the troops. Plainly delighted by his wife's presence, Washington seemed less austere; became something more of a human being in the eyes of the men who served him.

The general indicated the fruit and wine:

"Take your ease and help yourself to refreshments, Kent. Mr. Knox requested your presence."

"And your assistance, Philip."

"Certainly, Henr—sir. What can I do?"

"Find me at least one more good man to go with us on a mission of considerable urgency."

Philip picked up an orange, began to peel it clumsily. Breaking the skin with his thumbnail, he squirted juice onto his coat, further compounding his nervousness. *Us,* Knox had said. Then he recalled some reference to a scheme Knox was hatching; Knox had mentioned it back in September.

To cover his awkwardness, Philip slipped into a chair Knox indicated and dispensed with trying to eat the messy orange. Washington's shadow lay black and immense over the wall map. He put one finger on the outline of the coast:

"We face a perilous situation here at Boston, Kent. A situation which Mr. Knox with his special knowledge and abilities may help us remedy. I had hoped to be able to commission him colonel for this duty. That's temporarily delayed— the damn paperwork required to gain Congressional approval of an appointment is beyond belief. But Henry will still serve as commander of the expedition in question."

Washington knocked knuckles against the map. "Prolonged hostilities now appear certain. Especially since His Majesty has declared us in rebellion. At any hour we can look for Billy Howe to break his ministerial troops out of Boston to attack our positions—"

General Howe, Philip knew, had already replaced the well-intentioned but ineffective Thomas Gage as commander of the Crown forces locked up on the Boston peninsula.

"—and here—" Again Washington knocked the map, in its southeast quadrant. The heights of Dorchester, overlooking the Neck and the city. "—we are vulnerable."

Knox put in, "For that reason I intend to procure a train of artillery. The guns we need to fortify our defenses and insure that Howe does not break out. I must have one or two dependable men with me, Philip."

"Knox recommends you," Washington said with a keen look, while Philip thought of his wife, his son, his ailing father-in-law. "You are of course not compelled to undertake the duty—"

Two pairs of eyes fixed on him, waiting. Washington's remark wasn't entirely truthful. Those steady gazes left him no choice.

"If I can be of use, General, then of course—"

Washington's smile was wry. "A refreshing attitude, eh, Henry?" He swung back to Philip. "Mr. Knox learned that you plan to re-enlist, Kent."

"Yes, sir, that's my intention."

"Well, you are in a minority," the general grumbled. "It seems that most of our men have no desire except to retire to their chimney corners. In fact, such a dearth of public spirit and want of virtue—such stock-jobbing and versatility in

all the low arts to obtain personal advantage—such grubby self-seeking per-
vades this ill-formed army that I shouldn't be at all surprised at *any* disaster
which—"

The rising voice cut off abruptly. Somehow it heartened Philip to see the
general momentarily embarrassed by an excess of temper.

"However—" Washington cleared his throat. "You heard Mr. Knox say he
needs a pair of aides he can count on—"

"Can you suggest someone from your own unit?" Knox asked.

Philip thought, chose words with care: "I know a great many men. But I'm
not sure whether—"

"Whether they're trustworthy?" Washington broke in.

Philip's nod acknowledged the truth he'd been unwilling to speak. Then, an
inspiration:

"There is one man I met—he seems very courageous and forthright. He's
from your own colony, General."

That pleased Washington: "What's his name?"

"Experience Tait. I don't know anything about his military ability. But as a
friend, I can't speak of him too highly. When I couldn't find a physician, he went
to Watertown to deliver my wife of our son."

"For money?" Washington asked.

Philip smiled. "No, all he wanted was a drink afterward."

"A Virginian, all right," Washington said. To Knox: "Get him."

Knox nodded, said to Philip, "I'll arrange matters with your commandant so
we can leave as soon as possible."

"If I may ask—"

The silence of both men gave Philip leave to continue.

"—where will we be going? To one of the outlying towns?" Before the
outbreak of hostilities at Lexington and Concord, various patriot groups had
hidden a few small artillery pieces to protect them from possible British seizure.

Knox stared at his bandaged left hand while Washington unrolled a map lying
on the desk. Philip craned forward, bone-cold again. What Washington was
spreading was not a map of the Massachusetts colony but the whole eastern
seaboard of the continent. Philip began to understand why Henry Knox looked
grim.

"We need many more cannon than we can find in the barns and cellars of
Massachusetts Bay," Washington said. "There is only one place they may be
had—difficult to reach, doubly difficult to return from this time of year. But Mr.
Knox has volunteered to bring the cannon back regardless. You will be going
after the artillery pieces captured some months ago at the British fort here—"

The Virginian's big-boned hand dropped down to thwack a blue patch on the
map, far away from the Boston shore:

"Ticonderoga."

The drawing-room windows whined under the onslaught of the November
wind. The orange fell from Philip's suddenly slack hand, thumped the floor and
rolled to Knox's feet.

The fat young man picked it up and tossed it back to Philip with an empty
smile:

"I'm not surprised at your reaction. The roads are poor where they exist at
all—the distance is formidable—and there's winter to contend with. But we *will*
bring back the guns, because our cause is in extreme danger until they're in
place. I suppose we should again offer you the option of withdrawal—"

Philip shook his head. "No, I agreed to go. I will."

Washington and Knox exchanged brief smiles. But that didn't relieve Philip's awareness of the staggering problems of the venture to which he'd just committed himself. Sleet struck the windows like a rattle of small-arms fire, and the panes once again gave off a forlorn, whining sound.

III

ON THE eve of the new year, 1776, Philip Kent half believed that he'd been submerged in a nightmare from which he would never awaken.

How long he'd been working, he didn't know. Since eternity, it seemed. The axe felt twenty times as heavy as it should. He swung it up again, brought it down, chopped through the slushy surface of the ice—

And heard a terrifying crack just to his right.

"Better stand back!" Eph Tait yelled from a couple of yards away. "She sounds ready to go—"

No sooner was the last word out than Philip felt the ice of the Mohawk River give way. A large section dropped out from under one foot. He teetered wildly, off balance.

His right boot plunged into icy water. Eph Tait threw down his axe and leaped, pulling Philip back to safety with a yank. Tait let go and Philip sat down hard on his rump. The ice crackled again, but held. Philip climbed to his feet and rubbed his rear, grimacing.

"Better'n a river bath, ain't it?" Tait wanted to know.

"Not much."

"Some thanks I get," Tait said, grinning.

From one shore of the Mohawk to the other, shadow-figures—hired teamsters plus volunteers dragooned locally by the persuasive, determined Knox—continued to chop openings in the ice. The holes permitted water to flood up and freeze a new layer over the perilously thin crust on which the men worked. A high winter moon lit the landscape and the workmen with eerie touches of white. Behind Philip and Tait, the lights of the settlement called Half Moon gleamed on a point of land where the Mohawk and Hudson met. In Half Moon right now, Knox was undoubtedly engaged in his interminable haggling for more sledges, more horses and oxen, more drivers to push the bizarre caravan southward—

"All this work's a waste!" Philip exploded, his breath a cloud in the moonlight. He was still butt-sore; dull pain tormented every muscle. His rag-wrapped hands were stiff as sticks. "We'll never get them across such thin ice."

"We will with a good sharp freeze." Eph Tait slapped his friend's shoulder. "Come on, let's mosey back. I'd say we could draw our whiskey ration 'bout now, wouldn't you? Half an hour's rest'll do our bones some good."

"A half hour standing still and I'll be frozen to death."

"Listen, I'm the one oughta be complainin'!" Tait retorted as they crossed the slippery, moon-bright ice. On their right, the black line of trees on the Hudson's east bank showed an edge of silver. "You volunteered me for this damn duty! A real honor! 'Bout the only honor I'll get is if I get killed an' they bury me. Say, you 'spose Washington'd come to our funerals personal, Philip?"

"If he could, I think he would," Philip said absently.

"Least he could do for a pair o' fine gentleman volunteers, I'd say—"

As always, Tait's chatter helped relieve Philip's gloom, and the immediate prospect of a warming drink took his mind off his yearning to be back in Massachusetts with Anne and their son. He slogged on toward the bank where oxen lowed and men huddled around a log fire built near the sledges with their precious cargo lashed down by a webbing of ropes.

At first the journey with Knox had been a delight. Philip reveled in unexpected vistas of mountainous country; the vast, silent forests of York State blanketed with fluffy, fast-melting snow. They had reached Fort George in early December, then pushed north to star-shaped Fort Ticonderoga where the "noble train of artillery," as Knox termed it, waited for them.

Fifty-eight pieces. Four-pounders to twenty-four-pounders, Howitzers and some small coehorns and a few mortars including one giant that had been nicknamed The Old Sow. In size, the captured cannon ranged from a foot long to eleven feet; in weight, from a hundred pounds to over five thousand. A hundred and twenty thousand pounds in all, Knox calculated. To be transported through wilderness, south and then eastward, three hundred miles in the depth of winter.

Initially, the artillery—along with one invaluable barrel of fine-quality British flints and twenty-three crates of shot—had to be freighted down Lake George in a collection of pirogues and batteaux. A single big scow took the largest pieces. At Sabbath Day Point, the scow foundered and sank. But in shallow water. Bailing operations set her afloat again.

With the help of the wealthy York State patrician Philip Schuyler, already appointed a major general in the Continental forces, Knox secured eight specially built sledges and eighty yoke of oxen. But thawed, mushy ground prevented the caravan from getting underway immediately. Finally, late in December, snow pelted down—and the drivers began to lash their beasts forward, the sledges slipping and sliding on runners. New Year's brought the train of wrangling men, laboring animals and precious guns to the river junction—where capricious weather once again betrayed them. In hopes of strengthening a route to the Mohawk's southern shore, the hired men and local volunteers had been set to work making holes in the ice.

"Be damned if I ain't goin' home, and my team too," Philip heard a man complain as he and Tait approached the welcome warmth of the bonfire. "Twenty-four shillings a day ain't half enough when the animals won't be fit to work after this here trip's over. Hell, they'll probably be drowned 'fore it's done." Philip recognized a yellow-bearded farmer name Crenkle. The man had hired on with his oxen at Glens Falls.

"Twenty-four shillings is what you agreed to, neighbor," Tait said in an unfriendly tone as he picked up a dirty earthenware cup. He popped the bung of a whiskey cask resting on a trestle. "You should of bitched to Colonel Knox then."

"Don't give me that colonel shit," Crenkle said. "He ain't nothin' but a civilian. A lazy one to boot! Sittin' on his ass in the village—eatin' dinner while we work ourselves half to death on that blasted river—"

"No, sir. Not dining."

The voice whirled Crenkle around. In the firelight his breath plumed as he exhaled.

Cloaked, Henry Knox came waddling out of the darkness leading his fretful horse. Despite his girth and his pudding face, there was a severity in his eyes that made Crenkle step backward.

"I have been hunting men to serve in the stead of cowards and malingerers like you." Knox snatched a cup from Crenkle's hand and flung it away.

The cup shattered against the muzzle of a howitzer. Filthy, half-frozen men around the fire exchanged furtive looks. Some of the men were amused; others far from it. Their guilt showed.

"Drag home like a cur if you wish, Crenkle," Knox said. "But if you do, you've broken your contract. I will feel free to confiscate your oxen as a penalty."

"*Confiscate*—!" Crenkle screamed. "You ain't got any right whatsoever—"

"Why sure he does, brother. Here 'tis."

Philip spun, startled. He hadn't been aware of Eph Tait slipping off into the dark. Tait had returned as silently as he'd gone—bringing with him his Kentucky rifle that traveled carefully lashed in place on the sledge carrying The Old Sow. The long muzzle glittered with highlights from the fire.

"She's primed and ready to jine the argument," Tait advised the furious Crenkle. "What was you sayin' about the colonel's rights?"

"Damned high-handed bunch of army bastards—!" Crenkle began, wiping his beard with a wind-raw hand. But he sounded less than sure of himself.

Knox glared. "Get back to the river or go home. Now."

Muttering, Crenkle crept away from the campfire.

Toward the river.

Knox sighed in a disgusted way, tramped to Tait and Philip. "Tonight I sent a letter to General Washington, advising him of our delay. I assured him we'll cross the Mohawk the moment it's reasonably safe to do so. Can we hope that'll be soon?"

"Ice is still pretty weak, Henry," Philip said through stiff lips.

"We must risk it. We've another crossing down at Albany—and after we turn east, the hardest terrain of all. The longer we wait, the worse the danger of a blizzard."

Neither Philip nor Tait required convincing. Having ridden west with Knox and pored over his maps, they were well aware of the mountains separating the Hudson valley and Boston. There were no conventional roads or easy passes through the range. To be caught there in a full-scale winter storm might mean days or weeks of delay.

Eph Tait sighed. "We was goin' to lay off half an hour like the rest of 'em. But I guess we better not. Come on, Philip, let's go chop us some more ice."

"And watch that man Crenkle," Knox advised. "I'd count on him to sacrifice one of the guns—or any one of us—to save his scurvy hide."

IV

THE MOHAWK was crossed a day later, with the temporary loss of only one eighteen-pounder. Several hours' labor with pulleys and chains retrieved the sunken cannon.

By the end of the first week in January the straggling caravan reached Albany, a substantial town where a spirit somewhat more patriotic than Crenkle's prevailed. The ruddy-faced burghers turned out to cheer the arrival of the first sledges and half-frozen men.

General Schuyler was a resident of the district. His influence produced a

good-sized party of new volunteers who helped speed the guns across the Hudson, reasonably solid now thanks to a spell of much colder weather. On the crossing another large cannon drowned, but next morning it was raised back up through a fourteen-foot hole in the ice. In return for the help of the citizens who manned the salvage equipment, Knox christened the piece The Albany.

The caravan was far behind schedule. In November, Knox had told Washington that the entire overland journey of three hundred miles could be accomplished in fifteen days. On the tenth of January, the first teams were just starting their climb toward the snow-powdered spruces and pines in the foothills of the mountain barrier that still lay between the guns and the general who needed them so desperately.

V

AT A night camp, fresh snow ankle-deep on the ground, Eph Tait asked Philip how he'd come to be involved in the military struggle:

"I mean, once or twice I heard kind of a funny turn of phrase out o' you. Like you was foreign, maybe."

Philip held stiff palms toward the fire, ignoring a sullen stare from Crenkle across the way.

"I am, Eph. I was born in France. I learned English early, but sometimes I don't say a word quite the proper way."

"Be damned," Tait declared. "How'd you get to Boston?"

Philip shared the entire story with his friend. Described how his father's wife and son, the Amberlys in England, had tried to dispute his claim to his inheritance, then had cruelly hoaxed Philip and his mother into believing James Amberly had died. Because he had incurred the wrath of Amberly's one lawful son, Roger, Philip and his mother had been forced to flee the Kentish countryside. They sought sanctuary in London, hoping to hide in its crowds and teeming streets.

For a time, the plan worked. Philip learned the printing trade at a shop operated by a family named Sholto, met Dr. Franklin, the American, who encouraged him to emigrate to the colonies.

But in Kent, Philip had done more than make his half-brother angry; he'd crippled Roger Amberly's hand in a fight. The vengeful young man hired a professional assassin to track Philip and his mother. Again they were forced to flee.

This time, Philip followed Franklin's advice and chose new opportunity in a new land, instead of a return to their life of poverty in France. Broken-hearted because her dream of wealth and position for her son had been destroyed, Philip's mother died on the sea voyage.

In Boston Philip again took up the printing trade, with Mr. Ben Edes. As a result, he was slowly drawn into the patriot movement. He met Samuel Adams. The rich, dandified merchant, John Hancock. Paul Revere—

Philip exhibited a front tooth for Eph. A tooth carved out of hippo tusk and wired in place by Revere, who practiced dentistry to help support his family— when he wasn't grinding out engravings on popular subjects, working in silver, or riding express for the patriot committees.

Philip told Eph about the unexpected arrival of his half-brother Roger as an

officer in the British forces garrisoning the city. He even described how he'd helped an infantryman, a redcoat named George Lumden, to desert—and how he'd run Roger through with a British bayonet to save Anne Ware.

"I suppose secrets like those don't matter much any more."

"Wouldn't think so," Eph said. The gazes of both men were drawn almost unconsciously toward the steep, dark slopes where great evergreens soughed in the night wind. Tomorrow they would begin the ascent of those slopes.

Eph got tickled then, huddling closer to the fire and wrapping his hands around his body as he laughed:

"My Lord, I didn't realize I fell in with such fancy company. A duke for a papa—!"

"And his son's blood on my hands," Philip said somberly.

He had omitted only one major part of the story: his violently emotional affair with the young woman who was Roger's fiancee in England and, later, his wife. Alicia Amberly, daughter of the Earl of Parkhurst, had undertaken the difficult Atlantic crossing to be with her mortally wounded husband, who was being cared for by Alicia's relatives, wealthy Philadelphia Tories. In answer to a letter from Alicia, Philip had ridden to the Quaker city to see her, and for a time, he thought of resuming their liaison. Even thought of marrying the beautiful, passionate young girl.

Then, in a chance encounter with Franklin who had just returned from England, Philip discovered the hoax perpetrated by Roger and Lady Jane Amberly. Philip's father was still alive. And Alicia knew it. She'd only reestablished contact because Philip stood to inherit everything now that Roger was dead.

Though Alicia professed love for him, the revelation of her deceit was a turning point for Philip, bringing him at last to a sorting-out of his own thoughts and emotions. He returned to Boston to marry the girl he knew he really loved; and to fight in the army.

"To date, a not particularly distinguished career," he said at the end. "I'm not proud of some of the things I've done to survive. I've killed more than just my half-brother—"

"Figgered that," Tait said. "It shows in a man's eyes. Philip—you 'spose this crazy-quilt army's got any chance atall? I heard the lobsterbacks might even bring over hired Germans."

"So did I. To answer your question—I don't know, Eph."

"But you think all this is worth it, whatever happens?"

"I guess I do. Most of the time any more, I don't go that deep. I just go day to day."

"Smart, I reckon," Tait said, looking again to the star-silvered foothills above them. "Tomorrow ain't gonna be one of the better ones, I bet."

VI

"ANOTHER CHECKROPE! You up there—*tie her fast!*"

Philip's shouted order started the teamster moving. The man was behind him, near the top of the forty-degree slope. The hillside was layered with fresh snow; patterned in blazing white and deep shadow by the January sun falling between the huge trees. The sun was melting the snow's crust just enough to worsen the already treacherous surface.

On its third day in the roadless mountains, the artillery train was stretched out for several miles. Each descent of the rolling terrain had to be negotiated with special care, and proper distance maintained between the sledges in case of accident. Philip was about halfway to the bottom of the hill, tramping beside the sledge bearing The Old Sow.

Below, on level ground, another sledge carrying two coehorns was about to start upward again. Eph Tait ran alongside while the drivers lashed their balky horses. Over his arm Tait carried a number of heavy drag chains which he'd unhooked from the runners as soon as the coehorn sledge reached the bottom of the steep hill.

Now The Old Sow was being freighted down that same hillside, and four checkropes fastened to trees higher up were proving insufficient. One had already frayed and popped, causing Philip to yell at the man near the summit. The teamster was starting to string another rope around a thick bole. But slowly. Too damn slowly—

The drag chains under the Sow's sledge seemed to be having little effect. The sledge kept sliding faster. Foundering in the snow, the yoked oxen felt the push. Crenkle, their driver, didn't help matters by screaming obscenities and whipping them frantically with a supple stick.

The sledge lurched sideways, to the left. Philip jumped back to keep his feet from being crushed by the runners. Despite the chill air, he was awash with sweat under his filthy clothing.

"Crenkle, ease up with the stick, they're panicky enough," Philip bawled at the farmer. Crenkle threw him a defiant look and kept flailing.

The back end of the sledge lurched again, further left—toward a natural drop-off of about twenty feet. If even part of the sledge slipped over, oxen and all would go. The mortar might be cracked beyond repair—

"Hurry up with the rope!" Philip screamed, hand cupped around his beard-stubbled mouth. The man higher up still seemed to be moving with maddening slowness. He was just starting to secure the end of the rope that led all the way back down to the vehicle bearing the Sow. Six ropes in all were lashed to staples on the bed of the sledge. One had broken; only one more was available, trailing loose on the hillside, tracing a snake pattern in the snow.

Tense, Philip watched the sledge slide again. Only a couple of feet this time—

He whipped his glance back up to the man struggling with the rope. *Why couldn't he get it tied faster?*

One of the oxen bellowed, a terrifying sound that echoed through the mountain stillness. Philip spun, saw Crenkle flogging the left-hand ox, down on both forelegs. The rear of the sledge started another slide, straight toward the drop-off—

Just as the man fastening the checkrope around the tree finished his last knot, the sledge's back end swung all the way left, pointing toward the drop. The newly tied knots failed to hold. The rope snapped, uncoiled from around the trunk, end whipping free—

Another rope broke, leaving two in place. At that precise instant, Crenkle's maniacal beating of the oxen achieved results—disastrous ones:

The left-hand ox lurched up and lunged ahead. The other beast felt the pull and responded in tandem. The sledge was jerked forward too precipitously—no longer in danger of slipping over the drop, but given a sudden giant yank that started it sliding straight down the melted, slippery track—

The sledge picked up speed, spuming snow from the runners despite the drag

chains. Crenkle saw the sledge gathering momentum. His reason deserted him. Before Philip could react, Crenkle dropped his stick, jerked a hatchet from his hide belt, started chopping the traces.

"Don't release them, Crenkle!" Philip yelled. But the frightened farmer paid no attention. He hacked the last of the traces, stretched out his free hand and jerked the pin connecting the yoketree to the front of the sledge.

The freed oxen lunged to the right, off the dangerously melted path. An instant later, the sledge left Philip and Crenkle behind, then hurtled by the oxen, still gathering speed.

Philip reached Crenkle and knocked him down with one mauling fist. "You stinking yellow animal—!"

Crenkle snuffled, on his knees and trying to stop blood leaking from his nose. The sledge was a good way down the hill now, thundering toward the bottom where Eph Tait was just releasing the last drag chain from the coehorn carrier.

Tait heard the rumbling, turned his head. For a moment, sunlight made his bad eye glow like a star—

Time seemed to suspend. Philip was only marginally conscious of his legs pumping through the deep snow. He shouted incoherent warnings.

He saw Eph Tait frozen with surprise in the patch of sunlit snow; Eph's jaw dropping at the sight of the juggernaut hurtling toward him. The Virginian started to run.

The drag chains draped over his arm fell to the ground. Somehow he tangled his feet in one of them. Thrashing, he sprawled in the snow—

The mortar sledge hit the bottom of the slope and careened ahead. Tait threw an arm up in front of his face—

He disappeared as the sledge ran over him and slid on past the coehorns, losing momentum on the flat. The sledge's front end rose at the bottom of the next slope, the hillside soon braking its forward progress completely. In the snow behind, something grotesque and loose-limbed flopped.

Philip kept running toward his friend. Then the Virginian screamed.

Philip's beard-matted face distorted. Other teamsters were rushing to Tait's side. Squinting in the sunlight, Philip whirled and ran back up the hill in a shambling gait.

Above him, Crenkle crouched defensively, hatchet upraised. The defensive posture crumpled the moment Philip came close enough for the yellow-bearded farmer to see his almost bestial face. Crenkle threw his hatchet away, turned and jumped from the edge of the drop-off.

At the bottom, he struggled to his feet, flung himself on down the slope, vanishing into a thick stand of pines. Philip retrieved the hatchet, raced for the drop. A voice got through to him then; one of the men from the coehorn sledge:

"Leave him go, Kent! Help us with Tait. He's still alive."

Philip hesitated. The numbed hand holding the hatchet shook. In the distance, the pathetic Crenkle put more ground between himself and the caravan, a scurrying figure appearing and disappearing in sun and shadow.

The teamster at the bottom of the hill shouted Philip's name again. Making a guttural sound, he flung the hatchet down. With a last look at the tiny figure fleeing into the snowy fastness, he went to answer the summons. He never saw Crenkle again.

VII

FORWARD PROGRESS of the artillery train stopped. The sledge carrying The Old Sow had survived the runaway descent with no damage. Nearby, Philip and some of the teamsters erected a crude tent from fresh-cut branches and blankets.

Ten minutes after the tent was up, Philip crawled out of it backwards and let the end blanket fall. He blinked as his eyes adjusted to the blaze of the snow. The blinking didn't clear his vision.

A horseman was struggling down the slope where the Sow's sledge had come to rest. Philip watched the horse slip sideways, falter, then gallop forward, the mountainous figure of Henry Knox bouncing in the saddle.

Inside the improvised tent there was a tormented moan. Philip tried to hide his face by pretending to wipe his nose. But the other teamsters weren't looking at him. They studied the treetops, or gazed at the churned snow marked by Eph Tait's blood, or they simply stared at their rag-wrapped boots. Not a man said a word. The silence was broken only by the occasional whisper of the wind, the frozen creak of a bough, the soft thudding of the hoofs in the snow as Knox swung out of the saddle.

"I got your message and sent ahead for a doctor from Westfield," he said to Philip. He started toward the tent entrance.

Philip grabbed his arm:

"I wouldn't, Henry."

"I must see what attention he needs—"

"From here down—" Philip swallowed, touched his own waist. "No amount of attention is going to help."

Knox turned white as the snowfields. "My God. Is he awake?"

Forcing back tears, Philip nodded. "We dosed him with some whiskey. That stopped the worst of his raving. I even talked to him a minute or so. He—he knows how badly he's been hurt. He wants his rifle with him." Philip's stiff hand lifted in a sad, ironic gesture at the mortar sledge. Fastened to the bed by ropes tied to pins, Eph Tait's Kentucky rifle gleamed blue through a patchy dusting of snow.

"Well, fetch it if it'll be any comfort to him!" Knox said. "It'll take the doctor a while to trek here, so anything that—"

He stopped as Philip shook his head.

"Eph asked me to write his family later, Henry. He wants his rifle loaded."

Knox swayed. Philip had never seen him look so drained. He glanced around the little circle of York State drivers, face after weatherbeaten face, as if hoping one of the men would speak. Philip said to him:

"I'd say the decision's yours, Henry."

"No. No, it's his. Still—" Knox swiped at his face. "There is a moral question—"

"Then you tell him that, Henry. You look at what's left of him and tell him that. I won't."

Silence. The wind mourned through the pines. A branch broke loudly and fell.

"Get the rifle, would you please, Philip? I'll take it in to him. Unless you—?"

"We did our talking. You'll probably have to use more whiskey to wake him."

He turned, trudged to the mortar sledge, dimly aware of shouted curses and snapping whips beyond the crest of the slope down which The Old Sow had

plunged. A new sledge struggling for the summit. Maybe the messengers sent in both directions from the scene of the accident had missed one of the vehicles laboring through the woods. The noise almost seemed a blasphemy as Philip laboriously untied the frozen ropes, opened the ammunition box lashed down beside the rifle, loaded the piece and carried it back to Henry Knox.

Another groan sounded from inside the tent. Then Eph Tait cried someone's name. A woman's, Philip thought. Knox bent to enter, carrying the rifle. Philip walked away.

About five minutes later, leaning his forearm on the cold iron of the giant mortar, Philip heard the shot. Hideously loud; echoing and reechoing through the tree-clad ridges and valleys. He stared at the mortar's maw as if he could destroy it with a single glance. He started when someone touched him—

Knox.

The drivers were shuffling away from the tent. The end blanket flapped in the wind.

Drifting clouds started to obscure the sun. Whorls of white powder danced on the hillsides. At the western summit, the sledge coming up had stopped. The teamsters peered at the peculiar scene below. The wind sang again, a low, pained sound.

"I think we should bury him here, Philip."

"I think so."

"The rifle's to be yours. He told me. We'll dig a proper place and I'll say a few words and—" His voice broke. "—and then we'll get these goddamned guns going again."

"Yes. All right," Philip said, staring at nothing. Knox left him standing in a cloud of wind-driven snow.

VIII

THE ARRIVAL of the artillery in the village of Westfield produced almost a carnival atmosphere.

Townsfolk followed the sledges on both sides, and small boys couldn't be kept from jumping aboard to touch the marvelous cold solidity of the great weapons.

The Westfield citizens offered the weary drivers huge quantities of food and drink. The men accepted eagerly, nearly starved after their passage across the worst of the mountains.

In return for the hospitality, the people of Westfield begged Henry Knox to show off the artillery by firing the most spectacular piece of all, The Old Sow. The exhausted Knox obliged. Philip made himself scarce during the demonstration, taking refuge in the local taproom. But he still heard the boom of the mortar, and the subsequent cheers, applause and shouted insults to King George. Philip immediately helped himself to another ale. Like everyone else, the landlord was outside enjoying the celebration.

IX

"ANNE? ANNIE—I'm back!"

Yelling at the top of his voice, Philip climbed the stairs of the house in Watertown on the night of January twenty-sixth. The preceding day, the artil-

lery train had arrived in Framingham, its journey complete for all practical purposes. Philip had ridden ahead with Knox, who gave him leave to go see his family. Knox galloped on to the Vassall House to report to General Washington.

Filthy and almost drained of strength, Philip shouted his wife's name again as he reached the landing. He shifted Eph Tait's Kentucky rifle to his left hand, raised his other hand to knock—

And stopped, paralyzed by what he saw hanging on the door.

A poorly made wreath of black crepe.

Fears for Anne and little Abraham flashed through his mind. He stood motionless, aware of doors opening on the lower floor, heads popping out—the whole house had been turned into a honeycomb of emergency apartments. He was certain his wife or his child had died in his absence—

The door opened. Philip almost wept at the sight of Anne's fatigued face.

Her chestnut hair was disordered, her dress stained and wrinkled. Philip couldn't speak. He was afraid to ask the obvious question.

"The baby's well," Anne said quietly. "He's sleeping now."

"Then it's your father. Oh, Annie—"

Suddenly she was tight against him, unable to hold back her sobs. He let the valuable rifle fall where it would. Heedless of how he was dirtying her with his filthy coat, he hugged her; buried his bearded, unwashed face in the warmth of her hair. She cried loudly for a minute or so, then fought to get herself under control.

Philip retrieved his rifle, guided her gently into the dim-lit parlor, shut out the curious faces at the bottom of the stairs.

"When, Annie?" he whispered.

"The fourth of January. All during December, the illness grew worse. And you know how it's all but impossible to find a doctor. Mr. Revere finally located a retired, half senile old fellow and practically kidnapped him from Roxbury. He diagnosed pleurisy—just as I'd done myself, weeks before—and of course he couldn't prescribe anything except the usual emetics and laxatives and—well, when he hauled out this positively filthy bleeding basin and a fleam with every last blade caked with rust, I paid him and thanked him and told him to leave. I knew it was hopeless."

Anne's face was white; Philip understood why. Pleurisy was the name of a dreaded disease of the lungs and chest; more common in bad weather, it took a high toll of those who contracted it.

Anne looked around in a strange fashion, almost as if seeking her father in the gloomy corners. Then:

"Papa was fortunate in one way. He went peacefully—in his sleep. But dear God, Philip!—at the same time, there was no word from you. Nothing except rumors from Cambridge that Henry Knox was still on the road. Having difficulties—accidents—" Her agony poured forth in one strident cry: "*I was afraid you were going to die too*—"

Again he held her close, touched her, stroked her shoulders, trying to soothe away the remembered horror. All at once he heard the impatient gurgling of his son waking in the bedroom. Even as he listened, the gurgling turned to a yell. He felt a shameful, completely inappropriate urge to whoop.

This time Anne broke the embrace, dabbing at her cheeks. "I'm sorry I took on so. Really, the worst has passed. I just broke down."

"You had to bury him yourself?"

"Yes, I arranged it here in the local cemetery. Ben Edes helped. There was no telling when we could get back to Boston. Philip—at Christmas, Papa asked me to say goodbye to you. I'm sure he already knew what was going to happen—"

She started away, bothered by the baby's cry: "I must feed him—and you too. Why, you must have lost twenty pounds—"

She fought to hold a wan smile in place. That was so like her, he thought, filled with a wordless tenderness that somehow eradicated his exhaustion, his hunger, the unpleasantly cold, smoky stench of his clothing.

"There is one happy circumstance in all the grief," Anne added. "Papa left what money he has to both of us. And—oh wait, Abraham, wait, I'm coming!" she exclaimed as the squalling grew louder. "Papa said that if we could keep from spending all the money to live, we should use it to start your printing business one day. He thought well of you, Philip, he really did. He wanted you to know."

It should have been heartening news; something to bank away for the future. But he was again struck with grave doubts about that future.

He thought of Dr. Warren perishing in the redoubt.

Of Eph Tait buried in the wintry wastes of western Massachusetts, so far from the southern mountains from which he'd marched.

And he thought of Abraham Ware, who perhaps would never have contracted his fatal illness if he'd been warm and comfortable in his home on Launder Street, Boston—

Who would be the next to be scythed down?

When Philip speculated about the prospects for his infant son, the very act seemed macabre futility. Conceived in the joy of passion—born under a mantle of hope and love from his parents—what did the child have to look forward to save growing up in a country shattered by rebellion?

The struggle could conceivably drag on for years; wars often did in Europe. That America could win her fight seemed to him chancy at best. That she could win quickly was virtually unthinkable. There was no purpose in dwelling on the boy's future, or the inheritance either. Dead men had no use for handbills and calling cards. What printing equipment could you buy in a grave?

Possessed by pessimism, Philip felt a sudden, unexpected need to seize the small pleasures of the moment. The feel of his wife's warm shoulder beneath his arm. And something else:

"I want to see my son."

An hour later, Anne served a supper of cold lamb, fresh cheese, stale bread and hot tea. Though the fare was less than luxurious, there was plenty of it. Yet despite the poor rations he'd endured on the three-hundred-mile journey, he didn't feel like eating.

All at once, out of his need, fear, uncertainty, he reached for Anne's hand.

She looked at him and understood. At long last, a soft smile eased a little of the fatigue in her eyes. She was as uncertain and hungry as he.

Rising, she blew out the lamp in the corner of the parlor where they had sat down for their meal. Gently, lovingly, she took his other hand in hers.

"I should use a razor first," he said with an awkward little laugh. "Scrape off this bristle. It could do damage to a lady's cheek—"

"Don't worry," she said. "Just come—" She led him to the door.

In their large, high bed, their son sleeping nearby and cooing occasionally, she was warm and eager. Arms tight around his neck, she wept when he first kissed

her. The touching, the caressing, and then the rhythm of their bodies seemed to drive back some of the world's lowering darkness.

But afterward, he couldn't sleep.

He stole out to the parlor, lit a lamp and spent more than two hours composing one short letter to Experience Tait's wife in Albemarle County, Virginia. Even if it had cost every last shilling of Abraham Ware's money to have it posted and delivered, he would have paid.

___6
"The Seedtime of Continental Union"

"GENTLEMEN," SAID Dr. Benjamin Franklin, the tankard in his pudgy hand shimmering in the light from the hearth, "I give you our honored guest. By birth, an Englishman. By choice, an American. By disposition and God-given talent, a journalist of the first rank. In the manner of most authors who delve into politics in these treacherous times, he has chosen to see his pamphlet brought into the world anonymously. But to judge from the reception accorded it since publication one short week ago, I predict its distinguished creator will not long be able to conceal his identity. Certainly he may be named and honored by those gathered here. To a man, I believe we hold his inspired prose and irrefutable logic in the utmost regard."

Franklin turned toward the rather seedy-looking guest: a man with a large nose, a rough complexion, luminous sad eyes and the general air of one who, near age forty, recognized his own failure in life. Tonight, the guest smiled.

Dr. Franklin saluted him with the tankard:

"I give you Mr. Paine."

Stick ferrules hammered the floor of the private dining room of Philadelphia's City Tavern. *"Hear! Hear! Hear!"* Those among the twenty selected guests who lacked canes made noise with their boots.

Gradually, the hammering and stomping faded, replaced by a hubbub of conversation. In the fireplace, two halves of a heavy log fell, scattering sparks. Franklin sat down beside the guest of honor. While serving as commercial agent for various colonies in England, Franklin had apparently met Mr. Paine, and induced him to come to America after Paine suffered assorted disasters in customs collecting, corset manufacturing and marriage.

There were calls for a speech. Applause greeted the suggestion. Thomas Paine rose, flushing:

"Gentlemen, thank you most sincerely. But I've prepared no remarks. I only wished to enjoy dinner and fellowship with the men I consider the most enlightened of all those holding sessions at the State House."

More applause, cane-thumping, boot-stamping, mingled with jokes and laughter. At his table near the fire, Judson Fletcher was hellishly warm. He was starting to sweat out all the dark brown ale he'd swilled down. But he joined enthusiastically in the uproar.

Certainly it was a select group from the Congress gathered at the City Tavern

this rainy evening in late January. A select group of patriots—or a select group of the insane, depending on your side of the political fence.

Judson had gravitated to the group because Donald had been part of it. Around him sat politicians whose names were known in every one of the colonies. Franklin. The portly, high-voiced little Braintree lawyer, John Adams, seated at Paine's left. From Virginia, the Lee brothers, and gangling, red-haired Tom Jefferson, who occupied a chair just across the table from Judson. Once in a while, Judson was troubled by the realization that these refined, well-educated men were determined to push the colonies straight down one and only one perilous road.

John Adams jumped to his feet. "Then I will speak for you, Mr. Paine."

The Massachusetts lawyer always struck Judson as self-important. The guest looked relieved, though. Adams went on:

"To paraphrase Mr. Jefferson there, we as a Congress and as a people want neither inducement nor power to declare and assert a separation from Great Britain. It is the will alone which is wanting—"

"Oh, we have the will to gallop the other way, Wilson style," said Francis Lightfoot Lee, referring to the Pennsylvania sponsor of a Congressional resolution of January ninth passed by a coalition of conscientious conservatives and the frankly faint-hearted. According to Judson's somewhat bleary recollection, the resolution declared that the colonies had "no design" to set themselves up as an independent nation. Consequently the mention of Wilson's name produced a few hisses, including a loud one from Judson.

Tom Jefferson, relaxed and pensive with his long legs stretched out toward the flames, gave Judson a speculative look, then glanced away. Judson belched. *Wonder what that was all about?*

Adams was continuing:

"—but with the publication of Mr. Paine's pamphlet, a great step forward has been taken toward solidifying public thought. We owe him a debt beyond our collective power to repay."

Once more the diners noisily expressed their approval as the Braintree lawyer sat down, pleased.

Judson had to admit that Adams, who was perhaps the most determined exponent of independence in the Congress, hadn't exaggerated. In the days since the release of Paine's tract of some fifty pages and fourteen thousand words, it had become a publishing phenomenon. People literally fought their way into Robert Bell's small shop in Third Street to purchase copies; either the version in a deluxe binding, or the one in less expensive paper covers.

Judson had finally gotten hold of one of the latter just this afternoon. So far he hadn't done more than examine the title page. But he knew a little about the book's history.

Aitken, the local printer for whom Thomas Paine did menial shop work, had deemed his employee's material too inflammatory to print. But help and advice from Franklin and the ultra-radical Samuel Adams of Boston—not present to-night; even radicals like his own cousin John considered him a mite *too* radical—had led to the connection with Bell.

But Bell, who took the risk of bringing out the first edition, wasn't enjoying exclusive benefits—or profits—from his venture. All over Philadelphia, and in other cities as well, other presses were churning out copies. The eager public didn't care whether an edition was pirated or not. They just wanted to read it.

So did Judson. He was anxious to get away from this stultifying if augustly

populated room, return to his rented quarters in Windmill Street near the river and dive into Paine's pamphlet.

Scraping chairs and the opening of the doors to admit serving girls to clean up the litter of plates, cups and glasses indicated he might be getting his opportunity.

He judged the hour to be past nine. He hoped Alice wouldn't choose to spend the night with him. Her whims were unpredictable; dictated largely by how much claret she'd consumed.

She was damned attractive wench, of course. A welcome diversion despite certain puzzling, even alarming quirks of personality, and a history that was a total enigma—

But he didn't want Alice tonight. He was eager to go to bed with no companion save Mr. Paine's *Common Sense*.

Reaching for his hat and stick as the gathering broke up, he was startled by a hand on his sleeve:

"Judson? A word with you—"

Tom Jefferson stood well over six feet. He met his fellow Virginian's smile with a calm, almost remote expression. Judson's smile disappeared.

He had gotten on exceptionally well with Tom Jefferson ever since arriving in Philadelphia in mid-December. The other members of the Virginia delegation— the Lees, Ben Harrison, Jefferson's law tutor George Wythe, Braxton, Nelson— all were cordial enough. But Jefferson was closer to Judson's own age than the rest of them. Just a little over thirty, Judson guessed.

Not much for oratory, but reputed to be the best phrase-turner in Congress, Jefferson still spoke with a quiet directness that demanded a listener's attention. His laugh, when he was in the mood, could roar. Tonight he obviously wasn't in the mood—as Judson had noticed a while ago, when the wealthy young man gave him that odd look.

"By all means," Judson said with a slight bow. "Shall we go to the public room? I'd drink another ale before braving that rain."

Jefferson shook his head. "I believe enough's been drunk for one night."

Instantly Judson tightened up. The polite reply had delivered its barb—as he was sure Jefferson intended. Annoyed, Judson picked up a tankard left by someone else. He gulped the warm, flat ale remaining in the bottom.

That defiance out of the way, he wiped his lips with his lace-trimmed cuff and smiled engagingly:

"Then let's talk here, Tom. What did you want to discuss?" He suspected he knew.

Jefferson didn't avoid Judson's gaze. "You, Judson."

The smile stayed in place. "A fascinating subject! Go on."

"As you know, we've welcomed your presence and your liberal spirit in the Congress. In that sphere, you're as much a credit to Virginia as your brother."

Judson's smile soured then. "Shall we skip the preliminaries? I smell that compliment for what it is—a preamble to something less flattering."

Jefferson's lips thinned a moment. "Very well," he said. "We have received word of a rather distressing exhibition of patriotism at The Keg the other evening."

"It wasn't an exhibition of patriotism, it was a brawl." Judson cheerfully exhibited the bruises and healing scrapes on the back of his right hand. "I just went in the place for a drink. I had no idea it was the refuge of every young Tory in town. I had two or three, and then a couple of sweet-smelling chaps remarked

that German Georgie would soon make the Congress regret it ever convened—
by signing his treaties with the landgraves who are to supply him with German
mercenaries.''

Judson shrugged: ''One thing led to the next, and when I got done with 'em,
two of the pretty young gentlemen looked less pretty than when they first opened
their mouths.''

The lanky Virginian's nod was dour. ''So it was reported. I only want to
remind you, Judson—friend to friend—that we're engaged in deliberations of the
most serious nature. Our every act will be scrutinized for years to come—''

''A lecture, then. This is a lecture!''

''Judson, calm down.''

''No, by God, I won't listen to—''

''Yes you will,'' Jefferson said, so softly that Judson caught his breath. ''Your
private life is your affair. But publicly—''

''Publicly *what?*''

''We ask that you do nothing further to bring criticism to our cause.'' To ease
the situation, he smiled a quick, glowing smile. ''I don't doubt that in certain
yet-to-be-written histories, we're damned beyond redemption as it is.''

Jefferson seemed to relax then, the stiffness going out of his shoulders. But his
clear eyes watched, awaiting a response. Judson bridled his temper with difficulty.

''You keep saying *we,* Tom. You're not speaking personally, then?''

''Not entirely.''

''For the delegation?''

''And some others. Let's just say I was requested to pass the message along.
I didn't relish doing it—in case that wasn't obvious. But I agreed because, in
principle, the gentleman who asked me to do it was right.''

Cheeks livid, Judson blurted, ''Name the gentleman.''

''Judson, there's no point—''

''Name him!''

Jefferson sighed. ''Mr. Hancock—with the concurrence of Mr. John Adams.''

''Hancock! That pompous dandy—!'' Judson was sputtering.

But his anger cooled almost at once. The handsome and extremely rich Boston
merchant, formerly the chief financier of patriot activities in Massachusetts, was
the duly chosen president of the Congress. This was no mere slap on the wrist by
a nonentity. For a blink of time, Tom Jefferson's lean face seemed to be replaced
by that of Angus Fletcher—

Around the private dining room, shadows sprang up as the serving girls
snuffed candles. All the other men had gone. Winter rain struck the window
glass.

In a more temperate voice, Judson asked:

''You say John Adams also joined in the request?''

''You must understand why, Judson. What we're undertaking here in Philadelphia will be considered so heinous in some quarters of the world, our personal
motives and behavior must be above reproach.''

''In other words, we can drink and curse and whore as much as we like behind
closed doors, just so long as the public face is hypocritically spotless?''

Jefferson looked upset. ''If that's the way you care to phrase it, yes.''

''That's the only way I care to phrase it!''

Jefferson stifled a sharp reply. Then:

"Judson, the central argument makes sense, if you'll just reflect on it a while—"

"I'll reflect on it while I'm having a drink somewhere else!" He turned and stormed out, leaving Jefferson in the shadows by the dying fire, a red-etched figure, vaguely accusing. All he could think of as he rushed from the City Tavern was that he had once more been found wanting.

II

WINTER RAIN slicked the brick streets and gathered in wind-riffled pools that reflected the butter glow of chimneyed streetlamps designed, people said, by Dr. Franklin personally. Muffled in his cape, Judson headed for Windmill Street, cursing fluently.

One minute he cursed Jefferson, deputized by Hancock and Adams to chastise him. The next minute he cursed himself, for again failing to live up to what was expected of him. Whatever the hell that was!

Jefferson's warning couldn't be ignored. Though still young, the red-haired Virginian had already made a considerable name for himself because of his grasp of diverse fields of learning, from the natural sciences to the law. That Hancock had assigned him the task of speaking to Judson was proof of his rising status.

And once he cooled down a little, Judson had to admit that Jefferson's argument was probably correct. The Congress *was* engaged in momentous and difficult work. The faction to which Jefferson and Judson belonged saw independence as the last available option in the face of the king's continuous refusal to protect American liberties. But time and again, Judson had heard John Adams state that although he considered independence a cause with high moral purpose, the idea lacked support among ordinary folk in the colonies. If it were noised about that members of the independence group were thugs who bloodied the noses of Tories in public taverns, the legitimacy of the cause could be seriously hurt.

And right now, the radicals certainly couldn't afford that.

Opposition to independence among the Congressional conservatives led by Wilson and the London-trained lawyer, John Dickinson of Pennsylvania, was formidable and determined. The conservatives would seize on every remark or incident that might change minds and ultimately swing votes. No, Jefferson couldn't be faulted—

Especially now that Paine's pamphlet had finally fired the imaginations of great masses of people, and begun to sway them toward the viewpoint of the radicals. All at once, Judson felt like a moral pygmy among giants.

By the time he neared Windmill Street and the plainly furnished rooms he rented from an elderly tinker, his sense of shame had deepened even further. He vowed he wouldn't embarrass Donald again—for he had certainly done that too, along with alienating himself from the members of Congress whose convictions he shared. He would have to work hard to repair the damage.

Judson had undergone subtle changes in attitude since coming to the city beside the Schuylkill river. At first, appointment as Donald's alternate had been little more than a welcome escape from the turmoil at Sermon Hill.

Then there'd been a period of confusion; a couple of weeks of familiarizing himself with the routine of the Congress; of sitting in on his first committee

meetings, saying little. He was a junior member of two committees. One screened officer appointments for the twenty-seven new Continental regiments established the preceding November. The other supervised the newly structured Post Office Department, a Congressional creation which John Adams scorned as "frivolous" in view of the weightier matters to be considered.

Confusion and all, those first two weeks brought Judson a great sense of pleasure. He relished association with important men who had only been names before.

Then, because he did share Donald's politics, he began to take an active interest in the seesaw struggle between the conservative and radical factions. He was now definitely aligned with those who wanted independence but lacked the votes, or even an initial resolution to be voted upon. The conservatives were using every device and argument to block the introduction of the latter. Despite the king's rejection of the petition for conciliation, the conservatives and many of the moderates still believed that separation from England would not only be morally wrong for the colonies, but would also be economic suicide.

Judson climbed the rickety outer stair and let himself into the tinker's musty parlor. Flinging off his wet cloak and hat, he headed automatically for the sideboard, and the decanter of claret he kept for Alice.

Well, not only for Alice—

Midway there, he stopped, stung again with the conviction that, by his actions, he'd betrayed the men—and the cause—he supported without reservation. He ran his tongue over his teeth, scowled, turned away and lit a lamp.

He was again aware of some serious and fundamental flaw within himself. A weakness for the bottle was just one of its manifestations. Tonight, by heaven, he meant to start some corrective actions, however small. Such as forcing himself to leave the claret alone.

He took off his finely cut coat of plum velveteen, grateful that Alice wasn't on the premises. He carried the lamp to the bedroom and picked up Pain's pamphlet from the bedside table. Sprawling on the coverlet, he opened to the first page of text.

He read the whole book in less than an hour, relishing its polemical savagery. Then he went back to particular passages.

He laughed out loud at Paine's characterization of monarchy as *the most prosperous invention the devil ever set on foot for the promotion of idolatry.* He agreed with Paine's insistence on urgency: *The period of debate is closed. Arms, as a last resource, must decide the contest. By referring the matter from argument to arms, a new era for politics is struck; a new method of thinking hath risen. All plans, proposals, etc., prior to the nineteenth of April, i.e., to the commencement of hostilities, are like the almanacs of last year; which, though proper then, are superseded and useless now . . .*

He likewise concurred with Paine's assessment of the king's behavior:

Even brutes do not devour their young, nor savages make war upon their families.

And his scalp prickled when the journalist urged total separation from the mother country in phrases that rang like great bells:

The sun never shined on a cause of greater worth. 'Tis not the affair of a city, a county, a province, or a kingdom; but of a continent—of at least one-eighth part of the habitable globe—

Lying with the book resting on his hard belly, Judson thought of George

Clark, wandering the western wilderness. Paine shared some of George's vision. He devoured the rest of the passage again:

'Tis not the concern of a day, a year, or an age; posterity are virtually involved in the contest, and will be more or less affected even to the end of time by the proceedings now—

Just what Jefferson had been saying.

Now is the seedtime of continental union, faith, and honor.

Then, almost with reverence, he turned to the final page. Unblinking, he gazed at the seven superbly isolated words Paine had contrived to have set by themselves—his last tocsin and challenge to his readers.

Staring at the words, Judson's scalp prickled again. So rapt was his attention, he didn't hear the light footfalls on the outer stair, or the soft clicking of the latch.

But suddenly he was aware that the sound of the rain was louder. He jumped up, laid the pamphlet face down on the bed, open to that final, astonishing page. He walked toward the dark parlor.

He recognized the footsteps of his visitor. In a moment, she entered the perimeter of light cast by the bedside lamp. Alice—throwing back the cowl of her cheap cloak of gray wool. Just as lovely as she was every time he saw her.

And just as drunk.

III

"HALLO, LOVE," Alice grinned. She weaved a little, one sooty hand pushing back a lock of hair that might have been a tawny gold color if she had ever washed it. She was wearing her usual much-mended dark brown skirt, and a shabby low-necked blouse grayed by greasy smoke.

Judson concealed his annoyance. "Hello, Alice. I wasn't expecting you this evening."

"Meaning my company's not wanted?" Her smile, a shade malicious all at once, unsettled him. But that wasn't unusual.

She sidled forward, placed her roughened hands on his shoulders, bent to give him a teasing view of her naked breasts. "Ah, but yours is, love." The sight of her half-bared bosom started a familiar, tumid excitement.

She was a coarse girl; peculiar in many more ways than one. Maybe that was part of her fascination: she was a strange admixture of feigned refinement and gutter frankness.

At times she moved with the grace of the finely dressed ladies who took the air on Chestnut Street behind their jeweled vizards. But unlike those same ladies, she had a direct, unconcealed interest in matters sexual. She knew how to stir him. She wasted no time now, caressing his mouth with open lips.

Judson resigned himself, though not entirely unwillingly. He slipped an arm around her waist, smelling the tavern sweat mingled with the odor of the claret she drank from dawn to dusk—and later. He bussed her ear, murmured:

"You're still speaking of my company, correct?"

"Certainly, isn't that the dignified way to refer to this?" One hand crept below his waist to grasp and fondle.

Almost at once, her fingers produced the sought-for response. After she'd teased him a moment, she let go:

"Ah, but we have the whole night—I don't mean to go out in this damnable weather again. So how about a glass for a lady, Mr. Fine Fletcher of Virginia?"

He waved to the sideboard. "Lady you aren't. But help yourself."

"Not a lady? Don't lay wagers!" she laughed, flouncing off to the decanter with a peculiar look in her sky-blue eyes. He heard a mug clink. "Want some, love?"

He sank down on the edge of the bed, glancing with regret at Paine's pamphlet. "No, I don't believe—" Suddenly he saw Jefferson's face. "Hell, why not?"

He listened to the sound of claret splashing out of the decanter. She drank too much; much more than he did, and his consumption was far from moderate. On occasion, she used foul language, but it usually sounded awkward. She was ruining herself physically and mentally, and she couldn't be more than twenty-three or twenty-four.

Another curious thing: her cheeks were pitted. At one time she must have used the fashionable but ruinous cosmetics popular among highborn ladies. When and where had she been able to afford such concoctions?

Sometimes she made oblique jokes about a mysterious background in better circumstances. But Judson's questions about it always went unanswered. In fact he knew nothing about her except her one name, Alice, and that she worked serving the riffraff who frequented a particularly disreputable tavern near the docks. He'd stumbled into the place one night after Christmas, feeling especially blue with memories of Seth McLean's wife. In his stupor, Alice's flaunted body appealed to him. A direct proposition led to a quick coupling upstairs in a sleazy room under the eaves—for a fee. Half of it, she said, went to the landlord.

Still a bit drunk, he'd invited her to come to his quarters in Windmill Street some evening. For no fee. Two nights later, at two in the morning, she arrrived. He'd seen her at least twice a week since.

Alice carried the cups of claret back into the bedroom, handed him one, neglecting her tugged-down blouse, a casualty of their embrace. The half-circle of one rouged nipple showed like part of a flower. Alice toasted him, drank what he guessed was a full cup in four quick gulps.

"No trade tonight?" he inquired, mildly cynical.

"Nothing Peggy can't accommodate."

Judson paled. "Who?"

"Oh, the other slut the old bastard's hired on—a stupid wench from Jersey. Peggy's this fat—" She pantomimed the measurements. Judson wiped sweat off his forehead and lay back on the bed as Alice went on, "when she's with a customer, you can hear her grunting all the way downstairs. Disgusting," she declared with a sniff.

Then she laughed, harshly. Judson studied her beautiful blue eyes and wondered again whether she was quite sane.

Alice plumped down beside him. "I give the customers something more refined, don't I, love?" Drinking with one hand, she teased his groin with the other. "It costs you nothing—and in exchange, I get to sleep in a bed that isn't crawling with bugs. A lovely bargain, I'd say—"

"If you despise that place so much, why do you work there?"

"Oh, reasons," she said with a vague wave of the cup. "Where else should a poor countryman's daughter work?"

"I've never been convinced you're just a poor countryman's daughter, Alice."

"Then what am I?" she teased, tossing her head. Her hair glistened with that greasy sheen he found repulsive—when he was sober.

"A very attractive young woman who, for some inexplicable reason, chooses to stay wretchedly dirty when she'd glow like the sun if she bathed—"

"Pooh," Alice replied thickly. "Bathing's for rich folk."

"—and who," Judson continued with mock seriousness, "drinks somewhat more than is good for her—"

"Now *that's* a fine comment from a chap who tosses it down the way you do."

"Well, I'm not trying to kill myself with it."

Alice's slightly glazed blue eyes glowed oddly. "You're not?"

"Alice, tell me who the hell you are. What are you running away from? A husband? An indenture contract?"

"Nothing." She repeated it, louder: "Nothing. Listen, Mr. Fine Judson Fletcher—I could ask the same of you!"

He looked away.

"Oh, come on love," she said, more softly. "What's made you so cross with me this evening?" She reached past his thigh for the pamphlet. "Is this the reason for the chilly reception?"

"There!" he exclaimed. " 'Chilly reception.' Tavern trollops don't command such fine phrases—"

Examining the pamphlet's flyleaf, she ignored him:

"Oh, I see what it is. The book everyone's reading. We even had a helmsman tonight who had a copy. A lot of foolishness—just like the business with those dreadful old men at the State House. Why do you bother? Of course, if you hadn't come from Virginia to waste your time at that silly Congress, we'd never have met, would we, love? I'd still be tossing around in that nasty straw every night—instead of sharing a tidy bed. And sporting with a genuine gentleman—"

One hand between his legs, the other, with the cup, dangling down as she crooked her arm around his neck, she rubbed her mouth slowly back and forth across Judson's. Flicked her tongue along his upper lip. He smelled the wine, and her heat:

"We are going to make love, aren't we, Judson? You've improved your mind sufficiently for one evening, haven't you? Brains aren't everything—" Her hand grew bolder. "Master Cock-and-balls needs his exercise too—"

Damn, how she worked on him! Someone, somewhere, had taught her amorous skills in fine detail. He pressed his mouth tight on hers. They kissed a long, langorous moment, her tongue licking at his teeth, wet, sinuous—

But even embracing, he couldn't escape the past.

His hands constricted roughly on Alice's waist as he shoved her down on the bed. She dropped the empty cup and wrapped her arms around his neck. The cup thudded on the carpet. He heard the pamphlet slide off as well—

He didn't care any longer. She'd slipped her blouse down so he could kiss her breasts. The smoky smell of her skin excited him beyond all reason.

"Wait, wait, love. A little more wine first," she gasped, darting away.

Flushed, he stood up. She found the cup and walked into the dark parlor, her blouse pushed all the way to her waist. He heard the decanter clink. He tugged off his throat-stock, his linen shirt. He really didn't understand why he wallowed with this girl who meant nothing to him. Nor did he understand her. Each had built a wall beyond which the other was not permitted.

But penetrating the wall wasn't necessary for their main amusement. He

dropped his breeches, then his underclothes. Why the hell did it matter who she was? Physically, she hid nothing.

She had left her clothes in the parlor. She came out of the dark with long, langorous steps, her sky-blue eyes shining bright as the crystal of the decanter in her right hand. Her breasts bobbed at each step. Her lower belly glowed like finespun gold. Her body had a pale beauty that couldn't be marred even by the rings of dirt on her neck and forearms.

Standing next to the bed, Alice caressed the stem of the decanter in a lascivious way. She gazed at Judson's hips and smiled at the production of the desired response.

"I'm not the only one with mysteries, love," she giggled, seating herself on the bed. She cooed with mock disappointment as passion drained out of him suddenly.

"What do you mean, Alice?"

"I saw how you turned white when I mentioned the name Peggy."

"Like hell I did!"

"Who is she, darling? Your mistress in Virginia? A wife you're hiding from me? I don't honestly care, I'm just curious—"

His hand stabbed out. "Give me a drink."

"La, what a rude-tempered swain you are!" She held the decanter out of his reach. *Swain,* he thought. *Too educated by half to be only what she pretends—*

And yet, she played the part. She spilled some of the decanter's contents over her rouged breasts, letting the claret trickle down over her white belly. She sprawled back and uttered one of those wild, unnerving laughs that made him question whether she was of sound mind. What unhappy occurrence in the past had driven her to this unchecked, uncaring recklessness—?

Touching herself, she whispered, "Drink your fill, love."

Swiping the back of his hand across his mouth, he bent toward her.

Soon the rickety bed was creaking in steadily increasing rhythm. Alice raked him with her broken nails and cried her urgency with filthy street language. The decanter discarded on the carpet dripped the last of the claret onto Paine's pamphlet. The book lay open to that final page bearing just seven words, forgotten now; stained by the wine—

THE FREE AND INDEPENDENT STATES OF AMERICA

IV

THE MILD Pennsylvania winter faded under a mellow sun and the first balmy breezes off the river. Crowds on the streets grew more numerous as the temperatures moderated. Whether the Philadelphians wore the brocade of the wealthy or the craftsman's homespun, the livery of servants or the rags of youngsters hawking flowers or papers or fragrant bread up and down High and Chestnut Streets, chances were excellent that if they hadn't read Tom Paine's *Common Sense,* they had an opinion about it, or had heard of it at very least. As they'd heard the astonishing tidings couriers brought in from Boston:

By night, General Washington had fortified the Dorchester Heights with cannon brought from Fort Ticonderoga by his chief of artillery, a Colonel Knox. In a short span of hours between one sunset and the next dawn, two thousand men

had performed the herculean task of digging earthworks and moving the weapons into place.

And just in time.

General Howe had planned to break out of the city. American intelligence had picked up definite word of an impending attack. But a violent storm prevented it. Then all at once, Washington's guns stared down on the rooftops. By the morning of the seventeenth of March, Boston was empty of the king's soldiers. All had been loaded aboard ships and evacuated to Halifax along with at least a thousand Tory families. From Halifax, it was said, a major British thrust would be mounted.

Among the patriot faction in Congress, there was jubilation. The Continental army, conceived and authorized by the Philadelphia body, had won its first significant victory. If not on a battleground, then in the hearts of its partisans.

But fear mingled with the elation. Where would Howe strike? There was little doubt that he *would* strike. America remained "in rebellion."

Even more reason to declare independence, the radicals argued in the large and lovely white room of the State House. It was time to unite the thirteen colonies for a concerted effort against the Crown; a war unhampered by hesitation. A war to secure American liberty forever.

The conservatives still shrank from it. What was needed, Judson's fellow radicals agreed, was resolution to force the issue.

V

ALICE CONTINUED to visit Judson regularly. After that night in January, no more questions passed between them about the origins of the other, or about motives for the liaison.

Judson knew his own demons and strongly suspected that Alice had hers. But he decided that trying to force those demons into the light would probably serve no purpose. Would only cause trouble, in fact, since Alice seemed set on keeping them hidden. So he took pleasure in her highly sexed nature and at the same time worked to control his drinking. The results proved satisfactory. No more warnings were issued by Tom Jefferson, who treated him cordially again, though it plainly required effort. Jefferson's mother had died of an apoplectic seizure the end of March, and immediately, the tall Virginian began to suffer violent headaches that left his face bleached with pain.

For Judson, life was somewhat easier. When he held Alice in his arms after an hour of lovemaking, he slept deeply, free of dreams of Seth McLean's wife.

The Congressional committees labored from early morning till late in the day. One session in early April ran particularly long. Judson didn't arrive back at Windmill Street until shortly before midnight. As he opened the outer door, he saw a lamp burning in the bedroom—and Alice, standing in front of the ancient, flecked pier glass.

He called her name from the dark parlor but got no response. He started forward, heard her voice, pulled up short.

Quite drunk, Alice was watching herself in the mirror. She touched her bare body now and then. Tears ran down her cheeks. Her slurred words stunned and frightened him:

"Philip? Why did you go? Why didn't you love me enough, Philip?"

He crept back to the outer landing. There he made sufficient noise to attract her attention before he re-entered. He didn't let on that he had seen her haunted face.

Or heard her speaking some lost lover's name as if her heart would break.

___ VI

FROM THE south came alarming news. British vessels with troops aboard were cruising the coast of the Carolinas, obviously intending to launch an attack. The rebellion was no longer solely a Massachusetts problem, but an American one.

In Congress, the radicals continued to press their case in lengthy debates. Finally North Carolina empowered its delegates to support a declaration for independence. And at a meeting of the Virginia House of Burgesses in May, that colony followed suit. Even as riders on lathered horses brought word to Philadelphia that the British flotilla had dropped anchor off Charleston, South Carolina, and that an armed strike under the joint leadership of General Clinton and the newly arrived General Cornwallis was imminent, the ranking member of Judson's delegation rose to introduce a resolution.

Feeling a deep sense of pride because Virginia had finally provided the means for Congress to act, Judson sat with the other delegates and watched the handsome president of the body, John Hancock. On the wall behind Hancock's desk hung a drum, British swords and banners captured at Fort Ticonderoga. With appropriate protocol, Hancock recognized Richard Henry Lee.

Scowls appeared on the faces of John Dickinson and his fellow conservatives. They knew what was coming. To Judson, the morning light pouring through the chamber's tall windows had a luminous quality.

Having been recognized, the patrician Lee began to read the resolution modeled after the one adopted in his native state:

"The resolution embodies three propositions, the first being as follows. That these united colonies are, and of right ought to be, free and independent states. That they are absolved from all allegiance to the British Crown, and that all political connection between them and the state of Great Britain is, and ought to be, totally dissolved—"

The room was stuffy. Sunlight glared on the windowpanes, shone on the brass fittings of the chamber's two fireplaces. Men coughed, shuffled their feet, glanced at the narrow openings at the tops of the windows as if longing for more air. The windows were kept almost completely shut at all times, to prevent the frequently loud debates from being overheard in the street.

Despite the heat, the discomfort, Judson was suddenly aglow with a sense of purpose—of counting for something—that he had never experienced before.

While Lee continued to read, Judson glanced at Tom Jefferson. He sat hunched over, his palms pressed against his cheeks and his fingertips covering his closed eyes. Judson assumed he was suffering from another of the headaches that had afflicted him almost constantly since his mother's burial in Virginia. Across the chamber, Dr. Franklin kept his eye on John Adams, who sat with arms folded, taut, ready to spring up for the inevitable debate.

To Judson, never a religious person, the June morning had power to cleanse his soul. It was, somehow, a bright and sacred occasion—

Which rapidly degenerated into noise and rancor as proponents and opponents shouted to be recognized in order to debate the issue posed by the resolution.

VII

"DAMME, SIRS, I'll prepare no document designed for approval by a group!" Benjamin Franklin declared three evenings later, over coffee and tea cups at The Sovereign near the State House. "I can forsee the surgery that'll be done upon it."

"Ben, don't be so confounded stubborn!" John Adams said.

"On this, I will be stubborn. Let me tell you a story—"

"I hope it's pertinent," Adams snapped.

"Extremely. I once knew a fellow here in Philadelphia who desired to open a hatter's shop. He put hours of energy and effort into designing and finishing the most important feature of such a shop—the signboard for attracting customers. He meticulously painted a hat on it, and the inscription 'John Thompson, hatter, makes and sells hats for ready money.' Then the poor fool consulted his friends. One said that because of the drawing, the word 'hatter' was superfluous. Out it went with a stroke of the brush! Someone else said that 'makes' should be deleted, since people who purchased hats didn't give a damn who made 'em. 'Ready money' was wasteful wordage—everyone knew Thompson never extended credit. Thus his precious board was reduced to 'John Thompson sells hats.' Ah, said another helpful soul, but who will be dunce enough to believe you'd give 'em away? So all the hours of work and thought produced nothing more than a worthless piece of wood with all of its legend brushed over, save for 'John Thompson' and the hat drawing, which was poorly done in the first place. Spare me from editorial congresses of any sort!" Franklin concluded cheerily. "I'll yield the labor—and the later discomfort produced by the disemboweling of every other phrase—to our more eloquent and hardy gentlemen of Virginia."

"Not me, doctor," Judson declared when Franklin looked at him. He wished for a good drink of rum, instead of the weak tea he'd ordered. "I'm a poor writer at best."

"Then you, Tom." Franklin's curious spectacles with lenses of two different thicknesses flashed back the lamplight. "I'll be of what help I can, but you have both the skill for the writing, and the young man's vigor to withstand the editing."

Pursing his lips, Adams said, "But naturally you'll interject a few ideas."

Franklin beamed. "Naturally. Correcting others is easy. What do you say, Tom?"

Jefferson looked doubtful. From his waistcoat pocket he pulled a scrap of paper and laid it on the table. "My forte is composition of a particular and limited kind, gentlemen."

That produced laughter. Jefferson's spell of headaches had passed, and he didn't mind a joke at his own expense. His friends knew he was notorious as a maker of meticulous lists: the daily weather in Philadelphia; the delegates and where they stood on independence, day by day and week by week; or the list he'd just shown them. Leaning over, Judson saw that it itemized Jefferson's current living expenses.

As he put the list away, Jefferson added, "I'd really prefer not to carry the whole responsibility—"

"Damme, we have a committee, a committee!" Adams thumped the table. "Appointed this very day—!"

Franklin shook his head. "A committee never accomplishes anything save the wasting of time and the destruction of sound ideas. The committee can submit

the draft, but one man must write it. Else we'll never debate and vote by the first of the month.''

From the corner, the scowling Adams declared, ''And since a decision has been postponed until the Congress *is* presented with a document, a document we must have! *Ipso facto,* we require an author. Like Ben, I shun that role with a passion, and defer to you, Tom.''

''Why?'' Jefferson wanted to know.

''Reason the first—you are a Virginian, and a Virginian ought to appear at the head of this business. There is too much opprobrium attached to the name of Massachusetts. Reason second, because of my vehemence in favor of inde- pendence, I am suspected, unpopular and considered obnoxious.'' Adams sounded almost boastful, but Judson had to admit that the statement was correct. ''Reason third—and the most important—you can write ten times better than I can.''

''No more arguments,'' Franklin said. ''You're elected.''

Jefferson sighed. ''Very well, I'll try it. But there are complex questions. What about the condemnation of slavery we discussed? Though I own slaves myself, I think we should include it. But it's certain to be disapproved by most of the southern delegates—''

The discussion continued until almost ten, with little settled except Jefferson's role in preparing the necessary statement for submission to the Congress. After the gathering adjourned, Judson walked slowly back to Windmill Street, savor- ing the balmy June air.

He hoped Alice would visit this evening. He was anxious to tell her what had happened today: the appointment of the committee to draft a declaration of separation. He knew she wouldn't be very interested. But his intense enthusiasm, fed by the mounting tensions in the elegant white room of the State House, had to find an outlet—

In the deep shadow on the corner opposite his lodging-house, he stopped. On another corner, he saw a man leaning against a brick wall. A very tall man whose features were hidden by the darkness. The man wore a cloak and tricorn and seemed to be studying the windows of Judson's bedroom—

There, a lamp burned. Had Alice already arrived?

Some warning instinct turned Judson's palms sweaty. He hesitated only a moment before making up his mind. He started across the intersection toward the tall watcher—

Who promptly wheeled and hurried off down Windmill Street.

But not before Judson had seen the man's cloak bell out as he passed under a streetlamp. The lamp revealed something that flashed dull yellow—

Metal-work. On a pistol in the man's belt.

Alarmed, Judson climbed the shaky stairs to his door. He was suddenly extremely thirsty again.

VIII

ALICE SEEMED in a gay, playful mood. He hesitated to mention the watcher. He wondered whether the man had been there before.

Judson and the girl drank, then tumbled into bed. An hour later, Alice slept restlessly in the crook of his bare arm. The fragrant air of early summer, turned even more ripe by the smell of the river, stirred the curtains.

Somehow the lovemaking had had an unusual effect on him. Ordinarily he went right to sleep afterward. Tonight he was tense; but not unpleasantly so.

Maybe it was the gathering momentum of events in the Congress. Earlier, while they tossed down claret, he'd described his day to Alice, ignoring her obvious boredom. He couldn't possibly be bored. One way or another, the issue should be resolved in early July when Jefferson's draft declaration was presented by the committee—

Musing, he was a fraction late in hearing the stealthy footstep on the landing.

The door crashed in, the fragile latch booted to pieces by the hulking figure silhouetted against the moonlight.

"Stand fast in there!" a raspy voice commanded. Alice stirred. "I have a pistol."

And so the intruder did. It was the tall man Judson had seen earlier.

The man took a couple of steps into the parlor. "Light a lamp."

Judson hesitated, cold beneath the coverlet.

"I said light a lamp or I'll send a ball your way!"

Judson reached clumsily for the lamp and a sulphur match. In a moment a roseate glow lit the bedchamber. Alice rolled over on her back, muttering to herself. A section of the cover fell away, revealing her breasts.

Still in bed but with hands braced under him, Judson watched the tall man enter the room. Servant's livery showed under his open cloak. Lamplight gleamed on the brass-chased pistol. Judson didn't miss the way the man's supercilious eyes roved over Alice's exposed body.

"Get up and go to the inside wall," the tall man ordered. When Judson didn't instantly obey, the servant snarled. "Any further delay and it will be my distinct pleasure to kill you. A regrettable loss for the Continental Congress, eh, Mr. Fletcher?"

Naked and genuinely frightened, Judson pushed back the coverlet. He walked barefoot to the place indicated.

"It's taken a deal of searching to find her," the tall man remarked. "Months, in fact. We never imagined she'd go into the stews. Where you obviously took advantage of her. Ample cause for an accident, I'd say. However, if you remain quiet you'll come to no harm." He sounded as if he regretted the fact.

The tall man turned and called softly toward the landing:

"She's here, sir. It's safe to come in. Our Virginia gentleman is pacified for the moment."

A portly, elegantly dressed man of middle age almost tiptoed through the parlor. He gazed at the restless girl, horrified:

"My God, smell the wine on her! No wonder she doesn't wake up—" Face mottled, he swung on Judson. "By heaven, sir, if you've debauched her—"

"Debauched her!" Judson guffawed. The nightmare had turned ludicrous suddenly. "She's a tavern whore! Just who the hell are you?"

"Careful how you address Mr. Trumbull," advised the servant.

"Yes, but you've got the better of me. Who—?"

"Never mind. We know who you are, and that's enough."

The portly man bent over at the bedside and began to chafe Alice's wrists. She groaned, thrashed her head from side to side as if resisting the hands on her flesh. *Trumbull, Trumbull,* Judson's mind repeated. He'd heard the name before. The Trumbulls of Arch Street were a prominent Tory family. The head of it—the portly man?—owned a large, prosperous ropewalk.

"Alicia, wake up. Alicia; it's Uncle Tobias come to take you home—"

"Alicia?" Judson repeated. "Her name's Alice."

The portly man directed another hateful glance at him. Judson realized he must have been followed for some length of time. Days; perhaps weeks. The naked girl just opening her sky-blue eyes and pushing back a strand of dirty hair was—as he'd suspected—someone other than whom she pretended to be.

All at once Alice's eyes focused. She sat upright as if she'd been slapped. Her voice was a mixture of terror and fury:

"What are you doing here, Tobias? Get away—get out!"

The portly man paled. "Alicia, cover your nakedness! *What am I doing here—?*" A gesture to the servant with one ringed hand. The tall man watched Alice with quick alternating glances at Judson. "We have searched Philadelphia for months to locate you! What I am doing here is taking you back to Arch Street. To your aunt, who's been devastated—driven to her bed!—ever since you disappeared last fall. To find you working in a wharf den and consorting with a man who would destroy these colonies—!"

The sentence sputtered out. Tory politics and the morality of the well-entrenched made Mr. Tobias Trumbull speechless with outrage. But he managed to seize Alice's wrist again.

"I'm where I want to be!" She jerked her hand away. "Leave me alone."

"She's ailing," Trumbull gasped to his servant. "Robbed of her senses by grief—"

"Or by drink, and this lecher," the tall man said, pointing the pistol at Judson.

"Alicia, you must come home. We'll find the best doctors—restore you to health—"

"Get out of here!" Alice screamed in her best river-front bellow. Then she began to curse Trumbull with oaths that bleached his reddened cheeks. Even the tall servant looked surprised—and in that moment, Judson moved with long, swift strides.

The servant swore, leveled his pistol. For one dreadful moment Judson stared down the muzzle. He grabbed the servant's wrist, cracked it over his leg, caught the pistol and drove his bare knee in to the man's groin.

Judson jumped back as the tall man stumbled against the wall, teeth clenching. The servant recovered, lunged—

Only to halt as Judson took another long step back and aimed the pistol at his forehead. The servant glared.

Judson felt harrowingly sober, somewhat ridiculous—nude with a pistol in one hand—and not a little confused:

"Now before this charade continues, I want an explanation." To the portly man: "You claim to be her relative—"

"My wife is her aunt! She is Mrs. Alicia Amberly, widow of an officer in His Majesty's service and daughter of the Earl of Parkhurst."

"Earl?" Judson exploded, slack-jawed from this latest surprise. Alice had covered her breasts and was watching the scene like a trapped animal. She too was sober now, he judged. But still irrational. He had seen those sky-blue eyes glaze like that before—

He could hardly believe what he'd just learned. Still, if true, it would explain much about the girl's strange, contradictory personality—

Trumbull swung to Alice but pointed at Judson:

"Do you realize what sort of man you've fallen in with? One of those political cheapjacks who—"

"Now I understand why you know so much about me," Judson interrupted. "I've been spied upon."

"She has been hunted," the servant corrected, still furious.

· "For the most humane of reasons!" Trumbull exclaimed. "Sorrow over the death of her husband, Lieutenant Colonel Amberly, caused her to run away. Sickness of the mind made her seek refuge in—squalor, in—"

Suddenly Alice screamed out, "I ran because my lover deserted me, you stupid old fool! My *American* lover. He turned his back on me—*that's* why I ran—"

Judson was horrified by the wild brightness in the girl's eyes. He remembered Alice standing at the pier glass. Was *Philip* the American she'd loved—?

Again Trumbull could barely speak: "Alicia—what you're saying—it's against all propriety, it's—obscenity—a symptom of your derangement—" He lurched for her. "You will come home for care, for protection—"

She spat in the fat Tory's face.

Trumbull wiped the saliva from his jowl. For the first time, he turned pleading eyes to Judson:

"In God's name, sir—help me!"

Judson shook his head. "Why? The decision is Alice's."

"Her name is Alicia, you arrogant bastard!"

"The decision is still hers. You have no right to force her out of here."

The servant licked his lips. "He has debauched her, Mr. Trumbull. That's obvious now."

"I am here *by choice!*" Alice screamed again.

"Oh, God—child, please—" Trumbull was almost weeping.

Judson lifted the pistol, gestured toward the door open on the mellow June night:

"I think you'd better leave. At once. There is no law of which I'm aware that can compel her to go with you. I'm not holding her prisoner. So if she chooses to stay with me, there's not a damn thing you can do about it."

Livid, Tobias Trumbull said, "You'll do nothing to assist me when she obviously needs medical attention?"

"Nothing," Judson repeated. "Unless she agrees to it."

"No," Alice whispered, fingers like claws on the coverlet.

"I—" Trumbull swallowed. Then a bit more determination seemed to infuse his bloated face. "I do have one recourse in the face of behavior such as yours, Mr. Fletcher. Gentleman to gentleman—" The last word seethed with contempt. "I can demand satisfaction."

Judson's eyes raked the wheezing, overweight man. "Don't be an idiot. You're not up to a duel."

"Please—"

Alice was moaning now; moaning and swaying back and forth. Judson knew Trumbull was right about one thing: something in the girl's past had damaged her mind.

Abruptly, she burst into tears:

"No more quarreling!" She covered her ears. *"Leave me alone!"*

The awful howl turned Trumbull's face pure white. He glared at Judson again. Behind Trumbull, the servant smiled sardonically.

"Then you'll deny me satisfaction?" Trumbull asked. "You're not only a traitor but a coward, is that it?"

Stung by the insult, Judson shouted, "Goddamn it, if that's what you want, send your second!"

Instantly, he regretted the outburst. It was the wrong thing to do on several counts. Trumbull was a pathetically weak-looking man. Yet accepting the challenge gave Judson a perverse satisfaction, somehow.

The tall servant bowed. "I will call on you in due course, Mr. Fletcher. Come, Mr. Trumbull—" Gently, he took the shaking Tory's arm. "—the matter is settled. When you've disposed of this gentleman, Mrs. Amberly can be brought home comfortably."

At the landing the servant glanced back, still amused:

"Keep the pistol for a time, Mr. Fletcher. I'll reclaim it after Mr. Trumbull puts an end to your life."

The door with its splintered latch closed.

Judson stared at the brasswork of the gun. Sick and furious, he flung the pistol on the floor. It skidded, struck the wall.

He sat down beside—what had they called her? Alicia Amberly? It didn't matter. He was consumed with terror and pity. Her sky-blue eyes had an almost infantile quality now.

One hand groped out to touch his chin. She said in a tiny, plaintive voice:

"No fighting, darling. There's been too much blood and hurt already, dearest. Promise me—"

Suddenly she pitched against him, her bare breasts cold; so cold. Her hands worked at his shoulder muscles:

"Promise me there'll be no fighting, Philip. Promise!"

"Alice, I—I'm not—"

No use. She was crying again. Wild, gulping sobs that told him just how fragile her mental balance really was.

He became aware of a noise that had intruded at the edge of his consciousness some time ago, but which he only now identified: a thudding from below. The tinker.

A faint voice demanded to know the cause of the uproar.

"Nothing wrong," Judson shouted over Alice's hysterical sobs. "It'll be quiet in a moment—"

"—tolerate no unseemly behavior in my house!" The voice faded.

Judson stroked the girl's filthy hair and stared over her shoulder at the pistol lying near the baseboard. Several times he repeated the name by which he knew her. She didn't answer or even respond, only kept kneading his muscles and crying like a sick child.

___7
The Thirteen Clocks

AFTER THE departure of the surprise visitors, Judson threw on a robe and persuaded Alice to drink a bit of the only remedy he had to hand—claret. She held the cup between her work-reddened hands, gulping greedily. She shuddered. Some of the glassy quality seemed to leave her eyes.

Mightily relieved, Judson saw that she recognized him, and her surroundings.

"Alice—" Though the name seemed awkward in light of Trumbrull's revelation, he couldn't use the other with comfort. "—is that man really your aunt's husband?"

Her bowed head hid her face. "Yes."

"And you ran off from his home in Arch Street?"

"I was tending my husband who was—wounded while serving in Boston. He died and—please, no more, Judson," she finished in a whisper.

"But he said you were an earl's daughter. Is that true?"

"It was." Her mouth twisted. "Once."

"Who was Philip?"

"*Stop!*" she cried, hurling the cup at his head.

He dodged. The cup hit the wall, shattered. Once again the tinker thumped his ceiling and demanded quiet. Judson shouted ill-tempered assurances, then started pacing the bedroom. Alice had bundled herself in the coverlet as if she were extremely cold.

He saw how everything Trumbull said could be possible. The lines of her face were fine, delicate; or had been, before dissipation blurred them—

Alice stroked her arm. The flesh was prickled with tiny bumps. "Judson?"

He faced her, still dismayed by the information that had put a whole new perspective on their relationship. She'd meant next to nothing to him until the moment he discovered who she was, and what had driven her to her present state. Now he felt a new, deep concern. With it, he felt confusion about what to do.

"I heard a little of what they said, Judson. Talk of dueling—"

"That stupid uncle of yours wants satisfaction."

"Don't fight him—" She sprang naked from the bed, clutching at him. "Swear you won't! I've brought on too much ruin already—"

He caressed her hair. "Alice, I haven't much choice."

"You have the choice of saying no!"

Judson shook his head.

"*Why not?*"

"Because—" He could offer only one rather sour explanation. "—that's the way it is among gentlemen."

Although it was a truthful response, it seemed unsatisfactory. A moment later he understood why. He dared not admit the real truth. Deep in him, something wanted to lash out and maim—

He was ashamed and vaguely excited at the same time. Christ, how despicable he was!

"Then you won't promise—?" she began.

"The best I can do is try to get the poor fellow to reconsider and withdraw his challenge."

"If you face him, would—would you kill him?"

"He's fat, slow and twice my age. Yes, I think I would."

She stared into his eyes a moment longer, then limped back to the bed, covered herself and burrowed deep into the pillow. Her shoulders shook as she sobbed. The sound of her voice reminded him of Peggy McLean's on the night of the slave uprising.

He poured more claret for himself—that seemed the only antidote to this muddled situation—and crawled into bed with her.

He pulled her close, tried to comfort her. Gradually her hysterical crying

moderated and she fell asleep. Somewhere toward the hour when the stars paled, he did too.

When he awoke after sunup, his head aching, she was gone.

Every trace of clothing—every indication that she'd been in the room had disappeared, except two:

A strand of hair he found clinging to the still-warm bedclothes. And the tall servant's pistol gleaming in a ray of morning sun.

II

NEWS ARRIVING in Philadelphia during June's balmy weather heartened the patriots. The British flotilla at Charleston had been repulsed and heavily damaged, thanks to the accurate, steady fire of the Americans entrenched in a fort of palmetto logs on Sullivan's Island in the harbor.

And members of Congress began to converse in whispers about *Roderigue Hortalez et Cie.*, a mysterious private trading company just organized in France. The company had one express purpose: to speed shipments of war material, including barrel after barrel of vitally needed black powder, to the colonies.

Some speculated that King Louis XVI, no friend of Britain, had callously seized an opportunity to strike at his country's traditional enemy via the Americans. If that were the real reason for the abrupt birth of the peculiar firm, no one loyal to the colonial side would quarrel. Dr. Franklin reported to a few confidants that similar covert assistance might be forthcoming under the auspices of Charles III of Spain.

But what heartened the patriots most was a hope:

If France had moved with such dispatch to aid the Americans in secret, perhaps, with careful diplomacy, the French might be persuaded to openly ally themselves with the rebels. Franklin thought it not impossible at all. And he expressed complete willingness to take advantage of the centuries-old European rivalry.

But whatever the outcome in that area, the long-term prospects for the war looked a shade less grim now that *Hortalez et Cie.* was operating under the personal direction of a most unlikely manager—the author and court wit, Beaumarchais.

Judson absorbed the news in the corridors of the State House, or in whispered conferences in the great white chamber that grew more and more sultry as the weather warmed. The windows still remained almost completely shut as the Congress labored on, awaiting the completion of the draft declaration by the committee.

Concern for Alice had somewhat lessened Judson's interest in the cause. He was drinking heavily again. He spent a large part of his time searching the city for the girl. But she had left the waterfront tavern where she worked and dropped completely out of sight.

The days dragged. There was no communication from the Trumbull household. Then Francis Lightfoot Lee took Judson aside and politely informed him that the challenge by the Tory ropewalk owner had become a choice item of gossip in the city. On behalf of Judson's friends among the delegates, Lee hoped—trusted—some settlement less scandalous than a public duel could be worked out.

Judson promised to do what he could. He penned a careful note which he dispatched to Arch Street. In the note, offered to entertain Mr. Trumbull's reconsideration of the challenge. A day later, Judson's landlord handed him an answer when he returned from the State House.

He questioned the landlord:

Yes, the person who had delivered the reply was tall; and damned arrogant for a servant. Judson broke the elaborate wax seal and unfolded the parchment. He read the note, then crumpled it and threw it away.

Far from accepting Judson's offer, Mr. Tobias Trumbull re-stated his demand for satisfaction more strongly than ever. The unfortunate Mrs. Amberly could not be located anywhere. The Trumbulls feared for her safety—and blamed him. Therefore Judson would please take steps to choose a time, a place and the weapons by which they would settle their quarrel.

III

IN THE middle of the final week of June, there were signs of incredibly hot weather soon to come. On the afternoon Judson called at the rooms Tom Jefferson rented in a large brick house at High and Seventh Streets, the air had a hazy gray quality, minus any trace of wind.

The normally tidy parlor which Judson had visited on several occasions was a litter of crumpled foolscap. The young Virginian sat by a window, his beloved viola and some compositions by Purcell and Vivaldi gathering dust on a table nearby. One of Jefferson's arms was draped laconically over the back of his chair. A quill dangled from his inky fingers.

Across the room, Dr. Franklin occupied a settee. He acknowledged Judson's entrance with a cordial nod, then poked a finger at the sheet he'd been scanning:

"Tom, I find this wordy—'we hold these truths to be sacred and undeniable.' Wouldn't 'self-evident' serve as well?"

"Yes, that's good, scratch it in," Jefferson answered. He sounded tired and indifferent. Franklin picked up another quill, dipped it in a well and made the correction.

Noticing Judson's rather awkward pose at the parlor door, Jefferson laid aside the portable writing-box of highly polished wood that had been resting on his lap. He had designed the miniature desk himself, folding top and all. He lifted his long body from the chair, stretched, yawned.

"I only want to complete the damned thing and get on with the debate," he said. "Will you join me in tea this warm afternoon, Judson?"

"If you have it, I'd prefer something stronger."

Once more that vaguely accusing expression flickered across the Virginian's face, on which summer sunlight had brought out a considerable number of freckles. But he nodded politely, poured a glass of Madeira, his forehead glistening with sweat. Then Jefferson helped himself to tea from a pot.

Franklin tossed aside the foolscap sheet, pushed his spectacles up on his forehead, massaged the bridge of his nose:

"I would say we are approaching a finished draft." To the other man, with a smile: "What brings you here, Judson? Some additional thoughts for Tom to put in?"

"No, it's a personal matter."

"Well, before you launch into it, have you any final opinion about including a passage referring to slavery?" He indicated the discarded sheet. "Tom's still pushing for it."

Judson's brows hooked up as he sipped. The Madeira eased his edgy feeling. "You're talking about a passage condemning slavery?"

Jefferson nodded. "An instrument of oppression permitted, not to say encouraged, by His Majesty."

"It's going a bit far to blame the king for the blackbird trade, isn't it? He may permit it—but we practice it."

Jefferson stared out the window at the clatter of High Street. "Aye, a point. And in my own hands—and my conscience—are dirty on that score."

"If we include it, I predict the declaration will be voted down," Judson said with conviction. "Dickinson and his friends are fighting us for every vote. Even stated in temperate language, an anti-slavery clause would sink us for good."

"I loathe the trade," Franklin said. "I organized the first anti-slavery club in the whole of this city. But I agree with your assessment, Judson."

"I'm still not prepared to strike it out at this stage," Jefferson warned them.

Franklin's eyes narrowed. "Nor ever?"

"Only if it becomes crucial to success or failure."

Heaving his bulk up from the settee, Franklin mopped his neck with a kerchief and picked up his coat of brown velour. He draped it over his arm, saying:

"It will, Tom, never fear, it will. Gentlemen, I'll leave you to your private business."

As Franklin departed, Judson helped himself to another drink. He felt sure the Pennsylvania scholar knew why he'd called—and had deliberately absented himself from the discussion. The entire Congress knew about Judson's predicament by now.

"Tom, I'll come right to it. I'm going to face Trumbull."

"Didn't Francis Lee speak with you?"

"Yes."

"And urge you to reconsider?"

"I sent Trumbull a letter agreeing to forget the matter. In reply, he insisted we go ahead. We've arranged it for the third of July, in the morning, someplace up the Delaware. I come to you as a friend, Tom. I know very few people in Philadelphia, and I need a second."

Unhappily, Tom Jefferson ran a hand over his clubbed red hair. With a look that sent Judson's hopes plummeting, he answered:

"In other circumstances, I might do it. Now—it's impossible."

"Because of the reasons you mentioned back in January? The moral outrage it might cause—?"

Jefferson agreed with another nod. "You realize what may happen if you go ahead, don't you, Judson? President Hancock is well aware of the trouble. He has again made his feelings—his strong feelings—known to me. If you persist, in all likelihood you'll be quietly asked to withdraw from the Virginia delegation. I'm afraid I'd have to support that request. I'm sorry, Judson, but I fail to see how some tavern trollop is worth—"

White-lipped, Judson cut him off: "We needn't debate the details."

"Yes, we very much need to debate them. Damn it, Judson, no one among your close associates—least of all those of us from your home colony—can understand why you let yourself be drawn into such a shabby business. A futile, purposeless encounter over a woman who—"

"Tom, that's enough."

"On the contrary! You're being obstinate. You act damned near driven to this!"

Judson turned away. "Maybe I am."

"Well, it's a shameful waste. One day you're in the thick of things, working, debating, using your considerable intellect—the next, you're off swilling down so much strong drink you make Franklin look like a temperance lecturer! I puzzle over it, Judson."

Cold-eyed, Judson said, "Why bother?"

"Because—in a short time—" An eloquent shrug. "—you've become a friend. I try and try to understand what flogs you to these excesses—"

"So do I," Judson replied with a bitter smile.

"Have you found any answers?"

"Only one—and that not very satisfactory. I've concluded that in this world, certain men are stronger than others. The weaker ones are unable to accommodate themselves to normal behavior—and finding themselves not fitting the pattern, they're destroyed by the situation. Or destroy themselves—"

"Are you sure that's not merely the wine talking?"

"No." He tossed off the rest of the Madeira. "My father. On numerous occasions."

"It's idiotic to surrender to that sort of defeatist philosophy."

"I'm a misfit, Tom. I always will be. Recognizing that, I've at least carried out one of my father's wishes." Judson's eyes grew bitterly amused. "He cautioned me against ever marrying, since if I did, I'd surely pass along my waywardness to generations of helpless, suffering grandchildren—"

"Nonsense. You're indulging in self-pity."

Judson smiled again, this time with utter charm. "But that goes with being a misfit."

Jefferson refused to be diverted: "If we can bring about independency, Judson—if we can finish this war soon—"

"A pair of mighty tall *ifs*."

"Granted, granted. But think of what's to be won! All the chances you have to break out of this—this pattern you claim you despise—"

"I don't understand."

"Do you have any notion of the size of this continent, Judson? We're only crouching on the edge! It stretches from the Floridas to Hudson's Bay, and beyond. Out west, past the Ohio, the French fur traders have traveled a river that beggars the imagination! The Sieur de La Salle named it the Colbert but the Indians call it Big River. *Misi Sipi*." He was striding now, caught up in his vision.

"We're getting off the subject, Tom."

"No, no, we're not! This land mass is huge! Bountiful as well. Who knows the full extent of the wealth it holds between that big river and the Pacific? I tell you the Spanish are doing their best to learn the answers—with their presidios and missions in what they christened the New Philippines. Imagine if even a portion of that territory were ours! If the foreign flags came down—the lions and castles of Leon and Castile flying right now in the southwest—the area they're coming to call *Tejas*—think of the opportunity for settlement! Agriculture and commerce! The general increase of human knowledge! All I'm saying to you, Judson, is that with such vast lands still contested in the west, no man should feel hemmed in by his immediate surroundings. By the Lord, I don't intend to be.

Before I die, I mean to see a scientific expedition walk that whole wilderness to the Pacific!''

After a moment of silence, Judson said, ''I understand a little of what you're saying. One of my good friends has already traveled past the Blue Ridge. Sometimes I've thought I belonged out there with him—''

''Who is your friend?''

''George Clark.''

''George Rogers Clark?''

''That's right.''

''He's already made a distinguished name scouting with the Virginia militia. But leaving the opportunity in the west aside for a moment—''

''Yes, because the idea's unrealistic. I'll never get there.''

Judson's emphatic statement checked Jefferson before he could begin another sentence. His enthusiasm vanished, replaced first by a look of regret, then by an expression faintly stern and righteous:

''Very well, that may be so. But no matter what his condition or location, a man grown to adulthood is at least called to exercise self-control.''

''That's another lecture I've received from my father.''

Jefferson gnawed his lip. Then:

''In short, you won't try to moderate your behavior? Keep your eye on greater possibilities than what's up a skirt or down in the bottom of a glass?''

''I try.'' A pause. ''I always fail.''

''Does that mean you won't reconsider the Trumbull matter?''

''At this late hour—I can't.''

''Not even in view of the probable consequences? Hancock will almost certainly insist you withdraw and return to Virginia.''

''Let him.''

''Judson, what are you trying to prove about yourself?''

''I beg your pardon?''

''To whom are you trying to demonstrate your independence? Your manhood—?''

Judson set the Madeira glass down, noisily. ''I'm in no mood for subtle discourses—''

''Nothing subtle about it,'' Jefferson waved. ''I see you as you can't see yourself. Sometimes you permit your essential nature to shine through. A good mind, moral courage of the highest order. Then you seem to lose sight of those qualities. Or quell them deliberately. I think only a man overcome with loathing for himself acts that way. You've mentioned your father—is he one you're constantly—?''

''Good day, Tom.'' A muscle in his neck bulging, Judson started out.

''Wait! Listen to me! You'll destroy yourself, trying to prove something that doesn't need prov—''

The slam of the door shut out the rest.

Judson rushed down the stairs toward High Street, noisy with wagons rolling in from the country laden with farm produce. The astute Mr. Tom Jefferson had struck into the depths Judson didn't care to plumb. Very uncomfortable depths—

As he walked through the hazy gray afternoon, ignoring several stares directed his way—the forthcoming duel was a town scandal—an image of Alice loomed in his mind.

The Trumbulls had driven her to her pathetic state. That angry conviction was validation enough for what he meant to do.

The image of Alice dissolved into another. His father—

Yes, Jefferson had struck much too close to the truth. Whatever the causes, he was poisoned by a frequent, almost wholly uncontrollable desire to defy convention, or any authority; to choose one road when he knew another was the accepted way—

Who was to blame? As if it mattered any longer! Or would change anything—

Instead of returning to committee session, he turned in at the first available ale shop and lost himself in the airless gloom, safe for a while from the reality of the world outside. It wasn't long before his inner world was similarly deadened and remote.

IV

THUNDER SHOOK the State House. Bursts of lightning glared like infernal fire let up from the bowels of the earth. The storm ripped across Philadelphia, slamming rain against the tightly shut windows and reverberating through the chamber where John Hancock again occupied the presidential dais.

The air in the room was boiling. Judson's face streamed with sweat. He swatted at one of the mammoth horseflies that had somehow invaded the chamber to bedevil the perspiring men listening to John Dickinson defend his position:

"—and I therefore cannot in conscience support the resolution yesterday debated by this Congress sitting as a committee of the whole with Mr. Harrison as chairman—"

The fuzzy-sounding voice irritated Judson. He was starting to sober up, and didn't feel at all well. He wanted to leave, find a tavern, quench his thirst.

Exactly what day was it? He'd lost track—

With a jolt he realized it was the second of July. Tomorrow, unseconded, he'd face Trumbull. Perhaps the steady approach of the day of the duel was what had kept him in a constant stupor for the past week. That, and no word about Alice; she had utterly vanished.

He blinked, feeling more bilious by the moment. He changed the position of his chair noisily. He was aware of the disapproving stares of the Lees and George Wythe at desks nearby. Even Jefferson, nervously fingering a copy of his completed draft declaration, appeared less than friendly. Dickinson's damnably boring voice droned on.

Judson slouched, dull-headed, callously indifferent. To hell with all of them. He had no business in this lofty gathering. He was exactly what Angus Fletcher had always said he was. A wastrel—

What in God's name was that idiot Dickinson saying now?

"—I have long stood firmly against abuses perpetrated by His Majesty's ministers—"

A few canes rapped agreement. There was another crackle of thunder, then blinding whiteness outside the rain-rivered windows.

"—and in fact have publicly condemned those abuses in publications of which you are fully aware. But I see nothing save disaster in the resolution it is proposed we vote on today. To favor independency is akin to torching our house in winter before we have got another shelter. I beg you to consider the consequences of the total war which will surely follow such a declaration. Think of great cities such as Boston not evacuated quietly by His Majesty's armies, but

burned and razed to ruin. Already agents bring us reports that British officers are swarming across the frontier, rousing the Indian tribes as allies. What can that mean but butchery for the settlers who, for example, chose homesites in the western reaches of my own Pennsylvania? Furthermore, a war of long duration cannot but bankrupt both sides. Ruin England financially, and ourselves as well—''

"Dammit, this is tedious and insufferable yellow coward's talk!" Judson yelled, lurching to his feet. "I submit that we are not arguing what is or is not good business. We are arguing the choice of liberty or tyranny. Courage or cowardice!''

Shocked whispers ran around the chamber. Hancock glared and rapped for silence:

"If you please, Mr. Fletcher! You will be recognized in proper turn."

Flushing, Judson sat down. He felt queasy again. Received more than a few angry looks. Dickinson, obviously enraged, concluded with a single clipped statement:

"I cannot continue to be a party to these proceedings."

Stunned silence.

Upset, Hancock asked, "Are you indicating that you wish to absent yourself from further deliberations of this Congress, Mr. Dickinson?"

"I am."

In the pause, thunder boomed like cannon in the black sky. With an agonizing sincerity, Dickinson added:

"I am aware that my conduct this day will give the finishing blow to any brief popularity I may have enjoyed as a result of my defense of Englishmen's liberties. Yet I had rather forfeit popularity forever than vote away the blood and happiness of my countrymen."

John Dickinson sat down amid another flurry of cane-knocking, approval of his moral courage if not of his final stance. Judson stifled a belch. Thank God he wasn't burdened with such niceties of conscience—though he probably shouldn't have attacked Dickinson so rudely; should have waited his turn, framed a reasoned rebuttal—

A lightning-glare startled him. He whipped his head around as John Adams clamored to be recognized. On the white-shimmering surface of a tall window, he saw a ghostly image.

Lank hair.

Slack lips.

Haunted blue eyes—

Trembling, Judson covered his face. He broke out in a cold sweat, nauseous.

Tom Jefferson leaned close, whispering:

"Judson? Are you ill?"

"Drunk," someone else sneered.

"Spoiled sausage—" he said hoarsely. "Breakfast, I think—" His stomach began to churn more violently. Sourness climbed in his throat—

He stumbled up from his desk, hearing exclamations in the chamber. Hancock turned an unsympathetic eye on him as he ran toward the closed doors, afraid he'd be sick before he got outside.

His illness had nothing to do with breakfast. He'd eaten no sausage that morning, spoiled or otherwise. He'd eaten nothing. He had consumed four—or was it five?—pints of ale.

In the pouring rain in the Stae House yard, he vomited. When he tried to walk

back inside, he slipped on the steps, seeing Trumbull's porcine face in a light-ning burst. He sprawled on hands and knees, retching, delirious—

And then the step slammed up to strike his face.

Eventually he heard a voice. Familiar, somehow—

He rolled his head back; heard his name spoken again. Against the black sky he saw Tom Jefferson, rain-drenched. Jefferson leaned down to pull him to his feet:

"Stand up, Judson."

"Sorry," the younger man mumbled. "Sorry for the spectacle. Plagued bad sausage—"

Sadly, Jefferson glanced at Judson's befouled clothing. "Whatever the reason, it's the consensus of the delegation that you should withdraw. Immediately. I am sorry to tell you that, but you've exceeded reasonable bounds. Hancock is still in a fury over your interruption of Dickinson. Whatever his views, Mr. Dickinson is respected—and treated accordingly. Hancock would have come out and caned you if there hadn't been such important business before the chamber."

Thunder; roaring as if the earth would shake apart. The rain drove between them, and Judson hated Tom Jefferson's quiet power as much as he loathed his own weakness.

He wiped sourness from the corner of his mouth. "Sorry too. Wanted to be seated when the resolution—"

Jefferson shook his head. "It's done. You've been lying out here almost two hours."

"The voting's done?"

"Yes."

"How—?"

"Twelve for, none against, New York instructed to abstain. Tomorrow we begin work on the final phrasing of the document." Jefferson couldn't conceal his disgust. "But you have a more pressing engagement. You lent strength to this gathering for a time, Judson. I wish you'd had enough strength to see the venture to its end."

He turned and disappeared into the State House. The door closed loudly.

Judson felt humiliated; unclean. Still sick to his stomach, he stood with the rain pouring over him. It had washed the worst of the mess off his clothes but it could do nothing to cleanse the stench in his mind and soul.

V

AT FIRST light the next morning, Judson faced Tobias Trumbull and the tall, smirking servant in a maple grove beside the Delaware River. Judson's horse was tethered nearby. Further away in the mist, a large, splendid coach-and-four showed blurs at the windows: a few well-wishers come to offer Trumbull en-couragement.

Nervously tapping a thumb on the side plate of his pistol, the Tory wheezed:

"I ask you one more time, sir. Where is Alicia?"

"I haven't seen her and I don't know." Judson felt abominable. Hung over. His stomach was still unsettled. His hands shook.

"Liar," Trumbell said. *"Damned liar!"*

Judson almost struck the fat fool. Instead, he turned to the servant:

"Let's have done."

Pleased, the servant indicated a fresh slash on the muddy ground:

"Start back to back from this line. At the count, begin your paces. At ten, turn and fire."

Pistols held muzzle up, the two men took their positions. Judson was worried about his powder and the priming in this damp weather. The tall man called out:

"*One.*"

Both duelists started forward, walking away from each other. Judson consciously tried to steady his gun hand.

"*Two. Three.*"

Trees along the murmuring river dripped from yesterday's storm. Rising before daylight, Judson had found the streets already crowded. People were turning out to learn more about the incredible action taken in the State House. Independency had been voted, so everyone said—

"*Four. Five.*"

Judson fingered the cock of his pistol, aware of his own raspy breathing. *What had happened to Alice?*

"*Six. Seven. Eight.*"

Judson's boots squashed the sodden ground. Muggy with mist, the morning seemed funereal. An appropriate day to die—

Goddamn it, stop thinking that way! He had only to take his time; remain calm. Trumbull would surely miss—

"*Nine.*"

All at once, a torrent of rage against everyone and everything ripped through him, threatening to loosen the hard-won control of his pistol hand.

"*TEN*"

Fighting to stay steady, he pivoted. Watched the Tory ropewalk owner raise his pistol, aim—

Judson stood motionless, presenting the right side of his body, a narrow target. The tremor in Trumbull's forearm already spelled the outcome. The pistol discharged with a spurt of red, a lick of smoke. Trumbull took a backward step as Judson listened to the ball whiz past a good yard from his chest.

The stupid wretch, to push it this far—!

He could aim to wound and the affair would be settled. That would be the sensible way. Slowly, Judson swung up his dueling pistol, extended his arm full length, sighted down the muzzle. The tall servant tensed, clearly afraid his master might bolt.

Trumbull stood his ground, but only with obvious difficulty. Judson's face wrenched into vicious pleasure as he noticed a set stain at the crotch of Trumbull's trousers. He sighted for Trumbull's left shoulder, started to squeeze the trigger—

And saw not some ridiculous, craven Tory, but his own father, a spectre in the river mist—

Without conscious thought, Judson swung the muzzle slightly left and fired. Trumbull squealed, tried to dodge. But he wasn't fast enough. The ball caught him in the side of the temple, opening a splintery hole that looked black in the bad light.

Cries of shock and horror sounded from the coach. The tall servant fanned his cloak aside, his right hand diving toward his belt. Judson enjoyed a brief moment of self-congratulation. He had anticipated some such treachery. The tall servant drew a pistol as he stepped across the body of his fallen master—

But Judson had already produced a second pistol himself, from a hiding place under his coat. He held the pistol at full cock:

"My duel was with him. I shot fairly. Walk to the bank and throw your gun in the river."

The tall servant didn't move.

"Throw it away or I'll kill you," Judson shouted. "With those fine gentlemen in the coach as my witnesses that I was attacked first."

The bluff worked. Fuming, the tall man strode through the mud to the high grass along the shore. He flung his weapon into the water. Judson laughed, his face as white as a skull in the murk. He aimed the second pistol at the ground, fired, and when the explosion died away, tossed the weapon to a point halfway between himself and the servant.

"That's the one you promised to take back," he yelled. He walked to his horse, mounted quickly and booted the animal toward the rutted road leading to Philadelphia.

Despite the fairness of the duel, Judson had no illusions about the stories that would be circulated. He'd had no seconds—no witnesses of his own. Philadelphia would be hot for him now. He could become the victim of much more than slanted gossip.

The horse's hoofs shot up great sticky slops of mud on the road to the city. Feeling the aftershocks of the duel at last, Judson sweated and trembled and wondered numbly who, after all, he had shot to death beside the Delaware.

___VI

WEARY, HE unlatched the door to his quarters on Windmill Street—and pulled up short just inside the entrance:

"Alice! My God, what's happened to you?"

All filth and rags, she swayed in front of him.

"Judson—this was the morning when—"

"Where have you been? *Where?*" he exclaimed, rushing forward.

She fended his hands. He realized with a second shock that she was feverish. Her eyes failed to focus properly. Her shabby clothing was brown with mud; ripped in half a dozen places. There were ugly moist sores at each corner of her mouth.

"Never mind," she said, with an expression of such utter misery Judson could barely bring himself to look at her. "Is my aunt's husband—?"

"Dead." Judson swallowed. "I gave him a fair chance. Alice—" He walked toward her. "Let me get you into bed. Clean you up. You're ill. Christ, girl, have you just been wandering the street—?"

As he reached for her, she uttered one short, wild wail and dashed past him, out the door and down the stairs.

He ran after her, shouting her name. But she eluded him in the morning mist. He ran a block up Windmill Street in one direction, a block the other.

She'd disappeared.

Knowing that he could have done little to correct her unbalanced mental condition, he still felt a deep sense of responsibility for her safety. Not love; nothing like love. It was just that she had no one else to protect her against herself. As he had no one else.

He pondered alternatives. Should he take his horse and search again? No, he'd tried that before, with no success.

But he couldn't simply abandon her when she was clearly in a deranged state. Starting up the steps to get rid of his damp, mud-fouled clothes, he looked down, struck by something he'd missed before—

Marks of bare feet on the bleached plank steps. A toe; an instep; traced in something damp and reddish-brown.

He crouched, fingered it.

Blood.

How long had she been walking like that? In pain? He bent his head and wept his grief.

VII

HE SEARCHED for her the remainder of the day, unsuccessfully. At dusk, exhausted, he found a tavern. He barely heard the animated conversation—and loud arguments—that seethed over the latest rumors from the State House. Yes, the Congress *was* close to adopting a final draft of its declaration—

Uncaring, Judson drank himself steadily deeper into darkness—

And woke with a lump on his head, and his purse empty, in an alley two blocks from the establishment where he'd passed out.

Stumbling up, he staggered into the nearest street. A newsboy was ringing a handbell. Judson walked by, then caught the lad's cry:

"—alarming death of relative of Trumbull family!"

He snatched a sheet, read it over the boy's whining protests. The story was brief, the ink still wet:

A woman had been discovered floating near one of the river piers the preceding evening. A Mrs. Alicia Amberly, widow of the late Lieutenant Colonel Amberly of His Majesty's army, and niece by marriage of Mr. Tobias Trumbull who had likewise met his death the same day in an affair of honor. Trumbull's distraught wife had identified the drowned girl, apparently a suicide, as heiress to the fortune of the Earl of Parkhurst of Great Britain.

Judson flung the paper back at the boy and strode on, too drained to hurt any more. Now the issue was whether he himself wanted to survive amidst the wreckage he had created.

VIII

BUT THAT was another weakness among the countless ones afflicting him: he lacked the strength to expunge his guilt by doing away with himself.

He thought about it many times in the next couple of days, sitting alone in the silence of the rooms at Windmill Street, drinking. Outside, bell boys passed frequently, shouting that the text of the independency declaration had finally been approved by the Congress.

That finally stirred Judson out of his torpor. He found a coin, went into the street and purchased a broadsheet—another quick print job, he saw from the bleary type. Going back upstairs, he read the news:

On Thursday, the fourth, the *Unamimous Declaration of the Thirteen States of America* had been duly agreed upon, and signed by the Congressional president, Hancock, "in a hand big enough for John Bull to read it." Judson reckoned this to be Saturday morning already. Quickly he read on.

Official signing of the declaration by all the Congressional delegates would not take place for at least a month. A much-corrected copy of Jefferson's text had been turned over to a printer named Matlack for proper engrossing on a clean sheet of parchment. Additional copies were being rushed to the army and other major cities. On the eighth, the broadsheet declared, the people of Philadelphia would be made aware of the document's contents by a public reading in the State House yard.

Judson suddenly felt hungry. Hungry and awake. In no better spirits, but stubbornly alive. The high drama had reached its conclusion. He reckoned he'd go along to that reading and learn how it had all come out. As he poured himself still one more drink, he decided that a minor actor who had botched his small, almost insignificant role still had a right to be present for the denouement.

Despite the horrors of the past days, Judson couldn't help feeling a shiver of pride at the thought of what had been done in Philadelphia City. If he was of no consequence on the world's stage—and he knew he wasn't—at least he had been privileged to share a bit of the last act. The thought was enough to make him put the decanter aside and think of hunting up a bite of food to renew his strength.

Monday he would be in the Yard. Time enough after that to let the circumstances of his dismal existence reclaim him.

___ IX

A THOUSAND people or more jammed the area around the State House on Monday morning. The crowd packed the Yard and spilled out into the streets, everyone talking excitedly. Some looked fearful. Others boasted that now the colonies would whip King George's soldiers for fair.

Judson tethered his horse at a crowded hitch-post, wormed his way to the Yard entrance and gained a favorable position with some shoving and scowling. The attention of the crowd was focused on a circular platform normally used as a base for the telescopes of the Philosophical Society. But this morning, the person clambering up with parchment sheets in hand was no scientist bent on studying the heavens. Judson recognized a man he'd seen around the State House before: John Nixon, of the local Committee of Safety.

Judson scanned the faces, smiled in a weary way. Very few well-to-do people were present. Mostly plain folk of the working classes, to judge from their garb.

Then, a row or two ahead, he noticed three familiar backs: Tom Jefferson, Dr. Franklin, John Adams. They were talking in an animated way. Judson didn't want to be seen by them. Yet something compelled him to edge forward sufficiently to pick up some of the conversation.

"—and it ought to be celebrated by succeeding generations as the great anniversary festival!" Adams was saying. "It ought to be commemorated as the day of deliverance! Solemnized with pomp and parade! With shows, games, sports, guns, bells, bonfires and illuminations from one end of this continent to the other—from this time forward!"

Judson heard Jefferson answer, "You have a good right to be proud and thrilled, John. You were its chief architect."

"I never thought I'd see the hour come," Franklin said with a deep sigh. "Remember what I observed about the clocks?"

"Certainly," Adams told him. "That pulling thirteen colonies into concerted action was like trying to force thirteen clocks engineered by thirteen distinctly dissimilar clockmakers to chime all at once. Improbable indeed!"

"But not impossible, as it turned out," Franklin said. "We've done it, by God."

Said Jefferson with a wry smile: "Let us devoutly hope we survive the consequences."

"Come, come, Tom," Adams chided, "no flagging now! We must all hang together—"

"Or surely we'll all hang separately," Franklin said, amused.

Nixon clamored for the crowd's attention, finally got it. A wave of silence rippled outward from the round platform. The man's clear, strong voice sent each word through the gates and into the mob thronging the street:

"Herewith the unanimous declaration of the thirteen United States of America, voted upon by the delegates of the various states in congress assembled last July fourth—"

Applause, some cheering. Nixon waited. In the interval, Judson heard Jefferson say to Adams:

"I've seen some of the copies run off from the one at Matlack's. My God, what they'll think of us when those copies arrive in Boston or Richmond—!"

"What's wrong with them?" Adams asked.

"The spelling! The punctuation! They follow neither the approved draft, nor reason, nor the custom of any age known to man—"

Adams laughed, then shushed the young Virginian as Nixon resumed:

"When in the course of human events, it becomes necessary for one people to dissolve the political bands which have connected them with another, and to assume among the powers of the earth the separate and equal station to which the laws of nature and of nature's God entitle them, a decent respect to the opinions of mankind requires that they should declare the causes which impel them to the separation—"

Total silence now, the throng hanging on each syllable. Judson had the eerie feeling that he was being watched. He turned his head slightly, saw the tinker from whom he rented his rooms clinging to the top of the Yard's brick wall. The little old man frowned, his white locks blowing in the July breeze. He seemed to be trying to communicate something to Judson with his glance. Exactly what, Judson couldn't fathom. He returned his attention to the reading:

"We hold these truths to be self-evident, that all men are created equal—"
Cheering.

"—that they are endowed by their Creator with certain unalienable rights, that among these are life, liberty, and the pursuit of happiness. That to secure these rights, governments are instituted among men, deriving their just powers from the consent of the governed. That whenever any form of government becomes destructive of these ends, it is the right of the people to alter or to abolish it, and to institute new government, laying its foundation on such principles and organizing its powers in such form, as to them shall seem most likely to effect their safety and happiness—"

The crowd began to grow restive. Jefferson's stirring phrases were just a bit lofty for the common man's taste. But shortly, Nixon reached a section that stirred the people to frenzied huzzahs and hand-clapping. The speaker read off a

lengthy bill of particulars accusing *the present king of Great Britain* of a host of *injuries and ursurpations*. Each new accusation was greeted with an outburst more enthusiastic than the last; clearly, this was the section of the declaration that would prove the most popular, and be quoted most frequently in years to come:

"He has called together legislative bodies at places unusual, uncomfortable, and distant from the depository of their public records, for the sole purpose of fatiguing them into compliance with his measures. He has dissolved representative houses repeatedly, for opposing with manly firmness his invasions on the rights of the people—"

Judson's attention wandered a little, his eyes drawn upward to the bell tower of the State House where he thought he saw a figure scrambling against the blue summer sky. Again he swung to peer at the tinker perched on the wall. But the man was watching Nixon:

"For imposing taxes on us without our consent. For depriving us in many cases of the benefits of trial by jury—"

Judson began to be troubled by the tinker's earlier look. It had seemed to contain a warning. Of what? He wondered. When the reading concluded, he must find out.

"He has plundered our seas, ravaged our coasts, burnt our towns, and destroyed the lives of our people—"

As the sonorous accusations rolled on, Judson again felt the humiliation of having failed to carry out his role which his brother had arranged for him in good faith. *If only he'd sat through with the Congress to the end!* The Fletcher name—his name; and Donald's—would have gone down with the names of all those others who would eventually sign the clean copy—

Judson's mouth twisted. As he'd suggested to Tom Jefferson, not all men in the world could be great or important men. Some had to be flawed; failures—

The dreadful self-hate filled him again, relieved only by the rising volume of Nixon's voice. He had evidently reached the document's conclusion:

"We therefore, the representatives of the United States of America, in general congress assembled, appealing to the Supreme Judge of the world for the rectitude of our intentions, do, in the name, and by authority of the good people of these colonies, solemnly publish and declare that these united colonies are, and of right ought to be free and independent states. That they are absolved from all allegiance to the British Crown, and that all political connection between them and the state of Great Britain is and ought to be totally dissolved. And that as free and independent states they have full power to levy war—"

The crowd grew hushed at that sentence.

"—conclude peace—"

A stirring; whispers here and there; perhaps the conflict could be speedily resolved.

"—contract alliances—"

France, Judson thought. If only France could now publicly come to the aid of the fledgling country.

"—establish commerce, and to do all other acts and things which independent states may of right do. And for the support of this declaration, with a firm reliance on the protection of Divine Providence, we mutually pledge to each other—"

Judson glanced up, saw more activity in the bell tower; ropes bobbing.

"—our lives, our fortunes and our sacred honor."

Bedlam broke loose. People shouted, stamped the ground, wept and clapped.

Judson was punched, nudged, buffeted from every side as the crowd roared approval of all it had heard. He wanted to leave the Yard.

As he turned, so did Tom Jefferson, his red hair bright as fire in the sun. Their eyes met. Jefferson's looked abruptly sad.

He seemed on the point of trying to speak through the rising tumult, a tumult heightened by the first clangorous peals of the huge bell in the State House tower. Ashamed, Judson turned away.

Clang! Clang! The bell sang, each peal reverberating. As Judson struggled through the crowd, he thought he'd suddenly been afflicted with some malady of the ear. He heard echoes begin, sweeping from one end of the sky to the other. Bells of different pitch and volume, all responding to the signal of the first bell proclaiming liberty, filling heaven with their brazen music—

CLANG! CLANG!

The free and independent states of America. Judson wasn't embarrassed to wipe tears from his eyes. He would be forgotten. But he had been here.

CLANG! CLANG! CLANG!

Clambering down from the wall, the old tinker fought toward him, looking decidedly out of sorts:

"Mr. Fletcher—stop pushing, woman, this is important!—Mr. Fletcher, you left Windmill Street ahead o' me—"

"That's right, what of it?"

"Just 'fore I come down here, a party of gentlemen arrived. Huntin' for you." The tinker was obviously unhappy about this latest disturbance of his quiet life.

Judson scowled, his gray-blue eyes hardening. "I know of no gentlemen who'd seek me out."

"Not a one but didn't have a mighty ugly phiz. And a couple o' pistols, too. Tory gentlemen, I think they were."

Trumbull's crowd. He'd been lucky to avoid them thus far.

"I want no trouble, Mr. Fletcher! If you go back to the rooms, I'd at least wait until dark. I just won't abide any more rows, or damage to my property—"

Judson's decision was almost instantaneous. He shook his head:

"I don't believe I'll go back. I've no belongings of value there. And my account with you is in order, isn't it?"

"Yes, square. But what do you want done with 'em things of yours?"

"Sell them, burn them, I don't give a damn." He turned and strode swiftly through the crowd as the bells pealed across the sky. In moments, he was mounted and lashing a path through the celebrating mob, heedless of whom he struck with his flying crop.

X

BY EARLY afternoon on the eighth of July, 1776, Judson Fletcher was riding southwestward along the Delaware, bound home for Virginia.

He knew his father's strength of will. There would be no place for him at Sermon Hill. But he'd face that problem later. Virginia was the inevitable choice. It was the only land he knew.

Ah, but what did it matter where you lived when your only course seemed to be uncontrollable destruction of yourself and everything around you?

Still, as Jefferson had said, it seemed to him that there should be a place in the

world—in this country—where a man could find contentment. An ordered existence. Peace for a troubled spirit. Unfortunately Judson had no clear and positive idea about where such a place might be.

The brief exhilaration of the morning faded under the wearying rhythm of the horse. Tom Jefferson was right about something else. The patriots who had gambled their futures and their very lives on a sheet of parchment—the men who had pulled and hauled with such dedication to create union out of disunion—would want no name like Judson Fletcher's on their declaration. They would want no part of a man who was dishonorable and damned.

But why damned? *Why?*

Was he, as his father contended, the bearer of some contaminant impossible to overcome? Some fatal flaw of body and soul?—providing, of course, such a commodity as a soul existed! The old man termed it the devil's blood, but Judson reckoned *Fletcher blood* would be more accurate.

Whatever the name, was he absolutely powerless to escape the disastrous effects? Sometimes—as now—he felt so. But he could never puzzle out a certain answer. And just thinking about it was laborious and hurtful—

Do you suppose there's an inn at the ferry crossing ahead? I'm plagued thirsty—

Gradually, as he rode on, the last distant ringing of the bells of Philadelphia died away beneath the murmur of the hot July breeze.

What would become of the new nation? he wondered, trying to dismiss a sudden picture of Alice from his mind. What would become of him—?

Godamighty, he was thirsty!

And a great fool. The first question was certainly the only one of importance. The second—and its answer—counted for nothing at all.

BOOK TWO
THE TIMES THAT TRY MEN'S SOULS

__1
The Privateers

FEBRUARY ICICLES hung outside the parlor windows, fiery crystal that dripped in the bright sun. The light spilling into the room sparkled the dark eyes of the baby Philip Kent swung high over his head, then down again.

"Philip, you'll frighten him!" Anne said as she came in. The child, stocky as his father, and with the same thick, dark hair, disproved it with a delighted gurgle as Philip set him down gently, then brushed out a fold in the homespun smock Anne had sewn herself.

"He enjoys it," Philip grinned, moving two paces backward. He stretched out his arms. "Walk to me, Abraham. Walk to Papa."

Gurgling again, Abraham took three unsteady steps. He stumbled and sprawled, wailing.

Philip rushed forward. So did the two visitors. But Anne reached the baby first, snatched him to her breast and started out of the room:

"You're so used to tossing muskets around at top speed, you've forgotten how to handle something more delicate," she teased Philip. "I'll put him in the crib for his nap. Then we'll eat."

When she'd gone, George Lumden packed tobacco into his clay pipe and said, "A fine, strong boy, Philip. How old is he now?"

"Just turned sixteen months."

"I hope we're similarly blessed this spring."

Lumden was a soft-spoken, gray-eyed man with a large mole on his forehead. Formerly a British infantryman garrisoned in Boston, he had deserted to the American side—and an American bride—with Philip's assistance.

Reveling in the warmth of the two logs popping in the fireplace, Philip said to Lumden's visibly pregnant wife:

"So this will very likely be your last trip to Concord before the baby's born, eh?"

All vivid red hair and winter-pinked cheeks, Daisy Lumden nodded. She sat beside her husband, clasping his hand. "I wanted to see my father before it became impossible to travel."

Early in 1775, Philip had stayed at the farm Daisy's father owned out beyond the Concord River. The red-haired girl had been the cook in the Ware home in Boston. Lumden had been quartered there, as soldiers were quartered in houses all over the city, by royal decree. Romance had spurred his decision to join the hundreds of other redcoats who stole away, unwilling to take part in a war against people they considered fellow Englishmen.

"Even with the thaw, the trip up from Connecticut is difficult," Daisy added.

Philip stretched his cracked boots toward the flames of the hearth. How well he knew.

"I'll spend half my leave just riding to and from Morristown." A pause. "But you haven't told me how you're finding life in Connecticut, George."

"Satisfactory, more than satisfactory!" the ex-soldier smiled. "I obtained a small loan from my second cousin in Hartford, and I've put the training I got at my father's smithy in Warwickshire to good use—"

From a traveling valise, he produced a long, slender oiled-paper package.

"I'll never make a Continental soldier," he said. "But at least I can do my share in other ways. Here, I brought this for you."

Pleased and surprised, Philip unwrapped the package. Sunlight flashed on the gleaming metal of a new bayonet.

"I opened up a small forge, and I'm supplying them on contract to the army," Lumden explained with pride.

"A beautiful instrument." Philip balanced it on his hand. "And appreciated— as they weren't when we tried to hold Breed's Hill. I'd say a fourth of our men are equipped with bayonets now. More are getting them every day. Thank you, George."

Daisy patted a loose curl of coppery hair. "When Anne wrote that you were coming home, we thought it might be permanently, Philip."

He clucked his tongue. "I wish it were. But in January, I rejoined for three more years."

"You very nearly had no army left to rejoin," Lumden commented.

"That's true."

"In Connecticut, the criticism of General Washington has been bloody scandalous. Or it was until last month. People claimed he was such a poor commander, men kept sneaking away home by the hundreds."

"It's not the general who's lacking, it's the troops," Philip replied. Yet he had to admit that during the grim days of the autumn of '76 just passed, he too had again questioned the leadership ability of the squire from Fairfax County, Virginia. Now that he was home for a bit, the agonies of the preceding months had a dim, unreal quality; but the net effect lingered. The American army had failed miserably.

Washington had lost Long Island in August. Then came the humiliation of the

British capture of New York City, as the Howe brothers—General Sir William in charge of the ground forces, Admiral Lord Richard commanding the naval squadron blockading the rivers and landing the regiments—forced Washington's army into retreat after retreat.

Lumden said, "We understood Sir William and Black Dick Howe had the king's authorization to pardon the colonials."

"Yes, I think that's correct. But that was *before* Long Island. And of course the effort came to nothing because they had no authority *except* to pardon us for our supposed sins. No power to deal with the issues that caused all this."

Philip chuckled. "The whole rigmarole does have its comical side sometimes. The Howes tried to open negotiations with Washington but they refused to address him any other way than *Mister* Washington. To have called him general, you see, would have acknowledged that he had some authority! And that, in effect, would have recognized last July's declaration. Well, *Mister* Washington rejected all such correspondence—so the Howes tried 'George Washington, Esquire, *etcetera*'—arguing that *etcetera* could mean anything the recipient wished! Washington rejected those letters too. Finally the Howes got tired of dallying offshore and landed on Long Island."

"And the soldiers ran!" Daisy said, disgusted.

"In some cases," Philip agreed. "But for every one of those incidents, I could tell you three where little groups of men stood and died. Still, the problem of lack of training is having its toll. The majority of men just don't understand military life. God knows I don't enjoy obeying some fool's orders! A friend of mine who's in charge of the artillery once prophesied the problem. He said farmers and artisans probably couldn't be turned into a disciplined fighting force. And whenever it proves to be true, it's a disaster. When the British crossed to New York island and landed at Kip's Bay, for instance, the militia turned tail. Washington arrived on that beautiful white horse he rides. He swore like I've never heard a man swear before. And he laid about him with his own sword—"

"Attacking the enemy personally?" Lumden asked.

Philip shook his head. "His own men—who were running. He was in such a state, one of the staff officers had to lead his horse off the field. That kind of thing poisons the air. By the time we were pushed back across the Hudson into Jersey, and then marched south, the army was ready to fall apart. I think it would have if the general hadn't turned us out on Christmas to cross the Delaware."

"People began saying better things about Washington after that," Lumden commented. "It was a splendid victory!"

"George, you're acting and sounding like a patriot these days," Philip laughed.

"I am, a bit," Lumden said, reddening. "Loyalties do change. How many of those damned German mercenaries did you capture?"

"Over nine hundred. They're not the beasts they've been painted. They're hired to fight and they do it, that's all."

Lumden was correct in one comment, though. Public opinion of Washington had altered radically in the preceding thirty days. Only the general's desperate decision to attack Trenton's Hessian garrison—a garrison placidly celebrating Christmas and totally unprepared for attack—had kept the American army from collapsing under wholesale desertions brought on by demolished morale. Philip vividly recalled the cheerless cold of the December weather; the stomach-turning passage over the ice-blocked Delaware in open boats piloted by the men from Marblehead; the fast march to Trenton with his boots all but rotted away; kneeling and firing at the Hessians charging along Trenton's main street while the sleet

slashed over his bare, bloodied feet. Sent to the rear of the lines because he could barely walk, Philip had missed taking part in Washington's second small but decisive rout of the British at Princeton.

Though the memories, once called up, came back in detail, he could contemplate them with a certain hard calm. He had faced death often in the past year. And though he was always afraid before an engagement, his earlier morbid concern for his own welfare had disappeared. He supposed that was a result of experience; the toughening process of combat. Like Colonel Johann Rall's Hessians at Trenton, he did his job and hoped for a speedy end to it, so that he could come home for good to the little house Anne had rented here in Cambridge.

But the return wouldn't be immediate. At the moment Washington's army was in winter quarters, as were the forces of the king. Spring was sure to bring new campaigns. Against York State, some said. Against Philadelphia, others claimed.

Along with the Trenton and Princeton victories, the discovery that the Hessian mercenaries could be defeated had somewhat stiffened the army's backbone. But not enough, Philip had decided. As Knox had predicted, the Americans had not become an army in the true sense—

Anne brought cheer back to the room as she announced:

"Come, the meal's ready. I'm afraid the fare isn't very elegant."

"Seeing you both again is worth ten banquets," Lumden smiled, an arm around his pregnant wife's waist.

"But we must be off by mid-afternoon, George," Daisy said. "I want to be in Concord before it gets too dark."

"Of course, love," Lumden murmured. Anne and Philip exchanged amused glances over Lumden's domestication.

For a while, accompanying his wife to the carefully set table in the dining room, Philip could forget the squalid garrison life at Morristown, and the constant speculation about a spring offensive. He surrendered pleasurably to conversation with old friends, and to the costly but slightly gamy chuck of beef Anne had purchased for the occasion, doctoring it with a thick brown gravy to make it palatable.

II

FAREWELLS WERE said on schedule, about three. Philip and Anne waved their visitors away from the front gate. Lumden's hired carriage lurched out of sight up the rutted street.

Philip took his wife's hand, started back along the walk almost melted clear of snow. He noticed a curtain stirring at a downstairs window of the clapboard house next door.

"Our busybody's watching us again."

Anne laughed. "Mrs. Brumple is a dear lady, Philip. Eccentric, but dear."

"There's nothing more pestiferous than a widow with time on her hands. I know she spies on us in the evening—especially when we shut the curtains early and go to bed. Frustrated biddy!"

"But she's been very kind and helpful. She fixed a poultice when Abraham had the croup at Christmas."

"She's asked me twice how much money your father left us."

"Only twice? I've lost count of the times I've heard the same question—" Anne's brown eyes shone merrily. "I fend her off."

"I'm afraid I just act rude and say nothing."

"Oh, Philip, you mustn't. It's ever so much more satisfying to Mrs. Brumple if you hint that Papa left a fortune. That way, she has something to discuss when she visits the market, or sews uniforms with her church group—"

"I suppose." He wasn't convinced.

Back in the parlor, he warmed his hands at the fire. On the mantel rested his mother's casket and the little green bottle of tea. Above, on pegs, hung Experience Tait's Kentucky rifle and, higher still, the sword given him by his friend Gil.

"Would you like to rest a while till Abraham's done napping?" Anne asked.

He yawned, said, "I would, but there's work that needs doing." Somber, he kissed her mouth gently. "It's time I answered my father's letter."

Her brief nod and quick caress of his cheek said she understood.

III

SEATED AT a desk near their bed, a candle lit against the fading light of the winter afternoon, Philip unfolded the neatly inked pages of thin vellum.

The letter had been delivered in January to the Cambridge office of the postal service, after months in transit. It had been written in the early fall, and had reached Boston on a French packet that slipped past the British squadrons ranging the coast. When Philip had initiated the correspondence the preceding summer before marching south to New York, he had never imagined his letter stood much chance of being delivered to Kentland, his father's country seat, let alone a chance of being answered.

But now, re-reading the reply, he felt the same emotional tug as he had all the other times he'd pored over the words since his return home. His eye was drawn to the passage toward the end:

> It is a wondrous thing—nay, I may say a miraculous thing—to hear, after years of silence, that my well-loved son Phillipe Charboneau is alive and grown to manhood. Your brief missive to that effect burst like a sunrise into what has become a gray and tedious existence. My wife is ten months in her grave, and my other son, Roger, perished in Philadelphia, of wounds incurred in Boston Town, where he was serving with the army. The exact details of his fatal encounter remain elusive to this day.

Philip wiped his perspiring upper lip. Last summer he had written his father out of some deep, almost mystical compulsion to communicate with the man who had given him life. But that first letter to James Amberly had been guarded; had done little more than establish his existence in the colonies under a new and different name. He'd mentioned Marie Charboneau's death on the voyage to New England. But he'd said nothing about Lady Jane Amberly's treacherous hoax to cheat him of the inheritance his father had promised. Nor would he, ever.

And the identity of the slayer of Amberly's legitimate son would likewise remain his secret; his guilt.

To know, however, that Phillipe Charboneau has become Philip Kent—I do not overlook the significance of the last name; to know, I say, that he is happily wed, and has presented me with a grandson, cheers me as nothing else could. I am only regretful that circumstances, including my untimely illness when you were at Kentland, conspired to rob you of the portion I meant you to have from my estate. Your remark that you had burnt the letter to your beloved mother—the letter in which I pledged you that portion—was momentarily distressful. Yet on reflection, I grew to appreciate your act, drawing from it many favorable assumptions about the man you have become. With an ocean separating us, and a d——d debilitating war whose causes are better left undebated between father and son, I send you my warmest affections, a full measure of pride, and my renewed expression of astonished joy at hearing from one I had presumed dead. I hope conditions will not prevent the happy occurrence of communication from repeating itself.

> *With eternal fondness,*
> *Jas. Amberly.*

His father had omitted his hereditary title.

Philip found a fresh sheet, whittled a sharper point on the quill, then hesitated. He was still unsure how a duke was properly addressed.

At last he gave up speculating and again wrote *My dear father* as the salutation.

I too experienced great joy and pleasure when a French vessel succeeded in delivering your letter to our shores. Let me tell you at once that I wish only for your good health and fortune, despite the opposite positions in which we find ourselves as a result of the strife between our nations. Along with most of my countrymen, I hope that the trouble will be resolved, with due consideration to the interests of both sides, before much more time elapses—

Though wholly dedicated to the patriot cause, Philip could write that honestly; it was the prevalent view. Most men he knew looked forward to a resumption of amicable relations with England not to mention trade. Provided, of course, the Americans didn't lose the war.

In regard to your statement about the inheritance, I must say to you that I have no regrets about destroying the letter in question, as I determined at the time to renounce all claims except the one, most meaningful of all, whose renunciation circumstance, pride, and love would never permit. That I may address you as my father is reward enough, as many persons I met round about your estate, and also in London where I stopped briefly, spoke excellently well of your virtues and character. Not the least of these was the famous American savant, Dr. B. Franklin—

The quill scratched on as the candle burned down. Philip described his wife in glowing terms, then his son Abraham. After deliberating, he included one carefully phrased line about his service under General Washington.

He signed the name *Philip*, folded the closely written sheet and waxed it shut. He owned no special seal to mark the wax. He addressed the outside to his father at Kentland, Kent, Great Britain, not knowing Amberly's London residence.

Then he went to the kitchen. Anne was using the remains of the meal for the Lumdens to create a kettle of marrow soup.

Walking up behind her, he kissed her ear. She clasped his hand where it circled her stomach, pressed his forearm up against the softness of her breasts, leaned her head back a moment, her eyes closed.

"Annie," he said, "do you suppose we—?"

Mischievous, she gave him no time to finish, spinning around and kissing him soundly on the lips. "The answer is yes. The soup can wait. Your leave's too short as it is, and Abraham won't wake for a while yet—"

Laughing, he hugged her. "That wasn't precisely the proposition I had in mind—though it's a very good one. Would you like to go to Boston?"

"Now?" she exclaimed.

"Oh, we've things to do now," he smiled. "Tomorrow, perhaps. You could market while I look up Ben Edes and see whether letters can be posted to England."

"I'd love to! I'm sure Mrs. Brumple would care for Abraham for the day."

Philip grimaced. "I'm glad she's good for something besides asking impertinent questions and peering at our closed curtains." He tugged her hand. "Come on, let's pull 'em shut and give the old soul her evening's titillation."

IV

THE EXCURSION to Boston, though undertaken on foot along slushy roads, proved fortuitous in several ways. At North Square, Anne was able to fill her basket with two reasonably fresh loins of pork. And at another of the market booths there, Philip spent a few shillings on a brightly painted toy drum and sticks for Abraham. He ignored Anne's tart comments about disliking playthings that reminded her of the war.

Ben Edes' former shop had been looted and burned out by the British. But he had returned to a new location a few doors further down in Dassett Alley. There the young couple found their old friend busily working his hand press. He was once again publishing the *Gazette,* though without any assistance.

As soon as Philip and Anne arrived, Edes closed up shop and took them to the Green Dragon for tea and biscuits. At the table, Philip asked about outgoing mail.

"Oh, it'll take a spell for it to reach England," was Edes' reply. "But it should get there eventually. Here, I'll see to the posting—" He plucked the letter from Philip's fingers.

"I must pay you—" Philip began.

"No, it's a patriotic service to one of our army lads. Just like buying the tea and biscuits."

"You think the letter'll get through, then?" Philip asked.

"Well, I'm not positive. But there are plenty of New England privateersmen

coasting down south hunting for British ships to plunder. They drop mail for Europe in the Indies. From there, neutral ships carry it to the continent, and it crosses back to England. We might get lucky and make a more direct connection on a Frenchman going home light after dumping powder here.''

"The harbor is certainly crowded," Anne remarked. "On the way back from the market, we walked by the Sawyer Yard. I've never seen it so busy.''

Edes said, "These days the slogan is—if it floats, arm it. A new privateer puts out practically every day, seems like. Only problem is finding money to build and equip 'em. And men to sail 'em.''

He unfolded the copy of the *Gazette* he'd brought along, pointed to an advertising notice headed in bold type. Philip had heard that the launching of privately owned war vessels under letters of marque issued by the Congress was a move to help offset America's virtual lack of a navy. But something much more personal about the notice captured his attention:

> *An Invitation to all brave Seamen and Marines, who have an inclination to serve their Country and make their Fortunes.*
> ### The grand Privateer Ship ECLIPSE
> commanded by WM. CALEB, ESQ., and prov'd to be a very capital Sailor, will shortly Sail on a Cruise against the Enemies of the United States of America. The ECLIPSE is excellently well calculated for Attacks, Defense, and Pursuit—This therefore is to invite all those Jolly Fellows, who love their country, and want to make their Fortunes at one Stroke, to repair immediately to His Excellency Governor Hancock's Wharf, where they will be received aboard ECLIPSE with a hearty Welcome by a Number of Brave Fellows there assembled, and treated with that excellent Liquor call'd GROG, which is allow'd by all true Seamen, to be the LIQUOR OF LIFE.

The moment he'd finished reading, Philip said, "Annie, look at this. *Eclipse* is the ship that brought my mother and me from England.''

Edes' eyebrows lifted. "You know Will Caleb?''

"If it's the same man—''

"First-class captain. From up Maine way.''

"That's the one," Philip nodded, warming at the memory of Caleb's kindnesses to him aboard ship after his mother's burial at sea. "As I recall, though, Captain Caleb didn't take to sailors drinking—''

"Can't attract a crew without grog," Edes commented. "And Caleb needs more crews than one. He's going into privateering in a big way. Got *Eclipse* and another ship armed already. He's trying to raise money to build two more. Depending on his luck at sea, he and the people who buy in stand to lose a lot— or get rich.''

Anne glanced up from the paper. Her brown eyes took on a speculative look:

"Does this Captain Caleb have his commissions in order?''

"Think so. Two from the Congress on the vessels already afloat. Two more are supposedly guaranteed by the Massachusetts legislature soon as his new ships are built. A real enterprising fellow, Caleb is.''

"Where is his office?" she asked.

"The head of Hancock's Wharf, a little further up from where the ship's berthed.''

Crisply, Anne swung to her husband. "Philip, I think we might go along and look up your old friend."

"Whatever for?"

"To see whether we might put a bit of Papa's money to work for us."

"Annie, we're saving that!"

"So you can turn into my competitor one of these days," Edes joked.

"The money's just sitting there," Anne said. "And we don't need every last pound to live. If we had an opportunity to help the cause and make a modest profit at the same time—"

Skeptically, Philip cut in, "We're more likely to see that kind of investment sunk in the ocean and gone forever."

"At least it's worth investigating, don't you think? I do." Her emphatic nod left Philip smiling in spite of himself:

"Annie, sometimes you are the most surprising woman—"

"She's a woman," Edes said. "That explains it all."

Philip said to him, "I think she's just making up for her mother not being able to stay in the ship-building business because it wasn't permissible for women. Her grandfather owned Sawyer's—"

"Enjoy your fancied male supremacy, gentlemen," Anne said cheerily, rising. "I intend to look out for the interests of Kent and Son."

"Is that the name of my competition?" Edes asked.

Anne smiled her sweetest smile. "It will be."

"If she's your business manager, Philip, I might as well quit right now. There won't be a printing house in New England can stand up against the combination of you on the press and your wife on the ledgers."

"I think you could be right," Philip grinned as he rose to join Anne, who was obviously impatient to leave the smoky taproom. "Goodbye, Mr. Edes."

The printer looked mockingly mournful. "Remember me when I'm bankrupt and need a loan, will you?"

"How much interest can you pay?" Anne asked.

Edes laughed, then she did too, as she and Philip left.

They walked into the February sunlight. Melting snow ran in the street channels. Philip shook his head:

"Annie, I repeat—you are a damned astonishing woman."

"Why should you be astonished, darling?" She settled her market basket over her arm. "You know our plans as well as I do. You're going to get through this detestable war, which we're going to win, and you might as well open your shop with two or three presses instead of one—and have something left to hire a couple of apprentices. Captain Caleb just might make that possible. So it's all settled."

"Yes, I had that feeling a few minutes ago," he laughed, admitting privately with some chagrin that he wished he'd thought of the idea himself.

V

In a tiny loft office at the head of Hancock's Wharf, Philip introduced his wife to a momentarily dumbfounded Will Caleb:

"Lord, you were barely more than a boy when you crossed on *Eclipse*. I hardly know you!"

"Well, a good deal's happened since that voyage, Captain Caleb." Philip moved a chair into position for Anne beside the Maine seaman's cluttered work table. "Right now I'm on leave from a Massachusetts regiment down in Jersey."

"The army?"

"Yes."

Caleb had really changed very little, Philip decided. He had to be approaching sixty now. But he was still as trim and tanned as when Philip had sailed with him from Bristol. His beak nose and flowing white hair reminded Philip of the prow of one of the swift New England merchantmen on which Caleb had spent his life.

Caleb said, "If you're in the army, then you sure as hel—uh, your pardon, Mrs. Kent. You surely didn't come here to sign aboard one of my privateersmen."

"No," Anne put in, "Mr. Ben Edes mentioned that you were searching for investors to help underwrite the construction of two additional vessels."

Caleb's eyes narrowed. "You've money to put into such a venture?"

"Possibly—under a captain with an outstanding record," Anne told him. "Both Philip and Mr. Edes say you're every bit of that. We might be able to raise a sum of two hundred pounds if the proposition was suitable."

Philip almost strangled trying to protest. Two hundred pounds sterling represented just about two thirds of the total bequest left them by Anne's father. He'd been thinking more on the order of fifty. It was painfully evident—again—that his business affairs were now securely in the hands of his wife.

Captain Caleb likewise nearly broke out in a sweat at the mention of the amount. At once he unlocked a lower drawer of his desk and produced a bottle of rum and rolled-up plans. Anne declined the offer of strong drink but Philip, still nonplused, helped himself to a bracer. Caleb eagerly spread the inked drawings:

"You know anything at all about seagoing vessels, Mrs. Kent?"

"A little. My grandfather founded Sawyer's."

"The devil! That's where I'm going to have these two beauties built. Here, let me show you—"

Anne bent forward with interest. To Philip the drawings resembled a confusion of spiderwebs. He recognized a hull plan and elevation, but not much else. He rapidly became lost in Caleb's nonstop references to fore-and-aft rigging, hull displacement, sharper deadrise for greater speed and reduced tumble-home thanks to smaller-bore cannon, another weight-saving scheme.

"All the newest designs, Mrs. Kent. And the best long guns we can purchase. The idea's to crack on as much canvas as possible, for short cruises. Carry fewer provisions, less ammuniton—speed, speed! Catch those lumbering Britishers! If we hit, we'll hit big."

"What are the financial arrangements if you do seize an enemy merchantman, Captain?"

"Works like this. A prize crew brings the ship back to an American port—I can't afford agents in France and the Indies. Besides, the owners lose out if the prize is sold in a foreign port. That's standard in the Articles for any privateer."

"All right, that's clear."

"We publish the captured ship's name in the papers and wait fifteen days. There's a trial to determine whether she's legally a prize—formality, mostly. Don't imagine any Britishers are going to hop across the Atlantic to appear in court and fight the claim. Soon as the jurors condemn the captive as a prize, we pay off the trial costs and put her on sale—cargo *and* vessel. There's auction expense to be deducted, but that's a pittance. Whatever the auction brings, the

Articles for each privateer of mine state that no more than a third is divided among the captain and crew. The remainder's to be paid to the owners, in proportion, according to how much they put in."

Anne said, "I'd want all of that in writing. I mean the exact amount of ownership in each vessel."

"*Each?* You'd want to invest in both?"

She nodded. "A hundred pounds per new ship. The designs are excellent, so by dividing the investment we double the chance of a return, and halve the chance of loss."

"Anything you say!" Caleb beamed. "I've papers here to completely describe the agreem—"

"No, we're not prepared to negotiate today. But you're welcome to call at our home in Cambridge with the documents. Also your letters of marque which I'd of course like to see personally."

"I'll be there inside of a week! With two hundred pounds promised—"

"Not promised," Anne warned. "Available."

"Yes, yes, understood. But still, that'll be a big help. Enough so that I can pretty near raise all the funds for at least one of the new ships right away."

Anne rose and extended her hand in a business-like fashion. "Then do call at your convenience, and let's discuss the terms."

"Yes, ma'am, I surely—"

Footsteps on the stairs leading up from the wharf distracted them. A tall, swarthy man in a blue wool captain's jacket stalked into the office, carrying documents. The man was perhaps ten years older than Philip; in his thirties. He had dark, tight-curling hair, heavy brows and a small white scar at the outer corner of his right eye. The scar pulled the skin downward to lend the eye a peculiar slitted look.

Despite that, the man exuded cockiness. His expression had a certain arrogance that repelled Philip completely.

"Pardon me, Will. Didn't realize you had visitors." The man's nasal voice identified him at once as a New Englander.

"Potential investors, Malachi," Caleb said. "Mr. And Mrs. Kent of Cambridge—my associate, Captain Rackham, in command of *Nancy,* the other privateer I've already got on the water. I'll be skippering *Eclipse* till the new ones are built."

"Pleasure," said Rackham, bowing but obviously unaccustomed to it. Philip noticed how the man's eyes worked their way from Anne's face to the outline of her breasts. Uncomfortable, Anne fiddled with the cloth cover on her market basket.

Caleb didn't appreciate Rackham's somewhat brazen interest either. To divert him, he asked sharply:

"You've something for me, Malachi?"

Rackham showed the papers. "A good morning's work. Two more prize masters for *Nancy,* plus the cooper and the sailmaker you've been hunting for *Eclipse.*" He tossed the articles of agreement on the desk, then helped himself to rum. "But it can wait while we entertain our guests."

"We're leaving," Philip announced, taking Anne's arm and steering her toward the captain, whose rakish figure blocked the head of the stairs.

Rackham stared at Philip—considerably shorter—for a moment or so. Then he smiled with insolent charm:

"Shame. Thought we might all become better acquainted, seeing as how

you're planning to join our venture.'' He took account of Philip's tricorn hat with its black army cockade. "Serving with the troops, are you, Mr. Kent?''

He met Rackham's gaze without blinking. "That's right.''

"Stationed where?''

"Jersey. I'll be going back soon.''

He said it without thinking. An instant later he regretted the damnable frankness. Captain Rackham seemed to have become extremely interested in the contents of his mug of rum. But Philip saw the seaman's eyes flicker toward Anne with renewed interest.

Or was he only letting his imagination get the better of him?

Captain Caleb remained perturbed by the minor confrontation: Philip and his wife at the stairs, Rackham casually pretending he didn't realize he was blocking their way. Caleb reached out, gently but firmly pushed Rackham's shoulder.

The taller captain stiffened, his quick glare giving Philip a clue to his temper. Caleb, however, was clearly in charge. Rackham took the shove and stepped aside without protest.

"Philip, I wish you safety in Morristown,'' Caleb said.

"Thank you, Captain, I'll take that wish. Things may get pretty lively when the weather breaks. General Howe is slow-moving. But Lord Cornwallis is turning out to be fast and foxy—''

Caleb saw them part way down the stairs:

"Mrs. Kent, the pleasure's entirely mine. Be assured I'll call on you promptly with my proposal.''

"I'll look forward to it.''

From above, Captain Rackham called, "We'll both come if you wish.''

Philip said harshly, "That won't be necessary.''

Caleb glared at the other captain. Ignoring him, Rackham lifed his mug in a wry salute:

"Whatever you say, sir.''

As they left the head of the noisy wharf, Philip said, "Anne, I disliked that Rackham fellow on sight. A low, scurvy sort.''

"I agree. I didn't care for the looks he gave me.''

"Stay clear of him.''

"I intend to. I'll make sure I deal only with Captain Caleb. He's obviously a man of good character. If we're lucky, we stand to make a great deal of money.''

"Yes, aside from associating with Rackham, I think the gamble could be worth it. And I'm not saying that just because I have no choice.''

Despite his smile, he was troubled. In minutes, he had become less concerned about the financial risk than about Caleb's partner—who would be within a few miles of his wife after he had gone back to Morristown.

Anne sensed his worry. "Don't fret,'' she said, tucking her free arm around his. "I've handled worse than a ruffian sailor before. I can do it again if need be.''

Still, the February sun seemed a mite more chilly, and the prospect of financial gain from privateer shares much less appealing.

But he knew his wife. Anne was a determined woman. So he said nothing more about it.

__2
Deed of Darkness

SOMETIMES WHEN the summer's heat of Caroline County weighed too heavily in the cabin, Lottie liked to start their lovemaking outdoors. Tonight was one of those times. Judson heard her call from the darkness under Tom Shaw's apple tree that had failed to come to bud in the spring:

"Darlin', hurry up!"

Leaning in the cabin door, Judson tilted the jug of corn across the back of his thin forearm and drained the last of it. He dropped the jug beside the lolling yellow hound. The dog's tongue dripped moisture drop by slow drop.

A red-hued, steamy moon hung three quarters up from the horizon. Judson could hear Lottie preparing for him; soft sounds of her skirt and blouse being put aside counterpointed the harping of night insects. By now Judson had tired of Lottie. But he'd had no place else to live when he rode home from Philadelphia the preceding summer.

He hadn't considered stopping at Sermon Hill. Simply out of the question. To postpone the return to Caroline County even further, he'd bypassed it and spent a week in the stews of Richmond. There, in a brothel, he'd encountered an acquaintance from his home county. Once the red-faced young squire had gotten over his embarrassment at being recognized, he and Judson fell to drinking, and thus Judson picked up word that Lottie's marital status had changed while he was away. She couldn't go home to her mother and father; they had married her off solely to get rid of her and create a little more room in a squalid shanty still crowded with six smaller children. So, Judson's acquaintance related, Lottie had been forced to set herself up in business, accommodating any planter's boy with a few shillings and a randy feeling in his breeches. Judson went to see her and they reached an accommodation; an accommodation helped along by Donald's sense of responsibility.

Early on, Donald visited the cabin—Judson having made no special effort to conceal his presence. Donald politely asked his younger brother to go somewhere else besides Caroline County. On that occasion, Judson—as usual—was half drunk. He bluntly refused Donald's request, offering the very reasonable explanation that he had nowhere else to go.

That stoked Donald's anger:

"I don't care—and I don't want any of your damned impertinence. You've disgraced yourself, Judson. In Philadelphia you completely betrayed the trust I placed in you—"

"Oh, so you heard. I wondered."

"You've been back home three weeks. Express letters from Pennsylvania travel almost as quickly."

"Who wrote you?"

"It doesn't matter."

"Well, I hope you're not going to lecture me about killing that damn Tory— I assume you know about that too?"

"That information was also contained in the letter—" Judson's older brother sighed. "But I won't lecture. It seems you've gone far past the point where mere words will avail—"

"For Christ's sake stop talking like the old man."

In that wheezy, unhealthy voice, Donald said, "Nastiness seems to be your stock in trade, Judson. Let's get back to the issue. If you insist on spending your days here—"

"I told you I've no place else!"

"—then be so good as to be reasonably discreet. Keep yourself and your whore out of sight as much as possible."

Judson shrugged. "That won't be hard. I don't have a penny left. Before I came back and made my arrangement with Lottie, I spent my last on a little— ah—holiday in Richmond."

"Very well, then. I'll make a bargain with you. Don't flaunt yourself all over the county and I'll return from time to time—" He fished in his coat, pulled out a small purse that jingled in his hand.

Judson grinned suddenly:

"You came prepared for a little bribery!"

"Because I suspected you wouldn't go away," Donald admitted.

"Shrewd. You always were the clever one of us, Donald. The one Father half admired—"

"Have the decency to let that subject drop. I am sick to death of what you've permitted yourself to become. I should turn my back on you—just as every respectable citizen in this county will do—"

"When it's a chance encounter in public," Judson smirked, recalling the young squire in the Richmond brothel. The point escaped Donald. He went on:

"I should abandon you, but I find I can't. Not completely, anyway."

This time, Judson laughed aloud: "Then the bloodline *is* improving from father to son! The old man takes the opposite view. At least where I'm concerned."

"Spare me your hatred, for God's sake!" Donald flung the purse on the ground. "I will see you again—here—*if* you've kept your distance. As I say, I can't properly explain why I should take the trouble when apparently all you want is to go down to ruin—" The puffy face wrenched. "It's my curse to be unable to forget we're brothers. But believe me, Judson—any public scandal and I will forget. Forever."

Scooping up the purse, Judson bowed low. "You, Donald, have the misfortune to be an honorable man."

"No, damme—only a very weak and foolish one."

With that he summoned the black who'd been sent to wait out by the road. The black helped Donald mount and the two rode away—

The conversation came to mind this July evening in 1777 because Judson suddenly recalled that his most recent purse from Donald was almost empty. He took an unsteady step into the dooryard, wondering if his brother would pay another call soon—

More immediate concerns re-focused his thoughts. Lottie's voice whined in the shadows under the dead apple tree:

"What the devil are you doin', Jud? Stop thinkin' about it and come do it, sweet—"

How many Virginia gentlemen have their own private whores? he thought mockingly as he shambled toward her in the humid dark. *Raised from the depths of her foul degradation courtesy of my soft-hearted brother, she accommodates my every wish here on my splendid private estate—*

He glanced past the corner of the cabin, saw the white puff of a rabbit's tail.

The rabbit was hunting edible leaves in the pathetic garden patch Judson had tried to plant in the spring weather. Hardly any of the seeds had sprouted.

Dying. Everything dying—

In a year Judson had lost about twenty pounds. Gone from fashionable slimness to near-emaciation. His unkempt beard had sprouted fairer than his hair. His mouth, moonlit as he crossed the yard, looked softer than ever. Sweat ran down his bare chest toward the first swelling of an old man's belly. He wore only ragged trousers—

Well, what difference did it make? He had nothing to dress for; no purpose beyond sheer, perverse continuation of his existence. His days and nights passed in a haze that was like the haze of the summer moon. Indistinct, vaguely unreal—

For a year he'd roamed the back roads with the yellow hound; fished in creeks; worked as little as possible, and slept a lot. When he tired of that, he played one-hand card games with a worn deck he'd bought from a peddler's wagon. When his need or Lottie's grew too fierce, fornication brought a moment's release. But not much more.

And of course Donald's money bought distilled popskull from the dirt farmers in the county—

"Wish you'd save a drop of that corn for me," Lottie complained as he reached the tree. "I'm so damn dry—"

Judson dropped his breeches and squatted beside her, his hand reaching out to begin the wearying routine.

"Oh, we'll have that fixed in a minute, Lottie—"

She giggled, widening the spread of her legs to allow him a freer access. He ran one palm down the slope of her breast, aware of the premature sag of her flesh. Very quickly he tired of the fondling. He dropped over her and began to work.

Somehow, rolling and clutching at one another, they moved a short distance from the dead trunk of the apple tree. All at once, braced above her on his hands, Judson realized where they were. He wrenched away, sickened—

On coming home to Caroline County, he'd learned that Tom Shaw had been killed one night riding patrol. A fox had spooked his horse. He'd tumbled off the runaway, breaking his neck. Lottie couldn't afford to bury him anywhere but on his own property.

Now, seeing Judson's stark eyes blazing in the moon, Lottie giggled again. She reached between his legs:

"Come on, darlin', you don't believe all those church stories about souls flyin' around once the body's planted. The old fool don't know we're doin' it right on top of him—"

His face almost demented-looking, Judson stared at the crude wood cross just beyond Lottie's tangled hair. Lottie jerked her hand back:

"Listen, Judson Fletcher! You got me all worked up. You got to finish what you—"

He slammed at her cheek with the back of his right hand. Her head snapped over. She yelled, a low, hurt sound. He jumped up, ran from the grave to the far side of the dead apple tree, leaned his forearm on the rotting trunk, and his forehead on his arm.

Behind him, Lottie was panting, half frightened, half furious:

"You're turnin' into a crazy man. *A crazy man!*"

In the stillness of the summer dark, he said nothing to deny it. He was sick of her sluttish voice and sluttish ways—because of what they told about him.

His refusal to answer only angered her more:

"You gonna talk to me, or you gonna stand there staring like some stupid, moonstruck—?"

He whirled on her. She'd clambered to her feet, rushed at him, one hand lifted as if she wanted to use her nails on his cheeks; his eyes. When she saw his ugly stare, the hand lowered quickly.

"I've had enough of you, Lottie. Leave."

"*Leave?* This here's my property, not yours—"

"You want to be buried on your property, Lottie? That's the only way you're going to stay around here—buried beside that poor wretch lying yonder. I'll give you till dawn to pack up and get out."

He flung her hand away like some befouled object, snatched up his breeches and hurried toward the road. He didn't have a notion of where he'd spend the rest of the night. But he couldn't stand to spend it with her.

He heard her screaming at him:

"You'll be sorry you treated me like this, Mr. Judson Fletcher. You'll be goddamn sorry, I promise you—!"

He walked faster, pausing only long enough to tug on the filthy trousers. Threatening him, was she? Maybe that meant she was going to respond to his own, completely honest threat of physical harm—and get out. It was some small encouragement—

But he had to suffer the sound of her yammering voice for a good quarter mile before distance and the racketing night insects finally stilled it.

II

THREE MORNINGS later, Judson groaned and rolled over on the straw pallet in the cabin. The yellow hound was licking at his arm.

Judson heard rain through the hole in the roof near the fireplace, *plip-plop*, then another sound—the splash of the hoofs of a horse in puddles in the yard. Before he could stand up and pull on his breeches, the cabin door opened.

Supporting himself on his cane and favoring his bandaged left foot, Donald hobbled in. Outside, standing with two sets of reins in his hand—and getting soaked because that was his function at the moment—Judson recognized the house slave who always accompanied Donald on his trips from Sermon Hill. The young black had charge of Donald's horse and his own pony. His eyes shone, big and white in the steamy gray of the morning. He was peering toward the cabin, perhaps hoping for a glimpse of its notorious inhabitant.

"Shut the goddamned door," Judson said, holding his head.

"I will if you put your pants on and try to behave like something halfway human." Donald pushed the squeaking door closed with his cane.

Climbing into his trousers, Judson let go with a sour-tasting belch. "A little moral remonstrance before I get the monthly dole? Well, you can keep 'em both!"

Donald colored. But he refused to be provoked:

"The Shaw woman's left you?"

"That's right, I got a bellyful of her and told her to pack up."

"Certainly cavalier of you—considering it was her husband who owned this place."

Judson spat one quick epithet to show what he thought of that sarcastic quibble. He rubbed his eyes, yawned, asked:

"How'd you find out she was gone?"

"Very simple. She's already selling her fine wares in Richmond. A friend of mine came back from there yesterday. He said Lottie's informing everyone that you've lost your mind."

That brought a smirk to Judson's mouth. "Could well be, Donald, could well be. How's the lord of Sermon Hill taking the news?"

"I've been at some pains to keep it from him. That's not too difficult. He knows you're back but he doesn't talk about you."

"Never?"

There was a hesitation before Donald replied:

"No. Never."

"Jesus," Judson said, very softly.

Donald frowned. "Judson, this place is a sty. Since that slattern's gone, there's no reason you can't clean it up."

"Oh, God, don't start—"

"Why not? Some time, you're going to have to put an end to reveling in filth—indolence—"

"Right you are. The moment I find something for which I'm better suited" Judson yawned again, then shambled toward the crock where he kept the cabin's supply of mealy corn cakes. Lifting the lid, he found the crock empty. He remembered that he'd fried the last cake for his only meal yesterday.

Donald reached for the inevitable purse whose drawstring hung from his coat pocket. Fingering the string, he asked, "You do know they're constantly in need of men for the Virginia militia levies—?"

Judson scratched his navel. "The last thing I want to be is a Virginia soldier."

"Then what the hell do you want to be?—other than a drunken fool bent on slow death? You seem totally dedicated to rebelling against everything ordinary people consider normal or decent or—"

"Get out."

"No. You've got to look at yourself, Judson."

"Damn," Judson said with a weary shudder, "what's provoked you this morning? I've never begged you to come here, remember. I'd just as soon you leave."

Donald bit his lip. "Well—you ask what provoked me—the truth is, I had a most distressing note delivered to me at Sermon Hill last night. It upset me because I don't know how to reply to it."

"A note from who?"

"From Seth McLean's widow."

Rigid, Judson swallowed. "She's back home?"

"For nearly a month. With the assistance of Williams, she's gradually taking over affairs at the plantation. I haven't seen her. But I'm told her health and composure have been reasonably well restored. Unfortunately she heard some talk about you. Your—" A weary wave of the hand. "Present condition. She asked whether there was anything anyone could do to help." Donald's mouth pursed, sour. "You see why I'm in difficult straits regarding a reply? Obviously the answer is no."

Judson seized his brother's arm. There was a strange, prickling alertness tearing through the lethargy of sleep and hangover:

"Maybe I'll answer in person. I haven't seen Peggy since Seth was killed. I should call on her—"

Donald shook his head sharply. "I'm not certain that would be wise." Yet his skepticism seemed a trifle artificial.

"Dammit, listen—I'll behave myself. I swear I will. Just a brief visit. I owe it to her!"

Still doubtful, Donald said, "There's no guarantee she'd receive you."

"I think she would."

"Well, you certainly couldn't go in your present state."

"Are any of my old clothes stored at the Hill?"

"I believe so. In the attic—"

"Get one of the nigras to bring me an outfit. Sneak it out after dark if you have to—" Judson whirled to a wall peg where a scrap of pot-tin served as a bleary mirror. He raked his fingers through his fair beard. "I'll scrape this off. Clean myself up decently—"

"*Only* to pay your respects and express your sympathies about Seth."

The concern in Donald's voice spun Judson around again. Vaguely fearful and yet excited, he answered:

"Yes, what else did you think? I'll stay only ten or fifteen minutes. Just long enough to—*what the hell are you grinning about?*"

"Nothing, nothing. I'll see what can be done about the clothes—" He gestured to the young black being drenched in the dooryard. "Lemon can be trusted. But we'll need to take care that the old man doesn't find out. It may require a day or two—"

"As soon as you can!'"

Donald nodded, started out. Then he turned back:

"I hope it isn't necessary to remind you that she is a widow. Her status demands special courtesy."

"Stop worrying! I'll behave! I just want to see her, tell her—dammit, what is it now?"

With surprising gentleness Donald said, "You love her very much, don't you?"

After a moment Judson said, "I always have. Hopeless. But I can't help it."

All at once Donald seemed brisk; almost cheerful: "A visit might hearten her. And perhaps have a salutary effect on you as well."

Sudden understanding made Judson laugh aloud:

"*That's* why you came here today. For my benefit, not hers. Admit it!"

"Yes, you've caught me. I thought that if anything could pull you up out of your sorry state, it might be the name of Peggy McLean."

"Well, you were right. Though I continue to be astonished that you'd concern yourself."

Donald's smile faded. "I continue to be astonished myself. I don't suppose anyone can fully explain how it's possible to despise and love a brother at the same time. Or why one woman out of all the women in this world has the power to redeem a man."

Or ruin him, Judson thought as Donald went out into the rain.

The brief flash of despair passed almost instantly. Before Donald and the slave Lemon rode away from the dooryard, Judson was at work in front of the scrap of pot-metal. Teeth clenched, he hacked and chopped at the yellow growth with

his hunting knife. In the process he cut himself three times, and scraped his skin nearly raw.

But he couldn't recollect any discomfort he'd ever enjoyed quite so much.

III

REASONABLY PRESENTABLE, and mounted on a gray gelding Lemon had smuggled out of the Sermon Hill stables for his temporary use, Judson Fletcher rode up the lane to the McLean plantation the following Tuesday. Twilight etched the western horizon gold below bars of dark gray cloud. The rainy, stifling weather had passed in favor of a cooler spell. That too had a certain restorative effect on Judson's spirits.

He was infernally nervous, though. His belly was as fluttery as a young man's at his first plantation ball.

He was still determined to keep his promise to Donald. He would make the call a short one—

Provided Peggy McLean would let him in the house!

He cantered up the drive past lamp-lit windows, listening to the trees rustling in a light breeze. The sound lent a certain enjoyable melancholy to the occasion. As he crossed the veranda, he realized he hadn't been on this same spot since the night of the uprising. He almost dreaded the opening of the front door, for more than one reason.

He fussed a moment with the lace stock at his throat. He smoothed his ruffled cuffs, rubbed both hands back across his combed temples, checked the knot of the ribbon with which he'd clubbed his hair. Then he raised the knocker.

The shiny black face that appeared a moment later belonged to one of the house girls who'd sent him upstairs the night Peggy was raped. Astonishment, then delight registered in quick succession:

"Why, Mist' Fletcher! Good evening, sar."

"Good evening, Melissa. Is—is Mrs. McLean at home?"

"Yes, sar, she be out in the summerhouse."

"I wonder if I might speak with her?" With effort, he kept his eyes on the girl's, avoiding the parquet beyond. Even so, his mind saw grisly images of Seth's butchered body.

"Why, yes, sar, I think she'd be right happy to see you."

"I understand she's well and in good spirits?"

"After a long time home with her kin. Mist' Williams, he took good care of the place while she was away. But we mighty glad to have her back."

Melissa stepped onto the veranda, pointed toward the corner of the house. "Why don't you walk 'round and right on up to the summerhouse, Mist' Fletcher?"

That was precisely what Judson wanted to do. He wiped his moist palms on his trousers, forced a shake of his head:

"I believe it might be better if you told her who was calling. She might not wish company this evening."

Puzzled, the black girl said, "All right, sar." she started away along the veranda.

In the west, beyond the trees where the last light was fading to amber, a flight of swallows sailed gracefully. "I'll wait right here," Judson called. Melissa vanished.

He began to pace back and forth. Remember—a brief visit. *Brief!*

The darkness along the lane seemed to deepen. He kept peering toward the veranda's end. The black girl didn't return. His hope started to disintegrate—

"Mist' Fletcher?"

Surprised, he whirled. The girl had returned through the rear of the house. She stood in the open front door. For a long, dizzy second, Judson hung between wild hope and what he felt was certain refusal.

"Yes?"

A dazzling smile.

"Mrs. McLean, she say she pleased to see you. So you go right on 'round."

It was all he could do to keep from running.

___IV

THE MCLEAN summerhouse, a white-painted structure with a cupola and pine louvers to admit the breeze, perched on a knoll at some distance from the main house. As Judson hurried up the lawn, he saw lamps gleaming in the slave cabins at the rear of the property, blacks gathered in groups in the street between. Someone was clicking out a rhythm with beef bones. Someone else chanted a wordless melody. Up at the far end of the cabin street, a portly figure sat in a rocker that moved slowly back and forth to the tempo of the music.

Judson thought he saw the overseer wave, lifted his hand in response. To make such a small, ordinary gesture somehow filled him with a warmth and satisfaction he hadn't known in a long time.

A lantern glowed inside the summerhouse. But the louvers hid the interior. The closed door intimidated Judson all at once.

Inhaling the fragrance of the freshly cut lawn, he approached, straightened his stock again, knocked softly.

"Come in."

As he closed the door behind him, Peggy Ashford McLean rose from a wicker chair, putting aside a newspaper. Several more were neatly stacked at the foot of the chair. The sight of Seth's widow, her creamy skin given warmth and luster by the shaded lantern, almost petrified him.

Peggy wore white silk. The mourning period was over. Her flawlessly done dark hair caught the lantern's gleam. She was still slim; elegant; heartbreakingly lovely. Only her eyes had changed. They lacked the vivacity he remembered. Well, there was good reason for that—

Peggy's cheeks took on more color as she extended her hand. Her skin carried a faint tang of sweet balsam oil.

"Judson, how good to see you!"

"Peggy—" Words came hard. "You're looking exceptionally well."

"Thank you."

"I—I understand you're taking over the plantation."

"Yes, I'm finally learning something about it. Not without a good deal of struggle, I must confess. I'm afraid I never concerned myself before—"

She held back the rest of it; he thought he saw the horror of memory stain her eyes for an instant.

"Oh, but please sit down, Judson. It's terribly rude of me to keep you standing—"

"I can't stay long. I only wanted to call because I hadn't seen you since—" Inadvertently trapped, he got out as best he could: "—since Seth's passing."

"I remember very little of that night," Peggy said in a calm voice. She sat down, folding her hands in her lap. "That's turned out to be a blessing."

"Yes, I can see how—"

Again he faltered. To conceal how ill at ease he was, he took the indicated seat, a wicker lounge. He sat perched on the edge. Peggy picked up the conversation:

"Still, I know very well what you did to help. The debt can never be properly paid."

Another awkward silence. He suddenly felt he'd made a serious error in coming here. He'd wanted to see her; look at her a moment. But it was too painful. The sweet lines of her figure, the grace of her finely wrought face still had the power to torture him. But reopening the old wounds served no purpose—

Again it was Peggy who broke the silence:

"Would you care for refreshment? There's port on the table."

Even though his mouth felt dust-dry, he shook his head. "I don't believe so, thank you."

"I hope you don't mind if I pour a glass. I've grown to like a little something this time of evening."

"All right, I will join you," he said impulsively, standing and walking over to pour a crystal goblet for each of them. As he handed Peggy's to her, his hand accidentally touched her fingers. A shock vibrated through him. Damn, he'd better leave. And quickly.

He tossed off half the port much too fast. Peggy noticed. The lantern's flame cast shifting shadows. With night's coming, the breeze between the half-closed slats had grown a little more chilly.

"I'm told you've been home almost a year—" she began.

Another piece of touchy ground! How much did she know about his present situation? And Lottie Shaw? He inclined his head, trying for casualness:

"Yes, I spent a while in Philadelphia."

"But you're not living at Sermon Hill."

"No. No, I'm not."

"I did hear the sad news that you and your father had quarreled—"

He finished the port, felt sweat on his palms. The balsam scent teased his senses in a disturbing way. A ghost of his old, charming smile hid his turmoil:

"Oh, I think it was to be expected sooner or later. I've never fit in with this sort of life. I guess I'm too ornery to be tamed down by anyone, especially a father."

"But that's always been one of your chief charms," she smiled. Then she took a quick sip of wine, as if embarrassed. She set the goblet aside and lifted one of the papers from the floor, finding a refuge in safer subjects:

"I've been trying to catch up on the war news. The Richmond *Leader* reports that we have a new flag for the thirteen states."

"I hadn't heard. What sort?"

She tapped a finger against one of the narrow columns. "Thirteen alternating stripes of red and white, and in the corner, a blue field of thirteen white stars. The Congress approved the design in June."

"Sounds appropriate." Yes, dammit, he'd best get out. The intimacy of the sequestered summerhouse was too upsetting. He rose from the lounge, walked quickly to the port. "May I?"

"Of course." A pause. "The paper says things aren't going well for the army in the north—"

"Honestly, I'm all but out of touch—" His hand was shaking. He spilled some of the wine as he filled the glass.

"And we now have commissioners in Paris. Mr. Deane, Dr. Franklin—"

"I met Franklin in Philadelphia. A genius. Damned—uh—very jolly gentleman, too."

"So far, he and his associates haven't been able to promote direct assistance from any of the European countries."

"I suppose such negotiations take time," Judson answered in a lame tone, feeling more and more trapped by the moment. He could barely keep his eyes off the sculptured neck of Peggy's gown. Sweat filmed his forehead. His mind's eye flickered with images of her naked body on the bedroom floor.

He fought the memories, sipped the port in silence. Again she came to his rescue:

"That British general—the one they call Gentleman Johnny—"

"Burgoyne, isn't it?"

"Yes. The paper reports he may bring a great force of Germans and those terrible Indians down through York State this summer. There's turmoil in the west, too."

It had been months since Judson had thought of his friend George Clark. He brought up his name, said, "I wonder how he's faring."

"I understand he was back in Virginia last fall."

"He was? For what purpose?"

"My father told me he came to see Governor Henry in Williamsburg. He was asking for several hundred pounds of powder to defend the Kentucky settlements. The Indian tribes are raiding there, incited by the British at Detroit. There's an officer in charge at Detroit who pays silver for American scalps."

With genuine astonishment, Judson studied Peggy McLean again. He really hadn't appreciated how much she'd changed. The young woman he'd courted would never have been so matter-of-fact about a subject such as the Indian threat to American settlers on the frontier. In fact the Peggy of the past might have made a gay, tasteless joke about it—if she mentioned it at all. Perhaps the slave uprising hadn't been without some saving effects. There was a new, assured firmness in her manner. She had passed out of girlhood forever.

Pondering the change while he finished the wine helped relieve his disappointment on another score: not having seen George Clark the preceding autumn.

Ah, but George had probably been warned off:

Don't bother with Judson Fletcher any longer. He's ruined. Drunk all the time. Rutting with a white-trash woman—

He set the empty goblet on the table, a sudden, jerky motion. His head was buzzing a little. The summerhouse was confining; dangerous. Peggy was too lovely. He damn near ached for her—

"Yes," he said at last, "Donald did tell me the situation in Kentucky is very perilous. All the settlers have taken to the stockades for fear the men will be shot and the women rap—"

He closed his mouth abruptly. Then:

"Peggy, I believe I should be going."

She rose, hurrying toward him. Again he thought he saw something unusual in her eyes. Embarrassment over her own quick reaction—

She lifted one slender hand, as if to hold him:

"You mustn't leave without telling me what plans you have for the future."

The wine had gotten to him. "None at all. Donald sent me to sit in his stead in Congress. If you listen to the county gossips, you know I botched that. I humiliated Donald—and since returning, my life has been even more distinguished."

"Judson." Her cool, gentle voice caught him up short.

"What?"

"You needn't sound so bitter. You can't shock me. I've heard everything."

Something drove him to ask, "Including my relationship with Lottie Shaw?"

"Yes, that too."

"And you still permit me to come here?"

"Oh, I suppose by custom, I shouldn't—" She turned away, her cheeks coloring again. From the wine—or something else. "But much as I love my parents, I hope I'll never be so narrow and unforgiving as they are on occasion. Being married to Seth for even a few years was a blessing. I learned a great many things from him. Things you'd understand because you were his friend. Above all I learned kindness. Love—" Head bowed suddenly, she said, "I only grieve for the waste, Judson. The terrible waste of yourself."

Without knowing how it happened, he touched her.

Perhaps it was the isolation of the summerhouse; or the wine; or her loveliness and the haunting balsam tang that drifted in the soft lamplight. But standing close behind her, he touched the shoulders of her gown.

Leave, damn you! Before you do something you'll regret!

He didn't leave. He said:

"It was the only possible outcome after I lost you, Peggy. Though I didn't want to, I stayed away because I cared for your husband."

Head still bowed, she whispered, "Yes, I know."

"Of all the people along this river, I cared for George Clark and Seth McLean—and so I stopped caring for you. Or tried. You know I came to the house too often. Everyone knew it. I'm sorry for that, and I'm sorry for bringing it up now, but I can't help it—"

He was drowning in the scent from her skin. Against all prudence and judgment, he leaned down to kiss the back of her neck.

Instantly he realized his mistake. He let go of her shoulders—

The rest would never have happened if some impulse hadn't caused her to weaken just one instant. Swiftly, she reached down with her right hand to grasp his and pull it around to violent, startling contact with her breast. Her eyes were closed:

"I was a good wife to Seth. I couldn't be anything else. But there was only one man I really loved, ever."

The flesh beneath her gown seemed to heat his hand; then his whole body. She felt him stiffen. Her eyes flew open, alarmed. She broke away:

"Judson, forgive me—"

"There's nothing to forgive, Peggy."

"Yes—what I did just now—taking your hand that way—"

He saw how deeply it disturbed her. Peggy Ashford McLean had always lived by the moral code of the tidewater. Not welcoming it, perhaps. But accepting it. And that code, of which her parents were the symbols, explicitly forbade certain behavior—and a relationship with certain men. He was one of those men and always would be.

Shame reddened Peggy's cheeks now:

"Perhaps we had better say good evening—"

"Kiss me, Peggy."

"Oh dear God, don't—"

"No one will see. We're far away from the house—"

"Please go. In your presence I'm not as strong as I should be—"

And he had no strength at all, save the special kind she'd roused in him suddenly. If only he hadn't weakened! Hadn't indulged his habit; drunk the wine—

But it was too late for ifs. She was far too beautiful. And they were alone—

Clumsily he pulled her into an embrace. She fought back, tried to push him away even as his mouth crushed hard on hers, taking from it all the warmth and sweetness that had been denied him for so long. He felt himself roused again. So did she. With a small, terrified moan she wrenched her head to one side:

"It's wrong, Judson—this is wrong—"

"Admit you want what I do, Peggy." His voice was already slurred from the wine. He pressed her backwards, hands caressing her shoulders. Something savage was loose in him, mastering every thought but one; every intent but one—

"I don't dare admit that. If we were husband and wife—"

"We'll never be husband and wife. You know that."

"Yes. Yes."

"But at least we can pretend—"

This time he literally took her prisoner, his arms around her waist. She struggled very little as he kissed her. But for a moment her lips gave no response. Some dim corner of his mind comprehended what he was doing to her. Yet the stark, undammed forces within him overrode conscience. He kissed her cheeks, her eyelids while she whispered her fear, all the old morality of her upbringing crying out against the touching of their bodies, the increasing heat of flesh against flesh with confining clothing between—

Suddenly she clasped her arms around his neck. Her mouth came open under his. He picked her up—she was so light; so airy-light—and bore her to the lounge, his boots trampling the Richmond papers with their news of meaningless distant battles. She resisted hardly at all; a fist against his shoulder for a moment. Then it opened, defeated. The fingers slid to the back of his head—

To have put out the lantern would have betrayed too much. But as he lowered her gently to the lounge, he managed to shut the louvers on the side of the summerhouse facing the plantation buildings. He sat beside her, hands fondling her breasts free of the corseting—

Her gown a tangle around her hips, she let him bare her lower body and kneel over it. A terror filled her eyes all at once. She pushed her palms against him:

"I don't think I can. Not since—"

"Yes you can, love. Of course you can—"

"No, I'm afraid, I don't—*ah!*"

She uttered the cry as he pierced into her, aware of her fear but unable to stop himself. Tears ran down her cheeks.

She tried to feign feeling; response. But it was as if her body had locked into rigidity. The quick, almost brutal thrusts skidded the lounge back and forth an inch, then two, each motion painful to him but doubly so for her. He saw that in the stricken face pressed close to his; felt it in the taut, abruptly cold body. Who was she seeing with those staring, tear-brimming eyes? Not him. Another man who had stalked up to her bedroom on a night of fire and murder and taken her the same way. *Christ, almost the same way—*

Mercifully, it was soon over.

Panting, he drew back, realizing much too late the kind of choice she had made: on one hand, the impulsive thrust of her emotions; on the other, her scruples and—more important—a fear from which, God help her, she might never recover.

And it had been the wrong choice.

She wouldn't look at him. She kept her head turned aside on the lounge cushion, tears shining tracks down her cheeks. Drained and hating himself, he brought up one hand to brush at the tears. She pulled her head away as if his fingers were fouled.

"Peggy—"

"Don't say anything. Don't speak."

"I lost control, I—"

"It doesn't make any difference. You —you felt—how I couldn't—how—"

"That'll pass with a man who's gentle. I wasn't. I'm sorry. God, believe me, I'm sorry—"

"The sin's mine as much as yours. Please go."

"Peggy, there's no sin if two people want—"

"*Yes there is!*" she cried. "I've dishonored Seth!"

"Seth's *dead!*"

Her eyes flew open. For one blinding moment she gazed at him with absolute revulsion.

Then she said in a voice whose softness terrified him:

"*I am still his wife.*"

Struggling to conceal her exposed body, she stood and turned her back, tugging her underthings into place to hide the staining evidence of their mutual weakness. He heard her weeping, and that was how he left her—

He ran down the lawn through thte darkness, mounted the gelding, booted it along the lane. The weakness was his; *his!*

He'd vowed nothing like this would happen if he called. But he'd made a hundred vows in the past—a thousand!—and broken every one. Whatever he touched became wreckage. And now he'd wrecked the dearest object of all.

Forever, he was certain.

V

PACING THE Shaw cabin all that long night, Judson seethed with conflicting emotions. Shame. Condemnation of Peggy for leading him on, permitting him—

No, goddammit! *He* was responsible! He had virtually raped her.

Yes, of course, she'd wanted it—at first. But if he'd had the sense to remember the uprising—the strength to call a halt at any of several stages—

The yellow hound licked at his bare foot. Judson kicked the dog's ribs. The animal fell, yelping, then crept into the cabin corner, its tail curled under its hindquarters.

Judson couldn't sleep. It was agony for him to imagine what Peggy must be feeling as the sun rose on Caroline County. The deed of last night would probably blot her conscience for a lifetime. She was that sort of person.

Yet he'd gone ahead. *Gone ahead!* Just as he went recklessly ahead with any headstrong wish, no matter the havoc it caused—

He found a quill, a little ink, tore a scrap from an old ledger Tom Shaw had used for keeping a record of his pathetically small purchases of seed and other staples. In the dawn, Judson wrote a single sentence:

I abjectly beg your forgiveness.

He signed his initial, folded the scrap twice, put on his shirt and boots and rode to the McLean house where hands were already heading into the fields. He knocked at the front door. This time a different house girl answered.

"Please give this to Mrs. McLean at once."

The girl shook her head. "Mrs. McLean, she still in bed. She was up mos' of the night feeling poorly."

"Then give it to her when she wakens."

"Yes, sar, Mist' Fletcher, I will."

Destruction on destruction, he thought as he galloped down the lane. He had to escape. But the very hope was futile. There was no escape from the failures that were built into the flawed framework of Judson Fletcher. Perhaps old Angus was right after all; perhaps some poisonous perversity raged in his blood, uncontrollable. He wondered if some learned physician might explain it; doubted it. At any rate, if the lord of Sermon Hill was correct—and mounting evidence seemed to indicate he was—it might prove fortunate in the long run that Peggy's parents had chosen childless Seth over her other suitor—

At the cabin Judson found some corn left. He kicked the hound outside, latched the windows and the door and started drinking. When he woke up hours later, the hound was gone.

VI

A FEW days later, a McLean black rode over with an answer to Judson's note:

> *All shame and responsibility must be shared equally between ourselves. I deem it wisest—and safest—that we do not ever see one another again. P.*

So Judson didn't venture anywhere near the McLean plantation again that summer. He could never quite decide whether he was doing penance or suffering punishment.

But then, weren't they supposed to be the same thing? It certainly felt like it. The yellow hound never came back.

3
Reunion in Pennsylvania

"LET GO, Adams! Damn you, I say let go—!"

"Ah, come on, Royal. I only want to try your little cap."

"You stay away from me!"

In response, Philip heard a low, rumbling laugh.

Philip jumped up, spilling his wood trencher and the utensils—wood-handled knife and spoon; wrought-iron fork—into the dirt beside the four-legged brass cooking pot. Uneaten slices of fried salt beef were trampled as he and chubby-faced Lucas Cowper dashed for the flapped entrance of the wall tent assigned to their mess. At least the infernal salt beef ration, as appetizing as burned gun-powder, was no loss—

Philip whipped up the flap to see Mayo Adams backing the small-boned, dark-eyed Rothman toward the rear of the six-foot-square tent. Rothman's feet tangled in the bedrolls arranged on the ground. With an explosion of breath, he sat down heavily on the packet of new books his parents had shipped him. Philip was very nearly as alarmed over the welfare of the precious books as he was about that of the young man; the books provided Philip's only means of keeping abreast of trends in the printing trade.

Chuckling, Adams watched Rothman flounder. When the younger man diverted his attention to the book packet for a moment, Adams shot one hand toward the small knitted cap of black wool that Rothman wore fastened to the top of his head with pins:

"Don't be so skittish, Royal. Here, alls I want to do is try it on—"

Rothman bobbed his head to avoid the bigger soldier's hand. Scrambling to hands and knees, then crouching, he panted, "You can't. It's part of my religion and nothing to do with you!"

"Yeh, but I only seen a few Israelites in this army, and you're all a mighty sanctified lot—" He snatched again with one huge hand; again Rothman ducked just in time.

Adams claimed to have been a brewer's apprentice in Boston. The bunched muscles of his forearms showed he was accustomed to heavy work. His oafish face and squinty eyes indicated that the work didn't require much brainpower. Royal Rothman was nineteen, and frail. He had formerly clerked for his father, a prosperous Boston chandler.

"Listen, I'm gettin' peeved, Royal. I want to try it on—now *gimme!*"

A third time, Royal's agility saved his skullcap. Philip and Cowper grabbed the bull-shouldered Adams and spun him around.

"Leave him alone, Mayo," Cowper said, though it obviously required some courage because of Adams' size.

"Go on back and eat them slops they call food around here," Adams warned, his eyes smoldering suddenly. In the heat of the early August evening, the inside of the tent was as hot as a furnace. "This ain't none of your affair."

"Certainly is," Philip said, glancing past the big apprentice to the wooden horses; the racks where six muskets leaned. He judged the distance, adding, "When six people live together in one tent, everybody needs to tread a little easy. You've been ragging Royal ever since he came to camp."

Adams, who was fond of bragging about kinship with Mr. Samuel Adams—a lie already identified by the messmates for what it was—spat on the ground:

"Cause he's been nothin' but a nuisance. I'm gettin' a bellyful of livin' with a feller who jabbers half the goddam night, keeps a lantern lit the other half—"

"There is nothing wrong with praying *or* reading!" Royal protested.

"—*and* sports a fancy British monicker on top of it!"

On the defensive, the dark-haired young man shook his head. "I've informed you a dozen times, Mayo—my father gave me the name Royal when the colonies were still friendly to His Majesty."

"No damn skin off me," Mayo Adams grinned ill-humoredly. "I just plain want to try on your cap. Want to see if it'll make me as all-fired holy as you are."

"Nothing would do that, Mayo," Philip said. "Absolutely nothing."

Wearily, the big-bellied Cowper asked, "What's got you up, Mayo? Did you bribe one of your friends at the sutler's tent to give you more than your half pint of spirits for the day?"

"Go fuck a sheep, farm boy."

Lucas Cowper turned scarlet. But he kept his temper. "You wait outside, Royal," he ordered.

The dark-haired private scrambled past Mayo Adams' tree-like legs and disappeared with one hand still clutching the little black cap on the top of his head.

As Adams glared, Cowper said, "Now calm down and that's the end of it."

"Not by a damn sight! I'm tired of the rest of you treatin' me like I'm nothin'—"

"You act like something else, we'll treat you that way," Philip snapped, pivoting to escape to the slightly cooler air outside.

A massive hand crashed on his shoulder, the fingers constricting, jerking him around. From Mayo's breath it was evident that he'd consumed much more than the permitted quantity of gin. The huge apprentice towered over Philip, enraged—no novelty in these steamy days of inactivity:

"Suppose you say that where we got some wranglin' room."

Philip wriggled free of the hand. "For God's sake, Mayo, we're supposed to be fighting Howe, not each other!"

"Yeh, but nobody knows where old Billy's got to since he sailed out o' New York—and you're right here, Mr. Sassy Kent." Fists up, he lunged.

Frightened out of an earlier impulse to laugh in Adam's face, Philip barely had time to sidestep. He blocked the bigger man's fist on his forearm, ducked under the windmilling arms while he signaled Lucas Cowper with one quick glance. Adams grabbed Philip's throat. He shoved Adams' slab-like chest with both hands. Cowper bent just enough so that Adams fell over him backwards, cursing blue.

By that time Philip had reached the storage horses. He jerked out his Brown Bess with Lumden's bayonet locked to the barrel stud. Philip was the only man in the mess who owned one of the weapons. Now the way the bayonet extended his reach was a definite advantage. Leaning forward and down, he brought the tip to within a couple of inches of Adams' bobbing throat-apple.

Soaked with the sudden sweat of danger, Philip still tried to speak reasonably:

"Mayo, if you don't back off, and right now, I'm going to send you up to the hospital tents. You've got better things to do, don't you?"

Sprawled on his back, Adams eyed the steel under his chin. Some of the hate went out of his eyes. Some, but not all:

"Well—I guess I do. Let me up."

"Only if you go outside and walk around till you're sober."

Cowper put in, "And stay away from Royal, he does you no harm."

"I didn't sign up to serve with no damn Israelites!" Adams exploded as he clambered to his feet. "Robbers, usurers, every stinking one—"

"Outside," Cowper sighed, summoning courage to add a shove.

Huge and stooping, Mayo Adams swung his massive head around as he reached the tent entrance. His glower was no less unpleasant than it had been when he was baiting Rothman:

"This time you got me two for one. But I remember pretty good. Soon as we

see some action, you boys are gonna have more to fret about than Tommy's musket. You better watch your own backs, too."

He clumped out, leaving Philip and Cowper exchanging uneasy looks. Lucas Cowper wiped his forehead.

"Lord, Philip, I think the big fool's serious."

"I know he is," Philip said he returned the Brown Bess to the horse.

There had been arguments with the dull-witted Adams before. But they'd never climaxed with such an open threat. Damn, it infuriated him. As if they didn't have enough to wring out their nerves these summer days—!

He followed Cowper outside. Mayo Adams had disappeared down the noisy street that ran between the Massachusetts tents. Royal Rothman was righting the overturned cooking pot in which the six-man mess prepared its meals. He glanced at Philip and Cowper, almost apologetic:

"I thank you both for helping me."

Cowper waved it aside as he retrieved his trencher. "Royal, keeping a bridle on that straw-head is to our own benefit. Just as Philip said—men who have to fight together should stick together."

"That's granting we ever fight," Philip said with a nervous eye on the steaming August sunset.

All across the hillsides near the Neshaminy Bridge northeast of Philadelphia, heavy blue smoke from hundreds of cook fires hung in the humid air. Regimental pennons in the tent city drooped on their poles. Eleven thousand men were camped in the prescribed rows—and had been for weeks. A sea of canvas shelters—the largest belonging to the officers—rolled from horizon to horizon. There was constant din: men arguing or laughing or singing; the rumble of baker's wagons delivering the next day's ration of fresh bread; the rattle of musketry as some unit staged a sharpshooting contest to pass the time.

Philip picked up his trencher and utensils, then forked the dirt-covered salt beef and held it up:

"Want this, Lucas? Might taste better with some Pennsylvania grit on it."

"Nothing would make it taste better," Cowper said, throwing his own half-eaten slices into the coals under the cooking pot. Philip started off to dispose of his garbage, stopped when he recognized two men coming along the smoky, teeming street—the other two members of their mess.

One was Breen, a man from the village of Andover. He was about thirty-five, a lackadaisical tosspot who maintained that all his life, he'd had no occupation other than "unemployed." Breen wasn't his real name, he'd confided once. He'd used it to join the army and escape creditors and a common-law wife.

Breen's companion, Pettibone, was a short, spectacled man in his middle twenties. Before enlisting he'd taught school in Roxbury. It was to the somewhat prim teacher that Philip hurried:

"Did you stop to see about mail?"

Pettibone showed a letter. "I've one from my Patsy. Nothing for the rest of you, I'm afraid."

Philip was disturbed. He hadn't heard from Anne in over a month.

He knew that freighting the wagon-loads of mail to the army was a slow process. Sometimes a sack split and weather ruined hundreds of addresses. Many letters took months to be delivered, or got lost altogether. That didn't change the fact that he wanted word about Anne's well-being, and Abraham's. And about the progress of construction on Captain Caleb's two new privateering vessels.

In the first of two letters he'd received since his departure from Cambridge,

Anne reported that Caleb had called—without Captain Rackham; a relief. She had gone over Caleb's proposal, satisfied herself about the details and invested their two hundred pounds. But her second letter, posted in June, said nothing more about the venture.

After supper, Philip occupied himself with the little sewing kit Anne had prepared before he left. Seated cross-legged on the ground outside the tent, he stitched up a tear in the sleeve of his long hunting shirt. He was becoming an expert with thread and the steel needle and the open-topped pewter thimble. In the field, there was no other choice.

Royal Rothman had already gone inside, lit a lamp and started opening the packet of books from his parents. His collection thus far included an assortment of political pamphlets, a tattered copy of *Common Sense* which he claimed to have gone through over fifty times, and an edition of one of the most popular books of recent years, *Night Thoughts on Life, Death, and Immortality*.

It was a work of the so-called "graveyard" school of poets. Philip found its blank verse uninspiring, and its themes somewhat too morbid for present circumstances. What did continue to amaze and confound him was the popularity of English authors such as Reverend Young who had produced *Night Thoughts*. The war didn't seem to dampen American enthusiasm for British literature.

Momentarily, Royal came out again with his new arrivals. Philip looked enviously at a richly bound volume whose title he recognized at once. John Milton's century-old metaphysical epic, *Paradise Lost*, was enjoying a new burst of popularity; it was, Royal reported, the year's best seller in Boston. And the new edition which the younger man showed enthusiastically was one of the handsomest Philip had ever seen.

He ran his hand down one page, experiencing a pleasure that was almost painful. For a moment, bitterness swept over him, coupled with another intense wish that he could be home, free to pursue the trade he'd come to love. He voiced his feelings to Royal, with whom he'd discussed his ambitions before:

"If I had the money and equipment to print fine books, this would be the sort I'd want to bear my name."

"I'm sure you'll publish books like this one day, Philip."

Philip's shrug expressed his uncertainty. Royal laid the Milton aside, knelt beside his messmate, fanned out three inexpensively produced pamphlets.

"Here are the real treats—a new series by Mr. Paine."

Philip took the trio of pamphlets, noted that they all bore a common title—*The American Crisis*—and were numbered sequentially. He opened the first; it was just a few pages long. He flipped to the end, where the date appeared—December 23 of the preceding year—along with the author's pseudonym, *Common Sense*. Philip had heard that the famous pamphleteer was now employed as secretary to the committee of foreign affairs of the Congress. From that vantage point, he continued to use his pen to praise and encourage the patriots—and damn all Tories, British and domestic.

"Read the opening paragraph," Royal urged.

"I'd like to read the whole of all three when you're finished with them."

"Of course you may. But do look at the opening of the first. Some of the phrases are worthy of a Milton."

Philip turned back to the passage indicated:

> *These are the times that try men's souls. The summer soldier and the sunshine patriot will, in this crisis, shrink from the service of*

*the country, but he that stands it now deserves the love and thanks
of man and woman. Tyranny, like hell, is not easily conquered;
yet we have this consolation with us that, the harder the conflict,
the more glorious the triumph. What we obtain too cheap, we
esteem too lightly; it is dearness only that gives everything its
value. Heaven knows how to put a proper price upon its goods,
and it would be strange indeed if so celestial an article as freedom
should not be highly rated.*

At that point, Philip stopped and returned the papercovered essay with the
other two, saying:

"Mr. Paine certainly has a grasp of the mood of an army camp. He's doing his
best to keep spirits up."

And my own need it badly, he added in the silence of his mind. He wondered
again whether he would ever live to embrace Anne; hold his child; or pull the
lever on a flatbed press and watch a sheet come forth, miraculously inked with
the thoughts of the author.

Royal said, "My father's letter reports that Mr. Paine is planning a whole
series of these *Crisis* articles—written as the need arises. Someone will certainly
put them together in a book one day. Why shouldn't it be you, Philip?"

Philip smiled wearily. "Well, it's a mite early to consider that, seeing as I
have no press, no pressroom and precious little money."

But his eyes had brightened a bit; the suggestion had caught his fancy. Reality
quickly took control again:

"Very likely some printer who isn't with the army will seize on the idea
first."

"Yes, but a Kent edition could be finer and more handsomely prepared—and
I'm sure it would have a guaranteed sale. Look at all the different versions of
Common Sense that are circulating."

Philip nodded, enjoying the fantasy of a collection of Paine's essays offered
under his own imprint. He didn't even think about the legality of it. Every
respectable printer practiced piracy, despite copyright statues of various sorts in
force in the former colonies. Massachusetts Bay's law had been enacted in 1672,
Ben Edes had told him once. But it was largely ignored, and the penalty was
relatively paltry: a fine three times the manufacturing cost of the illegal edition.
Anyone could reprint foreign authors such as Milton and the Reverend Young
with absolute impunity. Exisiting copyright laws didn't apply to works by non-
Americans.

"All right, Royal," Philip smiled at last, "I'll consider an edition of Mr.
Paine one of my first priorities. But don't pin me to a calendar, please. Who can
be certain when we'll be back in Boston?"

Royal's somber nod showed that he caught the undertone of resignation and
apprehension. He scooped up his shipment and headed for the tent.

"I'll get busy reading so you may have these quickly—"

Philip barely heard the remark. He was staring into space, seeing the title page
of the Paine book as he would compose it.

Lucas Cowper, not the least interested in matters literacy, had paid no attention to the conversation, occupying himself instead with an ox horn he'd obtained at the camp slaughterhouse. He was fashioning a new container for his
powder. Left-handed, Cowper needed a horn that would fit snugly on his left hip;
an ox's right horn would have done him no good.

While Philip and Royal talked, Cowper worked away with the tip of his knife, carefully chipping letters from the bony surface. Now he held up the horn and displayed its legend to Philip:

LUCAS COWPER, HIS HORN, AUGUST 1777

"A handsome job, Lucas," Philip told him.

"I don't know about that," the other grinned. "But maybe it won't be stolen like the last one." He applied himself to a few finishing cuts to smooth rough edges of the letters.

Paine's phrase kept stealing back into Philip's mind. *Times that try men's souls.* It was certainly apt. Fear and frustration combined to harry the strongest man's nerve; erode his will; fill him with anxiety. In a few moments, Philip was almost regretting that Royal had brought up the subject of an edition of Paine. The tempting idea only reminded him of the impossibility of fulfilling any dreams or ambitions in the immediate future.

Stretching, Pettibone emerged from the tent to take the air after completing his letter to his wife Patsy. Breen appeared, having vanished to the sutler's for a while. As the regimental drums began to beat the night's tattoo, Breen announced disparagingly:

"More of them goddamn Frenchies comin' out tomorrow."

Philip looked up from his unfinished sewing. "Officers?"

"Fortune-hunters, more like. Figger to make a killin' sellin' their fancy selves to lead us poor ignorant clodfoots. Feller told me the Congress is gettin' mighty sick of them monsoors paradin' off the ships and askin' for high rank and lots o' pay."

"If there are more coming out tomorrow, I imagine we'll have an inspection," Philip said. "Maybe even a grand review. That'll break up the day, anyway."

Anything to break up the day—!

And the waiting.

___II

MAYO ADAMS hadn't come back by the time the last drumbeats died out across the Pennsylvania countryside. Philip lay sweating in his underdrawers, on top of his bedroll instead of in it. Breen's loud snores, augmented by the click of his wooden dentures, added to the other irritants—the heat; the boredom; the uncertainty about what might lie ahead—that kept Philip awake and restless.

Eventually he dozed off. A sudden clumping and heavy breathing shot him upright:

"Who is it?"

"Adams." Crawling past the other sleepers.

Adams still reeked of gin. General Washington believed that a certain amount of alcohol was necessary to a soldier, but that too much was disastrous. A man could only obtain more than the daily ration if he had a friend. Adams did.

"You gwan back to sleep, Kent. Let's hope you wake up tomorrow, huh?"

Chuckling, Adams passed on, a dimly seen bulk in the stifling gloom of the tent. He took his place on his roll at the rear corner. Philip settled down again, tense.

Not a sound came from Mayo Adams. But Philip had the uncomfortable feeling that the brewer's apprentice was still awake.

Staring at him.
Watching him.
And maybe thinking secret thoughts—?

III

TWO THINGS plagued the Americans encamped above Philadelphia. One was in the past, the other yet to come.

The first was the devastating plunge in morale produced by news from the north. Practically on the anniversary of the declaration of a year ago, the American defenders of Fort Ticonderoga had been forced to evacuate the position as untenable. Gentleman Johnny Burgoyne was marching south from Canada with eight thousand British soldiers, Canadians, and Iroquois tribesmen recruited by the king's agents.

Word of Ticonderoga's recapture had arrived in the Pennsylvania encampment in mid-July. Virtually every man took it as a grim sign. Horatio Gates, a capable American general, was supposedly moving to blunt Burgoyne's thrust. But there was no guarantee he could do it. God knew what bloodshed was being perpetrated in northern York State this very moment.

Then there was the second worry—the future.

The uneasiness sprang directly from no one knowing the whereabouts of General Sir William Howe, His Majesty's commander-in-chief in America.

For months, Howe had dallied at New York. First there were reports that he intended to go north to link up with Burgoyne. Then other reports said his objective was Philadelphia. All the while, his troops remained garrisoned in New Brunswick and Amboy, supplied from across the Hudson and capable of retaking the whole of Jersey—if they received orders.

Howe was too busy to issue orders. He was occupied with balls and fetes in the captured city. And, so the story ran, with his new blonde mistress, one Mrs. Loring.

The charming lady's husband, a fervent Boston Tory, had been appointed commissary-general in charge of American battle prisoners. The position permitted Loring to fatten his own purse by selling off prisoner rations at a profit. The scoundrel seemed happy with his lot—and not the least jealous when General Howe commandeered his wife for a bed-partner. Perhaps, in some bizarre way, he considered her surrender a duty to the Crown that was making him rich.

At last, in late July, Howe had moved—but in an unexpected direction. He and his Jersey army disappeared into the Atlantic aboard the three hundred ships commanded by Howe's brother. Somewhere on the ocean, that armada cruised out of sight of shore—and no one could say where the eighteen thousand British and Hessians would ultimately land. Nearly every day, new rumors reached the Pennsylvania camp—

Howe had been sighted off the Virginia capes—

No, he had not.

Yes he had, but the fleet was gone again.

Whatever the truth, it seemed obvious to Philip and his messmates that the plan to relieve Burgoyne had been abandoned. So what would be Howe's objective? A southern port? Philadelphia, where a nervous Congress was receiving a stream of foreign officers who had sailed to America bearing papers from Silas

Deane, the commissioner in Paris? The papers guaranteed the foreign officers high ranks in the Continental army in return for their services. *Guaranteed it!* Their American counterparts complained, with justifiable bitterness.

Some of the soldier-adventurers were reasonably well qualified. Washington had already appointed a skilled Polish engineer, Kosciusko, to a colonelship in that "learned" branch of the service. But many of the officers were not qualified for much of anything, and had only come to the new country in hopes of deposing some native-born officer—for profit.

And tomorrow, Philip thought, dozing again, a new contingent of Europeans was due to arrive.

Well, it *would* provide diversion. Something to break the endless tedium of the days spent waiting and wondering when Howe's flotilla would appear again; and where.

IV

THE DRUMMERS hammered in the blistering sun. The fifers tootled the melody of *The White Cockade*. Standing in the ranks on the parade field, his musket held at shoulder firelock position, Philip squinted across the sere grass toward the approaching horsemen. Out in front of Philip's company, the commander, Captain Walter Webb of Worcester, stood as straight as the spontoon he gripped in his right hand.

Philip wished he could wipe the sweat off his forehead. It trickled down both sides of his nose and into his eyes. He had trouble seeing the brightly uniformed officers cantering toward the Massachusetts companies.

Of course Washington was immediately recognizable because of his white mount and his customary blue and buff. But the two men beside him, riding out ahead of the staff officers, were unrecognizable blurs—

Until they drew up opposite Philip's company. Suddenly one of the two with Washington reined in. Philip gasped aloud at the sight of a long-forgotten face.

A youthful face. Aristocratic. Crowned under a tricorn by red hair far brighter than the commanding general's. But Philip was sure his own eyes were playing tricks—

No, no, there could be no mistake. It *was* the same face; a face he'd first seen in a howling blizzard near his mother's inn, when he'd come upon a thirteen-year-old boy struggling with two would-be kidnappers. The boy had been born to the French nobility; destined for a military career—

The Marquis de Lafayette caught Washington's attention, pointed. Next to Philip, Lucas Cowper said under his breath:

"My Lord, he's singling out somebody in this company!"

Washington stood in his saddle, spotted Philip. The general's face seemed to register recognition too; perhaps from that night in Vassall House before the expedition with Knox.

Washington said something to Lafayette. Instantly, Gil's face burst into a smile.

Royal Rothman, his cap concealed under his round-brimmed hunting hat, hissed from the front rank where the shortest men stood:

"It isn't me. It's somebody behind me."

"Damn if that froggy ain't wavin' at you, Kent," Mayo Adams said from directly behind. "How'd you git your ass in trouble this time?"

Unbelievably, Washington himself had now ridden back to consult with a staff officer. The main body of the inspection party rode on, Lafayette casting one glowing smile back across his shoulder. The staff officer wheeled his horse toward Captain Webb, who appeared ready to fall over in a faint from the sudden flurry of attention.

The staff officer dismounted, spoke with Webb. Philip could hear their voices but not the words. Then Webb's eyes literally bugged.

As the staff officer re-mounted and cantered away, Captain Webb turned to give Philip a disbelieving stare. Lucas Cowper whispered again:

"Philip, do you know that officer who went by?"

"Yes, I do."

From behind, Mayo Adams sneered, "Way it's going', Kent's liable to be suppin' with old George 'fore long. My God, I didn't know we were in such highfalutin company."

But Adams' jibes couldn't unsettle Philip now. He was too stirred by memories, by excitement, by the astounding reappearance of the young man who had given him the treasured sword—

The young man Philip had never expected to see again in all his lifetime.

Then he recalled something the young marquis had said the last time they met at Marie Charboneau's inn, just before Gil returned to Paris for more military training. Something about comrades in arms always encountering one another again on battlefields.

Comrades in arms. Gil had said they were exactly that because Philip had saved his life—

And the prediction had come true.

Officers began to shout orders to break up the review formation. Captain Webb barked Philip's name and headed straight for him:

"Kent, are you aware of the identity of that Frenchman? The one who singled you out?"

"Yes, Captain, I am. Let's see whether I can give you all his names—"

Philip's friends crowded around, listening. Even Mayo Adams lingered, a disgusted curiosity on his face. Philip recalled the names one by one:

"Marie Joseph Paul Yves Roch Gilbert du Motier—"

Webb continued to look utterly stupefied as Philip added:

"His hereditary title's Marquis de Lafayette. I always called him Gil."

"Pretty damn familiar!" Webb exclaimed.

"I was born in France, Captain. I knew him there. His family home was in the same province as mine."

"Well, I don't care what you called him then, you're going to have to call him sir when you go to supper."

"Supper?"

"Why d'you suppose that major rode over here? You're to clean up and report to the marquis' pavilion at six on the dot. And you'd better not forget the Congress just appointed him a major general."

That touched off an explosion of exclamations. Philip joined in:

"He can't be more than nineteen!"

"Looks younger, if you ask me. But he's still a general attached to Washington's personal staff. And the major passed the word that the old man's taken a strong liking to him. You'd best be on your good behavior."

Abruptly, Philip was overcome with apprehension. He was excited at the prospect of a reunion with his boyhood friend. But a meeting between a common

private and a freshly commissioned major general—that was something else entirely. He spent the rest of the afternoon nervously washing, shaving, sewing all the ragged places in his best shirt and trousers—and withstanding jokes from the men in his mess.

There were no jokes from Mayo Adams, though. He treated the whole business with silent contempt.

V

"UH—SIR?"

The young Frenchman seated inside the spacious officer's tent jumped up from his camp chair and ran around the table where exquisite china, silver and glassware had been set for two. The orderly held the entrance flap aside, but Philip hesitated, uncertain as to whether he should salute.

Gil seized both his shoulders, his face almost glowing as he exclaimed in French:

"My God, Phillipe—it is you! Ranks and titles are forgotten here. It is Gil and—no, no, I was told you were someone else! A new name?"

"Yes. Philip Kent."

"Gil and Philip, then! Long-lost comrades reunited!"

He embraced Philip so ardently, kissing him on both cheeks, that the orderly blushed.

Gil took Philip's arm. "Come in, come in—we will dine and talk. But what shall it be? French? Or the English I speak so badly?"

"My French is pretty well forgotten," Philip said with an apologetic smile. Though several years older than the handsome nineteen-year-old, he still had a feeling that he was the junior in the relationship. Even at thirteen, Gil had been a commanding presence; the tutor who gave Philip his first rudimentary lessons with the musket and spontoon. "But we can try, if you wish—"

"It's easier, easier," Gil continued in French as he pulled back a chair for his guest. "Be seated! Tell me everything! Where you live, your fortunes—everything."

"I'd like to. But honestly, Gil, it—it isn't necessary for you to entertain me this way—" He indicated the elegant table. "You're a high-ranking member of the staff. I'm only—"

"Only my friend. My savior," Gil said with utter seriousness. His hazel eyes held Philip's. "I remember very distinctly that I would not be here in the glorious new land of freedom if you hadn't happened along that road near Chavaniac when I was in danger. I'd be a major general of the worms, very likely. So let's have no more folderol about rank—" He grinned. "That is a direct order."

Philip laughed. "All right—General. I still have the sword you gave me. It hangs over the mantel in our home in Massachusetts—" The language was slow going, but Philip took his time, translating each phrase carefully out of the more familiar English. Gil's sandy eyebrows hooked up at the last remark:

" 'Our home.' You are married, then?"

"Yes, to a girl I met in Boston."

"Children?"

"One son. He'll be two in September."

"How marvelous, wonderful!" Gil reached under the bosom of his uniform,

pulled out a golden locket on a slender chain. "This is rather a delicate ornament for a soldier. But my own dear heart insisted I bring it with me—"

Proudly, Gil thumbed the locket open to display a beautifully done miniature of his attractive, fragile-looking wife. Philip judged her to be little more than fifteen or sixteen.

The marquis snapped the locket shut, signaled to the orderly, said in heavily accented English:

"Set the meal, please—and the wine. Then leave us." The orderly wheeled and hurried out.

"Gil, how in God's name did you get here?"

"Well, service to your new country has become popular in many parts of Europe. The splendid declaration against King George last summer—you've no idea how it fired the minds and hearts of Frenchmen!"

"And inspired some private help from your king."

"The bogus trading company? Yes, I've heard of it. Officially, of course, France takes no position in the war. As yet," he added in a significant way. "One may hope—"

He shrugged. "For the present, it's enough that volunteers may cross the ocean to offer their swords. In my case, I'm afraid King Louis felt the Lafayette name a trifle too prestigious for even that to be allowed." He made a face to demonstrate his displeasure.

"You mean it was suggested you shouldn't come?"

"*Suggested* hardly covers it. I was on garrison duty in Metz when word reached me about the noble declaration. I have never been so overcome—so moved. I decided at once to speed here to support your cause."

Finally relaxing a little, Philip smiled. "I also recall you didn't think too highly of the British."

"That's true—as well as an understatement. Unfortunately, members of my family were determined I should not risk my career in this venture—nor lend the Lafayette name to what remains, in official circles, an illegitimately conceived nation. King Louis even issued a writ forbidding my journey. Had the paper ever caught up with me, I'd have been clapped away in the Bastille until my enthusiasm for America cooled. As it was, I rushed overland in secret—I took ship at *Los Pasajes* in Spain—and I landed early in July in your Charleston."

"South Carolina?"

"Quite so. Then I traveled nine hundred miles more—in carriages I paid for myself—also on horseback when the carriages broke down. When I reached the Congress in Philadelphia, I was given a decidedly rude reception, at least in some quarters. A Mr. Lovell of that body remarked that French officers had a great fancy to enter American service without being invited. In short, I was treated like the rankest freebooter."

"We've had some of those show up, though."

"Nevertheless, it was an insult. Since I had come here out of the purest motives, and at my own expense, I demanded two favors of the Congress. To serve at my own cost, and entirely as a volunteer—requiring no rank or command. Though naturally I hope to have the honor of field command at some time in the future. I am well trained for it, after all." He still sounded a bit miffed. "And training seems sorely needed in this army. I was agog this morning. That is the only word—agog. No uniforms! Merely—forgive me!—those peculiar shirts such as you're wearing. Then I watched a bit of drill. An absolute shambles! A drill master's badly needed—"

"Gil, I'm afraid Washington has neither the money nor the talent to put together the kind of army you're accustomed to."

"Aha, but European officers are arriving who can do something about that! They must be given the opportunity! Else your cause—our cause—is surely lost."

Glum, Philip told him, "I don't doubt the general would welcome really good assistance."

"Yes, a magnificent man, magnificent! I told him I wished for nothing more than to be allowed to serve near his person till such time as he thought it proper to entrust me with a division." With an emphatic flick of one of his epaulettes, he added, "I did not *insist* upon a major generalship. However—" Another shrug, and a wink. "It is certainly a step in the right direction."

Philip smiled again. So did his friend. The orderly returned, followed by two Frenchmen: one a cook in a white smock, pushing a wood-wheeled serving cart, the other a liveried waiter who proceeded to serve the meal and decant the wine. Philip discovered that Gil wasn't exaggerating about paying his own way:

"I want no one in this command to think I am living in my accustomed style at their expense, Philip. Everything you see, I purchased. The venison, the wine—this uniform, the tent, even my horses and wagons. I am of the opinion that perhaps I have more dedication to the American purpose than some of your own rude Congressmen."

"I don't doubt it. More money, too."

"A hit, a most accurate hit!" Gil cried, clapping one hand over his heart in false pain.

There was no longer any barrier of hesitancy between them. Philip's uneasiness had completely vanished, and he fell to enjoying the excellent meal, the wine and the conversation with unashamed gusto. The talk was virtually continuous because both friends had much to tell.

Philip related all of his up-and-down history since Gil had ridden away from Auvergne that long-ago day. He only omitted the most unflattering parts—his killing of Roger Amberly and his dalliance with Alicia before he finally made up his mind about Anne Ware and the American cause.

For his part, Gil was ready with anecdotes about military life, as well as acid comments about the American commissioner in Paris, Mr. Deane, who was "frantically" issuing letters to European officers, promising them exalted posts and high wages—without specific authorization from the Congress. Presently, when the table had been cleared and a lantern lighted and hung at the open end of the tent, Gil offered a toast with brandy:

"To my comrade Phillipe—ah, I forget so easily. Philip! May he and his country live in liberty forever."

Unable to think of any appropriate sentiment to offer in return, Philip smiled, raised his glass and drank, supremely content for a few hours in the renewal of a bond that defied explanation or—seemingly—geography.

With a little more of the brandy under their belts, the friends could talk even more frankly:

"Gil, I don't want to sound pessimistic, but it strikes me that the outcome of this war is as much up to men like Johnny Burgoyne and General Howe as it is to us."

"Exactly! There has never been an engagement of forces in which that wasn't so. However, don't worry—the enemy will make all the incorrect moves, and we shall make all the proper ones."

Philip sighed. "I wish I shared your confidence."

Gil grew solemn. "Sham confidence—and a poor joke. Truly, I wish it were so simple. There is much tension and impatience on the general's staff because of the uncertainty in regard to Howe's position."

"He can't stay at sea forever."

Gil clapped him on the shoulder, breaking the dour moment:

"He'd better not, with two such stout fighters waiting to engage him!"

The boast was cheerful enough. But Philip was already certain his friend placed little or no confidence in the disreputable-looking American troops he'd reviewed earlier in the day. Philip couldn't much blame Gil, either.

The two talked late into the night. Tipsy, Philip finally meandered back toward the Massachusetts tents. On the way he took great pleasure in displaying Captain Webb's signed order to the guards who questioned a private's right to be abroad after tattoo.

He yawned as he neared his own tent. He was anxious to climb into his bedroll and sleep. But it wasn't to be. His messmates were still awake and fired questions at him almost until dawn. They wanted this or that bit of information about Lafayette; a history of his experience; an explanation of how he'd gotten to be general at age nineteen; his views on the possibilities for victory.

The only one who sat sullen, cursing frequently because he couldn't sleep, was Mayo Adams. Philip's evening out with his celebrated friend seemed to have increased the man's hostility all the more.

VI

ON SATURDAY, August twenty-third, the drummers beat out a different rhythm. The signal to strike camp.

Immediately, the tent city began to come down; the artillery and the Conestoga wagons began to rumble; work replaced indolence. Admiral Howe's fleet had been sighted off Chesapeake Bay. If the enemy troops landed, less than a hundred miles separated them from the much smaller American force. In between lay Philadelphia, where the Congress still sat in session. Every man in that body was a candidate for a hangrope if he were caught.

The Americans marched south. Philip was in low spirits because he still hadn't received any new letters from Anne.

VII

ON SUNDAY morning, it rained. But the clouds cleared by noon, in time for a good percentage of the forty thousand people now living in Philadelphia to turn out and watch the American companies march through. Philip didn't see Gil; he would be riding at the very head of the column, with Washington, and Henry Knox, and other senior members of the staff.

Captain Webb's command lived up to Gil's original horrified assessment of it. They were just as ill-clad as the rest of the units from the other states represented in the huge parade of eleven thousand men.

But one visible feature united them—a sprig of greenery, fresh-cut the night before by the carpenters and placed in each man's hat to signify the army's vitality—on direct order of the commander-in-chief. Quite a few grumbled that more than a couple of leaves on a twig would be required to bring the quarrelsome, heat-weary citizen-soldiers up to fighting trim.

Webb's company, where Philip marched, was at present a fifty-man unit, the second in line among four such companies forming the battalion. Two battalions comprised the regiment. And throughout its shambling ranks—marching was too dignified and precise a term—disorder in formation accompanied disorder in costume. Seldom did anyone step exactly in time with the drumbeats. And whenever the fifers struck up one of the popular marching songs of the day, the men bellowed out the words if they felt like it:

> "We are the troop
> "That ne'er will stoop
> "To wretched sla-ver-ee—"

People leaned from windows, huzzahing, fluttering handkerchiefs. They lined the walks of Front and Chestnut Streets that Philip remembered so well from the weeks he'd spent in the city. Now circumstances were much different. Burdened with the equipment of war—canteen, cooking gear, hand-carved wood drinking cup, sheathed hunting knife, cartridge box, lead, ball mold and, most important of all, his Brown Bess with the bayonet in place—he was leaving the great city not to return to Anne but to confront the immense might of Howe's army. He imagined the foe as a scarlet serpent a thousand times longer than the British columns he remembered from Concord and New York and Jersey.

Next to Philip was Lucas Cowper. Although he had a deaf ear for music, he tried to improvise the marching airs anyway—whistling them off key. Philip stared up at the housepeaks and the clearing sky, singularly uninspired. No doubt it was partly due to the long, worrisome silence out of Cambridge. Surely Anne would have written if anything had gone wrong—

The singing and the cheers didn't help his mood either. A dedicated enemy lurked to the south. His job—every man's job—was to obey orders and destroy that enemy. Philip was sure Gil would be all dash and zeal on a prancing horse somewhere up with Washington. He was glad his friend couldn't see him, or the rest of his company, as they struggled to keep time with the Massachusetts drummers and fifers.

Marching immediately behind Philip and Cowper were Mayo Adams and Royal Rothman, the latter looking extremely nervous. But no more than exschoolmaster Pettibone just ahead. Pettibone gazed wistfully at the faces of the young girls cheering themselves hoarse on either side of Chestnut. He was no doubt wishing one of them was his dear Patsy.

Only Cowper, whistling in his monotone, seemed phlegmatically content. And of course Breen, staggering next to Pettibone. Breen was drunk.

The older man had soemhow wheedled an extra ration of rum which he had proudly poured into his canteen before the march began. Now he found it necessary to slake his thirst frequently—no unusual sight among the soldiers. But Breen's step grew more erratic by the moment. Finally, swearing under his breath, Captain Webb dropped back and ordered Pettibone to hold Breen up.

Breen gladly accepted the support, doffing his filthy hat to the captain. His sprig of green fell off and was trampled.

Breen paid no attention, putting his hat back on, then extending his canteen to Webb. The captain slapped it down, colored when he saw people on the sidewalk point. He about-faced, returned stiffly to the head of the company. All jollity, Breen made an obscene gesture and continued to loll with his arm over the shoulders of the scowling schoolteacher.

Philip wasn't amused. It seemed bitter clear again that a victorious army would never rise from such a disorganized collection of hooligans, malingerers and sometime-patriots yearning for home. Yet if there was ever a day when an army in the true sense was needed, that day had arrived.

The complainers were right. Twigs worn on the order of the commanding general weren't enough to work the miracle.

Some of the men started a new song:

> *"Over the hills with heart we go,*
> *"To fight the proud insulting foe—"*

"Kent?"

The voice brought Philip's head around even as he tried to keep in step with the drums. Mayo Adams gave him a coarse wink. His eyes glittered like polished stones in the August sun.

"You doin' all right, Kent?"

"I'm doing fine, thanks."

"Well, good, good. Just don't want you to forget I'm right behind you, boy. Right behind you every step."

> *"Our country calls and we'll obey—*
> *"Over the hills and far away!"*

4

Retreat at Brandywine

"JEHOSHAPHAT, PHILIP —look there in the ditch!"

Staggering along the road among the hundreds of men fleeing through the early autumn dusk toward Chester Creek, Philip wiped sweat from his eyes and followed Lucas Cowper's pointing hand. Of the men from his mess, Cowper was the only one he'd seen since the full retreat began an hour ago.

Now he saw another. Pettibone, lying on the slope of the roadside ditch, a bloodied hole shot through the left side of his chest.

The schoolmaster had apparently come this far when the lines broke, only to drop and die. Through the dust and smoke billowing over the road, the last, almost horizontal beams of September sunlight pierced here and there; sufficient light for Philip to have a swift, harrowing glimpse of a fat green fly landing on Pettibone's lip. The fly crawled over Pettibone's lower teeth and into his mouth.

"Somebody's got to let his poor wife know," Cowper said, shaken.

Philip tugged Cowper's arm. "Later. Come on! Staring won't help him—or us." He had to shout to be heard above the noise.

All around them, men limped or ran through the mellow evening. Cursed or complained as they dragged themselves along, slowed by wounds or the plain disgust and bitterness of defeat. Cowper surrendered to the pull of Philip's hand. The two returned to the center of the road. Behind them, musketry rattled.

For most of the day the American center had held Chad's Ford on the east side of Brandywine Creek, against the fire of Knyphausen's entrenched Hessians. Then, late in the afternoon, red jackets began appearing on the wooded hills to their rear, northward, where the right wing was stretched out in a long defense line. The bulk of the British army, mysteriously absent from the field for hours, had somehow gotten around behind the American positions. Three divisions under Cornwallis streamed down the hillsides to attack.

General Sullivan's brigades vainly tried to hold them back. Knyphausen's Hessians moved at last, eastward, to ford the Brandywine. From that hour, when the sun was already starting down, the outcome was certain. The Americans had been prepared for an assault from the west, not for a two-pronged attack from both front and rear. Around Philip and Lucas Cowper was the terrible result—a retreat more clamorous and confused than the one at Breed's Hill. A retreat that might prove even more devastating than the steady withdrawal of Washington's troops at Long Island and New York—

Philip knew the battle was lost. Cowper knew it. So did all the other men on the road. Fright and humiliation showed on every face.

As the light kept fading, Philip thought he saw the shapes of soldiers moving among the trees on his left, about a hundred yards north of the road. More Americans retreating, he assumed.

He was so tired, each step almost required a conscious act of will. His shoulder ached from returning Hessian fire with the Brown Bess. He'd had no food since early morning. At three, he'd drained the last tepid water from his canteen.

"Where in Christ are we supposed to be going?" he yelled at Cowper, above a din of hoofs and wheels coming up behind.

"We're to cross Chester Creek, that's what Webb said."

"Then what?"

"I don't know, maybe they'll tell us at the creek—"

"Clear away, clear away!" men shouted. Hastily Philip pushed Cowper to the shoulder. The heads of charging horses loomed, great silhouettes against the sunset light piercing the smoke. At full gallop, the horses dragged a pair of jouncing howitzers.

The men nearby broke for both sides of the road. The horses and wheeled guns thundered past. Above all, it was necessary to prevent the capture of artillery. Men were expendable.

Back on the road, yearning for just one good breath in the smoke and dust, Philip grabbed at a skinny soldier loping toward the east:

"Who are you? What unit?"

"Pinter's Marylanders—"

"Is the whole line broken?" Cowper shouted.

"Damn right it is. Howe's liable to whip us all the way back to Philadelphia—"

Then the Marylander was gone, dodging and darting around less speedy soldiers. The man was plainly determined to save his own skin. Maybe he had more brains than the rest of them, Philip thought. More brains than any of the spectral pairs and trios stumbling east in the lowering gloom, too worn out or hurt or disheartened to run.

More artillery roared through. Horse-drawn field cannon this time. One soldier failed to heed the shouted warnings and fell in the path of the slashing hoofs. Sourness rose in Philip's throat as the horses, then the iron-tired wheels, kept straight on over the flailing victim, muffling his shrieks, leaving him twitching in the road, all blood and broken bones.

Cowper kept looking back. Philip jerked his arm again:

"Damn it, Lucas, you can't stop to help every man who's hurt or you'll wind up the same way yourself."

Resigned, Cowper resumed the shambling pace. And despite the seeming callousness of his words, Philip was just as sick over the carnage as the young farmer was. It seemed to him that those in command—Washington, the staff, even his friend Gil who was supposedly on the field today—must have trained themselves never to view a battle in terms of individuals, only in terms of units, tactics, strategy. If they ever looked at the soldiers one by one—looked at the Pettibones lying dead in the ditches—they could never remain strong enough to issue orders for the next battle. Their hearts would break with despair.

Bitter fury welled up in Philip then. Fury born of the chaos and his exhaustion; fury over the human loss and the scandalous defeat—

Why hadn't someone caught the surprise flanking movement of Cornwallis? Was Washington asleep? Or was he simply the bungler he was so often accused of being?

Letting his emotions blue his already failing alertness, Philip wasn't ready for the unexpected crackle of musket-fire that raked the road from the left. Men yelled, dove for the ditches. Philip and Cowper crouched down, fumbling to load their weapons. The men drifting through the trees north of the road had right-flanked suddenly. They weren't American stragglers at all. Philip glimpsed florid faces, mitre-shaped hats—

A jaeger company. Hessians who had thrust forward parallel to the retreat route and were now turning to attack.

Running for the ditch with powder trailing from his horn, Lucas Cowper's legs suddenly gave out. Only an instant later did Philip realize what had happened. The young Massachusetts farmer had been hit.

Cowper pitched head first into the ditch, musket fallen, horn fallen, bellowing in pain as blood poured from the place where a Hessian ball had shattered his upper left arm.

The Hessians were kneeling among the trees nearest the road, firing their rifles with precision. Philip jumped into the ditch, ducked as a ball hissed by, completed the loading of his Brown Bess without conscious thought. He raised it into position, shot, absorbed the slam of the stockplate against his already bruised shoulder, squinted through the failing light. A blond-haired German boy slumped against the trunk where he'd been kneeling. Philip hoped it was his ball that had opened a gushing hole in the boy's throat.

Cowper was moaning. Philip took a moment to look at the wound. He saw grisly muscle and bone showing through the blackened rent in Cowper's sleeve. The Hessians began advancing toward the ditch, where no more than a dozen men had taken cover to fight off the attack. The last of the September light glared on the steel of German bayonets.

On the road, Philip could still hear many more men running. He knew what they were thinking. Why risk your life in a skirmish that couldn't possibly change the day's outcome—?

"Into the ditch! Turn them back! *Blast you for a pack of yellow dogs—!*"

Struggling to re-load, Philip twisted his head to see who had shouted. An officer who had evidently come up from the west dismounted and pulled his saber. Whacking back and forth with the flat of the blade, the officer drove men into position to defend the ditch.

The officer was young; in his thirties. He wore a dingy assortment of clothing. A soiled dark red coat; a sweat-blackened cravat; limp, frowsy lace on his tricorn. He might have been good-looking, except for the wrath that disfigured his features.

He smacked heads, backsides, thighs, succeeded in forcing ten or twelve more soldiers to the ditch. Philip got off another shot but saw no direct result. The Hessian company was advancing through tall weeds across a long, ragged front.

The American officer leaped into the ditch near Philip, one of his boots accidentally slamming Lucas Cowper's right leg. Disgusted with the man's almost maniacal bravado—some promotion-hungry subaltern, undoubtedly— Philip turned on him:

"The man's wounded, you damn idiot!"

"Then he can't turn back the jaegers. But you can. Charge 'em with me!"

In other circumstances Philip might have struck the officer. But there was no time. Bent over, the man ran along the ditch, shoved the crouching Americans up over the lip toward the Hessians. When he'd gotten half a dozen of them started, he jumped out of the ditch himself, a grin of bestial glee on his face.

My God, he's serious! Philip thought, caught between an impulse to follow and another that urged him to tend to the fallen Cowper, who was weeping in delirious pain.

A yard or so out from the ditch, the young officer turned back:

"Are you all weaklings? *Come on!*"

He ducked as if instinct had warned him of a ball from the Hessian rifles—he was facing toward the road—then spun and went storming toward the mercenaries. He uttered such a bloodthirsty howl that Philip's spine crawled. The officer was either a complete madman or entirely without fear.

But here and there along the ditch, a few more men climbed out to follow the half dozen others. The Hessians immediately stopped their forward march, knelt to re-load—

Philip hadn't had time yet. But he had his bayonet in place. He watched the officer an instant longer. Out in front of all the others, the man was actually charging right toward the Hessians, ducking and dodging as the German rifles cracked and flashed.

Miraculously, the officer avoided being hit. He brandished his sword and kept up that worldless screaming that brought all of the Americans out of the ditch at last—Philip among them. The first ranks of Hessians started scuttling back toward the trees.

Across a front fifty or sixty yards long, two dozen Americans followed the officer in his crazed charge. A Hessian stumbled. The officer sabered him through the chest. A cheer went up from the Americans. Suddenly Philip caught the mood of savagery, found himself running as fast as he could, just like the others—

The Hessians—perhaps thirty in the company—completely abandoned any pretense of orderly formation, retreating from the wave of attackers who began howling like the officer. Philip sped through the tall weeds between the ditch and the trees. Almost all the mercenaries had already melted back into the forest.

One sergeant, his belly bulging the tunic of his uniform, didn't quite make it.

He stepped into an animal's burrow and sprawled. Philip reached the sergeant just as the man pulled his foot from the hole, supporting himself on his hands and one knee.

The Hessian heard Philip coming, turning his bulky body, raised a forearm to protect his face, shrieked:

"*Himmel—*"

Philip bayoneted him in the stomach.

In the near-darkness, American muskets spouted orange fire. Philip stepped on the Hessian's head, plunged on toward the trees where the saber-wielding officer had disappeared. But the light was so poor, he could find no more targets.

He passed a Hessian corpse just this side of the woods, saw another man running toward him, whipped up his Brown Bess to stab defensively—

A saber flashed as another musket glared to Philip's left. The saber clashed on bayonet steel, striking sparks. Philip absorbed the blow, dropped back a step, prepared to fight hand-to-hand—

Then he recognized the man who'd knocked his bayonet aside. The shabbily dressed officer.

Philip couldn't see the man's face clearly. But his voice was enough to suggest his pleasure:

"A little spirit and they turn tail. That's all it took, a little spirit—"

He breathed hard a moment, then shouted to those who had followed him: "Well done! Well done!"

To the right and left, the Americans who'd joined the charge, voluntarily and otherwise, offered each other loud congratulations. The officer's saber clacked back into its scabbard. The whole action had taken no more than three or four minutes.

Philip thought of Cowper, headed back for the ditch. The officer strode beside him through the tall weeds:

"Damme, if we'd had this kind of spirit at the creek, we might have carried the day."

Quite without thinking, Philip said an obscene word. "We don't need more spirit. We need some commanders who know where the hell the British are hiding. If intelligence had been proper, we wouldn't have lost."

The officer stopped suddenly. His voice iced:

"I'll convey your opinion to the commander-in-chief. But perhaps I should also convey the name and unit of the man making the statement."

"Philip Kent. Private, Massachusetts infantry."

"You've a ready tongue, Mr. Kent."

Beyond caring whom he offended, Philip shot back, "Maybe so. But I'll stick by what I said. We wouldn't be retreating if we'd known Cornwallis was coming at us from behind."

"*I am well aware of that, soldier! Do you think I like it any better than you?*"

The officer's tone brought Philip up short. He rubbed his eyes.

"No, sir, I suppose not. I'm sorry I spoke out."

The officer too seemed less angry:

"Don't be. What you said was blunt but correct. And I spoke too sharply. You fought well a few moments ago. All these men fought well—"

His hand lifted to indicate the little band he'd rallied to rout the Hessians. All at once he realized the men were gone. As quickly as they'd assembled, the anonymous soldiers had disappeared back to the road, rejoining the columns trailing east. The officer concluded:

"Let's put the whole conversation out of mind and just remember the engagement, eh?"

In the darkness a voice shouted, "General Wayne?"

"Here," the officer barked.

"I've caught your horse, sir."

"Right with you. Mr. Kent—" A hand clapped Philip's shoulder. "Bravely done."

And he tramped off toward the ditch, leaving Philip stunned and speechless.

Because of the man's sorry-looking uniform, Philip had had no idea he'd been following one of Washington's top field commanders. General Anthony Wayne, a young squire of this same Pennsylvania country through which they were fleeing, had a reputation for recklessness and quick temper. Philip was grateful that temper had moderated while they talked. Otherwise he'd certainly have been a candidate for disciplinary action.

He heard Wayne's horse pound away in the direction of Chester Creek. Again he remembered Lucas Cowper, started running.

There seemed to be fewer men on the road. Perhaps the main body of the retreating army had passed. He was uncomfortably conscious of the quiet of the nightshrouded countryside as he reached the ditch, clambered down to the bottom, oriented himself as best he could—

He had charged the Hessians on an oblique line from the point where Wayne first joined him. That meant Cowper should be somewhere to the left as Philip faced the road. He headed that way.

He'd gone no more than a yard or so when he heard sounds made by two other people. One was unmistakably Cowper; groaning. Another man was breathing hard. The man heard Philip coming along the ditch:

"Who's that?"

Sudden fear wrenching his stomach, Philip answered:

"It's Kent. What are you doing, Mayo?"

Mayo Adams stood up beside Cowper's shuddering body, a black hulk against the first stars. There was a vicious undertone in Adams' voice:

"I come across Lucas and decided to help myself to his canteen and cartridge box. Lost mine back at the crick."

"Don't touch him. He's hurt pretty badly."

"Shit, he's dyin'. He won't miss them things."

"I said get away from him and get back on the road." Philip raised his empty musket. The metal of the bayonet glimmered in the starlight.

Mayo Adams chuckled.

"Why, you still got a musket! Think I'll take that too."

"What happened to yours?"

"Dropped it a ways back, accidental, and couldn't find it again. And a feller can't get by without a musket, now can he? Sure glad I bumped into you this way. Nobody's gonna know whether the redcoats kilt only one of the bodies in this here ditch, *or two*—"

The sudden explosion of Adams' breath gave Philip forewarning that the bigger man was moving. But tiredness slowed his reaction time. His bayonet-thrust was poorly aimed.

Mayo Adams sidestepped, safe, and clamped both hands on the muzzle of the Brown Bess. He jerked hard. The musket tore out of Philip's fingers.

Adams swung the musket like a club, his meaty face awash with starlight for

a moment. The little eyes shone. Desperately Philip wrenched back out of range of the stock arcing toward his head—

Adams cursed when the blow failed to land. Philip dove forward, both hands fastening on the stock. He kicked Adams' shin. The bigger man swore and kicked right back. Philip almost let go under the painful impact. Adams wrenched and Philip lost his hold a second time.

The stock came hurtling toward his jaw. Once more he started to dodge. His left boot skidded on the slope of the ditch. Off balance, he fell. He landed on his spine, the wind knocked out of him.

Laughing, Adams dropped the Brown Bess in the weeds.

"Well, Kent, guess this here's as good a time as any to settle things, what d'you say—?"

Philip yelled as Adams' huge weight crushed his belly; Adams had simply dropped down on both knees. Big hands stinking of powder closed on Philip's neck.

Suddenly he felt something rigid under his right hip. His hunting knife, still in its belt sheath. If he could only reach it—

To do it, he first had to stretch out his right arm. And he was close to passing out because Adams' fingers were digging deep, cutting off his wind. The Boston apprentice squeezed, then let go; squeezed and let go. He hummed as he knelt on Philip's midsection, sporting with him.

Philip heard several men passing along the road only a short distance away. But they were moving fast in the darkness, making noise themselves. They'd never hear Adams' little hum of pleasure—

Philip got his arm straightened out. Then he doubled his right hand under; bent it so far he thought the bones in his wrist would snap. Almost as if the hand were a separate thing, he groped back toward his right hip. Pushing his knuckles against the ground, he forced the hand along until he touched his own body.

He extended his fingers—stretched them toward the hilt of the knife—

He couldn't reach under and free it. Adams' weight was too great, pressing him flat. The huge fingers worked on Philip's throat while Adams hummed. Dig and release. *Dig and release*—

"Your poor wife's sure gonna wonder what happened to you, Kent. She'll think some Tommy kilt you. Maybe I'll call on her one day and tell her what really happened. Tell her how you got smart with the wrong man—how you feel about that?"

Abruptly, Adams released his grip.

"Come on, you snotty little bastard, say somethin' ! "

Waiting, Adams slid off Philip's belly. Philip could only make raw, retching sounds. He tried to raise his right hip a little. He was too weak.

Adams seized his hair, yanked his head up.

"Listen, I told you to say somethin', you son of a bitch!"

Adams pulling him up was the mistake. Philip's tortured right hand closed on the hilt, freed the knife, brought it whipping up, the blade turning toward Adams' throat—

Adams saw the glare of the stars on metal. He stabbed his free hand at Philip's wrist—

Too late. Philip raked the knife edge over Adams' neck, pushing——

One startled, gurgling cry. Then blood spewed like a fountain.

The blood drenched Philip's forehead, his eyes, his cheeks. He rolled away as

the dead hand came loose from his hair. The warm, meaty stench of the pumping blood sickened him.

He flattened on his belly, burrowed in the grass of the ditch bank, wiping frantically at the mess on his face. He heard Adams fall.

Minutes went by. Philip lay panting, wanting to vomit. Gradually the nausea passed. He tried to stand. Still too tired. He'd had too much. He'd just lie here, forget it all—

He thought of Lucas Cowper.

He fought the shock and the overpowering lethargy as if they were enemies as real as Adams had been. At last he was able to stand up. Weakly; dizzily. But he was upright. He made four passes at the belt sheath before he got the knife back in place.

Clenching his teeth and shuddering, he forced himself to step over Mayo Adams' corpse, walk toward Cowper till he found him.

He knelt, touched sticky fingers to Cowper's lips. He felt faint breath.

"Lucas? Lucas, I'm going to pick you up—"

One hand curved under Cowper's neck. As he raised Cowper's head a few inches, the young farmer screamed and thrashed. The starlight whitened exposed bone in Cowper's ruined upper arm. Philip knew he had to get Cowper on his feet and moving or his friend would surely bleed to death. The responsibility somehow helped him find strength:

"We'll get to a hospital, Lucas. They'll have a hospital set up someplace ahead. Chester Creek, maybe. Don't worry, we'll get you there and get you fixed—"

He literally dragged Cowper to his feet. The young farmer cried out again as Philip maneuvered him. Finally Cowper's right arm was draped over Philip's neck.

Left arm around Cowper's waist, Philip crouched and retrieved his Brown Bess. Supporting Cowper's limp body, fighting the pain and dizziness in his own, Philip started to walk. Step by labored step, he climbed to the road and turned east in the September darkness.

II

AT CHESTER CREEK bridge, he caught up to a Conestoga wagon that had broken an axle. The teamsters struggling to repair it stopped long enough to help raise Lucas Cowper, unconscious now, to a place on top of the rolled-up command tents. When it became apparent that the battle was lost, the tents had been struck at headquarters not far from Brandywine Church.

The teamsters told Philip to pull himself up into the wagon too, and ride the rest of the way. He was glad to do it.

Only half aware of the repaired wagon starting to roll again, he leaned his forehead against the plank side and laid one hand on Lucas Cowper's feverish forehead. The wagon swayed and bounced as the drivers negotiated the rutted road. Each jolt made Cowper writhe, though he never woke up completely.

It took the wagon over an hour to travel beyond the village of Chester and reach the temporary night camp—and the hastily erected tent that resembled a corner of hell more than a hospital.

III

"RAISE HIS head so he can take the rum. That's good, Son? You awake?"

Stretched out on bloody planks placed on wood trestles, Lucas Cowper shivered and opened his eyes. Philip stood directly behind Cowper's head at the end of the crude operating table. An orderly was already at work ripping away Cowper's shirt.

Philip hardly dared look at the arm. It was a ruin of blood, severed muscle, bone slivers. Any time the orderly touched it, Cowper grimaced.

The surgeon was middle-aged. He wore a white apron stained as red as a butcher's. He pressed a brown glass bottle to Cowper's lips. Cowper choked. But some of the liquor got down his throat. Gradually, a little of the glaze left his eyes.

He heard the sounds of the tent. The sounds Philip tried not to hear—

The cursing of the overworked doctors. The grisly grind from the next table, where two surgeons twisted the wood handles of a T-shaped cylindrical saw whose toothed bit was boring a hole in a casualty's shaved skull.

And above all, there was the screaming.

The tent stank of urine, excrement, sweat, putrefying flesh. In the aisle to Philip's left, a severed foot and a length of intestine floated in a tub of pink-tinted water. Although exhausted, the surgeon treating Cowper tried to speak gently, patiently. His voice carried the soft rhythms of one of the southern states:

"Can you hear what I'm saying to you, son?"

Feebly, Cowper answered, "I—I can."

"You feel anything in that arm?"

"Hurts—plenty. Can't—move it—"

"Well, the ball destroyed too much muscle and bone. I'm going to have to take it off at the shoulder."

The surgeon held out one hand. An orderly dropped a new musket ball into the dirty palm. Grasping the ball between thumb and forfinger, the surgeon held the ball up where Cowper could focus on it:

"I'm going to put this between your teeth. I want you to bite down hard. Then you won't feel it so much." The surgeon's pale, stubbled face showed the lie behind the words.

All at once Cowper tried to struggle up:

"What did you say about my arm, doc—?"

"That I can't save it, son. I have to saw it off."

"Please don't. Oh God, *please!* I'm left-handed, doc. I need both hands to work a plow—I'm a farmer, *I can't run a farm with one arm gone—*"

Cowper was shrieking now. Philip turned away, closed his eyes a moment, tightened his hands on Cowper's shoulders as the wounded man tried to wrench himself off the bloody table.

"Goddamn it, you've got to hold him down!" the surgeon shouted to Philip. The orderly shoved the rum bottle between Cowper's teeth, up-ended it until Cowper fell back gagging and slobbering from the liquid gushing into his mouth. Against his will, Cowper swallowed several times. The wild wrenching subsided.

More wounded men were being carried into the tent on litters, put down in rows near the entrance. There were six surgical tables working; the steady grind of the trephining saw filled Philip's throat with bile again.

Cowper's lids fluttered closed as the rum began to take effect. The surgeon shoved the musket ball between Cowper's teeth:

"Bite."

Cowper didn't respond. Using both hands, the surgeon pressed his jaws together:

"Bite, son *bite*—that's it." He dashed sweat from his eyes. "Give me the saw."

An orderly passed him the instrument. It still showed stains from the last amputation. The surgeon walked around to the left side of the table, stumbling once. Another orderly caught him, held him until he was able to stand on his own.

The surgeon scrutinized the exposed shoulder joint for a moment, then put the center of the notched blade on the spot he'd selected. With quick back and forth motions, he began to saw.

Blood ran. Muscle parted. Bone rasped. Cowper turned white, started to writhe. An orderly clamped hands on Cowper's mouth so he wouldn't cry out and swallow the ball. *Grate* and *grate*, the saw cut deeper——

Philip expended every remaining ounce of his strength to hold the farmer's shoulders. At last, the awful rasping noise ceased. The severed limb thumped into the dirt beside the table.

The surgeon passed the saw to an orderly, wiped his forehead again, looked around, turned almost as red as his apron:

"Where the hell is the tar?"

"Had to heat up a new batch, sir. Here it comes—"

Two more orderlies struggled to bring up a small cauldron of bubbling pitch that had been heated on the fires burning in the hospital yard.

"Watch your eyes," the surgeon warned those around the table. An orderly took a stick and tilted up one side of the cauldron. Hot tar cascaded onto the bleeding stump just below Cowper's shoulder, cauterizing, sterilizing—

Cowper woke again, screamed and fainted.

The pitch slopped and hissed on the board table, clotted sticky-black on the end of the stump. The bloodflow stopped.

Cowper's chest barely moved, so thin was his breathing. Philip thought he couldn't stand there an instant longer—

"Apprecite your assistance, soldier," the surgeon told him. The man rubbed a red hand across his lips and gestured to Cowper's still form. "Clear him away and bring the next one."

His eyes returned to Philip.

"There's hot water outside. You can wash up. You look like you took a bath in somebody's blood. I hope it was one of the British."

IV

OUTSIDE, THE near-scalding water dipped from a kettle hanging over burning logs restored Philip to some semblance of sanity. But that was almost worse than the semi-delirium of his twenty or thirty minutes in the hospital tent.

Drying his face on a rag from the ground, he tried to shut out the almost continual din of shouting and screaming from the other side of the canvas walls. It was impossible—just as winning this accursed war was impossible—

A face, bright red hair, caught his attention from the other side of the fire. The Marquis de Lafayette's fine uniform was stained and torn in several places.

"Philip! I thought I glimpsed you when I rode in. Thank God you've survived the day—"

Gil hobbled around the fire. Only then did Philip see the bandage tied tightly around the trouser leg. A ball had torn the outside of Gil's left thigh a few inches below the groin.

Gil gestured to the hospital tent:

"Were you wounded in the action? I notice no evidence of it—"

Too tired to speak immediately, Philip shook his head. Then:

"Man from my unit lost an arm. I brought him here."

There was a strange despair in Gil's eyes. He tried to conceal it with a shrug and a weak smile:

"Well, as you can see, *messieurs les anglais* favored me with a gun-shot. It's trifling. I shall wait until the doctors finish with the urgent cases."

"Where were you when you were hit?"

"I do not know, exactly. General Sullivan's men were all around me. I was endeavoring to urge them to turn and stand when the ball knocked me from the saddle—"

His eyes shifted toward the bedlam of the tent; a man was baying like an animal. His face wrenched:

"I have never seen such chaos! Or such cowardice! A formal retreat is one thing—the enemy carried the day decisively. But these men run like hares. To control them—to command them—it can't be done!"

Philip sighed. "I guess that's why we keep losing battles."

"The laxity I saw when I first rode into the encampment will be our undoing!" Gil fumed. "Undisciplined children running helter-skelter, disobeying orders at their whim, cannot defeat the British. Only an *army* can defeat them."

Philip's face, still marked with dried blood at the hairline and around the ears, looked utterly weary and despondent:

"I know, Gil. And that's the one thing we still don't have."

Gil's silence represented total agreement.

V

THE BRANDYWINE position lost on the eleventh of September. For two more weeks the rival armies feinted and skirmished through the countryside around Philadelphia. Then the beaten Americans withdrew to erect a temporary camp at Pennybacker's Mill, on a creek that flowed down to join the Schuylkill. The first hint of autumn nipped the air as Philip and the men in his mess—now down to three with Pettibone and Adams dead and Cowper off in a recovery area—wearily raised their tent.

Philip had visited Lucas Cowper once. Although conscious, the farmer refused to speak or even acknowledge Philip's presence. A stained bandage was pinned over the stub of Cowper's arm. He lay staring at the roof of the recovery tent, never blinking. After asking a score of quiet questions and receiving no answers, Philip crept away, totally depressed.

He tried to remember that if every man in the army allowed himself to fall prey to an erosion of the spirit such as he was again suffering, the struggle was already

over for good. But it was hard to keep going; hard to be at all encouraged in the face of a shambles like the Brandywine. And its equally humiliating aftermath:

"It's 'ficial," Breen announced, late in the afternoon of the twenty-seventh. He'd just come from the sutler's.

"What's official?" Royal Rothman asked in a listless voice.

"Every man-jack in the Congress skedaddled out to Lancaster a week ago. And yesterday, ol' Cornwallis marched the grenadiers into Philadelphia."

"So the city's fallen?"

" 'Pears so, Royal. All the damned Tories should be mighty happy."

"What the devil happens to us?"

"Oh, we just go on drawin' our liquor ration an' doin' what they tell us. Be winter soon. Doubt there'll be much more fightin'."

Having listened in gloomy silence, Philip burst out, "Why don't we try to re-take Philadelphia, for God's sake?"

Breen shrugged in a laconic way. "Have to ask General George about that. But I wouldn't, even if I had the chance. I understand he's in mighty mean spirits. Maybe your Frenchy friend could tell you. I sure God can't."

Breen scratched his belly, hiccoughed, took a couple of wobbly steps toward the tent, pivoted back:

"Oh—and 'fore you ask, no, they ain't paying' us. Again."

"We haven't seen a penny in three months!" Royal protested.

Breen shrugged. "What's the difference? You can't hardly spend them bills they printed up for the paymaster. Only place they'll take 'em 'thout a bitch is the sutler's. I heard half the colonies—"

"States," Royal corrected primly. Breen ignored him:

"—is makin' jokes about the money. 'Not worth a Continental' is what they call somethin' absolutely not worth a damn."

Breen lifted the tent flap, acting unusually sober all at once.

"Sure's funny 'thout old Pettibone hangin' around. S'pose they'll send us some green replacements, Philip?"

"Eventually."

"An' Cowper—what the devil's that poor feller gonna do? He told me once his daddy couldn't work no more. Too old. So there wasn't nobody except Lucas to tend the farm."

"I don't know what he'll do. I don't want to think about it."

"You was there when they sawed—"

"Yes, I was there. Shut up about it!"

A moment of silence. Breen looked contrite:

"Sorry."

"Yes—me too."

Breen rolled his tongue in his cheek. "You're an allright sort, Philip. I don't 'pologize to no other kind, y'know. That's why I can admit I don't miss Mayo Adams one whit. Wonder what become of him?"

Philip studied the sky. "Took a British or Hessian ball, probably."

"Yeh, probably."

Breen pulled up his hunting shirt to scratch his stomach again. Philip noticed a wrinkled sheet of paper stuck in the older man's hide belt.

"Breen, what's that?"

Fuzzily, Breen peered down. "My bellybutton."

"No, dammit, *that*—" He pointed.

"Well, damme if it didn't clean slip my mind. Fer you—"

As he pulled the paper loose, Philip practically leaped for it:
"A letter?"

"Yessir, mail finally come through. Picked it up 'fore I bought my ration. Clean forgot I had it. Maybe it'll perk your spirits up some. Royal, when the hell you gonna start our cook fire? I'm hungry as a grizzly cub in April—" Blinking, he ambled on into the tent.

Philip almost whooped for joy as he examined the badly wrinkled letter. The handwriting was Anne's.

He tore the letter open, read the date—late July—swiftly skipped down the lines for the essential details, his spirits soaring:

His wife was well.

Abraham was growing, talking and in good health.

Captain Caleb's two new privateers werre nearing completion on the ways at Sawyer's.

The final paragraphs riveted his gaze and turned him cold.

> *I do not wish to put additional worry on you when your task is difficult enough, my dearest. But at the moment, there is no one else with whom I can share a problem that is proving troublesome.*
>
> *I have received two notes from Will Caleb's hired captain, Mr. Rackham, whom I am certain you recall. In each, he has invited me to Sawyer's to view the vessels under construction—which struck me as an altogether suspect invitation, considering his behavior that day last winter. Neither missive received an answer, of course. However, my silence did not end his improper interest. Indeed, it produced two visits from the obnoxious man, on our very doorstep here in Cambridge.*
>
> *Both were likewise of the briefest nature. I let him know I did not welcome his attentions. He seemed to treat the reply as a joke. I am honestly fearful the fellow is a reckless libertine, no doubt encouraged by the thoughtless talk of some women whose husbands are away serving; such women proclaim their loneliness to any available male who is not in his dotage. So upsetting were Rackham's smiles and hints, I have decided to ask our neighbor Mrs. Brumple to share the house with me. She craves company, and I believe her presence would help deter any further forwardness on Rackham's part.*
>
> *At first I hesitated to mention the matter to you, dear husband. Yet here I am pouring out my concerns in an unseemly way. With you so distant, a great portion of that strength of which I have sometimes foolishly boasted now seems altogether lacking—proof, if it were needed, that man and wife become a new whole, far different from what each might have been as an individual. What I am attempting to do, I suppose, is to reassure both myself and you that nothing is amiss—and that with Mrs. Brumple occupying the spare room, no further difficulty could arise.*
>
> *I can also promise you that at the first opportunity, I shall speak to Captain Caleb about his associate's unwelcome overtures. However, the captain is presently put out into the ocean with* Eclipse *for a week or two, during which time her guns and*

*procedures for operating same are to be brought into perfect trim.
I will contact him the moment he returns to Boston Harbor.*

*God protect you, my beloved, and may your son and your
eternally affectionate wife soon be blessed with your presence, or,
until that joyous day, further word that you are safe and well.*

> *Ever yours,*
> *Anne.*

The cool September breeze fluttered the page. Philip stared at the amber
clouds and a flight of wild geese streaming toward the southern horizon. But he
saw only the insolent face of Captain Malachi Rackham.

That night he actually thought about desertion; about damning this futile war
and hurrying home.

Tempting though the idea was, he put it out of mind because he knew that it
was wrong for him, no matter how anyone else chose to act. It was also wrong
because it would be the most foolish kind of weakness to give in to fears that
were, for the moment, of small substance. Anne was taking steps to deal with the
problem of Rackham. Those steps would probably prove effective.

The mere thought of desertion made him ashamed for other reasons, too. If he
did what many had already done—simply went home the moment he felt like it—
he would be one of those whom Tom Paine scathingly denounced as summer
soldiers; sunshine patriots. More important, if mass desertions continued, there
would soon not even be a semblance of an army left. And the larger purpose, of
which the army was the sole instrument of fulfillment, would be lost. He believed in what the army was fighting for, even though up till now most of the
fighting had been poorly done.

He had come to his belief over a long period of years, with much doubt along
the way. But he did have an unashamed conviction that the cause was just. To
leave would betray both the cause and the conviction.

And, finally, it would betray Anne.

A deserter who appeared suddenly in Cambridge would not be the man she'd
taken as a husband. He'd wait for the next letter. It would contain less disheartening news. Confirmation that Caleb had brought his captain to heel. Surely it
would—

With struggle, he almost convinced himself of that.

5

"I Mean to March to Hostile Ground"

JUDSON FLETCHER rode like a man pursued.

Lather streaked the flanks of his horse. He knew he'd already pushed the
animal much too hard, covering the sixty-mile distance with only very brief
stops. He'd been in the saddle most of the night, his stained coat not nearly warm
enough to protect him from the bite of the late October air.

From the east, first light gilded the shocked corn standing in the fields. A
yawning farmer loading fat pumpkins into a wagon gave him a startled stare as

he hammered along the dirt road, plumes of breath streaming from the horse's muzzle.

What if I'm too late? What if he's gone?

It was Donald, day before yesterday, who had dropped the casual remark that sent Judson speeding south. Donald had come by the Shaw cabin with another purse; the dole was delivered more grudgingly with every visit.

Judson's appearance had worsened over the summer. He'd lost more weight. He was lethargic; sullen; constantly unshaven.

Still, as always, Donald dutifully tried to spark some reaction from his brother with reports on various aspects of the war, starting with the loss of Philadelphia to General Howe's army in September. That had caused sharp criticism of General Washington even among his fellow Virginians, Donald said.

One bright circumstance offset the fall of America's largest city: the surrender of Gentleman Johnny Burgoyne's expeditionary force at Saratoga just a couple of weeks ago.

Expecting reinforcements in the form of troops under General Howe, Burgoyne had instead been virtually abandoned in the York State, while Howe pursued his conquest of Philadelphia—then settled in, presumably, to enjoy the favors of his mistress. Outnumbered three to one by the Americans under General Gates, Burgoyne asked for terms. It was the sole piece of encouraging news in an otherwise bleak cavalcade of disasters and defeats:

"Unless you wish to count the end of the verbal war over the Articles of Confederation," Donald told his brother. "I understand a draft is just about ready."

For over a year Congress had been debating the wording of a document that would organize the thirteen states into some kind of working relationship; stipulate areas of authority; divide financial responsibility for the war fairly—

"They finally worked out a plan where expenses of the central government will be apportioned according to each state's surveyed land, which I suppose is fair. We won't properly be a country until every one of the thirteen ratifies the draft Articles, though. Considering how long it's taken to get the material written and agreed upon, that may not happen till the next century! Even if the Articles are accepted, they leave much to be desired."

Judson's vague murmur was enough to prompt Donald to continue:

"Every state retains its sovereignty, and the Congress is granted jurisdiction only in certain limited areas. It can declare war—but can't wage it unless each state approves. There's a proviso saying Congress may borrow money, but not a single word about how the central government may *raise* money to repay the loans. In short, if the Congressional fiddler wants to play a tune, the states collectively pretty well tell him yea or nay."

"I'd hardly compare that kind of document to a military victory," Judson observed sourly.

"True. But what other accomplishments can we brag about?"

"Why not save your breath altogether?"

"I probably should. The Articles are a patchwork. Too many basic questions dodged while everyone's diverted by lofty sentiments about 'perpetual union.' The best you can say is that it's a start. It seems to me that a more clearly and thoughtfully drawn statement will be required before very long. Some sort of formal constitution—"

Judson's apathetic stare showed he'd completely lost interest. Donald smiled sadly:

"I'm not precisely enthralling you with all this, am I?"

Judson shrugged, as if to ask what else his brother expected. Donald sighed. Then:

"Well, perhaps something more personal will pique your interest. Your friend George has been at Williamsburg for a fortnight now—*by the Lord!* A response at last!"

It was true. Judson's blue eyes finally showed something other than contempt or indifference:

"What's he doing there?"

"Damme if I can tell you. Something big's afoot, though. He's been attending secret meetings with a special committee appointed by Governor Henry—Mr. Jefferson, Mr. Wythe and several other Burgesses. The meetings last for hours at a time. They must be debating something besides another request for powder to defend the Kentucky forts."

"Have you seen George personally?"

"Yes, I talked to him at the Raleigh Tavern before I rode home."

"How does he look?"

"Very fit. But worried. Conditions in the west are growing worse. All the tribes rising against the settlers—my guess is that George came east to raise some additional militia units. He wouldn't tell me specifically." A pause, as Donald eyed his disheveled brother. "He asked about you."

"What did you tell him?"

"Exactly what I tell Father. As little as possible. I imagine Tom Jefferson and some of the others talk more freely—"

Judson glanced away.

"George sent you his regards. Also his regrets that he couldn't stop by for a visit. I got the impression he'll be bound back for Kentucky soon after the secret meetings are concluded."

At that exact moment, Judson felt as if a door had opened; perhaps the last one remaining for him.

It was a desperate, perhaps foredoomed hope. But confinement on the tiny piece of cabin property had grown intolerable. Too often, he found his thoughts turning to the means for suicide.

He said nothing to his brother about the sudden idea that fired his mind and restored his energy all at once. But shortly after Donald had gone back to Sermon Hill, Judson was mounted and riding south.

Now, in the October dawn sparkling with hoarfrost, he pounded into Williamsburg. Flashed by the lovely rose-brick residences of the merchants and the gentry. Thundered through the farmer's market where a flock of geese honked and waddled to escape the flying hoofs. He rode straight to the yard of the Raleigh Tavern, its leaded windows reflecting the autumn dawn in diamond-shaped patterns of yellow fire.

Looking more like a scarecrow than a man, Judson dismounted and turned the exhausted horse over to a groom for feeding and stabling. As he walked toward the tavern entrance, he was acutely aware of the hammering of his heart.

In the dark-beamed foyer, he found a sleepy boy swishing a straw broom over the pegged floor. Judson's eyes showed huge gray circles of fatigue. His fair beard, scraped off in preparation for the trip, had already sprouted again, un-evenly. The sweep knew in a glance that Judson wasn't the sort of gentleman who belonged at the Raleigh.

"Son, you've a guest here—"

"Got eight or nine," the sweep replied, leaning on his broom. "Most are still in bed. And the landlord don't take kindly to loud talk at this hour."

Checking a burst of anger, Judson lowered his voice:

"The guest I'm referring to is named Clark. He hasn't left, has he?"

The boy took his time answering:

"Would you be meaning Major Clark, the militia commander from Kentucky?"

"Yes, dammit! Is he still here?"

"I tell you the landlord'll tan me if you keep on swearing and yelling—"

Judson glared. "Then stop being cheeky and answer me straight!"

The sweep took a step backwards, poked his broom toward the arch leading to the public room:

"Major Clark come down about twenty minutes ago to eat breakfast. Hops up way before daylight every morning. Guess that's the style out west. You'll find him around the corner by the fireplace, I reckon."

"Thank you very much!"

Boots hammering, Judson spun away. He'd made it in time. *In time!*

Suddenly he halted, catching a whiff of the wood fire burning somewhere on the other side of the wall. The aroma wasn't nearly as strong as his own sweaty stench. He must look a sight.

He stepped to the wall where an ornamental silver plate hung on display. He bent, examined his blurred reflection, tried to smooth his tangled hair. He'd lost the tie-ribbon on the frantic ride. God, he was totally unpresentable—

But there was nothing to be done. In the public room, a chair had scraped. Boots squeaked the plank floor as someone approached the arch. Judson straightened up with jerk, aware of the trembling of his hands as he confronted the tall figure of George Clark, red hair neatly tied at the nape of his neck.

"Judson—?"

"Hello, George."

"Good Lord, I couldn't believe it when I thought I heard your voice. You're the last person in creation I expected to see this morning! What brings you to Williamsburg?"

Judson's mouth went dry. His friend looked lean, clear-eyed, deeply tanned—and dismayed as he took in Judson's stained apparel and unhealthy pallor. All Judson could say was:

"George, it—it's fine to see you—"

He shot out an unsteady hand. George Clark clasped it in a hard, callused grip. Now that he'd ridden all this distance, Judson's courage failed him. He couldn't bring himself to tell his friend the reason for the trip.

He was afraid George would laugh in his face.

II

EVEN THE sweep leaning on his broom was sensitive to something awkward in the confrontation between the fine-featured young gentleman who looked as if he'd just crawled out of some hole in the earth, and the younger but somehow more poised frontiersman wearing a thigh-length fringed hunting shirt and leggings of deerhide. Apparently both were at a loss for words.

All at once Judson blurted, "Donald told me you were here. I rode most of the night—"

"By God that's a mark of friendship! My end of it's been sadly neglected, I'm afraid."

"I know you have pressing responsibilities, George. No time—"

"And too few men. And too little powder. And every tribe putting on the bloodroot—but come on, come to the table. Join me in something to eat—"

A bit reassured when his friend laid his arm over his shoulder, Judson accompanied George into the public room. As they approached a table near the fireplace, Judson said:

"I'm afraid you've lost me already. What was that word—? Bloodroot?"

"The braves use it to paint their faces for battle."

George pulled out a chair for Judson, signaled a yawning servant girl, slipped into his own chair in front of the immense breakfast he'd been eating. Half a loaf of cornbread and most of a crock of country butter had been put away, plus part of an eight- or nine-inch stack of griddle cakes dripping with clear colorless syrup.

"All the tribes are going to war against Kentucky," George explained. "The Mingos, the Shawnee, the Piankashaws, Delaware, Wyandots—the year of the three sevens hasn't been good to my part of the country. The year of the bloody sevens, Kentuckians are calling it."

The serving girl's shadow touched the table where George's browned hand closed around his coffee mug. George glanced up.

"My friend's hungry, my girl."

Younger than I am, Judson thought with despair. *Younger, and he acts twice my age. Twice as composed and sure of himself—*

"May I bring you something, sir?" the girl asked Judson.

"Only something to drink—" he began. When George's eyes widened in surprise, he added quickly, "What my friend's having. Coffee. Put milk in mine, please."

The girl shuffled away, yawning again.

"I was pleased to have the chance to talk with Donald when he was here," George said. "If he'd shed some of that weight, his gout might bother him less."

"Well, there's precious little pleasure for him at Sermon Hill besides eating and drinking."

"He's helping your father operate the plantation, then?"

"When he's not meeting here with the Burgesses."

George hesitated. "You're not at Sermon Hill—?"

"No." Judson's mouth twisted. "Father and I had one of our famous disagreements—this one a little more permanent than the others."

"How permanent?"

"I don't intend to go back to the place, ever. Furthermore, I'm not allowed."

"I'm sorry to hear that."

Judson waved, as if it didn't matter. "I rode off to Philadelphia to replace Donald in the Congress for a time—"

George nodded. "Tom Jefferson told me, during one of our meetings."

"What else did he tell you? That I botched my duties, the way I've botched everything in the last—?"

The serving girl's return stopped Judson in midsentence. Embarrassed by the outburst, George glanced toward the fire. Judson wiped his damp forehead, accepted the mug of steaming coffee, drank a third of it in a series of gulps. The coffee was nearly scalding and took some of the chill out of him.

It didn't lessen his tension, though. He was more and more convinced George Clark would reject his proposal out of hand.

"I always suspected I didn't fit in around here," Judson said finally. "Now, I know it." The words had a lame, whipped sound.

There was no reproof in his friend's eyes, only sympathy:

"Donald said your views on the slave question helped bring on the trouble with your father."

"It's much more than that. As I told you, I disgraced myself in Philadelphia. I shot a fat Tory to death when he challenged me to a duel—even though Jefferson and the president of the Congress warned me to steer clear of that sort of affair. There was also a scandal over a woman—" *And some things since that I'm too ashamed to speak about even to you.* "I'm not proud of any of it. Ever since I came back, I've done nothing but live day to day. No purpose, no ambition—"

He stared at his friend. It was impossible to conceal his hope any longer:

"I've thought a good deal about what you used to write in your letters. About the open country in the west—"

"It's very different than it was just a few years ago, Judson."

"The war, you mean."

"Aye. We're down to three settlements in Kentucky. Harrodsburg, Boonesborough and Fort Logan. All this past spring and summer, our people have lived like prisoners inside the stockades. When work parties go out to plant corn, other armed men go with them to stand guard. It's not safe to hunt or farm your own piece of ground. Everyone's taken refuge at the forts—"

George's mouth set, almost ugly. "There's a governor at Fort Detroit, Henry Hamilton, who's paying British silver for every scalp cut from an American corpse."

"I've heard of him."

"They call him the Hair-Buyer. He understands how easily the whole Northwest Territory can be taken if the tribes are properly incited. He also understands the value of the land. Which is more than can be said for some of our elegant Burgesses sitting here in Williamsburg pinching snuff from their silver boxes. I came back to try to remedy the situation."

Judson came closer to the issue: "Donald thought you might be raising a new levy of men—"

George Clark didn't answer immediately. He scanned the room as if searching for possible eavesdroppers. But there was no one else present besides the two of them and the girl dozing on her stool by the fire.

George clacked his fork back on his trencher, used a finger to dab a smear of syrup from the corner of his mouth. He leaned forward in his chair:

"Donald guessed correctly. After a great deal of argument and some table-pounding, I persuaded the committee of the Burgesses to authorize the recruiting of three hundred and fifty Virginians for the defense of Kentucky. They're giving me six thousand Continental dollars to buy ammunition and supplies."

"Where are you going to find the men?"

"Anywhere I can. Here. Pittsburgh—"

"I'd like to be one of them."

The sudden silence was strained. Judson thought, *He's going to turn me down—*

George Clark picked up his fork, dropped it again. In the kitchen, a man and woman argued over who had broken half a crate of eggs. A wagon creaked in the

street; a cow lowed, its bell clanking. The rhythmic slow swish of the sweep's broom going over and over the same square of floor sounded beyond the arch.

George frowned. "When you said you'd ridden all night, I thought there was probably some reason other than a wish to see an old friend."

"I want to go to Kentucky, George. I want to start again."

"I don't think you quite know what you're asking."

The words, gently said, almost broke Judson's heart. And instant later, they angered him. He slammed the coffee mug on the table:

"So I'm judged and found guilty before the fact?"

George still looked troubled. "I'm not sure I understand."

"You've listened to Tom Jefferson. And to Donald. You've heard how I failed at everything before and you've decided I'll fail again."

"Judson, for God's sake! That's a totally unwarranted accusation—!"

"Is it?"

"Yes!"

"Forgive me, George, but I think you're lying. Maybe out of kindness, but lying all the same—"

If so, George concealed it. "You simply don't realize—Kentucky is *not* the tidewater." His supple hand spread eloquently over the griddlecakes, the syrup pitcher, the cornbread loaf. "There's little or no food like this. Just a swallow of water from a canteen and a handful of dried corn from your haversack. On the trail, you live like that for days—maybe weeks."

"I can do it. I know I can."

Silence again. Finally George resumed:

"Judson, it's difficult to say this—"

"A turn-down. All right, do it and be done!"

"God, they weren't exaggerating. You're angry at everything."

Judson flushed. "I'm sorry."

"Then hear me out. You're my friend, Judson. The closest friend I knew when I was growing up. That can't be changed by anything that happens. But because you *are* my friend, I won't deceive or flatter you—despite your notions to the contrary. There is no peace in Kentucky! No freedom to roam, explore, settle where you wish. The tribes are raiding regularly from north of the Ohio. Killing and butchering any man they find alone. Or women and babies, for that matter. I hate to put it so bluntly, but I need soldiers, not gentlemen-adventurers."

"Do you think you can locate three hundred and fifty who meet your high standards?" Judson blazed.

George stiffened, but he controlled his temper, and his voice:

"If I'm lucky."

"And if you're not, you'll have to take somewhat less perfect specimens——"

"Judson, I can hardly stand to listen to this."

"To what?"

"Your bitterness. What in the name of heaven has happened to you?"

"What's happened, George, is that I'm dying."

He said it swiftly; softly. But George rocked back in his chair, hammered by the ferocity and pain of the statement.

"I mean it, George. I'm dying by days and by hours and by minutes—"

"So are we all."

"Not the same way. I'm dying from failing. Dying because I hold what seem to be the wrong beliefs. I'm dying from hating my father and being hated—"

"And dying from not being strong enough to overcome all that—and learn from it?" George asked quietly, with just the barest hint of condemnation.

Bleak-faced, Judson agreed:

"Yes. That too. But I have learned this much. I think I have just about one more chance left. One chance somewhere to pick up the litter of my life and prove I can be successful at something, however small or insignificant—"

George cooled visibly. "The defense of Virginia's western counties is neither small nor insignificant."

"George, I didn't mean—"

"What happens out there in the next year will determine how much land America holds when this war is settled. It will determine whether we'll be pushed back east of the mountains, forced forever to huddle here on the coast—"

"Believe me, I didn't mean to suggest—"

Abruptly, George relaxed again. "I know." A weary smile; a nod. "The fault's mine. I haven't been in the best of spirits lately—"

He picked up his coffee mug, drank. "However—that doesn't change the situation I'm facing. I need steady hands. Sharp eyes." He looked directly at Judson. "God forbid that I should sound like a Bible-thumper inveighing against the sin of drunkenness. But this much is the truth. In the forest, liquor will only get a man lost, or slain."

The quiet statements told Judson more about what Jefferson or Donald had said to George; and much more about the immensity of the change in his friend. This George Clark wasn't the young man who'd roamed the Virginia woodlands for sheer pleasure. He spoke like what he was a military commander.

Judson gave George the answer he hoped his friend wanted to hear:

"Then I'll swear off if that's what it takes. Never another drop—"

"It takes even more than that."

"What, then? *Goddamn it, I'm pleading for my life!*"

Judson had tears in his eyes. He only realized it after he shouted. The outcry roused the serving girl on her stool, brought a gray feminine head peeping out of the kitchen, stopped the swish of the broom from beyond the arch. Judson drowned in a red wave of shame, his cheeks burning—

He kicked against the table's trestle, shoved his chair back, frantic to leave. His red-haired friend was staring at him with a mixture of alarm and sorrow.

As Judson whirled toward the arch, George's fingers clamped on his arm. "Sit down."

The sneer was unconscious: "What the hell for? I'm not the sort you want. Clear-eyed. Pure-hearted—"

"*Sit down,*" George Clark said. "And if you really want to discuss it, stop that self-pitying whine."

Judson felt as if he'd tumbled into an icy brook:

"*Discuss it*—? Do you?"

"Yes. I think I've made it clear that it won't be easy to gather the men I need. So I have—motives for possibly accepting your offer."

Jubilant, Judson pulled his chair up again, planted his elbows on the table, pleaded with open hands:

"I'll be sober as a damn saint, George! You always said I should see the western lands—well, maybe this isn't the wrong time but exactly the right one. If you think there'll be any problem about me taking orders because we're friends—"

"I think that could be a very definite problem."

"No, no, it won't be, I give you my word."

"The word's easy. The deed's hard. I want you to realize what you're asking. Consider the effort just to reach Pittsburgh. It's hundreds of miles—"

"I'm strong—you saw how I got here. I rode all night—"

"And walked in white and trembly as poplar leaves in a windstorm. I'm not trying to be difficult, Judson, or hard on you—I could never do that easily because of all the fine times we shared. But the truth of what my men will be facing can't be dodged. Can you sleep in the open when there are ten inches of snow covering the ground?"

"Yes."

"Walk till there's no feeling left in your legs—then keep on walking?"

"I can, yes."

"Do you think you could kill a man without making a sound?"

Judson tried to smile. "The first part is no problem. I'll practice the second."

George didn't smile back. "The pay is negligible. Most of my funds will go for supplies."

"I don't care. Nothing can be any worse than the trap I've gotten myself into here."

"Can you fire a rifle?"

"One of the long Kentucky models? I've never tried but I'm positive I can learn. I'm fair with pistols. Always have been—"

Suddenly George Clark unfolded his lanky frame, tossed coins on the table: "Come on."

"Where?"

"I'll saddle my horse and we'll ride out in the country and find out how expert a marksman you are."

"With a rifle?"

"Yes."

George Clark had a peculiar, almost secretive expression on his face. Judson noticed it but failed to understand its meaning.

Once more the tall woodsman surveyed the public room. Satisfied, he led Judson toward the side entrance. In twenty minutes, they were cantering along under arching limbs that streamed down yellow and scarlet leaves in the brisk morning wind. The road was alternately dark and dazzling with sunlight.

He had a chance. One chance. He dared not let it slip out of his hands—

The hands that were white from gripping his rein hard, so George wouldn't see how he was trembling.

III

GEORGE CLARK shucked his leather hunting bag off his shoulder, dropped his powder horn on top, then laid his gleaming Kentucky rifle on the pile. From a sheath sewn into the side of the bag, he drew a bone-handled knife. He set to work stripping a square of bark from the trunk of one of the trees in the isolated clearing where they'd stopped. Judson marveled at the swift, sure movements of George's fingers—and silently cursed the continuing tremor of his own.

Kneeling in the thick layer of fallen leaves, George carefully inscribed a small circle on the moist inner surface of the peeled bark. He tucked his knife back in

his boot, dug under the leaves, scratched up some dirt. He rubbed the dirt all around the circular cut, then blew off the excess. When he held up the square, the dirt still clung in the cut outlining a round target.

"Ought to be able to see that," George said.

"Yes, I can see it fine." Judson couldn't remember when he'd been so jittery. Perhaps that was because the stakes had never been quite so high.

George carried the target across the clearing. He pinned it to a trunk with one stab of his knife. He left the knife humming faintly, ambled back through the rustling leaves. Off in the trees that ringed the clearing, their horses blew and stamped.

George waved Judson to his side. Both men hunkered down as George supported the long-barreled rifle on his palms:

"I'll show you how to load one of these beauties. It's slower than loading a musket, but your aim's far more accurate."

"So I've heard."

Judson eyed the blade-pinned scrap of bark across the clearing. The bark moved a little in the brisk wind. Damn, he'd never hit it. *Never—*

Yes he would. He'd hit it if he never did another thing.

Patiently, George took him through the routine. First he filled the rifle pan with powder from his smaller priming horn. Then he picked up the second, larger horn, scraped down at the end so the cut-off tip fit like a cap. He pulled off the cap section, held it up:

"One of these is an exact measure of powder."

He poured the coarse black grains into the barrel, then unlatched a perfectly polished rust-free plate in the side of the stock.

"Greased patches in here. You lay one over the muzzle opening—"

He did so, then fished in the bag for a ball. He inserted the ball over the patch. He loosened the ramrod clipped to the rifle and handed the rod to Judson:

"You seat both the patch and the ball with a good solid stroke."

Judson nearly dropped the ramrod. George smiled in a tolerant way. Judson got the ramrod positioned, shoved it down the barrel.

"More, Judson. More. Seat it all the way, good and firm. All right, that's got it—"

He placed the rifle in Judson's hand.

"Now cock and fire—and remember to use your sight. Keep reminding yourself that it's not a musket. You don't just shut your eyes and let 'er blow—"

He pointed to a spot on the perimeter of the clearing opposite the target.

"Try it from there."

Feeling as if he were walking to an execution, Judson headed for the indicated place. When he got the rifle to his shoulder, it felt immense. Despite the fall air, he was sweating. The inside of his mouth tasted like brass.

Off to his left, George leaned on the ramrod. The wind fluttered the fringe on the hem and sleeves of his hunting shirt. Judson squinted down the blue barrel. *Dammit, why couldn't he keep his hands from shaking—?*

The target seemed to be flapping a lot. Jerkily, he corrected his aim—

"Wait till the wind dies," George said. "One hit is worth half a dozen hasty misses if you're aiming for a Delaware who's been stoking himself on drum talk and Hamilton's rum."

When the target finally settled in place, Judson began to apply pressure to the trigger.

More pressure.

More—

He tried not to think of the importance of this one shot. It was impossible. His chance to pull himself out of the morass he'd made was staked on one lead ball—

Steady.

Steady—

He fired.

The recoil almost knocked him off his feet. A thunderous echo went rolling through the glade toward the fields of shocked corn. Birds screeched and beat their wings, rising from the treetops. Smoke blurred Judson's vision. He hadn't heard the ball chunk into the trunk. It was a miss. A complete miss—

Dismally, he lowered the rifle to his side. In a moment George Clark came trotting back aross the clearing with the scrap of bark:

"Well, you were wide of the bull."

Failure. Again.

Then, disbelieving, he saw the smile on George's face. George wiggled the tip of his little finger in the semicircle knocked out of the lower edge of the bark square:

"But at least you hit the target itself. Not many accomplish that on the first try."

"I never heard the ball land—"

"Did you expect to, with all the echoes?"

"George, that's not good enough. Put the target up again."

George flung the square away.

"Not necessary. With practice, I think you can handle a rifle well enough. I really brought you out here for another reason entirely. A much more important one."

Thunderstruck, Judson felt a burst of anger over the deception. He opened his mouth—

And shut it, thinking:

That's one thing you'll have to stop, boiling every time something doesn't please you—

George Clark walked toward another tree, his hunting knife back in his hand. Judson saw that peculiar, secretive expression again.

"Before we strike any sort of bargain," George said, "I want you to know the full extent of what you'll be facing if you come west."

"I don't understand. You already explained—"

"I'm not talking about the hardships. I mean the real purpose for which I'm recruiting men."

A white-tailed hare hopped halfway across the clearing, discovered them and went bounding away. Judson felt an ominous little tickle along his backbone. His friend looked positively grim.

"You said you're raising a levy for the defense of Kentucky. To protect the settlements against the Indian attacks—"

"I have one set of vaguely worded orders to that effect, yes," George replied. "Those orders are meant to be public knowledge. But I have a second set as well. Very much more explicit. And secret. Thus far those orders have been seen only by Governor Henry and the special committee of the Burgesses he appointed. Eventually all the men I recruit will know the contents of the second set of orders. But I think you should know them now, while you've still time to back out."

George started to cut a small chip from the tree to which he'd walked. "You

see, I came home specifically to present a plan I've been hatching for months. Governor Henry set up the special committee because he didn't want to make the decision by himself. The plan was approved—enthusiastically by the governor, somewhat less enthusiastically by the committee—just a few days ago. I declined to bring up the subject at the Raleigh—or anywhere in Williamsburg, for that matter. No man who serves with me will hear anything about the scheme unless we're in the place where no Tories could be listening. And every man who *does* hear is pledged to absolute secrecy. Clear?''

Judson nodded.

Below the first mark he'd cut on the tree, and to the left, George cut another. Still further left, he cut one more. He drove the tip of the knife into the highest of the three cuts:

''That's Detroit—the Hair-Buyer's headquarters. From there, trade goods—hatchets, scalp knives, rum—travel south to the two British-controlled posts in the Territory—''

He stabbed the second spot.

''Fort Vincennes on the Wabash River—''

Chunk, the knife bit the third place.

''And further west, on the prairies that form the approaches to the Big River, Fort Kaskaskia. The three sources of British strength in the northwest. The three points from which they intend to *take* the northwest—''

George shoved the knife back in his boot, walked slowly toward the center of the clearing.

''A strategy of cowering inside stockades, awaiting attack, is a strategy of loss, Judson—a strategy of futility. I proposed to Governor Henry that we actively fight for control of the northwest. Destroy British power in the three forts one by one.''

''Attack them?'' Judson asked.

''Capture them,'' George corrected.

''Can it be done?''

''That's what I sent two of my best men to find out during the summer.''

''Two of your own men went into British towns?''

''It wasn't all that hard. The towns are largely French-populated. The British only control the forts. Linn and Moore pretended to be neutral fur traders. They weren't molested once. But I guarantee you they brought back accurate drawings of the British fortifications at both Kaskaskia and Vincennes—down to the very number of portholes for the swivel cannon. The French don't care for King George's soldiers very much, you see. They remember that the *fleur-de-lis* flew over that part of the country prior to the settlement at the end of the French and Indian War. Consequently, the French at both posts talk freely. They confirmed that war parties being sent into Kentucky are directed from Detroit and equipped from the other two forts. Vincennes and Kaskaskia supply the tomahawks—and the promises of silver for every scalp taken. I plan to put a stop to that. Then, once those stations are secure, I'm going after our friend Governor Hamilton at Detroit. With the three forts fallen, there'll be no further threat of any conse-quence west of Pittsburgh. And no doubt about who possesses the land, once the inevitable haggling starts.''

''You mean haggling during peace negotiations?''

''Exactly. The war will end sometime. So concerning the northwest, the negotiations can have either a conclusion that's favorable to us, or one that isn't. I want to make sure it's the former. You know the saying about possession being

nine points of the law. That's why I proposed my plan, and why I fought for it when some members of Henry's committee called it too risky or too expensive. Every man who goes with me must understand my aim, Judson—"

George stared in a hard, challenging way:

"Despite the peculiar technicalities of our situation—for instance, I'm informed King George still hasn't declared war officially—"

"For fear it would mean we're recognized as a country," Judson said.

"Be that as it may, I know who the enemy is, and where. You would be signing on for much more than defensive duty. I mean to march straight to hostile ground, and put it under our new flag."

"So you've answered my question. You believe the forts can be taken."

"I wouldn't have argued with the committee for days, and staked my future on the outcome of the plan, if I thought otherwise. I wanted five hundred men. I got three hundred and fifty. If they're the right kind, I can bring it off."

Judson said, "I'd be proud to be one of them."

"I confess good judgment still leaves some doubt about whether I should take you on—"

"I swear to God I'll obey every order—keep myself straight—"

Because this is the last chance left for me.

George pondered only a moment:

"All right."

Judson let out a yell of pleasure, cut short by George's raised hand:

"If you don't honor that promise, I'll do what I would with any man who fails me. Send him home if it's possible. If it's not, leave him behind."

"Understood."

"Are you sure? I'll abandon the laggards in the middle of enemy country if necessary."

At that moment, Judson was stricken with doubt. *Could* he do it? Did he have the strength and will to endure—to perform as expected?

He knew how his father would answer the question. Angus Fletcher would totally reject the idea that his younger son could overcome his own nature. Even now, the old man's words whispered in his mind, unsettling him—

Devil's blood.

That was a convenient, if vicious, catchphrase for some terrible flaw in his character; but Judson no longer doubted the existence of the flaw itself. It was a foe waiting to destroy him. A foe as dangerous as any of those tribal warriors George described. An inescapable foe; one he must confront and defeat forever.

Was it possible?

He had grave and terrible doubt. But he had no doubt about the finality of the opportunity. That tipped the balance. He committed himself with a fervency that barely suggested a fraction of the fear and hope seething inside.

"Agreed. Every bit of it—agreed."

George Clark smiled then; a cordial smile. But still not the same sort of smile Judson remembered from their boyhood. It was the controlled smile of a military commander who could never again enjoy the same equal relationship with an old friend. And Judson knew full well that the responsibility for fulfilling the bargain was his, not George's. The prospect was both joyful and terrifying.

"Then let's be leaving," George said. "You'd best clean up your affairs at home—"

"I will, immediately."

"When you've done so, meet me back in Williamsburg no later than three

weeks from today.'' Again Judson heard that warning note in his friend's voice. "Three weeks at the outside. If you're not here, I won't wait.''

"I'll be here, you can count on it. Will we be heading across the mountains then?''

"In slow stages," George replied as they collected the rifle and gear. "I plan to visit quite a few settlements between here and the forks of the Ohio. Recruit my men as I go, and have them ready to leave Pittsburgh no later than next April or May. The tribes settle in for the winter pretty much the way the armies do, thank God. But we'll still have a fair piece of ground to cover before spring—''

He tapped the rifle. "While you're home, buy one of these. Oh, and perhaps a good compass. Do some practicing with the rifle.''

"George, I'll learn how to knock out a redbird's eye at a hundred yards," Judson promised.

"Two hundred," George said, perfectly serious. "And you'll do better if you imagine it's the eye of a redcoat on the parapet at Vincennes.''

But George's severe manner couldn't destroy Judson's feeling that perhaps, at last, he was negotiating a way out of his troubles. He knew one fact for certain. He wouldn't give George cause to regret his trust.

He'd die first.

__IV

JUDSON STAYED the night in Williamsburg. But he had no further opportunity to talk with George Clark. His friend returned to Governor Henry's office in the late morning and remained until well after dark. By that time Judson had already fallen into exhausted sleep in his rented room at the Raleigh. Next morning at dawn, he set out for home.

The golden radiance of the October sunrise filled him with a mystical feeling close to that which he'd experienced in June over a year ago, when Richard Henry Lee rose to introduce the resolution for independency. A long-forgotten passage of scripture popped into his head. With it came memories of how he'd learned his Bible—and then, later, consciously put it out of mind.

Verses had stayed stored in his mental baggage against his will. Because of his perpetual fear of displeasing Angus, no doubt. He remembered those dim Sundays of boyhood when he and Donald were dragged to the country church. He remembered how his father always sat perfectly rigid, and cast disapproving looks at Judson's slightest squirm.

But now, he didn't at all object to having a passage of scripture in his thoughts. The story from St. John fitted him in an oblique sort of way—

Lazarus, come forth.

And he that was dead came forth, bound hand and foot with graveclothes—

He couldn't recall the next part exactly. Some line or other about a face covered with a napkin. It had probably once made sense to the Hebrews, but he'd giggled when he first heard it. Earning a sharp thwack on the ear from Angus, right in the pew.

The rest came back easily, making his backbone ripple in an eerie way.

Jesus saith unto them, Loose him, and let him go.

Risen from the dead?

Well, not quite. But stirring. Stirring.

How ironic, Judson thought as he jogged along. A Bible verse he hadn't thought of in years—a verse forced into his head by the discipline of the man who hated and disowned him—brought him cheer and comfort in an unexpected place and time. Even mental pictures of his father's face couldn't dampen his happiness.

As he rode, he savored the sight of grouse in the fields, fleecy clouds in the sky. He hailed a small girl in a cottage yard. Proudly, she held up her calico kitten as he went by. He smiled as if the scruffy little animal was the most elegant of house cats. Perhaps the black tomb of his existence *was* freeing him at last, and he was going forth, alive, onto firm ground—

Not ground free of risk, certainly. George Clark's plan was perilous, and so was the territory involved. On the other hand, one of those Indians George talked about could surely die in exactly the same way as a Philadelphia Tory. The only problem was to deliver the shot straight and true.

He wished that he could tell Peggy McLean where he was going, and with whom. It might make her think a little better of him—if that were possible after the debased, drunken act he'd committed. However, even if Peggy would be willing so speak to him again—which he very much doubted—the idea was academic. According to Donald, Peggy hadn't been at home for the past four weeks.

Donald didn't believe she was visiting her parents. He'd remarked on how curious it was that no one at the McLean place, not even the house blacks, knew where the mistress had gone. If Williams knew, he wasn't saying. Perhaps her absence had something to do with the business affairs of the plantation.

Whatever the explanation, Judson hoped the absence didn't signify more of the same emotional strain that had tormented Peggy after the uprising; a need to flee a place where terrible memories lived—

But then everyone had such memories, didn't they? And, ultimately, the need to flee from them somehow? He did. A combination of luck, friendship and providential timing had at last combined to offer him a way out. Had there not been such a way—

Well, he didn't relish thinking about that alternative.

Actually, he was ambivalent about Peggy. On one hand he hoped he'd never again have to face her. Another part of him still wished she could somehow learn that he had earned George Clark's confidence. She didn't need to know how hesitantly, and with what reservations, George had finally extended that confidence—

Perhaps Donald would tell Peggy about it when she returned. That would be easiest for all concerned.

He turned his attention to less somber subjects. After he'd ridden some five miles more, a remarkable thought crossed his mind, making him smile broadly.

He'd been concentrating on how to approach Donald for a loan to finance a trip to Richmond—and purchase of the very best Kentucky rifle available from the local gunsmiths. Not once had he thought about, or felt a desire for, something to drink.

Still, a rum might refresh him. Perhaps there was an inn—

No. That was done. Let his palms crawl and his tongue taste of ashes and the craving bring all the horrors of hell. It was *done*. He'd promised

He knew the name of the worst enemy he faced—*Judson Fletcher*—and he meant to conquer him. By God he did!

As the October day turned radiant, he forced thoughts of drinking from his mind and let his soaring imagination fashion the sleek, deadly silhouette of the rifle he'd carry across the Blue Wall into the west.

V

AHEAD, THE familiar curve of the road signaled that he had barely a quarter of a mile to ride.

He was grimy, exhausted, butt-sore and hungry after the long trip, but still in an ebullient mood. He looked forward to easing out of the saddle, washing up, enjoying a solid night's rest and a little food from the cabin's meager stores. In the morning he'd begin to implement his plans. Contact Donald about the loan. Perhaps, if all went well, he'd be on the road to Richmond before the week was out.

He inhaled the fragrant, nippy air of the October twilight, a bemused smile on his face. He let the horse find its own way to the dooryard—

Where he pulled up short, jolted out of his reverie. A sorry-looking gray nag whose hock joints showed signs of bog spavin was tethered to the dead apple tree.

The gray swung its head, whinnied. Judson's palms prickled. A lantern glowed inside the cabin. He heard a woman's voice—

Lottie.

Damn, this was an unexpected complication. A quick alteration of his plans was in order. He'd have to ride downriver a ways, locate an inn where they'd accept his promise of payment until he had an opportunity to speak with Donald—

At the moment, though, his challenge was to avoid any sort of argument with Tom Shaw's widow.

Judson dismounted, caught the sound of footsteps inside the cabin. Lottie's voice had gone silent all at once. The door remained closed.

Why was she back? Had she found business poor in Richmond? Well, he'd commiserate. Even go so far as to ask that she forgive him for his outrageous act of throwing her off her own property, if that would satisfy her. Hell, he'd treat her like a princess if necessary.

The thoughts chased through his mind in the moments he stood beside the horse, patting its lathered neck. He took a deep breath, preparing to walk to the cabin—

The door opened.

"Lottie—" he began, and scowled.

He saw her, right enough. Dirty and disheveled as ever. But she was standing behind someone else. A man.

The man blocked the cabin door, worn boots planted wide apart as if to bar Judson's entrance. The fellow was somewhere in his thirties. Not bad looking, but going paunchy. He wore dirty white breeches, a ruffled shirt, a once elegant fawn waistcoat. He had a puffy, dissolute face that wasn't helped by a three- or four-day growth of beard.

Lottie clutched the man's arm, her face all nasty pleasure as she exclaimed, "Well, look who's back!"

"Evening, Lottie." Judson spoke calmly, determined to avoid an altercation. "I've been in Williamsburg a few days—"

"Then I guess we came home at exactly the right time, didn't we, Mr. Carter?"

Mr. Carter acted slightly tipsy. He gurgled something Judson didn't catch. Lottie went on:

"Mr. Carter an' me, *we're* livin' here now. You better not make any fuss about it."

"Don't intend to, Lottie." He'd guessed the laconic Carter's profession, if that was the proper word. The man continued to regard him with a peculiar stare that might have been animosity, or awe, or some of both. "I'll be leaving Caroline County soon. Just came to collect a few belongings. My other shirt, my—"

Carter interrupted. "Afraid we disposed of those right after we returned." The man affected polite speech, but handled it awkwardly. Judson had seen men of Carter's stamp in Richmond before. Why he and his whore had left there, Judson still couldn't imagine.

"We burned them," Lottie added, still baiting him.

Judson forced a shrug. "In that case I'll ride on."

Yet it required effort for him to check a mounting annoyance. He kept reminding himself that Lottie and her new-found companion weren't worth his trouble. He turned to amble back toward his horse.

"You ain't gettin' away from here that easy, Mr. Fine Judson Fletcher. Not after the way you pushed me off my own land."

"Yes, we've actually been waiting for you," Carter said. Judson didn't like the sound of it. "Lottie thinks you're due a comeuppance."

He tried to keep his smile easy, alert to the undertone of ugliness in the conversation. "I admit I treated you in pretty shabby fashion, Lottie. For that, I tender my apologies. But there's no point in starting an argument now. There's nothing to argue about—the cabin's yours. I'm bound away from this part of the country, so let's just say good evening and—"

"The hell!" Lottie fairly screamed, dashing past her slovenly friend and snatching at the bridle of Judson's horse

Judson was faster. Bridle in hand, he retreated two steps. The horse nipped at Lottie's hand but missed. She jerked back, glaring.

"I don't blame you for being angry," Judson said. "But believe me, I don't have the slightest desire to cause you further distress—"

"Doesn't make any damn difference what *you* got a desire for, I told you I wouldn't forget what you did."

Suddenly Judson stopped smiling. He had to impress on them that although he wanted no trouble, he wouldn't bear harassment:

"Lottie, keep quiet I'm going to mount up and leave, and you and your—ah—business associate can put the cabin to any use you see fit."

"I don't care for your tone," Carter said, taking a wobbly step forward. "What were you implying when you said business associate?"

God! Trifling with trash like these two tried his patience to the limit. He stood in the left stirrup, hoisted his right leg over and met Carter's stare straight on:

"I didn't see any point in using the word pimp, Mr. Carter."

Carter wilted under Judson's gaze; looked at the ground.

Judson yanked the horse's head toward the road, ignoring Lottie's burst of obscenities. At the sound of scuffling he reined in, swung around in the saddle just as Lottie pushed Carter aside and darted into the cabin. Carter's eyes flicked between Judson and the girl, out of sight in the dim interior. When Carter spoke, it was to her:

"He's agreed to ride on, Lottie. I don't think we need press—"

"Scares you, does he?" Lottie jeered, still unseen. "Well, you can turn yellow, but he's got somethin' coming for the way he treated me—"

Suddenly she was back in the door, again shoving the confused Carter out of the way. And Judson saw just how badly he'd miscalculated the extent of her wrath.

He tried to rear the horse back out of the line of fire. Both of Lottie's hands were clamped on a horse pistol that evidently belonged to Carter, who tried to grab it:

"Listen, we had enough trouble with the Richmond authorities, we don't want to be responsible for murd—"

The hammer fell, the powder ignited, the muzzle bloomed smoke and fire.

Judson ducked, but not quickly enough. The ball slammed his left side, knocked him from the saddle. All he could think of in that chaotic instant was George Clark's warning—

Three weeks at the outside. If you're not here, I won't wait.

He floundered in the dirt, hurting. The ball had hit just under his left armpit. Already he felt warm blood soaking his clothes. Coughing hard, he tried to crawl on hands and knees. Carter's voice had a frightened quality:

"Christ amighty, Lottie, you said he has friends and kinfolk in this county. They won't stand for—"

"Who's going to know who shot him when they find him lying dead by Plum Creek, like we talked about?"

Judson's hands weakened. He could barely support himself. He wanted to curse her. Wanted to curse himself for not getting away sooner. *Christ, it was intolerable, Lottie doing this to him when things had finally changed for the better—!*

In his mind, a vicious voice mocked his despair:

Why blame Lottie? Who caused it if not you?

Coughing harder, he spoke George Clark's first name aloud. He was stupefyingly dizzy. He heard his horse clatter away down the road, spooked by the shot. The dirt of the dooryard rushed up toward his blurring eyes and struck him, bringing the ruinous dark.

6
The Drillmaster

ANOTHER HORSE lay on the shoulder of the road, the sleet spattering from its still flanks and huge, distended eyeballs. Philip had already counted three others, starved and abandoned along the line of march. He averted his eyes and passed by the dead animal as quickly as his split, rag-wrapped shoes would carry him.

The sleet was starting to turn to rain. Ahead and behind, ghostly double columns of men plodded in the December murk. Royal Rothman, his face half concealed by a strip torn from the bottom of his coat, bumped against Philip to attract his attention.

Philip turned his head. Even that small effort was painful. He walked and breathed in pain. The worst was in his feet.

Sometimes they felt totally numb. Then, abruptly, sensation would return. Dozens of tiny knives seemed to be slicing his flesh. A while ago, he'd glanced down and seen blood staining the rags on his left foot.

Philip hunched his shoulders against the sleet, tried to catch Royal's words, had trouble because the chandler's clerk had almost lost his voice.

"They lied to us," Royal said. "They damn well lied."

Too weak and weary to argue, Philip answered, "It's possible. They said thirteen miles. Thirteen miles from Whitemarsh to the campsite."

"Thirteen hundred, more like," Breen said just behind them. "Fuckin' liars. Fuckin' incompetents, every one."

"I can't keep walking," Royal croaked.

"Here, put your arm around my neck," Philip said, "Lean on me a while."

A little extra weight made no difference. He had long passed beyond the point of caring about anything except taking the next agonizing step; then the next; and the next. Royal Rothman's body slumping against his was just one more minor hardship among all the rest: no food; no water; no decent clothing; no conviction that anyone really knew where they were supposed to be going—

The world consisted of this long, seemingly endless road where the edges of the mud ruts had frozen sharp as axe-blades, and were only now beginning to soften a little. But the frozen ruts had already done adequate damage during the week's march. Men sprawled at the roadside in the gray of the winter morning, their feet bleeding so badly they couldn't go on.

It did seem impossible that it could only be thirteen miles from their last permanent camp at Whitemarsh to the new one, somewhere on the bank of the Schuylkill River about twenty miles west and slightly north of Philadelphia. There, presumably, they would winter. Rest. Draw rations.

But a *week* to reach the place? God, that was incomprehensible—!

Or was it? Everything seemed incomprehensible of late.

In October, at Germantown, the army had come close to revenging the humiliation of the Brandywine. General Washington had implemented an attack plan against Howe's troops. But confusion about battle orders—and a sudden heavy fog descending—turned the near-victory into another rout. Philip had even heard that American units lost in the fog had fired on one another.

For an hour at Germantown, the possibility of success had been within their grasp. Officers said the troops had fought well. Then came the fog—and disaster. Seven hundred lost, they said, more than four hundred captured—

Supporting Royal, Philip staggered on between skeletal trees rising in the mist. They passed more men who had simply stopped; given up. Then an overturned baggage wagon with two of its wheels still revolving slowly. Someone had tried to move the wagon with only one horse. The spent beast lay thrashing and whinnying in the traces. Philip saw the spectral figure of an officer approach, lift a pistol to the animal's head. The shot boomed through the rain. Royal Rothman started to cry.

Up ahead, the ground appeared to rise. Philip picked up the sound of men splashing through water, then a few weak cheers. Word came back along the line from soldier to filthy soldier:

"It's Valley Creek."

"We've reached it."

"We'll be camping tonight—pass it to the rear—"

Wearily, Philip tried. While he was shouting at Breen, Royal slipped and sprawled face down in the mud. Philip motioned Breen forward. Together the

two lifted the younger soldier and carried him through the icy water of Valley Creek.

The rags on Philip's feet fell away, drifted off in the current. He refused to stop. All he wanted was the haven of the campsite that apparently waited at the top of the rise where thick tree trunks clustered in the murk.

A plateau, then. They were climbing to a plateau where there was wood for fires. There should be food, too. The prospect helped him drive his tired, hurting body the last few hundred yards. Perhaps their agony was coming to an end—

By nightfall, Philip knew the hope had been cruelly false.

A savage December wind swept across the rolling, two-mile plateau in the angle between the Schuylkill River flowing from west to east and the creek that came up from the south to join it. There were pines and oaks in plenty. But they offered scant protection from the wind.

And there were no supply wagons waiting.

When Philip, Breen and Royal tried to hammer pegs for their tent into the half-frozen ground, the pegs kept popping out. Exhausted, the three finally gave up, spread the rain-sodden canvas on the ground and crawled under it.

Philip listened to the pines moaning in the darkness. He had a dizzying vision of Anne and little Abraham sitting by a cheery fire in Cambridge. At least they were safe and warm. At least they would survive—

Even that assumption, though, was not without a certain hollow ring. Philip had received no further letters from his wife since the last one in the summertime.

Thinking about that for very long was too much on top of everything else: the army's failure; his bleeding foot; his ferocious, unremitting hunger—

Dinner for the night had consisted of the one, greentinged chunk of bread remaining in his haversack.

He shifted position under the soaked canvas, trying to get comfortable. The wind roared across the plateau, carrying the sound of officers shouting orders, horses and wagons crisscrossing the high ground. Units of the Continental army were still arriving.

Next to Philip, Royal began to cry again. Without even thinking about it, Philip reached over with one stiffened hand and patted the younger man's shoulder, trying to comfort him.

On Philip's left, Breen suddenly let out an assortment of curses. Then:

"Cap'n Webb said the general picked this place 'cause we could escape easy if we got attacked. Shit, you think Billy Howe's gonna come out in this weather to bother with us? He's gonna let us die in the goddamned place."

"Shut up, Breen," Philip said. "Try to sleep."

"And wake up froze to death? Not me!"

Breen hauled himself out from beneath the canvas, tramped away:

"I'm gonna squat under one of them pines."

Philip might have done the same, but Royal Rothman seemed to be suffering an attack of the chills. His body convulsed for perhaps ten minutes. Philip held him with both arms, trying to transfer what warmth he could from his own body.

Finally the convulsions stopped. Royal drifted to sleep. Philip dozed a little himself. All at once, Royal started up:

"Where are we? I dreamed it was Boston—"

"Lie down," Philip said. "I wish it was Boston too."

Awake and miserable, Royal asked, "Does this place have any name at all?"

"Captain Webb said it's called Valley Forge."

Royal collapsed against him like a child, burrowing against Philip's filthy coat and starting to sob again:

"I'm sorry, I—I shouldn't cry, it's—not manly, but—I can't help it—"

"Go ahead, Royal. There's nothing to be ashamed of. Christ, I'd cry too if I had any strength left."

Philip pulled the soaked tent canvas up over his head as the rain started falling again.

II

BY JANUARY, axemen felled enough timber for construction to start on a hut city on the plateau that took its name from a Quaker-owned iron works beside Valley Creek. The works had formerly supplied Washington's army; the British had stopped in September to burn it out.

The commanding general, who had finally moved into a fieldstone house near the junction of the creek and the river, ordered regulation army huts built by each unit. Philip and the men of his company spent their days laboriously putting up theirs according to the approved design: fourteen by sixteen feet, with a rise of six and a half feet to the steep timbered roof. They had a chimney chinked with cat and clay, but no windows.

And no meat, other than an infrequent issue of salt pork.

And no yellow soap to bathe their filthy, infected, foul-smelling feet.

And no drinking water save what they could carry from the partially frozen creek.

And no hope. Worst of all, no hope.

III

A KNOCK at the hut door brought Breen's head up where he lay dozing. Just as quickly, he lay down again and snored. Breen had spent three pence for a gill of peach brandy at the sutler's. Philip had purchased a quart of vinegar instead.

One of the camp physicians had told him vinegar would keep his gums from bleeding; prevent his skin from bursting open with countless sores. Philip hated drinking the vile stuff. But the doctor had apparently been right. Breen wouldn't waste his money on vinegar, and his already malodorous person had fallen prey to the scurvy. So had a good percentage of the eleven thousand men settled in for the winter in the hut city.

The knock came again, more insistently. With a disgusted sigh, Philip turned over the last of three firecakes heating on the stones next to the fireplace logs. That was their evening meal: peach brandy—or vinegar in Philip's case—and flour mixed with water, then cooked till it hardened. Wind whined in the chimney, blowing smoke back in Philip's face as he said:

"Will you see who's there, Royal?"

The younger man nodded apathetically, shuffled to the door on rag-covered feet. He opened the door to admit a gust of snow—and Captain Webb, who hardly resembled an officer any longer.

Webb was hatless, white crystals powdering his hair. He wore an old padded blue dressing gown he'd adopted for warmth on night duty. In the distance, above the wind's wail, Philip heard men bawling a contemptuous song around some campfire, to the tune of the marching air *Yankee Doodle*:

> *"First we'll take a pinch of snuff,*
> *"And then a drink of water—"*

Raising his head again, Breen focused his eyes until he identified their visitor. Then he passed wind, loudly.

Webb said, "I appreciate your gesture of respect."

"Think nothin' of it. You finally bringin' us some replacements? Food would be too much to ask—"

"I'm hunting for cards and dice," Webb snapped. "The general's making an inspection tour this evening."

"Likes to keep track of our luxurious livin' conditions, does he?"

"For God's sake, Breen, that doesn't help anything."

"Captain Webb's right," Philip put in. Breen shrugged, uncaring.

"You know how set against gaming the general is," Webb said, too tired— as they all were— to worry about breaches of discipline and courtesy. "Some bunch of nabobs called a Committee of Conference rolled in from York this afternoon."

"The Congress is sitting at York now, isn't it?" Royal asked.

"Correct. The committee's purpose is to inspect and improve on conditions here, if possible."

Another oath from Breen indicated what he thought of the whole idea. The singers in the distance were repeating their chorus with an even nastier intonation to the final lines:

> *"And then we'll say, How do you do?*
> *"And that's a Yankee supper!"*

"That won't be hard," Philip said. "I swear to God, Captain, if we don't get some decent food, there'll be a riot like nobody's ever seen before."

"And clothing," Royal added, pointing at his bandaged feet. The brown of dried blood shaded into the green of pus.

Philip hadn't spoken idly. For days now, as the bitter January sleet and snow continued without letup, certain sections of the hut city had taken to chanting *"No meat! No meat!"* for half an hour every evening. The poison of incipient rebellion was spreading through the entire encampment.

"There's nothing I can do about that tonight," Webb told them. "I just want you to look reasonably sharp if the dignitaries come this way."

"You know where you can put them dignitaries," Breen said, farting again. "Will you shut the fuckin' door before we freeze to death?"

Looking defeated, Captain Webb withdrew into the snowy darkness. Philip closed the door.

He almost said something to Breen about his discourtesy to the officer. But such talk wasn't uncommon, and was seldom punished. Besides, Philip identified it for what it was: not a disease, but the symptom of a disease. The problem Henry Knox had predicted still plagued them. They were amateurs at war, and except for a few isolated victories now forgotten, they had performed badly. Untrained as soldiers, they could hardly be expected to behave like soldiers.

Philip had no answer for the problem. But he knew it could only grow worse unless something drastic happened.

Saying little to each other, Breen, Royal and Philip ate their hard, blackened fire-cakes. Moments later, Philip experienced one of his frequent attacks of nausea because of the hut's almost insufferable stench. Their unwashed bodies, Royal's diseased feet—and Breen's stubborn refusal to expose himself to the winter air to urinate—created a stew of smells Philip could bear only so long. He drank another half cup of vinegar, put on his tattered coat and hurried out to the company street.

Head down, eyes slitted against the wind-whipped snow that had come at nightfall, he trudged aimlessly between the uniformly built log huts facing one another on both sides of the dirt avenue. The rows of huts were perhaps the only detail in all of Valley Forge that gave the encampment a semblance of order.

In the distance he saw an immense bonfire blazing near the artillery park where Henry Knox kept his cannon. He thought briefly of going to see his friend. But just as he did, he heard strident voices off to his left.

He peered between two huts, glimpsed lanterns a-bob in the next street. He thought he recognized the tall, angular figure of Washington, cloak flapping like wings at his shoulders. A party of officers and civilians had halted around the general. An argument was in progress.

Philip dodged between the huts, huddled against the logs, numb hands in his bottomless pockets. He heard one of the civilians say:

"—distressing and unbelievable filth, General. Corrective measures must be taken, and swiftly."

Suddenly Washington snatched off his tricorn and slammed it against his right leg:

"Corrective measures, sir? Why don't you gentlemen in Congress take corrective measures? Hire honest teamsters, instead of cheats who drain the brine from the salt pork barrels to lighten the load, then deliver us spoiled meat? Why don't you hire men who can draw accurate maps? Half the supplies we're sent never arrive because the drivers get lost for want of proper directions, and finally dump their grain sacks in empty fields to rot!"

Another member of the committee spoke up:

"Yes, those criticisms are fully merited. The Congress is aware—"

"I don't give a damn whether they're *aware*, I want to know what's being done to change things!"

"We intend to return with a full report."

"On the miserable state of affairs you've discovered?"

"Certainly we shall have to detail that, but—"

Another disgusted oath from Washington. "So instead of help for these brave men, I'll receive remonstrances and more remonstrances. Well, let me assure you and all the gentlemen of the Congress—" Even above the singsong of the wind, his furious voice could be heard a good distance. "—it's a much easier and less distressing thing to draw remonstrances in a comfortable room by a good fire than to occupy a cold, bleak hill and sleep under frost and snow. Some of my troops are not yet hutted—you tell *them* that the immediate result of your visit will be a report instead of food and blankets!"

Yanking his cloak across his chest to protect his blue and buff coat from the pelt of the snow, Washington glared at his critics:

"And where is that German officer you promised for my staff?"

Another of the Congressmen said, "Baron von Steuben is having his credentials examined by one of our committees."

"To perdition with your committees! I've heard his credentials and they're more than satisfactory. Get him into this camp with a suitable rank and ready to assist me. I need someone who can teach these men proper military drill! At least they can learn something while they're starving to death!"

"We shall do everything possible to expedite—"

The rest was blurred as the big general stamped past the front of the hut and out of sight, followed by the Congressmen and his officers with the lanterns.

Shivering by the hut wall, Philip thought about the reference to a German. Another of those volunteers?

Some, like Gil, had proved themselves brave and able; effective additions to the army. Others were held in contempt. But it was interesting to hear Washington tell a Congressional committee that he and his own staff lacked the ability to shape the Continental and militia units into a cohesive, well-trained force capable of fighting in the best European style.

Many at Valley Forge still called Washington a poor leader in combat. Yet Philip had heard few openly declare that they would refuse to continue to serve under him. Specific complaints were always directed at Washington's senior officers, or the Congress. The general himself somehow escaped most of the direct criticism.

But Philip could understand that. The man was an aristocrat; yet he cared about the welfare of the ordinary soldier. He had a rare forthrightness when it came to admitting and correcting his own mistakes, and the lowest private was aware of it. Perhaps that was why Washington was admired even when his battlefield ability was questioned. Perhaps that was why, despite almost intolerable conditions, Valley Forge hadn't yet succumbed to insurrection and mass desertion—

Returning to the hut, Philip settled down to sleep. As he was drifting off, he speculated about the German officer. A baron, they'd said. The Germans were generally considered excellent in the field. The hired Hessians were respected, even if they were openly cursed and universally hated. Now Washington was getting his own German. It remained to be seen whether the man could accomplish anything.

The last flames flickered out on the hearth. Philip listened to Breen's snores and Royal's wheezy breathing. The wind had picked up. It howled around the chimney and blew fireplace ash back into the cramped, fetid room. Thoughts about the German were replaced by thoughts of Anne—and the familiar worry:

Why hadn't she written? Was she safe in Cambridge? Did the silence spell illness? Or something worse—?

Under a violent gusting of the wind, the hut door flew open. Shivering, Philip leaped up to close it. He stared a moment into the snowy dark.

Annie, for God's sake write me. Else I can't go on here. I just can't go on.

____ IV

BARON FRIEDRICH WILHELM LUDOLF GERHARD AUGUSTIN VON STEUBEN set the Valley Forge camp to buzzing when he arrived in February. He was accompanied by a trio of aides and a lean Italian greyhound called Azor. The dog trotted after the new inspector-general of the army wherever he went.

Philip first saw von Steuben two days after he reached the plateau. He didn't quite know what to make of the officer.

The man rode well, looking huge and formidable in the saddle despite his middle age and a bandy-legged body. Some who had seen von Steuben hurrying through the camp on foot guffawed and said he waddled. They also said he could speak no English except the word "goddamn," which he apparently used quite often. He and his suite had reached the New Hampshire coast the preceding December, presenting themselves to the Congress as available for service to General Washington.

Encountering Gil one February twilight near the sutler's, Philip discovered that the Marquis de Lafayette was not impressed:

"That red uniform with the blue facings he sports? I have it on excellent authority that he designed it himself. And that medal—faugh!"

Gil's mouth pursed to emphasize his contempt. Studying his friend, Philip thought he detected more than a trace of jealousy.

"Have you seen it?" Gil asked.

"Yes. It is fairly large—"

"*Large?* It's gigantic! A sunburst big as a soup dish—disgraceful ostentation, disgraceful! The Star of the Order of Fidelity of Baden-Durlach, he calls it. Well, my good friend, I am not certain he ever fought for Baden-Durlach—let alone under Frederick the Great whom he's claiming as his 'close associate.' I am convinced his estate in Swabia is a fiction, just like the 'von' in his name—he probably added that himself, to enhance his credentials. He keeps prattling in that wretched French of his about having surrendered various 'places and posts of honor in Germany' in order to come here. But one can't pin him down as to precisely what places or posts! If he was ever more than a subaltern, I am King Louis! And yesterday—*yesterday* he had the effrontery to tell *mon ami* General Washington that the officers in camp have too many servants! That the soldiers must not be kept so busy shining boots and laying fires in our huts, but must learn soldiering instead! Can you conceive of such advice coming from him? A rascal, a pretender, a windbag equally as mercenary as Howe's Hessians? I understand his salary is incredible—*another* swindle of the Congress! Learn soldiering from a man like that? The very idea is an insult to the rest of us who have volunteered!"

"Well," Philip said when the tirade sputtered to its end, "I heard one of his suggestions, and it seemed to make sense."

"Pooh, that clock business?"

"Yes. I wonder why it never occurred to anyone else?"

Gil waved. "Because it's unimportant."

Von Steuben had reportedly made a scene when he discovered that not a single timepiece in all of Valley Forge was coordinated with any other. He had insisted that all clocks be synchronized with the one at Washington's headquarters. In Philip's view, Gil's too-curt dismissal of the idea was evidence that he wished he'd thought of it.

"I repeat—you'll learn nothing from a man who is patently an adventurer and a fraud," was Gil's final opinion before he and his friend parted. Philip hid his amusement at Gil's professional hostility, deciding he'd wait and see.

The wait wasn't long:

"Rothman, Kent, Breen," Captain Webb said when he showed up at the hut a few evenings later. "Turn out on the parade field tomorrow at six. With muskets."

Breen scratched his genitals. "Six in the evening?"

"Six in the morning."

"Jesus Christ, what for?"

"The baron is organizing a special company. One hundred men from all units, to whom he's going to teach musket drill and marching. The men will then teach other groups of a hundred. That damn Dutchman is trying to turn this army inside out! He rises at three in the morning to write a drill text—and I understand he's also developing a manual of procedures for officers." Webb clearly didn't care for that.

"Well, I sure ain't wakin' up at six—" Breen began.

"You'll wake up at five thirty," Webb cut in.

"—to take lessons from some fat-ass German," Breen finished, emphatically.

"Like it or not, I'm afraid you will. The order to form the company of a hundred is direct from the commander-in-chief. So you'll be there or you'll be flogged."

"Son of a bitch." Breen shook his head. "I guess I'll be there."

Royal Rothman actually looked pleased at the news. He reached up to the small black cap pinned to his hair, plucked out something, crushed it between his fingers, threw it away, then said:

"It might actually be worthwhile, don't you think, Philip?"

"It's bound to be more diverting than hunting lice or watching your feet bleed."

"Jesus Christ and the Holy Sepulchre," Breen grumbled as Webb bent to go out into the bitter February wind. "Six o'clock in the fucking morning."

___V

PHILIP SHIVERED in the dawn wind, gritty-eyed and yawning. The Baron von Steuben, his dinner-plate medal bouncing against his red-uniformed stomach, struggled to control his prancing horse. The greyhound Azor nipped at the horse's legs, causing the brown-haired, round-faced inspector-general to lash downward with his crop:

"Azor, goddamn—*nein!*"

The dog temporarily at bay, von Steuben pointed his crop at the blushing captain from New York, Benjamin Walker, who was serving as his interpreter. The baron blistered a stream of French orders at Walker. The captain nodded feverishly every second or so until the harangue concluded. The French was mingled with German phrases, and Philip could follow it only with great difficulty.

Next to Philip, Breen used a few highly obscene words to characterize the peculiar man on horseback. Walker overhead but chose to overlook it. Von Steuben didn't. If he failed to comprehend the specific words; he caught their general meaning. He fixed Breen with a glare that started the latter blinking rapidly.

Walker cleared his throat.

"Men, the general has instructed me to say that he is personally going to undertake your training. That he, ah—"

Walker licked his lips, hesitated, almost winced as von Steuben stared him down.

"He, ah, finds conditions in this camp—ah—appalling. He is equally shocked to discover there is, ah, no standardized set of procedures for marching and handling weapons."

Walker glanced at the general for further instruction. Von Steuben let fly with more French.

"He says he has noticed a difference between American troops and those of Europe, in that European soldiers will follow orders without question but—ah—Americans seem to want to know *why* first. So he will try to explain the reason for each maneuver as we go along."

Several surprised exclamations and even some applause greeted the announcement. Whatever his pretensions, Philip thought, the German had assessed the temperament of the soldiers correctly. Some of Philip's reservations began to fade. He rather liked the hard, capable look of the middle-aged officer—ostentatious Order of Fidelity and all.

"Now the first thing the general wants to see you do is the drill for loading and firing your muskets. On the count of one—"

In haphazard fashion, Philip and the others went through the drill's twenty steps, Captain Walker counting each one. By the time the young New Yorker had called *"Fifteen!"* von Steuben was scarlet. The conclusion of the drill, muskets at the shoulder in position to shoot, produced another torrent of French.

"The general wishes me to inform you that in his opinion, that is—ah—the most slovenly and time-consuming drill he has ever seen—"

Still more French.

"—in any part of the globe—"

And more.

"—in his entire life."

Von Steuben uttered a few guttural barks just to make sure the point got across.

"The general is going to introduce you to a new drill for the same procedure. A drill which will shortly be available in written form for you to study. The general's drill requires only ten counts—"

Suddenly there wasn't a whisper in the ranks. Walker had caught their full attention at last.

"—the idea being to save time so more shots may be discharged at the enemy in the same interval."

Walker bent down to pick up the musket lying at his feet.

"I will now demonstrate the drill, following the general's instructions."

Walker's face showed that he disliked the assignment intensely. Actually handling weapons during training was considered beneath the dignity of any officer.

Von Steuben noticed Walker's expression. He swore, cropped his horse to a standstill, leaped to the ground and waddled to his translator. He snatched the musket from the astonished captain's hands.

Then von Steuben jerked at the strap of the cartridge box Walker had picked up, slung the strap over his own shoulder, settled the box on his hip and stalked out in front of the hundred men.

He presented the musket for viewing by the soldiers, shouted, *"Ein!"* and immediately brought the firelock to half cock.

Philip saw jaws drop and eyes go wide. The demonstration was absolutely unbelievable. A high-ranking officer *off* his horse? Handling a musket *personally*—?

"Zwei!"

With thick but somehow swift fingers, von Steuben took out a cartridge, bit off the end of the paper and covered the opening with his thumb.

"Drei!"

He primed the pan.

When the entire ten counts were finished, von Steuben had armed the musket and brought it to his shoulder in half the time the normal drill required.

The stocky man stumped forward, eyes darting in search of a pupil. Bad luck brought Breen to his attention. Von Steuben literally jerked Breen out in front of the others, slammed the musket into his hands, flung the cartridge box strap over the confused victim's head and bawled:

"Ein!"

Breen managed to remember the first step—halfcocking the piece—but when von Steuben shouted the count of two, he grew fuddled. Turning red again, the German thrust his face up near Breen's and screamed, *"Zwei,* goddamn, *zwei!"*

Breen lost his grip on the musket. It fell to the ground. Apoplectic, von Steuben shoved Breen back into line and pulled out another man, a Marylander. He managed to get to five before von Steuben dismissed him with an even more torrential outpouring of French and German profanities. Some of the former— anatomically colorful—Philip could translate, with considerable amusement.

The baron proceeded to go through the entire drill three more times before dragging another man forward. Fortunately, the Virginian completed the count with a minimum of error. The German beamed—and so did most of his trainees, letting the smiles drain away the built-up tension.

While the February wind grew stronger, bringing a few snowflakes down, the hundred soldiers repeated the drill together ten times. Then ten more. And ten more after that. Von Steuben waddled briskly up and down the ranks, correcting the slant of a muzzle here, the grip of a ramrod there, occasionally slapping a student on the back but more often cursing.

Finaly, around ten o'clock, the baron remounted his horse. Walker ordered the hundred to prepare to repeat the drill one last time, while von Steuben called the count.

By then Philip had fairly well gotten the hang of it. He was amazed at how the drill did pare the time required for the vital operation. But the unison drill was still uncoordinated. By the time Walker had reached six, von Steuben was screaming and pointing at poor performers:

"Nein, nein!" Another storm of profanity, concluding with a thunderous, *"Viens,* Valkair, *mon ami! Sacre!* Goddamn *die gaucheries* of dese *imbeciles! Je ne puis plus!"* Growing almost incoherent, he shrieked, "You curse dem, Valkair—*you!"*

He wheeled his horse and went pounding away across the parade field, Azor streaking behind him through the slanting snow. Captain Walker once more cleared his throat.

"Ah—you men realize—I have orders—"

"Ah, go ahead and get it over with!" someone yelled. There was laughter at the captain's expense.

Flushing, Walker cursed and condemned the soldiers in a monotonous voice for the better part of two minutes.

Relieved when it was over, he said, "All right, let's resume the drill. One—!"

Philip observed von Steuben resting his horse at the far edge of the field.

Before long the baron was lured back by his own interest in the proceedings. By noon, alternately swearing and complimenting in his strange pidgin mixture of French, German and very occasional English, he had the entire hundred going through the drill with reasonable precision.

Philip noticed something else as they ran through the final counts—*shoulder firelock; poise and cock firelock; take aim and fire.* The weariness and despair on the faces in the snow-covered ranks seemed to have been replaced by something else. Something he too was experiencing. It gave him the first glimmer of hope for this conglomeration of unruly men nominally called an army.

He saw shoulders a little straighter. Fatigued, reddened eyes a little more alert. Hands blue-tinged with cold moving with a little more speed and deftness—

There in the February snow he saw—and felt—the stirring of pride.

VI

ON THEIR way back to their hut after the remarkable morning, the trio of Massachusetts men discussed the bizarre drilllmaster.

"I think maybe the man has a touch of genius," Philip said.

"Fucking maniac," was Breen's contribution.

Royal Rothman said, "I think he's both. I like him."

VII

So DID the rank and file of the army, as it turned out. Except with those officers such as Gil, who considered the baron's methods both unorthodox and degrading, von Steuben was soon the most popular commander in the camp after Washington.

The German ignored the jealous jibes and rumors circulated about him, and kept working. As the winter wore on, leavened at last by a growing trickle of supply wagons that brought in foodstuffs and clothing, the baron's original hundred taught new contingents of a hundred. Those hundreds taught hundreds more. By early March, Philip and even Breen had become busy and proficient instructors of all of von Steuben's lessons:

The new musket drill.

The new cadences that smoothed the execution of flanking and countermarching by masses of troops on the move.

The new marching formation—four abreast, instead of the traditional single or double file. This, the baron had explained, would allow the regiments to enter or retreat from a battle zone in an orderly way, as well as faster. Another obvious innovation, yet quite astonishing when it was suddenly introduced into an army that had never thought of it before.

The German also insisted that bayonet drill be taught—and demanded every soldier have one. Philip could imagine how that order alone increased business at George Lumden's forge back in Connecticut.

Uniforms began to look a little sharper. Although few had been completely replaced, the men took to maintaining them more carefully, sewing and patching

them instead of letting them simply fall to pieces. When wagonloads of soap became available, the men washed their clothes as well as themselves. It struck Philip that had von Steuben not arrived when he did, the next engagement of the army might have brought total anarchy—wholesale refusal to fight. Now there was actually talk of wanting to face Howe's soldiers; of wanting to discover how well the new techniques worked in battle.

Henry Knox expressed it when Philip encountered him one day in March:

"I thought no one could create a military force out of this rabble. But I do believe that strutting, egotistical German's done it."

The long, dark night of the winter seemed to be ending. The calendar ran on toward spring. Only one grave concern still infected Philip's waking thoughts and haunted his sleep.

He still hadn't received a single reply to his letters to Anne.

____ VIII

AT A special evening muster in the company street, Captain Webb read the message sent to all the troops from the gray fieldstone house near Schuylkill:

"Headquarters, Valley Forge. The commander-in-chief takes this occasion to return his warmest thanks to the virtuous offices and soldiers of this army for that persevering fidelity and zeal which they have uniformly manifested in all their conduct. Their fortitude not only under their common hardships incident to a military life, but also under the additional sufferings to which the peculiar situation of these states has exposed them, clearly proves them men worthy of the enviable privilege of contending for the rights of human nature and the freedom and independence of their country—"

Philip noticed Breen wearing a smug smile. And the older man joined with all the others in a round of cheers when Webb concluded.

Tramping along to the sutler's after the formation broke up, Philip said to his messmates:

"I don't think it makes a damn bit of difference what they say about his losses in the field. If we win the war and the general had ambition to be king of this country, he could ask and it would be done."

No one disagreed.

____ IX

ATTENDANCE AT divine worship every Sunday was, supposedly, mandatory. But skimpy crowds in the log chapel usually testified to the lax enforcement of the commanding general's order. The last Sunday in March was an exception. The eleven o'clock service was to be held on the parade field because a bigger than usual crowd was expected—without duress.

The predictions proved correct, solely because of the identity of the preacher. Even Breen went along to listen.

The morning, although gray, wasn't excessively chilly. Philip and Breen found places in the huge crowd of seated men—two or three thousand at least,

Philip guessed. In front of the gathering, regimental drummers had stacked their drums into a three-tier platform, on top of which boards had been laid.

The regular chaplains presided over the hymns and prayers. But the men were clearly waiting for the sermon, to be presented by one of Washington's most loyal and hard-driving officers, General Peter Muhlenberg, the Pennsylvania-born commander of the Virginia line.

When Muhlenberg mounted the drum platform with a Bible in one hand, a wave of surprised comment raced through the crowd. The general wasn't wearing his uniform today. Instead, he wore the somber black robes of his former calling.

There was hardly a man at Valley Forge who didn't know a bit of Muhlenberg's story: his training at a theological school in Europe—which he found too dull; his military service with the dragoons in one of the German provinces; and—this part was told most often—the Sunday morning in January of '76.

Ordained at last and fending to a small parish flock in the Blue Ridge, Muhlenberg had mounted his pulpit while his congregation thundered *Ein Feste Burg*. As the hymn faded away, he flung off his black robes to reveal a colonel's uniform. Then he launched into a blistering sermon directed principally at one sinner—King George III. That was his last official message to his congregation before leading the Eighth Virginia off to war.

A powerful, commanding figure against the gray sky, General Muhlenberg leafed through the front of his Bible. The tactic had its effect; the last talk quieted—though Breen still whispered questions:

"What kind o' preacher did you say he is, Philip?"

"Lutheran. It's a German denomination, mostly."

"Well, I hope he's good, 'cause I don't usually hang around this sort o' function—why, look yonder! What's he doin' here? His church don't meet on Sunday."

Philip peered past the men seated nearby, saw Royal Rothman lingering at the very back of the crowd, darting glances every which way, as though anticipating some kind of trouble. Philip smiled, shrugged:

"I suppose he wants to hear the general as much as we do. No law says he can't."

The sermon of the preacher-turned-soldier was very much worth hearing. Philip soon realized Muhlenberg had chosen his text with care. It came from the twenty-third chapter of Exodus, and was perfectly fitted to the mood of the troops—especially this growing sense of becoming an army worthy of the name.

Muhlenberg first read his text:

"Behold, I send an angel before thee, to keep thee in the way, and to bring thee into the place which I have prepared. Beware of him, and obey his voice, provoke him not. For he will not pardon your transgressions, for my name is in him—"

Then, skillfully, Muhlenberg began to weave military propaganda into his theology. He likened the Lord's angel to an army commander whose every order must be executed without question. Discipline and obedience—whether he who followed was a lowly private or one of the Children of Israel—would surely bring the desired rewards. Muhlenberg saved the biblical version of those rewards for the end, rolling them out from the drum pulpit to his rapt, wide-eyed audience:

"But if thou shalt indeed obey his voice, and do all that I speak, then I will be an enemy unto thine enemies, and an adversary unto thine adversaries. For

mine angel shall go before thee, and bring thee in unto the Amorites, and the Hittites, and Perizzites, and the Canaanites, the Hivites, and Jebusites—

"And I will cut them off!"

It required only a moment's mental translation for the men to understand the real names of the enemy: the light infantry; the grenadiers; the Hessians. The sermon's conclusion brought the soldiers jumping to their feet to applaud, embarrassing Muhlenberg and provoking the other chaplains to what amounted to glares of envy. No one ever applauded *their* sermons.

Breen admitted to being "a mite excited" by the message, and confessed he'd never quite considered obeying a superior to be as vital as Muhlenberg claimed.

But the sermon had still left him thirsty. Even though it was Sunday, he announced with a wink, there were ways—

Losing track of the older man in the crowd, Philip made a point to catch up with Royal Rothman:

"Didn't expect to see you, Royal. How did you like the general?"

"He's every bit as fine a preacher as I've heard. Though I must say, Philip, I was startled by the concept that General Washington—or Captain Webb— could be considered as important in the scheme of things as an angel."

"Still, it was pretty stirring stuff."

Royal nodded with a shy smile. "By the way—I've been meaning to say something to you. About an idea I've had for several weeks now. This printing house we've talked about—where you're going to publish a deluxe edition of Mr. Paine's *Crisis* papers—" He hesitated. "You haven't forgotten—?"

"No, Royal. Seeing my family again is the first thing I want when this war's over. My own business is the second."

"Good! Where do you plan to set it up?"

"In Boston."

"I mean where in Boston?"

The extremely serious tone of the question checked Philip's impulse to chuckle. "Why, I don't know, Royal. I hadn't thought that far. At the start, I'll have to rent space—"

"That's my idea. Rothman's is the second largest chandler's in the whole town. My father always has extra loft room. I'm sure you could strike a good bargain for renting some of it. My father's conscious of the value of a penny, but he's fair, and—" Royal almost blushed. "—I've even taken the liberty of writing him about you and your plans. I think he'd do anything for you, after—"

"After what?"

"I must confess I described how you and Lucas helped out when Adams was baiting me."

A vivid memory of Mayo Adams dying in the ditch after Brandywine stained Philip's thoughts a moment, destroying the high excitement and good feeling the sermon had produced. He forced the ugly recollections away, said:

"Royal, it wasn't necessary to say anything to your father. Or to extend special thanks of any kind."

The young man's brown eyes were round and intense. "I felt it was."

"Well, then, I think your idea's a capital one."

"Do you? Honestly?"

"I do. I'll need a good place to operate my press—but I won't be able to pay much. Loft space sounds first rate. I'll tuck the thought away and take it out again at the right time—"

The recurrent streak of pessimism that plagued him produced a final thought: "—if we all survive this business."

"We will," Royal Rothman declared as they reached the edge of the parade field.

"If we follow that angel, eh?"

Royal appeared embarrassed. "My father is a very religious man, Philip. He'd scold me ferociously for saying this. But if it's a choice between trusting an angel or General Washington, I'll favor the latter."

Philip laughed. "You don't have to make the choice. I'd say at the present time they're one and the same person."

__X

"*The shad* are out! The shad are running upriver!"

The cry in the company street one April morning brought Philip and his messmates tumbling outside. Excited soldiers were racing through the camp with the news:

"Thousands of shad—"

"Running right now!"

Under a chilly sky of pale blue, Philip, Breen and Royal located whatever implements they could—a pitchfork, a shovel, a broken tree branch—and joined the hundreds of men streaming toward the Schuylkill River. Some carried barrels, baskets or the all-important salt. The human tide poured down to the Schuylkill's banks, where an incredible sight stunned Philip:

The river was dark, almost black with the bodies of thousands of fish swimming toward its headwaters like a second, living surface underneath the first. The whole river seemed to churn. The passage of the immense schools filled the air with a strange, whispery hum.

All along the bank, men rushed into the shallows, clubbing and stabbing and grabbing with their bare hands while they yelped and swore like profane children. Fresh fish to be cooked or salted away was a miracle whose importance was almost beyond reckoning.

Philip peeled off the new shoes supplied him only a week earlier, darted into the water, felt the eerie movement of the shad around his ankles. He slashed downward with the pitchfork, brought up two fish on the tines. He raised the fork to show Royal, but the young man was flailing at the water with his tree branch, oblivious to anyone's delight but his own.

A major of dragoons galloped by on the bank, headed upstream to plant his horsemen in the river to turn back the fleeing fish. The strategy worked. The Schuylkill shallows soon boiled white with frantic shad trying to swim back downstream against thousands of others still heading the opposite way—

The starvation of the Valley Forge winter ended in the largest fish banquet Philip had ever seen.

That night the Pennsylvania air reeked of broiled shad and rang with singing, a sound unheard for months, except in protest. As the smoke of cook fires climbed to the sky, Captain Webb purchased an extra gill of rum for each of his men, and reported an item of camp gossip about Martha Washington.

Mrs. Washington had joined her husband at the Potts house in February. Since then she'd been a regular visitor to the camp hospitals—when she wasn't busy

taking instruction from a neighborhood farm woman on how to darn the general's stockings. Tonight, Webb declared with tipsy pride, he knew for a fact that the lady too had served shad.

"Picked up some other tasty tidings," Webb went on. "Still talk, mostly. But it's coming from the Congress in York. May be a big announcement in the wind—"

Relishing his control of a secret, he crooked a finger so Philip would lean closer. Then he whispered:

Something about the French coming into the war. Sending us ships. Soldiers, even. Don't breathe a word. Nothing official—"

He tottered away toward the next hut to tell another confidante the same secret.

All at once, Webb about-faced. Fumbling in his uniform pocket, he returned to hand Philip a wrinkled letter:

"This finally came down the line from headquarters. Got sent by mistake to an officer named Philemon Kent in Moore's Fourth Rhode Island."

Abruptly, Philip forgot how stuffed he felt from the excellent fish. He forgot everything except the letter.

Quills had scratched and re-scratched the names of different units across the face. The original address had been smeared by water; rain, perhaps. But the name *Kent* in Anne's hand was unmistakable.

He tore the letter open, held it near the cook fire to read. The date was the preceding November, 1777.

In the midst of pleasantries, endearments and news of their son, Anne reported that Captain Malachi Rackham had written her *another distressingly impertinent letter, which Mrs. Brumple, who is now moved in, considered alarming in its tone of familiarity.*

Philip went white at that; read on:

> But I do not, and neither should you, my darling. I did find the occasion to speak with W. Caleb concerning his captain's behavior, and Caleb assured me he would take corrective steps. He stated that while Rackham was a most able sailor, he was known to be of erratic temperament, and had only been engaged out of necessity, and with considerable reservation on Caleb's part. Evidently Mr. Rackham's chief problem is a conviction that he is irresistible to females—which only strikes me as proof that inwardly, he fears exactly the opposite is true, and must constantly disprove the suspicion. Since I discussed Rackham prior to the arrival of the aforementioned letter, it is evident that any efforts Captain Caleb may have made to curb R. have not availed. However, Mrs. Brumple's presence surely will, in the event the unpleasant gentleman should dare present himself here again.

XI

"HENRY, I'M going home."

Overflowing the seat of the crude wooden chair provided for his officer's hut, Henry Knox stared at his visitor in puzzlement.

Philip had arrived at four in the morning, after a sleepless night. Knox had come to the door wearing a shabby robe and carrying a lantern. Now the lantern flickered on the mantel of Knox's fireplace; the officers' quarters were duplicates of those of the enlisted men, except that they were somewhat larger.

The fat artillery colonel tented his fingers. "Philip, I can plainly see that you're overwrought. But I believe I misunderstood what you said."

"You didn't. I'm leaving for Cambridge. Now, before daylight—" He stabbed a hand through his dark hair. "I had to tell someone who'd understand. The two men in my mess wouldn't. They don't know Anne. Besides, I need—"

"Wait, Philip," Knox interrupted, sounding much less sleepy. "You are telling me that you've desertion in mind?"

"Much more than in mind. I'm going. Here, I received this last night. You can see it was written in November, then sent by mistake to another man in a different unit."

Knox scanned the letter, his normally placid face still showing some confusion.

"That I see very clearly. What I do not see is what there is on this page to bring you to such a state."

Quickly then, Philip poured out the story: the investment in Caleb's privateers; the first encounter with Malachi Rackham; Anne's subsequent references to him in her letters:

"I know her, Henry. Each time, she tried to reassure me that she wasn't worried. But she'd never have brought it up if—well, let's just say I can read what's behind the words, too. She's terrified of him. One look at him and you'd understand. He's handsome. Fancies himself a prize for the ladies. But there's a nastiness about him—"

The words trailed off. Philip had the dismal feeling that he wasn't getting through.

Knox confirmed it: "You still haven't explained why you feel you must commit a very rash and dangerous act."

"Because I'm afraid something's happened to Anne! It's April and that was posted in November. I've had no other letter from her—"

"Like everything else, the mails are plagued slow—"

"Not that slow." Philip paced, feeling trapped. "Not that damned slow."

Knox frowned again, lifting the letter. "Isn't there another person sharing your house? I noticed a reference to a Mrs.—"

"Brumple. An old lady next door. She moved in with Anne last year because Annie was already afraid of Rackham then."

"And so you've decided to return to Cambridge to look into it? Just like that?"

"I have to, Henry. I'm convinced—"

"You do *not* have to," Knox cut in. "In fact, it's not permitted."

The words hit Philip like physical blows. He could barely speak:

"For Christ's sake, I know it's not permitted! I'm telling you because—"

"Because you want me to sanction what you're going to do? I can't. I am an officer in this army."

"Don't talk like someone making a speech at a parade review—!"

"Then kindly do not shout!"

Silence. Finally Philip let out a long sigh.

"All right. I'm sorry. I need traveling money, Henry. Just a little, but I didn't know who else to ask—"

"The answer is no."

"Dammit, Henry, you've got to—!"

"Philip!" This time it was Knox who shouted. "It's not pleasant for me to employ the differences in our ranks—but you forget yourself. I agree with what you say to this extent. You may have cause for concern. *May.* There is no evidence to support any stronger word. But do you think you're the only man at Valley Forge with worries at home? Some have wives and children facing outright starvation because no one can operate a family farm—a family business! Others have lost loved ones and learned of it only months later, in letters that went astray just like this one. With the spring campaign ahead, no leaves are being granted for any reason."

"I don't give a damn what you say, I'm leaving," Philip exclaimed, wheeling for the door.

Knox lunged after him, spun him around, flung him against the mantel so hard the lantern nearly toppled off:

"You will get control of yourself!"

"Goddamn it, let go! I won't listen—"

"You will! Either go back to your unit or I will have you arrested and flogged."

Aghast, Philip stared at him.

"You're my friend. You're *Anne's* friend—"

"That makes no difference. You're being driven to this by fear and fear alone. If you desert, I'll have you hunted down at once—and brought back." Abruptly, Knox's tone changed. "You have a duty here. We all do. After the winter we've endured—the deaths—the near-rebellions—my God, and the work you've put in with von Steuben—learning, teaching others— To quit now for any reason save being brought down by an enemy ball is nothing short of treason."

"Treas—?"

Philip couldn't even get the whole word out. The accusation from his long-time friend seared him like an iron—

And crumbled the facade of the almost hysterical rationalization he'd constructed in his mind to justify what he planned to do.

"Friend or not," Knox went on, "if you go, I promise you I'll report it—and see you punished."

Numb, Philip picked up the letter that had fallen to the dirt floor. He felt drained—and dismally aware that everything Henry Knox had said was right. He stumbled toward the door:

"I'm sorry I came here—"

"So am I."

Philip spun to glare.

"Because we are friends, Philip. Ordering your arrest wouldn't be easy for me. But I will do it."

Philip started out. At the sound of his name repeated, he turned again.

Knox asked, "Where are you going?"

"To—" Philip swallowed. "Back to the hut."

"Is that the truth?"

"Yes."

Knox let out a long, relieved sigh:

"Good."

Philip closed the door behind him, avoided the suspicious stare of a guard posted at the head of the officers' street, walked with slumping shoulders through

the spring dawn, repelled all at once by what he'd wanted to do until Knox's rough treatment jarred him out of it.

At the same time, he felt trapped. Trapped and frightened.

He glanced up at the paling stars.

Annie, he thought. *Annie, are you all right?*

7

Rackham

UNCONTROLLABLE ANNOYANCE edged Anne Kent's voice:

"Abraham, for the third time—eat your porridge."

"Don't want to," declared the stocky, dark-eyed boy teetering on three worn books piled on his chair. He dipped his wood spoon into the bowl. With a wrench of his small wrist, he sent a gob of porridge flying across the kitchen.

Anne jumped up from the table. "Oh, Abraham, you're such a trial some-times—!" Her hands slapped against her skirt, bringing an alarmed look to the boy's face.

At once, Anne regretted the shrill reprimand. She believed in discipline that was firm yet loving. Whenever her son misbehaved, she tried not to raise her voice, even as a prologue to one or two quick whacks of his behind. But in recent weeks she'd been losing her temper more and more frequently.

She started around the table to make amends; substitute cajolery for insistence. But Abraham had already made up his mind about what he wanted—and didn't:

"Don't want to eat. Want Papa."

"Papa can't come home. Papa's in Pennsylvania at a place called Valley Forge. I've showed you his letters. The word that spells his name and yours. Kent—"

She bent to caress the boy's dark hair. But Abraham was still upset from her sharp outcry of a few moments earlier. He pulled away:

"I want Papa. No more porge. Papa!"

The tension and weariness plaguing Anne these cold winter days of early 1778 came out again unbidden:

"Stop it, Abraham! You can't see Papa because he's not here! Now eat your breakfast or I'll give you a spanking."

She showed him her hand to illustrate. It was precisely the wrong thing to do.

Abraham Kent, going on two and a half years old, hurled his spoon to the floor. With one stubby-fingered hand, he pushed the bowl off the edge of the table. The crockery shattered, splattering the gooey paste of oats and water all over the hem of Anne's dress. She slapped his hand:

"You're a wicked little boy!"

Abraham puckered up his eyebrows, turned beet color and bawled.

"My heavens, catch the child before he falls!" exclaimed a new voice. Mrs. Eulalie Brumple, tiny and frail, darted from the doorway through beams of watery sunlight and snatched Abraham to her shoulder an instant before he tumbled to the floor.

Ashamed and upset, Anne covered her eyes, turned away.

"I don't know who's in worse temper this morning, Mrs. Brumple, Abraham or me."

She felt the start of tears, fought them with all her will as the neighbor woman rocked Abraham back and forth, ignoring his sharp pulls of her mobcap and his repeated shrieks:

"Want to see Papa. *Want to see Papa!*"

"Here, here, that's no way for a young gentleman to behave," Mrs. Brumple said as Abraham yanked the cap down over her right eye. "Let's find that drum your father bought you, shall we?"

Abraham was diverted from his sobbing, and sniffled instead:

"Drum?"

"Drum," Mrs. Brumple repeated. "You can relieve your frustration by banging away to your heart's content." She glanced at Anne. "Not here, however. In the parlor."

Anne stared in dismay as Mrs. Brumple marched Abraham to the front of the house. In a few moments the toy drum began to rattle and thump.

The erratic rhythm grated on Anne's nerves. *But what doesn't these days?* she thought as she hung the tea kettle up to boil.

The kitchen in Cambridge was chilly this February morning. Anne had risen early, unable to sleep—again. She'd started another letter to Philip, determined to keep the contents cheerful, free of any indication of the growing strain she felt in his absence.

She'd written exactly one paragraph, describing how Cambridge's population had increased now that a huge number of Gentleman Johnny Burgoyne's redcoats and Hessians had been marched east after Saratoga. The enemy troops were locked up in compounds, pledged not to fight during the remainder of the war because Burgoyne had agreed to that as part of the terms of his surrender. Anne had broken off the letter in the middle of a sentence speculating about whether English transports would ever arrive to take the soldiers away, and then she'd simply sat staring into space, her body aching with an all-too-familiar tension.

As Abraham's drumming continued, Mrs. Eulalie Brumple marched back into the kitchen. The small-boned sixty-year-old lady with the hawk's eye and the firmly set mouth never walked anywhere, only marched.

But her presence in the spare bedroom was a comfort to Anne. Prickly as the widow Brumple might be, once she had moved a few belongings from her home next door, Anne had felt much less alarmed about the occasional, all-too-obvious overtures from Captain Rackham. Happily, she hadn't been bothered by the man since the autumn. She assumed it was because Rackham had finally put to sea in search of prizes.

Anne busied herself pouring tea for the two of them. She recognized the expression on the older woman's face and braced for another lecture.

"Mrs. Kent?"

"Yes, Mrs. Brumple?" Neither woman had yet breached the formality of using last names.

"I certainly hope you won't take offense if I mention another condition which I believe needs rectifying." Mrs. Brumple always preceded one of her declarations with some such empty apology.

"Won't you have some tea before it gets cold?" Anne asked, hoping to forestall the impending remarks on—what this time? Child guidance, she guessed. She was correct:

"In a moment. First I must speak my mind."

Dark circles showed beneath Anne's eyes. She sighed, sank down in a chair. "Go ahead."

"I'm not criticizing, I'm only trying to be helpful—"

"Yes, yes, I know. Go on." Anne had heard the preamble dozens of times.

"In my opinion it's a shame you can't in some wise show that dear young child his father's likeness."

"I don't have any pictures of my husband!" Anne exclaimed, almost to the point of tears. "We're not the sort of family that can afford to commission painters of miniatures!"

Mrs. Brumple considered that, then observed primly, "Perhaps it would have served you better to hire a third-rate artist—keeping him at the proper distance. of course; artists are all immoral rascals; I was once unwholesomely propositioned by such a person—than to have put so much money in two pirate ships which have yet to pay you a penny."

"They're not pirates, they're authorized privateersmen."

"Makes no difference, they've repaid not one cent of your investment."

Anne said nothing. Mrs. Brumple's statement was correct. Caleb's small fleet of prize-hunters, all of them reportedly in southern waters, had captured not a single enemy vessel. She was beginning to regret her decision to invest two hundred pounds in the construction of *Gull* and *Fidelity*. And not just because of the character of Captain Caleb's associate, who had relinquished command of *Nancy* and become the skipper of *Gull*. Caleb himself was sailing the other new privateer.

Mrs. Brumple went on, "A child does need to become familiar with his own father's face. What a pity your husband is not as vain as Brumple—"

The little widow always referred to her late spouse by his last name only. Brumple had evidently been a tailor who had achieved only modest success. Anne knew far more about his faults than his virtues, which were apparently almost non-existent.

"—Brumple was always presenting me with this or that little charcoal sketch of his likeness. He fancied himself handsome. The more fool he! May I have some more tea, dear?"

Anne poured the smuggled Dutch brew, not knowing whether to laugh at the little woman's pretensions or burst out sobbing in hopeless frustration.

"Naturally I would have welcomed all those portraits of Brumple if we'd had babies," the widow said. "But after the first several years of our marriage—years in which I reluctantly permitted Brumple to indulge in his constant pecking at my cheek and pawing at my smallclothes—that sort of thing always led to the inevitable conclusion which I only suffered as part of my female duty—where was I? Oh yes. I was speaking of how it became evident that Brumple and I were not going to leave heirs in this world. Believe me, after that I saw to it that he left my smallclothes alone! However—" She sipped tea. "My original contention remains valid. Little pictures of a faraway loved one can be valuable in helping a child remember the loved one."

Mrs. Brumple fixed Anne with a direct stare. "Is it possible you could sketch such a likeness of Mr. Kent?"

Anne shook her head. "I'm hard put to draw a straight line."

"Pity." Mrs. Brumple finished her tea.

A crash from the parlor brought Anne half out of her chair. The widow too:

"Oh dear, the boy's upset something. No, you let me see to it, you're much too tired to deal with him properly." She marched from the kitchen at quick step.

Anne felt resentful. But the reaction passed quickly. In her peculiar, flinty way, Mrs. Eulalie Brumple liked her neighbor—and loved Abraham. Anne, too, was basically fond of the old busybody. She knew that the widow's last charge was not maliciously spoken—and was entirely correct. She *was* worn out—

Worn out from coping with Abraham without the help of a father's masculine hand and voice. Worn out from lying alone too many nights, shivering despite the footwarmer she religiously took under the covers. Worn out worrying about whether two hundred pounds loaned to Caleb were gone forever. Worn out fretting about Rackham, whose name kept slipping into the letters she wrote Philip, despite her best intentions that it shouldn't. Worn out with the war that seemed to bring nothing but minor victories and major defeats for the American armies. Worn out with thoughts of Philip meeting his death on the point of a British bayonet. Worn out imagining how she would survive if he never came home, never held her again, never kissed her and made love to her—

Worn out. Beyond her capacity to endure it any longer—

She wasn't even aware that she'd pressed her palms to her eyes and started crying there in the pale February sunlight. She sat bolt upright at the touch of a hand:

"Mrs. Kent—let me tuck you in for a rest."

As it could on occasion, Mrs. Eulalie Brumple's face had softened. Her fundamental kindness was showing through the hard Congregationalist facade.

"Did you sleep at all last night?" she asked softly.

"Very little."

"Then come along."

"I'm sorry my tongue's been so sharp, Mrs. Brumple. I don't mean to be so curt with the boy, or you—"

"Now, now, let's have no apologies. I'll bundle Abraham up and we'll walk to the market. Come, my dear, stand up—"

Anne did. She was soon in bed, listening to the stillness of the house. A patch of melting snow slid off the roof shakes, a loud scraping. She was literally aching with exhaustion and the hunger for Philip's presence.

But no matter how she tried, she still couldn't sleep.

II

IT SEEMED an eternity since Anne had found anything the least amusing about the war. But here it was at last, reported at some length in a month-old copy of Ben Edes' *Gazette*.

The wet, gusty April night seemed momentarily remote. Curled up in a chair by the cozy fire, Anne laughed out loud, causing Mrs. Brumple to glance up from the scarf she was knitting for Abraham.

"Mrs. Kent, I certainly hesitate to criticize, but I believe Abraham is finally asleep—"

Giggling. Anne covered her mouth a moment. "I was being too noisy, wasn't I? But this is just delightful. Some chap from Connecticut—let's see—" She checked the paper. "David Bushnell's his name. In February he launched a whole flotilla of what they call infernals."

"What is an infernal, pray? Another name for a husband?"

"No, Mrs. Brumple! A keg of powder with a contact fuse. Bushnell set them afloat in the Delaware River above Philadelphia. His idea was to blow up the British ships anchored in mid-river. But because of floating ice, all the frigates were moored close to shore. The paper says the British were absolutely terrified of the kegs, though. The soldiers peppered away at them with muskets, trying to explode them."

Mrs. Brumple rested her knitting in her lap, her expression saying clearly that she thus far failed to find anything hilarious in the story. Anne went on:

"The part that amused me is the song composed by a Mr. Hopkinson from the Congress. It's called *The Battle of the Kegs*. Here, listen—"

"Brumple was always fond of light verse. It did little to improve his already frivolous mind."

But Anne couldn't be deterred:

"Sir William Howe and that doxy of his are sleeping when some of the kegs start exploding, you see. Hopkinson says—

> *"Sir William, he, snug as a flea*
> *"Lay all this while a-snoring.*
> *"Nor dreamed of harm as he lay warm*
> *"In bed with—"*

Anne's finger ticked against the page, her wan face merry:

"Ben Edes left two blanks right there, but I can imagine our soldiers hooting out the missing words. 'Mrs. Loring.' Here's the rest—

> *"Now in a fright, he starts upright,*
> *"Awaked by such a clatter.*
> *"He rubs his eyes, and boldly cries*
> *"For God's sake, what's the mat—?"* "

A knocking in the hallway interrupted Anne, and diverted Mrs. Brumple from whatever remark of disapproval she was about to make.

Being closest to the front door, Mrs. Brumple went to answer. Anne returned to the verse, laughing as she hadn't in weeks. The doggerel truly wasn't all that excellent, but she'd gone too long without finding anything to lighten her spirits. She barely heard Mrs. Brumple speaking sharply, and a man's voice replying. The exchange lasted less than a minute. Then the front door slammed.

Mrs. Brumple marched back to the fringe of the firelight:

"Well, I certainly didn't like that person's looks."

Anne glanced up. "Who was it?"

"Some sort of seaman. Terribly scruffy. He was inquiring for the Russell house."

"There's no family named Russell living in this neighborhood."

"I'm well aware of that. I think it was a subterfuge. I didn't care for the man's cut one bit, I tell you. Shifty eyes. Just like Brumple's."

Even though she realized Mrs. Brumple's concern was probably unfounded, Anne was troubled. She laid the paper aside, her earlier mood gone. For no reason she could adequately explain, the word *seaman* brought Malachi Rackham instantly to mind.

Before she went to bed she scanned the rainy street for a sign of anyone

suspicious. She saw no one. But she made doubly certain that the front and rear doors were bolted and all the windows latched before looking in on Abraham to see that he was adequately covered.

III

Two EVENINGS later, with the late April rain still pelting Cambridge, Mrs. Brumple collected her cloak, gloves and parasol to pit her Christian courage against the elements:

"You're certain you don't mind me leaving you this evening, Mrs. Kent?"

Anne smiled. "You're the one who's going to get soaked, not I."

"In the Lord's word—and General Washington's. Our prayer circle has reorganized. Not only to read scripture but to sew hunting shirts at the same time. We shall be convening every Wednesday evening from now on. I should certainly be home in an hour or two—"

"I'll be up, don't worry."

"I attend religious functions with a clearer conscience than I did when I was married," the little lady said as she tugged on her gloves. "Brumple sat in the pew with me every Sunday because he felt it was good for trade. Underneath, I always suspected him of being a freethinker. Good evening," she concluded, marching out the front door.

Despite the coming of spring, the house still felt a trifle cold. Anne kindled a small fire in the parlor, then sat down to her mending. She worked for nearly an hour, until her concentration was broken by sounds from Abraham's bedroom.

She put the mending aside, hurried to the back of the house. The boy was breathing loudly. As she watched at the bedside, he shifted position several times.

She felt his forehead. No fever. Perhaps he'd been thrashing because of bad dreams—

A loud, hollow clatter startled her. It echoed from the front of the house. She frowned. Who could be calling at this hour—?

Apprehensive, she hurried to the parlor, then to the bay of windows. She lifted a curtain. Outside, barely visible in the rain, a closed carriage sat at the curb. The horse was tied to the hitch post. She saw no sign of a driver.

Anne's palms turned cold. The logs on the hearth cast slow-changing shadows over the walls. She felt a peculiar, nervous fluttering inside her breast. Perhaps whoever it was would go—

More knocking. Louder.

"I say, Mrs. Kent, are you at home?"

"Oh my God," she breathed, recognizing the voice.

Terrified, she dashed for the front hallway. *She hadn't latched the door after Mrs. Brumple left—*

Three steps from the door, she stopped—too late. The door opened inward, spattering her with rain.

Like some hobgoblin, the tall man slipped inside. His tightly curled dark hair glistened. The hem of his cloak dripped. His right eye, so strangely drawn into a slit by the small scar, caught firelight from the parlor and glowed like a coal.

"Pardon me for just walking in, but I thought it possible you didn't hear the knock," said Captain Malachi Rackham.

IV

ANNE WENT numb as Rackham stared at her, that nasty, cocksure smile seemingly fixed in place. He swayed a little. She smelled rum on him—

A dreadful suspicion leaped into her mind. The man the other evening—the seaman—had he been sent to see whether she was alone? *Had Rackham been keeping watch—?*

No, no, that was too fanciful by half—

Or was it?

She tried to compose her features. But the fluttering sensation persisted. In a second, she became certain that her initial guess was correct. Rackham had waited to call until his man reported Mrs. Brumple's departure.

"See here, I didn't mean to shock you to total silence?" Rackham declared, pulling a face. "I stopped off because I thought you might welcome a report concerning your investment in *Gull.*"

He glanced beyond her to the empty parlor. "Are you at liberty to discuss it?"

"I—" God, why was her throat so dry? "I've been working in the kitchen. I've a cauldron of soup cooking—"

Rackham wrinkled his nose. "Odd. I don't smell it."

"I was about to put it on the fire when you arrived."

"Then you are at liberty for a few moments—"

He accidentally brushed her elbow as he slipped past into the parlor.

Rackham unfastened his cloak and dropped it over a chair. He swung to face her, one knee bent and his boot planted out in front of him. The pose of a man aping his betters. His clothing reinforced the impression. He wore dove gray breeches, an ostentatious coat of yellow velour, too much lace at collar and cuffs—

He flexed his hands behind him, warming them near the fire. "Come, come, Mrs. Kent! You can at least be hospitable to a man of whom you've spoken ill."

"Captain Rackham—" Anne struggled to keep her voice level. "—it should be evident many times over that you're not welcome here."

He shrugged, surveying the closed curtains at the bay of front windows. "That may be. But you'll have to put up with me for a bit, my girl, because you owe me a kindness."

"What do you mean, a kindness? I owe you nothing!"

Under the drooping right lid, the pupil of Rackham's eye seemed to burn. "But you do. I did not appreciate your speaking to Will Caleb about my letters and my visits."

"Oh? I'm so sorry. Be assured I'll speak to him again, Captain." She started for the hall. "You will please leave."

"In due course."

Still smiling, Rackham sat down and crossed his legs.

More frightened than ever, Anne stood in the hall, not knowing what to do. She realized Abraham had been wakened by the voices. His faint cry sounded from the darkness at the back of the house:

"Mama?"

"Go to sleep, Abraham," she called. "It's all right, I'm here."

There was a fretful murmur from his bedroom, then silence.

Slowly Anne looked back at the man lounging near the hearth. Rackham was studying her figure that her dress showed to advantage despite its shabbiness. He made no attempt to conceal his interest.

She glanced at the French sword hanging above the mantel. Could she pull it down fast enough, if necessary? The Kentucky rifle beneath the sword was empty; useless, except perhaps as a club—

Determined not to let her fear get the best of her, Anne folded her arms across her breasts, addressed Rackham sharply:

"Was it you who sent someone to the door two nights ago? A man pretending to be hunting a family named Russell?"

"Aye, I used a lad from *Gull* for that duty. Same one who watched the place tonight, then drove me out here in the coach."

"So you have been spying—!"

"Call it what you wish. We have private matters to discuss. I didn't want anyone else's company but yours, my dear."

Once more he showed his teeth in what he presumed was a charming smile. To Anne it resembled the grimace of a fanged animal. Rackham went on:

"*Gull* anchored in Boston harbor last Sunday morning. We took a mighty handsome prize off the Carolinas. As I remarked when I came in, I thought you'd be interested in that." He feigned readiness to rise and leave. "However, if you insist you're not—"

Despite her fear, Anne said, "A British prize?"

"Correct. With some sharp sailing and gun work on our part, she hauled down her colors mighty fast. The total proceeds of the auction come—ah, came to about half a million sterling pounds." He paused. "Care to hear more?"

The sum stunned her; left her confused and uncertain about how to proceed.

She had an overpowering urge to dash from the house; Malachi Rackham would never have spied on her, nor come all the way to Cambridge in the rain, out of sheer concern for the Kent investment. That was doubly obvious from the way he continued to glance at her breasts, the line of her hip, like a man anticipating a sumptuous dinner—

Yet if he wasn't lying to her—if *Gull* had indeed captured a merchantman— the prospects were dizzying, and she ought to know the whole story.

Rackham tried to resolve her quandry:

"Fetch me a port—or a rum if you have it—and I'll be happy to share the details."

"I'm sorry, I've nothing to give you."

"Ah, Mrs. Kent, that's where you are quite wrong." His smile left no doubt about his meaning.

"Get out," Anne said, livid. "At once."

"Belay that, if you please," Rackham chuckled. "I'm not your husband, after all. In fact I assume your husband is still far away—? Serving his country honorably while his wife remains unconsolable because her bed's empty—?"

"Get *out*!" Anne exploded, raising a clenched fist.

Rackham's veneer of sham politeness crumbled. He reached her in two swift strides, jerked her upraised hand down, leaned close until she nearly choked from the stench of rum:

"You listen here, Mrs. Kent. That very first day we met, I tabbed you for what you are—a lass who fancies herself stronger than any man she'll ever meet. And shows it. Well, permit me to tell you something. Captain Rackman is a fellow who doesn't hold with being put down in such fashion. I don't like being put down with haughty looks or nasty no-thank-you's at the doorstep. Still —I'll admit that's part of your charm—the fact you think I'm a nobody and don't bother to hide it. I expect that's the reason I made up my mind that morning on Hancock's Wharf that I'd take you—with your agreement or without."

"*Take—?*"

"Here, here, no silly prudery." The cocksure smile somehow acquired a malevolent twist. "I've been sporting a good twenty years with the gentle sex. Never had one of 'em turn me down. Till you."

"You drunken popinjay liar—!"

He grabbed her wrist again. "You watch your language, woman—"

Anne raked his face with her free hand, her nails leaving bleeding scratches. Rackham struck her.

She staggered, crying out. Her mind held one dreadful word—

Madman.

She didn't know what warped memories or conceits made him what he was. But she knew that every rebuff she'd given him must have festered weeks, months in the mazes of his head. She knew he was drunk, and dangerous—

"Mama?"

Abraham was calling again, frightened by her outcry. Anne struggled to her feet. But somehow, she couldn't avoid Rackham's hands. Big hands; hairmatted; sliding under her arms—

Rackham's thumbs pressed the fabric over her breasts. "Even in a temper, you're a soft, dear sight, Mrs. Kent. I can't properly explain it, but I've never fancied a woman as much as I fancy you. Perhaps it's because I'm not supposed to, eh?"

"Damn your eyes—*let me go!*"

That only provoked more laughter:

"Ah, stop, Mrs. Kent. You must want a man so bad you hurt from it. That little fellow you're wed to—he can't be much in the cock department, now admit—"

Writhing away from him, she spat in his face.

Again Rackham struck her. She tumbled at his feet, stunned. Abraham started to cry loudly. Rackham leaned down, his shadow distorting across the wall as he jerked her head up by a fist in her hair:

"I want to tell you about your property, Mrs. Kent. Your investment—a man who wants to do that should be treated right, eh? *Eh?*"

He yanked her hair. She uttered another hoarse yelp. Rackham laughed:

"Yes indeed, I want to invite you aboard *Gull* for a pleasant and diverting evening. As I say—you owe me. You got me roasted by that sanctimonious old bastard Caleb. But I'll forgive you—if you'll visit the ship and be nice and agreeable when we get there—"

Anne screamed deliberately, hoping to attract someone's attention outside. Abraham's terrified cries sounded as stridently as her own.

"Be quiet!" Rackman shouted, letting go of her hair and smashing the side of her head with his fist.

She lurched sideways, reaching clumsily toward the mantel; toward Philip's gleaming sword—

Rackham hit her harder. She fell, struck her temple on the floor, moaned, opened and closed one stretched out hand, then lay still.

V

ANNE AWOKE briefly to the sensation of motion.

She heard carriage wheels and springs creaking. The clop and splash of hoofs along a rutted road. Rain pattering overhead—

Through a slot window she glimpsed a distant farmstead, a yellow smear of lamplight in the rain. She realized she was leaning against the curve of a man's left shoulder.

She struggled away, only to have a sweaty-smelling hand clamp over her mouth.

The places where Rackham had hit her and the other place where she'd struck her head all hurt terribly. Rackham inclined his head to slobber a kiss on her face. She tried to wrench the other way.

That made him burst out with his damnable laugh—and hold her more tightly.

His left hand still covered her mouth. She bit at the fingers. He jerked them away, freeing his arm so he could squeeze her throat in the vee of his elbow, cutting off her wind:

"Screaming's useless, my girl. I told you it's one of my lads up on the box of this hired rig. Even at the dock in Boston, the sight of Malachi Rackham knocking some wench about to get her into a dinghy and out to his ship ain't—isn't likely to cause any commotion. The tavern trulls, they sometimes say yes, then start a squall on the pier, wanting a higher price. I've often been seen roughing 'em up a wee bit. So you won't get any help by yelling or—*bitch!*" he howled as she bit hard into the fleshy back of his hand.

He flung her to the floor of the rocking carriage, kicked her twice in the ribs, bashed her eye with his knuckles, bringing new, nauseous darkness swirling over her.

VI

A PINPOINT of light; dull orange.

And motion again. But of a different order this time. Gentler—

She recognized sounds. The lap of water against hull planks. The creak of a ship's upper and lower capstans being turned in tandem. Chain being pulled up by the messenger cables—

Anchor chain?

Anne Kent opened her eyes; saw her skirt and petticoat hiked around her knees. She was lying in a ship's bunk.

She shifted her throbbing head to the left, saw Malachi Rackham—and a cabin where a single glass-paneled lantern swayed overhead on a beam hook. The two large oval stern windows showed a spatter of lamp-gilded raindrops.

Rackham lounged in a chair beside an oak table. Both chair and table were bolted to the decking. Rackham lolled a drinking cup back and forth in one hand

as he watched Anne with an amused expression. His showy coat and breeches hung on a peg near his wall-mounted drop-front desk. He wore drawers of soiled gray linen, nothing else.

"Hallo, Mrs. Kent," he said, scratching the curled hair on his chest. It was as dark as that on his head. "Wondered how long it'd take you to liven up. Been an hour since I brought you aboard."

He held out the cup. "Little rum?"

"The—" She was so dazed, she could barely speak. "The ship's under way—"

"Oh, not quite as yet. But getting there, getting there. My pilot'll take us through the island channels as soon as the tide's fair. We may meet some foul weather, but I decided to risk it. I thought it'd be advisable not to tell Captain Caleb how we disposed of the prize we took with *Gull*. Caleb and me—I—we're only temporary bedfellows. As he'll find out shortly after he sails *Fidelity* back to Boston. The British prize I mentioned did bring a handsome sum at the sell-off. But not in American waters, I'm sorry to say."

Rackham feigned sorrow. "We encountered unfavorable winds, don't you see. Had to beat south to Saint Eustatius in the Leewards. Only safe harbor available—"

He was amused at his own reporting of the lie. He clucked his tongue:

"Yes, truly unfortunate. But the Dutchmen were accommodating, damned accommodating. We had the trial—the auction—the only problem being, as Caleb explained, that under the terms of our Articles, a prize disposed of in a foreign port means all the proceeds go to captain and crew. The owners, God pity 'em, miss out. We've already divided the share belonging to you and your husband. Understand now why I've such a loyal bunch of lads? They'll help me abduct a lady anytime."

Grinning, Rackham slopped down more rum.

Anne had to struggle to form a coherent sentence:

"You—you cheated Caleb—"

"Oh, no, Mrs. Kent! We couldn't help what happened. Unfavorable winds!"

"Liar. You—you planned something like that—all along—"

Rackham shrugged. "Well—it's possible. But it's done. Now there's an even more profitable prospect ahead. We'll be setting a coasting course for New York."

"The—British—the British hold—"

"New York? Indeed they do. Why do you think I'm heading there? The privateersmen are taking a lot of prizes, you see. I'm sure I can find a buyer for a spanking new beauty like *Gull*. A little work and she'll serve nicely as a transport to replace one of the captured ones. I wager plenty of Tory merchants in New York'll be glad to bid on her."

"The ship isn't yours to sell!" Anne cried hoarsely.

"Why, who's here to dispute my right—except you? And we've other matters to attend to, yes we do—"

Still grinning, he ran a hand down between his thighs and squeezed his crotch.

Anne felt gagging sourness in her mouth; felt an urge to scream and keep screaming and overcame it only with maximum effort.

"Right here—" Rackham was still fingering his groin. "—right here I've the machinery to keep your thoughts diverted to subjects more pleasant than ships and who owns 'em. Soon as I strike a good bargain for *Gull*, we'll have a grand holiday together in New York town. Live elegantly, I'll guarantee it."

"You—you'd sell out Caleb when he hired and trusted you—?"

Rackham's face wrenched. "Caleb's a fool who thinks as ill of me as you do. We only did business with each other out of necessity. Captains—good captains—they're mighty scarce. I was down on my luck, so I took the first arrangement offered. But every time that bastard looked down his nose at me, I remembered. Every time he ordered me this way or every which, I remembered—"

Slowly, like a muscular animal rousing from its den, Rackham laid the drinking cup aside. He stood up, unfastened the tie-knot of his drawers and let them fall.

"Just like I remembered every time you gave me the cool stare or the turndown. Aye—"

Rackham started for the bunk, his immense engorged maleness swaying on a level with Anne's eyes.

"—we'll have a fine and lively time in New York. We will provided you learn one lesson. I mean who is giving orders and who is taking 'em—"

"Traitor."

"You be quiet, you bitch."

"A traitor to the country that—"

Rackham chuckled, terrifying her to silence.

"Ah, you're a delicious one, Mrs. Kent. And why should I be at all angry with you? You've already called me more names than I can remember. Sure you have! It'll take me a month to punish you for each—"

He moved a step closer.

"A dollop of punishment, a dollop of pleasure—all at the same time, what d'you say—?"

He reached down, crooked his hand around his own reddened flesh. From beside the bunk, he crooned to her:

"Come on, now. Come on. Be good. *Give us a kiss—*"

This time Anne Kent screamed the wild wail of hysteria. But Rackham only laughed as he climbed on top of her.

VII

SHE AWOKE in the fouled bunk sometime near dawn.

She had never hurt so terribly in all her life. Not even at the height of her labor when she bore Abraham. She felt almost destroyed by the repeated punishings Rackham had inflicted on her all night long, beating her and forcing her legs apart each time, tearing and plunging in her until the pain became so intense that it turned to a perverted blessing; a sort of drug to deaden some of the anguish.

Disconnected thoughts flickered through Anne's mind as she tried to climb from the bunk, fell when *Gull* rolled sharply. She groped for the captain's table. It took her almost two minutes to pull herself to her feet.

Through the oval stern windows she saw the steepsided hills and valleys of the ocean.

And no land anywhere.

She brushed hair from one eye, leaned on the table, stared down at the blood

that had dried along the inside of her left thigh. On her breasts three vivid blue-yellow bruises showed.

She grew aware of intermittent sounds. The rush of water against the hull; the stamp of sailors feet overhead; a muffled yell—

In a weak voice she repeated her husband's name. Her child's. Her husband's again, as if the litany would somehow rescue her; waken her from this unbelievable nightmare of captivity and pain—

She hammered on the door. Tugged. Wrenched—

Bolted. On the outside.

She opened one of the oval windows, smelled the salt tang and watched the wake foaming white. *Gull* was running through a moderately heavy sea.

After staring at the water for a moment or so in a forlorn way, she latched the window, slipping and falling once more as she negotiated her way back to the table. She sank into the bolted-down chair, on the brink of another fit of uncontrollable weeping. She hurt; she hurt so terribly—

Then, out of her pain emerged a different sort of emotion.

Rage.

Rage at the vile way in which she'd been used.

Rage—and a determination not to surrender to despair while one breath was left.

All right, she said to herself. Think, now. Hard as it is, if you want to see Philip again—see Abraham again, ever—*think!*—

Rackham would return to the cabin eventually. But how could she get *out* of the cabin?

Only by eluding him. Disabling him, even.

If she managed to gain the deck, she might—*might* be able to convince a few of the crew to side with her; possibly put back to Boston. Rackham's boasts about the loyalty of his men might not apply to every single one—

A slim, almost impossible chance.

But what else was there?

She began to turn her head slowly, searching for a weapon; any weapon to hold Rackham at bay—

All at once she realized that she'd failed to see the one serious flaw in the scheme. Rackham would never allow her on deck more than a moment if he could follow her. *If he*—

Hair hanging down into her eyes, Anne Kent shivered. She wiped her mouth. She literally forced the completion of the thought:

If he were alive.

Remembering something, she raised her head. She stared at the lantern swaying from the beam hook. The lantern was paned with pebbled glass.

Rackham would notice a broken stern window instantly. But he might not notice a broken lantern pane—

Whimpering a little because the effort hurt so much, she knelt on the table. Groped upward—

The pitch of *Gull* nearly toppled her off. She managed to seize the lantern, twist it slightly. She bit down on her lower lip and struck her knuckles against the pebbled pane on the side away from the door.

She inhaled sharply. Someone was coming along the companionway!

She started to scramble off the table. The footsteps came closer—

Then passed by, and faded.

Panting, she waited a few moments. Then she hit the pane again.

And once more, harder—

Soon after, she lay in the bunk, her naked back to the door, her body curled not only to feign sleep but to hide her left hand that held the shard of glass. Her right hand bled steadily onto the stained bedclothing.

She lay as still as possible, thinking of Philip's face, and Abraham's. She tried not to dwell on how much she hurt. Or on how the pain might slow her; ruin her sole chance—

She lay with her eyes closed and her heart beating in a fast, irregular way and her ears straining for a sound of Rackham returning.

VIII

THE BOLT rattled. Anne tensed.

Her right hand hurt horribly. She'd gashed it breaking the glass and carrying the shards to Rackham's desk, closing its drop front to conceal all but the piece she gripped in her left hand.

She heard hard breathing as the door opened. Heard Rackham's heavy tread.

"Having a spot of rest, my girl?"

Philip, she thought, *pray for me. I've just one chance at him—*

"Come along, wake up, let's see how you came through the evening—"

Rackham's hand closed on her left shoulder, pulling her over. He groped past her forearm to pluck at a nipple—

And went white as Anne shot out her left hand with all her remaining strength, tearing the sharp edge of the glass across his face once, twice—

"Goddamn you for a deceiving whore!" he screamed, knees buckling. He slapped hands over his face. The glass had pierced his left eyeball.

Pink fluid leaked between Rackham's fingers. His slitted right eye began to quiver in involuntary spasm.

Anne started to crawl from the bunk. Rackham was teetering back and forth, cursing and pushing at his ruined eyesocket as if he could somehow stop the leak and bleeding. She ducked as he flailed at her with one arm. She dodged by him, ran—

She almost made it to the unbolted door. The deck tilted sharply. She lurched backwards against Rackham.

The lower half of his face was drenched red. His lips spewed unintelligible words. He grappled her around the waist, his spittle and blood running down her arm, her breasts, her belly—

Making wheezy sounds, Rackham hauled her around the table. Shreds of tissue hung from the hole in the left side of his face. His pulled-down right eye glared with beast's pain as he lifted Anne bodily, started to hurl her away from him toward the stern—

She dug fingers into his face, felt one slip into the pulpy socket. *Gull's* bow rose, coming out of the trough of a wave. Rackham's thrust carried him along, stumbling, screaming as Anne kept her clawing hold on his face.

Too late, Rackham tried to release her. They fell together, against the glass of an oval window that burst outward at the impact.

She let go then, both of them plunging toward the boiling white of the wake.

She heard Rackham's dreadful shriek of fear but had no time for fear; no time for anything save a last strident cry of the soul;

Philip, I love—

The water smashed her and took her down.

BOOK THREE

DEATH AND RESURRECTION

1
The Wolves

A CLOCK ticked in his mind. Ticked ceaselessly, hurrying him another mile, then another.

The clock drove him on when his exhausted body almost refused. It woke him early every day, false dawn or sooner, the time when the spring air was piercingly cool and cardinals were just beginning to swoop through the waving meadowgrass. A mouthful of dried corn from the haversack—a twists or two of jerked beef bitten off and washed down with canteen water taken from a bubbling creek—then he was off again, mounted on the big bay he'd purchased at the Will's Creek trading station.

He'd chosen the horse for stamina rather than speed. But as the days warmed, speed became his paramount concern. He began to push the horse harder than he should.

In small valleys between the ranges of mountains, he'd sometimes stop of an evening with settlers—one family, or several living in close-clustered cabins. He'd luxuriate in the comfort of a slab-wood chair beside a smoky hearth constructed of mud-plastered sticks.

And always, he'd ask the people a variation of the same question:

"Do you know the day of the month? I reckon it to be about the fourteenth, but I had a fever for three days after I crossed Savage Mountain and may have lost track somewhat—"

"It's the sixteenth."

And the clock ticked louder, a tormenting rhythm reminding him that it might already be too late. He'd be up and gone from the settlement before sunrise, ignoring the healed wound in his left side that still ached when the air was cold.

The first week or two, traveling across the Blue Ridge that turned all smoky

indigo in the twilight hours, then up through the meadows along the meandering Shenandoah, he'd wondered if the prophecies put to him before his departure had not been wholly correct. Maybe he *was* a madman to set out alone.

True, he was well enough equipped. And he faced little risk of Indian attack this far south. Most of the fury of the British-incited Six Nations was focused miles to the north, across the tier of tribal towns from the valley of the Genesee to the valley of the Mohawk in York State.

Yet there were many other ways for a lone man to perish in the wilderness.

And he was inexperienced; possessed no forest skills as such, only his rifle and a compass and a couple of sparsely detailed maps.

But he had an almost demonic will be succeed. To follow and find the man who had warily put trust in him; the man who now surely felt that trust betrayed. He kept going when rainstorms drenched him; stopped only when the fever and flux made his head spin and his bowels run until he was so weak he felt he could never stand up again.

But somehow he did, listening to the great clock buried in his mind; the clock ticking and ticking the hours and days like whip-strokes being laid on.

He followed the trails that wound up the dark, forested grade of Little Allegheny Mountain, then Savage Mountain where the fever felled him a second time and he lost another three days, too feeble to do more than lift corn kernels to his mouth.

At last he reached Allegheny Mountain, in the highest range. The wooded peaks looked almost black against the April sky. Bobolinks wheeled over him and hares jumped in the brush as he climbed the slope on horseback, sitting quite tall on the bay, the Kentucky rifle held one-handed across his thighs. He was never more than a foot or two from the rifle, even in the pleasant green valleys of cabins and small tilled fields.

As the clock beat, something burned out of him. An older self became a stranger.

After weeks on the trail, his deerhide trousers and shirt felt not stiff but supple; a second skin. His flesh took on a darker tone, changing from the dead white of the winter sickbed through the burned red of the first days of exposure to the sun and wind and beating rains. When April came to an end, his cheeks had a mahogany shine. Not a single extra ounce of flesh remained on his body. Strangely, the new gauntness didn't give him an unhealthy appearance, but the opposite.

On the downslope of Chestnut Ridge, beyond the Great Meadows where General Washington had once built a fort to withstand a siege by the French, the bay horse broke its leg stepping in a burrow. He shot the animal and left it in a grove of shimmering mountain laurel and went ahead on foot, along a trail that should bring him to the junction of the two rivers—the Monongahela flowing up from the south, the Allegheny rushing down from the north—

If his compass and maps were correct.

But it had to be May already. The breathtaking beauty of the mountains and the intervening green valleys no longer exhilarated him. The clock in his mind beat louder—

George Clark had said he would depart from the forks in mid-April or early May.

He was proud of having come this far alone. Proud of surviving on sheer persistence, with not one drink of liquor since he'd left the tidewater. Those times when he'd sickened and lay shivering in the night woods astir with unfa-

miliar, unseen creatures, he'd wanted a taste of alcohol so badly his throat burned.

But he had gotten through without it. He'd summoned up resources in himself long unused. There was deep satisfaction in finding them still present, ready to lend him the stamina and stubbornness he needed for the trek.

Yet even that pride was fading as he plodded on foot, fearing—knowing— he'd be too late.

The weather changed from spring sunshine to cool, windy gray as he followed gullies where black coal-veins showed along the eroded walls. He slept less and less every night, tossing by the small fire he always built with his chip of flint and his little steel bar and the supply of tinder shavings kept carefully dry in his haversack along with his powder and ball. Dozing, knowing he must rest but wishing he didn't need to. He'd hear a howling off in the trees, and occasionally see a glittering animal eye reflect the firelight. The wolves smelled him. They came to prowl close by. But the blaze kept them at a distance.

As he came out of the woods one gray morning, a farmer's wife guiding a plow on a poor, cleared patch of land reached for her musket lying a few feet away. She watched him warily as he approached.

He touched the floppy brim of his old loaf-crowned hat—a gift from a family for whom he'd chopped some wood in return for dinner at the start of his trail in Maryland. He tried to smile in a cordial way:

"Morning, ma'am. My name is Fletcher. I'm headed for the fort at the forks. Can you tell me how far that is?"

The lean, weary-looking woman, thirty or so but already minus most of her teeth, leaned on the plow handles while the dray horse clopped a hoof impatiently. He saw one of the woman's palms, ugly and moist with old and new blisters.

"At least thirty miles, give or take a few," she said. "Where you from?"

"Virginia."

"You bound to the forks alone?"

"That's right. I'd hoped to arrive by the first of May."

"You're two weeks late."

He touched his hat brim again. "Then I'd best not delay. Thank you—"

"You—"

He turned around at the sound of her voice.

"—you wouldn't want to stay a while? I could use help with the planting."

"I'm sorry. I can't."

"All right."

He started on along the fresh-turned furrows, hearing a faint rumble in the gray sky to the west. The woman wiped her forehead with her forearm, pointed toward the ramshackle cabin surrounded by stumps at the edge of the field:

"There's a spring out behind if you want to fill that canteen."

"Thanks very much, I will."

He said it quickly, his tone matching the impatience he felt. The clock in his head beat its warning. *He'll be gone—*

HE'LL BE GONE

As he bent to hold the mouth of his canteen under the stream spilling from the rock ledge behind the cabin, he wished suddenly that the earth could pour forth more than water. The old craving hit him, thickening his tongue.

Near the spring, an upright slab of wood bore a man's name carved out with the point of a knife. Evidently the father of the two small girls he heard chattering

and giggling in the cabin. Perhaps he should stop; help the woman in return for a few meals and a few nights of rest. Then turn around and go back east. He felt too incredibly tired to travel one more mile if, at the end, he failed to find his friend—

Now listen, he reprimanded himself. *You'll find him. You'll find him if you have to go all the way to the shore of the Kentucky country alone—*

But he had scant confidence.

His throat burned as he capped the canteen, walked around the cabin, waved to the woman at the slow-moving plow and set off through the forest while the May sky rumbled.

II

JUDSON ASSUMED that what had spared his life was the clean passage of Lottie Shaw's pistol ball in and out through the flesh of his left side. That and the cowardice of Carter, the man who was living off her diminished earning power following their flight from Richmond.

He had no way of knowing whether Carter had deterred Lottie from putting another ball into him and seeing him surely dead. In fact he had no recollection of anything in the hours immediately after the shooting.

Lottie and Carter had evidently left him where they planned: in the damp autumn leaves along Plum Creek. Somehow he'd stumbled up and away from there, guided by an instinctive sense of direction, until he reached the road that wound to the Rapahannock near Sermon Hill. He learned later that a field black spied him staggering along the road and summoned help.

He was borne to Sermon Hill in a wagon. There, according to Donald's subsequent report, he was looked at by Angus Fletcher.

The old man recognized that his son might be bleeding to death. He sent for a physician—and told Donald that Judson would be permitted to remain at the plantation until he recovered or died.

But Angus insisted Judson be put in one of the slave cabins. His principles would only bend so far.

III

JUDSON DID remember waking in the cabin, thrashing and yelling and feeling thick bandages wrapping his chest under an itchy nightshirt.

Flushed of face, Donald perched on a stool beside Judson's pallet. Gently, he tried to push his brother down:

"You'll kill yourself for certain if you flop around that way."

"I promised to meet George Clark in Williamsburg!" were Judson's first words.

"You *what?*"

Breathing hard, Judson explained in labored sentences. At the end Donald shook his head:

"You've been lying here the best part of two weeks. There is no way you can make that rendezvous."

"Send a message, then. You've got to!"

Donald agreed, and arranged it. But the black messenger returned in three days with the news that George Clark had already departed.

"Then—" Speech and even breathing still cost Judson considerable pain. "As soon as I'm up—a week or so—I'll follow him—"

Donald rubbed his gouty leg, shook his head a second time:

"It'll be more like a month before you're well enough to hobble. The wound was clean but quite deep." An ironic smile touched Donald's lips. "Father said you were to be given the best possible care. Do you know he summoned a second doctor all the way from Richmond because he felt the local sawbones didn't know enough? I've never seen him so shamefaced as when he told me he'd done it."

Judson was too astonished to say anything immediately. He gazed at the cabin's dirt floor, listened to the voices of blacks moving in the street outside, experienced alternate pangs of bitter mirth and exultation. Finally, he spoke:

"I can't conceive that I'd even be allowed at Sermon Hill. I'm surprised Father didn't order me floated in the river immediately, to save possible funeral expenses."

"Stop that," Donald said, angered. "He's a narrow-minded, vile-tempered old devil, and no one knows it better than I. But he's not a monster, just a man. And you *are* his son. So let's have no more vituperation. There's been enough hate on both sides too damned long."

Judson lay back, hurting. "Yes," he murmured. "Yes, I guess that's right—"

A moment later, he re-opened his eyes:

"When I am able to leave, I still intend to follow George."

"By yourself? That's insanity."

"Maybe, but I'm going. I'll settle with that Shaw bitch first, though."

Donald waved. "You'll be spared. She's disappeared, along with the flash gentleman who arrived with her while you were in Williamsburg. They either left you for dead or feared to finish what they'd started because they could guess the consequences. Father sent drivers searching for them. With pistols and muskets."

"*Nigra* drivers?"

"Three of his most trusted. He armed them personally."

"You can't be serious."

"I am."

"I'll be goddamned."

"Why should you be so surprised? Blood outlasts everything. Overcomes everything—including hatred. Blood and time are the world's two great healers."

Judson repeated it, bemused: "Blood—" He shook his head slowly. "Odd you should light on that word."

"It's common enough."

"But the old man thinks I've a bad strain running in me. Devil's blood, he calls it."

"He has the same kind." Again that ironic smile. "Don't tell me you've never noticed. Of course, I don't doubt he softened somewhat because you were shot. That made you vulnerable, you see. It's easier to forgive a wounded creature than one who'd raring up to snap at you. I wouldn't question it too much, I'd just be thankful. The hate's ruined both of you for years."

Sleepy, Judson sighed. "I feel too stinking rotten to hate anyone but myself. Yes, I—I'm grateful he relented. Would you tell him?"

"Of course. I doubt he'll have any reaction."

"I'm not looking for a reaction, just tell him."

"I will."

"Also tell him I'm going to follow George. It's the only way I can turn my life around. Even if I don't catch him, or—if something should happen to me on the way, I have to start over. Do you understand?"

Donald answered quietly, "I do. And that's a great virtue of this country. One of the things which makes a disheartening, tiresome war worth fighting."

"What are you talking about?"

"We've much to win besides all those lofty principles declared in Philadelphia, Judson. I've heard Tom Jefferson speak of it time and again—the country in the west. The chance it offers for people to begin again. Lord—" A brief sigh. "I sometimes wish I could go."

His eyes sought his younger brother's. "But I hope you haven't conceived this venture only to prove something to Father."

"No. As I told George, I tangled my affairs so badly in this part of the world, I have to leave or I'll die here."

Donald tried to joke, pointing at Judson's left side:

"I agree—it damned near happened, didn't it?"

IV

ON A bright morning in late March, Donald walked down to the river road with his younger brother.

Though still pale, Judson looked fit. He carried a haversack and the Kentucky rifle Donald had sent to Richmond to procure. Misty March afternoons when he could manage to keep his powder dry, he'd practiced loading and firing in a remote field. His target was a chunk of log set on top of a tree stump. Before too many days had gone by, he could hit the section of log, six inches high and four across, nearly every time.

Donald looked ponderously heavy and tired as he leaned on his cane at the point where the main road intersected the one leading from the great house. At sunrise, Judson had packed his haversack, tucked away the pocket money Donald had loaned him, dressed for his departure and left the cabin. Not once during his recuperation had he entered the main building at Sermon Hill, nor seen his father, except to catch glimpses of him riding the fields.

"I still think you are absolutely lunatic," Donald said. "But I also have come to the conclusion that with a spot of luck, you might find what you're seeking."

"I don't know what that is, Donald."

"Yes, but when you find it, perhaps you'll recognize it."

"You're more confident than I am."

"Brotherly intuition," Donald smiled. "You're not the same person I used to know—"

"Of necessity," Judson said. "I guess we drive out our demons the best way we can, just to survive. I don't really know where I'm going, but I know I can't stay here. That's a splendid declaration of purpose, isn't it?"

And he gave Donald a wry smile that hid a very real ache. The melancholy had overwhelmed him without warning on the slow walk down to the river.

"It's an honest one," Donald said. "By the way—I'll take care of your request that Peggy McLean be told."

Judson's head lifted sharply. "Is she back home?"

"Why, yes. In all the bustle of preparation these past couple of days, I must have forgotten to mention it. I ran into Williams. He told me. He said she returned about a week ago. She's been staying inside because her health is poor again, evidently."

Concern stabbed Judson. "What's wrong?"

"Williams professes not to know. It's very odd—you realize she's been away since last fall—? Williams said she let slip a remark about sailing home on a coasting vessel."

"A *coasting* vessel? Why in God's name would she risk a sea trip, north or south, when the British are everywhere?"

"So are the American privateersmen. But I agree, in wartime, a pleasure cruise anywhere is deuced peculiar—and a holiday the length of hers downright astonishing. Where could she go? Neither Philadelphia nor New York in the north, only Boston. Possibly Charleston or Savannah south of here—"

"I'm sure Peggy has no relatives in Charleston or Savannah," Judson said, trying to puzzle it out. "It seems to me she told me years ago that her mother had kin somewhere up in New England. Maybe my memory's faulty, though—"

"The sad truth is, the uprising is probably still affecting her. To the degree that wild jaunts offer the only release she can find. Williams said nothing about—" Donald sought the term he wanted. "—mental difficulties. But he's intensely loyal, so he wouldn't."

I doubt the cause is solely the uprising, Judson thought somberly. *I expect it's also a certain event that happened afterward—*

For a moment he entertained the notion of stopping at McLean's on his way out of Caroline County. But he rejected the idea. Nothing he could do now would ever make amends for the despicable act committed in the summerhouse.

His thoughts lingered a moment on an image of Peggy's face. Not without effort, he blanked the image from his mind as part of the past he had to shut out forever.

"Well—" He couldn't bear to protract the parting much longer. "—if you do have the opportunity, tell her where I've gone, and why."

"Be assured I'll do so. I know it will be months if not a year or more before we hear from you—"

"I promise I'll write when I can."

"Yes, but with the tribes rising, I doubt the post operates on any sort of regular schedule between here and Kentucky!"

And not at all from the British-controlled territory beyond, Judson added silently.

"I don't want to sermonize, Judson, but I do believe you've made the proper choice. I'm thankful that despite all the turmoil in the west, there's open land to which a man can go if need be—"

Tears glistened in the corners of his eyes. He wiped them away quickly. "God keep you, brother."

"And you," Judson answered, starting up the road.

"Oh, wait—damme! I'm forgetting everything—!"

Judson wheeled around, startled to see his brother pull a small black-bound book from his coat pocket.

"I saw Father while you were putting your things together. This is a present—"

Judson's jaw dropped. "Not for me—?"

"Don't be too overwhelmed until you examine it. It's what you'd expect of him, I think."

"I didn't expect anything."

"No, I mean the nature of the gift." Donald's thumb bent around to the gold stamping on the binding. Judson smiled that old, brilliant smile that could light his face:

"A New Testament. I see what you meant."

"Go on, open the flyleaf."

Judson took the book. Something caught in his throat when he saw the familiar handwriting, a little shakier with age than he remembered, but still recognizably his father's. The inscription read:

> *To my son Judson.*
> *Angus Fletcher*
> *March 29, 1778*

Judson's smile faded. His face grew almost stark as he stared at the words. Donald chuckled with false heartiness:

"Of course Father thinks you're even madder than I do. Yet all the while he's inveighing against your waywardness, I get the feeling that in some queer, perverse way he approves of what you've chosen to do."

Judson's eyes widened in fury. "I told you I chose it for myself, not to please him."

"Somehow I believe he appreciates that. I think it's the very reason he does approve. Maybe he recognized that you've become a man."

"I wasn't aware I was anything else."

"Oh yes," Donald said quietly. "Until a few months ago, you didn't deserve the name. Ah—!" A hand was quickly raised. "None of your temper, now. It's the truth. Most of us come to it in our own time and in our own way, and some never come to it at all. But you have. And while you didn't exactly turn out as Father wished—" A shrug. "Well, life is endless compromise. You wanted Peggy and couldn't have her. I loved my wife and lost her. Father wanted a dutiful pair of boys, appropriately Tory in sentiment—he still abominates the rebellion, you realize—and instead, he got one gouty old lump who barely manages to help him run the place and is on the wrong side politically to boot. He also got an atheistic rogue who has decided, God save us, to be one of those rude frontiersmen—"

Donald smiled. "Every father desires a lot from a son, I suppose. If he can't have everything, he settles for what good things do come about."

"I don't think Father really cares about m—"

"Dammit, now, no more! He does! He told me he is convinced you'll probably die of the ague after your first week of sleeping in the woods. But I swear he sounded just a mite proud when he remarked on it."

Judson started to speak, found he couldn't. He tightened his hand around the testament, tucked it carefully down into the haversack. Something in him fought to bring forth words; the hardest words, perhaps, that he'd ever uttered—

Something else resisted. For a moment his fine features showed the tormenting struggle.

Then, almost blurting it:

"Tell him I thank him very much for the gift."

"Certainly."

"And—"

My God, there were tears in his eyes!

"—and tell him I said—"

The tide burst through—older than all the terrible resentments built between them, timeless in its force and power:

"Tell him I said I love him."

"That, he will welcome most of all."

Judson grinned. "But he won't believe it, the old bastard."

They laughed together, clasped hands, and Judson turned west in the morning sunshine.

V

LATE IN the afternoon of the day he met the woman plowing in the field, Judson felt the first drops of rain. Before long, with thunder rumbling intermittently, the drizzle changed to a downpour. He was quickly soaked to the skin.

The woods grew darker, the faint trail increasingly difficult to follow. Squinting through the rain, he saw the way ahead blocked by an immense, lightning-felled tree.

He decided to bear to the left, go around. He was thankful for the deerhide trousers; brambles grew among the ferns.

The forest smelled of rich earth that steamed as the rain slacked off. But for several minutes, the fall had been torrential. Footing was hazardous.

He reached the rim of a gully perhaps ten feet deep. He started to work his way along it, keeping an eye on the position of the fallen tree on his right. When he was well past it, he'd cut back to the trail and—

Weakened by the rain, the gully's edge gave way under his left boot.

Judson flailed, toppling over with a yell that went echoing through the dense trees.

He struck the gully bottom, left leg bent back under his right knee. At the moment of impact, the leg was lanced with an excruciating pain.

He lay gasping for a minute or so. He searched the crumbled side of the gully until he located his rifle and haversack, both dropped during the fall. He braced his hands in the mud beneath him, straightened his left leg—

The fierce pain exploded again.

Damn! He'd twisted something, badly.

He floundered onto his chest, tried to push up that way. But the moment he gained his feet, he grimaced and clenched his teeth. He'd never get a quarter of a mile on the leg. Not till he rested it. Overnight, at least.

He attempted a few abortive steps, only to give up in exquisite agony. He was conscious of the clock ticking in his mind, every wasted moment spelling ever more certain failure to find George Clark at Pittsburgh. Christ, he'd *crawl* on—!

But good sense prevailed. The scant amount of time he'd gain if he kept going would be better spent letting the injury repair itself a little. Better to make his camp and start at daylight. By then, he might be able to move faster.

Trying to control his anger over the sorry turn of affairs, he clawed his way up the mud and rock of the gully side, retrieving his rifle and tossing it up to the rim, then the haversack. After what seemed an endless climb, he reached the top. He pulled himself over, resting his cheek on a fern while he gulped air. Thunder rocked the forest. Rain began to patter the back of his neck.

No damn possibility of finding dry wood now, he thought. The best he could do was drag himself to the nearest large tree—and hope that the lightning he saw flickering in the west would not strike the particular tree he selected. Actually, he couldn't very well avoid trees, they grew so closely here. One was no more or less dangerous than another.

Lugging rifle and haversack, he reached the big maple he'd chosen, settled himself so his spine rested against the trunk. The new leaves overhead would protect him from all but the heaviest rain.

The injured leg throbbed. What a blasted, damned piece of bad luck! He was so *close!* Less than thirty miles to the forks—

Still, there was nothing to be done except rest and wait for morning. He let his mind drift, trying to free it of frustration and fury. The patter of the rain and the murmur of the receding thunder had a soporific effect. His eyelids grew heavy. Leaning the back of his head against the maple bark, he yawned—

And popped his eyes open, disoriented, alarmed—

Blind—

No, no—he'd only slept. Till dark.

All around him, the woods were still. The silence was accentuated by the occasional, barely audible scurry of some nocturnal animal, or the drip of water from a branch. The air was cool, moist. He rubbed a hand across his mouth, reached down to the aching leg, squeezed it and winced.

Thirsty, he groped for his canteen. He had it tilted, ready to take a swallow, when he heard the sound—

A yipping bark that slid higher, into a howl.

Wolves. Somewhere out in the darkness.

He understood instantly how vulnerable he was. The howl multiplied, two, three, perhaps four predators blending into a weird chorus that set his teeth chattering. He couldn't run away from them. He had to stay here and defend himself here—

At least he had the rifle, and the hunting knife in his boot.

Thunder again, booming. He fumbled for the haversack, face and chest covered with a sudden sweat. Laboriously, he loaded the rifle, readied it in his lap while the howling grew louder.

As a new thunderclap died away, he heard another sound. The drip from the trees was quickening. The rain was starting again. Heavy enough to reach his protected position and soak him—

A streak of lightning zigzagged through the sky, showing him three black-nosed snouts not four yards from where he lay. Fangs shone white and animal eyes glowed until the lightning flickered out.

He swallowed, heard a wolf's guttural snarling; heard clawed feet moving across the wet earth—

He flung the rifle to his shoulder, aimed it blind in the dark, triggered it—

The damp powder in the pan didn't ignite.

Swearing, he fought to his feet. He almost yelled aloud at the agony in his leg. But he had to stand up. They were coming. Three at least. The Lord alone knew

how many more might be gathering further out in the impenetrable black of the woods.

He hunched his right shoulder, snaked his hunting knife out of his boot sheath, closed his teeth on the blade's dull edge and gripped the rifle muzzle with both hands. He concentrated all his attention on the sounds of the wolves closing, cruelly aware of the one central fact of his situation:

He would kill them, or he would be killed by them and never reach the forks of the Ohio.

The rain beat down harder, making detection of noises more difficult.

Well, he thought, *if this is the end of it, at least I needn't be ashamed of how it happened.*

He tried to buoy his confidence with a silent assertion that he would not *permit* himself to be killed.

Well and good. That didn't alter reality. He could very well die in the next few minutes even if he made a thousand resolves. The most disheartening part was realizing that if he did perish, George Clark would never know how he'd tried to catch up to him and honor his pledge to serve—

Strangely, though, when he accepted the possibility of dying, a deadly sort of calm swept over him. It helped him take a firmer grip on the rifle muzzle, and almost completely forget the terrible pain in his leg.

A snarling, clawing thing of fur and fangs hurled against him. Judson wrenched his head aside. The twisted leg gave way.

He lurched against the tree, slid, landed on his side, gashed the corner of his mouth on the knife clenched in his teeth. Fangs tore through his deerhide trousers. He brought the rifle whipping over and down. The wolf's jaws loosened as bone cracked.

Judson kicked at the flopping, clawing animal. Beat at it with the rifle stock, smashing, *smashing*——

The wolf let out a weak yelp and fell away from him—

Just as the other two converged, snapping, slavering—

He clubbed at them, kicked them while the rain fell steadily. He switched his rifle to his left hand, took the knife out of his mouth with his right, stabbing and clubbing simultaneously, hardly a man any longer; he was an animal almost as savage as his attackers.

His knife opened the throat of one of the wolves. The other clamped its jaws on his left arm, shredding flesh, starting blood running.

Crazed with pain, Judson dropped the rifle from his left hand, lashed his right hand over and buried the knife in the wolf's belly. In its death-throes, the animal bit him to the bone.

Judson screamed, jerked back against the tree, knocking his head hard. The gut-stabbed wolf twitched at his feet and lay still.

He panted, tried to close his left hand into a fist, could not. He felt warm blood trickling down over his knuckles.

But they were dead. All three, dead. He was safe from—

Lightning lit the forest. He let out a single short sob of despair.

The glow in the heavens showed him two more, jaws dripping. Thunder pealed as they crouched to spring.

2
The Guns of Summer

To PHILIP there was a peculiar and frightening familiarity about this moment. The heat reminded him of Breed's Hill. So did the dull glare of bayonets; the scarlet coats—

The British foot soldiers were advancing from the east, through steam rising after the most recent downpour. The sunlit vapor fumed up between the trees like some outpouring of infernal ovens, lending a spectral quality to the figures of the enemy.

He was awash with sweat. It ran down to the tip of his noise, rivered over his chest and along his legs, soaking clothing already wet from the June rain. He guessed their position to be somewhere to the west of the little Jersey hamlet of Monmouth Court House. While the ghost-soldiers marched toward them through the mist, the Americans waited in a north-south line on the east side of McGellaird's Brook, a ravine whose bottom resembled a swamp more than a creek.

The army of thirteen thousand had marched north from Valley Forge a week ago. Philip guessed that perhaps half that number of men were strung out in advanced positions to which they'd moved starting around seven that morning. Thus far, Philip's contingent had only light resistance.

The temperature in the woods had to be close to a hundred. Up and down the line men lay fallen, fainted away. A few others struggled to revive them, without much luck.

Philip's musket felt slippery in his hands as he squinted through the steaming air. Each breath he took was labored. He heard the British infantry drummers hammering the cadence somewhere behind the dim figures advancing in the steam between the thickly clustered trees.

Sword pulled and ready, General Anthony Wayne slipped along the rear of the American line. His sweat-sheened face showed an emotion that might have been frustration—or rage. From the brush where he crouched near Breen and Royal Rothman, Philip heard Wayne repeat the same command over and over:

"Hold fire. Hold fire until your officer signals."

The handsome, flamboyant young general—as dirty, stinking, sand-covered and fly-bitten as the rest of them today—passed within a yard of Philip. Wayne broke step, stopped a moment as recognition registered.

Philip was too weary to return Wayne's brief, comradely smile. But he did ask a question:

"Are we to hold, General? Our own drum signals don't make much sense."

Wayne's mouth wrenched. "As long as I have charge here, we'll not only hold, we'll attack. As for the signals—I'll be damned if any officer in this sector can make sense of 'em—or knows what our esteemed commander's up to. Order, counter-order, disorder—that seems to be the rule for the morning. Charlie Lee didn't want this action in the first place. So we'll just forget him, eh?"

Wayne smiled again, the kind of bravado grin that had given the young Pennsylvanian a reputation as a commander impatient with hesitation and virtually unconcerned about his personal safety. Philip watched the general move off through the sodden weeds, working his way south along the ragged line awaiting the redcoats.

They were much closer now. Philip could distinctly see facial features through the confused interplay of sunlight and steam. Far away, thunder rumbled. Another storm.

Or could it be cannon-fire?

In Breen's eyes—in Royal's—in the eyes of all the stubbled, sweating men watching the advancing enemy, Philip saw the same concern that kept a triphammer rhythm of fear going in his own chest.

The army had not formally engaged the British since leaving Valley Forge on the twenty-third of June.

And now the British had a new commander.

Unfortunately so did all the Americans holding advanced outposts in the field this morning. To a man, they distrusted the general who was supposed to be giving the orders. As Wayne had said, Charles Lee had argued against this pursuit. Despite all von Steuben's training, the Americans, Lee was convinced, were still no match for British regiments—

Very shortly they would resolve the issue. Resolve it in this patch of Jersey marshland where the tree trunks were surround by pools of water left from the huge storms that had alternated with intense heat and humidity for days on end. Philip watched the British closing in the ordered ranks he remembered so well from Breed's Hill—

Then suddenly, from behind the marching redcoats, he picked up a terrifying new sound.

"Oh Jesus," Breen exclaimed. "They're throwin' cavalry at us!"

Philip peered through the sweat blurring his eyes. The British infantrymen were flanking right and left. Into the openings burst the hard-riding vans of mounted units; men in green-faced blue coats and hussar busbies, their drawn sabers flashing—

"Queen's Rangers!" someone cried in fright.

The American officers up and down the line called the count for cocking and poising firelocks. Philip heard Walter Webb yell:

"Hold for the signal—!"

Looking inhumanly tall in their saddles, the Tory Queen's Rangers thundered between the trees, riding down on the Americans, sabers raised.

Philip watched one jouncing cavalryman's busby tilt askew so that it touched his right eyebrow.

Sixty yards away now.

Fifty—

Coming at the gallop, dozens of them, hundreds, a surging wave of blue coats and steel—

A man to Philip's left shrieked in panic, threw down his musket and began to run back toward the ravine. Webb shouted at him but let him go, whirling to concentrate on the cavalrymen. In the distance Philip thought he heard an American drum signal for a retreat.

Or was that thunder again?

Where was General Washington? Why had they been thrust forward like this under the over-all command of a man everyone considered a braggart, a fool, even a coward?

The Ranger horse came on.

Forty yards.

Thirty—

The great chargers rolled their eyes and bared their huge yellowed teeth

against their bits. In patches of sunlight, the sabers glared like a spiked wall rolling forward—

Finally—much too late, Philip feared—he heard the command bawled from company to company:

"Fire!"

II

A WILD but all too brief elation had greeted the news of the French alliance.

The agreement between the American commissioners in Paris and the government of King Louis XVI had actually been reached in early January. A treaty stipulated that France would come to the aid of the new country with men and material if and when war broke out between Britain and her traditional enemy.

Very few doubted that such a war was inevitable. According to the rumors reaching Valley Forge in the late spring, France actually seemed to be encouraging incidents that would provoke open conflict. A French armada commanded by Admiral Count d'Estaing had already sailed from Toulon with four thousand soldiers aboard. The soldiers were prepared to land on American soil if, by chance, their country and England were at war by the time the ships made a landfall.

Alarmed, the king's ministers in London had replaced the sluggish, luxury-loving Howe with a new commander in America, Sir Henry Clinton. Upon hearing the news of the French armada, Clinton promptly abandoned the prize of Philadelphia and began its evacuation in mid-June. Washington ordered the march from Valley Forge a few days later, moving the American army into New Jersey, an inferno of summer humidity and sandy roads and sudden storms.

Somewhere ahead of them Clinton zigzagged toward New York with his troops and his precious train of fifteen hundred wagons loaded with supplies and equipment. According to the scouts, Clinton was at present heading northeast, to reach the safety of New York via Sandy Hook. Only General Charles Lee and a few other senior officers were in favor of letting him go unmolested.

But thus far the pursuit had been a fiasco.

Washington pushed on without directly contacting the retreating enemy, listening meantime to the counsels of his various generals, and weighing each opinion. Everyone knew Anthony Wayne's terse advice:

"Fight, sir."

Von Steuben had theoretically brought the army to a new, higher pitch of readiness. Yet Washington had finally decided on a compromise. They would engage Clinton's rear guard only. If that action proved successful, the entire American force could sweep forward.

Regrettably, the general who demanded personal command of the exploratory action was thin, ugly, egotistical Charles Lee, nominally the highest-ranking officer after Washington.

Lee had seen service in Europe. He considered himself much more of a military expert than his superior. There was even talk that he had penned not-so-secret notes to the Congress denouncing Washington as "damnably deficient." Lee stubbornly maintained that the army to which he'd pledged his service could never win a major engagement against crack British and Hessian units.

Conscious of his rank and its perquisites, he still demanded command of the probing action aimed at Clinton's retreating troops. Washington reluctantly agreed—

And Lee began not a vigorous chase but a slow, aimless dallying. The men in the field this steaming twenty-eighth of June, 1778, were already aware that while Lee vacillated, Clinton had started his precious baggage train moving again. During the darkest hours of the preceding night, the quarry had begun to widen its margin of distance from the Americans.

Now, along an irregular front near tiny Monmouth Court House, the forward American units braced for what appeared to be a protective counter-stroke from Clinton's rear. And, as General Wayne had disgustedly noted, no clear-cut instructions had yet been issued by General Lee.

"Order, counter-order, disorder." Every man, it seemed to Philip, was left to fight as circumstance dictated.

Or flee.

Or die.

III

THE FIRST of the Tory Queen's Rangers had nearly reached the American line. Philip's musket bucked against his shoulder, cracking out flame and smoke.

His ball struck an officer's huge roan in the neck. The animal bellowed as it went down. A fountain of horse blood sopped the officer's breeches.

Three and four deep, the cavalry charged the line of erupting muskets. Some blue-coated men dropped. Others broke through to hack and chop with their sabers. The area immediately in front of Philip quickly became a melee of downed horses and mountless men, with other Rangers from the rear charging through as best they could.

And now came the frantic business of re-loading—

The officer Philip had unseated dashed to his right, grabbing at the reins of a horse whose rider had been shot. Philip saw this while he fumbled with powder and ball and tried to remember von Steuben's ten-count. All around him he heard screams, shots, curses, the sickening *chunk* of sabers striking exposed flesh.

The bloodstained officer gained the saddle, spurred the new mount forward. Sections of the American line began to break, the men scrambling toward the ravine. Philip and Royal Rothman held their places in a clump of shrubbery that afforded them only minimal cover. The smoke, the steam, the uproar of hoof-beats and shrieks and explosions constricted Philip's world to little more than a few yards of ground—

Just as Philip finished loading, the officer with the blood-reddened trousers tensed in the saddle, ready to leap his new horse straight over their heads in pursuit of the men fleeing to the ravine.

Royal Rothman jumped to his feet, took two short steps to the side, rammed his bayonet into the horse's belly as it went over. A hoof struck Philip's ear, drawing blood—

The big cavalry horse wrenched in midair. The Ranger cried out, his blade arcing crazily as horse and man tumbled. Breen was back-stepping and re-loading at the same time. He slipped in a muddy place. The falling officer's saber, coming down at a chance angle, cut Breen's neck from the right side.

Breen's head seemed to loll toward his left shoulder. Blood cascaded over his chest. The officer's bayoneted horse was down, thrashing, loosing its stinking bowels in its death-agony.

The officer pulled himself from under the fallen horse, staggered to his feet. Philip aimed his musket at the blue-coated back, decided instantly not to waste a shot, leaped over the dying animal with bayonet thrust out ahead.

The officer heard him coming, spun. A bar of steaming June sun lit young, frightened blue eyes. The saber flashed up defensively. Philip dodged under, stabbed his bayonet home and yanked it out.

The Queen's Ranger spilled forward into the mud. American muskets were crackling and flaming again.

"Have at 'em with bayonets!"

Off to his right Philip recognized Wayne's voice, very nearly a maniacal shriek. A riderless British horse went by, almost knocking Royal over. The horse tried to check at the edge of the ravine. Philip watched it tumble over—just as he heard other hoofbeats behind him—

More of the Rangers on the attack. He shot shoulder to shoulder with Royal. Their two balls killed one cavalryman, wounded a second. They jumped apart to let the horses race past. The dead Ranger hung head down, his boot caught in his stirrup.

Again Wayne ordered the bayonet charge. This time sections of the American line began to move.

Philip and Royal bent low, stumbling toward the trees. Philip gulped air. God, he was dizzy. The heat was enough to make anyone pass out—

Quickly he glanced up and down the line. What he saw restored his spirits and re-sharpened his senses. The American musket-fire had blunted, then broken the Ranger charge. A few last horsemen were wheeling to head back the way they'd come, retreating wraiths in the forest steam.

A ball whizzed past Philip's head. He ducked automatically, realized that the infantrymen who had stopped to permit the Ranger companies to charge through had now started a defensive fire.

But the Rangers—superb soldiers—had been *beaten!*

Philip and Royal converged on a kneeling infantryman who desperately tried to decide which of them to shoot. His face plastered with sweat and sand, Royal took advantage of the hesitation and dispatched the luckless redcoat with one stroke of the bayonet.

When the man fell, Philip glanced at his friend. There was something strange and terrible and old in Royal's eyes. A he smiled, the sand cracked from his cheeks and dribbled onto his filthy shirt. His teeth had the white look of a skull's.

Ahead, they heard Wayne's bellow. Out in front of all the rest, he was leading the bayonet attack. Philip and Royal staggered toward the voice, hunting for redcoats.

But in the steamy, uncertain light they were hard to spot. And now they too were pulling back.

Philip stumbled and sprawled in a pool of water. By the time Royal had helped him to his feet, they both heard a new, readily identifiable sound in the woods:

American drummers beating a familiar cadence.

Anthony Wayne came storming back toward them, shaking a bloodied spontoon:

"Form up in column of fours! *Column of fours!*"

"General, why are they beating retreat?" Philip shouted. "We've got 'em running—''

Wayne stopped long enough to mop his forehead with his sleeve. He was shaking:

"You go tell that to General Lee—you can probably find him having breakfast behind the lines! It appears we nipped Clinton's tail a little too smartly. A scout came through before we started the charge. He said Clinton's turning the main body of the army back against us. He's afraid of losing his wagons. We're *that close—''*

Wayne's index finger and thumb illustrated. His face was still white with fury.

"—consequently, Charlie Lee's called a retreat!"

He stalked on toward the ravine, screaming:

"Column of fours, goddamn you! *Retreat formation!''*

Wearily, Philip and Royal began to trot after the retreating general.

Philip's temples hurt. So did his chest. Sand and tiny insects tormented his exposed skin. He cursed long and loud, finally exclaimed:

"That damn yellow Lee still thinks we can't hold against the British!"

Astonished, he heard Royal echo his anger with one foul word after another. The boy, it seemed, was no longer a boy—

They loped back past the horse Royal had killed, to rally around two drummers signaling from the other side of McGellaird's Brook.

IV

THEY MARCHED while the sun blistered them. They marched on a road half mud, half sand, in a direction Philip presumed to be westward. Back toward Englishtown; back toward the main body of the army.

They marched along in a column of fours, cursing but keeping step. Every man in the ranks knew how close they'd come to blunting the British counterthrust and breaking through.

It seemed to Philip that the horror of Breed's Hill had been repeated with an eerie, subtle variation. This time the American bayonets could have won the day. At least in his limited sector—

Then, once again, the retreat signal. Not to keep them from defeat, but to prevent a victory. *Damn!*

They tramped along the sandy, hell-hot road, complaining bitterly.

The pullback had been orderly, and without casualties. Von Steuben had taught them that. He had also taught them a great deal they were unable to use, Philip thought in disgust.

Next to him, Royal said, "Do you suppose anyone will go back for Breen's body?''

Philip grimaced. "How can they? Looks like we're going to be driven back miles from where we started.''

"Will Captain Webb write Breen's family?''

Philip shrugged. "Breen never told us his real name. It would take a visit to Andover to find out who he really was.''

"For all his coarseness, he wasn't a bad sort.''

"No—'' Philip ached at the memory of the older man dying from the chance cut of the saber. "No, he really wasn't, he—''

"Look sharp!" Royal exclaimed. "Horsemen coming!"

A man behind suddenly groaned and pitched sideways, overcome by the heat. Royal jumped to grab him and support him as Philip caught a clatter of hoofs in the shimmering air down the road to the west.

At the head of their company, Captain Webb called for a left-face to the roadside. With fair precision the men executed the movement as von Steuben had taught them, holding their lines in the damp weeds at the shoulder. Royal lowered the fainted man to the ground and fanned him with both hands.

"Bet we got to fight here," someone said. "Bet the fucking British swungaround the flank and cut off the road—"

For a moment there was more cursing, and consternation until Captain Webb cried:

"Shut up and listen! Hear that cheering? That's not for the enemy—"

Men craned insect-bitten necks, jostling to see. And suddenly, out of the west, Philip heard it: a massed roar of voices.

The outcry grew louder and louder under the sweltering sky. A wave of sound, it rolled toward them along with a cloud of boiling dust in the center of the road.

A rider emerged from the leading edge of the cloud. Hatless, wearing blue and buff, he galloped his huge white horse in the direction opposite that of the retreat. *Toward* Monmouth Court House—

Behind Washington an entourage of officers rode full speed. The cheering was unbelieving loud.

The commander-in-chief glanced neither right nor left to acknowledge the bellow that rolled across the countryside as he passed. He paid no attention to the muskets thrust up in the air in rhythm with the huzzahs. Philip had only a momentary glimpse of the tall general's face before he disappeared beyond the dust streaming out behind the horses. But that glimpse was enough to give Philip pause.

Washington's profile had looked savagely scarlet. If not with sunburn, then with anger.

Almost stupefied, Royal and Philip gaped at one another. They heard yet another new sound, this time from the east. A different pattern of flams and ruffs—

Tootling fifes joined the drums. And from man to bedraggled man, cries ran along the roadside:

"Counter-march!"

"They say he caught Charlie Lee and blistered him with curses!"

"Called him a damned poltroon—a coward—"

"Lees's relieved. Washington's in personal command—"

"*No more retreat!*"

"All right, form up!" Captain Webb shouted, vainly trying to shove his men back onto the road as the uproar all but drowned him out:

"We're going back!"

"*We're going back!*"

"*WE'RE GOING BACK!*"

V

They were in an orchard, behind a hedge that rimmed its eastern perimeter. As far as Philip could tell, they were holding the orchard somewhere near the center of the American lines. They were south of the Englishtown road, still west of Monmouth Court House—and firing through the shrubbery as the British grenadiers advanced in those splendid, never-wavering formations.

Philip's hands were beginning to blister from the combined heat of the weather and the musket-metal. Royal was still alongside. Wayne was in over-all command of the orchard position; Philip could see him peering through the barely breathable powder-smoke that drifted from muskets and the cannon booming on their flanks. The entire afternoon had been mind-numbing. Endless shifts of position; charge and counter-charge.

Philip wearily pointed the musket through the hedge and picked off a fur-capped, perspiring grenadier coming toward him in rote step. The grenadier toppled forward, his bayonet stabbing into the ground. The soldier knew he was dying, but he clung to the butt of the Brown Bess to keep himself from falling, as if that in itself could undo the effect of Philip's shot.

Slowly, the grenadier's slippery hands gave out. He slumped to his knees, fingers sliding inexorably down the muzzle. Philip blinked twice. When his vision cleared, the grenadier had let go of his musket and lay on his back, unmoving. The upside-down weapon stood beside him in the earth like some obscene parody of a churchyard marker. Other grenadiers with bayonets at the ready marched past the corpse, never glancing down.

Philip wondered how much longer he could survive without water. Just to his rear, an older man flopped in the grass, felled not by a wound but by prostration that purpled his cheeks. The man's tongue protruded like a frog's as he compressed his hands against his belly and made retching sounds—

Philip had no energy for thinking of the danger of their situation. No energy to speculate about strategies, or the over-all success or failure of the engagement of the entire American army. Clinton had struck swiftly, throwing unit after unit against them across a broad front. But for Philip, the world had again constricted to a small patch of ground where he crouched behind the hedge, concentrating on the steps of von Steuben's ten-count drill.

Philip's flayed hands almost worked independently of his exhausted mind. He loaded, fired, dodged instinctively whenever he heard a ball hiss through the leaves—

The American fire broke the grenadier charge thirty yards from the hedge. In the smoke, Philip saw redcoat after redcoat falling. Suddenly someone stumbled against his legs.

Philip wrenched his head up. Saw Webb, a sooty ghoul who grinned and pointed a bleeding hand through a break in the foliage:

"We've hit Colonel Monckton, their commander."

Up and down the line, men picked it up:

"Monckton's killed—someone shot Monckton!"

As the grenadiers began to pull back, re-form for another charge, Webb's hand closed hard on Philip's shoulder.

"He's one of their kingbirds. Can you two bring him back to our colors?"

Gulping for air, Philip said, "Can try. Come on, Royal. Leave the musket. Stay low—"

The two of them crawled forward on their bellies, out past the hedge into tall grass. Occasional musket fire still crackled over their heads. All at once, Philip stopped.

He burrowed his elbows into the soft ground. His ears rang. He let his head hang like an exhausted dog's. Waves of nausea left him helpless.

"Royal, I can't," he gasped. "The damned heat—"

"It's only a little further," Royal panted, grabbing the back of Philip's hunting shirt and giving him a tug. "They want Monckton's body at the colors. You can make it—"

The perimeter of the orchard was a miasma of smoke and dimly seen sky. He was tired beyond the limits of comprehension. He rolled his head sideways, saw Royal watching him with almost wild-eyed intensity. The boy had lost his little black wool cap during the day, Philip realized.

"Come *on!*" Royal said.

Philip dug his elbows into the grass, pulled his numbed body forward a few inches. And a few more—

Royal Rothman speared out one hand, closed it clawlike on the powder-blacked uniform of the grenadier commander who lay with eyes and mouth open. Out of sight in the tall grass, the British drummers changed cadence to start the next advance.

"Help me pull him!" Royal pleaded. "If you don't, the grenadiers will catch up to us—"

Philip's right arm felt dead. He forced it to move by will alone, reaching down across Colonel Monckton's nose and open mouth to dig his fingers into sweat-drenched wool. Then he began to crawl backwards, feeling as if he were dragging the weight of the world.

His head buzzed. Buzzed and rang. Distantly, as though in a windstorm, he heard Royal's voice, now louder, now fainter:

"A little more. Only a little more, Philip. *Don't let go of him—!*"

"*I can't stand to look at him that way!*" Philip screamed, shifting his hand to the dead officer's face. One by one he pushed down Monckton's eyelids.

Just after he touched the corpse, something started his hand shuddering; then his whole arm. It was all so damned senseless. The heat; the slaughter—

He just wanted to give up. Stop. Rest. Close his eyes—

"Keep pulling, Philip! The grenadiers have spotted us. But we're close. *Pull!*"

He tried. God, he tried. He had no strength left. His arm shook uncontrollably—

What sort of man had this Monckton been? Surely he'd loved someone. A wife. Children. Surely he believed he was just as right as those on Philip's side. It was a waste. A wretched, damnable *waste*—

All that kept him tugging the corpse was a memory of Anne and Abraham on which he forced himself to concentrate.

He knew there was a purpose to the struggle beyond the immediate one. He knew because Anne had revealed it to him, little by little, in their first months of courting.

He'd believed in it when he married her. Did he now—?

Yes, he supposed so. But he was spent; so spent, the nature of the purpose was beyond his power to recall. What he clung to—what kept him floundering and flopping on his knees and elbows to drag the body were two faces. All else was stripped away; dross.

A woman. A child—*that* was why he was here. Why he had to fire his musket. Obey orders. Stay alive, so he could return to—

"Up, Philip! Drag him through! Quickly—I can see grenadiers aiming at us—"

A foot from the hedge, Philip struggled with the incredibly heavy body. He seemed incapable of raising it properly. Warning shouts rose from the American side of the hedge. He wondered about the reason, the instant before musket fire exploded behind him.

Royal shouted and flattened out, letting their burden drop. Dazed, Philip was a fraction slow. On hands and knees, he presented a clear target. He seemed to see Royal's sweat-shiny face across some great abyss of smoke and noise. Royal's mouth opened to utter a cry of warning. Something buzzed near Philip's ear. Leaves rustled, a dream-like sound—

The buzz was a grenadier ball. Royaly's yell dinned suddenly:

"For God's sake get down—"

Another musket-blast obliterated the rest. Philip felt something thump his right calf. There was searing pain.

A moment later his dazed mind finally recognized that something had pierced the top of his right boot. He flopped on his buttocks, propped up by one hand on Monckton's shoulder. Incredulous, he stared at the hole in the boot's thin, worn leather.

Something large and hurtful was lodged in the flesh inside that boot. All at once, another peculiar sensation made him grimace. His lower leg not only hurt like fury, it felt as if it had just been plunged into a pot of boiling honey—

Idiotic, he thought, blinking back a haze that wouldn't go away. It was in his mind. *Honey's never warm, never—*

He saw the redness pouring through the place where the ball had penetrated the leather. *My God, I'm hit,* he thought with a curious, light-headed detachment.

Royal shouted urgent warnings he couldn't understand. The drums of the advancing grenadiers hammered. Trying to focus his eyes on the glistening blood, he sagged over against Monckton's corpse.

Blearily, he came back to consciousness a few minutes later. Royal was slapping his cheek. His whole lower leg and foot burned fiercely. When he rolled his head sideways to squint down the side of his body, he saw his trousers soaked with blood where the fabric was stuffed into his boot-top.

"Get up, Philip. If you stay here you'll be caught or killed. We've got to get you to the surgeons."

"I—" Cracked lips formed thoughtless words. "I'm hit."

"I know you're hit! That's why we have to get out of here."

"Not sure—I can walk."

"Try."

"Tired. So damn tired, Royal—"

"Listen to the drums!"

"The grenadiers?"

"No, ours. We're pulling back."

"Don't think—don't think I—"

"You *have* to! I didn't drag you through the hedge to see you left for the enemy."

"Good of you," Philip mumbled, afraid he wasn't making much sense. "Good of you, Royal. But I'd rather rest. You go on—"

"You don't know what you're saying!" Royal panted, his face a barely

recognizable blur. He pressed his hands against Philip's cheeks. "Listen to me! I'll help you walk.''

"No, I—''

"Yes! You must walk! *Listen—!*'' So desperate that he was close to tears, Royal wrenched Philip's head from side to side, trying to rouse him from his wound-induced lethargy. "Do you want to spend the rest of the war on one of their prison ships in New York harbor?''

"No.''

"What kind of medical help do you think they'll give you? None! They won't see to your wound. They'll probably let the gangrene take over—rot your leg— do you want that?''

"No, but—''

"Then stop fighting me and *get up!*''

Savagely, Royal dug his arms beneath Philip's back. Philip saw Royal's musket lying on the ground. It seemed to bend and quiver like a snake even as he watched.

Royal almost dropped him. Philip thoughtlessly put weight on his right foot, cried out. But somehow, he got upright, Royal beside him.

Philip hooked his right arm around Royal's neck, bent his right leg at the knee. Something Royal had said drove him to the effort. *Gangrene—*

Mustn't think of that. Just hang onto Royal.

The younger man was panting now, his retrieved musket dragging from his right hand. They hobbled away from the hedge on Philip's one good leg and Royal's two, moving through the orchard.

After a few minutes, it was a little easier. Philip's head cleared slightly.

But why couldn't he feel anything in his right foot?

Sweat streamed down his neck. Mosquitoes and sand flies stung him. "Must be—hundred and ten—'' he mumbled.

"At least. Come on, we're making it—''

The drumming pulsed in Philip's ears. He felt ashamed of his lack of strength. Biting his upper teeth into his lower lip, he stung himself out of the dulled weariness that made him want to lie down again. In the nightmare of smoke and noise, of thudding drums and steadily reddening afternoon light, they crossed the orchard, the last stragglers in a column retreating to the next holding position. The two kept up as best they could.

Soon Philip completely lost track of his surroundings. He heard a clatter of hoofs, a creak of wheels—then Royal's jubilant exclamation:

"Here's a medical wagon! We'll have you aboard in no time.'' Royal raised his voice: "Driver, hold up! Wounded man—''

Royal's supporting arm inadvertently relaxed. Philip sagged forward onto his knees, then slammed face first into the dust, never feeling the impact.

VI

HE WOKE in the inferno of a medical tent, wishing he hadn't. It was like living Brandywine all over again, except that this time, the man writhing on the gory planks wasn't Lucas Cowper.

He tasted rum in his mouth. Bit the ball when he was ordered. Shifted and moaned softly as unseen pincers dug into the flesh of his calf just a few inches above his ankle.

Then he saw two spheres floating near; one huge, white and moist, the other smaller, red and wet—

"Got her out nice and clean."

The white sphere was the surgeon's perspiring face, the red one the flattened lead ball held in dirty pincers. The surgeon discarded the ball and the instrument, gripped Philip's shoulders.

"Hold steady, now. We're going to cauterize it with an iron."

Before Philip could move his lips, the heated metal touched his skin. He started to scream. From behind, a hand jammed his jaws together so he wouldn't swallow the ball held between his teeth.

A foul odor of burning flesh rose into his nostrils, starting uncontrollable gagging. At once, the ball was jerked from his teeth.

Rough hands seized the injured leg, held it. His calf and foot, numbed again by the searing iron, felt curiously thick. The surgeon's sticky face peered down. A lantern hanging above him lit droplets of sweat in his unpowdered hair.

"They're wrapping it with clean rags, and we've a crutch for you," he said. "One of your messmates is outside. He'll help you walk. We can't let you lie in here, we need the room for more serious cases. You understand—"

The man's exhausted voice indicated that he didn't care whether Philip did or not.

The surgeon barked over his shoulder, "Let's have his crutch! And one of the chits, so he can draw all the rum he needs to kill the pain."

"Is—will I walk all right?" Philip gasped out.

The surgeon wiped his hands on a filthy scarlet apron. "You saw the ball. It came out clean. I can't say whether or not there's muscle damage."

And that was the end of his attention, because another patient on the next table was shrieking as the bone-saw rasped back and forth. Philip's doctor ran to answer a cry for assistance.

Like some animal being shunted out of a pen, Philip was propped up on one foot, dizzy as he was. The crutch-pad was jammed under his right armpit. Then he was helped to the tent entrance, where Royal waited anxiously, his face indistinct in the glow of the lanterns flaring in the twilight.

Philip breathed hard. Moving was difficult. But he wasn't excessively uncomfortable. The rum, the cauterizing iron and the rag bandages had reduced his lower leg and foot to little more than a lump of meat, devoid of feeling.

"Come on," Royal said, maneuvering Philip's left arm over his back again. "I think I can locate our unit. Are—are you all right?"

"Little—out of my head," Philip answered truthfully. Something fluttered from his hand. "Royal—that paper—need it for extra rum tonight—"

Dutifully, Royal stretched and half-squatted, recovering the chit. Philip closed the fingers of his hand as if the bit of paper were a nugget of precious metal or a priceless gem.

He was too dazed to worry about the possibility of gangrene, or how his leg would feel when the mortifying effects of the hot iron wore off. He wondered if he would ever walk properly again, but he couldn't bring himself to think much about that, either. For that he was thankful.

VII

NOT LONG after dark, they were resting in another apple orchard, among several hundred men, quite a few of whom had light wounds. Philip was grateful the day's action had been called to a halt. He couldn't have hobbled one more step if General Washington had personally ordered him to do so under threat of court-martial.

Royal lay near him, sprawled on his side. Philip sat against the trunk of a tree, his right leg stuck out straight, the bandage that wrapped him from sole to mid-calf looking gigantic and grotesque in the dim light. His crutch rested across his thighs.

Royal had brought Philip his extra ration of rum. He sipped it from his hand-carved wooden drinking mug, taking a little every time the pain became hard to bear. With his other hand, he slowly slapped at sand flies deviling his cheek. It was all the effort he could manage.

Once twilight came on, the fighting had ended. In the steaming darkness Philip heard a dim buzz of many conversations. He wondered which portions of the field he and Royal had occupied during the frantic maneuvering of the afternoon. He supposed he'd never know—

He grew aware of Royal speaking in a tired monotone:

"—some say we whipped them. But I've heard just as many say it was a standoff. Clinton's gotten away in the dark with his baggage, and we'll never catch him now."

Philip could only utter a single wordless syllable to show he'd heard.

"They say we lost over a hundred dead from sunstroke, too."

Again Philip could do no more than murmur.

A lantern spread a widening glow off to their right. Several subalterns and a senior officer, shadow-figures, were slowly working their way among the resting men. Philip thought he recognized a voice that was asking a question for which no one had the answer.

Royal did, though:

"General Wayne?"

"Who spoke?"

"Over here, sir."

"Who is it—?"

The party of officers approached. Philip lifted his head, saw a disturbing double image of a bedraggled Anthony Wayne.

"Private Rothman, sir. I heard you ask about General Washington."

"Can't find him anywhere."

"One of the other fellows told me he'd already gone to sleep. Yonder under a tree at the far side of the orchard. He found General Lafayette lying exhausted and spread his cloak over both of them."

"Many thanks—"

Wayne started on, then hesitated, his eye fixing on Philip.

Wayne said, "I recognize you. Kent, am I right?"

Each word seemed to weigh a ton in his mouth:

"Yes, sir."

"You were at McGellaird's Brook."

"Yes, I was."

"Took a British ball, it appears."

"Yes, sir. Nothing—" He forced each word, hoping they were true. "—nothing too serious."

"Well, savor that rum, Kent. You and the rest of these men earned it." His handsome face broke into a prideful grin; the kind of devil's grin that had earned him his fierce reputation. "Today wasn't Brandywine, by heaven."

"No, sir," Philip said. "Thank God for that."

"We can thank the commander-in-chief while we're at it. God grant you a swift recovery."

Before Philip could offer a reply, Wayne strode off, a tall silhouette between the two resting soldiers and the subaltern leading the way with the lantern.

Philip closed his eyes, let his whole body go slack. No conscious effort was required. His right leg was throbbing again.

He brought his hand up; tilted the cup; dribbled rum over his chin before his tongue caught the rest.

Royal sighed. Then:

"Philip?"

"Uh?"

"Do you feel any better?"

"Some."

"Then I think I'll sleep a little myself."

"Good." It was barely audible.

After a moment's silence:

"Philip?"

"Mm?"

"Captain Webb told me General Washington ordered a huge celebration back in camp at Englishtown tomorrow. Said we'd behaved like a real army, and won a victory over the flower of the British troops." Royal's tone was unmistakably proud. "The flower of the British troops, those were his exact words. Captain Webb said there was very little panic, despite all the confusion at the beginning. I suppose a lot of the credit goes to that German. Maybe our luck's changing. Maybe we'll win against them yet—"

Philip's answer was a snore.

VIII

BEFORE A week passed, Philip knew something was seriously wrong with his right leg.

The wound had been re-dressed twice by army doctors. Each commented that Philip had been lucky to escape the kind of ravaging infection that produced gangrene, then amputation. But when Philip was told by the second doctor to test his weight on the wounded leg, he fell over in a child-like sprawl. The doctor avoided Philip's eyes when he was back up on his crutch. Philip demanded an explanation.

"I think the ball may have damaged internal tissues," the doctor said. "A great tendon, possibly. If it doesn't heal properly, you—you may have difficulty walking."

A cold lump clotted in Philip's throat. "For how long?"

"For life. Our knowledge of anatomy's inexact, you understand. But—"

Philip's ghastly whiteness made the doctor stop.

"You mean I'll have to get about on a crutch from now on?"

"I can't be certain. I saw a somewhat similar case after a pistol duel over cards at Valley Forge. The man was left with a permanent limp."

Tears of humiliation and rage sprang to Philip's eyes. "Jesus Christ."

"Here, here," the doctor said with false heartiness, clapping Philip's shoulder. "At least there's one benefit. You'll be mustered out very promptly now."

"To go home and live as a cripple?"

"I—I told you, soldier. I can't be positive one way or another—"

"I'm sorry, doctor, but I think you're lying."

The man said nothing, averting his gaze a second time. White-lipped, Philip hobbled out of the tent.

IX

THE JULY twilight was cool. After picking up the mail that had finally come north through Jersey to Washington's summer encampment at Haverstraw Bay, Philip started immediately for the bluffs.

The doctor's prediction had proved partially correct. Two days ago, Philip had started getting about for short periods without the crutch. The injured right leg no longer caused him much pain; the wound was healing, and evidently no bones had been broken.

But there was permanent damage. His foot was stiffer than before, lacking natural springiness. He had looked at the foot closely the last time it was dressed, and it seemed to him that the arch of the sole had flattened somewhat.

Tonight he leaned on the crutch. Without it, his progress was awkward, and the limp noticeable—just as his bitter, brooding silences had become noticeable to Royal and Gil and Captain Webb and others who knew him.

The doctors had also confirmed that he was no longer fit for fighting. His separation orders were being prepared. Before many more days passed, he would be free to return to Boston. It was ironic that the prospect filled him with so little joy, when it was all he'd wanted for so long.

But he'd never planned on returning to his wife and his son as a cripple.

Behind him, Philip heard singing around the cook fires. Even on the tiring march north from Englishtown—a march on which he'd been permitted to travel most of the way in a medical wagon—the spirits of the other men had improved dramatically.

True, the army had lost a prime chance to destroy Clinton's force. The enemy commander was now safe on the island of New York, some miles downriver. But for the first time, the Americans *had* fought like first-class troops. Even Gil said so, riding in the medical wagon and trying to cheer his friend. Washington, awaiting Clinton's next move and planning his own, expressed his pride in his men openly and frequently.

General Charles Lee, relieved of command and facing disciplinary action— perhaps even court-martial—had not been heard from on the subject.

To hearten the men even more, a courier had arrived at headquarters this morning bearing word that spread through the encampment by noon. The Count d'Estaing's frigates and ships of the line had been sighted off the Delaware capes!

Extra rations of alcohol were allowed, on Washington's order, and permission

was given for another all-out celebration. Perhaps, as Royal had said that night in the orchard, the fortunes of the Americans were reversing at last—

But that was of small importance to Philip just now. He was finally able to forget his own injury, and the problems it posed for the future. Forgetfulness came with concentrating on the two much-wrinkled letters he pulled from his pocket as he reached a secluded place where the cliffs dropped away to the wide, blue-black Hudson. The river flowed serenely, its surface pricked silver by the first summer stars.

Philip had practically snatched the letters from the postal clerk, noting only that one was in a man's hand, the other in a woman's. Clumsily, he lowered himself into the long grass and laid his crutch aside, unable to suppress a smile as he started to open Anne's letter.

All at once he noticed what he hadn't noticed before. The handwriting, though feminine, was not hers.

A moment after he tore the seal, the first thunderblow fell.

X

THE LETTER from the neighbor woman. Mrs. Eulalie Brumple, was dated the end of April. Phrases leaped out to sear him:

—*sad duty to report distressing events*—

—*and when I returned, she was not present*—

—*within hours I had begun to fear for her safety*—

—*a seafaring gentleman of your acquaintance has called, and believes he may have some clue to the perpetrator of what now seems a most foul act of abduction*—

—*hope this will reach you with dispatch, bringing you at least the small assurance that I will care for your son Abraham devotedly until some resolution of the situation is effected*—

One word burned Philip's brain and set him trembling.

Abduction.

XI

THE SECOND letter, dated the tenth of May, was from Captain Will Caleb. It told the rest of the dreadful story.

Returning from a voyage aboard *Fidelity*—a voyage capped by seizure of a valuable British prize—Caleb had discovered that his other new vessel, *Gull*, had vanished from Boston harbor with Malachi Rackham in command. Even Caleb's somewhat stilted phrasing—an indication, perhaps, of how difficult it had been for him to write the letter—couldn't conceal his fury:

> *The rogue likewise captured a prize off the Carolinas. To auction*
> *it, he sailed to the Leewards rather than an American port—his*
> *express intent being to defraud the rightful owners of their share,*
> *I am certain.*

> *Upon his arrival in Boston late in the month of April—I now fear with the foulest purpose in mind—he stayed not overlong.*
>
> *Word first reached me only to the effect that he had set sail for an unknown destination. I subsequently learned, through that network of seamen's intelligence which operates despite the presence of the army of a foreign tyrant, that said destination was the port of New York, where Rackham planned to compound his fraud and multiply his illicit gains by selling* Gull *to a new Tory owner—selling, in effect, what he neither owned nor had any right to sell.*
>
> *But I am ahead of myself, and will shortly explain how I come to use Rackham's name in past tense. Learning of* Gull's *abrupt departure, I repaired at once to Cambridge to report the sad turn to your most esteemed wife, hoping to offset the disappointment with my own happy news—that in command of* Fidelity, *I had secured a British merchantman whose sale here has increased your investment some thousand-fold, a right handsome profit—*

Racing on through the letter, Philip could not summon the faintest stir of delight at what should have been welcome news: he was modestly rich. It made no difference because of what he already sensed lay ahead.

> *In Cambridge, the good Mrs. Brumple relays to me the horrid story of the surprising disappearance of yr. dear wife, a most perplexing and puzzling affair, but only that—until more news came to me from New York—this very day.*
>
> *The news was brought by a neutral vessel, Dutch flag, which called at the aforementioned port last week.* Gull *did indeed put in there, but under mystifying circumstances.*
>
> *Her first mate, a fellow who was privy to Rackham's plan, was in command. The captain himself was lost at sea between Boston and* Gull's *destination; lost, I regret to report, along with a Massachusetts Bay woman of unknown identity whom Rackham caused to be brought aboard the night before he sailed.*
>
> *Evidently a struggle ensued, as both fell to their deaths from Rackham's own cabin. In the cabin was evidence of blood, and one window was shattered. The whole business is the talk of New York, and was narrated in detail by the Dutchmen.*

"God," Philip said in a stricken voice. "Oh dear God." He virtually forced himself to read the next:

> *Thus a perverse pattern has shaped itself; a pattern, I say, unguessed and unglimpsed till I recollected Mrs. Brumple's odd tale—as well as certain other incidents, viz., the unsavory and reckless interest of the d——d Rackham in Mrs. Kent.*
>
> *I will endeavor to find out whether my suspicion as to the identity of Rackham's companion has foundation, or, mercifully, is but grim coincidence. I debated long over whether to inform you of matters herewith reported. However, since Mrs. B. later told me she was writing an urgent message concerning yr. wife's absence, I felt I had better take the step.*

> *I trust Divine Providence will prove all worries ungrounded,*
> *and reveal the person who perished with Rackham to be some*
> *other—*

Philip couldn't read the rest. Captain Will Caleb's hope was fruitless. He knew it with a heavy, dead feeling; knew it as certainly as he stood shivering on the solid brink of the cliff.

Finally, he looked back at one passage in the letter.

Late April, Caleb said.

After his decision not to return home.

He damned himself and his idiotic sense of duty. He damned Henry Knox and he damned Washington and he damned the war most of all.

A lightning bug winked soft gold in the wind-stirred grass high above the river. What could he do?

Nothing. *It was too late—*

"Anne!" he cried, a small dark blur on the throw of the bluff. From the silent forests on the Hudson's far shore the frantic echo pealed back.

AnneAnneAnneAnne—

A sentry came running, musket at the ready, to see who had shrieked like a madman in the July twilight.

___XII

"I FEEL partially responsible—" Henry Kox said in a feeble voice. Philip had hobbled to Knox's quarters, a dead man who yet moved and thought. Solitude was unbearable; he needed to speak to someone. Share his grief with someone—

Or was it guilt he wanted another to share?

Realizing it, he was ashamed. Guilt was quite evident on Knox's round face. Forcing himself, Philip shook his head.

"Henry, there's no blame. You were right in everything you said at Valley Forge. And no one forced me to stay and take a British ball. But—"

The decision was spoken an instant after he made it:

"—I'm not waiting for the mustering-out papers. I'm going home now."

"Yes. I fully understand. Is there someone to care for your son until you arrive?"

Philip balanced on his crutch, tugged out the first letter. "The lady who wrote this, Mrs. Brumple. She can give Abraham her complete attention since—" His mouth wrenched. "—since there's no one to bury."

Knox frowned sadly, silent.

Philip stared down at his right leg in the new, larger boot that permitted a bandage to be worn inside. His voice sounded faint, almost like an old man's, as he went on:

"Once I met Dr. Franklin in Philadelphia. He told me a story from his boyhood. How he bought a pennywhistle, not knowing its small value and paying far too much. He said that afterward, he always judged everything in those terms—was he paying too much for a whistle?"

Suddenly, uncontrollably, tears streamed down Philip's cheeks.

"She's dead. I know that bastard took her aboard his ship. She probably died trying to get away from him—that would be like her. I know I had to stay. I know

we all had to fight for the country if we mean to keep it. But the price is too high, Henry. The whistle cost too much—oh, Christ—*Annie*—''

Not caring that it was unmanly, he covered his face and cried.

Henry Knox continued to stare in silent misery. At last he managed to say:

''I'm sure it's precious small consolation for your injury and your personal grief. But as Mr. Paine wrote in that famous pamphlet of his, anything worthwhile—worth having—ultimately commands a high pr—''

Philip swallowed back the tears, silencing his friend with a hateful stare:

''I don't want to hear any more, Henry.''

''Philip, you mustn't lose sight of the goal! You said it yourself—if we win this war, we secure liberty for—''

''Yes, Henry. Yes, goddamn it, I know *very well* what we'll secure. But doing it, you haven't lost the woman you love.''

___3
The Shawnee Spy

THE LOW-LYING sun set fire to the great bend of the river sweeping away west of the point of land where the American flag flew above the five-sided fort. The fort was constructed of heavy logs, reinforced on the landward faces with brick and stone. East of the fort, mercantile establishments, shanties and a boatyard straggled along the shore of the Monongahela. He saw it all through a haze of June humidity as he came down from Coal Hill some kind of walking corpse.

His deerhide shirt and trousers were stained and torn. Strips of the shirt were wrapped tightly around his upper left arm. The arm was bandaged in two other places, below the elbow and at the wrist. All three bandages, and the exposed skin above and below each, were filthy with dirt and dried blood.

The fair-haired man had a strange, almost maniacal glaze in his eyes as he limped along the street in the early dusk, dragging the stock of his Kentucky rifle in the dirt. There were men and a few women abroad, the men mostly in hunting outfits. Despite the heat, a couple of them wore fur hats with raccoon tails dangling down the back. One or two of the men were dark enough to have some black or Indian blood. Nearly everyone gave the stranger a stare. Several pointed to call a companion's attention to the shambling figure.

The man continued to move with that sleepwalker's gaze and gait. His passing stilled the voices of loungers on the shadowy porch of a two-story boardinghouse. The man seemed not to hear any of the clatter of the river settlement: the hammer and thud of mallets from the boatyard; the riffle of an evening drum from Fort Dunmore; the creak of a wagon almost overflowing with glistening black lumps of coal coming up behind him.

As the wagon went by, the man glanced up. The driver was instantly uneasy because the man's eyes burned with fever or hunger or something else. In a hoarse voice the man asked:

''Is George Clark here?''

The driver hauled on his reins, stopped his team. ''George Clark of the Kentucky militia?''

"Yes."

The drive pointed between crude buildings to the boat landing on the Monongahela. "Them's his five flatboats moored yonder."

The man with the rifle swayed, as if he were having trouble standing up. But his eyes were still afire.

"I didn't ask you about Clark's flatboats, I asked about him."

Fearfully, the wagon driver swallowed. "Try Semple's Tavern."

"Where is it?"

"Right down there."

Without so much as a thank-you, the grim figure stumbled on. The driver wiped his mouth and shook his head.

Judson saw. But he didn't give a damn what anyone thought about him. His sole objective was to reach the end of the journey, and stop. It wouldn't be too long, hopefully. A few more steps—

Lord! If only he could relieve his thirst with a swig of rum. Just one drink, to ease the tension in him; to moisten his raw, parched throat—

Since the night when he'd killed five wolves between sunset and dawn, emerging from the experience half alive, he'd wanted nothing so much as a strong drink. It would have eased his pain; mitigated the agony he felt at every step. But, of necessity, he'd gone ahead without it, pushing on—dragging on—toward the forks with the ache of clumsily bandaged wounds a constant companion.

Now, stumbling toward the door of Semple's, his thoughts grew confused. Why was he here? For a drink?

No, that wasn't right—

Dizzy, he swayed back and forth again. He knuckled his eyes, planted his feet wider until the spell passed.

He licked his upper lip, all peeled and split and hard. He blinked a few times, then realized someone was watching him.

The man was a dim figure in the fast-lowering dark. He was seated against the corner of the building. He wore buckskins with long fringing, and hide moccasins. An English dragoon pistol and a hunting knife were thrust into his belt. The man's face was completely in shadow. The sinking sun was behind him; and his features.

Oddly, the fellow hadn't so much as stirred when Judson showed signs of passing out in front of him.

Not that Judson Fletcher expected an outpouring of humanitarianism from the citizens of Pittsburgh. He knew he looked far too grimy and forbidding for that.

But as his mind cleared a little, he mentally remarked on the man's absolute lack of motion. Quite different from reactions of the other inhabitants he'd encountered while walking into the settlement.

In the few seconds that he and the seated man stared at one another, Judson noticed one more peculiarity. The man had his arms crossed over his chest, and his hands tucked out of sight next to his ribs.

Judson's scrutiny made the fellow nervous. He jumped up and disappeared around the end of the building. But not before Judson saw the back of a hand that was either a white man's burned extremely brown by the weather, or was naturally dark—

Well, he'd seen a few similar types in the little town already. He supposed it was possible for half-breeds to venture into Pittsburgh so long as they proclaimed themselves loyal to the American side.

Having decided the strange spectator was indeed an Indian—and cleared his

head a little more in the bargain—Judson shuffled on toward the tavern door and thrust it open.

He heard a blast of boisterous talk, saw a blur of faces in the sullen redness leaking through greasy windows. When he entered, heads turned. Some of the conversation diminished.

At the bar, in the shadow of a stag's horns hanging on the wall, a tap-boy drew foaming mugs of ale from a cask. The smell drifted to Judson clear across the room; set his tongue moving in his mouth.

Abruptly, the interior of the tavern seemed to tilt and distort. Again he fought to stay on his feet. Searched—but didn't find the face he sought.

He staggered forward between the tables, smelling the sweat of the long hunters, the teamsters and rivermen gathereed over venison and fish and hominy. He was aware of foreheads scratched; comments murmured about his ghastly appearance. None of that made any difference. Two emotions gripped him as he took his faltering steps:

Disappointment that his friend wasn't here.

And anger over his own consuming awareness of the rum and ale fumes.

As through a fog that receded ahead of him, stirred and swirled back by the motion of his weary body, he saw half a dozen rough-clad men watching him with particular attention from a table beside a window. The men had been poring over a map. As it became apparent that Judson was heading in their general direction, one of the men quickly folded the map and slipped it inside his greasy shirt. His eyes slid to the ravaged arm, then back to Judson's face, suspiciously.

Judson went by a table of three noisy men wearing homespun shirts. One of the three, in his cups, grabbed Judson's rifle.

"Stranger, where you come from? Looks like you tangled with—"

Judson wrenched the rifle away so violently the drunk nearly toppled out of his chair. The drunk's face and those of his companions sobered as Judson stared at them.

"Are you with Major Clark?" Judson asked, hoarse.

One member of the trio had enough courage to meet the glowing blue eyes. "You mean Colonel Clark? He's carryin' that rank now."

"I see. Are you with him or not?"

"Nah, we ain't. But them lads are." A thumb indicated the map-readers who sat silently, watching the exchange.

Judson's features lost a little of their hostility. "Obliged," he mumbled, shuffling on. The drinker who had seized the rifle swallowed as he eyed Judson's profile obliquely, then swung around and yelled for another rum, too loudly.

Near the table where the six were seated, Judson squinted into the smoke. "Have any of you seen Colonel Clark?"

"Yes," replied the man who'd put the map away. "He's off lookin' to the supplies."

Judson concealed his resentment of the curt tone, asked:

"Will he be coming back here?"

"In a while. Do you have business with the colonel?"

"That's right."

"He expectin' you?"

"I'll discuss the details with him personally," Judson said. The fellow who'd answered his questions shrugged. No one invited Judson to sit down.

He supposed he couldn't blame George's men for that. Who was to say he

wasn't some Tory sent to spy on the famed frontiersman? Still, the rejection rankled; his anger nearly burst out in a flash of cursing.

Just in time, he remembered the larger objective. With effort, he shuffled away from the six unblinking pairs of eyes and reached a small, unoccupied table along the wall.

It was blessed comfort just to stretch out in the hard wooden chair. The tap boy negotiated a path through the tables, appeared beside him:

"Something, sir?"

"I'm just waiting for—"

He stopped. His pain, his fatigue, his anxiety about the sort of reception he'd get from George, and the cool suspicion of the six men by the window combined in an instant to loosen the rein he'd kept on himself during the long, agonizing miles to Pittsburgh.

The boy tried to be polite: "Waiting, sir? For a friend?"

"Exactly right." Judson fished in his trousers pocket, touching coins. Something bleak and sad seemed to fill his blue eyes as he finished, "A friend you keep in one of those kegs. Bring me a rum."

As the boy started away, Judson added, "But just one!"

The boy glanced back, puzzled by the remark. Judson saw the six at the window whispering to one another behind the cover of lifted mugs.

Hell, they're drinkin, he thought. *I'm certainly entitled to one.*

He need that rum. It would relax him. Put him more at ease when it came time to explain to George why he was so late catching up to him. The boy returned shortly, Judson paid, then clamped both hands around the battered pewter mug, raised it and gulped.

Yes—better. His teeth chattered less after the very first swallow. Much less after the second.

The last daylight was leaching from the sky outside the window where the six still talked softly, their map spread again. One of the men was pointing to the map with the tip of a pelt knife that caught lamplight and flashed—

To his astonishment, Judson discovered that the contents of the mug had disappeared without his even being aware of it.

And no George yet.

Ah, but it was marvelous to stretch his legs. Feel the rum soothe the lingering pain, and his apprehension. The taproom seemed to grow noisier and more smoky. Extra lamps were lit now that full dark had fallen. Judson put away a second rum that tasted even better than the one before.

His spirits improved with remarkable speed. He had just about convinced himself that he should approach George's suspicious friends, identify himself and state his business. It certainly wasn't to his advantage that they'd backed him down at first. Hell, he was as valuable to George as any of them!

Yes, he'd speak to them a second time; he made up his mind to it. And if they grew insolent, he'd give them cause to regret it—

"Boy!"

The lad came scampering in response to the yell. "Yes, sir?"

"One more rum—and buy a round for that glum crew at the window."

Consternation among the six. Surprised, eyeing one another, they didn't know what to make of Judson's bold assault on their privacy. Leaning back in his chair, vastly amused and feeling like a new man, he allowed himself a loud chuckle.

When the boy brought a tray of mugs, Judson boomed a thanks, flung coins

onto the tray and tipped an extra penny. Then, holding his full mug, he shoved the tap boy lightly with it:

"Go on, now. Serve Colonel Clark's lieutenants. But they needn't reciprocate. They don't look the sort to understand good Virginia manners anyhow."

He saw a deep scowl at the window table. He responded to it by lifting his mug in a mock toast. Another of the frontiersmen rose from his seat, flushed. Two others pulled him back down because Judson was grinning. A tipsy, insolent grin, but a grin all the same.

His behavior was beginning to cause puzzled comment among others close by. Just as he raised his mug still higher, prolonging the pantomimed toast, he heard a voice at the window table. Belonging to which man, he couldn't say; the tap boy blocked his view. But the words were clear:

"—some common drunk, that's all. Not worth a quarrel—"

Judson fingers whitened on the mug handle. His cheeks turned livid as he slammed the mug on the table, started to jump up. At that instant, he was aware of heads turning near the door. Through the smoke he saw flame-red hair.

The first expression on George Clark's face was surprise. Then came brief bewilderment; next, disappoinment. And finally, disgust.

George saw Judson half risen from his chair, the rum mug in one hand. George's eyes grew sadly accusing. His cheeks were white.

Judson let go of the mug, paying no attention to the location of the edge of the table. The mug tipped, clanked on the floor, splattering the rum in a huge pool.

Judson tried to untangle himself from between table and chair. The drinks had addled him more than he'd realized. He slipped on the wet floor, sprawled on hands and knees, his rifle crashing beside him as he called his friend's name. The name came out as a slurred yelp.

Laughter, then. Scornful laughter, and loud.

Judson's temples hammered as fast as his pulse. His face felt hot. He fumbled for the rifle, staggered up, ready to call out those who'd laughed—

There were too many. Gaping, guffawing mouths ringed him. In stunned confusion, he saw the terrible consequences of his behavior—

The doorway of Semple's Tavern was empty. George Clark had seen him drinking and walked out.

___ II

A FULL moon haloed George's head as he stalked away from the tavern. Judson reached the doorway a good half minute after his friend left, and he would have lost him in the darkness save for that silvery light. George was moving rapidly in the direction of the boat landing.

As Judson lunged across the tavern yard, he heard voices raised behind him, and chairs overturned. But he gave little thought to George's friends who might consider him a threat to their commander. All that concerned him was the contempt on George's face the moment before he turned and stalked from Semple's.

Knuckling his eyes and fighting off the rum-fumed dizziness, he kept the dwindling figure in sight only a moment longer. Then George disappeared into the shadows under the log wall of a mercantile establishment.

Desperate, Judson began to run.

He dashed past the front of the darkened store and down along the same wall where he'd lost sight of his friend. Panting, he pulled up at the building's rear corner, conscious of a violin squeaking somewhere ahead.

He glanced back, saw George's half-dozen friends clustered in the spill of light at Scmple's doorway. He held his position in the shadows until five of them went back inside following a brief, noisy discussion. The alarmists in the group evidently lost the argument. But a sixth man set off toward the fort on the point.

Judson's breathing had a fast, panicky quality as he crept around to the back of the store. He lost his balance, nearly fell when he stepped into a deep wagon-rut. Cursing, he jammed the butt of his rifle into the rut while he searched the riverfront for a sign of his friend.

With a gasp of relief, he saw him—silhouetted against the mellow glow of lanterns shining inside the moored flatboats.

Five of the river craft were tied to the landing, three along one side, two on the other. Each boat was roughly sixty feet long, twenty wide, and squared off at the ends. Above the timbers of hulls that rose a good three or four feet higher than the moon-dappled water, walls and roofs enclosed most of the deck space. A great wooden steering sweep swung to and fro at the stern of each flatboat.

Windows and roof trapdoors on four of the vessels were thrown open, letting the lamplight show. Only one boat—the one farthest out in the row of three—was totally dark. From the others came an assortment of sounds: that scraping violin; voices; the bleating of sheep; the low of a cow. In one unenclosed section of deck, the horns of a massive bull caught moonlight.

But it was George Clark on whom Judson centered his attention. Near the head of the landing, George was walking back and forth with quick strides, pausing now and again to lift his head toward the moon. Judson was reluctant to abandon the protection of the shadows from which he watched. George's posture, and his pacing, were conclusive evidence of how angrily his friend had reacted to the sight of him drinking.

With the back of his free hand, Judson wiped sweat off his forehead. He had only two courses: either slink away and hide until his friend departed down the Ohio, or confront him and try to explain the circumstances that had caused him to break his vow. When Judson thought of all the distance he'd come—thought of the terrible fight with the wolves, and the brutalizing trek to Pittsburgh afterward—he really had no choice at all.

"George?"

George's trained reactions brought him whirling around in a defensive crouch. One hand dropped toward the long knife tucked in his boot. Judson called the name again, and stepped into the moonlight so the redhaired frontiersman could identify him.

George Clark's supple hand fell to his sides. On the flatboat where the violin sawed away, playing a reel, Judson was astonished to hear female voices, then children's laughter. His heart hammering, he walked toward the head of the landing where George waited, a slim, almost blade-like figure in the moonlight.

Never had such a short distance seemed so long. Judson's hands itched and shook. And he was bitterly conscious of the telltale reek of rum. But shock and despair had already sobered his mind.

George turned his head slightly as Judson approached. The moonlight fell across the red-haired Virginian's lean face. Judson trembled at the chill aloofness of his friend's features, and found himself wishing for one more drink.

He walked to within three feet of his friend, catching the pungent aroma of

pigs drifting from one of the flatboats. Aboard another, a child bawled suddenly. A woman's gentle voice murmured comfort. Those on a third boat blew out their lamps and pulled the roof trap shut from inside with a loud thump.

Judson started to speak, couldn't. A night bird sailed low over the Monongahela, moon-silver on its wings. For a brief moment the bird shone as a glowing dot against the woods on the far shore. Then darkness hid its flight.

George said coldly, "I never expected to see you, Judson. When you failed to arrive in Williamsburg—"

"I couldn't help that." God, how thick his voice sounded. "I was shot. A light wound, but I couldn't leave till I recovered. I—I came overland—"

"Alone?"

"Yes. I had a little trouble, but I made it all right. I traveled as fast as I could because I thought you might be gone from here already."

"Should have been. We were delayed at Redstone, up the river. To my surprise, I picked up twenty families who want to make the trip to Kentucky, danger or no." He gestured toward the boats. "Getting their belongings stowed took time."

"You can carry twenty families on those five craft?"

"Yes, and all my men. The boats are exceedingly roomy. And I recruited only a hundred and fifty. I even had trouble finding those. That's another reason for the delay."

"I saw some of your men at the tavern," Judson told him, then added a word that went straight to the issue: "Drinking."

George Clark uttered a long, almost sad sigh.

"Judson, if that remark is supposed to excuse what I witnessed in Semple's, I must tell you it won't. Those men can be trusted with their liquor."

"Meaning I can't be?"

"Meaning you gave your pledge. That was the only condition under which I accepted you."

"My God, I came miles and miles—!" Judson began.

"And look a good deal the worse for it." George pointed at the filthy bandages.

"Shouldn't I be entitled to one mug of rum, then?"

"You answer that," George shot back. "You're the one who gave the pledge. I'm afraid you traveled to Pittsburgh for nothing, Judson."

"For nothing—?"

Stunned, disbelieving, Judson was speechless for a moment after that. Then his anger burst out:

"You pious, arrogant son of a bitch! You're short of men, yet you'd turn me away for downing one drink!"

George's pale eyes flared in the moonlight. "How many?"

"Well—not one. But not many more. George—"

The other cut in sharply, "I told you in Virginia, we have serious military business down the Ohio. Where we're going, each man depends on all the others for his safety. I'm responsible for everyone in my party—I must have men I can trust not to weaken when the going's difficult. You knew that before you started west. You knew that when you ordered up liquor at Semple's. I am not being puritanical, only practical. Believe me, I didn't accept every recruit who presented himself these past months, and—"

Suddenly there was unhappiness on George's face. He pivoted away to keep from displaying it as he finished:

"And much as I might want to, I won't accept you."

At first Judson didn't know whether to guffaw in astonishment or drop to his knees and beg. Then, slowly, he understood that the rejection was final. He understood just how wide the gulf separating him from his boyhood friend had become. And he felt completely stripped of every hope he'd cherished since that day he and George had ridden into the country outside Williamsburg, and he had shot the Kentucky rifle with trembling hands, and given his pledge—

For a moment he almost seemed to see wispy, leather-skinned Angus Fletcher in George's place. Angus shaking his head. *The devil's blood will tell*—

He started to pull the little black-bound testament from the pocket of his hunting shirt, ready to fling the book at that tormenting image. But the mind-phantom disappeared. Only George remained, condemning him with austere silence.

The violin fell quiet. Sheep bleated. The river lapped the flatboat hulls with a tranquil rhythm.

"What the hell am I supposed to do, George?" Judson asked finally. "I've left everything behind. Everything!"

"I don't know," George admitted, weary-sounding now. "Perhaps you can find work here in the settlement."

"*Work!* Christ, I don't know how to do any work! But I can fight—"

"Not in the forest. Not on the Illinois prairie. Not craving spirits so terribly that it hampers your judgment, ruins your stamina, makes you worthless—" Abruptly, George bit off the loud reply. He went on more moderately, "If I could make the decision as your friend, I would. But it's not possible any longer. All I can do is invite you aboard my boat—" He indicated the dark vessel at the outer end of the three. "—pour you one more rum—"

"Now that the damage is done, eh?"

George winced at the bitterness. Softly:

"No, just—just for old times' sake. I'll loan you a little money if you need it, but—that's the end. Come on, let's not quarrel any more. The decision's made. I'd feel much better if you'd enjoy the hospitality of the boat for a bit—"

Ears ringing, eyes blurred, Judson still caught the guilt in George's voice. He tried to hate his friend. Tried to summon wrathful words again, but he was unable. *He* was the guilty one. *He* was the betrayer. Of everyone including himself.

A dreadful weight seemed to push down on his shoulders. Something George had said a moment ago rang through his mind, almost like a bell tolling for his own life:

But that's the end.

Lazarus, reborn for a few hours, had lacked the fortitude to survive. Angus Fletcher was right after all. Judson betrayed and destroyed at every turn. Never quite strong enough; never quite knowing why—

Well, at least there was the promise of a drink.

"All right. I'll accept the offer," Judson said with a wan smile. He and his tall friend started along the landing.

George moved with his customary silent grace. The bull bellowed and tossed its horns as they passed. Judson gazed at the swift-flowing river, thinking of the ruinous tide that coursed through him. That tide had swept him to a final chance—then, just as quickly, swept the chance from his grasp.

Uncomfortable in the awkward situation, George tried to make conversation:

"These are interesting craft, you'll find. They're one-way boats. Designed to

be torn apart again, and the lumber used for shelters once we reach the falls of the Oh—''

Judson barely heard his friend hesitate. He was ready to turn and flee, his guilt deepening moment by moment. He decided to tell George he'd changed his mind; intended to make his way back into the settlement at once. Just as he was about to speak, he grew aware of a peculiar tension in his friend's stance.

George had stopped talking—and walking—just where the square stern of his flatboat bumped gently against the landing pilings. The moon burned in the pupils of George's narrowing eyes as he raised a finger to keep Judson silent.

Wrenched from the morass of his own misery, Judson followed George's pointing hand. Up the plank sidewalls, past a latched wooden window to the slightly arched roof. Judson sucked in a breath. The trap lay back; open.

And, running to it from the far edge of the roof, was a track of small, glistening puddles of water.

George bent close to Judson's ear:

"Someone's inside. Crawled up from the other rail—from the river—''

"Who would it be?''

"No idea. But I keep my public orders aboard, locked in a strong box. I've wondered if some Tory sympathizer might try to steal them. The other set's here—'' He touched the belly of his hunting shirt. Then he tapped Judson's rifle:

"Is that primed?''

"Yes.''

"All right, look sharp—''

George sidled near the rail of the moored boat, one hand darting down to his boot. The blade of his long knife flashed as he raised it waist high.

"I don't care to jump through the trap and surprise our visitors in the dark,'' he whispered. "But maybe we can flush them out into the light—''

As Judson lifted his rifle with sweaty hands, George leaned forward and started hammering a fist on the sidewall of the flatboat.

III

THE MOMENT George stopped thumping, he heard sounds inside. Quick, light footsteps; then an oath, as something banged the deck planks.

"After my strong box, all right—'' George began.

Hands shot from the black square of the open trap. A tall-crowned hat with a flop brim seemed to levitate swiftly into the moonlight. By the time the lithe intruder hauled himself onto the roof, Judson recognized him.

It was the lounger from outside Semple's Tavern. The man who had concealed his hands. Judson thought he understood why—

The intruder's hat blew off as he scrambled for the river side of flatboat. Judson had a swift impression of a knife blade glittering in one brown fist, and metalwork shining on the pistol in the man's belt. George Clark leaped up onto the rail, then to the roof.

Judson jammed his rifle to his shoulder. He had a clear shot at the moon-silhouetted stranger. He steadied his grip, triggered the weapon.

An explosion—a dull glare of orange—

Then the aftermath of silence, signaling a flash in the pan. *Damn!* Either he'd lost most of his priming, or it had gotten damp—

"Stop!" George yelled, starting across the flatboat roof. He was between Judson and the intruder now, so that even with another weapon ready, no further shots would have been possible. Judson put a knee on the flatboat rail, stretched out his bandaged arm, clenched his teeth, dragged himself up to the roof as George lunged across it, knife in one hand, the other shooting out to catch the fringe of the intruder's hunting shirt.

The man let out a wild, terrified cry that instantly raised voices of alarm from the other boats. By sheer strength, George held onto the spy's shirt while Judson painfully hauled himself up to the roof. As he did, he saw the chiseled starkness of the intruder's face; saw black, moon-washed eyes blinking with rage and terror; saw dark, grease-dressed hair hanging straight to the man's buckskin collar—

The Indian fought as George tried to drag him back to the center of the roof. Judson gained his feet at the roof's edge, unsteady because the struggle had set the flatboat bobbing. All at once he saw something else stuck in the Indian's belt:

Folded papers. The orders from the strong box.

With a guttural yell, the Indian yanked his knife from his belt, swiped at George's throat with a bright arc of steel. Judson shouted a warning but George was even quicker. Releasing his hold on the captive, he jumped backwards.

His left boot landed in the trail of water left when the Indian stole aboard. George skidded and sprawled, hitting the roof with a loud clump. By then Judson was moving, peripherally conscious of clamoring voices, of boots pounding the landing as people poured from the other flatboats—

But all he saw was the Indian's throwing hand jerking back, then streaking forward.

The knife was poorly aimed. George wrenched his right shoulder up. The blade struck the roof where he'd been lying, skittered away.

The Indian's other hand closed on the butt of his English dragoon pistol. Crouching, he transferred the weapon to his right hand with startling speed, drew back the cock—

George Clark was a target too large and too close to miss. The Indian's teeth shone, clenched in a kind of death's-head grin as he extended his pistol arm full length. Frantically, George started to roll aside. But he was too late; too late—

Judson launched himself hard and fast. He had a dream-like sensation of almost flying across the roof. The Indian swung instinctively. The pistol discharged at close range. Judson doubled as the ball struck him in the gut.

Smoke drifted. Judson felt flowing warmth in his middle. Then pain.

He dropped to his knees, holding back a hurt cry. He heard the shouts of men clambering up the flatboat's side behind him, several bringing lanterns whose light flooded the roof. George Clark had regained his feet and caught the Indian. He wrenched one arm around the spy's windpipe. With his other hand he pressed his knife to the writhing captive's throat.

Judson watched with a dreamy sense of unreality, even though ferocious pain was eating through his midsection, and blood was washing down under his trousers into his crotch. He knew very well why he had endangered himself deliberately. It was more than friendship. It was the terrible need for absolution.

Curiously, despite the pain, there was tranquility in him. Paying the high price of expunging some of his guilt brought a light-headed feeling of release; freedom. For a moment a strange parody of his old, shining smile wrenched his mouth.

Harsh voices sounded as the flatboat men rushed by him across the roof:

"You all right, George?"

"Who'd you catch? Who fired?"

"Damn half-breed, looks like—"

Clear and strong above the clamor, Judson heard George's voice:

"See to Fletcher there. He took the Indian's ball."

George flung the captive into the hands of others as the lanterns tossed grotesque shadows back and forth across the swaying roof. In the pen area of a nearby boat, frightened sheep bleated louder than ever, quickly joined by squealing pigs, then a wailing infant.

George rushed to the men gathering around Judson, pushed them aside as Judson lowered himself clumsily to the roof. Breathing seemed difficult. The initial violent pain in his middle had subsided, replaced by a steady ache. From the waist downward he was bloodsoaked. He could feel the drenching along his thighs.

George knelt beside him, face pale in the starlight. Several of the other men seized the Indian, pressed pistols and knives against his body, struck him in the face, barked questions:

"You speak English?"

"What's your name, you red bastard?"

"Where'd you come from?"

"Say something or we'll shoot your damn head off."

In a rasping voice, the Indian snarled a word:

"Nen-nemki."

About to speak to Judson, George Clark glanced back over his shoulder.

" 'The thunder.' I've heard of him. Part English, part Shawnee—and one of Hamilton's roving agents. He was after the orders in the strong box."

"Got 'em, too. Almost," a man said, jerking the folded papers from the spy's belt.

Judson coughed. That worsened the ache in his belly. He rested his head against the flatboat roof, seeing George outlined against the moon. His friend's hair glowed like silver fire, and his voice had an odd, strained quality:

"You took that shot deliberately, Judson."

"You—" Speech required immense effort. "—you—would have gotten it—otherwise. And—"

More coughing, this time with a phlegmy sound.

"—it's more important—you get—where you're going than—that I go with you—"

"Let's have none of that kind of talk. We'll carry you to the surgeon at the fort—"

"What—whatever you say. Doubt—if it's worth the trouble, though—"

Over the muted conversation, rougher voices were continuing the interrogation of the half-breed. He fought in the grip of the men holding him, tried in vain to avoid the kicks to his groin, the yanks of his hair, the knifepoints raked along his exposed skin. George kept staring at Judson, stricken to silence.

Nen-nemki started to scream at his tormentors, an outburst of badly pronounced English:

"Goddamn long knives! Come just for pelts, there is land enough for all. But now, goddamn Kaintucks, you want the land too! Come with your women, come with your plows, come with your houses of log and steal our hunting fields, our deer forests, so we fight you for Great Father George! You can kill Nen-nemki—"

"You bet your damn greased-up hide we will," someone growled.

The Shawnee paid no attention, his shrieks silencing the clamor of the growing crowd on the landing:

"—but others will run the trails with guns from the Hair-Buyer, power from the Hair-Buyer. You steal the land, we throw down the red war belt until we die or you die—!"

Listening to the shriek over a steadily rising roar in his inner ear, Judson somehow felt sorry for the captive. Beneath the fury of the Shawnee's ranting was an almost pathetic undertone of misery and loss. Judson grieved for the savages in that strange moment, because he understood why the Shawnee cried his outrage. As the tidewater planters had gradually taken the freedom of the blacks, the frontiersmen too were taking what was not theirs: the lush woods and meadows Judson had seen only through the descriptions in George's letter; but on those lands, Nen-nemki's forefathers had roamed for generations—

Now George Clark and his boatloads of riflemen and pigs and children would ride the river westward. And if George's great plan succeeded, the tribes would have even less land than they'd had before.

Perhaps it had to be. But, oddly, there was little hate for the Shawnee in Judson, even though he knew the half-breed had mortally wounded him.

Judson couldn't hear the rest of Nen-nemski's harangue. The roaring in his ears had grown too loud. He felt an overpowering desire to rest.

Fingers touched his cheek. George's—

"We'll fetch you to the surgeon now, Judson."

"Still think—it's useless—" One hand struggled up to clasp his friend's, because he was all at once cold and afraid. "I'm—only sorry—I'll never—see Kentucky with you—"

Sudden darkness descended.

iV

HE WOKE on a straw pallet in a log-walled room at Fort Dunmore. George was there, and the post doctor as well.

The doctor hesitated a long time and cleared his throat twice before saying softly that the pistol ball couldn't be removed; that Judson was evidently bleeding internally; that an opium tincture had been forced down his throat to ease his pain; and that saving his life was next to impossible.

Judson listened in a detached way, light-headed. When the doctor finished, Judson whispered that his wound didn't hurt all that much, thanks to the tincture. He endured a fit of coughing, then asked George when he intended to head the flatboats down the Ohio. George said they would push off shortly after sunrise next day.

"I—" Judson swallowed, then smiled, his sweat-slicked face shiny in the flickering light of the room's one lantern of pierced tin. "—I'll live—long enough to see that, anyway."

George and the doctor glanced at one another. Despite Judson's feeble voice, he sounded certain.

How remarkable, Judson thought. He *did* feel peaceful. As if a struggle had reached an end, and he could rest in good conscience.

Before drifting off again, he mumbled a question about the Indian spy. George

told him that Nen-nemki had confessed. The Shawnee had indeed been dispatched by Hamilton at Detroit. His mission was to watch for signs of any substantial military force being assembled at Pittsburgh.

"I suppose Hamilton chose him because he's half white, and therefore less suspect. Nen-nemki did make one most revealing statement, though I doubt he himself understood its significance." George paused a moment. "Hamilton wants to know how many men might be coming to fortify and defend the Kentucky settlements."

"The Kentucky—? That—that means the British still haven't guessed—"

Judson stopped, realizing the doctor was still in the room. He started to mutter an apology, but George's icy smile said it wasn't necessary:

"Our true purpose? No, evidently not."

Judson breathed one more word—all he could manage:

"Good."

He remembered George staying with him a long time, hunched on an up-ended section of log with his hands locked around his ankles while his pale eyes watched with a mixture of guilt and regret. Judson woke occasionally, attempted to speak to the tall young man. He wanted to tell George to have neither regret nor guilt because he, Judson, had been the one with the tally of guilt that required erasing. That was one reason he'd lunged between George and the Shawnee with the pistol. One reason, but only one—

He couldn't muster enough strength to say what needed saying, though, and that saddened him. He floated in a foggy limbo where the pain was constant and, at times, close to unbearable. He made no outcry.

In one of Judson's wakeful intervals, one of George's men—a member of the six from Semple's Tavern—appeared to say than Nen-nemki had been hanged.

V

BARELY AWAKE, and having consciously willed himself to live the night, he asked to be carried to the shore in the morning sunshine.

He sensed a sizable crowd around the litter on which he lay; he could hear their excited voices. Though he couldn't feel it in his chilly hands, he knew he must be holding the small New Testament because he recalled asking for it.

Gradually, he separated other sounds from the hubbub: an almost continual thud of boots on the landing; the sharp commands of George's men making the flatboats ready for departure.

Judson saw next to none of the actual activity. His eyes were slitted against the bright daylight. He felt the sun on his cheeks but it was curiously heatless. From his chest downward, his body seemed thick. He knew he was bandaged and doped with the surgeon's tincture.

Time dragged. At last, a woman near him exclaimed, "Oh, they're going—!"

A round of huzzahs split the early summer air. Judson cried feebly, "Lift me up! Please, someone lift me up—!"

At last, he was heard. Hands grasped the end of the litter where his head lay, elevated it slowly. He was disappointed. He could see little more than a glare of sunlit water.

He blinked and kept blinking until, finally, in a welter of confusing shapes and colors, he discerned a glowing patch of red.

Red hair—
George Clark.

Where was he standing? On the roof of one of the flatboats? It must be so. The tall figure of his friend burned bright as an angel's in the sunshine. And it was receding ever so slowly.

"Man the sweep when we pick up the current!' a voice boomed in the distance.

Suddenly Judson was more afraid than he had ever been in his life.

His hands had turned to ice. He had to exert tremendous effort just to feel the grainy surface of the testament cover between his fingers.

Shining and fierce and powerful, the figure of George Clark floated off in the sunshine. The cheering started again. *Gone away,* Judson thought. *Gone away into the west I never saw. Gone away to—what were the names?*

Kaskaskia was one. He couldn't recall the other.

But he did remember that George had an important secret mission in the Northwest Territory. By paying the price of his guilt—a price that had needed paying for so many years—he had helped make George's journey possible. It was a good thing to think about. One good thing to balance against all the bad—

Faces drifted through his mind. A wrathful Angus. A disappointed Donald. Butchered Seth, and Alice, drowned. Vengeful Lottie. Sorrowing but stern Tom Jefferson—

Peggy. Lovely Peggy.

The memories disturbed his sleepy comfort. He'd brought others so much sorrow; done so much that was despicable. He had so few good memories. The best, perhaps, was having seen the nation born—

And there was George. There, he could be proud. He'd helped one of Virginia's finest captains set out to extend the boundaries of the new nation. That could be written down in the meager column opposite the much longer, blotted one.

He concentrated on the distant red-haired figure that now seemed to be floating in a gathering mist. With a shiver, he realized the mist was not external; it was within himself. He clutched the testament tightly, whispered the word, "*Father*—" while the cheering thundered.

The first of George Clark's flatboats swung into the bend at the forks and, with sweeps churning back and forth, caught the current that would bear the little army down the Ohio, into the west.

But Judson never saw. Slowly, he closed his eyes. His head lolled to one side, a faint smile fading away.

One of the men holding the litter said, "I think we can put it down now."

4
The Price of Heaven

ON A spring afternoon some eleven months later, two men climbed Breed's Hill overlooking the Charles and Mystic and Boston harbor.

The older of the two, Philip Kent, walked with a slight limp that contrasted

with the frolicsome skips and jumps of the small boy clutching his hand. The boy was dark-haired, handsome. His brown eyes sparkled as he surveyed the orchards and stone fences and wind-blown pastures of the peninsula.

The boy tugged his father's hand. "Papa, couldn't we have a race?"

"You know I can't run a footrace," Philip said in a sharp voice.

"But we run together sometimes."

"Only because you insist, Abraham. And only at home."

The boy frowned. "All right, but can't we go over to that other hill? I want to see the ships better—"

"You'll stay here. We won't be all that long."

"Papa, please—"

"I said *no!*"

The Marquis de Lafayette adjusted his tricorn against the slant of the sun. On one of the hat's upturned sides, Gil sported the white-centered cockade that symbolized the French alliance.

"My good friend," he said, "would it hurt to let your son roam? I shall be a little while examining the redoubt."

Philip shrugged wearily. "All right. You can run by yourself, Abraham. But no farther than the top of Morton's—" He pointed. "And stay in sight!"

Abraham gave a quick nod, a half-fearful look in his dark eyes as he watched his father's severe face a moment longer. Then he turned away.

Freedom quickly restored his spirits. He was soon racing through the grass on his way to the summit of Morton's Hill.

"A splendid lad," Gil remarked as he watched the diminishing figure. "Four years old, isn't he?"

"Not quite. In September. But he's bright for his age. Mrs. Brumple has already taught him to read a little."

The young Frenchman turned to gaze at the rooftops of Boston across the Charles. "Tell me. Are you and he—shall we say—on good terms?"

"I don't know what you mean by that. I'm his father."

"Do you spend time together?"

"I see Abraham whenever I can. And twice a week—Wednesdays and Sundays—very early in the morning, we both go out to Watertown."

Gil asked lightly, "What's the attraction there, pray?"

"My wife's memorial."

"Ah, certainly. My deepest apologies—I forgot—"

Recovering from his embarrassment, Gil pondered Philip's blunt statements silently. Philip was thankful, because he'd heard quite enough on the subject of Abraham from Mrs. Brumple. Only the other morning, she had launched into one of those well-intentioned but infuriating lectures that would have caused Philip to order her out of the house if he hadn't needed her to care for his son. Even now, he could recall the conversation—

"Mr. Kent, sir, you'll forgive me if I interject a comment—"

"Of course!" Philip retorted, displaying the bad temper that had afflicted him of late. "I forgive you for it constantly, don't I?"

A forced, belated smile didn't mitigate Mrs. Brumple's irritation. "I certainly never intend to be critical, Mr. Kent—"

"Yes you do, my good woman, so go right ahead."

Really, sir, this is intolerable—!"

Philip sighed. "I apologize. Please do continue."

"Well—all right. I've been meaning to speak to you about these continual trips to the place where your dear wife's memorial is."

"You sound as if you don't approve. I see nothing wrong in paying respects to Anne."

"But must Abraham go with you each time? Twice weekly?"

"Why shouldn't he?"

"Well, sir, this is a personal opinion—and you may find it odd coming from one who constantly deplored her husband's lack of piety. But I feel that your insistence upon Abraham visiting Mrs. Kent's memorial so often is harmful to him."

"Harmful?"Philip arched his brows. "In God's name, woman, how?"

"Sir, please accept this in the spirit in which it is offered. The Lord's name should never be taken—"

"Yes, yes, I realize! I'm sorry. Now please get to the point."

Mrs. Brumple clamped her lips together and nodded. Unhappily, Philip realized he'd roused her combative spirit:

"The point is this. A small boy should associate his father with cheerful events and surroundings, not exclusively with graveyards—no matter how revered the departed."

Philip replied quietly, earnestly, speaking the deep hurt that was always with him—and was especially painful during long, wakeful nights in his solitary bed:

"Mrs. Brumple, I loved Anne above all other people in this world. I repeat—her memory deserves to be honored."

"I wouldn't have it otherwise, sir! You miss my meaning entirely. Your visits have become a fixation! The boy barely remembers the dear lady, and he only thinks of you in connection with situations of sadness—bereavement. I cannot help but believe it will warp his nature if it continues indefinitely."

Curly, Philip said, "Thank you for the advice. I will give it serious consideration."

Ye gods, how the old goose annoyed him sometimes! He certainly *didn't* intend to give her words even a moment's serious consideration—

But now, standing with Gil and watching Abraham's whirls and turns in the long grass, the discussion slipped back into his mind, and he felt a twinge of guilt.

He'd seen the fear in his son's eyes when he spoke harshly to him a few moments ago. Perhaps he *was* giving excessive attention to mourning—and, more important, forcing the boy into the same pattern.

But dear Lord, he did miss Anne! Was it so wrong to pay homage to that undying affection?

Gil continued to study him with thoughtful hazel eyes. Somehow the glance prodded Philip to expand his defense of himself and his relationship with his son:

"I don't deliberately leave Abraham to his own devices, you understand. But I've all I can handle running the presses and watching those damned apprentices. Also, as you're well aware, I've sunk a great deal of money into the preparation of my first book."

Gil nodded, tugging the slim volume from the roomy pocket of his coat. The book was bound in lustrous brown leather over boards. Philip had invested in the paper and other materials necessary to produce the sort of book Royal Rothman had suggested—a deluxe edition of Tom Paine's *American Crisis* essays.

More essays were still coming from Paine's quill, of course. But Philip had collected all those previously issued as individual paper-bound pamphlets, re-set

them in a highly legible typeface, run off the sheets and sent them to a bindery. He was gambling on being able to eventually sell two thousand copies to private collectors and circulating libraries.

He had received the books from the bindery three weeks ago, and thus far had disposed of perhaps two hundred copies, on consignment to Boston book shops. Less than fifty had been sold. He had expected to do much better.

"If business doesn't improve," Philip said at length, "I may go out of the trade altogether."

"What?" Gil exclaimed. "You've only just started!"

Philip stared over the sunny hillsides shadowed by a passing cloud.

"Yes, but Anne's death changed a great many things, Gil." He swung to face his friend. "I didn't tell you everything when I showed you the shop this morning. Selwyn Rothman, whom you met, is pressing me for a long-term commitment. A lease on the space I rent by the month. I've put him off because I frankly don't know whether I want to continue. A few months after I opened the shop, I ordered a signboard to be hung outside the entrance to Rothman's loft. Although the sign's completed, I've never called for it. The sign painter's apprentice devils me about it practically every other day—"

Gil looked genuinely concerned as he returned the book to his pocket. "If you abandon your enterprise, what will you do?"

Philip shrugged, "I might have a stab at a different trade. In another city."

"Printing is all you know?"

"That's true. But without Anne, I've damned little heart for it."

"My friend, it saddens me to see you grieving so deeply," Gil said. "It makes you sound like an old man at twenty-five."

"Twenty-six. That's about half an average lifetime, don't forget."

"Still, you talk like a veritable ancient. I've been only a week in Boston, but I've noticed it almost constantly. A change since we last saw each other—a distinct and unhappy change."

"I'll remind you that any new business is taxing. Especially when you wonder if you should continue with it. I wasn't aware of sounding ancient, however."

Sensitive to Philip's sarcasm, Gil veered the subject slightly:

"I was quite impressed by your shop, I might say."

"Over and above the gamble on the book, I have to fight like the devil to get orders. Old Rothman's a fine gentleman, though. He's used all of his contacts to help me. But other people would pay him much more than I do for the loft space. So he's pressing me about a lease. Gently, but pressing nevertheless."

"The chandler is the father of the young man from your mess, am I not correct?"

"Yes. Royal's still with the army—"

Philip sat down on a stone fence, folding his hands around his knee. It seemed to him that he heard drumming in the sunshine; distant drumming. Voices crying *"Push on—!"*

He shivered. But the illusions refused to depart. He heard Anne's laughter—

He searched for the spot where he'd rowed to their very first picnic. Centuries ago, it seemed. Melancholy, his eyes lingered on the strip of beach.

"Philip, you mustn't think of giving up so quickly," Gil said suddenly. "I venture Kent's will prosper if you only give it time."

"I'm fearful no one can really prosper till we have peace again. And the war goes on."

"Ah, but in our favor! Such a change since a year ago! The splendid Colonel

Clark's victories—both British posts in the northwest taken, and that perfidious Hamilton forced to surrender at Vincennes! Captain Paul Jones sailing his *Ranger* into Whitehaven in England and spiking the very guns of their fort! Now the rumors of conciliation attempts being undertaken by Lord North—let us hope the Paris commissioners stand fast. Nothing short of independence. Full independence!''

Philip rubbed his right leg absently. ''They'd better not settle for anything less. Thank God for the French, anyway. Without your country, we wouldn't have a fraction of the negotiating power that we do now.''

It was true; especially since the preceding December, when King Louis XVI's council had elected to recognize the United States as a fully independent nation.

''So it is a bright picture!'' Gil said with false cheer. ''And I hope to brighten it more by taking this leave and returning to Paris. I am going personally to the king, to request a larger fleet, additional troops—believe me, Philip, it is only a matter of time before the war is decided in America's favor. Of course, until it happens, there will continue to be pulling and hauling on both sides—''

''They *have* captured Savannah. And they seem to be mounting a campaign down south.''

''Yes, but Clinton's strategy is most interesting. More important, I believe it is significant.''

''I honestly haven't paid that much attention—''

''Since Monmouth Court House, the British have not committed an entire army to the field anywhere. I think they scent stalemate or defeat in the wind—just as I scent victory. If not this year, then within twenty-four months. Thirty-six at most. I'd wager on it.''

''I hope you're right.''

''France's entrance into the war has turned this to a global struggle. The sort of struggle England can least afford. We are harassing her from the Indies to the Indian Ocean. She can no longer give full attention to you rebellious Americans—''

Gils' jab at his friend's shoulder, lightly delivered, produced no response. Nor did another forced smile. Philip continued to stare moodily at the sunlit hills, the ships at anchor, the raw buildings of the new Charlestown rising where the old one had burned.

Gil perched on the stone fence alongside Philip, frowning now:

''I begged George Washington's permission to sail from Boston in part because I wanted to see you, my friend. I'm afraid I almost regret doing so.''

''Well, I'm sorry. I wouldn't pretend I've been in the best spirits since I came home last summer.''

''One cannot mourn forever, Philip.''

Philip didn't answer.

Gil sighed, tried to start the one-sided conversation on yet another tack:

''I would like to see the remains of the redoubt where you fought.''

Philip raised a listless hand. ''There.''

''You won't come with me?''

''I'd rather not.''

''Damme, you are a gloomy one!'' Gil indicated the small figure scuttling across the sunny landscape. ''If you have no thought for yourself, have a thought for that child. You'll pardon me for saying so—'' Philip glanced around sharply, hearing the echo of Mrs. Brumple. ''—but sometimes you treat him as if he were some Hessian's brat instead of your own son.''

"I told you, Gil, I have a lot to do these days. For one thing, I'm rushing to finish a circular to promote the Paine book in other cities."

"Yet at the same time, you are uncertain whether it's worth the effort!"

Philip said nothing.

"No wonder the boy suffers," Gil murmured.

Philip jerked his head up, defensive again:

"Mrs. Brumple is a very adequate housekeeper. She feeds Abraham—sees to his clothing, his naps—he doesn't want for anything. Our—" The unconsidered word seemed to bring a shadow across Philip's eyes. "—our investment in the privateers paid off handsomely. Of course much of it's tied up in equipment and loft rental and the new book. But I'll always make sure there's enough left for Abraham's needs."

"His material needs. A woman you have hired as your housekeeper is no substitute for a father's attentions and affections."

Philip rose quickly.

"Did you come here to see the redoubt or to lecture me, Gil?"

Gil flushed. "The former. Again I beg you to excuse my impertinence."

Philip sighed. "If you'll excuse my temper. It must be obvious that I'm having trouble with it lately."

Gil asked softly, "With the boy?"

"With everyone."

The admission was a hard one, but truthful. The months since he'd come home from the camp at Haverstraw Bay had been confused, hectic—and miserable. Everything he had confessed to the young marquis he felt twice as deeply inside:

Once, he had looked forward to every step involved in establishing his business. The purchasing of two second-hand presses—the hiring of two devils—the long hours spent meeting delivery deadlines on his first hard-won orders for handbills and broadsides all seemed devoid of the joy he'd anticipated from the days when he first caught the excitement of the printing trade at the Sholto shop in London.

Reality, somehow hadn't matched his expectations. Without Anne to share it, his life was nothing more than a succession of tiresome days and fretful nights. It was an emotional strain to make his frequent visits to the cemetery in Watertown, though he felt he had no choice.

He'd erected a headstone in Watertown, alongside the one marking the resting place of Anne's father. He'd erected it even though no mortal remains would ever fill the grave—

Gil had been eyeing his friend speculatively for several moments. Now, finally, he jumped to his feet.

"Philip, I regret to say I must renege on one arrangement we made."

Philip's dark eyes narrowed. "What arrangement?"

"My promise to take your letter to your father the duke, and see to its smuggling across the Channel to England."

That, at last, got a strong reaction:

"You promised to do it! I haven't written him in a couple of years—"

"Yes, I realize that. However—" Gil pursed his lips, shrugged. "—you are not precisely being a cordial companion. I frankly resent being treated in such boorish fashion."

For a moment Philip believed his friend was wholly serious. Then he saw the faintly mocking gleam in Gil's hazel eyes. He didn't immediately comprehend the reason for it, though.

"Here I am," Gil continued, "faced with my final night in America—my ship due to sail shortly after sunrise—and I will go to this very fine late supper which has been arranged in my honor, but the whole evening will be spoiled by memories of my friend's glum spirits."

"If this is some elaborate joke, Gil, I fail to understand it. I'm not trying to ruin your damn supper party!"

"Never mind—just take my word, you have. I cannot do a service for someone who treats me so shabbily. However—" He arched his brows, studying the slow-sailing clouds. "—if, for example, you were to show your sincere interest in my well-being—"

"How?"

"By accompanying me tonight."

"*What?*"

"I said I would like you to accompany me to the supper party."

"Out of the question."

"You're engaged?"

"There's a cracked leg on one of my presses. I planned to go back to the loft yet this afternoon and start on the repair. I imagine it'll take me a good part of the evening—"

"Ah, pouf! Tomorrow will be soon enough."

"I've got to finish that blasted circular!"

"You are inventing excuses," Gill declared with an airy wave.

"That's not so, I—"

"Why bother with repairs and circulars if you intend to give up your trade?"

"I haven't definitely decided to do that—"

"But you're thinking about it. So neither repairs nor advertisements are that urgent. Besides," Gil hurried on as Philip started to protest again, "there's a practical reason for my desiring your company. The kind family issuing the invitation to me had also included another guest. A young woman who is the niece of my host's wife. Since I am a married man, the host and hostess have arranged for my partner for the evening to be a grand dame quite advanced in years. Some antique relative of Mr. Hancock's, I believe. But the other lady I mentioned—a young widow—is thus far without a suitable compan—wait, wait, hear me out!"

Philip had limped off along the stone fence to stare at the cloud-dappled sky.

Gil rushed after him, still speaking in that light, half-mocking tone:

"You needn't curdle up so! You might enjoy an evening of feminine companionship."

Gazing obliquely at Philip to see if he'd piqued his curiosity, Gil waited. Philip merely scowled. Gil went on in spite of it:

"The young woman is from Virginia. Her name is McLean. According to my host, she is pretty and quite intelligent. To have dinner with her, while possibly a pleasant diversion, should not be construed as an attempt at matchmaking, if that's what troubling you."

It was, in part, but Philip didn't admit it, saying instead:

"Hauling a stranger along, Gil—that's ridiculous."

"Let me decide that, please. Will you go?"

"No, of course I won't go. I doubt the lady would care to have someone like me for a partner. I mean—" He spread his fingers downward to indicate his right leg. His mouth twisted in an ugly way. "—I'd hardly cut a fine figure dancing."

"There is to be no dancing. But your concern is revealing. I've suspected you

were overly anxious about your injury. You probably pay it more heed than anyone else would.''

"I *am* a cripple.''

Gil shrugged again. "You are if you think you are. It is that simple, I believe.''

"To you.''

"So you definitely will not go?''

"I've already answered that.''

"In other words, you reject your friend and his interest in you?''

Philip uttered a long sigh. "If you insist on putting it that way, yes.''

"Very well. I shall have my secretary return your letter to the duke.''

"Damme, you promised—''

"Ah, but I have my price.''

"Lectures, supper invitations—*what the hell is this all about?*''

Suddenly the Marquis de Lafayette grew completely sober-faced. He looked much older than his years as he laid a compassionate hand on Philip's arm.

"It is about you, my friend. It is about your life, which must go on even though your beloved wife's has ended.''

Gil spun and thrust one hand toward Abraham scampering on the sunlit hilltop in the distance.

"Will you consign him to misery the remainder of his days just so you can revel in it too? I think that is decidedly short-sighted. And selfish. Earlier, I tried to suggest that every grief must have an end. You paid no attention—''

"My wife *died* because I was away when I should have been *here?*''

"*Why* should you have been here? Explain to me exactly—why? You professed belief in the army's purpose, did you not? You pledged yourself to that purpose, did you not? You committed yourself to helping deliver this new nation into freedom—freedom for each man to choose his own path without consulting kings or ministers. I am a foreigner, but I have the distinct impression that what has happened in this country in the last few years now means more to me than it does to you!''

"That's a damned lie. I believe it was worthwhile to—''

"Faugh, you do not believe it was worthwhile at all. Otherwise you would not throw it all away.''

"Throw *what* away, for Christ's sake?''

"The future that has been and is being so dearly and preciously won! You make a mockery of the struggle. You no longer care about the future! Oh, you run about pretending to be busy—you substitute frantic motion for authentic purpose—but you've admitted you've lost hope—abandoned yourself to wallowing in grief—even reached the brink of throwing away the career you once hoped to create for yourself in this country! If all of that weren't so, you'd clearly see, for example, that your behavior is creating an irreparable gulf between yourself and that boy. No, don't deny it—I saw how he looked at you a few minutes ago! In twenty years you'll have no son worthy of inheriting what you've begun, because what you've begun is already disappearing in apathy and bitterness. Your son's love will have disappeared too—and no doubt your son himself, when he's old enough to flee the moody creature who's a father in name only! I repeat, do not argue—I am not finished!'' Gil cried, cheeks scarlet now.

"I know I should not speak this way. It is none of my affair if you wish to entomb yourself, give up and rot in despair all your days. But a week in Boston has been quite long enough for me to see the pattern evolving. You are driving

that boy from you, and just as surely, you are counting as nothing all that's been spent to give him a future—a country to grow up in that is unlike any other this world has ever seen. Once, you faced death for that. Now you dismiss it! You dismiss out of hand all the decent men who have surrendered their lives for this new nation. You very conveniently forget they died not only for themselves but for you. More important, for that boy! You forget, and you spit on their sacrifice!''

Gil was trembling. He averted his head, as if ashamed. Philip tried to blunt the stinging accusations with sarcasm:

"Those are fine sentiments. But over-optimistic, don't you think? You're talking as if we've won.''

"*We have!* I am willing to take my oath on it! America will surely triumph now that its own army has shown fighting teeth, and allies are on your side—''

"Allies? We've only France.''

"I suspect there will be another soon. Perhaps not formally tied to America but declaring war on Britain nevertheless. I refer to Spain. However, you're dodging the issue.''

"Gil, I can't help how I feel!''

"But certainly you can. You are a man. Grieve inwardly if you must. Of course you will never forget your wife. But the world goes on. So must you.''

"I'd rather have lost the war than Anne!''

Hazel eyes pinned him. "You see? My indictment was entirely correct.''

"I—'' Philip hesitated. "Well, dammit, not entirely, but—''

"What you mean is, you want both the war won and your wife alive, and it has not worked out that way because things of value carry a high cost. One which must be paid despite our bitter reluctance. Mr. Jefferson named the price explicitly. 'Our lives. Our fortunes. Our sacred honor.' If you were not willing to pay it, you should have said so at the beginning—and stuck with the damned, cowardly Tories! It is a measure of what a weak, pathetic creature you are allowing yourself to become that you put those same sentiments into type—''

Gil snatched the slim book from his pocket and shook it at Philip.

"—you print them in hope of a profit, yet you're blind to the very words on the page! Mr. Paine knows Heaven sets the proper price on its goods. In your miserable self-pity, you have forgotten!''

He hurled the book at Philip's feet and stalked off.

II

STUNNED, PHILIP reached down for the volume that represented so much of his stake in the future—a future which, in his darkest moments, he was indeed ready to abandon.

As he straightened up, he saw Gil glaring at him. The young Frenchman turned his back.

Philip swallowed, remembering almost word for word the passage Royal had first shown him; the passage he'd set so carefully as he began work on the Paine edition.

What we obtain too cheap, we esteem too lightly; it is dearness only that gives everything its value. . . .

Heaven knows how to put a proper price upon its goods . . . .

*It would be strange indeed if so celestial an article as freedom should not be
highly rated. . . .*

But it was dearness and struggle that had given Anne her importance in life,
too. Now she was gone. Irretrievably gone. That was the loss, the price, that had
reduced him to confusion and depression and uncertainty about what he wanted
for himself in the years ahead—if indeed he wanted anything at all.

His temper in control again, Gil walked slowly back to his friend. With a
polite half-bow, he said:

"Once more I was grossly intemperate. But this time I offer no apology. The
words needed speaking."

"Gil, I—perhaps you just can't understand. Believe me when I say I feel
responsible for Anne's death."

"Then you have fallen into dire error."

Philip shook his head, resigned: "It certainly wouldn't be the first time—"

"I do remind you of this. If you cannot or will not lift yourself out of your
despondency, then you *will* be responsible for that young boy dying—even
though he lives physically to be a hundred years."

"Gil, this—"

Philip stared into his friend's face, still shocked and hurt by the assault, even
as he began to understand Gil's motives.

"—this is pretty damned thick stuff for you to spout just because I don't want
to have supper with some damned widow from Virginia."

"The dinner is incidental. Your willingness is not." Gil touched his arm,
adding softly, "Come—will you deny your old comrade in arms?"

A lengthy pause. Philip's face hardened a little.

"Let's get back to the basic issue. If I go, will you carry the letter?"

"Yes."

"Otherwise you won't?"

"No. You will have to see to it yourself. I will consider our friendship at an
end."

"You're not serious."

"Perfectly."

Philip remained silent even longer. The sound of the wind seemed to intensify,
then fade. Shaken, he began:

"What time—?"

He couldn't get out the rest, because Gil exclaimed:

"My coach will call at seven sharp!"

Feeling exhausted by the argument, and more than slightly traitorous to Anne's
memory, Philip let out a long, defeated sigh:

"All right. Seven o'clock."

"Splendid! *Splendid!* You don't even have to enjoy it. Just go. Now—"

Gil whirled him around by the shoulders, drawing Philip's attention to what
he'd perceived only dimly a moment before:

"—your son is calling you. Evidently he's found some object of interest."
Another of the billowy, slow-moving clouds darkened Gil's face. "Why don't
you go to him? Speak to him? This time, out of more than necessity?"

Philip stared at the summit of Morton's Hill as Gil added, "I shall stroll by
what's left of the redoubt and rejoin shortly."

All elegance, lace and gold trim that gleamed in the sun, the Marquis de
Lafayette walked off through the high grass.

___5
The Woman from Virginia

PHILIP CLIMBED awkwardly over the stone fence and started down the slope toward the base of Morton's Hill. He was continually conscious of his limp now, and certain that the other guests at the supper party would be also. What a blasted fool he was, to allow a moment's weakness to overcome his initial refusal!

Or was it weakness? Could Gil be right about the necessity for abandoning his excessive preoccupation with Anne's death?

The blatant bribery concerning the letter to James Amberly had been relatively incidental to Philip's change of mind. He could have found other, though less certain, means of posting the letter to England. He could not have endured the dissolution of his friendship with the marquis quite so easily.

The more he thought about it, the more convinced he was that Gil's threats were deliberate devices for breaking through to the heart of his personal crisis and jolting him, if possible, from the despair that had held him in its grip for months.

Still, the idea of dining beside some strange woman was unnerving. But he had said he would, so now he must suffer through. The evening was certain to be a disaster—

He was glad to be momentarily distracted from contemplating it. The distraction was provided by Abraham, waving and calling from the summit of Morton's Hill.

As Philip reached the depression between the hills, the boy pointed to something in the grass. Philip blinked against the sun, thinking he saw Anne standing on the hilltop, lovely as he remembered her from that first picnic in the pastures of farmers Breed and Bunker—

So long ago.

He heard the distant drums again. The distant voices—

Push on! Push on!

How that cry had terrified them, just before the redcoats stormed the redoubt where Gil was wandering, trying to mark its outline in the overgrown grass.

Philip started up the hill toward Abraham, still upset about the prospect of an evening in the company of some Virginia charmer. About all he'd learn from such a person might be a few details of the widening war in the southern states. He might not even learn that if she were a vapid creature who paid no attention to affairs of the country.

He thought about the long conversation just concluded. Realistically, Gil was correct in one of his comments. There *was* confidence abroad now. Philip heard it in every lane and coffee-house in Boston.

It was a boisterous, be-damned-to-you confidence risen phoenix-like from the humiliation of the early days of the war. It was a confidence forged in the bitter struggle to bring military discipline out of disorder. It was a confidence instilled by steady, courageous, honorable men like Washington, and bizarre professionals like Baron von Steuben. It was a confidence heightened by France's open and growing support of her ally, even though that support was birthed in expediency as the result of centuries-old hatred.

Whatever the motivation for the act, France had tipped the balance. The

bastard nation had at last been legitimized; recognized by another country. Surely others would follow suit—

Laboring up Morton's Hill, Philip hesitated at the halfway point, jerked back to the immediacy of his surroundings. There were too many ghosts stirring here; ghosts whose presence threatened to overwhelm him with grief—

Sweating suddenly, he stood with one hand at his brow to blot out the sun. He failed to notice Abraham's wigwagging arms fall to his sides, indicative of his disappointment as he saw his father come to a stop in the rippling pasture grass.

Philip was pale. The eerie drumming became a thunder that conjured up too many faces he wanted to forget.

Black-skinned Salem Prince and handsome Dr. Warren facing bayonets in the redoubt, and going down to death—

Eph Tait, begging for a rifle to end his own life in the winter-clutched mountains—

Lucas Cowper screaming as pitch on the stump of his arm seared his whole future out of existence—

A schoolmaster with a fly crawling in the moist, dead cavern of his mouth; never again for him the pleasure of shiny faces over hornbooks, or the companionship of a girl called Patsy—

There were more, thousands more, whose names and histories he would never know. Gil said they had died for him. He would have died for them if that had been his lot and luck. And collectively, they would have perished for a piece of paper drawn up in Philadelphia and flung at the world in magnificent defiance of tyranny; magnificent affirmation of everything in which a lovely, tender, strong-minded Boston girl had believed—

Everything *he* had believed.

Once.

A new thought struck him. Anne, too, had given herself. She was a casualty of war just as surely as the others were. He was certain that, to the end, she had kept her faith in the worth of the difficult struggle—

What we obtain too cheap, we esteem too lightly.

Heaven knows how to put a proper price upon its goods—

All those he remembered, including Anne, had known the value of the goal for which the nation fought. And had paid the price. Not by choice. But they had paid.

He stared down at his right leg and thought, *And so did I.*

Would he have had it otherwise? Seen freedom lost in return for personal safety and security? That was the fundamental question Gil asked. In concscience, Philip had to admit his answer was no. But in that answer, there was heartbreak—

"Papa? Come see—I've found a bird. I think it's a waxwing!"

Once more Philip shielded his eyes, shifted position for a glimpse of his son's face. He was disconcerted to see that the boy looked apprehensive. No doubt he expected an absent stare; or scowl and a reprimand—

"I'm coming, Abraham."

He resumed his slow ascent of the hillside, the phantom drumming a crescendo; the sound seemed to throb all around him.

Then, as he concentrated on the boy's tense, expectant face, it began to fade—

As did the horrible massed cry of those long-ago voices:

Push on! Push on!

Suddenly, there was no grimness at all in the voices dying away in the sunny wind. There was only a challenge. His mouth framed the words softly:

"Push on—"

It was what he must do. Put pain and grief behind as best he could, and live the rest of his life in the now, not the yesterday or the tomorrow that should have been

God, it would be hard. But the spur was there.

In the boy.

A good thing, he thought wearily. A good thing, or I never would do it—

He went as fast as he could to the top of Morton's Hill. When he reached Abraham's side, the boy pointed down:

"See, Papa, isn't that a waxwing?"

Yes, I think so."

"Mrs. Brumple showed one to me last week. She said they come and they go and nobody knows when or why—"

Studying the brown, crested bird pathetically flopping in the grass, Philip nodded in an absent way.

"He's hurt, isn't he. Papa?"

"Yes." Philip said, kneeling and starting to touch the bird. He pulled his hand back for fear of injuring the already mangled wing.

"Do you think we could make him well if we took him home?"

"Abraham, I don't know anything about caring for birds—"

He saw disappointment stain Abraham's round brown eyes again, added quickly:

"—but I'll venture Mrs. Brumple knows. If she doesn't, she'll pound every door in Cambridge till she finds someone who does."

"Yes, she knows just about everything." Abraham said, his jutting lower lip testifying to his bittersweet relationship with the elderly housekeeper. "She said cedar waxwings eat mulberries and cherries, I remember."

Philip stroked his son's hair, saw Anne's face shimmering like a double image over the boy's. So close he could almost touch her.

"I'll tell you one thing I'll bet she doesn't know, Abraham, and that's how to build a wood bird cage. It's the sort of thing fathers are supposed to do. Let's pick the bird up. You'll have to do it because your hands are smaller and softer. And we'll need something to carry him—I'll borrow Gil's hat. By the way, I've promised Gil I'd go to a supper with him tonight—"

His stomach knotted at the mere thought of it.

"—but I needn't repair that broken leg on the press until tomorrow, so we'll go along to Rothman's right now and ask Mr. Rothman for a packing crate we can chop apart. I'll build a slat cage for the bird and we'll take him home to Mrs. Brumple and let her ply her skills. If it's possible for that wing to heal, at least the fellow will have a place to recuperate comfortably. Are you agreed, Abraham?"

"Oh, yes, Papa, yes, let's go at once! May we call Gil?"

"Yes, we—"

Philip paused as he started to stand up. Still kneeling, he took his son's small hand in his larger one.

"Abraham."

The old uncertainty blurred Abraham's smile:

"What, Papa?"

"Abraham, you're a good son and I always want you to know I love you. I

haven't been in very good temper these past months, but I promise you that's going to change. I want to show you I love you, not just say the words.''

The boy flung himself at his father and wrapped his arms around his neck and held him tightly.

Philip pulled Abraham close, holding him around the waist, feeling the beat of life and warmth in the small, strong body. Presently he drew back, looked into his son's eyes, seeing for a moment the other flesh that had given the boy life: the remarkable chestnut-haired girl who had taught him to love liberty as much as he loved her.

"One more thing, Abraham—"

"Yes, sir?"

"From now on, I don't believe we'll be traveling to Watertown quite so often."

"To Mama's place?"

"Yes. I will go occasionally myself, but you need not. After all, you must have extra time to tend the waxwing. And you and I should do other things together—"

"I wish you would let me go to the shop with you, Papa."

"You like it?"

"Yes, the ink smell, and all the noise, and the boys who work for you— I wish you could find something for me to do there."

"Perhaps I can, Abraham. I'll try."

"I know I am not very old—"

"Big enought to carry an ink ball, I should imagine." He patted Abraham's cheek. "At any rate, let me make what visits to Mama's place are called for, eh?"

"Of course, Papa."

Philip was ashamed of the relief he saw in his son's face.

But he was gratified by the merriment that quickly replaced it.

___ II

AT DUSK, Gil's hired coach wound through the dimly lit Boston streets. The elegant young officer lounged on the forward-facing seat. Philip sat uncomfortably on the other.

He hadn't been so finely dressed in months. But putting together an outfit for the supper had required Mrs. Brumple to postpone care of the waxwing for an hour, and to make a quick trip to a haberdasher's. From there she rushed to a neighbor's, to borrow a decent pale blue shirt of the proper size, and a cravat of the same shade.

Philip's coat and velvet breeches of dark blue did not precisely match. But his white waistcoat and hose looked new-bought, which they were. Eulalie Brumple had fussed over him as if he were her child instead of her employer—"You'll forgive me for saying so, Mr. Kent, but your hair ribbon is not neatly tied. It looks every bit as sloppy as Brumple's always did. Come here!''—and despite his nervousness, Gil's arrival had come as a genuine relief.

But his anxiety was back full force now, heightened by a continued sense of betraying Anne's memory. Gil watched Philip drum his fingers on his right knee, then reached over to grasp his friend's wrist:

"Stop that! You're fidgeting worse than a green recruit going into battle."

"That is exactly how I feel."

Gil laughed. Philip glanced out the coach window for the first time in several minutes and exclaimed. "Where the devil is this party? Either your host and hostess are in financial straits—"

"I assure you they are not."

"Then your coachman's lost."

"Not that either. We are going to call for the young woman whom I mentioned to you this afternoon."

Philip jerked his gaze back from the row of houses rolling past outside. Quite without his being aware of it, the coach had proceeded to a North End street which was distinctly run down.

Scowling, he said, "When I agreed to come, I wasn't aware the bargain included calling for the widow in person."

"It didn't—then," Gil grinned. "I took care of that after we parted."

Irked and not a little confused, Philip gestured to the shabby houses. "This widow—she's staying in this part of town?"

"No, she is staying at our ultimate destination. The home of our host and hostess. The latter is Madam McLean's aunt on her mother's side."

"Gil, you aren't making sense! What the hell are we doing in the North End?"

"Well, there's a snippet of gossip attached to the answer to that. We are calling for Mrs. McLean where she boards her child."

"Her *child!*" Philip shouted. "You *have* got me into some old woman's match-making session!"

"Philip—"

"You've paired me off with some panting bitch who's lost one husband and is desperate to trap another to support her brat! I've a mind to climb out right now."

Amused, Gil restrained Philip with a hand on his arm:

"My friend, I am assured that Madame McLean has neither the desire nor the intention to go shopping for a mate among cold-blooded New Englanders."

"Then what's she doing boarding a child in Boston? Was her husband from here?"

The hazel eyes grew more somber as Gil answered, "He was not. Philip, please treat what I'm going to tell you in confidence. It is my understanding that the young woman's daughter was born well *after* her husband died. Born out of wedlock, I suspect."

"Then I've more in common with the baby than the mother," Philip grumped.

"I believe the child was brought into the world here in Boston, however."

"Not Virginia?"

"No. The child's mother comes of good stock. No doubt she wished to avoid scandal at home. I do know for a fact that she has made two difficult voyages from Virginia in order to see to the child's welfare."

Philip shook his head. "I still don't understand—" He pointed outside to the less than elegant dwellings with ramshackle stoops and grimy front windows. "Why is the child lodged in this area, instead of with prosperous relatives?"

"Why, simply because the widow's aunt and her uncle by marriage are too advanced in years to handle a bumptious infant. You'll see when you meet them. A private home would therefore be preferable over an orphan's asylum, I imagine—and no financial hardship for Madame McLean. She is reputedly quite well

off. So don't flatter yourself into thinking you'll be examined up and down for husbandly earning power! I promise you, Philip, it's a social occasion only—''

Scowling again, Philip said nothing.

"See here! Are you so ungallant that you can't help escort Madame McLean to the party in style?''

Philip's face turned bleak. He pointed to the new white hose showing at his calf.

"I hardly cut a figure that could be called stylish.''

"*Will* you stop that confounded self-pity?'' Gil barked, his smile humorless all of a sudden.

Regretting his irritation, he started to add something else. Just then the coach rocked to a halt, in front of an unprepossessing house on another shabby street.

"We have arrived. Philip —'' The hazel eyes caught lamplight from the windows of the residence. "—if I have erred, forgive me. I only arranged to call for Madame McLean because I thought you might be more comfortable making her acquaintance before we descend into the somewhat stiffer atmosphere of the party.''

"Well, I'm decidedly *un*comfortable. You fetch her out by yourself.''

"No, I will not.'' Gil said, gently nudging his friend toward the door one of the coachmen had handed open. "The snail must emerge from his shell sometime!''

Climbing down. Philip swore a blistering oath which Gil pretended not to hear.

III

As THEY ascended the steps, Philip tried to keep his shoulders squared. It was impossible. His right one sagged a little each time he put weight on that foot.

To make matters worse, he and the celebrated marquis were being peered at from numerous windows on both sides of the street. Within the house itself, Philip heard a high-pitched squalling.

"Plague on it!'' Gil muttered. "Sounds like her child's fretful. She'll not be ready—'' He let the knocker fall.

"How old is this offspring of hers?'' Philip wanted to know.

"Let's see, I was told—'' He thought. "A year? Something on that order—''

The door opened to reveal an obese man in his middle thirties. The man was either a member of the merchant class, or had attempted to dress like one when he learned who was to call at his front step. From the quality of the neighborhood, Philip suspected it was the latter.

Wig slightly askew, the poor fellow dry-washed his hands and hopped from one foot to the other as his distinguished visitor introduced himself and his friend. From somewhere upstairs, the devilish squalling continued as the obese man said:

"Come in, sirs, please do! I am Chadbourne Harris. My good wife and I board little Elizabeth—'' A piercing shriek made him gulp.

Harris had a comfortable enough home, Philip decided, glancing into the parlor that opened off the front hallway. But the air was tanged with an odor of cooked cabbage, which he detested. Opposite the parlor entrance, double doors

to a dining room stood slightly ajar. Philip spied a gleaming eye on the other side.

Goodwife Harris perhaps? Embarrassed to confront her distinguished guest in person?

Gil, however, was all activity and kindness as he passed small talk with the nervous master of the house. Harris kept fidgeting with his wig and getting powder on his fingers while the screaming continued upstairs. Philip noted a woman's hooded cloak of fine velvet lying on a hall stand. Of the woman herself, there was still no sign—

She appeared all at once in the lamplight of the upper landing, startling Harris, Gil and Philip because, over her shoulder, she carried the howling infant.

The young woman was elegantly gowned, with dark hair and fair skin. Her quite pretty features showed her distress. But she wasn't the least hesitant about coming downstairs. The little girl wearing a nightgown squealed and struggled on the widow McLean's shoulder.

"Mr. Harris," the young woman said, "is your wife nearby? I can do absolutely nothing with Elizabeth—"

"My wife? Ah—somewhere—I'll see—"

He bolted for the parlor, remembered something, hurtled the other way and jerked the double doors open to reveal a flustered woman whose girth nearly matched his.

"Mrs. Harris, Mrs. McLean requires you!"

Goggling at Gil—it was obvious which one of the visitors was the French officer—Mrs. Harris crossed to the younger woman and took the wailing infant. Philip got a brief look at the child's face: angelically beautiful, with fair hair and pale blue eyes. But the beauty was marred by the infant's rage and continual thrashing.

"Madame McLean," Gil said, "may I bid you good evening? I am your humble servant, the Marquis de Lafayette."

She curtsied prettily, though her pink cheeks showed her embarrassment at the child's behavior, and she had to raise her voice to be heard:

"It's indeed a privilege to meet a soldier and patriot of your distinction, sir."

The widow McLean's speech was softer, more rhythmic than that of New England. It had a pleasing sound; but Philip was more impressed at the way the young woman managed to maintain composure while her daughter was yelling.

He had to admit the lady from Virgina had a handsome figure, too. What drew his sympathy, however, was a certain quality in her eyes. A sad quality that didn't match her smile—

Gil was just about to present Philip when the child gave another cry and hit Mrs. Harris on the head.

"Elizabeth!"

Mrs. McLean ran to the older woman, seized the little girl's wrist and slapped it smartly. The child cried all the louder, while Mr. Harris gestured and grimaced, urging his wife to remove the source of the noise.

This Mrs. Harris did. The wail slowly diminished. The young woman brushed at a lock of dark hair that had loosened over her forehead. In her eyes Philip saw the sadness intensify for a moment.

Then she overcame it, and smiled again as she turned to her escorts:

"My deepest apologies to both of you gentlemen. Sometimes Elizabeth is so uncontrollable, I'd swear the child is an imp tutored by Satan himself." Her smile was dazzling now. But Philip sensed a grimmer undertone in the remark.

As Gil assisted Mrs. McLean with her cloak, he said:

"Permit me to present my dear friend, Mr. Philip Kent of Boston."

Fastening the ties of her cloak, Peggy McLean met Philip's eyes with cordiality, nothing more. He stepped forward to acknowledge the introduction—and realized too late that he had automatically put his weight on his right foot, revealing his limp. The young woman's glance dropped for an instant; she had seen—

Philip reddened, found it impossible to speak. Gil filled the strained silence:

"Mr. Kent is lately returned from the Continental army, where he served with distinction. He was injured in the battle of Monmouth Court House, in New Jersey."

"An injury in a noble cause, Mr. Kent," Peggy McLean said. "I have read that the army fought splendidly there. But for the lack of a few more officers with the courage of Virginia's General Washington and Pennsylvania's General Wayne, the enemy would have been destroyed."

Gil beamed. "Quite so. Philip and I have known each other many, many years, by the way. We fought together at Monmouth, and in other actions as well. Happily, my dear comrade survived to lend his considerable talents to that admirable enterprise for the promulgation of knowledge, the printing craft."

Even as Gil finished the embarrassingly flowery pronouncement, he swept the front door open and stepped aside to permit Peggy McLean to go through. Philip caught his friend's prompting glance. He raised his hand and let the young woman rest hers on top.

"Thank you, Mr. Kent," she said.

They descended the stairs together. Philip was conscious that he was shorter than his companion, and that, too, was unsettling. He recalled feeling the same way in his first days of courting Anne—

As he assisted the widow into the coach, it occurred to him that Gil had deliberately raised the subject of his limp in order to minimize it; keep it from being an additional source of tension during the rest of the evening. Climbing into the coach himself, he realized with relief that Peggy McLean didn't appear to be the least repelled by his disability. In fact, as the coach set off, the driver hallooing to warn a crowd of urchins out of the way, she put Philip further at ease by saying:

"This printing business which the Marquis mentioned—I assume it's located here in the city. Mr. Kent?"

"Yes, that's right. My firm's a modest one so far. Broadsides, advertising notices—"

"But I agree with the marquis—printing *is* a craft of great worth to society in general. Especially in these times, when all the states depend on the printed word for encouraging news."

"It is the owner of the firm who is modest," Gil broke in. "Philip has just published a very handsome library edition of Mr. Paine's *Crisis* papers."

"Indeed! I've read several of them. I admire the content as much as the prose. Is your edition doing well, Mr. Kent?"

"Not as well as I'd like. I'm preparing a circular to promote its sale by post to booksellers in other cities—"

"Perhaps I could take a quantity back to Virginia with me. I have friends in both Richmond and Williamsburg, and I'm sure I could prevail on them to place the circulars in the proper hands."

Despite himself, Philip smiled. "Why, that's very kind. I understand you do travel between your state and ours occasionally."

"Yes, when the weather's favorable and the seas reasonably safe. Tell me, what's the name of your firm? Is it a family firm?"

"Well, I have a young son, named Abraham after my late wife's father. Of course I entertain some hope that he might continue in the business. For that reason I christened the establishment Kent and Son."

"I wish both Kents much success and prosperity," Peggy McLean said, returning his smile with warmth.

Philip felt a peculiar sensation then. With a touch of surprise, he realized what it was. He was enjoying this young woman's amiable and literate conversation as he'd enjoyed nothing else in months. He even caught himself eyeing the swell of her figure beneath her cloak.

That produced another severe twinge of guilt. It was embarrassing to find himself responding to widow McLean's presence with even a flicker or physical pleasure—

Perhaps the evening wouldn't be so disastrous as he'd imagined.

Gil tapped Philip's shoulder, interrupting his reverie:

"By the by, my friend. That signboard for your doorway—have you made plans yet to put it up?"

"No, I—"

He cut the sentence off abruptly, realizing how skillfully he had been maneuvered into a trap. But Philip couldn't be angry. Behind Gils' smile and apparently innocent question lay genuine concern.

"I have been too busy to think much about it," he resumed. A moment later, the decision was made:

"I expect to call for the sign and have it erected within a week, though."

"First-rate! I'm sorry I shan't be here to watch."

Peggy McLean said, "Most business signboards here in Boston seem to have distinctive designs, Mr. Kent. Is that true of yours?"

"It has a design. Whether it's distinctive, I can't say. Just the name, Kent and son, lettered in gold, Kent at the top, the other two words at the bottom. In between, there's a green bottle painted black for about a third of the way up. The black represents tea. I was present at Griffin's Wharf when—"

"When Mr. Adams held his famous tea party," Peggy nodded. Her stock rose immediately with Philip, for whatever else she might be, she was no empty-headed beauty languishing disconnected for the world.

Sitting forward on the coach seat, aware that he was looking at her with perhaps too great a degree of interest—and sinfully enjoying it!—he went on:

"Yes, exactly right. During the cutting and dumping of the tea chest, my shoes got filled with the stuff. I put some in a green bottle to save it. I have it as a souvenir at home. I like the bottle's symmetry, but more important, I like what it stands for. So I chose the bottle for the signboard instead of something more typical such as a press or a book—"

He realized the coach had stopped. A large, impressive house loomed outside. All the downstairs windows were aglow with candles, and the rooms themselves shed brilliant lamplight into the street. Liveried servants sprang to the coach door. Glancing out the other side, Philip saw they had returned to the vicinity of the Common.

One of the servants handed Peggy McLean out. Philip followed, alighting with only a slight awkwardness. He was feeling less self-conscious by the moment.

Moving to Philip, Peggy McLean said, "I will need to pick up those circulars before I sail home, Mr. Kent."

"I can have them brought around to you."

"But I've never seen a printing shop. I should like an invitation to visit yours."

"You may have it, of course."

"I hope you don't think me too forward. Since my husband was killed some years ago, it's been necessary for me to involve myself in many areas not normally considered proper for a woman. With my overseer's assistance, I manage my own plantation, for example. I've found I have an interest in commerce—even a certain small aptitude for it. I like to broaden my knowledge of all areas of business—"

"Then you'll surely be welcome at Kent and Son, Mrs. McLean."

"Wonderful! We can work out the details over supper. And on my next trip to Boston, I'll give you a report on my success with the circulars."

"You'll be coming back reasonably soon?"

"Yes, Mr. Kent, most assuredly."

Standing perhaps a foot from him in the glare of a torch held aloft by one of the host's footmen, Peggy McLean looked at Philip a moment longer. Color rushed to her cheeks. She glanced away, adding:

"I wonder if I might have your hand to climb the steps—?"

Philip smiled. "Certainly."

When he lifted his arm and she touched him, there was a peculiar prickling all along his spine. And, within him, only a vestige of guilt.

Philip couldn't see the Marquis de Lafayette smiling broadly as he followed the couple up the stairs in the shifting light of the windblown torches.

___EPILOGUE
The World Turned Upside Down

ON THE nineteenth of October, 1781, some eight thousand British and German troops laid down their arms outside the tiny tobacco port of Yorktown in the state of Virginia, in token of the surrender of their commanding officer, General Charles Cornwallis, Earl of Cornwallis, to the combined American and French forces under George Washington and his ally, Count Donatien de Rochambeau.

The Hessians who had been besieged in Yorktown, trapped between the American army and the French fleet of Admiral de Grasse, stacked their arms with phlegmatic resignation. The British were a shade less gallant; embittered redcoats were seen to crack the butts of their muskets on the ground, and regimental musicians staved in the heads of their drums. Lord Cornwallis himself pleaded indisposition, sending a deputy to the ceremony.

General Washington refused to treat with the deputy. He insisted that Cornwallis' alternate speak with *his* alternate, an American general of lesser rank, Benjamin Lincoln.

During the unit-by-unit abandonment of arms and musical instruments, the

British bands played a peculiar assortment of music. Few were marches; some were airs with a distinctly melancholy strain. One, a popular nursery tune entitled *The World Turned Upside Down,* seemed ironically appropriate to the failure of the last thrust of the army of his Majesty. The army had swept up along the southern coast of the United States, hoping to win the victory that had eluded the British in the north.

At Sermon Hill, Caroline County, Donald Fletcher heard the story of the siege and surrender not many days later, from relieved residents of the district. There had been an ominous period of several months in which all the farmers and planters along the Rappahannock had feared they would be fighting redcoats from their own fields and verandas.

News of the surrender brought jubilation. And word of the playing of that particular children's melody tickled Donald's fancy as very little did any more.

Donald felt his age. His gouty leg kept him in constant pain. He did leave Sermon Hill occasionally, but not without enormous effort.

Donald's stomach had swollen to immense proprotions from his continuing refusal to cease his excessive eating and drinking. The task of operating the plantation after his father's death from a paralytic seizure in mid-1780 had become a burdensome routine without real purpose; only massive meals and massive quantities of port and claret could relieve the lonely sameness of his days.

So he enjoyed hearing every detail of the humiliation of Cornwallis, a humiliation most interpreted as the end of hostilities, even though peace was by no means official as yet.

Before the year was out, the gentry along the Rappahannock found their own world turned topsy-turvy by other unexpected happenings. Hints of the first one circulated about Thanksgiving time, and Donald, through his house blacks, soon managed to confirm that the rumors had a factual basis.

Williams, the overseer who had helped Seth McLean's widow keep her plantation operating as efficiently as was possible during the war, had been authorized to place the property on the market.

The actual owner, Peggy Ashford McLean, was away on one of her frequent trips to the city of Boston when the estate went up for sale. She returned to Caroline County in early December—and to the astonishment of Donald and everyone else in the district, she brought with her a new husband, plus two children.

One was her bridegroom's son by his first wife. The second was a little girl a few years younger, who was supposedly related to Peggy's distant kin in New England.

There were no fêtes, no gala balls to welcome the new couple, because they had expressed their desire for privacy, keeping to their great house except for Sunday worship at the little Presbyterian church six miles from Sermon Hill. The children were not present on those occasions.

Like most other persons of substance along the river, Donald at first harbored private reservations about the fellow Peggy McLean had married. A mere tradesman, it was said; a printing-house owner! Neighbors who came to visit Donald stated unequivocally that the Bostonian had to be a fortune-hunter. The opinion was widely held until Williams gradually let slip certain details to disprove the charge.

According to the overseer, Mr. Philip Kent had some wealth of his own, due

to successful investment in a privateering enterprise. His printing business was, if not yet overwhelmingly properous, at least successful.

And he had important personal connections.

He was a good friend of a wealthy Jewish merchant of Boston—there were several thousand Jews in America at the time, many quite affluent—and Kent's friend, Selwyn Rothman by name, was said to have been one of those who had quite literally helped stave off the total collapse of America's finances during the war. He and others had advanced the government huge sums from their personal treasuries. Rothman, it was reported, had given nearly as much as the Polish-born Haym Solomon and, like Solomon, had not demanded any definite terms for repayment.

Further, Donald learned that Rothman had helped Peggy McLean's new husband through his first difficult days of establishing the firm called Kent and Son. But what gave final approval to Kent's credentials was his widely discussed friendship with the Marquis de Lafayette. The Frenchman was a heroic figure in the eyes of Virginians, both because George Washington thought so highly of him, and because of his presence during the fighting at Yorktown.

Curious about the new liaison that was to result in Peggy Ashford McLean Kent's removal to a new home in the North, Donald made a difficult trip to worship services one drizzly Sunday morning. He noted that Peggy looked radiantly happy as she entered the tiny church on the arm of her new husband—who, Donald saw with some astonishment, was a good half a head shorter than his wife. Also, he limped noticeably.

Yet the Bostonian had a rather cocky bearing, and a certain pugnacious set to his dark features. To Donald he appeared a man of determination and quiet vigor.

In the churchyard afterward, Donald had a chance to greet the New Englander. He found Kent to be well educated, at least superficially. What continued to impress Donald the most, however, was Kent's steady, almost bold stare—as if he would cheerfully thrash any person who dared to question his right to marry a woman of such impeccable background as Peggy.

All smile and blushes—looking healthier, in fact, than he'd seen her in many a year—Peggy invited Donald to call at the McLean house that afternoon. He accepted.

In the carriage on the way back to Sermon Hill—Donald could no longer exert the effort or withstand the pain of riding horseback—he lingered on some far-from-godly thoughts which had teased his mind throughout the tedious sermon.

Peggy certainly seemed pleased with her new spouse. But Donald wondered about the more intimate details of the marriage. Having endured the nightmare of the uprising of '75—been raped, was the long and short of it—would she be capable of fulfilling what were euphemistically known as wifely duties?

And had the groom known the quality—or should one say "limitations?"—of the goods he had acquired?

Donald realized he'd never know the answers, and supposed they were none of his business. But he wondered all the same.

At the McLean house, he visited for an hour while the drizzle continued to fall from the December sky. He found himself enjoying conversation with this Kent chap, who had served with the American army for several years, and been mustered out after Monmouth Court House, where he had received the wound that crippled him. At one point, their talk was interrupted by the sudden arrival of the two children.

One was a rather stocky, dark-haired boy of about six. The other was a bad-tempered but lovely little girl of about three.

Philip Kent presented his son Abraham, but Peggy had scant chance to do the same with the girl, whose name was Elizabeth. The child seemed preoccupied with turning over small tables, pulling books from shelves and howling like a fiend when Peggy tried to discipline her—gently at first, then crossly.

Fortunately, the little girl caused so much commotion in the couple of minutes before Peggy seized her and carried her out bodily, both Peggy and her new husband failed to notice the absolutely thunderstruck expression on Donald Fletcher's face.

When Peggy returned, out of breath and murmuring apologies, Donald had concealed his surprise behind a bland expression. But he did ask a question or two about the little girl. She would of course become part of the new household along with the boy Abraham, Kent said.

Peggy supplied the information that the girl was an orphaned relation of the northern branch of Peggy's mother's family. Elizabeth had been raised in a private home in Boston. It was the child, Peggy explained, whom she had gone to visit by ship, twice annually at first, then more often. Donald concluded that the shortened intervals were probably prompted by a ripening romance with Kent.

During the discussion of the vile-tempered little girl, Peggy seemed to be staring at Donald in an odd, apprehensive way. Still privately agog, he struggled to keep his features bland, and to give her no cause to think he suspected much of her story was a lie. Soon she lost her air of tension. The visit ended on an equable basis—though Donald could still hear the little girl yelling her head off somewhere upstairs as he bundled into his coat and muffler. Just before he stepped off the veranda to the open door of his cartridge, he shook Kent's hand, then Peggy's. On her wrist he saw a pattern of red marks; she had been bitten.

Riding back to Sermon Hill for the second time that day, he asked himself if his senses had deceived him. But he was certain they hadn't. He didn't know whether to feel horribly sorry for the new Kent household, or to laugh at the unexpected twists and turns fate could take.

The rain fell more heavily throughout the rest of the afternoon. That evening, in Sermon Hill's huge and lonely dining room, he found he had no appetite for food. After the blacks had left him, he sat with a decanter and glass, his bandaged left leg propped on a stool and his eyes resting on one of the more recent and unprecedented additions to the furnishings of the house.

On the inner wall, its canvas glowing in the candlelight hung an oil portrait of Angus Fletcher.

The portrait was of immense size. It showed the old man dressed in elegant gentleman's apparel—a suit and accessories which, in fact, he had never owned, but which were added by the artist at Angus' insistence.

Throughout his entire life, the elder Fletcher had shown no concern whatever for his personal appearance. Indeed, he'd shown few traces of vanity at all, except for the vast and unspoken one of operating Sermon Hill exactly as he wished, and at a profit. Then, unexpectedly, he had commissioned the painting—one month after receiving the news that Judson had been shot to death in Pittsburgh.

George Clark was another hero to the Virginians along the river. After his victory at Kaskaskia, then the more incredible one at Fort Vincennes which his little army had approached in the dead of winter, across flooded prairies others

would have considered impassable, George Clark had sent Angus a letter. Donald had read the letter several times; it was still stored among his father's few personal effects in the office.

In the letter, the Virginia frontiersman paid glowing tribute to Judson's heroism. He made it quite clear that, except for Judson's sacrifice, the great enterprise in the west would very likely never have come about.

It was after the receipt of the letter that Angus Fletcher began making inquiries about qualified portrait painters—insisting on references and answers by mail to a series of questions. He finally selected an artist from Baltimore.

The artist boarded at Sermon Hill six weeks while completing the canvas. Angus sat willingly, though he put forward certain demands which the artist protested. Sermon Hill must be glimpsed in the background of the painting. In the middle distance, one or two figures must appear in a field, standing passively. Black figures; slaves.

The artist said all those stipulations would limit his thinking; hamper his artistic expression. But Angus' hectoring ways, and the high price he was paying, won out. So there Donald's father hung, resplendent in a white lace cravat such as he never owned in later life. And there were the docile blacks behind him, and Sermon Hill a whitish rectangle in the upper right.

The artist from Baltimore had professed to be an admirer of the well-known Boston miniaturist and portrait painter, John Copley, who had gone off to Italy before the war and was now settled in England—colonial migration in reverse! The artist told Donald that Copley had painted a number of the Boston radicals responsible for precipitating the conflict—Samuel Adams and the express rider Revere were two—and that in their portraits, Copley had striven both for verisimilitude and for composition that captured the essence of the subject's character. Thus Angus Fletcher had been posed with one fisted hand on his hip. And he was shown full face, so that the tough, lined countenance assaulted the viewer head on. Whether by accident or intent, the artist had brushed tiny highlights into Angus' pupils, lending them a suggestion of temper about to be unleashed.

At first, Donald had charged the whole business off to senility, plus Angus' abrupt if belated realization that he, like all men, would go to the earth in the end. Only gradually did it dawn on Donald that Judson's behavior at Pittsburgh had given Angus something of which to be genuinely proud; something which therefore made the old man worthy of memorialization in a family portrait. It was as if, for all his days, Angus Fletcher had harbored doubts about his principles, his style of life, his very worth—doubts which he had succesfully concealed. Donald came to the conclusion that he never wholly understood his father until the portrait was completed.

Now, with the winter rain ticking the glass of the dining room windows and the candles burning down in their graceful chimneys, Donald refilled his glass and regarded the protrait with a sardonic smile.

In the hours before Angus Fletcher had closed his eyes for the last time, he had rambled a good deal to his older son who sat by the bedside. Angus confessed his joy in Judson having partially redeemed himself by the way he died. But Angus again stated that he thanked the God he would soon confront that Judson had fathered no children. In spite of his manner of dying, Angus said with regret, Judson had been driven by the devil. Pride and grief wove together in that, Angus' final verdict on his second son.

It was a blessing that Angus Fletcher wasn't alive today, Donald thought, to have seen what he had seen at McLean's.

He understood at last Peggy McLean's long absence in New England before Judson's departure to the west. She had been bearing the child.

When had it been conceived? So far as he knew, Judson had visited Peggy only that one time after Seth's burial. Perhaps there had been additional meetings of which Donald was unaware.

Obviously others in the neighborhood would now suspect an illegitimate birth as one possible reason for Peggy's mysterious behavior. Donald thought that only the most perspicacious would identify the father, however.

He understood Peggy's apprehension during the afternoon visit, too. He was thankful he had done nothing to show he recognized the little girl's resemblance to his younger brother.

But there could be no mistake. Elizabeth had Judson Fletcher's bright hair and Judson Fletcher's bright eyes, and she bore a certain facial resemblance to Judson as well.

She had also inherited Judson's violent tendencies, it seemed.

And that fellow Kent was taking the child into his household! Donald wished him the strength and luck to survive the ordeal.

God, it was funny how the world revolved.

A collection of contentious, stubborn-minded colonials of all degrees of literacy, wealth and dedication had somehow defeated the military might of the globe's greatest empire. In the process, a new country had come into being.

And Judson, who had squandered most of his life in uncontrollable excesses, had redeemed himself in his father's eyes by dying a hero of sorts—

And leaving no heirs.

And now an angel-faced little harridan was carrying the Fletcher blood straight to the table of a Boston family. *Thank heaven I won't be around in fifty years to see what havoc that's wrought!*

Laughing aloud, Donald poured more wine while the rain beat harder on the house and the Fletcher eyes glared from the wall in the guttering candlelight.

___Afterword

AUTHORS SOMETIMES think (misguidedly) that once *The End* is written, all the important work has been done.

The truth, of course, is far different. The publication process is never completed—a real link is never created—until a book reaches the hands of a reader.

And a great many people collectively perform the indispensable job of seeing any new book out into the world where that happens. But those same people are usually overlooked in the author's haste to thank everyone from his postman to his dog.

So recognition and appreciation are due all those in the unsung sectors of publishing, from copyediting and production to marketing and sales, for their dedicated and enthusiastic effort on behalf of this series, and this writer.

JOHN JAKES

THE SEEKERS

For my daughter Ellen

"Ask these Pilgrims what they expect when they git to Kentuckey the answer is Land. have you any. No, but I expect I can git it. have you any thing to pay for land, No. did you ever see the Country. No but Every Body says its good land . . .

"Here is hundreds Travelling hundreds of Miles, they Know not for what Nor Whither, except its to Kentuckey, passing land almost as good and easy obtained, the Proprietors of which would gladly give on any terms but it will not do . . . its not the Promised Land its not the goodly inheratence the Land of Milk and Honey."

> 1796: MOSES AUSTIN,
> FOUNDER OF TEXAS,
> WRITING OF A JOURNEY
> FROM WYTHE COUNTY, VIRGINIA,
> TO LOUISIANA TERRITORY.

"I of course expected to find beaver, which with us hunters is a primary object, but I was also led on by the love of novelty common to all, which is much increased by the pursuit of its gratification . . ."

> 1827: THE JOURNAL OF
> JEDEDIAH SMITH,
> MOUNTAIN MAN.

Contents

CONTENTS

KENT AND SON

____1
Battle Morning

ABOUT FOUR o'clock Abraham Kent woke from a fitful sleep and realized he couldn't rest again until the day's action was concluded, in the Legion's favor or otherwise.

His heart beat rapidly as he lay sweating in the tiny tent. He heard muted voices outside; saw a play of flame and shadow on the tent wall. Campfires; burning brightly in the sweltering dark. No attempt had been made to conceal the presence of three thousand men on the north bank of the Maumee River. The Indians already knew that the general who commanded the army of the Fifteen Fires had arrived, and meant to fight. The only question was when.

Abraham had learned the answer to that the preceding evening. Sitting his mare in formation, he'd listened to the reading of the general order that announced a march at daybreak. Men cheered—principally some of the less disciplined Kentucky mounted militia, whose ranks numbered close to fifteen hundred.

On hearing the order, Abraham Kent felt both relief and sharp fear. Relief came from knowing that nearly two years of preparation, marching, fort-building in the wilderness of the Northwest Territory was finally reaching a climax. The general had repeatedly sent messages to the tribes, urging peace and conciliation even as he drove his Legion of the United States deeper into the lands north of the Ohio, constructing stockade after stockade en route. The reply of the tribes to the last message had been equivocal. So the general had let it be known he meant to attack.

Abraham Kent experienced fear on hearing the order because he'd never taken part in an actual engagement; not in all the twenty-four months since he'd arrived in Pittsburgh in response to the recruiting notices in Boston. Those notices

declared that the United States was raising a formal army for the first time since the Revolution.

There had been engagements as the American army twisted back and forth across the hostile country, earning the general the name *Blacksnake* from the Indian spies who watched the army's progress. Earlier in the summer, for example, a Shawnee war party had launched a ferocious attack on newly built Fort Recovery. When it happened Abraham was on duty at the general's base, Fort Greenville, a day's ride south. So he had yet to be blooded.

Today, the twentieth of August, 1794, that situation was likely to change.

He crawled out of the tent, his linen shirt and trousers already plastered to his body. For a moment he wondered whether he would see the dawn of the twenty-first.

Scouts had brought reports into the camp beside the river that upwards of two thousand Indians had gathered some seven to ten miles northeast, near the rapids of the Maumee where the British had brazenly erected a fort close to McKee's trading station. Warriors from all the major tribes had come: Blue Jacket's Shawnee, including the young warrior with the fierce reputation, Tecumseh, who had led the unsuccessful attack on Fort Recovery. Little Turtle's Miamis were there. The Wyandots under Tarhe the Crane. Captain Pipe's Delawares. All united to resist the Americans who were bent on taking the Indians' land—

Not a man in the Legion of the United States considered it anything but American land, of course. The vast expanse west of Pennsylvania, east of the Mississippi, north of the Ohio and south of the Lakes had been ceded to the new nation by Britain as part of the peace treaty of 1783. Yet in the following decade, the British continued to maintain their posts in the surrendered territory; kept urging the Indians to demand that the northern border of American expansion remain the Ohio River.

Small expeditionary forces had marched into the Northwest before, to try to settle matters. One, St. Clair's, had met death along the bend of the Wabash tributary where Abraham's commanding general had built Fort Recovery the preceding winter. Yawning and stretching as he walked past the men talking around the campfires, Abraham vividly recalled the stone-gray winter's day he had ridden as one of the eight hundred pressing forward to the site of St. Clair's defeat—

In the first drifting snowflakes, he had seen skulls and bones protruding from the frozen ground. As the new fort rose on the site during the early months of 1794, men working the earth dug up and counted the human skulls. Over six hundred of them. Six hundred of General Dicky Butler's soldiers, slaughtered—

Abraham ambled on through the steamy darkness, breathing the acrid wood smoke; listening to the strained, subdued conversations; seeing here and there a surreptitious jug passed, in violation of the general's edict forbidding use of alcohol in camp or on the march. Nineteen years old, the young soldier had wide shoulders and a stocky build; heavy brows and the dark eyes of his parents. He'd also inherited their dark hair, which he never bothered to dress since dashing about on horseback loosened all the powder. He stood five feet ten inches, taller than his father.

Abraham passed the end of an earthwork. Behind it, the general had deposited the army's baggage and wagons, in case they needed to be defended during a retreat. Outside a command tent Abraham saw aides conferring with Captain Zebulon Pike, who'd been put in charge of the rear position. He strode by the circle of lantern light, swatting mosquitoes that deviled his neck, and soon

reached the picket lines where the dragoon horses fretted and stamped in the pre-dawn heat.

A sentry thrust out his musket:

"Who goes?"

"Cornet Kent. I want to see to my mount."

The sentry saluted the junior officer, stood aside. Abraham ducked between two nervous stallions, found his mare at her tether, ran his hand down her neck, soothing her as if she were human:

"I hope they fed and watered you well, Sprite. You'll need to be lively when the sun's up. They say the Indians have taken positions among some fallen trees destroyed by a storm a long time ago. That'll be hard ground for galloping and jumping, my girl—"

The mare nipped at his caressing hand, but not viciously. Abraham smiled. In two years, he and the mare assigned him at Cincinnati had established a bond between them; the kind of bond infantrymen and other, lesser orders of human beings could never comprehend. Like the other dragoon officers, Abraham talked to his horse frequently. He knew Sprite recognized his voice if not the sense of his words. Now he almost spoke his fear aloud to the animal; almost launched into a monologue concerning the special reason he was apprehensive about the coming battle. He had admitted the reason to few other human beings; he admitted it to himself only with some shame—

Oh, he was a good enough soldier, he supposed. But his motive for enlisting— for making the difficult overland journey to Pittsburgh—had not been purely patriotic. He had no desire for glory in battle, and hence feared combat perhaps more than some officers did—

Noticing the sentry watching him, Abraham kept it all to himself. After one more stroke of Sprite's sweating neck, he turned and made for the river, feeling a steady pressure in his loins.

He was again thankful that his father's business had prospered sufficiently to permit him to go riding on the Common on a fine hired mount when he was growing up. Abraham was likewise thankful that his stepmother had encouraged the lessons in horsemanship. Except for that, he would never have been accepted for the dragoons.

But astride Sprite, and commanded by an excellent officer—a captain with the peculiar name Robert MisCampbell—Abraham knew that in the coming battle, he would be less of a target than those in the four Sub-legions who advanced on foot with bayonet-tipped muskets. Whether the general's combined infantry and cavalry stood a chance against the untrained but elusively swift tribesmen waiting somewhere up the Maumee, he couldn't say. That made him even more glad that he was going into danger on an animal he loved and trusted.

A trampled patch of corn and the charred smell of a burned Indian lean-to told him he was nearing the shore. He smelled the wet loam of the bottoms; heard night birds crying among the rushes. The stars were lost in a humid haze. He unfastened the buttons of his trousers and started to urinate in the river.

While in this prosaic but somewhat restrictive position, he heard slow footsteps along the bank.

He turned his head, choked back an exclamation as he recognized the man limping out of the darkness, a rangy silhouette against the distant fires.

Faced with the choice of saluting or closing up his trousers, he decided on the latter. Only afterward did he whip up his right hand in the respectful gesture due

the tall, somewhat rotund officer whose left boot and pants leg were almost entirely swathed in strips of flannel.

Major General Wayne—admiringly called Mad Anthony ever since his daring seizure of the British fort at Stony Point during the Revolution—rested a hand on the butt of one of the two pistols thrust into his belt and stared at Abraham Kent, whose face all at once felt hotter than ever.

II

THE GENERAL, appearing rather bedraggled in his old blue coat, leather sword belt and leg-bandages, smiled at last:

"Cornet Kent. Good evening to you. Good morning, rather."

"Good morning, sir," Abraham managed to say in a reasonably calm voice.

Wayne hobbled toward him; Abraham guessed the general must be close to fifty now. Supposedly his left leg still contained a piece of ball lodged there during the Virginia campaign at the close of the War for Independence. He had been called out of retirement to head the army sent west by President Washington to quell the Indian threat in the Northwest Territory once and for all.

Wayne's men loved him; Abraham was no exception. The Indians dreaded him because it seemed that he was never off guard; never slept; knew everything that transpired for miles around whatever position he happened to be occupying.

In gentle reproof, Wayne said, "I urged my men to get as much sleep as possible, Cornet. All my men."

"Yes, sir, but—well, sir, that's hard, facing an engagement as we are—"

To Abraham's relief, Wayne nodded. "As you can tell from my presence here, I understand perfectly. I hope our red adversaries aren't resting. I know they're not eating," he added with a thin smile.

Abraham knew the meaning of Wayne's last words, of course. The general's stratagem had been the talk of the camp for two days:

Via his scouts, Wayne had let slip word that he intended to fight, knowing full well that, by custom, the Indians would never eat on the morning of a battle. For that reason Wayne had carefully refrained from mentioning exactly when he intended to engage. Thus the enemy had probably taken little or no nourishment for almost forty-eight hours.

Wayne stumped closer. As always, the general's limp reminded Abraham of his father's, the result of a hit by a musket ball at the battle of Monmouth Court House. The general asked:

"Did the last pouches of mail from Cincinnati bring any word of your father, Cornet?"

"Yes, sir, I had a letter. He's recovered from the grippe that kept him in bed for a time. His business continues to do well."

"Success evidently runs in the family. Captain MisCampbell informs me you're an exemplary junior officer."

"That's good to hear, sir—thank you for telling me."

Wayne had acknowledged his acquaintance with Abraham's father when Abraham first reached the training camp at Legionville, down the Ohio from Pittsburgh. Part of Abraham's reverence for the general was due to his father having fought beside Mad Anthony in the Revolution. During the retreat after the American defeat at Brandywine Creek, Philip Kent had joined the reckless young

officer in a charge against some Hessians harrying the retreat route. And Philip often referred with pride to standing with Wayne a second time at Monmouth Court House.

Wayne stared at the dark-flowing river. "May I ask you a personal question, Cornet?"

"Of course, sir."

"It comes to mind because you are an excellent officer, and because I remember your father so well. Do you intend to make the army a career?"

Abraham hesitated a moment, then decided to answer truthfully:

"No, sir. I imagine I'll go back to Boston when the campaign's over."

"Perhaps that will be accomplished by this time tomorrow. There is a very great deal at stake in the next few hours—"

"I'm aware of that, sir."

So was virtually every man in the Legion. The Northwest Ordinance, passed by the Congress in 1787, had wisely promised the creation of new states—no less than three, no more than five—once the territory was pacified and settled. Each new state would be fully equal with those fifteen already established under the country's federal Constitution, which had become law when the ninth of thirteen original states, New Hampshire, ratified it in 1788. Abraham knew that thousands of settlers were waiting along the eastern seaboard for the chance to start new lives in the western territory. But they were held back by fear of the Indian menace.

Just as important, President Washington had recently sent Chief Justice John Jay to England to attempt to negotiate a new treaty with the king's ministers. The status of the Northwest was one of the points at issue. Under the peace settlement, the territory unquestionably belonged to America. But if Britain could in effect hold it illegally—hold it by means of Crown agents inciting the tribes in order to prevent an inrush of settlers—Jay could never hope to gain a re-confirmation on paper of America's claim to the land.

Picking up the conversation, Wayne said, "I'm sorry to hear the military will eventually lose your services, Cornet. Still, I'm not entirely surprised. Ever since you enlisted, I have frankly wondered why a young man of your background—your prospects for the future—would risk himself in an enterprise of this sort."

Caught off guard, Abraham replied haltingly, "Someone must if the territory's to be secured—"

"Oh, I'm not questioning your patriotism. But I've found that in the Legion, most of the men have at least one other motive for joining our hazardous venture. Wives they regret marrying, for example—"

"I'm single, General."

"Debts, then."

"No, I haven't that problem."

"I should imagine not." Bleak, tired eyes ranged the murmuring river where a heat mist was beginning to form. "Sometimes the motive for a man staying in the army is simply an inability to endure other, comparatively tame endeavors once the man has tasted battle—" That, Wayne's officers well knew, was the general's own spur.

Wayne turned slightly, his eyes reflecting the distant fires. Those glowing eyes prodded Abraham to another honest reply:

"Well, sir, in my case that doesn't apply either. I left home because my father and I were having our differences."

"Over what, may I ask?"

"My future. Specifically, my future with the family printing house. My father wanted me to study at Harvard a year or so, then join him in the business. I honestly couldn't decide whether I wanted that. With so much happening in the country—all this new land opening—it seemed, to use your word, a tame alternative."

"So you chose a period in the army to think things over?"

"Exactly, sir. I'm afraid my father and I had quite a few loud and lengthy arguments on the subject. On many other subjects, too. We don't see eye to eye on politics, for instance."

Wayne nodded. "I'm familiar with Kent and Son publishing tracts in support of Mr. Hamilton's Federalist views."

"Quite right, sir. And if you'll forgive my saying so, it's always struck me as damned odd that men who were so violently anti-British twenty years ago are now anxious to establish strong commercial and political ties with that country."

"A matter of economics," Wayne shrugged. "Think of the market in England for ship's timbers, for instance. Good northeastern oak and pine to build dreadnoughts for the most powerful navy in the world—who wants to lose trade like that? No wonder nearly all of New England's gone Federalist—"

"I'm a New Englander and I haven't, sir. I personally see nothing wrong with Mr. Jefferson's support of the revolution in France."

"You'll have to agree it's fallen into bloody excess."

"Yes, but—"

"And still Mr. Jefferson and many of the others in the Virginia junto continue to champion its democratic principles. If they exist any longer!—which I doubt. Ah, but let's not debate that. We have a more immediate enemy—"

Abraham wasn't quite ready to drop the subject, though:

"Part of the trouble at home comes from the fact that my father's grown wealthy. Achieved a status that encourages him to think like an aristocrat—"

"The father's a Federalist, the son isn't—and under those circumstances, a term of service in the army seemed prudent in order to maintain the domestic peace?" Wayne's voice had a wry sound. But Abraham's answer was straightforward:

"Exactly."

And that one word concealed much: the turmoil, the rancor that had shaken the Kent household until Philip had finally given grudging permission for his son to enlist under Wayne's command. Something compelled Abraham to add:

"The solution's only temporary anyway. I'm sure that when I go home, the arguments will start all over again."

Wayne didn't comment immediately. With a touch of chagrin, Abraham realized he had already poured out a good deal of what ought to be considered private information. But as long as the general was willing to listen, Abraham supposed the talk didn't hurt. In a way the confession relieved him. He seldom had a chance to air the problem that continually nagged at his mind. As he'd intimated, it was a problem for which a permanent solution would have to be found eventually.

Wayne brushed a hand absently over one cheek, squashing an insect. He smiled that weary smile again:

"Fathers and sons at loggerheads—that was the central issue of the war for independence, you know. The right of the new blood to run its own course—freely. Well, Cornet, if the army doesn't suit you as a career, and if you've no heart to spend your days in a prosperous Federalist printing firm—"

"I just haven't decided, sir," Abraham broke in. "My father wished for me to do so immediately. That's why I had to strike out on my own for a time."

Once more the relatively glib explanation hid other meanings. Abraham felt a momentary sense of his own shameful, innate weakness—

No, no, that was the wrong term. Unbearably demeaning. Call it not weakness but indecision born of family loyalty. He loved his father even though he resented Philip's strong opinions. And, deep down, Abraham supposed he'd eventually succumb to his father's wish that he join Kent and Son. But at his young age, he didn't want that decision forced on him by fiat—

So he'd run away. No other description would do. Again he was face to face with a suspected failure of character that troubled him often; a failure he struggled to rationalize away by convoluted explanations involving family love and devotion—

Listening to the night insects, he recalled abruptly where he was, and why. A coldness filled his belly. The question of his future might soon become entirely academic. There was a battle to be fought. Men died in battle.

As if hunting for stars behind the sky's haze, Wayne tilted his graying head back. "I can suggest an alternative to commerce or the army, Cornet. You could settle out here."

Mildly astonished, Abraham replied, "Why, yes, sir, I suppose I could. Truthfully, that's never occurred to me before."

"When we raised the stockade at the confluence of this river and the Aux Glaize—" The general was referring to the fort he'd christened Defiance. "—I was struck by the remarkable beauty and fertility of the land. Nature's dealt bountifully with it. A man could hew his house from these forests. Fill his table from the trails and streams—" A boot scraped a furrow in the loam of the bank. "—raise enough crops in this soil to provide for his household and have ample corn meal or flour left to transship across the Great Lakes, or back up the Ohio in exchange for the manufactured goods he needs. You know what they call me these days. One of the old Revolutionary war horses. I suppose I'll never shed the label—nor lose the urge to lead men. But I've found that life on the land can be very good. Very good. I own a rice plantation in the south—Hazzard's Cowpen, it's called. A gift of the people of the state of Georgia for my services during the rebellion—" His voice had grown dreamy, remote. "Yes, a man could do far worse than to stay here when the battle's done—"

Abraham had to admit the idea was intriguing. Escape to a homestead in the Northwest Territory would solve his problem with his father. As Wayne said, a man could live well. *If* the Indian threat were gone—

Abraham's brief enthusiasm faded as footsteps approached. Northward along the Maumee, his whole life could be decided in an instant. It could end in an instant. The recollection of that set his palms itching and started rivulets of sweat trickling down his neck to his linen collar.

He'd been foolishly carried away by Wayne's remarks. Even if he survived his first test in battle, the chance of pulling away from his father was a slim one. Philip Kent would not easily loose his hold on his son—

Abraham put the whole vexing question out of mind, turning along with Wayne as a wiry young officer approached. The officer carried his cockaded bicorn hat under his arm. Despite the semi-darkness, Abraham recognized one of the general's aides, William Henry Harrison.

Harrison saluted. Wayne returned it smartly. "What is it, Lieutenant?"

"The barber has arrived at the headquarters tent, sir."

"Ah, yes—" Wayne smiled again. "I don't want to lead the Legion with my hair unpowdered and disarrayed." The general's vanity, like his courage, was familiar to the men he commanded. But on the wilderness march, he'd had few chances to indulge his penchant for elegance. Care of his hair was one of the rare exceptions.

Stifling a groan and clamping a hand around his bandaged left leg, Wayne started to hobble off. The mist hanging over the Maumee had begun to turn a pearly color. A few drooping willow branches were discernible in the murk now. Dawn—

Wayne stopped, glanced back.

"Whenever I've had the opportunity to speak privately with one or more of my officers, I have acquainted them with a letter I recently received from the secretary of war—"

"General Knox is a friend of my father's, sir."

"Then your father is fortunate. Henry Knox is a sagacious man. He wrote to say that the nation has waited two years for this morning. So have the hundreds of thousands seeking to leave the seacoast. And those six hundred brave men whose remains will stay forever along the Wabash—they're waiting too. I trust each officer will carry that thought in his heart today."

Abraham could only give a quick nod as Mad Anthony leaned on William Henry Harrison's offered arm and labored back toward the camp where men were rousing around the fires. In the gray light Abraham heard the first drums beating.

III

ON THE way back to his tent for his sword and pistols, Abraham Kent was hailed from an officer's tent belonging to the Third Sub-legion. He angled through the noisy press of men turning out with their muskets and approached a handsome twenty-year-old. The officer held his spontoon in one hand while he crooked the index finger of the other.

On his blond head the young man wore one of the shaggy fur caps designed at Wayne's request by the tailors at Legionville. The cap in this case was decorated with a plume of the Third Sub-legion's particular color—yellow. The lieutenant kept beckoning with his finger:

"Come here, dragoon. We've a present for you."

"Not now, Meriwether—they're beating assembly."

But Lieutenant Meriwether Lewis, whom Abraham had frequently engaged at cards in winter quarters back at Greenville, set his spontoon aside and practically dragged the junior officer to the tent entrance:

"I hear. But you're out-ranked, Cornet. You're not permitted to reject a gift from a couple of Virginians who've taken so much of your pay."

"Stolen would be a better word," Abraham said with a grin not completely genuine.

Lewis spoke to someone inside the tent:

"This horse soldier's questioning our integrity, William. Suggesting we deal with sharp's cards—"

"Didn't know New Englanders were that astute," came the laconic reply of another lieutenant, a tall, red-haired fellow some four or five years older than the other two. Abraham was pushed bodily into the tent.

"Shut the damn flap before we're all cashiered!" the red-haired officer whispered. As he rummaged through the folds of his blankets, he added, "Don't tell me you're going to refuse a tot of prime Kaintuck whiskey."

Abraham's grin looked less forced. "I didn't realize that was the gift you had in mind, William."

Lieutenant William Clark, youngest brother of the famous frontiersman George Rogers Clark, displayed his jug:

"Most carefully smuggled in—at a cost of five new dollars per gallon."

Clark walked toward Abraham, stepping over the pile of sketch pads he was using to develop his natural aptitude for drawing and map-making. Clark's intelligence reports, illustrated with small charcoal scenes, were well known in the Legion—and reputedly brought General Wayne diversion while increasing his regard for the junior officer.

Clark propped a boot on one of two brass-latched wooden cases in which his friend Lewis, almost his match in height, collected mineral and botanical samples. Clark waggled the jug at Abraham again, his eyes losing a little of their mirth.

"If you can't use a couple of swallows on a morning like this," he said, "I'll be happy to down your share."

"Or I," Meriwether Lewis said.

Touched by the gesture of friendship on the eve of battle, Abraham looked at the two officers from Virginia—men with whom he'd spent many an enjoyable, if unprofitable, hour over the past twelve months. A shiver chased down his backbone as he thought of the massed might of the tribes awaiting the Legion to the northeast. He grabbed the jug.

"Yes, I can use it—on a morning like this," he said.

Somber-eyed, he drank while the Legionary drums beat steadily louder in the dawn heat.

2
The Charge

SHORTLY AFTER seven, with the sun spearing oblique shafts of light through the mist on the Maumee, the Legion of the United States assembled for the attack.

The Legion itself, four Sub-legions of foot preceded by a small mounted patrol, formed in columns of fours on the right flank, close by the shore of the river. Scott's Kentucky mounted militia would advance along a parallel route on the left flank, through the cornfields that stretched northeast between the river on one side and thick woods on the other.

Mounted on Sprite, whose restlessness seemed to match his own, Abraham gathered with the rest of MisCampbell's dragoon officers at the rear of the Legion columns. The commanding officer explained their orders in a few words:

"We'll be held in reserve, behind the lines, and ordered forward if they need us."

On hearing that, Abraham gave voice to the annoyance most of the officers expressed with scowls and grumbles:

"Sir, if the Indians are really waiting for us upriver—"

MisCampbell swiped at his perspiring cheek. "We believe so, Kent. But we're not positive. They were seen there on the eighteenth. They may have pulled back to the British fort."

"Even so, shouldn't the horse be going in first? If the terrain's as rough as I hear it is, columns of foot can hardly maneuver there."

"To the contrary, Cornet. Only columns of foot can maneuver well on such ground. A head-on cavalry charge with all those fallen trees lying every which way would be impossible. Perhaps General Wayne will utilize us for an assault on the flank—"

The captain's stern eyes softened, cynically amused. "Don't be so anxious to shed blood. I've done it, and it's far from pleasant."

Abraham saw some of his fellow officers grinning and turned red. He was the greenest of the lot, and he'd unwittingly demonstrated it. Fortunately discussion was cut short. MisCampbell shouted:

"Prepare your troops to advance and await the command!"

Tugging Sprite's rein, Abraham turned the mare back toward his men. All were dressed much as he was: shirt, trousers, boots. Sabers hung from leather belts. Pairs of primed and loaded pistols were snugged in saddle holsters. At least the Americans had learned something from the agonizing years of the Revolution. Wayne suited the army's clothing and equipment to the country and the temperature; there was no laboring under monstrously heavy packs and blanket-rolls, as Abraham's father said the British infantry had always done during the Rebellion.

The foot too were lightly dressed this morning, carrying only canteens and weapons. The trappings of rank—waistcoats, epauletted outer coats—had been left in heaps behind Captain Pike's earthwork.

The Indians fought with even less equipment, Abraham knew. They wore only hide trousers or waist clouts, and moccasins.

And paint.

He'd listened to descriptions of those ugly slashes of color with which the braves decorated their faces, arms and torsos. This morning, he'd probably see war paint with his own eyes—

Head aching from the heat and the whiskey he'd drunk with Lieutenants Lewis and Clark, he swung Sprite into line behind his troop's senior officer, Lieutenant Stovall. Abraham didn't care much for the chubby Marylander, reputed to be a sodomite. Stovall had made one advance, months ago, but Abraham's gruff reply and clenched fists quickly persuaded the young officer from Baltimore to seek his pleasure elsewhere.

Stovall occasionally bragged that his parents had hustled him out of his home city and into the army because of a scandal whose enormity remained a source of amusement to him. Abraham never learned the full nature of the scandal, but an incident a few weeks prior to the abortive seduction gave him a clue.

One of Stovall's treasured possessions was an expensive, rather large oval locket on a chain. A woman's locket; a curiously effeminate souvenir for a man in the army. In a rare hour of drunken camaraderie, Stovall had opened the locket and shown Abraham a miniature which even the young Bostonian, no prude, found shocking because it represented something he had never seen before: a full-figure miniature of a dark-haired young woman reclining on a drapery, nude.

One coy hand partially concealed a dusty triangle, which the anonymous artist had detailed with the same attention to eroticism he'd given to the young woman's

somewhat sleepy eyes, her wide mouth and her large breasts, carefully reddened at the tips.

The young woman in the portrait—she could be no more than sixteen or seventeen—had a voluptuous, puffy decadence that disgusted Abraham even while it aroused him. As Stovall snapped the locket shut, Abraham offered the expected ribald compliment, then asked:

"Is that your mistress, Lieutenant?"

Stovall chuckled, using his amusement as a pretext to touch the back of Abraham's hand:

"A gentleman never compromises a lady by answering such a question, dear boy. It's sufficient to say the locket was given to me by a charming creature who loves me deeply, and whose love is reciprocated."

Days later, Abraham brought up the locket in conversation with another officer. His scalp crawled when the officer identified the girl in the painting:

"His mistress? Yes, he intimates she is. She's also his sister, Lucy Stovall."

"Good Christ! I thought his remarks about a scandal in Baltimore were only boasts."

"To the best of my knowledge, I'm right in the identity of that pretty whore he carries around in his breeches. There was a scandal, and a juicy one. The girl's married now, to some chap named Freemantle—Stovall fairly seethes whenever he mentions him. In case it's not clear, Cornet, Stovall is a libertine of the worst sort. Don't let him catch you alone! I understand his family's damned rich, by the way. That probably helps buy official silence about his little escapades—"

"And helps bribe recruiting officers to look in the other direction?"

"And sign his papers in haste—yes."

After that, Abraham avoided the lieutenant, save for the one time he was unavoidably alone with him, and slyly propositioned.

Stovall's unpopularity was heightened by a condescending manner he displayed even to superiors—and to Abraham this morning:

"Damned silly of you to run about pretending to be a bloody firebrand, Kent." Stovall sometimes affected diction he imagined to be British; Abraham considered it a sign of Federalist leanings. "I've no desire to be potted by a bloody lot of howling heathen. Riding in the rear suits me admirably—"

Abraham couldn't resist a jab at the soft-featured officer:

"Off the field as well as on, eh, sir?"

Stovall colored, started to retort. MisCampbell's shouted command distracted him. Stovall reined his horse around and repeated the order loudly:

"*For-aaard!*"

In a moment they were moving with a jingle of metal, a slap of leather, a plop of hoofs in the black earth leading to the slope that angled down into the cornfields. Abraham still felt foolish because of his comments to MisCampbell. Perhaps that was the reason he'd dared to jape at a senior officer.

Why *had* he made those idiotic remarks about wanting to be first to charge the enemy? Was he secretly afraid he lacked courage? Yes, that might be the reason—

But admitting it didn't help his spirits one whit. A heavy lump had formed in his throat. Sweat continually blurred his eyes. Off to the far right, the Legion columns shimmered in the heat, their fur caps with different-colored plumes the only concession to military dress. Abraham felt heavy sweat on his chest and

under his arms as MisCampbell led the dragoons down into the tasseled corn planted by the Indians.

As he rode, Abraham's thoughts turned inward again. He knew why he hoped to do well in the engagement. He wanted some record of accomplishment, however slight, from which to draw the strength of experience if and when he confronted his father in a much different sort of conflict.

Once he acknowledged this in the silence of his mind, he felt a little better— though no less nervous. Guiding Sprite over the edge of the gentle slope, he noticed activity in a grove to the left. He saw General Wayne trying to lift his foot to his stirrup. Bending the flannel-swathed leg brought a grimace to Wayne's face, then tears. Two servants rushed forward to boost him up. Abraham distinctly heard Wayne's gasp of pain as he mounted.

But once in the saddle, the general looked fierce and formidable. No trace of the tears remained. The hilt of his sword and the metal-capped butts of his pistols twinkled in the dappled sunlight of the grove.

Abraham coughed in the dust raised by Stovall's gray just ahead. He felt a sudden pride in serving with Anthony Wayne. If he were to die this morning, at least he wouldn't be dying for a coward or an incompetent—

Or a sodomite, he thought, making a disgusted face as Stovall wiggled his fat rump in his saddle and complained loudly about the heat.

II

THE SUN climbed higher as they advanced. Stovall owned a precious wilderness rarity, a pocket watch with a cheerfully painted sun face on its dial. He kept close track of the time.

Eight o'clock.

Nine o'clock.

Nine-thirty—

Lulled by the rhythm of posting, Abraham grew drowsy in the heat. Sprite's flanks glistened with lather. He and the mare—in fact all of the dragoons and their horses—exuded a stench that grew riper with every passing moment.

Ahead and to the right, half the Legion had already vanished into a line of trees running at a right angle between the woods on the far left and the river. The trees, a living wall that hid all the terrain beyond, marked the end of the corn bottoms. As the Legion foot disappeared into the dark green gloom, MisCampbell called a halt.

The dragoons reined their horses. General Wayne and his command staff cantered past on their left, soon gone into the trees after the others. Lieutenant Stovall tugged out his pocket watch again.

"Ten o' the clock. The hostiles must have turned tail. Suits me perfectl—"

Abraham stood up straight in his stirrups as Stovall's sentence was punctuated by a rolling thunderclap of sound from the other side of the line of trees. Frantic orders rang along the end of the column of foot. The last of the infantrymen plunged into the woods at quick-step. Abraham saw smoke rising above the trees, but those same trees barred the dragoons from seeing the source of the firing.

"Turned tail?" a dragoon jeered at Stovall. "Doesn't sound like it!"

"No, I don't imagine Mad Anthony ordered musket practice just to while

away the time,'' said another. Stovall jammed his watch back in his trousers pocket, looking petulant.

That muskets by the hundreds were exploding beyond the trees was not in question. But suddenly a new sound was added to the din: massed voices—yells—of infantrymen charging.

A third sound made Abraham's scalp prickle. Wild, ululating yells that could only come from the savages entrenched in the fallen timbers. The battle had been joined—

A horseman burst from the trees, galloping straight toward MisCampbell. Bringing orders? So it appeared. Abraham's belly knotted. His palms turned cold despite the heat.

MisCampbell conferred with the arriving officer, then stood in his stirrups and drew his saber.

"Listen to me!'' he shouted, pointing his blade at the river. It shone like a brass mirror now that the mist had burned away. "There's another cornfield along the bank beyond those trees. We're to advance, drive into the enemy's left flank and turn it that way—'' In a shimmering arc, the saber flashed toward the forest on Abraham's left. Smoke rose from its depths too. More muskets crashed. The Kentuckians had engaged.

MisCampbell bent to listen to the courier again. Then:

"The foot's already in trouble among the fallen trees. So once we're in there, formations be damned. Just kill the red whoresons.'' Up went his saber, then down. *"For-aaard—!''*

The dragoons thundered toward the trees nearest the river. Abraham breathed loudly through his mouth as his rump bounced up and down in the saddle. Sprite's plaited mane stood out in the wind. She seemed eager to run—

MisCampbell plunged into the trees, a gloomy place made gloomier by drifting smoke. Above the drumming of hoofs Abraham once more heard sounds on his left. Muskets. Men shouting and cursing in English. Other voices screaming in tongues he didn't understand—

The line of trees was not deep. MisCampbell's men rode through in a matter of a minute or so, bursting onto level ground thick with ripe corn that grew nearly to the water's edge. The world seemed to race by as Abraham's mare carried him from semi-darkness to blinding sunlight. He gasped at the incredible scene of confusion and carnage on his left.

A vast area of the bottom was covered by the immense trunks of uprooted trees, some nearly rotted away. Here and there, two or three of the storm-blasted trunks lay across one another, creating natural barricades six to eight feet high. Among this titanic natural wreckage, men struggled; men with white skins, and others much darker—

Abraham saw bayonets flashing as whole squads clambered over the huge horizontal trees; saw red faces contorted in rage; red hands swinging war clubs and tomahawks and even firing muskets. The Legion and the Indians fought hand to hand in near-total disorder—

At least a thousand to fifteen hundred men were battling, Abraham guessed. He was barely able to hear MisCampbell's bawled orders in the din. Past the fallen timbers, the smoke thickened above the woods where the Kentuckians fought.

Screaming commands, MisCampbell turned the column's head, charging the dragoons left toward the nearest uprooted trees. As Abraham pulled his saber, Stovall swung left in turn. Abraham followed—and got a horrifying view of

hard-planed, reddish-brown faces waiting behind the natural fortifications; faces marked with slashes of yellow and vermilion.

Heads shaved save for single oiled scalplocks trailing down their necks, the Indian defenders—of what tribe, Abraham didn't know—raised muskets and aimed at the attacking cavalry.

Abraham bent low over Sprite's neck. He realized the dragoon formation would disintegrate the moment MisCampbell reached the first great trunks. So he chose a route for himself: a natural lane between two destroyed trees. The lane angled away to his left. Riding hard, he turned Sprite in that direction.

The smell of powder was chokingly strong. He heard the Indian muskets erupt, raised his head just a little as a sheet of flame leaped out directly in front of the first dragoons. MisCampbell's chest seemed to cave in, the white of his linen shirt stained with red blotches as several balls struck him at once. He pitched from his saddle, trampled by his men galloping behind him—

Then the first riders were into the trees, each man charging in a different direction, choosing his own enemy. Never before had Abraham heard such noise: the muskets blasting; the American foot soldiers grunting and cursing as they clambered over the tree trunks; the earth-shaking hoofbeats; the war cries of the Indians—and the shrieks of men on both sides dying of a ball or a bayonet or the blade of a scalp knife—

Abraham's mare dashed into the head of the lane he'd picked out. Stovall was racing down the same lane directly ahead. Sprite's flank scraped one of the tumbled trees. She almost fell. On the far side of the tree, two clouted Indians struggled with an officer of the Fourth Sub-legion. The man was fending off the savages with thrusts of his spontoon.

Abraham reined in, reached across the trunk, hacked down and sideways with his saber. The blade struck flesh. With a kind of hypnotic fascination, he watched the brave's neck spout blood over the beleaguered officer. The American took the hideous drenching—and grinned.

The other Indian tried to scramble away over the next tree. The officer ran him through the back with the long spontoon. Abraham's bowels felt watery as he nudged Sprite ahead, the dying Indian's cries of agony loud in his ears.

Abruptly, on his right a brave leaped to the top of another fallen tree. Abraham realized the warrior must have been crouching down—awaiting a victim. The Indian was tall, in his late twenties, with a distinctively handsome face and baleful eyes. He swung his spiked war club straight at Sprite's neck.

Abraham jerked the rein savagely. The mare reared, front hoofs tearing at the sky. The spike missed her by a fraction.

Sprite came back to earth with a terrific jolt. The Indian found a new, more convenient target: Lieutenant Stovall. A few yards ahead, his gray's front hoof had caught in a tangle of exposed roots. The Indian ran gracefully along the tree trunk, leaped as Abraham shouted:

"Stovall! Behind y—"

Stovall took the spike of the war club in the nape of his neck. He screamed a name—Lucy, Abraham thought it was—as he slumped over. His corpse bounced in the saddle.

Abraham kicked Sprite ahead, hatred dizzying his mind. Stovall was a despicable young man. But he was also a United States soldier, and he had been foully murdered. Holding his seat by clenching his knees against Sprite's heaving sides, Abraham jerked out one of the dragoon pistols and fired.

When the smoke cleared, Abraham saw the Indian laughing at him from the

other side of Stovall's horse. Fresh blood stained Stovall's shirt where the pistol ball had struck. The Indian had maneuvered Stovall's corpse as a shield.

Eyes glittering with hateful mirth, the Indian reached up as Stovall's boots came loose from the stirrups. He tangled his fingers in Stovall's blood-slimed hair, jerked, flung the body on the ground. In a moment the Indian was mounted and riding away, bent close to the animal's neck as he beat the grays ribs with moccasined feet. Abraham pulled his other pistol, shot—but the fleeing savage was already out of range.

Soon the Indian was gone in the smoke. Abraham rode past Stovall's corpse, unable to look at it. Vomit filled his throat. He swallowed several times and that way kept from getting sick. But nausea still churned his middle.

Pistols empty, he had only his bloodied saber for a weapon—and precious few enemies to use it on, he discovered. The Indians had withdrawn from the immediate area. In fact, as he reined in again, he saw scores of them retreating in a frantic scramble through the timbers at the far side of the battleground. Legion soldiers with bayonets gave chase, stabbing the fugitives in the back or shooting them.

Abraham began to shake. He controlled the violent trembling only with great effort. He'd been in combat five minutes or a little less, and already the field was clearing. As he scanned the tumbled trees, he realized that the cavalry charge against the Indian flank had been largely responsible for the sudden retreat. Wayne's strategy had been sound after all.

He heard a lieutenant calling for the dragoons to assemble in a relatively open area a short distance away. He spoke to Sprite to send her forward. The firing was diminishing quickly, but great blue layers of smoke still lay over the blasted trees. The grotesque and gory bodies of Americans and Indians were hideous to look upon.

As Abraham rounded the split end of a rotting tree, he heard a muffled groan, glanced down—

He saw an Indian, hardly older than he was.

Hunched over in pain—gut-shot—the young brave stared up at Abraham's bloodied sword, expecting death. Abraham's eyes locked with the brave's. Agony and humiliation filled those eyes, but no hatred. The Indian was dying.

Abraham had no stomach for administering a final stroke, merciful or otherwise. He rode on. The young warrior began to chant, a mournful, sing-song melody. A death-litany—?

The sight of the dying warrior lingered in Abraham's mind, sad and ugly. He felt ashamed as he remembered his foolish bravado earlier in the morning. To take pleasure in the death and suffering of battle struck him as inhuman, no matter how important or righteous the cause of either side seemed. He was oddly proud of having survived the short but fierce engagement. Yet at the same time he was sickened and shaken by everything he had seen and done.

III

THE BATTLE along the Maumee was won in under half an hour. It was won by superior numbers and, specifically, as Abraham had suspected, by the dragoon charge against the Indian flank. When Abraham rejoined his troop, he found that seven or eight men he knew well had died somewhere in the fallen timbers.

Not long afterward, he and the other dragoons found themselves in high grass overlooking a stockade beside the river. Above the fort, a British flag flew.

Closer to the hilltop position, McKee's trading station stood among a collection of deserted Indian huts and lean-tos. One of the men in Abraham's troop pointed in surprise:

"Stripe me if the yellow British ain't going to keep the damn gate shut."

He moved forward for a better look. About two dozen Indians, most of them wounded, were howling and beating on the entrance to the log fort. Red-coated sentries on the ramparts motioned for them to go away. That set the Indians to howling all the louder. Abraham recognized one of the angriest fugitives.

"See that one who's bloodied his hands hammering the gate?" he asked the officer beside him. "Unless my eyes are tricking me, I came close to killing him back in the timbers."

The bedraggled officer answered, "Don't you know who that is?"

Abraham shook his head.

"A scout pointed him out to me. He was fleeing like the very devil. On horseback."

"But who is he?"

"The Shawanese, Tecumseh. One of Blue Jacket's hottest bloods."

"I'm sure he's the one I shot at—"

"And missed, obviously."

"Yes."

"Too bad. A ball in his brain would have saved every white man on the frontier a mightly lot of grief."

Hardly hearing, Abraham continued to stare at the appalling sight of the allies of the Indians refusing them sanctuary in the fort. Presently the enraged braves slipped out of sight in the woods beyond the log stockade. Wayne had passed an order that they were not to be fired on.

That angered a great many of the Americans. Abraham felt only a profound sense of sorrow. The tribes of the Ohio country might be enemies, but you could only pity men whose pretended friends abandoned them in such fashion.

IV

BOLDLY, GENERAL ANTHONY WAYNE remained camped in the meadows half a mile from Fort Miami. Although the British commandant refused Wayne's demand for surrender, the redcoats stayed safely behind their palisade and didn't fire even a single shot when Wayne ordered McKee's station burned.

Next the Americans burned the huts around the trading post. Finally they set fire to the gardens and cornfields where the Indians raised their food for the winter.

On the way south again in the rain, the army still managed to light enough firebrands to start the cornfields along the Maumee blazing. While the wagons carrying wounded creaked and oozed through the muddy bottoms, pillars of black smoke climbed to the drizzly sky. Wayne had not only vowed to defeat the federated tribes—which he had done in thirty minutes—but also to leave them no means of survival.

Abraham rode Sprite through the rows of ripened corn, setting the tall stalks alight with a sputtering torch. His emotions were in turmoil. He knew that

destroying the corn was a military necessity. Yet doing it somehow made him miserable.

He felt that during the brief battle, he had come a little closer to full manhood. But the experience was not nearly as glorious and gratifying as he'd imagined it would be. He found himself thinking frequently of his family. Found himself calling on Lieutenants Clark and Lewis whenever he had a free moment, helping himself to quantities of their whiskey.

And he always avoided looking back at the smoky horizon as the triumphant army marched south in the waning summer.

V

A COMMOTION brought Abraham running from his barracks at Fort Greenville one brittle gray afternoon late in January. Dull silver light tinged the western horizon. Lamps had already been lit in General Wayne's neat house with its border of white picket fencing. On the ramparts, sentries were hallooing while other men lifted the great log bar that held Greenville's gates shut from the inside.

Crowds of soldiers had already gathered. In one of them, Abraham found red-haired Lieutenant Clark.

"Why all the excitement, William?" Abraham asked, shivering in his all-too-thin dark blue winter coat. He blinked as a couple of snowflakes tickled his eyelids.

"Party of red men coming in," Clark answered in his soft Virginia speech. Several officers dashed to the porch of Wayne's house. One pounded on the door.

The fort gates swung inward. A strange silence fell, broken only by the wind's whine. A file of about three dozen Indians straggled into the fort, looking considerably less prideful than their peers at Fallen Timbers. In fact Abraham had seldom seen so pathetic a sight as the half-dozen hunched old men who led the procession on horseback.

The protruding ribs of the horses testified to their near-starvation. The men wore ragged blankets, or filthy cast-off British army coats. They huddled together while an American interpreter in buckskin spoke to the leaders with words and signs. Among the soldiers gathered on the perimeter of the parade area, there were brief outbursts of contemptuous laughter, and a few obscene jests. The laughter soon died. The jokes drew little response.

How different from the day in late December, Abraham thought. Wayne had assembled the Legion and the Kentuckians in the post-Christmas cold to hear a reading of a proclamation from Philip Kent's old friend Knox, head of the Department of War. The proclamation said President Washington and the Congress *joined in commending Major General Wayne's men for the good conduct and bravery displayed by them in the action of the twentieth August last, with the Indians—*

Afterward, the cheering was long and loud.

Now some of those same Indians, hollow-cheeked and shivering, stood helplessly in the midst of their enemies under the lowering winter sky. They awaited the emergence of the White Captain from his cozy house. Abraham remembered the dreadful harvest of skulls on the Wabash; reminded himself that perhaps some of these very chiefs had caused that slaughter—

Yet he understood their reasons. Pitied them again as he recalled the way their erstwhile friends had denied them sanctuary after the battle. Ever since that simmering morning in August, he'd scorned himself for ever thinking that war, in whatever cause, could be ennobling.

Necessary, perhaps. But ennobling? Never.

Men drifted from group to group, identifying members of the Indian party:

"That's Half King's son, the Wyandot."

"And the Delaware, Moses. The only English letter he can write is M, they say—"

"Well," remarked Lieutenant William Clark, "this is what the general wanted. Beating them in the field wasn't enough. They had to be beaten in their bellies and their hearts and their minds before this country could be pacified. I'll venture this is only the start, Abraham—the first trickle."

"You mean more of the chiefs will come?"

Clark nodded. "Wayne will have a treaty with all the tribes before the year's out, mark my word."

"That'll mean furloughs!" a soldier behind them exclaimed. "Damme, I can't wait to fuck one of those Cincinnati whores, never mind how bad they smell—"

Someone else snickered. But only for a moment.

Abraham was thinking of something other than women. He was thinking that if the Northwest had indeed been secured, he could return home when his enlistment ran out at mid-year. The realization triggered a memory of Wayne's remarks about the opportunity in the new land.

But Abraham knew himself reasonably well now. He couldn't simply defy his father and never go home. He'd have to return to Boston at least for a short time.

The thought of the homecoming filled him with conflicting emotions. On one hand he longed to be among familiar comforts and familiar people again; on the other, he dreaded facing the owner of Kent and Son.

He dug his hands deeply into the pockets of his thin coat. The more he thought about Wayne's words that stifling morning beside the river, the more he questioned them. At the moment he could see very little in this western frontier that was attractive. Memories of shimmering meadows, abundant forests, whitewater brooks and plentiful wildlife all seemed lusterless here in the dull silver light of a January afternoon—

The front door of Wayne's small house opened, spilling lamplight in which a shadow loomed. The general hobbled out, tall and somehow awesome in spite of his infirmity. The Indians drew closer together.

"Yes, it's the end," William Clark said. He sounded relieved. A moment later he clapped a hand on Abraham's shoulder. "Care for some whiskey by way of celebration?"

"Very much so," Abraham answered, with more feeling than his friend understood.

VI

SOME THIRTEEN months after the defeat of the federated tribes, with the great treaty signed in Greenville's council house, men began to be released from Wayne's command. Abraham Kent was one.

Turning Sprite over to the new cornet whose mount she would become, he spoke with the unconsciously condescending air of the veteran addressing the green replacement.

"Take care of her. She's a splendid campaigner—" His natural manner broke through the feigned superiority; he smiled in a rueful way. "—better than I am, in fact. There's a great deal to recommend this western country, Cornet. But I don't have much fondness for the human price paid for settling the question of its ownership. I mean the price on both sides."

The new junior officer merely look puzzled.

"One final word of advice," Abraham added, with a broad wink. "It's in reference to the whiskey they freight up from Kentucky. Or Kaintuck, if you prefer. If you can survive the first few sips—and develop a fondness for it—you can face the worst life has to offer out here. The Kentucky brew, in case I don't make myself clear, is potent as hell. It's also necessary as hell."

He was only partially joking.

3
Clouds at Homecoming

AFTER THE magnificent dinner, Abraham held forth for a quarter of an hour.

He described how more than eleven hundred braves and sachems of the north-western tribes had come to Greenville the preceding August to listen to Wayne's passionate, if lengthy, speeches of persuasion. Dressed in a fine suit of brown New England broadcloth, he jumped to his feet as he launched into the closing of the general's last speech, which he'd memorized:

"—I now take the hatchet out of your hands—"

Abraham added gestures to the recitation, aware that four pairs of eyes were focused on him with varying degrees of attentiveness. One pair particularly— eyes at which he dared not glance—stirred him in a strange and surprising way. His voice strengthened:

"—and with a strong arm throw it into the center of the great ocean, where no mortal can ever find it!" A mimed throw dramatized the line. "And I now deliver to you the wide and straight path to the Fifteen Fires, to be used by you and your posterity forever. So long as you continue to follow this road, so long will you continue to be a happy people. You see it is straight and wide—and they will be blind indeed who deviate from it!"

Flushed, Abraham paused. He'd jumped up almost unconsciously, carried away with excitement. He sat down before going on:

"That was virtually the end of it. Wayne had won them—every important chief and brave in the Northwest Territory except one. A Shawnee named Tecumseh. He refused to come to Greenville because his father was shot to death by white hunters when he was a boy—and he saw his village burned on orders of George Rogers Clark just a couple of years later. The day after Wayne's speech, the chiefs began signing. They're to receive twenty thousand dollars this first year, half that in succeeding years in return for the land they've given up.

I've heard the area amounts to as much as twenty-five thousand square miles. The treaty line runs roughly east to west, from a river called the Cuyahoga to Fort Recovery. There, it angles down toward the Ohio. Everything south and east of the line is reserved for white settlement. The Indians must stay to the north and west—but Wayne very cannily granted the tribes the right to hunt and fish all the way to the Ohio so long as they conduct themselves peacefully. At the same time, he negotiated U.S. possession of sixteen choice parcels *within* the Indian territory. Altogether, the terms were complex to explain to the sachems. But they were eager to sign when the general finished speaking. I was listening outside the council house a good part of the time, and I've never heard such eloquent delivery."

"Nor I," said Elizabeth, seated on Abraham's right. He couldn't help turning red again.

He wanted to look into the girl's pale blue eyes; wanted to savor the sight of her fair, perfectly coiffed hair and the fetchingly rounded breasts that had barely been visible on her slim body when he left for Pittsburgh three years earlier.

But Abraham Kent had served in the army. He could discipline himself. Instead of making a show over Elizabeth's admiration, he acknowledged his stepmother's smile from the lower end of the table, and kept his eyes on her as she spoke:

"I agree, Elizabeth. We may have raised an orator as well as a soldier."

Peggy Ashford McLean Kent's smooth white hands rested on the polished surface of the great dining table imported from Mr. Phyfe's increasingly popular—and immensely expensive—New York shop. When Abraham departed for the west, the family had only been settled six months in the new home on Beacon Street overlooking the Common. Since his return a week ago, he had been dazzled by the opulence of the furnishings added in his absence.

"A soldier I'll never be, mother," he said now. Out of politeness, he always referred to the dark-haired, graceful woman from Virginia as mother, even though she was his father's second wife.

Peggy Kent had a gentle, lovely face, and eyes that occasionally revealed some private sorrow Abraham had never fully understood. She was taller than his father, but that hadn't proved an impediment to a happy marriage. Philip, the head of the household who was sitting silently at the other end of the table, more than made up in strength of personality what he lacked in height. Abraham fidgeted, aware of Philips' unblinking gaze.

Across the table from Abraham, thin and sallow little Gilbert, going on twelve, leaned forward and exclaimed:

"Tell us again about the fight at Fallen Timbers, Abraham."

"Come, I must have recited that four times already this week," Abraham grinned.

Gilbert was Abraham half-brother, the only child of Philip Kent's second marriage. He had a fragility to his bones and a luminosity in his eyes that showed him to be his mother's child. The brightness of his mind somewhat compensated for his lack of size and stamina.

He answered Abraham with a gay smile:

"Actually it's five. But I don't tire of it."

"Let's spare the family, then, shall we? I'll repeat the story in private."

"A promise?" asked the boy. He'd been named for his father's life-long friend Lafayette, the French nobleman who had fought valiantly for the American cause during the Revolution.

"A promise," Abraham replied.

"Abraham."

The voice from the head of the table was quiet yet commanding. Abraham turned, almost dreading to meet his father's eyes.

At forty-two, Philip Kent's strong features had acquired some of the lines of age. His neatly tied hair showed gray streaks. Abraham could never remember Philip using powder, or covering his hair with one of the wigs now rapidly passing out of fashion. This evening Philip wore an expensive suit of deep emerald velvet, a fawn waistcoat and snowy linen. He'd returned late from his business establishment—it occupied three floors in an old building near Long Wharf, and was already outgrowing the space—and hadn't bothered to remove traces of ink from beneath his blunt fingernails. Owner of the highly successful printing and book publishing firm of Kent and Son, Philip was by no means an absentee manager.

"Yes, papa?" Abraham said.

Philip continued to scrutinize his older son. There was something a bit forbidding in that stare, Abraham thought.

Or was that only his imagination? His guilt? In the short time he'd been back in Boston, he had seen Philip but briefly; the inevitable subject of Abraham's future hadn't yet arisen.

At last Philip spoke: "You favored us with some interesting accounts of your time in the west. But you'll forgive me if I observe that very little of what you've said is anything more than superficial."

Abraham frowned. "I don't understand, sir."

"Well, for instance—during the charge, were you frightened?"

Peggy clasped her hands together. "Oh dear, Philip, must he answer? You've a way of tossing people straight onto the griddle with your questions."

"My thought exactly!" Elizabeth agreed.

Her words drew a frown from Philip. But that wasn't all:

"Young woman, I believe I've made it abundantly clear that you have a great many thoughts of which I don't approve." His glance leaped to his wife. "Have you seen to the disposal of that trashy novel Elizabeth brought into the house?"

"Yes, she did," Elizabeth said, angry. With a slight turn of his head, Abraham saw the fire in the girl's blue eyes. Almost reckless, those eyes. An inheritance from her father, the family had long ago concluded—

Elizabeth's father had been a Virginia gentleman of good background but poor character. On the rare occasions when he was discussed in the Kent house, it was said that he'd been given to heavy drinking, and furious rages. Now Elizabeth showed more of that inheritance. She pouted; struck the table with one dainty fist:

"I should think at seventeen, I might read what I please."

"Not Mrs. Rowson's sinful novel," Philip declared. "*Charlotte Temple* is sentimental tripe. It dwells excessively on seduction, and is therefore unfit for young women of breeding. The book may have enjoyed a vogue in England. But I refused the opportunity—if you care to call it that—to bring it out in America under the Kent imprint. That summarizes my opinion, I believe." He addressed his wife again. "Is it gone?"

Peggy smiled a tolerant smile. "Yes, what Elizabeth told you is correct—I've seen to it."

"Good."

Abraham kept a straight face. The little dialogue just concluded only demon-

strated again the thickness of the shell of conservatism that had hardened around his father in the latter's advancing years.

Philip said, "Now, Abraham, back to the question—which I didn't mean unkindly, by the way."

"I realize, sir."

"A man who goes into battle without fear is the worst sort of fool."

"Then, happily, I guess I'll escape that label. I was terrified."

Gilbert's worshipful expression vanished. "You were?"

"Of course. At the same time, I still wanted to do well—wanted to acquit myself honorably." That pleased Philip. "But after ten minutes in the thick of the fighting, I'd frankly had enough to last me the rest of my life. I discovered there's nothing pleasant or uplifting about killing another human being."

"Yes, I discovered the same thing. On several occasions," Philip added, letting it go at that.

Abraham naturally knew most of the details of his father's history. Philip Kent had emigrated from England before the Revolution, as a result of trouble over an inheritance from his father—an English peer dead almost six years now. The duke had never married Philip's mother, a French woman of great beauty but low birth who had been an actress in Paris for a time. Philip frequently intimated that he'd had to defend his own life more than once in the uncertain years before he gave his wholehearted support to the cause of the Boston patriots. Philip's struggle for survival as a young man—and perhaps his bastardy—explained to Abraham why his father had acquired an aura of confidence, power, even arrogance that often intimidated others of his sex—his sons included.

Not that Philip was overtly truculent. the quiet air of absolute authority was simply part of his makeup. It showed in the challenging quality of his next remark:

"You've decided that soldiering is not a career you'd want to pursue, then?"

Abraham nodded. "Very definitely."

"So that leaves your future open to discussion. Excellent."

Abraham tried not to show how great an impact those words had on him. He felt as if a huge weight, long suspended over his head, had crashed down on him at last. He'd known he couldn't indefinitely postpone talking about what he intended to do now that he was home. Philip had just made that doubly clear.

But Gilbert didn't want to abandon war stories quite so quickly. The adoring look stole back into his eyes as he said to his half-brother:

"How many of the red men did you kill, Abraham?"

"I don't know."

"Didn't you count?"

"No," Abraham answered, curtly. He saw agonized faces; heard screams—

Elizabeth tossed her fair hair. "I'd like to know which is more immoral—Mrs. Rowson's novel of seduction or all this gory talk of slaughtering Indians!"

Philip shot the girl another irritated glance. Peggy, always the mistress of tact and diplomacy, rose from her chair before he could speak:

"Neither is appropriate at the moment, my dears. I'm sure the servants are anxious to clear away. Shall we take tea in the music room? Abraham, you haven't heard Gilbert play the harpsichord—"

Gilbert made a disgusted face.

"I'm looking forward to it," Abraham said.

"You'll be delightfully surprised. Gilbert can perform most of the hymns and

fugues in Mr. Belcher's *Harmony of Maine*. Or any of Mr. Kimball's popular songs from *The Rural Harmony*—he's really quite accomplished.''

Philip stood up. ''I prefer that Gilbert concentrate on his study of mathematics. If he continues to show the aptitude he's demonstrated so far, our business will never lack for managerial talent. In fact I've given some thought to having the sign repainted.''

Peggy looked startled. ''In what fashion?''

''So that it reads *Kent and Sons*—plural.'' With affection, Philip reached out to tousle Gilbert's curly hair. For a moment his stern countenance softened noticeably.

Gilbert smiled in a forced way. He appeared to accept the channeling of his life into a pre-determined course with almost complete resignation. But he grew a little more cheerful when Philip said to him:

''Let us postpone the concert, shall we?''

''Anything you say, father!''

''Why can't Gilbert play?'' Peggy asked.

''Because I want a word with Abraham alone—over a glass of port in the sitting room.''

Again it was more of a command than a statement, and it didn't sit well with Abraham, rankled as he was by Philip's remark about re-naming the firm. Elizabeth rebelled too, though against something else:

''I despise this ridiculous tradition of the gentlemen retiring behind closed doors!'' She rose, flinging her linen napkin on the table. ''Mama and I are expected to be docile slaves simply because of our sex—''

''Elizabeth!'' Peggy warned. ''You will refrain from the use of that word in conversation.''

''Oh, mama, stop!''

Peggy glanced pointedly at Gilbert. ''Please consider who is present—''

''Do you honestly suppose Gilbert hasn't seen the dogs coupling in every alley in Boston?''

''Of course I have,'' Gilbert grinned.

Already scarlet, Peggy gasped, ''Young man—!''

''This pious sham of not using certain words is disgusting!'' Elizabeth cried.

Philip's eyes were thunderous—like his voice:

''Nevertheless, you will not use them in Gilbert's presence—your mother's presence—or mine! This is my house, and it's my decision.''

''Yes, you make all the decisions, don't you?''

''See here—!''

''You also make it quite apparent that I'm an outsider.''

''Oh, Elizabeth, that's altogether unfair and unwarranted,'' Peggy said in a saddened tone.

''Is it? I don't believe so!''

The candles in the chandelier put glistening highlights in Elizabeth's pale blue eyes. Yet Abraham had the uncanny feeling that her tears were artifice. If so, they still worked. Philip looked taken aback:

''My dear child, your mother's quite right. You're as much a part of this family circle as any other person at the table. But the fact remains—you're much too forward and free-thinking.''

''I suppose next you'll be calling me a mad, bloodthirsty Jacobin!'' Elizabeth wailed, starting to rush out. As she left, she contrived to brush against Abraham. His arm tingled at the touch of her muslin-covered breast.

They all listened to Elizabeth clattering away upstairs to her room just down the hall from Abraham's on the third floor. A door slammed distantly. Philip sighed. Then:

"Peggy, will you please go to her? She continues to harbor the misguided notion that because I'm not her father, I care the less for her."

Peggy said softly, "We both know that's not true."

"At the same time, I demand decent behavior. Elizabeth quite often seems totally incapable of it."

"She just doesn't want to grow up and be ladylike," Gilbert said with a tentative smile.

No one responded. His large eyes lost their glow. His face fell.

Abraham knew full well that the problem was much deeper than Gilbert's over-simplification suggested. Elizabeth bore her father's last name, Fletcher. That she was illegitimate was no secret within the Kent family. The circumstances of her conception, however, were largely unclear to Abraham.

He did know that his stepmother had met Philip only after she had placed her infant daughter in a foster home here in Boston. Evidently Peggy hadn't wanted to expose the child—and herself—to scandal in her native Virginia. Beyond that, Abraham had pieced together certain other information from chance remarks at the family table or hearthside:

Peggy's first husband had been a Virginia planter named McLean. He was butchered in a short but apparently harrowing slave rebellion that swept Peggy's home district along the Rappahannock River in 1775. Elizabeth, born in 1778, had therefore been fathered by this Fletcher fellow after Peggy became a widow.

Sometimes Abraham wondered whether that slave uprising might be the cause of the silent grief that seemed to grip his stepmother occasionally. Walking abroad in Boston, he had seen Peggy turn pale at the sight of a free black man.

Philip had once confided to Abraham that Peggy had indeed suffered physical harm in the rebellion. To what extent, he didn't say. Abraham had speculated on the possibility of rape. That would account for Peggy's pallor and the sudden nervous starts which automatically—and unfairly—lumped all Negroes into a single category: persons to be feared.

If Peggy Ashford McLean Kent's past did include ravishment, how it had affected her intimate relationship with Abraham's father remained a mystery. He knew they shared one large bed. And his stepmother hadn't been so devastated that sexual congress was impossible for her. Gilbert was proof of that. Beyond the obvious, however, Abraham didn't deem it his business—or, to use Philip's word, decent—to speculate.

He did know that no children had come of Peggy's union with the murdered McLean. Growing up, he'd asked his father questions about the whole puzzling business. Philip refused to reply to most of them, stating that he did so out of respect for his wife's wishes. The past was buried and would remain so.

No one was forbidden from talking about Elizabeth's real father—though no one dwelled on him especially either. Over the years, Peggy had let slip a few tantalizing details about the man. The one mentioned most often—and most proudly—was that he had been shot to death in Pittsburgh in 1778, by an Indian spy attempting to abort George Rogers Clark's march to capture British forts in the Northwest Territory.

It seemed clear that the man had indeed possessed an unstable nature. It showed up, as it had for as long as Abraham could remember, in Elizabeth's dislike of Philip's discipline, and her occasional outright rebellion against it.

That was one thing in the household that hadn't changed in Abraham's absence—even though Elizabeth's appearance had changed remarkably. She had
quite literally grown up. Filled out. Become almost beautiful.

She was no blood kin of Abraham's. Yet he still felt vaguely guilty over the
sensual thoughts she inspired. Her frank glances had stirred him often during the
short time he'd been home.

Responding to Philip's request, Peggy said in a weary tone, "Yes, I'll go to
her—though I doubt my admonitions will have much effect. They seldom do any
more. Gilbert, you see to finishing your studies for the day."

Gilbert stuck out his lower lip. "I'd rather talk to Abraham about Indians."

"Your brother is going to talk to me," Philip said, starting from the dining
room. With each step, his right shoulder drooped a little—the result of the wound
he had suffered at the battle of Monmouth Court House. The way he had limped
ever since had also played a part in making him an assertive, sometimes domineering man, Abraham suspected.

Reluctantly he followed his father into the front sitting room. Servants had
already lit a fire against the December darkness. Philip warmed his hands in front
of the blaze. He didn't once glance back to see whether Abraham had followed.
He expected Abraham to be there, and Abraham was.

II

OVER THE mantel hung a long, beautifully polished and oiled Kentucky rifle that
Philip had acquired in the war. Above that, a focal point of the room, shone the
grenadier's sword given him by Lafayette. They had known each other as young
men in the French province of Auvergne; then, Philip's name had been Phillipe
Charboneau. He had adopted his new one on the voyage to America.

Gazing at the sword, Abraham recalled what his father had recently told him
about its famous donor. At first a supporter of the French Revolution, the
Marquis de Lafayette had lately rebelled against the savagery of the Jacobins. He
was now imprisoned somewhere in Europe—Prussia or Austria, Philip believed.
It was an irony of the great political upheaval that had polarized not only Europe
but the United States that Lafayette, finally rejecting the revolution, had still
been clapped into irons by its enemies because of his position before he changed
his mind.

Below the rifle and sword on the mantel proper stood a small green glass bottle
with a quantity of dried tea leaves in the bottom. This Abraham's father had
acquired on the night of Mr. Samuel Adams' famous tea party in Boston harbor.

The tea had accumulated in Philip's boots during the opening and dumping of
the chests. Later that same night he had put the tea in the bottle, to save as a
family souvenir. Years afterward, he'd adopted the symbol of the partially filled
bottle for the signboard identifying Kent and Son.

Despite the crackling fire, the sitting room was chilly. All at once Abraham
noticed the tea-bottle symbol on the masthead of a single-sheet, four-page gazette lying on a small table. The title of the paper was the *Bay State Federalist*.
That and a quick glance at its columns identified the paper's slant; Abraham
noted an unfriendly story referring to the ex-secretary of state, Mr. Jefferson, and
his *Jacobin cohorts*.

"I've a great deal to catch up on," he said while Philip poured two glasses of

port. "No one's bothered to tell me you've gone into the newspaper business as well."

Philip handed a glass to his son. "It's merely a weekly at the moment. Still, the more voices speaking out against these imbeciles who'd entangle us with the French, the better."

Abraham laughed.

"Pray tell me what's so amusing," Philip snapped.

"Forgive me, papa—it's just that your attitude's a bit surprising. I mean, you *were* born in France."

"The people living there now have collectively lost their minds. And some of the revolution's friends in America are in equally pathetic shape. I've heard educated gentlemen who should know better aping the French barbarians by addressing one another as 'citizen.' Proudly! Can you imagine—?"

He capped his little oration with a scornful sniff. Abraham sipped his port, then said:

"So your sympathies are entirely with Mr. Hamilton and his faction?"

"Indeed they are. Alexander Hamilton is the one authentic genius in the president's cabinet. An absolute master of financial affairs. It's Hamilton who untangled the debt mess left at the end of the war, you know. He and he alone put this nation on a sound monetary basis. I agree wholeheartedly with his contention that we must strengthen our commercial ties with England now that we've settled our differences."

"I'm not sure they're settled."

"You're wrong."

"No, papa. For one thing, the British haven't yet withdrawn from their forts in the northwest."

"But they signed Mr. Jay's treaty last year, agreeing to do so! They can't delay forever," Philip declared, seating himself as if the subject was closed. Abraham still looked skeptical:

"The treaty is all right as far as it goes. But as I understand it, the treaty said nothing about some vital issues still outstanding. Interference with our shipping—that absurd ploy of boarding American vessels to hunt for British seamen who've deserted. The real object as everyone knows is to seize Americans to fill the Royal Navy's press gang quotas."

"The treaty may have its weaknesses," Philip said, somewhat huffily. "But by and large, I approved of Mr. Jay's endeavors."

"I heard that others didn't. Quite a few others."

Philip waved. "Ignorant rabble."

"Is it true they burned Jay's effigy in various cities?"

"Yes, and stoned Hamilton when he spoke for the treaty in New York! But I can cite you an outrage closer to home. Do you know what those filthy Francophiles painted on the wall of my own establishment—right here in Boston? *Damn John Jay! Damn everyone who won't damn John Jay—!*"

Philip noticed his son smiling again. "You are easily amused, Abraham. Such outbursts against public order—deprecations of the effort of decent, patriotic men—they're a disgrace!"

He lowered his voice until it sounded almost threatening:

"I trust you haven't acquired a different view. Haven't fallen in with a pack of republican radicals during your army service."

Straight-faced, but marveling anew at the way wealth and position could alter

a man's politics and tame his passion for upsetting the status quo, Abraham answered:

"I don't believe so, sir. We were a little too busy with the tribes to discuss political theory."

"I had some doubts about permitting you to go off to military duty—as you well know. I allowed it because I suspected the outcome—that you wouldn't find it to your liking."

"You knew that ahead of time? How?"

Philip shrugged, as if the answer was obvious:

"I never liked soldiering either."

"I see." Again Abraham wanted to chuckle. But he didn't. Philip went on:

"I confess I'm not entirely happy to see the new territory secure. It only means the creation of new states. The settlers will be nothing but farmers—artisans—"

"Mr. Jefferson's sort of people," Abraham returned wryly.

"The fool is wrong to believe government should rest in the hands of all! Hamilton sees the issue correctly—"

"Only the rich—the well-educated—are competent to administer the affairs of the nation? Forgive me a second time, papa, but I thought that was exactly what you fought against in the late war."

"Times change! So does a man's thinking. However, I don't wish to discuss my views. I wish to discuss your future."

"I've only been home a week—"

"And I expect to give you sufficient time to acclimate yourself to civilian life. But I do want to inform you of one fact, Abraham." Philip looked so serious, Abraham lost even the slightest desire to laugh. He asked:

"What fact?"

"I am relying on you to join the printing house as soon as possible. I'll give you as much responsibility as I think you can handle, and—"

Quickly, Abraham raised his glass to interrupt:

"Papa, papa—wait! I'm not certain that's what I want to do with my life."

"A career with Kent and Son offers you everything!" Philip exclaimed. "Why wouldn't you want a comfortable, secure existence? Influential friends? A position of respect within the Federalist community—?"

"Perhaps because I'm not yet a Federalist."

"You'll change."

"How can you be so sure?"

The dark eyes caught the hearth's glare. "You are my son."

Softly, but without hesitation, Abraham said, "Yes—and that's the very reason I prefer to do exactly as you did."

"What do you mean?"

"The story, papa."

"*What* story?"

"The one you told me so often when I was growing up. How you refused to accept what was planned for you by your mother—how you struck out on your own instead. Made your own way. Will you deny me the same opportunity? It's a tribute to you that I want it that way—"

"I do *not* consider it a tribute," Philip said. Abraham felt a sudden hurt. "I will be exceedingly disappointed if you refuse to come into Kent and Son as your half-brother will surely do."

"Gilbert's a different case. Bright, but too frail for any kind of work except commerce. In a business he can use his true strength—his mind."

Philip sat in stony immobility for a moment. Then:

"If you don't care to accept my suggestion, be kind enough to tell me what alternative you've chosen."

"The truth is, I can't."

"And why not, sir?"

Silence.

"Answer me! *Why not?*"

"I—I just haven't found it yet. The alternative—"

Abraham's sentence trailed off in lame fashion. Philip's lip showed his scorn—and perhaps concealed pain as deep as Abraham's own. Philip turned defensive, sarcastic:

"You don't know what you want to do, yet you already know my proposition is unsatisfactory. Odd—"

"Papa—"

"*Damned* odd!"

Abraham set his unfinished glass aside. "Sir, I'd like to ask that we postpone the rest of this discussion."

"Until when?"

"Until I've had a chance to think things out."

Abraham was uncomfortable in the evasion. But he couldn't bear to continue the talk—the argument—now. His father was growing too angry. It showed in the seethe of his next sentence:

"I do hope you haven't entirely closed your mind against me."

"No—" Abraham faced away quickly to conceal the lie. "—no, of course I haven't. Goodnight, papa."

Philip rose and walked into the shadows near the front windows. He remained gloomily silent as his son left the room.

III

"GOOD NIGHT, Mr. Abraham," said the nasal-voiced octogenarian who served as footman in the Kent house. Climbing the stairs to his old room in the third story—a room only occupied for a short time before he left for Pittsburgh and Wayne's service—Abraham called a reply over his shoulder. The reply was more grumble than anything else.

Yes, he had lied to his father. No point in denying that. On the long, arduous journey home, he had thought a good deal about the future. He wasn't content to fit pliably into the mold prepared for him by Philip Kent.

In many ways service in the northwest had been an unsettling experience. It had shown him the world was not confined to paper and presses—all he had known as a child. His most vivid early memory of his father was sensory: the smell of ink in the first loft Philip had occupied; a loft above the chandler's store operated by the patriarch of the powerful Rothman family, now respected Boston bankers.

Some of what Abraham had told his father was true. He didn't yet know what he wanted to do with his life. Not in detail, that is. His central goal was much as he'd stated it: to strike out on his own. That was clearly imitative admiration

of Philip—though he realized his father would always refuse to see it as such. God, how the man had changed in just three years—!

During Abraham's first twenty-four hours in the house, he'd literally gaped at the lavish new furnishings—the obvious signs of Philip's continuing ability to pyramid his profits from his initial business venture: an investment in shares in privateering vessels during the Rebellion. The venture had cost Abraham the mother he didn't remember. She had been abducted by one of the privateer captains, and had perished at sea trying to escape from her kidnapper.

Abraham really hadn't appreciated how rich Philip had become until he'd been away from Boston a while, living in altogether different and less luxurious surroundings. Following his return, however, he very quickly found the wealthy household stultifying; too formalized and proper. That spurred him to make up his mind to go his own way.

Because he didn't want to hurt his father, he had tried to hide that truth just now. But he couldn't hide it from himself. So there remained two obstacles for him to overcome:

The immediate one of convincing Philip that he deserved the right to shape his own destiny.

And the more difficult because less clear-cut one of determining what that destiny ought to be.

With a shake of his head, Abraham realized he'd paused on the second-floor landing. As he started up toward the third, he heard his stepmother's voice murmuring in Gilbert's room. He called the obligatory goodnight. Then, aware of Peggy hurrying to the door to speak to him, he rushed on up the steps into the relative gloom of the cramped upper story.

Peggy didn't call out to summon him. She was a wise woman, and he admired her wisdom. She would sense from his quick passage upstairs that the interview with Philip hadn't gone well, and he wanted to retire undisturbed.

Servants had lit a small fire in the grate in his room. He could smell the wood smoke as he touched the latch, thrust the door inward—

"My God—!"

"*Sssh!*" Elizabeth Fletcher put a warning hand to her lips. "Don't be a ninny and make noise or you'll spoil everything."

Shaking a little, Abraham stepped into the room, closed the door.

"What the hell are you doing here, Elizabeth? Dressed like that—it—it isn't proper."

"Oh, don't start talking like the others!" Elizabeth exclaimed. "I've already had another tedious lecture from mama this evening."

She was standing barefoot before the hearth. Thus Abraham could see—most disturbingly—the details of her figure through the filmy material of her nightdress. Her young woman's breasts were clearly defined, nipples and all. And—was her pose deliberate?—he even glimpsed the area between her legs where the clearer outlines of her thighs joined, blurring into a hint of—Quickly, he looked away.

"Please do keep your voice lowered," she whispered. "Before I crept down the hall, I shut my own door with a great show of going to bed."

She walked slowly toward the turned-down coverlets, plumping herself on them. "Anyway, why shouldn't I be here? We're not brother and sister."

"I know, but—"

"And I'm already condemned as perfectly scandalous by the rest of them—" The pale blue eyes challenged him. "Excluding you, I trust."

"Yes. Yes, certainly," Abraham told her, dissembling desperately. He felt both awkward and terrified.

She patted the bed next to her leg.

"Then sit with me, and talk. There's no one else I can talk to in this house, you know."

He continued to stand motionless. She brushed back a lock of fair hair, her expression by turns defiant and devilish:

"Don't tell me you've never been alone with a woman, Abraham Kent. Not after three years in the army."

"Why, I—I've been with a woman several times." The truth of it was, it had happened just once. In the village of Cincinnati, on his way home, he had paid a whore. At the time the whole business had been quick and embarrassing, though in retrospect it had a certain nostalgic charm.

"So do sit down!"

He stared at her a moment longer, seeing something strange, even wicked, shining in her blue eyes. It was a reckless unconcern for propriety that lent her lovely face an almost unholy radiance in the flicker from the grate. Was this what she'd inherited from the Fletcher fellow who had carried on so disgracefully before his death?

The thought frightened Abraham all the more. Yet he didn't pull away, or order her out. Instead, he eased himself gently onto the bed. Elizabeth seized his cold hands in her warm ones. He felt the first hardness of arousal.

"Abraham," she said, her face close enough so that he could smell the sweetness of her breath, "you understand what they're trying to do to both of us, don't you?"

"They?"

"Well, chiefly your father. I didn't understand it myself for the longest time. Then, the older I got, the clearer it became. I've known the truth for—oh, almost two years."

"The truth about what?"

"About what your father wants. It's very simple. He wants everyone who lives under this roof—me, and now you—to bend to his notions of respectability. I admit he's been kind to me over the years. Yet in a way, I hate him."

"Elizabeth, that's a damned ghastly thing to say—"

"I can't help it, that's how I feel. Don't you realize he wants to trap both of us in the same trap? Neither of us must let that happen—we're not cut out for it!"

"What do you propose we do, may I ask?"

"We must fight him, Abraham. Secretly. Together—"

Suddenly she leaned against him, letting him feel her breasts through the thin gown.

Then she took his hand and placed it over one breast and squeezed his fingers, all the while staring at him with those strange, pale eyes.

IV

THAT MOMENT destroyed any doubts Abraham Kent might have had about Elizabeth's purpose in coming to his room so furtively. By means of an act Philip would be sure to find reprehensible, she would defy the authority he sought to exert over her.

Abraham had felt some of the same pressure in the painful interview with his father. Thus he was quite willing to let the eager instincts of his young man's body have their way, joining the girl in this private, ultimately pleasurable form of protest.

To his surprise, he discovered she wasn't a virgin. Her gown tossed aside, her pale thighs spread to reveal a gilded place, she kissed and teased him as expertly as that Cincinnati whore. She drew him down, then guided him with practiced hands curled around his maleness. As the rhythm of the coupling intensified, she groaned louder and louder against his ear. Wantonly, she locked her legs around the small of his back. The ferocious outpourings shook them both almost simultaneously.

Afterward, under the coverlets, she nestled naked in the curve of his arm. When he questioned her about her experience, she only laughed brightly and said it was of no importance. She rolled against him, gripping his cheeks with both palms while those intense blue eyes probed:

"We mustn't let them destroy us, Abraham. *We mustn't.*"

Limp from their union and captivated by her presence, he found it easy to say, "We won't."

"Promise?"

He heard a grotesque echo of Gilbert's voice when she spoke; another echo in his own reply:

"Yes, Elizabeth. I promise."

She uttered a small, satisfied laugh and leaned back against his arm.

She stayed with him an hour or more, until the house was utterly still, and then stole away. In the weeks that followed, as the new year of 1796 opened, she visited him by night whenever she could. No one in the house seemed to suspect, because the lovers carefully avoided one another except at those times when normal household activities such as meals brought them together.

But not many days had passed in January before Abraham realized that his problems had taken on a new dimension.

He was no longer merely defying his father.

He was falling in love with Elizabeth Fletcher.

4
The Storm Breaks

DURING LATE January and into February, Abraham's relationship with his father remained in a state of truce. He agreed to work regular hours at Kent and Son—the firm was expanding so fast that sufficient help couldn't be found—but at the same time, he made clear to Philip that his decision shouldn't be construed as a permanent one.

To reinforce the point, Abraham insisted on menial work and menial wages. He didn't want other employees thinking he was taking advantage of his status as the owner's son.

Despite all the conditions Abraham set, Philip seemed happy with the arrange-

ment. His face showed his pleasure whenever he walked into the press room and saw Abraham black-handed and smeary-cheeked from manipulating the leather balls that inked the type forms, or lugging huge stacks of newly cut paper.

Although new inventions were being introduced at an astonishing rate—duly reported in the columns of the *Bay State Federalist*—the equipment of Kent and Son remained similar to that on which Philip had first learned his trade in a shop in London in the 1770s. Kent's now owned four large flatbeds, each driven by human muscle applied to a screw lever. The presses were located on the first floor of the three-story structure near Long Wharf. Their weight had already caused a noticeable sag in the floor.

On the second story Philip maintained his own bindery, plus warehousing space. Kent and Son had just printed an inexpensive edition of Mr. Noah Webster's *Blue-Backed Speller*. This instructional book for school children was already more than a decade old. But it showed every sign of remaining the standard text for generations to come, and the warehouse was piled high with copies of the Kent version.

The building's third floor held Philip's cramped, rather dingy private office, a smaller press for his weekly newspaper, and another, even dingier cubby occupied by the paper's editor, Mr. Supply Pleasant.

Mr. Pleasant had advanced to journalism from a career as a public letter-writer hired for a few pence by the illiterate, or by those who wanted their correspondence inscribed in a fine, graceful hand. Abraham quickly developed a liking for the graying, pot-bellied editor. Whenever he had a free moment, he climbed the stairs to talk with Pleasant and scan the stories being set in type by Pleasant's one assistant.

Pleasant, in turn, soon sensed Abraham's dissatisfaction with his work downstairs. He raised the subject one blustery day in February:

"Your father's delighted that you're working for Kent's, Abraham."

"It's only temporary, I assure you."

"The book trade isn't to your liking?"

"No, that's not quite it. What I don't like is being expected to spend my life in the book trade."

Supply Pleasant leaned back in his chair, scratched his nose with a quill that left an ink stain between his eyes. He peered over the top of his steel spectacles:

"Then what career do you have in mind? Medicine? The law?"

"I don't know."

"A year's study at Harvard might help you decide."

"I doubt it."

"Well, many a young man takes a while to find his way. But surely you have some idea—"

"Frankly, Mr. Pleasant, about all I've been able to determine so far is what I don't want. I know I'm not a bookman or a scholar. I'm damned if I'd make a good soldier, either—"

Admitting all that was hard. In fact, he was vaguely ashamed that his accomplishments in Boston thus far consisted of doing his job without too many mistakes, and conducting half a dozen furtive meetings with Elizabeth. That last, and the attendant deception of his father and stepmother each secret hour required, were hardly things to be proud of; yet he was so completely and dizzily in love with the fair-haired girl, all else seemed unimportant.

Supply Pleasant chewed the stem of his quill a while, then picked up a stack of neatly inked foolscap sheets:

"Strikes me you're like a beggar at a banquet, Abraham."

"How so, Mr. Pleasant?"

"You're confronted with so many rare dishes, you don't know which to pick first. The country's a veritable cornucopia of opportunity—a veritable cornucopia!" Pleasant had a passion for flowery phrases, in conversation as well as in the paper. He wrote every word of the five columns on each of the four sixteen-by-twenty-inch pages of the *Federalist*.

He handed the foolscap sheets to the younger man:

"Sit ten minutes with this. You'll see what I mean."

"What is it?"

"A feature I've been preparing for some time. A review, if you will, of the remarkable accomplishments of our young country. Of course," Pleasant added after another bite of the quill, "my employer exercises his right to edit my copy. There *are* subjects which can't be mentioned. The very sensible metric measurement system, for example. It's certain to become a world standard—certain! But it's deemed an invention of the devil by good Federalists like your father. While other nations go ahead and adopt it, I predict we shall not—simply because the French Jacobins thought it up. Also—"

He pointed at the sheets with his quill.

"Mr. Jefferson's new plow. Experts claim it will revolutionize farming. Not only does it break the soil, it lifts and turns it aside more efficiently by means of the moldboard Jefferson added. I've put in some copy on the plow, but I'm sure Mr. Kent will scratch it out."

"Don't you resent that sort of interference, Mr. Pleasant?"

"Naturally I resent it."

"Then why don't you protest? Or quit? The first amendment to our Constitution in 'ninety-one guaranteed a man's freedom to speak—or publish—what he wishes."

"That's exactly how it is—Mr. Kent publishes what he wishes," Pleasant said with a resigned smile. "I don't quit because I like newspapering. And I'm not shrewd enough on matters of financing to operate my own gazette. You're too young to realize that much of life is compromise, Abraham. My idealism doesn't extend to my belly, which is empty several times a day, regular as a clock. Besides, your father and I have reached a state of accommodation. He only interferes on subjects related to politics."

"But slanted news is dishonest!"

"No doubt you're right. However, don't forget it was propaganda, not straight news, that rescued us from the morass of the unworkable Articles of Confederation and gave us our Constitution. If Messrs Jay and Hamilton and Madison hadn't published their eighty-odd *Federalist* essays in the New York papers a few years ago, we might still be a gaggle of fractious states instead of a reasonably stable federal union. Like all things, journalism has both its lofty and ignoble sides."

Abraham wasn't persuaded. But he was interested in the article Supply Pleasant had handed him; intrigued by its title and sub-headings:

THE YOUNG COLOSSUS!
A Succinct Review of the Conditions
Generating Unparalleled Prosperity
Under Our Federal Government!
Amazing Advancements

In The Mechanical Sciences!
Expansionist Fever Points To
Vast Population Increase!

"To return to my original point," Pleasant said, "there is enough happening in the United States to provide a young fellow with twenty lifetimes of satisfying labor. Give that a scan and you'll see I'm right. Not I must get to work and finish this review of *The Mysterious Monk*. I saw it last night at Powell's theater. A most diverting Gothic melodrama—"

Abraham hardly heard. Carrying the sheets in his blackened fingers, he retired to the back stairs of the building, found a little light under a grimy window, plucked an apple from his leather apron and began to read.

For a while he couldn't get past the opening sentence. He kept seeing Elizabeth's lovely and defiant blue eyes.

___II

FINALLY ABRAHAM managed to read the article to the end. Mr. Pleasant's piece was indeed a paean to the prosperity and intellectual achievement that seemed to be sweeping the nation.

Pleasant began by noting that the first census, authorized by Congress in 1790, had discovered a population nearing four million, of which, he reported in a dour aside, almost seven hundred thousand were slaves. The editor predicted that by the time of the next census—the year the new century opened—the country would probably grow to an astonishing five or six million people, particularly since there was now more room in which to raise families. The treaties maneuvered through the ministries of England and Spain by Mr. Jay and Mr. Pinckney had at last resolved some territorial disputes and brought a measure of stability to the northwest.

Jay's treaty had removed or reduced the British threat on the country's northern and western borders. Pinckney's Treaty of San Lorenzo, signed in Madrid, had established the Mississippi as the official western limit of the country—set the southern boundary at the thirty-first parallel—and, most important, given America free navigation of the river and free deposit of goods—the right to store and re-ship them without paying duty—at Spanish-held New Orleans for an initial period of three years. Settlers raising crops for profit would now have a secure and easy route to a major port.

The nation had adapted with reasonable ease to the new coinage of 1786. Abraham smiled at Pleasant's deliberate inclusion of the fact that Mr. Jefferson had thought out the system, based on the Spanish milled dollar; the editor wasn't as pliant as he pretended.

A general economic boom was accelerating the pace of commerce and invention. Mr. Whitney of New Haven, for instance, had virtually eliminated the old, tedious process of cleaning green seed cotton. His new gin enabled a single slave to separate out a remarkable fifty pounds of staple per day. As a result, the entire south was turning to a cotton economy; the commodity had at last been made profitable. At the same time, the luckless Whitney was spending a fortune to defend his patent against infringements by rival manufacturers.

As for "expansionist fever"—well, a whole array of startling developments

had made it possible for immigrants to travel into the newly won west faster and more safely than ever before.

Highways were a-building; a turnpike modeled after those in Britain had been opened between Philadelphia and Lancaster, Pennsylvania. Boone's Wilderness Road had been widened to accommodate wagon traffic. And the waterways swarmed with one-way flatboats and keelboats. Families going west gathered on the Pittsburgh docks faster than craft to transport them could be constructed. Wayne's victory had made a journey down the Ohio relatively safe.

Mr. Pleasant touched on other trends that promised to quicken the pace of migration even more. Men were talking of canal systems. Steam power was being harnessed for river boats. Fitch and Rumsey had already launched trial vessels on the Delaware and the Potomac—

With a sigh, Abraham turned over the last sheet. The editor had indeed painted a glowing picture. But in it, he saw no definite place for himself.

He carried the article back to Pleasant's office, hearing and feeling the thud and vibration of the building's presses. That noise, that motion was a manifestation of his father's power. It brought on the pessimistic thought that perhaps he never would find what he wanted.

On top of that, what he wanted most was something he probably wasn't supposed to have—

Elizabeth.

III

THE SHAME of conducting an illicit relationship and the intolerable sameness of the work at Kent and Son finally drove Abraham to decisive action. One balmy Sunday in March, he surprised the family at dinner by announcing that he and Elizabeth were going walking in the afternoon.

As he said it, he caught Elizabeth's quick, glowing glance of admiration. Immediately, his stepmother gave all her attention to the plate in front of her.

But to Abraham's surprise, Philip's reaction was exactly the opposite of what he'd expected:

"Certainly, if you wish." Philip smiled at his son. "I'm not quite the blind, insensitive fellow I'm sometimes credited with being. The interest you two have shown in one another hasn't passed entirely unnoticed."

In a panic, Abraham wondered how much his father knew. Peggy partially answered that:

"We've noticed how you gaze at each other at mealtime."

Abraham was still nonplussed, as was Elizabeth. Philip seemed almost as delighted as little Gilbert, who stared at Abraham with worshipful eyes. Abraham could no longer count the number of times he'd described the charge at Fallen Timbers to his half-brother.

"Have you strolled by Hartt's as yet?" Peggy asked her stepson.

"No—"

"It's quite the attraction, even though work on the frigate has been suspended." She was referring to the shipyard where the keel had been laid in 1794 for one of four large warships put under construction by the government. The ships had been ordered as a response to a threat to American commerce in the Mediterranean. Pirate vessels of the Barbary states had taken to harassing U.S.

merchantmen. A tenuous settlement had finally been reached with Algiers; it amounted to paying tribute in return for safe passage of American vessels in the area. At that point, work on the frigates being built at Boston, New York, Philadelphia and Norfolk had been stopped.

Still struggling to fathom Philip's easy compliance, Abraham said, "Where we go is less important than—certain things Elizabeth and I need to discuss."

"Then by all means discuss them," Philip exclaimed. "I'm delighted to see you giving some thought to the future. Along with these personal matters, I imagine you'll want to consider a decision about your livelihood."

Peggy shot a warning glance at her husband. Philip ignored it:

"Naturally I hope that will also be resolved in favor of a family association."

So that was the trap! Philip was confident that if Abraham settled down with a wife, he would instantly surrender—join Kent and Son. Abraham's jaw muscles hardened as he put down his napkin and rose abruptly.

"One decision won't necessarily lead to the other, sir."

Stung, Philip turned red.

"Then you are a damned fool, sir!" he shouted as Abraham left the room.

Too overwrought to look back, Abraham heard Elizabeth hurrying after him. He paused in the hall to get control of himself. Elizabeth rushed to his side, grasped his arm in silent approval. As they left the house and turned down sloping Beacon Street, both could hear Philip's voice raised in angry argument with Peggy.

IV

IN THE sunny warmth of the afternoon, they did wend their way to Hartt's. Abraham perched on a rotting nail keg, barely seeing the huge frigate sitting unfinished on the ways that ran down to the lapping water.

The great hull, over two hundred feet long, was only partially sheathed in the copper supplied by Philip's old friend Mr. Revere—the same gentleman who, years ago, had fitted Philip with a hand-carved replacement for a broken front tooth. Abraham's father now and then liked to show off his tooth of African hippo tusk. Revere had been able to complete that small project—which couldn't be said of his metalwork on the frigate.

Rated at forty-four guns and estimated to cost a staggering three hundred thousand dollars or more, *Constitution* sat in lonely splendor, guarded only by a couple of elderly watchmen. They paid no attention to the dozen people wandering through the yard to admire Boston's would-be contribution to national defense.

Abraham took Elizabeth's hand, stared into those blue eyes that, by turns, could be so intemperate and so loving:

"I wonder how long father and mother have suspected."

"What difference does it make, Abraham?"

"None. Actually, I'm glad the secret's out. Now I can talk to them about my intention."

"Which is—?"

"To marry you, Elizabeth. With their permission or without it."

She bent to tease his mouth with her lips, caressing him briefly with her tongue. A middle-aged couple hurrying by with two children loudly expressed their outrage.

"You still want to marry me even after enjoying what most men want from a wife?"

"How do you know so much about what most men want?"

"La, Abraham, don't be so frightfully stern! I'm fairly suffocated by all the righteousness in the Boston air! And the thickest cloud hangs over Beacon Street—as you well know. I want to get away from here." She touched his cheek. "With you."

Abraham pondered silently a moment or two.

"Elizabeth—I must ask you a hard question."

Her eyes clouded. "Ask it, then."

"I know growing up in the Kent house hasn't been easy for you—"

"Easier than running the streets and alleys, I suppose. But no, it hasn't. Your father isn't my father. Yet he insists on acting like—I'm sorry. What did you want to ask?"

He hesitated. She stamped her foot:

"Go on!"

"All right. My question is this. Would you marry me just to escape?"

"Good heavens, that is a foolish question! Please don't think me too conceited for saying this, but do you fancy you're the only man I *could* marry?"

He sighed. "No. You're a lovely girl. I've noticed the looks some of papa's gentlemen friends cast your way. I realize you could have your pick of husbands."

"Doesn't that answer your question, my darling?"

He shook his head. "Not entirely. I wouldn't want you to say yes in order to spite father—"

"Impossible! You saw his reaction at the table. I think he'll approve of the match."

"Oh, no. Not unless a commitment to Kent and Son is part of it."

"But it isn't, is it?"

The intensity of her whisper bothered Abraham; revealed again the depth of her dislike of Philip. Still, he said:

"No."

"Then don't make me out to be more wicked than you are, please."

"I don't understand."

"Are *you* thinking of marrying me because it would help you break with him?"

Chilled, he realized how accurate her question was. All the turmoil of the past weeks seemed to clarify in an instant. He understood at last, completely, that Elizabeth's pleas about resisting his father would never have taken root had not the ground been fertile. He needed a force to propel him to action; to help separate him from what he didn't want—even though he still had no clear goal to pursue afterward.

Glumly, he admitted, "Yes—in part. Don't misconstrue that. I do love you. Very much."

"And I love you, Abraham. You needn't be ashamed of admitting we need each other because neither of us can fight him alone."

"He isn't trying to influence me to join the firm out of malice—"

Her features froze. "Since he's your father, you're free to hold that view. But I see it differently. I'm not his child—and I refuse to jump at his every order."

He was tolerant of her last remark. Her reaction to Philip wasn't tempered by natural love, as his was. Yet even he could never remember a time when his

father hadn't terrified him just a little. Philip was a formidable person; a penniless bastard boy who, by sheer will and luck, had elevated himself from nothing to a position of importance in Boston. Abraham recalled one dreadful period of double intimidation; a dim time when Philip's authority had been supported by a harridan housekeeper. A woman named Brumple, long dead. Under Philip's orders, she had pushed Abraham this way and that—

He shook his head again, as if clearing his mind. There was no doubt that he had to escape Philip's dominance, or perish.

Once more he clasped Elizabeth's hand. He was heartened by the responsive pressure of her fingers. And her soothing tone:

"It's all right, Abraham. Marrying to escape him is no sin—"

He didn't answer. His gaze drifted back to the copper plating on *Constitution*'s lower hull. A highlight from the sun blinded him a moment. In the glare he saw a ghost-image of Elizabeth's blue eyes. Unsettling; defiant—

He loved her in spite of all he knew about her: that she'd been born with rebellious blood; a temperament that delighted in defying accepted standards and conventional family authority. It didn't pay to dwell too long on that side of her character. He had to remember only that she was lovely, and said she loved him—

"What we've decided raises another issue, though," he said. "I must support you, but I have no trade."

"We're both young and strong—" She clapped her hands and threw her arms wide. "We can do anything we wish! The country's vast now. There's room for us to search for the kind of life that suits us. I honestly don't care where we live so long as it's not Boston."

Abruptly, his mind jumped to a memory of Anthony Wayne's musings about the promise of the northwest, then to the article by Mr. Pleasant; specifically, his comments on the tide of migration sweeping through Pennsylvania and down the Ohio to the territory east of the Mississippi. Speculating aloud, he described what Wayne had said about the opportunity in the lands now largely cleared of Indian menace.

As he spoke, Elizabeth watched him with total attention. When he finished her voice was hushed:

"My father felt just as General Wayne does, Abraham. You know he was a lifelong friend of George Rogers Clark—"

"Yes."

"Mother's told me Clark wrote him many letters about the west. But he only got as far as Pittsburgh. We—we could go farther. Build our own home—why, I've read you can buy an acre of ground out there for as little as two dollars!"

"If you attend an auction sponsored by one of the speculation companies. They've grabbed up a lot of the acreage." His speech quickened, just as hers had a moment ago. "There are other ways—"

"Tell me!"

"Men who fought in the Revolution can claim parcels of western land the government reserved for veterans."

"Does your father own land like that?"

"I've no idea. I suppose if he ever did, he's sold it by now."

"Even if he hasn't, he'd never give it to us."

"You're probably right. Better we don't even raise the subject with him. Besides, when I was in the army, I saw a few people who simply moved in and settled where they wished. Squatters, they're called. They choose their land first

and worry about filing a claim later. If you go far enough west, you see, you'll find territory that hasn't been laid out into townships—or even surveyed as yet. Pick a parcel like that, and if you're lucky, no speculators will ever leave their comfortable eastern parlors to dispute your title—" He sighed all at once. "It's an exciting idea."

"Oh, yes!"

"But there's a drawback."

"I don't see any."

"The one I mentioned before. I've no trade I could practice out there."

"You know how to run a printing press."

"I've no particular desire to be a printer. Besides, it'll be a while before the west is civilized enough to want many newspapers and handbills."

"Frankly, I don't care what you do. Keep a store. Hammer at a smith's forge. Farm—"

"I doubt I'd be too successful at farming—"

"How do you know till you've tried? You're certainly bright enough to learn anything you want to learn. *If* you want it badly enough."

Standing, he put both hands on her waist. "I want only you. Let the rest happen as it will."

Again he thought he detected that strange glint of malicious delight in her sunlit eyes. He resolved not to worry about it. Who ever understood all the motives behind any action or decision? He was content that her passion matched his.

In a moment, emotion swept practical considerations out of his mind. The thought of the two of them launching out together beyond the mountain barriers had an almost magical attraction—

"All right," he said abruptly. "We'll try the new country."

She fairly leaped into his arms, hugging him while scandalized heads again turned their way. He felt the warmth of her mouth near his ear:

"Do you know a secret? I despise wearing stockings and shoes—isn't that funny? In the west, I won't have to, will I?"

"No." He laughted. "No, you can run barefoot any time you please."

Happy and confident, they rushed back to the Kent house to break the news.

___V

WHEN PHILIP heard Abraham's breathless declaration of the young couple's plans, he reacted swiftly and emphatically:

"Madness! Absolute *madness!*"

His strong, blunt jaw had drained of color. He stalked back and forth in front of the windows overlooking the street and the Common, where noisy children played in the sunlight. A chill had enveloped the sitting room all at once, it seemed to Abraham.

Peggy Kent, seated, tried to temper her husband's rage:

"Perhaps we should discuss the whole subject later, Philip. When everyone's a bit calmer—"

"What is there to discuss, woman? The very idea's preposterous!"

Consigned to a corner of a settee, Gilbert bounced to his feet:

"I think it's splendid, papa. I've read Mr. Pleasant's articles in your paper— men will be needed for all sorts of work in the west."

"Be damned to your impertinence!" Philip shouted. Gilbert turned white. Philip shot out one hand, pointing. "To your room—immediately!"

Hurt, Gilbert rose and hurried out.

Philip limped over and slammed the doors. Then he whirled to face his son. In moments, Philip had almost destroyed Abraham's confidence. But Elizabeth looked as determined as ever; and almost as angry as the head of the household.

Before she could say anything, Philip shook a finger in his son's face:

"The time to abandon this lunacy is *now,* young man!"

"No, I won't—"

"*Yes!* You're being totally impractical!"

"Papa, I refuse to listen to—"

Philip drowned him out: "Precisely what do you plan to do after you complete this romantic pilgrimage? Become one of Mr. Jefferson's noble and impoverished dirt-farmers?"

"By God, sir," Abraham said, reddening, "there's no shame in any kind of work so long as its respectable."

"Respectable poverty, that's what you want?"

"*I want to make my own way!* Thousands of others are doing it—with fewer wits and less strength than I have!"

"I question your statement about wits," Philip sneered. "You've lost yours." He faced Elizabeth. "This is entirely your doing."

"Philip, don't—!" Peggy began. Elizabeth broke in:

"You're vile to suggest that!"

"Do you deny it?"

"I won't deny Abraham and I want to leave Boston and live our own lives—"

"In preference to staying here and enjoying security? Wealth? The chance to mold opinion—the very course of this nation? You're a fool—" Philip spun to his son. "And so are you. At Kent's you have every opportunity to be of real service to the country—*and* earn a handsome profit at the same time! I—"

Suddenly Philip drew a deep breath. His anger seemed to melt just a little. He ignored Elizabeth standing beside Abraham, gripping his arm. His eyes sought his son's, imploring:

"—I beg you to recognize what you're throwing away."

"We're throwing away *nothing!*" Elizabeth exclaimed. "Arguing is useless. We plan to be married and go where we will!"

Again Philip started to yell, restrained himself only with obvious effort. While Peggy watched anxiously, he took a different tack. His voice shook as he raised both hands:

"A compromise, then—"

Abraham looked stunned when he heard the words. They were natural enough coming from a poor man like Supply Pleasant. When Philip used them, it signaled panic.

"No compromise," Elizabeth said.

"You must give me a fair chance to present my side. 'Abraham? You must!"

Abraham hated to see his father plead. It was sad and degrading, somehow. And yet, one tiny part of his mind took pleasure in it.

He said to Elizabeth, "We should at least be courteous enough to listen—"

"*No!*"

"Yes." Abraham said, with firmness.

"Thank you," Philip said. "If—if you've failed to see the sort of future you could have, the fault's mine. I must rectify that. Elizabeth—"

Forcing himself to ignore her hostile glare, he moved toward her, his right shoulder sagging at every step.

"—you've never been outside Boston. Abraham has seen nothing but the back roads and rivers between here and that damned godforsak—between here and the west. Let me show you what you'll be rejecting if you pursue the course you've set—"

Sounding more confident, Philip straightened his shoulders, even attempted a smile:

"I think after I've laid the alternative before you both, you'll quickly choose it in preference to your own plan."

Quietly, Peggy said, "Philip, I am not sure what you *are* proposing."

"A tour! A holiday! To the capital—perhaps even as far as your home state of Virginia—" There was a falsity to Philip's enthusiasm that still saddened Abraham. But he listened without comment as the older man rushed on:

"I'm in need of a change of scene anyway. The good weather is coming—the roads will be passable—we'll show these young people where the future of America really lies. In the cities! The solid seats of power along the coast! By God, I'll even write my old friend Henry Knox and arrange for Abraham and Elizabeth to meet the president himself! What do you say, Abraham?"

The son hesitated, sickened to see his father so desperate. At the same time, he was conscious of Elizabeth's tension as she held his arm. Her fingers dug into the fabric of his sleeve.

"I say nothing can change our minds," she told Philip.

"Not the prospect of being well off? Influential? Ah, we'll see. We'll see—!" He looked straight at Abraham. "As my son, I think it is your duty to grant me the right to prove my case."

"Oh, that's unfair, sir!" Elizabeth cried. "To play on his emotions—" She would have said more, but Peggy's sharp glance silenced her.

There was a long moment in which no one spoke. Then, very quietly, Philip said:

"Abraham?"

Abraham knew even before he replied that his father had outwitted him—because Philip knew his son couldn't refuse a plea of family love, family duty—no matter how expedient or meretricious its invocation. With mingled feelings of outrage and pity, he answered:

"All right, we'll accede to your wishes, papa."

"Splendid, excellent! We'll leave within a week."

"But don't expect miracles," Abraham cautioned. "Our minds are made up."

"Ah, we'll see!" Philip repeated, trying to restore a measure of gaiety to the discussion. Elizabeth's blue eyes burned with resentment.

As his anger drained away, Abraham was saddened by a new thought. The Bible, which Peggy had insisted he study as a boy, said something explicit about a man taking a wife, and cleaving to her, and leaving his father's house forever. He'd come to that watershed—and at the last moment, refused to cross.

Seated beside Peggy, Philip was already outlining his plans for hiring carriages, packing their belongings. He acted supremely confident. For a moment Abraham thought that his father might be right. Perhaps he *was* a fool to throw away so many advantages—

As if sensing his indecision, Elizabeth dug her fingers still deeper into his arm. Abraham looked at her, then away. The savagery of her glance terrified him.

═5

"Scenes of Life Among the Mighty"

WHEN EDITOR PLEASANT learned of the forthcoming trip, and heard Abraham describe its purpose, he broke out laughing.

"Why, it's almost as if he's taking you to a great museum, isn't it? One in which you'll be expected to sigh and gape respectfully at scenes of life among the mighty—"

Pleasant sobered, raised a hand. "I didn't mean to mock your father, Abraham. He's treated me well. But he's as stubborn as sin—and remarkably canny, as you'll discover if you haven't so far. Prepare yourself for a dazzling exhibition. 'Scenes of life among the mighty'—"

He scribbled it down with his quill.

"I'd rather like that. Damned if I'm not a shade jealous at being left behind!"

Pleasant's phrase stuck in Abraham's mind, constantly emphasizing the contrivance of the trip and tainting his attitude toward it. He didn't mention the remark to Elizabeth. He was afraid she might taunt Philip with it. That could earn Pleasant a reprimand, a cut in salary, the loss of his job, or, if Philip were really exercised, a thrashing. From his boyhood Abraham remembered a couple of occasions when Philip struck employees who displeased him.

The family set out in mid-April, in two carriages. Each carriage had its own driver and postillion. Luggage was lashed in place on top. An armed guard rode ahead, another behind; ugly fellows, but necessary because the rutted highways were known to attract thieves who preyed on rich travelers.

Gilbert was delighted by every new vista along the route. But Elizabeth complained constantly about the jars and jolts. At their overnight stops, she seldom ate more than a few mouthfuls of the evening's meal, and retired early. Her pale blue eyes sought Abraham's often, silently imploring him—warning him—not to be seduced. He had few chances to speak to her in private, and reassure her that he was on his guard.

As Elizabeth suffered under the rigors of the journey, Philip's spirits, by contrast, grew more and more ebullient. He was positively gay as they neared the nation's temporary capital, Philadelphia.

On their first full day in that splendid and impressive city, they drove out to see some of the fine Georgian homes, as well as the newer, neo-classic ones designed in what was coming to be called the Federal style. They visited Congress Hall, where the two houses of the legislature sat while in session. They returned to their lodgings to find a beautifully inscribed invitation from the appointments secretary of the chief executive of the United States.

President and Mrs. Washington would be delighted to receive the family of Mr. Philip Kent, the noted Boston publisher, at their quarters in the Morris mansion on High Street at four P.M. Thursday.

At last, Elizabeth seemed a bit impressed by the ease with which Philip's long-time friendship with the Boston bookseller Henry Knox, now retired as Secretary of War and gone to Maine, had opened the doors that shielded the mighty from those Philip scorned as "Jefferson's democratic-republican rabble."

II

ROBERT MORRIS had signed the Declaration; managed the fledgling nation's finances during the Revolution; founded the national bank. He was called the wealthiest man in the country. His house, turned over to the president and first lady for their own use, was a magnificent three-story brick mansion. In it, people said, everything glittered, as befitted an American Midas. The lamp fixtures outside glittered; the furniture and mahogany woodwork glittered; the largest brass door-hinge and the smallest bit of brass cabinet hardware glittered. It was no wonder the entire Kent family was in a state of nerves when their carriage pulled up in front of the Morris house at the appointed hour.

With obvious trepidation, Peggy remarked on the presence of half a dozen even more sumptuous coaches, and many servants lounging around them. Even Elizabeth's eyes sparkled at the sight.

Elizabeth had dressed with special care, as they all had. Her gown of white brocade silk shimmered in the mild sunlight of the spring afternoon. In her excitement, she stumbled going up the walk, losing one of her silver-embroidered high-heeled shoes, which Abraham gallantly retrieved.

Servants ushered the visitors into the parlor. Abraham's nervousness grew as the elegantly groomed guests, a dozen ladies and gentlemen, turned toward the newcomers.

The aging president approached the Kents, a small, plump woman at his side. Martha Washington exchanged curtseys with Peggy and Elizabeth while the tall Virginian who preferred Mount Vernon to Philadelphia greeted Philip and his party with impeccable politeness:

"I'm honored to welcome so distinguished a family, Mr. Kent. When General Knox wrote that you planned a tour, I decided we must surely meet—for social as well as for somewhat more practical reasons."

Washington, Abraham noticed, had an odd, rigid smile. Except when speaking, he kept his lips compressed. The gossipmongers said this was to hide false teeth that fit poorly, causing him continual discomfort. According to Supply Pleasant, a New York dentist had carved the president's dentures out of hippotamus ivory, the same material Revere had used for Philip's false tooth. Washington's were reportedly attached to metal bars that gouged his gums and lent his lower face a swollen look.

Philip said, "The honor is entirely ours, Mr. President."

"Come, let me present you to the rest of the gathering," Washington said. His lips parted sufficiently for Abraham to see that something—wine or tea—had badly blackened the artificial teeth.

Among men who were taller than he, Philip always seemed to stand more erect. That was the case now. His limp was hardly noticeable as he walked at Washington's side.

Abraham and the others met Robert Morris and his wife, then the tubby vice

president, John Adams, and his wife Abigail. Philip and Adams reminisced briefly about their long acquaintance; it had begun in Boston before the Revolution.

The famous Philadelphia socialite and beauty, Mrs. Bingham, was presented next. She graciously drew Peggy and Elizabeth into conversation after apologizing that her wealthy husband was indisposed.

Servants brought in refreshments—tea, port and trays of sweet little cakes. Before long, the gentlemen were gathered in one group, the ladies in another. The president led Philip and the others to a large, ornate key which hung on one wall of the parlor.

"I'm reminded that you are a good friend of the Marquis de Lafayette, Mr. Kent."

Philip didn't seem the least overawed by the towering president. Giving a crisp nod, he replied, "Perhaps you also recall we met when we were quite young, in our native province of Auvergne, in France."

Washington nodded. Then his gaze turned toward the great key. "My sympathies were with the revolutionaries for a time. As were those of our mutual friend." He gestured. "That is the key to the Bastille. Lafayette obtained it the day that evil fortress was destroyed, and later sent it to me."

"I understand the marquis is being reasonably well treated in prison," Philip said.

"Yes, so I've heard. But his circumstances grieve me all the same. France was our great ally once. Now I believe our courses have separated—perhaps forever."

The president was alluding to the political rift between the Federalists—some said they controlled Washington's thinking through Alexander Hamilton—and Jefferson, the Francophile, who had resigned his position as secretary of state and gone home to Virginia.

"Experience is a good teacher, if she is only heeded," Washington continued. "I would hope the next president of these states would avoid permanent alliances of any kind. Even though conditions have changed radically in France in twenty years, she still expects us to grant her favored status because of her past support. Our refusal may pose difficulties for us."

Philip set his port aside. "You refer to the next president, sir. The reports are true, then? You won't relent and seek a third term?"

Washington shook his head. "When a man passes sixty, a certain vigor departs. But I am sure your widely read newspaper, as well as you personally, will stand behind the gentleman I hope to see elected by year's end."

He laid a hand on the shoulder of the preening Adams.

"Among men of Federalist persuasion, Mr. Adams has no peers and no rivals," Philip answered smoothly. "Of course my paper will endorse his candidacy."

Robert Morris—and even Adams himself—murmured their approval.

Abraham was beginning to understand the pleasure his father took in associating with these opulently dressed, rather aristocratic gentlemen. They were the movers of the new nation. Abraham sensed an unspoken bond between them. They shared, and enjoyed, power. Philip was happy to be included.

President Washington faced Abraham. But his words were for the older Kent:

"And your son? Does he intend to carry on the family endeavor? Will my successor have his support along with yours?"

Philip's glance challenged Abraham. "I have every hope the answer to both questions will be affirmative."

Abraham's jaws clenched. A burst of laughter from the ladies kept him from speaking up, and mentioning his plan to travel west. With the rest of the gentlemen, he turned toward the women. He saw Elizabeth chatting in lively fashion with the beautiful Mrs. Bingham. He was delighted to see color back in her cheeks—

He decided not to re-open the argument with his father in such dignified surroundings.

III

THE KENTS stayed a week in Philadelphia, attending the theater and visiting tourist attractions such as Bartram's famous botanical gardens, the Charles Peale museum with its amazing display of mastodon bones, and the old State House where the Declaration had been presented by the self-exiled Mr. Jefferson. Then the two carriages resumed their journey south. Peggy had persuaded Philip to follow through on a chance remark the day the trip first came up. At her request, Philip intended to show the young couple the prosperous, populous state of Virginia where Peggy had spent much of her life.

The spring weather turned stormy. The roads became bogs. Progress was slow and the carriages stopped frequently. Alarmed, Abraham watched Elizabeth growing pale again. She was unable to travel for more than a few hours without succumbing to fits of nausea.

For the first time, he wondered about her health. She had always been slender and somewhat delicate. Now he asked himself whether she was suited for a long trip west, not to mention the hard work that would follow. Perhaps he shouldn't be so quick to reject his father's offer of a good job—

He didn't express his doubts to the girl. They were having enough trouble just making a few miles a day on the wretched roads.

Their route took them near the ten-square-mile tract of land straddling the Potomac River where the capital would eventually be located. The site had been chosen in a political horse trade. Former Secretary of the Treasury Hamilton had been instrumental in moving the permanent seat of the nation's government below the Mason-Dixon survey line in return for southern votes for some of his financial measures.

The special district, two-thirds in Maryland, one-third on the southwest side of the river in Virginia, was already being informally called "Columbia," in honor of the Italian navigator who had reached the continent in the fifteenth century. A French-born engineer named L'Enfant was drawing up plans for a modern city which everyone hoped could be occupied by the turn of the century.

Abraham found Virginia a green and pleasant state, full of handsome homes, large tracts under cultivation—and scores of black men and women owned outright by white planters. Though he was well aware of slavery's existence, seeing it first hand was something of a jolt. He'd been brought up in the only state in the union which had reported a slave population of zero in the 1790 census.

As the weather improved, so did Elizabeth's health. The Kents spent an enjoyable week and a half at an inn in Caroline County, responding to invitations

from families who remembered Peggy and her second husband from their trip to Virginia shortly after their marriage in 1781. The family even received a note by courier from a totally unexpected source: a gentleman who had heard of their presence from mutual friends with whom they'd dined.

When Peggy read the gracious note, Philip exploded:

"*What?* Visit that damned republican devil? I'd sooner take a vacation in hell!"

"Come, come, dear," Peggy soothed. "Mr. Jefferson is an old, old friend of my parents. It would be rude to refuse his invitation to Monticello." She teased him: "Are you afraid your principles would melt away in his presence?"

"I am afraid I might not be able to contain my temper!"

"I think we shoud go, papa," Abraham said.

"The decision is not yours," Philip answered in a brusque way. But after twenty-four hours of grumbling, he gave in. He justified his turnabout by saying a man should know his enemy.

The two carriages left the Rappahannock and turned westward toward Mr. Jefferson's county seat in Albemarle County. There, on the eight-hundred-foot *monticello*—little mountain—near Charlottesville, Philip confronted his intellectual adversary.

He soon had cause to regret agreeing to the excursion.

IV

NEVER IN his life had Abraham inhaled such a heady combination of fragrances— nor seen so many different kinds of trees.

Mr. Jefferson had arranged to receive them in the garden adjoining his orchard. A burly black servant who met the carriage pointed out the varieties: walnut and peach; plum and cherry; olives and almonds and figs. There were even a few of the exotic orange trees from the far Floridas. Deer could be glimpsed grazing here and there in the orchard. Only Peggy acted uninterested. She gave the slave guide a peculiar, nervous look from time to time.

On the carriage ride to the hilltop, Abraham had been startled to see that Monticello seemed to be in a state of disrepair. Now, at close range, his original impression was confirmed. Scaffolding rose everywhere. Slaves pushed barrows of bricks from the kilns on the property. Carpenters' tools made a racket in the soft morning air. Peggy explained that since the death of his wife and the decline of his political fortunes, the man who had played such a large role in shaping the new country had withdrawn from public life and now occupied himself with his two passions—architecture and agriculture.

Abraham touched Peggy's arm. Was the man approaching through the orchard Mr. Jefferson? Yes, she said, it was. The man's clothing instantly drew a disdainful comment from Philip, who was formally dressed. Jefferson, ten years younger than the president, and standing well over six feet, wore a linen shirt sticky with sweat, and workman's trousers tucked into dusty boots.

Jefferson's face had a gaunt quality, as if from illness or personal strain. But he greeted Abraham's stepmother warmly, taking both her hands in his:

"My dear Peggy! How wonderful to see you! When I heard you'd come home, I wanted to welcome you in grand style—" Chagrined, he indicated his filthy clothes. "—and look at me."

"You're remodeling the house, Tom—"

"Again," he said, and pointed. "Tearing down most of the facade. There'll be a new foyer and balcony, and an octagonal roof I've patterned after the Roman temple of Vesta. Unfortunately, a scaffolding collapsed yesterday. One of my nigras—the husband of my cook—nearly lost his life. We've been in a turmoil—so all my plans for setting you a good meal inside have gone away."

In the sunlight, Jefferson's graying hair still showed faint glints of its original red. He swung toward Philip, who was gazing at the blacks pushing the barrows. Jefferson had often spoken out against the evils of slavery. Yet he continued to keep slaves on his own property, making him vulnerable to the criticism of New Englanders.

If the former secretary of state understood the meaning of Philip's pointed stare, he was polite enough to overlook it.

"And this is your husband—" Jefferson reached Philip in two long strides, grasped his hand. "My honor, Mr. Kent."

"Mine, sir," Philip said.

Peggy introduced Abraham and wide-eyed Gilbert. Then she resorted to the convenient falsehood used by the family:

"And my niece who lives with us, Miss Elizabeth Fletcher."

Jefferson raked a muscular wrist across his sweaty jaw. His eyes lingered on Elizabeth's face. "Fletcher," he repeated. "A familiar name in the district where you grew up, Peggy. The Fletchers of Sermon Hill come to mind—"

Pale, Peggy answered, "There is no connection other than coincidence, Tom. Elizabeth is kin to my mother's people in Massachusetts."

"Yes, I suppose we have no monopoly on good English names in Virginia," Jefferson smiled.

Philip shifted from foot to foot, uncomfortable. Abraham had been a bit startled at his stepmother violating protocol by introducing Elizabeth last rather than first. Now he suspected the reason—fear. He recalled that Elizabeth's father had spent a short time in the Second Continental Congress, as an alternate for his older brother. Jefferson, attending the same Congress—had he known the long-dead Judson Fletcher? If so, it might account for his momentary surprise when Elizabeth was presented.

But any echoes of the past had been stilled by Peggy's statement and Jefferson's tactful acceptance of it. He led his guests to benches in the breezy shade. A moment later, a huge-breasted black woman brought a tray of refreshments into the garden. Abraham took a crystal goblet of tea with chips of ice floating in it. Philip gave Gilbert permission to run off and explore the orchard, but warned him to avoid the frantic construction activity near the house.

Jefferson sat down, resting his elbows on his knees and lacing his fingers together beneath his chin. Philip remained standing. Jefferson said:

"Your newspaper is well written, Mr. Kent."

Now it was Philip's turn to be startled. It took him a moment to reply, with a shrug whose involuntary impoliteness made Peggy frown:

"The *Bay State Federalist* is only a minor part of the activities of Kent and Son, Mr. Jefferson."

"Yes, but politically, it's the most important part."

"I'm surprised the paper has circulated this far south."

Jefferson's smile was vaguely pained. "Why, Mr. Kent, I never close my mind to the views of the opposition."

"A noble sentiment," Philip mumbled, put off by the other man's polite and winning manner.

"Not a sentiment—conviction!" The tall Virginian stood up. "The basis of our government is the opinion of the people, Mr. Kent. *All* the people—"

Philip stiffened. Jefferson returned the pugnacious stare with an equally steady one. He immediately began to undercut Philip's obvious irritation:

"So the very first object of government must be the maintenance of free circulation of ideas. From all quarters. If it were left to me to decide whether we ought to have a government without newspapers, or newspapers without a government, I shouldn't hesitate a moment to prefer the latter." He smiled that charming smile again, and drank his tea, leaving Philip nonplussed.

Jefferson turned his attention to Abraham:

"What's your role in Kent and Son, young man? Are you connected with the book side? Or the newspaper?"

"I work in the book printing department. But I don't have an official position. My—" He decided to test the water. "—my presence in Boston is only temporary."

"How so?"

Ignoring Philip's hostile stare, Abraham went on, "I served with General Wayne's Legion in the northwest. I was taken with the spaciousness and abundance of the country. I find the idea of settling where there's plenty of land—and few people—more appealing than city life."

He was about to add that the girl Peggy presented as her niece shared that opinion, and would share whatever future it led him to as well. But since neither Philip nor Peggy had raised the subject of marriage, he held back; the introduction of one more irritant wouldn't help the already strained situation.

"You plan to take up farming, then?" Jefferson asked.

"Quite possibly."

"Do you know anything about agriculture?"

"No. But I imagine a man can learn that, can't he?"

"Indeed he can—if he has the back for it."

Peggy's soft laugh was forced. A bird rilled in a nearby walnut tree. Philip didn't bother to hide his unhappiness over the course of the conversation.

Jefferson, however, showed genuine enthusiasm all at once. He snatched up a stick, sat down and started to trace a rectangular shape where the grass had worn away in front of his bench.

"I'm glad to hear your plans, young man. I think they're praiseworthy." As he talked, he changed the outline of the rectangle, angling it here, adding a jutting peninsula there. All at once Abraham realized Jefferson was drawing a crude map of the North American continent.

"We must fill the west with settlers as fast as we can. In the west, there's room for families to multiply. And an increasing population of farmers and craftsmen will strengthen America immeasurably."

"That is the democratic view,' Philip said in an arch way. "The French view."

Jefferson didn't rise to the bait:

"Unfortunately, the French have carried liberty to the stage of license—but yes, you're quite right. They have also shaped my views—as perhaps mine shaped theirs."

Drawing a vertical slash from the bottom of the rectangle two-thirds of the way to the top, he tapped it with the stick, saying to Abraham:

"Our boundaries extend only this far—the Mississippi. But beyond—" He moved the stick left, toward the irregular coastline. "—the land mass is immense. All of this territory is currently the property of Spain. In fact, a Franciscan named Serra has established missions all up and down this shore—"

He jabbed several times at the western perimeter, then moved the stick back to the right.

"But it's my conviction that the Spanish lands physically connected to these United States must one day belong to the United States. Somehow, somehow—!"

"And what about British land, sir?" Philip demanded. "What about Canada? Would you covet that too?"

"I might."

Jefferson cast the stick aside, standing again, splendidly tall and commanding:

"At very least, we must know for certain what natural riches lie between the Mississippi and the ocean. I've tried for almost a decade to generate funds for a trans-continental exploration—all the way to the Pacific. A few years ago, I almost succeeded. The Philosophical Society agreed to send Michaux, a French botanist. The president himself gave the largest single contribution—twenty-five dollars. Which shows you the popularity of exploration. Or should I say the insularity of those of us who live east of the mountains?"

"I'm not surprised you had trouble raising the money," Philip told him. "Such exploration is absolutely pointless."

"Indeed? Spain doesn't think it's pointless. She's been at it for several centuries."

"America's prosperity rests on the continuing development of eastern commerce."

"Partly, only partly," Jefferson argued. "A contemporary man must have manufactured articles—including a shirt on his back. But he also needs food in his belly. The northeast is poor farmland, and the south is going to cotton. The west, by contrast, is unbelievably fertile. We simply can't ignore that kind of natural wealth—"

As he spoke, his gaze lingered on the hazy blue hills in the west. Then he smiled again:

"But let's not quarrel over honest differences of opinion, Mr. Kent. The fact is, many Americans feel just as you do. That's why I wasn't able to implement my trans-continental plan in '93."

Philip said, "I also recall Michaux proved to be a spy intent on causing friction between America and Spain."

Jefferson looked rueful. "That's correct. When the less than pure-hearted botanist was recalled by President Washington, we had something of a scene about it. Just one of many," he added, with a trace of sadness. "Still, if I'm ever in a position to encourage a similar venture, I will. I believe our country's true future lies not in the east but the west."

For the first time, Elizabeth broke from the expected feminine role of polite listener:

"That's exactly what Abraham has been saying, Mr. Jefferson!"

"Then I'd encourage you to follow your instincts, young man. They're correct."

"I am *dis*couraging him!" Philip exclaimed, limping off to emphasize his pique. "I think the idea is utterly foolish."

"I don't know that either of us will have much of a hand in the decision, Mr.

Kent.'' Jefferson nodded to Abraham. ''Youth must be given its day—and its freedom to choose. Ah, but I think we've quite covered the subject—let me give you a tour of the grounds. And then, if you don't mind the dust and noise, I'll show you a little of the house, too.''

He lifted one hand toward Philip, palm up; it was both an invitation and a gesture of conciliation. Although Philip still looked flushed and upset, he didn't prolong the argument. He fell in step beside his wife as Jefferson led the way.

Abraham and Elizabeth dropped a few steps behind, allowing their hands to touch. She whispered softly:

''Mr. Jefferson said exactly what I hoped to hear, Abraham.''

''And I.''

''Those dreadful, stuffy people in Philadelphia—so rich and smug—I don't want to be like them. I don't want to spend my life in drawing rooms—or on a plantation veranda, for that matter—murmuring lies with a smile on my face.''

''Speaking of lies, I had the eerie feeling Mr. Jefferson recognized you.''

''I suppose he would have known my father, and I'm told I resemble him.''

''I feel a little sorry for papa. I expect he's kicking himself for his decision to come here.''

''He only did it as a courtesy to mama,'' Elizabeth sniffed, scornful. ''Your father was positively rude. There's no other word for it.''

''Rude because he fears Jefferson's right,'' Abraham said. His eyes were drawn to the blurred hills of the Blue Ridge in the west. But his mind went back to Supply Pleasant's mocking comments about the little series of exhibitions arranged for his benefit. How true the editor's jibe had turned out to be!

Ah, but Jefferson had given Philip a comeuppance. Under the spell of the Virginian's words, with Elizabeth at his side in the sweet-smelling lane between rows of trees, Abraham abruptly voiced a decision:

''I wavered a little in Philadelphia. But now I'm convinced we should do what we talked about doing in the first place.''

''I am too, my darling.''

He turned, noting that his father and stepmother were a good distance away in the orchard's dappled shade. Mr. Jefferson was pointing out something up in the branches of a cherry tree. But Philip was staring back over his shoulder at the young lovers who stood close together beneath leaves that seethed softly in the warm wind.

Abraham began, ''I have only one reservation—''

Her blue eyes flared. ''You're afraid to inform your father of your decision, is that what you mean?''

He was, a little. But it wasn't what troubled him:

''You haven't been in the best of health on this trip. A life somewhere other than a comfortable city might be too difficult for you.''

''Abraham—''

''No, hear me out. If I were responsible for putting you into unhappy circumstances, I'd carry it on my conscience all my days.''

''I am strong and completely healthy!'' Elizabeth said, with such fervency that Abraham was alarmed. She protested too much. It was another indication of her almost fanatic desire to escape the confinement of the Kent house.

She seized his hand. ''I'll go with you anywhere you want to go. And I'll thrive, I promise you. I'll thrive!''

What she said failed to put all his fears to rest. But her expression was so intense, he didn't dare voice further doubt.

So, with part of the burden temporarily lifted by her declaration, he closed his fingers around hers. Together they hurried to catch up to the older people.

V

THAT NIGHT, in the sitting room of the suite they had taken at the best lodging house in Charlottesville, Abraham and Elizabeth announced their determination to stick by their original plan.

Again Philip burst into a rage; again he hammered them with the same arguments. Hadn't they seen the desirability of being welcome among the rich and powerful—?''

Losing his temper, Abraham admitted that such a life had its charms—for those who valued them:

"Perhaps there's a reason you value them more than I, papa."

"Explain that remark!''

"There's still a touch of the aristocrat in your blood. Your father *was* an English lord, after all—''

Livid, Philip whirled on Peggy. "This is your fault!''

"Just a moment, sir—!'' she exclaimed.

"Don't deny it! You permitted him to be exposed to Jefferson's democratic rot—!''

"You agreed to come, Philip! No one coerced you!''

"Don't blow Mr. Jefferson's part in this all out of proportion,'' Abraham put in. "He did no more than articulate what I've been thinking for a long time.''

"He did more than that,'' Elizabeth said. "He told the truth!'' To Philip: "Which you, in your narrowness, can't stand to hear!''

Philip glared, "*You damned, ungrateful—*''

"*Stop it, sir!*'' Peggy cried, jumping up. She was angrier than Abraham had ever seen her.

Philip limped to Gilbert, who sat on a cane-backed chair, huge-eyed and frightened. He slipped his arm around the boy's shoulders:''

"At least I've one son who won't turn his back on me.''

"Oh, God, sir—that's *vicious!*'' Elizabeth practically screamed. "The closer you come to being defeated, the more your cruel, vindictive nature reveals itself!''

Philip's hand whipped upward, as if he meant to strike her. She ran to Abraham. Slowly, and with obvious effort, Philip lowered his hand to his side.

"Cruel?'' Philip repeated in a strangled voice. "Vindictive—? I thank you for your compassionate judgment. For your gratitude—'' His glance at his older son was scathing. "I thank you both. Gilbert, come with me.''

"Where, papa?''

"Downstairs. I'll buy you a sweet from the landlord before you're tucked in.''

Stunned and hurt, Abraham watched his father limp out with the boy. Peggy began to cry softly.

Elizabeth moved closer to Abraham, pressing her breast against him. She slipped her arms around his waist, squeezed hard, making a strange little sound in her throat. A suppressed laugh? he thought, horrified. No, surely not—

She buried her head against his chest. He couldn't see her eyes, ugly with triumph.

Philip didn't speak to either of them for the first forty-eight hours of the dismal journey home.

___6
Wedding Night

IN HIS youth, Philip Kent's connection with a religious faith had been all but nonexistent. Because of her brief career as an actress in Paris, his mother was automatically excommunicated from the Catholic church.

Philip's first wife, Anne, the daughter of a Boston lawyer, was a Congregationalist. But she and her husband had seldom attended services. His second wife had been raised in Virginia's aristocratic Episcopal church, but had adopted her first husband's faith—the dour Presbyterianism of the Scots—following her marriage.

Thus it was another sign of Philip's rising status and growing conservatism that by the time Abraham and Elizabeth were married in midsummer of 1796, Philip had reverted to British-rooted Anglicanism. The Kents owned a high-sided box pew directly across the aisle from the one belonging to the family of Mr. Revere's eldest son in the small but lovely Christ Church in the city's North End.

Here, on a mellow Saturday in late July, the rector united Abraham Kent and Elizabeth Fletcher, watched by an impressive gathering of notables.

Elderly Mr. Revere sat in his son's pew. Philip's friend General Knox, the obese ex-Secretary of War, had traveled down from Maine. John Adams and his wife Abigail, just returned from Philadelphia, were present. So was the head of the Rothman house, dark-eyed and handsome Royal, and his attractive Jewish wife.

A wealthy iron-maker named George Lumden had come all the way from Connecticut, along with his red-haired, bright-cheeked wife Daisy. The bridal couple understood Philip had helped Lumden desert from his British regiment during the troubled days before Lexington and Concord. Lumden had been quartered in the house of Abraham's mother, where Daisy was a lowly cook. Now she was rich.

Christ Church, in short, was so packed with persons of wealth and influence that ordinary well-wishers such as Mr. Supply Pleasant were hard put to find a single seat in a rear corner.

Abraham hardly noticed the dignitaries, however. His attention was divided between Elizabeth and his father.

Elizabeth's bridal gown and veil were the most expensive obtainable. Yet beneath that veil, her cheeks lacked color, as if the wedding were more strain than pleasure.

Philip looked just as he had for weeks—glum and displeased.

Peggy had been responsible for virtually all the wedding arrangements. She sat in the family pew with perfect poise. Yet her face showed signs of fatigue and tension. Philip's face might have been hewn from Maine granite as he performed the novel function of giving Elizabeth away to his own son and then retired to the pew, limping yet somehow haughty.

Only thirteen-year-old Gilbert seemed totally delighted. Gilbert had shot up in height without adding weight. His skin was the color of parchment. People often commented privately that Gilbert Kent resembled a worried, emaciated old man more than he did an adolescent.

But all that dimmed from Abraham's awareness as he stood beside Elizabeth. Her eyes sought his from time to time, large and startlingly blue despite the gauzy veil covering her face. He wished he could speak to her. Comfort her. Instead, he was forced to stand rigid, then kneel, then rise again while the rector droned his way through the service.

Unhappy about his father's attitude and concerned for his bride, Abraham got a jolt as the rector began reading scripture:

"So ought men to love their wives as their own bodies. He that loveth his wife loveth himself."

The words struck a responsive chord in Abraham's memory. Wasn't that the very passage he'd tried to recall months ago? At the time, he'd been unable to remember either the precise text or its source—Saint Paul's epistle to the Ephesians. A slight flush tinged his cheeks as he realized how widespread the knowledge of his rift with his father must be. Otherwise, why would the rector have selected this particular passage?

Sunshine slanted through large windows into the white-walled brilliance of the sanctuary. Elizabeth's fair hair shone beneath her veil. Her quick, sidelong glance told Abraham she too understood the significance of the text—and his discomfort.

"For this cause shall a man leave his father and mother, and shall be joined unto his wife, and they two shall be one flesh—"

Abraham longed to turn and see how Philip was taking it. He didn't dare.

"—let every one of you in particular so love his wife even as himself, and the wife see that she reverence her husband."

The rector closed his Bible, began to pray. In a tangle of emotion—soaring love, depressing guilt—Abraham steeled himself to endure the rest of the ceremony. He wanted it over so that he could speak to his father. The need had all at once grown almost compulsive.

The rector might as well have been praying in a foreign tongue for all the attention Abraham paid. Something else was troubling him now.

Shame.

Here he was, standing in God's house accepting a white-gowned young woman as his spouse—and he had already known her carnally. Sinfully, the rector would declare. The mere thought undercut the joy of the occasion, and increased his uneasiness.

Well, he said to himself at last, *I suppose even among these respectable people, there are few who have totally clean hands and a spotless conscience.* His father, for example, had killed other human beings in order to survive. Didn't the Bible promise that Christ would forgive error? Bless those who came to His altar with a humble and contrite heart?

Never what could be called a devout person, Abraham still found himself saying a short, fervent prayer. A prayer begging Heaven to grant him forgiveness and, more important, a good beginning to his life with his new wife—

The organ pealed. Lifting Elizabeth's veil to give her a decorous kiss, Abraham saw her lids flutter, as if she were faint. When he touched his mouth to her cheek, he was shocked by the chill of her skin. And he felt her trembling.

As he stood back, she smiled, but wanly. With a stab of dread he wondered whether his prayer would go unheard because they had both sinned.

II

IN THE dusk, the house on Beacon Street blazed with lamplight; rang with the voices of the guests. The voices grew louder with every quart of rum added to the great crystal bowls of punch. In a corner of the dining room, a small string orchestra scraped away, adding to the din.

Abraham paced back and forth in the downstairs hall. He was dressed in his best suit. From time to time he glanced anxiously up to the second-floor landing.

Luggage had already been carried to the hooded chaise awaiting the young couple at the ring-block out in front. Abraham had intended to pay for all expenses connected with their wedding journey. But through Peggy, he discovered that Philip had hired the chaise himself, just as he was financing this large, noisy party.

Since leaving Christ Church, Abraham had had no good opportunity to speak to his father. Outside the church, Philip had shaken his son's hand, murmured some word of congratulations, and gone immediately to his own carriage. Once the party started, Philip seemed to be everywhere—except alone, where his son might catch him for a private word. Abraham was hurt and angry at the way Philip seemed to be withholding his emotions—his affection—while he displayed his material generosity.

Through a doorway, Abraham could see his father's back. Philip was in the midst of a heated discussion with huge-bellied General Knox, Lumden the iron-maker, and the slender, elegantly dressed banker, Royal Rothman. Suddenly Abraham felt a tug on his arm. Startled, he turned to discover Gilbert—at thirteen already taller than his half-brother.

"Aren't you anxious to be away, Abraham?" Gilbert asked, trying to invest the question with a manly wickedness.

Abraham put on a smile he didn't feel. "Of course I am."

"Where are you and Elizabeth going?"

"That, Gilbert, is our secret."

"You must be sure to speak to papa before you leave."

Abraham frowned. "Yes, I do wish he'd take the trouble to say goodbye—"

Philip's haughty back—and his loud harangue about the danger of Jefferson standing for election and receiving enough votes to become vice president or, worse yet, president—gave him little encouragement.

"Oh, he definitely wants to speak with you." A mischievous smile curved Gilbert's colorless lips. "I have it on mama's authority."

But Philip still showed every sign of being engrossed. The older brother shrugged in a weary way:

"Mama may be expressing a hope, not a fact."

The slim, white-faced boy stepped closer. His expression showed a maturity beyond his years as he asked:

"You're unhappy with papa, aren't you?"

"I'd say it's the other way around."

"Well, I want you to know I think it's splendid you and Elizabeth made a match. Just splendid."

"Thank you, Gilbert. You're the first person to really sound sincere about it."

"You'll be a good influence on her, too."

"What?"

"I mean you'll keep a good tether on her, so she won't grow moody and tearful, and fly into her rages—yes, it's all turned out very well."

Abraham failed to share Gilbert's enthusiasm:

"I don't believe papa sees it that way. He still blames Elizabeth for our plans to move west."

"I think it's wonderful you're going." Gilbert's eyes brimmed with admiration. "I just wish I were strong enough to see the new country. I know I'm not. So I'll help papa look after Kent's. It's probably the only sort of life I'm cut out for anyway—" He touched his half-brother, fondly yet with a certain shyness. "I'd like to be as big as you—"

"You're taller."

"As strong, I mean. With good shoulders. Hands that can chop wood, or plow—"

"A fine compliment! Comparing me to a plow horse!"

Gilbert reddened. "I know I'm not saying this exactly right—"

"I'm only teasing."

"I just don't want you to have any bad feelings about leaving. You're doing what you were meant to do—"

"Let's hope so," Abraham said, uncertain.

"There's only a problem because papa needs someone to carry on the business. I'm the one. He'll get used to it one of these days, don't you worry."

Abraham was touched by his half-brother's words, even as he was a little saddened by their hint of sorrow. Suddenly Gilbert's eyes flashed past Abraham's shoulder.

"I told you!" he hissed. "Papa's coming—"

Abraham didn't face around. He waited, feeling his father's presence almost like a physical force. He prayed there would be no stormy scene—

Moments later, in response to Philip's toneless request, Abraham followed the older man past groups of boisterous well-wishers to the library. There, Philip closed the double doors. He swung to face his son.

Philip's dark eyes caught light from the single lamp on a small Phyfe table. Without knowing precisely why, Abraham shivered.

III

PHILIP SPOKE in a low voice:

"Before you and Elizabeth leave this house, Abraham—"

"Don't sound so grim, papa. We'll be back after our honeymoon."

"Only for a short time. This is a day of parting. Because you're my son, I felt we should have a moment alone. In addition to all the items your stepmother has provided for your new household, I am adding a family gift." He paused only a moment. "The sum of five hundred dollars."

"*Five hundred—!*" It took Abraham a few seconds to recover. "Sir, forgive me, but I don't understand."

"What is it you don't understand?"

"A gift like that. You don't approve of this match."

"Perhaps not," Philip agreed. He rolled his tongue in his cheek, and nearly smiled. "However, I'm not so insensitive that I failed to grasp the meaning of the rector's text. I'm sure he chose it deliberately. But let's not discuss that. The reason for the gift is very simple. Eventually you'll need funds to purchase land. Just as important, you'll need money for transportation. Wagon travel, river travel—I am informed they're not cheap."

"I've put aside most of my cornet's pay from the army for that, papa."

Philip stiffened. "Are you trying to say you refuse the gift?"

Abraham swallowed. "No, sir, of course not. I'm extremely grateful for—"

He hesitated over the rest. Emotion brought it forth:

"—for an expression of your love."

Features still stony, Philip seated himself in a chair. He placed his hands on the knees of his fine gray breeches. "I won't pretend I believe you're doing the right thing. Nor will I deny I want to keep you here for selfish reasons."

"Gilbert has a much quicker mind than I do. He'll be an asset to the firm after he gains a little experience. He'll be able to discuss finances with men like your friend Mr. Rothman, for instance. I get lost just doing a few simple sums—"

"Yes, even as young as he is, Gilbert shows great promise. But he is also not in the best of health. That may reduce his value to Kent's, though I sincerely hope not—"

Philip's dark eyes locked with his son's.

"I not only wanted to keep you in Boston for my own sake, but for yours. You have great strength and vitality, Abraham. But enthusiasm often blinds a young man's eyes to hard reality. I do believe you underestimate the rigors of life in the west. You yourself may be fit enough for it. But you are not one person any longer. You are two. A family—"

Refusing to dodge the issue, Abraham blurted, "Papa, this is no time for anything less than complete candor. Do you dislike Elizabeth so much? Would you rather I not have married her?"

Philip glanced away. "That choice wasn't mine to make."

"Please answer."

"No. To do so might be uncharitable."

"That makes it very clear that you—"

"Permit me to finish. I took your wife into my house when I married Peggy, and I have tried to give her every advantage you and Gilbert have received. I have tried to give unstintingly—regardless of my feelings. Elizabeth has good qualities. She's certainly beautiful, and I can readily understand why you would fall in love with her. But she's frail, like Gilbert. And sometimes her behavior, as you've seen for yourself, suggests a reckless, even unstable temperament. I don't mean any unkindness when I say she may be quite unsuited for the sort of existence you've both chosen."

Abraham struggled to forget that the same suspicion had troubled him on the family trip. He shook his head:

"I'm sure she'll get along with no difficulty, papa. We both will."

Philip sighed. "Youth's optimism. Seldom tempered by reason until—" He seemed to grieve as he studied Abraham. "Until it's much too late."

"Papa, I've said I appreciate your gift. But to present it along with these dire warnings—"

Philip held up his hand to interrupt: "Don't be angry with me. I realize the decision's made. I accept it. I would have struggled even harder—kept trying to persuade you to change your mind—except for one fact."

His eyes drifted toward the windows overlooking the dark Common.

"I would have been forced to employ the same weapon my mother employed with me. The bribery of love. And you needn't say I *have* employed it, because I know I have. But not to the extent—well, someday I'll tell you the story of what she wanted for me. How she almost destroyed me as a man by insisting I would destroy *her* if I didn't follow her plan for my life. Much as I loved her, I couldn't allow that, because I *was* a man. Experience does knock a few lessons into thick old heads, you see. Difficult as it is—"

Philip's voice had grown almost hoarse. He rose, limped toward his son, suddenly gripped his shoulders.

"—I let you go. With bitterness, yes. With regret, yes. But also with the deep and honest hope that your dreams won't be shattered. I can't help how I feel, Abraham—even as you can't help going your own way. We are all guilty of being human. If I have committed any sins against you, I have committed them only out of love—just as my mother did. What a paradox, eh? What a damned, terrible par—"

His voice broke. He embraced his son.

Head bent against his father's shoulder, Abraham heard the tears in the older man's voice:

"God keep you, Abraham. God keep you *and* your dreams."

With sadness and a strange sense of foreboding, Abraham held Philip close for a long, silent moment.

IV

WHILE PEGGY cried and Gilbert capered and a crowd of guests shouted good wishes along with a few somewhat ribald encouragements for the evening, Abraham and Elizabeth hurried into the hooded chaise for the start of their wedding journey. Abraham whipped up the horse and they rattled off through the summer dark with the shouts and laughter dwindling slowly behind.

Abraham's new sense of responsibility sat heavy on his shoulders for a little while. He was launching out on his own at last. And, as Philip said, he was a new, different man. He was accountable for his wife's future as well as for his own—

But with Elizabeth close beside him in the bouncing chaise, chattering gaily and caressing his arm from time to time, the responsibility quickly changed from an ominous burden to a joy. He tingled when Elizabeth pressed her lips to his cheek and whispered that she hoped they wouldn't take too long to reach the night's stopping-place.

Their eventual destination, some miles northeast along the coast, was the town of Salem. They planned to spend a week at the town's best inn, enjoying the sea air and taking in the sights of the booming seaport.

Salem's harbor was crowded these days with tall-masted ships whose enterprising captains were carrying the country's flag and the country's products to Europe and around the world. Some of the ships that transported beer brewed in Philadelphia and butter churned on Massachusetts farms voyaged as far as the Chinese port of Canton, there unloading another part of their cargo—American-grown ginseng, an aromatic root highly prized by Oriental physicians.

The same ships often returned to Massachusetts bearing Chinese opium for the

valises of American doctors, as well as pepper, madder dye, Turkish carpets, figs and other exotic goods from ports along the way. People said marvelous curiosities such as African monkeys could be seen on the Salem docks—and, nearby, evidence that the thriving ocean trade was creating fortunes overnight. Mansions were being raised by captains or ship-owners who often realized as much as a seven hundred percent profit on a single voyage.

Both Abraham and Elizabeth had considered Salem an ideal spot for a honeymoon. This evening, however, they only planned to go part of the distance, to a country inn where Abraham had reserved a sitting room with adjoining bedchamber. Amused, he supposed that when they got there, they'd probably find Philip had pre-paid the bill.

As the ferry bore them across the Charles to the peninsula, Elizabeth seemed to grow less animated. At one point, she pressed a hand to her stomach.

"Elizabeth, are you feeling poorly?"

"No, darling, don't worry."

He peered at the dim oval of her face, beautiful under the summer stars. "You're not telling me the truth."

"Only a minor dizziness. It will pass." She tried to smile. Her eyes reflected the glint of the rising moon on the river. "Caused, I'm sure, by the excitement of finally being married—"

But her face remained white. Abraham saw that when the ferryman lifted his lantern and motioned the chaise forward across the end of the scow that had dropped down to rest on the dark shore.

V

ABRAHAM LEANED over and blew out the lamp.

He heard rather than saw Elizabeth slip toward the bed from the concealment of the screen where she'd retired to remove her traveling clothes. The country inn was quiet, save for one last customer bidding the landlord a tipsy farewell beneath the open window.

The summer air was fragrant with the smell of scythed grass. The brilliant moon turned the planes of Abraham's chest white above the coverlet drawn to his waist. Expectantly, he swung toward the whisper of Elizabeth's bare feet—and caught his breath.

Her hair hung unbound, a waterfall of gold across her shoulders. The moon lit her eyes until they glowed like blue gems.

Her breasts, remarkably large and firm for one so slender, bobbed as she neared the bedside. The moonlight burnished the soft golden thatch below her smooth stomach.

Without embarrassment or hesitation, she raised the coverlet and slipped in beside him. Her bare hip touched his, a velvety sensation. Her hand stole over to grasp him as her other arm slipped around his neck. He pressed her to the pillows, his lips eager, hers responding, opening—

Transported beyond himself by the sweet smell of her clinging mouth, he seemed to float in a dazzle of summer moonlight that spilled over the bed. He stroked her body with mounting excitement. Felt the heat of her flesh as it warmed—

"Elizabeth. Elizabeth, dear heaven, how I love you," he murmured. His mouth sought her breasts as she caressed the back of his head.

"And I love you, Abraham. Husband," she laughed. "Isn't that a grand word? I love to say it. Husb—*ah!*"

She arched her back, rolling out of his embrace. Her left arm came up across her forehead, her wrist resting over her eyes. When he reached for her face— "Dearest, what is it?"—he felt an unexpected clamminess on her skin.

"A little dizziness again, that's all."

"The same as you felt on the ferry?"

"Yes. I'm sorry. The rains last week made the roads so rough—"

"And in my haste to get you here—" He tried speaking lightly, to hide his dismay. "—I drove too fast."

"I seem to be a poor traveler, don't I?"

"All the furor of the wedding—it's bound to be tiring—"

He tried not to let her hear his disappointment. But his body registered that disappointment. Reacted by cooling; changing; diminishing—

"Abraham, I wouldn't spoil tonight for anyth—"

He pressed tender fingers against her mouth. "Hush, hush. Don't fret about that." Again he feigned lightness. "It's not as if we're missing something we've never tried before."

"Yes, I realize. But even though we've been together, tonight is—well, important."

"Of course it's important. We're married at last. Here—" He shifted his body to let her rest in the crook of his left arm. "Lie back. Be comfortable. We have the whole week—and all our lives—for making love. One night missed isn't that important."

"Yes it is. I'll be fine in a few minutes," she promised.

"Elizabeth, don't worry!" he said, ashamed of his own inward bitterness.

He found himself wondering where she'd come by this physical weakness. Did it spring from the same source as her passion for rebelling against authority? From the same source as her vindictive streak?

From her father, that unstable man who had lived a profligate life, and only cleaned up a little of the blotted ledger by the manner of his dying?

Abruptly, he was ashamed of the speculation too. Yet he couldn't help feeling that something had robbed him—and Elizabeth—of the mutual joy that should have been theirs this evening.

Presently she stirred; started the love-play again. It lasted only a minute or so. She gave a small, and unhappy cry when her hand glided across Abraham's lifeless loins.

Without warning, whatever pain had seized her before struck her again. She doubled over, knees clenched against her belly, hands locked around her legs. For a confused moment, he thought of one possible answer. Pregnancy.

No, that was absurd. They'd had no opportunity to be alone since well before the southern tour. And once they agreed to marry, she stopped visiting his room secretly—as if the defiance that had driven her to his bed in the first place was no longer necessary, or even quite proper.

In misery, Elizabeth straightened her legs. She clutched her naked stomach, cried out. Then she began to sob an incoherent apology. Abraham didn't know what to do.

All at once she struggled up to a sitting position, left the bed. She staggered toward the screen on the far side of the room.

Abraham raced after her, reaching out to steady her. Almost screaming, she threw off his hand:

"I don't want you to touch me when I'm this way!"

He stepped back, horrified by the ferocity of her cry. Still hunched over, she started to weep in earnest:

"Abraham, I'm sorry. I didn't mean to raise my voice. But I'm ill. I can't bear for you to see me—oh, I'm so ashamed—"

She disappeared behind the screen. Abraham watched it totter and almost topple before she caught it. A moment later, he heard the ugly sounds of his wife being sick in a basin.

Standing naked in the moon-glare at the foot of the bed, he felt as if winter had closed in outside the open window. He recalled his father's warning, and experienced a consuming fear that Philip was right: Elizabeth *was* entirely unsuited to the sort of life awaiting them in the Ohio country—

Even more appalling was his certainty that he'd never be able to change her mind about the future.

He could hint, argue, plead—and he would. But he knew her nature; knew his efforts would prove futile in the end.

Frozen and frightened, he stood staring at nothing, listening to the terrible sounds of sickness from behind the screen.

═7
Wagon Road

THE WAGONER'S name was Leland Pell. He stood nearly a head taller than Abraham, thin but broad-shouldered, with immense, dirty, scarred hands. Wind and weather had burnished his cheeks to the color of mahogany. His eyes were brown, his hair the same, sleek and pushed straight back over his high forehead. Abraham judged him to be about forty. White stubble showed against the dark skin of his jawbone.

Pell's clothing certainly didn't justify arrogance. He wore old leather boots, linsey trousers, a faded blue flannel shirt, a broad-brimmed wool hat heavily stained with grease. At his feet crouched the fattest, ugliest bulldog Abraham had ever seen. The dog's wet eyes and underslung jaw looked downright threatening.

When Abraham first approached Pell in the tavern yard, the wagoner struck a pose. Thumbs hooked in his belt, he gazed at the sky with lofty indifference. Fortunately, Abraham had been warned to expect such behavior. A passenger in the coach from Lancaster to Harrisburg told him the wagoners considered themselves "sea captains of the road."

Instead of an answer to his question, Abraham got a continuation of the pose. Irked, he said:

"I asked you the price, Mr. Pell."

Silence.

Abraham shivered in the chilly autumn wind. Nearby, the Susquehanna flowed with a cold yellow sheen. Beyond, the western hills rose black against the clear blue sky of the changing season.

Pell's cronies inside the tavern shouted for him to come share whiskey and

cigars. The wagoner ignored the shouts, but finally deigned to glance at Abraham—then past him, to Elizabeth. Bundled in her heaviest traveling clothes, including a shawl and bonnet, Abraham's wife still looked frozen as she waited beside the five large trunks stacked under the tavern wall.

"Six pieces of baggage," Pell said, then grinned. "Counting your missus, I mean to say. She's the handsomest piece o' the lot."

Angered by Pell's insolence, Abraham pivoted away. "I'll find someone who wants to discuss business, not crack jokes."

"Suit yourself," Pell called as Abraham walked off. "But there ain't a wagoner on the old Forbes Road who'll take you on—haul you to Pittsburgh before the snow comes down. I know every one of 'em. Passengers ain't their business—and they all got full crews."

Abraham halted as Pell took a couple of steps in his direction:

"Only reason I'm even botherin' to talk is because my Conestoga needs two men. My second—he got a mite chopped down a while back. So far I ain't found a new second, y'see—"

Reluctantly, Abraham went back. If this was an elaborate game, he supposed he had to play it if he wanted to make a deal.

"What do you mean, he got chopped down?"

"Cut." Pell showed his right hand. "Lost three fingers in a fight. Dumb son of a bitch was nineteen years old. But up here—" He tapped his head. "More like six. Shoulders like an ox, though. I was right sorry to lose him."

Pell wiped his nose with the back of his hand, eyed Elizabeth again. "You was askin' about the price—"

"Several times."

"First of all, you realize no coaches can make it over the mountains to Pittsburgh?"

"That I already know. What's your price?"

But the wagoner wouldn't be hurried:

"And you also got to realize I'm a regular, not a sharpshooter. I get you there in good shape, fifteen steady miles a day. I don't shake your teeth out like them gypsies that pull a farm wagon outa the field and try to turn a fast dollar pushin' twenty, twenty-five miles a day—wreckin' everything aboard. Besides, don't look to me like too much speed would suit the lady. She don't appear any too strong."

By now Abraham's temper was raw:

"I want your price, Mr. Pell, not a discourse on customs of the road."

" 'Dis-course!' I don't believe I ever heard that word before. You must be a mighty educated young fella—"

"Your price!"

When Abraham shouted, Pell's brown eyes grew unpleasant:

"A hundred dollars. Cash."

"Ridiculous!"

Pell shrugged. "Shit, nobody's forcin' you."

"A hundred dollars—" Abraham repeated. "That's four times what it should be—"

"Sure, based on the fare from Lancaster to here," Pell agreed with a frigid smile. "But they's hard country 'tween Harrisburg and the old fort at the Ohio. You want to get to Pittsburgh 'fore next spring, mister, you ain't got but three choices. Shank's mare. Buy your own wagon and team—which'll cost you

plenty more'n a hundred. Or pay my price. I'm doin' you a favor the way it is—''

From his height, he downgraded Abraham with a single glance:

"I ain't even sure you're big enough to handle the chores on a Conestoga. Well, it's up to you. I already got nigh to a full load of freight, so you won't skin my ass any if you say no.''

The frosty smile revealed a mouth with only half the teeth left; and those were browned by tobacco. With another look at Elizabeth, Pell added:

"I need some segars. I'll be inside if you want me. Come on, Chief.''

He ambled toward the tavern door, the bulldog at his heels. Drool dripped from the dog's lower jaw. Pell paused at the entrance for one last bit of persuasion:

"You want to try to hire a smaller rig for them rough roads up ahead, go on. But I warn you, you'll spend six or seven times what I'm askin'. And you're liable to get to Ohio two years from now—and find somebody else squattin' on them twenty acres you say you bought. Your business, I guess—''

Shrugging again in that arrogant way, he started inside. The bulldog got between his boots. Pell kicked the dog's ribs. Chief yelped, fell, but finally trotted after the tall man as he vanished into the tavern's yellow haze.

Abraham stuffed his hands in his pockets, walked morosely to Elizabeth.

"You look cold,'' he said.

She tried to smile. "I'll be glad to reach the lodging house.''

"That man wants—''

"I heard. Abraham, let's find another way. He's loathsome.''

"But from what I've observed, he's not much different from any other wagon driver.''

He knew he was trying to convince himself. He could hardly blame Pell for staring at his wife. In spite of her pallor, Elizabeth was by far the prettiest woman he'd seen since the coach pulled into Harrisburg. Just about the only young woman, in fact.

He thought of Pell's warnings about squatters. Thought of his auction deed to twenty acres of prime bottom land on the Great Miami near Fort Hamilton. The deed would be next to worthless if he and Elizabeth found other settlers already occupying the tract of ground. Forged deeds weren't uncommon. It could take months—even years—to validate his claim in the frontier circuit courts.

Reluctantly, he said, "I'm going to accept his offer.''

"No. No, Abraham!''

He touched her arm. "We'll be all right.''

But Elizabeth wasn't reassured. She closed her eyes, shivering in the autumn wind.

Swiftly, Abraham stepped forward, supported her with both arms. "You'd better sit down a minute. I'll find a boy to help with the trunks. I can come back and see Pell later. Sit down, Elizabeth—we'll be at the lodging house soon. Then you'll be warm.''

"I don't think I'll ever be warm again,'' she said. The forlorn look in her blue eyes chilled him more than the wind off the river.

II

ONLY A closed pan of coals warmed the bed, and the lodging-house room, that night. Elizabeth put on a second bedgown over her regular one, then snuggled in the curve of Abraham's arm.

They had been traveling since early September, down to Philadelphia and then westward. But the hardest terrain lay ahead. He still questioned whether they should go on.

Elizabeth had already been stricken with spells of nausea and abdominal pain. Each time, for his benefit, she tried to conceal or minimize her discomfort. But she couldn't conceal the fact that she was losing weight. The coarse fare served at the coaching stops wasn't to her liking.

So, as they huddled together with their feet near the warming pan, he voiced his doubts:

"Perhaps we should turn back."

"My answer to that is the same as it was in Salem. Nonsense. I'm stronger than you think. I'll prove it."

"But things seem to grow a little more difficult every day. Dealing with clods like Pell doesn't make it any easier—"

"Are you saying *you* want to turn back, Abraham?"

Shamed, he answered quickly, "Only for your sake."

"Put it out of your mind, then. I'm sorry I carried on at the tavern. I was just tired. The Pell fellow is probably all bluff and boast."

In his mind's eye Abraham saw the arrogant brown eyes and thought otherwise. Elizabeth's first assessment had been the correct one. But he said nothing.

"We can deal with him," she went on, her voice firm. "With him and with any other difficulties we encounter. I want our children to be born out here, Abraham. It's beautiful country. Beautiful—"

Murmuring, she drifted off.

Abraham lay awake for more than an hour, listening to the noise drifting from the Harrisburg riverfront. Elizabeth had inadvertently raised another troubling question. Thus far, their efforts to conceive a child had failed.

Lately, he had even grown hesitant about making love to his wife, much as his body urged him to it. He was afraid that on top of the other rigors of the journey, the burden of carrying a baby would prove too much for Elizabeth.

Tormented by his anxieties, he stared into the darkness. His father's gift of five hundred dollars was dwindling. Another hundred paid to Pell would leave only three hundred and fifty in reserve.

And even if they got to Pittsburgh, there were many long, arduous miles yet to travel before they reached the land whose deed was tucked away in one of the trunks.

They had to make a start before bad weather closed in. Much as he disliked the idea, he'd look Pell up in the morning.

III

LELAND PELL'S Conestoga wagon measured twenty feet along the top, fourteen feet along the bottom, and could, he boasted, bear up to ten tons of crates and barrels through the Pennsylvania wilderness.

The wagon had huge, iron-tired wheels. The axles sat high off the ground, so they'd clear the stumps left standing in the cleared track that passed for a road west of the Susquehanna ferry. Inside, the wagon was comfortable enough. The heaviest goods were packed toward the middle, and the whole was covered over by tow-canvas stretched on twelve large hoops.

The German craftsmen of eastern Pennsylvania who built the four-wheeled land arks decorated them in cheerful colors. The wagon proper was painted bright blue, with flame red used on the gear, including the lazy board and the grain box. This box hung under the tailgate during the day. At night it was opened and placed on the tongue.

Pell owned not only his wagon but the six great black horses that pulled it. A couple of the horses weighed over three-quarters of a ton. Pell's pride in the animals was evident in the way he decorated them. Their chainlink traces were wound with bright red yarn. Five small bells hung from a wrought iron arch that rose above the hames of each horse. On the road, the thirty bells all chiming at random made a strange, wild music.

The horses were hitched in tandem. Altogether, wagon and animals stretched more than sixty feet. When the wagon was moving, the bulldog dashed back and forth beneath the bed, barking at the horses to urge them along.

Elizabeth spent most of her time in a nook Abraham had arranged inside. He rode the lazy board, a piece of stout white oak that pulled out from the wagon's left side to make a projecting seat. The seat was handy to the long lever which controlled the brakes for the rear tires; brakes that set the iron squealing and sparking when Pell screamed for more pressure on a steep downward grade.

No wagons overtook them. Pell knew his business. He clipped off fifteen miles almost every day, regardless of delays from fording streams or climbing and descending mountainsides.

Once or twice a day they did encounter freighters returning east. Pell greeted some of the drivers with an obscenely cheerful hail. Others he ignored; the despised, unprofessional sharpshooters. He never relinquished his position on the right side of the rough dirt road. Professional or sharpshooter, it was the other wagon that always pulled aside to let Pell pass. That said a lot about the man and his reputation.

After no more than a few days of travel, it became evident to Abraham that his wife was terrified of Leland Pell. Terrified even though the wagoner's behavior was fairly restrained when they made their night camps.

The camp routine seldom varied. First the horses were unhitched and tied to the tongue, three on each side, and the grain box was set out to feed them. While Chief barked at noises in the forest, Abraham and Pell gathered wood for a fire. Conversation during the meal was fitful.

Pell actually boasted about his illiteracy. He needed no education to turn a profit hauling freight back and forth across the mountains!

The wagoner knew the United States had won the war with Britain—he hadn't bothered to volunteer for the army, he announced—and he knew the president's name was General Washington, and that he'd fought along Braddock's old Pennsylvania road at some dim time in the past. Over and above those meager facts, Pell's knowledge of national affairs was scanty, and his interest nonexistent.

In one way, though, he was completely typical of people in all social classes, Abraham noticed. Pell still wasn't accustomed to thinking of the country as a single entity. Once or twice when he mentioned the United States, he did so in

the plural—"The United States are mighty big now, I reckon"—which was the common way.

Pell's chief recreation seemed to be smoking the long, thin, villainously black four-a-penny cigars favored by the Conestoga drivers. When the travelers sat beside the fragrant evening fire, Pell would light up one of the foul-smelling stogies, then flourish it or tilt it up between his clenched teeth as though it lent him a dashing air. Through a blue haze, his eyes frequently darted to Elizabeth's breasts.

Those sly glances angered Abraham. But since the wagoner did nothing more overt than that, he restrained his impulses to speak out. He and Elizabeth were dependent on Pell, after all.

Abraham had to admit Pell's physical strength was admirable. The tall man handled the sets of gears for each horse as if they were a fraction of their actual weight. Abraham panted and grew slightly dizzy the first time he tried to help Pell with the fifteen-inch back bands and ten-inch hip straps.

He'd gained weight and lost muscle tone during his months in the east—and this despite the hard work in Philip's press room. Good food and home comforts had taken their toll. But as they put more and more miles behind the wagon, Abraham's skin darkened, his belly flattened, and his general fitness improved. The winy October air, the rich blue skies, the bursts of autumn color on the hillsides lifted his spirits. Elizabeth too seemed invigorated; less pale.

Still, her presence clearly gave Pell something to think about.

"Kent,' he said, scratching his crotch unconsciously, "you s'pose you'd let your wife have a dance with me tomorrow night?"

It was a brilliant morning. Abraham was walking beside the left-hand wheel horse. Pell drove from a saddle on the horse's back, jerkline in one hand, long black-snake whip in the other.

Abraham stared upward, studying the odd smile on the wagoner's face. Thanks to Abraham's hard work, Pell had lost some of his contempt for the younger man. Some, but not all.

"We going to be someplace where there's dancing?" Abraham asked.

"Yep. Figger we'll be in the next settlement by dark tomorrow. Hell, we're gettin' near Pittsburgh—ain't you noticed the eastbound traffic heavyin' up?"

Abraham nodded to indicate he had.

"We only got one more crick to ford. There's some cabins and a dandy tavern just this side. I usually find lots o' my friends there. And when a bunch o' wagon men stop at the same place, we have dancin' with our whiskey. Provided we can rustle up a fiddle player, 'course.''

"What about women? They aren't necessary?"

"Sure. But we'll dance with each other if they ain't any whores around—wait a minute, now! Don't take on! I ain't puttin' your wife in the same stall as whores—"

"Thanks very much." But the sarcasm was lost.

"Yessir, I'd surely like to have a whirl with your missus. A real, clean-smellin' lady—"

Pell grinned, jerking the whip back over his shoulder, then laying it into the air above the heads of the lead horses. Pell was expert with the whip. He could give it an explosive crack—accompanied by an obscene bellow—inches from the horses' ears, never touching them.

"Well, Kent, what d'you say?"

"It's not up to me. It's up to the missus, as you call her."

"Yeh, but I want you to ask her. She won't pay me any mind."

"I'll ask her," Abraham agreed.. *And you'll get set on your butt by her answer, my friend.*

The wagoner rubbed his crotch again. "Good. I figured I ought to have your permission first. Sure wouldn't want to tangle with an educated eastern feller— I might get hurt, y'know? Talked to death by all them ten-penny words—"

Laughing, he popped the whip again. Abraham stopped to wait for the lazy board, furious at Pell's heavy-handed contempt.

IV

THAT NIGHT Abraham mentioned Pell's request to Elizabeth as they bedded down inside the wagon. Pell slept outside, wrapped in blankets, with Chief keeping watch.

Elizabeth's reaction was just what Abraham expected:

"I wouldn't let that filthy, illiterate ruffian touch me."

He chuckled, moving close to her for warmth. "That's why I didn't write his name in your program."

"As for this—celebration he's planning, I refuse to have any part of it. I'll spend the evening right here in the wagon. Have you noticed Pell's behavior the last couple of days? Somehow he acts almost—oh, I don't know. The best word I know is feverish."

"I expect he's just ready to tear loose and kick up his heels."

"In that case I suggest we have some protection handy. One of those pistols from the trunk—"

"I doubt if that'll be necessary," Abraham said. But next day, he wondered.

Smiling, he broke the news that Mrs. Kent didn't plan on dancing in the settlement tavern. Pell scowled:

"I don't smell good enough for her, mebbe?"

Abraham met the ugly brown eyes under the wool hat brim. "I didn't ask. I suggest that you don't either."

"Fuckin' high and mighty easterners," the wagoner muttered, lashing out with the whip. This time, accidentally or otherwise, he nicked the neck of one of the lead horses, drawing blood.

They rolled into the little settlement just before sunset. Pell cursed and stormed about, flinging off the gears and manhandling the six horses up to the tongue. While Abraham and Elizabeth ate a meager supper at one of the tavern's greasy tables, they could still hear Pell's profanity.

They left the table and started for the wagon just as Pell came in. The wagoner was greeted by shouts from half a dozen of his road cronies gathered at the plank bar.

All during the meal, Abraham and his wife had been conscious of the men staring. Pell's glance as he approached the couple just inside the doorway was more angry than lascivious. Abraham whiffed liquor. He took Elizabeth's elbow—and struggled to keep his temper when Pell jostled him.

Fingering the coiled whip at his belt, Pell stalked on toward the bar:

"Somebody drag that fiddler-boy's ass out of the woodshed. I been bouncin' on the road for days. I aim to stomp a little."

Stomp he did, along with the others, while the fiddle squeaked frantically. The

laughter and boot-thuds grew louder, the oaths more florid as midnight approached. Elizabeth fretted and tossed under the blankets, trying to sleep despite the racket.

Abraham sat up for a while, then crawled in beside his wife. He dozed off, only to be wakened by a shrill cry.

He bolted upright, shot out his hand—

Elizabeth was there.

He wiped his perspiring forehead. Torchlight flared in the tavern yard. As he scrambled out of the Conestoga, Chief barked at him. He shied a stone at the bulldog and trotted toward the confusion of firelight and shadow-figures around the tavern door.

Pell had parked the wagon a good distance from the building. So it took Abraham a moment to see what was happening. The drunken wagoners, their clothing in disarray, formed a ring around someone. One of the men held the torch, and by its light Abraham finally identified the person in the center of the circle. A tow-haired boy. He realized he must have mistaken the boy's high-pitched voice for a woman's.

Held by a couple of the wagoners, the boy struggled to break loose. He couldn't. All at once Abraham saw a demijohn dangling from the boy's right hand.

Hatless, Leland Pell staggered forward, flipping away the stub of a stogie. He backhanded the boy across the cheeks.

"Nothin' worse than a whiskey thief."

"Leave me go!" the boy squealed. "Ain't but a quarter of a jug left in here—"

A man jerked the demijohn out of the boy's fingers, shook it. "Goddamn liar. She's nearly full."

Another wagoner grabbed the boy's hair. "Full or empty, don't make no difference. You was sneakin' out with it—"

"Call the landlord," the boy pleaded.

"He's dead drunk,' a third man said. "And you, you little shithead, you're stealin' the liquor we paid for!"

"I played for you all evenin'! I'm entitled—"

Leland Pell's voice was slurred: "You played for free 'cause we said so. You're entitled to *nothin'*—" He drove his fist into the boy's midsection.

The boy doubled, retching. Pell seized the whiskey jug.

"You ever been to Pittsburgh, boy? You know how they take care of whiskey thieves in Pittsburgh? I'll show you. Sam, bring me a stick from the fireplace."

"What the hell you fixin' to do, Leland?" one of the drivers asked, apprehensive suddenly.

Pell weaved on his feet. "You shut up."

Abraham had jogged through the darkness and stopped near the group. All at once Pell saw him. Pell's stubbled mouth wrenched.

"An' you better crawl back to your wagon, Kent. This might be a little too strong for your lah-de-dah eastern belly—" Spittle flew from his lips as he wheeled around: "Sam, go get that stick 'fore I take after you with this whip!"

Terrified, Sam bolted inside.

Pell uncorked the demijohn, poured its contents over the writhing boy. Abraham's stomach flipflopped as Sam appeared with the stick. The end was afire—

He'd taken just one long step when Pell motioned the boy's captors away and touched the stick to the boy's soaked shirt. The alcohol ignited.

The boy shrieked. The shirt was afire across his shoulders. The flames leaped down his back, into his hair, as Pell laughed uproariously. Two of the wagoners stood aside to let the boy dash toward the nearby stream.

Abraham's mouth hardened. Pell didn't see. He was collapsing with mirth on a bench beside the tavern door.

The boy's screams pealed, even as the blur of orange grew smaller in the darkness. One of the wagoners was shocked to sobriety:

"That warn't called for, Leland."

Wiping tears from his eyes, Pell told him what he could do with his opinions. Abraham yelled at the men:

"Why are you standing there? Let's go help the boy!"

He started running toward the orange glow. Suddenly it dipped toward the ground; the boy was frantically trying to extinguish the flames by rolling along the creek bank.

Three of the wagoners responded to Abraham's shout, followed him. Two others drifted back inside, not quite sober enough to be ashamed. Pell's laughter boomed.

Halfway to the stream, Abraham heard another keening cry. This one he recognized instantly:

"Elizabeth—!"

One of the wagoners running beside him panted, "That's your wife's name, ain't it? Pell's been talkin' about her all evenin'. Dirty talk—"

"You see to the boy," Abraham shouted, pivoting and racing back toward the tavern.

The two wagoners had come outside again. Beyond the shifting circle of light from the torch one of them held, Abraham saw only the tethered horses. The Conestoga itself was deep in shadow. But he was sure the cry had come from within the wagon. He heard it again as he pounded across the tavern yard.

"He warned us to stay away," called one of the wagoners by the doorway. "You better too. He's murderin' drunk—"

Hardly hearing, Abraham dodged the bulldog snapping at his boots. From inside the wagon came sounds of a struggle—thumps and thrashing. Elizabeth screamed a third time.

Abraham hauled himself up the wagon's high raked front, tasted sourness in his mouth as Pell wheezed in the darkness:

"Come on, you sassy little bitch. Jest feel it once. Gimme your hand—"

Abraham bellowed, *"Goddamn you, Pell—"*

He started to climb inside, marginally aware of a body falling—Elizabeth?— then Pell's sudden, strident breathing. With one leg hooked over the end of the wagon, he could still see nothing of the interior. But he realized with quick terror that Pell could certainly see him against the glare of the torch.

Pell laughed again; a flat, wicked sound. A slithering noise warned Abraham to jerk his head aside—

Crack!

Had he not reacted so fast, the tip of Pell's black-snake would have put out an eye. As it was, he hung on the end of the wagon with his left cheek laid open, pouring blood.

The pain overwhelmed him in an instant. He fell toward the tongue and the hoofs of the snorting, stamping horses.

V

THE BACK of Abraham's head slammed against the wagon tongue. His vision blurred. One of the frightened horses kicked his ribs.

He rolled away, toward the front wheels, just as Pell leaped down, his boots stirring little clouds of dust when he landed.

Abraham couldn't see clearly. He was dizzy. Blood from the whip cut leaked into his left eye as he groped for the front axle, frantically dragged himself under the wagon bed just as Pell brought the whip down with maniacal force.

Abraham jerked his legs out of the way just in time. The whip raised another dust cloud. Distantly, Abraham heard men yelling and running; heard doors crash open. Residents of the settlement coming from their cabins. Overhead, Elizabeth screamed again.

In a moment of terrible lucidity, Abraham understood that most of the wagoners were too afraid of Pell to interfere. The same probably held true for the settlers. And he was certain Pell meant to kill him.

He shook his head, trying to overcome the dizziness. At the front end of the wagon, Pell dropped into a crouch, gesturing to Abraham with the whip.

"Come out from under there, you yella bastard!"

Pell was silhouetted against the torch at the tavern. His trousers hung around his knees. His suit of dirty gray underwear gaped open at his crotch. Abraham might have laughed at that, except for Pell's rage:

"I said come out! I'm gonna whip your balls off one at a time—"

Blood glistened on Pell's cheek; the raking marks of Elizabeth's nails, Abraham realized suddenly. The wagoner dropped his right wrist close to the ground, intending to lash Abraham's legs under the front of the wagon. It required a tricky horizontal strike—and by the time Pell stretched his whip hand behind him, Abraham was ready.

The whip shot forward with an explosive pop. Abraham took the cut on his right forearm—raised deliberately. The tip of the snake wound round and round his sleeve like a band of fire. Clenching his teeth, he closed his left hand on the whip, then his right. He yanked.

Pell was jerked forward. He crashed head first into one of the iron-tired wheels. Bellowing, he fell to his knees and let go of the whip's butt.

Abraham still had the end wound around his right arm. He reached upward and to the side, seized the hickory spokes of the left front wheel that Pell had struck. He dug in his heels and pulled himself—and the whip—out of Pell's reach.

He crawled into the open, stumbled to his feet beside the wheel, conscious of people gathering. Elizabeth's cries had changed to low, hurt sobs.

He lurched to the front of the Conestoga, the whole left side of his face bloody. For one nauseous moment he thought he might faint. He fought it, then noticed two odd things:

Not one wagoner stepped forward to lend Pell a hand. And the bulldog, growling, didn't attack as Abraham crept up behind the groaning man.

Pell was still on his knees. Abraham wrapped the whip around Pell's neck, pulled with both hands—

Pell tried to plead. Only gagging sounds came from his throat. He struggled, clawed over his shoulder at Abraham's fingers. But the fall against the wheel had weakened him. Abraham jammed his knee into Pell's back, tightening the rawhide noose.

Let him go, a voice cried in his mind. *Don't murder him, He's beaten—*

But he could still hear Elizabeth sobbing. He pulled harder.

His hands trembled from clenching so tightly; trembled and turned white as bone—

Mercifully, he blanked out during the rest.

He felt his fingers being pried loose. He blinked, relaxed his grip, stared down. Several torches showed him Leland Pell, cheeks purplish, tongue protruding. Pell's trousers were still tangled around his calves. His underwear hung open to reveal a tiny penis as dead as the rest of him.

Abraham felt so ill he almost wept:

"Somebody cover him up, for Christ's sake! And see to my wi—"

The bones in his legs melted. He tumbled to the ground, unconscious. One hand lay across the wagoner's distended right eyeball.

___ VI

DURING THE night, a man who claimed to be an apothecary cleaned Abraham's face in the tavern. He applied a stinging, sulphurous-smelling paste to the wound, then wrapped Abraham's head with an oval of rags, as though he were a toothache patient.

The man told Abraham he had already administered whiskey to Elizabeth. She was sleeping.

Abraham wanted to go to the wagon and see for himself. But he hurt too much. Exhausted, he let the groggy landlord spread a filthy blanket on one of the trestle tables, help him up, then cover him with a second blanket. In a moment, his eyes closed.

By dawn the other wagoners had disposed of Pell's body. Where, they didn't say. Nor did Abraham ask.

The landlord reported that the fiddler-boy had been treated by the same fellow who'd doctored Abraham's face:

"The boy weren't as lucky as you. Even after the burned skin sloughs off an' his hair grows back, his face'll likely be ruined fer life."

Sickened, Abraham shoved away the fragrant cup of coffee the landlord was extending. He tottered into the frosty air where his breath plumed. He saw Elizabeth peering at him over the front of the wagon, her face as pale as marble.

He started running. But a few long strides set his head throbbing. He walked the rest of the way, trying not to be aware of the horror in her blue eyes.

Stopping next to the wagon, he reached up. She put her hand down to find his. Her fingers were stiff; cold as the dawn air.

"Elizabeth, did he—?"

"He only touched me. Just—touched me, that's all." Her voice shook.

Her fingers constricted around his suddenly:

"Abraham, let's leave. Please, please, *let's leave this place!*"

Alarmed, he chafed her icy hands until she calmed down. He promised they'd drive down to the ford and cross the stream as soon as he made some necessary inquiries about the dead man's rig.

Staring through him, she said nothing.

He walked back to a silent band of thoroughly sobered wagoners gathered outside the tavern. The smell of their sweat was rank in the crisp air.

"I know the outfit belonged to Pell," Abraham said. "Did he have any kin?"

One toothless fellow spoke: "A wife and a flock of young 'uns in Harrisburg. But the woman turned Leland out a couple of years ago."

"She still live there?"

"Think so."

"Still under the name Pell? Not remarried?"

"Not so's we've heard."

Abraham nodded in a grave, tired way. "I'll get the rig to Pittsburgh. Make deliveries of the freight as best I can, then sell the wagon and the horses. After I deduct the hundred he charged me for the trip, I'll deposit the rest at the postal office. There *is* a postal office—?"

"Yes, sir," said the toothless man.

"I'll leave the money for Pell's wife. I'll leave it in her name. One of you see it gets back to Harrisburg."

Murmurs of consent. Abraham stumbled back to the Conestoga. Elizabeth had disappeared.

The eastern sky was empty of clouds. But in the west, gray banks promised rain, or even early snow, reminding him of the lateness of the season.

He climbed up the front of the wagon, glanced into the crowded interior. Elizabeth was sprawled on her blanket pallet, hands over her face. She was crying, almost inaudibly.

He thought about going to her; decided she might respond more favorably to the feel of the wagon in motion. As if in penance, the other wagoners helped him hitch up in record time.

Abraham dragged himself into the saddle on the left wheel horse, picked up the jerkline. He didn't have Pell's whip. He wouldn't have used it if he had.

Just as he was maneuvering the rig into the water at the ford, he heard a loud bark. He leaned out to the left, looked behind, saw the bulldog, tongue lolling, wet old eyes red in the dawn.

"Come on, Chief."

With a bound and another bark, the bulldog shot to his customary place beneath the bright blue bed. Abraham smiled, but the smile was empty. It made his face hurt.

He started the six horses into the purling stream. Listened—

Inside the huge wagon there was only silence.

__8
Ark to the Wilderness

THE BRIM of Abraham's hat and the shoulders of his thick wool coat were as white as the sugared buns he remembered with longing from breakfasts in Boston. Tonight, as he climbed the unlit stairs of the Pittsburgh rooming house in sodden boots, feeling thoroughly downhearted, he thought of all the splendid meals he had quite taken for granted as he was growing up.

What a contrast between the luscious aromas memory conjured and the stenches of this old building that creaked in the winter wind. He smelled tobacco.

Unwashed linen and unclean bodies. The ghastly fish stew served by the bad-tempered landlady for the evening meal—

Elizabeth hadn't eaten the wretched stew. She hadn't felt well enough to go downstairs with him. Poor health did have its blessings—!

Ah, that was a shameful thought. He should be, and was, desperately worried about his wife. Of late she'd been unusually pale and fatigued. He supposed it was the result of living cramped in a single combination bedroom-sitting room for most of the winter—and eating the landlady's swill when hunger overpowered good sense.

Even Chief, laboring up the rickety stairs behind him, looked bedraggled; moved with rheumatic slowness. The old bulldog acted as tired as he felt.

On the second floor landing, a single lamp shed a feeble light. Abraham paused, his attention captured by sounds from behind one of the closed doors. With bleak eyes he listened to the unmistakable rhythm of a bed being strained up and down. He heard a woman's strident moan—

At least one of the transient couples paying the landlady's gouging prices while waiting for winter to loosen its grip on the Ohio was managing to take comfort in each other.

The reflection was more sad than angry. Elizabeth had retired early every night for six or seven weeks. She seemed incapable of any affection save a prim, dutiful kiss now and then. How long had it been since they'd last lain in each other's arms? Centuries! he thought, though the truth was less melodramatic: early January—

He climbed on toward the third floor, Chief panting behind him.

Abraham blamed the dead wagoner for the apprehensive look in Elizabeth's blue eyes whenever he tried to touch her. She still refused to tell him exactly what Pell had done that night. But it was obvious that scars remained.

He blamed himself a little, too. He lacked the ability—the right words, the proper degree of tenderness—to cut through her moods; her aura of remoteness.

His failure in another area didn't help either. He had been totally unable to find a way for them to leave cold, crowded Pittsburgh with its heartless profiteers and its hordes of gray-faced immigrants who wore their hope like a badge. Again today he'd tramped the docks along the Monongahela; kept making inquiries and returning to the notice board even after the snow began to rage out of the northwest.

Yawning and shivering, he tapped the door of their room, murmured a few words to identify himself. He heard Elizabeth's slow, shuffling tread as she came to lift the latch.

The room was unbelievably small. They'd moved the ancient bed against the wall to make room for their trunks. Little extra space remained—and two scarred chairs, a plain table and a wash stand took up most of that.

As usual, the plank floor fairly radiated cold. Elizabeth was already robed for bed. He shut the door after Chief lurched in, flung off his snow-soaked hat and coat.

"Still no luck," he said, sinking into a chair. "Every man I approach seems to have a full load by the time I get to him."

"Nothing new on the notice board?"

"Nothing. We may have to buy another wagon and go along Zane's Trace after all."

Abraham referred to a new road cleared the preceding year. It ran from Zane's Station, on the Ohio's northeast-southwest salient, to Maysville, where the river

flowed generally westward again. Traveling by land part of the way to their destination would be possible, if extremely difficult.

Abraham and Elizabeth had arrived in Pittsburgh in the late fall, just as the first snows fell. After disposing of Pell's horses and wagon and seeing to the delivery of his goods, Abraham and his wife had agreed to make the remaining portion of their trip by riverboat. It was relatively safer, for one thing. The great number of boats shuttling upstream and down had sharply reduced the danger of Indian attack.

But even after recouping the hundred dollars paid to Pell, Abraham couldn't afford to buy his own flatboat. More important, the arks that plied the Ohio required more than one man to handle them, particularly if the boat was going on past Cincinnati to the shallow but treacherous rapids at the falls of the Ohio. A shared-cost, shared-labor arrangement was the only solution.

Now it seemed no solution at all. He'd trudged the docks literally for weeks, unable to find anyone who needed an extra man come spring. Part of the problem was the fact that a partner would also have to transport Elizabeth and their baggage. Space was precious on most of the riverboats.

Abraham sat motionless in the chair, listening to the whine of the February wind. Snow tickled at the windows. His eyes seemed to be focused on Chief. The bulldog lay under the foot of the bed, sleeping. But Abraham really wasn't looking at the animal. He saw instead the comfortable house on Beacon Street—

Aware of Elizabeth standing near him, he glanced up. Pointed to his sodden coat:

"I did buy a recent paper. Just came in with a pack train from Harrisburg. In December, John Adams was elected to the presidency. But the second highest total of votes cast by the electors went to Jefferson, so he's vice president. I doubt papa's happy about that. It shows the Democratic-Republicans are gaining strength and influ—"

He broke off, startled. Elizabeth was staring at him in a most peculiar way. There was a glow in her eyes such as he hadn't seen for months.

She was *smiling!*

He shot to his feet, seized her chilly hands. He could only infer the smile was the result of some new abnormality in her physical health or her mental state:

"Elizabeth, what's wrong?"

"Nothing, darling. In fact, for the first time since we set foot in this wretched town, I'm happy."

The smile grew. At first, he couldn't believe what he suspected. But that smile gave him encouragement. Happiness surged through him like a tonic, washing away his exhaustion, his frustration—

Yet he still didn't dare to believe it. Not until she spoke:

"I've been making a count of the days and weeks. I think enough time's passed so that I can say with fair certainty we're going to have a child."

"Oh my God, that's *wonderful!*"

He whooped, wrapped her in a hug, then leaped back. He'd practically crushed her—

She laughed; really laughed. Faint spots of color showed in her cheeks.

"Yes," she said softly, "I think so too."

Abraham whooped again, did a little dance step on the cold floor. Chief's head came up. The wet, ugly eyes opened. They were already closing by the time Elizabeth added:

"I just wanted to be sure before I raised any false hopes."

Abraham started pacing:

"I know there are doctors in Pittsburgh. We must get you to one immediately. No matter how much he charges—"

He stopped, faced her:

"And I think we should stay right here until the baby's delivered."

"Not see our own land till the autumn? I won't hear of it! I want the child born where we're going to make our home."

"But traveling just this far was taxing enough. And you haven't been yourself since the first of the year—"

"Because I'm going to have a baby! It—it frightens me more than a little."

"That's why you've been so—?"

He didn't finish.

"So cool? Yes. I suspected I might be pregnant right after New Year's, but as I told you, I vowed I wouldn't speak until I was positive." Her radiant expression dimmed as she surveyed the cobwebbed corners of the mean, dingy room. "I simply won't stay here once the weather breaks. It's a prison. And a filthy one at that."

She put her hands on his shoulders, smiling again:

"Besides, everyone we've talked to says river travel is much smoother than going overland in a wagon."

"Yes, I know, but—"

"We must double our efforts to find passage."

Her blue eyes narrowed. He had seen that prologue to an angry outburst many times before.

"I mean it, Abraham. I will not stay in this dreadful room, this vile town, any longer than is absolutely necessary. I'm strong enough to make the river trip—"

"I'm not sure—"

"I *am!* We *must* go!"

He doubted her claim about her strength. But he didn't doubt her determination. He knew further argument would be useless. So he gathered her into his arms while the snow of February, 1797, whined the lodging house windows, and he said:

"All right, Elizabeth. We will."

II

THE LUCK of the Kents seemed to change with the coming of sunshine and a late February thaw. The notice board near the docks, where new arrivals posted their partnership propositions, sent Abraham running to a wagon camp at the edge of town. There he located the Clappers, a family from the Genessee River valley in upper New York state.

The Clapper clan consisted of Daniel, the father, a barrel of a man with a gray-streaked red beard and huge, hair-matted arms; his wife, a leathery little woman named Edna, and their two youngsters. Daniel Junior was sixteen; tiny, doll-like Danetta, nine.

Yes, Daniel Clapper said, Abraham had read the notice correctly. He meant to sell his wagon—but not his horses or all the merchandise the wagon had carried—and invest in a one-way ark.

"What's your destination, Mr. Clapper? The notice didn't say."

"Destination?" Clapper combed out his beard with thick fingers. "Wherever it strikes my fancy to squat, I reckon. I'm a storekeeper, y'see—"

He led Abraham to the wagon, showed him an assortment of goods from bolts of cloth to kegs of nails.

"Had a right good location up New Hampshire way for eleven years. All of a sudden one day, I just got sick of it. We packed up our goods, toted 'em cross country and opened a new store near the falls of the Genesee. Kept that seven years—till the movin' fever come on me again. We been bogged down north of here for a whole month, waitin' for the snow to melt. I can't get out o' Pittsburgh fast enough—just *look* at all these damn people—!''

His wave encompassed fifteen to twenty cook fires glowing in the twilight among immigrant wagons of every description.

"I'm fixin' to go towards the Ohio land, where there's a tad more room," Clapper continued. "Got all I need to open me a store the day I arrive. Put up my tent, lay a board 'twixt two kegs and I'm in business. I'll sell what I brung with me till I can pick up more from the packets comin' downriver. I'll use my horses to peddle in the back country, an' there I am—set up as pert as you please!''

Abraham tried to put the conversation back on course:

"According to the sheet you posted, you need three men for your ark. One more besides you and your son—"

"I need some cash, too." From his coat pocket Clapper pulled two paper-covered pamphlets, opened the first, shut it again. "Wrong one. That's the river map with the islands an' hazards marked—I can't afford me one of them high-priced pilots—"

Tucking the pamphlet away, he handed Abraham the other one:

"This hear *Compleat Guide to the Western Territories* says arks run four dollar a foot. I need one about sixty feet, I guess, to haul the wife and Daniel and Danetta and my horses and goods.''

"That's about two hundred forty dollars."

"Yessir."

"I'd be willing to put in half."

"She wouldn't all go to waste, y'know." Clapper pointed at the pamphlet. "Says in there someplace that you can recover about a quarter o' what you spend for a boat if you tear her up and sell the lumber at the other end."

"Fine with me. Do we have a deal?"

"Hold on, Mr. Kent! We ain't covered all the details."

"What details?"

"Well, f'rinstance—are you travelin' all by yourself? I never seed so blasted many bachelors in one place in my life!''

"I'm married. I have my wife to take along—a small amount of luggage—a bulldog—"

Clapper scowled. "Does he bite?"

"Don't think so."

"Good. Miz Rachel hates mean dogs. That it?"

Abraham smiled. "Yes and no."

"What the hell's that mean?"

"My wife's expecting a child in the fall."

"Why, congratulations to you!" Clapper grabbed Abraham's hand and pumped it, squeezing so hard the younger man winced.

Pale, Abraham said, "Any more details?"

Clapper pondered. "Nope. It don't take me long to make up my mind about a feller's cut. Mr. Kent. If you're agreeable, it's partners."

"Partners," Abraham said, declining to shake the hand Clapper once again extended. Anxious to tell Elizabeth about their good fortune, he started away, then stopped short. He pivoted back to the huge tree of a man who was busy pulling a few chips of wood from his chest-length beard. "Mr. Clapper, there is one very important detail we didn't settle."

"What, Mr. Kent?"

"You still don't know where my wife and I want to go."

Clapper thought again, then shrugged:

"Don't much care. You can tell me if you want to."

"I've a deed to a plot of land on the Great Miami River, above Cincinnati."

"Used to call it Losantville 'bout ten years ago—I read that in one o' them guide books. I got a whole box of guide books about the new country—"

He jerked a thumb at his wagon. Over the end-board, a red-headed young man and a little rose-cheeked girl were watching.

"Where you're goin' sounds all right to me, Mr. Kent. Maybe I'll head on west, maybe I won't. Miz Rachel won't much care. She sighs a lot when we move, but she follers wherever I've a notion to go."

"You mean it really doesn't matter to you where you end up?"

"No, sir. I always like a place for a spell while I'm there. But then the itch sets in—can't explain it any better'n that. It's the goin', not the stoppin', I enjoy the most. Suppose that sounds crazy, huh?"

It did, but Abraham was too polite to admit it:

"I understand perfectly."

"Will you have a talk with Miz Rachel sometime? She sure as hell don't."

"How about this evening? I'd like to bring my wife over to get acquainted—"

"Bring her to supper! Miz Rachel don't mind fixin' for one more."

"Shouldn't you ask her?"

"Never ask a woman anything, Mr. Kent. She might tell you what she wants. Then wouldn't you be in a fix? Listen, you get a move on! The sooner we lay our plans, the sooner we'll be shed o' these damn mobs of people!"

Abraham vanished in the blue wood smoke of the cook fires Daniel Clapper continued to eye with disgust.

III

APRIL CAME, bringing longer days, warmer air, the first warbling birds, the first shoots of green on the coal-veined hills around Pittsburgh. To Abraham and Elizabeth, it seemed that the new season marked an end to their own long night of frustration and hardship as well.

To those with enough money, obtaining one of the huge flatbeds known as arks was no problem. Any of several yards along the two rivers could hammer one together in the space of about two weeks. Morning after morning, Abraham and Daniel Clapper watched theirs being constructed: a rectangular scow sixty-two feet long, twenty-two feet wide.

The ark hull was built of timbers ten inches square, carefully caulked to

minimize leakage. The entire deck was enclosed with four-inch planks that rose flush with the vessel's four sides.

A door in the larboard side near the stern was large enough to admit Clapper's horses to their appointed space. Forward of this, canvas hanging from the slightly pitched plank roof created temporary walls. One large area was set aside at the bow for communal dining and socializing. The partners agreed to pay extra to have a mud-brick hearth and chimney installed. The ark was quite literally a floating house and stable in one.

A ladder from below gave access to the roof through a trap door. From the roof's stern, a great steering oar nearly as long as the ark itself trailed into the water. She was a clumsy-looking craft, Abraham thought. He already felt confined just glancing into the canvas-partitioned sleeping cubicle he and Elizabeth would share. The ark had no windows, only small loopholes through which muskets could be poked in the event of an Indian attack from shore. But that danger was minimal, everyone said, at least above the falls.

The real hazards, according to Clapper's pamphlets, were sunken obstructions. Limbs and occasionally entire trees were swept away from the banks into the current. A few of the largest planters—trees whose upper ends protruded above the surface—and sleepers—trees with their upper ends submerged—were marked on Clapper's map, along with islands and sandbars. The map also noted a few well-known sawyers, submerged logs whose upper ends rose and fell in cycles as long as twenty minutes to half an hour. These were the most dangerous obstructions of all. Unfortunately, the map located only a fraction of them.

But that didn't intimidate the Clappers or the Kents. They watched families with just as little river experience confidently board their arks and set off around the bend of the Ohio in high spirits. One or two vessels a day departed from the Pittsburgh landings.

Finally, one brilliant morning in late April, so did theirs.

Abraham and Daniel Clapper leaned on the end of the great sweep. Daniel Junior cursed down below, struggling to calm the panicky horses. Edna Clapper, Danetta and Elizabeth were at the hearth, forward, preparing breakfast.

It was a smooth and auspicious beginning.

IV

THE OHIO was more beautiful than Abraham remembered it. Their journey, while requiring long, tiring hours at the sweep, was almost like a holiday in some respects. Every sundown, they anchored in midstream, as did all boats traveling up and down the river. The Kents—Elizabeth growing noticeably around the middle—shared the physical warmth of the hearth at the bow, as well as the less tangible but very real human warmth generated by the Clappers. Indeed, the younger couple already felt themselves almost part of the family.

Elizabeth was unstinting when it came to helping Mrs. Clapper with the cooking. And she did her share of the washing that hung on a line strung across the roof. All of them took pleasure in innocuous chatter about the sights of the day, or in the lusty singing of a few hymns—Daniel Clapper enjoyed hymns—after the spring sun went down. Chief grew fatter on the scraps Rachel Clapper fed him.

At night, lying close together in their cubicle while Daniel Clapper snored

noisily beyond the canvas partition, Abraham usually asked Elizabeth for reassurances that she was feeling well. Her spirits seemed remarkably improved but her color didn't.

She gave him the reassurances—truthful or not, he was unable to tell. He still felt occasional stabs of guilt over not being more sensitive to his father's warnings about the hardships they'd face in the west. He now saw clearly that he'd permitted his passion for Elizabeth, as well as their shared defiance of Philip, to lure him into the false certainty that love would sustain them in the face of all difficulties. Elizabeth's extreme fatigue every evening, and her parchment-white cheeks, were constant reminders that it just wasn't so.

Despite his concerns, the unvarying routine of the days and the continual pageant of towering forests and tiny settlements slipping behind them began to lull Abraham into a sense of security he enjoyed. A week passed without a mishap of any kind. He looked forward to one or two more such idyllic weeks before they reached the little frontier settlement of Cincinnati.

On a Friday evening, just at dusk, Abraham came up from below with two mugs of coffee freshly brewed by Mrs. Clapper. Her big, red-bearded husband was seated near the chimney. His legs hung down over the bow wall. Daniel Junior was taking his turn manning the sweep.

The river here ran straight and smooth. Some two or three miles ahead, Abraham glimpsed another ark preceding them. Half a mile behind, a two-way boat was being cordelled upstream against the four-mile-an-hour current. Its crew plodded along a clear stretch on the south bank, the long tow rope strung across their shoulders.

"Thankee," Clapper said, accepting the coffee. He squinted into the sunlight falling through the cathedral-like trees and burnishing the river. "Be dark soon. Time to drop anchor." He sipped from the mug. "Your wife seems to be weathering the Ohio mighty fine."

Abraham sat down; drank some coffee. "Did you think she might not?"

"She's a lovely lass, but she *is* a mite frail." Clapper stared at the younger man with disarming directness. "Surely you had doubts of your own."

"Yes. I did."

That seemed to conclude the subject. Abraham turned to another that had kept him curious for days:

"Have you come to any decision about your final destination?"

"No, sir, I feel the same as I did in Pittsburgh. We agreed to split up the ark an' sell off her timbers in Cincinnati. I'll decide where we're goin' after that. Told you before—it don't make a hell of a lot of difference. I know a little about plenty o' things, but not enough to be a success at any one. In a way, that's mighty fortunate—"

When he grinned, his teeth literally materialized in the midst of the red hair covering the lower part of his face.

"I can relax some. Don't have to feel the least bit ambitious."

Abraham smiled, nodded. Clapper had a way of putting an immutable period at the end of certain conversations. Though he would have liked to question the older man about the origins of his odd attitudes, he didn't. Instead, he contented himself with savoring the coffee and the sunlight scattering golden sparks on the river.

The sweep creaked in its mounting as Daniel Junior changed course slightly. Ahead, the other ark was coasting out of sight around a bend.

Clapper surprised him by saying, "What do you want out here, Mr. Kent? You don't exactly fit."

"Why not?"

"Fer one thing, it's plain you're more of an educated man than I'll ever be."

"I'm not sure about that, Mr. Clapper. There's all sorts of education—"

"You know what I mean, Miz Edna, she keeps sayin', Daniel, that young Mr. Kent's got all the marks of a real gentleman."

Abraham chuckled. "I suppose that means I'll be a bad farmer?"

Clapper sugared the truth with a smile: "Probably won't make it any easier."

"To answer your question, I first came out here with the army. I served in the campaign of '94."

"Under Mad Anthony?"

"Yes. I liked the look of the country. And when I got home to Boston, I decided I didn't care to stay in the east. Right now my wants are simple."

"F'rinstance?"

Abraham shrugged. "The obvious things. To see Elizabeth content. To raise a family. To be happy myself—"

"As a dirt farmer?"

"I'm not sure. We'll find out."

"Least you're honest."

"Mostly I guess you could say I came west because I knew what I didn't want."

"Life in a big city—"

"That's right."

He thought of Philip, but he let the reply stand without amplification. The river burbled around the ark's hull. A hawk swooped through the green gloom of the woods to starboard. Abraham took another sip of the potent coffee, said:

"I didn't give you much of an answer, did I, Mr. Clapper? Knowing what you don't want—having to search for something else you can't even name—that's a pretty poor excuse for taking up a new life. The only trouble is, in my case it's true."

"You needn't look so glum about it. You think any of the other young people pilin' down this river are any smarter 'n you in that respect? No, sir." Clapper shook his head. "All *they* know is the same thing both of us know—what they don't want. They hope to heaven there's somethin' different out here—"

He waved the mug at the bend where the ark ahead had disappeared.

"—but don't ask 'em to name it!"

"Puts them on a spot, does it?"

"Right smart! They can't answer. Not so's a feller who's been around can believe 'em, that is. Oh, you'll hear plenty of gab about how everybody's free an' equal in the western lands—free an' equal, yes, sir! The west is *demo-cratic,* ain't that what that Mr. Jefferson says? No rich nabobs to crowd a young man, or make him feel second best. Maybe a mite of that's true—"

He held index finger and thumb close together.

" 'Bout this much. I'll tell you something. If a man could be happy in the east, do you imagine he'd up and leave? Lord no! They can be loads o' reasons *why* he ain't happy. Money. Women. Mebbe he's ugly as that bulldog of yours—"

"I wouldn't wish that on another human being, Mr. Clapper."

The other man still refused to smile:

"Lots of times, a man can't be happy and just plain don't know why. He might have a bit of cash put by, even some regular schooling—"

"But he leaves anyway?"

"Yes, sir, 'cause he's so blamed unhappy. Mr. Kent, believe me, that's the whole reason. A man don't *never* cut the roots if everything's right with his world—or his head. Folks can turn it other side backwards all they want. They can shout *'Free an' equal!'* till they're blue. But just like your case—it really ain't a matter of goin' *toward*, it's a matter of runnin' *from*—"

Clapper encompassed the western horizon with a sweep of the cup:

"And once you catch the urge to run away, you never lose it. You must keep movin'—miserable as ever."

Abraham shivered. "That's a grim view."

"True, though."

"Well, if all you say about people being unhappy is correct—"

"It is!"

"Then we're fortunate we have room to run, aren't we? If we had to stay bottled up back east with all the grief you describe, I suspect we'd soon go crazy. So that makes the western country a blessing. And people moving into it—that's a good, healthy thing when you consider the alternative."

"Got to think that through a minute," Clapper informed him, dubious.

"In my case it's a blessing. I had to have somewhere to escape to, and that's a fact."

"Yeh, but you can't pin down what you're huntin'—you said so."

"I know. Still, I'm hoping I'll find something good—and be smart enough to recognize it for what it is."

"Something, something," Clapper parroted. Then, a snort: "You feel that way 'cause you're young."

"You don't feel that way?"

"Not no more. You want to keep hopin', Mr. Kent, don't ask questions of folks my age."

"Why not?"

" 'Cause you'll find that a mighty lot of the settlers swarmin' out here have stopped other places before. Lookin', always lookin'—for *something*. The ones that got ten or fifteen years on you—they already found out."

"Found out what?"

"*Something* don't exist. No place."

"But surely—"

"No. It don't." Without self-pity, Clapper added, "I found out. Now you understand why it don't make any difference to me where this boat's headed, or where it stops?"

"Yes, I do."

Clapper bobbed his head once, and drained his cup.

God in heaven, Abraham hoped Clapper wasn't right. He prayed he and Elizabeth wouldn't reach their tract of land only to come face to face with the futility of their flight—

No, surely the big man was in error; embittered by personal failures barely hinted at. To believe what Clapper said was too disillusioning—

The sudden, violent impact shattered his dour reverie. With a great crunch, then a prolonged grinding, the ark wrenched broadside to the current. Clapper almost pitched into the water.

Abraham's grab saved him. He dragged Clapper back as the bow of the ark came around, then lifted sharply on the larboard side.

Both men were nearly hurled off the roof as the ark rode up on some underwater obstacle, slid off and slammed down.

Below, the terrified horses neighed and kicked against the plank walls. The kicks were loud as gunshots.

"Sweep broke clean off, pa!" Daniel Junior yelled from the stern. "We musta hit a sawyer—"

"Damn! The log was probably way down when that boat ahead of us went by. Then she bobbed up—go see how bad we're busted up, Daniel."

Abraham studied the tilt of the roof. "We're taking water. She's listing."

Daniel Junior vanished below. Clapper began, "We better—"

"*Danetta!*"

Clapper and Abraham exchanged terrified looks. The cry came from Edna Clapper—and she wasn't given to excesses of emotion.

All Abraham could think of was the ark's brief but jolting rise and fall. *Where was Elizabeth when they hit—?*

He ran to the roof trap and scrambled down the ladder, hardly aware of Daniel Junior's urgent cries from the stern. Clapper came down the ladder after him. Chief was yapping. The horses kept kicking the ark walls, *bang, bang—*

Mrs. Clapper screamed for her daughter a second time.

Abraham batted canvas hangings aside, dashed forward through sloshing water and burst into the communal room at the bow.

"*Elizabeth!*"

Tumbled into an awkward position against the bricks at one side of the hearth, his wife didn't respond, or see him. Her eyes were nearly closed. One of her white hands constricted on the small mound of her belly.

Mrs. Clapper was kneeling beside her, partially concealing Elizabeth's legs. Abraham felt sick to his stomach as he watched Edna Clapper withdraw her hands from beneath Elizabeth's twisted skirt.

The hands were bloody.

"She fell," Mrs. Clapper said in a faint voice, as though holding great emotion in check. "When we hit, she fell against the fireplace—"

Suddenly her eyes smoldered:

"This is no place for men! *Find Danetta.*"

Anguish held Abraham rooted. He realized Clapper had come up behind him—and even the big red-bearded man seemed horrified into helplessness.

Edna Clapper turned her wrath on both of them:

"In God's name, will you hurry? Mrs. Kent is losing the baby!"

BOOK TWO
THE ENEMY LAND

1
The Cabin

"ONE FOR the crow, two for the cutworm, three to grow. One for the crow, two for the cut—"

Alarmed, young Daniel Clapper suddenly broke off the monotonous chant.

He and Abraham Kent had been marching side by side down the new checkrows plowed with the help of one of Daniel Clapper's horses. At every transverse row marking the cleared four-acre plot into yard-sized squares, man and boy dropped half a dozen kernels of seed corn. Now Daniel had stopped.

A moment later, Abraham halted too. Looked back. Young Daniel remained motionless, signaling with his eyes:

"Yonder, Mr. Kent. Injuns on the ridge."

Slowly, so as not to show his concern, Abraham Kent slipped the seed bag off his bare shoulder. He wore only buckskin trousers and soft moccasins padded with leaves for comfort. His glance traveled first to the edge of the plot, where Chief rested next to a smoldering stump. On the ground near the bulldog's paws lay Abraham's Kentucky flintlock rifle, his horn and his shot pouch. It would require a good run to reach the weapon. But it was primed and ready to fire, as always.

The wind this gray, thundery afternoon in late May, 1799, cooled the sweat on Abraham's chest in an instant. His gaze moved quickly on toward the cabin.

The windowless, twenty-by-sixteen building was half hidden by the inevitable trees that made clearing and planting even a single acre an exhausting task. Abraham had felled the smaller trees around the cabin. The larger ones showed the cuts where he'd girdled them to kill them. Several other stumps he was burning out fumed like the one at the field's edge, mingling their smoke with the reassuring column rising from the cabin chimney. The chimney's surrounding

log superstructure jutted from the end of the cabin facing the river. The offset cut down the danger of fire, but not much.

Near the cabin, their once-fat milk cow nibbled at a patch of grass. In one of Elizabeth's rare moments of good humor, she'd insisted on naming the cow Henrietta Knox.

Pretending to draw several deep breaths, Abraham finally completed the covert inspection. Once again he had cause to regret the location of his property: a good four miles above the settlement at Fort Hamilton.

Finally he turned. He wiped his forehead with his forearm to conceal his interest in the western ridge-line. Just as he spotted the four tiny figures, young Daniel let out a relieved breath:

"They're movin' again. They were just standin' and watchin' when I seen 'em first."

Abraham's heart slowed down. He picked up his seed bag.

"We can finish, then."

He licked his lips, resumed walking. Young Daniel followed along the adjacent row. But he didn't continue his sower's chant.

The Indian danger kept Abraham constantly alert. It terrified his wife. Although raids in the district were infrequent—and were usually limited to cow thefts or cabin burnings—they did happen. Occasionally they were augmented by atrocities. Usually the victims had chosen to live a good distance from a fort or village.

The atrocities were by no means confined to one side, though. Abraham knew several white men in the settlement around Fort Hamilton who would automatically shoot and butcher any Indians they caught on the trails that ran parallel to the river.

Trudging and scattering corn, Abraham said in a listless voice, "I suppose they were Shawnee again."

Young Daniel nodded. "Goin' back to their towns north o' here, I reckon. Pap says General Wayne never should of 'lowed them to hunt in the treaty lands. Only makes 'em resent what the gummint took away—and crave it worse every time they travel through."

Too tired to enter into a discussion of Indian policy, Abraham kept walking. A few spatters of rain landed on his bare shoulders. Although it couldn't be later than four o'clock, the silver-gray clouds sweeping out of the west were rapidly bringing near-darkness. The wind had turned gusty. A little less than half a mile away, the surface of the Great Miami showed white riffles.

When the rain began to fall harder, Abraham swore and closed his seed bag:

"We'd better wait till morning to finish, Daniel."

"All right," the gangly boy agreed. "Be back right after sunup."

"You want to rest in the cabin till the storm's over?"

"I would, but pap's waitin' for me to unload them tools we brung up from Cincinnati."

"I really appreciate your help, Daniel."

"Oh, hell, it's nothin'."

"I couldn't get by without it and you know it. I only hope to God I can raise four good acres this year, and give your father half."

"Mr. Kent, he don't expect you to settle up right away."

"Well, I'm going to, Daniel."

Abraham was sincere in his promise to repay Clapper the only way he could. Yet repeating the pledge depressed him too.

Even if four full acres of corn matured, half of the yield would barely keep the

little family over the winter, while the other half would hardly make a dent in the various debts he'd run up at the small store Daniel Clapper had established near the fort, simply by partitioning half of his large cabin and hanging out a sign.

Daniel was embarrassed by Abraham's sober expression. Without understanding its cause, he tried to dismiss it with a wave:

"Folks got to help each other, Mr. Kent. Otherwise none of us'd make it, isn't that right?"

"Yes," Abraham said in an absent way.

"See you in the morning."

Running, young Daniel disappeared into the trees west of the cabin. As Abraham watched the boy go, he noted that all the smoldering stumps were being drenched by the rain. He'd have to relight them tomorrow. Another chore—

That was the extent of life out here: chores. Seven days a week, indoors and out. The rigors of it had stripped all the fat from Abraham's body; thickened his muscles noticeably. But he felt tired every waking minute.

He put on his linsey shirt, grimacing at its wetness. He picked up his pouch, horn and flintlock, taking care to shield the lock in the crook of his arm. Burdened with those items plus the two seed sacks, he tramped toward the cabin.

Under the protection of one of the big girdled trees, he watched the clouds sailing out of the west and reflected on the understated truth of young Daniel's parting remark. Without mutual assistance, few settlers could survive the first year or so in the new land.

Abraham and Elizabeth had been fortunate in several ways. He often forgot that in his weariness and frustration—

Repairing the ark struck by the sunken log had been fairly easy, thanks to the help of some coarse-talking but genial boatmen who had come upstream, sail raised to a freshening wind, an hour after the accident. Elizabeth had indeed lost the baby, and been weak for more than a month. But the tragedy hadn't destroyed her ability to bear, thank God. The evidence of that was in the cabin.

On their arrival at Cincinnati, Daniel Clapper, that odd, cheerfully pessimistic man of small education and large wisdom had declared that he and his brood might as well open their store at Abraham and Elizabeth's destination, because it was "probably as good as anyplace else—in fact just the same as anyplace else."

So the Kents and the Clappers had ridden the thirty-odd miles north along the Miami in a hired wagon pulled by Clapper's two horses. On their property, the younger couple found the blessing of a half-faced camp, ramshackle but serviceable during the first weeks. People at the Fort Hamilton settlement said squatters had been on the Kent land the year before. But the squatters had moved on out toward the Wabash River country. No one in the settlement even remembered the squatters by name.

Leaning against the gridled tree and watching the rain fall, Abraham recalled that first hard summer and autumn. He particularly recalled his desperate rush to hoe a few holes in the ground between the trees and plant a small amount of corn to tide them over the cold months. The corn not only failed to grow, it failed to sprout.

By custom, all men in the district came to raise the Kents' cabin in September of '97. Since that time Abraham had taken part in six three-day cabin raisings for others.

During the winter of 1797–98, Abraham spent almost all of his remaining money for provisions to tide them through until spring. He bartered a clock

Elizabeth had brought from Boston to obtain the rifle they needed for protection. A number of settings of fine china were surrendered to storekeeper Clapper for a pair of cheaper pewter plates, seed and a plow. Abraham knew Clapper was getting the bad end of the bargain. No one out here would purchase that exquisite china off Clapper's shelf.

The last of the money paid for Henrietta Knox, who delivered the milk he and Elizabeth learned to drink sour, although they abominated the taste. There was no way to keep milk sweet for long; storing it in a crock in the cold, clear spring at the back of their property only retarded the souring a few days.

The following year, '98, Abraham had laboriously cleared a two-acre plot, planted it and harvested the corn. Half the crop was ruined by a disease that blighted the ears as they were forming. But at least the family had some food for the winter. The baby, born in the fall with the help of a local midwife, took its nourishment directly from Elizabeth's breast.

Under the bellies of fast-flying clouds, Abraham saw a wedge of birds streaming north. Plump and tasty passenger pigeons. When they stopped to roost, you could practically knock them out of the lower branches with sticks. Abraham watched the birds longingly. A cooked pigeon would have been a welcome change from their diet of corn mush and sour milk.

The movement of the birds against the strangely luminous gray-and-silver sky drew Abraham's mind back to the conversation with Daniel Clapper just before the ark hit the sunken log. Abraham had changed his thinking since then. He believed Clapper was, in part if not entirely, correct. The desire to see the other side of the hill *was* rooted in discontent, whether it took the form of a yearning for wealth the east denied, a second chance to repair a wrecked life, misery generated by crowded conditions in the cities—or even plain, cussed boredom.

In his case and Elizabeth's, the goal had been escape from Philip's domineering influence. Abraham could admit that freely to himself now, without shame. He *was* ashamed of his desire to see the Boston house again. He never revealed it to his wife.

Still, it was odd, he thought as he watched the gray rain pour down on his newly planted field—odd that unhappiness was the motive force behind so many people moving west. And my God—they were moving west by the thousands!

Just this past March, he'd gone to Cincinnati with Daniel Clapper and his son, to help them transport an unusually large stock of new staples and implements back to the store. Cincinnati was no longer the tiny frontier outpost Abraham remembered. It had boomed since the Kents and Clappers passed through in the late spring of '97. Population had spurted to over five hundred, not counting the Fort Washington garrison.

What astonished Abraham most was the river traffic. With boats tied up everywhere, pushing off at all hours only to be replaced by new ones coming down the Ohio, the river town actually looked more crowded than Pittsburgh. Almost all the transients were heading further west. Americans, Abraham concluded, were the damnedest bunch of perpetual malcontents civilization had ever seen.

As he strolled the packed, noisy piers, observing families as well as young bachelors armed only with hunting rifles preparing to set out, he recalled Daniel Clapper's dour prediction that most of the travelers would never find the ideal life they sought. Yet they took pleasure in haggling over flatboat passage, and spoke glowingly in the taverns of all the freedom and promise of the bountiful land waiting out ahead—

That country just *had* to be more attractive and comfortable than the coastal

belt, where a swelling populace was growing more and more alarmed over the undeclared naval war between America and her former ally, France.

From time to time a letter written by Philip or Peggy—a letter months in transit—expressed the Kents' open hostility to Philip's native country. The letters were further signs of how Philip's conservatism was hardening into unqualified pro-British sentiment.

The French Directory had been angered by Jay's treaty with England, the letters reported. And despite President Washington's specific warnings in his farewell address against all alliances with foreign nations except those alliances of the most temporary, expedient nature, Minister Pinckney had gone to Paris along with Commissioners Elbridge Gerry and John Marshall to attempt to secure a treaty guaranteeing friendship and, more important, commerce.

The commissioners were outraged by a request for an outright bribe to be paid to foreign minister Talleyrand, in return for consideration of the requested treaty. The bribe wasn't to be paid directly, of course. It was to be funneled through three intermediaries tactfully dubbed Messieurs X, Y and Z. All but the most illiterate passing along the Ohio had heard of—and by and large approved—the ringing toast that had become a catch-phrase. The toast had been given Minister Pinckney after his furious refusal to pay Talleyrand, and his return to the United States:

"Millions for defense but not one cent for tribute!"

That was a sentiment Philip Kent heartily endorsed in his letters—especially as it applied to post-revolutionary France. He was pleased, he wrote, that a Navy Department had at last been created. He was delighted that *Constitution* and the other frigates had finally been completed, and launched to oppose French harassment of American shipping.

Most of the settlers Abraham talked with in Cincinnati weren't articulate about the question of war. But they were quite aware of its possibility. Thus they had an added incentive to get as far away as possible from the vulnerable seacoast.

Perhaps some would end up at a destination that satisfied them. Or perhaps they'd pretend that was the case, anyway, so as not to confront their families—or themselves—with the sad truth of their error.

A few might actually better themselves. But no gentle Edens awaited them, Abraham was positive of that. The fact had come home to him long before the Cincinnati trip. It had come to him as he lay beside his wife during the summer and winter nights, his body hurting so badly from physical labor that he literally couldn't sleep.

Something else struck him in Cincinnati—struck with the power of a revelation:

He and Elizabeth were just as much prisoners of their surroundings as they would have been had Abraham taken a place and done Philip's bidding at Kent and Son.

Thousands were moving west but they could not. They had mortgaged their lives to twenty acres along the Miami River, and were consumed by the challenges of daily living: food, shelter, the Indian threat—

Survival.

He and Elizabeth would never see another place. At least not easily. Clapper said it made no difference—one was identical with the next. Still, what Abraham was denied, he somehow coveted.

After the excursion to Cincinnati, he began to think of the twenty acres in a new way. No longer was the land a haven. It acquired quasi-human characteristics in his mind—especially when he tramped to Fort Hamilton for supplies and

wound up accepting too much of Clapper's corn whiskey. Then the land became a true opponent. A captor whom he could and did curse aloud—

Even basic survival on the land was still in doubt. Abraham was succeeding, but only marginally; and that success would have been impossible without the cooperative spirit that tended to tie the settlers together, each helping the other.

The preceding autumn, for instance, Abraham had worked all night many a night at husking bees, since no man could husk a large corn crop alone. He had lent his time and his strength to those cabin-raisings, in return for the help he had received with his.

Yet even with human allies, he found the land a formidable foe. Many—like the vanished squatters who'd built the half-faced camp he and Elizabeth had originally inhabited—lacked the will and the wits to win against it. Abraham had done his best; given the struggle everything for nearly two years—and all he had to show was a meager four-acre plot, and no guarantee of a good crop on that.

It might be different if Elizabeth were stronger physically, he thought. *Tougher mentally—*

But as he stared into the heavying rain that hid the river and extinguished the last of his burning stumps, he admitted she was not. He'd have welcomed an occasional smile of pleasure at his small accomplishments; a word of encouragement about the tasks still to be done. Elizabeth seemed incapable of giving either. Somehow it doubled the rigors of his work.

A noise on a nearby tree branch diverted him from the gloomy meditation. He spied a fat squirrel perched where the limb joined the trunk. He found squirrel meat in a pot pie not too unpalatable. So he raised the Kentucky rifle to his shoulder slowly, and aimed down the acid-browned octagonal barrel. The trick was to avoid hitting the squirrel and destroying the flesh. Instead, Abraham would try to bark him.

The rifle exploded. Smoke curled. Chief began to snap and run in a circle as Abraham grimaced—it couldn't be called a smile. His ball had flown true. Smacked the thick wood where the branch met the tree. The concussion had spun the squirrel to the ground, where it now lay stunned.

"Stay back, Chief."

The bulldog reluctantly obeyed as Abraham picked up a stone and ran forward. He killed the squirrel with one quick stroke that broke its head open but left the carcass undamaged.

Abraham trotted to the end of the cabin opposite that where the chimney rose. He stowed his corn sacks in the little shed he'd built and chinked carefully. He tied Henrietta Knox to the bar on the shed door, although the rain was beginning to pelt down so hard that the cabin wall would afford her little protection.

The cow lowed uncomfortaby. Stamped and jangled her bell as Abraham felt her udder.

Full. Elizabeth hadn't milked her again.

Well, he'd have to do it when the rain let up.

More and more often this spring, Elizabeth seemed to be forgetting or ignoring important work. He never spoke of it, adding the burden to his other ones in the silent hope that doing so might make his wife less weary and somber. It never seemed to. Yet Abraham refused to give up the effort to lighten her load. At the same time, the lapses troubled him.

He returnd to retrieve his rifle, horn, pouch—and, by the tail, the squirrel. He slopped through the mud at the front of the cabin. From several feet away, he

saw the thick plank door standing slightly ajar. The thong that raised the inside latch dangled from the small hole.

He always insisted Elizabeth keep the door barred and the latchstring in, even when he was near the cabin. She refused, claiming the cabin was confining enough as it was. She shrugged off his statements that women had been murdered by stealthy Indians while their husbands worked only a short distance away.

As he reached the door, he heard one-year-old Jared Adam bawling. His scalp prickled with a belated realization:

Elizabeth should have come to the door when she heard the shot.

Fearful, he jerked the cabin door open as the blackening sky rumbled.

___II

ABRAHAM STEPPED out of the downpour, held up his prize:

"I picked off a squirrel for—"

His face froze in surprise.

Not one of the three tallow candles in tin wall sconces had been lit. The cabin was dark except for the flickering logs in the hearth.

Above the logs the family stew pot hung from a pole mounted across the inside of the chimney. A burned stench drifted from the pot. Elizabeth had been cooking corn meal into mush. All the water had boiled away.

There was an oppressive stillness. It was broken only by the rattle of rain on the hand-riven roof clapboards. By the tick of Chief's unclipped nails on the puncheon floor. And by Jared Adam's fretful crying, off to Abraham's right where the firelight failed to reach.

He saw his wife clearly enough. Her back bowed, she sat on one of their two block chairs—sixteen-inch hickory logs standing on end. Her hands were fisted on the knees of her soiled dress. Her blue eyes stared into and through the fire.

Angry, Abraham flung the squirrel on the puncheon table projecting from one wall. The squirrel struck so hard, the table's pole legs quivered. The dead animal's head stained the wood. He never noticed:

"Elizabeth."

No answer.

"Elizabeth, the baby's crying. Don't you hear him?"

An eternity seemed to pass before she turned her head. Tears shone on her cheeks.

He dropped his pouch and horn, laid his rifle beside the squirrel, rushed to her as the baby howled all the louder. His rage left him in an instant, replaced by grief. He gripped Elizabeth's shoulders, felt them trembling, whispered:

"What's wrong?"

Her voice was feeble:

"I—I don't know. I sat down—I'm so tired, Abraham. I felt so miserable all at once and—I don't know," she repeated in a futile tone.

Her face had a distinct pallor. She had lost weight over the past months. The bosom of her dress looked almost flat because her breasts sagged.

"Elizabeth, you're not carrying a child again, and haven't told me—?"

She shook her head. The fair hair that once had glowed so brilliantly was seldom washed these days; it hung dull and tangly at her shoulders. She began to rock back and forth.

"I don't know what's wrong, except I hate this place. I hate it, oh God, I *hate* it—"

Sobbing, she covered her face and turned her back on him. Unseen in the darkness, the infant still made his presence known with his damnable howling. Abraham came close to cursing him.

Struggling to keep his voice calm, he said, "I brought in a squirrel. Elizabeth, do you hear?"

She gave no sign.

"I thought a squirrel pie might be a welcome change. I'll fix it—"

"I'm not hungry."

"You've eaten next to nothing all week!"

"I don't know why," she said. "I don't know."

Terrified by her glazed eyes but not knowing exactly what to do, Abraham gripped her shoulders again, tried to lift her from the block chair:

"Let me put you to bed. I'll see to the boy—"

She offered no resistance. He guided her to the double bedstead in the angle of two walls. The bed's outer corner was supported by a pole similar to those beneath the table, but thicker. He lowered Elizabeth gently to the double deerhide spread over a thick matting of corn husks. Despite the padding, the bed was as hard as anything he'd ever slept on, the earth included.

Elizabeth started shivering. He covered her with one of their few luxuries—a hand-made Kentucky quilt in the simple yet beautiful Star of Bethlehem pattern.

In a moment or two, her shivering stopped. Abraham knelt. He suspected the chill and misery were products of her mind, not her body. He kissed her wind-roughened cheek:

"Don't fret, I'll have the baby quiet soon. Don't worry about a thing—"

She began to cry again:

"I don't know what's wrong with me, Abraham. I knew the corn meal was burning. I could smell it. I sat there and didn't care—"

"There's nothing wrong with you except lack of rest," he said. Neither of them believed it:

"No, Abraham, it's something else. I'm not strong enough for you. For this—"

"My God, don't say that! You've done so much work—"

"But I hate it, I despise it, sometimes I just don't want to go on—"

She controlled her crying; wiped her eyes; looked at him and spoke more lucidly:

"You've never heard much about my father, have you?"

"Only the talk at home. What has he to do with us?"

"He has a great deal to do with me, I think."

"What do you mean?"

"Mama told me more about him than she ever told anyone else, including your father. He was—a peculiar man. Wild and—and brave in some ways. But weak in others. He ran from whatever he disliked. Or drank to forget it. Perhaps—no, listen to me, Abraham, you must hear this—perhaps his nature was strength and weakness in one. Mama calls it the Fletcher blood."

"I've never heard her mention—"

"Fletcher blood. I have it. I know it's one reason I resented your father so, and insisted we come to this place."

"Don't forget that took courage, Elizabeth. Great courage."

The moment he said it, his mind showed him an image of Daniel Clapper. He

heard Clapper speaking of why men fled toward another horizon, then another, another—

"I don't have any courage left," she said. "Two years out here and—any that I may have had—it's gone. All I feel is hate. Tiredness, and hate—"

Her hand closed on his, an iced claw:

"I know what I am—"

"Stop."

"I don't want it to hurt you—"

"Elizabeth, don't—"

"Most of all I don't want it to hurt baby Jared."

A long silence. Then:

"How could it?"

"He has the same blood, doesn't he?"

Abraham felt a terror so deep and devastating that he couldn't speak for several moments. The child's howls dinned in the confined space, ceasing only when the baby gulped a breath. He tried to ignore the squalling; tried to quell the fear Elizabeth's strange ramblings generated. He soothed her forehead with a palm, and lied:

"You're feverish. You need rest."

She stared up into the darkness where the timbers of the loft floor were barely visible. He tucked the quilt around her throat and shoulders:

"I'll pile an extra log or two on the fire—it promises to be a foul night. Maybe you'll feel like eating something in a few hours—"

She closed her eyes. Tears ran down her cheeks as if she were in great pain.

"See to the baby," she whispered. "See to the poor baby."

She rolled onto her side, away from him. He covered his eyes, wondering if what she'd rambled about was true. Did some streak of inherited temperament drive her to these despairs that grew deeper and more frequent as the weeks passed?

Or was it the land? Some weren't strong enough to win the struggle with the land. Was she one of those—?

Forcing himself to activity, he placed two smaller logs atop the others, then walked across the cabin as flames leaped up beneath the stinking pot of burned mush. Jared Adam kept shrieking.

Abraham reached down for the bundled boy, raised him to his shoulder, felt the sopping wetness of the coverlet in which Elizabeth had wrapped him.

"Papa's here," Abraham whispered. "It's all right, Jared. Papa's here."

The infant cried less stridently. Chief tick-tacked across the floor to the cradle Abraham had hollowed from half a gum log and finished with crescent rockers pegged to the ends. The bulldog sniffed the aroma of urine permeating the crib, lumbered back to the corner where he always slept. Outside, Henrietta Knox lowed loudly, her bell clanking.

Abraham started for the trunk to find clean rags for the baby. After he'd discarded the soiled ones, he wrapped Jared carefully, then went back to the trunk for a dry coverlet. As he picked Jared up again, he glanced at the bedstead. Elizabeth lay motionless under the quilt. Her eyes were shut but he didn't believe she was asleep.

All at once he couldn't tolerate the ripe smells poisoning the air in the cabin. In spite of the downpour, he jerked the latchstring, stepped into the open doorway—

My God, how dark it was! And not even nightfall yet.

Gusts of wind blew cool rain in his face. He covered Jared's head hastily.

He pondered what his wife had said about the Fletcher blood. Despite a death some called heroic, Fletcher had been a tainted man. There was certainly mounting evidence of a similar taint on Elizabeth—

Had it passed to the baby boy on his shoulder? Unconsciously, he tugged up the blanket, all but hiding the dark-fuzzed skull.

Westward, the clouds had lowered. The western ridge had disappeared in the murk. The small amount of daylight remaining showed Abraham the damaging effects of the flash storm. All his checkrows were washed away. The rain had cut new channels in the ground. He would have to start again. The plowing, the seeding—everything.

With his wife lying silent behind him and Jared fretting on his shoulder, Abraham stared at the storm-raked field and almost shook with rage.

What an accursed land! It treated a man's hopes and a man's labors and a man's loved ones with inhuman indifference—

He stood there for almost half an hour, looking at the rain but seeing his mortal enemy.

2
Old Ghosts and New Beginnings

ONE AUTUMN Saturday a year later, Abraham walked back from Clapper's store to find the farm unexpectedly quiet.

He stopped at the edge of the property, frowning as he scanned it. His eye drifted from the cabin to the small barn built in the spring with the help of neighbors. Henrietta Knox grazed near the barn. From within came the mournful bellow of the ox he'd bought using money Daniel Clapper loaned him. He was deeper in debt than ever before.

His gaze moved on to the cultivated ground—eight acres now, the corn already standing in shocks that cast long shadows in the cool amber sunlight of late afternoon. In addition to the corn, he'd put in patches of turnips, which had done well, and watermelons, which hadn't.

He quickly shook off the lethargy induced by a generous amount of Clapper's whiskey. Elizabeth had planned to make soap today. The process took hours. She boiled wood-ash lye and fat which she'd saved, producing harsh, slimy lumps of soap that seemed to remove more skin than dirt. But Abraham saw no smoke rising from the chimney into the flurry of leaves whirled across the roof by the wind.

No smoke—nor any sign of activity in or around the cabin. He didn't see Elizabeth or their two-year old son anywhere.

He put down the jug of New Orleans molasses he'd obtained at Clapper's. Packet boats brought the sweetening up the Mississippi and the Ohio regularly now. He'd lacked the exact change for the purchase, so the storekeeper had snipped another piece from one of his few paper dollars.

A second close scrutiny of the property produced no evidence of trespassers. But just in case, he made sure his Kentucky rifle was loaded and ready to fire.

"Elizabeth? Jared?" His voice boomed back at him in the stiff wind—
Elizabeth? Jared?—unanswered. Henrietta Knox turned her head briefly, then
resumed chewing the brown grass.

Moving slowly toward the cabin, he saw Elizabeth's splint broom lying abandoned in the dooryard. Damn! She was supposed to stay locked inside while he
was gone.

Again he called her name. Again no answer. He prodded the cabin door open
with the muzzle of his rifle.

He saw nothing but darkness. Not a single tallow-dip was lit against the
coming dusk. The river murmured in the distance.

It was the letter, he decided. The damned, hurtful letter from his father. A
pack train had delivered it to Fort Hamilton thirty days ago—

During the past twelve months the elder Kent's letters had changed noticeably.
The tone grew steadily less cheerful, and items of interest concerning the east
and Europe had become more and more sparse. The last bit of information
Abraham could recall his father reporting with genuine enthusiasm was months
ago. Philip Kent's boyhood friend, Lafayette, had finally been released from
prison in Austria and allowed to return to France. There, living in relative
seclusion, he had resumed correspondence with his old comrade in Boston.

Of late, however, Abraham found himself relying almost totally on other
settlers for news—

News of President Adams' refusal to go to war with France, for instance.
Adams resisted war even though many in his political party—including Philip,
presumably—favored it.

There were new developments in France. By means of a coup, a military
leader had seized power. The soldier named Bonaparte was a man of vast
ambition, it was said. As first consul of his country, he announced his intention
to deal with the United States in an amicable way—no doubt to prevent an
American alliance with France's traditional enemy, Britain.

Bonaparte's avowed friendship might end the hostilities between American
and French naval forces. People in the east were suspicious of the new ruler,
though. Didn't he openly express his dream of a worldwide French empire?
Might he not press the Spanish to recede the vast Louisiana territory—including
the port of New Orleans—in return for France's surrender of portions of Italy?
The anti-French faction east of the mountains claimed such negotiations were in
fact underway in secret. Ultimately, Bonaparte could endanger the use of the
Ohio and Mississippi as commercial routes for the western part of the country.

Philip hardly touched on these matters. Abraham heard about them from men
gathered around Clapper's cracker barrel. When the recent, extremely brief letter
arrived via pack train, Abraham at last understood his father's silence on more
general subjects.

Philip wrote that in late February of this year, 1800, Peggy Ashford McLean
Kent had died of a wasting disease that shriveled her body and tortured her senses
for six months before death gave her release. Since reading the letter, Elizabeth
had lost her appetite, gone listlessly about her chores, paid little attention to Jared
and less to her husband.

They still slept side by side. But Abraham hadn't touched her in a month,
sensing her unspoken wish that he refrain. As a result, he often felt angry with
her. His anger found an outlet in Saturday visits to the settlement. She seldom
felt strong enough to walk with him. He usually came home more than a little
drunk—

"Elizabeth!"

This time he shouted. The echo rolled away through the trees and died under the murmur of the wind. Invisible in the brush that screened part of the river bank, someone answered:

"Papa?"

Exhaling loudly, Abraham hurried forward:

"Jared, you stay right there—"

What in hell was the child doing outside, unattended?

Abraham clambered noisily down through the brush. He heard Chief's feeble bark. The bulldog was ancient now, barely able to walk.

Once more Abraham searched the woods and the portion of the river bank visible to him. Still no sign of Elizabeth. Fear turned to wrath again as he parted a screen of low branches and discovered his son.

Moccasins off and feet dirty, Jared was seated on the ground, alternately scooping dirt from a hole and building it into a small mound. The boy looked up with bright blue eyes—the Fletcher eyes he'd inherited from his mother. Chief, lying a few feet away, lolled his tongue but made no effort to rise and greet his master.

Jared's tawny hair hung matted over his neck. His hide shirt showed rips at the elbows—more indications of Elizabeth's neglect. Almost fearfully, the boy continued to stare up at his stocky father.

"Why did mama leave you alone, Jared?"

Although Jared was only two, Elizabeth had been able to teach him to use rudimentary sentences. He answered with one:

"Don't know."

"Where did she go?"

The boy looked away. "Down there." A grimy hand pointed.

Abraham scowled. "The river? Whatever for?"

"Don't know. She said to play. Then she left." As if to show that he'd tried to do as he was told, he glanced down at the mound of dirt.

Abraham started to say something. A faint sound from the bushes behind Chief brought his head snapping around. His hand turned cold on the stock of his rifle.

Eyes fixed on the brush concealing the source of the rattle, he said:

"Jared, listen. Get up. Come to me."

Jared frowned. "Want to finish—"

"I said *come to me!*"

Abraham's palms were slick with sweat. He dared not look away from the brush for an instant—

Tears appeared in Jared's eyes. But he rose obediently and walked to his father—moments before the head of the snake jutted from the underbrush.

"Get behind me, Jared!"

The boy was gazing up at his father. He didn't understand the reason for the harsh command. The snake coiled out of the shadows, rattling—

The snake was sixteen or seventeen inches long. Its brown ground color was blotched with black. Its puffy head darted a few inches to the right, then a few inches to the left—

Abraham stepped around his son, jammed the rifle against his shoulder and fired.

Chief barked, struggled to stand up as Abraham's ball missed the head of the

pygmy rattler, blasting up a shower of leaves and dirt. The rattler's fangs glistened as its head shot forward. Chief yelped when the rattler bit.

By then Abraham had lunged forward. He drove the rifle's brass butt plate toward the front part of the snake's body. The snake whipped its head back a moment before the rifle struck. The blow cracked the snake's skull.

Using the rifle stock as a kind of shovel, Abraham hoisted the snake and hurled it away. On his belly, Chief tried to turn his head far enough to lick at his wound. The old dog was too stiff; his tongue wouldn't reach.

Jared clutched his father's leg:

"What—what was it?"

"A snake."

"What?"

"*Snake,* Jared. Dangerous. Hurt you."

"Didn't see it—"

"I know you didn't. That's the reason you should never play out here alone. That's why mama should never leave you here alone!"

The boy pointed to the floundering bulldog. "Chief's hurt."

Abraham doubted he could do anything for the animal. The bite of a pygmy rattler was seldom fatal to a grown man. But the venom might affect a dog—or a child—differently. He seized Jared's hand, pulled him away:

"If we leave him alone he'll be all right. Come with me and we'll look for your mother."

The wrath in Abraham's weary eyes made Jared obey without complaint.

II

"BABY? BABY,where are you—?"

Elizabeth's voice!

Running, he broke from the trees twenty feet from the river bank. When he saw her, a lump thickened in his throat.

He halted. Surveyed the area to be sure it was safe. He saw nothing to threaten the boy. He leaned his rifle against a maple, said:

"You wait here while I speak to your mother, understand? *Wait here.*"

Fidgeting, the boy nodded. Abraham turned around, grief-stricken at the sight of his wife wandering aimlessly through the reeds along the shore. The wind blew her dirty hair around her cheeks. Her plain, patched dress was soaked and mud-spattered from the knee downward.

Abraham deliberately made noise as he approached. She didn't seem to hear. Her fatigue-ringed blue eyes darted back and forth across the shallows:

"Baby? Baby, I know you're here. Don't hide from me."

"Elizabeth!"

The loudness penetrated her daze. She faced him, a peculiar half-smile curling her mouth. She hardly resembled the bright, fiery-spirited girl he'd taken into his bed in Boston. Barely into her twenties, she had become a pale, sagging old woman—

But she recognized him:

"Oh. Abraham dear. You've come back from the settlement."

He splashed toward her, his moccasins soaked in an instant. On the far bank of the Miami, the autumn-colored trees shimmered and flamed in the wind.

He gripped her arm. "Why did you leave Jared by himself? It isn't safe!"

"Please let go." She pried at his fingers with a cracked and reddened hand. "Please, Abraham. I only left him for a short time—"

"I shot a pygmy rattler up there. Right where the boy was playing!"

"Shot?" She shook her head. "I didn't hear any shot." Again that pleading smile. "But I've been busy searching for the baby."

His spine crawled. "What baby?"

"Ours, Abraham. Our baby—the first one. I don't remember the baby's name, but all at once, up in the cabin, I remembered the baby was lost on the river."

"You lost the baby on the Oh—" Sick and stunned, he couldn't continue.

"Please help me look, Abraham. I know the baby's here somewhere. Help me look before it's too dark—"

Tears started in the corners of his eyes. He fought to hold a rein on his emotions—the self-hate; the sadness. *How had this happened?*

He knew Elizabeth had been growing weaker and more distant month by month. But what had pushed her into this delusion? This retreat into a world of phantoms where the miscarried infant somehow cried out to her? Her mother's death? The hardships of the land? Both—?

Empty of anger, he curved his arm around her and tried to speak gently:

"It's growing dark. We should go back to the cabin."

"The baby's lost, Abraham!"

"I'm sure we'll find the baby tomorrow, when the sun's up. I'll help you search then if you'll come with me now."

She eyed the reeds and gleaming river. Then, with a sigh, she leaned against him:

"All right. I am tired. I would like to rest. I've been searching an hour or more."

In utter despair, he comforted her against his shoulder as they worked their way out of the shallows to solid ground. They walked up the shale slope to the tree where little Jared watched, white and wide-eyed.

The man, the woman and the boy plodded toward the cabin. Elizabeth's voice grew fainter in the shadows lengthening among the trees. She murmured sadly, absently, about the lost child that needed finding—

III

ABRAHAM LIGHTED one of the wall candles and tucked Elizabeth into bed. He got the fire going in the hearth, and then he and Jared left the cabin.

They hunted for Chief. They found him dead where he'd fallen. Abraham dug a shallow trench in the loamy soil. They laid the bulldog's body in it. Crying, Jared helped cover the grave with handfuls of earth.

They finished the work in almost total darkness. Abraham sheltered the weeping boy against his side on the way back to the cabin. He could feel little sorrow about the dog. Chief was old. Elizabeth was young. And she was dying too.

He knew some of the reasons: grueling work for which she wasn't suited; loneliness; the absence of amenities with which she'd grown up. Women grew old too soon on the frontier. Abraham saw such women every time he visited the settlement. Women of twenty-five or thirty with lusterless eyes, leathery hands,

browned, foul-smelling teeth. A few like Edna Clapper, were hardy enough to thrive. Those who weren't hardy, the land destroyed.

And I brought her here so she could be killed, Abraham thought as he approached the cabin. That was the moment he first admitted the land had beaten them.

He would not—*could* not—permit them to go on living as they were living now.

The unseen trees hissed in the wind, almost like laughter. He made up his mind that he'd find them a means of escape as soon as possible. He hated being defeated almost as much as he hated the land—

But accepting defeat was better than seeing his wife destroyed.

____IV

THE NEXT day was the Sabbath. Abraham opened the cabin door as soon as he got up. Elizabeth woke a few minutes later. The sight of the sunshine spilling onto the cabin floor seemed to put her in good spirits immediately.

She had been restless during the night. But she greeted him normally enough, making no reference to the incident on the river.

As they ate their morning meal, Abraham read a few verses from their Bible. Elizabeth listened with a cheerful expression. Yet he remained tense. At any moment he expected her to recall his pledge to search for the lost baby.

Nearly an hour went by with no mention of it. The nervousness persisted. He went for a stroll in the sunshine, kneading his knuckles against his chin as he walked.

God, what he'd give to be able to share the excitement and optimism reflected in the Saturday talk at Clapper's store. A few months before, a whole new century had opened. The successful settlers in the district discussed it with high hopes. President Washington's death the preceding year at age sixty-seven seemed to bring one era to an end and set a new and better one in motion.

A new president would be elected before this year was out. Many around Fort Hamilton predicted that Federalist John Adams was finished; would be replaced at last by a less aristocratic candidate—one who recognized the growing importance of the west and acted accordingly. The ideal man, of course, would be Mr. Jefferson.

Already there were sixteen states in the union. More would certainly be organized and admitted as the tide of migration swept on west beyond the Ohio country. The future looked splendid indeed—

Until you brought it down to a personal level, Abraham thought as he walked back into the cabin.

Elizabeth welcomed him with a smile. She was busy tending a skillet over the coals. Preparing the johnny-cake they'd eat for Sunday dinner even though they'd already eaten the same thing for breakfast. Jared sat silently in a corner, building bits of stick into a cabin. Abraham bent down to watch. The boy accepted his father's presence silently, without a smile.

Soon almost two hours had passed, with no reference to yesterday. Abraham relaxed a little. Apparently she'd forgotten—or, more correctly, the memory had somehow been locked away again in the recesses of her mind.

Still, he had been thoroughly shaken last night. He didn't intend to forget his silent vow to change their situation.

How he'd do it, he didn't know. As a first step, he'd ask advice from his friend Daniel Clapper. During next Saturday's visit to the settlement.

Having decided just that much buoyed him a little; it was a positive step. Out of it would come an eventual answer.

Not too late, he hoped.

V

"IT'S YOUR business how much you slosh down," Daniel Clapper said the following Saturday night. "But Daniel Junior's off at the camp meetin' with the girl he's courtin', an' I'm damned if I want to carry you home."

Abraham tilted the jug and poured more whiskey into a small earthenware cup. "I'll make it fine on my own, Daniel."

Clapper looked skeptical.

Abraham had already consumed two cups of whiskey while waiting for the other man to close up the store for the night and join him behind the curtain that separated business from daily living.

In addition to the family's everyday furniture and utensils, and curtained areas for sleeping, the rear half of the large cabin was crowded with goods for which Clapper had no room up front: boxes of slates and slate pencils; small kegs of gunpowder; cartons of foolscap paper—even a fresh shipment of books. Waiting for Clapper, Abraham browsed through them. He discovered three copies of a Kent and Son edition of *Pilgrim's Progress*. The moralistic work was popular among the settlers who could read.

He held the book a few moments, staring at it, then replaced it in its box, wishing he could put memories of Boston aside as easily.

Having built his cabin within sight of the others that formed the settlement around the palisaded walls of Fort Hamilton, Daniel Clapper had allowed himself the luxury of window openings with shutters. Away from a settlement, windows were a disadvantage. They could let in marauders along with sunlight and fresh air.

Now the red-bearded storekeeper pushed open one pair of shutters next to the stone fireplace. Abraham drew a deep breath between gulps of whiskey. The blazing logs in the hearth made the room stifling.

Clapper seemed to sense something important on Abraham's mind. His forehead furrowed as he watched his guest drink. Abraham didn't say anything. Clapper gazed outside again as a squad of mounted soldiers clattered toward the fort.

In the distance the horizon glowed orange. The light came from torches around the camp meeting tent. The week-long event was being conducted by a Bible-brandishing Methodist evangelist who'd ridden up from the state of Kentucky. People had driven rigs or come on horseback from as far away as thirty or forty miles, just to attend tonight's final meeting. Abraham could hear the shouts of praise and joy as the crowd replied to the evangelist's exhortations.

Clapper's wife Rachel and his daughter Danetta, as well as Daniel Junior and his young lady, were attending the four-hour service that combined hymn singing, hell-fire preaching, public confession of sin and the evangelist's promise of salvation. *Maybe I should be there,* Abraham thought, pouring one more drink—

Clapper stayed his hand:

"Listen, I been waitin' ten minutes! Speak your piece!"

"I need to ask your advice."

"Ask away."

"The reason is—I'm going to give up the farm."

With a sigh, Clapper ambled to the table. He poured a little whiskey for himself, then combed fingers through his long red beard.

"Figured it might be comin' to that. Of late you been lookin' mightly spiritless."

"It's Elizabeth I'm worried about. She—well—she's been acting strange."

"Expect you want to talk about it. Else you wouldn't bring it up, am I right?"

Slumping in his chair, Abraham nodded. He poured out the story, finishing: "She was hunting for the baby she lost on the Ohio, not Jared."

"Yep, I caught that drift."

Abraham peered into his cup. "I don't even know whether it was a boy or a girl."

"Don't know myself. If Miz Rachel knows, she's never said—and I ain't asked. I *do* know what she'll discuss and what she won't. Women things is on the won't list."

"I don't suppose a doctor could explain what's wrong with Elizabeth. Something in her mind, maybe. Her father was supposedly half crazy."

"Never heard that before."

"It's true."

"I told you once I thought she was a mite frail—"

"I remember."

"Why'd she ever agree to come out here?"

"Oh, a lot of reasons. I went along with them. Obviously we both made a mistake."

He filled his cup again, ignoring Clapper's frown.

"The point is," he said, "I've got to remedy the mistake before things get worse."

"So you're puttin' the farm up for sale."

"I think I should be able to get rid of it, don't you?"

"Lord yes! On my last trip south, the Ohia was blamed near solid with boats."

Abraham grimaced. "We're already being passed by—I saw that for myself when I went with you to Cincinnati."

"Don't get to thinkin' it's *too* civilized around here," Clapper cautioned. "The Shawnee, they're still burnin' farms and stirrin' up trouble. I musta seen a dozen of 'em when I was out peddlin' the first of the week. They been a lot more active ever since ol' Tecumseh's brother set up his town on the Wabash. Soldiers at the fort say Tecumseh an' the Prophet are preachin' some sort of wild scheme to pull all the tribes together, from New York State clean down into the Creek Nations."

"Why?"

"To push out the white people that took Injun land, why else?"

"The tribes signed a treaty with Wayne—"

"Not that Tecumseh. 'Cording to what you told me, he never set foot in the door at Greenville."

"That's true. We're off the subject. I'm going to sell the farm, but I don't know the next step. I hate like hell to crawl back to Boston and tell my father I failed."

"This father of yours—the one what printed the Bunyan book in the box yonder—he a pretty strong-minded soul, is he?"

"A banker friend of his once said my father could make Satan look indecisive."

"Sounds like an all-right sort. You an' Elizabeth *could* go back an' see him if things really got bad, couldn't you?"

"I'd rather not. I was hoping maybe I could find a way to make a living here in the settlement. Elizabeth might be more comfortable with more people around."

Quietly, Clapper asked. "Did the two o' you ever sit yourselves down and decide what it is you want?"

Abraham shook his head. "Pointless. We don't know. I've come to believe what you told me on the ark, Daniel—that most people who chase after some vague hope are only running away from problems."

"Absolutely right! Mebbe I got one answer for you, though—"

Abraham noticed a peculiar glint in Clapper's eyes. The storekeeper fingered his beard a while before he continued:

"The urge is on me again, Abraham. I want to pick up an' head out. Injuns or no, this part o' the country's gettin' crowded. Ten years ago there wasn't more'n three or four thousand souls settled north o' the river. Now I hear there's ten times that many. People are sayin' there'll soon be enough folks in the territory to make Ohia state number seventeen. I need elbow room, Abraham! Next spring, I'm goin'!"

"Does your family know?"

"Miz Edna's been watchin' me mighty close lately. She can feel it comin'. You're the first to hear, though."

Abraham thought a minute. "Are you suggesting maybe I could take over the store?"

"Yep."

"I don't know as I'd be any better running a place like this than I am at running a farm, Daniel."

"Hell, it's easy! Everythin' practically falls off the shelves—"

"Except that china I traded to you."

"Well, that's fancy stuff. The necessary things sell themselves—an' like you say, Miz Elizabeth might be easier in her mind livin' closer to the fort. Havin' womenfolk to visit with regular—"

Abraham did see how the plan could work. With a little more animation, he said:

"If the pattern of the last couple of years holds next year too, there'll be new families arriving in the spring. I could sell the farm to one of them, buy you out and pay you every penny I owe you—"

"I'll only sell you the building an' half my goods. I'll need some stocks to set up when I get where I'm headed."

"Got any idea where that is?"

Clapper grinned. "Nope. I'll light there same way as I lighted here. But once I take a notion to go, I want to git—fast. So I won't gouge you on the price, an' it'll be a fair deal all around."

For the first time in weeks, Abraham laughed aloud:

"By God I think I've found the answer, thanks to you."

Now it was Clapper's turn to stare into his whiskey cup. "Hope so."

"You don't think I have?"

The big storekeeper's eyes locked on Abraham's. "I don't want to discourage you, boy. You need *en*couragement—"

"But you think we won't find living here any easier than on the farm?"

"Easier, maybe. Not better. Even this far west, I see a mighty lot o' people movin' on, Abraham. Movin' on for the fifth an' sixth time—"

"I think Elizabeth can be happy here. I've got to believe that, Daniel. The only other choices are to go on west—and she's not strong enough—or to head home to Boston—and I'm not ready to give up *that* completely. The settlement will make everything right—"

"Sure," Clapper nodded. "Forget what I said."

A hymn thundered by scores of voices drifted from the camp meeting. Clapper squeezed his friend's shoulder:

"What's true for me ain't necessarily true for you. Things'll get a lot better if you move in here. Provided you don't pickle your liver in the meantime—gimme that cup!"

"No, let's have one more. To celebrate."

Abraham poured whiskey to the brim, raised the cup.

"I give you Mr. Abraham Kent, merchant."

Daniel Clapper raised his own cup but for some reason wouldn't look Abraham squarely in the eye.

VI

ELIZABETH GREETED Abraham's plan with complete agreement and overwhelming enthusiasm. As winter approached, she began taking better care of herself. She watched Jared more attentively; Abraham was busy making frequent trips to the settlement mill. There he had his corn ground, retaining what the family would need during the cold months and selling off the rest.

There were no repetitions of the search for the lost child.

During January and February, Elizabeth kept busy cooking, mending, doing laundry—and teaching Jared how to recognize and pronounce part of the alphabet. Watching his mother print large block letters on a slate, the little boy seemed happier than ever before. He enjoyed trying to say the names of the letters correctly. Elizabeth, surprisingly patient, encouraged him. Before long he had progressed to the letter M.

At least once an evening, Elizabeth's conversation returned to the forthcoming change in their lives. Abraham was glad. She was affectionate again. Amenable to lovemaking. Several times she clasped him with an ardor that reminded him of the first night she came secretly to his room.

According to the way Abraham figured it, new families should be starting up the Great Miami about the first of April, either to squat or to settle on ground whose deed they held. At the end of February he began thinking about the wording of a notice for the settlement's public message board. He felt confident that if he could find some squatters with money, he could convince them that buying his prime bottom land was a better investment than occupying free land someone else might eventually claim. Most good river acreage in the district was already taken, and that was in his favor.

The first of April 1801, began to loom as a magic date: the end of their hardships; the start of a new, more rewarding life. Abraham consciously avoided

thinking about Clapper's dour philosophy. For Elizabeth's sake, he couldn't permit himself to believe that disillusionment always waited, no matter how far a man roamed, or where he settled.

Occasional traders working their way through the ice-bound forests brought trickles of news:

Congress had at last convened in the district christened Columbia. There, the new capital city was rising, named in honor of the country's first president.

The unwieldly electoral college system had turned January's national election into a shambles. Jefferson and Aaron Burr deadlocked in a first-place tie with seventy-three votes each. John Adams, his popularity waning, ran third with sixty-five.

The tie vote threw the contest to the pro-Federalist House of Representatives. After thirty-six ballots and much behind-the-scenes maneuvering, Jefferson was named president in February, with Burr vice president. Whereupon, the traders said, certain devout Federalist ladies in New England buried their Bibles in their gardens, fearing secret agents of the "godless" chief executive would seize and burn them.

The results of the election reached the Great Miami in mid-March, just as the weather turned unusually warm and sunny. Elizabeth took to singing as she worked around the cabin. Abraham too was anticipating the day that symbolized a fresh start for the Kents.

Six days before the month ended, the Indians came.

3
The Burning

SHE TOUCHED his arm in the chilly darkness. Her fingers closed, rousing him from the fog of sleep. He felt her homespun nightdress touching his forearm; heard the murmur of the March winds. He heard other sounds he didn't recognize.

"Abraham—"

Her anxiety brought him upright, knuckling his eyes.

"What—?"

She covered his mouth with her other hand. "Be still and listen! There's someone outside."

His mind sorted out sounds: Jared breathing on the small bedstead he had built in the opposite corner; the low of the ox; the thump of a hoof on the side of a stall—perhaps that was Henrietta Knox.

Then, alert and alarmed, he made out a human voice, barely audible.

There was a louder thump, as of someone stumbling against a wall. Two voices overlapped one another; the second was angry.

The ox bellowed. Abraham wiped his upper lip.

"They're out by the barn," he said.

"Can you hear what they're saying?"

"Not clearly. But I don't think they're white men."

Elizabeth covered her face. "Oh God help us—"

"*Sssh!*"

As quietly as possible, he crawled out of bed. He struggled into his trousers. With the tail of his nightshirt still hanging out, he pulled on his boots. He guessed the time to be dawn. A thin line of light defined the edges of the cabin door.

His heart lubbed loudly in his inner ear. He crept toward his rifle propped against the wall, listening for the intruders. Either the men were being exceptionally quiet now or they were gone—

Another bellow from the ox told him his hope was false. His throat felt parched. He returned to Elizabeth. Knelt and whispered:

"Whatever you do, don't wake the boy. And stay inside with the door barred."

He could just discern the white oval of her face as she leaned close: "You're not going out there—?"

"Yes, I'd better. Maybe I can frighten them off."

"But I heard at least two voices!"

"Perhaps all they want is food."

"You mustn't go—you've only one charge in your rifle—"

"And this."

He groped a hand toward the puncheon table, found his long-bladed Barlow knife of English steel. He tucked the knife in his right boot.

"I'll be all right. They'll probably run as soon as I show myself—a lot of them don't own rifles or muskets."

"But some do. I've heard people at the settlement say—"

"*Don't raise your voice!* I've got to see what they're up to—suppose they take a notion to fire the cabin? I tell you I'll be all right," he finished, sounding more certain than he felt.

He patted her hand, stole toward the door. He raised the latchstring slowly to free the bar from its bracket. He inched the plank door open.

"Lock yourself in, Elizabeth."

He slipped outside.

He leaned against the cabin wall, drawing long, deep gulps of air. The leafless trees looked black and stark against the silver of the eastern horizon. A warbler trilled down by the river. The water purled over stones.

He heard the soft *chunk* of the bar being lowered back in place. Now he could move. Cautiously, he advanced to the corner of the cabin, then on around. The chimney jutting from the end of the cabin concealed the barn. He leaned toward the edge of the chimney, risked a glance—

He saw a black rectangle. Someone had opened the barn door. A moment later, a man laughed softly inside.

Questions tumbled through his mind. Were there really only two? How were they armed? He wished for his pistols, hanging on pegs inside. But they were useless, he remembered. He hadn't loaded or primed them since the last time he fired them—

So it came down to the ball in his rifle, and his long knife. Against whatever the intruders might be carrying.

He decided to wait them out. Running to the barn a clear target, would be foolish. He leaned his forehead against the chimney logs, listening.

He heard shuffling feet. An occasional word growled in an unfamiliar language. The two animals kept stamping. Time seemed to stretch out as the warbler sang down by the shore.

The light brightened. The outline of the barn became clearer. Suddenly Abraham sucked in a sibilant breath. A man had appeared in the barn door—

An Indian, right enough. Fat and toothless and old. His huge belly stretched his filthy army coat. The coat had been stolen from some other white man, Abraham assumed.

The old Indian trailed an ancient musket from one hand. A bedraggled wild turkey feather stuck up from the greased gray of his braided hair. He waved disgustedly for the benefit of someone still invisible in the barn.

Heart knocking faster than ever, Abraham kept one eye pressed to the chimney corner, hoping the poor light would prevent the Indian from spotting him. A second man lurched outside.

This one was younger, with a hard brown face and eyes like black stones. He wore hide trousers and shirt. His only visible weapon was a spiked war club.

From the way the younger Indian weaved on his feet, Abraham guessed the pair had stolen whiskey somewhere, and now wanted more. He presumed both were Shawnee or Miami, but he couldn't be positive. If he were lucky, they might abandon their search and slip away to try their thievery in another place—

The younger one barked words Abraham didn't understand. He lifted his spiked club, pointed it toward the cabin. The meaning was unmistakable.

The fat one seemed hesitant. He finally shook his head growled a reply that angered his companion. The younger one started walking—straight toward the jutting chimney where Abraham crouched.

He had to scare them off. But he didn't dare expend his one rifle ball to do it. He screwed up his nerve, took another deep breath—

Stepped from concealment, the rifle aimed at the breastbone of the younger Indian.

The fat one yelped in surprise. Abraham's nerve almost crumbled away when a cold smile curved the mouth of the younger one. The Indian was still a little drunk—

Abraham had seldom seen such hateful eyes.

"*Meneluh*," the Indian said.

Abraham shook his head to show he didn't understand. The young brave's smile vanished.

"*Meneluh, meneuh!*" A sharp gesture with his spiked club. "Drink!"

Abraham drew in a quick breath. Though the young Indian articulated English with difficulty, at least he understood it; perhaps from encounters with itinerant traders. Certain less than scrupulous white men had discovered a new and profitable market by introducing alcohol among the tribes. Heedless of long-term consequences, such traders were frequent visitors at the Indian villages, supplying rum and whiskey in return for pelts. If the savage had learned bits of English in such meetings, at least Abraham had a chance of communicating. Trying to do that was better than launching into a fight.

Aware of how his legs trembled, he shook his head several times, then said slowly and clearly:

"No whiskey."

The young brave grinned. "Whis-key. *Meneluh!*"

Abraham shook his head again. "No. No. I do not have any whiskey." He bobbed the rifle's muzzle at the trees. "Go. Go into the woods. Get off my land." He pointed at the ground. "This is mine." He jabbed his thumb against his chest. "Mine. The Shawnee can only hunt where there are no settlers—"

The scowling Indian clearly didn't comprehend the last word.

"No white men. White—" Abraham touched his face. The Shawnee continued to scowl. Abraham wasn't certain whether the next thought would have any meaning: "The treaty says—"

"Trea-ty!" The young Shawnee spat on the ground. Then he pronounced a name Abraham couldn't decipher.

"What?"

"Panther-Passing-Across. Panther-Passing-Across curses white man's trea-ty. Curses *you!*"

"Who—who is the Panther?" Abraham asked, still stunned by the violent reaction.

"Chief. Tecumseh. Other—" A garbled, obviously derogatory word. "—smoked *calumet* with Wayne." Derisively, he pretended to puff an invisible pipe. "Not Shawanese. Not Tecumseh. This land not his—not yours—not any man's to—" A hand darted outward. "Trade. Moneto gave to *all!*"

Another angry arc of the club made Abraham start. The fat old Indian giggled, revealing stumps of teeth in wrinkled gums.

"Moneto made land for all!" the young man repeated. "Cannot be—" Again the outward gesture. "Given." He pointed his club at the breaking light in the east. "Can *kesathwa* be given?" Supple fingers pantomimed falling rain. "Can *gimewane* be given?" He shook his head. "So land cannot be given. Not by one—not by many!"

The Shawnee began walking forward, sensing Abraham's gut fear now, and playing on it. He shook his head again, angrily. Then:

"Woods people who took Wayne *calumet*—sat with Wayne—" More unintelligible phrases, savagely spoken and plainly showing what the young brave thought of those Indians who had negotiated with the general. "—did not own this." He stamped the earth. "Moneto's land. For all. If we want—stay. If we want—go." A sly smile. "Look there—" The club jabbed toward the cabin. "Whis-key."

Abraham raised his rifle to his shoulder.

"No. I'll kill you. Do you understand? I'll *kill* you."

The Shawnee understood. Abraham jerked the rifle barrel toward the fields. "Get away! Get off this—"

He was unprepared for the sudden whipping motion of the brave's arm. The war club tumbled end over end toward his head. He lunged out of the way, stumbled, fell on his left side as the club struck the chimney logs and bounced away.

The young Shawnee reached the club in three long strides. He raised it over his head with both hands, brought it forward and down, the spike aimed at Abraham's torso. On the ground, Abraham braced the rifle against his hip and fired.

Inside the cabin, Elizabeth screamed. The ball only slowed the downward arc of the war club. Abraham rolled to the left. The bone spike raked his shoulder—

The club dropped from the Indian's hand. He seized the chimney logs for support, slowly sank to his knees. The shot had blown away his left eye and part of his cheek.

Vomit rose in Abraham's throat. The young Shawnee's trousers darkened as he urinated uncontrollably. On his knees, he moaned and slumped forward against the chimney. As he sagged all the way to the ground, his face left gore and bits of bone on the logs—

Abraham struggled to his feet, pulling his knife in case the fat Indian attacked.

Marginally aware of a second voice raised in the cabin—Jared's—he heard a sound that turned his bowels to water:

The rattle of the door latch.

"Abraham?"

Dammit, he'd warned her to stay inside! Always, always she defied advice, did as she wished—

"Abraham?" she called again. She came running around the corner of the cabin, hair streaming at her shoulders.

"Elizabeth, stay ba—"

The fat Indian's musket roared.

Abraham was facing his wife. He saw her literally fly backwards as the ball hit.

For a moment he stood numb, his gaze swinging back and forth between Elizabeth and the Indian. His wife lay on her back, a black hole oozing blood onto her right temple. The toothless old man lowered the musket as a curl of smoke drifted from the muzzle.

Howling, Abraham ran at the Indian, knife raised. The Indian wheeled and lumbered off around the barn, his grunts of fright trailing behind him.

Abraham pursued him only a dozen steps. Then he halted. Shock set his teeth to chattering. The Barlow knife fell from his fingers. He faced about; faced the sight of Elizabeth sprawled in her nightdress, her mouth open and her eyes too—

He knelt beside her, both palms on her cheeks. He heard Jared's voice from the cabin doorway:

"What's wrong, papa? Why is mama lying there?"

"Go back inside! *Close the door!*"

Frightened by the wild look of his father's face, Jared vanished. Abraham rocked back and forth on his knees, rubbing his wife's face:

"Elizabeth. Elizabeth—"

It became sobbing:

"Elizabeth, no. No, Elizabeth—"

The brightening dawn only heightened her waxy pallor; accented the color of the blood that flowed down past her eye to her ear, clotting in her fair hair. She had washed her hair to shiny brilliance just last night—

Still kneeling, Abraham cradled her corpse in his arms, speaking her name over and over. The cabin door stood slightly ajar. He never noticed.

Nor did he see the huge eyes of a small boy staring at the blood on his mother's face.

___II

IN THE pleasant March sunlight, Abraham walked the four miles downriver with Jared. His step was slow, his expression stony. The boy kept glancing up at his father, but never spoke.

When Abraham had finally carried Elizabeth's body into the cabin, Jared had repeated his questions. Abraham answered in a dull voice, saying Elizabeth had gone away from them and would not be coming back.

Jared's face showed his confusion: When Elizabeth's still form lay before him, how was it possible for her to have left the cabin—?

Then and now, as Abraham and Jared walked, a forbidding expression on the

father's face kept the son from voicing any of the fear and turmoil the morning's events had produced.

People stared at Abraham's white face and feverish eyes as he led the boy to Clapper's.

Waiting on a customer, Daniel Clapper immediately recognized that something dire had taken place. He bid the customer a quick good morning and followed Abraham into the rear of the cabin.

In a monotone, Abraham reported what had happened—producing a burst of tears from Clapper's wife. She recovered quickly. She hugged Jared to her shapeless bosom, drew the boy aside to comfort him.

Abraham said to Clapper, "I'm going back to take care of her body and to collect my things."

"Let me go with you, Abraham. You're in no state to—"

"Yes I am," Abraham said, his face animating into fury. He pushed Clapper's hand aside. "I'm going alone."

Seated on a chair with Jared on her lap, Mrs. Clapper said to her husband: "Don't let him, Daniel."

"I'm all right!" Abraham insisted. "I'll pack what Jared and I need for traveling and be right back."

Clapper goggled. "My God, boy—your wife just got shot an' you're goin' traveling?"

Abraham's eyes burned. "What good can I do her by staying here?"

A long silence. Then Clapper asked:

"Where you goin'?"

"East. Home. Away from this accursed place. I killed her bringing her out here."

"A couple of drunken Shawnee killed—"

"I did."

"Listen, Abraham, that little boy's scairt to death—look at him!"

But Abraham wouldn't. Jared burrowed his face in Edna Clapper's shoulder, began to cry.

Clapper stepped close to Abraham, whispered, "I know it's a grievous thing, Abraham, a grievous an' terrible thing. But you're carryin' on like a crazy man. You got to take hold of—"

Clapper stopped. Abraham's face was like a death's-head.

"I'm going *alone*, Daniel. I'll be back presently for Jared. Don't chase after me or you'll get hurt."

Pivoting, he ripped the curtain aside and disappeared into the front of the store.

No one followed.

III

THERE WAS a demon in Abraham Kent that morning; a demon whose hate lent him the strength he needed to do what had to be done.

First he dragged the young Shawnee down to the river. Keeping his eyes away from the destroyed face, he lifted the corpse and flung it in the shallows. He broke off a tree limb, waded out and prodded the body into the current. When it was floating, moving slowly in the sun-dazzled water Abraham threw the branch away and returned to the barn where he loaded his rifle.

The barn smelled of fresh manure. Abraham sighted down the muzzle to a spot between the horns of Henrietta Knox. The cow kept chewing slowly. Abraham began to tremble. At last he gave up, unable to pull the trigger.

He led Henrietta Knox outside. The ground was damp. The night's frost had melted, moistening the black earth. He rubbed the cow's back a moment, then let go of her rope and walked away. In similar fashion he brought the ox to the field and left it standing.

Inside the cabin, he spent an hour with Elizabeth.

He sat on the puncheon floor beside the bedstead, his eyes closed, his hand straying to her face occasionally. Soon her skin became so cold that touching it was unbearable. He rose, carried the newly packed knapsack out into the sunlight.

He deposited the knapsack on top of a stump that still bore the black traces of last fall's burning. He brought his rifle, shot bag and powder horn to the same stump. Back in the cabin, he used flint and steel to light tinder beneath the hearth logs.

When the fire was burning well, he broke off one of the pole legs of the table. He thrust the leg into the flames for a minute. Then he set the table afire.

As soon as it caught, he bent and kissed Elizabeth's cheek.

Coughing in the smoke, he walked outside and torched the barn. Then he picked up his gear.

He sniffed the fire as he walked toward the track leading to the settlement. He heard the cabin walls beginning to crackle, but he wouldn't look back at the puffs of black smoke. The smell was enough to remind him of how he'd erred; failed; lacked the strength and wisdom to deny Elizabeth's wish to start a new life in the west. The smell was enough to remind him of how much he hated this barbarous land that permitted only the hardiest to survive, destroying the others.

Henrietta Knox mooed at him as he hurried by the field where she stood in the glare of noonday. He wouldn't look at her either, nor could he have seen her clearly if he had. Tears blurred his eyes.

He hated the earth under his feet. God, how he hated it—!

And himself.

Blind to everything except his consuming need to escape, he stumbled on toward Fort Hamilton as the treetops around the cabin began to burn. Clouds of smoke billowed into the noon sky, shot through with fire.

IV

THE UNKEMPT strangers trudging up Beacon Street on a hot morning in early July, 1801, attracted the attention of everyone from housemaids bustling on errands to gentlemen climbing into carriages to be off for the day's business. There were whispers and stares—the pair hardly resembled Bostonians from this part of town—or any other!

One was a heavily bearded man of twenty-five or so. The other was a tow-haired boy whose face looked pinched and gray. The man carried a grubby knapsack on back straps, and a rifle in the crook of his left arm. He held the boy's hand tightly. It was hard to tell which of them wore the filthier coat and fringed trousers.

The pair caused no end of curiosity as they climbed the stoop of one of the

most substantial homes on the entire street. The man let the knocker fall three times.

A mobcapped girl opened the door. Abraham didn't recognize her.

The maid took a step backward, overpowered by Abraham's stench. He smelled rank for good reason. He'd obtained a small sum of money from a hasty sale of the farm to a Fort Hamilton speculator. The money had run out two weeks ago, as they approached Philadelphia. Abraham and his son had made the rest of the journey on foot, sleeping in the open, begging or stealing food where they could, and never bathing.

The maid's reaction was automatic:

"Beggars are not allowed at the front—"

"This is my home. I am Abraham Kent."

The maid caught her breath. She recognized the name. But her face showed her doubt and bewilderment. How could this greasy, bearded person in frontier garb be Abraham Kent?

The man's brown eyes piercing into hers were so terrifying, she didn't dare speak the question aloud.

"I wish to see my father. I wish to come in—*will you stop goggling?* I *live* here!"

He thrust her aside roughly, dragging the little boy after him like a mindless dwarf. In the middle of the front hall he put down his knapsack and rifle, wiped his nose with the back of his hand and demanded:

"Where is my father? And my brother? Have they gone to the firm already?"

The maid stammered, "Yes, Mr. Gilbert left an hour ago—"

"Is my father about the house, then?"

"Sir—sir—"

"What the hell's wrong with you, girl?"

She'd remembered some talk she'd heard about the whereabouts of Philip Kent's son. That would explain the crude, hideous clothing. She swallowed hard.

"If—if you are Mr. Abraham Kent from the west—"

His mouth twisted. "Don't I smell like it?"

"I know Mr. Gilbert wrote you two months ago—"

"Wrote what? My boy and I have been traveling for over three months. Any letter that was sent to me two months ago, I never received."

So weary he could barely stand, and maddened beyond endurance by the maid's fluttery behavior, Abraham raised his fist to her:

"Damn you, speak out! Where is my father?"

"Dead, sir," the girl whispered. "He died in his sleep on the thirtieth of April."

4
Problems of a Modernist

IN THE material as well as the intellectual sphere, Mr. Gilbert Kent was an avowed modernist.

He deemed that orientation eminently suitable to the new century, and to the

rapid changes taking place in the nation. He refused to close his mind to ideas simply because they had never been tried before, or were foreign to his experience.

His Beacon Street home, for example, boasted not one but three of the innovative banjo wall clocks introduced the previous year by Mr. Willard of Roxbury. He had adopted two new and novel fashions—regular bathing and the donning of clean underwear every day. He hadn't gone so far as to embrace the Napoleonic custom of a daily bath; once every two or three days seemed sufficient in a city that considered bathing the entire body bizarre.

His apparel would have found favor in fashionable circles in Britain. At eleven o'clock on a warm morning in midsummer, 1803, he approached Kent and Son wearing clothes that could only be termed impeccable:

His coat was one of the new, longer gentleman's models, lacking the severe cutaway so popular with conservative members of the business community. His shirt was linen, custom-cut, and featured the new detachable collar. His waistcoat was cut low to show off his stock and shirt ruffles. The basic ensemble was completed by snug boots over long pantaloons—the very combination said to be preferred by the elegant George Brummel, whose sartorial preferences were religiously aped by all in England's upper classes—including Brummel's intimate friend, the prince-regent.

To top off the outfit, Gilbert wore a dark, soft hat of beaver, the brim drooping slightly at front and back but rolled on the sides. The jaunty hat bobbed up and down briskly as he made his way through the crowds this humid morning. Most of the better dressed people on the street recognized the owner of Kent and Son. Those who didn't know him personally identified him from his costume precisely the way he wanted to be identified—as a modernist.

Perhaps in reaction to his late father's Federalist bias, Gilbert Kent was that rare creature—a New Englander who was also a Jeffersonian. After much thought and study, he had concluded the president was correct in his contention that all men, while perhaps not equal in their abilities, were certainly equal in their rights. He was convinced the country should be governed not by a coterie of highly educated aristocrats—to which group he would certainly have belonged by reasons of birth, wealth and talent—but by the consent of all, high-born or otherwise. He knew by heart—and despised—Alexander Hamilton's cynical expression of the opposing Federalist philosophy:

All communities divide themselves into the few and the many. The first are rich and well-born, the other the mass of the people. The people are turbulent and changing; they seldom determine rightly. Give, therefore, to the first class a distinct, permanent share in the government. They will check the unsteadiness of the second.

It was a persuasive argument, Gilbert recognized. But in his eyes it was nothing less than evil, for if it were espoused wholeheartedly, then the principles of American liberty became a sham and a deceit.

Gilbert's view wasn't a popular one in Boston. In the growing number of states in the west, and in their swelling populations, the great merchant families saw a threat to New England's traditional control of the nation's affairs. Gilbert Kent believed that to serve, not to control, was the proper function of the government in Washington—and the duty of the private citizen of more than average means. A subtle difference but, to his way of thinking, a crucial one.

Not that Gilbert Kent had anything against being successful in the private sector. He watched the Kent ledgers closely, usually examining them at midnight

or later, at home—he seldom slept more than four hours a night, to his wife's annoyance—and he seized every prudent opportunity to expand the family wealth. Indeed, he had just come from a meeting with that purpose.

The meeting had been held at the Rothman Bank. It was attended by a consortium of rich gentlemen of Boston. His father's old Revolutionary War comrade, Mr. Royal Rothman, presided. Before the meeting broke up, Gilbert pledged one hundred thousand dollars of risk capital to help finance the Blackstone Company, a new cotton-spinning firm going into competition with Slater's decade-old spinning works on the Blackstone River in Pawtucket, Rhode Island.

In a private session with Rothman after the other investors left, Gilbert informed the banker that he wanted his partnership to be a silent one. His shares were to be held by the bank so that future profits would go directly to the child his wife was now carrying, as well as to any other issue of their marriage.

Rothman naturally asked the reason for the arrangement. Gilbert gave a candid reply. He wanted his wife to have her just share of his estate when he died—

"And don't say it's too soon to think of that, Royal. I've already lived more than half the lifetime of many men."

"Go on."

"My wife has a number of good qualities, but self-denial isn't one of them. She buys whatever she wishes for herself or the house—heedless of the cost. I don't mean to sound unkind, but I don't believe she could manage and conserve a large sum successfully. I'd feel more comfortable if a part of the Kent estate was held in reserve, where she could never touch it. Indeed, I don't even want her to know about it. The profits of the printing house should be ample to sustain her should something happen to me."

"I wish I were as optimistic about the success of the Blackstone Company as you seem to be," Rothman observed with a wry expression.

"Oh, I'm very optimistic. Textiles will soon become the heart of New England's economy—along with shipping."

"The bank will naturally honor your request about the confidentiality of the shares."

"I'll visit my attorney next week and have him draw up the legal papers."

"Old Benbow senior is going blind. He should retire and turn your affairs over to his son."

"His mind's as alert as ever. He'll live to be ninety."

"Which you may not—at the pace you drive yourself."

Gilbert ignored him, using a quill to scribble *Benbow & Benbow* on a slip of paper. He tucked the slip in his waistcoat pocket and stood up, extending his hand:

"To the Blackstone Company. May it enrich my children and yours."

"It almost died a-borning," Rothman said with a thin smile. "I admire your progressive spirit, Gilbert. But I fear some of the other gentlemen found it incomprehensible—not to say dangerous."

Gilbert shrugged. "They gave in."

"Because you refused to commit Kent money otherwise."

"No, not until they agreed unconditionally to provide schooling for the children who'll be hired to operate the spinning machinery. I'd actually prefer to hire adults—"

"At least you're realistic enough to understand that's unprofitable. Children can be had for a fraction of adult wages."

"Still, it bothers my conscience."

"The other gentlemen salved it for you. Gave in to your demands for a free school—"

"Gave in grudgingly! I tell you, Royal, one day we'll have to face the question of profits at the expense of people. Children shouldn't be working twelve, fourteen, sixteen hours a day—"

"And one man should not own another?" Rothman added, having heard it all before.

"Yes, there'll be a confrontation on the slave question too, you mark me."

"I wish you wouldn't suggest we're somehow involved in slavery!"

"The next thing to it."

"Would you do away with factories, then?"

"How could I? They're being built everywhere."

"My dear boy, you're unreasonable! If a child takes a job at the Blackstone Company, that's entirely voluntary!"

"When a family is poor but much too large, and the young must be put to work at seven or eight or face starvation—you call that voluntary?"

"It's an imperfect world, Gilbert. We can either refuse to deal with it altogether, or content ourselves with altering it a little at a time. The trouble with you is, you've a strong streak of idealism *and* a sharp business sense. As the factory system grows, those two sides of your nature are becoming incompatible. Today you were lucky. You satisfied both."

Gilbert sighed. "I suppose it's the best that can be done. You will remember about the shares?"

"Certainly."

"I'll have Benbow senior call on you to settle the details—provided there's no reneging on the school!"

"Don't worry, I'll see that doesn't happen," Rothman assured him.

"I insist it doesn't."

"I know," the banker sighed. "In some ways, you are a very radical fellow."

It was true. But he was honest with himself about it. Much of what he thought and said and did sprang from a solid core of conviction. At the same time, his modernism was a mechanism, deliberately employed to show his much older peers in the business world that he was their match; perhaps even a step ahead—

Gilbert had been thrust into unexpected control of Kent and Son when his father died two years earlier. For a young man of eighteen to be in charge of his own affairs was not at all unusual. For a young man of eighteen to be solely responsible for a large and growing fortune as well as a prestigious publishing company was highly unusual. Therefore Gilbert had to demonstrate to the world— and to himself—that he was in every way capable of accepting the responsibility.

In a way it was fortunate that he had been a frail child. Of necessity, most of his time had been devoted to sedentary pursuits, chiefly reading. A year at Harvard before Philip's death only demonstrated to Gilbert that he'd already learned much more than his professors could teach him.

Close association with his father during adolescence had familiarized him with every phase of printing house operation long before Philip's sudden and sad demise. Philip had died resenting Abraham's decision to carve a new life for himself in the west. But Gilbert was there, ready and eager to take up the reins—

So, at age twenty, the modernist made his way along Boston's crowded thoroughfares until he came in sight of the familiar gold-lettered signboard with a tea-bottle design. He felt in excellent spirits until he reached the main entrance.

There, in the shadow of the swaying sign, he saw several large, dark splotches on the cobbles. His pale face lost its aura of good humor.

Tall and extremely slender—at nearly six feet he was a phenomenon in the Kent family—he ducked his head to keep his beaver hat from being knocked off by the sign and rushed through the front door to learn the cause of bloodstains at Kent and Son's doorstep.

II

THE PRESSES for the book-publishing part of the business still occupied the main floor. But now, instead of the four wooden flatbeds Gilbert remembered from childhood, six presses with cast iron frames crowded the long room. Gilbert had imported them from London.

Perfected in 1798 by the Earl of Stanhope, the new presses were operated by the familiar screw lever. But the iron framework all but eliminated breakdowns due to main members warping and splitting. Additionally, the iron could bear a greater load, critical to the inking and printing of the woodcuts Kent and Son was starting to incorporate in some of its school primers.

Twenty men and several apprentices worked busily in the press room. Among them Gilbert noted a singular absence. His parchment-pale cheeks took on an even whiter cast. On the second floor of the main aisle he detected still more bloodstains—and, behind one press, a pile of ruined sheets.

A jowly young man in a leather apron approached, moving slowly and refusing to look Gilbert in the eye.

"Good morning, Mr. Pleasant," Gilbert said to his press room manager, the son of the deceased editor of Philip Kent's *Bay State Federalist*. "I'm afraid I see evidence of a fight."

"Aye, and a royal one," Franklin Pleasant answered.

"What was the cause?"

"I don't know, sir. I was up checking the paper stores when it broke out. The other lads pulled the two apart after a couple of minutes. Regrettably, that was long enough for Tom Naughton to suffer a broken hand and an addled head."

Pursing his lips—usually the strongest indication of displeasure he allowed himself—Gilbert asked, "And the other combatant, Mr. Pleasant?"

"Well, sir—" Pleasant's eyes still avoided those of his employer. "He walked out."

"To go where?"

"I wasn't informed, sir. The truth is, your brother was in such an ugly mood, I didn't wish to ask. The lads said he tore into Naughton in what they call the frontier style—"

Gilbert sighed. "Just as on the other occasions? Kicking? Butting? Gouging eyes?"

Pleasant gave a somber nod.

Gilbert forced himself to the hardest question:

"Was my brother drunk again?"

"The lads say he stank of it. I don't doubt he traipsed off for more after he did his damage to Naughton. I—I have no right to speak about a relative of yours, Mr. Kent—"

"You certainly do. He works for you."

Less apprehensive, Pleasant went on, "Since you gave Mr. Abraham a job last year, he's done nothing but disrupt this press room."

"And it took him twelve months to shake off his despondency and reach the point where he'd even consider a menial job."

"I realize he suffered hard blows, losing his wife the way he did, then coming home to the shock of finding Mr. Philip dead and buried. But the fact remains, he can't get along here."

"Nor anywhere, it seems, except in the taverns."

"Yes, a couple of the lads have told me he consorts with the worst drunkards and trulls on the waterfront. Of course," Pleasant added hastily, "that may be no more than vicious gossip. Repayment for some of the difficulty he's caused—"

"It's not gossip, it's fact. Abraham's frequently gone from the house two or three nights in a row. I don't doubt he's visited a score of those poor women you dignify with the name trull. However—" Gilbert waved. "—it's not the facts that are wanting, Mr. Pleasant, it's the solution to the problem, eh?"

"Yes, sir."

"See you send Naughton an extra week's pay for his injuries. And my apologies."

"Oh, sir, the president of the firm needn't apologize to—"

"Enough, Mr. Pleasant. I want it done."

Pleasant looked pleased. "Very well, it shall be."

"Tell Naughton I rose later than usual this morning—well after seven. Abraham had already left the house. Sometimes, when I catch him at the table early, I can sober him up with coffee and a threat or two."

"Most days, he still manages a rum before reporting for work."

Gilbert's eyes strayed to the stains on the floor. "That would seem to be the case. It must have been an unusually strong draught today—" He cleared his throat. "Mr. Pleasant, be assured—and pass the word—that brotherly charity is not unlimited. Six brawls in as many months are five more than I should have permitted."

He indicated the working men, a few of whom were watching him in less than friendly fashion.

"Let it be known that I'll take immediate steps to bring Abraham into line. I'd hoped a job, however lowly, might help put his sad experiences out of mind. Obviously my hope was groundless. I will take steps," he repeated firmly, moving toward the stairs to the second floor.

A couple of the workmen waved and called a greeting. On normal mornings, most all of them did. Gilbert's reply was perfunctory.

He climbed to the third floor, to the cluttered office originally occupied by his father. There, along with his usual portion of day's work, he confronted the question of what to do about his half-brother.

He sympathized with Abraham, but he could no longer tolerate Abraham's sullen, destructive behavior. Nor, for that matter, could Abraham's son Jared.

He pondered the problem a while without success. Finally he put it out of mind and turned to other things. Often when a business difficulty needed a solution, he found that the answer came spontaneously if he mulled the subject, then forgot it for a few hours.

He prayed the process would repeat itself today.

III

GILBERT KENT'S first task was to check on the forthcoming issue of the firm's expanding newspaper, the *Bay State Republican*. Immediately on taking charge of Kent and Son, he had raised the paper's price to the prevailing six cents, added the job of general editor to his duties, and ordered a new masthead designed, sans the word *Federalist*.

The alteration in name and philosophic approach made him unwelcome in certain homes in Boston. But that was offset by generally widespread, if grudging, admiration for the courageous declaration of his own principles via the new name and the increasingly favorable coverage of the Jefferson administration.

Gilbert believed it was not only right but practical to provide an alternative to the viewpoint of most other New England papers. His judgment was rewarded by a slow but steady increase in circulation. Now the *Republican* appeared twice weekly.

With his coat off, his waistcoat unbuttoned and a quill in hand, he marked some minor changes on the foolscap copy describing the background of Commodore Edward Preble, newly named commander of the naval squadron Jefferson had reluctantly dispatched to the Mediterranean in an effort to get the Barbary states to end their outrageous piracy coupled with their demands for tribute. The tribute was supposed to guarantee the safety of American shipping. In fact, it didn't.

Gilbert inked a few rousing sentences at the end of the story, predicting that Preble would soon have the bandit-like Bashaw of Tripoli wishing he had not increased the sum he hoped to extract. Should some of Preble's crack marines storm Tripoli's shores, the Bashaw would regret his greed *and* his declaration of war on the United States.

He returned the copy to one of the two men who wrote for the *Republican:* "Very good, Mr. Morecam."

"Thank you, sir."

Gilbert watched Morecam work for a few minutes, then moved over to stand behind the other reporter. Neither appreciated his hovering presence, but neither protested. Shortly he went back to his office to see to the day's correspondence.

Much of it was inconsequential. But the pile contained two important items, the first being a lengthy letter from one of Kent and Son's best-selling authors, Mason Locke Weems.

Parson Weems as he was usually called—he was an ordained Anglican, and now a bishop—was a rare bird indeed: a theologian who doubled as a bookman— both writer and seller. Additionally, Weems had an uncanny sense of what the reading public would buy.

His *Life of Washington,* written to the popular taste in 1800, was already into several editions. Gilbert had negotiated to print a deluxe volume that was selling handsomely to the well-to-do who maintained private libraries.

Weems' letter reported on his progress in revising his text for yet another edition. The parson tiptoed around the question of *"embellishing"* the biography with some *"possibly apocryphal"* material.

Gilbert smiled. The good parson had raised the subject in his last letter too. Gilbert sensed Weems intended to invent anecdotes about the first president in order to add novelty to future printings.

His suspicion was confirmed as he read on. Weems said that *"reliable sources*

in Virginia'' had provided a story about young Washington hacking down a cherry tree, then manfully admitting his guilt when confronted by his father.

Gilbert sharpened another quill in preparation for a reply. He didn't allow himself the luxury of a male secretary. Even though his handwriting was small and difficult to read, he preferred to write his own letters to keep costs down.

In his reply, Gilbert tactfully suggested that George Washington's life was dramatic enough without *"apocryphal embellishments,"* and that Weems might do well to refrain from including such material, since it would only befuddle future generations hunting the truth. Since Weems was important to Kent and Son, Gilbert closed with an assurance that of course he would rely on the parson's *"honesty and good judgment"*—and accept the revised text exactly as submitted. He was cynically certain said text would include the invented material.

The second letter of importance was addressed in a hand Gilbert recognized at once; its owner had written him twice before.

With anticipation, he broke the letter open. It was dated the first of July.

> Dear Mr. Kent—
>
> The President has requested me to tender his thanks to you for your eminently fair and reasoned support of the purchase of the Louisiana Lands completed May second last by Minister Monroe in Paris. Your recognition of the importance of this Acquisition, and your praise of the treaty of cession in your most excellent Newspaper, have come to the President's attention, and are deeply appreciated.
>
> The President is particularly gratified that you share his view of the purchase, viz., that it is a transaction replete with blessings to unborn millions of men. As you might assume, contrary opinions expressed in various New England gazettes have distressed him.

Gilbert could well imagine Jefferson's ire over some of the extreme reaction. A number of northeastern editors claimed flatly that because the new land would eventually be parceled into states, the influence of New England was already destroyed—and therefore, the northeast should consider seceding from the union in order to establish itself as a separate country.

Gilbert had personally written two *Republican* editorials to prick that hysterical bubble, dismissing the notion of a "southern plot" to wrest control of the country from the easterners. The editorials hadn't increased his popularity among Boston Federalists. But then, it was his opinion that the party had seen its heyday. Incurring the wrath of its diehard supporters troubled him not at all.

He started to re-focus his attention on the letter. A sudden spasm in his throat prevented it. He coughed. Then again harder—

Damn! He hadn't been bothered with the cough for several weeks. Now it was nearly doubling him over.

He thrust the letter to the desk, gripped the arm of his chair with his other hand. He squeezed his lids shut, still coughing. Water trickled down his cheeks from the corners of his eyes. With the cough came the familiar chest pain.

As he rocked back and forth in his chair, he heard the voice of one of his writers:

"Mr. Kent? Shall I summon the doctor?"

Through sheer will he raised his head, opened his eyes:

"No, I—I'm over the worst."

His cheeks still shone from the tears. But the strangled feeling in his chest had lessened.

The reporter hesitated in the doorway. "Perhaps you ought to keep a window raised in here, sir."

"Air won't do a bit of good," Gilbert answered, wiping his eyes. "When one of those damned spells hits me, I can't get enough air no matter how many windows I throw open. When the spell passes, so does the struggle to breathe. The doctor tells me many people are afflicted with the condition and suffer nothing more than occasional discomfort all their lives."

He was fully recovered, and affable:

"Thank you for your concern, Mr. Morecam."

With a bob of his head, the writer vanished.

Gilbert cleaned his cheeks with a kerchief. God, how the infrequent but painful seizures angered him! He detested them because they impaired his ability to function at full efficiency. It was one of the few segments of his life he was unable to control.

Breathing normally again, he resumed reading:

> *The President is likewise grateful for your restraint in withholding an account of his special and confidential message to the Congress of January eighteenth last, even though he is well aware that certain details of that message reached you promptly as a result of your wide acquaintance with the legislators of your state. By now you surely know that the President's request for the sum of two thousand, five hundred dollars to fund an expedition into the remote Western reaches of the continent has been approved by the Congress. The purpose of the expedition is twofold—to expand our national commerce, and to perpetuate friendly relations with the Indian tribes.*

That amused Gilbert. The piqued Massachusetts conservatives from whom he'd heard about the January request complained they were being asked to indulge Jefferson's "literary pursuits"—and his desire to increase scientific knowledge of the vast land mass west of the Mississippi. Gilbert had assumed there was more to it, and still did.

Gazing at the letter, he wondered who had re-copied it for the author. Jefferson's aide was known to be a wretched speller, only able to approximate the sound of certain words. An ironical failing for one who held the title of secretary, Gilbert thought.

> *Now sir, it is my privilege to report that my letter is undoubtedly the last you shall receive from me in my present post, as the President has signally honored me by naming me commandant of the aforementioned Expedition. Together with my fellow officer, Mr. Wm. Clark of Virginia, whom I chose for his courage and intelligence as well as for his remarkable skills in drawing and*

map making, I have plans to embark with a small party of explorers from the settlement of St. Louis in the spring of next year. Our route will take us to the headwaters of the great river Missouri, and thence to the Pacific. Hopefully, we shall complete this last stage of our journey by means of the Northwest River Passage long rumored to exist.

I shall be leaving my present duties within a very few days to seek my companions, who must be good hunters, stout, healthy, unmarried men, accustomed to the woods and capable of bearing bodily fatigue in pretty considerable degree. I will also be making divers stops at the Federal arsenal for military equipment, at Philadelphia, Pittsburgh, etcetera for good calico shirts, lookingglasses, jewelry, beads, scissors and other items to be presented to the various tribal chieftains in the most friendly and conciliatory manner.

It is no longer possible to keep a venture of this magnitude entirely secret. However, a certain prudence is still necessary in view of the Nation's recent acquisitions in the approximate geographic area to be traversed by our Corps of Discovery. Your cooperation in referring to said Corps as a purely scientific body will be most deeply appreciated.

With kindest good wishes for your continued prosperity, and humble thanks for your many editorial expressions of support for the Administration, I trust I have the honor of remaining

> *Your obdt. friend,*
> *Meriwether Lewis (Capt.),*
> *Secretary to the President*

With a delicious shiver of excitement, Gilbert reread the closing passages of the letter, then smiled. The Federalist newspapers had exercised no restraint at all concerning Jefferson's secret message, growling about "frivolous and costly intellectual endeavors"—which proved they were exactly as confused as the president meant them to be. Some of Captain Meriwether Lewis' oblique phrasing, however, invested the undertaking with a significance—a purpose—Gilbert believed he understood.

He laid the letter aside, turned in his chair to regard his expensive beaver hat. Such hats were increasingly popular; here too it was the Englishman, Beau Brummel, who set the fashion. If Brummel adopted a beaver hat, every gentleman must have a beaver hat! Gentlewomen too—with suitable alterations in design, of course.

Gilbert's thoughts turned to the source of the fur which the hatters brushed and worked into such soft, lustrous nap. Montreal and the straits of Michilimackinac were already major gateways through which fur gathered around the lakes reached the European fur markets.

Most sought after were *castor gras d'hiver*—the winter skins of the beavers. The winter pelts were premium priced because only they yielded the superlative felt for the hats such as Gilbert wore. But other, less choice furs and skins were in demand as the growing middle and lower classes developed an appetite for small touches of luxury. From elk and deer came the leather for gloves. Muskrat

and raccoon and the hide of the fabled bison could be turned into modestly priced coats, coat linings and collar trim.

The British in Canada dominated the fur trade on the lakes and in the country along the Missouri. Hired Frenchmen wintered on the distant reaches of that unmapped river, trapping or trading for pelts. In the spring they took their bundles to Michilimackinac or to posts of the Hudson's Bay Company north of there. Though Michilimackinac now belonged to the United States, commercial licenses issued to the Canadians permitted them to use the island as a headquarters.

But a few of the French winterers—the men whose fathers and grandfathers had pioneered the trade years earlier—disliked all Englishmen, and journeyed down to St. Louis on the Mississippi to sell their catches to Americans trying to gain a foothold in the lucrative industry. Gilbert didn't doubt that one of the objectives of Jefferson's western expedition was the discovery of new routes to help American traders capture a larger share of the fur business. Because national rivalries were involved, a purpose like that would, of necessity, be kept secret until it was accomplished—

As would other details of the mission, simply because the president's monumental purchase—which some New Englanders called totally illegal—was sketchy on certain questions of boundaries. By exploring, Captain Lewis might help settle future disputes. Possession, as the old saying claimed, was still nine points of the law.

Establishment of territorial rights would blunt the thrust of Canadian expansion, too; balk the fur entrepreneurs already pushing their trapping parties west and south—

The Louisiana acquisition had made it all possible. It had also come as a stunning surprise to the country.

Minister Plenipotentiary Monroe had sailed to France the preceding January to investigate the possibility of buying the port of New Orleans, and perhaps some additional territory in the West Floridas, for no more than two million dollars. On arrival, Monroe was offered not merely the requested territory, but all of the Louisiana lands west of the Mississippi and north of the Gulf!

The turnabout in French policy—marking the abandonment of Bonaparte's vision of an empire in the western hemisphere—had two causes: the failure of the French military to suppress a decade-long slave revolt on the island of Haiti and, closer to home, the threat of renewed hostilities with Britain.

More than eight hundred and thirty thousand square miles were involved in the offer. Astonishingly, Jefferson quickly accepted it—and the price of sixty million francs, or about fifteen million dollars. The sum included the payment of some American war debts. By Gilbert's reckoning, the purchase itself amounted to something like three pennies per acre—which had to be one of the most remarkable real estate bargains of recorded history.

Gilbert had already read an edited text of the treaty of cession. For safety's sake, three copies of the full document had been rushed to the United States by three different couriers aboard three fast packets. The Senate had yet to ratify the treaty, however. And in the inevitable debate, old positions were being turned topsy-turvy:

The president, known to favor strict interpretation of the Constitution, adopted a somewhat broader view where the purchase was concerned. He argued that constitutional power to govern territory implied the right to acquire it. The majority of New England Federalists, normally loose constructionists, had like-

wise reversed themselves, insisting that nowhere in the Constitution was the president authorized to buy new land. Gilbert suspected Jefferson had made a pragmatic decision, bending principle to accommodate his conviction that the purchase would enrich the country in everything from minerals and timber—and fur-bearing animals—to much-needed land for settlement and agricultural cultivation.

From reading the edited text, Gilbert was well aware that the boundaries of the ceded land were vague, especially in the north and far west, where a vast mountain chain separated the inland prairies from the Pacific coastal region which a Boston skipper had explored in 1792. Discovering a great river that poured down out of the mountains—the western end of the legendary Northwest Passage, perhaps?—the skipper had christened it with the popular name "Columbia."

Gilbert admired Jefferson's labyrinthine thinking. With one stroke—the expedition—he could solidify the nation's claim to new territory *and* aid an increasingly important sector of the economy.

Suddenly he sat upright. Snatched Lewis' letter and scanned it.

He blinked several times. A smile slowly lifted the corners of his mouth. He just might have stumbled onto something—!

He rose quickly, tucked the letter into the pocket of his coat which lay neatly folded over another chair. He paced back and forth for a minute. Then he sat down. He tented his fingers and tilted his chair back, soothed by the faint and rhythmic *thump-thump* of the book presses churning out pages on the first floor. Despite his youth, he resembled nothing so much as a frail old man cogitating.

Gilbert knew what his critics said of him. That he had an almost driven desire to succeed—to be a good steward of the assets left by Philip Kent's passing. As a result, he sometimes behaved like a man three times his years. He never let it trouble him. Thinking without the passion of youth could be an advantage.

It proved so now, as he looked at Abraham's problems in an objective way.

He believed the problems sprang from three interrelated sources. The first was Abraham's obvious guilt about being responsible for his wife's death.

The second, perhaps as deep and fundamental as the first—although Abraham had never even mentioned it to Gilbert—was the rift between father and son when Abraham and his bride set out for the west. Philip's death during Abraham's absence had effectively prevented any healing of the wounds of either party.

The third source of the problems was Abraham himself.

Looking back to his own boyhood, Gilbert could recall very nearly worshiping his half-brother. His precipitous entry into the world of adult affairs had purified his thinking on many subjects; burned away old illusions. He could make a more accurate appraisal now: Abraham was a man of weaker character than their father.

Gilbert didn't consider it callous to form such judgments of the living and the dead. In all things, he tried to be rational. He knew it would have been difficult indeed for almost any young man, himself included, to have matched Philip Kent's mental and physical toughness.

To offset his limp, Philip had kept himself in perfect condition. He had constantly educated himself—a process made easier by his professional involvement with books and journalism. Gilbert, sickly as a child, had never faced the necessity of competing with his father on both fronts. Physically he was no match. That gave him leave to devote himself to keeping up with Philip's mind as best he could.

Abraham, sadly, had lived completely in Philip's shadow—and suffered by comparison. When Abraham married Elizabeth, stirring the so-called Fletcher temperament into the brew, no wonder explosions resulted.

Against that background, Gilbert analyzed the idea that had popped into his mind a few minutes ago. A mad idea, some would say; perhaps even Abraham himself! Yet Gilbert embraced it because he could no longer permit Abraham's behavior to go unchecked. Not only was his half-brother destroying himself with his drinking and trouble-making, he was harming his son. Perhaps irreparably.

As Gilbert sat and pondered, beams of slanting sunshine turned his cheeks to the color of warm ivory. His mind roved over tales told by fur factors who had made the difficult trip to the country's western outposts, St. Louis and Michilimackinac, there to bargain with the trappers whose wanderings had taken them into the country Lewis proposed to cross and map. The factors brought back astonishing, almost fanciful accounts of a sea of grass stretching west toward the mountain rampart. They spoke of gigantic herds of bison like those the Kentucky settlers had slain and eaten for years.

Out there, it was said, the red tribes were different from Indians of the east. They raised and rode horses, acquiring a dangerous mobility lacked by nations such as the Shawnee.

And now Mr. Meriwether Lewis was captaining an expedition to that very land. Abraham had soldiered with Lewis under General Wayne. Yes, and with the other one—the younger brother of George Rogers Clark. By God, it was perfect!

Even though the solution carried an element of risk, Gilbert didn't shrink from it. In the two years since he'd taken charge of Kent and Son, he had proved over and over that risk-taking could pay off handsomely. The only difference now was in the nature of what was at stake. Not money, but a man's life and sanity.

The question, then, was whether to consult Abraham first or present him with an accomplished fact. Thinking a few minutes more, Gilbert decided on the latter course. Abraham must have no excuse to back out; no more latitude in which to indulge his excesses. The press room was nearing the point of mutiny.

His mind raced. Much remained to be done before he went home for the evening. And much remained after that. He'd have to speak to Abraham as soon as his half-brother returned from whatever den he'd crawled into after the fight.

Beyond that, he needed to gain his wife Harriet's consent to her role in the plan. She had disliked Abraham and Jared—but particularly Abraham—since the day the two had come home after Elizabeth's death. The fact that Harriet was now in her eighth month of her first pregnancy wouldn't make Gilbert's job any easier. It would require extra effort on his part to make sure dinner this evening was composed and cordial—an appropriate forum for him to share his plan with his spouse before broaching it to Abraham.

Yes, he had much to do—

Commencing with the draft of a letter.

IV

HE FOUND fresh paper, inked his quill and began to scribble in that small, compressed hand others found so difficult to decipher:

> *My dear Captain Lewis,*
>   *I am in receipt of yours of the first instant, for which my deepest thanks. I hope I do not place you under an undue burden by tendering a most urgent request which, at the same time, could well work to your benefit—*

Ten minutes later, Gilbert stepped to the office door.
"Mr. Morecam?"
The reporter hurried over. "Sir?"
"Can you spare an hour from your duties?" Gilbert asked rhetorically. "You've a good hand—and I have a letter that needs to be copied three times—and kept entirely confidential. I want the letter to go to Pittsburgh, Cincinnati and Louisville, so that I'm certain it reaches the recipient—just like the purchase treaty, eh?"
"I'll be happy to make the copies, Mr. Kent."
"Bring them in as soon as you're finished and I'll see about the posting."
"By the regular mails? I can do that for you."
"Speed is essential. I want to engage private couriers."
Morecam goggled, contemplating the expense of that. Gilbert wheeled back into his office—and rushed out of the building an hour later. Seldom had employees of Kent and Son seen the youthful owner depart in such haste—and so early! A full hour before closing.
Nor had they ever seen such an intense luster in his dark eyes—or such touches of emotional color in his cheeks.
If Mr. Gilbert Kent the modernist was engrossed in another venture, it had to be a very important one indeed.

5
The Mark

"YOU MAY serve the plum pudding." Harriet Kent said to the girl in the striped cotton dress and gingham apron. "No hard sauce for the boy. But refill the milk pitcher."
On the side of the dining table opposite Abraham's empty place, Jared Adam Kent made a face:
"I don't want any more milk, Aunt Harriet."
The maid hesitated. The young woman at the foot of the table glared:
"Jared, I am growing tired of your impertinence. You behave like a dock boy instead of a child reared in a Christian home."

744

"Harriet," Gilbert said softly, pursing his lips.

"The boy is disrespectful! To me, to the servants, to everyone! He's a willful, headstrong child—"

As if to confirm it, Jared said, "I won't drink any more even if you whip me." He was handsome for a five-year-old, with long tawny hair and brilliant blue eyes. But his face had a fatigued, pasty look.

And his retort made Harriet furious:

"You see what I mean, Gilbert? He not only looks like his mother, he acts like her!"

Jared reacted with a stunned look, then with obvious anger. In a controlled voice, Gilbert said:

"Raking over the past is futile and cruel. Especially in front of—"

"I disagree. We've tiptoed around the issue too long. You've told me how his mother behaved. Defiant of everyone—"

"Please, stop," Gilbert broke in, aware of the hurt and hostility in the boy's eyes.

Harriet opened her mouth; hesitated; then glanced sharply at the maid.

"Bring the milk, Esther."

"Papa wouldn't force me to have it." Jared said.

Harriet leaned forward awkwardly; she was approaching the end of her term. Her huge stomach couldn't be minimized; not even by the expensive, high-waisted maternity gown of lavender lawn she wore over a matching petticoat. Gilbert pushed his chair away from the table, noting unhappily that his wife's features had taken on a familiar, pinched look. It had to do with her dark eyes. When she was angry, she tended to slit them, and frown. The contraction changed the proportions of her features subtly.

"Your father is not in charge of this household," she said to the boy. "Indeed, if he were present for meals a little more often—present and sober—he'd take you in hand."

Rapping his palm on the table, Gilbert said, "That will be quite enough, Harriet."

"Why? It's true—but you're always evading that issue, too." She gestured to the vacant place. "Abraham's gone more than he's here!"

"We had a great deal of work at the firm today. I asked him to stay late to help with it."

Harriet's pale lips compressed, branding the lie for what it was. She had an oval face, dark hair, fine patrician features. But bad temper destroyed the total effect.

Gilbert glanced at Jared. The boy sat on a pillow that raised him to table height. His downcast expression showed that he too disbelieved Gilbert's statement. Jared had seen his father's place empty too many evenings; watched Abraham come stumbling in from Beacon Street, unkempt and incoherent, too many times. Sadly, Gilbert reflected that Jared might not understand the word *sober*—or its opposite. But instinct surely told him his father's behavior was abnormal, and wrong.

The maid waiting nervously for a final resolution of the milk question started to speak to Harriet. Gilbert was quicker:

"We'll not have any more milk, Esther. Nor the pudding either. You may retire."

"Yes, sir." She curtseyed and left.

"Jared, be so good as to go up to your room," Gilbert said.

The boy started to protest, then took note of Gilbert's stern expression and slipped off the pillow. Irked by her husband's intervention, Harriet stared at him, spots of color showing in her cheeks. The color deepened when Jared blurted:

"You don't like papa, do you, Aunt Harriet?"

"That is not a suitable question for a boy your age! This house is partly his—"

"But you wish it weren't, don't you?"

"Jared, go," Gilbert said, soft but firm.

Jared paid no attention: "You wish we'd both leave and never trouble you again, don't you?"

"*Jared!*" Gilbert rose half way out of his chair.

Eyeing his uncle, Jared looked less pugnacious all at once. Gilbert sat down again:

"You owe your Aunt Harriet the same politeness she owes you. And please remember, she's expecting a child. That makes a person—well, rather cross at times. You do understand?"

Jared's tawny hair shone in the light of the chandelier candles. His blue eyes were almost venomous as tears sprang into them and he cried:

"I understand she doesn't want papa here—or me!"

He spun, dashed to the hall and clattered away up the stairs while thunder muttered in the distance.

II

THE MOMENT Jared had gone, Harriet vented her anger:

"I'm sick of the way you coddle that boy. You've said time and again how willful his mother was—and when he flaunts his temperament, you overlook it!"

"Harriet—"

"Must we suffer another Elizabeth Fletcher in this house? Abraham is bad enough, but—"

"The immediate concern is the father, not the son. I don't believe we should continue to discuss—"

"Why not? The boy resists the slightest imposition of authority! Absolutely refuses to behave as any respectable boy shou—"

"*God's sake, Harriet!*" he burst out, in such an unusually loud voice that his wife recoiled in her chair. "Is that all that ever matters to you—respectability? Did you look at that child? He's tormented with fear!"

"Of me?" she asked in an arch way.

"Of you *and* his father. Harsh discipline won't alleviate the problem. Nor will constant harping about his mother's faults. You'll only make him feel worth-less—and his behavior will get worse."

"Do you deny he's headstrong?"

"Of course not. But the way to cure it is with kindness, not rancor. He hasn't lived like normal children. Have you forgotten he saw his own mother murdered?"

"And whose fault is *that?*"

Gilbert uttered a dismayed sigh. "Is it necessary to place blame? It happened, that's all."

Harriet leaned forward again, a movement that emphasized her bulk and clumsiness:

"But it would *not* have happened if Abraham hadn't subjected his wife to the hardships of the west. Had he stayed in Boston, Jared wouldn't be a spoiled only child. He'd have an older brother or sister—"

"You're now blaming Abraham for Elizabeth losing her first baby?"

"Yes, he was responsible."

"Nonsense. Utter *nonsense!*"

Harriet's dark eyes suddenly became very bright. Her voice grew cool, malicious:

"Is it? My dear, you told me a few weeks after Abraham returned that Elizabeth was the one instrumental in their departure."

"I don't see how that makes him responsi—"

"He was manipulated because he's weak! As a man—the husband—he could have refused her unreasonable requests. He could have said no. But he didn't. And he was repaid for his cowardice by the death of his first child, and then by Jared—who has inherited the worst qualities of both his parents!"

Gilbert seethed. "I wish I'd never repeated one syllable of the story! You twist it all so terribly to fit your view of Abraham—justify your dislike—"

"He *is* weak," Harriet repeated emphatically. "God judged him so, and exacted punishment. You can see that in the way Abraham behaves—and his son too!"

Almost on the point of shouting at her, Gilbert controlled his temper with difficulty. He put the palms of his slim hands on the dining table. Through the strained softness of his voice he tried to show his wife how angry she'd made him:

"May we leave metaphysics out of this? The problem is tangible, urgent—and heaven has damn little to do with a solution."

"I would appreciate your refraining from cursing in my—"

"You drive me to it!"

He drew a deep breath, leaned back in his chair, finally went on:

"Harriet, it's absolutely pointless to debate who was responsible for what happened. That there's any debate at all is my fault. I was foolish to discuss past history and Abraham's confidences—"

"But you did."

Gilbert's mild demeanor seemed to harden:

"I do ask you, as I've asked you before, never to mention any of what I told you. Don't mention it in Abraham's presence—or, from now on, in mine."

"That has the distinct sound of a threat."

"No, no," Gilbert said hastily. "A request."

Harriet gave a sniff of disbelief. Gilbert's eyes fastened on hers:

"But it's a request I expect to see honored."

Harriet averted her glance. She pretended to be hurt.

Gilbert wasn't sure he'd succeeded in making his point. In public, Harriet accepted her husband's dominance, as did most wives of her station and circumstance. But the festering dislike she felt for his half-brother was an unusual factor in a marital relationship. In the privacy of the family, she might not bow to his politely phrased intimidation.

But he hoped she would. He was sure Abraham carried quite enough guilt without the burden being increased by his sister-in-law's spite.

During the ensuing silence, the tension between Gilbert and his wife gradually diminished. Finally he felt comfortable enough to try to return the conversation to its original course:

"The problem, Harriet, is not in the past but in the present. Abraham is not himself—"

"How long are we expected to suffer because of that?"

Gilbert struck the table. *"Enough!"*

For the second time, Harriet looked genuinely alarmed. He drew his hand back, wiped the damp palm on his trousers, swallowed once and went on.

"Let the past rest. I don't excuse Abraham's behavior, but I understand what drives him to it. I see nothing to be gained by punishing him—if indeed he deserves punishment, which I doubt. I see a great deal to be gained—I should say lost—if we fail to bring his son safely through this difficult period. You know very well that whenever Abraham walks in the door, Jared can't predict whether his father will hug him or hit him. We have a duty to alleviate that situation if we can."

"A duty I don't accept."

"But it must be accepted. It *must* be!"

Harriet obviously heard the strain, the emotion in her husband's voice. She seemed unmoved:

"Trying to help Jared is useless, Gilbert. He comes of bad stock, and he'll never overcome that."

"No, not if you keep telling him so. But I repeat—my first concern is with his father. I ask you to be tolerant just a short while longer. Just until I persuade Abraham to follow this plan I have in mind. Today I received an unexpected letter from Meriwether Lewis, the president's secretary. You'll remember Abraham served with him out west—"

Rapidly, Gilbert told his wife about the forthcoming expedition, and the chance he saw for Abraham to become part of it. By the time he mentioned the three letters he'd dispatched, enthusiasm had gone out of his voice, though. Harriet's face was growing more and more sour.

The moment he finished, she said, "The very idea is idiotic."

He pursed his lips. "Indeed. That's your considered opinion? Having thought it over for all of five seconds?"

"I don't need to think it over."

"Just condemn it out of hand? It may be an unusual plan, but it's not an impossible one."

"I disagree."

"Why?"

"Because I know Abraham. He'll have nothing to do with it. He'll laugh at you. Perhaps he'll even thrash you—that would be like him. He's a beast! Drunken, uncontrollable—what's the matter?"

Gilbert started to answer, then quickly lifted a hand to cup his mouth. The spasm of coughing went on for almost a minute.

At last, recovered, he asked:

"Why are you so averse to the plan? Why do you resist my efforts to help Abraham and the boy? Why do you detest them?"

"Abraham occupies too much of your time! I want this household to put attention where it belongs—on *our* lives. *Our* child!"

Unconsciously, her hand dropped to her swollen middle. Her features softened. She looked at her husband in a pleading way:

"Even if you can get him to agree, it still means we'll have to care for that vile-tempered little boy a year or more."

"That's true. But with Abraham gone, we might find Jared more tractable. I honestly think fear of his father has a great deal to do with the way he acts—"

"He has bad blood in him! He'll never amount to anything!"

"Help me give him a chance!"

After a moment's silence, Harriet sighed and struggled up from her chair. "Very well. Speak to Abraham. I want this intolerable situation resolved."

"I will speak to him," Gilbert nodded. "Tonight—when he returns."

She couldn't hold back a last thrust:

"If he returns."

She turned clumsily and waddled through the door that led to the kitchen and pantry, a sagging, somehow slovenly figure despite her elegant clothes.

Gilbert almost went after her. Instead, he forced himself to remain in the chair, one hand over his eyes. The verbal duel had drained and exhausted him.

Presently his angry feelings moderated again. His features smoothed out. He sat up straight. He brooded a good half hour before uttering a short sigh and rising.

His plans for a cordial, peaceful meal during which he would win Harriet's cooperation were in ruins. As he consulted the banjo clock and noted the lateness of the hour, he had to admit the prospects for the remainder of the evening didn't appear much better. Abraham might not come back until tomorrow—or next week!

The trouble in the household wasn't entirely Abraham's fault. Harriet exacerbated the difficulties. But much as he disliked certain facets of his wife's character, Gilbert couldn't place all the blame on her either. Jared Adam Kent *was* impertinent; rebellious; resentful of the most common and proper forms of discipline.

Though he felt he was being a traitor to his mother's memory, he again asked himself whether Harriet might be correct. Perhaps there *was* something bad in the child's bloodline. Something inherited from Elizabeth, who had in turn drawn it from that shadowy father about whom Gilbert knew so little—

Useless speculation. *Bury the past!* Hadn't he just urged that on his wife? Yet here he was, exhuming it as he desperately tried to fathom and resolve the turmoil Abraham and Jared caused.

The challenge lay in the present, not the past. With more than a little apprehension he fixed his mind on that fact. He left the table looking far older than his twenty years.

III

THE JULY evening with its threat of thunderstorms turned the air in the house sweltering and heavy. Gilbert loosened his stock and detached his collar as he crossed the hall to Philip's old library. Even lighting one lamp seemed to raise the room's temperature drastically.

Gilbert had converted the library into an office, with furnishings of dark wood. He slouched in the chair beside the littered desk and regarded the large oil portrait of his father hanging between the windows on the outer wall.

The portrait had been painted the year before Philip's death. Gilbert stared at the strong, almost truculent face on the canvas. Probed the painted eyes that appeared to defy the world. How would Philip have dealt with the problem of his older son—?

A boom of thunder roused him. The reverie was futile. No one could resolve the dilemma except Gilbert himself. That inescapable fact gave his eyes a remote, gloomy look as the curtains belled at the partially open windows. The lamp flickered. He heard the first spatters of rain on Beacon Street.

Gilbert loved his wife. He appreciated that pregnancy put her under a strain. Still, there *was* a sour, even cruel streak in her makeup that he wished were absent.

The coldness of her nature carried over to the marriage bed. She lacked spirit there; took no pleasure in making love. Though Gilbert had never been so indelicate as to question her on the subject, he suspected she'd been taught that sexual intercourse was basically sinful, to be indulged in only for the purpose of begetting children.

He found that disappointing though by no means unbearable. Perhaps because he'd always been less than robust, or perhaps because he was usually preoccupied with business affairs, he did not often experience a strong desire for sex. That reduced Harriet's reluctance to little more than an inconvenience. What he missed most in her was simple, straightforward affection.

For this and a number of other reasons, he had never considered their match perfect. But he'd learned at an early age that little in life was perfect, so he was reasonably content.

Harriet Lebow of New York City was one year older than Gilbert. She was the only child of a prosperous commodities dealer whose family had settled on Manhattan island four generations ago, when a majority of the residents were Dutch. The family originally spelled the name *Lebouwe*.

During his first year managing Kent and Son, Gilbert had found it necessary to float a loan for the new presses. The Rothman Bank provided the funds. With the money assured, Gilbert took a trip to New York to visit a machinery importer.

After inspecting one of the presses, Gilbert placed his order. He remained in the city a few more days, spending most of his time at the one place with which no rising American businessman dared be unfamiliar—the center of the country's expanding commerce, Wall Street. He was told an actual wall had once stood there, defense against attacks by Indians who lived in the woods at the north end of the island.

On busy Wall Street, Gilbert met Harriet's father through a mutual friend to whom he presented Royal Rothman's letter of introduction. The friend entertained Gilbert at the Tontine Coffee House building, which housed the growing Stock Exchange. Among the gentlemen gathered on the Tontine porch was the wealthy Lebow.

Later, Gilbert's friend provided some of Lebow's background. The commodities dealer had managed to keep his Tory leanings concealed during the Revolution. After the war, he built his fortune by speculating in the government certificates issued to soldiers in lieu of pay.

By 1783 these promissory notes had declined so sharply in value that their owners, pressed for cash, were eager to sell them to speculators like Lebow for as little as twelve cents on the dollar. Lebow, in turn, was gambling that the government would eventually untangle its finances and make good on a major part of its obligations.

Under Secretary of the Treasury Hamilton, it did—though as everyone knew, Hamilton had traded the location of the new capital city, Washington, for the southern votes necessary to pass his financial legislation. Mr. Lebow, now an

avowed Federalist, blessed Hamilton ever afterward. He prospered mightily as a member of what Mr. Jefferson sneeringly described as "the stock-jobbing herd."

While Gilbert was conversing with Lebow on the Tontine porch, Harriet called for her father in the family carriage. More introductions were performed. Soon Gilbert found himself making return trips to New York, first as a regular guest at the Lebow table, then as a prospective son-in-law.

Gilbert found Harriet intelligent and attractive, if overly concerned with matters of status and appearance. In the rational way his mind worked, he decided she would make an eminently suitable wife for a substantial businessman. She would also give him important connections in New York's financial community. Though her parents were both dead now, those connections remained intact.

He did love her—as much as a man of deliberately dispassionate temperament could love another person. He doubted that she loved him at all. He suspected love was alien to her experience—except as it applied to herself. Still, it wasn't a bad bargain—

Except at times like this, when Harriet's personality disrupted the entire house and created genuine ill-will among those living there.

A glare of lightning lit the office as Gilbert paced back and forth, still pondering the various approaches he might make to his half-brother. A quarter hour passed. Another. He was becoming convinced Abraham would be gone all night. He was almost relieved. Tomorrow or the next day, he'd be better rested. This evening he was edgy; prone to anger—

His relief was short-lived. At the end of a long rumble from the night sky, he heard irregular footsteps on the walk outside. Then an oath.

He didn't bother to glance out a window. He opened the double doors and waited in the dim hall, watching the front entrance.

In a moment, Abraham lurched through the doorway.

IV

GILBERT KENT was eight years younger than the shorter, stockier man who stood blinking at him in a vaguely hostile way. Yet Gilbert somehow seemed the older of the two.

Another lightning-burst lit Abraham's filthy, unshaven cheeks. His brown eyes looked addled. His ink-stained shirt, leather vest and homespun breeches bore an assortment of stains. He smelled of rum and vomit.

Gilbert said, "Come into the office please, Abraham."

Abraham slammed the door, started by, his step unsteady. "Spare me the lecture on self-discipline and deportment, will you? I've a terrible throbbing head—"

"That's not my doing." Gilbert seized Abraham's arm.

Abraham looked at his brother's hand resentfully. But Gilbert refused to let go:

"It's imperative that we speak privately. You can clean up later."

Releasing Abraham's arm, he re-entered the library, not glancing around. The sound of Abraham's shuffling footsteps signaled that he'd won the first skirmish. But he took no satisfaction. The major engagement remained to be fought.

Gilbert crossed to one window, then the other, opening them wide despite the rain that soaked the curtains. He could barely tolerate Abraham's stench.

Abraham rolled the double doors shut. He took a chair, turning it, Gilbert noticed, so that his back was toward the portrait of their father.

Gilbert glanced at the letter on the desk, then to his half-brother's sullen face.

"May I ask where you have been all day?"

"You can ask but you won't get an answer."

"Be so good as to speak to me in a civil way. Abraham! I'm your brother, not one of your tavern cronies."

Abraham covered his brow with a dirty hand. A small raw spot shone on one finger.

"I'm tired. Can't this wait?"

"No, I'm afraid not. This morning you completely disrupted operations at the printing house—for the sixth time. I don't count your innumerable verbal assaults on my employees."

"I didn't start it! That damned Naughton—"

"Whose hand you broke. A man can't set type with a broken hand."

Abraham pretended not to hear. "He made one sneering remark too many."

"About what?"

"About me not being fit to hold a job at Kent's."

"Don't sound so proud! Unfortunately, the remark appears to be correct."

"The bastard said I was only kept on because I'm your brother."

"In that, too, Mr. Naughton is regrettably accurate. I've given you repeated warnings, and you've disregarded every one. Therefore—"

Here was the delicate part; the first stroke of strategy so necessary to the working of his plan:

"—I've no choice but to discharge you."

That, at least, fully caught Abraham's attention. He raised his head. Stared in disbelief that changed to fury. A blue-white flash suffused the office, putting an eerie sheen on Philip's portrait.

"Thrown out? Is that it?"

"Yes."

"Out of the house too? That would make your wife happy!"

"I don't deny Harriet has little admiration for your gutter ways."

Abraham's jaw clenched. "I wonder how she'd feel if she saw you shot down, the bitch."

Gilbert turned scarlet. One hand closed into a fist. Abraham noticed. The harsh mask of his face seemed to crumble, revealing a man abruptly ashamed and vulnerable. Very softly, he said:

"Forgive me for that."

The scarlet faded.

"Certainly."

He walked over, laid a hand on Abraham's shoulder. He could feel the trembling; the physical manifestation of misery. Abraham's hand hid his eyes again. Gilbert asked:

"Would you let me pour you a rum?"

"That would help. That's all that seems to help any more."

Gilbert fetched the decanter and a glass from the cabinet where he kept liquor for business visitors. "I'll only pour you a small amount, because I want you to listen to what I have to say."

The older man accepted the drink, tossed it off quickly, extended the glass. Gilbert set the decanter on the desk beside the letter.

"I told you—no more until we've talked."

Abraham peered ruefully into the empty glass. Then he stretched his legs out. His body seemed flaccid; defenseless.

"All right. Lecture away."

"No lecture. Just facts. I can no longer tolerate your presence at Kent and Son. For the sake of efficiency, of morale—"

"Efficiency. Morale!" Abraham snickered. "Good old Gilbert! An eighty-year-old clerk in a boy's body."

Gilbert pursed his lips. "Unlike you, Abraham, I didn't have the benefit of good health when I was young. I had very little to do except follow father about and—and practice being old, perhaps you could say. On the other hand, I think every family needs someone with a clerk's mind, to keep its affairs in balance. The affairs of the Kents are definitely *out* of balance right now. They—Abraham, kindly stop staring into space and give me your attention! Destroying yourself is one thing. Destroying your son is quite another."

Abraham's gaze seemed to re-focus on the reality of the room. "Jared? What about him?"

"Have you watched him closely these past months?"

A vague gesture with the glass. "I see him when I can—"

"Once or twice a week? For a moment or two? Do you seriously believe that's enough?"

"I—" Abraham shook his head. "Who knows?"

"Even when you do speak to Jared, you're seldom sober. He's mortally afraid of you! Why, he—"

Shocked and angered, Gilbert stopped. The older brother was smiling in a strange, joyless way.

"You find this amusing, Abraham?"

"No. Oh, no. I was just thinking of a picture that comes into my mind sometimes. A picture of—"

He indicated the painting.

"I see him with his hand raised to me. He's angry, though I can't hear what he's saying. Father once told me that when he came home from the Continental army, wounded and unable to walk properly—came home to Boston with my mother dead—well, he said there was a period of nearly a year when he treated me very badly. By his own admission—treated me very badly! How unlike Mr. Philip Kent to admit he had faults, eh? In any case, I was apparently terrified of him—"

A humorless laugh. Silently, Gilbert waited.

"You know, Elizabeth always worried about the Fletcher blood being in Jared—"

"We are not discussing Elizabeth's parentage."

"Oh, no reflection on your mother—I just thought of it because—" He shrugged, wearily. "—because the Kent heritage has proved damned near as damaging. I'm acting the way my father did, if what you say is true."

"Isn't it?"

A lengthy pause.

"Yes." Once more he shielded his eyes. "God, yes—"

Pressing his advantage while Abraham's defenses were weakened, Gilbert pried the glass from his half-brother's hand. The rain beat heavily against the front of the house.

"I understand what you're going through, even though I can't condone your actions. You drink because Elizabeth died and you blame yourself—"

"Sufficient reason, don't you think?"

"—you hate the western country for what it did to her—"

"You're quite astute. Shall we drink to the land of opportunity beyond the Alleghenies—?"

His eye on the decanter, he started to rise. Gilbert pushed him back. Undeterred, Abraham took the glass from Gilbert's hand, raised it in a mock toast:

"To the great and glorious west—and the thousands of others it will ruin."

"What a strange enemy for a man to have," Gilbert said. "Land. You think it took Elizabeth, so you ran from it—"

"What the hell should I have done? Stayed there? The land *destroyed* her!"

"Land is land, Abraham. It can't be good or evil. Only the men who inhabit it have those qualities."

"No philosophic quibbles, thank you," Abraham snarled. "I've heard that argument till I'm fairly sick of it! Yes, I know two Shawnee came to the farm, and one shot her. But that's still the land as far as I'm concerned—"

Abruptly, he fixed his half-brother with a penetrating stare:

"Do you remember when we visited the president's home in Virginia?"

"Monticello? Yes, I recall a little of the trip—"

"In the orchard—I remember it distinctly—Mr. Jefferson went on at great length about the nation's future lying in the west. About the bounty of the land—"

Abraham spat.

"Of course it's very easy for a gentleman to find good in something he's never seen with his own eyes."

"You don't believe he was correct?"

"How can you even ask?" Abraham wiped his perspiring forehead. "I've mentioned the Clapper family to you, haven't I?"

"A few times."

"Did I ever tell you what Clapper said about the west?"

Gilbert shook his head.

"He said people went there not to seek something but to escape something."

"What?"

"Unhappiness."

"I think that view's wrong. Wrong and warped."

"Is it? I went to Ohio to escape his influence—" A hand jabbed toward the portrait. "So did Elizabeth."

"That doesn't make the generalization valid for everyone. Nor cancel the truth of Mr. Jefferson's words."

"I disagree—even though that makes me—what was your word? Warped—?" He shrugged. "You've been saying that in one way or another ever since I came home."

Gilbert bowed his head slightly, as if to avoid the scathing bitterness. Abraham exhaled loudly. Then:

"Well—perhaps you're right." One hand lifted absently to scrub at the stubble on his dirty face. "I can't help how I feel. I admit I'll never think of the western country without prejudice—"

"When a man allows himself to be defeated by an enemy, he has difficulty living with himself. Hides from himself. Destroys himself, sometimes—unless that enemy is overcome. If you had a second chance to defeat what you hate so much, you should take it."

"A *second*—? Gilbert, what the hell are you driving at?"

"I believe you understand."

"You're not suggesting I go west again?"

"That," Gilbert said, "is exactly what I am suggesting."

Violently, Abraham turned away. "Christ on the cross! Of all the insane, ill-conceived—"

Speechless, he couldn't finish.

On the precipice now, one misstep away from failure, Gilbert spoke with extreme care:

"I don't think you fully understand everything I've said. I want you out of this house. I want you out of Boston. I will see to it that you can't find decent employment anywhere in this city—believe me, I have the connections to do that."

"I know you do." Again Abraham shook his head. "What kind of monster have you turned into?"

"Call me that if you like. I have reasons for what I'm doing. I'm absolutely convinced you'll never hold your head up again—never drag yourself out of this slough into which you've fallen—unless someone forces you to best the enemy that bested you."

For a long moment, Gilbert was afraid Abraham still didn't comprehend one syllable, or his seriousness. Then, slowly, the older man lifted his head to stare at his taller brother:

"You've something in mind. Something you haven't mentioned."

"Indeed I do. Here—"

He snatched the letter from the desk.

"Sit down and read it through. I'll pour you another drink."

As he filled Abraham's glass, ashamed of resorting to such bribery, he heard the sheets crinkle. Abraham exclaimed softly:

"Meriwether—? This is from the president's secretary."

"Yes."

"I didn't realize you and he were in touch."

"Read it from the beginning," Gilbert urged.

He held out the glass. Abraham took it but didn't drink, concentrating on the letter. He read the sheets and dropped them on the floor one at a time.

A gust of wind blew rain against the back of Gilbert's neck. A carriage went rattling by in the aftermath of a thunderclap. Finally Abraham finished. The last sheet fluttered down. He drank the rum in a gulp, said:

"I don't understand why you wanted me to read that."

"Come, of course you do! You fit the specifications for the type of man Lewis wishes to recruit. Single, strong, in good health—"

"I am not precisely single. I have a son."

"Harriet has already agreed to care for Jared."

"She doesn't like me or Jared. And you'll soon have your own child—"

"I'll see she fulfills the promise. I swear that as your brother."

"What—" Abraham almost chuckled. "What kind of insanity has possessed you—?"

"A fear of the insanity that's possessing you."

He knelt beside Abraham's chair; rested one hand on his half-brother's forearm:

"You've our father's blood. He could never tolerate being beaten by anyone or anything. You hate the western country because of what it did to Elizabeth— right or wrong, that's how you feel. So what I'm saying is that you'll never be

whole until you *prove* you're stronger than what defeated you. If you don't do it—if you don't try to win back your self-respect—you'll end up in some Boston alley, and your son will despise your memory."

Abraham jumped to his feet. "I still say it's the maddest, most absurd—"

"It is *exactly* what you need!" Gilbert sank the last barb: "Unless, of course, you're willing to admit you're too weak and cowardly to set foot beyond the mountains a second time. *Do* you feel that way? Do you mean to say you couldn't survive?"

"I don't know, goddamn it!"

"Then find out! Look your devil in the face!"

Abraham bit his lip; gestured at the fallen sheets of the letter:

"I—I'd be gone a year. Maybe two—"

"Yes, the expedition could take all of that and more. What of it?"

"It wouldn't be good for me to be away from Jared for so long."

Gilbert had the feeling that Abraham was arguing every question except a central one—which he was being careful to avoid. Uneasy, he contented himself with countering the surface argument:

"You know damned well being close to your son in your present state is next to worthless. I tell you, Abraham, you lost more than your wife in Ohio. Without self-respect, no man can survive."

"Yes, you're right about that, anyway—"

"Gain it back! I know we can arrange it. You served with both officers in charge of the expedition—"

Abraham nodded, a strange, bemused look in his eyes. "And thought well of both, too. Brave men. Good soldiers—"

"I'm certain they'd take you on—"

He'd come to the turning point; he drew a long breath.

"—so certain that I've taken the liberty of writing Captain Lewis a letter." Disconcerted by Abraham's lack of reaction, he rushed on: "Three letters, in fact. Each a copy of the other, and already dispatched by courier. One went to Pittsburgh, one to Cincinnati, and the third to Louisville—*blast it, why are you smirking?*"

The bemused expression grew into a smile:

"Because your grand intentions and your efficiency will come to nothing."

"Even though Lewis is on the move, I'm sure one of the letters will reach him."

"That's not the point. I didn't particularly want to burden you with my personal problems—"

He reached for the decanter and glass. Spine crawling with inexplicable fear, Gilbert didn't protest.

"—but the truth is, you've trapped yourself. You've discharged me. Ordered me out of the house—to go back on those decisions would be difficult for a man of your principles. But I know Captain Lewis won't accept me. I fail to measure up to all of his lofty specifications."

"What the hell do you mean?"

Glass and decanter held in one hand, Abraham showed Gilbert the other. The small, raw sore Gilbert had noticed before gleamed in the lamplight.

"During my various jaunts around town in search of a bit of amusement—"

Not amusement. Punishment, Gilbert thought.

"—I've spent time with certain women—" He wriggled his hand. "Surely

you understand. I am not in the excellent health Captain Lewis demands. Even lying wouldn't conceal the evidence for long.''

Gilbert started to turn away.

"Look at the sore, damn you!"

Slowly, Gilbert swung around again. Abraham's hand held steady a moment, then dropped to his breeches.

"I've worse ones here. I've caught the pox.''

"Oh my God.''

The house shook with deafening thunder. Lightning lit Abraham's face, and Philip's on the canvas.

Gilbert sank down in the desk chair. He rested his elbows on the litter of papers and held his head.

Face locking into that odd smile again, Abraham said, "You're a remarkable fellow, Gilbert. How old are you?''

"What does that matter, for Christ's sake?''

"Just answer. You're twenty, aren't you?''

"That's right.''

"I marvel at your understanding of people. I suppose it was a necessity, eh? When our father died, someone had to take over the business and operate it successfully, else it would fail—and you're not the sort to accept failure readily, just as he wasn't. You've learned a great deal more than I did by age twenty— everything from accounting to dealing with press room helpers with bad tempers and worse morals. Well, I'm sorry none of your skills will avail this time, but they won't. I believe I'd better go upstairs. I expect you'll be wanting me out of the house immediately. Harriet wouldn't tolerate a man carrying the pox—''

Gilbert had grown light-headed. He sat watching his half-brother between the hands pressed to his temples. Abraham continued trying to make light of the situation, showing Gilbert the decanter and glass:

"I'll take these along if you don't mind. I'll pack up quickly—I wouldn't force you to compromise yourself by having to renege on the discharge, either. I—I do thank you for your good intentions.'' The last few words were barely audible.

"We'll consult a physician—'' Gilbert began.

"You know the pox can't be cured, only abated for a few months or a few years.''

Gilbert rose abruptly. "I won't let you leave.''

"You have no choice. I'm going up to get Jared.''

"You're not going to take *him?*''

Abraham's smile disappeared in an instant. "Of course I am. I wouldn't under any circumstances leave him with a woman who hates him the way Harriet does. That would be worse for Jared than living with a father who has the pox, don't you agree?''

"No, I don't. I won't permit—''

"You've nothing to say about it, Gilbert.''

Weaving a little, Abraham jerked the library doors open. The ringing in Gilbert's ears—his feeling of being disconnected from reality—intensified in that awful instant when Abraham swore and stepped back from the listener outside.

The glass and decanter slipped from his slack fingers, shattering. The splattering rum stained the hem of the maternity gown of lavender lawn.

"Well,'' Abraham said, and again, "Well. I can keep secrets from no one, it seems.''

Suddenly his face grew ugly. Harriet let out a small, startled cry as he thrust the sore-marked hand toward her face:

"You've snooped and heard about it, my dear. Now you can see the evidence for yourself."

For a moment Gilbert thought Harriet would faint away into the dangerous litter of glass. She clutched her immense belly, looking very nearly as pale and stricken as Gilbert himself. He stumbled away from the desk to intercede before things worsened—

Abraham acted first, shoving Harriet aside, not gently:

"I'm going to fetch my son. You'd be wise to stay out of my way."

6
Blood

ABRAHAM STARTED FOR the foot of the staircase.

Shadows clotted in the hall. The one lamp burning there had been extinguished by the gusting wind that came with the storm, slamming doors all through the house. The almost constant flickering of lightning cast a bluish tinge over furnishings and faces.

On the second floor, another door closed, loud as a pistol shot. A nimbus of yellow seemed to float across the landing. One of the maids, invisible behind the bobbing ball of light; the maid was bound for Jared's room, Gilbert suspected. Frightened of the storm, the boy cried out as Abraham climbed the first half dozen steps.

Hampered by her swollen belly, Harriet lurched after him. Hands on the railing, she dragged herself up two steps, then two more. She looked behind her:

"Gilbert—?"

"Harriet, come down!" he shouted, knowing somehow that the situation was careening toward an ugly conclusion.

Lightning glowed. Harriet's cheeks looked sweaty as she hung on the rail at the fifth riser, trying to locate her husband in the gloom of the lower hall. The wind played with distant doors, *crash* and *crash*. In Gilbert's old room, Jared's incoherent voice grew strident.

"Help me, Gilbert!" Harriet cried. "You can't let that filthy creature touch the child—"

Four steps above, Abraham spun around.

A drunken feelng overwhelmed Gilbert as he staggered around the shards of glass and the spilled rum. His pulse raced. His head buzzed. It was as if he had taken some unfamiliar drug that had coursed through his bloodstream in seconds, affecting his mind—

In the next burst of lightning, he saw Abraham's wrathful face:

"Such concern!" Abraham jumped down two steps, to tower over Harriet. "Such sudden and unexpected concern for a boy you've treated like scum. You'll pardon me if I don't believe your little turnabout."

Harriet cringed away "You depraved, bestial—"

"You're contemptible!" Abraham roared. "You pretend to protect Jared so you can revenge yourself on me! The worst dock whore has better morals than you, woman!"

At the foot of the stairs, Gilbert clenched his hands. The wild, dizzy feeling increased. Frustration and fear edged his voice:

"I don't care for your language, Abraham. This is Harriet's house, and if she wants you to keep away from the boy—"

"The boy is my *son!*"

Abraham whirled and started upward again. Harriet let go of the railing, groped toward him, managed to catch one of his boots:

"I won't let your diseased hands touch—"

Abraham twisted, kicking out the leg Harriet clutched. Gilbert leaped forward, trying to catch her even as he realized he was in the wrong position. Harriet sagged, tumbled down the stairs, struck his legs and sprawled. She shrieked.

Then, panting, she still managed to wrench her head around, seeking Abraham, blue-limned a few steps above:

"You—seem to have—a skill—for harming—women with unborn children—"

"God *damn* you!" Abraham howled, rushing down at her. He shoved Gilbert aside, bent and lashed her cheek with the back of his hand.

Gilbert heard the sickening thump as her head hit a riser. She arched her spine, dug fingers into the lavender fabric of her gown. She slid to the hall floor and lay there, eyes closed as she hugged her heaving belly.

Abraham's mouth dropped open, as if he himself were stunned by what he'd done. He stumbled down one step, one more. Incoherent emotion destroyed Gilbert's reason. He *knew* Abraham was going to strike her again—

He spun and ran.

In the front sitting room, lightning guided him to the mantel. He jerked the French sword from its pegs. He never recalled returning to the hall, was only peripherally aware of colliding with a woman. A face distorted by fright swam in lamplight as he passed in a rush—

Abraham crouched by Harriet, the sore-marked hand moving toward cheeks that glistened with perspiration. Harriet moaned, struggled to roll out of his reach. Gilbert raised the sword:

"Get away from her!"

"Gilbert, I'm sorry I—"

"Don't be a damned fool. Put that sword down. Give me a hand with her—"

"Don't touch her!" Gilbert cried. Lightning lit the sword as it slashed down, cutting edge foremost.

The maid with the lamp uttered a cry of alarm. Abraham tried to scramble out of the way, banged against the wall of the staircase, wrenched his head aside—

The blade hacked his left cheek, glanced off.

Abraham swore, jerking his head back and cracking it on the wall. He shot a hand out, clamped Gilbert's sword arm in a tight grip. The sword fell with a clatter.

The left side of his face streaming blood, Abraham pushed Gilbert hard. Gilbert nearly fell over the maid, who was kneeling beside Harriet.

The hall seemed to tilt as Gilbert skidded, windmilling his arms to regain his balance. His mind cried his anguish:

What has happened in this house? WHAT HAVE I DONE?

Unreasoning terror had driven him to attack—he, Gilbert Kent, who had never used a weapon in his life. The kneeling maid pressed her hand to Harriet's stomach. Ashen, she turned to search the hall's darkness:

"Mr. Gilbert? I think—I think the child is coming."

Gilbert lunged to the dining room door. "Esther? *Esther—!*"

A faint voice replied from the rear of the house:

"Yes, sir, what is it? I'm coming—"

"Run for Dr. Selkirk—*run!*"

"Yes, sir, at once—"

Someone slipped past him. The front door banged.

Gilbert wiped sweat from his eyes. Took one shaky step toward Harriet's convulsing body.

"Let's move her to the sitting room—"

"I think we'd best not move her at all," the maid said.

Slowly, Gilbert raised his head. His eyes sought his half-brother on the stairway. The maid had set her lamp on the floor. Abraham was visible at the edge of the circle of light, his bearded cheek bloody and one hand as well: he'd touched the deep cut.

That same hand left wet red marks on the wall as he braced himself then started upstairs.

Gilbert shouted his name.

Abraham turned. "I didn't mean to hurt—"

"Get out."

"Gilbert—"

"Leave this house. I've never harmed a living creature in my life, but if you don't go I'll pick up that sword and do my best to kill you."

Abraham started to answer. His dark eyes welled with a grief Gilbert perceived only dimly, and responded to not at all.

Thunder muttered. Lightning flickered. A second lamp was placed beside the first; another servant had come to help.

Gilbert couldn't bear to look at his wife more than a moment. His mind bore an image of white hands pressing against the great lump of her stomach—

Abraham's beard glistened with little drops of blood. He bobbed his head suddenly, left a red handprint on the railing as he resumed his climb to the second floor. On the landing, the ball of lamplight shone again. The unseen maid had rushed back from Jared's room.

"Leave *now!*" Gilbert demanded.

"I want my son."

He kept on, dragging himself almost as Harriet had, his reddened fingers smearing the railing. Gilbert darted for the fallen sword.

Bent over, he checked; straightened; glimpsed a pale oval at the top of the stairs; recognized Jared's face lit by the serving girl's lamp.

Abraham kept climbing toward the boy, his bloodied hand outstretched:

"Jared, come to me. We're leaving—"

Two steps below the landing, he closed his hand on the boy's gray ankle-length nightshirt. Suddenly Jared seemed to comprehend the meaning of the great red stains on the staircase wall and railing. He jerked back, cowering against the maid's skirt.

His sudden movement startled Abraham. He let go of the boy's garment. He and his son both looked down at the same time.

Jared's nightshirt was sticky with blood.

The boy flung his arms around the maid's legs, closed his eyes and screamed.

Abraham shouted at the boy—what, Gilbert couldn't hear above the thunder and Harriet's sudden wail and Jared's too. Again Abraham tried to touch his son. The boy literally flung himself away into the darkness. His shrieking rose and rose, a mindless keen—

Abraham's red-slimed hand was still stretched out toward the vanished boy. Dully, he blinked at it. A peculiar guttural noise tore out of his throat. He peered into the gloom of the landing:

"Jared—?"

In a hushed voice, the maid with the lamp said, *"For pity's sake, sir! Leave the poor child alone!"*

A last, low-pitched mutter of thunder died across the night sky. Gilbert leaned weakly against the pillar at the foot of the staircase. Abraham's hand fell to his side, staining his breeches. His shoulders slumped. He turned and came down the stairs, one slow step at a time.

Gilbert's head snapped up, his dark eyes venomous. But they found no venom in Abraham's as the latter went by; only dull horror and shame—

Gilbert pivoted slowly, his malevolent stare following his half-brother. Abraham reached the front door. Opened it, leaving a last bloodstain. He stumbled down the steps in the pouring rain, lit in bluish silhouette for a heartbeat's time—

The lightning faded and he was lost from view.

II

SLUMPED IN the chair beside his desk, Gilbert heard the library doors open.

On Beacon Street, the first glow of dawn reflected from wet cobblestones. He smelled his own sour sweat. Glanced up to see portly Doctor Selkirk rolling down his sleeves.

"There seems to be no injury to your wife, Mr. Kent."

Gilbert pushed up from the desk. It was an effort to speak calmly:

"Is she resting?"

"Quite comfortably. It wasn't an easy delivery, but I'm happy to say it was a successful one."

Gilbert almost wept. "The baby is—?"

"Alive. Alive and nicely swaddled by two of your household women." Selkirk, a middle-aged man with a lined face, covered a yawn. "The child is slightly underweight, as frequently happens in terms which are prematurely completed. Other than that, there are no problems. You may congratulate yourself on having fathered a splendid daughter."

Weak, Gilbert sank into the chair. "God, that's good news. Thank you, doctor."

Selkirk drew on his coat. "I'll catch a bit of sleep, then come back. Meantime, I suggest you have that gruesome mess in the hallway cleaned up. While it's none of my affair, I'm curious as to who bled so badly."

Gilbert's mouth had a dry, metallic taste. Sleepless for the entire night, he felt a hundred years old as he answered:

"I'd prefer not to discuss it."

Selkirk shrugged. "As you wish." He turned, ready to leave.

"Doctor—"

"Yes?"

"Did you look at the boy?"

"I did. He was talking—or, to be more precise, raving. About someone being hurt."

"You mean bloodied?"

"He didn't use the word. That was my inference, however."

"Did he—did he speak of his father?"

"As I indicated, *speak* is hardly the correct term. Surely you heard his outcries—?" Gilbert nodded. "I had trouble making sense out of them. Sometimes the boy seemed to be referring to a man who was hurt. At other times, unless I misheard, it was a woman. He was asking one or both to get up."

"Did he mention my wife's name?"

"No. He used the word mother once. I know his mother's dead—did the boy ever see her injured?"

Hoarsely, Gilbert said, "Yes."

"Obviously it left him disturbed. Whatever happened here tonight exacerbated the situation, I suspect. I dosed the boy with an opiate tincture. He's sleeping now. May I take the liberty of asking the whereabouts of his father?"

"I don't know his whereabouts."

"I gather he's not in the house—"

"That's correct."

"Will he be returning?"

"Not if I have any say." Concern for Abraham had disappeared in that moment when Abraham sent Harriet tumbling to the bottom of the stairs.

Outside, a produce cart clattered by. The two countrymen riding the cart were arguing about how much to charge for their cabbages at the day's market. Dr. Selkirk arranged his lacy stock, rolled his tongue inside his lower lip, then overcame his hesitancy:

"If I may make another comment, Mr. Kent—"

Gilbert looked at him.

"It is my conclusion that the boy—Jared is his name?"

"Yes, Jared."

"While I don't know all the circumstances behind his emotional condition, his behavior is far from normal. I believe he needs very careful attention. Affection. A feeling of security to overcome his fears. A new baby in the household will be taxing for you and your wife. It might be advisable to have his father look after him—"

"I'll see to Jared's care, doctor."

"But—"

"Thank you, doctor. Good day."

Looking baffled, Selkirk retired, closing the library doors. Gilbert laid his arms on the desk and rested his head for perhaps five minutes.

Then, by an act of will, he raised his head. His eyes accidentally touched the painting of Philip Kent.

Gilbert wished that he had as much courage and strength as that face suggested. Last night he had discovered a capability for blind rage and violence he had never suspected he possessed. The discovery—and the entire night—had been shattering. Abraham fled; Jared terrified and drugged to sleep; his wife delivered of the baby too soon—

He was deeply ashamed of his failure to cope with all that had happened. Ashamed too of his role in precipitating some of it—

A new thought popped into his mind. What would they call the child?

He was too weary to think about it. He slumped at the desk while the dawn brightened the ceiling and suffused the face of his father with light.

Philip couldn't help him. He was the one who would have to deal with all the problems sure to arise from the tragic events that had taken place in the house.

But his confidence had been shaken. He wasn't sure he could.

III

ON A steamy morning in the first week of August, Gilbert Kent—more haggard of late than his employees had ever seen him—looked up from some copy he was editing. The story dealt with progress in the construction of Boston's first Roman Catholic church, due to be completed and dedicated in September.

The reporter, Phineas Morecam, stood at the open door.

"Yes, Mr. Morecam? Any news?"

"No, sir, it's the same as the last five days in a row. The boys we hired spent all night combing the docks. The whole blasted city, in fact, from Roxbury to the North End. There's no sign of Mr. Abraham."

"Damn!" Gilbert tossed his quill aside. "How difficult is it to locate one man? Especially a man clearly marked by a wound on his left cheek?"

Morecam looked gloomy. "There are plenty of fellows who carry scars, sir. I hear that complaint from the boys practically every morning."

"But how many of those men will answer to the name Kent?"

"I know, sir—it should be easy. But it's not proving so. Maybe he's not giving his proper name."

"Has anyone seen him? His friends—?"

"Not since last week. Perhaps he's left Boston."

"You said that yesterday! *And* the day before!"

"Because it's a possibility, sir. He could be in some village miles from here—"

"The boys aren't doing the job. Hire men with horses. A dozen—two dozen if you need them. Have the men check every printer in the state! Printing's the only trade Abraham knows, and he's got to make a living somehow—I want him found!"

Morecam nodded unhappily, started out. Then he turned back to ask an obligatory question:

"How is Mrs. Kent faring?"

"She's recuperating splendidly, I'm happy to say."

"And your daughter?"

"Amanda is starting to gain weight thanks to the wet nurse we engaged. I believe both she and her mother have come through unscathed."

"That's wonderful. Does—does Mr. Abraham's son know his father has vanished?"

Gilbert nodded. "His reactions are strange. He acts neither happy nor sad. It's as if he's locked his feelings deep inside—"

And he's not the only one who has done that, Gilbert thought with a profound sense of guilt.

"Plagued odd, the whole business," Morecam said. "I should imagine it's disappointing, too, since you took such an interest in Mr. Abraham's welfare. Have you had a reply from Captain Lewis?"

"It's much too soon."

"Yes, I suppose." Morecam scratched his chin. "Do you have any idea why Mr. Abraham ran off?"

"None," Gilbert lied, turning away from the reporter. Surely his face was betraying him. His soul felt heavy as stone.

"Well, I'll see to hiring some men at once."

"Thank you, Mr. Morecam."

The reporter's footsteps faded, blending into the rhythmic *crumph-crumph* of the presses down on the first floor.

Gilbert stared out the grimy window, reflecting that there was but one source of joy left in the whole world: the tiny, gnarled and wondrously red face of the gnome-child that would, with luck, grow into girlhood and womanhood someday. He looked at Amanda often when he was at home. Suckled and cooing in her blankets, she was an astonishing creature. He held her with extreme care whenever he picked her up. His feelings at such times were as close as he'd ever come to a religious experience.

He already loved the child with a devotion that managed to scatter some of its warmth on Harriet. He was solicitous about her comfort. Never angry when she asked him—scathingly—about Abraham, usually coupling her inquiry with a declaration that she hoped he stayed away forever.

Gilbert was beginning to feel Abraham might do just that. Dear God, how many scars were left from that one night in July—!

He had seen a beast let loose within himself and had still not recovered from the experience. Very likely he never would, completely. In a peculiar way, his own violent outburst had drawn him closer to his vanished half-brother. They were more alike than he had ever suspected.

As a result, his new desire to find Abraham had become a fixation—even though Gilbert had no idea what he would do if his brother suddenly turned up.

Would he welcome Abraham back to the family? Harriet would resist—and the harm to Jared might make such an action doubly unacceptable. Gilbert didn't understand exactly what Jared felt about the events of that night—he refused to discuss them—but there was no question the boy's mental state had been affected. Perhaps permanently.

Why, then, did Gilbert pursue the search for Abraham? He had admitted the answer days ago.

Guilt.

The guilt was a constant, almost unendurable burden. And he couldn't share it with another human being; certainly not with his wife.

Like his own suddenly discovered capability for violence, Gilbert's guilt added a new perspective to his understanding of Abraham's actions after his return to Boston. He was able to see his half-brother's erratic behavior in a different, more compassionate light; was able to comprehend, and not just intellectually, how Abraham must have felt when Elizabeth died—

Staring through the fly-specked windows at slate roofs and church spires, Gilbert saw Abraham's eyes as they were a moment before he rushed into the rain that fateful evening.

Accurately or not, his memory told him Abraham's eyes had been filled with tears.

"Find him," Gilbert murmured to the yellow haze in the August sky. *"Find him—!"*

IV

BUT EVERY man and boy hired by Gilbert Kent ultimately failed in that assignment. By late September, he reluctantly concluded that Abraham had either left Massachusetts or—the possibility could not be escaped—done away with himself.

That only heightened Gilbert's sadness on the mellow afternoon when a special messenger brought a letter posted three weeks before, at the city by the falls of the Ohio.

From Louisville, where he had stopped with a river pilot, ten recruits and a Newfoundland dog christened Scannon, Captain Meriwether Lewis wrote to say that he and Captain William Clark would welcome former Cornet of Dragoons Abraham Kent into the Corps of Discovery that would start up the Missouri River the following spring. The letter was still in Gilbert's pocket as he walked slowly up the incline of Beacon Street in the late afternoon.

He had left Kent and Son early, unable to concentrate on his work. He'd roamed streets he couldn't remember, attempting to do the impossible—forget.

From the Common rang the cries of a band of small boys rolling hoops. Leaves streamed down from the trees under whose boughs his father had strolled while courting his first wife. The recurring cough brought Gilbert to a halt suddenly, a lace kerchief at his lips.

In a moment the spasm passed. He put the kerchief away and walked on.

The light had leached from the sky, leaving little more than a ribbon of bright amber beneath clouds lowering in the west. Gilbert drew Captain Lewis' letter from his coat. How pointless to carry it about, he thought. Harriet, occupied with baby Amanda, wouldn't be interested. A corner of the letter snapped in the autumn breeze as he remarked mentally that Abraham had certainly been right in one judgment:

Harriet's concern for Jared had only been pretense; a gambit to employ against Abraham in order to hurt him. Since Abraham's disappearance, she had barely spoken to the boy. Only from Gilbert did he ever hear a cordial word.

But it was to Jared's father that Gilbert's thoughts returned as he slowly ripped the letter into long strips, then tore each strip into smaller squares, finally letting the whole catch the wind and rise upward, blown and scattered in the fading amber light. The figures of the boys with their hoops were growing indistinct. Shadows covered the Common. Objectively, with no sense of superiority, he said to himself:

I have never been strong and never shall be. But poor Abraham—in many ways he was weaker than I. Well, all vessels have different flaws—as I have discovered.

But I am the only one left to help Jared survive.

That responsibility bore heavily on him as he resumed his slow progress up Beacon.

How different things might have been if Abraham hadn't caught some whore's pox. Perhaps the journey with Captains Lewis and Clark would have restored his faith in himself and his abilities—

Ah, but speculating on that was profitless. The chance was gone, just as the pieces of letter were gone in the clouds of dead leaves and debris whirled away by the twilight wind.

A servant girl from a house near Gilbert's went by. She carried a hamper of vegetables and a firkin of country butter. In response to her deferential greeting, Gilbert forced himself to touch the rolled brim of his beaver hat. A tall, emaciated figure in the dusk—an eighty-year-old clerk in a boy's body, wasn't that how Abraham had phrased it?—he gazed toward the lamplit windows of his own elegant home.

I must see that Jared does not merely survive, but grows into a sound, whole man—free of Abraham's legacy of failure and self-hate—

He had no illusions that it would be easy. Jared did carry the Fletcher blood. He lived in a household dominated by a woman who deemed him worthless, despised his very existence and seized every opportunity to show her feelings. As to the damage to Jared's young mind that dreadful night, who could say whether it would prove—as Gilbert often feared—irreparable?

Still, calmed by the beauty of the radiant light in the western sky, he knew he would try his best. One kind of blood—family blood; the blood of caring and compassion—must wash out the lingering traces of other, uglier blood that had marked the walls of the Kent house.

Was it possible? Though he vowed to try, it didn't seem so—

Then he thought of his father.

Gilbert stopped again, transfixed by the last golden sunshine under the darkening clouds above the Charles River. His eyes reflected the light like coins. From boyhood he recalled fragments of long conversations with Philip.

What was America if not the eternal promise of beginning again? Philip Kent had sensed that promise long before he first stepped on shore.

True, in his later years, he had rejected Jefferson's visions of an expanding nation. But to Gilbert that rejection was superficial, overridden by a deep and abiding kinship with Philip's most basic convictions. He and his father might differ on geography but they'd never had any fundamental differences about the promise of the land. They believed passionately in the enduring hope of change, renewal, rebirth that America's free air made possible—

His upturned face caught the last glimmers of the sunset. He felt a moment of almost supernatural closeness to his father. It was as if Philip stood near him in the shadows of evening, a presence at the edge of his vision, a powerful force that diminished his pain and strengthened his courage—

Unwilling to break the moment, Gilbert remained motionless, causing whispered comments from pedestrians hurrying by. Finally he roused himself, shivering in the sudden bite of the sunless wind. The aroma of wood smoke from chimneys enticed him homeward—with a quicker step now.

He would exchange trivial pleasantries with Harriet at dinner; rock and coo at baby Amanda for a few minutes afterward; and then he would speak with Jared. He would begin the long, hazardous and difficult job of raising Abraham Kent's son to manhood.

On his front stoop, Gilbert Kent paused one final time to stare into the western heavens, all clouds of ebony. His shoulders lifted, as if in anticipation of a struggle.

He turned and entered his house.

BOOK THREE
VOICES OF WAR

1
Jared

IN THE gloom of the vast building, the boy's breath plumed as he pointed to the plank-covered pits:

"Ten blocks of your best pond ice, Mr. Dawlish. Delivered to the house by six o'clock tonight. Six o'clock sharp. The poultry's due to arrive from the country by half past."

He extended a handful of coins. The ice house owner didn't take them:

"Anyone notice you two coming in here?"

The boy bristled. "Is that important? Money's money."

"Sometimes. Kent money ain't the most popular in Boston these days."

The slim but sturdy-looking boy stuffed the coins in his pocket and seized the hand of the little girl beside him.

Though only eight years old, in her cape and bonnet of purple velvet she resembled a miniature woman—as was intended. She had her mother's pale skin, brilliant dark eyes and hair. But her mouth was more generous, her expression more cheerful—never marred by the sourness the boy associated with Uncle Gilbert's wife, the girl's mother.

"Come, Amanda," the boy said. "Someone else will sell us ice."

Dawlish snatched the boy's forearm. "I'll deliver the order! Just do me a favor. Leave by the rear door."

Disgust showed on Jared Kent's rather sharp-featured face. He slapped the coins into Dawlish's hand and ushered Amanda toward the indicated door, walking with long, swift strides. Like his cousin, he was superbly and expensively dressed: nankeen trousers; a fine linen shirt with a frothy neckerchief; a vest cut straight across the bottom. Jared's uncle didn't insist he wear a striped

vest, the symbol of Democratic-Republican sympathies. Gilbert Kent frequently appeared in such a vest, though—scandalizing most of his Boston peers.

From beneath Jared's vest hung a fob, without which no gentleman, whatever his age, was well dressed. Jared lacked a watch to attach to the hidden end of the fob, but that didn't matter—only the fob's display counted.

He'd received the fob from his uncle the preceding Christmas. The obverse of the medal at the bottom of the broad green ribbon had been struck in the pattern of the tea-bottle symbol. There was also a Latin inscription:

Cape locum et fac vestigium.

The reverse bore the words Kent and Son, and the year. Jared liked wearing the fob as much as he hated wearing his tight-fitting jacket with its ridiculous short tails, a perfect duplicate of the adult male style.

As the cousins stepped into the surprisingly warm sunshine of a Saturday in early December, 1811, the varnish on the leather brim of Jared's cap glittered with highlights. He pointed suddenly:

"'Ware the cat."

Amanda hiked up her skirts and hopped over the dead animal rotting in the alley's drainage channel.

"Jared."

"Mm?"

"Why didn't that man want papa's money?"

Head tilted back, the boy was eyeing the slope of the roof at the rear of the ice house. Then he turned his attention to a pile of empty crates at the end of the building. His tawny hair, worn three inches long in the current youthful fashion, shone in the sun. His sky-blue eyes darted from the crates back to the roof. Finally he answered the question:

"Because Uncle Gilbert is about the only rich man in Boston who believes we should go to war, I guess."

Amanda covered her mouth. "Mama would take the birch rod to you if she heard what you just said."

"You're being silly. Tradespeople say 'I guess' all the time."

"But it's vulgar!"

With a grin, Jared leaned down, whispered:

"Shirt."

"Oh, don't!"

"Corset!"

"You *mustn't* say those words aloud!"

He laughed. "Going to report me to Aunt Harriet?"

The small, lovely girl shook her head in a serious way:

"No, you get enough punishment on your own. I hate it when she takes the rod to you."

"At the slightest pretext!" He started for the crates.

"It's no wonder. You're not polite to her."

"Amanda, she despises me. I'm sorry to say that about your mother, but it's true. Politeness has nothing to do with the thrashings—which I'm not going to allow much longer, I'll tell you. After all, I'm thirteen years old."

Stunned by the declaration, Amanda stood stock still. Jared strode straight on to the crates and climbed on the lowest one.

"Where are you going, Jared?"

He pointed. ''Up to Mr. Dawlish's roof peak. There should be a splendid view of the harbor.''

Holding her bonnet, Amanda looked upward. ''It's too steep!''

Jared shrugged. ''For you. Wait there.''

''No! I want to come with you.''

Jared glanced both ways along the alley. He heard a dray rumbling in the street that crossed one end of the narrow passage behind the ice house. But he saw no people. He crouched down on the crate, extended his hand, smiled a dazzling smile:

''All right. Take hold.''

Amanda was lithe and strong. In spite of her skirt she climbed the swaying pile of crates with little difficulty. Jared pulled himself up past the gutter, flung a knee onto the roof. A moment later he helped her up. He braced himself on the shingles, let her crawl ahead of him toward the peak. He saw her as a silhouette against the clear December sky.

Up here the wind tugged and gusted. Jared's cap blew off, skittered out of sight down in the alley. He paid no attention, amused at Amanda's panted complaint:

''If I dirty this cape mama will thrash me too. *Why* do you always have to do whatever comes into your head, Jared? If you'd just stop and think first—''

''That would spoil all the fun.'' His smile turned faintly bitter. ''I only do what your mother expects of me—''

''Don't be unkind again—!''

''I'm not. It's a fact.''

Clinging to the shingles, she breathed hard. ''But you know what gets you into trouble. And you go right ahead! You always have to see sights from a roof, or—or dash off to the next corner to look at what's beyond—''

''Because—'' Jared strained to keep from slipping. ''—because I usually don't like where I am at the moment, and I want to see where else I might go.'' His eyes hardened. ''I don't get caught all that often—''

''That's because—'' Looking back at him from the peak, Amanda drew deep breaths. ''—you're a boy. It's easy for you to go wherever you please. If I want to, I can't.''

''You're on the roof, aren't you?''

''It's too high.''

''No one forced you to climb up!''

''Oh, yes,'' she countered with utter seriousness. ''You did. I want to do whatever you do, Jared. But sometimes that's very hard for a girl.''

''You'd be wiser not to be such a good friend of mine,'' he said, still working his way upward by means of his knees and his elbows.

They hung over the peak side by side, gazing at a panorama of rooftops and, beyond, the piers of the South End where ships bobbed at anchor. Seaward, the harbor islands stood out with great clarity. The islands broke a horizon line that seemed incredibly distant.

The brisk wind gave Jared's cheeks a stiff, raw feeling. Yet the cold, pure light flooding down exhilarated him; produced a sense of freedom that was all too often lacking in the crowded street below.

Amanda's assessment of him was entirely correct. He *did* like to gaze on new sights—collect them, you could say. Maybe it was because he was always unhappy in the confinement of Uncle Gilbert's large, comfortable, but somehow unfriendly house on Beacon Street. Jared despised being at home—or in school—

anywhere, in fact, that he was supposed to be. He much preferred turning unfamiliar corners, or rattling through the ship yards, or hunting for coins in the muck beneath the piers.

"Oh!"

Amanda's cry jerked him back to reality. One of her tiny gloved hands shot out helplessly. A gust of wind had blown the bonnet from her head—the ties had evidently come unfastened during her climb. He saw the bonnet sailing into the next street.

She stretched both hands toward the vanishing hat. "It's gone!"

"Amanda, don't let go—!"

His warning came too late. She began sliding.

In panic, he grabbed for her elbow, missed. She slid further down the roof.

"Grab the guttering if you go over!"

Thankfully, she did. As he negotiated his way down the shingled incline, scraping his palms and his kneecaps, she hung from the edge of the roof. Then she disappeared. He heard a clatter as she struck the crates and toppled them.

By the time he slid over the gutter, dangled, then dropped, she was picking herself up from the cobbles. Ruefully she examined her cape. Mud and a long rip were her rewards for joining her cousin's little excursion.

She stamped a foot, as if that would somehow make the damage vanish. Her dark eyes filled with tears. Jared retrieved his sodden cap and wadded it in his coat pocket. To conceal his gloom over the little adventure ending badly, he scowled:

"Here, Amanda, it's only a cape. Don't snivel so."

"Do I care a penny for the cape? I'll get the rod and so will you!"

He pulled her against him; comforted her. She was probably right.

Eyes on the ice house door in case Dawlish came charging outside, he knelt. He began to dry her tears with his cuff. He noticed a raw place on the back of his left hand, which he'd scraped sliding down.

Blood oozed, bright scarlet. And the same thing happened that always happened when he chanced to cut himself. At the sight of blood, nausea churned his stomach and welled in his throat. For a seemingly endless moment, he was totally unable to move—

At last he wrenched his hand down, thrust it under his other arm, closed his eyes and applied pressure.

Puzzled, Amanda forgot her own difficulties. "Are you all right?"

"Yes. I—I'm fine."

Slowly he withdrew his hand. Thank God the scrape was superficial. The blood no longer oozed. His nausea lessened.

As usual, the reaction mystified and unsettled him. Why should the merest nick of a finger bring on that awful turmoil in his belly? That complete immobility?

Deep within himself, Jared had long ago answered the questions in a way that produced a feeling of utter hopelessness—and a secret conviction that Aunt Harriet was right in all she thought and said about him. He *did* have a quick temper; a wayward nature—and in some manner he couldn't fully comprehend or explain, he was being punished for it. Because he *deserved* punishment—

Jared could find no other way to explain the riddle of his uncontrollable sickness, always of short duration but always paralyzing.

He forced himself to glance to the ice house door. It remained closed. Evi-

dently Mr. Dawlish had retreated to another part of the big building and hadn't heard them clatter off his roof. That was one bit of luck, anyway.

"Are you sure—?" Amanda began.

"I'm perfectly all right. Let's be off."

He closed his bigger hand firmly around hers. The bedraggled cousins started for home, and the inevitable reckoning with Gilbert Kent's wife.

II

ON THE way, they passed a knife grinder singing a bit of New England doggerel:

> *"Our ships all in motion,*
> *"Once whitened the ocean,*
> *"They sailed and returned with a cargo.*
> *"Now doomed to decay,*
> *"They are fallen a-prey*
> *"To Jefferson, worms and embargo—"*

Though national and international politics held little interest for Jared, he had a good deal of knowledge about both subjects. His uncle discussed them often at meal time.

Thus he knew the three-year-old song was connected with the troubles currently besetting the United States; troubles that seemed to weigh more and more heavily on Gilbert Kent as one month succeeded another.

Almost alone among rich Bostonians, Uncle Gilbert had supported the former president, Mr. Jefferson of Virginia, just as he now supported Jefferson's chosen heir, President Madison. As a result, the Kent family had lost numerous friends.

Jared didn't understand all the reasons. But he did know that the bitter political feud between his uncle and men of similar position in the community went back at least to the early part of the decade; to what New Englanders termed the foul murder of the Federalist, Hamilton, by the Republican, Colonel Aaron Burr. Actually, as Jared understood it, Hamilton had not been murdered at all. He had died in a theoretically illlegal but perfectly fair match with dueling pistols.

Gilbert said contemptuously that because of "fossilized adherence to Federalism," Massachusetts and its neighboring states were becoming an alien island in the republic. He claimed most upper-class Bostonians were hysterics: falsely convinced that New England was being "submerged" by a "Virginia junto" which controlled the government.

Much of the current disagreement between Federalists and Democratic-Republicans had to do with the French conqueror, Bonaparte. Bostonians called him the Antichrist. In an effort to keep America from becoming embroiled in hostilities between the so-called Antichrist and his traditional enemies, the English, Jefferson had bottled up American shipping. Imposed something called the embargo. *Dambargo* was New England's name for it.

The embargo was the only one of Jefferson's policies that Gilbert had reluctantly disavowed. It was disastrous for New England's economy. Her merchants could not trade with England, France or any other foreign country. Her ships stood idle in port, protective barrels capping their masts. The other boys at

Jared's academy jeeringly referred to the barrels as "Mr. Madison's teacups"—Madison, then Secretary of State, supported and implemented the president's strategy.

Finally, the embargo was canceled—only to be replaced by the Non-intercourse Act. The Federalists considered it just as noxious as the embargo, since it still prohibited trade with Britain. That it also prohibited trade with France made no difference—France was the enemy, the Federalists shrilled, and why didn't America wake up to that fact?

Meantime, both Britain and France continued to interefere with American shipping. The British were particularly guilty. Their squadrons blockaded the American coast. Their frigates and ships-of-the-line stopped and boarded American vessels at will, supposedly searching for runaway English seamen who preferred to sail under the stars and stripes because American naval discipline was less cruel and capricious. The tensions at sea had all but nullified Jefferson's attempts at neutrality—and had produced an atmosphere in which the word *war* was mentioned more and more frequently.

New England wanted no part of a war with Britian. The rest of the country felt differently. Everywhere but in the northeast, people had cheered the preceding May when they heard the news of an encounter between a United States frigate and a British corvette.

The frigate *President* had mistaken the corvette *Little Belt* for a much larger and more infamous vessel, *Guerriere,* which had a long history of causing trouble for American ships in coastal waters. When *Little Belt* refused to answer *President*'s hail or raise identifying flags, there was a chase, then an exchange of salvos. The engagement ended with nine dead and twenty-three wounded aboard *Little Belt.*

Although the U.S. government offered to settle the resulting claims, many people said *President*'s action was completely justified, considering that three Americans had been killed, eighteen wounded and four alleged British deserters seized when H.M.S. *Leopard* stopped and searched America's *Chesapeake* in international waters in 1807. That four-year-old incident hadn't been forgotten. *President* had settled the score—and if the British wanted more of the same, they could have it! Were, in fact, begging for it. Despite diplomatic attempts to get the British to cancel their Orders in Council—the orders authorizing seizure of seamen on American vessels—the orders still stood.

So now, in 1811, practically all the nation except New England felt Britain should be called to account. Jared had heard Uncle Gilbert say that the settlers in the states and territories of the west were actually demanding war, to stop a rash of new forays by the Indian tribes supposedly taking orders from Canada.

Just a month ago, the activities of the tribes had driven the Americans to action. The prime troublemakers, the Shawnee Tecumseh and his brother the Prophet, who preached a mystical doctrine of Indian supremacy, had been fomenting a union of all the tribes; a union whose purpose was to halt the encroachment of white settlers. As Tecumseh's voice gained more and more listeners around council fires in the north as well as the south, General William Henry Harrison took to the field to stop him. In a stunning defeat, Harrison's small army routed Tecumseh's braves and razed his headquarters, the Shawnee village on Tippecanoe Creek in the Indiana Territory.

But Tecumseh was only at bay, not defeated. The Indian threat could materialize again—particularly since the British had a financial stake in driving the

Americans from the fur lands around the Great Lakes and beyond the Mississippi.

Furs remained the west's prime commodity. The expedition of Captains Lewis and Clark had only heightened the fever for exploration and exploitation of the Louisiana Purchase. Near the slopes of a great north-south mountain chain in the far west, Lewis and Clark said, beaver and other fur-bearing animals teemed. Thus America was in a race for control of the territory—

One evidence being the 1808 chartering of the American Fur Company headed by John Jacob Astor.

The German was already something of a national legend. Every boy Jared's age knew his name and his story.

A butcher's son, Astor had been born in a village called Waldorf, not far from the Rhine. He crossed the ocean and landed in America in 1785. His wealth consisted of seven expensive flutes which he hoped to sell at a profit.

The music business lost its appeal, however, as young Astor became interested in the growing fur trade. He made trading trips to the forests of upstate New York, returning with small collections of pelts. That was the beginning. Now he was incredibly wealthy, controlling his fur empire and his real estate holdings from a countinghouse in New York City's Liberty Street.

The Waldorf Astors would undoubtedly have been astonished to see how far their descendant had come in his lifetime, Gilbert said—but he predicted that Astor meant to go even further.

Long a familiar figure at the Montreal fur market, and closely connected with Canadian firms such as the North West Company, Astor knew the trade intimately. Gilbert believed Astor's formation of the American Fur Company was a naked grab for control of the fur business in the Louisiana lands—where the Canadians already operated freely. Gilbert supposed that if Astor's private ambitions were not at odds with the expansion plans of the United States—and on the surface they were not—Jefferson had been wise to throw his influence behind the granting of Astor's charter.

All in all, the reasons for a debate about war were many and tangled. None was considered valid in Boston, however—except in the Kent house. Gilbert steadfastly aligned himself with the American majority, and scoffed at those wealthy men who still talked of the New England states, seceding in order to form a separate country, friendly to England.

As Jared and Amanda neared the familiar streets in the vicinity of the Common, the boy recalled the elaborate dinner being arranged for tomorrow evening. The servants hadn't been told the names of the guests—nor had the cousins. The guests were supposedly arriving by private coach, from another city.

And the meal was scheduled for the unlikely hour of seven in the evening—after dark. Normally, dining began at two in the afternoon.

Could the mysterious preparations and the unidentified visitors have anything to do with all the talk of war?

III

ON BEACON Street, Jared pushed his cousin toward the curb suddenly. A dairyman's wagon went rumbling by, much too fast. Speeding vehicles were just one of the many manifestations of change about which Jared's aunt complained.

Jared supposed he should be grateful that Uncle Gilbert's wife tolerated him as part of her household. But he couldn't find it within himself to feel even a moment's gratitude. Aunt Harriet made it obvious that she'd thoroughly disliked Abraham Kent, who had disappeared and not been seen again since the year of Amanda's birth, 1803.

His aunt also seemed to know a good deal about Jared's mother. The boy had been told she was fair-haired and blue-eyed, as he was. Her maiden name had been Fletcher. Her roots went back to a fiery-tempered Virginia family.

Jared had long since conditioned himself to avoid thinking too much about the parents he'd never known, though that was difficult. Harriet Kent constantly reminded him of their flaws, and their unhappy ends—

Her attitude made the Beacon Street house a hostile place. But slowly, after much pain and inner turmoil, he had become resigned to that, and to his position in the house. No matter how kindly Uncle Gilbert treated him, he was an outsider; and an undesirable one.

Accordingly, he had come to realize that he would have to make his way alone, always fighting back his doubts about his ability to succeed at anything. His determination, however, only seemed to reinforce Aunt Harriet's feelings about him.

Whatever the source of his independent, even rebellious, nature, one thing was certain. He wasn't too young to indulge it—and much more completely than he had up to the present moment. Many young men ventured into the world at age twelve or thirteen. It might be time he joined their number. He was growing less and less willing to accept Aunt Harriet's criticism and discipline. The only reason he accepted them at all was Uncle Gilbert.

As he walked with Amanda, he pictured his uncle and felt a touch of sadness. Stoop-shouldered and already turning gray, Gilbert Kent was not yet thirty years old. A gentle, thoughtful man, he was burdened with too many worries. Everything from poor health and his complicated business interests to his lonely position as an opponent of men who should have been his friends—

Jared noticed a piece of paper blowing in the street. The type looked familiar. He picked up the paper and saw more evidence of his uncle's unpopularity.

The piece had been torn from the front page of the *Bay State Republican*. At the head of the central news column Jared saw a familiar black-ruled box surrounding four numbers set in a heavy face, in the style of a death notice:

$$\boxed{\textbf{6257}}$$

The number was carried on the front page of every issue. More symbolic than accurate, it represented the best available count of American seamen seized by the English navy as runaways from the King's service. The count had begun in the early 1790s, and the number had one objective—to inflame war fervor.

In the case of the person who'd bought this copy of the *Republican*, then ripped it up, it had inflamed something else. The words *Gilbert Kent Editor and Publisher* appeared in small type directly beneath the paper's masthead. Across them, another word had been crudely scrawled.

Turning around and seeing Jared stopped on the curb, Amanda skipped back. "Is that papa's paper?" she asked, brushing at the dried mud on her cape. She craned her head over. "Someone's scribbled on it—"

"A filthy word." He balled the paper and pocketed it quickly. Amanda was bright; she might understand the meaning of *traitor*.

"You mean a word as wicked as corset or shirt?" She tried to smile. But it was evident that her fear of returning home was undermining her spirits.

"Worse," Jared said. "Forget about it. We'd better decide what we're going to tell Aunt Harriet."

"Tell her?" The girl's eyes rounded. "You mean a lie?"

"Who said anything about lying? We'll just doctor the truth a bit! Now listen carefully. The alley was a mess of mud. I slipped and fell, then you fell trying to help me up. It's partly true, you know. We both tumbled pretty hard. We just won't mention that we started from Mr. Dawlish's roof."

Amanda looked dubious. "It's still fibbing. I never fib to papa or mama."

"Well, this is one time it's necessary! Even if we get away with the story, we'll probably take four or five whacks apiece, just for dirtying our clothes."

He gnawed his lip. But there was a sly gleam in his eyes:

"However—I won't fib unless you agree to it. So what's it to be? A fib to help me out? Or the truth—to get me in trouble?"

"That isn't fair! You mustn't make me take sides!"

A cloud hid the sun, throwing Jared's face in shadow. It was a handsome face, yet it turned ugly in the brief darkness. Something in him took pleasure in admitting that he did spite Harriet, and spite her well, by playing on the bond of affection between himself and his young cousin, whom he loved without reservation. He did it because it was one of his few means of striking back at his aunt; repaying her for the hurt she inflicted—

Abruptly, shame overwhelmed him. To use Amanda that way wasn't right, and he knew it. He squeezed her glove:

"See here. I wouldn't make you take sides for the world."

The cloud drifted away. So did the wrath on his face.

"Here's what we'll do instead. When we get home, you rush straight up to your room. Change those clothes while I handle the explanations. I'll insist what happened was completely my fault. I teased you so hard, you ran away—that's how you fell. I expect Aunt Harriet will believe it."

Amanda nodded in a grave way. "Yes, she might."

A bit startled, he smiled: "You agree very easily. You must think as little of me as your mama does."

"You know that's not so. But she—oh, I don't know how to say it right. She wants me not to like you."

His fair brows hooked together. "Does she tell you that straight out?"

"No, never. But she—I mustn't."

"Yes—" Jared's voice was flat. "Yes, you must. Go on, Amanda. What does Aunt Harriet tell you?"

"A great many bad things I know aren't true."

"That I'm disrespectful? Won't go to church? Slide through my studies at that wretched academy?"

"Things like that, yes."

Although he'd suspected as much, the confirmation hurt. It took him a moment to continue:

"And what do you say in reply?"

"Mostly I listen. I—I care for you, Jared. So I keep still and pretend I believe her." A hint of tears showed in her eyes again. "I suppose that's a kind of fibbing too. But I can't help it."

He touched her gently. "I never want to be the cause of your deceiving your mother and feeling bad—"

"I don't feel bad. Well—not too much." Her small, grave voice added years to the sound of the simple words. "It's just that—part of me belongs to her, Jared. Part belongs to you, and another part to papa—and you're both ever so much nicer than—well, I mean I try to be good with mama even when she speaks false, wicked things against you. But she makes me afraid. She says she won't love me if I stand up for you. I suppose all mothers act that way—"

He evaded the truth with a smile: "You know I can't speak from experience." A pause. "Does she talk to Uncle Gilbert about me?"

"All the time."

"Never when I'm present, of course."

"That's right, never."

"And—how does he take it?"

"Papa doesn't get mad very often, you know that. But I can tell that everything mama says makes him terribly angry because he puffs out his mouth—" She imitated Gilbert Kent's pursed lips. "—the way he does when something goes wrong at Kent's and they come to the house to tell him."

Quietly, Jared said, "I didn't realize I'd become such a burden to him."

"You haven't! He loves you just as I do!"

"But if Aunt Harriet's constantly carping about me, that's one more load he must carry—"

The blue eyes chilled. How careless and oblivious he'd been, not to sense that his aunt would actively work against him whenever he was absent—

With a gravity that outdid his cousin's, he said:

"No, I can't have Uncle Gilbert worrying on my account. Here's one more story—and this is the one I'm definitely going to tell." Rapidly, he repeated it for her:

After leaving Dawlish's ice house, he had insisted on climbing the roof. She begged him not to, but he went ahead. He slipped and fell to the alley. When she tried to help, he grew quarrelsome. Grabbed her cape, then pushed her down—

"*That's* how your clothes got all dirty and torn."

"It's just as much a fib as the other two stories, Jared."

"Yes, but it's the sort of fib your mother will believe without question. No mights, no maybes—"

"Are you trying to make her dislike you all the more?"

"Perhaps I am. Things can't go on as they are. I'm getting too old to stand for Aunt Harriet's punishments without—"

He stopped.

"Without what?"

"Without doing something about them."

"What can you do?"

He was silent a moment. Then, impulsively, he said, "Take myself away from her. Out of Boston—for good."

"Oh, no, Jared!" She clutched his arm. "I'd be so unhappy without you—you're the only true friend I have."

"But it's time I made my own way."

The thought had already solidified into a conviction. His mind raced at the new possibilities. Perhaps he could apprentice himself to a craftsman in another city. He'd need Uncle Gilbert's permission, though—

A sudden insight told him how to speed the arrival of that permission. Amanda seemed to sense what he was thinking:

"You're being so foolish! You want to take all the blame. You *want* to—!"

He patted her cheek affectionately.

"For eight years old, you're not only a beautiful child but a damned smart one."

"There you go cursing again—!"

"I'm sorry. Come along."

"Jared, you'll make me miserable if you go away—"

"And I'll stay miserable if I don't. If you really care for me, you'll let me do what I must."

Her dark hair shining as brightly as her silent tears, she hung her head and held his hand as they walked on toward the entrance to the Kent house.

IV

THE COUSINS were hardly given a moment's notice by the servants scurrying through the downstairs, arranging furniture, dusting, polishing—preparing for the Sunday evening guests. Disappointingly, there was no sign of Harriet.

Jared and Amanda went up to the third floor, to their respective rooms. Jared's had once belonged to his father. It was small—and made even smaller by his passion for collecting. Over the years he'd turned the room into a miniature museum and library; a junk shop, Harriet preferred to say.

Stacks of glass-fronted cases displayed all sorts of natural specimens: fossils, feathers, butterflies on pins, dried leaves and pressed plants. Tottering piles of books rose halfway to the ceiling, a huge and varied assortment. There were gazetteers and atlases of the country and the world—once, on a map of Ohio, he had marked a heavy charcoal cross on the approximate spot where his mother had met her death, then gazed at it for a quarter of an hour, and finally wept.

He had accumulated works of fiction and collections of essays too, including the very first volume ever published by his grandfather, Thomas Paine's *American Crisis* papers. On the top of one stack was 1809's international literary sensation, Diedrich Knickerbocker's *History of New York*. The pseudonymous author of the tongue-in-cheek narrative of the early days of New Amsterdam was a New Yorker himself, a Mr. Washington Irving. After hearing of Mr. Irving's manuscript, Gilbert had taken his private coach non-stop to Irving's home in an attempt to secure American rights to the work. To his annoyance, he had been outbid by another publisher.

But Kent's had scored a march the following year, successfully negotiating a contract to print an American edition of a rousing adventure tale, *Scottish Chiefs,* written by a woman named Porter. The book had done extremely well, salving Gilbert's disappointment at failing to land Washington Irving as a house author. *Scottish Chiefs* lay open on the bed; Jared was reading it for the third time.

He kindled a fire in the grate. As he finished, he heard Amanda's step in the hall. He peeked out to see her going down the back stairs, probably to the jakes at the rear of the second floor. She had already changed clothes.

He flung off his muddied coat, warmed his hands at the flames, re-examining his conviction that he must leave the house, and soon. He found no flaws in the idea—except one.

Where would he go?

Unbidden, thoughts of his father came, stirring a deep anguish. He knew so very little about Abraham Kent: that he'd served in the army under Mad Anthony

Wayne; that he'd spent a few years in Ohio as a farmer; that he'd brought his son back to Boston after marauding Indians killed his wife. Gilbert hinted that a quarrel with Philip Kent had driven Abraham out of the household the first time—and that a second quarrel with Gilbert himself had been responsible for Abraham's abrupt departure in 1803.

Jared's uncle refused to be explicit about details, but Harriet's invective made up for that. The boy's mental portrait of his father showed him a man who had been a failure. His image of his strong-willed mother was similar. Harriet made it clear she saw no hope for their son—and events often seemed to confirm that to Jared.

More often than not, his impulsiveness landed him in trouble. The little adventure on Dawlish's roof, for instance; Amanda could have been seriously hurt—

Perhaps he was destined to fail at everything he tried—and to be carried to that failure by his own temperament. The queer sickness he suffered at the sight of blood came to mind again. If there wasn't something wrong with him, why was he cursed with such an affliction?

Absorbed in the melancholy thoughts he was somehow unable to banish, he started at the sound of a voice:

"I was informed you had returned, Jared."

He turned. His aunt stood in the doorway, the birch rod in one hand.

"Good evening, Aunt Harriet, " he said politely. "I didn't hear you come in."

"The door was not quite closed."

She proceeded to close it. His heart leaped when she spied his mud-fouled coat lying in a corner. He was let down when the coat failed to keep her attention:

"You ordered the ice?"

Jared studied his aunt a moment. In a way, she was a beauty, Stunningly dark-haired, dark-eyed. But her face lacked the wholesomeness and good humor of Amanda's. On occasion it was a pinched, mean face—and this was one of the occasions:

"I asked you a question. Did you order the ice?"

"Ten blocks, Aunt Harriet. I did exactly as you instructed."

"How unusual."

He glanced pointedly at the stained coat.

"While you were gone," she said, "Mr. Tewkes paid a call."

He almost crowed with a perverse delight. From a totally unexpected quarter, here was an issue that would serve as well or better than the roof-climbing incident. Silas Tewkes kept a young man's academy in the North End. There, for a handsome fee from every pupil, the fussy old fellow taught Latin, sums and bits of natural science, history, philosophy and theology. Only the sons of wealthy citizens were welcome as pupils at the private school.

"Mr. Tewkes!" Jared repeated, rubbing his hands together in front of the fire. "That's a surprise."

"Don't act so cool and innocent! It's not a surprise at all—you surely know the reason."

"I suspect it."

"Well, it's going to earn you the rod."

Vastly pleased, Jared said nothing.

"Jared, it will be less difficult if you admit—"

"That I didn't appear for classes Tuesday or Wednesday? Of course I admit

it. There was still a little ice on the Charles. I went fishing. Tewkes is a dull old fart.''

He was delighted at Aunt Harriet's horrified gasp.

"You have a filthy mouth, Jared."

"I beg your forgiveness."

"Don't mock me!"

"Aunt Harriet, I'm sorry if I—if—" He could hardly keep from chortling.

"You dare to laugh! Silas Tewkes is a respected citizen and teacher! You've tried him sorely—when you've bothered to attend classes. And you've been absent repeatedly during the past several weeks, I discovered. He is thinking of dismissing you from the academy."

With a grand shrug, Jared said, "That's a bluff. Tewkes huffs and puffs, but he'll teach me till I'm a hundred if Uncle Gilbert keeps paying."

Harriet Kent tapped the rod against her skirt. "I have yet to report the visit to my husband—"

Smiling to soften his answer, he said, "I wouldn't do it. Uncle Gilbert seems in quite a state over these unknown visitors coming tomorrow. Who are they, by the way?"

"That is none of your concern. I find your defiant attitude intolerable—though not unfamiliar. You're just like your parents."

Here was an old, familiar weapon of attack; one that angered him as no other did:

"With all due respect, Aunt Harriet—don't bring them into this."

"You won't dictate to me what I will or will not discuss!"

"In this one area, yes, I will. For years I've listened to your slurs—"

"I only tell the truth!" she burst out. "Your father was a weak man. Unwilling to accept the standards of respectable behavior. That destroyed him, you know."

Jared's eyes burned. "The damned—"

"Stop that foul-mouthed talk!"

"—barbarous west everyone prattles about so glowingly—*that* destroyed him. Life out there is too hard for some people—"

Harriet's cheeks were mottled. She controlled her anger, but with difficulty; shook her head:

"It was his weakness. His weakness made him prey to your mother's foolish, rebellious—"

Jared took a step forward:

"Don't say any more."

"He took up a life in the west because *she* demanded it. They did it against all the advices of your grandfather, and she died as a result. Your father paid with his sanity and probably his life too. The night he left this house, he was insanely drunk. Bestial. And you've inherited the worst of both—"

Jared snatched at the rod in Harriet Kent's hand. Quickly, she retreated toward the marble fireplace. The color deepened in her cheeks. A tremor in her neck gave him a clue to the enjoyment she derived from baiting him.

For a moment they faced one another, eyes locked. All at once Harriet seemed to realize how tall Jared had grown; almost as tall as she was. Showing him the birch rod, she trembled:

"Stand aside. We'll discuss your parents another time—"

"We will not discuss them any other time, ever."

Harriet's mouth curled. "What a fine, proper boy we've raised! What a decent, respectful—"

A furious wave: "Don't use that flummery on me!"

"Flummery, is it—?"

"I never once begged for your not-so-kind attention!"

Scathing: "My! You've a masterful command of the language—"

"I haven't skipped all my classes with that pompous boot-licker."

"—but your expensive education seems to have generated no humility. Just the opposite. It's given you the desire—and the means—to flout your filthy temper and your arrogant views! I have no doubt—"

"Oh, be quiet, woman!"

"I have no doubt you'll ruin yourself the way your father did!"

His fists clenched at his sides:

"I'd rather be ruined, as you call it, than continue to live under the same roof with a mean-spirited bitch like you. Tell your husband *that,* why don't you?"

Harriet Kent whipped up the rod, intending to strike Jared's cheek. He caught her arm with one hand, seized the rod with the other.

Stepping back, he broke the rod over his knee and threw the halves onto the flames.

V

ASHEN, HARRIET whispered, "You're *exactly* like him! A *monster—*"

Jared stepped forward again, so close to her that he was overpowered by the citrus scent she wore. He fought to keep his hands at his sides:

"If you speak one more word about him—"

Harriet dodged toward the door:

"We're finished with words, Master Jared. I'll see you get your wish. *I'll have you out of this house!*"

Jared Adam Kent beamed:

"That would suit me admirably. *Admirably!*"

The door crashed shut.

He stared at it, the smile and the cocky feeling draining away all at once. He had widened the gulf, exactly as he'd planned. But it was less satisfying than he'd expected. Having given cruelty for cruelty, he felt unclean.

Sinking down on the bed, he held his head with both hands. The break had come sooner than he might have wished. But he'd been unable to control himself during the argument. That was disturbing—

Again the secret doubts swept over him. He wondered bitterly whether Harriet could be right. Was he taking the same kind of rash step his father had, at his mother's insistence? He'd heard it said that their confidence in their ability to survive in the west had been ill-founded. The results were death for Jared's mother—guilt and ruin for Abraham Kent—

Would he fail the same way? The fear of it grew consuming all at once—

And a distorted memory of his sickness when he stared at his own scraped hand seemed to turn the fear to a certainty.

Head starting to throb, he realized it was a little late for second thoughts about his decision. Fear or not, he'd have to face the consequences of the stormy scene just concluded. He must begin to think—and immediately—of a place to go. He

had to be ready when Aunt Harriet spoke to Uncle Gilbert, and Uncle Gilbert spoke to him—

He needed a destination—a means of escape—*something!*

The muddy coat forgotten, he leaned on the mantel and stared into the flames. No answer came.

2

A Mackerel by Moonlight

THE FOLLOWING morning, Jared delayed his arrival at breakfast as long as possible.

Normally, the first meal of the Sabbath would have been served early, to permit the family to attend church. This particular Sunday it was re-scheduled for the regular weekday hour—ten o'clock. Church was forgotten.

Jared felt intense relief as he entered the dining room. Uncle Gilbert was in his customary place, but Aunt Harriet was absent. He heard her out in the kitchen, shrilly warning the servants not to damage the Spode as they washed it.

So the best porcelain was to be set, eh? It was one more indication of the importance of the evening dinner party.

Uncle Gilbert sat at the head of the table, wearing a threadbare dressing gown and slippers. Harriet often complained about Gilbert's casual morning attire. Once Jared had heard his uncle reply that if a dressing gown and slippers were suitable for President Jefferson to wear while answering knocks at the door of the executive residence in Washington, he could dress the same way in his home with no loss of status. Harriet Kent used the word *status* often, with complete seriousness. When Gilbert used it, he did so jokingly.

"Good morning, Jared."

"Morning, sir."

"Sleep soundly?"

"Fine, thank you."

Gilbert's breakfast, hardly touched, was his customary slice of salt fish, piece of cornbread and glass of whiskey and water. At one side of the plate lay two piles of manuscript. The dark-haired, ascetic-looking owner of Kent and Son resumed reading. When he finished the page, he picked up his fork, absently ate a small bite of fish, glanced again over the top of his spectacles at his nephew, seated now. But he said nothing.

Gilbert looked almost as uncomfortable as Jared felt. His uncle took longer than usual arranging his fork, knife and spoons on his plate, the signal that he'd concluded his meal. He wiped his mouth and his hands on the hem of the tablecloth; utensils had made napkins unnecessary.

He coughed. Reached out; tugged the bell pull. Finally, fixed Jared with dark eyes made large by his spectacles, he brought up the subject the boy was dreading:

"You and I must have a conversation."

Jared wanted to be polite, but not overly defensive:

"I'm sorry I lost my temper with Aunt Harriet yesterday. She said unkind things about my father and mother."

Gilbert frowned. "She also said you were ready to strike her—which cannot under any circumstances be allowed or forgiven."

"Actually it was the other way around. She was going to strike me."

Expressionless, Gilbert digested that. Then:

"You've absented yourself from the academy twice this week, I hear."

"Aunt Harriet keeps you well informed, I hear."

Gilbert sighed, refusing to be baited by the bitter echo of his own words.

"She does. But even without that, your unhappiness lately has been quite evident. We must do something about it. Having said all I'm going to on the incident yesterday—specifically, that I won't tolerate a repetition—I'm prepared to sit down with you and discuss what's best for your future. I suggest we talk as soon as possible. This evening—after our guests depart."

"I'll be glad to, sir."

Jared could never stay angry at his uncle longer than a second or two. Gilbert's nature was essentially kind.

Not that he lacked strength of will. Jared knew he had that, in plenty. A weak man couldn't run a firm as large as Kent and Son successfully.

Yet Gilbert seldom raised his voice. Quiet reasonableness and a firm tone lent him just as much authority as bullying. Or more. Most people respected Gilbert's strength, no matter how they felt about his politics. And Jared knew better than to take Gilbert's mild warning about quarreling lightly.

In an effort to lighten the mood, he said, "May I ask who you're entertaining tonight, sir? From all the secrecy, I've wondered if it's someone who shouldn't be seen here." He forced a smile. "Mad old King George? Prinny?"

"The king and his dissolute son the prince-regent would be publicly welcomed in Boston," Gilbert said, returning the smile. "But they'd hardly call on us. I'm afraid I'm pledged not to reveal the names of our guests until they've left the city. You and Amanda will be served dinner upstairs, by the way."

Jared wanted to question his uncle further, but a serving girl entered, bringing his breakfast. It was the same as Gilbert's except for the beverage. Since his twelfth birthday, he'd been permitted beer in the morning instead of cider.

Gilbert returned to his reading while Jared picked at his food. A few moments later, Harriet came in from the kitchen, carrying a highly polished spittoon.

After a caustic glance at Jared, she paced around the table, for a place to put the gleaming brass pot.

"Really, Gilbert, you're occupying this room much too long," she said. "The girls need to begin preparing the table."

Gilbert sighed, removed his spectacles. "I'll take my manuscript to the library." He started to consolidate the two piles of paper.

"Why a respectable house must provide a place for men to spit their filthy tobacco is beyond me," Harriet complained, finally putting the spittoon beside the wall near the head of the table.

"There are spittoons all over Washington, my dear," Gilbert said. "The fad is spreading to some of the best homes in Boston."

"Not to ours, I trust! I never fancied I'd be forced to entertain one of those barbarous Kentuckians—"

Jared's hand went rigid, the fork halfway to his mouth. Hurriedly, he swallowed the bite, pretending not to see Gilbert frown slightly, and purse his lips. His glance at his wife, mild enough, still carried unmistakable warning.

Annoyed by the silent reproof, Harriet flounced out.

Jared's mind was afire with curiosity. A *Kentuckian* coming to dinner? Who could it possibly be? He determined to find out.

All at once his eye darted to a corner of the dining room. There right in front of him was the way to learn the identity of his uncle's guests—

"Finish quickly, Jared," Gilbert said as he left. "The day is going to be difficult enough, so try not to supply extra inducements for your aunt to fly into a temper."

He didn't act angry, merely resigned. Jared listened to the slow shuffle of his uncle's slippers as he proceeded to the library.

Gilbert did, however, shut the doors with a bang.

II

GILBERT KENT had always been a devoted student of the thinking and the habits of the former president, Mr. Jefferson. At considerable cost, he had copied one of the mechanical innovations the Virginian had installed at Monticello: a dumb-waiter.

Via a platform controlled by pulleys, the dumbwaiter lifted food from one floor to another. Carpenters had ripped out part of a dining room wall to install the shaft, which connected the downstairs with Gilbert's bedroom directly above. Jared had realized that, by means of the shaft, he might be able to hear the dinner conversation. He was so excited at the prospect, he quite forgot to be nervous about the coming discussion of his future.

Around three o'clock, he found an opportunity to slip into the dining room unobserved. In the kitchen, Aunt Harriet was yelling at the servants again. The roasting capons hadn't been properly stored in the ice delivered by Mr. Dawlish. One bird had spoiled—and she was going to take the cost out of the guilty party's wages!

Jared barely heard, busy unfastening the brass latch on the door of the dumb-waiter. He only opened the door a couple of inches. To open it more would invite discovery. He prayed no one would shut the door accidentally.

One of the servants in the kitchen commented that a Kentuckian would probably think a gamy capon very flavorful. Other servants laughed—which only made Harriet Kent launch into another tirade.

With a smile on his face, Jared stole out of the room.

III

"JARED, WHAT are you—?"

Angrily, he jerked his head around and put a finger to his lips.

Robed for bed, Amanda stood in the doorway. She blinked in dismay when Jared scowled. He sat on a chair pulled up to the opening of the dumbwaiter in Gilbert's bedroom. The room was plain, its furnishings wholly masculine. For as long as Jared could remember, Gilbert and his wife had occupied separate quarters.

"You scared me half to death," Jared whispered. "Why did you open that door?"

"Because it was closed."

"Don't you suppose doors are shut for a reason?"

"But papa's downstairs, Jared. He never closes this door unless he's in here by himself, read—"

"Keep your voice down! Leave or come in, as you please. But whichever it is, do it quietly! They've served the fruit and wine. Aunt Harriet will be leaving in a minute, so the gentlemen can talk."

The little girl darted a glance into the gloomy second floor hall. Then, curiosity mastering apprehension, she shut the door.

She padded across the carpet, her shadow long and distorted. Jared had turned down the single lamp always lit in the room after nightfall. Gilbert usually retired early, to work on copy for the newspaper or read one of the countless manuscripts submitted to the book department. With the bell pull at the side of his narrow bed, he summoned tea and cakes during the evening. The dumbwaiter brought them up—the same shaft that now carried hollow-sounding male voices to Jared's ear.

"Sit down. Here." He pointed to the floor near his knee. Amanda still looked a bit fearful. But she folded her legs beneath her, leaning her head against Jared's leg, her dark eyes large. She smelled pleasantly of soap.

"It's terrible to spy on grownups—" she began.

"You spy with your eyes, you ninny."

"Then what's the word for doing it with your ears?"

"Eavesdrop. Do be silent!"

"But who is down there? I saw Mr. Rothman's carriage drive up—"

"Yes, he came in the front way. The other two guests arrived in a coach that pulled into the alley. They used the rear entrance. At last I understand why," he added, with the smugness of one privy to a secret. "If your papa's guests showed their faces in Boston, they'd be mobbed—or worse."

"You still haven't said who—"

"Politicians! All the way from Washington. Very important men—hush! I hear Aunt Harriet leaving."

From below, a muddle of voices, one female, indicated the formal part of dinner was finished. Jared bent his head near the open door of the shaft, heard another door close distantly.

Glassware clinked—more wine being poured. Someone offered a compliment about the excellent capon. A loud spitting sound was followed by a *pling* as the jet hit the spittoon. Gradually, Jared began to sort out the voices.

He recognized Royal Rothman's easily. The middleaged Jewish banker was a frequent guest at the Kent table, because he was involved with Jared's uncle in business ventures. His bank provided money whenever Kent's needed to float a loan.

The voice of the spitter was rich and deep. His accent was definitely not that of the northeast.

The third guest spoke English with a foreign accent.

"—indeed generous of you to arrange this meeting, Mr. Kent," boomed the Kentucky tobacco-chewer. "The secretary and I felt the long journey and the inconvenience of traveling incognito were justified if we could sample the sentiment of New England first-hand."

"I'm flattered you chose to do it at my table, Mr. Speaker," Gilbert said.

"Mister who?" Amanda breathed.

"That's not his name, it's his title. Mr. Clay of Kentucky is a new member of the Congress. One of the Republicans called war hawks. He was just elected Speaker of the House. I don't know anyone in Boston who doesn't hate him."

A moment later, the cousins heard the voice of Royal Rothman. Despite surface politeness, his hostility was evident:

"Shall we address the issue, gentlemen? Mr. Kent and I wish to know whether there will be a war—which I would personally consider a national disaster. Mr. Kent must speak for himself—"

"In due course," Gilbert murmured.

Rothman went on, "You gentlemen in turn want to know New England's position. I trust I made that clear during dinner. And I believe I express the attitude of the entire business community."

"I'd be careful there," Gilbert said.

"Sometimes, Gilbert, I have the impression you actually favor a war. God pity you if you're that misguided! Your pardon, gentlemen. But I believe in being frank."

The heavily accented voice drifted up the shaft:

"Your candor is appreciated, Mr. Rothman. However, the Speaker and I are seeking somewhat more specific information."

Jared bent, lips to Amanda's ear:

"That man's name is Gallatin. He's in charge of the government treasury. Money. He's foreign-born. French, Swiss, something like that—"

"If we are forced into a second war for independence—" Henry Clay began.

"May we dispense with slogans, Mr. Clay?" Rothman asked curtly. "The issue is neither independence nor the one expressed in that other overworked phrase, free trade and sailors' rights. We know perfectly well what the main issue is. You and your associates—Mr. Calhoun and Mr. Cheves and Mr. Grundy and all the rest—you want Upper Canada, don't you?"

"That is the desire in the west, yes, sir," Clay returned, a chill in his voice. "It's a matter of—"

"Avarice," Rothman cut in. "Your constituents are greedy for the land. For the furs—"

"We are not acting out of greed, sir! We are acting on one of mankind's oldest principles—self-preservation! The lives of thousands of citizens of this country are being threatened. The British are inflaming the tribes of the entire Ohio valley!"

"The British foreign minister has repeatedly denied that charge."

"And I say Castlereagh's a damned liar, sir," Clay shot back, punctuating the retort with another loud spit.

The man did have a marvelous, resonant voice, Jared thought. He was a trial lawyer and, according to popular gossip, he'd trained himself as an orator by reading heavily, then going alone to a cornfield in his native Kentucky and speaking aloud for hours, discoursing on what he'd read. Most Bostonians wished he had never left that cornfield.

Secretary of the Treasury Gallatin spoke more moderately:

"We also have evidence that the Hudson's Bay Company is pledged to a plan to monopolize the fur trade—and is arming the savages with fusees to that end. You know how the British have coddled and encouraged that devil Tecumseh and his fanatical brother—"

"All of which," Gilbert said, "Castlereagh has denied."

Furious, Clay burst out, "If you gentlemen refuse to be reasonable about a clear threat to—"

"We will be reasonable if you will be truthful," Rothman said.

"Sir, are you calling me a liar?"

"I am saying every argument you put forward is spurious. Taken together, they resemble a rotten mackerel in the moonlight. It shines beautifully from afar. Up close, it stinks."

Clay snapped, "So brilliant, yet so corrupt—' Those were Congressman Randolph's exact words, I believe."

"I didn't claim the simile was original," Rothman said.

"But your choice of a source is regrettable. You're quoting an effeminate fool!"

"John Randolph of Roanoke is—"

"Half a man! Can you take seriously *anything* said by a scarecrow whose proudest claim is his descent from Pocahontas? Who struts into Congress wearing silver spurs, armed with a riding whip, and trailed by a damned slavering hound? Why, Randolph can't give a speech without stopping every ten minutes while the door keeper brings him a tumbler of malt liquor! Even that doesn't make his voice manly. He squeaks and squeals like a goddamned eunuch!"

Gilbert said, "Nevertheless, Mr. Speaker, John Randolph of Roanoke argues his positions in a compelling way."

"Not to Kentuckians he doesn't!"

"Ah, but you must grant he has a wit," Gallatin chuckled. "Adore him or despise him, you must admit that. I relish the time he was accused of lacking virility, and told his opponent, 'Sir—you pride yourself upon an animal faculty, in respect to which the Negro is your equal and the jackass infinitely your superior.' "

No one but Gallatin laughed. "I doubt if any black man would find that witty," Gilbert said. Gallatin harrumphed.

Rothman said, "We've strayed from the point. It's public knowledge that your faction wants Upper Canada, Mr. Clay, so we'll save time and eliminate distasteful acrimony—"

"It's you who were acrimonious, sir, not I! You brought up the mackerel by moonlight—*and* as much as called me a liar."

"Will you accept my apology so we can proceed?"

Clay grumbled something inaudible.

"Proceed from the assumption that war is inevitable," Gallatin suggested.

"Let's hope to heaven it's not!" Rothman cried.

"American liberty is again threatened on the land and on the sea," Clay declared. "There's just one way to teach Johnny Bull a lesson. At the point of a gun! From the mouth of a cannon!"

Once again Gilbert spoke, quietly but with authority:

"Since you raise the subject of guns, Mr. Speaker, perhaps some simple mathematics are in order. My newspaper keeps track of the state of the army. We have, I believe, not quite twelve thousand men in uniform—most of those green recruits. Moreover, the forces are widely scattered. A few at Michilimackinac, a few at Ford Dearborn out on the Illinois prairie—"

"The navy is in somewhat better shape," Gallatin said.

"You're joking," Rothman said. "Six frigates and scores of those worthless Jeffersonian gunboats—the whirligigs of the sage of Monticello? That's nothing

compared to six hundred British men-of-war, more than one hundred of which are ships of the line.''

Clay objected: ''But Britain still has her hands full on the continent.''

''And that is where *our* attention should be focused. On the true enemy. Bonaparte!''

''I must raise another hard question,'' Gilbert said. ''I don't mean to be rude. But have you gentlemen in Washington ever considered the danger to this country if Britain suddenly finds herself in a position to free large masses of men and great numbers of ships now committed to the struggle with Napoleon? We stand every chance of being crushed.''

Clay quickly overcame the argument:

''War will be declared before that ever happens, Mr. Kent. We'll overwhelm the British, not vice versa.''

''So you intend to have your way regardless of *any* consequences?'' Rothman demanded.

There was a strained pause. Jared leaned his head against the wall, his blue eyes large, his expression awed at the thought of men discussing the fate of millions of human beings over wine and the *pling* of tobacco hitting a spittoon.

''Answer me, please, Mr. Clay.''

''We will press ahead,'' Clay said.

''To disaster!'' Rothman predicted.

''Gentlemen, please,'' Gallatin put in. ''Once more we have drifted from the question Henry and I came here to discuss. It is no longer a matter of whether a war will be fought, but *how* it will be fought—''

''Why are you set on this hasty reckless course?'' Rothman roared, pounding the table. ''Britain has already shown some small sign of yielding eventually. Rescinding her Orders in Council. Stopping the impressment—''

''Don't forget Castlereagh is shrewd and slippery,'' Gallatin said. ''He may be playing for time.''

''I don't think so,'' Gilbert said. ''At least not according to what I hear from sources I trust. Visitors who've just returned from England. Aboard ships lucky enough not to be chased, stopped or fired upon, I might add!''

''Now you sound like a hawk,'' Rothman complained.

''I'm only stating facts, Royal. But like you, I believe we can bring the British ministries around. Convince them to change their policies. *If* we have time.''

''We don't,'' Rothman replied. ''And it makes no difference to Mr. Clay anyway. The west is hungry for land—nothing but land. Last year Jemmy Madison grabbed the West Floridas—''

''Annexed,'' Clay corrected.

''—and at the moment he's eyeing the East Floridas. You know who to blame, Gilbert. Your blasted Monticello squire started the fever. Now it's epidemic!''

Gilbert had no immediate answer. Gallatin said:

''Since New England is so important—indeed, we might say paramount—in commerce and finance, I must ask the position of gentlemen such as yourself, Mr. Rothman, in the event hostilities do break out.''

''Are you asking about loans to the government, Mr. Secretary? War loans?''

''I am.''

''You'll not get a dollar from Rothman's. I venture every other banking house in New England will say the same thing.''

''And you gentlemen will have a difficult time funding a war without New England money.'' Gilbert said.

"We will make do," Clay said in a flinty way. "We've obtained the answer we came for—"

Sounding dispirited, Gallatin said, "Indeed we have."

"I warned you what it would be, Mr. Secretary." Clay spat again.

Now that the hard truth had been brought into the open, Rothman attempted to soften it a little:

"I'm sorry, gentlemen. New England simply can't afford a war. We depend on overseas trade for marketing our goods. Jefferson nearly destroyed us with his embargo, and a war would bring complete ruin."

"That's sheer imagination—" Clay began.

"That is our position," Rothman countered, cold again.

"Thank God, it's not the position of the rest of the country. We *will* make do."

"You can't dismiss New England quite so quickly," Rothman warned.

"Why not, sir? Isn't she ready to set herself up as an independent nation?"

"Not as yet, sir. But if you and your cohorts persist—"

"I believe we have exhausted this subject, sir."

"No, we have not!" Rothman shouted. "I fought for these states in the Revolution, but I am not going to see your damned, unwashed mobocracy plunge them into a second, useless war with a people who should be our closest friends!"

"Is that patriotism speaking, sir? Or the balance sheet?"

"You damned poltroon—!"

"Royal, you forget yourself!" Gilbert exclaimed.

"To the contrary! New England is the bedrock of this nation—"

"No longer!" Clay thundered. "You are living in the past, sir! The west is the rising star!"

And may it sink to hell, Jared thought, the memory of his father breaking his concentration.

Downstairs, voices rose in a confusion of accusations and epithets until Gilbert cried, "Gentlemen, this is my house, not a tavern! Please act accordingly!"

That elicited another round of half-hearted apologies, and a degree of calm. The subject of war was dropped, in favor of perfunctory conversation about business in general, and Gilbert's newspaper in particular. Avoiding the question of whether the *Bay State Republican* would support a war, he tried to interest his visitors in some of the innovations he had in mind.

He spoke of his plan to launch a penny paper, undercutting the prevailing six-cent price in order to capture a larger share of the increasingly literate population.

He speculated about the possibility of employing boys to sell papers on the street in an organized way, not haphazardly, and of sending the same boys door to door to boost circulation even further.

When the troubles at sea cleared up, he said, he wanted to purchase a dispatch boat to sail out and meet incoming ships, so he could get the latest European news into print ahead of his competition.

By the time he started to discuss the possibility of modern invention being harnessed to improve printing equipment—"The prospect of a steam-powered press is staggering, gentlemen, and not at all out of the question."—his guests were murmuring that they must leave.

Chairs scraped. The goodbyes were stiffly polite. Jared closed the door of the dumbwaiter and caught his cousin's hand, hurrying her out of the room.

"They kept talking about war," Amanda said when they reached the stairs. "Do they mean men fighting other men?"

"Yes, that's what they mean."

"Will you have to fight?"

Startled, he realized her question raised an entirely new issue; injected a completely new factor onto the uncertain future.

"I don't know whether I'd have to. But I might want to," he answered.

At the back of the house, a coach clattered away. In the lower hallway, Royal Rothman was having a final word with his host. Jared heard the banker growl something about the rotten mackerel stinking worse than ever—

He patted Amanda's rump and started her up to bed:

"Tuck yourself in and put out your lamp—"

"Won't you come do it fo me?"

"No."

"Please—?"

His face oddly drawn, he shook his head.

IV

You DO have a passion for satisfying your curiosity—regardless of the possible consequences."

He drank, not realizing that his nephew took the remark as an accusation. An unconscious one, perhaps; but an accusation all the same.

"You must forget everything you heard, Jared. Mr. Rothman particularly would be badly compromised if it were known he'd even been in the same room with Henry Clay."

"I'll say nothing." *And I must tell Amanda not to, either.*

"The gentlemen are staying the night in Roxbury," Gilbert went on. "Under false names, of course. They'll start back to the capital tomorrow—" He sank into a chair and peered at the rum in his goblet. "I'm glad they came. I have a better perspective, meeting one of the leading war hawks in person. I believe war will come. And while Clay's motives are far from spotless, I believe it should."

"You do? You didn't make that clear during the conversation."

"Royal was already upset. I saw no reason to add to his unhappiness. I'll tell him my feelings in due course. He suspects them already—"

Another long swallow of rum. "I don't favor war for the reasons Mr. Clay does. Royal was correct—the hawk faction can only screech 'Canada! Canada!' It's their obsession. Impressment's a side issue—while to me it's the central issue. The same sort of issue which drove your grandfather to join all the others who refused to have their liberties abridged forty years ago—"

The eyes of both were drawn to the portrait of Philip. After a moment, Gilbert set his drink aside.

"But we have a different issue to discuss."

Tense, Jared murmured, "Yes, sir."

"I know you're not happy in this house. There's no need to dwell on why—"

"I *must* get away, Uncle Gilbert. I've no patience with school any more—"

"Oh, I think you've already had quite enough to carry you through life. The trouble is, I don't know what you *do* want. Where you hope to go, in the broadest

sense of those words. Is it an apprenticeship you're after? I can offer you that at Kent and Son.''

"But I'd have to stay on here, and I feel I shouldn't." Jared leaned forward. "Please understand—it has nothing to do with you."

"I understand." Gilbert covered his mouth briefly, coughed.

"I'll be less of a burden if I'm gone."

"You're no burden, Jared."

"That's kind of you to say, but I know otherwise."

"I've never particularly pressed you about joining the firm—"

"I appreciate that."

"From the time you were very small, I somehow felt commerce wouldn't interest you. I think you've inherited more than a touch of your mother's restlessness."

Jared tried to smile. "That Virginia blood you talk about?"

"This country is being created out of such restlessness. Created, expanded— it's not a bad thing."

"I've no desire to go into the west the way my father did," Jared said, his voice harder. "It's a brutal place. It killed him."

"Well—in part."

Gilbert didn't amplify the remark. He looked at his nephew with disarming friendliness.

"I know it would be wrong to urge you to stay and work at the firm. You can't abide your aunt—no, don't say anything. Don't pretend. That's a truth neither of us should hide from—though it's not necessary to delve into the reasons. As you well know, Harriet doesn't harbor warm feelings for you either. Regrettably, there's blame on both sides."

Jared nodded slowly. "I—I just want out."

"I'm willing—if we can find something suitable for you to do. You look surprised."

"I didn't think you'd agree to my going."

"I want to spare you *and* your aunt further quarrels you both might regret for the rest of your lives. I've let my temper carry me away a few times in the past— the night your father left, for one—and I've cursed myself ever since."

"You've hinted about that quarrel, but never described it. Was it—?"

"Bitter," Gilbert interrupted. "Bitter, hateful, viol—oh, but that's the past." He faced away. "It's enough to say that, ever since, my conscience has driven me to launch a search for your father at least once a year. Never with any success, alas."

He paused. "I'm wondering, though—"

The library lamps put pinpricks of light into his dark pupils.

"—suddenly I'm wondering whether the answer to your dilemma might not be a leaf from your father's book."

"What do you mean, sir?"

"I think I've mentioned that your father went through a period of conflict with his father and mine—" He gestured to the portrait. "As a temporary solution, your father chose the military service."

Jared turned cold at the implications of that. His negative reaction didn't come from cowardice as much as from his basic doubt about his own ability to survive in inherently difficult circumstances. But he kept silent, letting Gilbert continue:

"I wouldn't want to see you in the army. As you overheard, it's hardly worthy of the name. Its highest commanders are dodderers, incompetents or both. But

the navy, now—that's another matter. Though small, the navy's acquitted itself splendidly over the past ten years. From all I've heard, the officers by and large are first-rate—a match for any British captain afloat. And the half dozen frigates under sail must constantly replenish their crews as enlistments run out—''

"How old do you have to be to join?"

"For powder monkeys or cabin duty, they take boys from eight on up. You might have a chance at something better. A midshipman's appointment. I could perhaps direct a letter to the Secretary of the Navy—yes," Gilbert said with growing animation, "navy duty could be the answer. It would certainly suit the family tradition I've tried to keep alive."

"What tradition, sir?"

Gilbert didn't give a direct answer to the question. He walked to the portrait of Philip; gazed at it a moment, then said quietly:

"It's a pity you never knew him, Jared. A remarkable man. I loved him without reservation. When I was growing up, I was sickly—a disappointment to him, I'm sure. Yet he was unfailingly kind. The older I grew, the more I came to respect his convictions. I don't mean his conservative politics—most men become more conservative as they reach middle age. I'm talking about something deeper and much more fundamental. He used to say this country gave him hope when he had none. It gave him love when he had none—gave it twice over. Your grandmother Anne, and my mother. He said he always felt it was his duty to repay those debts—''

Jared looked at the strong face on the canvas. "I remember your telling me how brave he was."

"Brave in the most meaningful way. I'm sure he felt fear just as all normal men do—but in spite of that, he chose to fight for liberty when it would have been easier and more comfortable to remain a Tory. Beyond that, he pulled himself up in the world from nothing, and built a business. To make money, to be sure—but also because he believed the printing trade is of inestimable benefit to mankind. 'Take a stand and make a mark.' That was the sum of his life and his belief. He said those words to me shortly before he died. I've never forgotten them. I hope you won't either. That's why I had them inscribed on the fob I gave you last Christmas. In the navy, I think you could find the kind of fresh horizons you always seem to be hunting. Yet at the same time, you'd be giving as well as taking. Just as your grandfather did. Just as I try to do in my limited way. That's what I mean when I speak of carrying on the tradition he established."

In the ensuing silence, both gazed at the painting again. Then Gilbert became brisk; businesslike:

"Unless you say otherwise, tomorrow I'll draft a letter to Washington. I'll make inquiries as to the whereabouts of our frigates. And, if possible, learn whether one might be berthing in Boston soon."

Despite his earlier apprehension, Jared found himself warming to Gilbert's suggestion. Perhaps it was exactly what he needed: to test himself in hard circumstances. Perhaps that way, he could prove Harriet wrong—

Yet fear remained. What if he did say yes—only to fail?

He wouldn't! He swore that silently; fervently—

The idea of naval service wasn't all that ominous if he stopped to think about it. There were aspects that excited him. Small as it was, the navy had a certain dash. He vividly recalled the previous April when the city's own frigate, *Constitution*, Captain Hull commanding, had put in briefly to fill out her crew roster.

The town had taken on a festive air—and rocked with laughter at the story of a green farm boy who had apparently swallowed too much of the recruiting officer's rum. The country boy signed on believing he was to be the captain's gardener.

When he sobered up and demanded his rake and hoe, a light touch of the cat convinced him to accept the tools of a carpenter's mate instead.

Boston had an ambivalent attitude about *Constitution.* She would sail against the British if war came—and Bostonians detested that idea. Yet the locally built warship remained a source of intense civic pride.

Alas, there seemed little chance of serving aboard the city's own vessel. In August, *Constitution* had cleared the Virginia Capes, bound for the dangerous waters along the French coast. She was carrying the new minister to France, Mr. Barlow, and his family. The *Republican* had run an item about it.

But as Gilbert said, the Boston ship was only one of six frigates now in service. Perhaps Jared could find a place on another. The thought of it—of laying Aunt Harriet's convictions to rest—put a glow in his eyes—

Abruptly, the glow faded. Gilbert noticed:

"What's wrong?"

"Do you really think they'd take me? I have no experience with ships."

"Nor do half their recruits. You'll learn, and quickly. The life's hard. But most American captains aren't the martinets their British cousins are—and there are fewer cruel and unreasonable punishments for breaches of discipline. There *is* a real reason why English seamen desert and wind up on our ships, you see."

He scrutinized his nephew.

"Of course, in any service, one's expected to obey orders. As I've said before, you're much like your mother in some respects—"

"Aunt Harriet keeps reminding me of that."

Gilbert frowned, then shrugged off the retort. "The fact must be faced, Jared. It would be folly to consider the navy if you feel you couldn't do what's expected of you. *Without* resentment."

More moderately, Jared said, "I can follow orders, uncle." He hoped it was the truth.

Gilbert's expression softened. "I'm heartened to hear you say it. Perhaps life in this house hasn't been a fair test of that."

All at once Jared felt as if fetters had dropped from him. He recalled all the times he'd lounged along the Boston piers, watching the tall ships running in through the island channels, homeward bound from faraway ports. He'd never imagined that sort of life for himself. He was astonished at his oversight.

With enthusiasm, he declared, "I think the whole idea's wonderful. Please write the letter tomor—did I say something wrong? You're smiling."

"For no sensible reason. You said nothing wrong."

Absently, Gilbert passed a pale hand across his brow. He walked to one of the windows overlooking the Common.

Jared sensed an abrupt and extreme tension in his uncle. Gilbert's slow pivot from the window suggested physical labor. His eyes were sad; remote—as if he'd looked outside and gazed on something other than the Sunday evening darkness.

The boy waited, his hair glinting bright as metal in the radiance of the library lamps. He actually saw his uncle's eyes return from whatever private vision had bemused him—return and focus on Jared's face—and still with that sad air:

"I repeat, I had no reason to smile. I was struck by a thought, that's all. How everything changes and nothing changes. Some—"

His voice grew firmer as he composed himself.

"—some years ago, in this same library, I offered to write another letter for another—"

He hesitated. Jared contained his surprise at the glitter of tears Gilbert quickly dashed away with the back of one slim hand.

"—another man, in the misguided hope I could re-direct his life. I'll tell you the whole story one day. But not this evening. The—the dinner was quite tiring."

Jared accepted the falsehood in silence. Somehow he knew it was the recollection, not the argument about war, that had unsettled his uncle.

Gilbert went to his nephew. Put an arm around him:

"I trust I'll be more successful with the second attempt than I was with the first."

He removed his hand, averted his head.

"Now—"

Again the broken voice.

"It's best we retire, I think."

V

THE MOMENT Amanda heard the news at the dinner table, she wept—and refused to stop when Harriet ordered it. Harriet marched the little girl from the room and whipped her long and hard.

Yet Jared soon noticed that once he and his uncle announced their joint intention, Harriet treated him with unexpected cordiality. She was attentive, cheerful and permitted him to take as many holidays from the academy as he pleased.

He knew why. She was delighted at the idea of getting him out of the house.

Ordinarily, he might have hated her all the more. But he didn't because he was intoxicated by the winds of freedom he was scenting all at once. Strong, clean winds that blew frustration and unhappiness out of his life at last.

As the year 1812 opened, the inflammatory talk from Washington grew hotter still. Except in New England, the country seemed to be in a ferment of anticipation—

"Canada! Canada!"

"Free trade and sailor's rights!"

"SHOW THE DAMN BRITISH ONCE AND FOR ALL!"

Jared fully appreciated that in a war, men died. Yet he was young enough to accept the possibility without worrying too much about it. In return, he would escape from Beacon Street. He was getting the better end of the bargain, he felt.

If he stayed under Harriet Kent's thumb much longer, his spirit would wither and perish altogether—

Or erupt in some terrible act of rage and rebellion that could mar his life forever, as Gilbert said. By going to sea, he might escape all that. *And* answer some fundamental questions about himself.

Buoyed by a new sense of confidence, he found his fear lessening.

War was like that rotting mackerel in the moonlight, he decided. So long as

you stood far enough away to miss the stench, it gleamed with considerable attraction.

___3
The Frigate

IT WAS mid-May before Gilbert received a reply to his letter to Secretary of the Navy Paul Hamilton. The secretary apologized for his delay in answering, but as Mr. Kent could well appreciate, pressing matters occupied the department. Gilbert and Jared both understood the nature of the pressing matters.

Regrettably, Hamilton said, no appointments for midshipmen were available at the moment. Should Mr. Kent's nephew still wish to serve, he would have to do so as a ship's boy, receiving six dollars per month for an enlistment of one year. Mr. Kent would also understand that Mr. Hamilton could provide no information concerning the whereabouts of the larger United States vessels, but with luck, one of the frigates might soon put in at Boston or another New England port, and Mr. Kent's nephew could then apply.

Jared was disappointed. But the setback didn't change his plans.

On the eighteenth of June, President Madison declared war.

___II

BOSTON'S BELLS tolled in mourning. New England's Federalist press raged. The declaration had only been approved in the Senate by *six* votes!

Pastors took to their pulpits to decry the step. Toasts at conservative dinner tables condemned *The existing war—this child of prostitution—may no American acknowledge it as legitimate!*

Although the American army had to depend on the militia for immediate manpower, Governor Strong of Massachusetts, as well as the governors of Rhode Island and Connecticut, refused to permit their militias to operate outside their respective states—or obey any order of the federal government.

New England's fury mounted when packets slipped past the British vessels cruising off the coast and delivered news that seemed to confirm the declaration as a tragic mistake. On the twenty-third of June, Lord Castlereagh had suspended the Orders in Council—those hated edicts responsible for the harassment of American ships.

The news arrived too late. The army, such as it was, would soon be launching an attack on Upper Canada from its headquarters at Detroit. The commander was to be General William Hull, an outdated relic whose Revolutionary service hardly equipped him for modern frontier warfare. Few seemed worried. Hadn't Jefferson himself written that conquest of Canada was "just a matter of marching"?

In July, Bostonians could sneer at Jefferson's confidence with justification.

The key United States garrison on Michilimackinac Island, gateway to the western fur country, surrendered to an enemy force.

But worse was in store.

Rumors spread that the Shawnee Tecumseh would definitely align his braves with General Isaac Brock. The Federalists shook their heads. Brock had twice the wits and ten times the courage of that old fool Hull.

A pattern of hideous blundering began to emerge. The British on the frontier had of course received word of the declaration by special couriers. But while Hull was plodding northward through Ohio to Detroit, some dunderhead in Washington chose to send him the same news *by ordinary mail*. The British commanders knew war was definite eight days before Hull did. Thus they seized an American ship on Lake Erie and captured an unexpected prize—secret orders for the American general.

When Gilbert learned the whole unbelievable story, he penned the *Republican*'s first editorial in favor of the war. He demanded the firing of the incompetents in Washington who had informed Hull too late, and insisted on replacement of the general with a younger, more competent man. But he also voiced support for President Madison's decision, and the action of Congress.

The night the editorial was published, a dozen hooligans appeared on Beacon Street and hurled rocks at windows in the Kent house. Three were broken before Gilbert dashed outside, his father's Kentucky rifle loaded and ready to fire. He had taught himself how to use the rifle several weeks earlier, anticipating just this sort of nocturnal visit.

The hooligans screamed obscene insults and lobbed a few more rocks. Gilbert raised the rifle. Instantly, the small mob disappeared in the darkness. An hour later, still white from the incident and suffering sharp pains in his chest, Gilbert was rushed up to bed.

Against the advice of Doctor Selkirk, he was up and working twenty-four hours later.

III

ON THE twenty-sixth of July, sails appeared in the President Roads below Boston harbor. The sails belonged to the city's own frigate, *Constitution*.

She anchored and poured her tars into the streets soon after. They spread a story of an incredible feat of seamanship. Jared heard the particulars on the afternoon of the twenty-seventh, when he went to the recruiting office newly opened in a rooming house operated by a Mrs. Broadhurst in Fore Street.

He ran most of the way. *Constitution* hadn't filled out her crew roster before clearing Annapolis in early August.

IV

A PLANK table had been set up in the first floor parlor of the rooming house. After a few preliminaries, the officer behind the table asked:

"You're familiar with the ship for which we're recruiting, I take it?"

"I am."

"I mean to say, our recent exploits?"

"The town's talking of nothing else—though to be honest, nobody seems quite clear on all the details."

"I don't doubt there's considerable exaggeration in the retelling," the young officer commented. "Hardly necessary. The truth's remarkable enough." He helped himself to a drink from a jug of rum.

The young man was one of *Constitution*'s lieutenants, slender and tanned. Jared reckoned him to be twenty or twenty-one. And almost too handsome. His dark hair pinned up in a queue looked as glossy as a woman's. His brown eyes had a languid quality—maybe from rum. He had proffered the jug the moment Jared walked into the airless, musty parlor, but Jared had declined. Now he almost wished he hadn't. Somehow the officer made him self-conscious.

The young man put the jug down, his tongue creeping slowly along his pink upper lip. His eyes ranged over Jared's face. The boy grew even more uncomfortable; tried to distract the lieutenant:

"How long were you actually chased—?"

"Three days," the young man answered in a slightly slurred voice. "Three days and two nights. Almost sixty-seven hours." He didn't sound like a southerner, but neither did he speak with a New England accent. Jared decided he must be from one of the middle states.

"And you realize"—the officer punctuated the remark with a pointing finger—"not a man or boy aboard caught a wink of sleep during that entire time. You are not volunteering for a life of leisure."

"I understand that."

"Good—excellent."

The young man rose, strolled to the front window, his black pumps clicking on the scarred floor. Jared fidgeted. The room was depressing, its appointments old and shabby, in sharp contrast to the lieutenant's elegant white stockings and breeches and blue tailcoat. His huge half-moon hat lay on the table near a litter of forms. He gazed out the window a moment, then let the curtain fall.

"If you're prepared to work hard, you'll enjoy the privilege of serving under a damned fine sailor—"

"Captain Hull."

"Quite right. He's a fighter—but no fool. We came on the enemy three days out of Chesapeake Bay. Five of His Britannic Majesty's best—"

"I heard it was six."

"Exaggeration again. Five were sufficient to give Hull pause, I assure you. There were four men o'war and *Guerriere*, the frigate that's caused so much trouble recently." The lieutenant gestured in a languorous way. "Hull knew we stood no chance against those odds. Besides, the enemy had a slight breeze and we had none. But the captain vowed we wouldn't be captured." The lieutenant smiled. "Not quite the same attitude as you find in the army. There, it seems, they surrender the moment the enemy farts."

Jared shifted his weight from one foot to the other. He supposed this praise of the navy was intended to generate eagerness in new recruits, but in his case it wasn't necessary:

"I had no desire to join the army. My father was a soldier, but—"

"Was he!" the lieutenant broke in. "So was mine. Where did he serve?"

"In Ohio—when it was still the Northwest. He fought with Wayne at Fallen Timbers—"

"Remarkable! My father was there as well. Got himself killed, the poor wretch. Perhaps the two knew each other. Is your father still living?''

It was easier to simply say no than to give a complicated explanation about Abraham Kent's disappearance.

"Well,'' said the lieutenant, moving closer to Jared and squeezing his shoulder, ''we have something in common, don't we?''

The dark, languid eyes held the boy's. Jared felt acutely uncomfortable; said quickly:

"How exactly did you escape the five ships?''

For a moment the lieutenant acted annoyed. But he released Jared's shoulder.

"First we put men in rowboats, to tow us ahead. We gained a little headway, but not enough. And as soon as their wind died, the damn Britishers used the same trick. So next morning we began kedging. Do you know what that is, my boy?''

"I don't,'' Jared replied, growing irritated himself. To be called a boy by an officer barely out of his teens was demeaning.

Besides that, the lieutenant's half-lidded eyes had a disturbing way of focusing on odd places. Jared's mouth; his hands; and once, he was sure, his groin—

"You'll discover what it means if we sign you on,'' the lieutenant told him. "To kedge, a special anchor's fastened to the longest, stoutest hawser you can put together, using all the cordage aboard. Ours stretched half a mile—''

"I did hear someone talking about a long line,'' Jared nodded, anxious to conclude the business and get away. But the lieutenant was in no such hurry. Jared took it as another bad sign.

"The hawser's rowed ahead of the ship, don't you see, and dropped with the kedge anchor. Then the ship's pulled forward by men picking up the hawser and walking aft. That helped us move along in pretty fair fashion. Whenever one of the enemy got a little too close, Captain Hull ordered shots from four of our long twenty-fours. To set them up in the stern, we cut away—am I boring you?''

Jared's head jerked up at the abrupt change in tone. He had clearly angered the lieutenant—

Well, what of it? He was ready to walk out. He disliked the atmosphere in the dark, stifling room; and he disliked the officer even more—

Abruptly, he remembered his larger objective. He had no desire to fail at this early stage. So he held his temper and forced himself to shake his head:

"It's a fascinating story.''

"I should hope you'd find it so,'' the lieutenant sniffed. "We want our recruits to be enthusiastic—satisfied—in every way.'' Again there was a faintly lewd undertone to the words. Or perhaps Jared's nervousness was making him imagine it—

"As I was saying, we cut away the taffrail to make room for two guns, and two more were poked right out through the windows of the great cabin—Hull's cabin.''

"And you did get away at last—'' Jared said, hoping to hasten the end of the interview.

"By using every trick. To lighten us up, the captain dumped most of our drinking water. Ten tons, almost. He sent the topmen aloft to wet the sails. A wet sail holds more air than a dry one—another bit of information for you to store away in that handsome head.''

Feeling feverish and desperate for a breath of outside air, Jared pressed his

palms against his legs and struggled to feign interest. The lieutenant uttered a low chuckle. Was his pretense so obvious? Jared wondered.

"On the second night, we ran into a squall. Hull shortened sail just as we bore into the storm. He knows the Atlantic weather back and forth, you see. He predicted the squall would be a small one—"

I must get out of here! Jared thought wildly. Then, in his imagnation, he saw Harriet Kent.

How smug she'd look if he came home with excuses instead of an enlistment agreement. Though he was writhing inwardly, he stood his ground.

The lieutenant seemed to be enjoying his discomfort. Prolonging it—for sport. The young man tilted the rum jug again. Fastidiously dabbed his lips with a kerchief taken from his sleeve. Only then did he continue:

"The British, on the other hand, obviously feared a real blow. They hauled down everything. Shortly we lost sight of them—the squall hid us. Hull got busy and cracked on canvas. Sure enough, we were out of the squall soon, picked up a nice wind and showed 'em our heels. It was a hell of an effort, but every man did his part, without sleep and without complaint. And not twenty days ago, many of them were as green, as—" A pause. "—inexperienced as you." Another silence. "My boy, I'm disappointed."

"Why?"

"I expected you to be more impressed."

"But I am! I wouldn't have come here otherwise—"

"You can bet the Britishers were impressed. I'm sure there was plenty of cursing on their part that night—especially aboard *Guerriere*. Her captain, Dacres, is an old friend of Hull's, you know. They met in England some years ago, and they've a standing bet. If they ever engage, the loser presents the winner with a first-quality hat—"

Jared tensed. The officer was walking toward him again. He almost cringed from the touch of the supple hand on his shoulder:

"I've only told you all this in order to demonstrate the sort of effort that's expected from young fellows who sail with Captain Hull." The fingers constricted slightly. "Maximum effort and obedience. Absolute obedience to every command—every wish of your officers. But you and I will have no problem there, will we? We've already discovered we have things in common—"

Unwilling to suffer the fondling any longer, Jared jerked away. The lieutenant's dark eyes widened.

"Well. I see you have a ready temper." The smile was gone. "You'll have to curb that, else it'll be curbed for you."

Just a simple nod of assent required immense effort on Jared's part. A muscle in his jaw quivered. His eagerness to join *Constitution*'s crew had all but disappeared. He wondered whether the young officer was the sort of warped person he'd heard about but never met—one of those who disliked the opposite sex and preferred their own—

Even speculating about that, he couldn't walk out. He couldn't quite bring himself to throw away his first real chance to discover whether he was capable of surviving—and succeeding—in a difficult situation. So he endured the officer's pointed stare, and reminded himself that it was hardly fair to judge a company of more than four hundred sailors and marines by the actions of one.

The lieutenant resumed his seat, picked up a form. Jared's conclusions about the officer were abruptly shaken when a door opened down the dim hall leading

back from the parlor. He saw a fleshy young woman pulling up one shoulder of a bed gown to cover a heavy, red-nippled breast.

The young woman swayed. Drunk, was she—?

Livid, the lieutenant jumped up. He stalked two steps down the hall.

"I remind you, Mrs. Broadhurst, we rented these rooms for official business. Kindly keep yourself out of sight."

The blowzy young woman ran a palm down her thigh.

"But you said—"

"Presently," the officer whispered. Some unspoken communication seemed to leap between the two. With an undertone of savage force, he repeated the word:

"Presently."

The young woman kept rubbing her thigh. The lieutenant took one more step in her direction. She blinked, turned and lurched out of sight. The door closed.

The officer returned to the parlor. He smiled as if to dismiss the incident. But his eyes were humorless:

"You'll forget what you've just seen. As a personal favor to one of the officers with whom you'll be serving, Mr. —?"

Jared fought a shiver of fear. "Kent."

Relaxed again, the officer strolled back to the table. "Ah, that's right. You did mention your name at the start of our chat. I thought it had a certain familiarity. You did say your father fought at Fallen Timbers—?"

"Yes."

"An officer."

"A cornet in the dragoons."

"I don't recall the name in the letters my mother's kept almost twenty years. Still, there's *something* famil—" He snapped his fingers. "Are you perchance related to a Mr. Gilbert Kent of Boston?"

"He and my father are half-brothers."

"Then Gilbert Kent's your uncle,"

"Yes. Do you know him?"

"Do you know him, *sir?* You must begin to get accustomed to showing your officers the required respect, Kent."

Jared kept silent, but the muscle in his jaw quivered again.

"I know your uncle by reputation only. Although the citizens of this city crowded the docks to applaud our escape, their enthusiasm doesn't extend to their purses. Colonel Binney, the local naval agent, has exhausted his current allotment of government funds. No bank will grant him a loan. So Captain Hull's been reduced to begging donations in order to replenish our stores—principally our water. I was told that a Mr. Gray and a Mr. Kent jointly volunteered the sum of seventeen thousand dollars to furnish what we must have before we can weigh anchor."

"I hadn't heard that," Jared said, truthfully. The officer's eyes flickered. "Sir."

The lieutenant seemed more hostile now, very likely because he sensed how Jared felt about him:

"Don't expect your uncle's generosity to earn you any special favors. Only your responsiveness to the desires of your officers will do that."

Though severe, the young man still managed to invest the words with a faintly lascivious quality. Having seen the woman, Jared was totally confused. What sort of person *was* this lieutenant?

The lieutenant set about completing the requiring forms. Presently he handed them across the table.

"Read, then sign your name or make your mark."

"I can sign, sir. I've had schooling."

The lieutenant drifted to the window again, lifted the curtain, stared into the August glare.

"Yes, I should have guessed that from your rather quick tongue. Aboard ship, however, we're more interested in the strength of your body."

Jared's hand jumped. He barely managed to write his name in a legible way.

The officer took the papers, signed one copy. The street door opened. A man stumbled to the parlor entrance, his voice gruff:

"This the recruitin' place? Can't see a damn thing—"

The smell of gin was overpowering. But the lieutenant instantly exuded good humor:

"Come right in, sir. Your eyes will adjust in a moment—"

He handed Jared his copy of the enlistment agreement, then leaped forward as the ragged man swayed. Only the lieutenant's hands kept the drunk from pitching on his face.

The officer maintained a facade of friendliness as he helped the man to a chair, repeating an earlier speech to Jared almost word for word:

"You've come to investigate service under Captain Hull?"

"Mebbe."

"Well, you'll be joining a proud ship, sir."

"Just one 'at pays money an' hands grog around regular is all I give a shit about." The drunk belched, nearly toppling from the chair. The lieutenant cleared his throat behind one hand:

"Understandable, perfectly understandable. I'm sure you've heard of our escape from *Guerriere* and four other British vessels, though. We were chased three days. Three days and two nights—"

Jared folded the agreement, tucked it in his breeches, started for the parlor door. The lieutenant called after him:

"Report to the end of Long Wharf at dawn tomorrow. A longboat will be waiting to take new recruits out to the ship."

"I'll be there, sir," Jared said not looking back.

The hot, humid air of the street engulfed him. He sat down on the stoop, tugged the agreement out of his pocket and studied it without really seeing it. He had just signed away one whole year of his life. It was what he'd wanted when he walked into the recruiting office, but now he wondered whether he'd done the right thing.

The whole city—excluding the influential anti-war faction, of course—was hailing Isaac Hull as a hero; a master of naval tactics. Jared reminded himself that he was fortunate to be going to sea with a captain of Hull's caliber.

Yet serving with Hull also meant serving with that odd lieutenant—

He realized he didn't know the man's name. He looked at the signature at the bottom of the agreement.

Hamilton Stovall, 6th, Lt., U.S.S. Constitution.

He made up his mind to avoid Lieutenant Hamilton Stovall insofar as that would be possible within the confines of a two-hundred-and-four-foot frigate.

BY HIS own choice, Jared went to Long Wharf alone the next morning. He put everything at Beacon Street, from his Uncle Gilbert's prideful good wishes to his cousin Amanda's sobs, out of mind as he walked jauntily along, a small canvas bag dangling from one hand.

The bag contained a few personal articles, including his fob and a surprise gift from the family: a sharply honed knife of Spanish steel in a leather sheath. Gilbert meant for him to use the knife to scrape away the young man's beard that had started sprouting recently.

Sunrise etched a thin line of light along the horizon. Gulls wheeled overhead, occasionally swooping to snatch a tiny fish from the water. The air smelled salty and clean.

Eagerly, Jared searched for the officer supposedly waiting at the end of the pier, saw him—

It wasn't Stovall, thank heaven.

Out in the harbor, Boston's frigate bobbed gently, her tall masts catching the first scarlet out of the east. The breeze raised whitecaps around her hull. Jared could glimpse figures scurrying on the main deck.

His spirits lifted even more. That sleek, beautiful vessel with her intricately carved figurehead—a truculent Hercules—was his new home.

Having been raised in Boston, he had an advantage over country boys. He knew something about ships and their nomenclature. No one would have to tell him which mast was the mizzen, explain the system of watches and bells or point out starboard and larboard. With acquaintances from Mr. Tewkes' academy, he'd sailed the harbor in small pleasure boats, sometimes in heavy weather. He was confident he'd have no trouble with seasickness.

Another recruit had already arrived at the end of the pier. The drunk Jared had encountered yesterday.

As he approached the officer, he watched the poor fool from the recruiting office nearly fall off the pier ladder. He made sure his salute was smart, his name crisply spoken and his feet sure as he descended to the longboat heaving up and down in the chop. Within ten minutes, seven other recruits arrived. The longboat put out into the harbor.

Stovall all but forgotten, Jared gazed at the almost magical sight of the dawn-reddened masts growing taller and taller as the boat approached the frigate.

Twenty-four hours later, reality had replaced magic.

__VI

CONSTITUTION CARRIED a complement of thirty boys. They were outfitted in summer uniforms exactly like those worn by the older seamen: white canvas slops, cut wide through the legs to afford freedom of movement; wide-collared white blouses with flowing black scarves; round, flat-crowned black hats gleaming with varnish.

Most of the boys were younger than Jared. He was at first appalled, then amused, at the quantity and range of their profanity. To listen to a weather-browned ten-year-old cheerfully boast that he was already man enough to *shove the ramrod into a whore's muff* was startling, to say the least.

The boys were a rowdy, quarrelsome lot. They slept, as did the ordinary and able seamen, in canvas hammocks on the stifling berth deck. Hung up each evening from iron eyes in the beams of the gun deck above, the hammocks had to be taken down again in the morning and stored in special net racks along the ship's rails.

On his first night in the six- by three-foot hammock, Jared was cramped and uncomfortable. Barely able to breathe in the heat. The other boys kept him awake with chatter about their sexual conquests—an area of experience still foreign to him. They also exchanged opinions about the officers. Captain Hull and First Lieutenant Charles Morris were well liked. The rest were held in varying degrees of contempt; Sixth Lieutenant Stovall was mentioned as a "mean, dirty sod."

Some of the boys discussed duels of honor in which they'd taken part. Jared could hardly believe it, but apparently these near-infants occasionally settled disputes with pistols or swords. He got the impression the officers never interfered.

The routine of the frigate in port was less demanding than it would be at sea, he was told. But it was hectic enough. Four hundred and sixty-eight human beings jammed virtually every square inch of deck and gangway space. There was constant shoving and jostling and cursing as men and boys went about their duties.

In a day, Jared learned the ship's geography, from the magazine and shot locker in the depths of the orlop, up through the berth, gun and spar decks. He was assigned to the officer's wardroom, aft on the berth deck. His responsibilities included mopping the floor, maintaining the lamps, polishing the table and benches. When the officers ate, he ran food from the galley, forward on the gun deck.

He was fortunate to find a likeable companion assigned to the same job—a runtish, homely, but strongly muscled boy of twelve, Oliver Prouty. The boy came from Charleston, in the Carolinas.

On Jared's third night aboard, Prouty fought another boy barehanded for the right to hang his hammock next to Jared's. The southern boy's opponent, taller and older by a year, nevertheless succumbed quickly to Prouty's combination of punches, butts, kicks, gouges and bites.

The two fought by lantern-light on the berth deck. Just when Prouty was getting the best of it, two of his opponent's friends started to intervene. One raised a foot to stamp Prouty's spine while the other grabbed his hair. Jared snatched out the knife whose sheath he kept illegally tucked into his slops at his left hip.

He showed the knife and said, "Let them finish it alone."

The two boys fell back, eyeing the Spanish steel in Jared's hand.

Oliver Prouty finished demolishing his opponent's nose. He wiped his bloody hands on the other boy's blouse, then cheerfully helped his victim up:

"There, now. We change places, agreed?"

The other boy limped away, snot and blood dripping from his nose as he nodded weary assent.

Prouty slung his hammock in place just before eight clangs of the ship's bell signaled the end of the night watch and the beginning of the mid-watch.

"You've come aboard with one thing in your favor, Kent," Prouty said, putting his foot on a gun carriage and hauling himself up into the hammock.

"What's that, Oliver?"

"Being as tall as you are, nobody much wants to fight you. Still—'' with a lewd grin, he stretched out, hands laced under his head "—one chap I know has eyes for you in a different way."

Jared climbed into his own canvas bed. Down the row, a boy shouted, "Douse the fucking lamp!" It was doused. In a moment, Jared and Prouty heard the soft groans of a boy beginning to masturbate.

"Give 'er a thrust fer me, Davey," someone called. There was laughter.

Jared understood Prouty's last remark well enough. He'd been very conscious of eyes watching him with more than usual interest in the wardroom.

"You mean Stovall, I imagine."

"Aye, Mr. Handsome Stovall. He fancies himself a prize beauty, the shit."

"He's the one who signed me up."

"Lucky he didn't fling you down and try to bugger you. 'Course, on shore, he was probably sober—"

"Not quite. He was helping himself to the rum he was supposed to be serving to recruits."

"Well, beware of him if he's into the grog heavy. That's when he gets the urge. Thank the Lord I got an ugly phiz or I 'spose he'd be after me. You met Rudy—fourth down the line? Stovall got him to his cabin the night after we outran the five Britishers. Damn near raped the life out of Rudy, he did."

Aghast, Jared asked, "You mean you have to go along with something like that?"

"What's the choice? Accuse Stovall, and he'll up and call you a liar. Cap'n Hull has to take the word of another officer over ours. And then Stovall can make it miserable for you afterward."

"Doesn't the captain know Stovall's—tastes?"

"Think he does. But he just can't do anything unless an officer really steps out of line—in front of witnesses."

"He'd better not lay a damn hand on me," Jared said.

"Pray he doesn't. It's either give in or suffer a lot worse for refusing."

VII

THE EVENING of August first, Jared was on duty in the wardroom when Captain Isaac Hull said:

"Gentlemen, I've decided. We're going to sail."

Four of the five officers seated with him at the table expressed surprise. One voiced approval—the first lieutenant, Morris. Stovall raised a limp hand, a visual question mark:

"But we've yet to receive orders from Washington, sir."

"Damned if I want to receive 'em, Lieutenant," Hull replied. He was a short, pot-bellied man of thirty-eight, with ruddy cheeks. A bachelor, his genial, almost carefree manner belied his experience and toughness. Jared already knew a good deal about him:

Hull had been a sailor since age fourteen, having run away from home in Derby, Connecticut. His naval career was interrupted for a period of two years, during which he read law. He claimed he gave it up because he was a poor writer. Everyone else said it was really because he loved the sea.

He had trained on *Constitution,* as fourth lieutenant under Talbot, a famous

privateersman of the Revolution. He'd been to High Barbary, where Preble's squadron had twisted the tails of the arrogant deys and bashaws of the North African coast. And he'd achieved his captaincy through talent and hard work, not connections.

Mathematics were required for command of a bridge, so Hull had learned what he needed to know by diligent private study. He could be friendly with individual British captains, but he made no secret of his hatred of their country. His enmity dated from the time of his father's mistreatment on a prison ship anchored in New York harbor during the War for Independence.

Hull pressed the tips of his stubby fingers together, leaned forward to answer Stovall's objection:

"The navy department knows where I am, though I'd prefer not to hear from 'em. I wouldn't want to be handed anything smaller than this frigate. The way they're shuffling commands these days, it could happen. The longer we stay in port, gentlemen, the greater the danger you'll be deprived of my company—"

Muted laughter. Hull's eyes grew sober:

"—and the greater the danger we'll be blockaded by the English."

First Lieutenant Morris said, "I'm anxious to start hunting those bastards on *Spartan* and *Guerriere*." The two notorious ships had been ranging the coast and, almost daily, fishing boats slipped back to Boston with word that one or the other had seized and burned yet another American vessel.

Captain Hull broke a biscuit, munched half. "You forget one of those bastards is a friend of mine, Mr. Morris."

"Jimmy Dacres?"

"Aye. He owes me a hat and I mean to collect."

"All the more reason to weigh anchor!" Morris grinned.

"I agree. We're provisioned—we leave tomorrow."

Sixth Lieutenant Stovall was quick to change tack:

"I think the whole crew will be pleased. Certainly I am."

Hull said nothing, peering at his biscuit.

Stovall motioned Jared forward, indicated his cup which Jared had earlier filled with tea. Four of the others were drinking their daily ration of rum. But Jared had already heard Stovall profess—for Hull's benefit—that spirits dulled a man's mind. Hull hadn't seemed impressed. Jared thought the captain recognized Stovall for what he was—a bootlicker.

As Jared poured, Stovall contrived to brush his shoulder against the boy's hip. Without thinking, Jared jerked back. Tea jetted from the spout, staining Stovall's impeccably white breeches.

He leaped up, hand raised. "You clumsy whoreson—!"

"I'm sorry, sir," Jared blurted—only because form required it.

Hull shot out a pudgy hand, seized Stovall's arm:

"If you please, Mr. Stovall. It was an accident."

Seething, Stovall sank down again.

Hull said to Jared, "What's your name, lad?"

"Jared Kent, Captain."

"Signed on here in Boston?"

"That's right, sir."

"We have a benefactor named Kent—" Hull mused.

Jared saw no point in modesty; especially not with Stovall glaring at him. "My uncle, sir."

"Is that right! Well, we'd be thirsty as the devil without him—*and* stuck in this blasted harbor. His generosity was deeply appreciated."

Hull scratched at one rosy cheek. "Your uncle's quite a wealthy man, I understand. Publishes books?"

"And a newspaper."

"Peculiar to find such a man—a Bostonian, that is to say—supporting what some call the west's war."

"My uncle believes it's Boston's war too, sir." Conscious of Stovall watching him, he went on, "New England ships can't sail out in peace until the British stop trying to control the oceans. But that doesn't seem to occur to most New Englanders. My uncle says that's tragic."

Hull nodded. "Your uncle is perceptive. I'm delighted to have you aboard. I hope we can show you some lively action—and His Majesty's ensign being hauled down."

"I hope so too, Captain."

Still avoiding Stovall's stare, Jared cleared plates and utensils and left the wardroom. In the galley, he told Oliver Prouty what had happened.

"Oh my Lord, Jared," the homely boy sighed. "You messed up his uniform?"

"Not intentionally."

"He'll have your back under the cat for certain. I told you there's nothing Handsome Stovall fancies more than his fine appearance."

"Ollie, I have a strange feeling about him. A feeling he's not quite right in the head."

Prouty nodded. "There are plenty of odd stories afloat. That he's a bastard—I mean a real one. That he's rich as hell, and loves to gamble for high stakes. I even heard he got in his cups once and said everyone would be astonished if they knew who his father and mother were."

"Famous people?"

"Don't think he meant that. His father was a soldier out west if I recollect—"

"Yes, Stovall told me that at the recruiting office."

"His mother had another name—Free something. I guess he meant to suggest they were relations."

"Cousins?"

"Closer."

"That's not allowed."

"Christ on the mount! I know that!"

Jared grinned. "You know a lot for someone so young."

" 'Round the Charleston docks you don't miss much when you're on your own. I had nobody to raise me but a grandma—half blind and no teeth, poor old woman. I went to sea when I was nine. It was either that or starve—"

For a moment the twelve-year-old looked more like a gnome ten times that age.

"If even half the tales about Stovall are true, it's no wonder he's crazy," he added. "He'll settle up with you, don't think he won't."

A memory of Stovall's eyes flickered in Jared's mind. His hand stole unconsciously to the concealed knife.

"I'll be on my guard."

____ VIII

ON AUGUST 2, 1812, *Constitution* raised sail and put Boston behind the fierce eagle that spread carved golden wings across her stern.

As Jared had anticipated, seasickness didn't trouble him. He experienced an hour of mild nausea when the frigate first reached open water, but after that, he felt perfectly fit. He quickly developed the sea legs necessary to maintaining balance on the crowded, constantly tilting decks.

Almost every man aboard was eager to come in contact with the enemy. *Constitution* was still the target of disdainful remarks from British captains—and from the admiralty in London. War or no, that kind of talk got around among the seagoing fraternity.

The frigate was a joke on more than one count. Badly designed, His Majesty's naval architects sniffed. Far too much white pine, especially in her fished masts. And live oak for hull timber? Who ever heard of that?

Jared thrilled to the first morning on the open sea. He marveled at the agility of the topmen who scrambled aloft to work the yards, only their dexterous hands and feet separating them from a fall to death in the water. They cracked out the flax canvas with astonishing speed; and there was a lot of it—forty-two thousand square feet.

As the great sails were set, the frigate seemed to leap ahead, boiling up a snow-colored wake astern, splitting the cobalt summer sea at her bow. Hercules glowered at the horizon, the painted symbol of her readiness to do battle.

Once the coast vanished, the training of the crew—especially the several dozen recruits ultimately rounded up in Boston—began in earnest.

Gun drills perfected the teamwork required to open the ports, run out the cannon, load, fire and reload in minimum time.

Though rated as forty-four, *Constitution* actually carried much heavier armament: thirty twenty-four-pound long guns, for accurate distance firing; twenty-four thirty-two-pound carronades, of shorter range but capable of throwing a much heavier load of metal. One long eighteen-pounder brought the total to fifty-five guns.

The enemy Hull hoped to find was *Guerriere*. Her name meant "female warrior," and she was rated at thirty-eight. What interested the American sailors more was a recent report that she was only shipping sixteen carronades, reducing her close-range firepower.

Such comparisons were dismissed by the British. Their traditional skill and daring would always carry the day. They considered the American navy insignificant, and American captains upstarts—except on land, where friendship such as Hull's and Dacres' were both common and completely permissible.

All in all, the officers and men of *Constitution* had a good reason to yearn for an encounter with *Guerriere* or a ship of similar rate.

The frigate stood eastward for two days, raising no enemy sail. Hull changed course, bearing northwest toward the Bay of Fundy. On the tenth, *Constitution* intercepted a lightly armed British brig outward bound from Newfoundland to Halifax. A second brig was overtaken and captured the following day. Both vessels were burned, and their crews set adrift in longboats. The brigs were of too little value to be sailed back to American waters by prize crews.

A few more equally minor encounters put Captain Hull in a bad temper, and finally caused him to set a course for the Bermudas, where he hoped to find bigger prey.

On the eighteenth, off Cape Race, Newfoundland, *Constitution* overhauled a good-sized brig. She proved to be *Decatur*, a fourteen-gun American privateer. When her captain came aboard, he said he had assumed Hull's ship to be an enemy frigate. As was customary, *Constitution* had showed no colors until the other vessel was identified.

The American captain told Hull he had eluded a real British frigate only the day before. Within an hour, the news spread through the ship. Oliver Prouty repeated it to Jared:

"The captain thinks he's on to Jimmy Dacres. *Decatur* outran a frigate slower than we are. A big one, too—it must be *Guerriere!*"

Excitement gripped the ship all through the night. Next day, at three bells into the afternoon watch, *Constitution* was plowing through a heavy sea. Men aloft searched for signs of a sail—

But Jared, below, had forgotten all about the pursuit. He had just been dispatched from the galley, carrying a lunch of salt beef, suet, biscuits and hot black coffee.

The lunch was for Sixth Lieutenant Stovall, who had stood the watch till dawn, and was now indisposed in his cabin.

4
The Devil's Companion

JARED'S HAND turned sweaty as he knocked. He glanced along the dim starboard gangway. Overhead, he heard men moving. But the gangway was empty and still; the officers' sector of the berth deck totally deserted.

The sea boomed against the hull. He started to knock again; hesitated. Perhaps Lieutenant Stovall had fallen asleep. Perhaps he wouldn't have to face—

"Come in."

Jared stood unmoving, his left hand white on the handle of the wicker basket. The second time, the voice was less languid:

"I said come in."

Reluctantly, he did.

It took his eyes a moment to adjust to the feeble light of Stovall's single lantern. Tobacco smoke coiled slowly in the tiny cabin, fanned to motion by the opening and closing of the door. Through the haze Jared saw the young lieutenant lounging in his bunk, his throat stock undone, a long-stemmed pipe clenched between his perfect teeth. He didn't look a bit ill.

Stovall set aside the wooden lap desk on which he'd been playing some form of patience with an oversized deck of hand-colored cards: crimson diamonds, purplish-red hearts, blue spades, green clubs. As he swung his legs out of the bunk, two of the court cards slipped to the floor.

He leaned down gracefully; picked up the cards. One was a heart king with the face of President Washington, the other a queen in the form of a classical goddess. He replaced the cards in the deck.

With a straight face, he said, "I trust you won't put me on report, having

discovered me with this—'' He waggled the deck. ''New England divines call it the devil's picture book, don't they? Alas, I'm more comfortable as a companion of devils than of divines.''

Jared kept his head down, knowing he was being mocked. He set the basket on the small bolted-down table.

''There is your meal, Lieutenant Stovall.''

''Thank you, Mr. Kent. I wasn't up to the wardroom. Caught a touch of grippe in the damp night air, I think.''

Jared took a step backward.

''If that will be all—''

''Not quite.''

Stovall's manner was cordial enough. But his dark eyes had a bright, cold gleam. Walking slowly toward the boy, he talked with his pipe clenched in his teeth:

''I had no idea you would be on duty, Mr. Kent—''

Jared believed that was probably a lie, but said nothing.

''I thought they might send the lunch with that coarse Prouty fellow. However, since you're here—improperly dressed, I might add—''

Before the boy could stop him, the lieutenant tucked the bottom of Jared's blouse into his slops. For a moment he felt warm fingers probing past the waist of his pants—

Stovall withdrew his hand, sat in the chair beside the table, examined his pipe. It had gone out. He knocked dottle into his palm, carelessly discarded it on the floor.

''—since you are here, I say, we should perhaps discuss your clumsiness in the wardroom. Tea, as you know, leaves an abominable stain. You quite ruined my best breeches.''

The dark eyes slid to Jared again. The boy felt a strangling tightness in his throat; a sense of being utterly cut off from the world. He spoke with difficulty:

''As the captain said, it was an accident—''

Stovall sat up straight. ''An accident, *sir.*''

Jared's cheeks reddened. His hands shook a little. But he gave Stovall what he wanted:

''An accident—sir.''

Stovall licked his lips, his eyes moving again. To Jared's throat; his arms; his chest.

''I am prepared to be forgiving—''

''Captain Hull seemed to think the matter settled. Sir.''

''What Captain Hull thinks and what I think are not the same thing. You will sit down, Mr. Kent—''

Stovall vacated the chair.

''—while we consider whether reparations are in order, and if so, what kind.''

''Begging the lieutenant's pardon, the steward and the cook instructed me to come straight back to the galley after—''

''I take orders neither from the steward, who is a syphilitic sot, nor the cook, whose swill would win this war instantly if it were served to the enemy three days in a row. That a human being should be expected to eat suet—Christ! What barbarity!''

Then he smiled. ''You will sit down.''

Jared slipped into the chair. Stovall strolled to the door, leaned against it, his handsome face a pale oval in the smoky gloom. The single hooded lantern

swayed gently from one of the beams supporting the gun deck. Jared knew with a dismal certainty that it wasn't going to be easy to get through that door again.

Hamilton Stovall returned to the bunk. He picked up his cards, began to shuffle them as he perched on the bunk's edge.

"You don't seem to be adjusting to naval discipline too well, Mr.—*turn and look at me, please!"*

Jared swung his legs from one side of the chair to the other.

"Every time you're given an order, I notice a certain—shall we say—hostility? Perhaps you don't even realize you're reacting that way. But as I advised you once before, you won't do well in the service until you curb your rebellious temperament. Of course—"

A slow, limp gesture.

"—in other, more informal circumstances, your lively nature might have a certain charm."

Stovall's hands, somehow seeming quite independent of the rest of him, resumed the shuffling of the deck, pulling cards from the center and bringing them to the front. The rustling sound began to torture Jared's nerves.

He worked up the courage to speak again:

"May I ask the lieutenant the purpose of this—?"

"Damn your impertinence! I told you the purpose. We are discussing the damage done to my breeches. You will sit there and listen until I dismiss you!"

The cards moved again, whispering in counterpoint to the crash of the sea against *Constitution*'s hull. Abruptly, Stovall smiled:

"I want us to settle our difference amicably. You already know I consider us to be kindred spirits. Like you, I am not all that fond of the fuss and protocol of the navy. I accepted a commission out of necessity, frankly. A suitable position in my family's iron finery in Baltimore won't be available until my grandfather passes, bless his soul."

There wasn't a shred of feeling in the last remark. Jared knew Stovall was toying with him. Short of outright insubordination, he didn't know how to put an end to it.

"I don't intend to get myself killed in this war, I promise you that. I believe I mentioned that my father died in the army almost twenty years ago—of carelessness, I presume. That's the only reason a clever man comes to harm in a war. I am not careless. On the other hand, navy life can broaden a young man's perspectives on the world. It can be salutary in developing—oh, how shall I say it? Many traits—?"

The soft rippling of the cards stopped. Stovall tossed the deck down, stood and rummaged beneath the bunk bolster. With his back turned, he said:

"Mr. Kent, have you ever had a woman?"

Jared's spine crawled. He couldn't answer.

Stovall swung around, a metallic object gleaming on a chain in his right hand.

"Damme, you're a rude lout!" he exclaimed softly, "You will answer any and all questions put to you by officers of this ship!"

He took two long strides forward, planting his boots wide apart. Jared's mouth turned dry at the sight of the bulge beneath Stovall's tight trousers.

"I repeat—have you ever had a woman?"

"N—no, sir, I haven't."

"Don't you think about it? Many young men your age are fathers."

"I think about it, yes—"

"Do you think it would be pleasant?"

"I—I imagine so."

"Louder, Mr. Kent. You're whispering."

"I said—I imagine so."

Stovall flicked a catch on the oval locket. One side fell away to reveal the most astonishing miniature Jared had ever seen: a reclining nude; a voluptuous woman. Her fingers hid only part of the dark triangle between her legs.

"Lovely creature, isn't she? Her name is Mrs. Freemantle."

He leaned down toward the seated boy, his breath ripe with the smell of the tobacco he'd been smoking.

"Does the sight of a naked woman excite you, Mr. Kent? Make you imagine those pleasures and sensations you've never experienced before?"

Jared jerked his head up, so that he didn't have to stare at that obscene picture cupped in Stovall's hand. He said in a hoarse voice:

"Not really, sir."

Stovall's right brow hooked up. "Indeed? Why not?"

"I expect it would be better to—to wait for the real thing."

"You're a clever one," Stovall chuckled. "Practical, too, since we've no women on board." He snapped the locket shut, tucked it into the pocket of his breeches. "Still, Lord Cock can be a most impatient master. Surely at night, you sometimes feel his yearnings. His strainings—"

Stovall's hand dropped toward Jared's knee; touched it lightly.

"Surely you understand there are ways in which discreet gentlemen—pledged as friends—can relieve—"

"Take your hand away."

"What's this? *You* giving orders to *me?*" The fingers caressed his leg.

"I'm just telling you—take your hand away, or—" Jared swalloed.

"Or what, Mr. Kent?"

"Or I'll kill you."

Stovall's eyes widened. Jared braced for a blow of the lieutenant's fist. Instead, the young man guffawed:

"Kill me, will you? How, in heaven's name?"

"With—with my fists or any way I can," Jared said, having decided at the last second not to reveal his one small advantage.

Stovall let go of his leg, slapped him on the shoulder. Jared wrenched away.

"By God, Mr. Kent, those blue eyes tell the truth. You've spirit. Style! Imagine!—telling an officer you're going to kill him. That's incredible brass! But I admire it—"

He picked up the cards from the bunk.

"—I admit it because it's so atypical. The deeds—the lives of most men are so pathetically small and ordinary. Scruples hamper them—scruples being another name for fear. I never permit myself to be cowed that way. When I gamble, it's for thousands, not pennies. I don't shrink from the pleasures cowardly little men call vices—I seek them out!"

He gestured flamboyantly with the oversized cards. Jared's earlier suspicion had become a conviction. Although the lieutenant might put on a respectable face for his superiors, he was dangerously deranged. The boy pressed his palms against his knees to keep the lieutenant from seeing how badly he was shaking.

"That's why I do admire that chap Bonaparte," Stovall went on. "Everyone else damns him, but I appreciate the scope of his ambition. His willingness to abandon himself utterly to a grand vision. For the same reason, I rather admire our highly moral captain, surprising as that may sound. His escape from those

five Britishers was magnificent! No mundane fellow could have accomplished it—or would have tried. We gambled everything—risked everything for a single puff of wind, a quarter mile of distance—we staked our lives and damn near broke our backs, *but we won—!"*

Abruptly, Stovall drew a deep breath and riffled through the deck. Jared watched with mingled fascination and horror as he plucked out a blue-tinted spade—a knave represented by a scowling Indian chief with upraised tomahawk. Stovall twirled the card back and forth between thumb and index finger:

"I'm telling you all this, dear boy, to show you that we are much alike—"

Flick, the knave's face was hidden.

"We should be, we *will* be intimate friends—commencing now."

Flick, the savage popped back into sight.

"I have a certain desire that you can satisfy, and it will be to your advantage to do so. As the special friend of an officer aboard this ship, you would be able to obtain certain favors. Preferred duties. Further, anyone who affronts you would have to deal with me. Do you understand what I'm saying?"

"Yes, but—I won't have any of it."

"I'm afraid you've no choice." Stovall released the knave. It fluttered to his feet. "You are expected to obey orders."

He took hold of Jared's shoulder again. "Come, now. No more sparring. Pull off your trousers and climb into that bunk."

Jared shot from the chair, throwing Stovall off balance. He jerked his right knee up, striking the bulge at Stovall's crotch.

The lieutenant staggered backwards; let out an almost feminine scream:

"You filthy little bastard! I'll have fifty laid on you with the cat!"

"You know twelve's the limit, you damned—"

"Oh yes? You'll take a hundred!"

Jared backed swiftly around the table, spun and ran to the door.

"Come here!"

In the distance, Jared heard another man yelling. On the gun deck above, feet thudded suddenly. He had the door halfway open when Stovall's fist struck the back of his head.

His forehead slammed into the edge of the door. He gasped as Stovall pushed him aside, booted the door shut, whirled him around by the shoulders—then back-handed him across the face three times.

Strong as he was, Jared couldn't match the lieutenant's height and weight. He tried the tactic of a knee to the midsection a second time. Stovall jerked backwards at the waist, avoiding the knee. His fist pounded Jared's temple. The boy staggered, fell.

Stovall kicked Jared's belly, doubling him in pain. Then Stovall crouched, hands reaching for his throat. The clamor of voices grew louder overhead. *Constitution's* gangways echoed with a hammer of running feet.

Jared's arms were crossed over his aching belly. Stovall seized his neck. Jared slid the fingers of his right hand beneath his left forearm and down to his waist. He tugged the Spanish knife from its sheath, jerked it into the light where Stovall could see it shine.

The lieutenant dropped his hands to his sides, macabre amusement twisting his mouth:

"Damme, the pup has teeth!"

Jared's right hand trembled. It took will to steady it. He held the knife between

himself and Stovall. In a moment, staring at the steel glitter, the lieutenant ceased smiling.

Jared twisted the point of the knife in a small circle. He was too frightened to speak, but Stovall understood quite well. He rose slowly, retreated a step; another—

"You touch me again and I'll cut your face," Jared whispered. "Whatever else happens, I'll cut your face to pieces."

Stovall turned pale, began to curse, monotonous, obscene oaths that gave Jared an odd sort of hope. He'd struck a vulnerable spot—Stovall's vanity.

Jared dragged himself to his knees, then stood, back against the outer wall of the cabin. He had perhaps three feet to travel to the closed door. He moved his right foot, eyes never leaving the lieutenant. At any moment he expected another attack.

He dragged his left foot after his right, inching down the wall. The beam lantern swayed, flinging Stovall's shadow back and forth. The lieutenant's cheeks glistened with sweat.

Another step to the right. One more and he'd break for it—

Stovall's body tensed slightly, telling Jared the attack was coming. He raised his right hand higher, at the same time elevating the point of the knife. The blade's angle was about forty-five degrees.

Stovall's eyes flicked to the steel. He recognized the risk. One misstep, or a fall, and Jared could impale his face—

Rage overcame reason. Stovall whipped up his right fist. Too late, Jared saw the strategy: knock down the hanging lantern; force him to maneuver in darkness. He whirled toward the cabin door—

Stovall's smash was stopped in midair as someone knocked.

"Lieutenant Stovall? Captain requests all officers to the wheel at once. We've sighted—"

Jared jerked the door open and bowled past the goggling master's mate.

As if demons were after him, he plunged forward to the ladderway amidships, sheathing the knife as he ran. He streaked up to the gun deck and burst into the light at the waist. In the heavy sea, spray broke across *Constitution*'s rail. He'd never felt anything so welcome as that chilly salt water showering him while he scuttled up the steps to the fo'c'sle.

The Atlantic showed whitecaps with deep troughs between. Towering white clouds hid the sun, yet some of its light leaked through, putting a glare on the slopes of the swelling waves. Everywhere, men were shouting; running; going hand over hand up the ratlines.

Still blinking, Jared stumbled ahead through the press of seamen and marines. A glance over his shoulder revealed Captain Hull near the wheel. Some of the men on deck looked half dressed, but Hull's uniform was, as usual, impeccable: black silk stock; straight-cut jacket; tight white breeches over his bulging paunch.

The captain paced back and forth, fiddling with his fob. Finally he demanded the glass from the sailing master. One long look, and he began shouting orders.

Jared hurried around the foremast. He had trouble with his footing on the spray-slicked deck. He stumbled into a topman hurrying to the shrouds. Took a cuff on the cheek from the angry seaman, and almost fell.

The man rushed on. Jared searched for someone he knew; spied Oliver Prouty and a half dozen other boys just beyond a group of marines with rifles. Gathered between the fo'c'sle carronades, men and boys were watching a sail that jutted above the horizon off the larboard rail.

Once more Jared risked a look back; saw Sixth Lieutenant Stovall, now in full uniform, climb up from below.

Stovall spotted Jared. His expression made it plain the boy would be punished. Jared guessed the lieutenant would charge him with a long list of infractions, so he could be given the maximum penalty for each.

As if to confirm it, Stovall touched fingertips to the forward edge of his braided half-moon hat, a mock salute. Then he pivoted and walked smartly toward Captain Hull, the center of a growing crowd of excited men aft of the mizzen.

II

STILL LIMP from what had happened in Stovall's cabin, Jared joined the other boys. Oliver Prouty elbowed a place for him, then leaned out over the rail. He pointed at the scrap of sail:

"Caught sight of her at two sharp. I've already laid six bets that she's a Britisher."

The ship hidden below the horizon appeared to be bearing east-southeast. If that were true, her course would take her across *Constitution*'s bow. Jared stared at the sail in a vacant way.

The Charleston boy noticed; brushed windblown hair out of his eyes; took hold of his friend's arm:

"You're white. What the hell's wrong?"

"I—" Jared wiped his mouth. "I had to pay a visit to Stovall's quarters."

Oliver Prouty blinked, searched the aft part of the spar deck. "I see him near the wheel."

"Looks mad as the devil, too," one of the other boys said.

The sea blinded Jared with its glare as he swung around. Positioned between the sailing master and First Lieutenant Morris, Stovall was attempting to get Hull's attention. Jared knew what the Sixth Lieutenant wanted to say.

Hull wasn't interested. Eyes shielded with one hand, he watched the setting of canvas in preparation for pursuit of the other vessel. There were scores of men aloft. But all the masthead flags had been hauled down.

Once more Stovall spoke to Hull. The captain's dumpling face reddened. He said something sharp to the lieutenant. Jared thought he could make out two words:

Not now.

Stovall withdrew, scarlet. Oliver Prouty bent his head close:

"What happened in his cabin?"

"What do you think?"

"You mean he—"

"He tried."

"And you hollered."

"Worse than that. I had my knife out, ready to cut him up."

"Jesus! You're in for it."

Jared nodded. "At this point, I'd probably be better off jumping in the ocean. He'll have the cat on my back as soon as he can."

"Well," Prouty said, "that ship's bought you a little time. Hull won't put his mind to anything else until we've learned whether she's friend or foe. If they beat to quarters—"

"*When* they beat to quarters," said another boy. "From the size of that sail, she's got to be a big ship—and you've already wagered she's British."

Prouty nodded. "So little Isaac will fight. Look at him! He's so excited, he can't stand still!"

Prouty's expression grew sly. "Suppose we do engage. You can always hope some metal from the enemy's cannon puts Lieutenant Handsome out of commission. Or that *something* happens to him—"

Jared looked at his friend, comprehension slow in coming. Prouty's eyes were unblinkingly cruel.

"I never thought of that. Lieutenant Stovall could be one of those killed, couldn't he?"

"With things confused—cannon going off—marines sniping from the tops—any man can be killed—" Prouty snapped his fingers. "That quick."

Slowly, Jared moved his gaze to another of the young, tanned faces around him.

Then to a second.

A third.

A fourth—

What he saw in those faces was chilling. He recognized an unspoken promise. The boys would protect him with their silence.

He ran a hand over his forehead. That Hamilton Stovall was both unbalanced and vengeful, he didn't doubt for a moment. And it would be so easy. During gun drills, he'd seen how much smoke just a few of the cannon produced. Imagine the smoke from an entire broadside; clouds of it, to make faces indistinct; conceal one quick stroke of the Spanish knife—

God, he was tempted.

Prouty sensed his hesitancy:

"If you don't do something, I can tell you what'll happen. Stovall will have you punished so hard, you'll be lucky not to be crippled for life. Even if you take the cat and pull through, you'll be looking over your shoulder the rest of the voyage, wondering when he's going to come at you—"

Prouty's hand closed on Jared's forearm.

"Do it, Jared. *Do it.*"

Jared started to say yes. An image of his uncle flashed into his mind. His shoulders slumped.

"I can't, Ollie. I want to, but I can't."

Scowling, Prouty studied his crestfallen friend. After a moment, he gave a resigned shrug:

"All right. It's your skin. You know you're being a fool."

"I know. I'll just have to take my chances."

Waves thundered against *Constitution*'s hull. All sails set, she bore off on a course to intercept the stranger. As Jared watched the horizon, he could almost feel Hamilton Stovall's eyes on his back.

__5
"Her Sides Are Made of Iron!"

BY HALF-PAST three, no doubt remained. The sails of the ship *Constitution* was chasing identified her as a member of the frigate class.

By four, her hull was in sight. Jared could make out small figures scurrying on her deck. From the wheel, word was passed that the captain had definitely identified the stranger as *Guerriere.*

The American frigate drew closer, running in front of the stiff northwest breeze. Her bow rose and plunged in the heavy swells. The deck tilted at increasingly extreme angles.

About half past four, Hull ordered tampions removed from the muzzles of all cannon.

At a quarter of five, he began rattling a stream of orders. The topgallants, staysails and the flying jib were hauled in, the topsails reefed a second time, the royal yards sent down and the courses sent up. A final order started the drummers beating to quarters. All over the spar deck, men and boys joined in three loud cheers.

Everyone scrambled to battle stations. Jared kicked off his shoes just as the others did; bare skin held a bloody deck more firmly than leather. He stripped off his shirt; lint festering in a wound could bring on gangrene—and amputation. As he took his position on the fo'c'sle, he almost forgot about the ominous presence of Lieutenant Hamilton Stovall, aft.

About half the boys were assigned to running back and forth between the orlop and the upper decks, bringing shot and leather buckets of powder to the guns. Jared, Prouty and three other boys formed a chain on the fo'c'sle to pass the powder and shot to the forward gun crews.

Constitution plowed ahead under shortened sail. Topmen came scrambling down as the last of the drumrolls died away under the steady crash of the waves. The gunners were busy checking the breeching ropes of the fo'c'sle carronades. The ropes, secured to the rail timbers through eyebolts, prevented the cannon from recoiling too far.

Working next to Jared, Oliver Prouty seemed in high spirits:

"Just heard they're double-shotting the twenty-fours down on the gun deck. Round and grape'll bloody the fucking British quick enough!"

Jared shivered. He had never seen grapeshot used. But he'd heard about the effects of the small iron balls wrapped in canvas around a wooden dowel, then secured to a wood disc that slid into the cannon's muzzle; the whole split and flew apart when fired, filling the air with murderous fragments of metal.

Guerriere showed every intention of fighting. She'd already backed her main topsail, and was no longer making headway. Captain Hull bounced up and down on the balls of his feet, alternately observing the enemy through his glass and snapping orders.

Constitution bore down on the other ship, approaching with her bowsprit pointed at *Guerriere's* starboard bow. Jared heard one of the fo'c'sle gunners complain that Hull was playing a dangerous game. From her current position, the American would only be able to fire a couple of the twenty-fours mounted in the bow. *Guerriere,* on the other hand, would be able to rake with a full starboard broadside.

The clang of the ship's bell told Jared it was five o'clock. A moment later, men began to point and curse. A familiar and despised scarlet ensign was being run up each of *Guerriere's* three masts.

Slow matches wrapped around iron linstocks curled acrid smoke into the air beside each gun. Jared judged the frigates to be less than two miles apart. The Britisher was rolling violently in the white-capped swells.

All around him, he smelled sweat. Saw hands raised to rub watering eyes. Marines in groups of seven—one to fire, six others to reload the rifles for the marksman—were climbing quietly to the fighting tops.

Amidships, Lieutenant Morris called out, "Shall we give her a shot to catch her attention, sir?"

Hull's voice carried all the way forward:

"Mr. Morris, I will tell you when and where to fire. Stand ready—and see not a single shot is thrown away."

The frigates drew closer together.

Closer—

Jared saw a single puff of smoke erupt from *Guerriere*. A second later, he heard the slam of the explosion.

Almost at once, the enemy's entire starboard side poured out smoke and thunder. Men aboard *Constitution* jerked their heads up—the Britisher's shot would hit high if it hit at all.

Not a single round found a target. The accuracy of the guns depended on the precise moment of firing, Jared knew. Someone aboard the enemy had miscalculated—given the order to fire just as the starboard side rose on the up-swell of a wave.

He whirled around, saw and heard the British cannon balls raise huge, noisy geysers of water—every round having traveled all the way over *Constitution's* masts.

Guerriere immediately began to wear around to bring her larboard batteries to bear. Hull shouted so everyone on deck could hear:

"Men, do your duty now! Your officers can't command you every minute. You must each do everything in your power for your country—!"

Then he called for flags.

Wild cheering broke out as the three jacks traveled up their lines to snap in the wind at the three mastheads. On the mizzen, a huge seventeen-star ensign unfurled. New eighteen-star flags, recognizing the addition of Louisiana to the union in April, had yet to be supplied to the navy.

On Hull's next command, the forward gun crews swung into action. Smoldering linstocks dipped. The bow chasers boomed. But the shots dropped into the sea well short of the enemy.

Jared was fascinated by the agility of the gunners. When fired, the twenty-fours recoiled like juggernauts, their carriages slamming backwards from the open ports and jerking the breeching ropes so taut Jared fancied he could hear the thick lines whine. The moment the recoil spent itself, a member of the gun crew shoved the rammer into the muzzle. Once all sparks were swabbed out, reloading could safely begin.

Because *Constitution's* first shots had missed, the bow chaser crews grumbled about their error as they worked. They'd mistimed their fire by a second or so, and profanely swore it wouldn't happen again.

Guerriere had come about. Her larboard batteries began to spout smoke and orange fire. Some shot plopped into the water midway between the two vessels.

But a few rounds struck quite close to the American, raining water on Jared and the men nearby. Jared heard a peculiar thudding amidships, pivoted to see a gunner leaning over the high rail, pointing down at the hull.

"That one hit us! But the ball bounced right off."

Grinning, he whirled back to the disbelievers in his crew:

"I swear to God it bounced, lads. With that live oak, it's like her sides are made of iron!"

For almost an hour, the battle continued without much result. *Guerriere* kept wearing in order to rake with her starboard guns, then with those on the opposite side. But Hull was quick to respond, tacking and half-tacking so that most of the salvos fell short, or hit the sea where *Constitution* had been only moments before. Occasionally Hull ordered one or two shots. But no more.

As the inconclusive chase wore on, Jared grew increasingly nervous. So did the men at the fo'c'sle guns. They were openly impatient with Hull's tactics. *Constitution* was making slow headway, using the interval between the enemy's broadsides to bore in closer and closer. But the captain still refused to commit the frigate's full firepower.

The light was beginning to fade from the towering clouds. Getting on toward twilight, Jared thought. Perhaps there'd be no decisive end to the engagement—

A strange quiet descended. *Guerriere*'s guns were silent. She seemed to be standing completely still. Hull called for the main topgallants to be set. As men clambered aloft, he bawled another order:

"Sailing master—*lay her alongside!*"

Jared's throat tightened. At last, Hull was taking the offensive. In moments, he felt the frigate surge forward—on a course that would carry her directly past the enemy's larboard side—and larboard cannon.

Bells clanged six o'clock. Steadily, *Constitution* drew up nearer the stern of *Guerriere*. Evidently some of the American fire had done damage; Jared saw hands aloft at the enemy's mizzen, furiously re-rigging lines.

Out across *Constitution*'s starboard rail, he watched the frigate come abreast of *Guerriere*'s stern and pass it. Perhaps the distance of a pistol shot separated the vessels. He could pick out the braid-decorated uniform of the lean captain, Dacres, on the enemy's quarterdeck.

Guerriere's larboard cannon began firing, stern batteries first. The sea echoed with the rolling thunder; fiery bursts at the muzzles brightened the darkening day.

Geysers shot skyward between the ships. The American's hull thumped several times as more enemy shot caromed off. Then a round struck amidships and penetrated with a tremendous crashing of timbers. Men screamed in pain.

Shot ripped several of *Constitution*'s sails. Hull sent more men up to repair the damage. Impatience edged the voice of Lieutenant Morris:

"Sir, we have men badly hit on the gun deck. When can we fire?"

"Not yet, not yet!" Hull shouted back, clambering up on an arms chest in order to see the enemy more easily.

The fo'c'sle gun crews tried to encourage one another during the enforced inaction:

"They got blind men firing them guns. Can't hit a thing."

"Must be 'cos they got no sights on their pieces the way we do."

"I seen three more rounds bounce off our sides, just as pretty as you please—"

Slowly, inexorably, *Constitution* drew abreast of the British frigate, whose

gun and spar deck cannon continued to boom intermittently. Overhead, the frigate's canvas whined and cracked in the wind.

Gunners standing to the right of their pieces blew on the smoldering lengths of cord to raise sparks, then lowered their hands as close to the priming pans as they dared. Jared stood motionless not far from one of the carronades, the powder and shot relay having suspended activity because of the lack of American fire.

One of the carronade gunners gave his quoin a kick, making sure the elevating wedge was firmly in place. On *Guerriere,* Jared now saw faces clearly; he could even judge the relative ages of men. My God, how close the frigates were running! Why didn't Hull—?

"On the next one, sir?" Morris shouted.

"On the next one!" Hull replied, still balanced atop the arms chest, watching the slow rise of the rail in relation to the enemy's hull.

Suddenly he flung up his arms:

"Now, sir—*pour in the whole broadside!*"

Jared had never heard such noise. The deck shook beneath his feet as the foward gun deck batteries fired, then the midships batteries. The carronades on the fo'c'sle roared, and recoiled, billowing smoke from the depths of scorching-hot barrels. Starting at the bow, *Constitution* threw everything on her starboard side.

Almost immediately, jubilant shouts rang from the tops. The marines aloft were the first to see the damage double-shotting had done to *Guerriere's* masts and rigging. Jared saw it for himself when some of the thick smoke cleared.

He saw another kind of damage, too. Aboard the enemy, men writhed on the deck and tumbled out of the rigging. A new sound blended with the last of the American cannon fire—cries of agony from the wounded and dying aboard *Guerriere.*

Bouncing up and down on the arms chest, Captain Hull yelled even louder: "By heaven, that ship is ours!"

The captain seemed oblivious to the fact that, in his excitement, he had split his trousers from crotch to knee.

Men laughed. But not for long. In less than a minute, *Constitution's* batteries reloaded and fired a second broadside.

Hurriedly passing shot and powder buckets again, Jared coughed and gritted his teeth against the acutely painful roar of the fo'c'sle pieces. The carronades recoiled wildly on their wheeled carriages, checked only by the humming ropes. His world shrank to a small piece of deck, smoke-choked, filled with deafening crashes, lit by bursts of orange that glared, then quickly dimmed. In the hellish light, Oliver Prouty's dirty, grinning face resembled some imp's.

Through rifts in the smoke, Jared saw men fallen on the deck. He saw blood, and felt the old, puzzling nausea begin to build in his belly. He fought it, but it grew stronger moment by moment, almost paralyzing him. His only relief came from avoiding a direct look at the wounded.

For the next fifteen minutes, *Constitution* ran alongside *Guerriere,* suffering few hits from the enemy guns but doing devastating damage with her own.

II

SHORTLY AFTER six, *Constitution*'s broadsides broke *Guerriere*'s mizzen several feet above the deck. The Americans cheered as the huge mast began to topple, cordage and all.

Jared watched screaming men plummet from the yards and rigging. Some fell in the sea. Others landed on the deck, the luckier ones dead or unconscious, the rest broken and twitching.

Near the wheel, Captain Hull continued to bob up and down, his linen underdrawers showing through the tear in his trousers. As *Guerriere*'s mast crashed across her rail, Hull waved a fist:

"Huzzah, boys! We've made a brig of her! Next time we'll make her a sloop!"

III

THE BRITISH gunners still seemed unable to inflict much damage on *Constitution,* but the American fire was highly effective. As he passed shot and powder forward, the procedure almost automatic by now, Jared tried to figure out why.

When the smoke blew away enough to permit it, he studied *Guerriere*'s badly ripped hull, noting the exact moment at which her cannons went off. At last he saw the difference:

She tended to fire as she rolled upward on cresting waves. Hence the principal damage she did occurred aloft. *Constitution*'s gunners, on the other hand, usually fired on the down-roll, taking their toll on the enemy's deck, and hulling her in the bargain.

A few more men aboard the American frigate had been wounded. Jared still avoided looking at them; the nausea, barely manageable, was with him every moment.

Except for the humiliating sickness—and a growing ache in his arms and shoulders—he did his job as if he'd been at it for years. The first few broadsides had terrified him. Now he hardly glanced up as the batteries roared.

Constitution changed course again. She swept across *Guerriere*'s bow, then put her helm hard to larboard. Orders were barked—stand by for another broadside!

The frigate began to veer back before the wind. Her larboard gun crews readied their slow matches. Oliver Prouty swiped his face with his wrist, peering into the gray billows around the tops:

"We got some of our braces shot away. She's not falling off fast enough—"

The significance of that escaped Jared until a few moments later, when he heard alarmed cries aft. He whirled, squinted through the smoke—and saw a sight that froze him:

Like the prow of a phantom ship materializing, *Guerriere*'s jib boom and bowsprit appeared in the smoke.

Prouty yelled, "She's going to hit us—!"

The enemy's bowsprit thrust against the American's larboard stern quarter with a prolonged grinding noise. The impact splintered the taffrail and crushed the stern longboat.

Almost instantly, the British frigate dropped into *Constitution*'s wake—or tried. A man pointed:

"She's fouled the mizzen rigging!"

A moment later, sheets of fire seemed to leap from *Constitution*'s fighting tops. The marines aloft raked the enemy's deck with their rifles.

Tangled, the two ships bobbed on the swells, their rails not six feet apart. A voice screamed from the foretop:

Someone near *Constitution*'s wheel—Jared couldn't see who—took quick action:

"Boarders away!"

"Come on, Jared!" Prouty exclaimed, pulling his friend aft.

They scrambled along the gangway amidships, men running behind and ahead of them; all except the few hands responsible for the sails had left their stations and headed for the cutlass racks.

The rifle fire from the tops thickened the smoke even more. Above the din, Jared heard men shriek aboard *Guerriere* as the marines hit their targets.

But the enemy, too, had sharpshooters aloft. A man just in front of Jared took a ball in the shoulder and pitched against the rail. Jared made the mistake of glancing at him. Blood stained the man's blouse; big, bright patches of blood—

"Keep moving or you'll be trampled!" Prouty screamed behind him, shoving. Jared dashed on.

They seized cutlasses from their assigned racks. A few yards aft near the larboard rail, Lieutenant Morris doubled over suddenly, gut-shot by a ball from a British pistol half a dozen feet away. A lieutenant of marines clambered up on *Guerriere*'s fouled bowsprit, searching the blowing smoke for his commanding officer:

"Captain Hull? Shall we boar—?"

A ball hit his forehead, drove him to the deck. Jared swallowed the bile in his mouth, closed his fingers tight around the cutlass hilt. At the enemy's rail, he could see the British sailors milling. One side or the other would seize the advantage at any moment, and cross the bowsprit—

He watched Captain Hull bend over the fallen Morris. The first lieutenant grimaced, took Hull's hand, struggled to his feet. The front of Morris' coat was a red ruin. Bone-pale, he pressed his hands against his wound. Slimy red coils showed between his fingers—

Jared gagged. Morris' stomach had been torn open. Yet he was up and moving, literally holding his own entrails.

Hull spun away, sword drawn, as if he intended to lead the boarders personally. Morris reached for the captain's shoulder with one gory hand. Hull whirled, in a fury until he saw who had taken hold of him.

Morris ripped one epaulette from Hull's uniform, then the other.

"Now—" he gasped. "Now you won't make such a prize target—"

Hull understood, clapped a hand on his lieutenant's arm. Both men disappeared as heavy clouds of smoke rolled across the stern.

The din of rifle and pistol fire had become continuous. Jared and Prouty pushed and shoved, but a crowd of men, uncertain as to their orders, prevented forward movement. Jared's left foot slipped. He didn't dare look down. The deck was slick with blood. Men lay everywhere, wounded or dead—

Jared's ears began to ring. All the blood started him trembling violently.

Prouty pushed him:

"What the hell's the matter with you? Go to the left! Around the wheel! These simpletons may want to stand here, but I want to get aboard *Guerriere!*"

Jared swayed; let Prouty circle away from him, past the wheel on the starboard

side. The crowd was beginning to break up, move toward the stern. Jared stumbled after his friend—and came to a halt again a few steps aft of the wheel.

A dead seaman lay at his feet, blouse pierced by three balls. Jared was so mesmerized by the sight of the man's bloodied torso, he completely forgot his own danger—until another British ball chewed the deck a yard to the right.

Flying splinters stung his cheeks and throat, jolting him back to reality. The tumult of confused voices and small arms fire—suddenly blending with another long, crunching noise—made his head throb.

Aboard *Guerriere*, the wails and groans of the wounded were unbelievably loud; a chorus of condemned men howling in hell. Jared's eyes stung; the smoke was thick again. He could hardly see anyone.

To larboard, the smoke parted slightly. Jared lurched in that direction, saw another sailor spin around and fall. The grinding noise grew louder—the sound of the two frigates tearing apart, driven off from each other by the heavy waves.

Rigging broke. Wood snapped. Jared stumbled into lines tumbling from overhead. *Guerriere* separated just as the Americans were massing at her bowsprit, finally organized to board.

Watching from a good twenty feet away, Jared spied Oliver Prouty at the fringe of the boarding party. The Charleston boy was scowling and flourishing his cutlass. He dropped to his knees with a stunned look as a chance shot from one of *Guerriere*'s two remaining tops blew away the back of his head.

"Ollie!" Jared screamed, slipping and sliding aft and to larboard at the same time. In a second, more smoke hid the boarders.

A hand from the smoke caught his arm.

"Let go, goddamn y—"

The yell died in his throat. Standing beside one of the aft guns, Sixth Lieutenant Stovall glared at him. In his other hand Stovall held a navy pistol.

Writhing, Jared tried to free himself from the lieutenant's grip. He saw the round, black eye of the barrel pointed at his forehead. And behind it, Stovall's crazed smile:

"Everyone will think it was a British ball, won't they, Mr. Kent?"

He shoved Jared backwards, away from the rail.

"Won't they?"

Jared swung his cutlass as Stovall cocked the pistol. The lieutenant dodged the downward sweep of the blade. It struck something that vibrated. Jared heard the creak of carriage wheels—

Its right breeching rope severed by Jared's cut, the cannon by which Stovall had been standing swung away from the rail. The left breeching rope snapped; the cannon was loose—

Stovall saw it coming, rolling slowly as the left side of the frigate lifted. Stovall released Jared's arm. Both leaped back—but not before Jared swung his cutlass a second time.

The tip barely nicked Stovall's jaw. Then the runaway cannon rumbled between them, the wheels narrowly missing Jared's bare feet.

Stovall slapped a hand against his nicked chin as the deck tilted even more sharply. He stumbled to starboard, lost his footing, dropped his pistol, flailed wildly with both hands, seeking something to check his fall.

His hands closed on the muzzle of the cannon. He screamed.

A foul odor mingled with the reek of powder. The rest happened incredibly fast.

Already on his knees, Stovall pitched forward. As his hands slipped off the

metal, the right side of his face slammed against the breech below the firing pan. His second, piercing shriek testified to the searing heat. The cannon slid out from under him and rolled on to come to a jolting stop against the far rail.

In the smoke, men were still swarming aft on both sides of Jared. Several had leaped clear of the runaway cannon, but not a one paid any attention to the fallen lieutenant midway between the two rails; he was just another floundering casualty.

Screaming again, Stovall writhed on his back, both hands clutching his right cheek. All at once a stain spread at his crotch.

He fainted. His hands fell to his sides. Jared saw reddened facial tissue. The odor of burned flesh was overpowering—

Guerriere's batteries roared. *Constitution* shivered as round shot burst the rear wall of Captain Hull's great cabin. In a moment, flames licked upward over the stern. A fire crew assembled, disappeared in the gray billows—

The two frigates had separated completely. Jared snatched up Stovall's pistol, discharged it at the barely visible bow of the other ship. As far as he could see, he hit nothing. No wonder. His hand was trembling.

In despair, he threw the pistol away. He turned toward the bow, walking as best he could on the treacherous deck. *I should go back,* he thought. *Go back and make certain Stovall's dead—*

He couldn't. He was too weak from the shock of what had just happened. Too overcome with sickness from the sight of bleeding men. He let the cutlass drop from his other hand. He fell against the rail as the opposite side of the ship rose. He seized the rail, thrust his head over, violently sick—

When he raised his head, he saw *Guerriere* astern—and blinked in disbelief. Not one of her three masts remained.

Her deck was a litter of broken wood, ripped sail, tangled cordage. On the quarterdeck, her captain was being supported by two of his officers. Even at this distance, Jared clearly saw the large, dark stain on the back of the captain's uniform.

"She's done, by heaven!"

Hearing Hull shout somewhere in the smoke, men all over the ship began to cheer. But not Jared. He remembered Stovall. And Oliver Prouty—

Ollie was dead. *Dead.* How could that be?

Tears came to his eyes.

They were gone a few moments later when he stumbled back to the spot where Stovall had fallen.

The ship's sixth lieutenant was nowhere to be seen.

IV

IN THE lowering light, the two frigates continued to roll in the heavy sea, guns silent. *Constitution* was damaged but *Guerriere* was totally out of action. As the smoke gradually cleared, a tatter of white became visible on the enemy quarterdeck.

An officer strode to Isaac Hull's side. The little captain was grimy now. During the engagement his other trouser leg had split.

The officer called Hull's attention to the wigwagging white square. "I believe she's asking quarter, captain."

"Well she might. There's not a stick left standing for showing a flag—white or any other kind. What the devil is that man waving, Lieutenant Read?"

"As nearly as I can make out, sir, a tablecloth."

Isaac Hull's face looked as merry as Jared had ever seen it:

"Take a boat. Find out whether she has actually struck."

"I'm sure she has, sir. But I'll go at once—"

Hull caught him as he left: "Read—"

"Sir?"

"See to Jimmy Dacres. I watched him take a ball in the back when she fouled us."

The captain was no longer smiling.

V

SHORTLY AFTER seven o'clock, a returning boat brought *Guerriere's* captain alongside. Hull himself went to the ladder as men assisted Dacres up to the victor's deck.

Near the top of the ladder, Dacres paled visibly; Jared saw it from his place at the rail. He was crowded among men and boys eager for the sight of a British captain surrendering to one of the Americans his admiralty scorned. But all Jared could think of was Stovall; and the way he'd botched his one chance to put an end to the threat Stovall represented—

Captain Hull put on his half-moon hat, stepped to the head of the ladder:

"Dacres, give me your hand. I know you're hurt."

James Dacres replied with an oath. Hull backed away, waiting until the wounded skipper negotiated the rail.

Dacres approached Hull with an unsteady step. Blood stained his coat front and back. He looked ready to faint. Yet he managed to give his opponent a salute:

"My compliments, Captain Hull." He groped downward, grudging admiration and bitterness mingling in his voice: "You've earned my sword—"

Suddenly Dacres' head jerked up. Hull had stayed the hand struggling to unfasten the blade:

"No, Jimmy. I won't take a sword from one who knows how to use it so well. I will, however, trouble you for your hat."

Dacres almost smiled. But the cries of anguish still drifting across the chop from the foundering *Guerriere* prevented that. Dacres took off his half-moon hat, handed it to Hull. The American captain slipped the hat beneath one arm.

"Come to my cabin, Jimmy. I'm told they've put out the fire. We'll get our surgeon to dig out that ball you took."

"Not until my wounded are looked after."

"Of course. I'll see they're brought aboard at once." He took Dacres' elbow. "Isaac, let me ask you a question. What have you got for men in the tops?"

"My marines? Only a parcel of green bushwackers."

"Backwoodsmen?"

"According to your admirals."

Dacres caught the irony, shook his head. "You outsailed me. You outgunned me. Why the hell you weren't hulled as I was—"

"Live oak," Hull interrupted. "Your architects hold it in contempt, remember?"

Dacres flushed. "Be that as it may, one battle isn't the war."

As Hull led him to a ladderway, the British captain suddenly glanced back at his ship:

"You can't put a prize crew aboard her, can you, Isaac?"

"I doubt it. She's too badly riddled." Hull pointed. "With the sea so heavy, she's shipping water through her gun ports. I'll have to blow her up tomorrow."

Captain Dacres looked as grieved as if he'd lost a relative, Jared thought.

"One favor, then."

"It's yours."

"In my cabin there's a Bible. Given me years ago by my mother. I've carried it ever since I first went to sea."

"I'll see it's recovered and restored to you," Hull said, handing Dacres into the care of two seamen who helped him down the ladder.

Before Hull followed, he moved briefly among the men standing nearest to him. He shook a hand here, murmured a word of praise there. He never reached Jared. A shout summoned him to the surgeon's quarters, where Lieutenant Morris was being attended. Hull waddled to the ladderway and vanished, torn pants first, stained coat sans epaulettes next, round face last of all.

God, Jared admired the man's skill and courage. As innocent-looking as a rustic, Hull had been masterful during the engagement. If there were a few more captains like him, the outlook for America might not be as gloomy as many of her citizens believed—

By this time Jared had regained a measure of calm. He started asking questions, and discovered Sixth Lieutenant Stovall had been taken to the surgery. The news reinforced his sense of having failed at the critical moment, and kept him from sharing the festive mood that accompanied the process of cleaning up the frigate. He didn't drink the extra ration of grog ordered for all hands. And he slept poorly.

No one hung up a hammock in the place Ollie Prouty had occupied only twenty-four hours ago.

VI

ON AUGUST thirtieth, *Constitution* dropped anchor a mile and a half southeast of the Boston light.

A few hours later, she moved to Nantasket Roads. She sent a boat ashore with news of her stunning success—and with a request that facilities be readied for the prisoners and wounded from *Guerriere,* whose ruined hull had been torched and sunk at sea.

The party returning from shore brought a curious report. Despite New England's hatred of the war, most of the city had paradoxically gone wild with joy at word of the victory.

Constitution's triumph offset discouraging news from the west: in mid-August, General William Hull had surrendered Detroit to General Isaac Brock without firing so much as one shot. The officer in charge of the landing party said people were already clamoring for General Hull's court-martial. Captain Hull made no mention of the fact that the general was his uncle. Jared had to learn it from a seaman.

In the ten days since the engagement, everyone had taken to calling the frigate

by a new nickname—Old Ironsides. A new pride had kept the crew working cheerfully at their duties. The atmosphere had somewhat restored Jared's spirits, too. He slowly forgot the grim sea burial of the dead from both sides—fourteen Americans and seventy-nine British.

He took added encouragement from what he learned from boys who worked for the surgeon's mates. Yes, Lieutenant Stovall was alive. But the pain of his injury kept him unconscious most of the time. He had suffered severe facial burns in an accidental fall against a hot cannon.

"You have anything to do with that?" asked one of the boys with whom Jared talked.

"Would I tell you if I did?"

The boy studied Jared with foxy eyes. "Not if you was smart."

"What's to become of Stovall, Harry?"

"He'll be transferred to a hospital in Boston, then sent home when he's well enough."

Jared relaxed a little. That ended the immediate threat. He assumed Stovall would still be recuperating when *Constitution*'s crew went ashore for the huge civic welcome being planned.

Jared intended to be part of that welcome—though in truth, he was less than satisfied with his performance during the battle.

Yes, he'd stood in the thick of the fighting and carried out his duties well enough. But he'd failed miserably when confronted with the opportunity—at the time, the necessity—to get rid of Stovall. Blind chance had done it for him; he could take no comfort.

And the troubling sickness had recurred. At the critical moment with Stovall, it had undone him. That seemed an ominous sign.

So on balance, he was disappointed. Rather than resolving basic questions, the events of the past days merely continued and even sharpened them—and brought back the feeling that he might never escape the bent for failure that seemed to be his inheritance from his mother and father. The gloomy feelings persisted all through the flurry of preparations for going ashore.

He was on deck when *Constitution* warped into Long Wharf and began unloading prisoners and wounded. The fresh air improved his spirits a little. If there had been no fundamental alteration in his doubts about himself, at least he could be proud of outward changes that had accelerated during the past month. He stood more erect now, shoulders back, blue eyes shining in the sun. If he was not yet physically a man, he felt as if he were—even though his fourteenth birthday wouldn't come until October.

While the wounded were carried off, he and the other boys told each other how bold they'd been in combat. They bragged of the feminine conquests they planned to make in the city. Jared's boasts were even emptier than those of his shipmates. And all at once, he was silenced by the sight of Stovall being carried down the gangplank on a litter.

A bandage swathed most of the lieutenant's skull and the right side of his face. Jared swallowed. Even lying helpless, the young officer had the power to stir terror—

He told himself his fear was foolish. He'd repaid the lieutenant in kind, and they were even and quits. He'd probably never see Stovall again—he should focus on that, not on his failure to take the officer's life.

The last of the prisoners filed off. Crowds began to stream up Long Wharf to welcome the sailors. Soon the entire dock was jammed with people.

Jared set off among them with his chin up and his eyes a bit harder, a bit colder than they'd been on that morning he first boarded his ship—

A hundred years ago, it seemed. Could it really be only a month—?

In that time he had done and seen much. But dizzying change was the way of the world these days, Uncle Gilbert said. Finally, in the noisy throng on Long Wharf, he allowed himself a touch of pride. Perhaps some things hadn't changed. But others had—

The boy was dead. Long live the man.

6
Heritage

JARED STRUGGLED up Long Wharf against the human tide rolling toward the *Constitution*. Because he wore a uniform—newly laundered slops, blouse and scarf, varnished black hat—he was automatically a candidate for congratulations, boisterous backslaps, squeezes, pokes, pinches and pats. In the face of such enthusiasm, the going became difficult. He curled his left arm around the small canvas bag containing souvenirs for the family, lowered his head and kept shoving his way to the head of the pier.

People around *Constitution*'s gangplank rushed aboard. Some of the women ran to the sailors still on the ship and grasped them in ardent embraces. Hanging onto his hat and looking back, Jared wondered enviously whether he could find some attractive young woman to favor him with a kiss. Or something more—

As if the wish had conjured bad luck, he found himself approaching a woman, but hardly a desirable one. He was out of the heaviest press now, and had room to maneuver. He sidestepped to avoid a direct confrontation. The woman's dress and cap were filthy. Most of her teeth were gone, even though she didn't appear to be thirty. A whore, he was certain.

The woman changed course to intercept him:

"Here's one of the lads from the frigate!"

Her remark was directed to a short, wide-shouldered man lurching along behind her. Jared paid no attention to the fellow; he was too busy avoiding the whore's outstretched hands.

Rum fumes barely masked the stench of the woman's body. But she wasn't so drunk that she couldn't move quickly. Darting in front of Jared, she seized his shoulders and gave him a wet buss on the cheek.

Jared tolerated it, but with difficulty. The woman's incredibly dirty fingers and rouged, pox-pitted face turned his stomach. The woman's companion laughed—a wheezy, consumptive sound—and tapped her shoulder. His voice was slurred by drink:

"Back off, Nell. The lad's not old enough to buy what you're selling."

"Oh, he looks plenty old enough to me." The whore simpered, showing her discolored gums. "Want to come up the street a ways? I'll pleasure you for half the usual price. It's a special rate for any of the brave lads from Boston's frigate—"

"Let go of me, please," Jared said, concerned that the encounter might turn ugly. The whore reached for his groin. Her man restrained her:

"Nell, he said no. Leave him be."

"Thank you, sir, I'm obliged," Jared said while the whore grumbled.

For the first time he got a clear look at her companion; the woman's pimp, obviously. He was about forty; stocky, with untrimmed hair, whiskers and beard shot through with gray. He smelled even worse than the whore.

Because of the man's position and the angle of the sunlight, only the right side of the man's face was visible beneath his hat brim. But that was quite enough to make Jared queasy. The man's skin was covered with seeping sores. His right eye had gone milky with blindness—altogether, a ghastly specimen. But not unusual around the docks.

The pimp gave him a muzzy grin. Extended his right hand:

"Privilege to meet any of the lads who—"

Abruptly, the pimp stopped. Withdrew his scabby hand. He stared at the boy in an intense way, saying nothing.

The whore was anxious to rush on and find another customer. The pimp lingered.

"Boy—?"

Jared would have left instantly but he didn't want to provoke the drunken man. He held a hand over his brow to cut the sun's glare. Even so, he still couldn't see much of the man's face.

"Yes?" Jared said.

"Would you tell me your name?"

"Why?"

"Because you resemble someone—I mean to say—someone I once—"

"It's Prouty, Oliver Prouty," Jared said. It was the first name that popped into his head.

"Oh." The pimp nodded slowly. "Mistake, then—"

"Yes, sir. Good day."

Shivering, Jared turned and left.

The pimp tugged off his hat and fanned himself, staring after the tawny-haired boy. The pox sores glistened in the sunlight. The disease-blinded right eye shone like a white marble.

"He lied to me—" the pimp murmured, sounding more sorrowful than angry. The whore rushed back to him. "For Christ's sake, let's get to the ship!"

"But the boy didn't give me his right name."

"What difference does that make?"

Collecting himself, the pimp brushed a hand against his watering left eye. "None," he said softly. "None."

He put his stained hat on his head. The shadow of the brim blotted his face again, hiding the badly healed ridge of scar tissue on his left cheek.

He pulled a bottle from his coat pocket, swigged and followed the whore down Long Wharf.

II

JARED HAD hoped Uncle Gilbert and Amanda might bring a carriage to meet him. When he searched the street at the head of the pier and failed to find them, he was disappointed.

He could understand Aunt Harriet not coming; she wouldn't care whether he was alive or not. But Uncle Gilbert wasn't that way. Jared told himself his uncle must not have known the exact time of *Constitution*'s docking.

He knew the excuse wasn't valid—especially for a newspaperman. But he needed some kind of balm for his let-down feeling. His step was much less jaunty as he set off along a narrow street.

He'd gone no more than a few blocks when a voice challenged him:

"Hello. Are you off the Boston ship?"

Jumping across the refuse channel to the dark doorway, Jared peered at the person who had spoken; a girl, lounging in the shadows with her forearms crossed over small breasts barely concealed by a thin blouse.

Unlike the whore on the wharf, this one was reasonably attractive. Brown-haired, with a clear complexion and clean skin.

And she had most of her teeth.

"Yes, I am," he told her. "I'm headed for my home."

Wondering if this might be a deadfall, he glanced along the mean, littered street. No one else was in sight. Half a block away, a tavern showed closed shutters, as if the patrons had all departed. To welcome the frigate, perhaps—?

He felt reassured when the young woman smiled at him:

"Are you in a terrible rush? I could make you happy to be on land again."

Lazily, she dropped her arms and let him see her breasts covered by the thin blouse. The dark circles of her nipples showed clearly. Temptation set off peculiar sensations within Jared. Excitement and shame mingled as he felt the unconscious response of his body to the girl's.

"I have no money," he said truthfully. "We've yet to be paid."

"Surely there's something in that little bag to take a girl's fancy."

"Nothing of value. Two bracelets of tarred cordage, plus a four-inch splinter from our ship's mast."

"Would you show me one of the rope bracelets?"

She said it so gently, he couldn't refuse. He opened the canvas bag.

The brown-haired girl turned the crude bracelet in her fingers, then smiled again.

"If you swear this comes from the Boston frigate, it would be acceptable payment. I mean, today's a special day, isn't it? Everything about it should be special. For you. For me too."

He eyed the souvenir he'd tied and tarred himself. If he gave one away, there would only be one left—and that one must go to Amanda. Much as he despised Aunt Harriet, to neglect her would only provoke trouble.

Nervously, Jared hooked a finger in the collar of his blouse. He was perspiring. Partly from excitement, partly out of fear.

Why couldn't he present the souvenirs privately? Aunt Harriet didn't need to know she'd been shorted—

"All right," he said in an unsteady voice.

"The bracelet's mine?"

"Aye."

She seemed genuinely pleased, and bent to kiss his cheek lightly as he passed from the blue shadow of the street to the deeper shadow and mystery of the shabby ground-floor room.

III

WHEN HE emerged an hour later, a greater mystery had been solved—pleasantly if a little clumsily this first time.

The young whore had never even told him her name, leading him straight to her narrow bed and helping him undress. The moment she drew off his underclothes, he confronted her with an enormous erection—and a deep red face. But she laughed with delight, wriggling free of her own garments.

She lay back, one hand closing gently until he tingled with a tension altogether foreign to him before.

"Come, lie down with me," she said. "You'll find it nice, I think."

As he slipped down beside her, she pressed his erection against her tuft and left it straining there, stroking his cheeks with her palms, then opening her lips against his. Her tongue caressed the inside of his mouth, arousing him all the more.

Her breasts touched his chest. He started breathing heavily. He'd watched dogs coupling in the street a few times, but he'd never imagined a similar act between humans could produce such marvelous sensations—

Kissing, fondling, she guided him between her thighs, then began to slide up and down beneath him. He clasped his arms under her back, awkward in his movements until he found the proper angle. Soon she was breathing as loudly as he. She began to moan against his throat—

The explosion of his loins was matched by her own violent wrenchings; up and down; side to side. After that came a delicious lassitude. They lay close together, he feeling sad, somehow. He put his lips aginst her warm ear and whispered that he loved her very much. She laughed again, touching his nose and saying she loved him too.

Leaving her, he whistled as he walked. The odd sadness had passed.

Perhaps he'd experienced it because he knew their lovemaking was an exchange of pleasure for a price, nothing more. Yet the act seemed far too beautiful and moving to be of such fleeting significance. For a moment he wished he could see the girl again. He wished their declarations of love had been real ones, not lies born in the heat of the moment—

What foolishness!

Even so, her face lingered in his thoughts. He suspected it always would.

He whistled louder. Why feel bad? Hadn't he learned one of the things a man must know?

At an intersection, he paused and looked back. The brown-haired girl was waving goodbye from her doorway. The little bracelet of tarred cordage jiggled on her wrist.

He waved in return, then hurried on.

IV

AT BEACON Street, Amanda came to answer the door. When she saw Jared, she squealed with delight.

He dropped the canvas bag, caught her around the waist and whirled her above the stoop, nearly causing the driver of a dray to run his team onto the sidewalk.

Amanda was as pert and lovely as ever. He hugged her fiercely. The touch of her soft skin against his cheek made him feel he was truly home.

"Dear Jared!" she gasped when he released her. "How fine you look in that uniform!"

"Not fine enough for anyone to come greet me at the pier. Other families were there. But not mine. That demands an explanation, by God!"

"Oo, do sailors swear that way?"

"I know a hundred other words—all worse!" he teased, making a terrible face. Amanda covered her mouth and giggled.

Jared feigned anger:

"See here!—I meant what I said. Why didn't anyone meet me? I might have had an arm blown off—even been killed! Didn't anyone care?"

"Of course we care, Jared. But we already knew you were all right."

That caught him short: "You did?"

"Papa sent one of his reporters to the pier when some sailors from your boat—"

"Ship."

"What's the difference?"

"You're too little to understand."

"I am not, I am *not!*"

"Amanda!" he said sternly. "Go on!"

She huffed, then said, "Well—these men came to town a day or two ago—"

"The first shore party."

"—and papa's reporters gave one of them money for a list of the dead and wounded." She pronounced the last word to rhyme with "sounded."

"The word is "wounded.""

"I don't think it's the same word I saw in the paper."

"Yes it is." He spelled it.

She look dismayed. "Mercy, it is the same word."

"Wounded," he repeated. "As in moon, loon—you're not quite as grown up as you think, Miss Amanda!"

Perfectly serious, she asked, "Will I ever be?"

"I doubt it."

He said it too dourly. She started to weep.

"Amanda, for God's—for heaven's sake, stop that! I was only teasing!"

She bawled all the louder.

"Oh, God," Jared groaned. They were attracting stares from pedestrians. He grabbed her arms. "Amanda, you're grown up. You're *very* grown up. There!— I said it. Now stop. You seem to forget I'm the one who's supposed to be upset!"

Instantly, the tears vanished. "I was trying ever so hard to make you forget that."

"By crying? Typical woman's trick!" He pinched her chin with gentle affection. "Well, it worked. Let's go inside."

As he caught his cousin's hand, she said:

"Papa even made the reporter bring the list here, Jared. He's been in bed for the last four days."

"In bed?" Frowning, Jared closed the front door. Harriet Kent's voice drifted from the back of the house; she was hectoring one of the servants. "He's ill?"

"From too much work, the doctor says."

She led Jared into the front sitting room. Outside, he hadn't noticed the boards nailed across two of the windows.

"We've had visitors," Amanda told him. "Twice! The last time, they broke the glass with stones. I was so scared—!"

"Why were the windows broken? Because of Uncle Gilbert's position on the war?"

"I think so. Papa's hired watchmen at the printing house—"

She glanced toward the hall, where footsteps rapped.

"Amanda, were you the one squealing and shrieking outside—?"

Her back to the hall, Amanda stiffened at the sound of Harriet's voice. Jared did too. Amanda's small fingers knotted in her skirt.

Dressed in mauve and looking paler than usual, Harriet Kent darted a hand to her bosom:

"Jared!"

"Good morning, Aunt Harriet."

"We had no idea when to expect you—"

He set his canvas bag on a highly polished table. Harriet didn't allow her best furniture to be used so casually—the exact reason he deposited the bag where he did.

Her eyes flicked to the table. Her lips compressed. That delighted him. On the surface, however, he was polite:

"It all depends on when the pilot comes aboard to steer us in. He came aboard first thing this morning. Where's Uncle Gilbert?"

"At the printing house."

"But Amanda said he's ill—"

"When did that ever stop him from doing exactly as he wished?"

Jared indicated the boarded windows. "You've had unexpected callers."

Harriet sank into a chair. "Every time Gilbert writes one of his editorials, he's pilloried in the opposition press, abused on the street—or we're visited by vandals. The strain is getting to be more than I can bear."

Jared concealed his disgust. "Evidently the strain's been worse on Uncle Gilbert."

"It's his fault, not mine, if he chooses to endanger his health by working long hours for an unpopular cause!"

Jared was aghast at her lack of feeling for her husband. He was angry, too. Not only because of the callous way she spoke of Gilbert; but also because she didn't even trouble to ask one question about how he'd gotten along on the frigate.

Instead, she stood up, marched straight to the polished table, removed his canvas bag and set it on the floor.

"Your uncle and I have parted company on political matters, Jared. I now attend Federal Street Church, where I find Mr. Channing's sermons more to my taste."

"I see."

Jared knew of the church, naturally. Its pastor, the Reverend William Ellery Channing, was Boston's most popular preacher. He'd taken a pacifist stand on the war. Jared wasn't surprised that Harriet Kent would show her vindictiveness by refusing to attend the Kent family's church, and by displaying herself publicly, alone, in a place of worship whose pastor was more attuned to the thinking of those whose admiration she coveted. Christ, he didn't know how Gilbert stood the woman!

In a few moments, the joy of homecoming was wholly gone; destroyed by the sight of those ugly planks hammered over the empty window frames, and by Harriet's hauteur.

His black mood drove him to pick up the canvas bag:

"Here, Amanda, I brought you something."

"What is it, what?" she exclaimed, dancing up and down.

"A bracelet of rope from *Constitution*." He slipped it easily onto her small wrist. "I made it myself."

He swung around.

"I'm sorry I have nothing for you, Aunt Harriet."

Her eyes showed her hostility. "I wouldn't expect it of you, Jared. You are your mother's child, not mine."

She whirled, her skirts belling, and vanished into the hall.

Scarlet-cheeked, Jared kicked the canvas bag. Amanda hugged him and thanked him for the present, oblivious to the hatred that had crackled between the boy and the woman only a moment earlier.

___V

THE SKIES grayed in the early afternoon. A chilly rain began to fall, hinting of autumn. Gilbert returned a few minutes after six, to be greeted by a complaint from Harriet: some of the kitchen help were unhappy about preparing and serving large meals in the evening. In most other wealthy homes, by nightfall the kitchens were quiet, the day's work largely done. Why couldn't Gilbert try to change his habits? Learn to dine in the early afternoon, as respectable people did—?

Gilbert was wan; thinner than a month ago. But Jared's presence put him in high spirits. He refused to let Harriet's harangue bother him:

"My dear, you and the servants will wait in vain for that kind of change in me. We are Kents first and foremost. Respectability, if any, is incidental."

Harriet wasn't amused. "So I've discovered."

"Jared, come along to the table! I want to hear all about Hull's victory—"

Gilbert wrapped his arm around his nephew's shoulder, walking him past Harriet's vindictive eyes. "By God, I've never seen the old town in such an uproar. Do you know they're going to give you a parade down State Street? And a dinner at Faneuil Hall?"

"Not me, surely," Jared laughed.

"You're part of the crew, aren't you?"

"When is the dinner?"

"September fifth. In the evening," Gilbert added, for Harriet's benefit. "Even Royal's planning to attend, much as he loathes the war. The curious dualism of Boston continues! Bursts of patriotic fervor on one hand—widespread refusal to help the government on the other—"

Gilbert coughed as he slipped into his chair at the head of the dining room table. Amanda took her place opposite Jared, elbows on the tablecloth. That earned her a smack on the wrist from her mother. Jared wondered whether Harriet's choice of wrists was accidental. She slapped the one on which Amanda wore the bracelet.

Harriet sat down at her end of the table. Her husband virtually ignored her:

"Before you begin, Jared, what news do you want to hear?"

"About the war? I only know General Hull surrendered Fort Detroit—"

"Without shooting at the enemy once! Something much worse happened about the same time—the middle of August—but the reports took weeks to reach the eastern seaboard. Immediately the fort at Michilimackinac fell, Hull ordered Fort Dearborn evacuated—that's at the foot of the lake in the Illinois country.

Sixty-six men, women and children dutifully obeyed Hull's stupid order, and left the fort. They were promptly massacred by Indians lying in wait.''

Jared shook his head. ''That's horrible. I suppose the Indians were equipped by the British?''

''Undoubtedly. If it weren't for *Constitution*'s splendid performance, morale in the country would be nonexistent.''

''Did you know Captain Hull's going on leave?''

''I did not.''

''His brother died suddenly.''

''Will Hull resume command when he returns?''

''No, *Constitution*'s going to put to sea before that. I don't know this for certain, but I heard Hull's already been reassigned to the Boston Navy Yard, and Captain Bainbridge will command our ship.''

''I want to hear about the fight!'' Amanda said.

Harriet leaned forward. ''Such an interest on the part of a young girl is not suitable or—''

''Oh for God's sake, Harriet!'' Gilbert said. ''We all want to hear Jared describe the battle.''

''You needn't include me,'' his wife retorted. ''You'll forgive me if I retire. I'm not feeling well.''

Lips pursed, Gilbert stared after her as she left the room. They listened to her rush upstairs. Amanda seemed relieved that her mother was gone. She fairly bounced on her chair:

''The battle, Jared—!''

''Wait, dear,'' Gilbert said. ''I want to ask one question.'' He looked at Jared. ''Are you planning to sail out with Bainbridge?''

''Certainly, sir. My enlistment runs for a year.''

''Then you and I must have a chat after dinner.''

It was said lightly enough. But from the forthrightness of Gilbert's eyes—their dark color heightened by the unhealthy hue of his skin—Jared knew something serious was afoot.

Amanda responded to the exchange by pouting:

''And I'm to be sent to my room, I suppose?''

Gilbert pondered. ''Not necessarily. I believe it might be well if you joined us.'' He showed more animation as the maid brought in their plates. ''Now, Jared—every detail. From the moment you first sighted the enemy.''

Jared obliged his uncle, omitting only his trouble with Stovall and his strange sickness. While the problem of the sixth lieutenant could have been described in a reasonably rational way, the other could not.

And since Jared was positive his uncle couldn't explain the ominous flaw, he saw no reason to bring it up.

VI

BECAUSE THE rain had chilled the house, a fire had been lit in the sitting room hearth. Gilbert pulled a heavy chair up near it. Amanda snuggled at his feet, fondling her bracelet and yawning.

Gilbert's right hand moved gently, caressingly over her shining hair. In his other hand he held a goblet of port. But he drank very little of it.

Jared reveled in his uncle's recognition of his maturity; Gilbert had poured wine for his nephew without any reference to his age. He finished the first glass quickly, helped himself to another and resumed his seat, crossing his legs. His polished boots reflected the firelight. He had changed to civilian clothes for dinner. His fob hung below his trim purple jacket.

"I appreciate your thoughtfulness in bringing me that bit of wood from your ship," Gilbert said. "I'll treasure it."

"It's really of no value, uncle—"

"On the contrary. And the fact that you chose that sort of gift says something interesting about you."

Amanda yawned again. The goblet sparkled with fiery highlights as Gilbert raised it toward the mantel where the French sword hung above the Kentucky rifle. The green glass tea bottle shimmered directly below the gun.

"You are—instinctively, it seems—a Kent. A collector of mementos. That's good. But in other ways, you've changed remarkably in a very short time—"

Though Gilbert spoke matter-of-factly, Jared was disturbed. He had a strange feeling the conversation was about to take a gloomy turn. The rain ticked against the planks nailed over the windows. By the light of the fire, Gilbert looked weary and withered—

Jared tried to fend his uncle's comment with a smile:

"It's mainly because my voice has gotten deeper, I think."

"No, it's more than that. The way you carry yourself, for instance. I've been told danger can gray a man overnight. If that's true, I see no reason why it can't pull a boy from childhood to manhood in a month."

Gilbert set the goblet on a table beside his chair. Amanda had closed her eyes. Careful not to disturb her, he rose and approached the mantel.

"I am not a man of particularly morbid temperament, Jared. But all of us are mortal, and in my case, the time granted me on this earth may be shorter than that granted to others. *May* be," he repeated, a hand raised to silence his nephew's automatic protest.

"I say that only because my physician has said it to me. I don't like to borrow trouble. I've always believed, however, that those who are blind to future possibilities are certain to be punished by them."

"Amanda told me you were ill again," Jared said. "Do you mean to say it— it's more serious than we know?"

"I've no idea whether it is or not. I just have—oh, call it a premonition."

That was the moment Jared knew his uncle was concealing something:

"Uncle Gilbert, please tell me the truth. What has your doctor said?"

Gilbert waved. "The usual nonsense about too much work. The strain of trying to convert others to my viewpoint—a lot of twaddle. I'll probably live to be an old horse."

Jared stared into his uncle's eyes and didn't believe it. Neither did Gilbert, he realized with a jolt.

"But since you *are* old enough to discuss such matters, it's wise for us to at least recognize the possibility that I could be removed from the affairs of this family at any time."

With a glance, Jared tried to warn his uncle that Amanda had awakened. She was listening, her head leaning against the chair, her eyes large. Gilbert appeared not to notice that, or Jared's warning:

"In the event, what would be your attitude about a career with the firm?"

"I'll have to answer you honestly—"

"I'd have it no other way."

"I don't know if I'm the sort to run a printing house."

"Very well. Should anything happen to me, you must then rely on my general manager, Franklin Pleasant. He would be a good steward of the Kent interests until such time as you might decide to throw your lot with the firm—or, barring that, sell it. Naturally I'd hate to see it sold. But I won't force you into a mold of my own devising. Your father was almost—never mind, that's extraneous. Do you understand what I'm saying?"

Jared nodded slowly. He hesitated to speak what was in his thoughts. But his uncle's frankness and the fireshot darkness conspired to make his mood as somber as Gilbert's:

"I think you're saying decisions should not be trusted to Aunt Harriet."

"Yes. God forgive me."

"I still think it's premature to imagine something will hap—"

"Perhaps, perhaps," Gilbert interrupted. "But indulge me a little while longer, if you please. It's often struck me that a man's life is something like one of those gambling games the clerics abhor. In cards, for instance, the outcome depends partly on what you're dealt and what you draw by chance. At the same time, you have the opportunity to make choices—to show skill or lack of it; boldness or cowardice—in your disposition of the hand. A man also has certain things given to him. His capacity for learning. Sometimes his health—but those factors needn't control him completely. They needn't defeat him if they capriciously take charge for a while. That happens in this world, despite our best efforts to order our own lives—"

Jared remembered Stovall; remembered Ollie Prouty's death.

"I know."

"I want to share some thoughts about your life, Jared. How you might control and guide it in the years to come. As I said before, I'd never tell you exactly what to do, for reasons we won't go into. But whatever you do and wherever you go, I do want and expect you to remember one thing. You are a Kent. A member of a family not content to simply prosper without concern for this country which makes prosperity possible for all. Everything we are—you are—is summed up in our odd penchant for collecting little souvenirs of the times in which we've lived. I've noticed the books and scientific samples in your room, for instance. During your absence, your aunt wanted to store them away. I said no. Those things are signs that you're a Kent—as is that splinter of wood you brought home."

He returned to the mantel. "As a Kent, I want you to share the reverence I have for these objects—"

A hand encompassed the sword, the rifle, the bottle.

"—because they are the sum and symbol of the way your grandfather pledged his life to what he believed. Many men—and women—pledge themselves to nothing but their own self-interest. That's not the Kent way. Not my way, and I hope not yours. If Kent and Son must vanish one day because you choose another course, don't let these objects vanish—or what they represent. Guard them as you would your own life. Humor me in this, Jared—promise me you will revere and protect what you see before you."

In a whisper, Jared said, "I will."

And the voice of his doubt whispered in turn, *If I am strong enough. If I am not what my father was—*

He was conscious of Amanda's upturned face, evidently still unnoticed by

Gilbert. With an almost mystical fascination, she stared at the bottle and the fire-lit weapons.

"See that you live up to the words on that fob as well."

"I'll try."

"Finally—take care of your cousin. I fear you are the only one who can do that adequately."

Jared opened his mouth, ready to tell his uncle Amanda was listening. Young as she was, she apparently sensed the reason Gilbert spoke as he did; she understood his references to poor health and the possibility of death. Nestled against the chair, she had tears in her eyes.

Jared said, "I'll take care of her, sir."

Gilbert walked to the front windows, stared at the rainy darkness beyond the one remaining glass.

"If we survive and win this war—as we must—there will be great challenges for a man who is willing to look for them without fear. We are gaining new territory all the time. The pace of invention and technical progress is astounding. The United States can expand, and prosper. Despite greed and faulty thinking and all the cruelties and aberrations of the human condition, this nation can become something unlike any other state or kingdom in the world's history. Your grandfather recognized that, I have tried to, and I want you to do the same. I hope you will not be drawn into selfish byways, but will stay on the high road— the road of cause and contribution and commitment. In the Kent family, that's a kind of religion. Those are its altarpieces—"

Jared's gaze followed the slender hand back to the mantel.

"—and you are called to be one of its priests. Strong men of conviction will be needed, Jared. They are always needed, but they will be needed more and more urgently in the years ahead."

He began to pace. "The country's still in its infancy—growing, experimenting. Like a child, it could fall and flounder—and be abandoned by the march of history. Many questions over and above the immediate ones of this war remain to be resolved. The nation's survival depends on their resolution. One is the matter of the franchise. I have thought long and hard on it, and I've concluded that although the men who founded this country had great wisdom and courage, in some respects they were narrow traditionalists. Influenced by an English heritage—a heritage of aristocracy. It was natural that American aristocrats should lead the drive for independence. It's easier to find leaders among the rich simply because the rich can concern themselves with issues larger than making a living. But we've gone past that stage. If the principles of freedom Mr. Jefferson expressed so well are to have any validity, all men must have the basic right to control their government through their elected officials. *All* men, not merely those who meet their state's voting requirements—so much money, so much property, so much education. Such requirements must be abolished or the democratic ideal is a sham."

"Did President Jefferson really believe in freedom, uncle? He still keeps slaves down in Virginia, doesn't he?"

"Yes, he does. Like all human beings, he's a study in contradictions. I doubt he'd ever favor granting the vote to a black man."

"How do you feel about that?"

"I'd be horsewhipped for saying it, but I feel it must come. First, however, the whole slavery question must be addressed—and God knows where that confrontation will lead."

"Would you even let women vote?"

"Oh, no, I draw the line there! Men are temperamentally suited to the tasks of the world. By their very nature, women are domestic creatures."

Unseen by her father, Amanda scowled. Gilbert went on:

"Another problem is this dreadful business of the northeast seceding—or talking about it. Some of my acquaintances claim that since the Constitution grants only certain powers to the central government, it therefore implies that the states retain all others—including the privilege of deciding whether to remain in the union or withdraw. However, that same document begins with the words, 'We the people.' It does not say, 'We of the several states.' Once founded by the consent of all, the union can't be sundered at the whim of a few. Any other interpretation could tear this country apart. Men must recognize that danger. Be prepared to counter it—"

Again he pointed to the fob Jared was wearing.

"No matter where you are, or what you are, I expect you to be one of those men."

Stunned into silence by everything his uncle had said, Jared simply stared into the dark, sunken eyes. At last, Gilbert smiled:

"I think that's quite enough for one evening. Shall we have another glass of port?"

"You didn't finish the first one, sir."

"So I didn't! My mind wanders lately. Damned annoying—"

He passed a palm over his forehead. With a start, Jared saw that his uncle's brow was wet with sweat. He was breathing in a raspy way. He groaned softly as he lowered himself into his chair, tousling his daughter's hair.

Jared said, "She's been listening too, uncle."

Gilbert looked at him. "Yes, I was aware."

"You were? I thought—"

"I wanted her to hear. She's just as much a Kent as you are, Jared."

He bent and kissed his daughter's cheek. The rain rattled on the planks. Jared helped himself to more wine, wondering whether he could ever live up to all his uncle expected of him.

VII

ACCOMPANIED BY a harpsichord moved in for the occasion, the baritone sang every verse of the song Jared now knew by heart:

> "The first broadside we poured
> Swept their mainmast overboard,
> Which made this lofty frigate look
> Abandoned-O—
> Then Dacres he did sigh,
> And to his officers did cry,
> 'I did not think these Yankees were
> So handy-O!' "

Jared reflected dully that the songwriter had gotten things a bit mixed up; *Guerriere*'s mizzen, not her mainmast, had gone down under the first salvos.

Two more verses, he thought. *Then the toasts begin. We're going to broil here half the night.*

But most of the several hundred men gathered in Faneuil Hall were enjoying the performance, tapping or stamping the beat of the drinking song to which new words had been set. Copies of the lyrics were available all over Boston in a fast-selling broadside.

With appropriate fervor, the baritone launched into the final verse:

> *"Now fill your glasses full,*
> *Let's drink a toast to Captain Hull,*
> *So merrily we'll push around*
> *The brandy-O—*
> *For John Bull may drink his fill,*
> *And the world say what it will,*
> *The Yankee tars for fighting are*
> *The dandy-O!"*

Loud applause greeted the end of the song, and earned the baritone several bows. Jared sat back in his chair, folded his arms and closed his eyes. The hall was an inferno, and the dinner had made him sleepy. He ached for a breath of outside air, hot as it was. But since he couldn't make a spectacle by walking out, a surreptitious nap was the next best thing.

A voice droned from the dais. Another was still droning when he woke up to discover nothing had changed, except for the temperature, which seemed more hellish than ever, and the quantity of pipe and cigar smoke, which had reached asphyxiating proportions.

In his place of honor, Captain Hull still looked quite alert and attentive, however. His cheeks gleamed like polished apples and his dress uniform was resplendent. At his right hand lay a velvet box containing a commemorative medal struck in gold at the order of the Congress. Silver medals had been struck for the officers. All of them were present on the dais except for Morris and Stovall, who were still under medical care.

"Won't they ever stop?" one of the boys at the table whispered as yet another well-dressed gentleman rose to offer a toast.

"That's only sixteen so far," a second boy said.

"Fourteen," said the first.

"It damn well seems like a hundred and fourteen!"

A gentleman at the next table shushed them. The speaker raised his glass:

"Our infant navy! We must nurture the young Hercules in his cradle, if we mean to profit by the labors of his manhood!"

Every man in the hall stood up, and drank. Many stamped or shouted, "Hear!" The boys were required to stand but not to drink. Only the hardiest topers among them kept pace with the toasts, and that group didn't include Jared.

The guests resumed their seats. Waiters brought more wine to each table. Jared perked up slightly when Gilbert, seated at the extreme left end of the dais, stood up with glass in hand. Jared noticed a few sour expressions when his uncle rose.

"Christ, he's white as chalk," a boy whispered as Gilbert cleared his throat. Jared sat forward, wide awake and alarmed. The boy was right.

Gilbert held his glass aloft.

"To unconditional victory! We have suffered the injuries and insults of des-
potism with patience, but its friendship is more than we can bear—"

A groundswell of grumbling greeted the extreme anti-British sentiment. But it
hushed the instant the glass fell and broke.

Gilbert swayed, his eyes rolling up in his head. His fisted left hand jammed
against the center of his chest. In the silence, his gasps could be heard in every
corner of the hall.

Jared jumped up. Gilbert toppled, smashing china and dragging the tablecloth
after him as he slid to the floor.

____ VIII

IN THE sharp air of late October, *Constitution* put to sea. Jared Kent was aboard.
So was a new sixth lieutenant.

After the frigate passed Boston light, Jared looked back at the blur of the
channel islands. Uncle Gilbert had suffered a seizure from which he had not yet
recovered. His heart rhythm remained irregular. He'd been unconscious when
Jared slipped in to kneel at his bedside and bid him a silent goodbye.

As the familiar coastline receded and the noisy routine of shipboard began in
earnest, Jared remembered the responsibility with which Gilbert had charged him
on the night of his homecoming. Gilbert had spoken of a premonition, too.
Although the doctor continued to refuse comment, Jared still had the feeling his
uncle had known much more about his own failing health than anyone in the
household realized.

In a way, Jared was thankful Bainbridge had put to sea in company with
Hornet, a twenty-gun sloop of war. Shipboard gossip said they were to rendezvous with Captain David Porter's *Essex,* thirty-six guns, then proceed south to
search for enemy convoys bound around Cape Horn on their way to the Far East.
Dangerous duty—but preferable to remaining behind while Aunt Harriet raved
and wept over the injustice of her husband being struck down at age twenty-nine.

Constitution swept out into the Atlantic. But distance couldn't relieve Jared of
worries about his uncle—

Or about his own ability to cope with the future, if he came home from the
cruise to find himself the surviving male of the Kent family.

CARDS OF FATE

__1
Mr. Piggott

IN THE dressing room adjoining her bedroom on the second floor, Harriet took off the bandeau that held her breasts in place when she dressed. She added the bit of lingerie to the pile of petticoats and the long-waisted, lightly boned corset lying on the floor.

Harriet's upstairs maid had been ready to assist her in undressing, of course. The lascivious girl undoubtedly wanted to see what sort of nightgown her mistress had chosen—so she could gossip about it with the other servants. Harriet refused the help. Her bed apparel this evening in mid-July, 1813, was solely her affair.

A moth circled the chimney of the lamp on her dressing table. She studied the beating beige wings. She felt exactly like that poor creature—frantic—though only her quick breathing and her racing heart betrayed her state.

With the greatest of effort, she'd endured the ceremony performed by the Reverend Channing in the front sitting room. She'd feigned composure during the modest reception afterward, chatting with guests and concealing her inner turmoil. But she wasn't at all sure she could stay calm now. She faced the rest of the night with disgust, even outright fear.

Outside, the hooves of a carriage horse clopped rapidly. Beacon Street was becoming a raceway for commercial vehicles and young bloods on horseback. The hoofbeats set off a wistful yearning for the safe, quiet days of her childhood in New York. Being a woman certainly had its undesirable aspects—

Undesirable? Why not be truthful? The word was loathsome.

She had often expressed her loathing during the initial years of her marriage to Gilbert. By the time she became pregnant with Amanda, it was unmistakably

clear to him that physical intimacy repelled her. After the child was born, he left her alone.

But her current situation reminded her all too vividly of her first wedding trip. Reminded her of the revulsion; the anguish—

Like a prisoner, she was sentenced to that again tonight.

Well, it was the price she had to pay for marital respectability. But she refused to gaze at the mirror and confront the reality of her own body; especially the breasts her opaque cotton chemise concealed from sight but revealed in contour.

Her lips compressed angrily. She snatched at the moth, crushed it between her fingertips and flung it aside.

Seating herself, she began to comb out her long, dark hair.

Something else stunned and angered her suddenly. She leaned forward, touched the top of her head. In the mirror, she saw gray hair.

She'd never noticed it before. She counted only six or seven strands. But they upset her horribly.

Gilbert was responsible for that gray hair! He'd wrenched her whole life awry last December when he died. He had been bedridden ever since his collapse at the Faneuil Hall dinner in early September. On Christmas Eve, his heart had simply stopped beating while he slept.

The household was in a turmoil for days. Immediately, Harriet found herself coping with problems normally the purview of men: funeral preparations; arrangements for burial of the body at the family plot in Watertown—there had been no end to the aggravations. She recalled one of the worst—the necessity of sending servants all over Boston just to find a fashionable mourning costume for Amanda: a black cashmere dress with white frills; a white mull cap; gray stockings.

The whole period was a dreadful ordeal. But she got through it—only to be plunged into another. At the end of February, that wretched Jared had come home.

He'd been discharged from service along with most of his crew because *Constitution* was to be laid up in the Navy Yard indefinitely, for repairs. Having taken part in a second major engagement—the capture and sinking of the British frigate *Java* off the coast of Brazil—the boy was decidedly changed. Harriet had noticed a difference in him when he returned with Captain Hull. But at the second homecoming, the change was even more marked.

Physical maturation was part of it, of course. Abraham's son had grown taller. The relatively soft flesh of childhood had turned to muscle. But the change went deeper than mere passage through normal adolescent development.

Jared carried himself differently. With confidence; even a certain air of authority. Harriet could recall years gone by when she had deliberately intimidated him—and taken secret pleasure in the way it visibly withered his spirit; lent his eyes a nervous, unhappy quality—

Now her sharpest admonishments produced little response—other than a cool, almost hostile stare. It was harder than it had once been to make him lose his temper. She found the boy's new self-assurance infuriating. She regretted that she'd lost her power to make him feel terrified and demeaned.

Mercifully, Jared wasn't underfoot too long after his return. At his own request, he went to work at the firm under the supervision of Mr. Franklin Pleasant, a jowly, phlegmatic man who seemed to understand the ins and outs of the coarse, controversial trade in which her husband had been involved. Mr. Pleasant had taken over operation of the company pending a decision from

Harriet as to whether she wished to put Kent and Son up for sale. On several occasions he begged her not to sell. His pleas carried little weight. He was a tradesman and always would be; why, the fellow didn't even have a diploma from one of the lesser colleges!

Although Pleasant gave her a weekly report, Harriet paid scant attention to the business. She was aware that the list of titles to be published in the fall had been reduced. And she knew circulation of the *Republican* was off sharply. No one could match Gilbert's way with words, Pleasant said. Even those details failed to interest her.

Gilbert's demise had brought one benefit, however. It had put an end to those horrid visitations by anti-war hooligans who threw stones. To make doubly sure, she had given Mr. Pleasant definite orders that there were to be no more articles or editorials stating or even implying support of the war.

That action helped her in another sphere as well. She was once more accepted and treated cordially by members of Boston's better families.

Except for minor naval victories of the sort Jared talked about with quiet pride, the war was proving a disaster. The New England Federalists took smug satisfaction in having foreseen that—

To punish the upstart nation, Britain had clamped a blockade on Chesapeake and Delaware Bays the preceding December. The blockade had been extended to the mouth of the Mississippi and the ports of New York, Charleston and Savannah in May. Though New England's harbors were still open, the northeast felt the effects of the blockade in shortages of everyday goods, and in rising prices.

In consequence, the outcries from press and pulpit grew louder. They culminated in gloomy predictions of American defeat. As if to confirm the predictions, news reached the city that the much-touted Captain James Lawrence had lost the frigate *Chesapeake* to the British just thirty miles from the Boston waterfront.

Through most of the month of June, Harriet was forced to endure Jared's defense of the defeat: Lawrence might have lost his frigate, but not his fighting spirit! Dying, he had exclaimed, "Don't give up the ship!"

In vain, Harriet tried to convince the misguided boy that such sloganeering was foolish. It certainly hadn't helped save Lawrence's life—and it gave the country a false confidence. President Madison was steering the ship of state straight onto the rocks of military and economic disaster—all Harriet's friends and their husbands said so. The sooner America pleaded for terms, the better!

During one such argument, Harriet almost succeeded in goading Jared into a rage. But he controlled his temper and replied, "You—and your friends—are entitled to your opinion, Aunt Harriet." She seethed over the little exhibition of self-control.

The war made daily living difficult. Even a family as well off as Harriet's had trouble buying the necessities—and if they were available, prices were cruel. Managing household affairs by herself was a strain. Perhaps that was part of the reason she'd succumbed relatively quickly to the marriage proposal of a man she had only met in March, at Reverend Channing's church.

What she had liked immediately about Mr. Andrew Piggott was his gentility. He wore the proper clothes. Cultivated the proper people. Disavowed and damned the war. He was educated—a graduate of Yale down in New Haven. That wasn't Harvard; but one couldn't have everything.

More important, Mr. Piggott didn't misuse his education by wandering into philosophical byways and espousing radical causes, as Gilbert had.

Piggott told her he had become a man of independent means when an uncle in

Albany left him an inheritance. Harriet made a few inquiries around town and found no evidence to contradict Piggott's claim that the uncle was a prosperous fur factor associated with Mr. Astor. She had to admit the inquiries were superficial; in her eagerness to end the lonely struggle that was widowhood, she accepted Piggott's credentials almost at face value. He was urbane; polite; and appeared to be welcome in the best circles.

She wasn't totally imprudent, though. Mr. Piggott first proposed in June. She put him off. She needed to satisfy herself that he wasn't marrying her in order to take possession of the assets of Kent and Son. She questioned him about it several times. Repeatedly, Mr. Piggott assured her that he wished to live a gentleman's life, not soil his hands in business. He would be perfectly content to let Franklin Pleasant operate the company until Harriet decided about its disposition.

He also disarmed her by confessing to two vices. He liked liquor, he said. And he enjoyed card-playing. In fact, when he wasn't squiring her to salons, dinner parties, or the Federal Street Church, he spent most of his time at the Exchange Coffee House, hunting up other affluent and respectable gentlemen he could engage in a marathon game of solo. At other times, the game was shemmy—the one French invention whose origins Mr. Piggott, a good Federalist, overlooked.

The games were always played in private rooms rented for the occasion, he said. His fondness for cards would never cause a scandal. Everything was conducted with the utmost discretion.

Another investigation seemed in order. Harriet called on Franklin Pleasant, and he in turn sent out one of the *Republican*'s writers. She got back a report that yes, Mr. Piggott did involve himself in card games organized at the Exchange; games in which the stakes were rumored to be quite high. But he seemed to have the income to support his passion.

Finally, then, Harriet accepted the proposal, telling herself she could wean Mr. Piggott from his not-quite-respectable pastime after they were man and wife.

She had yet to learn the extent of Mr. Piggott's interest in sexual matters. It was a topic one didn't discuss prior to marriage. Tonight would surely shed some light on that repellent subject, however—

As she finished brushing her hair and walked to the wardrobe to select a gown in which to greet her new husband, she resolved that in the boudoir, too, she would rule. She had accepted Mr. Piggott because he seemed a decent, pliant man of good social connections; a man who would understand her wishes and accede to them. She meant to make sure he did—

A noise in the outer room startled her. The latch!

She darted back to the dressing table so he wouldn't see her in her chemise. "Andrew? Is that you?"

"Indeed it is." He had a deep, mellow voice. A little too mellow right now, she decided. He had imbibed somewhat heavily at the reception.

"I won't be ready to receive you for at least a quarter of an hour."

He laughed. "Don't trouble yourself with bed clothes, my dear—"

Andrew Piggott appeared in the dressing room entrance, gazing at his wife with alarming directness.

He was about Harriet's age, with good features and a ruddy complexion. His eyes tended to be squinty, and he carried a fair amount of flesh on his frame: some might even describe him as portly. But that mellow voice charmed everyone, compensating for the small signs of self-indulgence: a florid nose; the beginning of a paunch.

Harriet caught her breath as he studied her. Mr. Piggott had already discarded his dark green clawhammer tail coat with its elegant black velvet collar. She saw it on the bedroom floor behind him. He stood before her in his pea-green waistcoat, fluffy stock, fawn trousers and gaitered pumps. His eyes moved slowly from her throat to her breasts.

Undone by the sudden interruption and his candid stare, Harriet crossed her arms over her bosom.

"The clothes will come off soon enough anyway," Piggott said with a genial smile. The dreaded moment had come—too quickly.

Harriet Lebow Kent Piggott was terrified.

II

"I WISH you would retire and permit me—" she began.

"Nonsense." Piggott waved. "We're married now. Very enjoyable affair, too."

"I noticed you dipping into the punch quite often."

Piggott's eyes grew a bit less cordial. "That's my business, I think. By the way—your nephew refused to say more than a couple of words to me."

Turning her back, Harriet hurried to the wardrobe.

"You can be sure Jared will hear about that." She was less than confident that a reprimand would do any good, though.

"Not necessary," Piggott said. "If he persists in his rudeness, I'll speak to him. We will come to an understanding, I promise."

Piggott's tone made Harriet glance around. His smile remained fixed. But his eyes were humorless.

"I mean to say, if he doesn't show proper respect for his new father, I'll take him aside and thrash him."

"Jared has grown to be a very strong boy—"

"Headstrong is more like it. Sea duty quite inflated his hat size, I think."

"He's like his mother now. She was an arrogant creature—"

"Well, I can deal with him. Gentlemen at Yale don't spend all their hours musing over the classics! They've been known to fight free-for-all—"

Piggott rubbed the fingers of his right hand against his palm, as if in anticipation. Then he walked toward her.

"Time enough for that in the weeks to come. At the moment our concern is pleasure."

Harriet was afraid she might swoon. She noticed a disgusting lump under Piggott's trousers. She groped behind her for a gown—

Piggott seized her around the waist, pulled her to him, sounding a shade annoyed:

"Let's not concern ourselves with false propriety, my dear. I trust you *are* happy to be Mrs. Piggott—?"

"Of—of course."

His dark eyes focused behind her, on a shelf of the wardrobe.

"Not sufficiently happy to wear one of my wedding gifts."

His clasping fingers hurt her waist. She writhed away, spun to the shelf, plucked down the pair of white linen tubes decorated with bright red ribbons:

"I have certain standards, Andrew—"

"Pantalets are coming into fashion."

"But false pantalets are worn only by dancers and harlots."

He nodded, his face enigmatically empty of emotion:

"I'll forgive your reluctance. If you're less reluctant in bed—"

He took hold of her waist again. She realized that he might be drunk. She smelled the ginned punch on him, blending with the odor of his cologne. As he dragged her against him, she felt something stiff press her flesh through the chemise.

Her mouth went dry. Her eyes blurred. She gasped.

Visibly annoyed, Piggott stood back.

"What's this? You *are* reluctant."

"No. No, it's—a vaporish dizziness. Just give me a moment—"

She moved quickly to the dressing table, sank down, eyed Piggott in the glass. His features had hardened—exactly as his flesh had hardened beneath his trousers. He stared at her in an accusing way; he wasn't deceived by her lie.

He took two steps, came up behind her, deliberately thrust that bulge against her back while his hands slipped under her arms. He started fondling her breasts. She blurted the first thought that came into her head:

"Has Amanda retired?"

Piggott jerked his hands away. He laughed, a harsh sound.

"Amanda, Jared—who else shall we discuss, Mrs. Piggott?"

"I only wanted to know—"

"Is that what you propose to do this evening? Talk? It's not what I propose to do!"

"I thought—I thought you respected my wishes—"

"Yes! But I remind you that we're married. I have rights."

In a faint voice, she said, "And I'll permit you to exercise them—"

"Well! That's generous of you! My dear, there's no *permitting* about it."

Seeing her shocked expression, he forced another smile. But the way he raked a hand through his thick black hair revealed his anger:

"To answer your blasted question—yes, Amanda has gone to her room." Piggott ran his tongue over his lower lip. "Quite a fetching little creature now that she's started to fill out. She's begun to bleed, I assume—?"

"*Andrew—!*"

"It's a fact of life, isn't it? And she has, hasn't she?"

Harriet swallowed. Not even Gilbert had ever posed such a frank question. It was all she could do to answer:

"In—in April. Prematurely."

"Thought so from the way those breasts are popping out. Your daughter's going to be a beauty. I've noticed the way she glances at men. Teases them with her eyes—"

Harriet could hardly believe what she was hearing; Piggott sounded almost lustful.

"—I venture she'll be tumbled before she's twelve. And enjoy it!"

"That's *vile!*" Harriet cried. "Such talk isn't suitable even between husband and wife."

"Then shall we try something that is suitable between husband and wife? You've jabbered enough!"

He dragged her up, wrapped one arm around her waist and drove his tongue between her lips.

III

WHAT HAD begun as a day of nerves and worry ended as an utter nightmare.

Mr. Piggott wouldn't be denied. He carried her bodily into the bedroom, refusing her even the decencies of drawing the curtains or dimming the lamps. The harder she struggled, the rougher he became.

He flung her on the turned-down bed and sprawled beside her, nuzzling her throat, her temple, her eyelids—

Thick-fingered hands rubbed and pinched her nipples. He pulled up her chemise, forced one hand between her legs.

"By God you're a prime one," he groaned as he fingered her. "But I'll have you craving more before we're finished, Mrs. Piggott—"

He seized the bodice of her chemise, tore it. She lay exposed on the bed, her nipples wrinkled as prunes. She was incapable of speech. She rolled her head from side to side, making small, incoherent sounds.

Piggot shed his clothing. He had soft white skin. He pulled her legs apart and flung himself over her body.

Harriet's dry flesh hurt when he assaulted her. Piggott could feel that. But he kept thrusting in spite of it. His fingers found her bosom again. Harriet moaned under the hard caress of his thumbs—

Piggott moaned too, jerking back and forth as the rhythm quickened. Harriet felt a muscle jump in her awkwardly bent left leg. Piggott's whole midsection seemed to pummel her. And there was not even darkness to conceal his noisy rutting—

He jammed his hands beneath her buttocks and squeezed:

"Ah—*ah*—"

When he withdrew and rolled on his side, she dragged herself toward the opposite edge of the bed. He shot out a hand, seized her hair:

"Where are you going, Mrs. Piggott?"

"To find—clothes. I trust you'll—allow that. You've satisfied yourself—"

"Not by half, my dear!"

He told her what he wanted next.

"Dear God, you must be mad!"

"Mad for a taste, Mrs. Piggott," he laughed.

She had no strength to fight him. The buzzing in her ears became a roar. She tried to pretend he wasn't doing what she felt him doing: a filthy, unnatural act—

There was no rest for her until well after two in the morning. Piggott assaulted her twice more. The last time seemed endless. He'd worn himself out, yet he wouldn't halt the pounding that tortured her body and numbed her mind. After the first time, he'd blown out the lamps. But that no longer mattered.

Finally, he convulsed; groaned; withdrew. He crawled under the covers, chuckling:

"For a wife, Mrs. Piggott, your behavior is exceedingly odd."

"Yours—" She could barely speak. She lay on her side, her spine toward him. She clutched her stomach, the stickiness of him an abomination between her legs.

"—yours is an animal's."

That generated a deep laugh. *How had she misjudged him so badly?*

Until today, his caresses had been discreet, almost hesitant. Seldom had he done more than peck her cheek. His frantic desire for—*copulation* was the only word she allowed herself to think—gave him a bestial quality.

And he was laughing about it!

The mellow voice boomed in the darkness:

"I am always a gentleman in public, Mrs. Piggott. But in the bedroom, I have my appetites—yes, I do. D'you honestly believe they've never heard of fucking at Yale College?"

"Oh, your vile mouth. Your vile, vile—"

"Be quiet, woman! You make me sick."

"I—I will never again permit—"

"Oh yes you will. This is one area of our marriage in which I mean to call the tune. I've quite a few more novelties to show you."

"Novelties? *Indecencies!*"

"Call 'em what you will, Mrs. Piggott. We shall indulge, never fear. Good night."

After a noisy plumping of his pillow and a few moments of heavy breathing, he began to snore.

Harriet Lebow Kent Piggott lay rigid in the warm air of the bedroom. She listened to the wheels of another carriage speeding along Beacon and wondered how she could have been so deceived. So misguided as to have married the kind of debased man who slept beside her now in perfect contentment.

What a ghastly mistake she'd made. What a ghastly—and irrevocable—mistake.

___IV

NEWS OF some encouraging developments in the west reached Boston in the autumn of 1813.

An officer of talent had at last replaced the bunglers who had led the western army. William Henry Harrison, the same man who had routed the Shawnee at Tippecanoe, was commissioned a major general of militia by the alarmed Kentucky settlers, then given a national command by Secretary of War Eustis in September. With the rank of brigadier general and a force of some ten thousand soldiers, he was ordered to retake Detroit.

But it remained for a twenty-eight-year-old naval officer, Captain Oliver Perry, to make that possible. Perry handed a crushing defeat to the British blockade squadron at Put-in-Bay on Lake Erie. The dispatches said the flagship of Perry's small flotilla flew a pennant inscribed with Lawrence's dying words aboard *Chesapeake*. But the dispatches also carried an even more positive slogan that was soon on the lips of every literate citizen. At the end of his bloody three-and-a-half-hour battle, Perry had sent a message from his heavily damaged ship to General Harrison somewhere on the Sandusky River. In it he wrote, "We have met the enemy and they are ours."

Sweeping the British from Lake Erie permitted Harrison to advance on Detroit. He found the enemy had evacuated it and slipped across the river to Upper Canada. Harrison followed. A battle at Moravian Town on the north bank of the Thames River caused only a few deaths on either side. But one of those deaths brought great relief to the western settlers. Never again would the Shawnee Tecumseh terrorize the frontier.

Harrison and Perry helped end the threat of an Indian confederation manipulated by the British. They cleared the enemy from the northwest. The redcoats withdrew all the way to the Niagara frontier.

Harriet Piggott read the news items in the Kent paper from time to time. But they had no power to excite or even interest her. A much more personal battle was being waged in her own household.

On a Tuesday in late October, Franklin Pleasant called. The face of the graying general manager was unhappy:

"Mrs. Ken—forgive me. I meant to say Mrs. Piggott—"

Wan, Harriet lifted a hand to wave aside Pleasant's embarrassment:

"I wish it were Mrs. Kent again, Franklin. I don't doubt the whole town's laughing about the way a foolish widow was victimized."

"I pay no attention to that kind of nasty gossip," Pleasant declared. "However, a problem has arisen at the company, and I thought you should know. Actually there are two problems. Let me take the more serious one first."

Harriet's dull-eyed silence showed she expected the worst.

"This morning," Pleasant said, "I was served with papers. One of our six book presses is to be removed. It seems your husband—"

"Who has not been in this house for three days."

"Yes? Well, I believe I might have some grasp of the reason. Evidently he's been engaged in another of his gaming sessions."

"Cards?"

"Aye. At the end of a losing streak, he—"

Pleasant swallowed.

"—he refused to retire gracefully. It's not my place to say it, but Mr. Piggott's fondness for alcohol evidently leads to rash decisions. He insisted on continuing in the game. To finance his play, he signed a chit wagering the press I mentioned."

"*Wagering the press?*" Harriet whispered. "Is that legal?"

"The claimant sent a lawyer to Kent and Son this morning, and I asked the same question. I'm afraid it is quite legal. I verified that by consulting Mr. Benbow before I came to see you."

"Who is the claimant?"

"I've since discovered that too. His name means nothing, but he's known for loitering in the coffee houses—striking up friendships with prosperous-looking people—and drawing them into games for high stakes."

"Which he wins by cheating?"

"There is that suspicion—but no evidence has ever been brought forward. Very likely his victims are too humiliated—"

"And our lawyer can't block this—act of robbery?"

"He cannot. Had Mr. Piggott won his game, there'd be no problem. But he continued to lose. The press will be taken from the premises, and sold."

Harriet covered her eyes. "Oh dear God, Franklin. It's all my fault—"

Pleasant touched her hand. "Don't score yourself. We all make errors in judging other people. You were—you'll forgive me—not at all yourself during those weeks in which you kept company with your present husband. Mr. Gilbert was dead. It's only natural you'd want someone to fill his place. But what's done is done. We can make do without the press. I'd urge you to speak to Mr. Piggott, however. Insist that he refrain from similar wagers." Pleasant's smile was feeble. "Else he's liable to strip us to the walls."

After a moment Harriet said, "I'll speak to him."

"Good."

"But I have no legal means of compelling him to do anything."

"You mean—there was no agreement signed before marriage to limit his access to your property?"

Sadly, she shook her head. "I believed his lies about wanting no part of the business. Kent and Son is as much his as it is mine."

"Then—if I might suggest—"

He stopped, red-faced.

"Yes?" Harriet prompted.

"I *am* correct in assuming you're not entirely happy with your husband's character, am I not?"

Harriet almost burst out crying. She cried often these days. Piggott had dropped his mask of gentility. He treated her as a chattel. He was absent from the house more than he was present. But almost every time he returned, he demanded his rights in bed. Of late she'd taken to retiring to her room by five o'clock, and locking the door.

"That hardly covers it, Franklin," she said. "I have been duped. I was a willing, even eager accomplice, but the fact remains—I have been duped. And I don't seem to have any legal recourse."

Pleasant's eyes turned shrewd:

"Perhaps we can establish one."

"What do you mean?"

"Only that I'd like your permission to have one of our reporters do another bit of probing into Mr. Piggott's background and behavior. A little more thoroughly this time. It may yield nothing. But if there's evidence of immorality at these card games, for instance—women present—"

He shrugged, his cheek still deep pink.

Harriet said, "You have my permission."

"I'm happy to hear you say that. Now we come to the second matter. The day before yesterday, Mr. Piggott called on me in person—"

"Whatever for?"

"To inform me ahead of time that the press would be attached, and that I should not cause any difficulties. I'm afraid he and your nephew got into quite a heated argument. They do dislike one another—"

Harriet pressed her shaking hands into her lap:

"Intensely. Tell me exactly what happened."

"Mr. Piggott had been imbibing. To be honest, I didn't believe what he said about the press. I thought it was a drunkard's joke—else I'd have consulted Mr. Benbow before today, I guarantee you. In any case, Jared was working close by. There were—remarks exchanged. At one point, Master Jared completely lost his temper. I thought he was going to attack your husband. I prevented an actual fight, though—"

In the midst of her misery, Harried felt a brief twinge of pleasure hearing about Jared. But the pleasure faded quickly:

"What did my husband say?"

"First he maligned Master Jared's character—unjustly. The boy has worked hard and done well in the press room—" The statement displeased Harriet, but she said nothing. "I told Piggott as much, too. He then made one utterly indecent reference to your daughter. About her—physical appearance. I hesitate to say more—"

Dread closed over Harriet then. On several occasions she had noticed Piggott watching Amanda closely. Amanda was a beautiful child. Much too beautiful for her own good.

Pleasant was waiting for a reply. She composed herself;

"You needn't say any more, Franklin. I understand."

"That was the remark which sent Master Jared into a fury. Mr. Piggott had to flee for his own safety. I—"

Pleasant started. Harriet had buried her face in her hands, weeping uncontrollably.

"—I agreed with Jared to say nothing about it. But when the disposal of the press proved to be anything but a joke, I changed my mind—"

His voice trailed off. Harriet gave no indication that she'd heard.

"Good afternoon, Mrs. Piggott," he whispered, picking up his hat and stealing out.

V

"BE DAMNED to you, woman!" Andrew Piggott exclaimed.

"But you have no right to wager—"

"*I said be damned to you!*" Piggott shouted, raising his hand to her.

Harriet dodged away. She had asked her husband to come to the library when he returned to the house two days after Pleasant's visit. She hoped privacy would allow them to have an amicable discussion. The hope was misplaced from the beginning. Piggott had proceeded to grumble about needing a change of linen. He barely listened to her pleas. Now, at the end of the confrontation, he got control of himself and lowered his fist, saying:

"We share tenancy of all the assets of this family, Mrs. Piggott."

"I'm sure you made certain of that before the wedding," she said in a bitter voice.

He smiled. "I did. And I couldn't afford to be embarrassed during the game in question. I had to find some way to recoup—"

"So you gambled something which wasn't yours, and lost that too!"

He fussed with his stock. "Your shrillness is annoying. I'm going upstairs and then I'm leaving. I'm overdue at the Exchange Coffee House. Met a couple of Maryland gentlemen there only this morning. They're in metal refining. Pig iron into wrought—think that's what they said. A new version of something called a puddling furnace has been perfected on the Continent but they can't secure any information about it because of the blockade. They're hoping to put an inquiry agent aboard one of the neutral ships calling at Boston. Most agreeable chaps—"

"What's the point of all this?" Harriet demanded.

"Why—just that we're playing this evening, Mrs. Piggott."

"With *your* money!"

At the library door, he gave her a murderous look.

"With ours, if I choose. And there's not a damned thing you can do about it, my dear."

He raised his beaver hat to his forehead, tipped it and walked out.

2
Act of Vengeance

AMANDA KENT couldn't keep her mind on the book she was supposed to read by Monday, as part of her study of what the mistress of the dame school termed "fine literature." The book was a handsomely bound edition of a long poem that had something to do with a lady and a lake. The story took place in Scotland, but Amanda only succeeded in reading part of the first canto. The poem was as dreary as the weather!

She wandered to the library window. Watched dead leaves blowing across the Common. Noticed a few snowflakes in the air. Pedestrians passing the house looked chilly and uncomfortable.

Despite the darkness of the day, no lamps had been lit as yet. It was a Saturday afternoon in early November, and no one was home. No one, that is, except the servants. But they were virtually invisible. Very faintly, back in the kitchen, Amanda could hear cook singing to herself. The rest of the house was silent.

Amanda picked up an unfamiliar newspaper. Mr. Franklin Pleasant had brought it to the house only the day before. Of late, Mr. Pleasant called on Amanda's mother quite often. Amanda had asked why, but Harriet refused to answer, saying only that Mr. Pleasant's visits would soon change their lives for the better.

What could that mean? she wondered, idly scanning the front page of the paper which mama said had been started up in competition to Kent and Son's *Republican*.

Amanda found the family newspaper totally boring, packed as it was with paragraph after paragraph about the war. This new one, the *Boston Daily Advertiser,* seemed a little more lively. One story had to do with Indians in the Mississippi Territory; that was down south, wasn't it?

The Indians were called Creeks. Amanda hadn't heard the name before. It struck her as funny. But there was nothing amusing about the paper's vivid description of a massacre of white settlers at a place called Fort Mims. Near the end of August, a fanatical Creek faction, the Red Sticks, had slaughtered at least two hundred and fifty men, women and children.

Amanda wasn't familiar with the word "fanatical." After reading of the grisly activities of the Red Sticks, however, she thought she understood its meaning. The paper declared the Red Sticks would rue their butality. A man named Jackson, a major general of the Tennessee militia, had raised two thousand volunteers to fight the Indians. The *Advertiser* stated that the former congressman and judge whose nickname was Old Hickory would punish the bestial savages in fitting fashion.

Amanda enjoyed several delicious shivers while reading the article—and another giggle over that nickname. Imagine a soldier being described as an old tree. Americans had such a passion for funny names!

Another item on the front page diverted her for a few moments. It described the death of a well-known New England witch, Moll Pitcher, who lived out in Lynn. The story said Moll had been famous for her ability to predict the future, locate lost articles and brew love potions.

With a sigh, Amanda put the paper down. How she wished she had a potion! Several, in fact. One to correct each of the unhappy circumstances that were

making day-to-day existence so miserable. Glumly, she walked back to the window, planting her elbows on the sill and twisting the bracelet of tarred rope.

Amanda had grown taller in the first half of 1813. Mama said she'd soon have to wear a bandeau with her chemise, to contain those fleshy bumps that had appeared shortly after that hateful flow began—

If she'd had access to magic potions, she'd certainly have used one to stop the strange and alarming changes taking place in her body. Though mama assured her the flow was perfectly natural, it made her head hurt whenever she got it. And it was an untidy nuisance besides.

Another magic potion to restore her flat chest would have been welcome, too.

Then one more—to bring papa back. If only he were here, he'd set things right in the house. In its vast and almost incomprehensible finality, her father's death had left an empty place in her existence. No one, not even her cousin Jared whom she worshipped, could fill it.

But if no potion were available to restore her father to life, she'd certainly wish for one to put her mother in better spirits. Amanda often felt guilty because she loved her mother out of a sense of duty, rather than spontaneously and with joyful abandon, as she'd loved Gilbert. Still, she hated to see Harriet unhappy, because that unhappiness affected the entire household. And mama had been miserable ever since her marriage during the summer.

Well, it was no wonder! How could she be happy as the wife of that Mr. Piggott with his syrup voice! His squinty eyes—?

And his hands. Amanda despised his hands most of all. They strayed in a too familiar way over her arms and shoulders whenever she was unlucky enough to be alone with him. He pretended he was touching her because he was affectionate; because he wanted to be a second father to her.

She didn't believe him. She was sure papa would never have touched her breasts and then claimed it was an accident.

Yes, a potion to forever banish Mr. Piggott from the house was perhaps the most desirable potion of all, provided she could have her real father back at the same time. What a pity the witch had died! If she hadn't, Amanda fancied she might very well have gone all the way to Lynn to consult her.

She did count it a blessing that Mr. Piggott played cards. That pursuit, which all preachers condemned, took him away from Beacon Street for long periods. In fact he hadn't been home during the past week and a half except for brief visits to change his clothes.

Late in the evening two days ago, Jared had revealed a piece of shocking news about Mr. Piggott. The family—except for Piggott, of course—was gathered in the front sitting room just before Amanda went to bed. All red in the face, Jared told his cousin that Mr. Piggott had gambled away one of the company's printing presses.

It was the first time in a long time that Amanda had seen her cousin genuinely angry. Since coming back from the navy, Jared didn't act like his old self. He spent most of every day and often part of the night at the printing house, and when he was home, he said very little. He no longer proposed deliciously dangerous adventures, such as climbing the roof of an ice house. He was obviously trying to behave properly, but he frightened Amanda a little because he looked so severe. He seemed to be keeping all his feelings locked up inside himself—

He didn't keep them locked up while describing what Mr. Piggott had done, however. He growled that Piggott had better not do anything like that again. In

a way, Amanda was glad to see her cousin angry. He was more like the Jared she remembered—

The rest of the evening was puzzling, though. Instead of expressing anger toward Mr. Piggott, mama grew upset and argued with Jared. He had no right to reveal such matters to Amanda, she said. And besides, the loss of the press was a good thing. It had opened her eyes to the need for drastic steps. Ever since then, Amanda had been trying to form a mental picture of someone hurrying along the street taking drastic steps. But she still couldn't imagine what such steps looked like.

The same evening Jared blurted the news about the press and incurred Harriet's wrath, he stole into Amanda's bedroom after she was tucked in. Like a conspirator, he led her to his own cluttered room and latched the door. From under his pillow, he took something that both frightened and fascinated her.

A pistol.

He'd bought it with his wages, he said. He meant to keep it down at Kent and Son, in case Piggott dared to gamble away any more of the firm's equipment. He looked quite angry and determined, and when Amanda reminded him that mama said Mr. Piggott had the legal right to gamble a printing press, Jared turned red a second time, flew into a fury and called her stupid.

She was hurt. Yet, oddly, she was comforted too—just as she had been earlier. Jared was Jared again—

He told her courts and lawyers were useless in dealing with rascals such as Piggott—only he used a much more wicked word than *rascals*. He said courts and lawyers actually helped men like Piggott steal what wasn't theirs—but no one was going to steal from the Kent family.

Mr. Piggott might have a *legal* right to bet a Kent press in a gambling game. But the next lawyer who showed his face at the firm with such a claim would answer to a higher law. The law of possession—

When he said that, he raised the pistol.

It was all rather mystifying to Amanda. So many large words and complicated concepts. But Jared's feelings certainly weren't secret any longer. She begged him not to do anything that would land him in trouble. The red faded from his face and he promised he wouldn't. But she knew he was fibbing. She had never seen his blue eyes so unpleasant.

Amanda hoped there would be no trouble. No more terrifying shouts and thumps from behind the closed doors of the library as mama and Piggott screamed at one another.

She hoped there wouldn't be any more gambling of the kind that provoked Jared, either. But that hope was probably foolish. Just yesterday, mama had let slip the admission that Mr. Piggott was again involved in a card game somewhere in the city. This particular game had been in progress for more than a week, and mama was worried. Amanda had suspected the reason for Piggott's prolonged absence, naturally. She prayed the man was wagering money and not printing presses—

Oh, it was such a dreadful muddle! And to top it off, she just couldn't work up enough interest to finish Scott's tedious poem by Monday. That would earn her a bad mark—

Life had been so good until papa died! Why couldn't he come back? Tears appeared in the corners of her dark eyes. Leaning on the sill, she twisted the cordage bracelet one way, then another—

With a little cry of fright, she straightened up. She saw a familiar figure

lurching toward the stoop. It was Mr. Piggott, red in the cheeks and clutching his hat against the wind!

Amanda bolted out of the library, raced across the dim hall, started up the stairs. Piggott opened the front door before she'd climbed half a dozen steps. He called her name.

She felt a blast of cold air on her neck. Letting go of the heavy rail of the stair, she turned. Saw her stepfather silhouetted against the gray light of outdoors.

He closed the door. Its click echoed loudly in the still house.

"Amanda dear? Come here a moment."

He stood in the deep shadow by the closed door; she could barely see him. But his voice was quite loud; harsh. It started her heart beating fast under her frock of yellow percale. She climbed another step. Her high-topped cloth shoes seemed to weigh pounds apiece.

"Do you hear me, child? *I said come here.*"

Piggott shuffled out of the shadows, looming in the cross-light from the library. Digging her nails into her palms, Amanda descended the stairs.

Where were the servants? Why had she been caught by herself like this—? Oh, if only she were a witch from Lynn! She'd cast a spell and strike him dead—

At the foot of the stairs, she stopped. He approached, bent down, laid a hand on her forearm. She was certain she was going to faint dead away.

___ II

PIGGOTT DROPPED his hat as he squatted beside her. She wriggled but he wouldn't release her. He acted quite agitated:

"Where is Mrs. Piggott, Amanda?"

"Mama's gone out."

He looked relieved. "Do you know where?"

She hesitated before answering:

"She didn't say."

"You're lying to me, child." His fingers tightened. "I want you to tell me where Mrs. Piggott has gone, and how long she'll be away."

"I don't know how long—"

"Ah!" He smiled in a sly way. "But you do know where?"

"No, I—"

"No lies! I am your father, remember."

"You're not!" Amanda cried. "You're not and you never will be! Mama went to Mr. Benbow. About *you!*"

Shrieking the last word, she wrenched free and leaped toward the stairs. Piggott caught her, ripping her silk sash as he dragged her back.

Amanda stumbled, sprawled across the lowest stair. Piggott crouched, clasped both arms around her, pulling her against him. She smelled the bad odor from his mouth; and his cologne; and rum.

"She went to the attorney's? Why—? *Put your hand down! If you dare strike me—*"

"Mr. Piggott?"

Pinned on the stairs, Amanda saw him go rigid. He released her, leaped up and whirled toward the dim spill of light from the dining room. Amanda recognized Florence the downstairs maid.

"I heard someone cry out," Florence said. "Was it you, Miss Amanda?"

"Yes, he—"

"She fell," Piggott interrupted. "Leave us alone."

The maid looked uncertain: "But if Miss Amanda's hurt—"

"I'll see to the child. Get out of here!"

Florence fled. The door to the kitchen crashed shut, sealing off the light.

Piggott breathed loudly. He leaned toward the ten-year-old girl, cupped a hand beneath the small swell of her right breast:

"In other circumstances I'd strip you naked and give you a hiding you wouldn't forget, my girl—yes, and something else, too."

Amanda tried to cringe away from him. Away from that wicked, fondling hand. But Piggott was too big. And she was trapped on the stairs, pinned between the man on her left and the wall on her right.

All at once he drew his hand back.

"But I've no time. I'm going upstairs for a valise—"

Amanda thought the front door had opened. Piggott apparently failed to hear; his voice was very loud:

"—and if you call the servants or interfere in any way, I'll punish you as you've never been pun—"

"Punish her for what, Andrew?"

He straightened up as if he'd been whipped.

Amanda scrambled past his legs, hurled herself at the dim figure near the front door:

"Mama—*mama!*"

Sobbing, she wrapped her arms around Harriet's skirt. She felt her mother's hands on her hair. Those hands trembled almost as badly as her own.

"What was he doing, Amanda?" Harriet asked.

Controlling her tears, Amanda gasped, "Making me tell—where you'd gone."

"You have some special need to know that, Andrew?"

"None of your damn business, Mrs. Piggott."

"He said he's going to pack, mama—"

"Is that right?"

Harriet approached the foot of the stairs. Piggott had moved up to the fourth riser, an indistinct hulk in the chilly darkness. Some of Amanda's terror passed, driven out by the strange, almost happy tone of her mother's voice:

"You're leaving, Andrew? Good. You'll save me considerable trouble."

"Trouble? What the hell are you talking about?"

"Legal proceedings."

"Yes, I heard you'd gone to see that old bastard Benbow—"

"Amanda told you?"

"He forced me, mama."

"That's all right, dear—don't worry. It's typical of Mr. Piggott to threaten a child. But we won't be bothered with him any longer—"

Hugging the wall near the front door, Amanda watched Piggott jump down two steps, whip up his fist. Harriet darted out of range. Piggott called her a filthy name.

"Curse all you want, Andrew. That won't change anything. I have indeed been to the offices of Benbow and Benbow. I've passed certain information about you into their hands—"

"What information?" For the first time, he sounded shaken.

"How you lied to me before our marriage. You're not from a well-connected

family. You never attended any college. You're a tanner's boy from South Boston—''

"You set spies on me?''

"Yes, and it was long overdue. This card game that's occupied you all week—''

"What about it?''

"That too has been observed from the street outside. Women have been seen going in and out of those rented rooms. Women of bad character. I won't be more specific in Amanda's presence. But I have ample grounds for a bill of divorcement. Mr. Benbow senior will undertake the suit on my behalf. I have been victimized, Mr. Piggott. Deceived and victimized—''

"It's no less than you deserve, you harpy!'' Piggott roared, darting down the last two steps. Harriet lunged aside as Piggott lashed the air with his fist.

"Get out!'' Harriet breathed. "Take your personal belongings and get out of my house. If you try to claim any of my property, Mr. Benbow will have a warrant drawn for your arrest.''

Piggott laughed then; loudly.

"You've developed a surprising amount of courage, Mrs. Piggott—''

"Henceforward, my name is Mrs. Kent!''

"Well, that's all you'll have *henceforward*—your name. After our—our chat last week, I had a feeling you might go to your lawyer. So I haven't worried too much about the size of my wagers with the gentlemen from Maryland.''

"The card-players—?''

"We started with cards. Then we changed games. We tried a new one just introduced in New Orleans by a young sport named de Mandeville.''

"What has this to do with—?''

"Hear me out, Mrs. Piggott. I want you to hear every detail before I go. The game is played with dice—do you know what dice are, Mrs. Piggott?''

"Of course I do. You will stop calling me—''

"The gentlemen told me the game's a variation of hazards—very popular in English coffee houses, where Mr. de Marigny de Mandeville picked it up. The New Orleans gentry call it crapaud, after Johnny Crapaud, which I gather is a scornful name for Creoles. Wouldn't you like to know how I fared at crapaud, Mrs. Piggott?''

"Damn you, *get out!*'' Harriet cried, raising her own hand.

Piggott rushed at her, struck her forearm with his fist. Harriet let out a low cry. Piggott seized and shook her:

"You'll damn me ten times over before this day's done, woman!'' He let go, stood back, his smile vicious. "My luck ran against me. I kept losing. Heavily. But the gentlemen were quite pleasant about it. They accepted my note wagering the assets of Kent's. They suggested the idea, actually. It didn't pain me greatly when I lost the final rolls. As I say, ever since our chat, I suspected you were going to act against me—''

In a whisper, Harriet said, "Wait, sir.''

"—I suspected some ploy like this bill of divorce. I'm sorry to inform you, madam—''

"Wait. You said the assets of Kent's—''

"—because of my losses, you no longer own—''

"*What assets of Kent's?*'' she screamed. Amanda covered her ears, buried her face against the wall.

The kitchen door banged open again. Amanda heard a scurry of feet as several

servants rushed to discover the cause of the new commotion. She wouldn't uncover her eyes, though. She was too frightened.

Piggott boomed all the louder:

"The printing house, woman. The whole goddamned printing house!"

Silence.

Four of the servants watched from the dining room doorway, not daring to speak. Piggott chuckled:

"Need I point out that I was still your husband when I signed my vote? Your interview with your blasted Mr. Benbow is a mite tardy."

"You—you lost—?"

"Everything."

"God in heaven," Harriet said softly. "Oh dear God in heaven—" Suddenly her head came up. She stalked him. "You did it to spite me. You did it because you knew—"

"Suspected," Piggott broke in. "Suspected, my dear. Same thing, though, I suppose. There was precious little disappointment in losing what I didn't own in the first place. But there was a great deal of pleasure, I don't mind telling you. Of course, if the final rolls had gone the other way, I'd have taken the gentlemen's money and left here with it. Whichever way the game came out, I'd already decided to leave. I can do so now with immense satisfaction. You'll have to sell this house. Dismiss these cattle who fawn and wait on you—"

One of the servants, the young gardener, took a step forward. Florence held him back. Harriet began crying:

"It isn't true—"

"It is, and it's what you deserve."

"No. It can't be legal—"

"As legal as the first wager. Entirely legal. If you don't believe me, go down to Kent and Son this minute. My friends should be there with the same attorney who was engaged after I lost the press playing shemmy. They're taking possession this very afternoon."

"You're lying. *Lying to me—!*"

Piggott could no longer contain his rage. He ran at Harriet again. Through fingers pressed over her eyes, Amanda saw the man lift his right arm to his left shoulder, then slash outward with his fist. He struck Harriet's cheek, a loud, pulping blow.

She fell. Amanda screamed, "Mama—!" and rushed toward her as Piggott roared:

"If you dont believe you've nothing left, go down there and see, you fucking bitch!"

The family's young gardener slipped from the group of servants, flung off Florence's restraining hand, wiped his fingers on his leather apron:

"You'd better take your things out of here quick, Piggott—"

"Put a hand on me and I'll break your spine," Piggott said.

The young gardener blinked, hesitated. In that moment, Andrew Piggott spun and ran up the stairs two at a time. His laughter floated behind him, heavy, rich, triumphant.

III

AMANDA PUSHED past Florence, knelt at her mother's side. Cheeks wet from crying, she chafed Harriet's hands:

"Mama, get up. Please get up."

"We'd best help her into the sitting room, Miss Amanda."

"Yes," Harriet breathed. "Help me up, Florence—"

Her bonnet fell off as she tried to rise. She clutched the maid's hand, pulled herself to her feet. Amanda gave her the bonnet. Her eyes widened in surprise as Harriet put the bonnet on, struggled to fasten the ties beneath her chin.

"Come rest, mama—" Amanda begged.

"I must go to Kent's. Now. This instant."

"No, mama, wait—!"

"This instant!" Harriet repeated, turning and moving unsteadily toward the front door.

She jerked the door open, spilling gray light over the stricken servants and the almost hysterical child. Her steps remained unsteady as she descended the front steps and disappeared. A moment later, Amanda heard a heavy rumbling, the snap of a whip, the rattle and ring of shod hoofs on the cobbles—

A shout:

"Watch out, woman!"

The unseen horses neighed wildly. Then, through the open door, Amanda saw them plunge past, pulling a dray loaded with big barrels. The frantic driver was hauling on the reins and jamming a boot against the brake lever—

The wagon shot out of sight, sparks spurting from the rear tires. Dazed, Amanda didn't immediately understand why the servants gasped and rushed outside. But when the young gardener's voice drifted from the street—"Christ save us!"—she realized something terrible had happened.

IV

AMANDA SLIPPED through the doorway, blinked and shuddered in the bitter wind sweeping along Beacon Street.

The servants had all left the stoop. She saw them down on the walk, to the left, huddling over someone fallen half into the gutter.

To the right, the dray was stopping; the driver had gotten his frightened team under control. He leaped down, raced back, his leather cap flying off, his boots clattering.

He checked at the edge of the crowd as people appeared from nowhere to surround the servants, hide Amanda's view of the fallen body—

Her mother. Harriet's bonnet lay on the sidewalk, stained red.

The dray driver shrank from the hostile eyes of the servants.

"She—she come along the curbstone," he stammered. "All of a sudden, she—fell right in front of the horses. I couldn't stop in time—"

Standing abruptly, Florence said, "We must carry her inside."

"I don't know," the young gardener said. "It might hurt her worse to move her—"

Florence cried, "We can't leave her lying in the cold—on the street—all these people staring—!"

Sounding reluctant, the gardener said, "All right."

"Is she breathing?" the dray driver asked him.

"Just barely."

V

THE SERVANTS lifted Harriet gently and bore her up the steps into the house. On the stoop, Amanda got a clear view of her mother's head. It seemed to loll at an odd angle. Her cheeks were bruised and bloodied. Still numb from watching the awful scene with Piggott, Amanda couldn't quite believe what she saw.

The servants put Harriet in the front sitting room, on blankets spread on the floor. One maid rushed out of the house to fetch a doctor. Then the gardener dashed past Amanda who was watching from the hall, afraid to go in.

The gardener ran upstairs. In a minute or so, he came back swearing. He informed the others that Andrew Piggott had vanished. Out the back way, most likely.

"Why isn't mama getting up?" Amanda said in a hushed voice.

The gardener began, "Her neck is—" Florence silenced him with a sharp look.

Then the maid said to Amanda, "She can't get up, child. She's hurt. You'd best go to your—"

She broke off as one of the other girls motioned.

Florence knelt down. Put her ear close to Harriet's mouth. When she rose, tears tracked her cheeks.

She came toward Amanda, hands extended as if to gather the child to herself and comfort her. Gazing past her, Amanda saw the gardener pick up another blanket and cover Harriet's face.

"Amanda—" Florence could barely contain her misery. "—come with me to your room. You mustn't stay and look—"

Amanda knew then. She knew the second blanket meant permanence—

She tried to rush to Harriet's body. Florence barred her way.

"No, child!"

Amanda's grief burst out in a wild cry:

"Jared! *Jared, come help me—!*"

She fell against Florence's skirt, wailing hysterically.

3

Act of Murder

"JARED? WE got a visitor. It's that damn lawyer."

Jared barely heard the first words. But the last one struck him like an icy shower. He almost dropped the stack of untrimmed sheets as he deposited them on the pallet behind one of the thumping flatbed presses.

He straighted up, the sound of his own breathing loud in his inner ear. His heartbeat quickened as he turned toward the open front door. Snow swirled there. He'd been too busy to notice when it had started falling from the dull Saturday sky.

He scowled, recognizing the short, portly man just closing the door. In one hand the man carried a valise Jared had seen before.

"You'd better fetch Mr. Pleasant," he whispered to the pressman who had spoken to him.

The pressman reached for a rag to wipe his inky hands. Jared grabbed the rag, flung it aside:

"Right now!"

The pressman didn't protest being ordered around by a fifteen-year-old boy. He knew there was trouble looming. The presence of the well-dressed gentleman surveying the first floor work area charged the atmosphere with tension.

Jared felt the tension with mounting intensity. His temper had flared when he spoke to the pressman. That mustn't happen again. He had to stay calm until he learned the reason for the lawyer's call—

Instantly, his resolve was threatened. He could feel anger starting to simmer. A dull ache spread across his forehead as he studied the lawyer's expression. Smug. Disdainful—

One by one, the four other presses stopped. Two apprentices who had been cuffing each other quit suddenly. The pressman raced for the stairs.

The portly gentleman continued to scrutinize the room. Lanterns hung from the ceiling beams stretched Jared's silhouette across the floor as he walked toward the front. He recalled with bitter clarity the last time the man—and his infernal valise—had been on the premises. A large, empty section of floor space was a constant reminder of that visit.

"Good afternoon," the portly man said. His gaze jumped past Jared's shoulder, a deliberate affront. The boy reddened.

"What do you want?" Jared demanded.

The portly man condescended to look at him again. "I'll communicate that to the manager, if you don't mind."

"You'll tell me first! My aunt's the owner."

The portly man was amused:

"Not any longer, I'm afraid."

A knot twisted in Jared's midsection. Surely he hadn't heard correctly—

The man brushed by and strolled down the aisle between the presses. Jared almost grabbed him; then literally fought his hand back down as the man passed. The lawyer seemed unperturbed by the hostile stares of the men and boys on both sides of the room. Jared thought of the pistol he'd gotten in case something like this happened again—

No. Forget the pistol.

Only hours after buying the second-hand weapon, he'd decided the purchase was rash. He'd gone to the gunsmith's when the first press was taken; gone there with an almost drunken feeling of fury. But then, with the gun in his possession, he'd realized his mistake—

For weeks, up until the lawyer called the first time, Jared had consciously struggled to keep a check on his temper. To disprove, through new patterns of behavior, his old fears about himself. He hadn't succeeded completely. But he had made large strides, and he took pride in the fact. Then the lawyer arrived—

and afterward, he bought the gun, and stored it in a niche up in the second-floor warehouse section.

That's where it must stay, he said to himself now. *Don't even think about it—*

Footsteps hammered on the stairs. No one moved save the portly gentleman, who propped his valise on one of the rails separating the central aisle from the work areas. The man opened the valise, fished out papers.

Franklin Pleasant appeared on the stairs, his waistcoat unbuttoned, his cravat undone. The pressman who'd gone to find him was right behind.

Wary, Pleasant approached the portly man:

"I trust you're not here to attach more of our equipment, Mr. Elphinstone."

"I'm flattered you remember my name, Mr. Pleasant."

"As I'd remember any thief's."

Elphinstone met Pleasant's glare with a smug smile:

"I deplore your animosity, sir. I am only an attorney, hired by my clients to conduct business on their behalf. I have no interest in removing another press—"

Franklin Pleasant looked relieved. Having lulled him, Elphinstone closed the trap:

"I have come to inform you that new owners are taking over this establishment."

Pleasant gripped the rail, his knuckles white. The ache in Jared's head worsened instantly.

"You must be insane," Pleasant said.

"Is that right? Be so good as to scan this document. Particularly the attached note. Signed by Mr. Andrew Piggott in the presence of my clients, and duly witnessed by two residents of the rooming house where Mr. Piggott and my clients were gaming. The document—and the note—will stand up in any court of law in this state. They're just as legal as the note Mr. Piggott signed in connection with the press."

Outside, Jared heard wheels grind to a halt. A restless horse stamped and blew. Laughing voices blended with the slam of a coach door. Footsteps approached the front entrance.

Jared didn't look around. He was watching Pleasant's face.

The manager leafed through the legal sheets. Fingered a slip of paper waxed to the last one. Pale, he let his hand fall to his side.

Elphinstone snatched the legal-size sheets and began to fold them. Pleasant looked at Jared, but his words were addressed to everyone:

"Elphinstone's right. This time Piggott's lost the whole place."

Despite the effort of will that had held him white-lipped and silent, Jared felt his anger loosed like a flood within him. In a tick of time, his mind swirled with distorted images of Uncle Gilbert. His throbbing head rang with remembered words: the promises he'd made about protecting the Kent interests. A faint inner voice of warning faded as he lunged forward with a shout:

"I don't believe it!" He seized the lawyer's collar. "You're a damned, deceitful liar—!"

Elphinstone squealed as Jared shoved him against the rail:

"Take your hands off me or I'll have you clapped in jail!"

"You'd better do as he says, Jared," Pleasant warned.

"But that paper can't be legal—!"

Pleasant shook his head. "The last one was."

Beyond Elphinstone, Jared saw an apprentice's head whip toward the front

door. The sound of the door opening had barely registered in Jared's mind. Now he noted a startled look on the apprentice's face—

And heard a voice that numbed him:

"It's legal, Mr. Kent. You are now working for me."

Two men, elegantly dressed, stood at the front entrance, framed against the background of a carriage and swirling snow. Jared's blue eyes locked onto the man nearest to him; the other fellow, older, was a blur.

All Jared could see of the first man was half a face. A glowing brown eye. The young visitor wore a white silk bandana tied around his forehead. The edge of the bandana made an oblique line that ran from the left side of his forehead across his nose and right cheek to the curve of his jaw.

Perfectly relaxed, the visitor used a lacquered stick to knock snow from the brim of a beaver hat in his other hand.

"Mr. Kent and I are old acquaintances," the young man announced to the goggling employees. "Permit me to introduce my companion—Mr. Walpole, general manager of the Chesapeake Iron Finery, Baltimore. My name is Hamilton Stovall. My family owns the refinery—and now, it seems, a Boston printing house."

II

"JARED—"

Pleasant's voice sounded remote. The boy's ears were filled with a roaring again, as of a huge wind unleashed. He could have sworn the earth shook—then realized it was only the frantic, heavy rhythm inside his own chest. The scope of the monstrous duplicity began to register—and with it came an overwhelming sense of failure—

I should have killed him. I didn't, and because I didn't, this has happened—

"—who is this person?"

Stovall said, "Why, I'm the fellow who became acquainted with Mr. Kent's uncle by marriage. Played cards and dice with him—"

"Not by accident," Jared breathed.

"Oh no, dear boy," Stovall smiled, tapping his lacquered stick against his flawlessly cut mauve trouser leg. "Ever since my untimely separation from the naval service—"

His free hand touched the bandana hiding half his face.

"—I've laid plans for a return to New England. We are trying to secure information on the new modification of the Cort furnace being used in Europe. And it's impossible to get an inquiry agent aboard an outbound ship down in our part of the country. I could as easily have visited Providence to make arrangements, but I chose Boston for a special reason—which Mr. Kent of course understands."

Again Pleasant whispered:

"What's he talking about?"

"I—"

Jared licked his lips, trying to still the shaking of his hands at his sides.

The pistol. Remember the pistol—

Without thinking, he glanced at the stairway. Stovall noticed. Jared forced his eyes back to the young man with the stick; saw him for a moment as a blurred

image. He had to leave the pistol where it was. *Had* to, or he'd only compound the damage he'd already done—

But reason's voice was faint, its promptings overwhelmed by humiliation and guilt. Jared watched lawyer Elphinstone sidle along the rail, out of his reach. He clenched his fists so tightly they ached.

Pleasant was waiting for an answer. Jared finally finished the sentence:

"—I served with Mr. Stovall aboard *Constitution*. He was sixth lieutenant."

"Tell them what happened," Stovall said affably. But there was hate in his glaring eye. "Tell them how you caused me to fall against a cannon that broke loose during the action with *Guerriere*. How my face came in contact with the heated barrel. My face and my hands—"

Tucking his stick under his arm, he showed his palms. Jared and the others saw the ruin of puckered scar tissue.

"Even having recovered, I'm no longer welcome where I was welcome before. Hostesses—young ladies—decline to invite me to their levees—" Despite an effort to control his voice, it grew louder. "Thanks to you, Mr. Kent, I'm disgusting to look at. Do you wonder I planned to return to Boston from the first moment I awoke in the hospital?"

"You can also tell them why we had trouble," Jared said.

"That's not neces—"

"He talks about young ladies but he fancies men and boys."

The older man, Walpole, spoke at last:

"Take your stick to the young liar, Hamilton!"

Stovall rapped the lacquered wood against a scarred palm; a heavy sound.

"It's a shotted stick, Mr. Kent. It could ruin you for life—as you've ruined me. However, since my family now controls this company, I have a duty to behave as befits an owner. To put a curb on my temper, no matter how filthy and false your accusations. I'll defer physical punishment in favor of what's already been exacted—"

He started forward, a slow, languid walk that held every eye in the room.

"I readily admit I thought of hiring men to waylay you, Mr. Kent—I can't be imprisoned for a thought, can I? I decided that was entirely too coarse. Too quick. I wanted something more lasting. It struck me nothing could be more suitable than destroying you by destroying your family. I entertained various means. But a few inquiries in the local coffee houses showed me one that was ideal. The stupid sham gentleman who married your aunt is rather notorious. More to the point, so is his passion for gaming."

"So you made his acquaintance—"

"Actually," Stovall cut in, "a sharp we hired made his acquaintance first. The sharp—shall we say—tested Mr. Piggott's skill at cards? The sharp was the chap who won the press. When he reported Mr. Piggott to be the soul of gullibility—especially after a few rounds of rum—Mr. Walpole and I contrived a seemingly accidental meeting at the Exchange—"

"Contrived to cheat him too, I don't doubt!"

Hamilton Stovall smiled. "That, my dear boy, you'll never know."

"Of course Piggott was cheated," Pleasant fumed. "Marked cards. Weighted dice—"

Stovall waved. "Immaterial. The games are over. What remains is—this—"

The stick shimmered as Stovall tapped the legal papers in Elphinstone's hand.

"Our proof of ownership. It was quite easy to tempt Piggott into his last,

excessive wager. Plenty of that strong drink I mentioned—a few apparently spontaneous suggestions during the heat of the betting—''

Slap went the stick against the paper.

''—and Kent and Son belongs to the Stovalls.''

From behind Jared, Pleasant burst out, ''We'll fight you, by God! Our attorney Benbow—''

''He'll be able to do nothing.'' Elphinstone waved the document. ''Nothing!''

The pressman who'd run upstairs stalked to the rail:

''Damned if we need any lawyers to settle this—''

Stovall spun and rammed the ferrule of his stick against the pressman's throat.

The pressman gasped, his right hand flashing up to the stick as other employees started forward, fists ready.

''You had better restrain yourself, my friend—''

Again Stovall jabbed with the stick. The pressman turned scarlet, grabbed the stick at the mid-point.

''—else you'll rot in jail for assault.''

''It's not an idle threat!'' Elphinstone exclaimed. ''I'll see to it!''

''Let go of the stick, Joe,'' Franklin Pleasant said. ''These—gentlemen and I will retire to the office upstairs and discuss—''

''There's nothing to discuss!'' Jared shouted. ''Stovall and his cronies, they're—''

''Jared, be silent! For the sake of every employee of this company, don't say another word. Joe—let go of the stick.''

The pressman scowled. But he obeyed the manager. Stovall examined the finish on the stick as Jared wiped his sweating upper lip. He glared at Pleasant:

''I won't let you just surrender—''

''*Be silent!*'' Pleasant directed the warning not only to the boy but to all the confused and angry men and apprentices. ''I am still manager here—''

''In the employ of *the Kents!*''

''My dear boy, you forget—that's all changed,'' Stovall said, strolling past Jared and pushing through the gate in the rail. A huge, tow-haired pressman blocked his path. The young Marylander raised his stick. Sweating, Franklin Pleasant shook his head. The pressman retreated.

Stovall gave a short, brittle laugh and walked on, tucking the stick under his arm again:

''The firm of Kent and Son is now irrevocably part of the assets of the Stovall family—to do with as we please. We may wish to change the politics of your paper—''

He rapped knuckles against the screw lever of a press.

''—suspend publication of your books and your gazette altogether—''

He approached a type font, grasped the top of the case, pulled. The case crashed to the floor, scattering hundreds of bits of metal.

''—or raze it to the ground.''

Trembling, Jared cried, ''You goddamned, conniving—''

Pleasant grabbed his shoulder: ''I demand that you hold your temper! Nothing will be gained—''

Jared flung off Pleasant's hand and sprinted for the stairs.

THE RAGE in Jared Kent was out of control. He knew Hamilton Stovall wouldn't be making boasts if he lacked the legal means to back them up. Let Pleasant quibble and delay. He wouldn't.

As he reached the second floor, he heard contentious voices erupt below. Pleasant was shouting. Some of the pressmen too. And the lawyer—

The voices faded as Jared raced between the towers of books in the warehouse area. At the wall niche in the back, he stood on tiptoe, groped, pulled down the pistol. The English box-lock piece was a good fifteen years old. Six stubby barrels clustered around a seventh, central one. A plate above the trigger guard on the right side carried the maker's mark, and his name, Nock.

Jared had loaded and primed the pistol before storing it in the niche. He pulled the lock back to cock position; the first shot would discharge central barrel and one adjoining. He hid the pistol under his shirt, then sped for the stairs again. Stovall would never take the place. *Never!*

On the third floor, one of the *Republican*'s reporters glanced up from his copy.

"What's all the row downstairs, Jared? Pleasant fairly tore out of the office—"

Jared didn't bother to answer. He dashed into the cluttered office once used by his grandfather, then by his uncle. Mr. Pleasant had installed a convenience lacking until his occupancy—a small Franklin stove that heated the room to oven temperature.

Breathing hard, Jared jerked open the doors of the free-standing stove. His reflection in the smoke-stained windows looked like a goblin's. He snatched sheets of newspaper copy from the desk, tossed them onto the fire.

Then invoices. More foolscap copy. A book. Another—

He moved with incredible speed. He pitched everything on Pleasant's desk into the stove. Finally the grate could hold no more. Flames shot from the stove's front as the fire grew—

Let Pleasant prattle about lawyers! Let him *discuss!* Jared knew it was too late for any of that to help. He knew Stovall.

"For Christ's sake, Jared, what are you doing? *Catch those things—!*"

The reporter lunged into the office, jerked back as Jared pulled the seven-barrel flintlock from his trousers.

"I don't want to shoot you, Tommy—"

"Have you gone mad?" The reporter pointed. Two smoldering books and a pile of blazing sheets had fallen out of the overflowing grate. Smoke was curling from the ancient flooring. "You'll burn the place down!"

"That's just what I intend."

The reporter's sweaty face glistened as the fire brightened. Smoke hazed the office now. The tawny-haired boy—taller than the reporter—crouched with the seven-barrel pistol in his right hand, and something akin to lunacy in his bright blue eyes.

The reporter whirled and fled down the front stairs:

"Fire! *We've a fire up here!*"

Jared darted behind the Franklin stove. He touched the top gingerly, gave it a shove. The stove tipped forward, crashed, spilling the contents of the grate. Jared's face broke into a ghastly smile as the flames spread to the desk, one wall—

The heat was intense. Coughing, Jared backed out of the office. Ran to the head of the stairs—

Men were coming up. He recognized the loudest voices. Stovall and his companion—

He waited, the back of his neck hot from the flames. The blaze wasn't yet bright enough to illuminate the lightless stairs. He barely made out dim figures appearing on the landing halfway between the two floors.

But someone down there saw him clearly:

"He's got a gun—!"

Jared thought he saw a patch of white on the landing; the silk bandana. He aimed the seven-barrel, pulled the trigger. The central barrel and another went off simultaneously, a second after Hamilton Stovall wrenched someone in front of him.

The other man—Walpole—shrieked. Flung his arms wide and fell back to the landing, blood darkening his coat where one or both of the balls had struck. Jared felt the old, devastating nausea sweep up from his belly—

"Murder!" Stovall cried in the confusion below. "The boy's done murder!"

Jared revolved the barrels on the spindle, readying another shot. His hands shook. The nausea was almost overpowering—

Fire shot from the office door, burning the wall on either side. Stovall had cheated him again.

"Murder! He's done murder! THE PLACE IS BURNING—"

Stovall's shout thundered as Jared ran for the rear stairs.

He emerged in the alley behind the building. Fat, wet snowflakes struck his hands and face. Their coldness sobered him a little.

But in his imagination, he still saw Walpole falling, his coat bloodied—

Jared careened across the alley to a fence. He dropped the pistol, shot out his hands. He could find no purchase on the fence planks. He fell to his knees, his palms raking over the wood. Splinters stabbed his skin as the shuddering shook him, spasm after spasm—

Once the trembling passed, he scrabbled in the snow until he located the pistol. He stuffed it into his trousers, stumbled for the end of the alley.

There he stopped. He glanced right, to the intersection of the narrow cross-street and the one that ran in front of Kent's. At the intersection, he saw men racing by, heading for the printing house in response to voices crying fire.

He turned and gazed up through the pelting snow to a rear window on the top floor. The window glowed orange. The fire had spread all the way to the back—

Jared's mouth twisted into a peculiar smile. His ears buzzed. His belly ached. But the trembling was over, and he still felt the intoxication of the rage that had seized him just before he bolted upstairs.

I did what had to be done, he thought. *Better that Kent and Son burn than fall into the hands of someone like Stovall—*

He wasn't entirely oblivious to the consequences of his actions, though. He'd shot Stovall's accomplice. For that, they could hang him—

Like some pursued animal, he spun and ran to the left, slitting his eyes against the snow. The darkness of the narrow street soon hid him.

IV

OBSERVED SURREPTITIOUSLY from the blackness of the Common, the house on Beacon Street seemed quiet enough. The snow was falling harder now.

Jared hurried along Beacon to the end of the block. Cutting left, then left again, he approached the house through the small backyard.

His teeth were chattering and his soaked shirt stuck to his skin as he crept from the darkness into the stairwell behind the pantry. Beyond a door to the kitchen, he heard voices. Two or three servants, talking softly. He started up the stairs, testing each riser so it wouldn't creak.

Fortunately the servants had lit a fire in his room on the third floor. With the door shut, he pulled off his sodden shirt and warmed himself a moment.

On hands and knees, he groped under his bed. He dragged out the small canvas bag he'd brought home from sea duty. Backing up, he knocked over a stack of books.

The books thudded on the carpet. Jared tensed, listening—

A half minute passed.

A minute.

He stood up, carefully opened his wardrobe, found a fresh shirt, a few underthings—

His hand went slack. The clothing spilled to the floor. Blinking, he knelt to pick it up. In that moment, the dizzying anger that had possessed him for the past hour faded—replaced by a full realization of what he'd done.

He had destroyed Kent's.

Destroyed it!

Part of the blame was Stovall's. But only a small part. He, Jared Kent, was the truly guilty one. Surrendering to rage and unreason and the stunning shock of seeing Stovall again, he had behaved as he always did: At the moment when coolness counted most—the moment of crisis—he had been unable to deal with the situation except in one, destructive way. He had failed again.

And the new Jared he'd worked so carefully to create—the Jared who could be proud of his self-control—proud of finally giving the lie to everything Aunt Harriet said about him—he had destroyed that Jared Kent along with the printing house.

What a fool I was, he thought, still kneeling but seeing nothing around him. *A fool to think I could change—that I had the strength to change.* He remembered the terrible nausea moments after the pistol discharged. The punishing sickness was proof once again that all his old feelings about his worthlessness were correct; and that for the past months, he had only been deceiving himself—

An almost animal cry burst from his lips then. He buried his head in both hands.

After another minute or so, he lifted his head; drew a long breath.

All right. It's done. You are what you are. Now you have to save yourself as best you can—

He fumbled with the clothing, stood up unsteadily, trying to assess the situation calmly. That Stovall, his intended victim, had let someone else die in his place only compounded his problem. No magistrate would put much importance on Jared's contention that he meant to shoot the man who had cheated his family. Murder was murder. He'd be sought and arrested if he didn't run—

Despairing, he gazed down at something he'd pulled from a drawer in the wardrobe without being aware of it. The medal and the broad green ribbon—

868

His feeling of having betrayed Gilbert's trust was sharp and hurtful. He touched the tea bottle on the medal's obverse. Rubbed his thumb slowly back and forth over the raised Latin legend.

Take a stand and make a mark.

Well, I've made a mark, he thought. *But it's not one to be proud of—even if it is the only kind I'm capable of making.*

And because of it, what kind of life is left for me—?

The door opened suddenly. Jared's hand constricted on the medal as he whirled:

"Amanda!"

It took him a few seconds to realize that her face looked raw; her eyes puffy.

"Come in and close the door!"

With a peculiar, lethargic slowness, his dark-haired cousin shuffled into the room. He shoved the fob into his bag, then added the sheathed Spanish knife and a few more items of clothing.

"You mustn't tell anyone you've seen me here, Amanda."

She didn't respond. But she recognized the contour of the pistol butt showing beneath his shirt:

"Is that your gun, Jared?"

"Yes."

"Why are you putting things in the bag?"

"Because I'm leaving, and you mustn't tell Aunt Harriet you saw me."

"Leaving? Where are you going?"

"Away from Boston. As far as possible as fast as possible."

He jerked the drawstring tight on his bag. Then, seeing that his curt tone had alarmed her, he dropped to his knees beside her, touched her face.

"I don't want to leave. I must. I'll be all right. Promise me you won't tell your mama—"

Amanda whispered, "Mama's dead."

"Dead?"

His hand fell away from her cheek. His mouth hung open. He understood why her face was tear-reddened. Yet he somehow couldn't believe what she'd told him:

"I hope you're not making up a story. Death is a very serious—"

"She's lying in the sitting room this minute! Florence said I mustn't look at her. She said I had to stay in my room until someone takes mama away. But I heard a noise in here—"

"Where's Mr. Piggott?"

"I don't know. I was alone when he came home this afternoon. Then mama came home, and there was a terrible fuss. Shouting and cursing and crying—Mr. Piggott hit her. Then mama ran out into Beacon Street. A wagon was coming along, very fast. She fell in front of it—"

"Oh my God."

"Mr. Piggott ran away just like you're doing."

The boy was speechless. Amanda flung her arms around his neck.

"Please don't go away and leave me, Jared. I'm frightened of Mr. Piggott. What if he should come back?"

Jared guessed the reason for Piggott's abrupt flight. And for the quarrel. Harriet must have found out about her husband's last, disastrous wager.

"Jared—?"

"I doubt he'll come back."

"Why won't he?"

"Never mind!"

Her eyes brimmed with tears. "Don't talk to me that way, Jared. *Don't be cross—*"

He patted her arm clumsily. "I'm sorry. I'm—upset, that's all." He stood. "I must go—"

Yet he couldn't move. His eye traveled from his cousin's face to the cheerful hearth, then to his display cases. On one of the glass fronts, the fire twisted his image into an ugly distortion.

Murderer—

By his own hand, all the underpinnings of his world had been cut away—

But Amanda was no better off. He looked at her, small and lovely, watching him with fear and uncertainty—

How would she survive?

In the answer to that, he saw both a heavy responsibility that had fallen to him, and one slim opportunity to redeem himself a little. He put gentle hands on her shoulders.

"Amanda, you must listen carefully—"

"I will."

"There's been trouble at the printing house. I think I killed a man." Her eyes grew huge. "That's the reason I must go away. I'll be arrested and sent to prison if I don't. I think you'd better come with me."

She was slow to grasp the idea:

"You mean—away from here—?"

"Yes. Tonight. I'll take care of you. That is—" Bitterness showed in his eyes. "—I'll try. I *am* old enough—"

"But I don't understand why—"

"Your mama isn't here to protect you, and I promised Uncle Gilbert I would." *And if I don't keep that promise somehow, I'm finished.*

Seeing her reluctance, he added, "Mr. Piggott might come back—"

"That's not what you said a minute ago."

He struggled to keep his voice quiet and firm: "I was wrong." He hated to lie. But he knew of no better means to persuade her to accept his protection than invoking Piggott's spectre.

He sensed her wavering:

"I looked outside, Jared. It's snowing—"

"Goddamn it, I know it's snowing!"

"Oh, don't lose your temper! Don't swear at me—"

"I apologize. Please, Amanda—no more tears. Let's go to your room. Find some clothing. A warm coat—"

She held up her hand. For the first time, he noticed the cordage bracelet.

"Will you let me take this?"

"Yes, yes—but hurry!"

She fought as he tugged her hand:

"What's happened to you, Jared! Your face is funny. You don't look like yourself—"

And what do I look like? What I am?

MURDERER—

"Stop talking and come along!"

He said it with such ferocity that she obeyed without another question. As they passed the head of the stairs, he glanced down. He saw no one on the second

floor; heard nothing. The house seemed an enormous well of silence. Silence that mourned the passing of the dead, and the destruction of the living.

V

TWENTY MINUTES later, two figures emerged from the darkness around the Beacon Street stoop.

Jared had decided to risk stealing out the front way in order to satisfy himself about Aunt Harriet. He'd crept to the door of the lamp-lit sitting room; seen the body beneath the blanket.

Leaving Amanda shivering in the dark hall, he stole in, his eye turned warily toward the passage leading to the kitchen where voices still murmured.

He lifted the blanket. Stared. Let the blanket fall. There was no satisfaction in seeing her dead.

"I'm cold, Jared," Amanda said as they slipped across the street to the Common. He'd insisted she put on her heaviest coat and fur-lined bonnet. But already her teeth were chattering almost as badly as his. He tried to make light of it:

"Oh, you won't be cold for long. I know a cozy stable in the South End. We'll stay there tonight, very snugly. In the morning we'll slip across the Neck to Roxbury. We'll have a wonderful adventure—"

What a pathetic sham! But Amanda was young enough to believe him— almost. She sniffled, clutching his hand tightly.

From the Common, Jared looked back at the Kent house, its windows shedding warm light into the moving pattern of snowflakes. The sight engulfed him in a pessimism blacker than any he'd experienced before. Hope was futile. He could never be anything more than what he was: the inheritor of weakness and unbridled emotion; a creature possessed by the past, and carrying its curse forever into the future—

He turned away. Lowering his head against the wind, he guided Amanda into the dark.

VI

HAMILTON STOVALL stood across the street from the printing house, watching it burn.

In the distance, a clanging bell and the clatter of hoofs signaled the approach of a fire wagon. The snow continued to fall, but Stovall, bareheaded, seemed perfectly comfortable as he gazed at the flame-filled windows.

Close by, lawyer Elphinstone looked as if he were freezing. A man ran up to him, spoke briefly. Elphinstone bobbed his head, approached his employer:

"Hamilton?"

"What is it?"

"The doctor that boy fetched just looked at Walpole. He's going to pull through."

"I suspected he would. I examined the wound myself."

"Is that why you were so slow to send for the authorities?"

Stovall said nothing.

"How did he get in the line of fire, Hamilton?"

"He stumbled."

"Oh. I understand only one of the balls struck him—"

"Yes."

"Well above the heart, luckily."

Stovall's uncovered eye glistened with reflections of the blaze now threatening the adjoining buildings. Noisy men milled in the street. The fire bell clanged louder. Stovall seemed oblivious to everything but the flames gutting Kent and Son.

"Going to be a total loss," Elphinstone muttered.

"I imagine it's well insured."

"Will you keep the money, or rebuild?"

"I haven't decided." After a moment, he added, "Has anyone seen the Kent boy?"

"No. I expect he's fleeing for his life. He heard you shout murder. He undoubtedly thinks Walpole's dead."

Hamilton Stovall's mouth curved up at the corners. His brown eye glared as the fire shimmered on the white silk of the bandana.

"Let him," he said.

4
Ordeal

THE ROAD led on toward a town whose lights gleamed faintly in the darkening day.

Jared wished they could push on to that settlement. There, they might find a public house like the one in Philadelphia where he'd worked part of a week scrubbing floors and washing ceilings. The labor had left him stiff and sore every night, but it had given them a temporary haven in the stable attached to the public house—plus a quantity of biscuits and meal for the next stage of their journey.

Now the biscuits were eaten, and the meal too. They had to stop again. But going on to the town was impossible. He was too tired and weak. And Amanda was beginning to make small, fretful sounds that indicated her own exhaustion.

She was nearly as disreputable looking as Jared himself. Her cheeks were pale. Her dark hair hung tangled around her shoulders, picking up snow-crystals beginning to blow out of the northwest.

The draw-cord of the canvas bag was slipping from his shoulder. He tugged the cord up close to his collar as he surveyed the first of two farmhouses ahead. The houses and outbuildings were set about a quarter mile apart, and windows in both dwellings were lighted.

"Might as well try the first one," he said.

Amanda didn't respond. She acted dazed. Her hand moved aimlessly, brushing snow from her sleeve, then fingering a rent in the front of the coat that had

once been clean and fashionable but now, in December, bore the marks of hard use.

"Come on, Amanda."

She murmured something that might have been an argument or a complaint. Jared took hold of her elbow, guided her around the worst of the ruts in the road to the first farmyard. An almost sensual joy possessed him when he thought of resting behind solid walls.

They'd taken no more than a couple of steps toward the house when a huge brindle animal shot around the corner. Amanda screamed. The shepherd charged them, barking. The sound seemed loud enough to reach to the end of creation—

"Run!" Jared yelled, turning and starting away. An instant later, he heard his cousin's second outcry, whirled back and saw her on the ground, floundering.

The shepherd came on, teeth bared. The dog made straight for Amanda.

Jared lunged, caught the girl's arm, literally dragged her to him. The watchdog jumped at his legs. Jared kicked, struggling to pick his cousin up at the same time. Somehow he avoided the snapping jaws and reached the road.

The dog stopped at the edge of the property, but kept barking. Jared cradled his cousin in his arms and staggered down the road, unnerved by the yapping of the animal, by the thought of the harm Amanda could have suffered—and by disappointment.

"There, he didn't hurt you," he panted. Amanda kept moaning softly against his neck. "Amanda, stop that! You're all right."

"Yes. Yes, but the dog scared me—"

"He scared me too." The barking stopped abruptly.

Jared glanced back. He could barely see the huge animal as it padded toward the house. He set his cousin on the ground.

"We'll try the next place. There are lamps in the back—see?" He pointed. "Let's go around that way—"

She stumbled as they started into the second yard. Jared caught her and held her up. Night was coming fast. The wind was stiffening, driving the snow harder. The ground was already covered with a white crust.

A memory of the warmth of the Boston house tormented Jared for a moment. He put it ruthlessly aside. He could allow himself no weakness; no regrets. They had come a good distance, but they had to go even further, surviving day by day and hour by hour—

He led his cousin down the side of the shingled house. They must keep on; never falter; never stay in one place too long. This was still civilization. He was still a murderer—

He'd considered it an accomplishment just to reach Philadelphia before the worst weather began. But he'd been nervous working at the crowded public house. Even with the war going on, Philadelphia attracted a great many visitors. What if someone from Boston recognized him—?

So they'd taken to the road again, putting more miles between themselves and the threat that Boston represented. As yet, Jared had no clear destination in mind. He knew he'd have to choose one eventually. Eventually, but not tonight—

The snow was growing steadily thicker. It reminded him that it wouldn't be as easy to steal food in deepest wintertime as it had been on the long trip down to the Quaker City. He hoped they wouldn't have to resort to thievery tonight. He hoped begging would serve instead—

The rear porch creaked under his feet. Amanda refused to climb up with him. She stood in the yard and stared at him with a slack expression. Her thin fingers

kept plucking at the tear in the coat. God, how despicable he was to subject her to this—!

His still hand rapped on the door. Inside, he heard a man's guttural voice. Then a woman's, a little lighter, not so foreign-sounding. A small boy asked a question and the woman shushed him. Boots clumped.

The door opened to reveal a man in his late twenties, plainly dressed, with curly blond hair and blue eyes. An old flintlock glinted in his hands. The young man peered at Jared, then glanced beyond him, wary.

"*Ja?*"

"Good—good evening," Jared stammered. "My—sister and I—" He stood aside so the farmer could get a clear look at Amanda down in the whitened yard. With fair glibness, he slid into the tale that had served them before: "We're on our way to Pittsburgh—"

"Alone? No von else?"

"Just the two of us. We're from Rhode Island—" He didn't intend to tell anyone they came from Boston. Who could say how far Massachusetts law might reach? "Our parents died in a fire, so we're going to Pittsburgh to live with our uncle."

The young man's eyes remained suspicious. His wife appeared behind him. Despite her youth, she was rough-skinned and stooped. Jared was almost dizzy inhaling the aroma of fresh bread that suffused her kitchen.

"Children, Karl?" the woman asked.

"*Ja.* Dey say dey're going to Pittsburgh—"

"Look, I'm not armed in any way—" Jared raised his hands. He'd concealed the Spanish knife and the London-made pistol in the canvas bag on his shoulder. "There's nothing to fear. We'd only like permission to sleep in your barn."

The woman's face softened. "The barn will be frigid in a storm like this. We could let them come in, Karl—"

Jared was quick to capitalize on her sympathy:

"If there's any way I could work for you for a day or so, I'd be glad to, in exchange for a little food to take with us—"

"De roads are very bad dis time of year," the farmer advised him.

"I know, but we need to get to Pittsburgh as soon as we can."

The young man set the butt of his flintlock on the floor. Jared felt relieved.

"Might find one of de wagon men in town who'd take you," the farmer said.

"Town?" Jared repeated.

The young man gestured in the direction of the lights glimpsed on the road. "Langaster. But I cannot gif you charity, dis is a poor household—"

"I told you I'd work! Please, can't we come in? My cous—my sister's nearly frozen."

For a moment he thought the farmer would say no. Had something hinted to the young man that the visitors weren't brother and sister? Jared's light eyes and Amanda's dark ones, perhaps? Just as the farmer was about to speak, his wife touched his arm.

The man glanced at her, shrugged and stepped aside.

"*Ja,* all right. But you sleep in de barn."

"Karl—"

"No, dey go to de barn."

"That's fine," Jared assured him.

"If you can help me split wood, I maybe gif you some corn—"

"Amanda, come on!" Jared cried, darting down the steps into the blowing

snow. His excitement at having found them a sanctuary disappeared as he gazed at the dim oval of her face. Her eyes were tear-filled.

"I want to sleep, Jared," she said, teeth still chattering.

"We will! These people are going to let us stay in the barn. But first we can go inside."

"You better carry her," the woman said. "She don't look so well."

Wearily, Jared picked his cousin up and bore her to the porch and into the lamp-lit kitchen where the smell of fresh bread drifted, indescribably rich and sweet. *One more step taken,* he said to himself as the farmer closed the door against the wind's whine. *Don't worry about tomorrow or about the day after— be glad you've found a place away from the storm—*

But as he set Amanda on her feet and started brushing snowflakes off her brows and eyelashes, he thought again of the immense distance still ahead of them; thought of all the cheerless roads yet to be walked; of all the strange doors that might or might not open when he knocked—

It seemed too great an effort to ask of any human being, let alone two who were not even adults.

But Jared was able to banish that kind of pessimism very quickly. All he had to do was remind himself of what lay waiting for him back in Boston. Hungry and tired as he was, he showed firmness in guiding Amanda to the chair the farmer's wife pulled out from the table. Her son, a blond copy of his father, was awestruck by the visitors.

Jared spoke because he knew he must:

"I'd like to thank you for doing this. We've come a long way today."

The farmer stood his flintlock in a corner, saying nothing. His wife broke the tension with a smile:

"That is very clear. Please—sit down and eat."

II

JARED AND Amanda stayed four days with the German couple. Jared split eighteen cords of wood for the farmer, whose name was Konigsberg. The young man never quite lost his suspicion of the visitors. But his wife, whom he called Hilde, accepted their stories at face value, and treated them generously. By the time the cousins set out with Konigsberg on his weekly trip to Lancaster for supplies, the woman had persuaded her husband to give them not only a good-sized ration of corn, but some bread and a thin blanket as well:

"That will keep you a little warmer on the way to Pittsburgh, *ja?*"

III

THE WAGON creaked and swayed. From the head end, Jared heard the teamster cursing. His whip popped like a gunshot.

The driver, Francis Quilling, had agreed to take them to Pittsburgh on this, perhaps the last trip he could make before the roads became impassable; he had agreed because Jared would provide the extra strength needed to free the wheels from deep, muddy ruts.

Quilling was a garrulous man, and a braggart. No one made shrewder invest-
ments than he did. His house was one of the largest and finest in Lancaster,
envied by everyone. His seven children were all supremely intelligent; paragons
of Christian virtue. And during good weather, he wouldn't lower himself to take
help along on one of his runs; he could do it all, no assistance required.

But he did admit that in early winter, particularly after the sun shone for a
while, boggy places presented a problem. If the wagon mired, Jared's job was to
jam pieces of plank beneath the iron tires, then help Quilling push the wheels
while the straining horses pulled the wagon forward over the boards.

It was just before sunset. Amanda sat staring at her cousin in the wagon's dim
interior. Quilling had allowed Jared to take a short rest because the ground
hereabouts was frozen hard.

As Jared yawned, Amanda touched his hand:

"Where are we going, Jared?"

"Why, you know very well. Pittsburgh. Be there in a couple of days, Mr.
Quilling said."

"And after that?"

"I don't know."

"Can't we stop in Pittsburgh?"

"We'll have to, until the river opens up again."

She shook her head. "I mean for longer than that."

"No, we've got to keep going."

"Where?"

"I don't know yet, Amanda!"

"But I'm tired!"

"Then sleep. Put your head down."

"I mean I'm tired of walking and being dirty and hungry—"

"We'll find a place to stop," he said, sounding confident.

"I don't believe you. I don't think you know where we're going. You're just
pretending. Telling me lies. Aren't you? *Aren't you?*"

He didn't reply. She rolled away from him, covering herself with the blanket
given them by the Konigsbergs. He stared at her filthy hair, accused by her
silence but unable to admit his guilt aloud.

IV

AN OLD poster preserved on the wall of an emporium in Pittsburgh provided the
first hint of an answer.

Even in winter, the boat yards at the head of the Ohio didn't shut down. Work
was done indoors, in sheds that protected the river craft under construction. Jared
found a job as a boy-of-all-work in the noisy Suck's Run yard at Boyd's Bluff,
across the Monongahela from the busy town. All during January and into February, he ran nails and lumber to the laborers sawing and hammering on flatboats
and keelboats that would take to the water when good weather came.

At the end of his fourteen-hour day, Jared rode the ferry raft back to Pittsburgh. The ferrymen worked in pairs, using long poles to push away floating
chunks of ice. The trip was always tedious because Jared was always exhausted.
All he wanted to do was clean the sawdust and shavings from his hair and his
body, then go to bed and sleep.

With his wages, he and Amanda had been able to take a room in a shabby boarding house whose owners, an elderly couple, obviously weren't too scrupulous about their guests. Jared was never questioned about why he and a small girl were traveling together.

Jared's pay was low, so the room was tiny. He slept on a blanket on the floor while Amanda occupied the bed. The landlady set a fair table, though. And Amanda had a place to stay during the day, safe from the none-too-savory men who drifted in and out of the downstairs parlor.

Occasionally Jared spent a little of his money to bring his cousin a newspaper. Apart from that, entertainment for Amanda was non-existent. Confined in the room, she grew even more sallow and unhappy. Only Jared's return in the evening revived her spirits.

Two or three times a week she questioned him about their destination. He always gave the same answer:

"I still don't know."

Then they saw the poster.

Jared worked six days a week. One Saturday evening, he took Amanda to a store to buy her some penny candy. As the cousins walked in, the storekeeper was conversing with a couple of rough-looking types lounging in chairs by the cracker barrel.

The storekeeper came to wait on them. Amanda's eyes glowed as she surveyed the candy spread out in small wooden trays. But Jared's attention had been captured by the poster tacked to the wall:

March 17, 1811
Premier Voyage
Down the Ohio and Mississippi!
The Unique and Remarkable
STEAM-BOAT
"New Orleans"
constructed by
Mr. NICHOLAS J. ROOSEVELT
Associate of the Celebrated
Steam Pioneer
Mr. ROBERT FULTON
Captain A. Sack, Pilot

Busy counting out licorice pieces, the storekeeper didn't pay much heed to Jared. The boy continued to gaze at the name of the vessel. Certain things that he'd read and been told about the south came back to mind. How warm it was there. How gentle and easy a life—

True, the Indians had been active in that part of the country. But the military was moving against them. The name of the steamboat suddenly seemed to provide exactly the sense of direction he needed.

The storekeeper accepted Amanda's coin and turned to her cousin:

"That was quite a day."

Startled, Jared said, "What?"

"The day they launched *Orleans*. Never saw such crowds in this town." He scratched a white eyebrow. "But you sound like you come from back east—"

"We do."

"They got steamboats on the New York rivers, don't they?"

"Yes, but I've never seen one."

"Well, old *Orleans* was mighty handsome. Had a great big wheel in her stern. We sent her off with a hurrah you could hear for miles. She was supposed to make trips between here and the mouth of the Mississippi. Turned out she wasn't built quite right. She didn't have the power to get through the falls of the Ohio very easy—and once she did, she never could come back upstream past Natchez. She's hauling cotton down there, they say. There's a lot of talk about putting bigger steam boats on the Ohio soon. Then you'll see goods being carried like you never saw before—"

The storekeeper broke off; swung around. One of the men from the cracker barrel, burly and thick-lipped, had walked to the counter. Pretending to examine a tin of tobacco, he was actually staring at Amanda in an oblique way.

"You want to buy that, Rafe?" the storekeeper asked. "If you don't, then don't shake it. Ruins the tobacco."

"I might want to buy it," the man answered, nibbling at his lower lip. All at once Jared comprehended why Amanda was being scrutinized.

Though still only ten years old, she was maturing rapidly. Her face promised beauty in adulthood. And her breasts, already grown large for one so young, showed clearly beneath her dirty coat.

Jared tugged his cousin's hand. From Amanda's expression, he knew she was aware of the man's interest. It obviously upset her. Jared doubted that she understood the reason for the attention, though. As he led her past the burly fellow, he heard the tobacco tin rattle back on the counter. Fingers closed on his arm:

"Ain't seen you two in this store before, have I?"

Jared wrenched loose. "Does it make any difference?"

"Leave them be, Rafe," the storekeeper warned. His tone made clear that Rafe wasn't exactly his favorite customer.

The burly man grinned, his eyes lazy-looking in the lamplight. "Hell, I was just bein' cordial—"

"You can be cordial with folks your own age."

"Now Morris, don't carry on so. If I got a mind to greet somebody—"

"Let me put your candy away," Jared said, seizing Amanda's wrist. The chunks of licorice dropped into his other hand. He opened his coat. The butt of the London-made pistol and the sheathed Spanish knife were clearly visible at his belt—as he intended.

He tucked the candy into his pocket. As far as he could tell, the older man wasn't armed. At the sight of Jared's weapons, the man's interest cooled rapidly:

"Shit, you're makin' a fuss for nothin', Morris—" He ambled back to his crony.

Outside, Jared realized just how upset Amanda was:

"Why did that man stare at me like that?"

"Because—" He didn't hesitate long. It was time she understood. "—because you're very pretty."

"No I'm not. I'm all dirty."

"Makes no difference. You're a handsome girl, and you look older than you really are. That's why I insist you keep the door locked while I'm over at the yard. And why I never want you to speak to men when I'm not around."

As they tramped toward the boarding house in the winter darkness, Amanda seemed to brighten:

"You're not teasing me?"

"No."

"We're so raggedy—I never thought anyone would look twice at us."

"Not me, Amanda. You."

"Did he really think I was pretty?"

"You saw how he gawked."

She nodded, actually smiling a little. Then she shivered. "Mercy. Imagine!" A moment later: "You're *sure* you're not teasing?"

"Believe me, Amanda—some men lose their heads over pretty girls, and you're going to be one of the prettiest. That'll be nice for you, but it'll also be a problem."

In the light from the front of a hotel, he saw her lips still curved in that thoughtful smile.

But it vanished quickly enough:

"I want my licorice."

"Here. Want to know something?"

"What?"

"I know where we're going."

"You mean we can't stay in Pittsburgh?"

"Don't start that again. I've already said no."

"Why can't we?"

"Just because."

"Oh, I'm sick to death of hearing that, Jared!"

"But you'll like where we're going."

"Tell me and see if I will."

"We're going down south. A city called New Orleans."

"Is it far?"

"Not very," he lied. "We should be there by late spring or early summer."

"Is it warm?"

"Yes, it is."

"Did you just think this up, Jared?"

"Why, no," he said, trying to summon a smile himself. "I've had it in my head several days now."

"Liar."

He laughed and rumpled her hair.

New Orleans. The more he turned it over in his thoughts, the more certain he was that the poster had provided an invaluable inspiration. He'd decided long ago that they'd never go into the west—into the country where his mother had died and his father had failed.

But the south—that was different. It was a mellow, gentle land. He'd heard that New Orleans was a splendid old city, full of wealthy folk who spoke Spanish and French and lived in a grand style. From the storekeeper's remarks about river commerce, and from what he knew personally about the frantic pace of boat construction, Jared suspected that New Orleans was also a thriving commercial center. If Mr. Fulton's steamboats made their appearance on southern rivers as they had in the east, travel and shipping time would be cut drastically. More and more cargo would be moving up and down the Mississippi. Someone who was industrious should be able to find work easily at a major port—

So, for the first time in weeks, each of the cousins had something to be happy about. Amanda had her licorice. And Jared had his destination.

V

IN LATE February, he quit his job at the Suck's Run yard. It hadn't been profitable employment. His small salary barely met expenses. Thus he was immediately forced to look for a means of financing the next stage of their journey. After several days of combing the docks, he managed to sign onto a keelboat making a run to Louisville, at the falls of the Ohio.

But the captain was parsimonious. Jared would be allowed rations and sleeping space for one, not two. He didn't quarrel. By now he was used to sharing everything with his cousin.

Soon after the boat got under way, he realized again that Amanda had ripened to the point where she was bound to attract the stares of older men. Despite her disreputable appearance and her pale skin, the luminous beauty of her eyes and the curves of her swelling figure drew many a sly glance. Jared kept his pistol and knife visible at all times.

Amanda seemed conscious of the attention. Once Jared caught her returning a man's rough greeting with a coquettish smile. That evening he lectured her severely. She was too young to experiment with her newly discovered abilty to interest the opposite sex!

Amanda retorted that she'd only thought it might be fun to see how bad-smelling, bearded men reacted to a little friendliness—

"Besides, I was only teasing."

"They don't know that. You tease them too much and they'll want to try—"
Uncomfortable silence.

"Try what, Jared?"

"Never mind."

"Are you trying to say they'll want to do what men and women do together?"
Jared actually blushed. "Do you know about—?"

"Of course I do."

"How?"

Now it was her turn:

"Never mind."

"Damn you for an impudent little minx—!"

"Don't you dare curse me, Jared Kent!"

"All right, I'm sorry. But you pay attention to what I'm telling you about—"

"Pooh! If any man starts to—to hurt me or something, I'll just tell him he mustn't. If he thinks I'm pretty, he'll do what I say."

He would have guffawed except for the fact that she was serious. He replied the same way:

"You may be able to twine men around your finger when you're twenty, Amanda, but it won't work when you're only ten. You mind what I say. Don't lead them on."

She made a disappointed face. "Oh, very well."

But her eyes were still merry. She was entranced with her new-found power. God help me, Jared sighed silently, I've forced her to learn too many hard lessons too early. His familiar sense of guilt put him in a bitter and depressed mood the rest of the evening.

___VI

THE KEELBOAT glided on down the Ohio, and Jared found himself studying the terrain with a peculiarly intense fascination.

In the misty meadows and towering trees that moved slowly astern on both sides of the river, he saw primitive beauty. At the same time, the vistas of silent forest and shining river filled him with loathing.

Occasionally, on clear days, he glimpsed game on shore. Great prong-horned deer. Fat pheasants. Wild hogs. He began to understand why people would seek this new country, content to huddle together in small settlements of the kind the keelboat passed from time to time. The boat's coming was always announced by a blast of an old bugle owned by a member of the crew. When the bugle pealed, men and women in the settlement ran down to the shore and held their children up to see the vessel. Jared felt sorry for the children—and the parents. The older people usually waved with great animation. But they had a lonely, haggard look about them. Perhaps that was why they waved.

There was a strange duality in Jared's interest; a duality that didn't escape him. The great forest did impress him with its stark splendor. He could tell the land would be beautiful the moment the weather warmed. He could visualize the greening boughs; the bursts of wildflower color—

Yet he hated all he saw.

He tried to find a rational explanation for that feeling. On the surface, it seemed simple. The land had lured his mother and father with false promises of ease and abundance. They had found reality far different. The land had subjected them to the same hardships it worked on anyone who came to challenge its dominance. They had not been strong enough to endure, and they had been destroyed.

Jared loved the memory of his parents to the extent that it was possible for him to do so, knowing so little of them. But what had happened to them had happened in the past. It seemed insufficient to explain the loathing and unease that gripped him in the present.

One morning, unable to sleep, he went out on deck just as the light was breaking. He yawned and rubbed his eyes in the red dawn—and blinked suddenly at movement in the brush on the left-hand shore.

An animal stood there, its hindquarters concealed by a spray of ferns. Its great shoulders and head were fully visible. It resembled some huge, sleek, tan-colored cat. Its eyes caught the rising sun for an instant, burning like pieces of iridescent crystal—

Jared shuddered.

In its jaws, the cat held the remains of a smaller, darker animal.

A raccoon? A possum?

No way of telling. The prey was dead; crushed; nothing more than mangled meat and brown, blood-stained fur. Jared put the back of his hand against his lips, feeling the sickness rise—

With immense grace and power, the cat turned and loped away from the shore, and then Jared understood.

The land was like the cat. He and all the others who came to it were prey. Some survived. Some could not.

He was one of the latter. Bone-deep, he knew that.

Times beyond counting, Aunt Harriet had told him that he was what his parents had been: flawed. He had seen countless evidences of his own. Wasn't

the tremor in his belly, stirred by the sight of the bloody carcass in the cat's mouth, just one more?

He was the child of Abraham and Elizabeth, knowing with a certainty that he bore their weaknesses. Sometimes he tried to tell himself the conviction was irrational. Yet he believed.

If he challenged the land, it would destroy him. That was why he and Amanda had to flee to New Orleans; to civilized comforts. It wasn't merely a matter of being far from Boston. He probably could lose himself anywhere out here. But he would not—

He understood, on that scarlet morning, the real reason he hated the land. He hated it because it made him afraid of himself.

___VII

LOUISVILLE IMPRESSED Jared as a prosperous, if faintly pestilential, place. A profusion of ponds dotted the forests of oak, hackberry and buckeye that surrounded the town. But Louisville proper was as lively as Pittsburgh, and the warehouses and docks testified to its importance in commerce. Kegs and barrels containing everything from whiskey and flour to corn and lard were piled high on the wharves. Chickens and turkeys squawked in great tiers of wooden cages. The river men who carried and handled the goods kept the taverns and bordellos noisy all through the night.

Jared found temporary work unloading and uncrating newly arrived shipments at a general store. The store's signboard read *Audubon & Rozier, Merchants.* Mr. Ferdinand Rozier was the only partner in evidence. During the week and a half that Jared worked for Rozier, he learned that the man's former associate preferred fine art to business. Audubon and his wife had moved down the river to Henderson a few years earlier. There, Rozier said, Mr. Audubon had no doubt abandoned storekeeping entirely, in order to make sketches and paintings of what interested him most—wildlife; birds, chiefly. Rozier laughed at that. There was no market for portraits of birds! He was convinced his former partner was destined for failure.

Rozier agreed to pay some of Jared's wages in trade. Provisioned again, he and Amanda set off along the Cumberland Trail during a warm spell in early March. In forty-eight hours, the weather changed. Sleet began to slant down from the sky.

The cousins were struggling along a heavily wooded stretch of road at twilight. Great tree limbs soughed in the wind. Within minutes, the sleet completely soaked their clothing.

They hunted for a farm that might offer shelter, but found none. They were forced to spend the night in the open.

The storm continued until the following morning. When the light broke, Jared's head was hot and his eyes had a glazed look. Though not ill, Amanda was almost as miserable.

"We—we've got to hole up a while," Jared gasped as he and his cousin started out. The whole world seemed gray, wet and forlorn. "Anyplace—I'm not feeling good—"

The sunny visions of New Orleans were gone. Instead, he saw only his cousin's drawn face—or feverish imaginings:

Hamilton Stovall strutting through the main floor of Kent's—

Stovall's general manager dying in a welter of blood—

The printing house afire—

"Take my hand," Amanda said, sniffling. Jared was terrified by the sickly whiteness of her skin. What if she caught a chill and died just because he'd dragged her all this way—?

They managed to negotiate another half-mile of road, passing a bogged and abandoned freight wagon. Jared's eyes watered and blurred. The world seemed to consist of gargoyle trees against a sodden sky—

Suddenly Amanda exclaimed, "There's a creek ahead!"

"I don't see—"

"And a cabin!"

"I can't make it out—"

"Here, hang onto me. I'll lead you—"

It was the longest distance Jared had ever walked. Or so it felt. His head ached. One moment he burned; the next, he froze. After an interminable time, they reached the creek and crossed.

The water soaking his feet felt warm—another indication of how sick he was. As they stumbled across the dooryard of the cabin, a damp rooster scolded them from a small shed nearby.

Jared's voice had a wheezy sound:

"Knock on the door, Amanda—"

She did, loudly. In a moment the door was opened. Swaying, Jared heard a young girl speak:

"What do you want?"

He tried to focus his eyes; saw only shifting gray shapes.

"Who is it, Sarah?" a woman called.

Before the girl could answer, Jared lunged forward. Not intentionally; his legs simply gave out. He fell toward the door, his hands scraped by the rough logs on either side. The last thing he heard was the girl's shriek of fright.

Adding her wail to the commotion, Amanda threw herself on top of her cousin. Sobbing, she begged him to get up. But he lay motionless, his head and chest resting on the cabin's puncheon floor, his legs extending into the yard where the sleet beat down.

5

Reverend Blackthorn

"JARED?"

On the other side of the small fire he'd built at sundown, the boy rolled onto his belly.

"What?"

"Are you feeling all right?"

Jared peered through the flames at his cousin, who was even more wan and pinch-faced than she'd been just a few weeks ago. He tried to make his lie convincing:

"Yes."

"You look funny."

"I'm fine."

She regarded him in stoic silence. He tried to recall when he'd last seen a smile on her face. It was in Kentucky, he decided. At the cabin on Knob Creek, below Louisville, where he'd collapsed from sickness and exhaustion in early March.

The cabin belonged to a farmer and his family. Jared and Amanda stayed with them almost two weeks. The farmer's wife put cooling poultices on his sweating skin, and brought him slowly out of his lethargy with generous helpings of food and attention. At the end of his recuperation, Jared was convinced he'd beaten the disease.

But now it was mid-May, and since leaving the cabin on Knob Creek, he'd suffered a similar illness twice more. It had shaken him with fever and chills; watered his bowels, left him limp—and forced them to stop for a day or so each time.

From the way he felt at the moment—weak and shivery—he might be in for still another attack. Apparently Amanda saw it coming too.

Across the fire, she locked her frail arms around her knees. Her shoes were splitting apart at the soles. The hem of her muddied skirt was ragged, and so was her fine coat. She stared dully into the darkness of the Tennessee woodlands beyond the perimeter of light.

She was the same young girl who had left Boston with him, yet she had changed. Almost without his being aware of it. It was more than a matter of growing an inch or so; more than the pronounced development of her figure. She no longer protested about the hardships they were undergoing. She shared the work of building evening fires. Sometimes lately, he gazed at her and thought he was looking at a grown woman. Her strength seemed to be increasing while illness drained his away—

Trees newly leafed rustled in the night wind. The cry of an owl drifted through the clearing. Unseen nearby, a small river purled over stones.

"I'm so tired tonight," Amanda said at last. Not complaining; stating a fact. "I'll be thankful when we get to New Orleans."

Bracing on one elbow, Jared shoved his long and dirty yellow hair off his forehead. As he did, he felt the clamminess of his skin. He tried to sound encouraging:

"I'll bet we make it before the end of June."

"Those men with the wagons—the ones who came over on the ferry with us—"

"What about them?"

"They said there was a town near here."

He nodded. "Nashville."

"I think you should see if someone will put me to work while we're there."

"*You*—?" He laughed; a kind of croaking sound.

She jumped up tearing a burr out of her dark hair.

"Don't make fun of me, Jared Kent!"

"I'm not—" He forced a straight face. "But I'm the one who works."

"I can wash floors and carry water just as well as you can! Besides, you're sick."

"I am not."

Stamping her foot, Amanda showed some of the animation he remembered from another time—another world:

"You're fibbing. I can always tell when you're fibbing—" She circled the fire to kneel beside him. "Do you know what I'd really like? To stop for good—so you don't keep getting sick—"

"Amanda, the answer is no."

"I've heard that till I can't stand it any more!"

Jared sat up, trying to keep his temper. He held out his hands to warm them at the fire. His nails were cracked and grimy. His hair hung nearly to his shoulders. His cheeks were sunken, his good looks all but destroyed by paleness and the fever-glint in his eyes.

With a sigh, he said, "You know I won't stop anywhere around here. This is the kind of country where mama died."

"Yes, I've heard that too. Over and over! I still don't understand—"

"Because you're too young. Let's not argue. We're going where life doesn't demand so much of people. It's warm in the south. New Orleans has soft air— balmy winters. I didn't stop in Louisville for the same reason I won't stop more than a couple of days in Nashville. I despise this country, and you'll just have to accept that."

Unsatisfied, she flounced back to her original place. "Oh, I don't understand you, Jared. Why does it make any difference where your mama and papa lived?"

"It does, that's all! You don't know what this country did to them. I do. We're going to find a better place."

She shook her head. "You don't make sense."

"I'm tired—so let's drop it!"

His anger produced another unhappy look from the girl. She started to reply, but didn't. She sat down, arms crossed on her knees, her face stony.

Jared's ears rang as he stumbled around the fire, feeling ashamed all at once. He dropped down beside his cousin, tried to cradle her against his shoulder. At first she resisted. But the loneliness and the chill of the spring night proved stronger than anger. She huddled close.

"Take my word, it's better that we go on to New Orleans," he said. "The worst part's over. The warm weather's coming. And the wagon men said General Jackson whipped the Red Sticks for good a month or so ago. The trace from Nashville should be safe to travel—"

"We *could* stop," she said quietly. "We could if you didn't hate everything so much—"

"We're going on." His tone carried a note of finality, warning her to say no more.

She sighed again. "All right. I know better than to talk to you when you're sick."

"Dammit, I'm not—"

"Jared, be quiet and cover up."

She pulled up the thin blanket given them by the Konigsbergs in Pennsylvania. Then she changed her position so that he could lean against her shoulder. She started to stroke his forehead. Spent and dizzy, he didn't protest—

Unquestionably, the fever was back, brought on by continued exposure to the elements, and poor food. Their diet lately had consisted of creek water, wild berries, and occasional corn filched from the cribs of isolated homesteads.

Her hand moved slowly, comfortingly across his damp skin. "You know what I'm thinking about now?" she asked in a drowsy voice.

The fire seemed to afford very little warmth. His bones felt locked in ice, and his teeth clicked as he answered:

"No."

"Knob Creek. I could have stayed there the rest of my life. It was such a nice, warm cabin—"

"But too small for permanent boarders. We were lucky the Lincolns took us in as long as they did."

Lost in her memory of bright lamps and kindness, she mused on, sounding almost happy:

"I could have gone to blab school with Sarah—it would have been such fun, being in a schoolroom where everyone reads their lessons out loud at the same time. I could have taught her little brother, too. Taught him his letters—Abraham was fascinated with letters. Always trying to draw them on his slate with charcoal, or in the mud with a stick. He'll be smart when he grows up, I think. For five years old, he was very quick—"

"He was," Jared nodded, shuddering. The owl hooted again.

"He liked me. He kept asking me to write words for him. We could have stayed somehow—"

"No. I heard Lincoln and his wife talking about moving to Illinois or Indiana, where the soil's better for crops."

He did remember Tom Lincoln and his wife Nancy with fondness, though. They had been much more open and generous than the German farmer in Pennsylvania. For a moment he almost wished Amanda's dream could have come true—

"I only hope New Orleans is as nice as you say, Jared."

"It will be," he murmured, not at all certain.

"I never want to be cold again. I never want to be hungry again. I've had enough."

"Well, we finally agree on something. I have too. Now go to sleep."

II

WHEN AMANDA closed her eyes and began to breathe regularly, Jared eased away from her. He didn't want to move, but the fire needed more wood.

He covered her with the blanket. Circled the embers, stumbling once—the fever was rapidly growing worse. He was sweating heavily.

He shuffled into the darkness at the edge of the clearing. It seemed to take an eternity to gather a small quantity of loose brush. As he worked, he glanced occasionally at the stars visible through the treetops.

He hadn't learned the geography of the heavens well enough to use it to judge direction with complete accuracy. He tried to recall the conversation of the teamsters coming across the ferry further up the Cumberland. The men said the north-south stream near which they'd camped was a small river known as Stone's. It emptied into the Cumberland. A few miles west of the point where the rivers met should be the town of Nashville. There, Jared hoped to find a place where they could rest out of the weather for a day or two.

He'd also have to find some chores to do again. He almost smiled, thinking of Amanda's insistence that she hire herself out. Lord, how she'd changed in only a couple of months!

Once supplied with food, they'd head south along the trace, the Chickasaw Road, that would take them nearer New Orleans. And by summertime, there might be an end to the weariness and hunger and pain—

He dumped a last armload of green sticks on the fire and coughed as smoke clouded up. God, how he ached! His face was wet with perspiration—

He mustn't weaken now. They had survived the winter, and he was thin and hard because of it. He didn't know how many miles they'd traveled since leaving Boston, but it must be an incredible number. What seemed ironic was the possibility that something entirely uncontrollable might defeat them. Not the danger of animal predators. Not unscrupulous humans, either; but sickness. The sickness that had gripped him intermittently since late February, and threatened to reduce him to helplessness again—

He stumbled a second time as he returned to his cousin. He lay down beside her and tugged part of the blanket over his legs. The back of his head rested on the hard ground. He stared at the stars. They blurred and changed position too quickly as the fever mounted—

III

HE OPENED his eyes. Felt the brush of the May wind on his face. Saw, as if through gauze, the high, budded limbs of trees against the rosy sky.

Dawn.

He heard the soft rush of Stone's River. And another sound, totally unexpected—

The stamp of a horse.

He lay still, trying to clear his throbbing head. Where was his pistol—?

In his canvas bag. But his knife—

He felt its reassuring hardness at his belt.

Only then did he lift the blanket so as not to disturb Amanda. He rolled on his side, scrambled up—

A lean man hunkered beyond what was left of the fire: a few red coals glowing amidst white ash. The man wore a filthy beaver hat with a hole in it. Behind him, a swaybacked gray horse fretted, tied to a low branch.

"Morning, boy. Trust you don't mind sharing your fire with another traveler—?"

At the sound of the voice, Amanda stirred, sat up. Jared put his hand behind him, moved it back and forth, a wave of warning. He heard her quick intake of breath. She understood. She got to her feet, hid behind his back.

"Who are you?" Jared asked. "Where'd you come from?"

The man chuckled. "Why, I might ask both questions of you."

He rose, dusted off his hands—big, hard-looking and bruised. As he turned slightly, faint eastern light pinked his face beneath the brim of his beaver hat.

Tufts of gray hair showed around the man's ears. His linen and stock had a yellow cast—like the teeth he displayed in a smile that struck Jared as false. The man's fingers hung nearly to his knees. His abnormally long arms looked powerful.

He extended his right hand in greeting. Jared didn't offer to shake:

"I want to know where you came from."

Frowning, the man lowered his hand. His arm brushed the flap of a coat pocket aside. A small black-bound book stuck out of the pocket. A testament—?

The man jerked a thumb over his shoulder. "Came up Stone's from Nashville.

I'm headed for a little place I own a few miles east of here. Left Nashville late, and without supper. So when I saw the fire—''

He shrugged. ''I stopped to get warm, that's all.''

The glow of dawn set small fires in the pupils of the man's sunken eyes. Jared had grown through the winter. He was approaching six feet; but the stranger was taller. The man's slumping shoulders tended to minimize his height but not his aura of strength.

''Hardly expected to find two youngsters camped in these woods,'' the man said. ''You realize we're all trespassing—''

Jared said, ''I didn't see any signs posted.''

The man swept his hand in a wide arc. ''Belongs to the judge all the same. Oh, but I doubt he or any of his niggers will be out this far this early. We can eat breakfast in peace and go our respective ways.''

Just then Jared noticed two other odd things about the stranger. Bruises showed not only on his hands but on his throat. And part of his right earlobe was missing; a half-moon of tissue had somehow been torn away.

The man swept off his disreputable beaver. ''My name is Blackthorn, Reverend William Blackthorn. Who do I have the pleasure—?''

''Never mind. Amanda, let's get our things together.''

''You mean you're not going to eat?'' Blackthorn's heavy brows hooked together. He gestured to the bags hanging on his saddled horse. ''I'd be happy to split some of my biscuits and wild honey—''

''No thanks, we're going on to Nashville.''

Jared got busy folding up the blanket while Amanda peered at the stranger, her dark eyes sleepily curious. The man acted polite enough. But for no reason he could pin down, Jared didn't like him.

The Reverend Blackthorn sniffed. ''Traveling on an empty belly certainly isn't good stewardship of the health the Almighty granted you, boy. Strikes me that you and your ladyfriend—''

''My sister,'' Jared snapped, angered by the lingering emphasis the Reverend put on the last word.

''Is that a fact?'' Blackthorn ran a palm down the side of his patched trousers. ''You're fair and she's dark—and you're shoots off the same tree? Wondrous are the ways of God. Eh, boy?''

The sunken eyes—greenish, Jared noticed—seemed to stray past him again. He stepped to Amanda's side. He wondered whether the Reverend actually deserved his title. The bruises, that bitten place on his earlobe—those hardly seemed appropriate for a man of the gospel.

Blackthorn scratched his groin. ''How old are you, girl? Fourteen?''

''You're way off,'' Jared said, stuffing the blanket into the canvas bag. He had trouble speaking; the fever thickened his tongue and made his teeth click.

''Am I, now? Remarkable! I'd have sworn she was a young woman—''

Blackthorn's eyes flicked back to Jared. ''It's strange indeed to find two persons your age abroad in the Tennessee wilderness. Run away from home, did you? Or maybe you're indentured people? Give the slip to your masters?''

''None of your affair, Reverend.''

''Here, now!'' Blackthorn's voice roughened as he approached. ''That's no way to speak to a pilgrim who only seeks to share your fire—''

''We're leaving. The fire's yours.''

''You don't look well, boy. Don't sound it, either. Your teeth are knocking so

loudly, I'm surprised it doesn't wake the judge in his bed. Are you sick too, girl—?''

Blackthorn reached around Jared, brushed his fingers across Amanda's forehead. She retreated quickly:

"Don't you touch me!"

Jared's hand dropped to the hilt of the Spanish knife. He made sure the man saw the move.

"Come!" Blackthorn exclaimed. "I meant no disrespect to your—ah—sister. I only intended to see to her health—in the manner of the man of Samaria."

His eyes fastened on Jared's, hostile despite the yellow smile. "I'd hardly say your behavior's Christian, boy—"

"And you don't act much like a preacher."

Blackthorn rubbed his chin with one bruised hand. "I am. At the same time, I claim to be the best free-for-all fighter in half a dozen counties. I've had some setbacks in Nashville. Circumstances make it necessary for me to move on after a stop at my cabin for a few belongings. Traveling takes money if a man wants to sleep under a roof and partake of decent food. No doubt you have a little money—"

Dropping his pretense of cordiality, he extended his hand.

"Give me that canvas bag."

Dizzy with fear and fever, Jared jerked out the knife. He was totally unprepared for the astounding speed with which Blackthorn moved.

The man grabbed Jared's arm with both hands, twisted. Jared's fingers opened. The knife fell into the coals. Bobbing down, Blackthorn closed his big yellow teeth on the back of Jared's hand.

Jared yelped. Blackthorn let go, stepped back, wiping his lips.

"All's fair in free-for-all, boy. Now may I examine that bag?"

Jared launched himself with fists up. Blackthorn side-stepped, brought his knee up savagely. Pain erupted in Jared's groin.

He tumbled into the ashes and embers, yelped again, rolled away. Amanda's cry of terror sounded above the chatter of birds and the burble of the river.

On his back, Jared started to get up. Blackthorn dropped on Jared's belly with both knees. The tall man's face twisted with glee as he jabbed his thumbs into the outer corners of Jared's eyes:

"I can pop 'em neat as grapes," he breathed. "There's several in Nashville who can testify to that—"

The thumbs dug deeper. Jared kicked, to no avail. Tried to tear at the massive wrists against his jaw. Futile—

The edge of a thumbnail scraped Jared's left eyeball. Wildly, he hammered at the tall man's forearms. He couldn't dislodge the huge hands.

"Shame to blind someone so young," Blackthorn panted. "Shame to rob you of the sights of God's bountiful creation. But you're not Christian—"

He wrenched his left knee over, drove it into Jared's crotch a second time. Jared screamed.

Amanda leaped on Blackthorn, trying to claw his face.

"Goddamn you for a spiteful child!" Blackthorn roared, battering her with one fist. Amanda sprawled, the wind knocked out of her.

Jared jerked his head to escape the darting thumbs. Blackthorn pounded his nose twice. Already dazed, the boy watched the tall man and the rustling trees blur and distort—

Gasping, Blackthorn lurched to his feet. One huge boot lifted; Jared saw the

hobnails on the bottom. Blackthorn stomped his stomach, leaving him retching and half conscious.

"Now I'll have that peek in your bag."

Amanda crawled toward her cousin, repeating his name. Jared locked his hands over his middle, thrashing from side to side. He *had* to get up—

He heard Blackthorn open the canvas bag, dump its meager contents: the pistol; the fob; the blanket; items of dirty clothing—

"Nothing!"

He flung the bag on the ground.

"You've not been Christian, either of you. I think I'll repay that in kind before I ride on—"

He pointed down at Jared. The bruised hand seemed huge, the fingertip even bigger:

"I'm glad I didn't take your sight. I want you to watch what happens next. William Blackthorn's fought boys and made 'em grow up right while they bled. Done the same thing for girls in a different way—"

The gray-haired man tossed his hat on the ground and unfastened the buckle of his belt.

Frantic, Jared drove his right hand toward the knife lying in the ashes. Blackthorn paused in unbuttoning his trousers, raised one leg and brought his boot down on Jared's fingers.

Again Jared cried out. His limp hand flopped into the coals. He smelled burning hair, pulled his hand back as pain seared it—

"Amanda—*run!*"

She tried. But the stranger was faster. He caught her around the waist, laughing. Her shrieks stilled the birds in the nearby thickets. Blackthorn's horse stamped and blew noisily.

Still laughing, the Reverend tumbled to the ground, the girl trapped in his arms. Jared dragged himself to hands and knees. He tried to move fast but he couldn't. Blackthorn flung Amanda on her back, fastened hands at the throat of her dress and ripped.

Jared kept crawling toward the big man as he straddled Amanda's thighs. Blackthorn plucked aside her gray chemise, fondled the small nubbed mounds of her breasts. He bent down, nuzzling her cheek:

"Thy lips, o my spouse—drop as the honeycomb—honey and milk—are under thy tongue—"

Jared realized the crazed preacher was quoting scripture. He careened to his feet, took one faltering step and fell.

Wailing, Amanda pounded fists against Blackthorn's ribs. But he overpowered her by sheer size and weight, ripping and tearing until her body was bared below the waist.

"—the smell of thy garments is like—"

Jared saw a bruised hand draw out a huge, stiffened penis; press it down on the tiny mound where a few dark hairs had sprouted to signal the start of womanhood.

"—is like the smell of Lebanon—"

Blackthorn wedged a knee between Amanda's thighs, forced them open.

"A garden—enclosed—is my sister," he grunted. *"My—spouse—a spring shut up—a fountain—sealed—"*

Blackthorn jerked his hips forward. Amanda cried out and arched her back. Jared started crawling again, around the fire toward the interlocked bodies.

Amanda struggled feebly now that Blackthorn had penetrated her. The girl's eyes were closed. Her palms pressed against the ground. The tall man's trousers and drawers hung around his calves. His coat tails flapped over his humping buttocks.

Jared heard the shrill, hurt screams of his cousin; tried to shout:

"You—filthy bastard—I'll kill—"

Pain weakened his braced arms. The ground lifted toward his eyes with a strange, terrifying slowness—then slammed his face.

Time went by. How much, he didn't know. Once more he fought upward, catching a glimpse of Amanda. Her dark hair was fouled with dirt. She bit her lips and flailed her head back and forth and beat the ground, the cordage bracelet bouncing, *bouncing*—

Blackthorn convulsed. Groaned. Withdrew his dripping, bloodied organ and panted for air.

He pinched Amanda's chin between his fingers. His green eyes glowed in the sunrise. His yellow teeth bared in a grin:

"Now," he breathed, "Now you're worth something. Many a man won't pay to pleasure himself with a virgin your age. But once a girl's torn, that's another story. You'll finance my travels nicely—"

The words whined and echoed in Jared's mind as he pitched onto his side, blacking out. When he awoke sometime later, the gray horse, its owner and his cousin were gone.

IV

BEDRAGGLED AND heartsick, Jared ranged the clearing, trying to discover some sign of the trail Blackthorn had taken. On the clearing's east side he found a few low branches broken off. He knelt over them, gulping air and fighting off tears of rage.

He still could hardly believe the inhuman act he'd witnessed. But there was no denying Amanda had been abducted. By a lecher—a maniac—who called himself a man of God.

Guilt overwhelmed him for a moment. When Amanda had needed him most, he'd failed her. Just as he always failed. He couldn't excuse the failure on the grounds that he was ill—or that Blackthorn was too strong for him. He was supposed to take care of her—and he'd let her be kidnapped.

Well, now he had another responsibility. To *find* her—

The boy stumbled on through the brush for several hundred yards. He lost the trail. There were too many broken branches; too much brush disarranged by animals.

He shouted Amanda's name, heard it boom through the stillness of the woods. On the way back to the clearing, he had to sit down once. The physical punishment he'd taken at the hands of the self-styled preacher had left him almost without strength. He sat very still, cursing himself silently—oath after damning oath.

In the clearing, he collected the few belongings spilled from the canvas bag. The stranger had found nothing worthy of theft except Amanda. He'd left Jared his knife, his pistol, his clothing—

Stuffing them into the bag, he almost missed the fob partially buried in the

ashes of the dead fire. He flung the fob on top of the other things and jumped up—too fast. He swayed, sickeningly dizzy.

When the spell passed, he dragged the bag to the trees along the river. There he sat down again, trying to order his thoughts.

What Blackthorn wanted with Amanda, he couldn't imagine. Surely the man wasn't so vile and deranged that he'd do what he said—use her; sell her as a whore to pay for what he called his travels—

Travels, Jared said to himself. *Start there—travels.*

The man had left Nashville. There was a strong intimation of trouble connected with the departure. Blackthorn also had a cabin in the vicinity—

Where?

He needed to find someone who could tell him that—without delay.

Another of Blackthorn's remarks surfaced in his mind. A reference to someone named the judge, living nearby—

He glanced back toward the clearing, trying to guess where the judge's house might be. Toward the south or in the other direction?

He decided to go the latter way, to the winding Cumberland River. If he found no house, he'd work southward again.

Groaning, he stood up. He stumbled to the edge of Stone's River and checked the position of the sun. He set off as fast as his bruised, aching body permitted, trying to shut from his mind the images of Amanda's rape. She wouldn't be eleven until the summer—and Blackthorn had savaged her—

Better that he'd slain her outright!

No, don't think of that.

Find the house of the judge.

Someone—*anyone*—to tell you where Blackthorn might have gone.

V

THE TREES grew thickly here, screening the source of the sound Jared was too dull-witted to identify. He was weak; damnably weak. The fever and Blackthorn's pounding made him stagger like a drunken man. Branches stung his face as he stumbled toward brighter light that indicated an end to the dim woods—

He emerged on open grass. He took a few more steps, blinded by the sunlight. He scuffed a boot in dirt. He was standing on some sort of smooth track—

Only then did he recognize the thundering sound on his left. A horse—

In a whirl of dust, a big bay stallion with a black-skinned rider pounded along the track. Jared had walked directly into the rider's path. The frightened black saw him, frantically reined in—

"*Whoa, Truxton! Hol' up—!*"

Jared hurled himself toward the far side of the track. Halfway there, he stumbled and went down.

Sharp front hoofs dark against the sky, the bay stood on hind legs, neighing wildly—

The last thing Jared saw were those hoofs slashing down toward his head.

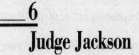

6
Judge Jackson

A SWEET smell drifted through the dark of Jared's waking mind. He didn't know the origin of the pleasant odor then, and it wasn't until later that he learned it came from the blossoms on scores of apple trees surrounding the two blockhouses.

A passage connected the main blockhouse and a similar one for guests. It was in this last that he opened his eyes, resting on unbelievably clean linen.

He discovered his battered ribs and hand were bandaged. He blinked, saw a slender, sinewy black woman drift into his line of sight and bend over him. Her cheeks glowed. So did the whole room. May sunlight fell through one large window whose shutters had been opened all the way.

From Jared's right, beyond his range of vision, fragrant blue smoke drifted. The black woman felt his forehead.

"Well, his eyes are open, Miz Rachel. Fever's gone, too."

Jared twisted his head to see the source of the smoke: a plainly dressed woman running to stoutness. At one time she might have been quite pretty, but sagging flesh, and strain suggested by her melancholy eyes, had left little more than a hint of beauty. She pulled a corncob pipe from between her teeth and laid it on a small table.

"I'm not so sure the young man will be thankful to be awake when the judge comes home," the woman said. To Jared: "Truxton is the prize horse in my husband's stable. You nearly lamed him by dashing out of the trees onto the race course."

Jared tried to sit up. The effort hurt. He tugged the wool nightshirt from under one arm. It itched ferociously.

"I didn't mean to startle the horse," he said. "I'm sorry it happened. Is the animal all right?"

"Yes."

"I was pretty worked up. Not thinking clearly—"

"Sick, too," said the black woman.

Jared nodded "I was trying to find help because my cousin was kidnapped—"

The white woman and the Negress exchanged quick glances.

"Where 'bouts?" asked the latter.

"We were stopped at a clearing on your property. Near the river, south of your race track. How did I get here?"

"Grooms brung you in. You were mutterin' something fierce," the black woman said.

"Early yesterday," said the white woman.

"Yesterday—!" Jared started to struggle upright again. The white woman pressed him back. She had strong hands.

"Last evening, the judge fetched the doctor from Nashville to look you over. The doctor said you weren't to get out of bed for three days."

"I can't lie here!" he exclaimed. "I've got to find my cousin!"

"What's your name, boy?" the Negress asked.

"Jared Kent. My cousin Amanda—"

"A girl?" the white woman interrupted.

He nodded. "She's not yet eleven. She and I met a man in a clearing—"

The black woman raised a hand. "Hold on, you're sashayin' way too fast. You and this cousin—you're not from these parts?"

The white woman picked up her pipe. She tapped cold dottle into her palm, walked to the window and let the dottle blow away in the pouring golden sunlight.

"I should think that's obvious from his speech, Clara. Where do you come from, Master Kent?"

"New England."

He said it carefully. He didn't know the identities of these people. Yet there was something about the white woman's name that struck a responsive note in his mind. What was it?

They were watching him. He finished his thought:

"We have no relatives left back there, so we were heading for New Orleans—"

"You've relatives in New Orleans, then?"

"No, not a one."

A growling in Jared's belly told him it was empty. But food didn't matter—nothing mattered except the horror of what had befallen Amanda. And he'd been sleeping a day and a half! Who could say where Blackthorn might have gotten to by now?

"I just can't do what that doctor said," he told the white woman. "I don't mean to act ungrateful, but I can't, Mrs.—"

"Jackson. Rachel Jackson."

Jared was startled. Of course that was it. The judge whom Blackthorn had mentioned was Judge Andrew Jackson, the Tennessee soldier. He should have guessed that was who Blackthorn was talking about. He remembered an account in the *Republican* that stated Jackson's home was near Nashville. It was the name Rachel that had almost brought the memory to the surface. From pressroom gossip, Jared knew a few things about this woman who was Jackson's wife.

"Mrs. Jackson," he went on, "I have to go after the man who—attacked my cousin."

Clara frowned, glanced sharply at her mistress. Mrs. Jackson asked:

"How was your cousin attacked?"

"She was raped."

The woman turned pale at the forbidden word. "And, as you said, she was then carried off—?"

"Yes, ma'am."

"By whom?"

"A man who claimed he lived in a cabin near here. A man with part of his right ear torn out. He pretended to be a minister. Acted friendly. That was a trick, so he could catch us off guard and steal our belongings—"

Quickly, Jared searched the puncheon-floored bedroom. He spotted the canvas bag sitting in a corner. The Negress noticed his concern:

"Everything's there. We took your clothes out, though. Boiled 'em good 'cause they were crawlin'."

"Tell me the name of the man," Rachel Jackson said.

"He called himself Reverend Blackthorn."

"Exactly what I suspected," Mrs. Jackson whispered. "That trash—!"

"You know him?"

"Sure we do," Clara said. "William Blackthorn isn't any more of a preacher

than I'm a brood mare in the judge's stable. Only way Blackthorn got the title reverend was by givin' it to himself.''

Jared looked puzzled. ''Why would he do that?''

Rachel Jackson said, ''Visiting evangelists who hold camp meetings are popular up in Kentucky and Ohio. Blackthorn has a certain talent for eloquence, and if he rides into a hamlet a hundred miles from here and identifies himself as a preacher, it's doubtful anyone asks to see his credentials from a divinity school. I'm afraid he found that masquerading as a minister could pay handsomely. The evangelist keeps the offering money after expenses are met, you see. Blackthorn leaves several times a year and comes home with enough cash for three or four months. The Nashville clergy have sent out circulars to the larger towns, but it isn't possible to warn every settlement in two states. I pity the poor people who've been taken in by his sham piety.''

''Around here, nobody's fooled,'' Clara said. ''Why, just this past year, Blackthorn's been in the stocks for fightin' and raisin' hel—the devil. Like Miz Jackson says—trash.''

''If he was bound for his cabin, he won't be there long,'' the judge's wife added.

''How do you know, ma'am?''

''Because three days ago, a number of gentlemen in Nashville arranged to have him run out of town.''

''Yes, he hinted about that. I didn't know whether to believe him.''

''It's true. William Blackthorn is a vicious, illiterate brute. Half crazy, I think. He's gouged out more eyes and bitten off more fingers than anyone can count.''

Jared showed his wrapped hand. ''He tried that with me. He hit me enough so that I couldn't stop him. He talked about taking Amanda with him, on what he called his travels. I didn't understand then—''

''Now you do,'' said Clara in a grim voice.

Jared nodded. ''He carried on about selling Amanda. Selling her like a who— a prostitute,'' he amended. ''I couldn't believe any man would do a thing like that.''

''William Blackthorn would,'' Rachel Jackson said. ''I pity you, but I pity your little cousin more. Ten years old. Imagine—!''

''She's well developed for her age. Blackthorn mistook her for older.''

''When the judge be back, Miz Rachel?'' Clara asked.

''Nightfall or later.'' She turned to the boy. ''My husband is major general of the state militia—''

''Yes, ma'am, I know. Some teamsters I met at the ferry on the Cumberland said that he and the militia had beaten Weatherford's Creek Indians—''

''At the Horse Shoe Bend. There's talk the judge may be given a major generalship in the regular army and put in command of the Seventh Military District. The war with the British is going badly in the north and east. Now there's fear of an attack by sea, somewhere down on the Gulf. Mobile Bay, New Orleans—those may need to be defended. The judge is setting some affairs in Nashville, in case he receives orders from Washington.''

''The judge ought to be receivin' orders to rest for a year!'' the black woman declared.

Rachel Jackson smiled sadly. ''You know he'd tear any order of that kind to pieces.''

''But he shouldn't be so active in his condition! It's bad enough that he's got a ball in his lung from duelin' Mr. Dickinson—''

"I can't score him too severely for that, Clara. He published his card in the paper because of me. Because of what Dickinson said—"

"Any man shot once would rest a while! But he's carryin' a double dose of lead!" The black woman explained to Jared, "One of the Benton brothers shot the judge in the left arm last November. Another duel. Then he drank bad water while he was chasin' the Indians, and he says it's fluxed his bowels for life."

All of that confirmed what Jared had read about the Tennessee lawyer and soldier. Judge Jackson, as he preferred to be called, was a gamester; a brawler; a man who settled affairs of honor by dueling, illegal though that might be. Jared wasn't overly interested in the judge's health, however. Amanda was all that counted. If he had to hobble, he was going to hunt for her. He announced that intention—

And Rachel Jackson again shook her head:

"No, young man. You'll obey doctor's orders—and speak to the judge when he returns."

"Ma'am, I can't wait for—"

"Indeed you can. If William Blackthorn actually went to his cabin, he's probably left again. Didn't you hear me say he was ordered to leave the vicinity of Nashville? He was given twenty-four hours—I suspect he's already taken your cousin out of the area. Still, if it will put your mind at ease, I'll have Culley, one of our nigras, ride over to Blackthorn's cabin immediately. He'll be back before the judge is, I expect. When the judge gets home, you can discuss your plans with him. I'm sure he'll take a personal interest—"

She smiled, somehow emphasizing the melancholy of her eyes:

"My husband doesn't mind flouting the law and putting a pistol ball through a man's head. But free-style fighting—Blackthorn's forte—is intolerable to him. The judge was one of those responsible for getting Blackthorn out of Nashville."

The black woman patted Jared's hand.

"You rest. I'll bring you up some food."

The two women left the room. Presently he heard a mule clatter by beneath the window of the log house.

He obeyed the women's orders because they made sense. He realized he was still too weak to travel any distance with speed.

Yet inactivity tortured him. In his mind, he re-lived every moment of the rape for which he blamed himself. Over and over, he promised himself he'd kill Blackthorn when he saw him.

And see him he would. Somewhere. Somehow.

II

WHEN HE woke again, around dusk, he discovered a mug of molasses and a dish of berries in honey on the table beside the bed.

He spooned out some of the fruit and honey mixture, relishing its flavor. The molasses he found thick and unpalatable.

As he ate, he tried to recall what he knew about the judge's wife. Some scandal having to do with her marriage, wasn't it? A scandal twenty years old or better—

Slowly it came back. She had been married to another man. He had divorced her. Jackson, a rising Tennessee lawyer who had suggested the name for his own

state, promptly married the young woman, only to discover that her husband hadn't obtained a divorce decree at all. He'd merely petitioned for, and received the grant of, an enabling act that would *permit* divorce if he could show reason why the marriage should be dissolved.

The first husband—Robards, Roberds, something like that—had churlishly waited two years before seeking the actual divorce. His grounds became his former wife's illegal and adulterous marriage to the young Jackson.

If Jared recalled the story right, the charge was technically true. The story was frequently circulated in Boston, because Jackson had served in the national legislature, and because the tale illustrated, for easterners anyway, the crudity of western mores.

The double humiliation of his wife being divorced *and* branded an adulteress supposedly weighed on Jackson's mind. Though he and Rachel had been remarried in legal fashion after the divorce, a stigma remained. Insulting remarks about living with a fallen woman were one of the main reasons Jackson was prone to calling out so many men. Jared wondered whether it might also be a reason for Rachel Jackson's strained look—

In any case, Jackson's propensity for shedding blood—his own as well as that of his opponents—was well known in the east. And mocked.

As Jared was finishing the berries, the black woman brought in a lamp to light the room.

"Is the judge back?" he asked.

Clara frowned. "No. Culley is, though."

"Did he find—?"

She shook her head. "Just like we figured—he's gone. The place is stripped bare. Culley said the tracks of Blackthorn's horse were 'bout a day old."

"Surely someone knows where the man was headed!"

"I don't," Clara answered. "Mebbe the judge will."

The door closed with a soft click. Jared pressed both hands over his eyes.

III

A RAPPING noise wakened Jared sometime later. He started up in bed, seeing a long, grotesque shadow on the wall.

The figure at the foot of the bed was hardly less grotesque. Jared had never seen a man quite so spindly, with such narrow, almost feminine shoulders and long, high-waisted legs. The man leaned on a cane. Even glanced at, he was a veritable exhibit of afflictions: a left arm held stiffly at his side; a hunched posture—perhaps the ball lodged in his lung pained him? Pox marks pitted his face. One cheek bore a white, badly healed sword scar.

Yet for all his ungainliness and his general air of physical ruin, the judge—for surely this must be he—had a strangely commanding aura as he stood tapping his cane and studying his uninvited guest. A crest of thick white hair rose above his forehead. His unblinking eyes were a glacial blue. When he spoke, his voice was rather high; almost shrill. But Jared had absolutely no urge to laugh.

"I've heard your story from Mrs. Jackson, Kent. If you'd lamed Truxton— one of my best studs—one of my main sources of income in his racing days— I'd pitch you out of that window yonder."

"I apologized to your wife for frightening the horse—"

"She told me."

"You're Judge Jackson?"

"I suspect," the other said in a dry way, hooking a chair with his boot and pulling it to the bedside. "Surely no one else could be such a catch-all of ills and aches and old bullets."

He settled into the chair, leaning forward with palms resting on the cane head. The blue eyes pinned Jared.

"I understand you ran afoul of Blackthorn—whom we should have caned till he couldn't walk."

"Yes, sir. He raped my cousin—"

"A young girl, I'm informed."

"Ten."

Jackson sniffed. "She isn't the first."

"Your wife sent a black man to the reverend's cabin—"

"Don't call him reverend! Satan has more right to the title than he does! The only place William Blackthorn's fit to preach is hell, and it's a shame he's taking so long to reach his destination. Yes, the girl's gone. Blackthorn too."

"They thought you might know where."

"I do not, because if I did, I wouldn't be here. I'd be on a horse going after him. I'd see he never maimed a man or molested a child again."

Jackson laid a bony hand on Jared's arm. "I appreciate your anxiety. We'll do our best to locate the blackguard. I presume you'll go after him—?"

"Wherever he is, Judge."

Jackson ruminated a moment, scratching the tough white skin of the sword scar.

"I believe you. I'm not overly fond of easterners, which I understand you are. But you've got a certain look about you—determined. It could fool many into thinking you're a Tennessean. That's a compliment, in case you missed it."

Jared couldn't even articulate a thank-you. The judge made him more than a little nervous.

Jackson's stare remained fixed and hard. "How old are you, Kent?"

"Sixteen this coming October."

"And you trudged all the way here from the east?"

"That's right."

"Did you have any money?"

"Only what I made working along the way."

Jackson thumped his cane on the floor. "By God, at your age that's quite an accomplishment! You must have had a mighty good reason to undertake such a trip."

Worried that he might face this kind of questioning, Jared had barely heard the judge's praise. He kept his voice as level as possible:

"Yes. Our kin—my cousin's and mine—are no longer living. We were making our way to New Orleans."

Jackson scrutinized him a moment.

"What are you running from?" he asked abruptly.

In confusion, Jared answered, "Is it that obvious—?"

"No youngster would travel as far as you have without a compelling reason. You said your kinfolk are dead—"

"That's the truth."

"Are you a runaway apprentice?"

"No, Judge."

"In trouble with the law?"

Jared knew he couldn't lie successfully for long. He nodded. "The Massachusetts law."

"Serious trouble?"

"I shot a man."

Silence. Then:

"In good cause?"

"Yes, sir."

Another pause, even longer. At last Jackson shrugged:

"Well, I've done the same. We won't pursue it unless you want to—"

"I'd rather not, sir."

"All right. I like your cut so we'll leave the matter closed. However, I'd advise you to steer shy of the Gulf Coast for a while."

Relieved, Jared said, "Your wife did mention possible military action there—"

"I have a feeling the British will attack somewhere on the Gulf. The numbskulls in the department of the army have thus far botched all engagements with the enemy, and I reckon it's going to be up to the west to do the work right. It'd be just like Johnny Bull to sneak around the back way, thinking we're napping out here. If I get command of the Seventh District, we won't be napping."

Again he stabbed Jared with those glacial eyes:

"Were you ever in the military?"

What in the world did that have to do with Amanda? the boy thought, resentful. But the judge's intimidating stare, plus Jared's feeling that he owed the man politeness, made him answer the question:

"The navy, for two cruises, under Captains Hull and Bainbridge on *Constitution*."

"Well, our seamen have acquitted themselves better than the fools and charlatans in charge of the army. By the Eternal, if they just give me a chance, I'll show those redcoats how Americans can fight!"

The emaciated man—nearly fifty, or at least looking it—screwed up his features into a caricature of menace. Only Jared guessed Jackson was serious:

"I despise Englishmen damned near as much as I do the butchering Cherokees and that lot." He touched the old scar. "I got this in the Revolution—"

Abruptly, Jackson compressed his lips and shook his head.

"You'll forgive me. I've been thinking about nothing except the Red Sticks for months, and now that we've cleaned up that business, the other enemy's on my mind."

Still trying to be courteous, Jared said, "I understand. My grandfather was in the Revolution too, as a matter of fact."

"Was he!"

"At Monmouth Court House, a British ball gave him a limp for the rest of his life."

"I acquired this charming mark when I was fifteen, riding dispatch in the Waxhaw district of South Carolina. Some of Tarleton's dragoons caught me. One of his snotty subalterns sabered me because I wasn't properly deferential. My brother Hugh died of wounds in the war, and my brother Robert of illness. My mother went aboard one of those British prison hulks to nurse the American captives and contracted ship fever and *she* died—"

"I'd say you have plenty of reason for wanting to do the British damage."

"I hate every goddamned one of them!" Then he smiled, wryly. "I do tend

to get carried away on the subject. However, I realize another subject is of more importance to you. So if you'll forgive my preoccupation with my enemy, we'll see what we can discover about yours—''

He stood, leaning on his cane and coughing, his head averted toward the open window. The mellow darkness billowed the scent of apple blossoms into the room. Distantly Jared heard soft, slurred voices singing an unfamiliar melody.

Cane tapping, Jackson hobbled toward the door.

"I'll do all I can to find out whether our bogus reverend gave any indication of his destination, following the expression of our communal will that he remove himself—''

Jackson turned, whipped the cane across in front of his chest in such a swift arc that Jared jerked back even though the cane's tip was several feet from his nose.

"Remove himself or be shot down like the dog he is!'' Jackson exclaimed. "Too bad we gave him a choice!''

He yanked the door open.

"I'll order several of my best niggers to make inquiry in Nashville tomorrow. In the meantime—''

He pointed the cane at Jared.

"—you don't give my wife any cause for worry. Take what you're fed and stay abed as you're instructed and we'll all get along splendidly.''

IV

JARED CHAFED under the enforced delay that resulted from Judge Jackson's absolute domination of the estate he called the Hermitage. The property, six hundred and forty rolling acres with a slave population of twenty, was centered around the crude but somehow comfortable two-story blockhouse attached to the other, similar one in which Jared recuperated.

He was invited to the main house as soon as the doctor removed a few of the bandages and pronounced him well enough to get up. The Hermitage proper consisted of one huge room on ground level. The room had a mammoth hearth, a puncheon floor and massive smoke-blackened joists overhead.

Upstairs, Judge and Mrs. Jackson and their miscellany of children—three or four, Jared was never precisely sure—had their quarters. One of the small boys was named Andrew Jackson, Junior. Jared couldn't keep the names of the others straight, since they were usually all mixed up with the slave children with whom they played. He did learn from Clara, who controlled the kitchen attached to the back of the house, that all the children were adopted. To add to the burden of being publicly called an adulteress—a burden already turning her into a recluse—Rachel Jackson had proved barren. Clara said scandalmongers called it Divine punishment. But never within the judge's hearing.

Various men in military uniform came and went on horseback at all hours of the day and night. Jared soon decided the judge seldom slept. At the end of Jared's fifth day at the Hermitage, Mrs. Jackson informed him that the judge had indeed been named to a generalship in the regular army as a result of his spectacular rout of the Creeks. Plans were being made for his early departure to the south, where he still anticipated a British thrust.

Several times Jared wandered into the main house, searching for the judge and

failing to find him. He began to fear Jackson had forgotten his promise about gathering information on Blackthorn's possible destination. Then, one noon, he was abruptly told that a huge banquet was being prepared for evening. "Last meal the judge figures to eat here for a spell. You too, I guess," Clara smiled.

Jared stuffed himself sampling everything set out on the thick plank table in the lower room: slabs of bear and venison; tender meat from ducks and wild turkeys; heaping bowls of vegetables and fresh, mealy cornbread; maple sugar lumps tied on a string for a confection—and the strongest coffee he'd ever tasted. The judge spent most of the meal railing against the British.

Afterward, he cleared the lower room of blacks, the assorted small boys and his wife. But he instructed Jared to remain.

Jackson produced a stoneware jug, pointed to a chair.

"Pull that up here close to me, Kent."

Looking like a long-legged bird, he folded himself into his own chair with a groan. He tilted the jug over his forearm, swigged, then wiped the neck and handed the jug to Jared:

"Treat it with respect. That's the sweetest sipping since God made Eden. Tennessee whiskey. I reckon you're old enough. Go on! Take a good slug—"

Jared tilted the jug over his arm, hopefully showing the grace Jackson displayed. But he slopped liquor on his sleeve as the judge added:

"—because I have glum news."

Some of the whiskey scalded down Jared's throat. With unsteady hands, he held onto the jug. The judge's expression was unsmiling.

"Yes, sir?" Jared prompted

"One of my niggers finally caught a whiff of Blackthorn's trail."

Jared waited.

"Before he left town, Blackthorn visited the bar of the City Hotel. He boasted that he'd be glad to leave. Said a man could do better where there's less law. He mentioned the sort of place he meant. St. Louis."

Jared wiped his mouth, feeling the whiskey burn his belly. He set the jug on the puncheons near the ferrule of Jackson's cane. The tall man looked wasted and weary. Clara had told Jared that while the judge was off commanding the militia against the Creeks, his body had pained him so greatly, he could neither sit down nor rest in bed. So he'd ordered a sapling spiked to a pair of posts in his tent, and spent hour after hour standing, one arm and then the other hanging over the sapling for support.

"St. Louis—" Jared repeated. "That's a long way off."

Jackson's eyes showed more animation:

"Northwest, all the way to the Mississippi. But if you've the gumption to go there, maybe you can catch the bastard."

Jared nodded, his face unhappy. "I'll go."

"I thought you would." Jackson picked up the jug, drank. "St. Louis is the capital of the new Missouri Territory. Your best source of information would be the governor."

"I'll remember that."

Jackson pointed a skeletal finger.

"Don't get your hopes too high, though. If Blackthorn's gone any further, you're pretty near done. By yourself, you'd have as much chance of locating him west of St. Louis as you would of finding the Ouragon."

Jared frowned. "The what?"

"Oh, that's what they call the damn river that's supposed to cut from the

Missouri to the Columbia but doesn't. A myth—the Ouragon. You'd better make a speedy departure, Kent. Get to St. Louis before Blackthorn fades away just like the dreams of finding the Ouragon did, once the beaver men started heading up the Missouri to see what the country was really like—'' He sniffed. "You do realize Blackthorn could have been throwing out a false scent, too?''

"And not be there, but someplace else? I do.''

Jackson whacked the ferrule of his cane on the floor. "All right, then. You know there's a chance it's a blind trail. But don't look so damn grieved! It might not be. You've got a scent to follow—which you didn't have before. That'd be plenty for a Tennessean!''

"Well, I'm not a Tennessean!'' Jared shot back.

"That's very plain, Kent, very plain. I changed my estimate of you since that first night we talked. It's no less complimentary, mind—just different.'' Jackson didn't speak with malice; only bluntly. "I've glimpsed you around the property once or twice. Your whole manner fairly yells your dislike of these parts. You're not one of those goddamned, ass-kissing Federalists, are you?''

Jared tried to give as stern a stare as he was receiving:

"No, sir! The opposite. I just never wanted to wind up in the west. My—''

He hesitated, then poured it out, relieved somehow, yet pained:

"—my father homesteaded in Ohio for a couple of years. I was born there. My father failed as a farmer. After Indians killed my mother, he went back east. He never got over the failure, either. He turned into a drunkard, disappeared—I never saw him again.''

Jackson's craggy features seemed to soften. "And then you had to come back out here to escape the law. I can appreciate why you don't think much of the west—and less of your present situation.''

Jared was thankful he didn't have to amplify his answer; didn't have to explain that what really tormented him was not his parents' failure but his fear that he was doomed to repeat it in a land that invited failure. He'd certainly made a good start, losing Amanda as he had—

After a moment, he said, "Regardless of how I feel, Judge, I'm going to try to find my cousin.''

He thought he saw a flicker of approval in the judge's eyes. "You know,'' Jackson said in a surprisingly gentle voice, "you're nothing special in these parts, Kent.''

"What do you mean?''

"I mean, it must seem to you that the whole world has its eye turned on you. Because of the trouble back east—''

Jared nodded at the uncomfortable truth.

"That's not so. Out here, what a man is counts for more than what he was—''

And what I am is my parents' child.

"—and for good reason. If you checked the history of people who settled in Tennessee, for instance, you'd find plenty of cases just like yours. Some came here for land. Some came because they had a yearning to see new country, and when they got tired or the yearning wore itself out, they stopped. But quite a few came here because they had to—and that's where you fit. You're a westerner, like it or not.''

Then I'm condemned.

But all he said aloud was, "I guess I am.''

"Hell, boy, it's not that grim! This is a bountiful land—''

"Oh, yes, I've heard that—often."

"Don't sound so sour! It's the truth! I love the land out here—and the people. They may lack manners, but that lack's more than made up in fortitude. I've had some dealings with your part of the country, you know. I was in the Congress and the Senate a while, until I got my belly full and came back here to spend six of the happiest years of my life, on the bench of the state supreme court. I hated the capital about as much as you hate the idea of going to St. Louis. When I used to walk into a room crowded with all those rich, educated politicians cozying up to each other, trading favor for favor, vote for vote like they belonged to some private club, I could feel them looking down their noses at me. Backwoodsman! they were thinking. Not fit to help run a country! Back east, some of our *gentlemen* don't put much stock in common people. Got to keep those poor, dumb backwoodsmen in line! They don't know what's good for themselves, so the members of the private club will have to show 'em. In Tennessee, it's different. We *believe* in the kind of government Mr. Jefferson professed to admire but somehow never managed to put into practice. I'd like to see a western man in the presidency one day. A man who understood what the freedom of this country's all about—by the Eternal, I would! Salt of the earth, westerners—"

Jackson sounded almost sad. He shook his head:

"The only blood relations I have in all the world."

After a moment, he went on, "You know I'm exaggerating. Blackthorn's a western man—the worst kind. I think the east has a bigger quota of Blackthorns, though. Only difference is, they do their killing and maiming with words and money—"

Not wanting to launch into an argument, Jared said, "I'll agree with you from the standpoint of kindness, Judge. I've been wonderfully treated at the Hermitage—"

Jackson shrugged, brushed a bony fingertip across one eye. "Nothing special about your welcome here. Rachel takes to lost boys. You've seen the pack we're bringing up. Pity she couldn't bear her own," he sighed. "She's a wonderful woman—as I'm constantly forced to remind the sons of bitches who defame her. Well—"

He braced both hands on the top of his cane and stood, wincing in pain.

"Are you sufficiently well to ride, Kent?"

"I think so. Most of my aches are gone—"

"Nothing broken, thank God. You were lucky Blackthorn's thoughts were on your cousin. Else you couldn't go after him. He'd have crippled you."

"I'll give him plenty of his own if I find him," Jared promised.

Jackson smiled. "By the Eternal, I think you will." He laid a lean hand on the boy's shoulder. "Culley will have a horse for you at sunrise."

"Oh, Judge, I can't pay for—"

"Who said pay? I'm making an investment!" He flourished the cane. "An investment in the punishment of the good reverend. I'm investing a horse and food and some sturdy frontier clothing and five dollars in gold Culley will wrap in a kerchief. I'll be off for Nashville before daylight myself. We're mustering men—" His eyes actually looked merry a moment. "The Tennessee regulars could use you, Jared Kent."

"You know I've got other fighting to do, Judge."

With myself.

With my fear—

"Yes," Andrew Jackson said. "Bend down and pick up that jug and let's drink to it, what do you say?"

V

AT DAWN, Clara filled him with a hearty breakfast. Culley gave him the kerchief containing five gold pieces, then brought the horse to the front of the Hermitage.

Rachel Jackson handed Jared an unexpected gift—a black-bound Bible with a ribbon marker in it.

"The judge has left for Nashville—" she began.

"Yes, he told me he was going early."

She smiled in a melancholy way. "He's not the most religious man who ever walked the earth. At least not so you would notice in public. He might think you need a jug of whiskey more than you need that book. But perhaps it'll sustain you better than whiskey in the weeks ahead."

A bit uncomfortable, Jared ran a hand over the pebbled cover of the Bible. "Mrs. Jackson, I thank you very much. For everything."

"I pray you'll find your cousin in St. Louis."

He tucked the Bible into his canvas bag. "I will." Their expressions said neither of them fully believed it.

Jared swung up into the saddle. "Goodbye, Mrs. Jackson."

"Goodbye, Jared. God guide you in your search."

7
Pursuit to St. Louis

ON THE twentieth of July, 1814, Jared Kent approached St. Louis from the south, riding Jackson's sorrel mare along the west bank of the wide, sun-glaring river. He'd followed the river shore since ferrying across two days earlier.

Necessity had turned him into a passable rider. The sorrel was a gentle animal. Even so, he'd been thrown three times during his first two days on the road. Having thus demonstrated her mastery, the horse settled down and Jared traveled the rest of the distance without mishap—if you discounted the brutal aches at the end of each day. By early July his body was more limber; accustomed to the up-and-down rhythm of riding.

He reined into a grove of cottonwoods on a slight rise overlooking the Mississippi. From there he surveyed the town ahead. St. Louis shimmered in the intense heat.

Sweat slicked Jared's body under the heavy shirt and trousers the Judge's wife had appropriated from one of the slaves at the Hermitage. His untrimmed hair was tied at the nape of his neck with a thong. His hands and face had turned a dark brown from exposure to the elements, and the skin was marked with dozens of insect bites that itched ferociously. He looked tall and fit sitting there. But he

didn't feel fit. The insides of his legs were still raw from long hours in the saddle. And during every one of those hours, guilt and the sense of his own inadequacy had been his constant companions.

He dismounted. As he scratched at a puffy bite on the back of his left hand, he gazed at the canvas bag hanging over the sorrel's flank. The Bible that Rachel Jackson had given him had gone unread across all the miles of forest and prairie. Although he'd sat in the family's box pew at Christ Church often enough in his boyhood, he'd never been especially religious, nor particularly attuned to the meaning of the Scriptures, the prayers and the preaching. He doubted there was much God could do to help him in the present situation. The outcome had probably been decided way back in Tennessee, when his blundering cost Amanda her freedom. Very likely his long journey had been for nothing—

Or almost for nothing. It absolved him of a little of his guilt. But only a very little.

Caught in the pessimistic mood, he gazed westward to gentle hills blurred by the midsummer haze. For miles on end, long prairie grass whispered in the wind. A lifeless landscape. Lifeless as his own hope, perhaps—

He tethered the mare and clambered down to the bank. He knelt and cupped river water in his mouth. It was warm; cloudy with silt. But it refreshed him.

He poured several handfuls over his head, shook off the excess, then went back up the slope to the mare, still a little surprised at the size of the town less than a mile away.

He'd expected a frontier hamlet. Instead, he saw two-story houses, church steeples and sizable commercial buildings. How large was St. Louis? Several thousand at least, he guessed.

Mounting up, he continued along the river bank. Insects buzzed loudly and constantly. The mare kept flicking her tail to drive away fat green flies.

Presently horse and rider reached the low limestone flat that provided a natural setting for the buildings overlooking the river. Along the St. Louis waterfront, Jared counted more than forty river craft tied up: long keelboats, flatboats, broadhorns, some of their muscular crewmen loitering in the blistering sun. Black men in tattered clothing unloaded cargo into wagons and carts. Here and there, elegant gentlemen in frock coats and beaver hats opened snuff boxes or puffed long cigars while overseeing the arrival of goods.

In mid-river, a ferry scow carrying six horsemen and a small wagon floated toward the docks. Over on the Illinois side, another wagon was waiting, this one big and canvas-topped. Near it, half a dozen miniature figures—a man, a woman, four bonneted little girls—watched the ferry's progress.

Anxious to cross the river, Jared thought somberly. *Can't wait to enter the promised land—the fools.*

On the trip from Nashville, he'd passed other families like the one on the ferry. The people carried their worldly possessions in rickety wagons or packed in bags on a string of horses. They usually greeted him with enthusiasm. He was going in their direction. The best direction; the *only* direction—

West.

Leaning to the left, Jared spat in the dirt.

Then he gave a gentle tug to the mare's rein and turned up into the town proper, following a procession of three high-wheeled oxcarts.

Coughing in the dust that clouded up behind them, he listened to the French and English curses of the sweating drivers. He smiled at the monotonous profanity. Unlike that family waiting over in Illinois, the cart drivers had been

around St. Louis a while. They knew the realities. For them there was no dream here, only a laborious job of coaxing and whipping dumb oxen one more block—

He passed a large limestone warehouse displaying a signboard that said *Manuel Lisa*. The business of the warehouse was apparent from the bales stacked in rows outside. Jared wrinkled his nose at the gamy stench of the furs.

He spent an hour jogging around the frontier town. He had to admit he'd seldom seen a place so sharp in contrasts, or so bursting with rowdy life.

Even the houses contrasted. There were old French residences, identifiable by the logs being set vertically, rather than horizontally, American style. There were newer buildings of Spanish stucco; even a few homes so squarely built and neatly bricked, he would have sworn he was back in Boston.

Many of the people in the busy streets appeared quite well-to-do. Others had the scruffy look of riffraff. And he was surprised to see quite a few Indians in blankets, beaded shirts and quilled trousers of animal skin. Many of them congregated at an open-air market. Bartering for the various items of trade goods on display, they offered birchbark sacks and skins that held commodities unknown to the boy on horseback.

Near the market, he passed a small jeweler's shop. The proprietor blocked the doorway as if reluctant to permit his three Indian customers to enter. The jeweler held a tray of glass eyes. The Indians were examining them with great interest.

A few moments later, Jared was forced to the side of the street by a half dozen whooping red men on horseback. They thundered by brandishing tomahawks and shooting arrows at a couple of mongrel dogs racing ahead of them. Jared thought it a cruel and disgusting exhibition—until he watched a couple of the arrows bounce off the flank of one of the dogs. He realized the arrows were blunt.

Though scowling, the whites on the street made no move to interfere. Jared suspected the reasons. The Indians came to trade with the local merchants, so they contributed to the town's economy. They also came armed. He hadn't seen one savage without a tomahawk.

Having retraced his route to the part of town nearest the river, he rode by a crowded café, a billiard parlor in which someone shot off a pistol, then a ramshackle building. From a second-floor gallery, a young woman in a gaily patterned wrapper beckoned to him. She opened the wrapper to show him her small breasts, smiled and ran her fingers down below her waist. She held up two fingers, questioningly.

Jared shook his head. She closed the wrapper and cursed him—whether in French or Spanish, he couldn't be certain.

Everywhere he rode, he searched faces. But his pessimism was deepening. What if Blackthorn had only been making idle conversation in Nashville? He could have ridden hundreds of miles for nothing.

He consoled himself with one thought. If Blackthorn had said nothing at all, he'd have been completely balked—with nowhere to search; no way to temper his stinging guilt.

A decent-looking tavern called the Green Tree offered him a room and a stable for the sorrel. A small black boy promised to rub her well and feed her amply. In the crowded taproom, Jared ate a platter of unfamiliar but tasty fried catfish washed down with strong beer.

To pay for everything, he handed the landlord his last dollar. The man placed the coin on a wood block. With expert strokes of a cleaver, he proceeded to chop the dollar into eight wedges. Bits, the westerners called them. He took six and returned two.

Jared ordered a second glass of beer and walked back to his table. The taproom was jammed with all sorts of people. Near him, several well-dressed gentlemen rose while one introduced two new arrivals: a beak-nosed older man identified as a Mr. Moses Austin. The younger man with him was his son Stephen. The group fell to discussing the current state of lead mining. Jared assumed the mines must be located somewhere in the vicinity.

The olive-skinned tap boy brought his beer. After a careful glance behind him, the boy leaned over and whispered in broken English:

"M'sieu Fink is presenting another show at eight tonight, Boston."

Jared's blue eyes widened. "How do you know where I'm from?"

"You come across the river, didn't you?"

"Yes."

"It's plain you're a Yankee—"

"And my home's Boston."

"Oh! Now I see. In St. Louis, the Spanish and my kind of people—"

"French?"

"Yes. To us, any American is a Boston. Until now I never met one who really was from that place. Listen, m'sieu—Fink's performance is at Lester's barn. Anyone can tell you how to find it. Cost you two bits for the wildest show you have ever seen."

"I don't know this man you're talking about."

"You don't know Mike Fink? Only the meanest damn fellow on the river. And the best shot! He puts on a splendid exhibition—" The boy's voice dropped. "For the climax, his woman, Mira Hodkins, she takes off every last stitch and places a can between her legs, so—" A quick gesture; a lewd smile. "Then Fink, he shoots it out. Unbelievable—!"

"I'll pass," Jared said. "I've got business to look after."

The boy shrugged, "Up to you, Boston. Not my fault if you don' know what's good." He walked off. Jared smiled and shook his head and gulped beer.

On his journey he'd acquired a fondness for strong drink. It helped ease worries about Amanda, not to mention the assorted aches and pains at the end of a day's riding. Though he wouldn't be sixteen until the fall, he felt twice that old.

The events of the past year had worked a great change. It showed in the way Jared carried himself; in the strength of his sunburned, insect-bitten hand curled around the beer glass; in the wary alertness of his blue eyes as he surveyed the patrons of the tavern and listened to the polyglot conversations he couldn't understand.

The beer made him sleepy. He went for a walk, still sweltering. He found a general store that sold newspapers, returned to his steaming room on the second floor of the tavern and latched the shutters to minimize the glare of the sun.

Using rags and the tepid water from an ewer on a stand, he washed. Then he flopped on the bed and scanned the front page of the *Missouri Gazette*.

His pressroom training made him critical of the typographical errors he found. He was contemptuous of the generally uneven inking. And much of the paper's content was local material, not of interest. Only a few items dealt with the war.

One article announced peace negotiations due to open in early August in Ghent, Belgium. Among the American delegates were Clay of Kentucky—Jared could almost hear the ring of the spittoon the night he'd crouched beside the dumbwaiter shaft—and John Quincy Adams, son of the former president. Whether the peace commissioners would be able to come to terms with Castlereagh's representatives was a moot question, the article said.

With a sigh, Jared folded the paper, laid it on his belly and closed his eyes. The war seemed far away, hardly touching this town on the edge of civilization. And he had other things to think about; all of them tainted by his guilt at having failed Uncle Gilbert in so many ways.

He slept for an hour. Then he tugged on his shirt and checked the powder and ball in his pistol. In the stable he asked the small black boy where he might find the governor. He was given directions to a farm a short way out of town:

"Gubnor Clark, he spend mos' of his time there in the summer."

Jared's brow hooked up. "Clark? What's his first name?"

"William. You know—the captain what went all the way to the ocean—?"

Surprised, Jared thanked the boy and went to saddle the mare.

II

TALL AND slightly stooped, General William Clark, governor of the Missouri Territory, welcomed Jared in the sitting room of the small but pleasant farmhouse.

Jared's horse had been taken away by a slave who tied the animal in a walnut grove at the rear of the property. The large open windows of the sitting room brought a banquet of aromas: the warm fragrance of summer grass; the sweet odors of flowers blooming all around the cottage. Sounds drifted in as well: slave children laughing at play; the buzz of bees in a hive near the house; the rustle of catalpa trees in the late afternoon wind.

The sitting room was plainly furnished, yet comfortable. Several things indicated the character of the man who made it his home. A russet-colored hound slept under a window. A rifle and game bag stood in one corner. An Indian calumet hung over the hearth. The windows opened onto the west where hills and sky blended into a hazy line below the disc of the sun.

"I knew a man named Kent many years ago," William Clark said. His voice still carried gentle Virginia accents. "At Fallen Timbers. He was from the east just as you are—"

"My father served at Fallen Timbers, General. Abraham Kent."

"You're Abraham's son?"

"Yes."

Clark's face broke into a grin. "By heaven, this makes an occasion!"

He fetched cups and a whiskey decanter from the mantel.

"How is your father? I've not heard of him since we soldiered together—wait, I did see one letter. Addressed to Merry Lewis—"

Clark's voice grew a little more somber when he mentioned the other man. Preceding Clark as governor at St. Louis, Meriwether Lewis had died on the Natchez Trace under mysterious circumstances some years earlier. There had been rumors of suicide brought on by mental depression.

Clark poured liquor. "As I recall, your father proposed to go with us to the Pacific. Merry and I welcomed the idea. But we heard nothing more."

Jared fidgeted on the Philadelphia settee, an elegant import perhaps added by Clark's wife. "My father died unexpectedly," he lied.

"I'm exceedingly sorry to hear that, Mr. Kent."

The general passed Jared his whiskey. He had removed his blue officer's coatee with its horizontal herringbones of braid. He lounged at a window in his shirtsleeves, sipping his drink.

"I must say you don't resemble Abraham very much."

"I'm told I take after my mother's side."

"Ah." Clark wiped the back of his hand across his sweating forehead. "You're a long way from home. Your family's business was printing and publishing, wasn't it?"

"Correct."

"You didn't find that to your taste?"

"The firm changed hands."

"Financial problems?"

"Something like that."

"Is it still operating as Kent's—wasn't that the name?"

"Kent and Son. Perhaps, I don't really know. I left Boston before the matter was settled. My cousin and I—a young girl—started for New Orleans—"

Clark looked startled. "By yourselves?"

"Yes."

"New Orleans is a long, long way from New England. Many people twice your age wouldn't even think about hazarding such a journey. Are there members of the family down south, may I ask?"

Jared had learned to avoid the trap the question posed:

"Distant relatives. We got as far as Nashville when we ran into trouble—"

In guarded language, he told the story of Amanda's kidnapping. He omitted the rape, finishing:

"The man responsible called himself Reverend Blackthorn. When they ran him out of Nashville, he mentioned coming to St. Louis. I assume he would have brought my cousin along—"

"He could have sold her as a bound girl anywhere along the route—"

"I realize. Still, I had to come looking for her. Judge Jackson said I should ask you whether you know Blackthorn, or have heard of him."

Clark pondered. "Blackthorn. We've no preacher in the city by that name."

Jared felt his worst fears confirmed. A few words from Clark and his journey was reduced to a futile exercise.

Clark saw his pain, said quickly, "He might have taken another name. A lot of men do that on the frontier. Describe this Blackthorn for me."

Jared had no trouble recalling the greenish eyes; the yellow teeth; the damaged earlobe. "—and he's a tall man. Exceptionally tall. With big hands, and a fondness for what they call free-for-all fighting."

"Of which we have more than enough," Clark smiled. "I wonder if it could be the fellow who went by the name Wilford Black."

Jared's blue eyes glinted as he sat forward. "Does the description fit?"

"Perfectly. We had this Black in jail a few months ago. He maimed an Osage brave who'd come in to trade some wild honey. There were witnesses to the fight, but afterward the Osage couldn't be found. Between the time of the attack and Black's arrest, there was a gap of several hours. The judge handling the case speculated that Black had killed the Osage in that interval and done away with the body. But without evidence, the most the court could do was throw Black in jail for a short time for disturbing the peace. I don't honestly know whether he's still in St. Louis—"

Jared was on his feet. "You didn't hear anything about a young girl with him, did you?"

"Nothing."

"Do you have any idea where he was staying when he was arrested?"

Clark thought again, his profile sharp against the sunlight falling through the western window.

"A place called Mrs. Cato's. Down near the river."

"A boarding house?"

Clark compressed his lips. "Not exactly. A brothel."

Jared set the whiskey aside unfinished. "I'd best ride back to town and inquire. I thank you for your help, General."

Clark waved. "Black may well have left us by now—no loss. We have too much scum in St. Louis. A town on the edge of civilization—and a river town at that—just normally attracts a bad element—"

Including murderers, Jared thought. What would Clark do if he knew he were talking to one?

As he turned to go, Clark put a hand on his arm:

"Mr. Kent—"

"Yes?"

"May I ask your plans if you fail to locate Wilford Black?"

"I have no plans," Jared confessed.

"Will you stay in St. Louis?"

"I doubt it."

"There are a good many fur traders looking for *engagés.* Hired men to go up the Missouri during the winter—"

"That's the last thing I'd do, General."

"You dislike this part of the country?"

"Intensely."

"Well—" Clark shrugged. "It's your affair. However, I must pass along one caution. Should you be lucky enough to find your man, remember that we have courts. Don't take justice into your own hands."

"General, I'll be honest with you. I couldn't make any promise about that. Blackthorn's mean and unpredictable—"

"So was Wilford Black, if they're one and the same. Still—"

"I'm sorry, General. I'll have to deal with him my own way."

"And we'll have to deal with you if it's the wrong way."

"Understood, sir."

Clark's eyes were unsmiling. "I hope so."

Jared wheeled and left.

III

MRS. CATO'S establishment stood on a dark, grubby street a block from the Mississippi. With his seven-shot tucked into his belt, Jared approached the dilapidated building shortly after the sun set around eight o'clock.

The street sloped down toward the lights of moored river boats. From a passage on his right, Jared heard sounds of struggle. He glanced around, perceiving two dim figures. One was a man on his knees; the other was battering him with both fists. Jared had no intention of interfering. His interest was centered on two lanterns above a high stoop. The sign of Mrs. Cato's, a man at the Green Tree had told him.

His heartbeat quickened as he approached the rickety steps. He climbed to the door, raised one hand to knock. Suddenly there was a ferocious crash inside. A woman screamed.

Jared tried the door. Unlocked. He stepped into a lightless foyer.

The racket grew louder. Men were shouting, laughing, cursing; women were shrieking; furniture broke and glass shattered. No one was in the foyer to question his presence.

He slipped forward until he was opposite a large doorway on the right, the source of the noise. In a lamp-lit parlor, half a dozen men in fringed buckskin and several women in gaudy gowns surrounded an immense, greasy-haired man who seemed bent on destroying the place. Jared gaped at the brawl from the darkness.

One of the women, older, was struggling to get hold of the big fellow doing all the damage. As he weaved on his feet, he battered away anyone who tried to grab him. Only the older woman, a dumpy harridan with dyed red hair, seemed serious about it. Some of the others were actually handing the man chairs or bottles which he proceeded to hurl against the walls, producing more squeals and laughter from the onlookers. As the big man lurched back and forth like a ship tossing in a sea of hands and heads, another man brandished a rifle and whooped encouragement.

The wrecker bellowed at the top of his lungs:

"—no damn snot-nosed French bastard calls me a *Kaintuck!*"

The dumpy woman managed to seize his shoulder. He knocked her hand away. The woman screeched, "Elijah Weatherby, I'll have the military on you!"

Thoroughly drunk, the big man in buckskin laughed louder than anyone else:

"Go ahead, Mrs. Cato, get 'em! I'll toss 'em all in the river! I'm from Tennessee—" He let out a wild cry, half crow, half bark. "—and calling me a *Kaintuck* is the worse insult I ever—*leggo my leg, you bitch!*" He lifted his knee to shake off a whore who was hugging his calf like a treetrunk. She fell to the floor, giggling.

The big man accepted a small table from one of the other men. He began to break off the table's legs:

"Yessir, I'm from Tennessee! That means I'm half horse—half alligator—"

Crack.

"—an' part snapping turtle—"

Mrs. Cato seized the leg he'd dropped. She bashed him over the head. The Tennessean hardly blinked.

"—the original yella blossom of the forest! A ringtailed roarer, by God! Men see me comin'—"

Snap went another leg. Mrs. Cato howled obscenities.

"—they step outa the way! They know I can crow like a rooster, neigh like a stallion—an' jump ten feet in the air and bust their heads with my heels!"

Snap, snap—that was the end of the table. Men scrambled for the pieces, holding them up as souvenirs. The whores fought to take them away as the Tennessean kept bellowing:

"—I can stand three bolts of lightning without a blink! Look a panther to death! Put a rifle ball into the moon pretty as you please—!"

Jared ducked as someone in the melee flung another whiskey bottle. It sailed over his head and shattered in the dark behind him. On the floor of the parlor, he glimpsed the unconscious form of a slight, well-dressed man with a goatee. The Frenchman who'd set the big man on his rampage—?

Jared's eyes had adjusted to the poor light in the foyer. At the rear, a staircase led upward. On the second floor, voices complained about the noise. Jared

looked speculatively at the stairs as the Tennessean, overwhelmed by two of the whores trying to kiss him, tumbled over backwards. He fell on top of the Frenchman, still whopping with laughter.

Mrs. Cato extricated herself from the crowd, rushing straight toward Jared in the dark foyer:

"Abel? Abel, fetch the soldiers before Weatherby puts me out of busin—"

She saw Jared and clutched her throat.

"Jesus and Mary, you scared me to death! I thought you were my nigger boy—" Breathing hard, she looked around. *"Abel, where the hell are you?"*

"Mrs. Cato—"

"Leave me be, damn you! That fool's demolishing my parlor. I should be whipped for ever letting a Kaintuck in the front door—"

Jared grabbed her arm as she swept by. "I want to speak to you!"

Mrs. Cato started to curse again. She saw his face in the light from the parlor. Something in the starkness of his expression made her catch her breath.

"You had a man staying here a while ago. Went by the name of Wilford Black—"

"He's still here. Second door on the right, upstairs."

Then she was gone into the gloom: "Abel, I'll switch your black ass if you don't answer me—"

Jared ignored the sounds of carnage in the parlor, wiped his lips with the back of his hand and drew his seven-barrel English pistol from his belt. He climbed the stairs two at a time, thinking one uneasy thought:

If there was ever a time you needed a cool head, it's now.

IV

THE UPPER hallway smelled vinegarish. At the far end, a dim candle in a tin wall sconce provided the only illumination. Behind a doorway on his left, he heard the steady thumping of a man and woman making love.

As he tiptoed along, a door opened further down. A bearded face poked out: "Who the hell's makin' all the racket downst—?"

The man saw Jared, who had stopped in the center of the hallway, the seven-barrel in plain sight.

Jared raised his free hand to signal silence. The bearded fellow eyed Jared's face, the pistol—and disappeared.

Jared stole up to the second door on his right. He leaned his head against the wood, his breathing thin and reedy. He heard irregular snoring.

Good.

He crouched, examined the crack at the bottom of the door. He detected light inside. That was good too. He wouldn't be operating in total darkness.

He wondered why the occupant of the room had gone to sleep with the lamp lit. And the door—it was unlocked.

He inched it open slowly; saw the answer to both puzzles. The tiny room had a sour odor compounded of whiskey and sweat. Its occupant, dressed in a filthy nightshirt, sprawled on the bed. A jug lay on the floor near the man's dangling right hand. He had evidently fallen asleep in a befuddled state; left the latch off and the lamp burning—

Jared's jaw clenched. He could feel anger starting to seethe within him. He

fought it; swallowed once; slipped through the door. At the bedside, he bent over, lowering the seven muzzles of the loaded pistol to within an inch of the head of Reverend William Blackthorn.

Then he pulled back the cock—a loud sound against the background of shouts, oaths, shattering furniture downstairs.

"Wake up."

V

HE REPEATED it, louder. The ungainly man on the bed mumbled; fluttered his eyelids—

The lids lifted. Jared stared into black dots at the center of greenish pupils.

The man stiffened, hands pressing the filthy sheet. Jared leaned one knee on the edge of the bed. Next to the head of the bed, he glimpsed his own blurred image in a smoke-stained pane of glass that showed a vista of rooming-house roofs.

"Oh God in heaven—"

Blackthorn could only get that much out before Jared pressed the seven barrels against his forehead.

"You recognize me."

"Let me get up—"

"No. Where's my cousin?"

Blackthorn's right hand closed into a fist.

"You better not do that. Where's Amanda?"

"She—she's not here," Blackthorn gulped.

"God damn you, I can see that! Answer my question straight or I'll blow your goddamned head onto that pillow."

"Do that," Blackthorn breathed, "you won't ever find out."

"You bastard—!" Jared exclaimed, grabbing and twisting Blackthorn's patched, rancid nightshirt.

The hand's constriction shifted Jared's weight ever so slightly as he knelt. Blackthorn felt the change. His green eyes opened wider.

Realizing his mistake, Jared started to straighten up. In that instant, Blackthorn jammed his right fist upward and out. The fist struck Jared's gun wrist, knocking his hand aside. His trigger finger jerked. Two charges thundered at once, the balls ripping the pillow where Blackthorn had been lying a moment before.

Breathing loudly, Blackthorn seized Jared's head, twisted his own head sideways and sank his teeth into Jared's throat.

The pain was hideous and stunning. Blackthorn let go, drove a knee into the boy's groin. Jared staggered back from the bed, coughing. Blackthorn's bare foot whipped up, kicked the pistol out of his hand.

Then Blackthorn pounded him in the belly. Jared crashed against the wall. Blackthorn lunged again, teeth and lips bloodied from biting Jared's throat. Jared saw the blood; choked—

Blackthorn picked him up bodily and hurled him across the room.

Jared shot his hands out, smacked his palms against the wall on either side of the windowpane. His head crashed through, his shoulders—

His hands stayed his forward motion. He pushed off from the wall as he fell. The shards of glass in the frame barely missed his eyes. He knocked his head on the sill and hit the floor. A fragment of glass cut his left cheek.

He snatched at the sill, hauled himself upright. Without thinking, he rubbed the left side of his face.

A door closed. Bare feet thumped, receding.

Jared stared at the bright red smears on his palm and fingertips. The old, overpowering nausea churned his belly—

He bit down on his lower lip, lurched forward, dizzy. He fell across the bed, fighting the sickness that turned his bones watery.

Stand up! he screamed at himself. *Stand up—Blackthorn's running—!*

He pushed up from the bed, sourness in his throat as he saw the red handprint on the gray sheet. He wanted to bury his head, hide from that harrowing redness—

On hands and knees on the bloody bedding, he spoke Amanda's name aloud. He started to shake; he screamed it:

"Amanda—"

No physical pain, no mental anguish had ever been worse than the next few seconds. Jared Kent literally drove himself to a standing position again; blundered around the room until he found the pistol; palmed it in a trembling hand— his right. Not bloody, thank God. He couldn't bear the sight of his left hand. He kept it by his side as he stumbled down the hall toward the staircase.

He shoved past a man and a girl, both naked. How much time had passed? Half a minute? More—?

From the head of the stairs, he saw Blackthorn making for the front entrance. Only Mrs. Cato and her slave boy stood between the man in the nightshirt and escape.

"Stop him!" Jared shouted.

The smash of another bottle testified to a situation still out of control in the parlor. Almost faster than Jared could comprehend, men and women appeared at the parlor entrance. One was the man Jared had seen brandishing the rifle.

The black boy was in Blackthorn's path. The running man seized the boy's shoulders, flung him aside—and lost his balance when the boy screeched and hung onto his arm.

Jared was halfway down the stairs. Blackthorn glanced wildly over his shoulder, regained his balance, shot out both hands and ripped the rifle away from the astonished onlooker.

Blackthorn whirled and pointed the rifle at Jared on the stairway.

Already twisting the multiple barrel to its next position, Jared locked it in place in the seconds Blackthorn's finger squeezed the trigger. Jared's pistol exploded first.

William Blackthorn shrieked and slapped a hand to his stomach. A black hole marked his nightshirt just above his waist.

He dropped the rifle, tottered forward and slammed on his face, his nightshirt tangled around his buttocks. Mrs. Cato took one look at him and fled for the front door. As Jared stumbled the rest of the way down the stairs, he heard her yelling on the stoop:

"Get the soldiers! A man's been shot—"

If I've killed him—Jared thought. *Oh, God, if I've killed him—*

___ VI

BOTH HANDS were bloodied now; how, he didn't know. He knelt over Blackthorn; rolled him onto his spine. The man's lips flecked with spittle. He had difficulty focusing his eyes on Jared's face.

The noise in the parlor had stopped. Even the Tennessean's voice was stilled as all the people from the parlor crowded the doorway.

"What did you do with Amanda?" Jared said to the dying man.

Blackthorn pressed his hands against his bleeding belly; grimaced.

"Sold her, you son of a bitch."

"*Sold her!* To who?"

Blackthorn's tongue licked at the corner of his mouth.

"Trappers heading—up the Missouri. Told them she was—my indentured girl—"

Hearing that, Jared almost wept.

"—made—a sweet profit, too—" The green eyes were vicious with hate and pain. "—enough to keep me half a year, until you—"

Blackthorn arched his back, shutting his eyes.

"Oh Jesus, you hurt me. I think you killed me—"

The eyes opened again, deranged:

"They'll fuck her bloody till they trade her. The better she's used, the better the savages will like her. Up in—Sioux country—plenty of young bucks and old chiefs take to—a white girl. She'll bring plenty of pelts—"

Jared seized Blackthorn's cheeks, marking them with blood:

"Tell me the name of the men who bought her!"

Blackthorn's eyes streamed tears as he arched his back again. When the spasm passed, he worked his lips—

And spat in Jared's face.

The warm, sticky stuff trickled down the boy's chin. Blackthorn said through clenched teeth:

"You find out who—bought her—"

Like a madman, Jared struck Blackthorn's jaw, smearing the blood already there.

"Oh God, it hurts me!" Blackthorn cried, rolling from side to side, lifting one shoulder, then the other in an effort to lessen his pain. The tears coursed down his cheeks, mingling with the blood, a pink wetness. "It hurts me, it hurts me something awful—"

Yellow hair hanging over his forehead, Jared watched Blackthorn die. A squad of mounted men clattered up in front of the bordello in response to Mrs. Cato's alarms. The tall Tennessean who had destroyed the parlor belched and draped an arm over one of the wide-eyed whores.

"Dunno who that boy is," the man said in a thick voice. "But bless his heart for takin' the heat off me. Mrs. Cato won't worry so much about her furniture if there's a man lyin' murdered in her hallway—"

Jared was numb. Numb and beaten. On his knees beside Blackthorn's corpse, he pressed his bloody palms against his thighs and stared at the rifles of the soldiers rushing through the front door.

__8
The Windigo

GENERAL WILLIAM CLARK personally took Jared's deposition next morning. The boy repeated the story of Amanda's abduction, and what Blackthorn had told him about selling her to white traders heading for the country of the Sioux tribes. In the afternoon, he was summoned to the governor's presence again.

"I can find no witnesses to corroborate the alleged sale of your cousin," Clark told him.

Jared simply looked at the general across the latter's desk.

Clark seemed disturbed by the young man's lackluster stare:

"See here, Kent! I should think you'd show some interest in this inquiry—"

"I heard what you said, General," Jared answered in a dull voice.

Still ruffled, Clark said, "I'm trying to establish the facts in the case. You did shoot a man dead."

"He was going to shoot me. And he deserved it."

"That doesn't condone it. I remind you, the rifle Black or Blackthorn aimed was empty."

"I had no way of knowing that. I'm just sorry he died before he told me the names of the men who bought Amanda."

"If anyone really did. I've had investigators at the fur houses of Manuel Lisa and the Chouteaus all morning. Those gentlemen know virtually everything that happens in the local trade. They've heard nothing about a girl, or a transaction, such as you describe. However—"

"I doubt if Blackthorn would have advertised the transaction, General."

"That's true. You didn't permit me to finish."

"I'm sorry," Jared said, without feeling.

"I was about to say I do have evidence that a girl resembling your cousin was in St. Louis."

Jared's head lifted abruptly. "What evidence?"

"The statement of Mrs. Cato. She said Black had a girl with him for a short time after his arrival. A quite well developed and handsome young girl. She was poorly dressed, and showed signs of having been injured or abused—bruises, that sort of thing. She seemed to obey the dead man without question. Mrs. Cato got the impression she was mortally afraid of him."

"Did you find out whether the girl was wearing a cordage bracelet?"

"She was. Mrs. Cato noticed it because tarred rope is hardly what any woman would consider fashionable."

"Didn't Mrs. Cato wonder about Blackthorn having a young girl with him?"

"In her—ah—profession, the lady is not greatly concerned about the history or the morals of her guests. She accepted the man's story that the girl was a relative, and she thought no more about it when the girl disappeared in a few days. So Mrs. Cato's deposition does give credence to yours—"

Again Jared said nothing. He stared at his hands. So much had been destroyed so quickly—

The firm in Boston belonged to the Stovalls—if they'd kept it. Perhaps Kent and Son already had another name; another owner. The objects from the mantel—the tea bottle, the French sword, the Kentucky rifle—had probably been

sold for junk. He thanked God his Uncle Gilbert was in his grave, and couldn't see the straits into which the family had fallen—

Because of me.

The destruction he'd brought down on the Kents only confirmed the feelings about himself that he'd had for so many years. Aunt Harriet always said he was made of the same flawed clay as his mother and father. He believed it today more than he ever had before.

He'd come into the west just as his father had, and the land had defeated him—and that, too, held no surprise.

Now there was the news about Amanda. It should have cheered him. It didn't. He suspected she was dead. Either at someone else's hand, or by her own.

He could hardly bear to think of her alive in the circumstances Blackthorn had described. He wished she were with him, if only for a moment, so he could tell her how sorry he was for what he had done to her—

"Kent?"

He glanced up. "Forgive me, General. My mind wanders. You were saying—?"

"I was saying that Black is no loss to the community. But if the law takes that posture, there's no reason to have law. Nor can I permit you to go scot free, regardless of how much provocation you had in attacking the man you killed."

In a tired voice, Jared began, "It was self defense—"

"The magistrate who hears your case will certainly take that into account. After you've served your sentence for disturbing the peace, I'll grant you an extra ten days' grace. In that time, you're to remove yourself from St. Louis. Don't come back."

"How long will I be in prison?"

"A minimum of ninety days—you find something amusing, Mr. Kent?"

Jared's mouth lost its bitter curl. "No, sir. I was just thinking it might as well be ninety years."

Clark was thrown off guard; moderated his tone:

"Come, you act as if your life's over—"

"Yes, sir. That's exactly how it feels."

II

THE STIFLING summer dragged on. Jared grew to hate the small, gloomy cell in which he was confined. The jailer allowed him the Bible Mrs. Jackson had given him, but he never opened it. His only reading matter was an occasional copy of the *Missouri Gazette,* which usually contained dismal news from the east.

A United States naval victory on Lake Champlain and the resulting British retreat into Canada were more than offset by the devastating success of another enemy probe into the Potomac district. In late August, the British marched on Washington virtually unopposed. The president and his cabinet had already fled when the enemy arrived, but the capitol was torched. So were the new White House and all of the departmental buildings save the patent office. Several private homes went up in flames along with the Navy Yard, which was deliberately destroyed to prevent it from falling into British hands.

A violent storm and the mustering of fresh American troops combined to push the enemy out of the city by the first of September. But the secretary of war was

forced to resign because of the debacle. He was replaced by Monroe, who also held the post of secretary of state.

In mid-September, a British thrust at Baltimore was repulsed. Fort McHenry withstood an all-night pounding by the cannons of an enemy flotilla. Witnessing the bombardment from one of the British vessels on which he was being held prisoner, a young lawyer and sometime poet, a Mr. Key, had been moved by the sight of fire in the heavens: the British employed the spectacular but relatively harmless Congreve rockets during the bombardment. Key wrote a patriotic poem about the successful resistance by the Americans in the fort. Jared read the poem's opening lines—*"O say can you see, by the dawn's early light—"* with the same interest he'd have had if he'd been perusing a description of events on another planet.

The conflict was dragging on too long for both sides. Britain was occupied with a renewed Napoleonic threat in Europe. The Americans were realizing that the war had perhaps been ill-advised in the first place. Even western papers such as the *Missouri Gazette* were expressing hope that the commissioners at Ghent might reach a peace accord by year's end.

It didn't matter; nothing mattered. Jared was consumed by his sense of failure—

Failure to deal with Stovall.

Failure to protect Amanda.

Failure to make Blackthorn reveal the names of the men to whom he'd sold the girl.

Worst of all—the cause, the wellspring of all the other failures—was his own seeming failure to be something other than what his father had been; to find the strength to overcome the taint he carried.

For one brief moment at Mrs. Cato's, he thought he might have mastered some of his own weakness. When he'd slashed his cheek on the broken window, and seen blood, and felt the familiar sickness, he'd still been able to function. He had *willed* himself to function.

Hardly conscious of that small victory at the time, he had thought of it occasionally since. But he found it laughably, pathetically insignificant in the light of everything else that had happened.

Night after night, he lay awake on the pallet in his cell, condemning himself and praying to a God with whom he wasn't on very familiar terms. A conviction that his cousin was dead never left him—because he saw no way that she could survive. But if by some perverse chance he was wrong, and she had indeed been bartered to an Indian, he prayed she'd find a means for suicide. She had already suffered more than many women did in a lifetime.

He thought about suicide for himself, too. Somehow he lacked the courage. Count that one more failure.

Other than the Bible, the only personal belonging he kept with him in his cell was the worn green ribbon and medal; the fob given him by Uncle Gilbert. He often stared at the Latin inscription and the tea-bottle design, alternately cursing himself for the way he'd besmirched the statement of his grandfather's purpose, and pondering whether the medal might unlock some answer about what he must do next. It didn't.

Toward the end of his term, his jailer announced a visitor.

Jared glanced toward the wooden door and his mouth dropped open. Huge and formidable-looking in buckskin leggings and a fringed blouse decorated with

beads and quillwork, there stood the Tennessean who had all but destroyed Mrs. Cato's parlor. A long white feather stuck up from the back of the man's head.

From outside the cell, he said, "Mr. Kent, aint' it?" He sounded far less truculent than when Jared had first seen him.

Jared laid the fob on his pallet, stood up. "Yes."

"I'll trouble you for the musket," the jailer said.

"Christ, you think I'm gonna shoot him?" the Tennessean grumbled.

"Hand it over or stay out."

Reluctantly the man surrendered his short-barreled gun. It was decorated with a curious piece of metalwork: a fork-tongued sea serpent with curling tail, all done in bronze and screwed to the wood just beneath the lock. The big man shook a cautionary finger:

"That's a genuine North West trade musket. I've had it nine years. Handle it real gingerly or I'll handle you so's you won't get over it."

The Tennessean ducked his head and entered the cell. The jailer, noticeably pale, closed the door.

Jared guessed his visitor to be thirty-five or forty years old. He had high cheekbones; tanned skin heavily marked with lines; eyes whose dark color and deep sockets lent him an air of melancholy now that he was sober.

He acted ill-at-ease. When he spoke again, his tone was surprisingly gentle:

"I come to pay some overdue thanks, Mr. Kent. I owe you a hell of a lot."

Jared shrugged. "I don't recall you owe me a thing."

"Oh yes I do. The night you shot that man, I was crazy drunk. I didn't mean to harm nobody, mind you—I was just havin' a frolic—but Mrs. Cato, that old whore—she'd have hauled me up before the law for certain if you hadn't been around. You kind of took her mind off me. Not completely, o' course. To cover the damage I done, she made me pay half my profit from winterin' last year. That put me way behind in makin' up my assortment."

"Your what?"

"Assortment."

"You've lost me, Mr.—"

"Weatherby. Elijah Weatherby."

Unconsciously, he stroked his shoulder-length gray hair before extending his hand. The hair glistened with some kind of grease. Jared shook reluctantly. Weatherby's palm was slick. But his grip was strong.

"An assortment's what you take to trade when you're spendin' the winter amongst the Injuns." Weatherby perched on the stool Jared had vacated, all but hiding it with his huge frame. "Red men'll trade prime pelts for the damnedest trifles. Don't sound sensible, but it's so. They don't have any trifles, y'see, but they can get hold of a heap of furs. Supply 'n demand is what the Chouteaus call it. I used to work for them, but now I'm a free trader—got my license from the governor an' all—and I still sell my bales to the Chouteaus every spring—" He massaged his jawbone, leaving a greasy residue. "I'm puttin' my assortment together right now. Spendin' every last penny I got, too. Only thing I won't take along is the trade whiskey they make up special at the distilleries here in town."

Jared started to insert a question about why he was being told all this, but Weatherby simply kept talking, perhaps out of nervousness:

"I ain't a man of outstandin' morals, Mr. Kent. But I don't hold with poisoning people. Trade whiskey's nothin' more than river water with some plugs of tobacco and pieces of soap thrown in. Oh, and some red pepper an' dead

leaves to darken it up proper. A whole barrel of that slop gets cut with just two gallons of alcohol an' two gallons of strychnine—''

''Strychnine's a poison!''

''That's what I said, ain't it? The strychnine makes up the scant amount of alcohol. The braves want to get drunk on *somethin'*. Also, they don't consider it good whiskey 'less they have a healthy puke after drinkin' some. The tobacco takes care of the puke.''

Weatherby noticed Jared's puzzled stare. He grinned in a shamefaced way. ''I guess I'm ramblin'—''

''It's pleasant to have a visitor after being cooped up alone for a couple of months, Mr. Weatherby. But I can't see that what you're saying has anything to do with me.''

''Well, yes it does. How much longer you gonna be in here?''

''Another couple of weeks. Why?''

''Mm. That'd work out just fine.''

''What are you talking about?''

Weatherby reached to the back of his head, plucked the white bird feather from his hair and began to twirl it in his fingers. Jared thought the feather was an affectation, like the man's flamboyantly beaded shirt. He learned later it was the fur trade's universal symbol of wintering. Less hardy men only ventured into the Indian lands from the spring to the autumn. The feather thus became a badge of stamina and status.

''Roundabout,'' Weatherby resumed, ''I heard the story of what that man called Black done with your little cousin—''

''Sold her to some trappers going up to the Sioux tribes, he said. I almost don't believe it.''

''I believe it. There's nothin' a Mandan chief prizes so much as a woman with white skin. Same goes for the dog soldiers out amongst the Tetons.''

''What in God's name are dog soldiers?''

''A special bunch of young braves picked to take charge of a buffla hunt. They're mean as sin—an' when you consider that the Teton Sioux are already about the wickedest of all the Dakota Injuns, you got a fair idea of what a dog soldier's like. Compared to one o' them, a Mandan Sioux's an old woman.''

''So you're telling me there's a ready market for my cousin.''

''Afraid so. That ain't what fetched me here, though. I—well, what I wondered—y'see, it's like this,'' he said with an explosion of breath. ''I lost my last partner this past February. A Frenchman, Marcel was his name. He got all messed up with a buffla dance. That's where a whole lot of Injuns and mebbe some real important visitors sit in a circle in a lodge. The old men make big drum medicine. Then their young wives come up behind the circle bare-ass naked except for a buffla robe. Each wife picks a man—not her own, y'understand— and goes outside with him, an' right there in the snow they make the two-backed beast—with everybody's one hunnerd percent approval.''

''That's incredible.''

''The truth! I been in the snow myself. Seen a dozen, two dozen couples humpin' away not six feet apart. It's part of the religion. 'Sposed to attract the herds in winter time. Get 'em to come close enough to the village so the braves can ride out an' lay in some meat. Well, the point is, my partner Marcel, he took a fancy to the squaw that picked him out. So he's livin' with the Mandans now, sort of a second husband to this young woman. I ain't found anybody but rum-sots to replace him—''

Weatherby raised a hand quickly. "Don't get me wrong. I drink some myself."

Jared almost smiled. "I know."

"But I only do it when I'm in town and havin' a frolic. To get right to it—"

Jared fervently wished he would.

"—I need a partner for *this* winter. I'm goin' back up toward the Sioux villages. You look like a sober, steady sort, and you ain't yella, that's plain from what happened at Mrs. Cato's. If you was of a mind to go with me, mebbe we could hunt for your cousin—"

He left the last words hanging, his tone punctuating them as a question.

"I expect my cousin's dead."

Weatherby frowned. "Well, by God. You mean you give up on her?"

"Don't you think I should?"

"I dunno about should. I didn't 'spect you *would*." He rubbed his chin. The melancholy cast of his expression started resentment simmering in Jared.

Weatherby clucked his tongue. "Yeh, I had you pegged for a different sort. I mean, you stepped up to the mark pretty smart at Mrs. Cato's. Plugged that bastard cool an' clean right while he was aimin' square at you." The trapper slitted his eyes. "How old are you, boy?"

"Sixteen."

"Plenty old enough for me to teach you the trade. Where you hail from?"

"Boston. Look, Mr. Weatherby—"

"Boston! Ain't that way up by the Atlantic Ocean someplace?"

"Yes, it is. I—"

"An' you come all the way out here with that little girl?"

"Actually she was stolen in Tennessee. We were heading south."

"Godamighty! You musta rode a thousand miles or more."

"I guess. We walked a good part of it."

"I sure wouldn't have any doubts about takin' on a youngster who could do that," Weatherby declared.

"Thanks, but I'm not interested."

"I sort o' got that idea. Appears I made a mistake—"

The big man rose, jamming the feather in his hair.

"You goin' back east when you get out?"

"I can't go back east."

"Why not?"

"Because—because the law wants me."

"Thievin'?"

"Something else."

"Murder?"

Jared didn't answer.

Weatherby's reaction was unexpected and puzzling. First he shrugged. Then, with a remote look, he said:

"Hell, I done a lot worse than that."

"I didn't say I'd—"

"Yes you did—by not sayin' anything."

"And you've done worse?"

"I sure have."

"For instance?"

"Well, for one thing, I left a woman and four young 'uns in Tennessee. I come out here eleven years ago. I couldn't stand farmin' fifty acres month in,

month out. Got so bad I couldn't sleep nights, thinkin' how I had to escape. It was like hands on my neck, stranglin' hands, that feeling. I was locked up on fifty acres and I'd see the same sights all my days—well, I begged my wife to come along. She said no. So one night I—just left. I ain't proud of it. But I had to do it or I would have died.''

Strangely moved by the hoarseness of Weatherby's voice, Jared found his own softening:

"That's still not as bad as killing a man. And I've botched up a whole lot of other—"

"I ain't finished." Weatherby stared at him. "You know what a windigo is, boy?"

"No."

"Big medicine with the Injuns. Scares hell out of 'em. I'm carryin' that name now.''

Some remembered agony shone in his eyes. Suddenly he glanced away.

"What I'm sayin' to you is, the country west of here forgives just about anything a man wants or needs to have forgiven. I heard a preacher say once that God forgives His wayward children, so maybe God's part of the prairies an' rivers, because a man can sure find a mighty lot of forgiveness—"

"Mr. Weatherby, I'm leaving St. Louis—"

"I know that! It's no secret Clark ordered you to hightail."

"I expect to head south, where I was going when Blackthorn stole my cousin. New Orleans—"

"Down where it's soft an' easy, huh?"

"Listen, I'm not asking advice from you or anyone!" He was angered by the Tennessean's contemptuous stare. "My mother was butchered by Indians in Ohio. My father failed when he farmed there—"

Weatherby shrugged:

"So?"

"What the hell do you mean—*so?*"

"So what's your point, is what I'd like to know."

Jared flushed. "If it's any of your business."

Weatherby blinked, then said in the mildest of voices, "Well, fuck you for a snotty pup,'' and started out.

Ashamed, Jared exclaimed, "Weatherby—"

The tall trapper turned back.

"Yeh?"

"Look, I—I'm sorry for that remark. I do appreciate your asking me to throw in with you. But there are—quite a few reasons why I can't.''

Weatherby studied the boy. Crooked an index finger and scratched his upper lip. Finally said quietly:

"You want to talk about any of 'em?"

Jared was stunned. "Why should you be interested?"

"Oh, I dunno—" The man's deep-hued cheeks actually turned darker, the equivalent of a blush. "Mebbe because I never quite got used to bein' without sons an' daughters. I don't feel natural 'less I'm worryin' about young 'uns. Told you I had four in Tennessee—an' I must have sired me three times that many off all the squaws I hung out with over the years. Seems to me like we're kind of a pair, Kent. You got nobody real close an' neither have I—"

He searched Jared's eyes a moment. Then:

"I ain't so good with fancy phrases, but I got a feelin' soon after I come in

here that you're hurtin' pretty bad over somethin'. It's a lot better to speak it out than to drown it with whiskey like I'm in the habit of doin'.''

Oddly touched, Jared said, ''You read me pretty well, Mr. Weatherby.'' He lifted a hand toward the stool. ''I'd be pleased if you kept me company a while longer.''

III

THE TRAPPER bobbed his head and resumed his seat:

''All righty, get it off your chest.''

Jared looked at the wall as he started to talk:

''The plain truth is, I'm scared of this country.''

''Scared! Why on earth—?''

''I told you. My father tried farming, Indians killed my mother—the west destroyed both of them. I—''

He turned and gazed straight at the older man, pent-up tension draining away. It was a relief just to be able to share the torment with someone:

''—I've made a lot of the mistakes my parents did. My father and mother weren't tough enough to beat this country, and I don't think I am either.''

Weatherby digested that for a moment. Then he inclined his head very slightly to one side and puckered his lips to express his doubt.

''I'd say you're crazy.''

''What?''

''You heard. Crazy. I don't know what your pa was like, but I know this. There ain't one man in fifty in St. Louis—no, nor west of here, neither—that could travel a thousand miles haulin' a little girl like you done an' live to tell of it. 'Specially at sixteen. Most of 'em would have quit 'fore they got halfway.''

Perplexed, Jared shook his head. ''I didn't think it was anything special. We had to do it—''

''You just take my word, boy. Unless your pa was a hell of a lot bigger an' better man than it sounds like, you got him beat a mile.''

Jared scrutinized Weatherby, trying to decide whether the trapper was flattering him. He saw nothing in the man's demeanor to indicate that was the case. Yet he couldn't quite believe what Weatherby said—

The older man sensed the boy's doubt:

''You think I'm funnin' you. Tell you what. When you get out, you haul yourself down to Manuel Lisa's warehouse, or the one the Chouteaus run. You tell any trapper you bump into that you walked all the way from the Atlantic to St. Lou' by way of Tennessee. Tell 'em you tracked the man who stole your cousin, an' killed him instead o' lettin' him kill you. You'll see how fast you get work. Why, you'll have so many offers, your head'll whirl!''

''But it wasn't that big a thing—''

''You ain't got much pride in yourself, have you, boy?''

Jared glanced up suddenly. Started to speak; hesitated; then said:

''No, I guess I don't.''

''Well, it's time to start havin' some! I'd be proud to call you my partner.''

That was when Jared recalled something Judge Jackson had said. Something about the accomplishment of reaching Nashville on his own. At the time, he hadn't paid much attention. But he remembered it vividly now.

He remembered Governor Clark expressing astonishment over the journey, too. He began to feel a little heartened—

Do you suppose we never know we've fought some battles until they're over? he asked himself. *Maybe I do have some reason to hold my head up—*

The thought pleased him. True or not, it lent him a touch of courage he'd lacked for a long time.

Weatherby said, "Tell me something."

"Sure."

"Your cousin—did she make the whole trip, like you say?"

"To Tennessee? Yes. Then she obviously came this far with Blackthorn—"

"How'd she get along?"

"When she was with me, not too well—at first. By the time we left Louisville, though, she'd toughened up a lot. She—"

He stopped, sensing the trapper's intent. Weatherby said:

"What you're saying is, she's got the stuff too. That oughta give you some hope that she's still alive. Hell, I bet you taught her plenty about how to get along—and did it without even knowin' it."

Jared would have liked to believe that, too. But skepticism brought a bitter laugh:

"You're just softening me up so I'll throw in with you. I haven't got a cent."

"The money was to be my part. I was only askin' for a strong back an' a strong belly. I think you got both of 'em—only somebody or something has whipped you so bad, you talked yourself into believin' the belly part ain't there. You think it over. I mean really think about what it took to get all the way out here. Think about that little girl, too. Whether you really want to act like she's dead when there's a chance she ain't. If you change your mind, I'll probably still be roomin' at Ungerleider's Hotel when they let you out."

"Do you honestly think we could find her, Mr. Weatherby?"

"I know we could have a damn good shot at it."

Jared stared down at the fob on the pallet, confused, his emotions churning—

Weatherby put a hand on his arm.

"Listen here. I can hire me a dozen no-goods. But I don't come across ones like old Marcel—or you—very often. I ain't never kissed any man's boots to make him feel good. When I say somethin', I mean it. Life's too goddamn short to have it any other way."

Weatherby turned and hammered on the cell door. When the jailer let him out, he snatched back his trade musket and disappeared, calling over his shoulder:

"That's Ungerleider's Hotel. Anybody can tell you how to find it."

IV

JARED KENT sat cross-legged on his pallet a long while afterward, running his finger across the surface of the fob medallion and scrutinizing the Latin inscription. The ball of his thumb began to work back and forth over the raised letters.

He *did* want to believe what Weatherby had told him. He wanted to believe that he had passed through a testing fire without even being aware of it. Making mistakes, yes; dreadful ones—

But surviving.

And what had the trapper said about the country where he traded? That it

forgave almost anything a man wanted or needed to have forgiven—? Perhaps that was one reason why people sought the land by the hundreds and the thousands—

Jared's thumb stopped, resting on the tea bottle again. Was it possible Amanda could be alive? His thoughts raced; back to Tennessee just before Blackthorn's appearance. He recalled the night beside the fire when he'd been struck by the new strength in her.

But God above, she'd been raped! And who knew how many times since then Blackthorn—and others—had abused her?

Still, he had to admit in the privacy of his conscience that he *was* guilty of inventing reasons for going south and abandoning the search—which was another way of saying he was guilty of giving in to his fear.

Maybe he didn't need to give in any longer. Maybe on the long, arduous journey from Boston, step by step and mile by mile, he'd trampled an enemy underfoot *and never known it—*

If he didn't quite believe it yet, he had the desire to believe, and the desire lifted his spirits in a way that had been foreign to him for months.

He stared at the medal.

Assuming Amanda was dead—or that he couldn't find her, which was just as likely—he was the only Kent left. What was he to do with his life?

Weatherby offered him a chance to learn the fur trade. He'd find no similar opportunity ready-made in New Orleans. If he could go with the trapper and not be afraid of the land—not be afraid because he had already won one battle against it—

Then wouldn't he be a fool not to accept Weatherby's offer of a new start? He could provide for himself. Perhaps even prosper—

His thumb began moving on the medal again.

He was the last of the Kents.

Not Abraham Kent.

Jared.

Not a poor creature tormented to failure, but one who had walked a thousand miles—

Before he was sixteen years old.

He had always believed everything Harriet Kent said about him. But he knew she had hated him. Perhaps some of the things she'd said were born of her hate; not altogether true—

Desperately, he sought for proofs of the possibility in the past. Once more he thought of his father.

After Abraham Kent had failed, he had gone home. To despair. To ruin and, presumably, death.

But he, Jared, failing in Tennessee, had kept on—

Perhaps he wasn't doomed to repeat the past. Perhaps he needn't be its lifelong prisoner. As Weatherby said, that was one of the promises of the western land: it forgave, and let a man begin again—

He was not Abraham.

He was *Jared—*

Unless he ran away.

He looked at the medal.

Take a stand and make a mark.

Who was right? Weatherby? Or Harriet—and the voice of self-doubt that had been his companion for as long as he could remember—?

Was there a possibility Amanda was alive?

And had he made too many terrible mistakes, and put himself beyond all chance of self-forgiveness? Weatherby claimed he had sinned great sins. How could they possibly be worse than Jared's own—?

Alternating between bursting hope and cynical despair, he paced and fretted for nearly an hour. He still did not know clearly what he should do—or whether he was capable of anything except helpless retreat.

Evening deepened outside the bars of the cell. From the riverfront he heard the sounds of the town's lusty life: horses drumming; men singing; a gun going off—

Weary of self-examination, he sought diversion. The only thing that offered it was a newspaper. He shouted through the small grille in the cell door—

No answer. The jailer had gone off to supper.

Frustrated, he ran a hand through his yellow hair. His eye fell on Rachel Jackson's Bible.

He picked it up. Turned pages aimlessly. Came at last to the ribbon that marked a place in the Old Testament. He supposed the marker had been inserted randomly, and he was just about to flip to the next page when something caught his attention.

Someone—the judge's wife, evidently—had inked brackets around a passage in—

He tilted the Bible so he could make out the page heading in the dying light of sunset. Ezekiel. The thirty-fourth book.

The brackets marked the sixteenth verse. He read it and realized the position of the ribbon marker was no accident. He read the verse a second time:

I will seek that which was lost, and bring again that which was driven away, and will bind up that which was broken, and will strengthen that which was sick—

With a shiver, he sat down on the stool and began reading at the head of the chapter.

When he reached the sixteenth verse, he closed the Bible and held it on his knees. Jackson's wife must have suspected he would falter, hesitate and question along the way. And so she had carefully marked those few words. In the Lord's promise to His people, Jared saw, at last, a clear sign of what he himself must do.

I will seek that which was lost—

Bring again that which was driven away—

Failure to carry out that command would forever break the vow he'd given Uncle Gilbert. Failure would make the precious medal a mockery—

Only one question remained, then. But it was of such magnitude that it wracked him all through the sleepless night:

Could he do what must be done?

Was he strong enough?

Was he Jared Kent—?

Or Abraham's helpless, doomed son-and-twin?

Even in the ruddy light of a new morning, there was no sure answer.

V

WHEN JARED was released, he reclaimed his few belongings and put the Bible and the fob with them in his small canvas bag. In a deserted street near the jail, he squatted down in the shadows. He drew a long breath, then did something which two Indians wandering by watched with amazement.

Using the Spanish knife, Jared pricked the ball of his left thumb.

He sheathed the knife and squeezed his thumb until the blood ran freely, bright red—

The nausea churned up from his belly, horribly sour in his throat. He gripped his left wrist with his right hand and forced himself to stare at the small wound— at the blood—his teeth locked together, his forehead sweaty, for some five minutes.

During that time, he felt faint. Felt the urge to hide his hand behind his back; shut out the sight of that awful redness—

But he watched the tiny wound until his trembling stopped and the nausea receded.

The prick in his thumb clotted. He stood up, pale but satisfied on one score.

This strange, debilitating enemy might be with him to the end of his days. But at least he saw the affliction in a truer perspective. Not so much a curse— punishment for unworthiness, real or imagined—as a burden whose origins, though they might be rational, would be forever hidden.

That, he could endure.

Walking with long, swift strides, he started for the fur warehouse of Manuel Lisa.

VI

THE CLERK checking through the bales outside the warehouse looked at Jared as if he were a lunatic. With an annoyed shake of his head, the clerk turned his attention back to his ledger:

"I haven't got time to answer fool questions about Indian fairy stories—"

Jared stepped around in front of the clerk. The clerk's head lifted. He met Jared's blue eyes and almost dropped the ledger.

"You'll tell me where I can get an answer, then," Jared said.

Nervous, the clerk glanced past the boy, pointed his quill:

"Maybe—maybe old Jeanette. See her over there?"

Jared followed the direction of the pen; saw what he hadn't before: beyond two gaudily quilled and beaded trappers cutting the bindings on bales of summer pelts, a figure hunched against the warehouse wall, seated in the shadows and almost lost within them.

"She's half Osage, half French. She speaks pretty fair English. But she's—"

The clerk tapped his temple with the quill.

"She's waiting for her husband. A free trader." The clerk went "Huh!" softly, either in pity or derision. "He disappeared up the Mizou ten years ago and never came back."

Nodding, Jared pivoted away.

He walked by the trappers to the deep shadow along the wall. Though it was full daylight, and the October sun was warm, a chill settled over him as he

inspected the old woman sitting cross-legged, her clothing layered on her frail body in filthy pieces, no two of which matched.

The old woman's face was like a finely detailed map, crosshatched with dozens of delicate lines. Her hair was almost pure white. The hands resting in her lap were emaciated. She smelled of dirt and human waste and tobacco.

Jared crouched down in front of her. The old woman's eyes were closed. But in her lap, one hand moved; fumbled with the flap of a worn pouch; reached in for a small, moist gob of tobacco.

Without opening her eyes, the woman slipped the tobacco between her lips and up against one of her diseased, toothless gums.

He said softly, "Jeanette?"

The ancient, leathery jaws began to work the tobacco. Her closed eyelids seemed lifeless.

He repeated her name.

She looked at him. Jared caught his breath.

The old woman's eyes were brown and clear. He saw no hint of madness in them, but neither did they hold any emotion. They seemed like natural objects— great stones; a river; the earth itself—that had no need of human feeling.

"Jeanette," he said a third time, "my name is Kent. The clerk said you might tell me something I need to know."

Slowly, so slowly, the lined jaws worked the tobacco and the old eyes remained fixed on his, unblinking.

The wrinkled lips opened, no more than a slit:

"Ask."

"I met a man. He used a word—he said it meant something very bad—"

Her voice was thin, a thread of sound, and raspy:

"What word?"

"Windigo."

She uttered a strange, chant-like syllable, and swayed from side to side. Her eyes seemed a little more animated.

"The devil. The great devil who walks in the dark. Accursed. A monster. Not fit to look upon."

"Not a real person?"

"Some men—a few—whom the Father-spirit chooses to hate—they become like the great windigo."

"But what is it that makes them so terrible? Do they kill—?"

"The great windigo kills. He kills out of pain and anger that the Father-spirit has made him what he is."

"Have you ever seen him?"

She was silent almost half a minute, the brown eyes opaque again; unreadable.

"The great windigo? No. I have seen two men in my life—maybe three—who became as he is. Accursed."

"Why are they accursed?" Jared persisted, feeling he was drawing close to something he might be better off avoiding. The old woman was undoubtedly senile. Yet somehow, he feared her—

"Because they have done what the great windigo does," she said. "They have eaten the flesh of a human being."

VII

JARED'S THROAT felt thick. He fought for a breath of air in the foul-smelling shadows. The old half-breed woman looked at him, and he thought that she saw him for the first time:

"The Father-spirit in heaven made the windigo so man would be humble and thankful. When the great windigo walks, higher than a house, with fire burning here—" One hand touched an eyelid. "—so bright it lights the night, an ordinary man knows the Father-spirit has showered him with love. An ordinary man is humble and thankful even if he is weak and evil, because no matter how terrible a man's lot, he will bless it forever if he meets the windigo."

In a whisper, Jared said, "Thank you."

Her right hand lifted from her lap, her palm a crosswork of lines.

"Do you have a little snuff for me?"

"I don't, I'm sorry. I wish I did."

She became agitated:

"Have you seen Langlois?"

"Lang—?"

Jared stopped. Did she mean her husband?

"He will be back by sunset, they say. I told him I would be waiting here."

Jared stood up. Grasped her open hand and pressed it gently:

"Yes, I heard he was coming back."

She relaxed, and seemed to smile.

"You have heard that? I am glad. That means he is truly coming. I will go on waiting."

Jared turned away, shaken and full of pity for the old Osage woman. But he understood why Weatherby had revealed his shameful secret.

VIII

JARED STAYED at the Lisa warehouse the better part of an hour, speaking to several men. Then he asked directions to Ungerleider's Hotel. He set off at a run, hoping he was not too late.

9
"I Will Seek That Which Was Lost"

ON THE first of November, 1814, Elijah Weatherby and Jared Adam Kent boarded a keelboat that would take them several hundred miles up the Missouri River with Weatherby's assortment.

In the assortment were the standard twenty-five-yard bolts of coarse woolen cloth called strouding. The Indians fashioned it into clothing. There were several

bolts each of calico, melton and cotton cloth; two dozen three-point Mackinac blankets, prized by the Indians for their warmth; and a collection of carefully packed kettles, needles, threads, axes, awls, hand mirrors, animal traps, shot and powder.

The assortment also included less utilitarian items which the Indians favored for personal adornment: cheap combs; a rainbow of ribbons; falconry bells; and white, red, gray, black and purple shells polished and strung to make wampum.

Weatherby had used the last of his funds to buy three dozen silver trinkets. There were gorgets and halfmoons, some bracelets, and fifteen pairs of enormous silver earrings, which Weatherby said the vainer braves wore with great pride. Weatherby had also bought two horses and enough food for three months.

II

THE KEELBOAT pushed up the Missouri under a favoring wind. Jared stood at the bow on the twelfth day of November, 1814. His new buckskins were stiff; sweat and exertion had yet to lend them the desired pliability.

The early evening was warm; unusually warm and dry for this far north and this late in the season, Elijah Weatherby said. But the sun was darkening rapidly, Jared noticed. Huge black clouds spilled out of the northwest. In the clouds, lightning flickered.

He gazed at the fast-flowing, muddy Missouri for several minutes. He was struck by the way his own fate and his father's had been so closely linked with rivers.

A river had taken the older brother or sister he'd never known.

Another had flowed by the place where he was born, and where his mother died.

A third had meandered past the dreadful patch of ground where he and Amanda met Blackthorn.

He'd followed a fourth to St. Louis.

And still one more was bearing him toward an unguessable future.

The west was growing chiefly because of the rivers. The seekers of escape and the seekers of dreams poured forth from the east, and the rivers in their silent, eternal power carried them; changing the nation; changing the lives of its people, including the Kents—

He lifted his gaze from the river to the land. He was spellbound by the vista. The prairie seemed to stretch away endlessly on both sides of the Missouri, broken only here and there by small groves of trees. On the starboard side, he saw bison—for the first time—two or three thousand, a great mass of hide and hair and horn moving slowly along the bank.

The majestic motion of the herd, the wind-lashed water and prairie grass, the turbulent, white-lit clouds folding in upon themselves as the storm advanced made him feel as he had long ago, times when he'd clambered to a Boston roof or dashed to the end of a pier and beheld sea and sky together, immense and breathtaking—

My God, he thought. *How beautiful it is.*

The wind blew harder now, flattening his hair against the top and sides of his head. He strained to keep the distant horizon in focus, no longer despairing, but thrilled; expectant—

In searching for Amanda, maybe he could find a place where he belonged—
A place where I can be happy.
I see what Weatherby meant. Out here, there is *room for hope to begin
again*—

His fear of the land had begun to wane when he had ceased to fear himself so
much. He no longer felt contempt for the family he'd glimpsed at the ferry on the
Illinois side of the Mississippi. He no longer pitied the men and women and tiny
children huddled in wagons or riding on mules or horses—or walking—he'd
passed on the trails up from Nashville. He understood them.

He was one of them.

The clouds had darkened the sky overhead. The keelboatmen hauled down the
sail and pitched the anchor overside, preparing to ride out the storm.

Thunder blasted. Lightning hit the river about a mile ahead. Open-mouthed,
Jared watched as the forked whiteness licked down a second time, striking the
earth in front of the plodding buffalo. In moments, fire ignited.

It spread quickly, fanned by the wind until a monumental wall of scarlet rose
toward the heavens. Even on the keelboat, Jared felt the heat.

The silhouettes of the frightened buffalo passed before the scarlet wall, stampeding. The earth shook. The sky turned black and so did the surrounding land.
Only that towering rampart of flame lit the stygian gloom—

Marveling at the sight, Jared was unprepared for the slash of the rain. With a
yelp, he headed below. He was soaked by the time he got there.

The rain lasted a quarter of an hour, then slacked off abruptly. In five more
minutes it was over. He returned to the deck, the wind cool against his cheeks.

The clouds cleared. A gold sunset burnished the river and the wet prairie. To
starboard, billows of smoke marked the site of the drenched fire. The distant
reverberation of the stampeding buffalo blew along the wind.

He felt a presence at his elbow.

"What you lookin' at?" Weatherby asked.

In a hushed voice, Jared answered, "Everything."

"Makes a man feel right clean again, don't it?"

Weatherby had that sad, remote look in his eyes, Jared noticed. It brought
something to mind; something that had needed saying for a couple of weeks.

"Elijah—"

"Uh?"

"You know one of the reasons I decided to come with you?"

Weatherby shook his head.

"I talked to some other fur men before we left St. Louis."

"Did you tell 'em where you come from?"

Jared smiled. "I did. I said I'd come on foot and on horseback and by wagon
and keelboat all the way from Boston. I had three solid offers to hire on."

"Knew you would."

No longer smiling, Jared went on, "I also asked about the windigo."

The words seemed to crush Weatherby like a blow. But after a moment, he
straightened up and faced his younger companion:

"So you know the story I spun about my Frenchie partner was a lie."

"I found out you had a partner who was French—"

"But he didn't disappear because of no buffla dance. We was in the mountains
last winter—"

"You don't have to tell me."

"I want to. It was snowin' to beat hell. We lost the pack horses with all the food. Then my partner, old Marcel, he—"

For a moment it seemed as if Weatherby couldn't continue.

"—well, there was a rock fall, and Marcel, he was broke up pretty bad under it. There was no way he could live, an' no way I could carry him out. It was all I could do to keep myself alive. I had to make the filthiest, meanest choice a man could be asked to make. I'll say this. Old Marcel, he helped me make it. I was ready to die with him but he wouldn't have no part of that. He—finished himself with his own gun. Then I was able to walk out of those mountains seventeen days later. Alive because I had flesh to eat."

III

EVEN NOW, Jared experienced the horror that had gripped him outside Lisa's warehouse.

Presently the trapper said, "There ain't much worse a man can carry on his soul, Jared."

"I'd guess not."

"Sometimes I can't carry it all, so I frolic, like I did at Mrs. Cato's. Now you see why I told you what I did? That any mistakes you made ain't nothin' compared to mine? But I swear—there *is* somethin' of God in this land. I know it, dumb as I am. I can't read nor write, but I know that much. A man's born like a cracked jar, and livin' don't improve the condition. There's never a way to repair the jar so it's perfect. But somehow, it's so clean and blessed beautiful out here, you're—"

"Forgiven."

"Yes. Maybe it's because there ain't many souls in these parts yet to see the crack in the jar. Maybe it's because you're so busy keepin' alive, the crack ain't very important. Even after last winter, I can stand up and start over."

"You showed me how I could do that, Elijah."

Weatherby managed a smile. "Then I'm good for somethin', I reckon."

"Listen, I'm counting on you to show me a lot more. I intend to make some money in this fur business."

"Fair enough. I don't guarantee it, but we'll give 'er a Tennessee try. I do promise you one thing, though. A year or so out here, and there'll be a fire in your soul like you never felt before. A fire to make that burnin' prairie look like sparks in brushwood."

Jared smiled back. "You've a poetic turn of mind, you know that?"

"Wouldn't go quite that far. But a fur man spends a lot o' hours inside his own head. Most times, there's nobody else for company—"

"And what kind of fire is it that's going to burn me up?"

"Why, the one that made me commit a great sin an' leave my woman and my youngsters. You keep hankerin' to see past the next hill, then the next, and one day it gets so bad, you can't stay in the same place more'n a week without goin' crazy."

"I had a curiosity about new things once upon a time. Somewhere along the way, I lost it."

"Well, you wait. The fire'll stoke up hot and you won't be satisfied till you've set eyes on the mountains—then the ocean—"

"You've seen the Pacific?"

" 'Course I have. I've et and smoked with the Haidas on the very shore of it. I've been a while in the earth lodges of the Pawnee and I've worked trap lines in the country of the horse tribes, too—the Cheyenne, the Blackfeet, the Crow. You'll see wondrous sights out where we're goin', Jared—"

There was silence broken by the whisper of the wind and the lap of the Missouri against the hull.

"Y'know," Weatherby continued, "I really did mean what I said in jail. I think you got the stuff."

"Kind of soon to tell, isn't it?"

"Oh, no. I've had three partners and I reckoned their good points and bad points mighty quick. Old Marcel, he was the best of the lot, God keep him. But I'd be proud to call you my kin."

Moved, Jared couldn't reply immediately. Finally, very softly, he said:

"The feeling's mutual, Elijah."

Weatherby clapped his hands. "By damn, I think we *will* make some money! You may even find an Injun girl you fancy. A lot of 'em are right pleasing."

And start the Kents growing again? It was an unexpected idea, but a warming one.

Rain-washed hills gleamed amber as the last clouds passed. A single shimmering star lit the pale blue far overhead. In his mind, he saw the passage from Ezekiel.

I will seek that which was lost, and bring again that which was driven away, and will bind up that which was broken—

He had it in his power to begin the family anew. He must do it as best he could. Whether a hope of locating Amanda was justified was another matter—

Once again Weatherby exhibited his uncanny faculty for sensing what was in Jared's mind; perhaps because Jared's eyes were focused on the remotest point on the river.

"I think we'll find her, Jared."

"Sometimes I think so too. Other times, I wonder."

"From all you told me about her, I'd say she's got too much life in her just to lie down an' die. I got a powerful feelin' she's still alive somewhere out yonder."

"I've almost come to believe that myself."

"Even if we don't find her, you got to remember it's the tryin' that counts most. It's the tryin' that makes a man worthy of the name."

Jared nodded slowly. His hand moved to his belt and touched the fob tied there by the raveling ribbon.

But his eye remained fixed on the horizon.

EPILOGUE
In the Tepee of the Dog Soldier

AMANDA KENT opened her eyes.

In the first seconds of wakefulness, she noted details of her surroundings without recognizing their significance. She floated in a pleasant state of lassi-

tude, fascinated by the colorful geometric designs daubed on the skin lining of the tepee. The lining stretched from the ground to perhaps a height of five feet.

Amanda was lying on one of three beds arranged around the tepee wall. Hers was positioned to one side of the oval entrance, which was closed. The entrance faced east, away from the prevailing winds.

On the other side of the entrance were the two beds for the tepee's regular occupants. The head of one abutted the foot of the other. All three beds were similar in most respects: two poles had been staked parallel on the ground, and the space between filled with dried prairie grass, then covered with hides. But only one of the beds had an angled backrest of closely spaced willow sticks. The top of the backrest's frame was connected by a thong to a tripod directly behind it.

Perhaps twenty poles, most of them toward the rear, formed the skeleton of the tepee, which was reasonably large, and filled with a delicious warmth that prolonged Amanda's sense of euphoria. Three very long poles, again in a tripod arrangement, shaped the tepee's basic structure. Additional poles spaced around the perimeter, plus a cluster at the back, stretched and braced the hide covering. Outside thongs staked into the ground helped keep the tepee standing in high winds.

Slightly behind the center of the dirt floor, a small fire burned—buffalo dung, though Amanda did not know that. She was only conscious of a peculiar aroma she had never smelled before. From the various poles hung items that obviously belonged to the tepee's owner:

A large, ornately painted parfleche. A shield of bull buffalo skin decorated with a crude representation of a bird with a great curving beak and immense wings. A willow bow reinforced with sinew. A quiver of arrows. A medicine bag.

A long thong hanging from the smoke hole suspended a bundle of saplings above the fire. The smoke, rising straight upward, cured the saplings that would become iron-headed arrows—

Awareness was returning slowly. Amanda recalled that it was fall, and the evening was chilly. Hence the fire. Overhead, she saw that the smoke wings had been opened about halfway to permit air to circulate. Where the smoke drifted into the darkness, she glimpsed a few faint stars. She heard, then recognized, sounds—

Heavy thumping, as of hide drums beaten.

Stamping; rhythmic clapping; the chant of many voices.

Occasionally a man or woman shouted something in an unfamiliar language. Or a child squalled. Or one of the dozens of dogs she had seen in the encampment barked—

Encampment—

She remembered where she was, and why.

With a low cry, she lunged upward to a sitting position, all at once feeling the thongs that bound her dirty wrists and ankles. As her angle of vision changed, she saw an object previously hidden by the willow backrest. A huge horned skull, the bone yellowed, the eye sockets black and terrifying—

She almost screamed aloud as it all came back.

The traders had brought her here. On a keelboat much like the one she remembered from another, almost unreal period in her life.

After the boat, the traders used horses. There were four of the white men, led by an immense, reddish-bearded fellow with a veined nose. His name was Maas.

She had slept at the foot of his bed on the boat, and whenever he had wanted her beside him, he had dragged her up by the hair.

The scream gathered in her dry throat. She fought it. She was sickened by the filthy feel of her skin. Something crawled beneath her arm on her left side, under the greasy buckskin dress that had replaced her other clothing.

She ached from the days of traveling across the empty grassland, sometimes permitted to ride behind Maas when he was in a good mood, but most of the time walking, connected to his saddle by a halter looped around her neck. Gazing down at her unwashed feet, she saw half a dozen healed cuts.

When the traders had finally reached the encampment earlier in the day, they had met with the Indians in the open. Amanda was relegated to a position some yards from the large group surrounding the whites, and from there watched Maas communicate with the ferocious-looking brown men in a combination of their tongue and hand-signs. There was much display of, and haggling over, the contents of the bales the white men had brought with them.

One moment was unforgettable: when the crowd parted abruptly, and she saw a tall, well-built but cruel-looking Indian gazing at her.

The Indian, in his twenties, made more hand-signs at Maas. The final sign was a finger jabbed in her direction.

Maas grinned, nodded—and she knew without being told that she now belonged to the Indian, who wore a bonnet of eagle feathers.

The bonnet was a kind of cap with thongs hanging down. Some of the feathers projected from the back of the cap. Others were attached to the thongs. Each feather had an ornamental tip of white weasel fur. What struck her was the absence of such bonnets on most of the other young men.

She saw several bonnets on older Indians. Some of those bonnets had trains of feathers that reached all the way to the ground. Instinct told her the Indian who had pointed to her was very powerful and much respected—thus the honor of the bonnet—but because he was younger, his bonnet was not yet as impressive as those worn by his elders.

Tonight there was a celebration in progress outside the tepee. At dusk, Amanda had seen chunks of the carcass of some kind of animal being dragged toward blazing cook fires. She remembered an Indian carrying a hairy hump, its underside gory. Another proudly displayed what appeared to be a tongue.

Then Maas had come to her, and officially informed her that she had been sold to the young man in return for buffalo hides gathered in the hunt two days ago. The young man was the son of one of the tribal elders, Maas said. He had counted coup many more times than any other young man of the tribe. The number of feathers in his bonnet attested to that. At birth, the young man's father had christened him with a name that anticipated this prowess—

Here Maas reeled off guttural syllables, than gave them an approximate English translation: Plenty Coups. The trader said Plenty Coups was further distinguished by belonging to the dog soldiers, the elite group that controlled and directed the all-important buffalo hunts.

In cynical fashion, Maas wished her well with her new owner.

Amanda was not permitted to take part in the feasting and celebration. She was led away by several young women, one of whom carried a sapling, and struck her in the face several times before supervising the tying of the thongs in the tepee. Amanda was deposited on the hide-covered bed. Miserable and exhausted, she fell asleep—

Now she was awake. *Remembering*—

Very little spare flesh remained on her rapidly maturing body. She had trouble recalling her last solid meal.

But that was of trifling importance. What mattered was the man who had bought her. He would surely come to her before the night was over. No doubt he'd do what she dreaded: strip her dress away, lower his body on top of hers, and heave back and forth until he had satisfied himself.

A sharp memory of the first time it had happened set her to shivering. She remembered faces—one of them fondly. She remembered blue eyes, tawny hair, kind and gentle hands that had helped her when she faltered—

Tears came to her eyes at the thought of her cousin Jared. Where was he now? New Orleans, she hoped.

She gazed at the bracelet of tarred rope, partially hidden by the thongs around her wrists. The bracelet was her last tangible link with the past—and Jared. As she looked at the blackened cordage, she knew she'd never see him again. But she'd keep the bracelet until she died.

She blinked the tears away as her mind conjured the other face. The man who called himself a preacher. The man who had inflicted the horrifying, unexpected hurt on her body years ago, in Tennessee—

The day Blackthorn carried her off to his cabin, she wanted to die. She wanted to close her eyes and never wake again—especially after he raped her a second time, on the floor of his squalid shanty. She'd screamed; tried to flee from him. But he was too big and quick, even with his trousers fallen around his ankles. She remembered the bite of splinters against her bare buttocks, and the immense, ravaging feel of him jamming up inside her, filling her with a hateful, slimy wetness—

When they left the cabin, she was tied hand and foot. She lay on her belly behind his saddle, praying for death.

For days, jolted and bruised as Blackthorn rode toward St. Louis, that was her only wish: to die. To end the shame and pain that had become her lot. Virtually every evening on the long, nightmarish trek, he had undressed her and thrust into her. She fought him each time, shrieking and scratching and crying out to God to let her die and escape the torture. The harder she resisted Blackthorn, the harder he ravaged her—and he usually beat her afterward as well.

Then one night, in the stuffy little boarding-house room in St. Louis, she was feeling so ill and so hurt that she vowed she'd throw herself out the window if Blackthorn touched her again. But she didn't, because a peculiar insight came to her.

What triggered the insight was another memory: the memory of a man's sly eyes in a Pittsburgh store. And words her cousin had spoken. Words about how men fancied her prettiness. The memory was tangled with the comforting feel of her cousin's hand, and the taste of licorice—

Thus when she saw the preacher's eyes looming over her, she recognized a gleam in them that reminded her of the eyes of the man in Pittsburgh—

That night, she didn't struggle so much. She let Blackthorn have his way without quarrel. Though he was startled and suspicious, he seemed to enjoy himself a bit more.

From that hour, she didn't even protest when the bogus preacher fondled her growing breasts, or spread her legs with his huge hands and lowered himself between. She pretended submissiveness—total fear of him—which wasn't hard to do. As a result, he beat her less often.

When Blackthorn sold her to Maas, she began to realize the real value of her

new insight. She never resisted when Maas wanted her in his bed. And if he wasn't kind to her, neither did he abuse her excessively.

Slowly, a little of her confidence came back. Even if she *was* relatively helpless, trapped among strangers, she had a weapon; a way to mitigate her suffering—

Now another man had bought her. A man totally unlike the preacher or the trader. This one was young, arrogant. His fierce eyes frightened her. And she couldn't even speak his language—

She heard a sound. Rolled her head sideways, alarmed.

The oval door-cover of the tepee, located about a foot above the ground and hinged by a thong at the top, had been lifted aside. She glimpsed figures against the firelight. Then a silhouette blotted the glow—

It was not Plenty Coups who stepped through the three-foot opening. It was the young woman who had struck Amanda with the sapling.

The young woman let the oval door-cover fall back into place. Outside, the hide drums pounded, and rattles kept the rhythm. Men yipped and barked, stamping in some ritual dance to celebrate the successful buffalo hunt. She heard one of the trappers bawl a few lines of a song in English, then discharge a gun—

The young Indian woman gazed at Amanda with unconcealed hatred. Though on the plump side, she wasn't unattractive. Her plaited black hair was clean and glossy. She wore moccasins and leggings beneath a dress of elkskin that reached below her knees. Across her shoulders and bosom, a separate yoke with long fringe gleamed and winked as she approached the younger girl. The yoke was decorated with tiny glass and porcelain beads worked into an intricate pattern. Maas had brought a bale that contained several large packages of such beads—

On the grass and hide bed, Amanda watched the Indian woman bend down beside her. The woman took Amanda's chin between her fingers. Then, with a syllable of contempt, she reached for Amanda's breasts and felt them one by one. It hurt. The woman meant that it should.

Next the woman explored Amanda's legs and genitals, as a white woman might handle a purchase of doubtful worth. Somehow, Amanda understood what the woman was thinking about her:

That she was little more than a child.

That it was humiliating for Plenty Coups to want her—and barter for her.

Amanda knew instinctively that the Indian woman belonged to the young man in the bonnet.

The girl's fear sharpened as the other woman rose and shuffled to the fire. There she reached up, pulled down one of the saplings from the drying bundle. It was relatively thick. She tested it against her palm; it was stiff.

She lowered the end into the fire. Looking over her shoulder, she smiled.

White-lipped, Amanda watched the Indian woman heat the end of the stick until it shot off wisps of smoke and turned a cherry color. Flame spurted from the stick's end. Hastily, the woman pulled it from the fire. The flame died but the cherry color remained.

The woman walked back to the bed and thrust the stick at Amanda's right eye.

She screamed, twisted her head away, felt the heat of the stick as it plunged into her tangled hair. She smelled her hair burning.

The Indian woman seized her jaw again. Forced her head around. Amanda kept her eyes closed, writhing and struggling. The Indian woman knelt on her stomach. Heat bathed her face as the woman jabbed the stick toward her right eyelid—

Abruptly, the weight was gone. She heard scuffling. A series of heavy oaths, then the crack of a palm against flesh. The Indian woman cried out. Amanda opened her eyes—

She saw Plenty Coups, half-crouched and furious. The woman lay at his feet, the print of his hand still vivid on her cheek.

The young man drew back one of his moccasined feet, kicked the woman in the stomach. She wailed and seized her middle. Then she raised one hand and, to Amanda's astonishment, showed no anger—she wept, and pleaded.

Plenty Coups kicked her again.

And again.

With swift, fluid motions, he signed her toward the oval door-cover. The shamed, sobbing woman crawled to it and dragged herself through. The door-cover fell back in place. Plenty Coups uttered a grunt of satisfaction.

He walked to within a pace of Amanda and stood gazing down, faint amusement leavening the harshness of his mouth. But he was still an imposing figure, and a forbidding one, clad only in his moccasins, his ceremonial bonnet and a peculiar clout decorated with an ornate feather bustle. Amanda had seen similar bustles worn by a few of the hardiest-looking young men in the encampment, and had assumed the bustles were symbols of some position of honor.

Plenty Coups' body was coated with sweat, as if he had been dancing with the other celebrants. He unfastened the knot that held the bustle in place. After a lingering glance at Amanda's body, he circled the fire and hung the bustle on the pole next to the one bearing his decorated shield.

From the opposite side of the tepee, Amanda stared at the bright, hard musculature of the Indian's body; at the shining black strands of his shoulder-length hair revealed when he removed the bonnet and carefully suspended it by a thong on another pole.

Then Plenty Coups unfastened his clout. He turned back toward her. She saw his maleness standing out in a clump of black hair. His prideful smile grew, just as he was growing—

Deep within herself, she felt the old urge to close her eyes and escape this endlessly repeated nightmare. But just as quickly as the desire seized her, she resisted. Life was precious. That was what she had come to realize in the dreadful days after the preacher had stolen her. Life was precious, and she would not give it up easily, no matter what else she might be forced to surrender—

Yet the panic and terror persisted.

To fight it, she summoned another memory as Plenty Coups walked slowly back to the grass bed. Dimly, she perceived a glittering length of metal jutting from his hand. A knife—with which he slashed the thongs binding her wrists and ankles. The point of the knife just missed the cordage bracelet.

But she saw that through a haze overlaid with a picture of a comfortable, shadowed room where a fire burned in a hearth, and a sword hung above a mantelpiece; a sword and a long gun like Maas and the trappers carried. On the mantel proper stood a small green bottle. Just in front of it and slightly to one side, a gaunt man—her father—spoke with great seriousness.

She didn't know what he was saying, except for one sentence—

You are a Kent.

It was said to Jared, who hovered wraith-like at the periphery of the vision. But she knew it applied to her as well. She was not a lump of clay, nor a person without a name or identity—

You are a Kent.

She clung to those words, and to the compelling impression she had of the objects on the mantel. They were important to her father; immensely important. Therefore they were important to her—

She knew their location. Boston. Where papa had died. And mama—

Boston was the city from which she'd fled with her cousin Jared, beginning the long journey that had ended in such totally unexpected fashion here, in the middle of a vast prairie, far from the sheltered and comfortable existence that had once been hers—

You are a Kent.

She must never forget that. When she wanted to die, she must remember—

As she did now.

The blind panic lessened a little.

Plenty Coups knelt beside her, slipping his knife out of sight beneath the hides on the bed. She kept concentrating on the images in her mind. She knew, without quite knowing how or why, that the precious objects glimpsed in her imagination were the tangible symbols of the reality of her earlier life, and must be sought one day, and reclaimed, if it were possible—

How would it be possible? she thought, despairing again. She was a prisoner. Bedraggled; hungry; not even certain of her exact age any longer—

Even as the young Indian reached for her, the image of her father seemed to burn within her mind.

You are a Kent.

She *must* live; *must* struggle against the hopelessness, the—

Plenty Coups seized her arm. He was scowling as he dragged her upright, pressed his other hand to her buckskin dress and began fondling her breast roughly.

She bent over his forearm and bit him.

Astonished, he yelped. She shoved. He toppled over backwards, almost singeing his hair in the fire. He came scrambling up, dark eyes murderous. His right hand shot under the hides, seeking the knife.

Amanda clambered to her knees, watching the sharp blade swing upward, then down toward her shoulder—

She shot up her left hand, caught the powerful wrist—

That in itself would never have stopped him from cutting her. What stopped him was the way her expression changed. Though she still felt terror, she willed herself to smile.

Baffled, he wrenched free of her grip. He shook the knife at her several times, plainly unfamiliar with this sort of behavior from a member of the female sex.

She grasped his left hand, placed it carefully on her breast.

Then, still holding his hand, she moved it back and forth. Gently.

And smiled.

She thought she saw comprehension in his eyes. Comprehension—and outrage that stunned him to inaction.

To capitalize on the momentary advantage she sensed, she let go of him, seized her left arm with her right hand, shook her arm—then scowled and shook her head. The young Indian looked thunderstruck.

Once again she guided his left hand to her breast, letting it rest easily.

There was a moment in which she thought she'd failed; thought that the gap between his world and hers was too wide, and he could not understand what Maas and the preacher had come to understand—and that even if he could, he would refuse to accept her terms.

But slowly, the mouth of Plenty Coups lifted at the corners. His eyes filled with hard, grudging admiration.

He laughed loudly.

So did she.

He was handsome when he laughed, she thought. She was capable of admiring him even though her heart was beating fast and her breathing was strident.

The young Indian's eyes moved to her mouth, then down her throat to her breasts. He laughed again, this time in almost childlike pleasure. He recognized her willingness to fight—something his mate probably never did. It delighted him. She experienced a moment of joy as she realized again that, young as she was, she could protect herself with her wits, and her body—

The Indian's erection, shriveled during the byplay with the knife, quickly reasserted itself. He picked Amanda up in his arms. His face was quite close to hers, his eyes mirthful. But the cruelty she had seen in them before was gone.

He bore her to the bed with the willow backrest, putting her down with great care. Then he touched her buckskin dress.

She nodded, and reached for the hem.

The drumming outside grew louder, the laughter and chanting more shrill. Naked, she reclined on the hides with her shoulders braced against the backrest. Plenty Coups slipped his arms around her waist and kissed her breasts one by one. Though she was still frightened and a little repelled by what was about to happen, it no longer held the terror it once had. She was able to stroke the side of the young Indian's face.

He crouched above her for a moment, then lowered his hips toward hers. As he pushed himself against her, firmly, yet not so hard as to hurt her, she closed her eyes.

She blanked her mind as he penetrated her, thinking two connected thoughts—

Thoughts which gave her hope for a certainty that, one day, she would escape from the snare in which fate had trapped her:

I will live.

I have found a way.

I will live.

Afterword

OLD-FASHIONED kindness and courtesy sometimes seem sadly absent from our world. Yet I discovered those qualities in abundance among a group of people often accused of lacking them.

I speak of the ladies and gentlemen of the broadcast media with whom I came in contact on a promotion tour to launch the American Bicentennial Series. I would like to thank all of them for their interest in the series, and for making the author feel very much at home in front of their respective mikes and cameras:

In Philadelphia, Edie Huggins and Stu Crowner; Abbott Barkley; Bill Jones; Connie Roussin and Bob McLean; Bob Perkins; and Ralph Collier.

In Cleveland, Eric Braun; Alan De Petro and John Slowey; Marcia Corsaro; and Merle Pollis.

In Detroit, Vic Caputo and Beverly Payne; Jan Gorham; Jerry Whitman; and J. P. McCarthy.

In Minneapolis and St. Paul, Jere Smith; Glen Olson; Nancy Nelson and Warren Miller; Jerry Wasley and Marcia Fleur; and Bill Carlson and Dave Higgins.

In Chicago, Bob Hale and Joe Turner; Jorie Lueloff and Phil Walters; Bob and Betty Sanders; Ralph Howard; Chicago Ed Schwartz; Karent Agrest; Mike Edwards; and Jim Conway and Steve Stein.

In Dayton, Ted Ryan and Toula Stamm; Gil Whitney; and my good friend Ken Hardin.

Special thanks go to Priscilla Russo of Pyramid Publications and Randie Levine of Accent on Broadcasting, the two charming ladies whose hard work and careful planning made it possible for me to meet all the good people mentioned above.

JOHN JAKES

About the Author

JOHN JAKES was born in Chicago. He is a graduate of DePauw University, and took his M.A. in literature at Ohio State. He sold his first short story during his second year of college, and his first book twelve months later. Since then, he has published more than 200 short stories and over 50 books—chiefly suspense, non-fiction for young people and, most recently, science fiction. He has also authored six popular historical novels under his Jay Scotland pseudonym. His books have appeared in translation from Europe to Japan. Originally intending to become an actor, Mr. Jakes' continuing interest in the theatre has manifested itself in four plays and the books and lyrics for five musicals, all of which are currently in print and being performed by stock and amateur groups around the U.S. The author is married, the father of four children, and lists among his organizations the Authors Guild, the Dramatists Guild and Science Fiction Writers of America.